ALSO BY RICHARD HOLBROOKE

Counsel to the President
(with Clark Clifford)

To End
a War

HOLBROOKE

TO END
A WAR

RANDOM HOUSE

NEW YORK

Grateful acknowledgment is made to the following for permission
to reprint previously published material:

Éditions Bernard Grasset: Excerpt from *Le Lys et la Cendre* by
Bernard-Henri Lévy (Paris: Éditions Bernard Grasset, 1996). Reprinted
by permission of Éditions Bernard Grasset.

Harcourt Brace & Company and Faber and Faber Limited: Excerpt from
"The Hollow Men" from *Collected Poems 1909–1962* by T. S. Eliot.
Copyright © 1936 by T. S. Eliot. Copyright © 1964, 1963 by T. S. Eliot.
Rights outside of the United States are controlled by Faber and Faber Limited.
Reprinted by permission of Harcourt Brace & Company and Faber
and Faber Limited.

Random House, Inc.: Fifty-one lines from "New Year's Day" by W. H. Auden.
Copyright © 1941, 1969 by W. H. Auden. Four lines from "Danse Macabre"
by W. H. Auden. Copyright © 1940, 1968 by W. H. Auden. Both poems are
published in *Collected Poems* (New York: Random House, Inc., 1945).
Reprinted by permission of Random House, Inc.

Photo of Joseph Kruzel (p. vii): Scott Davis/U.S. Army Visual
Information Center

Library of Congress Cataloging-in-Publication Data
Holbrooke, Richard C.
To end a war /
Richard Holbrooke.
p.   cm.
Includes bibliographical references and index.
ISBN 0-375-50057-X
1. Yugoslav War, 1991–   —Diplomatic history. 2. Yugoslav War,
1991–   —Bosnia and Herzegovina. 3. Yugoslav War, 1991–   —Personal
narratives, American. 4. Holbrooke, Richard C. 5. Bosnia and
Herzegovina—History—1992–   I. Title.
DR1313.7.D58H65   1998
949.703—dc21   97-45741

Random House website address: www.randomhouse.com
Printed in the United States of America on acid-free paper
24689753

This book is dedicated to three cherished colleagues
who did not reach Dayton.

Robert C. Frasure

Joseph Kruzel

S. Nelson Drew

No words men write can stop the war
Or measure up to the relief
Of its immeasurable grief. . . .
May an Accord be reached, and may
This aide-mémoire on what they say,
Be the dispatch that I intend;
Although addressed to a Whitehall,
Be under Flying Seal to all
Who wish to read it anywhere,
And, if they open it, En Clair.

—W. H. AUDEN, *New Year Letter*

Contents

BOOK III: DAYTON (November 1–21, 1995)

BOOK IV: IMPLEMENTATION

List of Maps

Note to the Reader

BETWEEN 1991 AND 1995, CLOSE TO three hundred thousand people were killed in the former Yugoslavia. The international response to this catastrophe was at best uncertain and at worst appalling. While both the United States and the European Union initially viewed the Balkan wars as a European problem, the Europeans chose not to take a strong stand, restricting themselves to dispatching U.N. "peacekeepers" to a country where there was no peace to keep, and withholding from them the means and the authority to stop the fighting. Finally, in late 1995, in the face of growing atrocities and new Bosnian Serb threats, the United States decided to launch a last, all-out negotiating effort. This is the story of how, belatedly and reluctantly, the United States came to intervene and how that intervention brought the war in Bosnia to an end.

In the last two years, many people have asked me what the negotiations were really like. This cannot be answered with a dry account of positions taken and agreements reached. The fourteen weeks that form the core of this story were filled with conflict, confusion, and tragedy before their ultimate success. The negotiations were simultaneously cerebral and physical, abstract and personal, something like a combination of chess and mountain climbing. This was not a theoretical game between nation-states, but a dangerous and unpredictable process.

This account of the Bosnia negotiations is written from the perspective of the negotiating team, but to broaden it I have interviewed many of my former colleagues and associates, as well as other experts on the region, who offered their own recollections of important events. Physical descriptions, anecdotes, and the personal background of participants are integral to the story; in diplomacy, as in architecture, details matter. Many events happened far from the negotiating team, in Washington, in the Balkans, in the United Nations, and in the major European capitals. I have included most of them, but, by necessity, they are discussed in less detail. Of special importance were the parallel negotiations with Moscow, conducted primarily by Secretary of Defense William Perry and Deputy Secretary of State Strobe Talbott, which resulted in the unprecedented deployment of Russian troops to Bosnia under American command as part of a NATO-led peacekeeping force.

Government service is always a collective effort; we were only part of a much larger team headed by President Clinton, Vice President Gore, and Secretary of State Warren Christopher, without whose support we would have failed. A list of acknowledgments can be found at the end of this book, but it is not long enough to credit everyone who made the shuttle and Dayton possible. The opinions and views expressed in this book are solely those of the author and do not necessarily represent the official views of the Department of State or the United States Government.

Today, public service has lost much of the aura that it had when John F. Kennedy asked us what we could do for our country. To hear that phrase before it became a cliché was electrifying and led many in my generation to enter public service. For me it was the Foreign Service, which I joined right after graduating from college. Less than a year later I found myself in Saigon. It seems like yesterday, but this was almost thirty-six years ago. I do not wish to suggest that in some distant "golden age" all was altruism and that today idealism is dead. Such easy myths may satisfy, but they are not true; every era has both heroes and scandals. But in an age when the media pays more attention to personalities than to issues, Americans may conclude that public service is either just another job, or a game played for personal advancement.

The public sector contains countless men and women who, whether liberal or conservative, still believe in hard work, high ethical standards, and patriotism. This book is dedicated to three of them. As this story demonstrates, public service can make a difference. If this book helps stimulate a few young Americans to enter the government or other forms of public service, it will have achieved one of its goals.

My own government experiences over the last thirty-five years have led me to conclude that most accounts of major historical events, including memoirs, do not convey how the process appeared at the time to those participating in it. This derives, in part, from the historian's need to compress immensely complicated and often contradictory events into a coherent narrative whose outcome the reader (unlike the participants at the time) already knows. Other, more subtle factors are also at work: the natural tendency of memoirists to present themselves in a favorable light; a faulty memory or incomplete knowledge; and the distorting effect of perfect hindsight. A memoir sits at the dangerous intersection of policy, ambition, and history, where it is tempting to focus on instances of good judgment, and to blur or forget times when one made a mistake.

Hindsight tends to give historical narrative a sense of inevitability. But there was nothing predetermined about the outcome of the Bosnia negotiations. In August 1995, when they began, it was almost universally believed that they would fail, as all previous efforts had. And we knew that if we failed, the war would continue.

RICHARD HOLBROOKE
New York
April 1998

Prologue

THE FIRST TIME I SAW SARAJEVO, I placed my feet for a moment in the cement footprints pressed into the sidewalk on the spot where Gavrilo Princip stood when he fired the bullets that killed Archduke Franz Ferdinand. This was in the summer of 1960. I was hitchhiking across southeastern Europe with a friend, and I was nineteen years old. Suddenly, a guide appeared and offered to translate the words engraved in Serbian on the wall above the footprints. "Here, on June 28, 1914," read the plaque (or so I remember it), "Gavrilo Princip struck the first blow for Serbian liberty."

I can still recall my astonishment. "Serbian liberty?" What was this all about? Every college student knew Princip's act had started Europe's slide into two world wars and contributed to the rise of both communism and fascism. How could anyone hail it as heroic? And "Serbia" didn't exist as an independent country; it was part of communist Yugoslavia, teeming, or so it seemed to a nineteen-year-old in Eastern Europe for the first time, with grim-faced soldiers and policemen. I never forgot that first brush with extreme nationalism, and it came back to me vividly when Yugoslavia fell apart.

By the time I saw Sarajevo again, in 1992, thirty-two years had passed. Bosnia had become the worst killing ground in Europe since World War II, and a new phrase had entered the English language: "ethnic cleansing." With Bosnia on the brink of collapse, I visited the region twice on fact-finding missions for the International Rescue Committee. On the second trip I finally returned to Sarajevo, traveling illegally across Serb lines in a Danish armored personnel carrier. The trip was far more dangerous than I had realized. The city, no longer a beautiful and cosmopolitan combination of Muslim, Catholic, and Eastern Orthodox cultures, had turned into a desperate hellhole, under heavy mortar, artillery, and sniper attacks. Children gathered twigs for firewood, and people piled shattered buses into makeshift barriers as protection against the constant sniper threat.

When I reached the war-torn city, I ran into John Burns, the great war correspondent of *The New York Times,* and asked if he could take me to Princip's footprints in the pavement. Impossible, he said with a laugh: they had been destroyed by the Bosnian Muslims. But the spirit behind their inscription had been revived—murderously so.*

---

* According to Rebecca West in *Black Lamb and Grey Falcon,* the inscription, engraved on "a very modest black tablet," read, "Here, in this historical place, Gavrilo Princip was the initiator of liberty, on the day of St. Vitus, the 28th of June, 1914." In *The Unknown War,* Winston Churchill referred to this inscription as "a monument erected by his fellow countrymen [which] records his infamy and their own." West, pro-Serb throughout her famous book, objected to Churchill's characterization, and described the words on the plaque as "remarkable in their restraint . . . [and] justified by their literal truth."

TO END
A WAR

CHAPTER 1

The Most Dangerous
Road in Europe

(August 15–21, 1995)

For all of us there is a twilight zone between history and memory;
between the past as a generalized record which is open to relatively
dispassionate inspection and the past as a remembered part of, or
background to, one's own life.

—ERIC HOBSBAWM, *The Age of Empire: 1875–1914*

THE MOUNT IGMAN ROUTE TO SARAJEVO was often described as the most
dangerous road in Europe. Parts of the road, a narrow, winding red-dirt track
originally used only by farmers and shepherds, were controlled by Serb machine gunners, who regularly shot at U.N. vehicles trying to reach the Bosnian
capital. The roadbed itself had little foundation and no reinforcement along its
sides, and in several of its narrower sections it was difficult for two cars to
pass each other. The wreckage of vehicles that had slid off the road or been hit
by Serb gunners littered the steep slopes and ravines. In the summer of 1995,
however, with the airport closed by Serb artillery, the two-hour drive over
Mount Igman was the only way to reach Sarajevo without going through
Bosnian Serb lines.

The chief European negotiator, Carl Bildt of Sweden, had been shot at
crossing Serb territory only weeks earlier. He urged us not to use the Igman
road. But without visiting Bosnia's beleaguered capital we could not carry out
our mission. On August 15, we made our first attempt, taking a United Nations helicopter from the Croatian coastal town of Split to a landing zone high
on Mount Igman, after which we would drive in armored vehicles to Sarajevo.
Our helicopter was unable to find a break in the heavy clouds over the landing
site. After circling for several unpleasant hours, we returned, frustrated and
tired, to Split.

Hearing that we could not reach Sarajevo, Bosnian Foreign Minister
Muhamed Sacirbey, accompanied by the senior American diplomat in

Bosnia, John Menzies, drove over Mount Igman to meet us at the Split airport. Known to most Americans via television as the eloquent face of his embattled new nation, Sacirbey was perhaps proudest of the fact that he had been a first-string defensive back at Tulane University. He was tough, strong, and fit. Still, the long and bumpy road trip had tired him, and he was as exhausted as we were. To avoid being overheard, we squeezed into the cabin of our small Air Force jet as it sat on the tarmac, and briefed him on our plans. I stressed that while our mission had the full backing of President Clinton, and represented a last, best hope for peace in the Balkans, there was no guarantee of its success. Our discussion finished as darkness fell over the Balkans, and we flew on to Zagreb, the capital of Croatia, to meet Croatian President Franjo Tudjman. After a day in Zagreb, we arrived in Belgrade on August 17 to meet the key actor in this stage of the drama, President Slobodan Milosevic of Serbia.

Although I knew the other major leaders in the region, this would be my first meeting with the man who, in our view, bore the heaviest responsibility for the war. I approached the meeting with great uncertainty and was guided by my deputy, Robert Frasure, who had spent many hours negotiating with Milosevic earlier that spring.

Frasure's main bargaining chip with Milosevic had been the economic sanctions that the United Nations had imposed in 1992 against the "Federal Republic of Yugoslavia," the name by which Serbia and Montenegro called themselves even though the four other republics of the original Yugoslavia—Slovenia, Croatia, Macedonia, and Bosnia-Herzegovina—had declared themselves independent nations. The sanctions had seriously damaged Serbia's economy, and Milosevic wanted them ended. But for more than sixteen months he had refused to offer anything concrete in return for our suspending or lifting them.

Our first meeting with Milosevic, on August 17, lasted almost six hours. He was smart, charming, and evasive. As Warren Zimmermann, our last Ambassador to Yugoslavia, put it: "Milosevic makes a stunning first impression on those who do not have the information to refute his often erroneous assertions. Many is the U.S. senator or congressman who has reeled out of his office exclaiming, 'Why, he's not nearly as bad as I expected!' "[1] But despite his cleverness, Milosevic was playing word games devoid of substance—and he knew it. Without budging, he focused on inconsequential changes in draft documents over which he and Frasure had been arguing since the beginning of the year. His goal remained to get the sanctions lifted at no cost.

Our most important point concerned whom we would negotiate with. The United States, we said, would never again deal directly with the Bosnian Serbs who rained artillery and racist rhetoric down upon the Muslims and the Croats from their mountain capital of Pale. "You must speak for Pale," I said. "We won't deal with them ever again."*

Frasure thought the meeting had gone well. Nonetheless, it left me dissatisfied. I decided to see Milosevic again the next morning to make clear that we would not continue the cat-and-mouse game he had played with previous negotiators. To emphasize this, it was necessary to change the ground rules a bit. Our entire team of six people had attended the first meeting, but Milosevic had had only two people with him—his new Foreign Minister, Milan Milutinovic, and his chief of staff, Goran Milinovic. Nine people were simply too many to establish the sort of direct relationship necessary for a frank dialogue.

Early on the morning of August 18, before our second meeting with Milosevic, I met with Frasure and Rudy Perina, the senior American diplomat in Belgrade,† in the garden of the ambassadorial residence. As we walked between the imposing old stone house and the tennis court, under magnificent chestnut trees and presumably out of the range of prying microphones, I said that I "planned to throw a controlled fit" to make clear to Milosevic that what he was doing was unacceptable. Because of this plan, I added that the next meeting needed to be smaller.

Apologizing to Rudy, I asked him to drop out of the meeting. Returning to the house, I asked the other two members of our team—Joseph Kruzel, the Senior Deputy Assistant Secretary of Defense; and Lieutenant General Wesley Clark, the Chief of Plans for the Joint Chiefs of Staff—to drop out as well. I would take only Frasure and Nelson Drew, an Air Force colonel who, as the National Security Council staff member on our team, represented the White House. Frasure concurred in this suggestion.

Nothing generates more heat in the government than the question of who is chosen to participate in important meetings. My request ran against a diplomatic custom I greatly respected—that the senior resident American diplomatic representative should normally attend every official meeting with a head of government. But although unhappy, all three men agreed without objection. It could have been a difficult moment; I was deeply gratified by this early sign of our cohesiveness as a team.

---

* Many earlier negotiating efforts of both the United States and the Europeans, including an American probe as late as January 1995, had dealt with the Bosnian Serbs as a separate entity.

† Our diplomatic presence in Belgrade was unique in the world: it was a fully functioning diplomatic mission, yet it was accredited to no one. Neither the United States nor the European Union recognized the claim of Serbia and Montenegro that they still constituted the "Federal Republic of Yugoslavia." However, because of the value of continuing contacts with the Serbians, we maintained an Embassy in Belgrade even though we did not recognize the country it was in.

· · ·

Less than an hour later Frasure, Drew, and I were seated in a high-ceilinged meeting room in the Presidential Palace—one of Tito's old offices—in Belgrade. It was a room we would come to know well in the next seven months. Like other such meeting rooms in communist and former communist countries from Beijing to Bratislava, the room tried to make up for its lack of charm by a drab giganticism. The three of us sat on a long sofa. Milosevic took an armchair a few feet from where I sat at the end of the sofa. Foreign Minister Milutinovic chose another soft chair facing us directly, and Goran Milinovic, always the loyal staff officer, sat at the edge of the group, taking notes.

As we talked, I thought of the difficulties and dangers we would face each time we tried to reach Sarajevo. It was annoying that we had to depend on U.N. helicopters, the uncertain weather—and that awful road.

"It is disgraceful," I said, "that President Clinton's peace mission has to travel to Sarajevo by such a slow and dangerous route. In order to negotiate we must be able to move rapidly between here and Sarajevo. We have already been in the area for almost a week and we haven't been able to get there. It is ridiculous. You claim to want peace. I ask you now to arrange for us to fly to Sarajevo or to guarantee that we can use a safer land route without any interference from the Bosnian Serbs."

Milosevic stared at us for a moment with a penetrating gaze, as if no one had ever made this request before. Then he replied in his excellent English, "You're right. I'll try." He spoke sharply in Serbian to Goran, who almost ran out of the room. Milosevic said, "I'm sending a message to General Mladic. Let's see what he can do."

Bob, Nelson, and I watched with fascination. We were constantly looking for clues as to how the enigmatic relationship between Milosevic and Mladic worked. This was the first time we saw what was to become a recurring pattern during the diplomatic shuttle: direct communication between Milosevic and Ratko Mladic, the commander of the Bosnian Serb forces, who had recently been indicted by the International War Crimes Tribunal for direct or indirect responsibility for the murder of thousands of Bosnian Muslims and Croats.

Less than twenty minutes later, Goran returned and handed a piece of paper to Milosevic. "Mladic says the airport is too dangerous," Milosevic said. "He cannot guarantee that you would not be shot down by Muslim or Croat soldiers." This was an absurd statement: everyone knew, I said heatedly, that the only danger to people at the Sarajevo airport was from the Serb gunners ringing the hills around it. But Milosevic was not finished. "Mladic says you can fly to Kiseljak and go in by road from there. You will be completely safe."

I knew that road. Its flat terrain and paved surface made it a much easier drive than the route over Mount Igman. But the road ran through Bosnian Serb territory—"Indian country," as Bob Frasure called it. I had traveled that road as a private citizen almost three years earlier, on December 31, 1992, huddled in the forward seat of a Danish armored personnel carrier, trying to appear inconspicuous under a U.N. helmet and a heavy blue flak jacket. We had been stopped a half-dozen times by heavily armed Serbs who poked machine guns around the inside of the APC while checking our ID cards (to make things worse, mine was a crude forgery).* Less than two weeks later, the Serbs had killed a Bosnian Deputy Prime Minister during a search of a French APC on the same route.

"We can only consider using that road," I said, "if you give us your personal guarantee that we will not be stopped by the Bosnian Serbs."

"I can't give you that guarantee," Milosevic said, "but I'll ask Mladic for one—"

"That's out of the question, Mr. President. We can't possibly accept guarantees from Mladic, only from you."

Sitting next to me on the long couch, Bob Frasure leaned over and whispered, "We have no choice except Igman."

That night we flew to Split. Four days earlier, we had stayed in the lovely old Kastile Hotel, directly on the water, where we had dared Joe Kruzel and Wes Clark to dive in from their third-story windows. The two men had leaped into the water, proud of their courage. But the Kastile was forty minutes away from the airport, too far for our exhausted team, and we opted for a dreary hotel with chalk-white walls and blue lights near the airport.

On the short bus trip from our plane to the hotel, Kruzel and Frasure hung on the hand straps and improvised a reggae lyric in anticipation of the trip we were going to make the next day; its refrain was something about "Goin' up Mount Igman, mon, tryin' to make da peace, mon." It wasn't much to listen to, they cheerfully admitted, as they danced in the bus to their own song. We ate dinner in the bleak hotel dining room, almost alone and unnoticed. I sat with Frasure, Kruzel, and Clark; my executive assistant, Rosemarie Pauli, sat at the next table with Nelson Drew.

We talked at length about a mutual friend, Frank Wisner, who had recently become Ambassador to India. When it came to personnel in the State Department, Frank was always the first person I consulted. When I became Assistant Secretary of State for European and Canadian Affairs in the summer of 1994, he recommended for the deputy's job Bob Frasure, who had worked for him in the Bureau of African Affairs ten years earlier. After one meeting with Bob, then finishing a tour as America's first Ambassador to Estonia, I offered him the job and asked him to reorganize the European Bureau's Central European

* See chapter 3.

division so that it reflected the new emphasis we wished to place on that region.*

Frasure, fifty-three years old, was a craggy, cynical professional diplomat who loved his work, while grumbling continually about it. He walked—almost shuffled—with a slight stoop, as if he were about to fall over, but he had enormous energy, great patience, and a strategic sense unusual in career Foreign Service officers. His cables were widely read in the Department of State not just for their content but for their wit and descriptive powers. His reports of negotiating with Milosevic over lengthy dinners of lamb and plum brandy were classics for both their conciseness and their humor—two qualities not much in evidence in most State Department telegrams.

Bob's greatest joy was to retreat to his farm in the Shenandoah and, with his wife, Katharina, and his two daughters, Sarah and Virginia, paint his barn. At the end of 1994, with the situation in Bosnia continuing to deteriorate, Secretary Christopher—who greatly admired Frasure's cool detachment, fierce loyalty, and patriotism—suggested we add to his portfolio the job of chief Bosnia negotiator. Although Bob had earlier said he did not want direct responsibility for Bosnia, he accepted this enormous additional burden without complaint. But by the summer of 1995 he was visibly worn out by the constant and frustrating travel to the Balkans, and we had agreed that after this trip he would remain at home to backstop our efforts. Frasure wondered constantly if, in its post-Vietnam, post-Somalia mood, our nation would have the nerve and strength to stand up to what he called the "junkyard dogs and skunks of the Balkans." He believed in the need to use airpower, but doubted that the United States had the political will to do so.

Joe Kruzel was shorter and stockier than Frasure. At fifty, his sharp mind combined in equal measure theoretical and practical ability. He often wore his eyeglasses on the lower part of his nose and peered over them, in a manner that emphasized his academic background. He was equally proud of his undergraduate days at the United States Air Force Academy and his Ph.D. from Harvard. Kruzel had a certain playfulness into which he could switch effortlessly from his somber, serious demeanor. After our dinner in Split, Joe volunteered to rewrite our presentation for the Bosnians. Reading his memo the next morning, I saw he had slipped in a one-liner, perhaps to see if we were paying attention: "We will need a mini–Marshall Plan (you know Minnie Marshall, George's sister)."

* To reflect this priority, we abolished the outdated Office of Eastern European Affairs on our first day in office in September 1994, and created in its place three new offices that reflected the post–Cold War realities of Europe. One combined the Nordic countries and the three newly independent Baltic states. We also banished the phrase "Eastern Europe" from our official vocabulary, replacing it with the historically and geographically more accurate "Central Europe." Unfortunately, most people, including the media, still use the outmoded phrase.

As we talked, General Wesley Clark joined us. He was in a complicated position on our team. A West Pointer, a Rhodes scholar from Arkansas, and a Vietnam veteran, he had been one of the fastest rising officers in the United States Army—the youngest brigadier general at the time he got his first star. He had a personal relationship, although not close, with another Rhodes scholar from Arkansas who was now our Commander in Chief. With three stars, Clark was at the crossroads of his career; this assignment would lead him either to a fourth star—every general officer's dream—or to retirement. Assignment to a diplomatic negotiating team offered some exciting possibilities, but it could be hazardous duty for a military officer, since it might put him into career-endangering conflicts with more senior officers. Clark's boyish demeanor and charm masked, but only slightly, his extraordinary intensity. No one worked longer hours or pushed himself harder than Wes Clark. Great things were expected of him—and he expected them of himself.

Of the people at the hotel that evening, the one I knew least was Samuel Nelson Drew, a forty-seven-year-old Air Force colonel who had recently joined the National Security Council staff. In civilian clothes he seemed less like a military officer than an academic. He had a doctorate from the University of Virginia. A devoted family man with a strong Christian faith, he had worked for almost four years at NATO headquarters, where, among other responsibilities, he had headed a special crisis task force on Yugoslavia.

In our first meeting with Milosevic, Nelson hung back, saying almost nothing. But near the end of dinner, Milosevic began to pay close attention to him. Sensing that he could become a vital part of our team, I took Nelson aside that night, and urged him to speak up more. As we prepared for the next day's trip, he seemed subdued, and spent part of the evening writing a long letter to his wife.

On Saturday, August 19, we ate breakfast early and returned to the French air base. The French helicopter had room for only six passengers, but we were seven, counting Rosemarie Pauli and General Clark's executive assistant, Lieutenant Colonel Dan Gerstein. So Rosemarie, who had visited Sarajevo on two earlier trips with me, offered her seat to Gerstein.

The helicopter ride was relatively uneventful, although swooping between hills and looking for breaks in the clouds can never be entirely routine. Nelson Drew, seeing the savage land for the first time, stared silently out the small window. After about ninety minutes, we landed in a soccer field at Veliko Polje, near the Mount Igman pass. Our greeting party was headed by Lieutenant Colonel Randy Banky, the senior American military liaison officer with the U.N. forces in Sarajevo. Two vehicles waited for us on the soccer field—a large, heavy French armored personnel carrier, painted U.N. white, and a U.S. Army Humvee.

General Clark talked to Colonel Banky for a moment. Then he turned to me and yelled over the roar of the helicopter, "Have you ever been in one of our new Humvees? You ought to see how much better it is than the jeeps you were used to in Vietnam."

The French armored personnel carrier, or APC, would take the rest of the party to Sarajevo. As we walked to the APC, I asked Kruzel what the attitude of the Pentagon would be if the United States sent troops to Bosnia as part of a peace settlement. "They wouldn't like it," he said in his half-sardonic, half-joking style, "because it would disrupt their training schedule."

Another American introduced himself at the doors of the APC: Pete Hargreaves, a security officer in the American Embassy in Sarajevo. The doors on the back of the massive vehicle swung open and everyone took seats on the side benches, Bob Frasure at the front left, the others facing each other, Gerstein and Hargreaves in the seats nearest the back doors. "Think hard about how we handle the meeting with Izetbegovic," I said to Bob Frasure. He gave an ironic laugh and, as I turned back toward the Humvee, the doors of the APC slammed shut.

Clark sat to my right in the backseat of the Humvee. Colonel Banky and the driver, an American sergeant, took the two seats in front. The vehicle was heavily armored and the windows, which could be opened, were almost two inches thick. Nonetheless, Clark insisted that we buckle our seat belts and put on flak jackets and helmets. In the August heat, our colleagues in the APC did not take these precautions.

For almost an hour we traveled toward Sarajevo through seemingly peaceful woods, although the road was bumpy and in poor condition. The French military, in whose sector Sarajevo and Mount Igman fell, had recently begun upgrading the road and patrolling it with tanks, part of the new and powerful Rapid Reaction Force (RRF) that French President Jacques Chirac had established to show the Serbs that France wanted a more aggressive policy.

The road emerged from the woods and reached a steep incline above the Sarajevo valley, where, hugging the mountain wall, it suddenly narrowed. On our left was a nearly vertical wall, to our right a sharp drop-off. We were approaching the most dangerous part of the road, where we would be directly exposed to Serb machine gunners. But in these well-armored cars we felt safe. It was about 9:30 in the morning.

The Humvee rounded a corner. On the left, a French convoy going the other way had pulled over against the inside wall to let us pass on the outside. As we approached the last French tank, we saw a soldier yelling and gesturing, but we couldn't hear what he was saying through the thick windows. Our driver got out of the car, looking puzzled. "I don't understand this guy," he said. "He's speaking French." I jumped out of the Humvee to help, but I couldn't quite grasp what the French soldier was saying, something about a vehicle behind us going over the edge of the road. I thought that I had misunderstood him. Behind us was—nothing. I signaled Clark to join me. The APC must be far behind us, I thought. Then it hit me.

Clark and I ran back about thirty yards. About six inches of red clay seemed to have broken off the edge of the roadbed. We could hear voices in the woods below. But we saw nothing except a few flattened trees. Somewhere below us lay the APC with our colleagues.

Wearing the heavy flak jackets and helmets—mine over a business suit—we jumped off the edge of the road and started down the steep incline. We were less than ten feet below the roadbed when two enormous explosions went off. Small-arms fire broke out around us. From below and above people cried out in French, "Mines! Get back on the road!" Grasping roots to pull ourselves up, we scrambled back onto the road.

The shooting continued. Far below in the distance lay villages with a clear line of fire. We had no idea if they were Serb or Muslim. I ran back to our Humvee and asked the sergeant to turn it around in case we had to get back to the relative safety of the woods and the soccer field–helipad. We tried to set up our portable satellite dish to establish communications with the outside world, but the vertical rise of the mountain made contact impossible. Colonel Banky had disappeared.

Finally—it seemed like an eternity but was in fact less than ten minutes—a French corporal ran up to us. The missing APC, he said, was not immediately below us, as we had thought, but beyond the next hairpin turn.

At that moment we realized how bad the situation was. Until then we had expected to find our colleagues injured but, we hoped, not seriously. I had not allowed myself to think of any worse possibility.

Wes and I started running down the road, twenty pounds of extra weight cutting into our necks and chests. We rounded the hairpin turn and followed the road for almost a kilometer. Finally, we ran into a cluster of French vehicles on the road, including a medical vehicle that had, by chance, been coming up the road. They were grouped at the spot, we now realized, where the APC had *bounced over the road* and continued to somersault down the mountain. Below us trees had been flattened as if by a giant plow.

The shooting died down and rain began to fall. In addition to five Americans, four French soldiers—the driver and three other men who had been in the APC—were missing. We established a weak radio contact with the Embassy in Sarajevo through the Embassy radio net, but because we did not know exactly what had happened, we asked Sarajevo to hold off reporting anything to Washington. It was not quite 4:00 A.M. in Washington, and whatever had happened, there was nothing for them to do until we knew more.

Since I was the only person on the mountain who spoke both French and English, I stayed on the road to work with the French while Wes descended. We anchored a rope around a tree stump so that he could rappel toward the vehicle, which French and Bosnian soldiers had already reached. Huge plumes of smoke rose from somewhere below us. We could hear Clark yelling through his walkie-talkie that he needed a fire extinguisher urgently. I looked around frantically; there was none.

A French jeep drove up and stopped. A solitary figure was seated upright in the backseat, covered in blood and bandages. His face was unrecognizable. I asked him who he was. He mumbled something unintelligible. "Who?" I asked again. "Hargreaves . . . your . . . security . . . officer . . . sir," he said, very slowly, talking in a daze. I climbed into the jeep and asked him if he wanted to lie down. He said he didn't know if he could make it. He thought his back was broken. Two French soldiers helped me ease Hargreaves out of the jeep and lay him on a cot on the road. I got down on my knees next to him. He was having great difficulty speaking. I understood him to be saying that he should have saved people, that it was his fault, that his back was broken. I tried to calm him down. Desperate for information, I started asking him, one by one, about our team.

"Frasure. Where is Ambassador Frasure?" I almost shouted.

"Died." He could barely say the word.

I stood up. Three years as a civilian in Vietnam had exposed me to occasional combat and its awful consequences, but this was different. This was *my* team, and my deputy was apparently dead. But there was no time to grieve. Wes Clark was still far below us on the mountainside, and the only thing I knew was that Hargreaves believed that Bob Frasure was dead.

I got back on my knees. "Joe Kruzel," I said. "What about Kruzel?"

"Don't know. Think he made it."

"Nelson Drew?"

"Gone. Didn't make it." Hargreaves started to cry. "I tried . . ."

"It's not your fault," I said hopelessly. "There was nothing you could have done." It was a refrain we would repeat regularly to Hargreaves over the next three days. His first reaction—typical of a highly committed security officer—was guilt for his failure to protect those for whom he was responsible.

Clark struggled up the hillside, using the ropes. He looked ten years older. "It's the worst thing you've ever seen down there," he said. By the time he reached the APC, he said, it was already on fire, apparently from live ammunition it was carrying that had "cooked off" and exploded. Bosnian soldiers in the area had reached the APC first, and had taken two Americans, tentatively identified as Joe Kruzel and Dan Gerstein, to the nearest field hospital. Wes had seen charred remains of two other bodies, probably Bob and Nelson.

As we stood on the road absorbing this unspeakable news, a jeep drove up and stopped. A tall, thin French officer stepped out and introduced himself as General René Bachelet, the commander of Sarajevo Sector. He began issuing instructions to his troops. Behind him came another French medical unit and the first Americans, three security officers from the embassy.

By now, journalists in Sarajevo had picked up some conversations about the accident on the internal radio network of the French military and had begun to report a confused and inaccurate version of the accident around the world. It was time to talk to Washington. Asking the American Embassy security unit to take their orders from General Clark, I left for Sarajevo with General Bachelet. On the road we passed the wreckage of several other vehicles that had been hit or had slid off the mountain; one had gone down only a week earlier, killing two British aid workers.

The American Embassy in Sarajevo had recently moved out of crowded and vulnerable rooms in the Holiday Inn. It now occupied a small villa next to the U.N. military headquarters. The communications equipment—secure telephone lines, radio links, and telegraph facilities—were crammed into one tiny, windowless room. It was from there that we now attempted to coordinate our activities. John Menzies, a brave young career diplomat from the United States Information Agency who was awaiting final Senate confirmation to become Ambassador to Bosnia, had already alerted Washington to the tragedy. Shortly after 2:00 P.M. in Sarajevo (8:00 A.M. in Washington) the State Department Operations Center—the indispensable nerve center that keeps all senior State Department and other officials around the world linked to one another twenty-four hours a day—set up, in its usual efficient manner, a conference call with the National Security Advisor, Tony Lake, and his deputy, Sandy Berger; Deputy Secretary of State Strobe Talbott; and the Chairman of the Joint Chiefs of Staff, General John Shalikashvili. (Both Secretary of State Christopher and Secretary of Defense William Perry were on vacation.) I described the scene, stressing that our information was incomplete and that General Clark was still on the mountain.

The Associated Press, Reuters, and UPI had all reported that the French APC had hit a Serb land mine. It was important to correct this as quickly as possible, in order to prevent runaway journalistic speculation and pressure for a military response. I asked Washington to include in its initial announcement a flat statement that the tragedy had been caused by a road accident. We agreed that the officials designated to tell Mrs. Frasure and Mrs. Drew the news prepare them for the worst, but not confirm their husbands' deaths yet. Finally, I asked that someone call my wife, Kati—we had been married for less than three months—and tell her the news personally, so that she would not hear an incomplete version when she woke up.

Clark soon arrived with a vivid description of his efforts to retrieve the remains of the two men, who he was now certain were Bob and Nelson. We called General Shalikashvili again to discuss arrangements for bringing the bodies and the injured home through the American Army hospital in Germany. As I was talking to Shalikashvili, Menzies came into the tiny communications room. "Kruzel is dead," he said quietly, his long arms hanging motionless at his side. "Didn't make it to the hospital. Massive head injuries."

This was, in some ways, the worst moment of the day for us. We had barely absorbed the terrible news about Bob and Nelson, but we thought Joe and Dan Gerstein had made it. Now all three of our senior colleagues were dead. And the thought of Joe—funny, sardonic, wise Joe—dying helplessly as he was driven to the field hospital was simply too much. I asked General Shalikashvili to tell the others in Washington and turned the telephone over to Clark.

A short time later President Clinton called from Jackson Hole, Wyoming, where he was taking a short vacation. I did not realize then that it was his forty-ninth birthday. "Mr. President," I began, rather formally, "we have the sad duty to report that three members of your negotiating team died this morning in a vehicle accident on Mount Igman . . ."

With Strobe Talbott listening in silently, the President made some comments about the terrible nature of the loss, both personally and for the nation. I told him that he could be especially proud of the actions of his fellow Arkansan, and put General Clark on. Wes gave the President a sense of what he had found at the site of the APC, and said it was "like the Boston Road" in Arkansas, a steep and dangerous route both men knew well.

The President asked what effect the tragedy would have on the negotiations, and when we would be ready to continue the mission. "You sent us here as a team, Mr. President," I replied, "and we want to come home as a team. Then we will be ready to resume our mission."

"That's fine," the President said. "Come home as soon as you can, but make clear publicly that our commitment to the peace effort will continue and that you will lead it. And see Izetbegovic before you leave." Knowing we were focused on our loss, the President was thinking ahead for us. He wanted to show publicly that the tragedy would not stop the peace effort.

"All of us, including Bob and Joe and Nelson, would want to continue," I replied. The President, in reporting to the nation from Jackson Hole a few minutes later, said publicly, "What they would want us to do is to press ahead, and that is what we intend to do."

The next few hours were a blur of action that felt meaningless; we kept thinking of how the smallest changes might have prevented the accident, yet it was already permanently imprinted on our lives. We found Gerstein alive in the makeshift French hospital in the basement of the Sarajevo Post Office Building; he was banged up but in surprisingly good shape. He told us a little about the terrible scene inside the APC: how it had slowly started to slide over the edge, how no one had time to speak or get out, how he had grabbed a metal pole above his head and pressed his face hard against the outer walls of the APC as it tumbled—he estimated twenty to thirty times—four hundred meters down the mountain; how it had come to a stop and he had climbed out the top hatch, then, hearing Pete Hargreaves moaning, had gone back to help him escape.

Then, Gerstein said, he and Hargreaves went back to the APC one more time and pulled Joe Kruzel out through the hatch just before the ammunition exploded. He last saw Joe as the Bosnians took him to the field hospital. It was his impression that the others had been knocked unconscious in the violent initial bouncing and tumbling of the APC, and that they never had a chance. Hargreaves himself had survived by wedging himself under his seat, after almost being thrown out the back doors as the APC fell.

We wanted to leave Sarajevo with our fallen and injured comrades that evening. But the injured could travel only by air, and this produced an ironic result: the very permission to use the Sarajevo airfield that had previously been denied us by the Bosnian Serbs—and that could have prevented the accident—suddenly materialized, arranged swiftly by the French directly with Mladic. As we went through that dreadful day, the French and British arranged to send helicopters to the Sarajevo airport to take us out.

Menzies sent word to President Alija Izetbegovic that we still wanted to see him, but, given the circumstances, we asked him to call on us at the Embassy rather than receive us in the normal manner at his office. At precisely 6:00 P.M., Izetbegovic and Sacirbey strode up the steps of the American Embassy. Menzies, Clark, and I greeted them outside the front door in front of a large throng of journalists, and escorted them into a conference room, where General Bachelet joined us.

Several people in Washington had suggested that we conduct substantive conversations with Izetbegovic, but it was clear that the circumstances were not appropriate for a serious discussion. With the press listening, I thanked the French and the Bosnians for their help during the long day. The Bosnians, having lost so many people in the war, seemed relatively unmoved by three American dead. Finally, slightly annoyed with Izetbegovic, Menzies pointedly said that, while we fully recognized how many Bosnians had died, these were the first Americans to lose their lives in Bosnia. This seemed to impress Izetbegovic, and he offered some words of condolence.

The helicopters would be at the airfield shortly. Light was beginning to fade in Sarajevo and the weather was deteriorating. We started for the airport, where there was one more terrible task to perform: the formal identification of Joe Kruzel. Then, as we stood at attention in a light drizzle, a French honor guard escorted three simple wooden coffins, each draped in an American flag, onto a French helicopter. The rain intensified. It was almost dark, and the clouds seemed to be descending toward us, obscuring the mountains that ringed the airfield. The flight out would be hell.

I turned to General Clark. "We've had enough for one day," I said. "Let's try again tomorrow. We'll spend the night in Sarajevo."

We slept, but only briefly, on Army cots in the Ambassador's office. Endless phone calls to Washington, to family and colleagues, filled the evening and the night. Sacirbey, who was distantly related to Joe Kruzel through a cousin of his American wife, came over and stayed for hours. Too exhausted to think, we were unable to sleep until, well after midnight, we had drained ourselves of the event.

On Sunday, August 20, we set out once again for the Sarajevo airport. This time without an honor guard, we loaded the three coffins onto a French helicopter and the two injured men onto a British helicopter. Although I had spent hundreds of hours on helicopters in and since Vietnam without fear, that French helicopter suddenly, irrationally, scared me. I started toward the British chopper. Clark said, "We should go with the coffins all the way." Wes and I had not been separated for what seemed like days, and we boarded the French chopper together.

The helicopters rose noisily into the air. With my knees pressed into one of the coffins, we flew on to Split. To distract myself, I tried to read a John le Carré novel I had been carrying with me, *The Secret Pilgrim*, but could not focus on the page.

Rosemarie Pauli had taken over the arrangements in Split from a confused and chaotic combination of military and civilian personnel. She had worked for me in Germany as well as Washington, and I had complete confidence in her ability. We needed to transfer the two men and the three coffins from the helicopters to a special American military plane, carrying medical equipment and military doctors, that would fly us to Germany. I gave Rosemarie only one instruction: make sure that the movement of Gerstein and Hargreaves, who were both on stretchers and looked awful, was done far from the television cameras and with dignity. All this Rosemarie accomplished with her usual skill. Shattered by the loss of our three colleagues, and aware that she would have been in the APC if there had been room for one more person in the helicopter, she carried out her responsibilities calmly and efficiently until we reached Andrews Air Force Base the next day.

As we changed aircraft at Split, we spoke briefly to the press, telling them we would resume our shuttle diplomacy in about a week. I expressed particular outrage at a statement by the Bosnian Serb leader, Radovan Karadzic, that we had taken "an unnecessary risk" by using the Mount Igman road rather than crossing Bosnian Serb territory—a deliberately nasty reference to the Serb offer to use the Kiseljak road. I called the tragedy "an accident, but an accident of war."

Air Force doctors quickly examined Gerstein and Hargreaves as we flew to Ramstein Air Base in Germany. The Supreme Commander of NATO, General George Joulwan, an old friend from Vietnam, had flown to Ramstein from his headquarters in Belgium. He stepped forward, saluted as we disembarked, and embraced me. Then we stood at attention as the three coffins received the first of many official American salutes on their way to their final resting places.

I knew the American military hospital at Ramstein well from my time as Ambassador to Germany, most unforgettably from an afternoon spent visiting the Americans wounded in the ambush in Mogadishu, Somalia, in October 1993. The raw courage and patriotism of those young men, several of whom had lost their sight or limbs during the fighting, were still vivid in my mind. Now the same doctors treated Gerstein and Hargreaves as we took our first showers in two days and prepared to return home.

At 12:15 P.M. the next day, August 21, we landed at Andrews Air Force Base. As our large C-141 pulled slowly up to the spot where so many of America's triumphal and tragic returns have taken place, the injured men were taken off the plane separately, out of sight of the television cameras. Clark, Rosemarie, and I walked into a silent crowd of friends and family. I could see some of our closest colleagues—Warren Christopher, Bill Perry, Strobe Talbott, Madeleine Albright, Tony Lake, Sandy Berger, Peter Tarnoff, and others—sitting immobile in chairs behind a velvet rope. A place had been saved for me next to my wife, who silently squeezed my hand as I sat down.

We had brought our comrades home, and it was time for others to carry on with the heartbreaking but necessary rituals of remembrance and farewell. Suddenly, exhaustion hit us. As we squinted into the bright midday August sun at Andrews and an Air Force band played "Nearer, My God, to Thee," the coffins were unloaded and placed by an honor guard into three hearses.

Christopher, Lake, and Perry talked movingly about the men who had died. We embraced one another and sought out the wives and children of Bob, Joe, and Nelson. Then, for a few moments, we stood around in a daze, not sure what to do next. Peter Tarnoff, the Undersecretary of State, found me and said gently he would take Kati and me home. We drove into Washington together with Peter, a close friend for over thirty years, and Brooke Shearer, Strobe Talbott's wife. Dropping us off, Peter suggested we take the rest of the day off, and asked if I could come to the State Department the next morning to meet with Warren Christopher.

BOOK ONE

BOSNIA
AT WAR

Twelve months ago in Brussels, I
Heard the same wishful-thinking sigh
As round me, trembling on their beds,
Or taut with apprehensive dreads,
The sleepless guests of Europe lay
Wishing the centuries away,
And the low mutter of their vows
Went echoing through her haunted house,
As on the verge of happening
There crouched the presence of The Thing.
All formulas were tried to still
The scratching on the window-sill,
All bolts of custom made secure
Against the pressure on the door,
But up the staircase of events
Carrying his special instruments,
To every bedside all the same
The dreadful figure swiftly came.

—W. H. AUDEN, *New Year Letter*

CHAPTER 2

"The Greatest
Collective Failure . . ."

(1991–93)

America, eternally protected by the Atlantic, desired to satisfy her self-righteousness while disengaging her responsibility.

—HAROLD NICOLSON, *Peacemaking 1919*

We do not interfere in American affairs; we trust America will not interfere in European affairs.

—JACQUES DELORS, President of the European Community, 1991

Europe took part in [the war] as a witness, but we must ask ourselves: was it always a fully responsible witness?

—POPE JOHN PAUL II, speaking in Sarajevo, April 13, 1997

IN EARLY 1995, IN AN ARTICLE PUBLISHED IN *Foreign Affairs,* I referred to the former Yugoslavia as "the greatest collective security failure of the West since the 1930s."[1] Although the article had been approved through the formal State Department clearance process, the phrase was not universally welcomed in the Administration. While it was intended to apply to events between 1990 and the end of 1992, there was concern that some people might also apply it to events as late as 1994, halfway into the Clinton Administration's first term.

Yugoslavia undeniably represented a failure of historic dimensions. Why and how had it happened—and just at the moment of the West's great triumph over communism?

There was, of course, no single, or simple, answer. But five major factors helped explain the tragedy: first, a misreading of Balkan history; second, the end of the Cold War; third, the behavior of the Yugoslav leaders themselves; fourth, the inadequate American response to the crisis; and, finally, the mistaken belief of the Europeans that they could handle their first post–Cold War challenge on their own.

I. Bad History, or The Rebecca West Factor. Many books and articles about Yugoslavia have left the impression that the war was inevitable. The most famous of all English-language books on the region was Rebecca West's monumental travel book *Black Lamb and Grey Falcon,* first published in 1941. West's openly pro-Serb attitudes and her view that the Muslims were racially inferior had influenced two generations of readers and policy makers. Some of her themes were revisited in modern dress in Robert Kaplan's widely acclaimed 1993 best-seller, *Balkan Ghosts: A Journey Through History,* which left most of its readers with the sense that nothing could be done by outsiders in a region so steeped in ancient hatreds. According to numerous press reports, the book had a profound impact on President Clinton and other members of the Administration shortly after they came into office.*

Thus arose an idea that "ancient hatreds," a vague but useful term for history too complicated (or trivial) for outsiders to master, made it impossible (or pointless) for anyone outside the region to try to prevent the conflict. This theory trivialized and oversimplified the forces that tore Yugoslavia apart in the early 1990s. It was expressed by many officials and politicians over the course of the war, and is still widely accepted today in parts of Washington and Europe. Those who invoked it were, for the most part, trying to excuse their own reluctance or inability to deal with the problems in the region. Some of the most surprising renderings of this view came from Lawrence Eagleburger, the

---

* Kaplan wrote of West, whose work he called "this century's greatest travel book": "I would rather have lost my passport and money than my heavily thumbed and annotated copy of *Black Lamb and Grey Falcon.*" For a perceptive analysis of the negative effects of West and her followers, see "Rebecca West's War," by Brian Hall, *The New Yorker,* April 15, 1996.

An example of the power of Kaplan's book came on October 17, 1995, during an appearance by Warren Christopher before the Senate Armed Services Committee, when William Cohen, then a senator from Maine, said: "Back in 1993 . . . the President was given a copy of *Balkan Ghosts,* Mr. Kaplan's book, and apparently had a change of heart . . . after reading about history's cauldron into which we might be stepping, and I think that particular book needs re-reading as we ponder exactly where we are going with this policy." (See also *On the Edge: The Clinton Presidency,* by Elizabeth Drew, p. 157.)

In his account of his years as editor of *Oslobodjenje,* the Sarajevo daily that published throughout the war, Kemal Kurspahic wrote: "At a time of crucial decisions [President Clinton] simply read the wrong book, or more precisely drew the wrong conclusions from *Balkan Ghosts* by Robert Kaplan, which led to the comforting thought that nothing much could be done in Bosnia 'until those folks got tired of killing each other' " (*As Long As Sarajevo Exists*).

Kaplan claims that he did not intend to have this effect. His book is primarily about Greece and Romania. It devotes less than four chapters out of seventeen to the former Yugoslavia, mostly Serbia, mentions Sarajevo only once and Mostar not at all, and has only twelve references to Bosnia. In his preface, Kaplan says that "nothing I write should be taken as a justification, however mild, for the war crimes committed by ethnic Serb troops in Bosnia, which I heartily condemn."

former American Ambassador to Yugoslavia, who succeeded James Baker as Secretary of State near the end of 1992. Eagleburger regularly expressed his frustration with those Americans who called for action in stark terms. In September 1992, for example, almost two months after journalists had first filmed the atrocities being committed by Serbs against Muslims in prison camps in western Bosnia, he said:

> I have said this 38,000 times, and I have to say this to the people of this country as well. This tragedy is not something that can be settled from outside and it's about damn well time that everybody understood that. Until the Bosnians, Serbs, and Croats decide to stop killing each other, there is nothing the outside world can do about it.

It was, of course, undeniable that the ethnic groups within Yugoslavia nursed deep-seated grievances against one another. But in and of itself, ethnic friction, no matter how serious, did not make the tragedy inevitable—or the three ethnic groups equally guilty.* Of course, there was friction between ethnic groups in Yugoslavia, but this was true in many other parts of the world where racial hatred had *not* turned into ethnic cleansing and civil war. There had been periods of intense ethnic conflict in Yugoslavia, most recently in World War II. But the fighting between 1941 and 1945 was part of the larger killing field, triggered by Hitler's ambitions, into which all of Europe had turned. Though the Serbs nursed an ancient enmity stemming from their defeat by the Turks on Kosovo Field in 1389, the three groups had lived together for centuries. Serbs, Croats, and Muslims worked together in every walk of life. There was no noticeable physical or ethnic difference between them, and, in fact, there was considerable intermarriage. Many people told me that until the collapse of their country they did not even know which of their friends were Serb and which were Muslim. Throughout the war, I heard frequent accounts of old friends sending each other personal messages and gifts and even helping each other escape across the battle lines. As Noel Malcolm wrote in his 1994 *Bosnia: A Short History,* "Having travelled widely in Bosnia over fifteen years, and having stayed in Muslim, Croat, and Serb villages, I cannot believe the claim that the country was forever seething with ethnic hatreds."†

Yugoslavia's tragedy was not foreordained. It was the product of bad, even criminal, political leaders who encouraged ethnic confrontation for personal,

---

* As journalists reported at the time, the American government had concluded by the early summer of 1992 that the Serbs had carried out close to 90 percent of all the atrocities in Bosnia and Croatia.

† Page 252. Malcolm's *Bosnia: A Short History* was the first serious English-language history of Bosnia, and argued convincingly that Bosnia had its own history and continuing identity. Malcolm undermined the conventional wisdom that the war was the inevitable result of ancient hatreds. It is unfortunate it did not appear earlier.

political, and financial gain. Rather than tackle the concrete problems of governance in the post-Tito era, they led their people into a war. Observing how racial hatred was deliberately inflamed, Warren Zimmermann wrote in his memoir of his ambassadorship:

> Those who argue that "ancient Balkan hostilities" account for the violence that overtook and destroyed Yugoslavia forget the power of television in the hands of officially provoked racism. While history, particularly the carnage of World War Two, provided plenty of tinder for ethnic hatred in Yugoslavia, it took the institutional nationalism of Milosevic and Tudjman to supply the torch. . . . Yugoslavia may have a violent history, but it isn't unique. What we witnessed was violence-provoking nationalism from the top down, inculcated primarily through the medium of television. . . . Many people in the Balkans may be weak or even bigoted, but in Yugoslavia it is their leaders who have been criminal. The virus of television spread ethnic hatred like an epidemic throughout Yugoslavia. . . . An entire generation of Serbs, Croats, and Muslims were aroused by television images to hate their neighbors.[2]

Malcolm similarly observed:

> Having watched Radio Television Belgrade in the period 1991–2, I can understand why simple Bosnian Serbs came to believe that they were under threat, from Ustasa hordes, fundamentalist jihads, or whatever. . . . It was as if all television in the USA had been taken over by the Ku Klux Klan.[3]

II. The End of the Cold War. Josip Broz Tito gained power in Yugoslavia by fighting the Nazis and held it for an astonishing thirty-five years. In 1948 came the event that defined Yugoslavia, Tito's historic break with the Soviet Union. From then on, the West was ready to overlook or minimize all other problems within Yugoslavia because of the strategic importance of supporting an anti-Soviet state, albeit a communist and undemocratic one, in such a vital area of Europe. Yugoslavia would receive special treatment from the West for the next forty years.

By the time Yugoslavia started its final agony in 1991, momentous events elsewhere obscured what was happening in the Balkans. The Berlin Wall had been torn down and Germany was unified; communism was dead or dying in Central Europe; the Soviet Union was breaking up into fifteen independent nations; and, in August 1990, Iraq invaded Kuwait, setting in motion the U.S.-led coalition that liberated Kuwait early the following year. Yugoslavia, having lost its strategic importance in the eyes of most Western policy makers, fell to its death almost ignored by the West.

The Former Yugoslavia

Serbia and Montenegro remain under a single Federal structure, and call themselves the Federal Republic of Yugoslavia; the other former Yugoslav Republics are all independent states. Kosovo is an "autonomous province" within Serbia.

III. The Internal Yugoslav Drama. It was famously said during Tito's time that Yugoslavia had six republics, five nations, four languages, three religions, two alphabets, and one party. But after his death in 1980, the Communist Party weakened. Like many other autocratic leaders, Tito had not permitted the development of a strong successor. An increasingly ineffectual central presidency rotated annually among the six semi-autonomous Yugoslav republics.

In the rest of Central and Eastern Europe, democracy and democratic ideals had been the strongest weapon in the struggle against communism. But in Yugoslavia it proved to be extreme nationalism. Thus racists and demagogues—often communists or former communists—rallied people on the basis of ethnic consciousness. Those who wanted to retain a multiethnic state or work out a peaceful new arrangement giving more autonomy to the republics were either driven out of the country or silenced—sometimes brutally.

The crisis began in Catholic, Western-oriented Slovenia, the smallest and wealthiest of the six Yugoslav republics. In 1989, as the Berlin Wall came down, Slovenia began a series of direct challenges to the central government. Kosovo, an "autonomous" region in Serbia whose Albanian majority lived under harsh Serb rule, teetered on the edge of secession and open revolt.

In Serbia, Slobodan Milosevic, the most agile Yugoslav leader, saw his opportunity. Renaming the Serbian Communist Party the Serbian Socialist Party, Milosevic took up the cause of Serb nationalism. In 1989, on the six hundredth anniversary of the Serb defeat by the Turks at Kosovo, Milosevic went to the legendary battlefield and delivered an inflammatory speech before one million Serbs. (When I asked Milosevic in 1995 about this famous speech, he heatedly denied that it was racist, and charged Ambassador Zimmermann with organizing a Western diplomatic boycott of the speech and the Western press with distorting it. Unfortunately for Milosevic, however, his words and their consequences are on the record.)

IV. Post–Iraq American Fatigue. In the spring of 1991, the Yugoslav crisis became acute. The victory in the desert against Saddam Hussein had been the result of superb coalition leadership by the Bush Administration, but dealing simultaneously with both Desert Storm and the death throes of the Soviet Union had exhausted Washington. As Zimmermann noted dryly in his memoirs, "Even a great power has difficulty in dealing with more than one crisis at a time."[4] In addition, the American presidential election was only a year away. American policy makers did not wish to get involved in Yugoslavia, and many considered the situation insoluble. In the words of David Gompert, a senior National Security Council staff member at the time, the Bush Administration knew "a year before the fighting began that Yugoslavia was being led toward the abyss by a few demagogic politicians, [but] simply knew of no way to prevent this from occurring. . . . The Bush national security team that performed so well in other crises was divided and stumped."[5]

In June 1991, Secretary of State James Baker made his only visit to Belgrade, a day trip jammed between an important meeting with Soviet officials in Berlin and an emotional trip to Albania, where one million Albanians cheered him in the streets of the capital.

Baker's perception of the situation was reflected in his personal report from Belgrade to President Bush that night, which he quoted in his memoirs: "My gut feeling is that we won't produce a serious dialogue on the future of Yugoslavia until all parties have a greater sense of urgency and danger. We may not be able to impart that from the outside, but we and others should continue to push."[6]

This was a crucial misreading. The Yugoslavs, who knew exactly how urgent and dangerous the situation was, had been waiting to see if the United States and its allies would intervene. Once they realized that the United States, at the height of its global influence, was disengaged, they proceeded rapidly on their descent into hell. Only four days after Baker left Belgrade, Croatia and Slovenia both declared their independence. Two days later, on June 27, the first (and shortest) of the Balkan wars—the Yugoslav invasion of Slovenia—began. Three more wars—between Croats and Serbs, Serbs and Bosnians, and Croats and Bosnians—were to follow, killing hundreds of thousands of people, displacing over two million more, and destroying not only the country of Yugoslavia, but dreams of what President Bush called a peaceful "new world order" in Europe. Long after he had left Belgrade, Ambassador Zimmermann reflected on the tragedy: "The refusal of the Bush Administration to commit American power early was our greatest mistake of the entire Yugoslav crisis. It made an unjust outcome inevitable and wasted the opportunity to save over a hundred thousand lives."[7]

The United States was now in the position of supporting something that no longer existed. Given their Yugoslav expertise, the key figures in shaping American policy should have been Eagleburger and National Security Advisor Brent Scowcroft, who had been a military attaché in Belgrade early in his Air Force career. Questioned about this in 1995, Scowcroft said, "Eagleburger and I were the most concerned here about Yugoslavia. The President and Baker were furthest on the other side. Baker would say 'We don't have a dog in this fight.' The President would say to me once a week 'Tell me again what this is all about.' "[8]

V. Atlantic Confusion and Euro–passivity. For the first time since World War II, Washington had turned a major security issue entirely over to

the Europeans. In his memoirs, Secretary Baker is unapologetic about this decision: "It was time to make the Europeans step up to the plate and show that
they could act as a unified power. Yugoslavia was as good a first test as any."[9]

In fact, Yugoslavia was the worst possible place for a "first test" of a new
American policy to "make the Europeans step up to the plate." To be sure,
with the Soviet threat gone and Germany united, Europe had to begin to assume a larger role in the Atlantic partnership, as they themselves wanted. But
for over a half century Europe had been unable to "act as a unified power"
without American leadership. The Bush Administration's stellar performance
in 1989–90 on one of the last great Cold War issues, German unification, had
been one of the brightest chapters in American foreign policy in the entire century; without Washington's steadfast and visionary support, it would not have
happened, given the opposition of Britain and France. Yet only a year later the
same officials who had made it possible turned their backs on the first
post–Cold War challenge in Europe.

The Yugoslavia crisis should have been handled by NATO, the Atlantic institution that mattered most, the one in which the United States was the core
member. The best chance to prevent war would have been to present the Yugoslavs with a clear warning that NATO airpower would be used against any
party that tried to deal with the ethnic tensions of Yugoslavia by force. The
United States and the Europeans could then have worked with the Yugoslav
parties to mediate peaceful (although certainly contentious and complicated)
divorce agreements between the republics. But Washington did not see it that
way. As David Gompert candidly observed of his own colleagues:

> The U.S. Government's handling of the Yugoslav crisis from 1990 to 1992
> contradicted and undermined its declaratory policy regarding the centrality and
> purpose of NATO in post–Cold War Europe, [which] implied NATO responsi-
> bility to respond to precisely the sort of conflict by then raging in the
> Balkans. . . . Predictably, the attempt to hold the Yugoslav crisis at arm's length
> did not spare the United States the effects of, or responsibility for, the failure that
> followed.[10]

Europe's own miscalculation was equally grievous. It was encapsulated in
a memorable statement by the Foreign Minister of Luxembourg, Jacques
Poos, whose country then held the rotating presidency of the European Community (later renamed the European Union). "The hour of Europe," Poos declared, "has dawned."

The day after the war between "Yugoslavia" and Slovenia began, six days
after Secretary Baker's June 1991 trip, Poos led a mission of the European
Community "troika"—the Foreign Ministers of the previous, current, and next

presidencies of the E.C.—to Belgrade. Poos did no better than Baker. But the process revealed the disarray between the United States and the Europeans.

So determined was Baker to keep the United States uninvolved that he flatly rejected a proposal from Assistant Secretary of State Thomas Niles to send an observer to the talks between the Yugoslav parties sponsored by the Europeans, fearing that even such a minor action might imply a possible American role.

In this sorry sequence, Europe and the United States proved to be equally misguided. Europe believed it could solve Yugoslavia without the United States; Washington believed that, with the Cold War over, it could leave Yugoslavia to Europe. Europe's hour had *not* dawned in Yugoslavia; Washington *had* a dog in this particular fight. It would take four years to undo these mistakes—four years before Washington belatedly and reluctantly, but decisively, stepped in and asserted leadership, with European support. But this did not happen until after even more severe strain within the Atlantic Alliance, and historic disasters in Bosnia.

The Yugoslav-Slovene war started on June 27. It was short and, by the standards of what was to come next, almost a lark. Within ten days, after light casualties on both sides, Milosevic ordered the Yugoslav Army to withdraw. A few days later, at a meeting on the Adriatic island of Brioni, Dutch Foreign Minister Hans van den Broek, the senior European representative, presided over an agreement that effectively gave Slovenia its independence, but left the situation more explosive than ever. As Laura Silber and Allan Little put it, "The Brioni Agreement was hailed as a triumph of European diplomacy. It was nothing of the sort. It left every important item of contention unresolved. . . . The diplomatic triumph belonged to Milosevic and [Slovenian President Milan] Kucan, who had, between them, agreed on Slovenia's departure from the federation . . . and, in effect, destroyed federal Yugoslavia."[11]

The Kucan-Milosevic deal was a characteristic example of Milosevic's tactical flexibility and superb negotiating skills, and served his long-term purposes in ways not well understood at the time. Slovenia's departure from Yugoslavia made it easier for Milosevic to create a Yugoslavia dominated by the Serbs, since it removed from the country a republic with almost no Serbs.

Croatia, with hundreds of thousands of Serbs within its boundaries, was not ready to accept such an outcome. Croatian President Franjo Tudjman had long dreamed of establishing Croatia as an independent country. But the boundaries of his "country," drawn originally by Tito to define the republic within Yugoslavia, would contain areas where Serbs had lived for centuries. In the brief war in Slovenia the Yugoslav Army seemed to be defending the territorial integrity of Yugoslavia; when that same army went to war only a few weeks later against Croatia, it had become a *Serb* army fighting for the Serbs inside Croatia.

The Croatian-Serbian war began with irregulars and local incidents, and escalated rapidly to full-scale fighting. In August 1991, an obscure Yugoslav Army lieutenant colonel named Ratko Mladic joined his regular forces with the local irregulars—groups of young racists and thugs who enjoyed beating up Croats—and launched an attack on Kijevo, an isolated Croat village in the Serb-controlled Krajina. There had been fighting prior to Kijevo, but this action, backed fully by Belgrade, "set the pattern for the rest of the war in Croatia: JNA [Yugoslav] artillery supporting an infantry that was part conscript and part locally-recruited Serb volunteers."[12] Within weeks, fighting had broken out across much of Croatia. The JNA began a vicious artillery assault on Vukovar, an important Croat town on the Serbian border. Vukovar and the region around it, known as eastern Slavonia, fell to the Serbs in mid-November, and Zagreb was threatened, sending Croatia into panic. (The peaceful return of eastern Slavonia to Croatia would become one of the central issues in our negotiations in 1995.)

After exhausting other options, the European Community asked the former British Foreign Secretary Lord Carrington to take on the task of bringing peace to Yugoslavia. Carrington, an urbane man of legendary integrity, told me later that he had never met such terrible liars in his life as the peoples of the Balkans. As the war in Croatia escalated and Vukovar crumbled under Serb shells, Carrington put forward a compromise plan to end the war.

Again the United States stayed away. No American negotiator entered the effort; Washington's support for the Carrington plan was confined to tepid public statements and low-level diplomatic messages. In mid-November, United Nations Secretary-General Boutros Boutros-Ghali appointed Cyrus Vance as the United Nations negotiator, and asked him to work closely with Carrington. Because Vance was a former Secretary of State, many people believed the United States was now somehow involved—an impression the Bush Administration did not discourage.

The appointment of Cy Vance quickened my own interest in Yugoslavia. I had worked for Vance twice—first in 1968, during the Paris peace negotiations with North Vietnam, and again when I was Assistant Secretary of State for East Asian and Pacific Affairs during the Carter Administration. We had been close allies in the Carter years, and I had great respect and affection for him and his family. Vance was a born mediator. Even in his mid-seventies, he still brought intensity and meticulousness to his work, with enough focused energy to outlast people half his age. Furthermore, Vance brought to the table something Carrington could not offer—the possibility of a U.N. peacekeeping force in Croatia if there was an agreement to end the fighting.

The Germans Recognize Croatia. As the Vance-Carrington effort commenced, the European Community addressed one of the most controversial decisions of the war: whether or not to recognize Croatia as an independent nation. For months Germany had been pressing the E.C. and the United States to recognize Croatia. Vance and Carrington opposed the German position vigorously. They both told me later that they had warned their old friend and colleague German Foreign Minister Hans Dietrich Genscher, in the strongest possible terms, that recognizing Croatia would trigger a chain reaction culminating in a war in Bosnia. They reasoned, correctly, that Bosnia would have to follow Croatia's lead and declare independence next. Once Bosnia did this, Vance and Carrington predicted, the substantial Serb minority within Bosnia would then rebel against living in a state dominated by Muslims. As one Yugoslav later put it, each ethnic group would ask, "Why should I be a minority in *your* state when *you* can be a minority in mine?" War would be inevitable.

Genscher, the senior Foreign Minister in Europe, ignored the warning of his old friends. Uncharacteristically flexing Germany's muscles during a critical Foreign Ministers meeting in Brussels in mid-December 1991, he told his colleagues that if they did not support him Germany would simply recognize Croatia unilaterally. Faced with a threat of a public break in European "unity" just when the historic Maastricht Treaty was proclaiming the dawn of a new, unified Europe—a treaty whose prime mover had been German Chancellor Helmut Kohl—the other Europeans yielded to Genscher. To Carrington's annoyance and embarrassment, the British did not even send their Foreign Secretary to the meeting, leaving it to a deputy to represent London at this critical occasion.

The United States opposed the E.C. decision, but without noticeable vigor: as Baker admitted in his memoirs, "our central focus for months to come would be on managing the peaceful dissolution of the USSR."[13] Even the unfailingly polite and generous Warren Zimmermann was critical of his superiors on this point, later describing Washington's telegram of instructions on recognition "perfunctory, . . . enough to show we had done something, but not enough to produce results." The State Department's statement, Zimmermann wrote, was "weak and nuanced, [designed] mainly to avoid ruffling the Croatian community in the United States."[14] Washington itself would recognize Croatia a few months later.

In recent years, I have been asked repeatedly whether or not the German decision to recognize Croatia triggered the war in Bosnia. This question is complicated. On the one hand, I believe the German decision was a mistake. On the other, many other actions taken in 1991 by the outside powers proved to be more serious errors. In the end, while the German decision probably hastened the outbreak of war in Bosnia, the conflict would have occurred anyway once

it was clear that the West would not intervene. To blame Bonn alone for causing the war in Bosnia evades the responsibility of many others. Germany was
scapegoated for what happened in Bosnia by people seeking to deflect attention from their own failures.

Given Germany's history in the region—the Nazi associations with their
puppet state in Croatia during World War II, and the death camps in Croatia,
where both Jews and Serbs had died—Bonn's position also raised concern
that Germany, united for the first time since 1945, was about to embark on a
more activist, perhaps more aggressive, foreign policy in Central and Eastern
Europe. But I see no evidence for the theory that German policy was derived
from either its history in the region or a plan for new German assertiveness in
Central Europe. During my ambassadorship in Germany, I came to know
Genscher and many of his former Foreign Ministry associates well. They were
among the most civilized and progressive people with whom I have ever
worked. They understood the terrible history of their country under the Nazis,
and were deeply committed to making a democratic Germany the key to a
democratic and peaceful Europe. I felt—and so stated as Ambassador—that
with the end of the Cold War it was desirable for Germany to develop a more
active foreign policy, one that would be commensurate with its size and economic strength.

President Clinton, who had visited Germany several times as a student and
had studied German, welcomed Germany's emergence as a major participant
in shaping European policy. Better to work for the gradual re-emergence of
Germany as a European power, this time prosperous and democratic, he felt,
than to bottle it up and risk an abrupt reaction later.

Thus, while the decision on Croatia was wrong, its importance should not
be overstated. In fact, Alija Izetbegovic's remarkably bold statement to the
Bosnian Parliament on February 27, 1991—almost ten months *before* Germany recognized Croatia—foreshadowed the problems to come: "I would
sacrifice peace for a sovereign Bosnia-Herzegovina," he said, "but for that
peace in Bosnia-Herzegovina I would not sacrifice sovereignty." As Silber and
Little observe, "To the Serbs, this was a war cry."[15]

Vance got an agreement to stop the fighting in Croatia at the beginning of
1992. By February he had overcome resistance from the local Krajina Serbs,
gained Milosevic's support, and formally recommended to the United Nations
the deployment of 12,500 U.N. peacekeepers. Within days, the U.N. had voted
to send to Croatia the second-largest international peacekeeping force ever deployed.

It was a substantial achievement, but there was a cost. Almost one third of
Croatia now lay in areas supposedly protected by the United Nations but in

fact controlled by the Serbs. Ethnic cleansing of the Croats from these "United Nations Safe Areas" by the Krajina Serbs—who contemptuously proclaimed an independent "republic" on the same terrain—proceeded under the passive eyes of a thirty-nation U.N. peacekeeping force. Vance and Carrington had stopped a war, but the feeble U.N. follow-up left a legacy of pent-up Croatian nationalism that would explode in the Krajina three years later, just as we were beginning our shuttle diplomacy.

CHAPTER 3

A Personal Prelude

(1992)

With other men, perhaps, such things would not have been induce-
ments; but as for me, I am tormented with an everlasting itch for
things remote. I love to sail forbidden seas, and land on barbarous
coasts.

—HERMAN MELVILLE, *Moby-Dick*

A PRIVATE TRIP

ON MARCH 3, 1992, BOSNIA DECLARED ITSELF an independent nation. The
United States and the European Union recognized it on April 6. Backed by
Belgrade, the Bosnian Serbs demanded that Bosnia withdraw its declaration
of independence. Izetbegovic refused, and fighting began, first as local skir-
mishing. The war had finally come to Bosnia, and with such savagery that,
alerted by a few courageous journalists—notably Roy Gutman of *Newsday,*
John Burns of *The New York Times,* Kurt Schork of Reuters, and Christiane
Amanpour of CNN—the world woke up during the summer of 1992 to the
fact that an immense tragedy was taking place, as the cliché went, "in Europe's backyard." An ugly new euphemism entered the English language,
courtesy of the Serbs: "ethnic cleansing." It meant the killing, rape, and forced
removal of people from their homes on the basis of their ethnic background.
Both Muslims and Croats were targets of Serb brutality. But even with a new
United Nations peacekeeping force that entered Bosnia in 1992 to assist in humanitarian relief, the catastrophe only worsened.

Almost by chance, I began to edge into an involvement in the region. In the
spring of 1992, I saw the Bosnian Ambassador to the United Nations,
Muhamed Sacirbey, on television calling on the world to save his nation. Impressed with his passion and eloquence, I phoned him, introducing myself as
an admirer of his cause, and offered my support. Sacirbey thus became my

first Bosnian friend, although neither of us imagined that someday we would be negotiating together for his country's future.

Sacirbey was one of the bright hopes of the fledgling Bosnian government. Married to an American, he was until 1992 as American as he was Bosnian; his enemies in Bosnia attacked him for speaking his native language with an American accent. But when the new nation needed an effective spokesman at the United Nations, Bosnia's founder-President, Alija Izetbegovic, chose Sacirbey, whose father, a distinguished doctor in suburban Washington, D.C., was his close friend.

It was an inspired choice. The terrible television pictures from Bosnia were deeply moving, but Americans needed to identify with an articulate Bosnian who could personalize his nation's cause. I was only one of many who, moved by his forceful public appearances, offered help. Unfortunately, he was less popular with government officials in both Washington and Europe, who regarded him as inexperienced, even immature, when it came to serious policy issues. He loved journalists and television cameras, and often gave dramatic sound bites without considering their consequences. But he was fun to work with, and enjoyed a teasing, almost fraternal relationship with many Americans, including myself once we began working together in 1994. By the time he was promoted to Foreign Minister in 1995, Sacirbey was one of the two most important Bosnians with whom we dealt on a regular basis. The other was his archrival, Prime Minister Haris Silajdzic.

In the summer of 1992 all that lay in an unimaginable future. I was still a private citizen when in early August I received a telephone call from my old friend and tennis partner Winston Lord, who had been the American Ambassador to China,* and was now vice chairman of the International Rescue Committee, a private refugee organization on whose board I also served. Lord asked if I would be interested in joining an IRC fact-finding mission to Bosnia. Within a few minutes Robert deVecchi, president of the IRC, called: Would I be able to leave within a week?

THE FIRST TRIP

We left for Croatia on August 11, 1992. Our core group consisted of deVecchi; John Richardson, an Assistant Secretary of State in the Nixon and Ford Administrations; and Sheppie Abramowitz, an old friend and refugee expert whose husband, Morton Abramowitz, had served with great distinction as Ambassador to Thailand and Turkey and was now the president of the

---

* In 1993, Lord became Assistant Secretary of State for East Asian and Pacific Affairs, the same job I had held during the Carter Administration.

Carnegie Endowment for International Peace. The Abramowitzes and I had worked closely together on the Thai-Cambodian-Vietnamese "boat people" refugee crisis in 1979–80.

As we approached Zagreb, I started keeping a journal. Rereading it for the first time four years later, I was struck by how this trip shaped my subsequent understanding of the situation:*

August 12, 1992: We are going blind into a war zone, since almost no one has yet seen much inside the area, and then only in the last few days. We are going to try to get into the death camps that have gotten so much publicity, but this may be hard; it seems unlikely that the Serbs will let us see anything that further damages their already horrible reputation. . . .

ZAGREB: At first glance from a car, Zagreb looks like an ordinary Central European town, with an old section that evokes the Austrian imperial roots from which it came, and newer sections of ugly and banal buildings. At the Inter-Continental Hotel, we find the sort of scene that usually signals a story of high drama—an odd-looking collection of people congregating in the hotel lobby: a large man with a flowing mane of white hair; journalists; several Arabs or Iranians whispering to each other in a corner; military personnel in various uniforms.

August 13: After a day of briefings in Zagreb, I can see that the situation is far more complicated and more difficult than other problems I have seen, even Cambodia. It is the peculiar three-sided nature of the struggle here that makes it so difficult. Everyone says that most people did not want this to happen. Yet it did. Everyone says it must stop. Yet it doesn't.

The U.N. refugee briefing yesterday was depressing. Maps filled with the numbers of refugees in each sector lined the room. Our host, Tony Land, a bearded Englishman with a wry sense of humor and a keen sense of the impossibility of his task, gave us a fine explanation of the situation. But when we ask him about the prison camps, he surprises us. "We are absolutely amazed at the press and public reaction to all this," he says. "For six months we have seen Sarajevo systematically being destroyed without the world getting very upset. Now a few pictures of people being held behind barbed wire, and the world goes crazy. We have seen more deaths in Sarajevo than in the prisons . . ."

This turns out to be a widely shared view among the international field-workers. On one hand, they are right—the war is deadlier than the camps. But to the extent that television pictures rouse the world to attention and action—they are, for example, the reason we are here—the pictures of the camps will help Land do his job. . . .

Noon: The difficult trip to Banja Luka has begun. As I write this, we are sitting in a long line of cars and trucks at the Croatian border, about 60 kilometers from Banja Luka, on the edge of the "Serbian Republic of Krajina"—the Serb-controlled areas of western Croatia. The town just ahead of us has life in it, but

---

* The excerpts that follow are edited for repetition and digressions, but are otherwise unchanged.

an air of tension—little sound, no one raises their voices. A moment ago we heard machine gun fire, and smoke is rising in the near distance. Our driver has just nervously asked me to stop videotaping from our car window. The mood is subdued and edgy.

Five P.M.: We have arrived in Banja Luka after a trip across land wasted by war. There is no electricity in the town. Our rooms at the Hotel Bosna are small and hot. Heavy gunfire breaks out just outside the hotel. No one can see where it is coming from, and in the street people keep going, on bike or foot, as though nothing has happened.

Later: The afternoon begins with a scary incident—I am hauled out of my hotel room by Serb policemen because someone reported that I had illegally videotaped inside the U.N. warehouse. Stalling in my room for a moment, I quickly erase the offending footage and go with a young UNHCR employee to see a Serb security officer at the warehouse, Our interpreter-guide explains to the nasty-looking Serb security man that I am not a journalist, etc., and after an angry talk, everything seemed to be under control.

Our young guide illustrates the dilemma here. When I ask him what his background is, he says, "I don't know what I am." He goes on to explain that his immediate family (parents, in-laws, grandparents) is a mixture of Croatian, Serb, Armenian, Russian, Muslim, and Slovenian. "What can I do?" he asks. "I have three choices: to leave, to join the army, or to help people. I choose the third—for now. . . ."

August 14: An extraordinary day! It begins with loud noise and shooting outside our hotel rooms. We go outside to find armed Serbs conducting a "mild" form of ethnic cleansing right in front of journalists with television cameras. We tape the whole scene. At close to gunpoint, Muslims are signing papers giving up their personal property, either to neighbors or in exchange for the right to leave Bosnia. Then they are herded onto buses headed for the border, although they have no guarantee they will actually be able to leave the country. Some leave quietly, others crying. This is the end of their lives in an area their families have lived in for centuries.

After this terrible scene, which leaves us shaken and subdued, we pile into white UNHCR vehicles. A few miles north of Banja Luka, we begin to see terrible signs of war—houses destroyed all along the route. As we progress toward the front lines, the destruction increases. We encounter the occasional house left completely undamaged in a row of ruined ones—its occupant a Serb, not a Muslim. Such destruction is clearly not the result of fighting, but of a systematic and methodical pogrom in which Serbs fingered their Muslim neighbors. This is how it must have been in Central Europe and Russia a century ago, but now using modern weapons and communications.

We are guided through this horrorscape by a tiny and vivacious young Montenegrin from the UNHCR named Senja, who spent a year in Ft. Collins, Colorado, as an exchange student. Whenever we hit a roadblock, she firmly orders us to stay in the car and take no pictures. Then she hops out to talk our way past the awful-looking guards, lounging around with their weapons.

The men in this country act as if they would be impotent if they didn't carry guns. Weapons have empowered people who were until recently gas station mechanics or shopkeepers. I have never seen so many weapons on so many men, even in Vietnam and Cambodia.

We drive to Sanski Most, crossing a difficult checkpoint at a bridge. As we reach the local Red Cross offices, the most frightening incident of the day occurs: an angry-looking man in a sloppy uniform, wearing Reeboks and smoking a cigarette, starts yelling and waving a semi-automatic around wildly in our direction. He seems drunk. He wants to "borrow" our vehicle, then dump us at the edge of the town—or worse. After a heated argument, Senja insists we be taken to the local police station, where she tells us to stay outside while she goes in alone. For a tense hour we wait, watched with open hostility by the heavily armed men lounging in front of the police station. We worry about Senja, but finally she emerges from the police station, saying urgently, "We have to leave immediately. These people are very angry and very dangerous." And we take off rapidly for Zagreb, relieved but mystified. . . .

August 15: We have flown to Split. After checking in at a lovely resort hotel on the sea, we set out for a refugee holding area just across the Croatian border in Bosnia, climbing through a typical Mediterranean landscape, with steep rocky mountains, seaside houses, and small villages. The towns could be in Italy, just across the Adriatic, but the militia makes me think more of Lebanon.

We arrive in Posesje, a town just inside the Bosnian border. The refugee holding area is a dreadful mess. In a school and its grounds are about 3,000 Muslim refugees who have fled from Serb-controlled areas of Bosnia and were stopped by the Croatians from crossing the border into Croatia.

Under a broiling sun, with several women crying out their stories at the same time, the refugees tell us for hours of the ordeals they and their families have lived through. Women gather around to recount how their men are still missing, how they were taken away and never seen again. No young men around. It is overwhelmingly oppressive. We return, depleted, to Split.

For a change of pace, we go to the ancient Roman ruins, near the main street. At this time of year Split is usually filled with tourists, but now there are only a few, mostly German, who seem a dreadful, walking insult to the terrible events happening a few miles away. We visit Emperor Diocletian's palace, a small part of which has been converted into a church.

As we look around, an unforgettable scene takes place, in sharp contrast to the rest of the day. Two nuns appear and sit down at the organ. A young girl starts singing, rehearsing for a wedding. Her beautiful voice fills the little church, echoing off the ancient stones. We stop, transfixed. The horrors of Bosnia are both far away and yet right here. We cannot tear ourselves away. If these moments of love, family, and tradition could last longer, perhaps they could fill the space that war possesses in this self-destructive land.

August 16: Zagreb. Dinner is again at the buffet of the Inter-Continental, where we are joined by Steve Engelberg, an impressive *New York Times* correspondent. He offers some opinions: those who might replace Milosevic would probably be worse; Vance did a terrific job stopping the Croatian-Serbian war; there is a serious danger of a European Islamic radical movement if this war is not stopped soon.

NEW YORK: **August 23, 1992:** The trip is over. As always, New York's problems are so demanding that it is hard to get people to worry about misery thousands of miles away. But I do not agree with the argument that we cannot afford to deal with these faraway problems when we have difficulties at home. Such thinking leads to an unacceptable global triage. Our society is still rich enough to deal with the outside world, even after the end of the Cold War.

The trip had hooked me. Not since Vietnam had I seen a problem so difficult or compelling. I told Strobe Talbott, then a columnist at *Time,* that if there were a change in Administrations Bosnia would be "the worst kind of legacy imaginable—it would be George Bush and Larry Eagleburger's revenge if Clinton wins." Before the trip, *The Washington Post* and *Newsweek* had both asked me to write about my trip. I was now anxious to do so. The *Newsweek* article, in the issue of September 17, 1992, marked my first effort to propose a course of action in Bosnia:

By its inadequate reaction so far, the United States and, to an even greater extent, the European Community may be undermining not only the dreams of a post–Cold War "common European House" but also laying the seeds for another era of tragedy in Europe.

Not that such a dire future is inevitable. . . . If the Europeans and the United States act with boldness and strength, worst-case scenarios do not need to occur. . . . [But] if the war continues, and the Serbs succeed in permanently reducing the Muslims to a small state or "cantonment" within a Bosnia that has been divided between Croatia and Serbia, the immediate consequences will be terrible—and the long-term consequences even worse. In the short run, the Muslims will have been removed from areas in which they have lived for centuries, with countless thousands butchered, often by their longtime neighbors. Hundreds of thousands, perhaps over one million refugees will have been thrust into a world community already staggering under enormous refugee burdens in Africa, Southeast Asia, and South Asia. . . . Most observers believe that nothing is likely to deter the Serbs except actions that raise the costs of their genocidal policies to an unacceptable level.

What might this mean in practice? First, international (presumably United Nations) observers should be deployed along the borders and in Kosovo and Macedonia immediately, *before* fighting spreads to these two critical regions. . . .

Another possibility would be to change the rules of the present embargo on all combatants—which in practice heavily favors the Serbs, who control the old Yugoslav military-industrial complex—so that the Bosnians can obtain more weapons with which to defend themselves. . . .

Other actions, including bombing the bridges linking Serbia with Bosnia, and attacking Serb military facilities, must be considered. Such actions may well increase the level of violence in the short term. But since the West does not intend or wish to send its own troops into the war, it is unfair to deny the Muslims the means with which to defend themselves. . . .

Every day that the killing goes on the chances of preventing the long-term tragedy decrease. What would the West be doing now if the religious convictions of the combatants were reversed, and a Muslim force was now trying to destroy two million beleaguered Christians and/or Jews?

THE 1992 CAMPAIGN

In 1988, I had supported Senator Al Gore during the primaries, traveling with him from time to time. Although his campaign started late, it got off to an excellent start, but it ran into immense and, as it turned out, insurmountable obstacles when it hit the primaries in some of the key northern states, especially New York, where I lived through some difficult days with him, his campaign team, and his close-knit family.

I told Gore I would support him again if he ran in 1992. When he decided not to run—in large part because of the aftereffects of an automobile accident that almost killed his young son—I was uncommitted until several close friends began to draw my attention to Governor Bill Clinton of Arkansas, whom I knew only slightly.

The first was Strobe Talbott, who had been Clinton's housemate at Oxford when they were both Rhodes scholars. Strobe, a friend since he had covered the State Department during the Carter Administration, could not get involved in the campaign since he was still at *Time*—but his wife, Brooke Shearer, went to work for Hillary Clinton, and traveled with her during much of the campaign. Another journalist I knew well, Joe Klein, then with *New York* magazine, later with *Newsweek* and *The New Yorker,* who had written a series of columns drawing national attention to Clinton, told me the Arkansas Governor was the most exciting Democrat in a generation. The third was Samuel Berger (universally known as Sandy), a partner in a leading Washington law firm and a former colleague in the Vance State Department.

I met Governor Clinton and his wife, Hillary, at several New York events in the early fall of 1991, and introduced him at one. After a breakfast meeting with a very smart and, it seemed to me, very young aide named George Stephanopoulos, I called Sandy Berger and told him I was ready to support Governor Clinton in any way I could.

Berger predicted that President Bush would try to portray Governor Clinton as inexperienced and unqualified to deal with national security issues—a technique that had worked well for Republicans in many recent campaigns, including Reagan's 1980 win over Jimmy Carter and Bush's defeat of Michael Dukakis in 1988. To prevent this, Sandy wanted to form a small group to work on national security issues early. The core group Berger had in mind would consist of the two of us and his old boss from the Vance State Department, Tony Lake. Sandy thought that Tony, who was teaching at Mount Holyoke, would have more time available than either of us, and, if he took leave in the fall, might be able to devote all his time to the campaign while we assisted him. Lake was at first reluctant, however, because he was planning to write a book about the campaign, not participate in it. Sandy asked if I would call Tony and help persuade him to accept the challenge.

I was pleased to do so. Tony Lake and I had been close friends for a long time. We had entered the Foreign Service together in 1962, studied Vietnamese together, and served in Vietnam together. Twice in our careers, with his support, I had succeeded him, first as the aide to the Ambassador in Saigon, then as an assistant to the number-two person in the State Department, Nicholas Katzenbach, during the Johnson Administration. I had been the head of the search committee that had given him the job as the director of International Voluntary Services, a small private organization similar to the Peace Corps. He had made the arrangements for my wedding, in Saigon, in 1964; I was godfather to his second child. If we were no longer as close as we used to be—given the effects of time and diverging career paths after 1980—we had remained in constant touch and worked together for thirty years.

Shortly after our talk Tony went to Little Rock to meet the candidate. The meeting was a success, and Tony quickly got started.

The Clinton campaign message was, famously, focused on the economy. Still, it was not wise to leave Bush's leadership in foreign policy unchallenged—a mistake that had badly damaged Dukakis in 1988. To deal with this dilemma, the team proposed to Governor Clinton and Senator Gore a two-pronged approach on foreign policy. On the negative side, they would criticize the Bush record; we did not think it as invulnerable as was commonly believed. On the positive side, Governor Clinton would present positions that would show him as slightly more forward-looking than Bush. As this strategy took shape in the summer of 1992, the issue that presented itself most starkly—because it fit both parts of this strategy—was Bosnia.

The tragedy in the former Yugoslavia was suddenly emerging into world consciousness. About the same time that I made my first trip there in the summer of 1992, the world began to see shocking film of emaciated prisoners in northern Bosnia, looking at the unblinking camera through barbed-wire fences, scenes straight out of World War II—yet happening now.

Governor Clinton attacked. Criticizing the Bush Administration for "turning its back on violations of basic human rights" and "being slow on the uptake," he called on President Bush to show "real leadership" and urged air strikes, supported by the United States if necessary, against the Serbs if they continued to block the delivery of humanitarian goods to the people trapped in Sarajevo. President Bush fired back, attacking his opponent for a "reckless approach that indicates Clinton better do some homework." However, by early August, partly in response to the criticism, the Bush Administration had adjusted its policy, urging the United Nations Security Council to use force, if necessary, to deliver humanitarian aid to Bosnia. But Clinton pressed on in a speech in Los Angeles on August 14 (the same day, by coincidence, that I was in Banja Luka), promising he would "make the United States the catalyst for a collective stand against aggression." "In a world of change," he said, "security flows from initiative, not from inertia." None of this made much of an impact on the American electorate, but it got a lot of attention in Europe.

As I told Tony and Sandy, these were correct and brave positions, both morally and politically, and both men deserved praise for proposing them. There was only one concern, I said: Would *President* Clinton carry out what *candidate* Clinton proposed? Proud of getting Governor Clinton to take these positions, Lake said he was confident they would be part of the policy if Clinton was elected. With this in mind, after the trip, I wrote a memorandum to the candidates on August 23:

To: Governor Clinton, Senator Gore (through Tony Lake and Sandy Berger)
From: Richard Holbrooke
Subject: Former Yugoslavia

... Whatever happens the rest of this year, the next Administration is certain to be confronted with a problem of staggering political, strategic, and humanitarian dimensions. I therefore want to bring the following points to your attention:

1. The Bush Administration's reactions have been weak and inadequate. . . .

2. The attention of the press, the efforts of the international relief community, and the belated response of European leaders and President Bush may have slowed down the more awful aspects of the situation, but only slightly. . . .

3. Your public statements have made a real difference, especially in pushing the Bush Administration into doing more than they otherwise would have done. They have also been interpreted as a sign that, if elected, you will follow a more vigorous policy against Serb aggression, which is the right signal to be sending to all parties. . . .

This is not a choice between Vietnam and doing nothing, as the Bush Administration has portrayed it. There are many actions that might be done now, including: dropping the arms embargo against the Bosnians, stationing U.N. observers along the Kosovo and Macedonia borders. . . . Doing nothing now risks a far greater and more costly involvement later.

In the weeks after Clinton's election victory, I heard little from my campaign colleagues; people with whom I had spent hours were now closeted in transition meetings in Little Rock or otherwise inaccessible. Asked by a Washington-based representative of the Presidential Transition Task Force what I hoped to do in the Clinton Administration, I replied that unless offered the position of Deputy Secretary of State, which was highly unlikely, I would prefer to remain a private citizen in New York and undertake special negotiating assignments for the Administration—a sort of troubleshooter role. Ever since my experience in Paris in 1968 as a junior member of the Vietnam negotiating team under Averell Harriman and Cyrus Vance, I had wanted to test myself against the most difficult negotiations in the world. At this time, I said, the toughest seemed to be Bosnia; I would be interested in becoming the American negotiator for that problem, a position that did not exist in the Bush Administration.

In those weeks Strobe Talbott and Brooke Shearer stayed in close touch. After Strobe turned down the ambassadorship to Russia for family reasons, the President-elect asked his former Oxford housemate to serve as a senior advisor on relations with the former Soviet Union.* It was a perfect job for him; he had unwittingly been preparing for it most of his life, studying Russian language and history, and writing a series of important books on U.S.-Soviet relations. I helped him draft terms of reference that would give him a larger role than that of previous senior advisors on Soviet affairs, a position that had existed in many earlier administrations, but always as a one-person shop. With the Soviet Union broken up into fifteen independent nations, the existing Bureau of European and Canadian Affairs could not handle the extra responsibility. We proposed creating a separate office to oversee relations with the former Soviet republics, closely linked to the old European Bureau. Despite some grumbling from the bureaucracy, it was put into effect over the next year under his leadership and with the backing of Secretary Christopher.†

CHRISTMAS IN CAMBODIA, NEW YEAR'S IN SARAJEVO

In mid-December, Tony Lake called to tell me that he was going to be the President's National Security Advisor. People who did not understand our

---

* Brooke Shearer was named Director of the prestigious White House Fellows Program, which she dramatically revitalized and revamped, making it more engaged in current events and more diverse in its selection process. In the second term, she became senior advisor to the Deputy Secretary of Interior.

† Because the United States had never accepted the incorporation of the three Baltic states, Estonia, Latvia, and Lithuania, into the Soviet Union, responsibility for them was left in the European Bureau.

complicated relationship had suggested that Tony and I were competitors for this position, but the truth was otherwise. As Tony and Sandy both knew, I had supported Tony for this job. His experience as Henry Kissinger's assistant in the Nixon White House—a position he resigned in 1970 to protest the invasion of Cambodia—had given him the perfect background for this demanding job. Besides, as I told Tony, I did not wish to compete with him; I wanted to work with him, as we so often had in the past, always with success.

Standing in the kitchen of a friend's house during a New York dinner party, I congratulated Tony and offered him whatever assistance he wanted. When he asked what would interest me, I repeated my conversation with the official from the transition team, and mentioned Bosnia. We ended by reminiscing about the long road that had led from Saigon to his new job—the job of his dreams—and Tony closed by promising he would keep in close touch.

Feeling detached from the excitement swirling around Washington, I decided to make a trip unusual for the holiday season, but fitting my mood. I spent Christmas Eve in Bangkok, floating down the river on a restaurant-boat with a group of Thai officials and Senator and Mrs. Sam Nunn. It was one of those strange cross-cultural experiences Asia offers Americans: we sang Christmas carols and listened to a Thai businessman demonstrate his love of the United States by reciting to us, word for word, President Kennedy's Inaugural Address. The next morning I flew to Phnom Penh, Cambodia's exhausted capital, to spend Christmas Day with Tim Carney, a Foreign Service officer who had been assigned to work on the U.N.-sponsored elections. During the day I talked at length with the senior U.N. representative in Cambodia, Yasushi Akashi, who had done a fine job in a nearly impossible situation. At the time these were simply interesting personal conversations with friends, but they later took on another, deeper meaning: when my diplomatic mission began in 1995, Akashi was the U.N. Secretary-General's senior representative in the former Yugoslavia, and our previous association proved valuable. And Carney, who became Ambassador to the Sudan, would later be part of our planning team for the final negotiations, advising us on how to supervise an election just after a war.

After another day in Southeast Asia, long one of my favorite parts of the world, I left for Zagreb, thinking that perhaps no one else on earth in 1992 would spend Christmas in Cambodia and New Year's in Bosnia. As my oldest son, David, said, "Who else could possibly want to do such a crazy thing?"

First Brush with the Krajina. On December 28, 1992, the afternoon I arrived in Zagreb, I was invited to meet the Foreign Minister of Croatia, Mate Granic. This was my first meeting with a man who was already a key figure in the negotiations, and with whom I would later spend many hours. Balding, immaculately dressed, charming, and polite, he greeted me and almost immediately began to explain why, if the United Nations did not fulfill its obligations under the Vance plan and restore the Krajina to its rightful owners, another war between Serbia and Croatia was inevitable.

Granic seated me on a sofa—"in the exact spot where Cy Vance sits," he said, with obvious pride—and took out a huge map of his country. Then, in a controlled but intense manner, Granic described how the Serbs had used the Vance Plan as cover to drive the Croats out of their lands in the Krajina. "Over twenty-five percent of our land is occupied by the Serbs," Granic said. "Before the war there were two hundred and ninety-five thousand Croats in the Krajina. Now there are only three thousand five hundred. This is our land. This is our country. The Serbs have cut our country almost in half. This is wholly unacceptable to us."

Granic's mild, almost deferential style was in sharp contrast to his words. If the Serbs did not return the Krajina peacefully, he said, his country would have to go to war again. As Granic's hands moved quickly over the large map in front of us, outlining Croatia's "lost territory," it occurred to me that this must have been how the French felt about Alsace-Lorraine, annexed by the Germans after the War of 1870–71, until they regained it after World War I; as Henry Kissinger had written, the effort "to regain that region had sustained French policy for half a century."[1]

Granic left the impression that a war to regain the Krajina would take place no later than the summer of 1993. In fact, it would be two and a half years before Tudjman attacked. I would never forget that conversation, however, which first alerted me to the absolute implacable determination of the Zagreb government to regain every inch of their territory.

A Wooden Statue. While in Zagreb, I visited several refugee camps, accompanied by Stephanie Frease, a dedicated young American refugee worker from Cleveland who spoke Croatian perfectly. One of her parents was Serb, the other Croat, and until the wars began, she had lived in Cleveland almost unaware of the enmity between the two peoples. We visited a refugee camp in Karlovac, about an hour from Zagreb, where we listened to chilling accounts of how the Serbs had carried out ethnic cleansing in Bosnia. Story after story reflected the confusion of the Muslims; they described how some of the Serbs with whom they had lived and worked for decades turned on them in the summer of 1992. Stephanie struggled through tears as she translated.

Among those we talked to was a young man who identified himself only as a baker from Sanski Most. Suddenly, he fished a plastic bag out from under a thin mattress, and handed me two carefully wrapped wooden figures. "I carved these with a piece of broken glass while I was at Manjaca prison camp," he said, "to show how we had to stand during the day, with our heads down and our hands tied behind our backs." The small figures seemed to burn in my hand with their pain and intensity. Mumbling something about their power and beauty, I started to hand them back. "No," he said. "Please take them back to your country, and show them to your people. Show the Americans how we have been treated. Tell America what is happening to us."

When I returned to New York a week later, I took the wooden statues with me to an interview on the Charlie Rose show, and showed them on camera. Within days, the editor of *The New York Times Magazine,* Jack Rosenthal, asked to print a full-page color photograph of one of the statues, along with a short description of how I had received it. In 1993, the IRC reproduced it on a bronze plaque, which they gave annually to someone who had made a contribution in the field of refugee relief. The baker got his wish—and in 1995, the IRC honored me with the award.

Sarajevo. After the visit to the refugee camp, Stephanie and I flew to Split, staying with the IRC field officer there, then set out, on December 30, for the interior of Bosnia. We spent the day driving through the steep and rocky ravines that had always made Yugoslavia such difficult terrain for military operations, stopping frequently to talk to international relief workers—an inspiring group of men and women from many lands—and listen to stories of families torn apart by the war.

As dusk fell, we drove on to Vitez, where we planned to spend the night, look at refugee operations, and return to the coast. Once again, however, chance changed my plans. When we arrived in Vitez, there was a telephone call waiting from Lionel Rosenblatt, who by coincidence was at that moment only one hour away in Zenica, and had discovered that we were headed in his direction. Lionel was traveling with Sylvana Foa, the press spokesperson for the UNHCR. They were going to try to get into Sarajevo the next day, and asked if we would like to join them. Of course, we said yes.

Rosenblatt, the most dynamic person I knew in the refugee field, had ranged across the globe over the previous two decades, going wherever the problems were greatest—Cambodia, the Turkish-Iraqi border, Somalia, and now Bosnia—trying to rally public attention and support for the plight of refugees. His small nonprofit humanitarian organization, Refugees International, had made a name for itself by pressuring—or, not to put too fine a point on it, harassing—governments around the world into doing more for their unwanted refugee populations.*

---

* Full disclosure: after leaving the government in 1995, I became chairman of the board of Refugees International.

In order to get to Sarajevo the next day, we had to drive to Zenica that night. Under a moonless sky, on a sharp curve on the road between Vitez and Zenica, our vehicle hit a sheet of ice, spun a full 360 degrees, and finally bumped up against a dirt embankment only inches short of a twenty-foot drop into an icy stream. Catching our breath, we drove on to Zenica, where we found Lionel and Sylvana dining at the grimy International Hotel, seated among assorted military personnel and civilian aid workers.

To get into Sarajevo, we would have to travel through Serb-controlled territory in United Nations armored personnel carriers. Under the agreement reached between the U.N. and the Serbs, who controlled the road, we needed U.N. accreditation papers. Everyone else in our group had such papers, but I did not.

With his usual ingenuity and bravado, Lionel solved the problem. From his bag, he fished out a motley collection of mug shots and, after some deliberation, picked one out. Lionel, it turned out, carried a collection of pictures for just such an occasion. "This ought to do the trick," he announced as I looked in astonishment at the photograph, which I did not think looked at all like me.

In the morning, Lionel obtained a blank U.N. identity pass from another one of his many friends—he seemed to know everyone—and created a U.N. identity card for me, using a cigarette lighter to seal some plastic he had found. Watching Lionel's performance with a combination of admiration and apprehension, I thought of Milo Minderbinder, the character in *Catch-22* who sold eggs to both sides during World War II.

Equipped with this highly dubious identification, we drove to Kiseljak in our own vehicle. This was as far as we could go without U.N. authorization; the final stage of the trip, which crossed Serb lines, would be in a U.N. armored personnel carrier. After buying food at a store near the U.N. base, with the thought of giving it away in Sarajevo, the four of us jammed into a Danish armored personnel carrier; I sat in front, under a huge helmet, trying to look invisible. Four or five times as we proceeded toward the Bosnian capital we were stopped at Serb checkpoints, where men and women—some heavily made up for New Year's Eve parties—poked rifles around the inside of the APC and inspected our IDs. It was only much later that I realized how dangerous the trip had been.

The Danes dropped us off at the Post Office Building in Sarajevo, where the press and most international aid workers worked. As we climbed out of the APC and blinked into the weak afternoon sun, a black limousine passed slowly by, followed closely by a U.N. tank, painted white, and hordes of journalists. Looking through the heavily tinted windows of the limousine, I saw, but only for a moment, a tired-looking Cy Vance staring straight ahead on one side of the car, and U.N. Secretary-General Boutros Boutros-Ghali on the other. Vance did not see me through the dark tinted glass, nor would he have recognized me, in my heavy flak jacket and helmet, bundled up against the biting cold and caked in dirt. It was a strange feeling to see my old boss behind the plate glass of an armored car just as I arrived in Sarajevo in an APC—so close, yet so far away.

Two days in that hellhole left impressions for a lifetime. That winter, people burned their books and furniture (usually starting with the closets and bookshelves) to keep warm. Some food was reaching Sarajevo, but it was poorly distributed, especially to the outlying areas. The cold was biting and debilitating. It sapped one's strength so quickly that every other activity, such as collecting food from a distribution center, was extremely difficult. The shooting (small arms, machine guns, mortars, snipers, artillery) was almost continuous, and had a destructive effect even on the extraordinarily brave people of Sarajevo. The international community of relief workers and journalists was huddled in three miserable locations—the Post Office Building, the shattered and grotesque Holiday Inn, and the airport, all of which were under frequent sniper fire. Every street was littered with destroyed vehicles, lying on their sides and blown apart, and I saw not a single building that was not damaged. There was no running water anywhere except at a few outside locations, some of which were sniper targets. The Serbs had destroyed several parts of town, the Muslims others; in some areas the two sides were separated by only a block.

In the midst of this inferno, the U.N. agencies, including the U.N. military (known as UNPROFOR, or United Nations Protection Force), negotiated the content and size of each relief convoy with the Bosnian Serbs, who permitted about half of what was needed to reach the city, just enough so that the world did not demand decisive military action. It was as if the U.N. were negotiating with the city's executioners as to whether Sarajevo's death would be by starvation or freezing, slow or fast. By allowing the Bosnian Serbs to determine what got in, the U.N. had, in effect, become an unintentional accomplice to Serb policy. In its press releases, the UNHCR boasted about the amount of food it had brought in, not the inadequacy of the system or the rising death toll.

From my journal:

1 A.M., January 1, 1993, Sarajevo—As this strangest New Year's Eve reaches its end, I am in an ice-cold room at the Holiday Inn, with no water, one small electric light that goes on and off without warning, listening to the sound of sniper fire (or is it celebrating?).

This Holiday Inn has to be one of the most peculiar hotels ever. Its cavernous lobby/atrium is freezing cold, dark, and dismal. The upper stories are shot to hell, with gaping holes to the outside world. The upper stories are closed to guests, since the fighting inside the Inn left them in shambles, and there is still blood all over the rooms.

No elevators or service, obviously. We carry our bags up to our freezing rooms. We eat in the hotel dining room with John Burns of *The New York Times,* the very essence of the old-time foreign correspondent. I first knew him in Asia. He is courageous, maybe even slightly crazy-courageous, and just the man for a New Year's Eve in Sarajevo. Other reporters pour in, and the room gradually fills with a noisy, smelly crowd of smokers, universally criticizing Boutros-Ghali for his press conference performance today. He actually said he could think of at least ten places on earth that were worse than Sarajevo—a very peculiar and ill-advised statement to make anywhere, but especially here.

After dinner, Burns invites us to go with him to a local New Year's Eve party. Thus ends 1992, in a crowded, noisy, and very smoky place called The Hole in the Wall—because to reach it one has to walk through a hole in a wall made by a mortar round. It is crammed with young people dancing, shouting, drinking, and trying to forget the nightmare around them. A mixture of reporters, U.N. people, and young Sarajevans who work with them or know them. They dance feverishly to the Rolling Stones, throw beer at each other at midnight, and hug each other continually. . . . The girls are beautiful, but the whole thing feels hopelessly melancholy. Was this how the Spanish Civil War felt, a romantic lost cause?

Midday, January 1, 1993—At 7:30 we rise, don't bother to dress since we slept fully clothed; don't bother to wash since there is no water; and go down for breakfast—an excellent cup of tea, some stale cheese and two awful slices of bologna. A big storm is forecast. I debate leaving early, can't make up my frozen mind, and, after checking out of the Holiday Inn (cash only), drive in an armored car to the PTT, where we can see children foraging through the debris and begging in the freezing cold. . . . Automatic weapon fire can be heard frequently as we cross the city. We pass the newspaper offices, once a proud tower, now reduced to almost total rubble. But from the basement people are still putting out a daily paper.* A man sits in the debris of the one of the public buses, holding his head in his hands, presumably drunk from the previous night.

In a "soft skin" (an unarmored vehicle) we race to the airport, weaving across the bridge where sniper fire has killed so many people, snaking through checkpoints, past overturned trucks and buses, and over icy roads.

2:30 P.M.: We are still at the Sarajevo airport, waiting amidst growing confusion and tension. In the last hour, the British and Canadian planes have been cancelled; a U.S. Air Force plane refused to take us out; there are reports that the Bosnians are massing in the hills around the airport, and that the UNHCR has ordered the evacuation of all of its personnel from Sarajevo immediately.

As in Vietnam, much of war is mindless waiting, but waiting in wartime is strangely paradoxical. One's senses are sharper because of the heightened sense of danger, but at the same time, there is an extraordinary waste of time and effort.

---

* The story of this brave newspaper, *Oslobodjenje,* is told by its former editor, Kemal Kurspahic, in *As Long As Sarajevo Exists.*

Zagreb, later: Weary almost beyond description, we get out of Sarajevo, just ahead of nightfall. Our Canadian plane crew, obviously in a great hurry to leave, shovels us aboard. The crewman in the belly of the C-130 yells at us, "O.K. Hold on. We're going to do a zoom takeoff!" and quickly buckles himself in. The plane leaves the ground quickly but does not rise at first, hovering about six feet off the ground until almost reaching the end of the runway. Then, with a tremendous thrust of power, it seems to go almost straight up in the air, soaring over the hills filled with Serb snipers and, perhaps, massing Bosnian troops.

Landing in Zagreb, we head directly for the Inter-Continental Hotel. Never had a shower seemed so wonderful. I turn on the television and hear CNN proclaiming the start of a major offensive.

I returned to New York full of a sense that something had to be done rapidly. My friend Leslie Gelb, then a columnist for *The New York Times,* warned me that Clinton's team, in the midst of a delicate minuet about their own interrelationships, did not want to hear anyone's views on Bosnia. Anticipating this problem as I sat freezing at the Sarajevo airport, I had written in my journal: "If I don't make my views known to the new team, I will not have done enough to help the desperate people we have just seen; but if I push my views I will appear too aggressive. I feel trapped."

THE 1993 MEMORANDUM

On January 13, 1993, one week before they were to assume office, I sent a long memorandum to Warren Christopher and Tony Lake. It began:

Bosnia will be the key test of American policy in Europe. We must therefore succeed in whatever we attempt. The Administration cannot afford to begin with either an international disaster or a quagmire. Despite the difficulties and risks involved, I believe that inaction or a continuation of the Bush policies in Bosnia by the Clinton Administration is the least desirable course. Continued inaction carries long-term risks which could be disruptive to U.S.-European relations, weaken NATO, increase tension in Greece and Turkey, and cause havoc with Moscow. . . .

No one with whom I talked last August expected the Bosnians to last this long. . . . An important reason the Bosnian Muslims are surviving is that they are beginning to get significant weapons shipments from Islamic nations, apparently including Iran. These are coming through Croatia, *with Croatian complicity.** . . . Four key points about these *not-so-secret* secret shipments to the Muslims:

---

* All italics in the original memorandum.

—first, the Croats, who do not want to let the Muslims become too strong, have not allowed them to include heavy weapons or artillery;

—second, every weapons shipments has a Croatian "weapons tax"; that is, the Croats siphon off some of the weapons for their own army and for the HVO [the Bosnian Croats] in Bosnia-Herzegovina;

—third, there is now strong evidence that small but growing numbers of "freedom fighters" or mujahideen are joining the Bosnian forces, although, as one might expect, the strict fundamentalists from the Mideast and the loose, secular Muslims of Bosnia do not understand each other or mix well;

—finally, these shipments will continue—and they will increase.*

I suggested four objectives for the new Administration: first, "to save as many lives as possible in Bosnia"; second, "to make containment of the war a top priority"; third, "to punish the Serbs for their behavior . . . and to brand certain individuals war criminals"; fourth, "to use this crisis as an opportunity to strengthen the U.N. system." We should act, I added, "in concert with other nations," even creating "some sort of ad hoc military coalition, [but] avoid getting dragged into a ground war in the region."

At the time the incoming Administration was trying to decide whether to support peace proposals put forward by Cyrus Vance and David Owen, the former British Foreign Secretary who had replaced Lord Carrington as the European Union negotiator. The Vance-Owen plan proposed dividing Bosnia into ten "cantons," some of which would be Muslim-controlled, some Serb-controlled, and some Croat-controlled. It had been attacked by many American commentators as a sellout, another Munich, and a precursor to the breakup of Bosnia.

---

* When I wrote these paragraphs in January 1993, no one could have imagined that this matter would re-emerge four years later as the subject of numerous journalistic inquiries and six congressional investigations, and become a major issue again during Tony Lake's attempt to become CIA Director.

These investigations were premised on the theory that secret arms shipments to the Bosnians from Iran had *begun in 1994,* and that the Clinton Administration had somehow acted illegally in not stopping them. It is especially noteworthy, therefore, that the activities in question were already taking place two years earlier, during the Bush Administration, with the clear knowledge of American Embassy and U.N. officials in Zagreb, and were even mentioned in newspaper stories at the time.

The events that were investigated took place in April 1994, when I was still Ambassador to Germany, but in late 1996 I was asked to testify several times as to my subsequent knowledge. The United States had played no role in the covert assistance to the Bosnians and the Croatians, but when asked for his views by President Tudjman, Ambassador Galbraith, under instructions, had not objected. This was the correct policy decision, although it was sloppily executed. As I stated in sworn testimony before the Senate Intelligence Committee, the "covert" support given to the Bosnian Muslims by Islamic nations (including Iran) had helped keep the Sarajevo government alive at a time when its survival hung by a thread. For the United States to have continued to object to such assistance without providing something to replace it would in my opinion have been unconscionable.

There was already deep division within the new team about Bosnia. The Joint Chiefs of Staff, led by its formidable Chairman, Colin Powell, was especially opposed to American involvement. The Vance-Owen plan was flawed, but if the United States killed it without coming up with a plan of its own, the consequences would be far worse, so I recommended that Washington give qualified public support to their plan:

> If Vance-Owen leads to a temporary cessation of fighting and relief to the Muslims, and offers the new Administration some breathing room to put a [full-fledged] policy into place, it should be welcomed. It will not solve the problem, only perhaps let the world think it is solved for a while. If the Vance-Owen plan is rejected, we must face the fact that the negotiating track is effectively dead— and that using it as an excuse for inaction or insufficient action is no longer acceptable.

I ended the memorandum with a series of specific recommendations, actions that the United States should consider, especially if the Vance-Owen plan was either rejected or if it failed. This was the most provocative part of the paper:

> LIFTING THE ARMS EMBARGO TO BOSNIA: I favored lifting the arms embargo to the Bosnians before I visited the region, and am still in favor of it, if it can gain UN Security Council approval. But this might be difficult to obtain (and create strains with Moscow). . . .
> I would therefore [also] recommend consideration of something that I know will cause many people heartburn: that we allow covert arms supply to the Bosnian Muslims, *so that Bosnia's outside support no longer comes solely from the Islamic nations.* Such a policy requires sophistication within the USG, including Congress, and, if it involves the US directly, a legal finding. It would undoubtedly leak, as our support to the Afghan resistance leaked long before it was openly acknowledged. But this might be the best way to help the Bosnians *quickly* without provoking a new round of escalatory steps from the Serbs. It does, however, carry the serious drawback of showing the United States evading a Security Council resolution that it previously supported. This concern could be lessened if our actions were accompanied by public efforts at the UN to change the embargo, or if *we acted only through third parties,* as we did in Afghanistan.
> DIRECT USE OF FORCE AGAINST THE SERBS: Bombing the Bosnian Serbs and even Serbia proper if necessary would send the proper message. However, the actions must be effective, both militarily and politically! . . . If done only to show the world we are "doing something," minor bombing—like the enforcement of the no-fly zone—might be a quick public relations success, but it would be followed by a long-term disaster.

ESTABLISH AN AMERICAN DIPLOMATIC PRESENCE IN SARAJEVO: This would be a dramatic step to show the world where we stand. An American Embassy can be very small; symbolism counts.

KEEP UP THE PRESSURE ON THE WAR CRIMINAL ISSUE: This policy, while belated, is useful. Name more names. Set up a separate staff to create more pressure on this front.

No one replied to this memorandum. Finally, some weeks after the Inauguration, I called Lake to ask if he had received it. Yes, he said, they had gotten it; it was "useful," but it contained some suggestions that would "undercut us at the U.N." We argued the issue briefly, but hopelessly. I told Tony again of my interest in special duty on Bosnia, but he did not respond; a few weeks later the Administration appointed Reginald Bartholomew, the former Ambassador to NATO, as special negotiator on Bosnia.

CHAPTER 4

Bonn to Washington

(1993–94)

Life is lived forward, but understood backward.
—SØREN KIERKEGAARD

AN UNEXPECTED ASSIGNMENT

MY PHONE RANG IN NEW YORK AT 6:45 in the morning. It was June 8, 1993. Since the Inauguration, I had kept in sporadic contact with various people in the Administration, but not on Bosnia, an issue that was placing great strain on the new foreign policy team. In January, Peter Tarnoff, calling on behalf of Christopher, had asked if I wished to be considered for Ambassador to Japan, a country to which I had made almost one hundred trips. I would be honored, I said, to let my name go forward. I heard nothing further on the matter for almost five months.

There had been one exception to my disengagement from Bosnia. In February, soon after Tarnoff called to discuss Tokyo, I asked for a private meeting with Tony Lake. I felt obliged, almost compelled, to offer some unsolicited thoughts on Bosnia.

Tony and I ate lunch, served by a Navy steward from the White House mess, alone in his office in the West Wing. I urged him to press for a greater American effort to stop the accelerating catastrophe in Bosnia. He protested, arguing that while people were still dying in large numbers, "you don't know how many more people would now be dead if it were not for our efforts." I replied that this was true but irrelevant. Even if, as Tony claimed, the situation was better than if the Bush Administration were still in office, it still fell far short of what it should be, and of what the world had been lead to expect by Governor Clinton's campaign rhetoric, which he was once so proud of having written. Agitated, Tony said he was doing his best and asked me to be patient. The meeting ended coolly and inconclusively.

A few weeks later, Warren Christopher went to London, Paris, and Bonn with a proposal to lift the arms embargo and conduct air strikes against the Bosnian Serbs—"lift and strike," as the idea was termed. The European reaction was, predictably, negative. The Administration began to reel, destabilized by this rebuff and troubled by the deteriorating situation on the ground. As the chances of American involvement visibly declined, the Serbs became bolder. Croat attacks on Muslims also increased. Soon a war-within-a-war between Bosnian Croats and Bosnian Muslims broke out at Mostar and other multiethnic towns. Meanwhile, the press was flaying the Administration for its weakness. Although no one wanted the United States to get involved in a ground war in Bosnia, public opinion was divided over what to do. Deeply frustrated, Christopher publicly referred to Bosnia as "the problem from hell."

After Tarnoff's call in February I heard nothing but rumors about the Embassy in Tokyo. A delay of several months on appointments was not uncommon in the Clinton Administration, but it was disconcerting, and increased the chances of leaks. In April, Walter F. Mondale turned down an offer to become Ambassador to Russia and indicated to the White House his interest in Tokyo. On June 4, with the issue still undecided, Elaine Sciolino wrote a front-page article in *The New York Times* describing the awkwardness of a situation in which "two old friends and allies," one of them a former Vice President of the United States, the other a former Assistant Secretary of State, had been cast as "reluctant warriors in an unseemly contest that pits political eminence against diplomatic experience." Mondale, one of the most decent people I ever worked for, called me immediately to let me know how much he regretted the whole business. He ended by saying, "We'll all get through this thing."

"I have good news and bad news." I was still half-asleep when Christopher began the conversation on June 8 with uncharacteristic mischievousness. "The bad news is that the President has asked Fritz Mondale to go to Tokyo. [Pause.] The good news is that he would like you to go to Germany."

To say I was stunned would be an understatement. The idea of serving in Germany had never entered my mind, and no one had ever mentioned it as a possibility. "I know this is rather sudden," Christopher said, "but we need your decision as quickly as possible." In tongue-tied astonishment, I was able to ask only one question: "Chris, how did the President reach this decision?"

"I have no idea," Christopher replied. Then, with apologies, saying he had to board a plane, he hung up.* Thus began a sequence of almost accidental

---

* More than three years later, while I was researching this book, Sandy Berger told me that when the *Times* article appeared, Sandy knew immediately that the long uncertainty over Tokyo was about to end with the choice of the former Vice President. Hoping to see both of us serve the new Administration, Sandy suggested to the President that he send me to Bonn, which was still open.

events that would lead me, via a convoluted and rocky path, back to the Bosnia assignment for which I had once volunteered.

Curiously, even though it was only one hour by plane to the war zone, Bosnia rarely came up during my year in Germany. The issue was handled entirely by Charles Redman, a senior Foreign Service officer who had replaced Ambassador Bartholomew as the Bosnia negotiator. Although I welcomed Redman each time he came to Bonn, I stayed away from the process, barely glancing at the endless telegrams on the situation in Bosnia. I now felt detached from the issue, knowing I could do nothing further about it, and was immersed in my fascinating new job.

But all was not well in Washington. Bosnia was beginning to damage American foreign policy throughout Europe. The press was merciless in its coverage of the Administration. The pressure reached into the highest levels of the government, and in the fall of 1993, to my great pleasure, Warren Christopher promoted Strobe Talbott to Deputy Secretary of State as part of a dramatic reorganization that greatly strengthened the State Department's senior management. At the same time, less happily, Les Aspin was forced out as Secretary of Defense, ending a brief and difficult tenure in the job that he had dreamed about for such a long time. Tragically, his forced departure from the Pentagon turned out to mark the end of his impressive career; he died less than two years later from a brain clot. As Frank Wisner wrote me from India, despite his enormous achievements, Aspin's life was unfinished. His many friends could not think of Les—his clothes always rumpled, his quick mind always asking questions, his cheerful mood masking deep uncertainty and loneliness—without an immense feeling of sadness.

By early 1994, stories were circulating widely in Washington about growing problems in the Bureau of European and Canadian Affairs. In the spring both Tarnoff and Talbott called and asked if I would consider leaving Bonn to take it over. I told them that, having served as Assistant Secretary of State for East Asian and Pacific Affairs fifteen years earlier, I was not interested in returning to Washington for a similar job; I loved my job in Germany and wanted to stay at least another year. But Peter and Strobe kept calling.

Finally, in May, Talbott played his ace: both the Secretary of State and the President wanted it to happen. This dramatically changed the nature of the request; I believed strongly that if the man who had given me the assignment on the Rhine wished to take it away, it was his prerogative; a presidential appointee owes the President his complete loyalty in such matters.

After a private meeting with Christopher in Rome, I agreed to take the job on one condition: that I could chose all my deputies. I asked to delay my return long enough to complete a full year in Germany and participate in President Clinton's trip to Bonn and Berlin.

. . .

Talbott and Tarnoff had listed three priorities for the new job: revitalizing the European Bureau, shaping a coherent policy on the enlargement of NATO, and Bosnia. I told Strobe I had one major concern. There were about thirty people in the State Department with the rank or equivalent rank of assistant secretary; this level of government no longer carried the authority it once had. But, in order to succeed on such contentious issues as Bosnia and NATO, I would have to operate in a rather assertive manner. If I were to operate in a routine manner, putting process ahead of substance, I might make fewer enemies but would have less chance of accomplishing their goals.

When I laid out this "lose-lose" dilemma to Strobe, he laughed. "We assume you will be aggressive," he said. "That's why we need you. We'll back you up." This time it was my turn to laugh. "How long have you been in Washington?" I asked, amused. "Anyway," Strobe said, "*I'll* back you up—and you'll finally be part of *our* team."

The President Visits Germany. Ambassadors dream of a presidential visit during their tenure. Although it is a logistical nightmare, the security requirements beyond any outsider's imagination, it can make a huge difference to policy. It is an unforgettable experience; ambassadors can dine out for the rest of their lives on tales of chaos and near disaster, their own brilliance in preventing some terrible calamity, and their moments with the President.

At the time of President Clinton's trip to Germany in July 1994 I was still in Germany, awaiting Senate confirmation hearings for my new post. The highlight of the trip—and one of the highlights of my government career—was President Clinton's visit to Berlin on July 12. He was the first U.S. President to visit Berlin since unification, and I proposed that he and Chancellor Kohl walk through the Brandenburg Gate from West to East as a symbol of the new Germany. Once inside what was once East Berlin, the two men would address as large a crowd as we could assemble.

The plan worked perfectly. On a nearly cloudless day, Clinton and Kohl and their wives walked together through the gate and into a roaring crowd of over one hundred thousand people, many waving small American flags, supplied for the occasion by local businesses. President Clinton's speech was short and eloquent. Gigantic video screens, something unimagined in Kennedy's day, carried his face as well as his words deep down Unter den Linden. I saw Germans, including two ministers, with tears in their eyes as the President spoke in his passable German. It was probably the last great American moment for the people of Berlin, a city with an open love affair with the United States, which had given us some of the most memorable moments of the last fifty years: the Berlin Airlift, the Wall, the confrontation between Soviet and American tanks at Checkpoint Charlie in 1961, Ronald Reagan's "Mr. Gorbachev, tear down this wall" speech, and above all, John F. Kennedy's *"Ich bin ein Berliner"* address in 1963.

As the speech ended, the President characteristically plunged into the crowd, but the security lines broke down and almost caused a friendly riot. The Secret Service went into high alert and tried to rush the President back to his car, where Mrs. Clinton was already waiting, but he was enjoying himself hugely. Once back in the car, he said that Berlin had been one of the best experiences of his presidency, "the second-largest crowd, after the Inauguration, since I became President."*

"Well, then you'll let me stay," I said jokingly.

"No way," he replied amicably. "We need you back home. Anyway, you can't top this."

During the drive from the airport to the hotel in Berlin, and again the next morning, I spoke directly to the President about my new assignment. He made the usual comments about doing well, but he added something no one else had mentioned. "When you come back, I want you to get out there with the press a lot," he said. "You're good at it, and we are in real trouble." Hillary Rodham Clinton later told me the same thing in even more explicit terms.

Driving to another meeting in Berlin that day, I mentioned my conversation with the President to Warren Christopher, who said he agreed completely. But despite Christopher's comment, I expected difficulties. No question was more sensitive in the government than how to deal with the press. It was, in a sense, another lose-lose situation: keeping a "low profile" was good policy within the bureaucracy, but without public support for a controversial policy it would fail, and public support required making oneself available to the press. The risk was of being accused of seeking personal publicity, sometimes by the same journalists who had sought the access.

The European Bureau. After a routine confirmation hearing, I was sworn in as Assistant Secretary of State for European and Canadian Affairs on September 13, 1994. I passed up the large ceremony and reception that normally goes with such an event in favor of a very small event in the large front office of the Secretary of State, with just a few friends and family, and went directly to work after the ceremony.

Selecting the right personnel is 50 percent of the decisions one makes in a job. Do it wrong, and you will pay for it for the rest of your tenure, in ways both tangible and invisible. By then I had chosen Bob Frasure. I had to make

---

* This number was later passed on a few occasions, most notably during his extraordinary trip to Ireland in December 1995.

one more important personnel decision: choosing a senior deputy. Since assistant secretaries have to spend a great deal of time on the road, the senior deputy has to have the confidence of the Secretary of State and his senior aides. After some thought, I offered the job to John Kornblum, then the State Department's senior European hand.

Kornblum became my indispensable alter ego, able to take over issues I did not have time for, and an articulate spokesman for the Bureau's point of view when I was out of the country. John steadily gained the respect of the Secretary and his inner team, and when I left the government in 1996, the President and Secretary Christopher selected him as my successor. Later, they appointed him Ambassador to Germany.

My first meeting after being sworn in was on Bosnia, as was my last, seventeen months later. In between I worked on many other problems, some of which—like NATO enlargement, the Baltic states, Albania, Cyprus, Turkey, Ireland, and the turmoil in Central Europe—were both interesting and important. But there was rarely a day when Bosnia did not overwhelm every other issue, never a day when we did not feel that we were, at best, only one more disaster from the abyss. At that first meeting, both Warren Christopher and Strobe Talbott had said that they felt we were heading into a terrible new phase of the Bosnia crisis. They were right.

CHAPTER 5

From Decline to Disaster

(September 1994–August 1995)

> We stand face-to-face with the terrible question of evil and do not
> even know what is before us, let alone what to pit against it.
>
> —CARL JUNG

THE NEXT ELEVEN MONTHS WERE EXTREMELY DIFFICULT. Even as we made
progress on a wide range of issues important to the shaping of America's
post–Cold War relations with Europe—notably NATO enlargement and relations with the former Soviet satellites of central Europe—Bosnia continued to
deteriorate, raising serious questions about the nature of America's post–Cold
War commitment to Europe.

My first few weeks in Washington were dominated by NATO enlargement.
After intense internal debate, we forged a position in nine weeks, just in time
for Christopher to present it at the Foreign Ministers meeting in Brussels at the
beginning of December 1994. We announced that NATO would begin a formal dialogue in 1995 with all potential NATO members and other nations affected by the decision, including Russia. Under our timetable, no nation
would be invited to join until 1997, with actual membership slated for 1999.
The process would be careful and methodical—too slow for those, like Zbig-
niew Brzezinski and Henry Kissinger, who wanted NATO to accept new
members immediately, and too fast for those, including George Kennan and
Sam Nunn, who feared the effect of enlargement on Russia, and did not believe NATO should expand at all. Despite such challenges to the policy from
both sides, the Administration stuck to its original schedule for the next three
years—a remarkably steady course in the face of difficulties and objections
from both sides. In May 1997, in Paris, President Yeltsin signed the NATO-
Russia Founding Act, which established a new relationship between Russia
and NATO. Six weeks later, NATO formally invited Poland, Hungary, and the
Czech Republic to join, and kept the door open for other members later.

There were other achievements during my first year in Washington, including American-sponsored solutions or breakthroughs on several second-tier is-

sues that could have escalated into first-class crises. These included a serious Greek-Albanian border dispute and quarrels over political prisoners, and problems between Hungary and its two neighbors Slovakia and Romania over the treatment of their Hungarian minorities. Under American pressure, the European Union approved a controversial but important Customs Union with Turkey in the spring of 1995 and moved Cyprus into the first tier of countries to be considered for future membership. And under President Clinton's skillful personal touch, relations with Russia and its temperamental President moved steadily forward despite a series of sharp challenges.

But these steps toward an undivided and secure Europe lay in an uncertain and troubled future in the fall of 1994, when America's policies were facing great difficulties and challenges. There could be no time for self-congratulation over NATO or any other issue in the desperate nine months between November 1994 and the end of July 1995, as Bosnia went from low point to lower point, culminating in the terrible events at Srebrenica. The value of the Administration's other achievements in Europe would be dependent, after all, on what happened in Bosnia.

Pinpricks. At the end of November, the Serbs attacked Croat and Muslim positions in western Bosnia, using warplanes based at a military airfield in Udbina, in the Serb-controlled part of Croatia. This was a remarkably bold escalation of the war: not only was the use of an aircraft itself a violation of United Nations "no-fly" provisions, but these planes had crossed an international border between Croatia and Bosnia. From London, where I was at the time of the incident, I urged Christopher to insist that NATO destroy the Serb planes and the Udbina air base. The next day, NATO released photographs of large holes their planes had made in the runway at Udbina, and proudly announced that it had launched the largest air raid in Europe since the end of World War II. Twenty-four hours later it became apparent that the "massive attack" was simply a series of minor air strikes—later contemptuously but accurately labeled "pinpricks" by the press. The runway could be repaired within a day or two, and was. The United Nations, which had agreed to the NATO air strikes, reverted to its former passivity, and the Serbs prepared to wait out the winter before attacking again. It was a shameful moment that left Bob Frasure and me deeply distressed.

Sarajevo. In early January 1995, I visited Sarajevo and Zagreb. The trip gave me new insight into the political mess within Bosnia. The Federation—the Croat-Muslim entity that had been negotiated in Washington the previous March—existed only on paper, and friction between the Croats and the Muslims was enormous. Sarajevo itself was not under attack, thanks to a four-month winter cease-fire announced by former President Jimmy Carter after a hurried trip to Sarajevo and Pale in late December. But President Izetbegovic told me that the cease-fire had been agreed to by both sides only because of the difficulty of fighting in the winter, and he predicted that the war would resume with even greater intensity well before the four months ran out.

Izetbegovic presented an astonishing picture of determination in the face of his difficulties. Sitting in his unheated and ill-lit Presidential Palace, its *interior* walls pockmarked with bullet holes and broken plaster, its windows partially replaced by heavy plastic sheeting, he showed no sign that he would ever yield or move his capital to the safety of nearby Tuzla. That evening, Prime Minister Haris Silajdzic and I walked alone through the frozen streets of Sarajevo, as he told me of his youth in a multiethnic city where, he said, he did not even know the religion or ethnic background of his friends. "That city I knew and loved is dying because the West has not stopped this war," he said bitterly.

In March 1995, Tudjman insisted that the Serbs give up control of the Krajina, the border sections of Croatia that had been seized in 1991 and were now "administered" by the United Nations—an international presence that had become a cover for continued Serb ethnic cleansing of a once-mixed Croat-Serb region. If the Krajina region was not returned to him peacefully, Tudjman warned, he would attack it soon, no matter what the risks. This was precisely what Croatian Foreign Minister Granic had warned me about in December 1992, during my first private trip.

American and British intelligence had long predicted that if the Croatians attacked in the Krajina, the Serbs would defeat them. Secretary of Defense Perry and General Shalikashvili gave this assessment directly to the Croatian Defense Minister, Gojko Susak, in a meeting that I attended in Munich on February 4, 1995, telling him that the Serbs would defeat any Croatian attack, either with their own local resources or with support from the regular Yugoslav Army under Milosevic's control. Later, after the success of his own forces, Susak enjoyed teasing me about the Munich meeting.*

In March 1995, I flew to Zagreb to try to persuade Tudjman not to launch the attack. Tudjman not only agreed not to attack the Krajina Serbs, but said he would announce it publicly if he could meet with Vice President Gore the following week, when both men would be in Copenhagen for an international conference. A week later, on March 12, Tudjman and Vice President Gore met

---

* From my notes of the meeting in Munich with Susak: "A grim meeting. Perry told Susak that we continue to feel that his government was making a mistake. Perry suggested that his country was sliding toward war and it might not turn out well for them. General Shali warned him that the JCS assessment of the balance of forces was far more pessimistic than Zagreb's. My own instinct is that the Croatian gamble might pay off, although the risks are high."

in the chaotic atmosphere of a huge conference hall in Copenhagen. Logistics were a nightmare; at one point, as we moved from meeting to meeting, the Vice President almost bumped into Fidel Castro, whom he was trying to avoid. Gore told Tudjman that the United States strongly opposed the use of force to settle the problems in the Krajina, and Tudjman pledged that he would not attack—provided the region was returned to him peacefully. The Gore-Tudjman announcement was widely hailed as a step away from the abyss, and for the time being, war was averted. But in the end, the Croatian assault in the Krajina was only delayed, not prevented, and the American intelligence judgment as to what would happen if the Croatians attacked proved—fortunately—to be profoundly wrong.

The Frasure Mission. By March the "Carter cease-fire" had begun to crumble, each side blaming the other. Frasure was by now in the midst of intense negotiations with Milosevic that were enthusiastically supported by the Europeans. Several times he came close to a compromise that would suspend the U.N. economic sanctions in return for a partial recognition of Bosnia. But each time Bob returned home empty-handed. Finally, in late May, Frasure recommended that we back off and allow the new European Union negotiator, former Swedish Prime Minister Carl Bildt, who had just replaced David Owen, to take the lead for a month or two, after which we would reassess the situation. No one imagined that this short period in which the new European negotiator took the lead would coincide with some of the most disastrous events of the war.

A Personal Interlude. This may not have seemed the best time to get married, but on Sunday, May 27, that is exactly what I did, marrying Kati Marton, an American writer and journalist, in her native Budapest. It was a wonderful wedding, beautifully arranged and hosted by Ambassador Donald Blinken and his Budapest-born wife, Vera. We held the ceremony and reception in the garden of the Ambassador's residence, a building that during the Cold War had symbolized America and freedom to Kati and her parents, brave journalists who escaped from Hungary in 1957, after having been jailed by the communists before the Revolution of 1956.

Our wedding preparations were shadowed by the drama in Bosnia. Two days before the ceremony, NATO bombed Bosnian Serb positions in retaliation for the increasingly blatant Serb shelling of Sarajevo and the other "U.N. Safe Areas," which were anything but safe. The air attacks were slightly heavier than the previous "pinpricks," but not by any standards serious or sustained. In response, the Bosnian Serbs raised the stakes dramatically: they seized more than 350 U.N. peacekeepers and, calling them "human shields" against further attacks, handcuffed them to trees and telephone poles. The world's press was invited to film these men standing miserably in the broiling sun. Images of French soldiers waving white flags of surrender were broadcast around the world, to the horror of the new French President, Jacques Chirac.

The television pictures were appalling. That the world's greatest powers would be brought to their knees by such thugs seemed to me inconceivable. As Kati and I prepared for the wedding, I kept in close touch with Washington. A high-level White House meeting was scheduled for early afternoon on May 27; I realized with a start that it would be taking place at exactly the same time as our wedding.

A few hours before the ceremony I made one final call from Budapest to Washington, and was connected by the Operations Center to Madeleine Albright, John Kornblum, and Tom Donilon, Christopher's chief of staff, who were preparing for the White House meeting. Giving advice to Europeans, whose personnel were at great risk, was difficult for the United States, which had no troops in the field. The nations with peacekeepers in exposed areas, including the British, the French, and the Dutch, feared that any retaliation against the Bosnian Serbs would result in the murder of hostages and other peacekeepers, and sought to negotiate their release, an approach I feared would weaken the U.N. and strengthen the Serbs. I argued that NATO should threaten new air strikes if the hostages were not released. I closed the conversation with my colleagues by asking that my views be presented at the meeting. "I recommend," I said, "that we give the Serbs forty-eight hours to release all the hostages unharmed, and tell them that if they don't, we will bomb Pale. And then do so if necessary. I recognize that the Europeans will oppose this because they fear reprisals, but not one U.N. soldier has been executed, and the Serbs cannot be permitted to defy the entire world community any longer. I am convinced that they will cave if the threat is credible." The silence on the other end of the line suggested that my colleagues in Washington thought that, with the wedding only a few minutes away, I had lost my mind. "I'm serious," I said, "but now I have to get married."

During our honeymoon, as Kati and I tried unsuccessfully to ignore the Balkans, the Bosnian Serbs released the peacekeepers unharmed. But there was substantial, if circumstantial, evidence of secret deals between the U.N. and the Bosnian Serbs. The release of the hostages came in stages after a secret meeting on June 4 at Zvornik between the top U.N. commander, French general Bernard Janvier, and the Bosnian Serb commander, General Ratko Mladic. It was not clear what assurances, if any, the Serbs got from the U.N. commanders, but a suspicion spread rapidly that the Serbs and the local U.N. commanders had made a deal never to use NATO airpower in Bosnia again.

While Milosevic and the Pale Serbs said publicly that they had received such assurances, French and U.N. officials denied it. To this day, Washington has never been sure of what actually was agreed to, but after the hostages were released, the intensity of the Bosnian Serb military effort increased dramatically, with no further U.N. or NATO air strikes.

The senior U.N. official in the former Yugoslavia, Yasushi Akashi, who had originally approved the air strikes, told his staff that the events of May had "finally shown" their "ineffectiveness." This was a repudiation of the British commander in Sarajevo, General Rupert Smith, who had tried to put a more muscular policy into effect. U.N. Secretary-General Boutros Boutros-Ghali removed from General Smith the authority to ask NATO for air strikes and said he would personally make all future decisions on an individual basis from New York, thus further reducing the chances of more air strikes.

A debate now broke out within the Western alliance over whether or not to stay in Bosnia. Some governments with troops in Bosnia, including Canada and Great Britain, began talking openly of withdrawing. On June 2, an American pilot, Captain Scott O'Grady, was shot down flying an F-16 over Bosnia. He survived, escaping a week later to become, briefly, an American hero.

While Prime Minister John Major supported the continuation of the British presence, a majority of his Cabinet favored withdrawal before the beginning of another harsh Balkan winter. In France, President Chirac took a more assertive position. His much older predecessor, François Mitterrand, had shown the pro-Serb sentiments of many Frenchmen of his generation, steeped in the history of Serb resistance to Germany in two world wars. Chirac was different, in both style and substance; he felt that the situation in Bosnia had reached a dead end, and that the Western powers either had to strengthen their forces and punish the Bosnian Serbs, or else withdraw. Under prodding from Chirac, the British, French, and Dutch announced on June 3 the creation of a new Rapid Reaction Force to strengthen the U.N. in Bosnia. But it was not clear, perhaps not even to its creators, whether the Rapid Reaction Force was designed to keep the U.N. in Bosnia or to help it get out quickly. The existing middle ground, Chirac correctly perceived, was indefensible, both politically and militarily. If the British withdrew, the French position would be impossible. To keep the British in Bosnia, Chirac judged that greater American involvement and support were essential. If this did not happen, Chirac would support withdrawal.

Chirac thus put the Administration in a tight bind, but one that was important in forcing us to start dealing with the reality—that one way or another, the United States could no longer stay uninvolved.

OpPlan 40–104. As it happened, there was a little-noticed, but critical, exception to American policy against sending troops to Bosnia: President Clinton had pledged that American troops would be used to support a U.N. withdrawal. As the situation in Bosnia deteriorated in the spring of 1995 and many countries began talking openly of withdrawing from the U.N. force, the Pentagon and NATO completed OpPlan 40-104, a highly classified planning document that covered every aspect of NATO's role in supporting a U.N. withdrawal, from bridge building to body bags.

Immediately upon returning from our honeymoon on June 8, I asked the Pentagon for a briefing on 40-104. At first they resisted, claiming the plan was a NATO document, but finally Lieutenant General Howell Estes, the chief Pentagon planner, came to my office and laid out before Kornblum, Frasure, and me a plan that left us stunned. As Estes, who was not its author, told us, it was bold and dangerous—and had already been formally approved by the NATO Council as a planning document, thus significantly reducing Washington's options. It used twenty thousand American troops, some of whom were assigned to carry out a risky nighttime U.S. heliborne extraction of U.N. troops from isolated enclaves, an operation likely to produce casualties. As soon as General Estes finished our briefing, I rushed to Christopher's office and insisted that he and his inner team get the same briefing. When he heard it, Christopher was equally amazed.

General Estes's briefing convinced me that it would no longer be possible to stay out of Bosnia. To assist in the U.N.'s withdrawal, which would be followed by an even greater disaster, made no sense at all. Using American ground troops to fight the war was equally out of the question. Something had to be done or else a Serb victory, and additional ethnic cleansing, were inevitable. It was a terrible set of choices, but there was no way Washington could avoid involvement much longer. I still favored air strikes, but there was fierce opposition to this in most parts of the government and throughout Europe.

When OpPlan 40-104 came to the attention of senior officials, there was some confusion as to its status. Although President Clinton had promised that U.S. troops would support a U.N. withdrawal, he had never formally approved (or been briefed on) OpPlan 40-104. But it had already been endorsed by the NATO Council. According to complicated Cold War procedures that had never been tested, if the NATO Council gave the order to assist the U.N.'s withdrawal, the planning document would become an operational order, adjusted for specific circumstances. Thus if the U.N. withdrew, OpPlan 40-104 would trigger the immediate deployment of twenty thousand American troops in the heart of the Balkans as part of the NATO force. The operation, which would have an American commander, would be impossible without the participation of Americans.

The President would still have to make the final decision to deploy U.S. troops, but his options had been drastically narrowed. If, in the event of a U.N.

withdrawal, he did not deploy American troops, the United States would be flouting, in its first test, the very NATO process it had created. The resulting recriminations could mean the end of NATO as an effective military alliance, as the British and French had already said to us privately. It was not an overstatement to say that America's post–World War II security role in Europe was at stake. Clearly, we had to find a policy that avoided a disastrous U.N. withdrawal. That meant a greater U.S. involvement.

M. Chirac Comes to Town. Jacques Chirac arrived in Washington on June 14 for his first presidential visit, demanding American action in Bosnia. It was not for nothing that he had acquired the nickname "Le Bulldozer." He was direct, intuitive, and blunt where his predecessor, François Mitterrand, had been opaque, intellectual, and elegant. The trip was supposed to be one in a series of semi-annual U.S.-E.U. summits, and Chirac was accompanied by Jacques Santer, the new President of the European Union. But it quickly turned into a Bosnia crisis session and the rest of the agenda—including economic, trade, law enforcement, and environmental issues—was swept away.

The day began with the "pre-brief," a normally routine session to prepare the President, but it quickly degenerated into an angry and contentious discussion of Bosnia. The presentation given by members of the National Security Council staff was, in my view, misleading as to the situation, and especially the degree of American "automaticity" in assisting a U.N. withdrawal. When I started to offer a contrary view, the President, obviously disturbed that he was receiving contradictory information before an important visit, cut me off sharply. Then, as various people offered differing views, Christopher and I had to excuse ourselves in order to go to the French Embassy, where Chirac was expecting us for lunch. In the car, I expressed my astonishment at what had just happened. Christopher, much sobered by the meeting, agreed that we had to talk to the President again as soon as possible.

The rest of the day was chaotic. The President met alone with Chirac for well over an hour instead of the scheduled twenty minutes, while Vice President Gore, Christopher, and half the American Cabinet milled around in the Cabinet Room, chatting with our perplexed European Union visitors. Clinton then sent Chirac on an impromptu trip to Capitol Hill to see Senate Majority Leader Bob Dole and Speaker Newt Gingrich, hoping that he would be able to persuade the Republican leaders to give the Administration greater support on Bosnia. Chirac's meetings, while cordial, changed nothing. Then he returned to the White House for a small dinner, which we spent, for the most part, in conversation about subjects other than Bosnia.

After Chirac left, I stood in the main entrance hall, in front of the North Portico, with Christopher, Berger, and Albright. The President and First Lady danced alone to the music of a Marine Band ensemble that had played during dinner, then walked over to us. It was a beautiful June evening, and the White House exuded all its special magic. I looked at Christopher, concerned that we would lose the moment. The President joined us and broke the ice. "What about Bosnia?" he asked suddenly.

"I hate to ruin a wonderful evening, Mr. President," I began, "but we should clarify something that came up during the day. Under existing NATO plans, the United States is already committed to sending troops to Bosnia if the U.N. decides to withdraw. I'm afraid that we may not have that much flexibility left."

The President looked at me with surprise. "What do you mean?" he asked. "I'll decide the troop issue if and when the time comes."

There was silence for a moment. "Mr. President," I said, "NATO has already approved the withdrawal plan. While you have the power to stop it, it has a high degree of automaticity built into it, especially since we have committed ourselves publicly to assisting NATO troops if the U.N. decides to withdraw."

The President looked at Christopher. "Is this true?" he said. "I suggest that we talk about it tomorrow," Christopher said. "We have a problem." Without another word, the President walked off, holding his wife's hand.

I hoped that the day with Chirac marked a turning point in the internal debate. The President continued the discussion the next day on the flight to Halifax, Nova Scotia, for the annual G-7 Summit, which Canada was hosting. He began to press his advisors for better options; he understood how odd it would be to send troops to Bosnia to implement a failure. This was not acceptable; another way had to be found.

In late June, Tony Lake convened several meetings to consider the problem. He did not invite me, but other participants kept me informed. Disturbed by this exclusion, I consulted Vernon Jordan, one of the wisest men in Washington and a close friend of the President. I had promised Kati I would leave the government within a year; now I told Jordan that I was considering departure before the end of the summer. If Bosnia policy was going to be formulated without my involvement, then there was little reason to stay. Jordan reacted strongly, telling me that I could not "abandon Clinton" at such a moment of crisis. Jordan then talked to various people in the Administration, including the President and Christopher, and the situation eased slightly.

Meanwhile, events in Bosnia were moving faster than the policy-review process in Washington. As the Administration deliberated, the Bosnian Serbs attacked. This time their action would go down in history.

Srebrenica. Emboldened by his successes in intimidating the U.N. peacekeepers, General Mladic now focused pressure on the three isolated Muslim enclaves in eastern Bosnia—Srebrenica, Zepa, and Gorazde—that had been completely surrounded by Serb forces since early in the war. They had been designated as "United Nations Safe Areas" by Security Council resolutions in 1993, but there was nothing safe about them. A small number of U.N. peace-keepers had been sent to each enclave, but they were bottled up, unable to re-lieve the siege conditions of the three towns. By the summer of 1995 all three towns were swollen with Muslim refugees from the surrounding areas. Mladic decided to eliminate the enclaves from the map in order to secure the entire eastern portion of Bosnia for the Serbs.

On July 6, 1995, Mladic's forces began shelling Srebrenica, allegedly in re-taliation for forays into Serb territory by Bosnian Muslim forces based in the enclave. Three days later, the Serbs took thirty Dutch peacekeepers hostage. On July 10, they took the town, and the rest of the Dutch soldiers, about 370 people, became hostages. The next day Mladic entered Srebrenica and an-nounced that he was "presenting this city to the Serbian people as a gift." He added, "Finally, after the rebellion of the Dahijas, the time has come to take revenge on the Turks in this region"—a reference to a Serb rebellion against the Ottomans that was brutally crushed in 1804. Mladic's identification of modern-day Bosnian Muslims with the Turks of 191 years earlier was reveal-ing of his dangerously warped mind-set.

Over the next week, the biggest single mass murder in Europe since World War II took place, while the outside world did nothing to stop the tragedy. Mladic's forces killed thousands of Muslims, most of them in cold-blooded executions after the town had surrendered. Precise details of what was hap-pening were not known at the time, but there was no question that something truly horrible was going on. By coincidence, I had an additional source be-yond the official reporting to confirm our worst suspicions about Srebrenica. My younger son, Anthony, who was then twenty-five, showed up in Tuzla to assist the State Department in interviewing refugees. He had been working in a refugee camp in Thailand when Refugees International president Lionel Rosenblatt asked him to rush to Bosnia to help with the emergency. Anthony and Lionel arrived in central Bosnia in late July, just as the first desperate sur-vivors from Srebrenica and Zepa reached the safety of the airfield outside Tuzla. They were soon joined by Assistant Secretary of State for Humanitar-ian Affairs John Shattuck and Assistant Secretary of State for Refugees Phyl-lis Oakley.

With Anthony assisting, Shattuck and Oakley interviewed shell-shocked survivors of Srebrenica—and heard the stories that were to horrify the world: how the Serbs, directed by General Mladic, had rounded up all the Muslims in the town and piled them onto buses; how most of the men were never seen again; how people were herded into a soccer field and killed in large numbers; how there were still men in the thousands trying to escape through the woods toward Tuzla. Then Shattuck and Oakley returned to Washington to press the government to greater action. Anthony stayed in Tuzla, calling me regularly with vivid stories of the continuing drama. Several times, in his characteristically blunt and passionate style, Anthony yelled into the phone that Washington had to do something, that I should "get my ass in gear." In fact, I had spent long hours unsuccessfully trying to find a way to stop the tragedy in Srebrenica and Zepa. My recommendation—to use airpower against the Bosnian Serbs in other parts of the country, as well as Srebrenica—had been rejected by the Western European nations that had troops at risk in Bosnia, and by the Pentagon. On July 13, the same day the Serbs began killing Muslims systematically in the soccer stadium, Chirac called President Clinton. He said that something had to be done, and proposed that American helicopters carry French troops into Srebrenica to relieve the town. This proposal had already been discussed through official French channels, and run into fierce opposition not only from the British and the Pentagon, but from Chirac's own generals. It had no chance of acceptance.

There was no more energy left in the international system. Everywhere one turned, there was a sense of confusion in the face of Bosnian Serb brutality. The first line of resistance to any action was the Dutch government, which refused to allow air strikes until all its soldiers were out of Bosnia. Through every channel available, in London, Paris, and NATO headquarters, we pressed for some response. It was useless. For a week I called our Ambassador in the Netherlands, Terry Dornbush, instructing him to press the Dutch to allow air strikes, but to no avail. The other Europeans had reached their limits; with their own soldiers also at risk, they were not going to agree to any action that endangered the Dutch. The Serbs knew this, and held the bulk of the Dutch forces captive in the U.N. compound at the nearby village of Potocari until they had finished their dirty work at Srebrenica. According to the International Committee of the Red Cross, the death toll of Bosnian Muslims in Srebrenica between July 12 and July 16, 1995, was 7,079. Most of the victims were unarmed, and most died in ambushes and mass executions. For sheer intensity, nothing in the war had matched, or ever would match, Srebrenica. The name would become part of the language of the horrors of modern war, alongside Lidice, Oradour, Babi Yar, and the Katyn Forest.

The London Conference. The destruction of Srebrenica was an enormous shock to the Western alliance. But there was more in that terrible month. On July 19, emboldened by the events in eastern Bosnia, the Krajina Serbs attacked the Muslim enclave in the farthest corner of northwestern Bosnia, the Bihac pocket. Bihac, an agricultural area jutting deep into Croatia, had been cut off from Sarajevo throughout the war, but it was less than an hour by car from Zagreb, and its fall would have changed the balance in Croatia and made Croatian recapture of the Krajina much more difficult.

The war was escalating dangerously. In the east, the last two enclaves, Zepa and Gorazde, lay open to Mladic's rampaging forces. In the far northwest, Bihac seemed about to be cut in half. Tudjman was preparing to reopen the war in the Krajina, despite the agreement he had reached with Vice President Gore and me in March. Sarajevo was under renewed attack. Washington was still uncertain about what to do next. After judging Srebrenica the "worst humiliation for the Western democracies since the 1930s," Speaker Gingrich offered an unhelpful view. "There are twenty ways to solve this problem without involving a single American directly in this thing," he said. I agreed with his assessment of Srebrenica, but could not imagine any of the "twenty ways" that Gingrich said he had in mind.

Chirac complained publicly that France was "alone," and added, "We can't imagine that the U.N. force will remain only to observe, and to be, in a way, accomplices in the situation. If that is the case, it is better to withdraw." Chirac did not mention, of course, that the U.N. forces were commanded by a French general. Prime Minister John Major publicly rejected Chirac's continued proposals to relieve Srebrenica and reinforce Gorazde. Instead, Major proposed an international "crisis meeting" that he would chair in London on July 21.

Washington reacted with a flurry of activity. General Shalikashvili rushed to Europe to meet his NATO counterparts, and then joined Christopher and Perry in London for Major's conference. To my great frustration, I could not attend the London meeting because of a serious ear infection. Grounded by the chief State Department medical officer, I watched from Washington as Christopher and Perry struggled to give the U.N. force in Bosnia greater authority—indeed, to head off a U.N. withdrawal.

The London conference was one of those remarkable events in which something unexpectedly positive emerges from an initially unpromising idea. The British did not have a clear goal for the conference, nor did the United States when Christopher and Perry accepted the invitation. But in that dreadful month of July 1995, when the situation in Bosnia was at its low ebb, the very act of bringing together all the Foreign and Defense Ministers of NATO, as well as the Russians, produced its own result, which was to play an important role in the eleventh-hour revival of NATO.

The conclusions of the London conference were not drafted until Christopher was airborne. But by the time he landed in London, his team—Chief of Staff Tom Donilon, John Kornblum, Bob Frasure, and Policy Planning Director Jim Steinberg—had produced a document with two important policy changes:

- First, NATO would draw "a line in the sand"—the evocation of President Bush's 1990–91 language on Iraq was deliberate—around the enclave of Gorazde.

- Second, the decision as to whether or not to use airpower, and how much, at Gorazde, would be made by NATO only, thus removing the U.N. from its dreadful "dual key" authority in regard to Gorazde—but not other parts of Bosnia.*

But in London, Christopher found initial reluctance on the part of the Europeans to such measures. In two private meetings with Prime Minister Major, he took a tough line. He found a partial ally in the new Foreign Secretary, Malcolm Rifkind, and the new Defense Minister, Michael Portillo, who overruled their subordinates and accepted Christopher's draft. Because it identified a place where NATO would make its final stand, London was an important benchmark, a sort of bottoming out at the last possible moment. Bill Perry later put a framed photograph of himself, Christopher, and Shalikashvili taken during the conference in a place of honor in his office, and labeled it "Turning Point." But that could not be foreseen at the time. The results in London were understandably greeted with skepticism by a world just beginning to learn what had happened in Srebrenica and familiar with earlier Western assertions of resolve that had evaporated before the cruelty of the Bosnian Serbs.

London did not go as far as many, including myself, wanted. For one thing, it doomed Zepa, now directly in the path of the Bosnian Serb Army. In addition, neither Sarajevo nor Bihac was yet covered by the new tough language. (This was partially corrected by General Joulwan and our Ambassador to NATO, Robert Hunter, who, in a tumultuous all-night session a few days later, forced the NATO Council to broaden the terms of engagement to include Sarajevo.)

The Croatian Offensive. In early August, the Croatians launched a major offensive to retake the Krajina. It was a dramatic gamble by President Tudjman—and it paid off. When it finally took place—still against American recommendations—the offensive was a complete success. The Krajina Serbs unexpectedly gave up their "capital," Knin, without a fight. President Tudjman had won his bet: contrary to American and British predictions, Milosevic had not come to the aid of the Krajina Serbs. For the first time in four years, the Serbs had suffered a military setback.

The Croatian offensive proved to be a wedge issue that divided not only Americans and Europeans, but the top echelons of the American government

---

* This was a system that required both the United Nations and NATO to "turn the key" to authorize NATO air strikes. In practice, the "dual key" was a "dual veto."

itself. Most officials saw these military thrusts as simply another chapter in the dreary story of fighting and bloodshed in the region. They felt that the duty of our diplomacy was to put a stop to the fighting, regardless of what was happening on the ground. For me, however, the success of the Croatian (and later, in similar circumstances, the Bosnian-Croat Federation) offensive was a classic illustration of the fact that the shape of the diplomatic landscape will usually reflect the balance of forces on the ground. In concrete terms, this meant that as diplomats we could not expect the Serbs to be conciliatory at the negotiating table as long as they had experienced nothing but success on the battlefield.

Zagreb's almost uncontested victory began to change the balance of power in the region. The abandonment of the Croatian Serbs by Milosevic eliminated one of our greatest fears—that Belgrade would re-enter the war.

Joe Kruzel reflected the general view of our team in his last message to Washington, sent the night before he died. "For the first time," he wrote, "I realize how much the Croatian offensive in the Krajina has profoundly changed the nature of the Balkan game and thus our diplomatic offensive."

Bob Frasure had also shared this view. At our lunch with President Tudjman in Zagreb on August 17, two days before the Mount Igman tragedy, one member of our team tried to persuade Tudjman that he should halt the offensive immediately, as Washington wanted. Frasure passed me a note written on his place card, which I saved and later gave to his wife, Katharina—it was the last note I ever got from him:

Dick: We "hired" these guys to be our junkyard dogs because we were desperate. We need to try to "control" them. But this is no time to get squeamish about things. This is the first time the Serb wave has been reversed. That is essential for us to get stability, so we can get out.

This view was not accepted by most of our Washington colleagues, especially the military and the CIA, which still feared, and predicted, a military response from the regular Yugoslav Army. The true importance of the Croatian offensive was thus not taken into account during the policy review that occurred in Washington in early August, well before our shuttle began so tragically.

The Policy Review and the Seven-Point Initiative. In early August, the President chaired three meetings in three days on Bosnia. Christopher was in Asia, and I was traveling in the western states with Kati. Tarnoff and Talbott represented the State Department and kept me closely informed. Finally, the President decided on a two-stage strategy: First, Lake and Tarnoff would go to seven European nations, including Russia, as presidential emissaries, and present a framework for peace. Then I would begin a last-ditch, all-out negotiating effort.

The Lake-Tarnoff presentation was produced through the usual interagency drafting process. My absence from Washington was later to result in a flurry of press speculation that I had been cut out, but in fact I'd deliberately remained at a distance, not only because of my family commitments, but also because participating might have reduced my negotiating flexibility later.

The final product contained seven points, ranging from the general to the specific. It called for (1) a "comprehensive peace settlement"; (2) three-way recognition among Bosnia-Herzegovina, Croatia, and the Federal Republic of Yugoslavia (Serbia and Montenegro); (3) the full lifting of all economic sanctions against Yugoslavia if a settlement was reached, and an American-backed program to equip and train the Croat-Muslim Federation forces if there was a settlement; (4) the peaceful return to Croatia of eastern Slavonia—the tiny, oil-rich sliver of Croatian land on the Serbian border that had been seized by the Serbs; (5) an all-out effort to pursue a cease-fire or an end to all offensive operations; (6) a reaffirmation of support for the so-called Contact Group plan agreed to in June 1994 by the Foreign Ministers of the United States, Great Britain, France, Germany, and Russia—dividing Bosnia into two entities, 49 percent of the land going to the Bosnian Serbs, 51 percent to the Croat-Muslim Federation; and (7) a comprehensive program for regional economic reconstruction.

By sending his National Security Advisor, the President, who had been criticized for excessive detachment from Bosnia policy, was saying: this is it—the real, and perhaps last, American push for peace. I had little difficulty with the broad outlines of the initiative. But several specific aspects of the proposals troubled me. I decided to hold off on making my views known until after the completion of Lake's trip to Europe.

The "Handoff." Strobe and Peter had warned me to be prepared to cut my trip short, and on Saturday, August 12, after only a few days in Colorado, I returned to Washington, repacked my bags, and left for London, where Lake and his team were waiting. On August 14, I arrived in London for a "handoff" meeting in the American Embassy. For the first hour we met alone.

The meeting was quietly emotional. Tony and I had been linked by close personal and professional ties through five Administrations. "This is the kind of thing we dreamed of doing together thirty years ago when we started out in Vietnam," Tony began in a low, intense voice. "I'm going to be with you all the way. And if this thing fails, it's my ass more than yours."

Tony briefed me on his talks with the allies and the Russians, which had gone well. They were pleased that the President was engaged so deeply. I told him that the framework he had proposed in his tour of Europe was fine, with an important exception: I could support neither his proposal to give the Serbs a wider corridor of land at Posavina nor the suggestion that we abandon Gorazde. Both of these ideas had been part of an attempt to create "more viable borders" for the Federation by trading Muslim enclaves for Serb concessions elsewhere. The Pentagon insisted it would not defend enclaves and slivers of land if it were called upon later to implement a peace agreement. Nonetheless, I told Tony that the United States could not be party to such a proposal. "This would create another forty thousand or more refugees," I said, "and we cannot be a party to that, especially after Srebrenica." Tony asked if it was not true that Izetbegovic had once told me he knew that all three eastern enclaves were not viable and would have to be given up. Izetbegovic had, in fact, made such a statement to me earlier in the year, but that was before the loss and horrors of Srebrenica and Zepa. "A trade is no longer possible," I said. "After Srebrenica, we cannot propose such a thing." After another meeting with the rest of our team and a call on several senior British officials, we shook hands warmly and parted, Tony and Sandy Vershbow heading west and home to Washington. Our team—General Clark, Rosemarie Pauli, Bob Frasure, Joe Kruzel, and Nelson Drew—flew to the Balkans to begin the negotiations that we hoped would end the war.

BOOK TWO

THE SHUTTLE

(August 22–October 31, 1995)

Tonight a scrambling decade ends,
And strangers, enemies and friends
Stand once more puzzled underneath
The signpost on the barren heath
Where the rough mountain track divides
To silent valleys on all sides,
Endeavouring to decipher what
Is written on it but cannot,
Nor guess in what direction lies
The overhanging precipice.
Far down below them whence they came
Still flickers feebly a red flame,
A tiny glow in the great void
Where an existence was destroyed;
And now and then a nature turns
To look where her whole system burns
And with a last defiant groan
Shudders her future into stone.

—W. H. AUDEN, *New Year Letter*

CHAPTER 6

Pale's Challenge

(August 22–28)

The inscrutability of history remains the salvation of human freedom and of human responsibility. The failure of prediction permits us to act as if our choices make a difference. For no one can prove that they don't, and there is no other way that we can vindicate human dignity and contrive a moral existence.

—ARTHUR SCHLESINGER, JR.[1]

AT 10:00 A.M. ON AUGUST 22, the day after our return from Sarajevo, Secretary Christopher convened his senior team to discuss Bosnia. As usual, we met in his working office, a small room directly behind his large, formal office on the seventh floor. When I first visited the State Department during college spring break in 1961—a trip that inspired me to join the Foreign Service the following year—Dean Rusk used the large room as his office, but most recent secretaries of state preferred the more intimate surroundings of the back office, and Christopher used the ornate larger room almost entirely for formal meetings with foreign officials.

Although the State Department's unique bureaucratic culture has survived every one of its leaders (and defeated some), the personal style of each secretary deeply affects the way the Department reacts to events. Warren Christopher's style was methodical and cautious. He was, as the press often said, a lawyer's lawyer. He rarely talked about himself, but once offered a revealing comment to a journalist about his style: "I always thought that I would do things in a conservative way to maximize the progressiveness of my policy positions. . . . If you are courteous and prudent, you can advance causes and advance ideas that would be unacceptable for others."[2] Highly successful in his Los Angeles legal practice, he went to Washington in 1977 as Deputy Secretary of State to Cyrus Vance, and carried out a number of key assignments, most famously the complex negotiations over the release of the fifty-two American hostages in Tehran at the end of the Carter Administration. Unfailingly polite, adept at concealing any annoyance or impatience that he might be feeling, Christopher preferred to let others take the lead in recommending a course of action, while he focused on the risks it entailed. As a result, those advising him often divided into two groups: advocates of action, and "doubting Thomases" who argued the dangers of the proposed policy.

Christopher reached his conclusions only after careful deliberations, which included not only the substantive officials responsible for the issue, but a core group of trusted senior aides who sat in on almost every discussion. He would listen quietly, ask a few clarifying questions, more in the style of a judge than an advocate, and generally withhold his views until the end of the discussion. When he took a strong stand on an issue, he carried great weight within the government.

That morning, August 22, Christopher's core team crowded into the meeting. Peter Tarnoff, Chief of Staff Tom Donilon, and Director of Policy Planning James Steinberg squeezed side by side on the sofa; others, including Strobe Talbott, Wendy Sherman, who held the critical position of Assistant Secretary for Legislative Affairs, and my senior deputy, John Kornblum, took seats on the chairs scattered around the small room. Latecomers sat on a narrow bench under a window that overlooked the Potomac and the Lincoln Memorial. Christopher sat, as always, behind his desk in the corner, sometimes leaning back against the bookcases, but usually taking careful notes on a legal pad. I sat in the chair closest to Christopher's desk, which was by custom saved for the primary action officer in the meeting.

The mood was understandably subdued. Our first need was to assemble a new team. I said that Christopher Hill, the brilliant, fearless, and argumentative country director for the Balkans, was ready to take the place of his good friend Bob Frasure, as we had planned before the accident. We left the designation of the NSC and Defense representatives to Lake and Perry.

Christopher noted that we lacked the legal expertise that would be essential if the negotiations got serious. He suggested adding to the team Roberts Owen, a distinguished Washington lawyer. Bob Owen, whom I had known since he had served as the Legal Advisor to the State Department during the Carter Administration, was calm, witty, and always cheerfully ready for the most demanding tasks, though he was almost seventy. Everyone marveled at his eternal youthfulness; he looked at least ten years younger than his age. Christopher's inspired idea gave our team something it was to need continually: an experienced and wise international lawyer.

Our meeting broke up quickly, and we left for the Fort Myer Memorial Chapel at Arlington National Cemetery to begin the painful ceremonies that would remain engraved on our consciousness for the rest of the Bosnian peace mission.

The wives of all three men had chosen Arlington for the final resting place of their husbands. The first of the services was for Bob Frasure. Even though all were painful, Bob's funeral was made particularly heart-wrenching by the eloquent yet unreachable anguish of his sixteen-year-old daughter, Sarah.

"One question I will always ask myself is 'Why?' " she said, speaking, in a voice breaking with pain, from the altar above her father's casket. "I took him for granted. I never told him how much I loved him, and I never showed him how much I cared about him. Now I will never wake to hear him making pancakes on a Sunday morning."

The mourners in the chapel could hardly breathe. We filed out in silence broken only by the sounds of soft crying, and slowly followed Bob's casket to a grave site high on the hill above Washington, where, in an eerie and disquieting hush, it was blessed by a priest. I placed a flower on top of Bob's casket, said good-bye, and turned back toward Washington for another meeting.

The Principals' Committee began its meeting an hour after we had left Arlington on August 22. These meetings—somewhat misleadingly named because the real principals, the President and Vice President, rarely attended them—were supposed to be the primary decision-making forum in the Executive Branch. In theory, the views of senior officials, including any disagreements, were then brought to the President for final policy decisions. In fact, if a clear consensus was not reached at these meetings, the decision-making process would often come to a temporary halt, which was followed by a slow, laborious process of telephoning and private deal making. People hated to take their disagreements to the President; it was as though a failure to agree somehow reflected badly on each of them, and consensus, rather than clarity, was often the highest goal of the process.

During my first ten months as Assistant Secretary, most high-level meetings on Bosnia had a dispirited, inconclusive quality that often left Bob Frasure and me depressed and frustrated. Although no one could ignore the crisis, there was little enthusiasm for any proposal of action, no matter what it was. The result was often inaction or half-measures instead of a clear strategy.

This was not the case, however, immediately following the tragedy. The loss of three friends infused our meetings with a somber sense that there was no turning back. In addition, the President was now imparting to everyone his own sense of urgency. Not for the first time, I observed the value of—indeed, the necessity for—direct, personal presidential involvement to overcome bu-

reaucratic stalemates or inertia and give policy direction and strategic purpose.

We met in the Situation Room, the windowless basement room in the West
Wing of the White House that has been the scene of so many historic crisis
meetings over the last thirty years. First-time visitors are usually surprised at
how small and unimpressive this room is. Movies always make the room seem
larger and fancier, but the real thing is small, with low ceilings, three plain
wood-paneled walls, and the fourth partially covered with a dreadful gray curtain. The end wall holds clocks showing the time in various parts of the world,
and above another wall floats a television screen, through which officials can
participate on a secure U.S. government network. The table is small, with
seats for only about ten people.

As chairman of the Principals' Committee, Tony Lake sat at the head of the
table, with the Secretary of State and the Secretary of Defense flanking him.
The rest of the principals arrayed themselves along the table according to
rank, and second-tier personnel took seats along the walls. The room was usually overcrowded, giving a physical sense of intimacy rarely reflected in the
tone of the meetings themselves. When she could not get to Washington from
New York for the meeting, Ambassador Albright hovered above us on the television screen, a disembodied but effective participant. She told me once that
when she attended the meeting by television she had the sense of observing
and participating simultaneously, thus affording her a degree of detachment
that made her comments seem more perspicacious and convincing.

Completing the Team. Tony ran through a review of the issues in preparation for the next day, when the President planned to meet with us after a special memorial service at Arlington. As we broke up, Tony pulled me aside and
said he wanted to assign Brigadier General Donald Kerrick to our team as
Nelson Drew's replacement. Kerrick, whom I knew slightly, seemed an excellent choice.

We now lacked only a new civilian Defense Department representative.
Perry said he was thinking of letting General Clark represent both the civilian
and the uniformed sides of the Pentagon. I disagreed, saying it was vital to
have a representative of the civilian side of the Defense Department in whom
the Secretary had personal confidence.

In pressing this seemingly minor point, I was influenced by my experience
as a junior member of the American negotiating team that met with the North
Vietnamese in Paris in 1968–69. Despite an extraordinary delegation—
Averell Harriman as leader, Cyrus Vance as his co-head, and Philip C. Habib,
the outstanding career Foreign Service officer of his generation, as number

three—the team in Paris never had full backing from Washington. The military representatives on the negotiating team fought with Harriman and Vance, and sent frequent "back-channel" messages to the Pentagon that undermined the negotiators. Although Secretary of Defense Clark Clifford and Deputy Secretary of State Nicholas Katzenbach supported Harriman and Vance, they were mistrusted by Secretary of State Dean Rusk, National Security Advisor Walt Rostow, and our Ambassador in Saigon, Ellsworth Bunker.

Watching that episode in Paris as a twenty-seven-year-old junior Foreign Service officer had been unforgettable, but not enjoyable; I had seen Governor Harriman, a historic figure who had negotiated directly with Stalin and Churchill, reduced to fury and frustration by what he considered the excessive detail of his instructions from Washington, and by internal intrigues with the military and with Bunker. No other experience was more important to me in preparing for the Bosnian mission; I would not tolerate any similar internal divisions within our team, and the negotiating flexibility we needed could come only with the full backing of all the key members of the Principals' Committee.

Perry, himself a veteran of the Vietnam era at the Pentagon, was sympathetic to my concern, and chose James Pardew, who as director of the Balkan Task Force at the Pentagon had been Joe Kruzel's closest aide on Bosnia. I did not know Pardew, a former Army officer, but said we would be delighted with anyone in whom the Secretary of Defense had confidence.

So our seven-person core team was set: myself, General Wes Clark, Bob Owen, Chris Hill, General Kerrick, Jim Pardew, and Rosemarie Pauli. It would remain unchanged through the next six months, although many other people became vital parts of the effort as we gathered momentum—and the support of Washington was at all times critical. As I was soon to discover under conditions of the highest stress, I could not have wished for a stronger team to replace our fallen colleagues.

The Europeans. The next day, August 23, Peter Tarnoff and I met in the Secretary's Conference Room with representatives of the European nations who had come to Washington to pay tribute to our three comrades.

Dealing with the Europeans was delicate and nettlesome throughout the Bosnia crisis, and put an unprecedented strain on NATO and the Atlantic Alliance just when the Cold War ties that had held us together had also disappeared. Our steadfast allies, who had looked to the United States for leadership during the Cold War, were ambivalent about the American role in post–Cold War Europe, and especially Bosnia. They had long called for greater American involvement but at the same time, they feared that they would be publicly humiliated if the United States took the lead. Our col-

leagues in the Contact Group—France, Germany, Great Britain, and Russia—
were disturbed that we planned to negotiate first and consult them later, reversing the previous procedure, in which the five nations tried to work out a
common position *before* taking it to the parties in the Balkans—a system that
was cumbersome and unworkable.

Jacques Blot, Deputy Secretary-General at the French Foreign Ministry,
mentioned that Izetbegovic would be visiting Paris early the next week, and
proposed a Contact Group meeting at that time. The French could be famously
difficult, but among the Europeans they now had the strongest, most assertive
foreign policy. They had paid for their involvement in Bosnia with the heaviest casualty toll, over fifty killed. We needed French support to succeed, and I
was convinced we could handle any problems that might arise if we met in
Paris. If we meant our high-minded rhetoric about partnership, we had to find
ways to work with the French. So, despite the aversion of some American officials to any event held in France, I agreed immediately to Blot's suggestion.

Keeping the Atlantic Alliance, the main pillar of American foreign policy
for over half a century, from coming apart over Bosnia was one of our greatest policy challenges. After a year as Ambassador to Germany, I was especially committed to repairing the strains that Bosnia had caused. We needed to
work in partnership with the Alliance on a large number of other issues—the
enlargement of NATO, a common policy toward the former Soviet Union, the
Mideast, and Iran, terrorism, human rights, the environment, and organized
crime—but Bosnia had begun to adversely affect everything. I addressed this
problem in a blunt personal note to Christopher on August 23:

> The Contact Group presents us with a constant conundrum. We can't live
> without it, we can't live with it. If we don't meet with them and tell them what
> we are doing, they complain publicly. If we tell them, they disagree and often
> leak—and worse.
>
> In the end, we must keep the Contact Group together, especially since we will
> need it later to endorse and legitimize any agreement. . . . On August 20, [one
> member of the Contact Group] told me in confidence that [his government] now
> believes that "at least one member" of the Contact Group is passing details of the
> Contact Group meetings directly to Belgrade. . . .*
>
> Any temporary Euro-annoyance with less information can be managed. It
> must be outweighed by our need for speed and security. . . . But we must never
> forget that we will need them *all* if there is ever a settlement—the E.U. for eco-
> nomic assistance, our NATO allies for the new post-U.N. peacekeeping force,
> the U.N. for legitimizing resolutions, the Islamic Conference for additional aid,
> and the Russians and Greeks for their influence (however limited) on Belgrade.

* This was a reference to Russia.

The Memorial Service. Our edgy meeting with the Europeans provided a sharp reminder of the unsentimental world to which we would soon return. But first there were more sad ceremonies at the Fort Myer Memorial Chapel. The next was a service in honor of all three men. There would be only one speaker: the President.

Any gathering with a President, even a tragic one, has a distinctive quality. The Fort Myer chapel was now infused with a combination of mourning and anticipation. Numerous security personnel, seemingly oblivious to the purpose for which we were gathered, added to the strange feeling, so different from the previous day's despair.

Four hundred people crowded into the nondenominational chapel. The President awarded each man the President's Citizen Medal, and then met privately with their families. He was masterful in such meetings, and afterward Katharina Frasure told me that he had comforted them and shared their loss in a very personal way.

Emerging from the chapel, the President spoke directly and movingly to the widows and children, saying the three men had "made reason their weapon, freedom their cause, and peace their goal." Praising them as "quiet American heroes," the President said that "Bob, Joe, and Nelson were in Bosnia because they were moved by the terrible injustice and suffering there."

When the President finished speaking, the audience stood in total silence as he came down from the podium and went up to the families, briefly holding hands with each of the three wives and six children. Then his senior advisors and the negotiating team followed the President down a narrow corridor, and into a small room with white cinder-block walls and shelves of inspirational books.

The meeting at Fort Myer proved to be an important benchmark. Although scheduled almost as an afterthought to the memorial service, this casual, quietly emotional meeting with the President was exactly what the Administration needed to restart the process and pull itself back together.

Pulling up chairs haphazardly, we gathered in a circle. The formality of meetings in the White House, with every seat carefully assigned by rank, was abandoned. Some people, having crowded into the room only to find that there were no more seats, stood against the walls.

The President asked me to review the status of each of the seven points Lake and Tarnoff had presented on their European trip two weeks earlier. We moved quickly past the more general points to focus on several more problematic issues.

Lake had told the Western Europeans that we "would pursue cease-fires or an end to offensive operations on the ground." This was, of course, contrary to

the emerging view of the negotiating team, which I explained: the Croatian offensive was valuable to the negotiating process. The time would come when a
cease-fire was desirable, but right now the trend on the battlefield was, for the
first time, favoring the Bosnians. Unless given specific instructions to the contrary, I said, we would not seek a cease-fire yet. To my relief, no one took issue
with this.

Lake had also said that the United States was ready to update the Contact
Group map to "incorporate more viable borders and distribution of territory,"
consider proposals to widen the Posavina Corridor, and provide the Serbs "de
jure control over the eastern enclaves" in return for the Bosnians and Bosnian
Croats receiving more area around Sarajevo and other territory in central and
western Bosnia that would create a more compact and coherent Federation
territory. Finally, Lake had told our European allies that because the beleaguered enclave of Gorazde would be difficult to defend and would add to the
difficulty of peace-plan implementation, we would seek to steer both parties
toward solutions that would "trade Gorazde for other substantial Serb concessions." I had already told Lake, in London, that I would not propose this, but
my position was still unknown in Washington.

I outlined why we should not press Sarajevo to trade away Gorazde or recommend a widening of the Posavina Corridor. The Bosnian government
would never voluntarily give up Gorazde following the massacres at Srebrenica and Zepa, nor should we put ourselves in the position of advocating
the creation of tens of thousands of new refugees. The Pentagon representatives in the room, who had previously been adamant on this point, said
nothing. Breathing another sigh of relief, I quickly moved on.

Finally, we came to the last point in Lake's original presentation, the comprehensive program for regional economic reconstruction. This provoked the
first real discussion of the meeting, one that we would often remember later.

The issue went far beyond Bosnia. Everyone in Washington recognized the
sea change that had come over congressional attitudes toward foreign assistance. Traditionally hostile to foreign aid, Congress had been especially brutal since control of both houses had passed to the Republicans seven months
earlier.

A huge economic reconstruction program was essential to any Bosnia settlement. Some people treated this as little more than rhetoric, but lasting peace
in the region required rebuilding the interdependent economy that, until four
years earlier, had existed in a single Yugoslavia, with a single economic infrastructure—railroads, highways, industry, etc. This would require not just
rhetoric, but significant American leadership and resources.

However, because of the congressional repercussions of any new budgetary
obligations, Lake and Tarnoff had not been allowed to indicate the size of

America's eventual contribution to a civilian reconstruction effort in Bosnia. Our obvious inconsistency on this issue was troubling. On the one hand, the United States wanted to remain the world's leading power; on the other, the Administration was reluctant to ask Congress for the resources to ensure that leadership—and Congress was even more parsimonious. This was wrong; even in an era of budget constraints and huge deficits, the nation could afford expenditures it considered vital to its national interests.

I suggested that an appropriate amount for the first year might be $500 million. My comments provoked a stirring among some of my colleagues. Perry said that an even higher figure—perhaps $1 billion for the first year—would be appropriate.

"If we can get peace, we should be prepared to put up a billion dollars," the President said emphatically.

Cautionary notes from several sides of the room came from people who had been bruised in budget battles with the new Congress. One person warned that since we were having difficulty getting "even $10 million for Ecuador," huge sums for Bosnia would be virtually impossible. The President turned to the White House Chief of Staff, Leon Panetta, a former Director of the Office of Management and Budget, who outlined the immense problem any supplemental request would confront. Panetta saw—and accurately predicted—the extraordinary budget crisis that was to erupt between the Gingrich Republicans and the Executive Branch later in the year, a confrontation so severe that it would ultimately close down most of the U.S. government for over a month.

I made one last attempt to underline the importance of the reconstruction effort, but a consensus had formed, as it often does in such meetings. It was clear that the amount of American assistance would be far less than desirable.

This exchange ended the meeting. The President asked us to return to the region quickly, and keep going until we had achieved something. Then, after greeting each new member of the team personally, he clapped me on the shoulder, pulled me aside for a moment to say he was counting on us, and was on his way back to Wyoming.

Leon Fuerth and the Sanctions Issue. On the morning of August 24, we said good-bye to Nelson Drew, and in the afternoon we walked in silence behind the horse-drawn casket of Joe Kruzel. By this time we had been to Arlington four times in three days; the week had turned into a blur. I asked the negotiating team to meet at the Officers' Club at Arlington between the two funerals so that we could begin planning our trip, which was only three days away. Because the United Nations sanctions against Serbia were always a central issue, Leon Fuerth joined us.

Fuerth, Vice President Gore's National Security Advisor, was one of those powerful but rarely seen people who play major roles behind the scene in Washington. Originally an arms-control expert, he had been a respected member of the national security community before he joined the staff of a young Tennessee Congressman named Al Gore in 1982. In 1993 the Administration gave Fuerth an important responsibility in addition to his duties as the Vice President's closest foreign policy advisor—implementing American policy worldwide on economic sanctions.* It was unprecedented to give such an assignment to a member of the Vice President's staff. But when sanctions against Bosnia became a critical issue in 1993, the Principals' Committee took responsibility away from State, apparently because of a failure to manage it properly, and gave it to Fuerth—an old friend with whom I had worked closely during Senator Gore's 1988 presidential campaign.

For months sanctions had been the subject of a heated dispute within the Contact Group, with the United States and Germany on one side, and Britain, France, and Russia on the other. Milosevic hated the sanctions. They really hurt his country, and he wanted them lifted. This gave us a potential lever over him, but by the fall of 1994, London, Paris, and Moscow wanted to lift all or most of the sanctions in return for almost nothing. Washington had a different view, although it was not held unanimously. Some officials believed we should offer Milosevic a small incentive, in the form of some sanctions relief, to "jump-start" the process; others, like Fuerth and Madeleine Albright, opposed any softening of our position without a significant reciprocal action by Milosevic. Although we had some tactical differences, I also opposed giving Milosevic relief without getting something tangible in return.

Since the end of the Cold War few issues have caused greater tension with our major European allies and Russia than sanctions. But to the credit of Vice President Gore, Leon Fuerth, and Madeleine Albright, the decision to take a hard line on sanctions proved correct; had we not done so, we would have begun the negotiations with almost no bargaining chips.

Friday, August 25, was my last day in Washington before the resumption of the shuttle. I spent it in endless meetings with foreign ambassadors and colleagues in the Department. But there was one more essential act of mourning and rebuilding. The tragedy on Mount Igman was deeply personal for the European Bureau, which had lost a truly beloved colleague. It needed to pull itself together. So, in the early afternoon, I invited the entire Bureau to join

---

* Fuerth's mandate, while focused heavily on Bosnia, also covered sanctions against other countries, including Iran and Iraq.

Strobe Talbott and me in the Dean Acheson Auditorium on the ground floor of the Department to decide how we were going to cope with the tragedy. I described the accident in detail, hoping to dispel some of the misunderstandings or rumors so endemic in such a situation. I asked everyone in the Bureau to give John Kornblum full support, and said that we would not replace Bob at this point. We would simply do the best we could; history would judge us by our results.

Several people asked how Bob's family was coping. Strobe told them of the extraordinary strength that Katharina Frasure was demonstrating, and described how the previous day she had visited Pete Hargreaves in the hospital, to tell him that she realized he could not have saved her husband. (Strobe, who had visited Hargreaves with her, said it was one of the most inspiring moments of his life.) Finally, I asked my colleagues to consider what permanent memorial we should set up for Bob. Then, after asking everyone to stand for a moment of silence for Bob, Joe, and Nelson, we went back to work.*

I flew to Long Island to spend the weekend with Kati. We had been married less than two months. The author of a recent book on extremists in the Middle East, she was concerned that rejectionist Bosnian Serbs—the "Hamas wing of the Serbs," as she put it—would try to kill us, especially if we were making progress toward peace. The risk was real, but we had no choice; the negotiations could not succeed unless we went to Sarajevo.

We were scheduled to leave for Europe on Sunday, August 27, but before we left, there was one last television interview, with NBC's *Meet the Press*. All through the week, the Bosnian Serbs had continued to make provocative statements, and had even exchanged fire with U.N. troops. This interview provided an opportunity to issue a clear warning that there were limits to American forbearance. Such a statement, however, required coordination within the government. On Saturday afternoon, therefore, I called Tom Donilon, Warren Christopher's chief of staff, for advice. He suggested that, while carefully avoiding a specific commitment that might be repudiated by others, I send a strong signal that we would no longer ignore hostile actions by the Bosnian Serbs. He volunteered to "protect" me within the government if anyone objected later.

Donilon, the only senior official at State with real political experience, brought a needed focus and crispness to the decision-making process. A proud "working-class kid" from Providence, Rhode Island, Tom joined the Carter White House in 1977 at the age of twenty-two, one of the youngest and bright-

---

* In 1996, the State Department established the Robert C. Frasure Memorial Award to "honor an individual who exemplifies a commitment to peace."

est of a group of outstanding political operatives assembled by Vice President Mondale's chief of staff, James A. Johnson.* In 1993, Donilon, who was then a partner in the Washington office of Warren Christopher's law firm, went to State as an aide to Christopher and emerged, somewhat unexpectedly, as the new Secretary of State's closest advisor. Although almost unknown to the public, Donilon was widely respected by the press and within the government; he was literally indispensable to the smooth functioning of the State Department.

At 6:00 A.M. on Sunday morning, an NBC crew arrived to set up their equipment in the sitting room of our weekend house in Bridgehampton. My new family stumbled sleepily over wires and watched in dismay as the crew turned the house into a makeshift television studio. The interview covered many issues that would be critical in the next few months. With Brian Williams moderating, the conservative columnist Robert Novak challenged the heavy emphasis we put on the fact that the leaders of the Bosnian Serbs, their "president," Radovan Karadzic, and General Ratko Mladic, had been indicted as war criminals by the International War Crimes Tribunal. "Do you think it's helpful to call [Karadzic] a war criminal?" Novak asked in his famous baiting style, as always on the attack. "Do you think it's helpful in the negotiations?" I replied:

> It's not a question of what I call him or what you call him. There's an international tribunal going on. And let me be clear on something. At Srebrenica a month ago, people were taken into a stadium, lined up, and massacred. It was a crime against humanity of the sort that we have rarely seen in Europe, and not since the days of Himmler and Stalin, and that's simply a fact and it has to be dealt with. I'm not going to cut a deal that absolves the people responsible for this.

Doyle McManus of the *Los Angeles Times* asked the question we had prepared for: "What leverage do you have on [the Bosnian Serbs]?" I answered:

> I'd rather not go into the diplomatic details. I think secret negotiations have a right to remain somewhat secret. But I do want to make one thing clear. If this peace initiative does not get moving, dramatically moving, in the next week or two, the consequences will be very adverse to the Serbian goals. One way or another NATO will be heavily involved, and the Serbs don't want that.

---

* In 1981, Johnson and I formed a consulting firm, which we sold to Lehman Brothers in 1985. Jim later became chairman and CEO of Fannie Mae and chairman of the John F. Kennedy Center for the Performing Arts.

I spent the rest of the interview trying to avoid saying what this meant—was I threatening NATO air strikes? What were the criteria for success? Under what circumstances would we send in ground troops?

Most newspapers covered the interview positively the next day. *The New York Times* ran a front-page article under the headline "U.S. Officials Say Bosnian Serbs Face NATO Attack If Talks Fail"—a headline justified by neither my interview nor the text of the story, but useful in creating the impression of a tougher policy than in fact existed. The *International Herald Tribune,* a newspaper to which we attached special importance since it was available in the Balkans, ran a similar headline: "U.S. Warns of Air Strikes Unless Serbs Negotiate."

With the interview completed, I spent the rest of the day trying to relax, even finding time to go to the local horse show, where my stepdaughter, Elizabeth, was competing. Good luck calls from Gore, Christopher, Lake, and Albright brightened the day. Some friends came over in the early evening for a long-planned housewarming party, in the middle of which, with most of the guests still there, I left for the Islip airport, where the Air Force plane carrying our new team stopped to refuel and pick me up. Boarding the C-20—the military equivalent of the Gulfstream III—we settled into our seats with nervous jokes and tried to get some sleep before Paris.

The Final Outrage. At 8:00 A.M., we landed at the military airport outside Paris. Waiting on the tarmac was our Ambassador to France, Pamela Harriman. It was typical of her that she would meet us, even at such an early hour, as a sign of support and in order to brief us immediately on the French point of view; some Ambassadors never made such an effort, no matter what the circumstances. We drove into Paris through heavy traffic, as she outlined a complicated schedule involving meetings with the French, the Contact Group representatives, and President Izetbegovic, who had asked to see us late that evening. I had time for a brief nap before our first meeting, a courtesy call on French Foreign Minister Hervé de Charette. As I woke up, I turned on CNN and heard terrible news: a Bosnian Serb mortar shell had killed at least thirty-five people in a marketplace in Sarajevo. It was the second-worst incident of the war against civilians in Sarajevo. Watching the small screen fill with scenes of new carnage, I wondered if this was a deliberate response to my public warnings of the day before, which had been widely reported in Bosnia. It seemed possible and, as I noted at the time, "I felt doubly awful."

Public reaction came quickly. From Pale the Bosnian Serbs accused the Bosnian Muslims of staging the incident to draw NATO into the war. The Muslim leadership called for the suspension of the American peace initiative "unless the obligations and role of NATO are clarified." United Nations Secretary-General Boutros-Ghali issued a statement that, typically, meant almost exactly the opposite of what it seemed to say: he "unreservedly condemned the shelling" and ordered his military commanders to "investigate this attack immediately and take appropriate action without delay." In fact, this was a device to avoid taking action.

None of this mattered much. What counted was whether the United States would act decisively and persuade its NATO allies to join in the sort of massive air campaign that we had so often talked about but never even come close to undertaking. Would our threats and warnings, including my own on *Meet the Press* the previous day, finally be backed up with action?

Even before we knew the exact casualty toll—thirty-eight killed and more than eighty-five wounded—I felt this was the final test for the West. Was this a deliberate Bosnian Serb attempt to show the world that our threats were empty? Or was it simply a single mortar fired by a single angry person? And the key question: what would we do in response?

Within a short time, Strobe Talbott, who was acting Secretary of State, called. He felt that a military response to the latest outrage was "essential," and wanted to know if the negotiating team agreed. He asked a key question: what effect might retaliatory air strikes have on the negotiations? "Your advice could be decisive," he said. "There's a lot of disagreement here."

I did not need to think about my reply. The brutal stupidity of the Bosnian Serbs had given us an unexpected last chance to do what should have been done three years earlier. I told him to start NATO air strikes against the Bosnian Serbs—not minor retaliatory "pinpricks," but a serious and, if possible, sustained air campaign, which was now authorized by the "London rules." It would be better to risk failure in the negotiations than let the Serbs get away with another criminal act. This was the most important test of American leadership since the end of the Cold War, I said, not only in Bosnia, but in Europe.

Our telephone conversation was about how to respond to the newest Bosnian Serb atrocity, but it was also part of a controversy that had gone on for thirty years about the relationship between diplomacy and airpower. This issue had haunted American decision makers since 1965, when the use of airpower against North Vietnam had been one of the most controversial aspects of that most controversial of all American wars.

Vietnam was, of course, the seminal event of our generation. By 1995, its shadows were lengthening, but they had marked almost every contemporary official and politician in Washington—some as student radicals, others as Vietnam veterans; some as doves, others as hawks. There was irony in my support of air strikes. As a young Foreign Service officer working on Vietnam,

I had disagreed with the air campaign against North Vietnam. To many of those opposing the use of airpower in Bosnia the lesson of Vietnam and Kuwait was that airpower would be ineffective unless backed up by ground troops—a political impossibility in Bosnia. But the comparison was dangerously misleading: Bosnia was different, and so were our objectives. While we had to learn from Vietnam, we could not be imprisoned by it. Bosnia was not Vietnam, the Bosnian Serbs were not the Vietcong, and Belgrade was not Hanoi. The Bosnian Serbs, poorly trained bullies and criminals, would not stand up to NATO air strikes the way the seasoned and indoctrinated Vietcong and North Vietnamese had. And, as we had seen in the Krajina, Belgrade was not going to back the Bosnian Serbs up the way Hanoi had backed the Vietcong.

The August 28 mortar attack was hardly the first challenge to Western policy, nor the worst incident of the war; it was only the latest. But it was different because of its timing: coming immediately after the launching of our diplomatic shuttle and the tragedy on Igman, it appeared not only as an act of terror against innocent people in Sarajevo, but as the first direct affront to the United States. As we sleepwalked through a busy schedule in Paris, my mind drifted back over the many failures of Western leadership over the last few years, and I hoped—prayed—that this time it would be different.

CHAPTER 7

Bombing and
Breakthrough

(August 28–31)

The time will come when those few hours will say much about war
and peace in Bosnia, the role that the United States played in the
outcome, the real importance of France, and perhaps the world
order that will reflect it.

—BERNARD-HENRI LÉVY, *Le Lys et la Cendre*

Paris, August 28, 1995. With the Administration facing some of the most
important decisions since it took office, the "Principals," including the President and Vice President, were all on vacation. As the hours and the days
blurred into one continuous crisis session, the deputies were in charge—so
much so that they began teasing each other about it. "We joked," Strobe Talbott, who was acting Secretary of State, recalled later, "that it was 'deputy
dogs' day,' and how we felt like the kid in *Home Alone*."

There was, of course, no joking about the issue at hand. It would prove to
be one of the decisive weeks of the war, indeed a seminal week in the shaping
of America's post–Cold War foreign policy. Led by Sandy Berger, who was
acting National Security Advisor, the team included John White (acting Secretary of Defense), Admiral Bill Owens (acting Chairman of the Joint Chiefs
of Staff), George Tenet (acting Director of the CIA), Undersecretary of Defense Walter Slocombe, and Undersecretary of State Peter Tarnoff. The only
Cabinet-level official not on vacation was Madeleine Albright, who shuttled
feverishly between Washington and New York trying to overcome the reluctance of U.N. officials to take action. The rest of the team spent much of its
time hunched over the oak table in the White House Situation Room, eating
cold pizzas and trying to forge a united front with our NATO allies and the
U.N.

Pamela Harriman. We delayed our departure for Belgrade a day while we pressed Washington for air strikes, and set up makeshift offices at Ambassador Harriman's magnificent official residence on Rue du Faubourg St.-Honoré. Less than two hundred yards from the Élysée Palace, where the French President lived, the huge eighteenth-century *hôtel particulier* and large gardens would have been a powerful weapon for any diplomat; Pamela Harriman knew how to use it especially well.

Pamela Harriman was no ordinary custodian. Her nearly legendary life was endlessly revisited by breathless journalists, but the gossip obscured the fact that she had done a superb job in Paris. The French, initially impressed only with her glamorous background, which had included many years in Paris in the late 1940s and early 1950s, came to realize that she was a huge asset in the relationship. Believing France the key to Europe—an ironic position for a person who had spent most of her life as a British citizen and who, moreover, was the daughter-in-law of Winston Churchill—and using her ability to reach almost anyone in Washington by phone, she gained greater access for French officials to important members of the U.S. government than ever before.

She had married Averell Harriman in 1970, after both her second husband, the celebrated Broadway producer Leland Heyward, and Harriman's wife, Marie, had died. It was famously part of this story that Pamela Digby Churchill and W. Averell Harriman had had a prior relationship during World War II, when she was still married to Randolph Churchill and Harriman was President Roosevelt's personal representative in London. Almost eighty when they were reunited, Harriman was rejuvenated by his marriage to Pam, who was then fifty. During the fifteen remaining years of Harriman's life, Pam created a wonderful final act to his long and storied career. One day, near the end, as we sat in his house in the Westchester hills near New York City, I asked my old boss if there was anything he regretted in his life. Harriman, rarely given to introspection, snapped back without a moment's hesitation, "Not marrying her the first time."

As Harriman aged slowly but inexorably, Pam began to play a more prominent role. When he died in 1986, Pam continued their joint efforts on her own. A number of articles and, finally, two books portrayed her in an unflattering light, as cold and ambitious, but, although upset by the books, she pushed on, ignoring her critics.

We remained close friends and political allies throughout this period, both before and after Governor Harriman's death. Now the meeting with Izetbegovic in Paris had given us a chance, after more than twenty years of friendship, to work together during a crisis. Even in the midst of such an intense day, I could not help but take a moment to ask her if it had occurred to her how extraordinary this was. "Of course," she said. "And Averell would have been so proud of both of us."

. . .

During the day, on August 28, I met twice with Izetbegovic and Sacirbey, once at the Hôtel Crillon, the second time at the great house on the Rue du Faubourg St.-Honoré. At the first session, Izetbegovic was still in the suit he had worn to his official meetings with his French hosts, but for the second meeting, he changed into a sort of paramilitary outfit, complete with loose khakis, a scarf, and a beret bearing a Bosnian insignia. I watched with amusement as his car drove across the courtyard of the residence, where our Ambassador awaited him at the front door, dressed in one of her trademark Courrèges dresses. Each was rendered momentarily speechless by the sight of the other—Pam, towering like a Parisian landmark over the diminutive Bosnian, not realizing for an instant that this strange person, dressed like an aging Left Bank revolutionary, was his country's President; and Izetbegovic, having one day earlier left a shattered city under siege, looking up at this astounding vision in silk.

When we finally settled down, Izetbegovic demanded that NATO launch strikes against the Bosnian Serbs immediately. Sacirbey went further, saying his President would not see us again until NATO began bombing, a position he repeated in a telephone call to Strobe Talbott. I told Sacirbey that while Strobe and I supported his desire for bombing, such threats were unacceptable.

What Do the Bosnians Want? To determine our negotiating goals, we needed to know what Izetbegovic and his government wanted. This proved far more difficult than we had expected, and began a debate that would continue for years, one that went to the heart of the matter—the shape of a postwar Bosnia-Herzegovina, and whether it would be one country, or two, or three.

That evening, for the first time, I posed to Izetbegovic and his colleagues the most important question that would need to be addressed: do you want us to negotiate a single Bosnian state, which would necessarily have a relatively weak central government, or would you prefer to let Bosnia be divided, leaving you in firm control of a much smaller country?

We would return to this issue repeatedly—and after the end of the war it would take center stage as people debated whether or not the attempt to create a single multiethnic country was realistic. Many in the West believed—and still believe—that the best course would have been to negotiate a partition of Bosnia. At the outset we were ready to consider this approach, even though it ran against the stated policy goal of both the United States and the Contact Group—but only if it were the desire of *all three ethnic groups*. Most Bosnian Serbs would want to secede from Bosnia and join Serbia itself—this was after all the issue that had led to war. Similarly, most of the Croats who lived along the strip of land in the east bordering Croatia would, given a free choice, seek to join Croatia. But there were also many Serbs and Croats in towns and villages that were ethnically mixed or isolated who could not survive in anything other than a multiethnic state. There was no easy answer to this crucial question: to divide Bosnia-Herzegovina into two independent parts would legitimize Serb aggression and ethnic cleansing, and lands that had been Muslim or Croat for centuries would be lost forever to their rightful inhabitants. On the other hand, trying to force Serbs, Croats, and Muslims to live together after the ravages and brutality of the war, after what they had done to one another, would be extraordinarily difficult.

The key voice in this decision had to be the primary victims of the war. But Izetbegovic was not prepared to discuss the future shape of Bosnia when I first brought it up in Paris on August 28. He was focused on the necessity for immediate NATO bombing, and wary of negotiations, which had thus far resolved nothing and resulted only in broken promises. Furthermore, the Bosnians had not resolved this question among themselves. Having put all their effort into survival, they had never functioned as a government in the normal sense of the word, nor clearly defined their postwar aims. Yet despite his obvious ambivalence and confusion, even in his first response, he gave an indication of where he wanted to go: Bosnia should remain a single country, he said, but he would accept a high degree of autonomy for the Serb portion.

Prime Minister Haris Silajdzic, with whom we had a similar discussion a few days later in Zagreb, had the same overall goal in mind, but a far different structure. He wanted a stronger multiethnic central government, with, not surprisingly, a powerful prime minister. Silajdzic spoke with passion about the need to re-create a multiethnic country, although he referred to the Croats with such animosity that I did not see how he could ever cooperate with them. This internal disagreement between the Bosnian President and Prime Minister was disturbing, and was to repeat itself often in the coming months.

At the center of this tangle was the remarkable figure of Alija Izetbegovic. He had kept the "idea" of Bosnia alive for years under the most difficult circumstances. It was an extraordinary achievement, a tribute to his courage and determination. At the age of seventy, after surviving eight years in Tito's jails and four years of Serb attacks, he saw politics as a perpetual struggle. He had probably never thought seriously about what it might mean to run a real country in peacetime. Any form of compromise, even minor gestures of reconciliation to those Serbs who had not wanted war and were ready to re-establish some form of multiethnic community, was not easy for Izetbegovic. His eyes had a cold and distant gaze; after so much suffering, they seemed dead to anyone else's pain. He was a devout Muslim, although not the Bosnian ayatollah that his enemies portrayed. But although he paid lip service to the principles of a multiethnic state, he was not the democrat that some supporters in the

West saw. He reminded me a bit of Mao Zedong and other radical Chinese communist leaders—good at revolution, poor at governance.

Three Signals from Pale. Tuesday, August 29, dawned with press reports from Washington that the Clinton Administration was urging NATO and the U.N. to respond militarily. In an editorial, *The New York Times* objected. "Diplomacy is clearly the better course," it wrote. "Mr. Holbrooke risks becoming the latest intermediary to fail at Balkan diplomacy, but he is right to try."

In Pale, the Bosnian Serbs seemed to realize they had blundered badly by shelling the marketplace. Trying to reduce the chances of air strikes, they took three revealing steps. First, they issued a statement welcoming the American peace initiative. This meant nothing, but it was a sign that Pale felt isolated and overexposed.

The second signal came directly from Karadzic, who in a fax asked former President Jimmy Carter to return to Pale to negotiate an immediate cease-fire and start peace negotiations. In public, the Administration was properly polite about Carter's role. Nicholas Burns, the State Department spokesman, said the letter to Carter "contains some potentially positive elements which we are examining carefully." In fact, however, we saw the letter as a clever attempt to lure the United States back into direct negotiations with Pale, something we had flirted with and rejected six months earlier as dangerously unproductive. Bob Frasure had been the primary architect of the strategy of negotiating solely with Milosevic; although it had not yet borne fruit, I was persuaded, as were my Washington colleagues, that it was the correct approach. While we did not want to elevate Milosevic to statesman status, we planned to negotiate only with him and, at the same time, hold him strictly accountable for the behavior of the Bosnian Serbs.

Fortunately, Carter's main contact with Washington on Bosnia was Harry Barnes, a respected former Ambassador to India, Chile, and Romania with whom my colleagues and I had worked for many years. Barnes understood that opening a direct channel to Pale at such a critical moment would undermine our strategy. After talking to Tarnoff and me, Barnes drafted a reply from President Carter to Karadzic that kept him at arm's length and ended this channel for the time being.

Pale's third and oddest effort to make direct contact came through Mike Wallace, who called me in Paris. He told me that he was in Pale, where he was taping a profile of Karadzic for *60 Minutes*. He said that they had been watching CNN together—the thought made me laugh—when an interview with me appeared and Karadzic told Wallace he would like to meet me. When Mike told him we were old friends, he asked Wallace to try to arrange a meeting the following day in Belgrade to discuss peace.

One of the toughest people in television, Wallace was trying to promote a good story, an exclusive. I laughed and told him that I would love to help him win another award, but that we would no longer meet with Karadzic unless he were part of a delegation headed by Belgrade. Mike repeated our position to Karadzic, sending a useful signal through an unexpected channel.

In view of what was about to happen, it was more than fortunate that we rejected these three probes from Pale. Had we opened any of these doors, the course of the next three months would have been significantly different.

Dîner Chez Harriman. In New York, Ambassador Albright continued her vigorous campaign with those United Nations officials she could round up; fortunately, Secretary-General Boutros-Ghali was unreachable on a commercial aircraft, so she dealt instead with his best deputy, Kofi Annan, who was in charge of peacekeeping operations. At 11:45 A.M., New York time, came a big break: Annan informed Talbott and Albright that he had instructed the U.N.'s civilian officials and military commanders to relinquish for a limited period of time their authority to veto air strikes in Bosnia. For the first time in the war, the decision on the air strikes was solely in the hands of NATO—primarily two American officers, NATO's Supreme Commander, General George Joulwan, and Admiral Leighton Smith, the commander of NATO's southern forces and all U.S. naval forces in Europe.

I asked our Ambassador in London, Admiral William Crowe, who had been Chairman of the JCS under Presidents Reagan and Bush, to make the case to his senior British counterparts for bombing, while at NATO Ambassador Robert Hunter and General Joulwan carried the case forward with our allies. We also gained vital support from the NATO Secretary-General, Willy Claes. This mattered: Claes, the former Foreign Minister of Belgium, was relatively new to his job, and this was a major decision for him; he was, after all, now advocating the biggest military action in the forty-five-year history of NATO, amidst a notable lack of enthusiasm from most of his fellow Europeans. Claes made one of those bureaucratic decisions whose importance is lost to most outside observers. Instead of calling for another formal meeting of the NATO Council to make a decision, Claes simply *informed* the other members of NATO that he had authorized General Joulwan and Admiral Leighton Smith, the commander of all NATO forces in the Mediterranean, to take military action if it was deemed appropriate. As it turned out, Claes's bureaucratic maneuver was vital; despite the decision of the London conference in July, the NATO Council would have either delayed or denied air strikes.

Izetbegovic would be busy with official events until after a dinner speech, so, to fill our evening, Ambassador Harriman put together a last-minute dinner for the delegation and a few French and Bosnian officials, including Sacirbey, who brought with him several friends, one of whom was the popular French *philosophe* and writer Bernard-Henri Lévy.

Although dinner was served, as always, in the impeccable manner that was Pamela Harriman's hallmark, it quickly degenerated into what must have been one of the most disjointed soirees ever held at the residence on the Rue du Faubourg St.-Honoré. The telephone never stopped ringing, and Wes Clark and I were constantly called from the table to discuss with Washington, Brussels, or New York some new problem in the effort to start the bombing. Finally, just as Lévy was leaving, he noticed an unannounced visitor in khakis and a paramilitary beret sitting quietly in a corner in one of the grand reception rooms.

With a keen and cynical Gallic eye, Lévy described the dinner in his bestseller *Le Lys et la Cendre,* published a year later. Because Lévy was one of only two or three outsiders who ever saw the negotiating team in action, his journal notes are worth quoting in some detail—although I hope that Lévy, whom we found engaging as well as engagé, later understood that we were not, in fact, as crazy as we seemed to him that frantic evening:

> Sacirbey and I both went to the residence of the American Ambassador, the lovely Pamela Harriman. I knew Pamela Harriman slightly. . . . I had had an opportunity to appreciate her pleasant intellect, her attentiveness to others, her way of feigning ignorance to force you to talk and reveal yourself to her. And her charm. Her strange beauty that evaded the attacks of age.
>
> At my table were two people whom, I must say, I couldn't place right away. Facing me, stuffed into an olive-green uniform dripping with decorations that seemed to have come from the wardrobe department of *Platoon* or *Full Metal Jacket,* was General Wesley Clark. . . . On my left was a civilian in his fifties, jovial, athletically built, with wire-framed eyeglasses. . . . He called Mohammed "Mo" and Sacirbey, in turn, unfailingly called him "Dick." At first I found him rather rude, since he was constantly leaving the table to go and answer the phone. This was Richard Holbrooke himself, the head of the peace mission, the "bulldozer diplomat," who, it was said, might be in the process of stopping the war in the Balkans. . . .
>
> After Holbrooke had gotten up for the eighth or ninth time to answer telephone calls . . . I remember saying to myself, "What is going on here anyway? Does he have St. Vitus' dance? And who is he trying to impress, getting up eight times in a row in the middle of dinner?" . . .
>
> It was now midnight. Pamela Harriman, who up to now had been the perfect host, began to look pointedly at her watch, as if she were suddenly in a hurry for us to leave. . . . We let ourselves be swept along in the commotion, almost a rush for the door, the reason for which we had absolutely no idea. . . . And whom did we find, lost in the immense [formal living room] that was even more imposing because it was otherwise empty? Over there, under the Renoir, perched casually

on the arm of a chair, talking on the phone in a low voice—a small scrawny guy, wearing a sort of loose-fitting jacket that looked from a distance like a painter's smock or a pajama top . . . was Bosnian President Izetbegovic. . . .

The Ambassador came over, utterly embarrassed. She let us talk for two or three minutes more . . . and then took him gently by the arm and led him over to join Holbrooke, Clark and the others. . . . My last image was of Pamela Harriman, very dignified, strangely earnest, followed in silence by Izetbegovic in his quasi pajamas and the American diplomats, all of them seemingly in awe, bathed in a wan light that made them look like conspirators caught in the act.

Of course, the next day, I had the key to this strange scene. I then realized that the Bosnian president had left the [official French] dinner, dropped by his hotel to shower and change, and then had come to join the other main actors as the major air strikes against the Serbs were launched.

I then understood that this was what Holbrooke had had on his mind during dinner, while we had been somewhat annoyed at what we perceived to be his self-importance . . . when in fact he was probably in the process of settling the last details of choreography. . . .

The time will come when those few hours will say much about war and peace in Bosnia, the role that the United States played in the outcome, the real importance of France, and perhaps the world order that will reflect it.[1]

Lévy was almost correct. The final decision to start the bombing had not yet been made, but was fast approaching—hence the drama and tension of the evening. After Lévy left, Clark spread out on the floor of the residence huge maps of Bosnia. Under Harriman's van Gogh and Picassos, Izetbegovic wandered aimlessly over the maps, trying to orient himself, while Clark's aides tried to keep the corners of the map panels aligned. The mere sight of maps, as Jim Pardew put it, "energized" the Bosnians into a deeply emotional state. Izetbegovic told us that the territorial issues—"the map"—would be far more difficult to resolve than the constitutional issues. At the time, I did not fully appreciate what he meant, but when we finally got down to serious map discussions more than two months later he was proved all too correct.

Just after midnight, after another telephone call from Washington, I pulled Izetbegovic aside. "Mr. President," I said, "we have some good news. Acting Secretary Talbott asked me to inform you that NATO planes will begin air strikes in Bosnia in less than two hours." I shook his hand warmly, but either because he was exhausted or because he had seen previous NATO bombing "campaigns" turn out to be meaningless pinpricks, he just smiled his strange smile, and slipped out into the Paris night.

The Bombs of August. Operation Deliberate Force began on August 30 at 2:00 A.M. local time. More than sixty aircraft, flying from bases in Italy and the aircraft carrier *Theodore Roosevelt* in the Adriatic, pounded Bosnian Serb positions around Sarajevo. It was the largest military action in NATO history. French and British artillery from the Rapid Reaction Force joined in, targeting Lukavica barracks southwest of Sarajevo. Unlike earlier air strikes, when the U.N. and NATO had restricted themselves to hitting individual Serb surface-to-air missile sites or single tanks, these strikes were massive. Planned by Admiral Smith and his brilliant Air Force commander, Lieutenant General Michael E. Ryan, the targets had been picked months in advance. General Ryan had prepared his forces for a possible bombing campaign for several years. I had examined the bulky photoreconnaissance books during a visit to Smith's headquarters high in the hills above Naples over a year earlier, and knew that NATO had photographs of thousands of targets, ranging from tiny bunkers to the new, sophisticated Serb surface-to-air system that had significantly increased the danger to NATO pilots in recent months. When the assignment came, he and Smith carried out the mission with great skill and astonishing success.

Press and public reaction was highly positive. Izetbegovic, his doubts temporarily erased, said, "The world has finally done what it should have done a long, long time ago." Senator Dole, calling the attacks "long overdue," backed them fully. Roger Cohen, *The New York Times*'s Sarajevo bureau chief, began his article: "After 40 months of awkward hesitation, NATO today stepped squarely into the midst of the Bosnian war." *The Wall Street Journal* began its news story: "The U.S. and its NATO allies, after four years of disagreement and feckless intervention . . ." The *Financial Times,* whose coverage of Bosnia had been unsurpassed, editorialized that "Western policy would not have had a shred of credibility left if there had not been a tough response." Rethinking its editorial policy overnight, *The New York Times* decided that the bombing was "a risk worth taking in this particular situation and for the purpose of sustaining the specific diplomatic initiative now under way." A *Times* article by Steven Greenhouse especially caught my eye, since it attributed to unnamed senior Washington policy makers a view at variance with mine: that "it would not be the smartest thing [for Mr. Holbrooke] . . . to show up in Belgrade this week to meet with President Slobodan Milosevic of Serbia right after NATO planes bombed his Bosnian Serb brothers . . . [because] the large-scale bombing might cause Serbian nationalists to pressure Mr. Milosevic to tell Mr. Holbrooke to go away—and derail the peace initiative."

The most insightful commentary came from the Paris-based American columnist William Pfaff. He saw instantly what it would take others months to discern: that the NATO bombing marked a historic development in post–Cold War relations between Europe and the United States. "The humiliation of Europe in what may prove the Yugoslav endgame has yet to be fully appreciated in Europe's capitals," he wrote on September 1 in the *International Herald-*

Tribune. "The United States today is again Europe's leader; there is no other. Both the Bush and Clinton administrations tried, and failed, to convince the European governments to take over Europe's leadership."

Operation Deliberate Force came after a magnificent effort, quarterbacked by Berger, Talbott, and Albright on the civilian side, and Admiral Owens, John White, and Walt Slocombe for the Pentagon. When it was all over and we could assess who had been most helpful, my Washington colleagues usually singled out Kofi Annan at the United Nations, and Willy Claes and General Joulwan at NATO. Annan's gutsy performance in those twenty-four hours was to play a central role in Washington's strong support for him a year later as the successor to Boutros Boutros-Ghali as Secretary-General of the United Nations. Indeed, in a sense Annan won the job on that day.

The President, who was still in Wyoming, did not make any telephone calls himself, but he made it clear that he wanted a military response. He told Sandy and Strobe that he wanted "to hit them hard," and was ready to make calls if necessary. This evidence of the President's own determination was vital in persuading the Europeans and the U.N. that action was unavoidable.

After all the years of minimal steps, the historic decision to "hit them hard" had been made remarkably quickly. What, therefore, had caused such a sudden and dramatic change of heart, after months in which there had been no NATO action, even in response to the horrors of Srebrenica and Zepa?

Different vantage points may produce different answers to this question. When I asked my colleagues later, they cited four factors: the sense that we had reached the absolute end of the line, and simply could not let this latest outrage stand; the grim, emotional reaction of Washington after losing three close and treasured colleagues on Mount Igman; the President's own determination; and the strong recommendation of our negotiating team that bombing should take place regardless of its effect on the negotiations.

From the vantage point of the Europeans, the issue undoubtedly looked different. They had opposed massive bombing in the past because they feared their soldiers would be taken hostage by the Serbs, and because they saw the stakes in Bosnia differently. The last British troops had been removed from the Gorazde enclave just before the bombing began, thus extracting the most vulnerable forces from positions where they could be taken hostage. But because many other U.N. peacekeepers remained vulnerable, there was still great concern about, even opposition to, the bombing as it began. Despite the rule changes for bombing that came out of the London conference, I have no doubt the Europeans would have blocked or minimized the bombing were it not for Washington's new resolve. We knew from the moment the bombing started, therefore, that there would be a continued disagreement with our

NATO allies and the U.N. over its duration and its scope—and that the United States would have to keep pressing.

History is often made of seemingly disparate events whose true relationship to one another becomes apparent only after the fact. This was true of the last two weeks of August. As our negotiations gathered momentum in the weeks following the bombing, almost everyone came to believe that the bombing had been part of a master plan. But in fact in none of the discussions prior to our mission had we considered bombing as part of a negotiating strategy. Lake himself never mentioned it during his trip to Europe, and in private he had shown great ambivalence toward it. The military was more than skeptical; most were opposed. Later, the Administration was praised for—or accused of—having planned what the Chinese might have called a policy of "talk-talk, bomb-bomb." In fact, this would not have been a bad idea—both Frasure and I had long favored it—but it simply did not happen that way. It took an outrageous Bosnian Serb action to trigger Operation Deliberate Force—but once launched, it made a huge difference.

By 3:00 A.M., with the bombing under way for almost an hour, I tried to get some sleep, but General Clark came to my room with a distressing piece of news: the U.S. Air Force did not want us to travel to Belgrade because of the danger of flying in or near the war zone. Clark explained that the Air Force was especially worried that we might be shot down by Serb missiles.

This was absurd, I told Clark, and asked him to ensure that, one way or another, we got to Belgrade in the morning, even if we had to fly around the combat zone. We simply had to get there immediately to see the effect of the bombing on Milosevic and the Pale Serbs.

I rose at 7:00 A.M. on August 30 to find that during the night Clark—who seemed to operate on even less sleep than the rest of us—had persuaded the Air Force to take us to Belgrade. After a one-hour delay to coordinate a new flight path with NATO, I told him that we should start for Belgrade without confirmation that we would be able to land, and divert to Zagreb if necessary. The flight east toward the Serbian capital was very tense, even after we received word that we would be cleared to land. We spent the journey trying to figure out a response to every possible contingency we might face in Belgrade. Would Milosevic refuse to see us? Keep us waiting for a day or more? See us but refuse to discuss anything except the cessation of the bombing? Negotiate more intensively? We covered every possibility—except the one that actually occurred.

One historical analogy, however inexact, came to mind: the gamble Nixon and Kissinger had taken when they mined the harbor of Haiphong just before the May 1972 Moscow summit. Even though they felt they were putting the summit, the centerpiece of their global diplomatic strategy, on the line, they decided to proceed with the attacks on North Vietnam. While I did not agree with the action, I respected the cool calculation involved in taking such a risk, and the fact that it had succeeded—that is, it did not wreck the U.S.-Soviet summit. Without overdramatizing the comparison, I mentioned it to my colleagues as our plane began to descend toward the military airport outside Belgrade.

Rudy Perina was waiting for us. As we drove into the city, he said there were no signs of public reaction to the bombing, which had now been going on for almost eight hours. The meeting was on, but Rudy had no idea what to expect. As we drove to the Presidential Palace, I could feel my stomach muscles tightening, as they often did before a high-risk, high-stakes meeting.

The Patriarch Paper. We had not been in Belgrade since Mount Igman, and Milosevic opened our August 30 meeting with words of sympathy about our three lost comrades. In particular, Milosevic talked about Bob Frasure, whom he knew better than Joe and Nelson. I was startled to hear Milosevic talk in detail about Bob's family, his farm, and his dreams for the future, and I realized, for the first time, that he and Bob must have spent a lot of time discussing personal matters.

Then, abruptly, Milosevic shifted gears. "I've been a busy man while you were away," he said, and, reaching into his breast pocket, he pulled out two sheets of paper.

"I have listened carefully to your public statements," he continued. "I have been meeting with the Bosnian Serb leaders—Karadzic, Mladic, Krajisnik, Buha, all of them—all weekend and again yesterday. This is the result." He handed me the document. Not being able to read it—it was in Serbian—I handed it right back.

"This paper creates a joint Yugoslav–Republika Srpksa delegation for all future peace talks," Milosevic said, using their own name for the Bosnian Serbs. "I will be the head of the joint delegation. And this document has been witnessed by Patriarch Pavle, the leader of the Serb Orthodox Church. Look here." Milosevic pointed to a single signature centered below two vertical rows of signatures, at the bottom of the second page of the document. Below the signature was the Eastern Orthodox cross.

For a moment I did not dare to believe it. For sixteen months, the Contact Group had argued fruitlessly with Milosevic over how to get the Bosnian Serbs to participate in negotiations under the Contact Group plan. Now we had the answer to the question we had asked for those sixteen months: who would speak for Pale? And the answer was: Slobodan Milosevic. Washington's decision to negotiate with Belgrade and try to isolate Pale had produced its first success—only a procedural one, to be sure, but a real breakthrough. Genuine negotiations were about to begin.

The document—which we afterward referred to as the Patriarch Paper, as though it were the title of a Robert Ludlum thriller—gave Milosevic virtually total power over the fate of the Bosnian Serbs. They agreed to the establishment of a six-person negotiating team, with three people from Yugoslavia and three from Pale. Milosevic proudly pointed to the most important clause in the Patriarch Paper: in the event of a tie vote on any issue, the head of the delegation would make the decision. And who was the head of the joint delegation, Milosevic asked rhetorically? We already knew the answer to this—Slobodan Milosevic!

As Milosevic explained this remarkable document, I whispered to Chris Hill, "If only Bob Frasure could have seen this." Chris told me later he'd had the same thought at exactly the same moment.

Milosevic was now at his most charming. Lighting up a huge Monte Cristo cigar, he proposed that I convene an international peace conference immediately, where he could meet Izetbegovic and Tudjman and "settle everything." Such a conference was, in fact, what Washington wanted, but our talks in Paris had made it evident that the Muslims were not ready. Besides, the bombing had just begun. "We will have a conference sooner or later," I said, "but not yet."

I questioned the positions of the Bosnian Serbs. "How do you know that your friends from Pale will—"

Milosevic showed momentary anger—real or feigned, I could not tell. "They are not my friends. They are not my colleagues. It is awful just to be in the same room with them for so long. They are shit." Milosevic pronounced the last word with an Eastern European accent, so it sounded like "sheet," but I was impressed with his undiplomatic command of the English idiom.

For the next eight hours, we discussed almost every issue that we would later negotiate to a conclusion in Dayton. For the first time, everything was on the table, including several issues that had never been discussed before as part of the peace process.

War Criminals ... and the Bombing. Not until we had talked for almost two hours did Milosevic finally bring up the bombing in Bosnia. I was struck by his lack of emotion on the subject, in contrast, for example, to his passion on the subject of lifting the economic sanctions against Serbia.

If we stopped the bombing, Milosevic said, Mladic would stop the shelling of Sarajevo. Such an offer would be favorably received in the U.N. and most

NATO capitals, and by the military; they had little enthusiasm for the bombing, and had already lost a Mirage fighter jet: two French pilots were missing and presumed captured.

I told Milosevic that if he could guarantee an end to the siege of Sarajevo, I would consider "recommending" a *suspension* of the bombing. Milosevic, repeating his performance of ten days earlier, immediately asked his faithful aide, Goran, to contact Mladic. We ate while waiting for Mladic's reply. The meal was, as usual, several different preparations of lamb, accompanied by potatoes and vegetables, and, for variety, some pork.

As we ate, Goran returned with an answer from Mladic. Milosevic read it aloud: "Mladic says that he promises to stop actions against the Muslims in Sarajevo if both NATO and the Muslims stop actions against his forces."

Typically, Mladic had tried to slip in a condition: the Bosnian Muslims would have to cease their own military activities throughout the country. This they would not do, as Milosevic well knew. He made no effort to argue Mladic's case, but turned back to a discussion of other matters. I decided to bring up, for the first time, a critical issue.

"Mr. President," I began, "there is one matter I must raise with you now, so that there is no misunderstanding later. That is the question of the International War Crimes Tribunal."

Milosevic started to object, but I pressed on. "Mr. President, two of the men who signed the Patriarch agreement are indicted war criminals—Radovan Karadzic and Ratko Mladic. They cannot participate in an international peace conference of any sort. Under international law they will be arrested if they set foot on the soil of the United States or of any member of the E.U." I also stressed that what had happened at Srebrenica and Zepa would have to be investigated.

Milosevic argued about the events surrounding the fall of the two eastern enclaves; he continued to deny any involvement in or prior knowledge of the attack. I told him we knew that Mladic, who considered himself an officer of the Yugoslav Army, had received support from their units situated just across the Serbian border from Srebrenica, from an army under Milosevic's command. "I want to be sure, since this is the beginning a serious negotiation with you as the head of a united Yugoslav-Srpksa delegation," I said, "that you understand that we will not, and cannot, compromise on the question of the war-crimes tribunal."

"But you need Karadzic and Mladic to make peace," he replied.

"That is your problem. Karadzic and Mladic cannot go to an international conference. They will be arrested if they set foot in any European country. In fact, if they come to the United States, I would gladly meet them at the airport and assist in their arrest. You have just shown us a piece of paper giving you the power to negotiate for them. It's your problem."

Milosevic continued to object to the exclusion of Karadzic and Mladic from the peace process. "We should not decide this now," he finally concluded wearily. "As for Srebrenica, I repeat: I had nothing to do with it, and I didn't know it was going to happen." Then he said he would agree to allow international investigators to travel to the enclaves to gather on-site information on what had happened—a significant concession if he meant it.

We needed a break to alert Washington to the Patriarch Paper, which Milosevic wanted to make public. As I left to call Washington, I sought to dampen the upbeat mood, which had been fueled by a certain amount of scotch, wine, and plum brandy. "We'll be back soon, Mr. President," I said, "but remember, NATO planes are in the air over Bosnia as we speak."

"Yes, Mr. Holbrooke," he replied. "And you have the power to stop them."

The Press. When we arrived at the Presidential Palace in the morning, a large number of journalists were waiting outside. This had not happened before Mount Igman, before the bombing. I made a short, impromptu statement, saying that "President Clinton has sent us on a mission of peace in a moment of war." An even larger group of journalists was waiting when we left the presidency building eight hours later. We realized that a big and aggressive press corps would henceforth be following our efforts—a significant development that we would have to take into account.

By this time Milosevic had released the Patriarch Paper, and it was necessary to make some public comment about it. Deliberately seeking to downplay its significance, I said the document was "an important procedural breakthrough, but only a procedural one." In our effort to prevent optimism, we were almost too successful; John Pomfret of *The Washington Post* got it just about right, describing it as "a conciliatory move" and a "significant advance," but *The New York Times* did not even mention the document for several days.

We asked Washington not to sound too upbeat. Bosnia was not a good place for the conventional Washington "spin," that natural American style of making everything look as good as possible. I believed it was best to underplay signs of progress and minimize optimism, while simultaneously seeking to establish a sense of new American commitment and engagement. If the glass was filling up, I would prefer that we said it was still almost empty.

Thus, our original plan to maintain "radio silence" and let Washington speak for us fell by the wayside. We did not even have a press officer with us—unprecedented for a major negotiating team. But as the pace picked up, the need for carefully calibrated nuance that was more likely to be understood by journalists in the region than Washington-based reporters required a major change in our approach to the press. The six-hour time difference created a special problem; our day was half over before most Washington officials got to the office, and they would often be asked to react early in the day to incomplete early-morning accounts of our activities on radio and television, before they could coordinate with, or sometimes even find, us. Considering this unexpected problem, Tom Donilon, Nick Burns, and White House Press Secretary Mike McCurry asked us to take the lead with the press. We continued to travel without a press officer, and, on over two hundred different flights, allowed a journalist on our small plane only twice. Relations with the press were admirably handled by Rosemarie Pauli and by the USIA press officers in the local Embassies. I encouraged every member of our small team to talk directly to journalists whenever they wanted to, provided they worked from a single script. The change in the way we dealt with the press would have far-ranging and positive consequences. The system worked well, a remarkable tribute to the dedication and discipline of our small group. With only a few relatively minor exceptions, the coverage of our efforts by the press based in the region was accurate and fair.

We returned to the Hyatt Hotel from Milosevic's office late in the evening. The sense that real negotiations had begun at last had given us a huge lift, and we stayed up half the night, reviewing our options and calling Washington and Brussels. In a handwritten note Jim Pardew captured our mood. "I've now put down the hammer I was using to beat down my own optimism," he said. "This may work."

The scene at the hotel that evening also had its comic aspects. In an effort to prevent our hosts from eavesdropping on our private conversations, General Clark had brought into the hotel a bizarre setup designed, in theory, to allow us to discuss highly sensitive matters inside our hotel rooms. Clark's team set up a small military tent inside a hotel room. Inside the tent they installed an air blower that emitted a continuous loud noise designed to "defeat" anyone trying to listen to our conversations. So, one by one, we huddled inside the tent inside the hotel room making secure telephone calls to Washington over an antiquated telephone system. But the noise from the air blower was so loud, and the secure telephone circuits often so weak, that we had to shout to be heard on the phone, thus making it easy for any listening devices (or anyone in the general vicinity) to pick us up.

The military's second device will remain forever enshrined in our memories, and we teased Wes about it endlessly long after we had abandoned it as unusable. This was a collection of bulky plastic "nose and mouth cones," which we placed over our faces so we could speak to each other in privacy. The cones smelled of old rubber, and worked only intermittently. Placed next to one another at our small conference table, they were linked by messy wires that ran like spaghetti across the table. Sitting at the table, elbow to elbow, we talked to each other through these smelly devices, which we held over our faces. At two in the morning, after a day that was ending with a diplomatic breakthrough in Belgrade nineteen hours after its uncertain and tense beginning in Paris, these smelly, ineffective devices broke the tension. As we joked and took ceremonial photographs of everyone wearing his cone, Rosemarie came in and told us that we were yelling so loud that everyone in the hotel corridors could hear our supposedly classified conversations.

The next morning, August 31, we met briefly with the Belgrade representatives of the British, French, German, and Russian governments. The British representative, Ivor Roberts, was erudite and charming, and I respected him for his intellect and his knowledge, although he seemed excessively pro-Serb. He was impressed by the Patriarch Paper, but cautioned me, in an eloquent letter, never to forget that the Serbs felt that history had victimized them. Don't put them in a corner, Roberts urged, or they will lash back. The clear subtext was that the bombing was a mistake. I thanked Roberts for his views, and thought again of Rebecca West. The Serb view of history was their problem, I told Roberts later; ours was to end the war.

After breakfast we flew to Zagreb to give briefings to President Tudjman and Muhamed Sacirbey on the talks in Belgrade. Tudjman immediately saw the full implications of the Patriarch Paper. "Sanctions worked," he noted, "and we should keep up the military pressure."

NATO was doing just that. August 31 was, in fact, the busiest day of military action in NATO history, with planes ranging across all of northern and western Bosnia. The bombing was spreading into areas far beyond Sarajevo, areas that had nothing to do with the mortar attack. The Bosnian Serbs were stunned. I knew there would be great pressure from the U.N.

Although we clearly were not ready for a full-scale international peace conference, I wondered about some intermediate step, one that would show progress. What about a short meeting, under American auspices, of the three Foreign Ministers—something that had not taken place in over two years?

I asked both Tudjman and Sacirbey what they thought of the idea. Without hesitation, Tudjman said he would send Foreign Minister Granic to Geneva whenever we wanted. Sacirbey also agreed to go, although he expressed skepticism that anything could be accomplished without Milosevic present.

The idea of convening a meeting of the three Foreign Ministers provoked a serious debate within our delegation as we flew back to Belgrade that evening. Not everyone on our delegation supported the idea. Our designated skeptic, Bob Owen, was—well, the most skeptical. "What will we accomplish?" he asked. "We have no position papers, no idea of what the parties will agree to. I'm not sure we are ready for this yet."

But the Patriarch agreement and the bombing had greatly strengthened our hand. It was time to see how much we could get from a preliminary meeting. We would be able to observe how the delegations interacted with one another and internally—good practice for the full-scale conference that still lay in the uncertain future. I asked Owen to start drafting the outlines of an interim, or partial, agreement. We did not consult or inform Washington.

A great deal of any good negotiation is improvisation within the framework of a general goal. After the tumultuous events of the last three days, a concept of how we should negotiate had begun to form in my mind. Although Washington wanted us to get the three Balkan Presidents together as quickly as possible, it was far too early to do this. But it was worth trying to reduce the huge differences between the parties with a series of limited interim agreements, which we could attempt to negotiate through shuttle diplomacy, then unveil in a series of quick one-day meetings at the Foreign Minister level. This might create a sense of momentum toward peace, and narrow the differences to the point where we could bring the three Presidents together.

Our negotiating team had already developed an internal dynamic that combined bantering, fierce but friendly argument, and tight internal discipline. Complete trust and openness among all seven of us were essential if we were to avoid energy-consuming factional intrigues and back channels to Washington. This presented difficulties for representatives of those agencies—the NSC, the JCS, the Office of the Secretary of Defense—that often distrusted or competed with one another and whose representatives normally sent private reports back to their home offices each day. (While Harriman and Vance could not solve this problem in 1968, Kissinger had famously solved it later by cutting everyone else out of the process, producing dramatic results in the short term and great animosity later.) We succeeded in avoiding this problem, in part because our team was so small, and in part because we shared all our information internally and developed close, even intense personal relationships. I told my colleagues that if we could not come up with a single position, each member of the team could make his viewpoint known to Washington directly—provided only that he shared his dissent with the rest of us. This system worked, and was a key ingredient in the success of our small team.

CHAPTER 8

The Longest Weekend

(September 1–4)

The historian must . . . constantly put himself at a point in the past
at which the known factors will seem to permit different outcomes.
If he speaks of Salamis, then it must be as if the Persians might still
win; if he speaks of the coup d'état of Brumaire, then it must remain to be seen if Bonaparte will be ignominiously repulsed.

—JOHAN HUIZINGA

OUR DIPLOMATIC SHUTTLE REACHED NEW INTENSITY. With a travel schedule that changed every few hours, we moved so unpredictably across Europe
that Washington often did not know where we were. Driven by the bombing
and by the sense that it was now all or nothing, we felt ready to take on almost
any challenge—so much so that in the midst of the Bosnia shuttle, we took on
an additional, related problem: the two-year-old crisis between Greece and the
former Yugoslav Republic of Macedonia, where five hundred American
troops were deployed to prevent hostilities.

It hardly dawned on us that the Labor Day holiday was starting in the
United States. Our own weekend would take us to Belgrade, Bonn, Brussels,
Geneva, Zagreb, Belgrade, Athens, Skopje (the capital of Macedonia),
Ankara, and back for a third time to Belgrade. During those four days we
would:

- arrange and announce the first high-level meeting among the three
  warring parties in two years;

- meet our Contact Group colleagues (and a half-dozen Central European heads of government) in Bonn;

- spend most of a night at NATO headquarters in Brussels arguing for
  the resumption of the bombing;

- meet representatives of the Organization of the Islamic Conference in
  Geneva to get Muslim support for our efforts;

- negotiate a draft agreement with Milosevic and Izetbegovic for the high-level meeting—the first such agreement that would ever hold;

- resolve the dangerous situation between Greece and the former Yugoslav Republic of Macedonia;

- plead for the resumption of the bombing, while holding off another invitation to Jimmy Carter to step into the negotiations.

FRIDAY, SEPTEMBER 1

NATO suspended its bombing in Bosnia at 5:00 A.M. on Friday, September 1. I had told Washington that we would support a short halt so that the U.N. commander, General Bernard Janvier, could negotiate with Mladic—but only if the pause would end promptly if the Bosnian Serbs did not agree to lift the siege of Sarajevo. With considerable prescience, Hill and Pardew warned that my position could cause a serious problem: it would be hard to resume the bombing once it was stopped, they feared, because the U.N. and some Europeans would try to prevent its resumption no matter what the circumstances. As if to prove Hill and Pardew right, U.N. headquarters in Zagreb, hiding its own desire for a total bombing halt behind our highly conditional support for a brief pause, told the press that the pause was at our request, a line that prompted a strong criticism of us by *New York Times* columnist William Safire.

The afternoon before the bombing halt began, we met General Janvier in his headquarters in Zagreb. Janvier, a small, unhappy-looking man, gave the impression that he wished he were somewhere else, and politely offered evasive nonresponses. He was clearly waiting for us to disappear, as had so many other negotiators in the previous three years, so that he could get on with his work. His demeanor suggested that he thought he could negotiate successfully with Mladic if only we would leave him alone.

Milosevic received us at Dobanovci, one of the many hunting lodges Tito had maintained around the country. About thirty minutes from downtown Belgrade, it was a collection of modest buildings set among large fields and forests, on the edge of a lake, not as fancy as Tito's more fabled retreats. We sat at a long table outside the main house, eating and drinking almost continually. Milosevic had added to his entourage Nikola Koljevic, a short, plump, and hard-drinking Shakespeare scholar who had taught English literature in Michigan. Koljevic held the title of "Vice President of Republika Srpska," but he was not trusted by the hard mountain men of Pale, the leaders of the Bosnian Serb movement, who viewed him as a Milosevic stooge. Koljevic liked to quote the Bard selectively to support his positions, frequently making statements like "The quality of mercy is not strained" or "The fault, dear Brutus . . ." Trying to keep even in the Shakespeare contest, I would offer up half-remembered phrases such as "Cry havoc, and let slip the dogs of war" or "There is a tide in the affairs of men."

The meeting at the hunting lodge rambled on for twelve hours, with a break during which we returned to our hotel for a short press conference. Milosevic had changed the venue in order to create a more relaxed atmosphere. There was heavy drinking for much of the day, which clearly affected Koljevic, but I saw no evidence—then or later—that the alcohol affected Milosevic's judgments. The Americans drank little, and I began a policy of accepting Milosevic's frequent offers of drinks only when we reached agreements.

Jim Pardew later called it the day of "bonding with the godfather." Milosevic could switch moods with astonishing speed, perhaps to keep others off balance. He could range from charm to brutality, from emotional outbursts to calm discussions of legal minutiae. When he was angry, his face wrinkled up, but he could regain control of himself instantly.

Near the beginning of the meeting, I suggested that we take a walk, accompanied only by General Clark. As he led us through the woods and fields behind the hunting lodge, he talked with nostalgia about his trips to New York as a banker—"I want to smell that wonderful New York air again," he said, and he seemed to be serious. He described his career as a successful Yugoslav businessman during the late Tito era, and, for the first time, he talked to us about the need for regional economic cooperation, ignoring his own central role in the destruction of Yugoslavia. When we returned to the villa, we asked him about his famous 1989 speech at Kosovo that ignited Serb extremism. He vigorously denied that this was his intent, and repeated his accusation that Ambassador Zimmermann had sought to turn international opinion against him by organizing a diplomatic boycott of the speech. But Milosevic made an interesting admission: "I was wrong not to meet with Ambassador Zimmermann for so long," he said. "I was angry at him, but I should not have waited a year." Chris Hill, who knew the history in detail, defended Zimmermann and reminded Milosevic that the speech had been inflammatory by any standards.

Over the lunch table, I proposed that the three Foreign Ministers meet in a week to start the peace process. Milosevic agreed instantly, and asked only that the United States, not the full Contact Group, be in charge. He would leave all details of location and timing to us. He criticized the Russians, saying that they presumed to a far greater influence in Serbia, based on historic Slav-Serb ties, than was justified. He was scornful of Moscow's attempts to pressure or bribe the Serbs with aid—"tons of rotten meat, and crap like that," he said. Since the Russians were his strongest supporters within the Contact Group, this was obviously said, at least in part, to have an effect on us.

Using a secure telephone system Clark had set up on the veranda of the lodge, I called Talbott and told him that we had a "little surprise" for Washington: all three countries had agreed to send their Foreign Ministers to Geneva in about a week for a U.S.-sponsored meeting. It would be the first meeting at such a high level in over two years. We asked him to get the British, French, Germans, and Russians on board immediately so that the meeting could be announced in four hours. Strobe was completely supportive, and said he would call us back as soon as he could.

Four hours is normally far too little time to coordinate such a complicated matter. But Strobe and John Kornblum, working frantically, accomplished it on schedule. Calling dozens of other Washington officials and the many foreign leaders, they gained rapid agreement from London, Paris, Moscow, Bonn, and the E.U.'s Carl Bildt for the Geneva meeting. Just over two hours later, as we sat anxiously on the patio outside Belgrade, Strobe called back with a characteristic opening line: "All set, pal. Everyone is on board." His dedicated executive assistant, Victoria Nuland, later told me it was the most satisfying day she had ever spent in public service, "because we worked together as a team and everything went off like clockwork on a big issue."

I had told Strobe that the Geneva meeting should be chaired by Secretary of State Christopher. He had discussed this with both Christopher and Donilon before calling back. Their reply surprised me. "The Secretary wants you to run the Geneva meeting," he said. "He has other matters to take care of. Besides, if he comes, the other Contact Group Foreign Ministers will insist on participating, and with all the grandstanding it could become hard to focus on the main event."

Government offers small moments like this, whose full import one realizes only later. Few Secretaries of State would have given up the chance to chair such a meeting. But it was characteristic of Warren Christopher, who firmly believed in delegating both authority and responsibility downward to key subordinates, provided they operated within established policy guidelines.

Nick Burns made the first announcement in Washington. A few minutes later, we made a short press appearance at the Hyatt in Belgrade. Our greatest regret, I began, was that Bob, Joe, and Nelson, to whom we had dedicated our shuttle effort, could not be with us for this announcement.

After the press conference, we returned to the villa. Milosevic's Foreign Minister, Milan Milutinovic, was openly fearful about the Geneva meeting. Pulling me aside during one of our many breaks, Milutinovic—smooth, affable, beautifully dressed, at ease in the language and style of international diplomacy, with its elaborate circumlocutions and nonconfrontational evasions—had just become Foreign Minister, and said he could lose his job ("Even my head," he joked weakly) if anything went wrong. Everything, he said, had to be "one hundred percent" agreed upon before we got to Geneva;

once there he would have no authority or flexibility. "The Master," he said, gesturing toward Milosevic, "will pull all the strings."

SATURDAY, SEPTEMBER 2

We flew to Bonn in the morning for a Contact Group meeting and an international conference on the future of Central Europe. The meeting and the conference both took place in Germany's state guest house at Petersburg, high on a hill above the Rhine overlooking the German capital, in the same rooms in which I had first met Chancellor Kohl.*

The Europeans. Carl Bildt was enthusiastic about the idea of the Geneva meeting, which he would co-chair. Although the selection of a Swede as the chief European negotiator, replacing Lord David Owen, carried no special meaning to most Americans, in Bildt's native land there was high symbolism in the selection of one of their countrymen (especially a former Prime Minister) to represent the European Union only a few months after Sweden had formally ended over 150 years of determined neutrality by joining the E.U. Bildt's selection had been the result, in large part, of our suggestions; even during our frequent arguments, a result of the pressures we faced, Bildt and I remained close friends. Tall, elegant, and witty, Bildt was to play an important role over the next two years before returning to Swedish politics. We had an unusual relationship for two diplomats—quite the reverse of the normal pattern in international diplomacy of outward cordiality masking animosity: we argued often but remained good friends, and made a productive team.

Everyone supported the Geneva meeting, but some of the Europeans were irritated because we had acted first and informed them later. This was particularly true of Pauline Neville-Jones of Great Britain, one of the most forceful people in the Contact Group. Strong-willed and dedicated to her work, she placed enormous importance on proper procedures, and vividly expressed her unhappiness that we had arranged the Foreign Ministers meeting without getting prior approval from the Contact Group. She and her German and French counterparts also said the meeting should be held in a U.N. building, rather than at the American Mission in Geneva. However, the Russian Contact Group representative, Deputy Foreign Minister Igor Ivanov, accepted an American venue immediately—on the condition that the next meeting be hosted by his government.

---

* I also met privately with leaders from Hungary, Poland, the Czech Republic, and Slovakia on NATO enlargement. The most difficult session was with the authoritarian Prime Minister of Slovakia, Vladimir Meciar. Two years later, Poland, the Czech Republic, and Hungary were invited to join NATO, but Slovakia was left behind because it still restricted internal freedoms.

Such arguments over the location and "hosting" of meetings may seem comical, but they were a constant and time-consuming subplot of the negotiations. In fact, disagreements over substance were rarely as intense as those concerning procedure and protocol. These minidramas had relatively little to do with Bosnia, but were a manifestation of the confusion within the European Union over how to forge a common foreign policy position. From a procedural point of view, Pauline Neville-Jones certainly had a point. However, as I had written Christopher ten days earlier, if we consulted the Contact Group prior to each action, it would be impossible for the negotiations to proceed, let alone succeed. Now that the United States was finally engaged in Bosnia, we could not allow internal Contact Group squabbles to deflect us.

The Russians. That day, Foreign Minister Andrei Kozyrev demanded publicly that Russia be made the third co-chair of the Geneva meeting. If Moscow secured an active role in the negotiations, it could cause a serious problem, given its pro-Serb attitude. But we felt that Moscow's primary goal was neither to run nor to wreck the negotiations. Rather, what it wanted most was to restore a sense, however symbolic, that they still mattered in the world. Strobe Talbott sometimes called this "the Rodney Dangerfield syndrome"; the Russians felt they "got no respect" anymore, and looked for ways to be seen as one of the "big boys." We felt that, despite occasional mischief making, Moscow would be easier to deal with if we gave it a place co-equal with the E.U. and the United States as a co-chair of the Geneva meeting than if we tried to downgrade it.

Meshing overall policy toward Russia with the search for peace in Bosnia was never simple. We spent much time calibrating and recalibrating our activities to promote both objectives simultaneously. In the end the effort succeeded, and produced, among other things, a historic arrangement that put Russian soldiers under an American commander in Bosnia.*

Behind our efforts to include Russia in the Bosnia negotiating process lay a fundamental belief on the part of the Clinton Administration that it was essential to find the proper place for Russia in Europe's security structure, something it had not been part of since 1914. There was a constant power struggle in Moscow between old-style officials who had served the communists—the so-called *nomenklatura*—and a newer, post-Soviet leadership that was just starting to emerge. The United States sought to encourage the latter. Sticking to this policy in the face of the 1993 coup attempt, the war in Chechnya, Boris Yeltsin's uncertain health, and officially sanctioned corruption took patience and determination, particularly because of constant attacks on the policy by

---

* See chapters 14 and 15.

American conservatives, who unfairly attacked the Administration, and especially Strobe Talbott, for being "soft on Russians."

As we left Bonn, a remarkable but invisible drama was playing itself out over whether or not to resume the bombing. Some U.N. and NATO commanders hoped to avoid resumption no matter what the outcome of the Mladic-Janvier talks. This was particularly true of General Janvier himself and, surprisingly, Admiral Leighton Smith, the commander of NATO's southern forces and Commander in Chief of all United States naval forces in Europe. Even though he carried out his assignment with precision and skill, Smith did not like the bombing; using the same phrase that Secretary of State James Baker had made famous four years earlier, Smith told me he did not have a "dog in this fight."

General Clark, on the other hand, believed the bombing should resume. This put him in a difficult position. For a three-star general to make unwelcome suggestions to men with four stars on their shoulders was not normally a wise career move, but after Mount Igman Clark was committed. As the personal representative of the Chairman of the JCS, he had the authority to make suggestions—but only suggestions—to senior officers, and report directly to General Shalikashvili. This awkward situation came to a head on Saturday afternoon, September 2, in an Embassy car on the Cologne airfield as Clark and I were about to board our plane to Brussels. As Clark explained to Smith why the bombing might have to resume, I could tell by the noises emanating from Clark's cell phone that he was being scolded by a very angry, very senior American naval commander. Genuinely worried about Clark's future, I grabbed the phone from his hands and told Smith that if Mladic did not comply with our demands on Sarajevo within the next few hours, I would insist on the resumption of the bombing. Smith, fuming at Clark, remained unconvinced.

In my view, Smith was edging into an area of political judgments that should have been reserved for civilian leaders. But Smith saw it differently: he told me that he was "solely responsible" for the safety and well-being of his forces, and he would make his decision, under authority delegated to him by the NATO Council, based on his own judgment. In fact, he pointed out, he did not even work for the United States; as a NATO commander he took orders from Brussels.

Clark and Smith never got along well after that telephone call. To ensure that no damage would be done to Clark's career, Strobe, Sandy Berger, and I all talked to General Shalikashvili. When, a year later, Clark received his fourth star and became Commander in Chief of the United States Southern Command in Panama, General Shalikashvili told me that Clark's performance in Bosnia had, in the end, been the key factor in his promotion. In 1997, Clark was chosen as Supreme Commander of NATO, succeeding General Joulwan. Ironically, the very thing that had once threatened his career, his service with the negotiating team, proved to be crucial to the assignment of a lifetime.

Problems such as these are not uncommon between the military and civilians in the government. I disagreed with Smith on this issue, but, as the person directly responsible for the safety of the NATO forces, his position was entirely rational. One must never forget in such circumstances what is at stake: the lives of young men and women. The wrong decision could send his men to their death or capture, as had happened in Somalia less than two years earlier. On the other hand, other lives were also at stake: those of the United Nations peacekeepers, over one hundred of whom had already been killed, and countless civilians on all sides. If negotiations failed, the war would continue—and even more United Nations troops might die while American leadership in Europe continued to decline.

At the NATO Council. With the friction between our delegation and Admiral Smith rising, we moved on to NATO headquarters in Brussels. As we arrived, confusion reigned: People milled around Secretary-General Claes's offices as he talked by phone to his military commanders, trying to find out how General Janvier's talks with General Mladic had gone. General Joulwan had been ready to support a resumption of the bombing, but had been pulled up short by Admiral Smith, who had already called to complain about Clark.

The bombing pause was now thirty-six hours old. I felt that the bombing should resume after no more than seventy-two hours unless Mladic accepted every detail of the conditions for the relief of Sarajevo, which was unlikely. But at NATO headquarters, many Ambassadors did not wish to resume the bombing.

By chance, the NATO Council was about to debate the issue when we arrived. Claes and Joulwan asked me to delay our departure in order to convey our views directly to them. We agreed immediately.

The Council convened in the early evening. After Ambassador Hunter made some introductory remarks, I said we confronted in its purest form "a classic dilemma in political-military relations, one we faced but never solved in Vietnam: the relationship between the use of force and diplomacy. The NATO decision to bomb was necessary, given the provocation. It is now essential to establish that we are negotiating from a position of strength. . . . If the air strikes resume and hurt the negotiations, so be it."

The questioning from the NATO Ambassadors continued for hours. As the clock passed midnight, Clark and I moved to a conference room and talked first to Admiral Smith, then at length with the White House, where Talbott, Berger, Admiral Owens, Sandy Vershbow (the NSC's senior European hand),

and Slocombe were tracking both the NATO debate and the talks between Janvier and Mladic. The news from Bosnia was shocking, but not surprising: Janvier had received an insolent proposal from Mladic—and publicly deemed it acceptable. He was immediately supported by Admiral Smith. "Our dilemma," Berger said, "is that Janvier and Smith have accepted a bad proposal from Mladic. He has played them for fools." We told Washington that while Smith did not want to resume the bombing, he would if ordered to by NATO. Berger and Talbott called Joulwan, Smith, and Claes to press for action.

With the NATO Ambassadors locked in a hopeless bureaucratic deadlock, NATO Secretary-General Willy Claes came through for the second time in a week, ruling on his own authority that a new NATO Council decision was not needed to resume the bombing. Claes's contribution during this week was hardly recognized at the time, and virtually forgotten within weeks, as he faced a personal scandal that forced him from the top NATO job. A Flemish Socialist and former Belgian Foreign Minister, Claes was best known as an amateur orchestra leader, a pursuit his critics used as a metaphor for his reputation as a weak man given to searching for a consensus at all costs. Our Ambassador in Belgium, Allan Blinken, had assured us this was not true, and predicted that Claes would surprise us. Blinken was right. Before Claes was forced to resign as NATO Secretary-General because of charges that he and his party had received bribes from a helicopter company—allegations that, two years later, had still not received a full and proper judicial hearing—he made a major contribution to a historic new policy.

SUNDAY, SEPTEMBER 3

Our team split up. Sending most of my colleagues to Zagreb to see Tudjman, I flew to Geneva to meet with the Organization of the Islamic Conference, which had long felt its pro-Bosnian positions had been ignored by the West. We met at the American Mission to the United Nations in Geneva, where our Ambassador, Daniel Spiegel, deftly led me through the meetings. The presence of the Ambassador from Iran, whom I ignored, made the meeting somewhat strained, but I was pleased to hear strong support from several nations, notably our NATO ally Turkey, Pakistan, and Malaysia. I had complete trust in Spiegel, who had been an assistant to Secretary of State Cyrus Vance during the Carter years and had then become a lawyer in Washington, and turned over to him the delicate task of arranging the logistics for the Foreign Ministers meeting, which was only five days away.

Early Sunday morning, Vice President Gore called Izetbegovic to say that the United States did not believe that the pause should continue. His call was designed to reassure an increasingly disturbed Izetbegovic that we were not abandoning him, while we continued to fight for a resumption of the bombing. Meanwhile, I flew from Geneva to Belgrade, where my colleagues had already begun a meeting with Milosevic. Owen and Hill had produced a short set of "Joint Agreed Principles" for Geneva. We used as our starting point the Contact Group plan of 1994, which divided the country into two "entities," giving the Croat-Muslim Federation 51 percent and the Serbs 49 percent of the land. Our long negotiating session, accompanied by a meal consisting of various kinds of lamb and sausages, ended with partial agreement on a draft we would discuss with Izetbegovic, who was visiting Turkey, the next day. By the time we returned to our hotel, called Washington, and went to sleep it was 4:00 A.M. Our colleagues in Washington were still struggling to get the bombing resumed.

Jimmy Carter. Early Sunday morning in Washington, at about the same time as my meeting in Geneva with the Islamic representatives, Talbott received a call from Jimmy Carter. In an effort to head off a resumption of the bombing, Radovan Karadzic had reached out again to Carter. Using as his channel a Serbian-American plastic surgeon from Beverly Hills who knew the Carters well, Karadzic said that he would stop the attacks on Sarajevo in return for a United Nations guarantee of the safety of the Bosnian Serb Army. It was a difficult situation for Strobe, one of the most polite people in Washington, and always respectful of the former President, whose administration he had covered as a journalist. But, determined to protect the negotiations, he told Carter that the Karadzic channel had to be shut down at least until our efforts were given a fair test. The Administration, Strobe told Carter, would not accept any offer from Karadzic, no matter what it was. Carter was not happy; a CNN camera crew was already standing by outside his office, and he had hoped to announce that he had reached an agreement with Karadzic. After several difficult talks with Strobe, he agreed to hold off.

MONDAY, SEPTEMBER 4: THE MACEDONIAN QUESTION

It was Labor Day in America, and we were starting the longest day of the entire shuttle. The battle over resumption of the bombing was still unresolved. We did not have an agreed text for Geneva yet, and to discuss it with Izetbegovic we had to follow him to Ankara, Turkey, where he was making an official visit. But on our way to Turkey we decided to take a side trip to Athens and Skopje to tackle the bitter dispute between Greece and the former Yugoslav Republic of Macedonia (FYROM) over the name of the country and its national flag.

The world's press tended to treat this as a comic issue. But to the two countries, the name and the flag of the new country were serious, and Washington and Western Europe feared that the tiny landlocked country would be the next flash point in the Balkans.

FYROM had explosive problems with all its neighbors—almost 30 percent of its population was Albanian, its language was virtually identical to Bulgarian, and, since it was supporting the economic sanctions against Serbia, relations along that border were also tense. The most threatening situation was to its south, with Athens, which felt that the new country posed a direct threat to Greece's very identity by attempting to co-opt Hellenic culture and a sacred name. Greece felt that by calling itself the "Republic of Macedonia," the government in Skopje was trying to create the basis for a future annexation not only of Greek culture and history but perhaps even parts of Greece's northernmost province, which had always been known as Macedonia. To the people of the former Yugoslav Republic of Macedonia, however, the name and the flag defined the identity of a new state carved—like Slovenia, Croatia, and Bosnia-Herzegovina—out of the old Yugoslavia. The new country added to the tensions by adopting an ancient Greek symbol, the sixteen-point Star of Vergina on the tomb of Philip of Macedon (the father of Alexander the Great), as the central motif of its national flag.

In February 1994, Greece imposed an economic blockade on the new country to its north, crippling its economy, which had already been hurt by its support for the sanctions against Serbia. The situation was so explosive that the United States made its only exception to the policy of not sending troops to the region, and sent 550 American soldiers to FYROM on a United Nations peacekeeping mission in order to prevent the war in Bosnia from spreading to the south and igniting a general Balkan conflict.

For more than two years, two tenacious negotiators had worked side by side to resolve the dispute: Cyrus Vance, representing the United Nations, and Matthew Nimetz, a New York lawyer who had served as Counselor to Secretary Vance during the Carter Administration, as the American negotiator. Inching through the maze of complex issues, they had come within sight of ending the dispute several times, only to see one or both sides back away from the final concessions required for settlement.

The idea that we try to settle this issue came from Chris Hill and Marshall Adair, the Deputy Assistant Secretary of State who covered Greece and Turkey. They suggested that we fly to Athens and Skopje to see if we could use the momentum of the Bosnian shuttle to end the dispute. We were greatly encouraged in this risky venture by the advice of Greece's Ambassador in Washington, Loucas Tsilas, who urged us to try for a breakthrough.

Hill and Pardew flew to Skopje in secret on September 1 to see President Kiro Gligorov. They returned with an upbeat report. "When I learned that you were coming today, I decided that now is the right time for an agreement," President Gligorov told them. He said he was ready to drop his long-standing insistence that the Greeks agree to end the embargo before the two sides sat down for a final agreement.

Greece was the member of NATO and the E.U. with the most positive feelings toward Belgrade—primarily because of a common religious heritage—and Milosevic had been careful not to alienate Athens by recognizing Macedonia. He predicted that no agreement between Athens and Skopje was possible in the foreseeable future. As he spoke, I privately hoped we would stun him with a breakthrough. We did not tell him we were going to Skopje.

We landed in Athens late on the morning of September 4. As our cars maneuvered through the crowded streets with the help of a sizable police escort, Chris Hill and the acting Ambassador, Tom Miller, wrote out by hand a short announcement that we hoped the two sides would make later that day. At the Greek Foreign Ministry, our first stop, an unruly group of journalists knocked one another down, shoved tape recorders into our faces, and backed into glass doors as we entered. Once behind closed doors, we found Greek Foreign Minister Karolas Papoulias openly hostile to any movement. He neither believed that Gligorov was ready to make a move, nor did he care. "You can never trust those people," he said. "Never."

Discouraged, we drove to the so-called Pink Villa, the luxurious new home of Prime Minister Andreas Papandreou in the suburbs north of Athens. The gardens were still unfinished, and the house had provoked controversy because of its opulence, but Papandreou did not care: he had built it as a present for his young new wife, Dimitra, whom he had married in 1989 after a long public affair that had led to a bitter breakup with his American wife, Margaret.

Papandreou was nowhere to be seen when we arrived. Instead, we were met by Mrs. Papandreou, who was wearing an almost transparent silk pajama suit that barely concealed important parts of her impressive anatomy. Greeting us warmly, she apologized for her husband's delay, and promised he would see us shortly. Mrs. Papandreou had a reputation as a sort of Greek Imelda Marcos. Whatever the truth about her past, I had previously observed the genuine tenderness that existed between her and her aged, frail husband. I knew she would not sit in on the meeting itself, but would have great influence on him. Taking her aside, I said we were carrying a message from Gligorov that offered her husband a unique opportunity to make history. If we achieved a breakthrough, it would greatly enhance the chances for peace in Bosnia. The new Mrs. Papandreou was highly controversial, and given her costume it was easy to see why, but I felt that she had her husband's best interests at heart and understood my message. She showed no interest in the details of the issue, but seemed focused on her husband's welfare and his place in history.

The word "legendary" is much overused, but it certainly applies to the seventy-six-year-old Andreas Papandreou, whose life had encompassed so much Greek-American history. As a Greek-born American citizen, he earned a doctorate in economics from Harvard, served in the United States Navy during World War II, and then taught at Harvard, the University of Minnesota, and Berkeley (where he was chairman of the economics department). He was part of Adlai Stevenson's advisory team during his two runs for the presidency. Then he returned to Greece and fought his way into power, surviving a long period in the political wilderness after right-wing pressure forced the resignation of his father, Georgios Papandreou, in 1965, two years before the military coup. He won the prime ministership fifteen years after his father had been forced out of it, and then lost it following a series of corruption scandals—only to make another astonishing comeback, regaining it again in 1993. To conservative Americans, he was anathema, an American turncoat. To Greeks, both those who followed him and those who hated him, he was the dominant political figure of the era.

He emerged from a back room, frail and moving slowly. His hands were thin, and his handshake all bones. But his mind was alert and he was cordial as he ushered us into his study. His wife plumped up some pillows behind his head, whispered something to him, and left us alone with him, his Foreign Minister, and his diplomatic advisor, Dimitrius Karaitides.

We outlined Gligorov's new position. Unlike his Foreign Minister, Papandreou was immediately interested. But Papoulias objected. First he said that it would require the approval of the entire Cabinet. This was a phony issue, and I said so, noting that the Prime Minister seemed to agree. Finally, Papoulis turned to Hill with a gleam in his eye. "When did you last see Gligorov?" he asked. "Because if it was more than twenty-four hours ago"—Papoulias knew it had been three days earlier—"his word is worthless."

The deal we were offering did no damage to Greece's basic interests. On the contrary, it gave Athens what it wanted on the flag; removed the economic embargo, which was hurting both nations; and left open the issue of the country's name—an issue that negotiators could continue to discuss without prejudice to the position of either side.

As the Foreign Minister argued, Papandreou began to tire. Time was running out. We still had to see Gligorov in Skopje, and then meet Izetbegovic in Ankara. Papandreou seemed unable to decide. He appeared sympathetic, but no longer possessed the strength with which he had for so long dominated the Greek scene. I decided to make one last effort, addressing in highly personal terms this proud man's long and complex love-hate relationship with the United States.

"Mr. Prime Minister, you and I have something in common," I began. "We both began our involvement in American politics working for Adlai Stevenson in 1952—only I was an eleven-year-old distributing bumper stickers, and you were a senior member of Stevenson's economic team. We both grew up despising Nixon. But we must admit that it took a Nixon to go to China, and it took a Sadat to go to Jerusalem. History will remember their courage and vision. Today, Mr. Prime Minister, you can do the same thing—and at no cost to your nation's interests, only benefit. And you can start us on the road to peace in Bosnia, on the eve of the Geneva meetings. But only you can do it."

The Foreign Minister glared at us, and spoke in Greek. Trying to convey a sense of urgency, I tried one more idea that had come to mind as Papoulias warned that Gligorov's word was worthless.

"Mr. Prime Minister, your Foreign Minister does not believe you can accept the word of the leaders in Skopje. But let the United States act as the guarantor of Skopje's pledge. Let us hold Gligorov's pledge 'in escrow.' "

Papandreou looked puzzled. "You do not have to accept Gligorov's word for anything," I explained. "We will fly to Skopje now, hear Gligorov out, and call you from his office to tell you whether or not he has given his word, and whether the Americans think it is reliable. You do not need to accept anything directly from him, only from the United States."

There was a long pause. Then, in a very frail voice, the old man said, "I like you. I want to do something to help peace in Bosnia, and to help you and your country. I will trust you. Call me from Skopje, from Gligorov's office."

It was time to leave. It was clear Papoulias would try to undo our progress as soon as we left, so I asked Tom Miller to be present at the Pink Villa when we called from Skopje. Then I bade good-bye to the old man whose life had reflected every up and down in the stormy drama of U.S.-Greek relations since World War II. I saw him last standing at the door of the Pink Villa, waving weakly.

We flew to Skopje to lock up the deal, hoping to rush through the meeting and go to Ankara. But Gligorov had other ideas. Even though he had given Hill and Pardew his new offer three days earlier, now he wanted to make us sweat awhile. We were learning that reneging on earlier offers was a basic style in the Balkans. These old men—Gligorov, like Papandreou, was in his seventies—were stubborn, but they would yield to pressure from the United States, if applied at the right moment.

Gligorov went over every detail of his earlier discussions with Hill and Pardew. Once Tito's Finance Minister, Gligorov had almost literally invented his country in late 1991 and early 1992. He wanted the embargo lifted, but would rather let his people suffer than betray what he viewed as his sacred mission to protect his nation's identity. Finally, he yielded, and I rose hurriedly to call Papandreou. But Gligorov wanted to stretch out the process, and demanded that we eat first. A large meal of meats and Lake Okhrid trout, a famous local fish, materialized. As we ate, I excused myself and called Tom Miller at the Pink Villa. Papandreou, he said, was so excited that he had not taken his afternoon nap, and was pacing up and down anxiously waiting for the call. I told Papandreou that the deal was done, and suggested we announce it simultaneously in Washington, Athens, and Skopje. He agreed, asking only that the Americans make the announcement in all three capitals.

I called Strobe and Sandy, who were in the Situation Room, totally preoccupied with the struggle over the resumption of the NATO bombing. They hardly had time for the breakthrough on Macedonia, but suggested that I call George Stephanopoulos, the President's senior advisor, who was also the key Administration connection to the Greek-American community. When he heard the news, George's voice—normally flat, unemotional, and analytical—broke for a moment. He said he would immediately call key members of the Greek-American community, starting with Senator Paul Sarbanes of Maryland. I also asked him to call Papandreou directly on behalf of the President. As we ended the conversation, his voice broke again, just for a moment, and he said, "God bless you and your team. This is truly wonderful."

Nick Burns made the announcement from the State Department, while Macedonian Foreign Minister Stevo Crevenkovski and I held a short press conference outside the Presidential Palace in Skopje. At Papandreou's request, Tom Miller made a similar announcement in Athens—more evidence of the deep desire in the region to let the United States take the lead in forcing solutions to long-standing problems. We stressed the special role of Vance and Nimetz, who had labored so long on the problem. The main newspapers caught the importance of the agreement; *The New York Times,* for example, reported the end of "a four-year dispute that had threatened to break into war." There were still some unpleasant scenes a week later when the two negotiators in New York both threatened to walk away from the September 4 agreement, but the two sides signed a formal agreement resolving the flag issue and lifting the embargo. Negotiations on the name of the new country continued, but the danger of a war on Greece's northern border had disappeared.

It is often said that timing is everything. It was only later that we realized just how true this was in regard to the Greece-FYROM question. Papandreou was hospitalized in November, resigned the prime ministership in January 1996, and died on June 22. Gligorov was nearly killed in an assassination attempt on October 3, 1995. The window had closed; the deal could not have been made even a few weeks later.* Had we not made our side trip when we did, the issue, a flash point in one of the most unstable regions of the world, might still be unsettled today. Yet as a result of the breakthrough, tensions dropped dramatically, and the economies of both countries benefited substantially. By 1998 Greece was the largest investor in Macedonia, and its second-largest trading partner.

Our intervention had demonstrated anew two central truths of the region: the United States was the only country that could force all the parties to a solution; but to do so, we had to be assertive.

By the time we reached Ankara it was 9:00 P.M., too late to meet with President Suleyman Demirel, Prime Minister Tansu Ciller, or Izetbegovic, who were already at an official dinner. We repaired to the residence of the American Ambassador, Marc Grossman, for a meal with some leading Turkish officials and businessmen. Grossman, perhaps the outstanding career diplomat then serving in Europe, had foreseen the problem, and arranged for us to meet with Izetbegovic and Sacirbey after their state dinner. This meant that the long day would be even longer, but we had no choice; the negotiations for Geneva had to be completed in Ankara or we would run out of time, making a catastrophe likely.

Meanwhile, the drama had grown over the resumption of the bombing. Throughout Labor Day officials in Washington and New York kept the telephone lines going nonstop to Brussels, Naples, Zagreb, Sarajevo, and the other Contact Group capitals. As we called Washington repeatedly, our delegation became increasingly concerned. Knowing the high regard in which General Kerrick was held by his colleagues at the NSC, I asked him to speak directly to Berger to emphasize the urgency of the situation.

At NATO, both General Joulwan and the stalwart Willy Claes had received the erroneous impression from Janvier and Smith that Mladic had made important concessions. This astonished us and Joulwan. In fact, Janvier had been rudely treated by Mladic, but the French general, still trying to avoid resumption of the bombing, tried to portray his discussions as "progress." Joulwan joined us in pressing for action.

As Washington, Brussels, New York, Zagreb, and the major NATO capitals argued over the bombing, two dramatically different documents arrived from the Bosnian Serbs—one seemingly conciliatory, the other blatantly provocative. The first struck me from the outset as a phony, but it almost derailed our efforts to get the bombing resumed; the second made the decision to resume easier.

---

* Gligorov made an amazing recovery and resumed the presidency within a few months, but by that time Papandreou was no longer functioning in Athens.

The first was a strange, short letter from "Vice President" Koljevic. Writing to Yasushi Akashi, the civilian chief of United Nations operations in the Balkans, Koljevic said that he was prepared to "accept conditions" of General Janvier's letter. That was all. In a telephone call to Washington as we waited for Izetbegovic at the Ambassador's residence in Ankara, I argued that this letter was meaningless on at least two levels. First, Koljevic, a creature of Milosevic's, had no authority in Pale. Second, the omission of any definite or indefinite article preceding the word "conditions" was, I argued, a dead giveaway. Where was a word like "all" or even "the" preceding the word "conditions"? I pointed out that the author of the letter was a Shakespeare scholar, and knew perfectly well the exact meaning of words in English. We were startled that anyone in the United Nations or Washington was taking this silly letter seriously.

The second letter of the day was from General Mladic—and it was chilling. Addressed to General Janvier, Mladic's letter was five pages of single-spaced ranting that suggested its author was out of control. He accused Janvier of reneging on the "long hours of agreeable talks in Zvornik" a few days earlier, of which, he said, "there are TV and phone records." In a remarkable passage, Mladic charged that the NATO bombing was "more brutal" than that of the Nazis against Belgrade on April 6, 1941, a famous date in Yugoslav history. "Hitler stopped the bombing on April 7 and 8 to allow the burial of victims after the Christian custom," Mladic wrote, "while NATO deliberately targeted our churches and cemeteries during the burial of the killed." The letter continued with a series of wild threats against U.N. personnel.

Mladic followed his threats with a ludicrous peace offering. "I assure you," he wrote, "that Sarajevo is running no danger from the Republika Srpska Army." Mladic called for "an urgent meeting between the warring sides' Commanders to sign an agreement on complete, lasting, and unconditional cessation of hostilities in the former Bosnia-Herzegovina. Until this meeting I declare a one-sided cessation of hostilities in the Sarajevo region."

When we saw Mladic's letter, we assumed it resolved any questions about resuming the bombing. What answer other than a resumption of the bombing was appropriate under the circumstances?

But Mladic's combination of peace offering and threats gave Janvier and other U.N. officials pause. The French general, who had spent an almost sleepless night and morning in meetings with Mladic, had come away from the meetings publicly expressing the view that "there could be room for negotiation with the Bosnian Serbs." A U.N. spokesman in Zagreb described Mladic's letter "as the first step toward full compliance."

Our reaction to these signs that the U.N. was looking for an excuse to avoid resumption can easily be imagined. But as Clark, Kerrick, Pardew, and I called Washington to express our outrage, Izetbegovic and Sacirbey arrived at Grossman's residence. It was already after 11:00 P.M. Temporarily leaving the drama over the resumption of bombing aside, we turned again to the draft document for the Geneva meeting.

The scene that now unfolded in Grossman's living room was memorable. Everyone was tired, especially the seventy-year-old Bosnian President, but we had important issues to discuss. As we talked, the telephones were constantly in use, as Clark or one of the other members of the delegation spoke to Washington, Naples, or Brussels about the bombing or, on several occasions, aspects of the Athens-Skopje deal, which was just beginning to get public attention.

The central issue that evening concerned names—the name of the country, and the name of each of the entities. Having spent the day in Athens and Skopje discussing the name and flag of another former Yugoslav republic, we were especially sensitive to, and increasingly weary of, the obsession the leaders in this region had with words and names. An outright military victory was no longer possible for either side, but the leaders of all three sides were willing to let their people die while they argued.

I watched Izetbegovic carefully. He and Sacirbey sat next to each other in the middle of the room. They studied carefully the draft that we had negotiated in Belgrade, entitled "Joint Agreed Statement of Political Principles." They were not happy with it. Despite the late hour, Izetbegovic had replaced his normal vagueness with a tougher, more focused attitude. He squinted and stared at the drafts Bob Owen had given him as if searching for verbal tricks that might destroy his country. He repeated phrases slowly in English while Sacirbey translated them, arguing heatedly over what they might mean.

Well after midnight, we had narrowed the discussion down almost entirely to two sentences—but they were critical to the future of Bosnia. The previous day in Belgrade we had obtained substantial concessions from Milosevic in a sentence that recognized for the first time that Bosnia would "continue its legal existence with its present borders and continuing international recognition."

In these twelve words, Owen and Hill had obtained three key concessions from Milosevic that had been unattainable for years:

- First, by accepting the words *"continue its legal existence,"* Milosevic agreed that the state of Bosnia had a legal existence—moreover, an existence that was deemed to "continue," thus clearly implying a retroactive acceptance of Bosnia's claim of independence, denied by the Serbs throughout the war. This was the first time that the Bosnian

Serbs had explicitly conceded Bosnia's right to exist as an independent country.

- Second, *"with its present borders."* Speaking for both Serbia and the Bosnian Serbs, Milosevic had accepted the existing boundaries of Bosnia, thereby officially ending territorial claims on Bosnia by Serbia, and rejecting the separatist goals of Pale.

- Third, *"continuing international recognition."* Had Milosevic only acknowledged international recognition, there might have been uncertainty as to what was being recognized. But the use of the word "continuing" eliminated a possible ambiguity; "Bosnia" would be the same country that had been recognized by many nations and sat in the United Nations. We felt that this phrase represented a huge breakthrough, amounting to de facto recognition of Bosnia by the Serbs.

But there were also some problems with the draft:

- First, Milosevic had opposed allowing the country to keep the name "Republic of Bosnia and Herzegovina." He demanded "Union" or perhaps "Confederation," names we knew Izetbegovic would reject.

- Second, Milosevic insisted that the Serb portion of the country be referred to as "Republika Srpska (R.S.)." The use of the name that Karadzic and the Pale Serbs had given themselves was certain to be a big problem for Sarajevo.

As Izetbegovic stared at the paper in front of him, he did not acknowledge the unprecedented concessions we had wrested from Milosevic. But as we expected, he was unhappy at Milosevic's attempt to change the name of the country, and strongly opposed to the use of the phrase "Republika Srpska."

I reassured Izetbegovic that the United States would never agree to Milosevic's desire to use "union" or "confederation." We urged Izetbegovic to let us propose to Milosevic that the country be called, simply, "Bosnia and Herzegovina." Izetbegovic objected. We argued that many countries, including Japan, did not have "republic" or "kingdom" or some other description of their political structure before their name. "Giving up the word 'republic' is giving up nothing, especially compared to the fact that Milosevic has now effectively recognized your country within its present boundaries," Owen told Izetbegovic.

The second point was more difficult. "That name [Republika Srpska] is like the Nazi name," Izetbegovic said. We replied that the name meant nothing, and that the governing—the overriding—sentence was the preceding one that recognized Bosnia and Herzegovina as a country "with its present borders"—

that is, a single country, of which R.S. was a part. "In our country," Owen noted, "some states, including Texas and Massachusetts, call themselves 'republics' or 'commonwealths.' It doesn't matter, as long as they acknowledge that they are part of one country, and are so recognized by the rest of the world."

Izetbegovic continued to object for over an hour. From time to time, I left the room to speak to the White House about the bombing. It helped that Izetbegovic saw that I was fighting hard for something he desperately wanted—the resumption of bombing. But it was still difficult for him to agree to a document that contained the name Republika Srpska.

It was one in the morning. "We understand your problems with this," I told the President, "but it is the best we can do with Milosevic at this time. We do not believe that the name Republika Srpska, awful though it is, means much as long as you get everything else—international recognition, defined borders, acceptance of your legal status. You had none of this before. We can't get 'Republika Srpska' out of the draft. I'm sorry, but this is as much as we can do."

A long pause. Some discussion among the Bosnians. Finally, the answer from Sacirbey, while Izetbegovic sat silent and unhappy. "This is bad for my President, but we will try to accept it. It will be very difficult for him to explain to his people."

When Izetbegovic and Sacirbey left Ambassador Grossman's residence, it was well after 1:00 A.M. We turned back to Washington for one last, extraordinary series of telephone calls. One by one, Kerrick, Pardew, and Clark told their superiors in Washington why the bombing should be resumed. Then I had my last shot at my friends. Berger, Talbott, Slocombe, Owens, and Vershbow were still in the White House Situation Room. I had a mental picture of the group, eating pizzas and hero sandwiches, huddled together all day—still Labor Day!—while we had raced across Serbia, Greece, Macedonia, and Turkey. In fact, they had been at it now for three straight days, missing almost all of their long-planned Labor Day weekends with their families. (Berger and Talbott had canceled their plans to attend the wedding of Madeleine Albright's daughter.)

Yet no decision had been made, and within the Situation Room we sensed several different views. I later learned that Talbott and Berger, who both supported the bombing, had thought earlier in the day that its resumption would be relatively easy, but that as the day progressed, opposition from various quarters, including the U.N. field commanders and the French, made the situation far less certain. In Ankara, we were unaware of the impact that CNN was having: one of its star correspondents, Peter Arnett, had been taken by the Bosnian Serbs to positions outside Sarajevo, where he had filmed scenes he was told were the beginning of the withdrawal of heavy weapons from the area around Sarajevo, as Mladic had promised in his ranting letter. This was a standard Bosnian Serb tactic: showing unilateral and phony "compliance" in an effort to head off NATO action—but it had worked for years. As a result, General Rupert Smith, the British commander of U.N. troops in Bosnia, was now recommending that the bombing *not* resume—an astonishing and dismaying change of position.

"Let me be clear," I said. "It is very late here now, and we are perhaps overly tired, but we have an absolutely unanimous point of view: the bombing must be resumed. If it is not, we will do our best, but our chances for success in the negotiations will be seriously reduced. The Bosnians are barely on board with our Geneva draft, and when we see Izetbegovic again in the morning for a last review of the draft, the bombing must have resumed."

I wanted to end on a high historical note, unusual for this sort of conversation. "If we do not resume the bombing, it will have lasted less than forty-eight hours. It will be another catastrophe. NATO will again look like a paper tiger. The Bosnian Serbs will return to their blackmailing ways." There was a short silence at the other end of the phone. Don Kerrick, who was listening in on an extension, looked at me, smiled, and gave me thumbs-up sign. I concluded: "I know how difficult this is, and what I am about to say may sound melodramatic, but history could well hang in the balance tonight. I truly believe that you may never take any decision as public officials more important than this one. Give us bombs for peace. Give us a resumption of the bombing by morning."

CHAPTER 9

Geneva

(September 5–8)

There is no process by which the cross-hatched complexity of acted history can be reproduced faithfully in the written word.
—C. V. WEDGWOOD, *History and Hope*

WHEN WE AWOKE IN ANKARA ON TUESDAY, September 5, we still had no idea if the bombing would resume. Calls to NATO headquarters were uninformative, and it was too early to call Washington, even Strobe Talbott, who was notorious for rising at an ungodly hour. With uncertainty hanging over our heads, we drove to the residence of Turkish Prime Minister Tansu Ciller for a meeting that Izetbegovic would join. Then we planned to fly to Belgrade to close the Geneva agreement with Milosevic.

Turkey had once shared a common history with Bosnia. Even today, when Serbs and Croats speak disparagingly of the Bosnian Muslims, they call them "Turki," in memory of the distant time when the Ottoman conquerors had come to the southern Balkans. Izetbegovic respected the Turkish leaders, especially President Demirel, and their support for any postsettlement activities in Bosnia, such as improving the quality of the Bosnia-Croat Federation military forces, would be important.

En route to Ankara the previous evening, we had discussed Cyprus, the long-running problem that had caused so much tension between Greece and Turkey, especially since the 1974 Turkish invasion. The image of Cyprus, its two hostile ethnic groups divided for twenty-one years by an ugly wall that cut the island in half, would haunt us during the entire Bosnia peace effort. Was this how Bosnia would look after we were done, even if we succeeded in ending the war? It would be better than war, but it would hardly be a real peace. Haris Silajdzic and some of the better-informed journalists often raised this specter with us. Aware of the problem, our team talked frequently about the need to avoid letting Bosnia become another Cyprus—that is, allowing a temporary cease-fire line to harden into a permanent partition line.

.   .   .

When Izetbegovic arrived, we held an unusual trilateral session with Ciller—not a normal grouping, but one that helped reduce the edge from the previous night's difficult meeting. Izetbegovic was clearly troubled, and seemed unsure whether to go forward with the text he had accepted the previous night. He was deeply annoyed that the bombing had not yet been resumed, and linked his final acceptance of the draft for Geneva to the resumption of bombing. Waiting for word from NATO, I thought this an entirely reasonable position.

After the meeting, Sacirbey and I headed for the Ankara Hilton, where we were scheduled to hold a joint press conference. As we drove through the streets, Strobe called. Reluctant to discuss sensitive matters over an open cellular telephone yet anxious to give us some much-needed good news, he talked in an improvised code: "The Smith Brothers and our jolly friend have made a new decision that makes our conversations of last night OBE."

What did he mean? It took a moment to understand that he was trying to tell me that the two (unrelated) Smiths, Admiral Leighton and General Rupert, and General Joulwan ("our jolly friend") had agreed to resume the bombing, and thus our discussions of the previous evening were now "OBE" (overtaken by events).

The persistent efforts of officials like Willy Claes and General Joulwan in Brussels, and Berger, Talbott, and Admiral Owens in Washington had paid off. Once again, the Bosnian Serbs had brought down upon themselves something that they could have prevented—fortunately for us. It is impossible, of course, to say with certainty what effect a failure to resume the bombing would have had on our efforts. After the peace settlement, some European officials argued that the negotiations would have achieved the same results with or without the bombing. I am glad that we did not have to test this proposition.

On the plane from Ankara to Belgrade, Hill and Owen predicted that Milosevic would not accept several of the key provisions in our Geneva draft. With three days to go before Geneva, they said, we faced a stalemate. We had pushed Izetbegovic as far as he could go, and could not go back to Sarajevo, literally or figuratively, to ask for changes. But would Milosevic agree to the document we had hammered out in Ankara? The views of Chris and Bob, who had done most of the negotiating with Milosevic on this issue, worried me. On the plane, anticipating a contentious meeting, we agreed that I should see Milosevic alone—my first private meeting with him.

Leaving our colleagues in the main sitting room, he and I went into the room next door as soon as I arrived. We sat side by side on a sofa. "This is what we agreed to with Izetbegovic," I said, handing him the Ankara draft. "We cannot change it."

Milosevic, who prided himself on his legal training and ability to read and absorb highly technical material with great speed, scanned the document rapidly. Even Bob Owen, a great lawyer and a demanding taskmaster, had been impressed with how quickly Milosevic assimilated every nuance of documents written in English. This skill made Milosevic all the more dangerous as a negotiator; he would regularly try to slip into documents words or phrases that seemed innocuous, but contained potentially deadly traps.

Milosevic objected to several phrases. He wanted the country to be called either the "Union of Bosnia-Herzegovina" or, perhaps, the "United States of Bosnia-Herzegovina." I countered that we should drop the use of "Republika Srpksa," a suggestion Milosevic termed "absolutely impossible." He retreated gradually from his initial demands, and, after thirty minutes of argument, accepted the document without any changes.

I walked with Milosevic back into the main room, where my colleagues had been listening to the Serb Foreign Minister lament his fate in having to go to Geneva. Handing the document to Owen, I said, "We have an agreement." He looked astonished, and gave me a thumbs-up sign.

Were I allowed to revisit the negotiations, this is where I would probably start. In its entirety the document represented significant gains for Sarajevo, as both Milosevic and Izetbegovic knew. But I regret that we did not make a stronger effort to drop the name Republika Srpska. We underestimated the value to Pale of retaining their blood-soaked name. We may also have underestimated the strength of our negotiating hand on that day, when the bombing had resumed. In retrospect, I think we should have pushed Milosevic harder to change the name of the Bosnian Serb entity. Even if the effort failed, as Owen and Hill predicted, it would have been worth trying.

Geneva was still four days away. Leaks could be fatal, since they would trigger public pressure in Sarajevo to ask for more. To maintain maximum secrecy, we faxed a copy of the agreement to Talbott's office in Washington and asked him to hand-deliver it to a few senior officials; it was a sad truth of modern Washington that no reporting sent through normal State Department channels—no matter how it was "slugged" for distribution—was safe from the risks of uncontrolled distribution and leaks.

We spent the night in Belgrade, then headed for Zagreb, where we reviewed Geneva with a decidedly uninterested Tudjman. He had only one thing on his mind: regaining eastern Slavonia from the Serbs. Repeating our warnings not to use force, we promised to include eastern Slavonia in any international negotiation. Tudjman welcomed this, but refused to eschew public threats.

We had an agreement. But before Geneva, we had to pull together our allies and the Contact Group, which had little idea of what we were up to. Clark and Pardew headed for Brussels to help NATO plan for deploying a force in Bosnia if we achieved a peace agreement. Hill flew to Paris to join Peter Tarnoff, who was briefing senior French, British, and German officials. I drew what appeared to be a pleasant assignment: at the urging of Tony Lake and Ambassador Bartholomew, a visit to Rome to calm down some very unhappy Italians.

My first stop in Rome was a call on an old friend, Foreign Minister Susanna Agnelli. Universally known as Sunni, she had been appointed to the post by the government of Lamberto Dini in part because of her personal stature. A former mayor and senator, the sister of Italy's most famous businessman, Gianni Agnelli, and the author of a best-selling memoir with the delightful title *We Always Wore Sailor Suits,* Sunni Agnelli combined aristocratic bearing with casual informality. Her giant white mane of hair and her imposing height added to her presence. She approached her job as she had probably approached almost everything else: with a relaxed confidence in her own intuition. She conveyed an impression of great amusement at the passing parade of overly intense men formulating policy. We had known each other for years, but only socially. I liked her, and expected, as did Bartholomew, a friendly call between old friends that would resolve a relatively minor problem—Italian pique at their exclusion from the Contact Group, which, as I had repeatedly tried to explain, was not our fault.

It was no social call. Flanked by her staff, one of whom glared at me through thick glasses, she lit into the United States for failing to keep her country adequately informed or involved. Reading from notes prepared by her staff, she said that we had reneged on Lake's commitment to get Italy into the Contact Group. Pleased that she was venting their frustration, her staff occasionally fueled the fire with short comments.

Only a few hours earlier, I had been in the ugliness of Belgrade and Zagreb, trying to end a war that threatened the stability of Europe. Now, in one of the most beautiful cities on earth, the capital of the only NATO nation with a common border with the war zone, a Foreign Minister whom I liked and knew as a friend was reading us the riot act. Bartholomew, one of America's most accomplished ambassadors, was as astonished as I was. He had said that my trip would mollify the Italians, but it seemed only to inflame them.

We explained that Lake had made no commitment to bring the Italians into the Contact Group, something that was beyond our capability. Her aides insisted that he had made a promise. Perhaps there had been a misunderstanding, we suggested gently: it was not Washington that objected to Italy's membership in the Contact Group, it was the European Union members of the

Contact Group. We stressed that the United States wanted Italy, the only NATO nation bordering the war zone, to play a greater role in the region. Tony had said only that we would seek to convene a larger group (the "Contact Group Plus") from time to time.

This was nothing less than the truth. Britain, France, and Germany liked the prominence that came from being senior members of a prestigious international negotiating group. (Never mind its ineffectiveness.) To allow Italy to join, they felt, would not only dilute it but create pressure to add Spain, the Netherlands, and other nations with troops in Bosnia. We later learned that senior diplomats from Paris, London, and Bonn had met privately and decided not only to keep Italy out of the Contact Group, but to tell Rome that Washington was the culprit.

I could not solve Italy's Contact Group problem, but, trying to ease the tension, I suggested we hold a special meeting of an "expanded Contact Group" in Rome in October, provided that we could get the rest of the Contact Group to agree to meet in Rome. She accepted immediately. When we had finished, Bartholomew and I met with Prime Minister Dini, who presented a position identical to Agnelli's. Recognizing by now that there was little we could do in the face of this profound misunderstanding by our Italian friends, I repeated our offer to hold a special meeting in Rome, stressed how important Italy was to the United States, and left.

Exhausted by our continuous shuttle, now in its eleventh straight day, I returned to the graceful ambassadorial residence in Rome for a quiet dinner with the Bartholomews. The visit had not been the pleasant, relaxed stop among friends in the Eternal City that we had expected. But in the end, the trip had been useful, since it would lead to more involvement by the Italians in the Bosnian peace effort. In fact, the Italians did end up hosting several key meetings in Rome, including a dramatic Balkan summit in February 1996. In 1997 they finally became members of the Contact Group. None of this would have happened if we had not taken such a strong pro-Italian position.

GENEVA

We arrived in Geneva on Thursday, September 7, and drove with Ambassador Spiegel directly to the U.S. Mission. I was impressed. In four days, he had somehow arranged everything and produced a room and table that fit our needs so well that we copied it exactly for all subsequent meetings, including the final negotiations.

In diplomacy, details matter. During the 1968 peace talks with the North Vietnamese in Paris, we had famously wasted more than two months arguing over the shape of the negotiating table, while the war continued. I had watched as two great American diplomats, Averell Harriman and Cyrus Vance, were humiliated and furious; I was determined not to let such an event happen to us. With this in mind, I had asked Spiegel to construct a round table large enough to seat no more than nine people—one representative from each of the five Contact Group nations, plus a seat for Co-chairman Carl Bildt, and one seat for each of the three Balkan countries. The chairs had to be close enough to one another so that there would be no room at the table for the Bosnian Serbs or anyone else. I asked for nameplates without country names, and the national flags of only the five Contact Group nations and the European Union. I was struck by the parallel with 1968: Hanoi's insistence that the Vietcong get a seat at the table separate from the North Vietnamese had been the reason for the argument over the table shape in Paris.

On the day before the meeting, NATO intensified the bombing, hitting the Lukavica barracks southwest of Sarajevo, and bombing ammunition dumps, communications equipment, and other facilities. I was pleased to see a column in *The Washington Post* by Charles Krauthammer, a constant critic of American policy, concluding that "U.S. policy on Bosnia is finally on track." In a phrase more perceptive than he may have realized, Krauthammer wrote that the bombing should continue until "(a) the Serbs have made concessions at the bargaining table . . . or (b) we run out of targets."

There was great tension that night in Geneva. So far, we had achieved nothing except the deal between Greece and the former Yugoslav Republic of Macedonia. Now, for the first time, everything was on the line. I called on Milutinovic and Sacirbey separately. The Serbian Foreign Minister was, as always, the essence of a smooth, affable diplomat. But when I asked him about the Bosnian Serb delegation, he waved his hand dismissively and said that they were staying at another hotel. He did not care to deal with them. Sacirbey was much more troubled. The agreement was not good for his country, he told me, and his President was taking "a lot of heat" for it back home.

September 8. We thought everything was agreed to; the agreement had been accepted by everyone two days earlier. We planned to meet, approve the agreement formally, discuss the future informally, and then meet the press. But nothing goes according to plan in the Balkans—and, for a day, the U.S. Mission in Geneva turned into part of the war zone. The troubles began fifteen minutes before our Contact Group colleagues were due to arrive, when Sacirbey called to say that he would not come to the meeting unless his government could retain the name "Republic of Bosnia-Herzegovina." They were getting heavily criticized in Sarajevo, Sacirbey said, and needed this last-minute change.

This was the first instance of a recurring pattern in the negotiations—second thoughts or changes in position by Sarajevo after it had agreed to something. I could sympathize with it, but Izetbegovic had made an agreement in Ankara, and if we tried to renegotiate it in Geneva, Yugoslav Foreign Minister Milutinovic would refuse; as he had repeatedly told us, he had no authority and could make no decisions.

In no uncertain terms, I told Sacirbey that if he precipitated a failure in Geneva, the United States would hold him responsible, and only the Serbs would benefit. It was a harsh conversation—the most difficult I had had with Sacirbey—and it was overheard by several other people. Later on, after it was leaked to the press in an exaggerated form, it became part of negotiating folklore that the chief American negotiator was a "bully" who had yelled at everyone. But in fact, such emotional exchanges were extremely rare, and usually deliberate. Whatever my tone, Sacirbey was convinced that it was in his interests to appear at the conference on time. But to protect the process, I later asked Warren Christopher to call Izetbegovic and Silajdzic in Sarajevo to calm them down. He did so immediately, explaining to both men that the first sentence of the Geneva agreement represented a "powerful recognition" of Bosnia's status that more than made up for their concessions on the names.

Shortly after 10:00 A.M., the delegates convened around Dan Spiegel's small round table. Carl Bildt sat to my right, and Russia's Deputy Foreign Minister Igor Ivanov to my left. Directly across from us sat the three Foreign Ministers, and behind them hundreds of journalists. Without warning, I rose and walked around the table to the three Foreign Ministers. "Would you all join me in a handshake for the world?" I asked. Astonished but unable to avoid it, Sacirbey, Granic, and Milutinovic rose and posed awkwardly for the photograph that would be seen around the world as a sign of momentum toward peace. Then we asked the press to leave and settled down to business.

As soon as I gaveled the session to order, we ran into a problem. The leader of the Bosnian Serb delegation, Republika Srpksa "Vice President" Nikolai Koljevic, rose from his seat behind the table. "I protest this arrangement," he said. "My delegation should be seated at the table, and we will not participate in this meeting if we are denied our rights." This was precisely what the seating arrangements were designed to prevent. I was thankful that there was no room for Koljevic at the table. I replied that, according to the Patriarch Paper, Foreign Minister Milan Milutinovic spoke for the Bosnian Serbs. Koljevic angrily persisted, and when I looked at Milutinovic, expecting him to silence Koljevic, he looked away. I immediately called for a recess.

We had set aside a set of small rooms just off the main conference room for private meetings. Taking Milutinovic into one of them alone, I asked him whether this was a game that he and Koljevic had devised. If it was, I said, the meeting would break up and the consequences would be serious. "If not," I said, "you must get your 'friends' under control."

Nervous and unhappy, Milutinovic said he could not control the little Bosnian Serb. "Only my Master can do that," he added. Then he made a suggestion that surprised me. "I think if you talk to him firmly he will understand."

I asked Koljevic and his colleague, "Foreign Minister" Aleksi Buha, to join us in the tiny room. With Milutinovic watching in silence, I told them that if they continued their protest they would deal themselves completely out of the process. "Walk out if you want to," I told the astonished Serbs. "But if you do, we will continue without you, and Bosnian Serb influence in this process will be eliminated. I doubt President Milosevic will be pleased, but it's up to you."

Koljevic seemed to deflate in front of our eyes. Suddenly he was everyone's friend, a man of peace who wanted only to be allowed to quote a few lines of his beloved Shakespeare before fading away. He proposed that he be allowed to rise one last time from his seat behind the table, concede that Milutinovic spoke for him and his colleagues, and then remain silent.

I said we would agree to his request, provided he said nothing substantive, and that Sacirbey and the Croatian Foreign Minister, Mate Granic, both agreed in advance. The confrontation had been intense, but it was over in less than thirty minutes. When we resumed, Koljevic followed his script, pathetically quoting the Bard and "relinquishing" his right to speak, after which we finally started the meeting.

The rest of the meeting was routine. Each person at the table made a speech; as is usual on such occasions, they were of little consequence. Given the chance to perform before an audience—even without journalists present—the three Foreign Ministers reverted to sterile and accusatory rhetoric.

That afternoon, at the InterContinental Hotel, flanked by Carl Bildt, Igor Ivanov, Pauline Neville-Jones, Jacques Blot, and Wolfgang Ischinger, my colleagues and I faced over four hundred journalists, with live broadcasts on CNN and several European networks. We did not invite the three Balkan Foreign Ministers to the press conference, knowing that their natural proclivity to argue would divert attention from the Joint Agreed Principles. Before reading the agreement, I made a personal statement:

> Our first thought this morning when we walked into the room and found that the Foreign Ministers of Bosnia, Croatia, and Serbia were in the room for the first time in so many months, that they were willing to shake hands and reach a common agreement which, though limited, moves us toward peace . . . our first thought—all of us—was: if only Nelson, Joe, and Bob Frasure could have seen this day.

I faltered for a moment, and Carl Bildt graciously picked up the same theme, saying of Frasure that "his excellence, knowledge, and humor made a lot of this possible."

The Joint Agreed Principles of September 8 were only a first step toward peace, and we did not want to oversell it. The bombing and the war were still going on. I stressed the limitations of the agreement:

> The statement takes us an important step closer to peace. Yet, important as it is, this statement does not constitute the end of the tragedy in the Balkans. Far from it. . . . The hardest work still lies ahead. The [two] entities have yet to develop a design for a central connecting structure. . . . In addition, the parties need to define their internal borders within Bosnia in accordance with the 51–49 principle. We should be under no illusions that these will be easy tasks.

After the press conference, I asked every member of our team to meet with journalists individually or in small groups organized by the European Bureau's energetic press officer, Aric Schwan, who had flown to Geneva to assist with the media. We wanted to be sure that the story was properly reported; most especially, we wanted to be sure that everyone understood that the next step was to fix the major omission in the Geneva agreement—the lack of any agreement on a central government. Without this, the agreement could easily be construed as having partitioned Bosnia, when the exact opposite was our goal.

We were through the first phase of the negotiations, and the world was taking notice. Yet, despite some overly optimistic reporting, we were still far from our goals. We planned to resume the shuttle within a week, but as we headed home we had no clear plan as to how to proceed.

The Siege of Sarajevo Ends

(September 9–14)

In one of his many public statements, the leader of the Bosnian Serbs, Montenegrin Radovan Karadzic, said that the Serbs in the past period, when everyone was on their side, had been subjected to "genocidal extermination," whereas now, over the last year, when so many are against them, they are suffering the least.

Of all the innumerable absurdities and untruths that have been uttered, this statement truly takes the cake. For more than forty years Bosnia was inhabited by Bosnians, and we did not distinguish between Serbs, Muslim, and Croats, or at least such distinctions were not paramount in their mutual relations. Throughout that period, to the best of the Yugoslav and world public's knowledge, there were no detention camps for Serbs in Bosnia, no brothels for Serb women, no Serbian children had their throats cut. . . . But according to Karadzic, the Serbs were somehow unhappy then. And now, in the war, with so many dead, . . . now, according to their leader, the time has come when they are suffering the least. . . . Ethnically pure states are an impossibility in today's world, and it is ridiculous to try to create and maintain such a state, even when there is just one nation.

—MIRA MARKOVIC (Mrs. Slobodan Milosevic),
in her newspaper column, January 20, 1993[1]

AFTER THIRTEEN DAYS ON THE ROAD—the longest of all our shuttle trips—we planned to spend at least a week in Washington. There were personal reasons for this, but, with major policy issues to be decided, we also needed a few days to develop a consensus on some key issues.

Events in Bosnia, however, were moving too fast for a coherent policy review, and after only one working day in Washington we were on our way back to the region. This time we would negotiate the end of the three-year siege of Sarajevo—and unexpectedly meet with the world's two most wanted indicted war criminals, Radovan Karadzic and Ratko Mladic.

On Sunday, September 10, even as we regrouped in Washington, Janvier met again with Mladic in the border town of Mali Zvornik. The meeting had been arranged by Presidents Chirac and Milosevic, both of whom wanted another bombing pause as soon as possible. Chirac was anxious for the release of the two French pilots who had been captured during the bombing. Janvier went to the meeting expecting Mladic to offer the withdrawal of Bosnian Serb heavy weapons from the hills around Sarajevo. But once again the meeting did not go according to the U.N. plan. Instead, Mladic threatened to attack the remaining "safe areas," and refused to negotiate until after the bombing had ended.

Mladic's behavior opened the door for two of the most unexpected and important tactical decisions of the NATO air campaign—to attack vital military targets near the largest Serb city in Bosnia, Banja Luka; and to use Tomahawk cruise missiles. Thirteen of these expensive radar-guided missiles were launched against important Bosnian Serb military centers in western Bosnia, far from Sarajevo and Gorazde. Although a few seven-hundred-pound warheads were hardly as powerful as the hundreds of two-thousand-pound bombs that were being dropped by planes, the psychological effect of such sophisticated weapons, previously used only in the Gulf War, was enormous. The damage, however, was more than psychological: one of the missiles knocked out the main communications center for the Bosnian Serb Army in the west, with devastating consequences.

Karadzic seemed increasingly desperate. In a letter addressed to Presidents Clinton, Yeltsin, and Chirac, he combined pleading, outrage, and threats, calling the attacks against Banja Luka "bizarre" and "barbaric." If they continued, he said, the Bosnian Serbs would "reconsider participation in further peace talks." NATO, he went on, "has declared war against the Republic of Srpska. . . . Time is rapidly running out."

Although Karadzic's letter seemed to me to confirm the effectiveness of the Tomahawks, the strikes added to the tension within NATO. On September 11, at a special meeting of the NATO Council, France, Spain, Canada, and Greece criticized the attacks in western Bosnia, claiming that they represented an unauthorized escalation.

There was also a wintry blast from Moscow. Even before the Tomahawks, Yeltsin had written President Clinton on September 7 to express concern about the bombing. Now, the use of cruise missiles, the quintessential Cold War weapon, rattled the Russians deeply. They could not, they announced angrily, "be indifferent to the fate of the children of our fellow-Slavs." (The Pentagon immediately denied that any children had been killed in the air strikes.) Russian diplomats threatened to withdraw from the Contact Group. Defense Minister Pavel Grachev called Bill Perry to warn that the strikes could lead Moscow to reconsider its military cooperation agreements with NATO, and even threatened "to help the Serbs in a unilateral way" if the bombing continued. The next day, Russia proposed a U.N. Security Council resolution to condemn the bombing, but Ambassador Albright swiftly headed it off.

This strong Russian reaction to the bombing could not be entirely ignored. Perry and Grachev had already begun discussions about Russian participation in a post–peace agreement force in Bosnia. Beyond the Balkans lay the larger issue of Russia's relations with NATO, a volatile issue ever since President Clinton had announced our intention to enlarge the Atlantic Alliance. With tensions mounting, the President and Christopher sent Strobe Talbott to Moscow immediately for "quiet consultations." His trip proved timely and effective. After his forceful explanation that the bombing was consistent with NATO's authority and essential to the negotiations, the Russian concerns, while not eliminated, abated considerably—thus clearing the path for the continuation of the Perry-Grachev negotiations.

As the bombing continued, Croat and Bosnian Muslim military forces enjoyed their best week since the war began, even though there was still no military coordination between them. In the week after Geneva, the Croats took the town of Donji Vakuf, thus opening up a large area in western Bosnia. Karadzic charged that the NATO air strikes had assisted the offensive. But while the air strikes had undeniably aided the Federation, there was no truth to Karadzic's charge; in fact, such coordination was the ultimate nightmare of many NATO officers, the "slippery slope" toward the deep military involvement they feared and opposed. The truth remained as simple as it was ironic: the air strikes would never have occurred if Pale had not made a historic misreading of President Clinton and the United States.

We were approaching circuit overload when the Principals' Committee met at the White House on the afternoon of September 11. The President attended part of the meeting, and his presence made a huge difference, giving our discussion focus and enabling us to reach some important conclusions quickly.

Tony Lake wanted us to convene an international peace conference right away. Others began to support him, but I resisted; we needed to allow the Federation offensive to continue, and the gap among the three sides was still too great for face-to-face meetings of the three presidents. Our next diplomatic goal, I said, had to be to fix "the major flaw in the Geneva principles"—the lack of "connective tissue between the two entities."

"Has the NATO bombing reached the point of diminishing returns?" the President asked.

The question was an indication of the heavy pressure the President was under to end the bombing. "No, Mr. President," I replied. "There may come a time when continued bombing would hurt the peace efforts, but we're not there yet. The negotiating team believes we should tough it out. Our leadership position is getting stronger. We should use it or we will lose it. It is hurting the Bosnian Serbs, and helping us. As for Milosevic, he is not making a big point of it."

Christopher agreed. "The bombing should continue," he said. "It would be a mistake to back off now."

"Okay," the President said. "But I am frustrated that the air campaign is not better coordinated with the diplomatic effort."

This was an astute observation. The same point troubled me deeply; there was no mechanism or structure within the Administration capable of such coordination. It was, in fact, the role of the NSC to coordinate such interagency issues. I wanted to tell the President that this problem required immediate attention. But relations among the NSC, State, and Defense were not something an Assistant Secretary of State could fix. In fact, we later learned that Admiral Smith had ordered Admiral Ryan, who was in charge of the bombing, to have no contact with the negotiating team.

Unexpectedly, Bill Perry suggested we consider another unilateral bombing pause. This caught Warren Christopher and me slightly off guard. Why would the Secretary of Defense propose a bombing halt just when his forces were dramatically expanding the scope of the bombing? To people not familiar with the ways of the Pentagon it may have appeared inexplicable. But the huge military establishment often operates at several different levels at once. Correctly understood, the Pentagon's behavior was less surprising. The military did not like putting its pilots at risk in pursuit of a limited political objective, hence their desire to end the bombing as soon as possible. At the same time, if asked to continue the bombing, they would seek to make it as effective as possible. Thus their desire to use Tomahawk missiles and F-117s, the airplane least detectable by radar. In addition, the Navy and the Air Force both wanted to publicize, especially to Congress, the value of their new weaponry. For the Navy, this meant the Tomahawks, which were launched from naval vessels in the Adriatic. For the Air Force, it meant the expensive and controversial F-117, whose value had been questioned by some Pentagon critics.

Warren Christopher objected first. Because he was normally so soft-spoken, Christopher was especially effective when he raised his voice or showed emotion. "We must carry on the bombing until it has achieved real effectiveness," he said firmly. "The Serbs must be impressed with our willingness to bomb on a continuous basis if necessary." Christopher was supported by Lake, Albright, and myself.

Almost immediately a more serious problem arose. Admiral Owens, the Vice Chairman of the JCS, made a remark that surprised Christopher and me. In his calm, methodical, and authoritative style, Owens said NATO would run out of new authorized "Option Two" targets within two or three days. Of course, Owens said, the bombing could be continued by hitting old Option One and Two targets again. However, this would have diminishing value, and put the pilots at continually greater risk as the Bosnian Serb anti-aircraft gunners became more proficient. To attack Option Three targets, a much broader group that included Serb troop concentrations and equipment throughout Bosnia, we would need to return to both the NATO Council and the U.N. Security Council for permission. But everyone in the room knew that the chances of getting approval from our NATO allies to attack Option Three targets was close to zero.

On the drive back to the State Department after the meeting, Christopher told me that he doubted that the military had really exhausted all its authorized Option Two targets. But there was no way to question the military within its own area of responsibility—the military controlled the information and independent verification was virtually impossible.

Only moments earlier the President had observed that the bombing should be calibrated for political and diplomatic purposes, but in fact the opposite was suddenly the case; the military had rewritten our negotiating timetable. My immediate concern was that if the information became public, as so often happened after White House meetings, it would weaken our negotiating hand. If the air campaign was really going to end within a few days, we had to continue the bombing long enough to negotiate something in return. "If NATO runs out of targets before we resume our talks with Belgrade, we won't have a chance to get anything in return for the bombing," I said. "Let's not stop it for free." Christopher agreed. "Let's be sure the negotiating team has the benefit of the leverage of military force for as long as possible," he said.

Confronting this new time pressure, Christopher asked that the negotiating team leave for Belgrade the next day, four days ahead of schedule.

Before leaving the next day, I called Admiral Smith in Naples to ask how much longer he would be willing to continue the bombing. Smith replied that, assuming routine weather, he thought he had about three more days of new targets, after which he could keep the bombing going only by returning to targets that had already been hit—or, as Smith put it in his best salty old sea dog style, "cleaning up a few stray cats and dogs." The meaning behind the message was clear: Smith did not wish to let the bombing be "used" by the negotiators, and would decide when to stop based on his own judgment. This was hardly the best way to integrate diplomacy and military pressure, but we had no choice in the matter.

·   ·   ·

We slept little as we flew to Belgrade on the night of September 12–13. As we prepared for the meetings, I raised a sensitive issue: What should we do if asked to meet the two indicted war criminals who led the Bosnian Serbs, Radovan Karadzic and Ratko Mladic? Should we meet with them at all, and, if so, how should we deal with them? It was one of those rare questions that combined political and tactical considerations with questions of morality.

There was a history here. Karadzic and Mladic had met in the past with Western negotiators, including Vance, Owen, and Lord Carrington. Jimmy Carter had spent a great deal of time with Karadzic only seven months earlier, and remained in regular contact with him by phone and fax.

Nonetheless, I felt deeply uncomfortable about the prospect of sitting down with indicted war criminals. But in the end I decided it was justifiable under these circumstances. In reaching this conclusion, I was deeply influenced by the stories of Raoul Wallenberg and Folke Bernadotte, two legendary Swedes—both the subject of biographies by my wife, Kati—who had negotiated, respectively, with Adolf Eichmann and Heinrich Himmler in 1944–1945. Each man had decided to deal with a mass murderer in order to save lives. History had shown the correctness of their decisions, which had resulted in the rescue of tens of thousands of Jews before the two men themselves were killed—Wallenberg in a Soviet prison, Bernadotte at the hands of Israeli terrorists in Jerusalem in 1948.

We concluded that it was similarly acceptable to meet with Karadzic and Mladic if it would help the negotiations. As our plane descended toward the military airport in Belgrade, we decided we would not ask to meet the two men, but would see them if Milosevic suggested it. However, we would set certain conditions. We would not meet with any Bosnian Serbs—indicted or unindicted—if they presented themselves as a separate delegation or tried to negotiate on their own. At the same time, I said each member of the team could decide whether to participate if either man showed up, and whether to shake hands with them.

We landed in Belgrade in the late morning on September 13. Two hours later we were back at Milosevic's villa outside Belgrade. He was anxious to get started. An ABC television crew, led by correspondent Sheila McVicker, filmed the opening moments of our meeting for a *Nightline* special they were producing, and then retreated to the garden. As soon as they left, Milosevic complained about the expanded bombing. "Your planes are giving close air support to the Muslims and Croats," he said. I told him that he was misinformed on this point, but I readily agreed—in fact, with a certain pleasure— that the bombing, even though it was not coordinated with Federation ground troops, had the effect of helping the Muslims and Croats. "The Serbs brought it down upon themselves," I said.

Milosevic said the situation on the ground needed "calming." He thought he could get the Bosnian Serbs to agree to a cease-fire throughout the country in return for a cessation of the bombing. Then, he said, we should convene an international conference as quickly as possible to end the war.

Milosevic's proposal for a nationwide cease-fire was new. I knew this was what Washington wanted, but it was premature as long as the offensive was progressing. "A general cease-fire is out of the question at this point," I said. "But we can talk about one for the Sarajevo area."

We were struck by the change in his tone. Clearly, the Croat-Muslim offensive in the west and the bombing were having a major effect on the Bosnian Serbs. Milosevic seemed in a rush. Unfortunately, so were many people in the West. Not for the first time, I thought: the chances for a viable peace will improve if the bombing and the offensive continue, at least for a while.

At about 5:00 P.M., Milosevic unveiled his big surprise. "Karadzic and Mladic are in another villa, about two hundred meters away," he said. "They can be here in ten minutes. Why don't we ask them to join us so you can negotiate directly with them?"

I was grateful we had prepared ourselves for this moment. At that instant, however, I felt a jolt go through my body. It is not an exaggeration to say that I simply hated the two men for what they had done—including, indirectly, causing the deaths of our three colleagues.

"Let's talk awhile first," I said, trying not to appear anxious. "Are you sure that we can accomplish anything? Why don't you see them first while we wait here?"

Milosevic said he was sure we could make progress if we used his "technology"—by which he meant the theatrical style with which he loved to dazzle and outmaneuver other politicians in the Balkans.

"Mr. President, in that case, we are ready to meet with them, but with two conditions. First, they must be part of your delegation, you must lead the discussions, and you must control them. Second, they must not give us a lot of historical bullshit, as they have with everyone else. They must be ready for serious discussions."

"They will agree," Milosevic said. "No bullshit. Let me get them." He told an aide to send for the Bosnian Serbs. We asked the ABC crew waiting outside to leave, without telling them why. Then we had drinks on the patio and waited for the men from Pale. The lawns blended into trees not far away. In the early August evening there was still plenty of natural light.

After about twenty minutes a couple of Mercedes sedans pulled up in the driveway. Two men stepped out of the first car, trailed by others. As they approached us through the trees in the fading summer light, their unmistakable silhouettes jolted me again: one, in a suit, tall with a wild shock of hair; the other, short and burly, in combat fatigues, walking as though through a muddy field.

Before the Bosnian Serbs could reach us, I turned to Milosevic and said, "We'll take a walk while you explain the ground rules. We'll return when you can assure us they have agreed." We retreated into the woods about one hundred yards behind the main house, where we waited nervously and reviewed our strategy. Ten minutes later an aide came running up to us and said Milosevic and his guests were ready.

I did not shake hands, although both Karadzic and Mladic tried to. Some of our team did, others did not; it was their choice. We sat down at a long table on the patio facing each other, and began to talk. Arrayed next to Karadzic were other Bosnian Serbs whose names were familiar to us, including Momcilo Krajisnik, the Speaker of the Bosnian Serb Assembly. Karadzic, speaking partly in English, began complaining immediately about how unfair the bombing was. He said he was ready for a nationwide cessation of hostilities, but only if the Federation agreed not to "take advantage of it." I said the United States supported a general cease-fire in principle, but not at this time. We were here only to discuss the situation around Sarajevo.

As Karadzic replied, I looked at Mladic. Hollywood could not find a more convincing war villain. He glowered—there was no better word for it—and engaged each of the Americans in what seemed to us, when we compared notes later, as staring contests. Nonetheless, he had a compelling presence; it was not hard to understand why his troops revered him; he was, I thought, one of those lethal combinations that history thrusts up occasionally—a charismatic murderer.

Despite his size, Karadzic was not an imposing figure at this meeting. He had a sad face, with heavy jowls, a soft chin, and surprisingly gentle eyes. He had studied psychiatry in New York and understood English well. He was quick to launch into a self-pitying diatribe against NATO and the Muslims, whom he accused of mortaring their own marketplace on August 28 in order to lure NATO into the war. He referred several times to the "humiliation the Serbs are suffering."

After a few minutes of Karadzic's harangue, I turned to Milosevic. "Mr. President," I said, "you assured us that this would not happen. If it continues, we are prepared to leave immediately." Karadzic responded emotionally. "If we can't get anything done here, I will call President Carter," he said. "I am in regular contact with him." We already knew, of course, that Karadzic had invited the former President to get involved again. Karadzic started to rise, as if to make a telephone call.

For the only time in the evening, I spoke directly to him. "Let me tell you something," I said, my voice rising. "President Carter appointed me as Assistant Secretary of State. I worked for him for four years. Like most Americans, I have great admiration for him. But he is now a private citizen. We work only for President Clinton. We take orders only from President Clinton. That is all there is to it."

Karadzic sat down abruptly, and Milosevic said something to him in Serbian. For the rest of the meeting, Karadzic was on his best behavior. As Pardew noted later, Karadzic played the "facilitator who kept the Bosnian Serbs on track"—something we assumed his psychiatric training had prepared him for. He showed no sign of the qualities that had led even a cautious observer like Ambassador Zimmermann to label him the "Himmler of his generation."[2]

Karadzic calmly proposed that the Americans produce a draft agreement. I asked Clark, Owen, Hill, and Pardew to work on a document that would end the siege of Sarajevo. As my colleagues hunched over pads of paper, Milosevic and I walked around the garden and talked about other matters. "You know, that was smart," he said, "what you said about Jimmy Carter. Those guys"—he meant the Bosnian Serbs—"are so cut off from the world they think Carter still determines American policy."

Dusk had fallen by the time my colleagues produced a first draft. Seated on a low brick wall about seventy-five feet away, Milosevic and I watched as General Clark began to read his draft to the Serbs, pausing regularly for translation. We could not make out his exact words, but the deep, booming voice of the Serbian interpreter drifted toward us. The scene was unforgettable: Clark standing under the tall lamp, reading from his draft, the Serbs clustered around, listening intently, the familiar shapes of the two main Serb protagonists outlined in the shadows. Occasionally we could hear other Serb voices getting louder.

As Milosevic and I chatted, Milutinovic ran over to us and said something to Milosevic. "We better join them," Milosevic said. "They're in trouble." Everyone was standing, but Milosevic pulled up a chair and sat down. After a moment's hesitation, I did the same in order to establish some rough equality between us.

Karadzic, clearly angry, said that our draft proposal was unacceptable. Suddenly Mladic erupted. Pushing to the center of the circle, he began a long, emotional diatribe. "The situation is explosive, worse than at any time since the war began," he said. "There is no justification for the bombing. NATO is supporting the regular Croatian Army inside our nation. It's worse than the Nazis. But they cannot destroy the spirit of the Serb people. Neither can the United States. The bombing is a criminal act." Then, a memorable phrase: "No one can be allowed to give away a meter of our sacred Serb soil."

This was the intimidating style he had used with the Dutch commander at Srebrenica, with Janvier, and with so many others. He gave off the scent of danger. It was not hard to see how frightening this man might be, especially on his own home ground. I did not know if his rage was real or feigned, but this was the genuine Mladic, the one who could unleash a murderous rampage.

Turning my back on Mladic and Karadzic, I rose from my chair and looked down at Milosevic. "Mr. President," I said, "we had an agreement. This behavior is clearly not consistent with it. If your 'friends' "—I said the word with as much sarcasm as I could—"do not wish to have a serious discussion, we will leave now."

Milosevic paused for a moment, perhaps to gauge if this was a bluff. Perhaps he sensed that it wasn't. NATO planes were bombing Bosnian Serb territory as we spoke. It was our moment of maximum leverage, and I was not bluffing about leaving, although we were acutely conscious of the fact that we might lose our best negotiating chip, the bombing, within two or three days.

Milosevic spoke sharply in Serbian to his colleagues, and they began to argue. Motioning my colleagues to follow, I walked to the other end of the patio, where we waited, listening to the sounds of an increasingly angry debate under the lamps.

It was over in a few minutes. Milosevic came over to us, asked us to rejoin him, and said that the Bosnian Serbs were ready to negotiate on the basis of our draft.

Our draft began with a Bosnian Serb commitment to "cease all offensive operations" in the Sarajevo area and remove all heavy weapons from the same area within a week. They also had to open two land routes out of Sarajevo, one the Kiseljak road, to unimpeded humanitarian road traffic. The Sarajevo airport had to reopen within twenty-four hours. In return, NATO would stand down its bombing for seventy-two hours, but resume the bombing if there was no compliance.

I left most of the negotiating to my colleagues, intervening only when necessary to break an impasse. I did not wish to diminish my role by spending too much time with Karadzic and Mladic, and I trusted my colleagues completely. I called Christopher and Tarnoff to describe the remarkable scene unfolding at the villa, and wandered around with Milosevic, talking about next steps in the peace process. Food was set out on a table on the patio, and Milosevic invited me to eat dinner with him and Mladic. I sat with the two men briefly, but left without eating, returning only after Mladic had left. Commenting on this later, Milosevic said I had insulted Mladic by not shaking his hand or eating with him, and this would not make the negotiations any easier. "If that is true, so be it," I replied, and repeated an earlier theme of our meetings: "We expect you to make this process work."

The Bosnian Serbs argued over almost every word, but sometime after midnight we had what we wanted: after four years, the siege of Sarajevo would be lifted. There was still one important procedural matter to resolve. The Serbs insisted I sign or witness the document. I refused, explaining that we had no formal authority to reach any agreement concerning the activities of NATO or the U.N. We wanted a document with only Serb signatures—and Milosevic and Milutinovic as its witnesses. This was something of a diplomatic innovation—a document drafted by us but signed only by the Serbs as a unilateral undertaking. None of us was aware of diplomatic precedent for it, but it fit our needs perfectly. After it was signed and witnessed, I explained, we would deliver it to Janvier with a "recommendation" that NATO and the U.N. suspend the bombing. The Bosnian Serbs protested vigorously, but they had no choice, and after another long debate, they agreed to the format we had proposed.

At 2:15 on the morning of September 14, after more than ten hours of negotiations, the Serbs signed the document we had written. We watched as one by one they affixed their signatures to the paper—first Karadzic, who signed without hesitating; then the "Vice President of Republika Srpksa," Nikola Koljevic, followed by Krajisnik. Mladic signed last. He had long since stopped participating in the negotiations, and sat slumped on a couch on the far side of the room away from his colleagues. One of Milosevic's aides carried the agreement to him. He reached out for the pen, scrawled his name on it without looking at it, and sank back into the sofa. He looked utterly spent.

Finally, Milosevic and his Foreign Minister signed the document as witnesses. We got up to leave, carrying the precious original with us. If it held, the long siege of Sarajevo would be over. Karadzic came over to me and grabbed my hand. "We are ready for peace," he said in English. "Why did you bomb us?"

"I think you know," I said.

I was beginning to get a sense of the Pale Serbs: headstrong, given to empty theatrical statements, but in the end, essentially bullies when their bluff was called. The Western mistake over the previous four years had been to treat the Serbs as rational people with whom one could argue, negotiate, compromise, and agree. In fact, they respected only force or an unambiguous and credible threat to use it.

CHAPTER 11

The Western Offensive

(September 14–20)

It's farewell to the drawing-room's civilised cry,
The professor's sensible whereto and why,
The frock-coated diplomat's social aplomb,
Now matters are settled with gas and with bomb.

—W. H. AUDEN, "Danse Macabre"

WE BELIEVED WE HAD MADE THE BEST possible deal in Belgrade, though I still wonder what might have been accomplished had we been able to continue the bombing for another two weeks. There were few second thoughts in Washington, however, where the reaction was astonishing. Buoyed by enthusiastic expressions of support during a long night of telephone conversations with Washington, we left Belgrade for Zagreb just after dawn on September 14 to deliver the Serb agreement to General Janvier. The United Nations command were sticklers for proper procedures, and we did not have formal authority to conduct a negotiation on their behalf. To minimize the U.N.'s sense of injured pride, we told Janvier that we were simply transmitting a "unilateral undertaking" by the Bosnian Serbs concerning Sarajevo, along with a recommendation that the U.N. suspend the bombing. But we asked him to wait until after we had talked to Izetbegovic, whom we planned to meet in Mostar that afternoon.

Janvier, whose own negotiations with Mladic had been a well-publicized disaster, seemed stunned by our success. But he recovered gracefully, thanked us, and said he would request a twelve-hour bombing "pause" and await the outcome of our talks with Izetbegovic. In military terminology a pause is different from a suspension—it is a brief period when planes are not flying, while the operational orders for the bombing are still in place.

From U.N. headquarters, we raced across town to brief Tudjman, who showed no interest in the Sarajevo agreement. He was focused entirely on the military offensive in western Bosnia. The Bosnian Serb Army was in disarray, and there were reports that some Serb soldiers had shot their own officers. At least one hundred thousand Serb refugees were pouring into Banja Luka or heading further east to escape the Federation advance.

Anger in Mostar. Bracing ourselves for a difficult encounter with Izetbegovic, we flew to Split and drove for three hours through the mountains to the medieval city of Mostar to meet Izetbegovic. We knew the Bosnians would be unhappy; from their point of view, stopping the bombing after only a few weeks in return for ending a four-year siege was a poor bargain.

One of my most vivid memories from my trip to Yugoslavia in 1960 was the beautiful sixteenth-century bridge linking the two parts of Mostar. It was perhaps Yugoslavia's most famous symbol of multiethnic harmony. When I last saw the high-arched bridge in 1992, it was crumbling under continuous shelling by the Croats, pathetically protected by automobile tires hung over its sides on ropes. Two years later, in September of 1994, when I visited Mostar with General Charles Boyd, the Deputy Commander in Chief of U.S. Forces in Europe, the bridge was gone, replaced by a narrow, swaying metal footbridge hundreds of feet above the Neretva River, which Boyd and I cautiously crossed, stepping over gaping holes in the steel planking.

When our negotiating team arrived on the afternoon of September 14, the fighting between the Croats and the Muslims in Mostar had been over for more than a year, as a result of intense efforts by Warren Christopher and U.S. negotiator Charles Redman. Their creation, the Federation, existed—but only on paper. As Silajdzic put it, the Federation was "a house with only a roof, a roof full of holes." The damage from that Croat-Muslim war was still palpable in Mostar, where the multiethnic city had become a cauldron of hate.

With Croat and Bosnian forces advancing against the Serbs in western Bosnia, there should have been a marked improvement in the situation in Mostar, far to the south. But there wasn't. Along the line dividing the two halves of Mostar, there were only rubble and tension. The hostility of the people was evident from their stares and gestures. The Croat portion of the city was held by organized gangsters. Each part of the city was patrolled by heavily armed men in police and paramilitary uniforms. When we had toured the "confrontation line" in 1994, Boyd and I had walked between armed Croats and Muslims men only ten or fifteen feet apart who drank and talked to one another, joked, and even played cards—but with the safeties off their weapons. It was one of the saddest and most tense walks of my life.

Now, a year later, little had changed. As our heavily armed convoy weaved through the streets, around wrecked vehicles and barricades, to reach the Muslim sector, where our meeting would be held, I was again appalled by the senselessness of the war.

. . .

The meeting with Izetbegovic was even worse than we expected. Christopher had called Izetbegovic earlier in the day, urging him to support the agreement, but the Bosnian President told the Secretary he wanted to withhold judgment until he saw us in Mostar. He showed no appreciation that the long siege of his capital city was over. He would prefer to let the people of Sarajevo live under Serb guns for a while longer if it also meant that the NATO bombing would continue.

Haris Silajdzic showed even greater fury. For the first time I saw in the normally urbane Prime Minister a tendency to explode that would re-emerge, sometimes disastrously, at tense moments in the negotiations. Calling the cease-fire "totally unacceptable," Silajdzic demanded that the bombing continue. As Silajdzic continued to complain vigorously, Izetbegovic signaled me to leave the room with him. Once alone, he told me he understood why the United States had taken its position, and would reluctantly support us. But, he said, he could not publicly endorse a bombing suspension yet. (There was a large press corps assembled outside our meeting place.) First, he would have to return to Sarajevo and, as he put it, "work with my people." He would have to show them that he had forced us to produce something "better" than the present agreement. In other words, he wanted us to return to Belgrade and "strengthen" the agreement.

I said that I sympathized with his dilemma. I told him, in confidence, that the bombing would have ended within days anyway and that his choices, like mine, were therefore limited. We returned to the larger meeting, where Silajdzic demanded several changes in the agreement. I agreed to negotiate all of these with Milosevic as soon as I returned to Belgrade, after a Contact Group meeting scheduled for the next day in Geneva. We parted amid confusion, in a mud-filled alley surrounded by journalists using long "boom" microphones to try to pick up our farewell comments. True to their promise, the Bosnians were reserved in their public comments, but they did not go so far as to attack the agreement.

Geneva. The next morning, I asked Bob Owen and Chris Hill to drive to Sarajevo with Silajdzic to reassure him and begin discussion of a postwar constitution. For both Americans it was their first trip over Mount Igman, and when they reached the scene of the accident, they got out for a moment to pay tribute to their fallen comrades and, as Hill told me later, take a look at that "godforsaken and worthless place."

The rest of us flew to Geneva for another round of Contact Group ritual. With the pace of negotiations so intense, I wanted to postpone the meeting, but we were locked in because we had agreed to let the Russians host it in lieu of a meeting in Moscow. The meeting was large and messy, but it received heavy publicity, which was all the Russians cared about. Igor Ivanov, the Russian Deputy Foreign Minister, chaired the meeting. Usually affable, Ivanov occasionally exploded in anger, but regained his composure quickly. He did not understand English as well as he thought he did, and rarely used an interpreter. This led to some misunderstandings, which the German Contact Group representative, Wolfgang Ischinger, helped smooth over.

All four nations pressed us to convene an international peace conference. I replied that the differences between the sides were still too great, but we would get there eventually. Instead, I suggested we invite the three Foreign Ministers to another meeting, similar to the one in Geneva, to be held during the United Nations General Assembly session in New York near the end of September. We needed an agreement on the creation of central governmental institutions—the "connective tissue" between the Serbs and the Federation—that had eluded us at Geneva. If we could achieve that, we could begin to plan "the big one"—a full-fledged peace conference with the three presidents.

Belgrade. We flew back to Belgrade on the afternoon of September 16 to convince Milosevic to accept changes in the cease-fire agreement. The bombing had been suspended since 10:00 A.M. on September 14, but we made it clear to Milosevic that it could resume. President Clinton had made a strong and simple public statement, at our request, to underline this threat: "Let me emphasize that if the Bosnian Serbs do not comply with their commitments, the air strikes will resume."

Milosevic asked General Momcilo Perisic, the Yugoslav Army chief of staff, to join the meeting. Perisic was a sullen chain-smoker who looked like a living Cold War relic. Milosevic said that Mladic was in the hospital for removal of kidney stones. I silently hoped that they would be the kind of medical problem that Chinese and Soviet leaders sometimes discovered in their political opponents, stones from which there is no recovery. Perhaps reading my thoughts, Milosevic offered to let us visit Mladic in the hospital to prove he really was sick. I declined.*

We presented to Milosevic and Perisic the requirements for continuing the halt in the bombing: first, we wanted the French Rapid Reaction Force to protect the roads into Sarajevo; second, "humanitarian" goods would henceforth mean *all* civilian goods, including cement, glass, shoes, and radios, which the Serbs had previously prevented from reaching the Bosnian capital; third, we

---

* We were never sure of the truth about Mladic's illness, although we did confirm that he had been hospitalized. One theory, widely held around Belgrade, was that Mladic did not want to withdraw the heavy weapons from around Sarajevo, and was sent to the hospital so that he'd be sidelined while the deal was made. In any case, Mladic soon returned to the field to rally his troops.

needed assurance that a drafting error made during the long night of September 12–13 concerning the size of artillery that must be removed would be corrected. This mistake, the result of fatigue by a member of our military support group, had already been reported around the world as a "major concession" by the American negotiators. Finally, we told the Serbs that henceforth the United States and NATO, not the U.N., would decide if they were in compliance.

Throughout this long discussion, I shuttled between the smoke-filled dining room in the villa and an American military field telephone on the patio, through which we had opened a continuous line to Sarajevo and General Rupert Smith, the British commander of all U.N. forces inside Bosnia.* Milosevic and Perisic argued over some of our demands, but eventually they agreed to all of them. Still, the same issue that had undermined so many previous cease-fires remained: making sure the orders agreed to at one level were carried out at another. The Serbs had become expert at pretending that they could not control their field commanders.

To prevent this, we demanded the name of a Serb field commander in the Sarajevo area with whom General Rupert Smith could negotiate starting the next morning in Sarajevo. Perisic offered the name of General Dragomir Milosevic (no relation to the Serbian President), who, he promised, would appear for discussions in Sarajevo the next morning. From Sarajevo, over a poor telephone connection, Smith told me dryly that he doubted he would ever see the Serb general.

Smith and I spent over an hour speaking on the ancient field telephone that night, and Wes Clark took over whenever I had to return to the villa. The obsolete military telephone system—there were no direct telephone lines between Belgrade and Sarajevo—was difficult to use, and several times the system got so overheated that we had to wait in silence while it cooled down. From Sarajevo, General Smith impatiently questioned our negotiations. I understood why he might mistrust Serb promises—so did we—but, like Janvier, Smith seemed slow to realize that this new situation offered a unique opportunity to break the Serb siege of Sarajevo.

We had been with Milosevic for almost seven hours. As Owen and Hill waited for me to conclude my conversation with General Smith, they tried to talk to Milosevic about constitutional issues. But no matter how hard the polite but persistent Owen tried, Milosevic avoided the subject. Finally, Milutinovic pulled me into a corner of the dining room. "Listen," he told me, "tell your colleagues that my President will not discuss these issues in front of

---

* Smith reported to Janvier, whose command in Zagreb covered all U.N. military activities in the former Yugoslavia, including Bosnia, Croatia, and Macedonia.

General Perisic. Hold off, and he will talk about them later." Such deep distrust among close compatriots was as common as plum brandy in the Balkans.

When Milosevic accepted all of our demands that evening, NATO's bombing
was truly over. Although it could have started again if the Serbs challenged the
agreement, the threat of resumption kept the Serbs in line. We got our first
proof of this the very next day: to General Smith's surprise, General Milosevic appeared on schedule, and the withdrawal of Serb heavy weapons from the
Sarajevo area began shortly thereafter.

The following day, to dramatize the end of the siege of Sarajevo, we did something that had not been attempted during the war: we visited all three Balkan
capitals and met all three Presidents on a single day. This was more than a
stunt; we were entering a new phase of the negotiations, where the ability to
visit all three capitals in a single day was essential.

Our first stop on Sunday morning was Zagreb, where the topic was the
gathering momentum of the Federation offensive—although, of course, the
Federation was never mentioned; as far as the Croatians were concerned, this
was their operation. Two more important towns had fallen: Bosanski Petrovac
and Jajce. The Bosnian Serb communications network in the west remained
out of commission, although the Serbs were struggling to repair it.

With many of the roads toward the Serb strongholds lying open before his
forces, Tudjman had to decide: should he continue the offensive, and, if so,
how far should he go? His government was receiving mixed signals from the
United States, and he was confused.

Tudjman's confusion about the American view was understandable. Two
days before I returned to Zagreb, Galbraith had presented to Defense Minister
Susak a formal message—a démarche, in State Department jargon—asking
the Croatians to halt the military campaign. Galbraith, who did not agree with
the démarche, had asked for a revision, but his appeal was overruled by Washington, and he unhappily delivered it. At almost the same time, in separate
meetings with Croatian Foreign Minister Mate Granic in Washington on September 12, Lake and Christopher recommended that the advance stop as soon
as the confrontation lines were "stabilized."

I did not agree, as John Kornblum told Washington. Simply stated, after
four years of Serb aggression, the Federation forces were finally gaining territory lost at the beginning of the war. As a matter of both simple justice and
high strategy, we should not oppose the offensive unless it either ran into trouble or went too far.

Like so many issues, the policy dispute began with a flawed intelligence assessment. Almost every morning's "daily intelligence report" brought to top
Washington officials new warnings of the dangers posed by the offensive. The

"experts" predicted that the more successful the Croatian-Bosnian offensive, the greater the chance that the regular Yugoslav Army would re-enter the war. These opinions were based not on secret intelligence of Yugoslav plans, but on a long-standing belief in the intelligence community about the military superiority of the Serbs and their cohesiveness.

By mid-September, having spent more time with the Serbian leadership than any other Americans, we had come to a different opinion. We concluded that Milosevic had virtually written off the Bosnian Serbs—as he had the Krajina Serbs—and would not intervene militarily to save them. In our opinion, there was only one move that might bring Yugoslav troops back into Bosnia: closing the narrow five-kilometer-long corridor at Brcko, an action that would physically cut off the majority of the Bosnian Serb population from Serbia.

Washington's desire to stop the offensive became public just as we met privately with Tudjman. In a front-page article in *The New York Times* filed from Belgrade—an article which, significantly, quoted Washington officials—Chris Hedges wrote,

> United Nations and American officials said they feared that the assault could draw Serbia directly into the war. . . . "All the lights have been red, irrevocably red," the [Washington] official said. "It risks blowing the whole thing out of the water." The message from Washington, this official said, was "quit while you're ahead."

The next day, White House Press Secretary Mike McCurry put the same message on the record. "There's fighting going on in western Bosnia," he said. "We wish they would suspend that fighting and turn their attention to the discussions that Ambassador Holbrooke has been conducting." I would have preferred a different message from the White House, but McCurry, a highly skilled press secretary, would not have made these remarks without guidance from the NSC.

While Washington wanted the offensive to stop, we never had a clear instruction, only the general sense of our senior colleagues, who left to us the exact calibration of the signal. Remembering again how Harriman and Vance had been "overinstructed" during their negotiations with the North Vietnamese in 1968, I was grateful that Washington was giving us such flexibility and support. Later, Tom Donilon told me that most of the credit for protecting our flexibility was owed to Warren Christopher, who, despite his own views, argued that Washington should back its negotiators.

Galbraith and I saw Tudjman on September 14. Tudjman wanted clarification of the American position. He bluntly asked for my *personal* views. I indicated my general support for the offensive, but delayed a more detailed exchange for a second meeting so that I could discuss it with my colleagues and Washington.

Galbraith and I met Tudjman alone again on September 17. At the same time, by prearrangement, Clark, Hill, Kerrick, and Pardew met with Susak. Peter and I sat side by side on an ornate sofa, embroidered with gold trim, while Tudjman sat at my right in a Louis Quinze armchair.

I told Tudjman the offensive had great value to the negotiations. It would be much easier to retain at the table what had been won on the battlefield than to get the Serbs to give up territory they had controlled for several years. I urged Tudjman to take Sanski Most, Prijedor, and Bosanski Novi—all important towns that had become worldwide symbols of ethnic cleansing. If they were captured before we opened negotiations on territory, they would remain under Federation control—otherwise it would be difficult to regain them in a negotiation.

Banja Luka, I said, was a different matter. As we spoke the road to this largest Bosnian Serb city appeared to lie open to the Croatian offensive, although it was not at all certain that the city could be taken. We knew that Susak wanted to go for it as quickly as possible. On the other hand, I told Tudjman, the city was unquestionably within the Serb portion of Bosnia. Even if it were captured, the Federation would have to return it to the Serbs in any peace negotiation. Finally, capturing Banja Luka would generate over two hundred thousand additional refugees. I did not think the United States should encourage an action that would create so many more refugees. I concluded my comments with a blunt statement: "Mr. President, I urge you to go as far as you can, but not to take Banja Luka."

Since we were encouraging military action in three specific areas while objecting to it in Banja Luka, I was conscious, of course, that we could be accused of applying a double standard. But these three towns were smaller and less charged with emotional and historical baggage, and they could be retained in a negotiation. And the number of refugees that would be created weighed heavily on my mind.

Even while encouraging the offensive, Galbraith and I expressed great concern over the many refugees already displaced. We told Tudjman that there was no excuse for the brutal treatment of Serbs that followed most Croatian military successes. The abuse of Serb civilians, most of whom had lived in the area for generations, was wrong. Using a provocative phrase normally applied only to the Serbs, I told Tudjman that current Croatian behavior might be viewed as a milder form of ethnic cleansing. Tudjman reacted strongly, but did not quite deny it; if our information was correct, he said, he

The Western Offensive, August–September 1995

SLOV.

Zagreb

Karlovac

C R O A T I A

HUNGARY

SERBIA

EASTERN SLAVONIA

Vukovar

KRAJINA

Bihac
Pocket

Bosanski Novi
Prijedor

Bosanski Samac

Sanski Most
Bosanski
Petrovac

Omarska
Banja
Luka

Doboj

Brcko

Udbina

BOSNIA-HERZEGOVINA

Jajce

Tuzla

Mali
Zvornik

Srebrenica

Knin

Kiseljak

Zepa

Rogatica

Sarajevo

Pale

Split

Mt.
Igman

Gorazde

Mostar

Foca

MONTE-
NEGRO

Dubrovnik

Podgorica

0   20 miles

0   20 kilometers

Direction of
Croat-Muslim
Offensive

Bosnian Serb–
controlled area
as of July 1995

Croat-Muslim
Federation–
controlled area
as of July 1995

would put an immediate stop to it. On the critical question of whether or not to take Banja Luka, Tudjman was noncommittal, although he made a strange and troubling proposal—that we "trade" Banja Luka for Tuzla, the most Muslim city in Bosnia. Galbraith leaned over to me and whispered, "This is one of his obsessions. No one else agrees with it." I told him it was inconceivable, and it was never revived—but it had provided a momentary glimpse into his heart.

Tudjman's proposal reflected his deep hatred of the Muslims and his dream to unite all Croats in one country, under one flag—under his leadership. He knew he could not rearrange international boundaries while the war continued, but he was testing the idea of a substantial land swap that would restructure the entire region. Under this scheme, Zagreb would gain de facto control of much of western Bosnia, which was closer physically and economically to Zagreb than to Sarajevo, while the Serbs would control much of eastern Bosnia, leaving the Muslims with a landlocked ministate around Sarajevo. We called this the "Stalin-Hitler" scenario, recalling the division of Poland in August 1939. We had repeatedly asked Tudjman to repudiate rumors of such a deal—one version of which had received wide publicity after he had discussed it informally at a dinner in London in May 1995.

Tensions were growing again between the Croats and Muslims. That same day we received alarming news: after taking the town of Bosanski Petrovac, the two sides had turned on each other, and three Croats had been killed by Muslim soldiers. Something had to be done immediately.

I asked Tudjman if he would agree to meet with Izetbegovic under American auspices to forge a common position. Sacirbey had previously suggested that we convene such a meeting, but the idea of an American Assistant Secretary of State convening two heads of state, who already knew each other well and met regularly, seemed both presumptuous and odd. The alarming incident at Bosanski Petrovac changed that: the explosive situation could undo everything that the Federation offensive had gained.

Return to Sarajevo. On this three-country day, we wanted to take our small jet into Sarajevo to show our confidence in the cease-fire. But the U.S. Air Force felt it was too dangerous, so, from Zagreb, we flew to the American air base in Aviano, Italy, and switched to a C-130 military cargo plane. For this flight, the Air Force was taking no chances: the crew captain, a colonel from Germany, made us don flak jackets and helmets as we crossed the coastline, and the pilot discharged chaff to confuse hostile radar as we descended into the Sarajevo valley. I sat in the cockpit with the pilots, looking for the spot on Igman where the APC had plunged off the road, and soon spied a barely discernable vertical slash of flattened trees descending from the road. We stared at it in silence for a moment before we bounced onto the runway.

I cannot describe my feelings as we returned to the very spot from which we had lifted off with the bodies of our three colleagues exactly four weeks earlier. This time the sun was out, and so was a very large press contingent, behind a rope. I said a few words and quickly moved on. On the way into the city in our armored cars, past the overturned buses and shattered buildings, we saw streets with pedestrians for the first time in months. A few people waved at the American Embassy vehicles. By the time we reached the presidency building, several hundred people had gathered across the street. As we got out of our cars, they applauded, and a few waved small American flags. The siege of Sarajevo was over.

Inside the building there was no cheering. Izetbegovic was sour and Silajdzic visibly unhappy. When I tried to discuss rebuilding Sarajevo, they ignored me. They did not believe the Bosnian Serbs would actually withdraw their heavy weapons; after all, they had not done so before. I was not pleased with this response. "You are concentrating only on the small picture," I said to Izetbegovic. "If the Serbs violate, we will resume the bombing. But if they comply, you must be ready to move forward toward peace and reconstruction."

The situation had changed too fast for these brave but isolated men to recognize how much progress had been made. Further pressure would only cause further problems. I dropped the rest of our agenda, and we parted grumpily. As we walked out, Sacirbey told me I was spending too much time with the Serbs—a standard Muslim refrain.

Our delegation went to see General Rupert Smith to encourage him to take a firm line with the Bosnian Serbs. We had a chance to break them in the Sarajevo area right then if Smith would take an uncompromising approach to implementing the agreement reached two days earlier. "This is the time to challenge the Serbs," I said. "We finally have a written arrangement and a mechanism with which we can go back to Milosevic and force compliance. We can hold the threat of resumed bombing over their heads." Smith was well known for being more aggressive than Janvier, but he hesitated. He did not want to be held responsible for what he felt was excessively rigorous enforcement.

"We must do things our way," Smith said stiffly. "Perhaps you do not understand." He went to the map and began a lengthy explanation of the battlefield situation. He still feared retaliation. "And of course we have the usual troubles communicating our instructions to all the troops," he said. By this he meant that the various nationalities serving under him reacted unpredictably to instructions. "They are conditioned to do things a certain way," he said dryly. What he meant was: some U.N. troops do not follow my orders.

As we were leaving, Smith pulled me aside, suddenly much friendlier. "Let me be clear," he said in a voice so low no one else could hear. "I cannot control the French commander of Sarajevo Sector.* He gets his guidance directly from Janvier, and you know what that means."

We returned to Belgrade, again via Italy. If anyone was counting, observed Chris Hill, we had been in four different countries (and in Italy and Serbia twice) during the day. But we still had another three hours of talks with Milosevic ahead of us, accompanied by another heavy dinner. Milosevic seemed unconcerned about the general military situation. When Pardew and Clark told him that the Bosnian Serb forces in the west had fallen apart, he did not argue. Instead, he urged us again to convene an international peace conference in the United States as quickly as possible.

Milosevic was proud of his knowledge of America, and particularly admired the motorcycle daredevil Evel Knievel. Referring to one of Knievel's most famous (and unsuccessful) stunts, I responded, "You can't leap the Grand Canyon in two jumps. It's too early for a conference. The gap between the sides is still too great to bring you together." Milosevic shrugged; he would keep trying.

The House with Only a Roof. The next morning, September 19, we convened the Tudjman-Izetbegovic meeting in Zagreb. In the two days since we had arranged the gathering, its urgency had increased because of an unexpected military setback for the Croatians. Regular units of the Croatian Army had encountered heavy Serb resistance and high water while trying to cross the Una River on the Croatian-Bosnian border. For the first time since the offensive began, Croatian casualties had been significant, some twenty-five killed and fifty still trapped on the opposite bank. The Danish battalion in UNPROFOR, caught in the middle of the fighting, had suffered two killed and eight wounded. Furious at this violation of an international border by the Croatian Army, General Rupert Smith called to tell me that he was considering a request for NATO air strikes *against the Croatians*—more a proof of his understandable rage than a real possibility.

This first serious military setback visibly changed the Croatian mood. The aggressiveness two days earlier had been replaced with a more cautious attitude. In addition, the Bosnian Serb Army had begun to stabilize its lines, encouraged by Mladic's return to the front from his Belgrade hospital bed. Intelligence reports said Mladic was digging in east of Banja Luka with heavy artillery—ironically, weapons redeployed after being withdrawn from the

---

* Ironically, the man he was referring to was General Bachelet, who had been so helpful to us on Mount Igman.

Sarajevo area in accordance with our agreement. Banja Luka, swollen with refugees, still lay near the Croatian front lines, but already it seemed less open to a quick strike. The Federation would have to fight for it, which meant a big artillery battle; the Croatians, having prevented the Muslims from obtaining heavy artillery throughout the war, had the only long guns. Thus the decision on Banja Luka lay almost entirely with Tudjman.

The September 19 meeting between the two Presidents, held in a large conference room in Tudjman's palace, began badly. Izetbegovic was three hours late from Sarajevo, and this left Tudjman fuming, though the reason for the delay—bad weather, bad roads—seemed understandable enough. Except for Galbraith, none of us had ever seen the two men together before, and their intense personal animosity was worse than we had imagined.

Tudjman began aggressively. His appetite for conquest had diminished since his troops had been trapped on the river, but his anger at his Bosnian allies was ugly. "*We* have suffered the casualties, and we liberated eighty percent of this territory ourselves," he shouted contemptuously across the table at the diminutive Bosnian President, as forty people listened in astonishment. "Now you demand we turn over to you towns that belong to Croatia, that Croatians freed. You insist we capture areas and then turn them over to you. This is simply unacceptable." Izetbegovic shrank back into his chair, saying nothing. I watched in horror, listening through earphones to a frantic simultaneous translation. As Galbraith observed later, "It was like observing a therapy session through a one-way mirror."

Sacirbey, seated next to me, whispered urgently, "You've got to stop this. Take over before it's too late." I asked permission to make a comment, and both Presidents abruptly turned toward me. It was suddenly clear that they wanted the United States to tell them what to do—a strange moment, which we often recalled later. An aspect of the Balkan character was revealed anew: once enraged, these leaders needed outside supervision to stop themselves from self-destruction.

I began by reminding them that the main purpose of this meeting was to bring the two parts of the Federation back together. With the recent territorial gains, there was a real chance for success—but only if the Federation worked. Fighting between Croats and Muslims at Bosanski Petrovac, and the tensions over who would control each newly recaptured area, benefited only the Serbs. We could not go to a peace conference with a divided Federation.

I repeated my objections to the capture of Banja Luka, stressing that I was talking *only* about Banja Luka, and not about the rest of the offensive. Izetbegovic said nothing. This was Tudjman's decision. Listening for a moment, Tudjman turned to Izetbegovic, and asked, quite calmly, "Shall we agree with Ambassador Holbrooke?" With a shrug, Izetbegovic agreed.

Surprised at the speed with which the issue had been resolved—and the equally rapid change in Tudjman's mood—I proposed we make a joint announcement immediately after the meeting. Tudjman suggested that we make the announcement ourselves, and not in the presence of either Izetbegovic or himself. As usual, the leaders wanted to leave the impression that the Americans had pressured them to do what they probably would have done anyway.

As we left the meeting, I pulled Defense Minister Susak aside. "Gojko, I want to be absolutely clear," I said. "Nothing we said today should be construed to mean that we want you to stop the rest of the offensive, other than Banja Luka. Speed is important. We can't say so publicly, but please take Sanski Most, Prijedor, and Bosanski Novi. And do it quickly, before the Serbs regroup!"

The press was waiting outside the Presidential Palace. I told them that the two Presidents had asked the United States to announce that the offensive would not be aimed at Banja Luka. I pointedly made no mention of any other targets. However, most news stories that day left the impression that we had forced the Bosnians and Croats to "halt their victorious sweep through western and central Bosnia."* Normally we would have tried to correct these stories, but since they sent the public message Washington wanted, we left them uncorrected.

Months later, Roger Cohen would write in *The New York Times Magazine* that preventing an attack on Banja Luka was "an act of consummate Realpolitik" on our part, since letting the Federation take the city would have "derailed" the peace process.

Cohen, one of the most knowledgeable journalists to cover the war, misunderstood our motives in opposing an attack on Banja Luka. A true practitioner of Realpolitik would have encouraged the attack regardless of its human consequences. In fact, humanitarian concerns decided the case for me. Given the harsh behavior of Federation troops during the offensive, it seemed certain that the fall of Banja Luka would lead to forced evictions and random murders. I did not think the United States should contribute to the creation of new refugees and more human suffering in order to take a city that would have to be returned later. Revenge might be a central part of the ethos of the Balkans, but American policy could not be party to it. Our responsibility was to implement the American national interest, as best as we could determine it. But I am no longer certain we were right to oppose an attack on Banja Luka. Had we known then that the Bosnian Serbs would have been able to defy or ignore so many of

---

* *The Washington Post,* September 20, 1995, p. A1. One exception was Stephen Kinzer of *The New York Times,* who got it right.

the key political provisions of the peace agreement in 1996 and 1997, the negotiating team might not have opposed such an attack. However, even with American encouragement, it is by no means certain that an attack would have taken place—or, if it had, that it would have been successful. Tudjman would have had to carry the burden of the attack, and the Serb lines were already stiffening. The Croatian Army had just taken heavy casualties on the Sarva. Furthermore, if it fell, Banja Luka would either have gone to the Muslims or been returned later to the Serbs, thus making it of dubious value to Tudjman.

There was another intriguing factor in the equation—one of the few things that Milosevic and Izetbegovic had agreed on. Banja Luka, they both said, was the center of moderate, anti-Pale sentiment within the Bosnian Serb community, and should be built up in importance as a center of opposition to Pale. Izetbegovic himself was ambivalent about taking the city, and feared that if it fell, it would only add to Croat-Bosnian tensions.

After meeting in Zagreb in the late afternoon with British Foreign Secretary Malcolm Rifkind, who was touring the region, we flew back to Belgrade that night for dinner and one more session with Milosevic before returning to Washington. It was still September 19. We needed Milosevic's agreement on a framework for the New York Foreign Ministers meeting, which we planned to hold September 26. Milosevic said that he would like to see us again before the New York meeting, and requested that I either return to Belgrade, or send Owen and Hill to discuss the draft agreement.

By the time our meeting with Milosevic ended, Rifkind had reached Belgrade, and, after midnight, I went to the British Embassy to brief him again on our talks. I was so tired I fell asleep while we were talking, but Rifkind graciously pretended not to notice. I even dozed off while answering a question.

Strobe Talbott had suggested that before I return to Washington, I send Warren Christopher a personal assessment of the negotiations—a "scene setter" for the meeting of the three Balkan Foreign Ministers on September 26 in New York. Christopher intended to make New York the scene of his first personal involvement in the negotiations, and Strobe particularly wanted me to explain why the military offensive was helping the peace process; there was, he said, a growing disagreement between us and Washington on this critical point. In another example of his honesty, Strobe included himself and Christopher in the group that "needed convincing." My informal handwritten note, sent by fax on September 20, was my first written message from the shuttle, after more than a month on the road:

> I suspect that the most dramatic phase of the offensive is coming to an end,
> and that the recent fluidity of the front lines will gradually be replaced by a re-

turn to a relatively stable front line. . . . Contrary to many press reports and other impressions, the Federation military offensive has so far helped the peace process. This basic truth is perhaps not something we can say publicly right now. . . . In fact, the map negotiation, which always seemed to me to be our most daunting challenge, is taking place right now on the battlefield, and so far, in a manner beneficial to the map. In only a few weeks, the famous 70%–30% division of the country has gone to around 50–50, obviously making our task easier. . . .

We recognize that two potential targets should be ruled off limits: Banja Luka and eastern Slavonia. On Tuesday [September 19] in Zagreb we succeeded in getting both Tudjman and Izzy to say to us simultaneously that they would not go to Banja Luka. Both used "the American peace plan" as the excuse for this sudden burst of restraint, even though it seems likely that they did not want to go for it anyway. . . .

After these two "prohibited zones," the issue of how far is enough [for the offensive] gets murkier. In the past we weakened our credibility by flashing so many "red lights" that no one knew which ones we meant. . . . If they take Sanski Most or Prijedor, both of which are in Federation hands in the Contact Group map but which Milosevic has said he will not yield in a negotiation, it would make our job easier. . . .

Finally, a word about our support. It has been superb all the way, the best I have ever seen in an important negotiation. While I resent some of the blind quotes of a personal nature in several recent articles, I know they do not come from the core team that is supporting us. You, Strobe, Peter, Tom [Donilon], John [Kornblum], Nick [Burns], and now Beth Jones* have been magnificent. Many thanks from all of us. See you in Washington.

---

* Elizabeth Jones, a career diplomat later appointed as Ambassador to Kazakhstan, had been added to our Washington backup team for a few months.

CHAPTER 12

Drama in New York

(September 18–26)

"I like the Walrus best," said Alice: "because he was a *little* sorry
for the poor oysters." "He ate more than the Carpenter, though,"
said Tweedledee. . . . "Well!" [said Alice] "They were *both* very
unpleasant characters."

—LEWIS CARROLL, *Through the Looking-Glass*

WE WERE DETERMINED TO AVOID REPEATING in New York the chaos of
Geneva. Yet, partly because of my own error of judgment, the New York Foreign Ministers meeting was nearly a complete disaster.

The drama surrounding New York would have surprised most journalists
and outside observers, who had begun to impart a sense of inevitability to the
negotiations. Their optimism was fueled by Administration officials who believed that when they talked to the press it was always necessary to emphasize
the positive—which inevitably meant *over*emphasize the positive. Still, overstated or not, there was good news for the first time in four years. The city of
Sarajevo was coming back to life. The aura of invincibility that surrounded the
Serbs had been shattered. Milosevic, who had started the war because Bosnia
had declared its independence from "Yugoslavia," had formally conceded in
Geneva that Bosnia was an independent country, and had accepted its existing
international boundaries.

Under these circumstances, Izetbegovic and his colleagues should have
looked forward to New York as a chance to take another step forward. But they
were disorganized and unfocused.

Meanwhile, Milosevic's first priority was the lifting of economic sanctions
against his country. He favored an early international conference at which the
three Presidents would sign an agreement of "no more than two or three
pages" and freeze the contending armies in place. He wanted to keep the political provisions of any peace agreement ambiguous and limited, and restrict
the functions and authority of a central government. His goal was to create a

situation similar to Cyprus or the two Koreas—a land in which a temporary dividing line becomes a permanent one.

This was not what we had in mind; if and when we invited the three Balkan Presidents to a conference, it would be with the clear intention of reaching a comprehensive peace agreement, not another weak, meaningless set of general principles that would be forgotten or ignored as soon as the conference adjourned.

Not for the first or the last time, Tudjman was the critical variable. He had a clear sense of what he wanted: first, to regain eastern Slavonia; second, to create an ethnically pure Croatia; and third, to maintain maximum influence, if not control, over the Croat portion of Bosnia. The Croatian President disliked both Milosevic and Izetbegovic, but his leverage over Sarajevo was substantial; the Croats in Izetbegovic's government, including the most important, Federation President Kresimir Zubak, usually followed "guidance" from Zagreb. The veteran British journalist Misha Glenny, who had covered the Balkans for years, was one of the first to recognize publicly the importance of Zagreb. In a perceptive article for the *New York Times* op-ed page published just before the New York meeting, entitled, "And the Winner Is . . . Croatia," Glenny praised our negotiating efforts but noted that, under any peace settlement, "Sarajevo will be utterly dependent on Croatia economically." He concluded: "The champagne corks can be opened in Zagreb—nowhere else."

Washington: The Bureaucratic Game. We had spent only one working day in Washington in the last three weeks. When we returned, we found that interest in our activities had increased substantially. Agencies and individuals that had paid us little attention now wanted to be part of the process. For example, the Agency for International Development (AID), asserting that it would have to carry out the reconstruction program, sought a major role in the negotiations. Some agencies or bureaus wanted to place representatives on the delegation; we fended them off on the grounds that our plane was too small. Tony Lake talked about creating a committee, under NSC direction, to oversee our efforts.

We were concerned that if the unprecedented degree of flexibility and autonomy we had been given by Washington were reduced, and we were subjected to the normal Washington decision-making process, the negotiations would become bogged down. At the same time, our small team was tired and understaffed. With only five days left until the New York meetings, we needed help, but I did not want to increase the size of the core team or relinquish our autonomy.

Faced with similar challenges in earlier crises, some administrations had created secret bypass mechanisms that kept information and authority within a small group—but also deceived or cut out everyone else. Most famously, when Kissinger was National Security Advisor, he had frequently ignored the entire State Department—once making a secret trip to Moscow without the knowledge of the American Ambassador, and regularly withholding almost all information about his secret discussions with China from the Secretary of State. We did not want to arouse the kind of distrust and intrigue that, as a result, had marred the Nixon-Kissinger period—an atmosphere Kissinger told me that in retrospect he regretted.

To avoid this classic bureaucratic dilemma, John Kornblum set up a small, informal team to support our efforts. As we envisioned it, the group would be, in effect, an extension of the negotiating team, but located in Washington. We drew on people outside the European Bureau, but insisted they work solely for Kornblum on this particular project. This meant that its participants, with the prior agreement of their superiors, would have to agree *not* to process drafts through the regular interagency "clearance process," which, while essential to the normal functioning of government, was too cumbersome and time-consuming for a fast-moving negotiation.

What Kornblum and I proposed was highly unusual, and could be derailed by forceful objections from a number of people. But Warren Christopher, with the strong encouragement of Talbott and Donilon, protected us. Christopher believed firmly in backing his negotiators, even if he did not agree with all their positions; this was fundamental to the man and shaped his attitude toward his role as the captain of the State Department. He, Strobe, and Tom regularly held off efforts by others to get involved in too many details. Without their support, the process would probably have resembled the one that had taught me such a strong negative lesson in Paris in 1968.

Sandy Berger also protected the negotiations. Several times a week, he chaired Deputies' Committee meetings on Bosnia. At every meeting, Kornblum would bring the national security apparatus up to date on our activities, while keeping at arm's length efforts to interfere in them. Sandy handled this deftly, keeping everyone sufficiently involved so that the Kissingerian problem—cutting people out—was avoided.

Kornblum's core group consisted primarily of lawyers: Jim O'Brien, who was part of Madeleine Albright's Washington office; Tim Ramish, the legal adviser for Europe; Miriam Sapiro, a lawyer on Jim Steinberg's Policy Planning staff; John Burley, a lawyer in the European Bureau; Laurel Miller, a lawyer in Bob Owen's firm who worked pro bono; and Lloyd Cutler, the former Counsel to both Presidents Carter and Clinton, who gave the group the perspective of a senior outsider.

Kornblum ran this backstop operation with skill. He had long been the Foreign Service's most experienced German hand, and was widely respected for his intellect. But in the Foreign Service "brilliant" is often a subtle code word for "arrogant," and, with his sharp wit and fierce advocacy, John had made some powerful bureaucratic enemies during his long career. Because he had gone without a promotion for a lengthy period, under State Department regulations he was within a year of being forced into early retirement—a result not of any career problems, but of a State Department budget so sharply reduced by Congress that promotions at higher levels had virtually ceased. This strange regulation had originally been designed to force deadwood out of the senior Foreign Service, and was now driving out some of the country's most qualified diplomats simply because they had been promoted early and then run into a general promotion slowdown caused by budgetary constraints.

From the beginning, we worked as a seamless team; I could turn a problem or a meeting over to him in midsentence and he would pick it up without a moment's pause. I felt a strong intellectual kinship with him, and greatly respected his superior knowledge of Europe.

On September 21, the day after we returned from the region, Tony Lake convened a meeting in the White House. He said that the "red lights" that Washington had conveyed to Zagreb and Sarajevo to end the offensive were extremely important and should continue to be emphasized. I wondered if Lake was aware of our conversations with Tudjman and Izetbegovic about continuing the offensive. Kerrick, Clark, and Pardew had kept their home offices informed, and my message to Christopher and Talbott the previous day had discussed the subject in detail.

"I want to be frank in the privacy of this room," I replied. "We asked them not to take Banja Luka, but we did not give the Croatians and the Bosnians any other 'red lights.' On the contrary, our team made no effort to discourage them from taking Prijedor and Sanski Most and other terrain that is theirs on the Contact Group map. The map negotiations are taking place on the battlefield right now, and that is one of the reasons we have not delayed our territorial discussions. It would help the negotiations greatly if these towns fell."

"I am very concerned that we will be blamed publicly for encouraging more fighting and more bloodshed," Tony said. "We should emphasize peace. This may not be your view, but you should say it in a way that doesn't exacerbate differences on other fronts, like with the Russians."

Christopher said he agreed with Tony as far as public statements went. I had no problem with that; the negotiating team had been careful in public, so much so that journalists in the region continued to think, and report, that we were trying to stop the entire offensive. But I refused to try to stop the offensive.

I was puzzled by Tony's comments. Was he objecting to the position we had taken in Zagreb, or was he simply worrying that it might leak? It was never clear, either to me or to my colleagues, including Christopher, who told me later that his only concern was that we not seem publicly to be encouraging the offensive.

After the meeting, Christopher, Lake, and I spoke briefly by telephone with the President, who was traveling in California. "I want you to make an all-out effort for peace," the President said. He asked me to return to Bosnia as soon as the New York meeting ended. Late that evening, in a radio call-in show with Larry King, the President was asked about Bosnia. "I feel better than I have in a long time," he said. "I feel good about the process, but I want to caution the American people that this is Bosnia and we have a long way to go."

Congress. The Hill can never be taken for granted. Without its support, it is virtually impossible to construct and carry out policy on a controversial issue—and nothing is more controversial than placing American troops in harm's way. Now that there was a real possibility of deploying American troops to Bosnia, Congress wanted to be heard. Bob Dole had made Bosnia his personal project, but he was relatively quiet at this point; since he had long attacked the Administration for weakness, he was not in a position to oppose a stronger policy. Other critics of the policy, like Senator Joe Lieberman and Senator Joe Biden, who were both Democrats, held their fire, waiting to see what would happen next.

The first warning shot came on the same day as the White House meeting, September 21, during what was supposed to be a routine hearing by the Senate Armed Services Committee to approve a second tour of duty for General Shalikashvili as Chairman of the Joint Chiefs of Staff. It was fortunate for the Administration that the first person to testify on American troop deployments was Shalikashvili, rather than a civilian; his low-key style and ramrod bearing, combined with his unquestionable patriotism and integrity, made him the most credible witness we could have.

Leading the skeptics were three of the Senate's most independent-minded Republicans: John McCain of Arizona, John Warner of Virginia, and William Cohen of Maine.* "Administration officials," reported *The New York Times* the next day, "were surprised by the breadth of Republican opposition to their intentions." The *Times* noted that Shalikashvili "seemed momentarily taken aback by the criticism," but he responded to it vigorously. "We cannot come in and out of the alliance and choose to lead when it's to our benefit, and let them take the lead when we don't wish to," he said. "Absent America's leadership role, things still don't get put together right."

The Senators kept Shalikashvili under polite but persistent pressure. "Why can't the Europeans carry out these peacekeeping duties themselves?" asked McCain, a former Vietnam prisoner of war whose courage and integrity were

---

* Cohen became Secretary of Defense during President Clinton's second term.

unsurpassed in the Senate. Cohen worried about "the consequences to NATO itself if U.S. forces are caught in a cross fire and American public opinion turns against the operation." These and similar questions gave clear warning that an intense effort on the Hill would be necessary.

Just before our team returned from the region, Kornblum had invited French and Russian officials separately to Washington to discuss a postsettlement military and civilian structure. The British also began discussions with us on the same subject. From the outset, there was agreement that the senior military commander on the ground would have to be an American, or else Congress would not approve U.S. troop deployments.

But what about the chief civilian in Bosnia, the person who would have the difficult task of implementing whatever settlement was reached? Not surprisingly, the Europeans wanted this position for one of their own. There were good arguments on both sides of this issue, but it was not decided on its merits, or on the basis of Bosnia itself. The critical variable would be who paid for the civilian effort.

Here domestic politics collided with Bosnia policy, and the timing could not have been worse. As Leon Panetta had predicted exactly a month earlier during the discussion at Fort Myer, the Administration and Congress were heading into the biggest budget confrontation between the two branches in this century—one so serious that by November it would lead to a shutdown of most of the U.S. government. The President's domestic advisors warned that getting *any* funds approved for Bosnia would be extraordinarily difficult. The only exception to this would be the military budget. The Europeans, members of Congress told us, must pay for reconstruction in Bosnia.

Under these circumstances, Berger and the Deputies' Committee decided that the chief civilian had to be a European. In taking this decision, they recognized that we would significantly reduce our control over one of the most important aspects of the effort. But there was really little choice. Reluctantly—because civilian implementation would be just as important as the military effort—I agreed with Sandy's conclusion. We informed the Europeans, who began to look for the right person to head the civilian effort.

The situation also gave U.N. Secretary-General Boutros-Ghali a chance to start the U.N.'s disengagement from Bosnia, something he had long wanted to do. After a few meetings with him, I concluded that this elegant and subtle Egyptian, whose Coptic family could trace its origins back over centuries,*

---

* See *Egypt's Road to Jerusalem: A Diplomat's Story of the Struggle for Peace in the Middle East,* by Boutros Boutros-Ghali, which contains frequent references to "my own awareness of my family's long tradition," and "its many generations [of] rich tradition of service to the country" (pp. 6, 7, et al.).

had disdain for the fractious and dirty peoples of the Balkans. Put bluntly, he never liked the place. In 1992, during his only visit to Sarajevo, he made the comment that had shocked the journalists on the day I arrived in the beleaguered capital: "Bosnia is a rich man's war. I understand your frustration, but you have a situation here that is better than ten other places in the world. . . . I can give you a list." He complained many times that Bosnia was eating up his budget, diverting him from other priorities, and threatening the entire U.N. system. "Bosnia has created a distortion in the work of the U.N.," he said just before Srebrenica. Sensing that our diplomatic efforts offered an opportunity to disengage, he informed the Security Council on September 18 that he would be ready to end the U.N. role in the former Yugoslavia, and allow all key aspects of implementation to be placed with others. Two days later, he told Madeleine Albright that the Contact Group should create its own mechanisms for implementation—thus volunteering to reduce the U.N.'s role at a critical moment. Ironically, his weakness simplified our task considerably.

Countdown to New York. On September 22, I met for almost three hours with our backstop team to review the planning for the New York Foreign Ministers meeting. I asked them to try for a huge leap beyond Geneva—an agreement on the framework of a central government for Bosnia that both the Bosnian Serbs and the Federation would accept as the sole sovereign entity. Owen and Hill, with support from Jim O'Brien and Miriam Sapiro, had produced a draft agreement, which established many essential institutions: a division of responsibilities between the central government and the two entities, the Federation and Republika Srpska; elections for both the presidency and the national assembly; and the creation of a constitutional court. I explained our strategy to a reporter at the time: "If we can get a cease-fire, we'll take that. If we can get some more constitutional principles, we'll take them. If we can settle Sarajevo, we'll do it. We're inventing peace as we go."

Our plan was first to negotiate with Foreign Minister Muhamed Sacirbey in Washington, then to turn back to Belgrade. As at Geneva, nothing could be left unresolved prior to the meeting itself. Sacirbey wanted a strong presidency, with every detail of the final political structure spelled out in New York, whereas I continued to follow a step-by-step approach: find areas of agreement, lock them in with a public announcement, and then return to the region for another round of negotiations to narrow the differences further.

It was increasingly obvious that Sacirbey's distaste for Silajdzic was coloring his own behavior. After a day of contentious discussions with Owen and Hill, during which tempers flared repeatedly and Sacirbey threatened several times to "go public," the two men warned me that the Bosnian Foreign Minister would try to go around the delegation and get other American officials—

particularly Strobe, Madeleine, or Tony—to change our positions. Sacirbey also worked the Congress vigorously, often criticizing the Administration in conversations with Senators, some of whom promptly told us. As Strobe put it, "He goes public anyway, and he can't get around you."

Sacirbey's behavior irritated American officials during this trip. Many of his points had merit, but he left people uncertain of his goal. It was not entirely clear what drove Sacirbey: was he was trying to show his colleagues (and enemies) back home that he was a true Bosnian patriot despite having spent most of the war in New York, was he positioning Izetbegovic for the struggle back home, or was he simply freelancing for the media?

As Sacirbey worked the town, Strobe Talbott was with his main Russian counterpart, Deputy Foreign Minister Georgi Mamedov, a witty and sophisticated man. The Talbott-Mamedov channel, low profile at the time, was the modern version of the special channel between Washington and Moscow that had existed from 1941 through the end of the Cold War, and now constituted the main vehicle for negotiating important issues between the two countries, including NATO enlargement, economic assistance, presidential summits, and sensitive political issues.*

Bosnia was a central part of this dialogue as we entered the second month of our shuttle. On Friday, September 22, hoping to reduce the tensions between the Russians and the Bosnians, Strobe invited Sacirbey to meet Mamedov privately in his office.

Strobe began with an imaginative attempt to lighten the tension and create a bond between the two men. "You have something in common," he told them. "You both have Muslim heritage and the same name!" (Mamedov was a slavicized version of Muhamed, Sacirbey's first name.) Sacirbey was surprised. "So, you're one of us?" he asked. Mamedov, of part-Azeri background, laughed. "Well, by way of Baku," he replied.

Unfortunately, the rest of the meeting did not live up to this promising start. Each man had a position to defend, and, while pleasant, the conversation did not produce any breakthrough on either side.

During our last meeting in Belgrade, Milosevic had suggested that someone from the delegation return to Belgrade before the New York session to put direct pressure on the Bosnian Serbs—part, he said, of his "technology." Although it was Milosevic's responsibility to deliver the Pale Serbs, there was value to his suggestion. I asked Owen, Hill, Pardew, and John Burley from State's Balkan desk to return to Belgrade after only two days in Washington.

---

* Although it had existed in other forms for decades, Henry Kissinger gave "The Channel" its name when it was conducted by him and Soviet Ambassador Anatoly Dobrynin. See *White House Years,* by Henry Kissinger, p. 141.

The three men reached Belgrade on Saturday, September 23. Milosevic, upset by some of the changes Sacirbey had proposed, asked them to meet with Karadzic and Krajisnik. This was the "technology" that Milosevic so enjoyed. But, as the discussion progressed, the Americans realized that the Pale Serbs had not really accepted the central concession to which Milosevic had committed them at Geneva—that Bosnia would remain a single state. Karadzic demanded the right to vote for secession, and, showing an unexpected flair for metaphor, said that a single Bosnia would be "a wooden oven which would burn itself up the first time it was used." He attacked every provision of Owen's draft designed to create national structures. He objected to the election provisions, refused to discuss the "competency" of the central government, and insisted that the Bosnian Serbs have a separate foreign policy and their own embassies. A meeting that was supposed to be mere "technology" turned into another marathon sixteen-hour negotiation, during which the American team rejected every Karadzic effort to legitimize a divided Bosnia.

Reaching an impasse on Sunday afternoon, Owen and Hill asked Milosevic, who had left the Americans alone with the Bosnian Serbs, to return. While the Americans waited in the gardens, Milosevic engaged in his usual routine of outmaneuvering and intimidating the rest of the Serbs. He then summoned the Americans back into the room, and produced an agreement close to the one we had negotiated with Sacirbey. Owen and Hill agreed, however, to drop the word "direct" in the clause describing elections for the presidency and the national assembly. They also agreed to soften the language on the functions of the central government.

Calling just before they left Belgrade on Sunday, September 24, Owen and Hill told us that despite some "minor changes" the basic elements of the Further Agreed Principles were intact. I congratulated them and requested that they fax us the new draft right away. By this time, I was at the Waldorf-Astoria in New York to meet foreign ministers from other countries, accompanied by Rosemarie and Christopher Hoh, who worked for Chris Hill. Anticipating a day of intense communications with the field, I asked Philip S. Goldberg to go to the State Department early Sunday morning to handle telephone calls, then come to New York later in the day. Goldberg and Hoh were two of the best younger American diplomats: candid in private, reliable, and dedicated.

Sacirbey remained in Washington that Sunday morning for a meeting with Lake, Tarnoff, Fuerth, Kerrick, and Sandy Vershbow. Sacirbey said the draft agreement he had negotiated in Washington was fine, but he warned that Izetbegovic was upset about the Owen-Hill-Pardew trip to Belgrade. "The negotiating team has been contaminated by the Belgrade air," Sacirbey said. He was not joking. "My President is not going to tolerate your people going to Belgrade all the time. The optics are bad. You must spend more time in Sarajevo." He was not moved when Tarnoff noted that Owen and Hill had spent two days with Silajdzic in Sarajevo on the document, as well as an entire day with Sacirbey himself in Washington.

Peter called immediately to alert me to the problem, but it still seemed just another Balkan bluff; I did not see how serious it was. By this time, Owen, Hill, and Pardew had started home in their small military jet. But as the negotiators flew west over Europe, Izetbegovic announced that Sacirbey "has been instructed not to attend" the meeting in New York, less than forty-eight hours away. "The Serbian side has demanded wholesale changes which radically alter the agreement," Sacirbey told the press waiting outside the White House. A White House press spokeswoman, Mary Ellen Glynn, trying to downplay the difficulty, called it "part of the ups and downs of shuttle diplomacy." As far as I could tell, however, this was all "downs."

More bad news followed immediately, in the form of a fax from Belgrade with the revised draft agreement. As soon as he saw the changes, Phil Goldberg warned that, while not substantial, they would be treated as "big" in Sarajevo. Later, we learned that Sacirbey had never sent the changes he made in Washington on September 22 to Sarajevo for approval. I felt the New York meeting slipping out of our hands.

In diplomacy process can often be as important as substance. This is especially true early on, when longtime adversaries are prone to maximize differences rather than reach out for agreements. Such was the case at that moment; we had been sloppy in not planning a stop in Sarajevo for Owen, Hill, and Pardew. Now we were paying the price. I blamed myself for three basic errors. First, I should have asked our team to reject any changes, no matter how small, in Belgrade. Second, even though we saw far more of the Muslims than the Serbs, many of our meetings were outside Sarajevo, and we had unintentionally left a public impression that we were spending more time with Milosevic than Izetbegovic; our team should have gone to Sarajevo. We also erred in thinking that Sacirbey could speak for the entire Bosnian government.

We needed to find a way to get the Sarajevo government back on track quickly, or the New York meeting would collapse, unleashing a cycle of disagreements and perhaps even a re-escalation of the war.

I had a desperate idea. Could we turn the Owen-Hill-Pardew team around in midair, and get them to Sarajevo in time to save the New York session? Goldberg and I realized our colleagues had not yet reached their refueling stop in Ireland. Goldberg gave the Operations Center and the National Military Command Center an urgent task: find the plane, get us in touch with it, turn it around.

We were in luck; Goldberg and the OpsCenter found the Irish official who ran the VIP room at Shannon; he knew us well from our frequent stopovers. The plane had just landed, and the official soon located our colleagues.

As we talked, Hill and Owen, unshaven and ragged, huddled around a green "Dial Your Relatives in America" shamrock-shaped pay phone, located next to the "Ladies' Toilet."

"Chris," I said, "you have to go back to Sarajevo. You have to go back. We will lose the agreement unless you get Izetbegovic back on board." They were halfway home, utterly exhausted. Now they were being asked to turn around in the middle of the night. It was not hard to sense Hill's fatigue and unhappiness. "Chris," I said, "let me talk to Bob."

I could hear Hill ask Owen if he wanted to talk to me, and, more faintly, Owen's dry, dignified voice saying, "Not much." Then he came on the phone. Anticipating his first question, I told him I had already talked to the Secretary of State and he shared my view. This provoked audible snorting at the other end of the phone, and a comment that they had allowed only "minor changes" in Belgrade. "Bob," I shouted into the phone, "there is no such thing as 'minor changes' in the Balkans!"

Although exhausted, they turned around and headed back across Europe, stopping in Ramstein, Germany, to switch to a C-130 flight to Sarajevo. After a sleepless wait, they were told that the only available transport plane was in Italy. After more difficulties at the Italian air base, they boarded a British C-130 and headed for Sarajevo at 7:30 A.M. Before leaving Ancona, Hill called Goldberg and me through the OpsCenter. It was 2:30 in the morning in New York, and both Phil and I sleepily understood that the call's primary reason was to make us share their exhaustion. "Do you realize how difficult this is for us?" Hill asked.

Hill said later he would never forget my answer. Just as I had visualized him at the shamrock-shaped pay phone in Shannon, he imagined me in a fancy suite at the Waldorf. "Look," I said, "you're in Ancona and I'm up at 2:30 A.M. We're all inconvenienced. We're having a difficult time here too. Now go get the Bosnians on board."

Owen, Hill, and Pardew finally arrived in Sarajevo on Monday morning, September 25. The meetings highlighted the widening split within the Bosnian government. An angry Haris Silajdzic immediately chastised them for dealing only with Sacirbey. "Do not believe," the Prime Minister said, "that you can reach an agreement without me."

The Bosnian government's opposition was caused not by the language changes in Belgrade but by a change of heart on the part of Silajdzic. After thinking further about the draft language he had approved on September 15, Haris told Owen and Hill that he now felt it was "too American"; the presidency was too powerful. He now favored a more "European" system; that is, one with a strong prime minister and a weak presidency. Silajdzic's annoyance was directed at Sacirbey, not the Serbs; he felt that the draft approved by the Foreign Minister, Izetbegovic's political ally, had been designed to weaken him. So deep was Silajdzic's anger that he insisted on a separate meeting with the three Americans, and refused to participate in their session with Izetbegovic.

To solve this impasse, Owen and Hill redrafted the New York document in such a way as to gain the support of both Bosnian factions and still be acceptable to the Serbs. They fell back on our standard approach of deferring the most difficult issues and focusing instead on general principles embraced by all, which could be made more specific later. As soon as we heard from Owen that the Bosnians had accepted the revised draft, Christopher called Izetbegovic to thank him. Izetbegovic assured him that Sacirbey would now attend the New York meeting.

But once unleashed, the cycle of demands for changes in the agreement could not easily be stopped. As soon as he read the revised election language from Sarajevo, Phil Goldberg said, "The Serbs will never accept this." He was right again. Hill sensed this as well; as he changed planes in Ancona on his way back to New York, he called the OpsCenter and left a short message: "Tell Holbrooke to call Milosevic over the elections provisions. They are going to cause a big problem."

It was now midday on Monday, September 25, and everyone was converging on New York. With concern in Washington rising, Christopher and I went to the teleconference room of the U.S. Mission to the United Nations, along with Madeleine Albright, to brief the President and the rest of the principals. Then Christopher, Albright, and I met with the three Balkan Foreign Ministers for a courtesy call. The meeting was short and perfunctory. To the press, Christopher was upbeat; but once they had left, the meeting became tense, with Christopher urging agreement, and then closing down the meeting before the three Foreign Ministers could start arguing with one another.

Working from my Waldorf hotel suite, Don Kerrick, Phil Goldberg, and I spent most of the next six hours on the telephone, alternating between Milosevic and Izetbegovic. Milosevic argued that he had reached an agreement in good faith with Owen, Hill, and Pardew and that he could not change it again. Milosevic was most adamant on the question of "direct" elections; having gotten it out of the draft, he did not want it to reappear. He also objected to elections by "popular vote," another clause that had been reinserted in Sarajevo.

Between phone calls, I saw Sacirbey. The meeting came closer to physical violence than any other during our long negotiations. I asked him if, for the sake of overall progress, he and his government could drop the "direct" clause for presidential elections. Even the United States, I pointed out, did not elect its president directly. Sacirbey said that without the precise word the Serbs could create "sham elections."

"That's nonsense, Mo," I said. "The Geneva principles guarantee international supervision of the elections. This is not the defining test of a democracy." Nothing in the draft precluded direct elections, I told Sacirbey; if we did not get them now, we would insist on them in the next round.

Sacirbey asked to call his President. We gave him some privacy, and he talked with Izetbegovic. When we resumed, he was angry and immovable. Without the direct-elections clause, there could be no agreement.

The atmosphere in the room grew tense. Sacirbey enjoyed a spirited, rowdy relationship with many of us, and we often expressed ourselves in rather rough-and-tumble terms. But this time the mood slipped over the edge, and the exchange became ugly. Without warning, Sacirbey slammed his jacket down on the sofa, stood up, and started for the door, yelling that the United States was betraying his country. "If you leave in this way, you will do your country immense damage," I responded, following him. He was in a rage, and for a moment it seemed to Goldberg and Kerrick that he was going to hit me. Kerrick stepped quickly between us, then moved smoothly into the hotel corridor to block Sacirbey's departure. As Sacirbey started out the door, he saw two dumbfounded journalists in the corridor watching this amazing scene. The sight of the journalists, and Kerrick's physical presence, seemed to calm Sacirbey slightly, and Don eased him back into the room. We shut the door again and managed to finish the meeting on relatively civil terms, but without any progress.

I called Izetbegovic as soon as Sacirbey had left. "Mr. President," I said, "we are on the brink of a disaster. You will gain a great deal from this agreement, and we will negotiate later to get direct elections. You are giving up nothing." He said he had to have the direct-elections clause. It was already after midnight in Sarajevo, and Izetbegovic disliked working at night. I gave up, ending with the hope that we could make progress in the morning.

Milosevic was, in this area as in so many others, the exact opposite of Izetbegovic. He enjoyed late-night drama, perhaps in part because his stamina and ability to hold liquor often gave him an additional edge over others at that time. Seeing we were in a hole, he stuck to his guns on the elimination of the direct-elections clause.

Kerrick, Goldberg, and I were drained. I called Christopher and asked if he would make a last-ditch call to Izetbegovic with me very early the next morning.

Tuesday, September 26. I arrived in our staff room at the Waldorf at 5:30 A.M. and was joined by Goldberg. It took almost an hour to reach Izetbegovic. When we finally connected, Christopher and I asked him to defer the question of direct elections, provided Milosevic would give up the reference that appeared to limit the role of the central government. After a few minutes of discussion, Izetbegovic agreed. We thought we were out of the woods.

The meeting of the Balkan Foreign Ministers was scheduled to start at 10:00 A.M. in the twelfth-floor conference room of the United States Mission to the United Nations on First Avenue, facing U.N. headquarters. The room, although less imposing, had been set up to resemble the one in Geneva. Fearing a repetition of Sacirbey's last-minute dramatics in Geneva, I sent Phil Goldberg to the Bosnian's offices to make sure that Sacirbey showed up on time. At 9:30 A.M., as our European colleagues were arriving at the twelfth floor, he called. "We've got a big problem," he said, speaking in a low voice. "Mo isn't going to agree. You'd better speak to him."

Sacirbey came on the line. He would attend the meeting, but he could not accept the agreement. I told him that there had to be a misunderstanding; the Secretary of State had just talked to his President, and everything was all set. No, said Sacirbey, "*I've* just talked to *my* President, and he told me not to agree."

It was Geneva all over again—a last-minute problem with the Bosnians. Racing down one flight of stairs to Albright's office, where Christopher had set up headquarters for the morning, I told him, Madeleine, and Tom Donilon what had happened. Moments later Goldberg arrived with Sacirbey and brought him directly to Albright's office.

Warren Christopher was famously a polite man who almost never raised his voice or showed personal discourtesy of any sort. But we were about to see an amazing sight. Sacirbey walked in smiling, said, "Hello, Chris," and stretched out his hand. Christopher ignored it, holding his own arms stiffly at his side. "What the hell is going on here?" he said in a voice just barely containing his fury. "I made an agreement with your President just two hours ago."

Taken aback by Christopher's anger, Sacirbey tried to explain that the Bosnian government had overruled Izetbegovic, but the more he talked, the more resistant Christopher became. "This cannot stand," he told Sacirbey. Albright, whose close relationship with Sacirbey dated from his U.N. ambassadorship, tried to reason with him, but to no avail. After fifteen minutes of useless argument, I pointed out that over one hundred journalists and officials from five nations were waiting for us upstairs. We had to join them.

Warren Christopher opened the meeting with brief remarks urging the parties to seize "this moment in history [to] end the fighting and end it for good." The photographers clicked away, and the press was ushered out. Immediately, to the surprise of nearly everyone in the room, I adjourned the meeting, whispered to Granic and Milutinovic that we had a problem with Sarajevo—this brought a gleam of real pleasure to the Serbian's eye—and asked the Contact Group to join us downstairs. We gave each of the Foreign Ministers a private "holding" room on the same floor.

Still furious, Christopher left for meetings across the street at the United Nations. Before he departed, he told Sacirbey that the situation would have to be cleared up right away if Sarajevo wanted to avoid serious consequences to its relations with the United States. I met with Carl Bildt and the four Contact Group representatives, who were distressed at having been shunted around. Apologizing, I invited them to talk to Sacirbey, but their efforts to move him got nowhere.

Sacirbey was scheduled to deliver his speech to the U.N. at 11:30. I asked him not to reveal to the press that we were in a state of crisis. He promised— and walked out onto First Avenue into a sea of journalists, whom he promptly told that he would not accept any agreement that did not provide for "direct elections."

The Contact Group waited, eating sandwiches in the office of Madeleine Albright's deputy, Edward "Skip" Gnehm. When Sacirbey returned, he seemed buoyed up by his public appearance at the General Assembly. Speaking in the great hall had taken some of the edge out of him. He now presented himself as the person who could solve the problem. Christopher returned from his other meetings to rejoin the fray. After coordinating with Tony Lake, we told Sacirbey that President Clinton would speak to the nation at 3:00 P.M. He would either announce the agreement and praise the Bosnians, or he would state publicly that New York had failed because of Sarajevo's stubbornness.

Asking for a private room, Sacirbey called Izetbegovic to relay our ultimatum. For a long time we waited. Then he emerged. "If President Clinton will say in his statement that he strongly opposes partition," he said, "we will agree." Since this was an existing American position, we assented on the spot. We also promised to pursue the cause of direct elections in the future. We went back upstairs to hold a brief formal meeting with the Croatian and Serbian Foreign Ministers, who had been waiting for four hours, and adjourned.

At 3:50 P.M. on September 26, the President announced the agreement from the White House pressroom. "There is no guarantee of success," he said, "but today's agreement moves us closer to the ultimate goal, and it makes clear that Bosnia will remain a single internationally recognized state. America will strongly oppose the partition of Bosnia."

As soon as the President finished his short statement, we met with the press. We could finally show the skeptics that we were building a central government, at least on paper. We had agreed on a three-person presidency, a parliament, a constitutional court, and other important attributes of a national government. A great bridge had been crossed—but with more difficulty than we had expected, revealing even more clearly than before the troubling divisions within the Bosnian government.

We announced our return to the region in two days to resume the shuttle. To journalists who asked if we were now going to get a cease-fire agreement, I was noncommittal. The truth was, we didn't know.

CHAPTER 13

Cease-fire

(September 27–October 5)

When the people vote on war, nobody reckons
On his own death; it is too soon; he thinks
Some other man will meet that wretched fate.
But if death faced him when he cast his vote,
Hellas would never perish from battle-madness.
And yet we men all know which of two words
Is better, and can weigh the good and the bad
They bring; how much better is peace than war!

—EURIPIDES, *Suppliant Women*

Your Place or Ours? No one wanted to relive the near disaster in New York. But despite the drama and difficulties, the September 26 agreement, with its unprecedented provisions for a central governmental structure, went a long way toward answering those who had criticized the Geneva agreement as a partition deal.

As we embarked on the evening of September 28 on our fourth trip to the Balkans, shuttle diplomacy had begun to lose its momentum. The three Balkan Presidents would soon have to be brought together in an all-or-nothing, high-risk negotiation. But none of the three key issues for such a meeting had been determined: its timing, its connection to a cease-fire, and where the peace talks would be held. Washington would leave the first two issues to us, but the third required a presidential decision, and our team had a serious disagreement with most of Washington.

Before we left for the region, there was the usual round of meetings with Foreign Ministers and other officials. The most important session was with French Foreign Minister Hervé de Charette in his suite at the United Nations Plaza Hotel in New York. De Charette did not share President Chirac's friendly, open style, or his admiration for American culture. He was a classic high French official, elegant, aloof, always sensitive to real or imagined insults toward himself or France—a distinction that he did not seem to acknowledge.

Yet even though his mission was to show that France still stood at the pinnacle of influence in Europe, on the day before our meeting he said to a group of reporters: "As President Reagan once remarked, 'America is back.' " De Charette was under pressure from his colleagues to show that the Foreign Ministry still mattered. To the annoyance of many professional French diplomats, we had been handling sensitive issues directly with Chirac's small but efficient staff at the Élysée Palace, headed by Jean-David Levitte, a brilliant young diplomat who served as Chirac's de facto national security advisor.

My meeting with de Charette was a microcosm of the complicated relationship between the United States and France. De Charette began with a complaint. "The French press," he said, "is saying that the United States had taken over the negotiations and left France standing on the sidelines." He expressed suspicion that we were already secretly arranging a peace conference in the United States. "It must be held in France," he said. "If not Paris, then in Évian on the Lake of Geneva. We can seal the resort hotels off from the press, and provide a calm and controlled atmosphere." He added that the European Union had agreed that France should host the peace talks—something both Germany and Britain firmly denied when asked a few days later.

I assured a skeptical de Charette that no decision had been made on the location or timing of the talks, but told him frankly that I favored an American site. De Charette proposed that we start the talks in the United States and move them to France after a predetermined time, say, two weeks. I said I did not think this would work, but added that perhaps we could consider a formal signing ceremony in France. As we left his hotel suite, de Charette took my arm and said, "This is very important to me and to France."

The issue of where the talks should be held had become the subject of a fierce internal dispute within the Administration. Our team's unanimous preference was for the United States, but this was a distinctly minority view in Washington. Most of our colleagues, with the exception of Tony Lake, wanted to hold the talks in Europe, preferably in Geneva, a city that symbolized to me unproductive diplomacy from the Indochina conference of 1954 to the endless rounds of Mideast and Cold War diplomacy. If we had to end up in Europe, my preference was for Stockholm, where Carl Bildt would be our host. At my request, Bildt started planning, in complete secret, for a conference at a resort hotel on Saltsjöbaden, an island not far from the Swedish capital.

The final decision would have to go to the President. Worried that the battle was already almost lost, I decided to appeal directly to Vice President Gore, who did not interfere casually in the normal processes of government. Gore returned my call while I was in a car on the way to La Guardia Airport. For security reasons, he asked that we talk on a land line, and so, from a pay phone at the airport, I made my case. Gore, who seemed surprised by my intensity on this issue, said he would consider it favorably. But, as we headed for Europe, the likelihood of a U.S. site seemed low.

The C-130 lumbered into Sarajevo from Italy at 8:00 A.M. on September 29. In the twelve days since our last trip there had been a visible improvement in the city. In the shadows of the shattered buildings the city streets were animated, even crowded. Streetcars were functioning, and barricades of wrecked cars were being dismantled. It is an unusual experience for a government official to see a direct and immediate connection between his efforts and the lives of ordinary people, but as we drove through the city we felt that the negotiations had already begun to make a difference.

For the first time, we raised the possibility of a cease-fire—without advocating it. Izetbegovic said he was not ready yet: the military trend in western Bosnia was still running in his favor. In fact, we agreed with him.

The U.N. Dilemma. In the first thirteen days after the lifting of the siege, General Rupert Smith had not opened either of the main roads leading out of Sarajevo, though this was one of the guarantees we had obtained from the Serbs on September 14. One of the roads ran through a Serb portion of Sarajevo that had been closed throughout the war, forcing all traffic to detour through a tiny, winding, and dangerous street. The Bosnian government publicly criticized the U.N. for leaving it dependent on what Silajdzic called "that notorious street."

The Bosnians were right. Frustrated, General Clark and I went to Smith's office after the meeting with Izetbegovic and urged him to open the main roads and dismantle all checkpoints. "General," I said, "you have a written commitment from the Serbs that these roads will be opened. If they resist, you can use force—but I don't think that will be necessary."

It was a replay of our last meeting. Smith, while far tougher than either Janvier or his predecessor, General Sir Michael Rose, did not appreciate our unsolicited advice, and responded forcefully. He was ready to run his own vehicles out of Sarajevo, but the U.N. had long been doing that. The risks, he said, would be his—not ours. He told us, as he had before, that he did not really control the French forces in Sarajevo Sector who would have to open the road. There were mines everywhere. He needed backing from Zagreb and U.N. headquarters in New York, both of which were passive or negative. Fighting was certain to break out. It would take time. And so on. As for the checkpoints, Smith thought eliminating them was impossible. "Bosnia is a country," he said with a dry laugh, "where every boy grows up with the dream that someday he will own his own checkpoint."

We understood Smith's predicament (and forevermore quoted his memorable line about checkpoints), but even Clark, who had great respect for his fellow general, was disheartened. If we failed to implement the September 14 agreement, its value would quickly be eroded by Serb encroachments and U.N. passivity.

To demonstrate America's determination to uphold that agreement, I asked John Menzies to send his Embassy staff on daily road trips from Sarajevo to Kiseljak. This was not, of course, a real test of the agreement, since the Serbs would not fire on a vehicle with an American flag and U.S. Embassy license plates, but at least it would show that the United States, for the first time in years, was using these roads.

The "Menzies patrols" produced several minor confrontations and small gains that demonstrated anew the necessity of applying continual pressure on the Serbs. Embassy staffers reported that the Serbs still maintained an armed checkpoint just outside Sarajevo. After a vigorous protest to Milosevic, who at first did not believe we cared about "such chickenshit," the checkpoint was opened and the barrier raised. This was an example of the new American approach. We would stand firm on every point, no matter how small.

Most American officials viewed Prime Minister Haris Silajdzic as the Bosnian leader with the broadest vision—an eloquent advocate of a multiethnic state. But his power struggles with Izetbegovic and Sacirbey and other members of the Bosnian government often isolated him. His colleagues complained that he was difficult to work with. He carried a serious additional burden: Tudjman and Milosevic distrusted him. Nevertheless, Silajdzic was one of the two most popular Muslim politicians in Bosnia, along with Izetbegovic.

My own feelings about Silajdzic shifted frequently. There was something touching about his intensity and energy, and his constant desire to improve himself intellectually. Although always busy, he seemed alone—his wife and son lived in Turkey. Silajdzic was the only Bosnian official who seemed genuinely to care about economic reconstruction of his ravaged land. His unpredictable moods worried us, but his support would be essential for any peace agreement. Chris Hill got it right: "If we have Haris's backing, we'll still have problems with Sarajevo," he said, "but they will be much reduced."

John Shattuck and Human Rights. The next morning, September 30, we flew to Belgrade, stopping first at the Zagreb airport for a short meeting with Ambassador Galbraith and John Shattuck, the Assistant Secretary of State for Democracy, Human Rights, and Labor. Wedging themselves into the plane's cabin, they gave us a vivid description of their trip the previous day to the Krajina in Croatia, and to Bosanski Petrovac and Klujic, two towns in western Bosnia that had fallen to Federation forces. They had passed "endless" streams of Serb refugees fleeing eastward to escape the advancing forces of the Federation. At Klujic, two miles from the front, with the sound of big guns in the distance, they had visited a mass grave site, the first to which any Americans were given access. Shattuck had given a press conference criticizing Zagreb for creating a new refugee flow, this one composed of Serbs driven out of *their* ancestral homes in the Krajina. His press conference infuriated Tudjman.

The Human Rights Bureau faced a long tradition of resistance from the regional branches of the State Department on bureaucratic grounds. It was not surprising, therefore, that some people initially opposed Shattuck's involvement in Bosnia. But I disagreed: his trips could focus public attention on ethnic cleansing and other war crimes, and increase the pressure on Milosevic to stop these practices. After much discussion, Christopher had agreed to let Shattuck travel in the region under our direction, an arrangement that prevented the creation of overlapping negotiating channels.

Shattuck masked his determination with a dispassionate manner. He had taught at Harvard Law School and served on the board of Amnesty International, and he understood the media, to whom he made himself easily accessible. In the end even the skeptics in the European Bureau, who initially argued that human rights should be handled by the Embassies in the region, saw the value of John Shattuck's highly publicized, highly focused efforts.

John and I intentionally did not travel together. But in my meetings with Milosevic we added a new demand: that Shattuck be allowed to visit war-crimes sites and towns. Shattuck's trips would be a constant public reminder that even as we sought peace, we were not abandoning the quest for justice. When Milosevic saw we were serious, he agreed.

Arkan. Shattuck and I were particularly concerned with the activities of Zeljko Raznatovic, popularly known as Arkan, one of the most notorious men in the Balkans. Even in the former Yugoslavia, Arkan was something special, a freelance murderer who roamed across Bosnia and eastern Slavonia with his black-shirted men, terrorizing Muslims and Croats. To the rest of the world Arkan was a racist fanatic run amok, but many Serbs regarded him as a hero. His private army, the Tigers, had committed some of the war's worst atrocities, carrying out summary executions and virtually inventing ethnic cleansing in 1991–92. Western intelligence was convinced he worked, or had worked, for the Yugoslav secret police.[1]

The only mechanism for dealing with such problems was imperfect but vital: the International War Crimes Tribunal, located at The Hague. When it was established by the United Nations Security Council in 1993, the tribunal was widely viewed as little more than a public relations device. It got off to a slow start despite the appointment of a forceful and eloquent jurist, Richard Goldstone of South Africa, as its chief. Credit for pumping up its role in those early days went to Madeleine Albright and John Shattuck, who fought for its status and funding. Other nations, especially its Dutch hosts and the Germans, also gave it substantial support. During our negotiations, the tribunal emerged as a valuable instrument of policy that allowed us, for example, to bar Karadzic and all other indicted war criminals from public office. Yet no mechanism existed for the arrest of indicted war criminals.

Although the tribunal had handed down over fifty indictments by October 1995, these did not include Arkan. I pressed Goldstone on this matter several times, but because a strict wall separated the tribunal's internal deliberations from the American government, he would not tell us why Arkan had not been indicted. This was especially puzzling given Goldstone's stature and his public criticisms of the international peacekeeping forces for not arresting any of the indicted war criminals.* Whenever I mentioned Arkan's name to Milosevic, he seemed annoyed; he frowned and his eyes narrowed. He did not mind criticism of Karadzic or Mladic, but Arkan—who lived in Belgrade, ran a popular restaurant, and was married to a rock star—was a different matter. Milosevic dismissed Arkan as a "peanut issue," and claimed he had no influence over him. But Arkan's activities in western Bosnia decreased immediately after my complaints. This was hardly a victory, however, because Arkan at large remained a dangerous force and a powerful signal that one could still get away with murder—literally—in Bosnia.

Belgrade and Zagreb. Our Zagreb airport meeting with Shattuck and Galbraith completed, we were back in the familiar sitting room in Belgrade by late afternoon on September 30. "The time for a cease-fire is now," Milosevic said. Like Izetbegovic, he insisted that any peace conference be held in the United States.

When we returned to Zagreb early the next morning, October 1, Tudjman lashed out against Shattuck's criticisms of his government. "This is not correct behavior between nations who are partners and friends," he said bitterly. I replied simply that Shattuck had an obligation to tell the story the way he saw it, and we would not muzzle him. Besides, Serbs who had lived for generations in the Krajina and western Bosnia should be allowed to remain in their homes in peace.

---

* The first military action against an indicted war criminal did not come until June 10, 1997, when British troops in Prijedor captured one Bosnian Serb and killed another who had been named in sealed indictments by Goldstone's successor, the Canadian judge Louise Arbour.

With pressure for a cease-fire building, we urged Tudjman to do as much as possible militarily "in the next week or so." Again we focused on three key towns in the west: Sanski Most, Prijedor, and Bosanski Novi. This might be the Federation's last chance to capture them before we started negotiating. I urged joint operations with the Bosnians. "The Bosnians can't take territory on their own," Tudjman said, as he so often did. He was right, of course, but part of the reason for this was that throughout the war the Croatians had denied the Bosnians access to heavy artillery.

Tudjman also wanted the conference to be held in the United States. At least there was one issue on which all three Presidents seemed to agree. But would Washington agree to an American site?

Sofia Side Trip. We were moving toward a cease-fire for which we were not prepared, and a peace conference whose location and structure were still undecided. Hoping to slow down the process, we decided to take a long-delayed side trip on October 1 to Bulgaria, a neglected part of the region. I had promised the Bulgarian Prime Minister during a meeting in New York a week earlier that we would visit his isolated nation to show that we recognized and appreciated the cost of its support for the embargo against Serbia.

The visit excited the Bulgarians. Finally someone from Washington was paying attention to them. Because we ran late in Zagreb, our meeting in Sofia with President Zhelyu Zhelev did not start until after 8:30 in the evening. Finally, at 10:00 P.M., he gave an enormous dinner in our honor, with leaders of about twenty political parties. When we expressed astonishment at the number of parties represented, Zhelev, a former dissident, said that these were only the leading factions, out of a total of over two hundred parties.

The dinner ended about midnight. We returned to our Stalin-era VIP hotel, now a Sheraton, for a surprise birthday party for my overworked assistant, Rosemarie Pauli, arranged by her fellow travelers and Bill Montgomery, our Ambassador in Sofia. Although we were exhausted, as usual, it was good to be away from the intensity of the three Balkan capitals and Washington.

The October 2 Cable. It was after 1:00 A.M. when I settled into my room, a huge, ill-designed suite, to call Strobe Talbott. I told him that with the Bosnian Serb military in the west stiffening, the front lines seemed to be less fluid. If the offensive ran out of gas, it would be time for a cease-fire. But, I told Strobe, we could not announce a cease-fire without announcing the location of the peace conference at the same time.

This linkage was not self-evident, Strobe said. Could we separate the three issues—cease-fire, peace conference, and location? I told him that we would then find ourselves in contentious and time-wasting negotiations within the

Contact Group. We had to bypass this step with a package announcement. Strobe said that Washington was still opposed to holding the talks in the United States. If they failed, the costs would be too high for the Administration. "It's about nine to one against you," Strobe said dryly, "and I'm afraid right now I'm one of the nine." He said that Lake was still the only person in the senior team supporting an American venue. A White House meeting was scheduled for the next day to make a recommendation to the President. "Strobe," I said, "let me make our case by phone."

"Look," he replied, "I don't think it makes sense for you to participate by phone; as a practical matter, it won't work well, and you won't be at your best in that format. But I have a suggestion: send us a careful, reasoned telegram stating your case. I will ensure it gets a fair hearing at the meeting." The suggestion was characteristic of Strobe: generous and fair-minded. He believed in settling tough issues openly, and he was willing to encourage a message whose content he did not support—in contrast to many officials who made deviousness, even with close colleagues, a way of life and rationalized such behavior as "necessary to get the job done."

So I sat down in the high-ceilinged sitting room to draft the cable. For the rest of the night, I wrote and rewrote, calling Donilon at 4:15 A.M. and Kornblum thirty minutes later to get a better understanding of the arguments against our position. When we boarded the plane early in the morning, I asked my colleagues to review my draft and took a much-needed nap.

By the time we landed in Sarajevo on the morning of October 2, we had distilled a sharp, focused, and unanimous message from my draft. This message would be our best shot at an issue we felt was absolutely critical. Unfortunately, because of concern about protecting the President's deliberative process, the White House would not permit direct quotation in this book from the message we sent that morning—a message that Strobe later called "the most effective cable sent so far in this Administration in terms of changing people's minds."

In the message we argued that we had already invested so much national prestige in the effort that our priority had to be to maximize success, rather than to reduce the cost of failure. A meeting site in the United States would give us physical and psychological control of the process; any other site would reduce our leverage dramatically. To those who claimed that failure on American soil would be more costly politically—the case most frequently advanced against us—we argued that the Administration's prestige was already fully on the line in the eyes both of the American public and of the world, and that failure would be no more costly in New Jersey than in New Caledonia. Failure, although quite possible, was not something we could worry about now.

The American peace initiative, which had already brought a lifting of the siege of Sarajevo and other benefits, had been a powerful signal that, as de Charette had said in New York, "America is back." The choice of venue would be *the* key indicator of how serious and committed we were. We ended by predicting that the Europeans would complain about an American site, but that they would respect our wishes and come along, and that—contrary to fears being expressed in Washington—it would not have an effect on the fundamental relationships we had with the Europeans and Russia.

A few hours later, Lake called Kerrick to report that while the White House meeting had "moved the ball forward," it had been ultimately inconclusive. Some officials still worried that a U.S.-based conference might somehow draw in the President against his will. But there was also good news: on the basis of the telegram and a talk with Bob Owen, Christopher had decided to support an American venue. So did Perry. Tony ended the phone call by asking Don to gather more arguments in favor of our position before the next meeting.

Meanwhile, on the Front. The best time to hit a serve is when the ball is suspended in the air, neither rising nor falling. We felt this equilibrium had arrived, or was about to, on the battlefield. On the trip from Sofia to Sarajevo, after an intense discussion, we decided to shift from "exploration" of a cease-fire to its advocacy. We feared that the Croat-Muslim offensive would soon run out of steam. General Mladic was highly visible again and trying to rally his forces. And we were concerned by the growing friction between Zagreb and Sarajevo, which had caused Zagreb to halt its advance and threatened what had already been achieved. John Pomfret reflected our concern in *The Washington Post* on October 3, reporting that "Croatian forces [have] stopped fighting, allowing the Serbs to concentrate their formidable firepower on the Bosnian army."

When we met Izetbegovic on October 2, he was buoyed by encouraging reports from his generals, and was even more resistant to a cease-fire than he had been three days earlier. The Croatians remained ambivalent, even unenthusiastic, about continued fighting, which they felt would gain ground only for the ungrateful and uncooperative Bosnians. Galbraith, Clark, and I continued to urge Susak to take as much territory as he could, especially Sanski Most and Prijedor.

October 3 ended with the astonishing news that President Kiro Gligorov of Macedonia had barely survived an assassination attempt in Skopje; he was in intensive care after hours of neurosurgery to remove shrapnel lodged in his head from a car bomb. Gligorov's driver had been killed, and it was not certain Gligorov would survive. We sent Gligorov wishes for speedy recovery and asked Washington to send him an emergency medical team.

October 4, Sarajevo. The United States Senate confirmed John Menzies as Ambassador to Bosnia-Herzegovina. Ambassadors normally take their oath of office in the State Department, but since Menzies was already in Sarajevo, we decided to swear him in immediately and to turn the swearing in into a high-profile event that would reaffirm our commitment to Bosnia.

The event was held in a building that resonated with history, the Konak House, where Archduke Franz Ferdinand and his wife, Sophia, lay in state after they were shot on June 28, 1914. The handsome nineteenth-century mansion, with its polished parquet floors and plaster molding, had not been used since the war began but it had survived in surprisingly good condition, with only a few mortar hits on its upper floor. Ghosts seemed to hang in the air of the old building, and as we walked up its elegant stairway, I was moved by the continuity of history. "This is where the twentieth century began to disintegrate," I whispered to Joe Klein, who was following us for *Newsweek*. Government officials, foreign Ambassadors, generals, Muslim mullahs, Serb Orthodox priests, Catholic prelates, and members of the fast-disappearing Jewish community in Sarajevo had assembled for the first genuine multiethnic ceremony in four years. Jammed into the elegant ballroom, many wearing ethnic or religious costumes, they reminded me of the famous photograph, taken minutes before the assassination, of the doomed royal couple descending the stairs outside the City Hall, flanked by costumed dignitaries.

After the short formal ceremony, Izetbegovic made a speech welcoming Menzies, and John spoke briefly. I closed my remarks by saying that Konak House's "historic failures impose a special obligation on all of us who are gathered here today." There was a warm mood among the guests, mingling as if in prewar Yugoslavia. This, I thought, was the perfect moment and place to raise the question of the cease-fire—better than the grim and grimy Bosnian presidency building, where we were scheduled to meet that afternoon. I suggested to Izetbegovic and Sacirbey that we meet in one of the private side rooms at once. The other guests, still drinking and talking, watched in amazement as we closed the doors and disappeared.

Only General Kerrick joined this meeting. I chose Don in order to emphasize the role of the White House, which he represented. We sat on four small gilded chairs in the corner of a large room, our knees almost touching. Stressing that Don was one of our nation's top military intelligence officers, I asked him to give President Izetbegovic and Foreign Minister Sacirbey an intelligence assessment of the military situation.

Kerrick and I had not discussed this meeting in advance. But he played his part perfectly. Quietly and authoritatively, he said that the Federation had probably reached its point of maximum conquest. He said he was concerned Tudjman would not support further territorial gains, lest they go mostly to the

Bosnians. Finally, Don reminded the Bosnian president that in all wars there were times for advance and times for consolidation, and in our opinion this was a time for consolidation.

Izetbegovic listened carefully and uncomfortably. His generals, he said, were still reporting advances in the west. "Your generals may be reporting advances that have not happened," Don said. "Our own information is quite different. According to our best intelligence, the Federation now controls around fifty percent of the land. You would be risking a great deal if the Serbs took back some of your recent gains."

"Mr. President," I said, "this is a crucial moment. Our advice is given to you in friendship and sincerity. I hope you are right and we are wrong. But if you are wrong the price to your country will be enormous. If you want to let the fighting go on, that is your right, but Washington does not want you to expect the United States to be your air force. If you continue the war, you will be shooting craps with your nation's destiny."

Sacirbey mumbled something to Izetbegovic—a translation, we learned later, of the phrase "shooting craps with destiny." Izetbegovic said he would consider the issue immediately with his senior military and civilian colleagues. Would we meet him at the presidency building at 2:00 P.M. to get his answer?

While we waited, Christopher and Lake called to report on the results of a short early-morning meeting at the White House. Tony was upbeat: he had successfully "precooked" the issue of where the conference would be held, and resolved all remaining internal differences. The President would formally approve—and the Bosnia peace conference would be held in the United States.

Nothing could have recharged our depleted energies as much as Washington's last-minute reversal. All the pieces were now in place for the final push to stop the fighting and bring the parties together.

Accompanied by Carl Bildt and Igor Ivanov, we reconvened at the Bosnian presidency building at 2:00 P.M. to discuss the draft constitution and the elections. Such discussions would not resolve the major issues, but they were useful in making the Bosnians contemplate what their government would look like in case of peace. Bildt and Ivanov then left for other meetings, leaving us alone with Izetbegovic and his colleagues.

Izetbegovic was flanked by his military and civilian advisors, and it was clear that they had been arguing up to the moment we arrived. "My military leaders don't want me to stop," Izetbegovic began, looking directly at Kerrick. "They don't agree with your judgment of the situation. But I will agree to a cease-fire if the Serbs meet certain conditions." First, he said he would not agree to a cease-fire for at least another five days. Second, he would accept the cease-fire only if the gas and electricity were turned on in Sarajevo, and the road to Gorazde opened before the start of a peace conference.

One had to admire his conditions. They skillfully straddled the distance between our position and that of his hard-line generals. Restoring the electricity required that the Serbs remove the many mines scattered around the electricity pylons leading into Sarajevo. He would buy more time for a revived military offensive. Getting gas to Sarajevo was a different matter: Sarajevo's gas was controlled by the giant Russian state-controlled firm Gazprom, which did not wish to turn on the pipeline to Bosnia until it had received a large cash payment for long-overdue bills. In the next few weeks, this unexpected side issue would greatly complicate our efforts and, ironically, bring Sarajevo and Belgrade together in a united front against Moscow and the man behind Gazprom, Russian Prime Minister Victor Chernomyrdin.

October 4: Belgrade. We quickly drafted a cease-fire agreement incorporating Izetbegovic's conditions and flew to Belgrade, leaving Hill and Pardew in Sarajevo to facilitate communications with the Bosnian government. We felt we had crossed a psychological divide in both Sarajevo and Washington, and wanted to see how far we could get in Belgrade. Milosevic was in an upbeat, almost celebratory mood. As he read the draft cease-fire agreement with his usual speed, he joked and continually offered us drinks, which I turned down. "Not until we have an agreement," I told him.

We soon began to argue over details. Milosevic gave us a large room in the front of the building, in which we set up word processors. We opened a direct telephone line to our Embassy in Sarajevo through the State Department Operations Center in Washington, and kept it open for several hours. Members of our support team typed and retyped the proposed cease-fire agreement as changes flew back and forth. When Washington heard that we were in the final stages of negotiating a nationwide cease-fire, Christopher, Lake, Tarnoff, Donilon, and Kornblum all joined the telephone marathon. At one point while I was talking to Christopher, Milosevic wandered into the room, drink in hand, and asked whom I was talking to. Hearing that the Secretary of State was on the line, he indicated a desire to speak to him. This was clearly not the right time for the two men to have their first conversation, and I mumbled an excuse.

For hours Milosevic and the Bosnians haggled long-distance, through us, over small changes of wording in the agreement, with Chris Hill relaying each of Milosevic's suggestion to Sacirbey. As the night progressed, we all became increasingly exhausted—except for Milosevic, who seemed to be enjoying himself thoroughly. In Sarajevo, Hill could not locate Sacirbey. Finally, after one of Sacirbey's unexplained disappearances, the normally dignified Roberts Owen slammed his fist against the wood paneling in our room in Belgrade and uttered a string of unlawyerlike oaths. From then on, he was affectionately known as "Mad Dog" Owen, or simply "Mad Dog."

At about one in the morning, we finally had a document acceptable to both Sarajevo and Belgrade. Izetbegovic had his conditions, almost exactly as he had demanded. Milosevic signed the document with a flourish. We still needed the signatures of Karadzic and his Bosnian Serb colleagues, who were waiting in a villa outside Belgrade. This task we left to Milosevic, who promised to return the document, "signed, sealed, and delivered," before we left in the morning. We stumbled back to our hotel, entering through the basement to avoid the press, and called Washington with the news. We would still have to get Izetbegovic and Tudjman to sign the next day.

October 5: Belgrade, Sarajevo, Zagreb, and Rome. In the morning Milosevic delivered the document signed by the Bosnian Serbs. After briefing the British chargé, Ivor Roberts, we raced (laboriously, via Italy, as usual) to Sarajevo to get Izetbegovic's signature.

Izetbegovic's withdrawn and unhappy face told the story. Flanking him were several members of his Cabinet and military. I assumed from the mood in the room that a number of his colleagues objected to the cease-fire. Izetbegovic took the document and read it carefully. We pointed out that Milosevic had agreed to most of Sacirbey's changes, including the immediate exchange of all prisoners of war and a tightening of the language regarding the restoration of full gas and electrical service to Sarajevo.

We were running far behind a difficult schedule: we had to fly to Zagreb to see Tudjman, then get to Rome in time for the first "expanded Contact Group" session we had promised the Italians. As Izetbegovic argued, Rosemarie handed me a note warning that we had five minutes left to make our "window" for the last flight of the day, after which we would be unable to get out of Sarajevo until the next day.

Izetbegovic's visceral fear of the cease-fire had to be resolved quickly. He studied it in silence, his eyes narrowed. Finally, pointing at the Serb signatures, he said emphatically that he could not affix his signature to the same piece of paper as his enemies. I asked Ambassador Menzies to make a photocopy of the document with the Serb names covered up, and again presented it to Izetbegovic for signature.

Still he hesitated. I pushed a pen toward him. "Mr. President, you can end four years of fighting in your country with a single signature," I said, "and on your terms."

His colleagues watched him in silence as he stared at the paper. Suddenly, he looked at me suspiciously. "Where is the American signature?" he said. "I don't see your signature on this document."

I grabbed his pen and took the paper from his hands. "Here it is, Mr. President," I said, and scrawled my name on the document in the lower left-hand corner. "We must leave immediately. If you don't sign now, the war will continue." I started to rise.

Izetbegovic took the paper. His hands shook as he held it. Finally, slowly and reluctantly, he signed the document. We shook hands and raced for the airport, taking the document with us and leaving Ambassador Menzies to call Washington with the news.

CHAPTER 14

Choosing Dayton,
Getting Ready

(October 5–25)

How did a snake get in the tower?
Delayed in the democracies
By departmental vanities,
The rival sergeants run about
But more to squabble than find out.

—W. H. AUDEN, *New Year Letter*

WE KEPT THE CEASE-FIRE SECRET long enough for President Clinton to break the news. At 11:00 A.M. on October 5, he announced "an important moment in the painful history" of the former Yugoslavia. A general cease-fire would take effect in five days, he said, if the gas and electricity were turned on in Sarajevo. This would be followed by talks among the three Balkan Presidents, which would take place in the United States.

At the very moment the President spoke, our team was in Zagreb, urging Tudjman to capture more territory before the cease-fire took effect. The Croatians had virtually stopped their advance, and Sanski Most and Prijedor still lay inside Serb lines. "You have five days left, that's all," I said. "What you don't win on the battlefield will be hard to gain at the peace talks. Don't waste these last days."

Tudjman requested that we delay the start of the peace conference until the beginning of November, so that it would not interfere with the Croatian parliamentary elections. We agreed. As it turned out, we needed every minute of that extra week to get ready.

Before leaving the region, we laid down three conditions for the negotiations:

- first, that each President come to the United States with full power to sign agreements, without further recourse to parliaments back home;

- second, that they stay as long as necessary to reach agreement, without threatening to walk out; and

- third, that they not talk to the press or other outsiders.

All three Presidents agreed to these conditions, although Izetbegovic and Sacirbey objected to the third provision, claiming that they had important friends in Congress and the press with whom they had to keep in touch. We said that serious negotiations were incompatible with the sort of outside contacts they had in mind. Milosevic, reading the document, protested mockingly that we were trying to make him a prisoner. Although this document had no official standing, the three parties generally stuck to its terms—until the final dramatic hours in Dayton.

Akashi. Our last call in Zagreb before returning to Washington was on U.N. Secretary-General Boutros-Ghali's senior representative in the former Yugoslavia, Yasushi Akashi, whom I had known since my two visits to Cambodia in 1992. Akashi had been harshly treated by the press and castigated by critics of the U.N. for his weakness. But it was not entirely his fault: he was operating under tight constraints imposed by Boutros-Ghali. Furthermore, Akashi was virtually ignored by General Janvier and the U.N. military.

We asked Akashi to make his first priority the quick reopening of the electrical lines, which had been cut and mined. Then we bade each other goodbye, almost emotionally. I felt sorry for Akashi. He was leaving Zagreb with his previously distinguished record blemished, but his mission had been doomed from the start because of limits imposed from New York. The United States was delighted with his replacement: Kofi Annan, who was already flying to Zagreb to take up temporary residence. Since the August bombing crisis, Annan was the U.N. official in whom we had the greatest confidence, and his arrival was good news.

Rome. As our team flew to Rome, Warren Christopher called each Contact Group Foreign Minister to propose that the talks be co-chaired by the United States, the European Union, and Russia at the "Holbrooke-Bildt-Ivanov level." He would participate only when required. Christopher was concerned that if he attended the entire conference, the other Foreign Ministers would also insist on attending, which would make the negotiations unmanageable.

The Europeans accepted the American decision to host the talks without complaint, with the exception of the French. To mollify them, Christopher kept open the possibility of a signing ceremony in Paris. Rifkind expressed concern, verging on anger, at the French position, stressing that the British government had never agreed to Paris. But not wishing to turn this into a public problem, he said that the British would be content to host an "implementation conference" shortly after a signing ceremony.

The expanded Contact Group meeting was designed to satisfy the Italians. Foreign Minister Agnelli began it on October 5 with a dinner in the Renaissance splendor of the Villa Madama, the official guest house of the Italian Foreign Ministry. For someone who had eaten breakfast in Belgrade and lunch in Sarajevo, the scene was disorienting, so enormous was the distance between Rome's classical grandeur and the ugly realities we had just left.

The Europeans who were not part of the Contact Group praised American diplomacy and leadership. But there was a clear undercurrent of resentment among some Contact Group members over American "unilateralism." When I noted that the U.N. seemed reluctant to try to open the roads around Sarajevo, Pauline Neville-Jones exploded, charging that I was trying to "set the U.N. and the Europeans up" to be blamed for a failure. I was unprepared for this outburst. I was not interested in discussing the possibility of failure, I said. We needed to lay the groundwork for a success in which we would all share. For that, the most rigorous enforcement of every detail of every agreement was essential. I expressed myself acidly, criticizing those mired in bureaucratic maneuvers at such a critical juncture in European history. It was probably unwise of me to rise to the bait, but I was trying to lay down a strong marker against unproductive procedural proposals. With her usual grace, Sunni Agnelli moved the discussion to less turbulent issues.

Despite this tense beginning, the Rome meetings were useful. The next morning, October 6, the Italians formally convened an expanded Contact Group meeting, followed by a special, even larger meeting designed to promote economic recovery of the region—the first time we had focused on the long-term economic needs of the region.

With Italy having finally hosted a Bosnia conference, Moscow wanted its moment in the limelight. Each major European nation wished to host an international meeting, designed in large part to demonstrate to its domestic audience that it was involved in the peace process. John Kornblum termed this phenomenon "conference proliferation," and we complained constantly about it as time-consuming and redundant. However, we recognized that these meetings were important for European-American unity.

Albright and the U.N. The United Nations intended to request a place as a fourth co-chair of the negotiations. Madeleine Albright and I were strong longtime supporters of the United Nations, but we both felt that the U.N.'s participation in the talks would further complicate them. In the end, we agreed that the U.N. representative, Thorvald Stoltenberg, would participate in the negotiations only when they involved eastern Slavonia, and over the next three weeks Madeleine held the U.N. at bay in its quest for a larger role. Telling the U.N. that its involvement would weaken the search for peace was painful, especially for those of us who had grown up believing in the importance of the world body. But Albright stepped up to the task without complaint, and performed with a toughness that was productive if not always popular. In this period, our working relationship became progressively closer and more effective. As she often put it, we had been "joined at the hip" on every key European issue. She also felt a special kinship with my wife, Kati, like herself a product of a Central European refugee family.

The struggle over the U.N.'s role foreshadowed the American determination a year later to oppose Boutros-Ghali's quest for a second term as Secretary-General. More than any other issue, it was his performance on Bosnia that made us feel he did not deserve a second term—just as Kofi Annan's strength on the bombing in August had already made him the private favorite of many American officials. Although the American campaign against Boutros-Ghali, in which all our key allies opposed us, was long and difficult—especially for Albright, who bore heavy and unjust criticism for her role—the decision was correct, and may well have saved America's role in the United Nations.

Albright and Talbott were also deeply involved in another complicated aspect of the cease-fire agreement—the effort to open the gas lines to Sarajevo. The Russians controlled the pipeline through Gazprom, which did not want to start the gas flowing until it received $100 million in unpaid bills. The Bosnians were furious; most of the debt, they said, was for gas that had been siphoned off by the Serbs. More important, they did not have the money.

To solve the impasse, Milosevic sent his Prime Minister to Moscow with a personal plea to Prime Minister Victor Chernomyrdin to open the gas lines immediately and work out the back payments later. Silajdzic also flew to Moscow, hoping to gain credit in Sarajevo for getting the gas turned on. Meanwhile, our Ambassador in Moscow, Thomas Pickering, struggled with the Russian Foreign Ministry and Gazprom through several long nights. Talbott and Leon Fuerth activated the Gore-Chernomyrdin channel, the key working-level mechanism for American-Russian cooperation. Participating in this frustrating subplot through constant telephone calls—the remarkable final conference call included Pickering, Albright, Menzies, Tarnoff, Donilon, Chris Hoh, Nick Burns, and me, all in different locations—I had the impression that for the Russians the issue was financial, not political; the famously powerful and greedy leaders of Gazprom were simply trying to squeeze the Bosnians for back payments, and only Chernomyrdin himself could break the logjam. Still, the gas was not turned on, and the fighting continued. While slamming Moscow for what it regarded as blackmail, Sarajevo took advantage of the cease-fire delay to accelerate the military offensive, which had picked up last-minute momentum.

The Birth of IFOR. On the same day that the President announced the cease-fire and we met in Rome, Secretary of Defense Perry concluded a special two-day session of the sixteen NATO Defense Ministers in Williamsburg, Virginia. The announcement of the cease-fire gave added urgency to his effort to forge a consensus on the first peacekeeping force in NATO's storied history. With surprisingly little difficulty, the ministers gave Perry support for a structure without precedent—one that would enforce a peace agreement and include both NATO and non-NATO troops. NATO's Supreme Commander, General Joulwan, told the ministers he wanted a force of fifty to sixty thousand troops, with separate American, French, and British operational zones. The United States would contribute about one third of the troops, at an estimated annual cost of close to $2 billion. The peacekeeping force would be called the Implementation Force—or IFOR.

Perry also planned to meet with his Russian counterpart, Marshal Pavel S. Grachev, in Geneva two days later to pursue a visionary goal: bringing Russian troops into a Bosnian peacekeeping force. Moscow bitterly opposed the enlargement of NATO, and we were often at cross-purposes over Bosnia, where the Kremlin resented and feared the reassertion of American leadership. Not since World War II had Russian, American, and other Western European forces served together under a common command. But President Clinton, Perry, and Strobe Talbott, the President's most influential advisor on Russian policy, believed that if Russia participated in Bosnia, it would be a historic step in the development of cooperation between countries that had been Cold War adversaries only four years earlier.

Site X. Tom Donilon took over responsibility for finding an acceptable place—which we code-named Site X—for the talks. He assigned the job to the Assistant Secretary of State for Administrative Affairs, Patrick F. Kennedy, an intense, no-nonsense official with over twenty years of government experience as an administrative specialist. Kennedy, with whom I had worked during the Carter Administration, came to my office on October 10 with his aide, Ken Messner, to find out what kind of site we wanted. I repeated our mantra: physical arrangements could make a difference; every detail mattered. Site X would have to hold nine delegations—each Balkan country, the five Contact Group nations, and E.U. representative Bildt. Ideally we wanted an area we could seal off from the press and all other outsiders, close enough to Wash-

ington so that senior Administration officials could visit, yet sufficiently remote, as Michael Dobbs later put it in *The Washington Post,* "to discourage
Balkan warlords from running off to television studios in New York and Washington every time the negotiations hit a snag."

The President's retreat at Camp David was too close to Washington, too
small, too "presidential," and too closely identified with the 1978 negotiations
between Egypt and Israel. Hearing our requirements, Kennedy observed that
a military base would best meet our needs. After Wes Clark and I called Jan
Lodal, the Principal Deputy Undersecretary of Defense for Policy, Bill Perry
ordered the Pentagon to help Kennedy find Site X immediately.

Kennedy quickly narrowed the search to three sites: the Navy base at Newport, Rhode Island; Langley Air Force Base in Norfolk, Virginia; and Wright-
Patterson Air Force Base in Dayton, Ohio. When the possibility of Newport
arose, Senator Claiborne Pell called to offer us access to some of the great
houses along the water in his home state. Though the idea of Milosevic,
Izetbegovic, and Tudjman wandering around The Breakers was amusing to
contemplate, the facilities at Newport were too spread out. Unable to make the
site inspections myself, I asked Rosemarie Pauli to help Kennedy. As they
drove around Wright-Patterson, a sprawling base that contained twenty-three
thousand government personnel, Kennedy noticed five visiting officers' quarters (VOQs) grouped around a central parking lot, only a few feet apart. He
and Rosemarie decided that while some of the rooms would need substantial
improvement, in all other ways Wright-Patterson filled our needs.

And so Dayton was chosen for the talks, to everyone's surprise. At the time,
it did not sound like an impressive place for a major international conference.
As Dobbs wrote in *The Washington Post,* "Camp David it isn't." When we told
Milosevic the news on October 17, he protested, half-jokingly, that he did not
want "to be locked up like a priest"—a remark that later leaked to Roger
Cohen of *The New York Times,* much to Milosevic's annoyance. The Europeans, used to negotiations in more opulent settings, literally had no idea
where Dayton was, and expressed open unhappiness with a site "somewhere
in the middle of America." Carl Bildt worried about the hawkish imagery of a
military base. But I thought that reminders of American airpower would not
hurt.

Studying Camp David. We could find no exact precedents for the negotiations on which we were about to embark. The closest model, of course, was
the Camp David talks in September 1978, when President Carter forged the
historic agreement between Egyptian President Anwar Sadat and Israeli Prime
Minister Menachem Begin that ended thirty years of armed hostility and wars
between Egypt and Israel. As we flew around the Balkans in October, I distributed to every member of our team Carter's own account of those thirteen

days, as well as the section on Camp David in Cyrus Vance's memoirs, *Hard Choices,* and William Quandt's *Camp David: Peacemaking and Politics.* Dan Hamilton of the European Bureau also interviewed Quandt and Harold Saunders, who had been Assistant Secretary of State for Near Eastern Affairs at the time of Camp David, about every detail, no matter how small, concerning the talks, including eating arrangements, telephone connections to the outside world, and the handling of the press. Of greatest interest to us was the question of personal relations between the leaders at Camp David. Had the Americans been able to create any sort of personal rapport between Sadat and Begin? Could we do so at Dayton? Do people become more malleable after being cooped up for days? Will sheer fatigue make tempers flare?

I phoned President Carter and listened in fascination as he described how he had tried without success to get Sadat and Begin to talk directly to each other. He had then reverted to "proximity talks," a diplomatic technique originating in Mideast negotiations held in the 1940s at the U.N., in which the mediator moves between the two parties, who rarely meet one another face-to-face—a sort of "shuttle diplomacy by foot." We already assumed that this would be our pattern, and always referred to Dayton as "proximity peace talks." Carter recounted his constant efforts to reduce the personal distaste between the two men. His most memorable effort was a field trip to the Gettysburg battlefield, where, he hoped, being at a site of wasted sacrifice would produce a breakthrough. No such thing happened, of course, and Carter sat in the car between Sadat and Begin for hours, their knees touching, while they ignored each other.

Preparations. By the second week of October, preparations had become frantic. Several task forces framed positions on every issue from elections to the creation of a joint railroad commission. Robert Gallucci, the former Assistant Secretary of State for Political-Military Affairs, was given responsibility for coordinating implementation of civilian activities if an agreement was reached.

Our strategy for Dayton was both ambitious and simple: we would never have a better chance to end the war in Bosnia—and therefore we sought to address as many issues as possible in the final agreements. What was not negotiated at Dayton would not be negotiated later. We recognized that implementation would be at least as difficult as the negotiations themselves, but we rejected the minimalist theory that we should negotiate only those matters on which implementation would be relatively easy. Later we would be criticized for being overly ambitious, but the alternative would have been a "small" agreement, not much more than a cease-fire—and an opportunity lost, perhaps forever.

While the preparations continued at home, teams spread out across Europe to conduct three simultaneous negotiations. First, Slocombe, Kornblum, and

Clark flew to Brussels to gain more support for a multinational NATO-led force. Observing the response to their trip, Perry said that NATO had finally "emerged from a long dark tunnel of indecision and irresolution."

Second, Perry and Talbott continued their negotiations with Moscow on Russia's role in a peacekeeping force. President Clinton discussed this with Yeltsin by phone on September 27 and in person with Kozyrev one week later; Perry, Slocombe, and Talbott saw Marshal Grachev in Geneva on October 8. The Russians wanted to participate in any military force in Bosnia, but they wanted it led not by NATO but by either the United Nations or some special coalition in which they played a role equal to that of the United States. Although the President, Perry, and Talbott had explained repeatedly to the Russians that this was impossible—"a deal breaker," as Strobe put it, because it would destroy the key principle of NATO, unity of command—the Russians did not budge.

The third negotiating track remained in the Balkans. I was already committed to a Contact Group meeting in Moscow, and the French had insisted that we stop first in Paris. We timed our travel so we could hold the Contact Group meeting in Moscow, join Talbott and Slocombe for the discussions on the Russian role in peacekeeping, and then return to the Balkans for a final "pre-Dayton systems check."

The fighting in western Bosnia intensified as the cease-fire approached. NATO planes swung back into action, attacking a Bosnian Serb command bunker after the Serbs shelled a U.N. base southeast of Tuzla and killed a twenty-nine-year-old Norwegian peacekeeper. Both sides tried to make last-minute gains, with the Federation forces having much the better of it. Facing the end of the fighting, the Croats and the Bosnians finally buried their differences, if only momentarily, and took Sanski Most and several other smaller towns. But Prijedor still eluded them. For reasons we never fully understood, they did not capture this important town, a famous symbol of ethnic cleansing.*

---

* In March 1997, I attended a showing at the Council on Foreign Relations in New York of a powerful documentary film, *Calling the Ghosts,* that recounted the brutal treatment two Bosnian women from Prijedor had suffered during their incarceration at the notorious Omarska prison camp. Following the film, the two women angrily asked me why they were still unable to return to their hometown. I told them we'd repeatedly encouraged an assault on Prijedor. They were astonished; they said General Dudakovic, the Bosnian commander, had told them personally that "Holbrooke would not let us capture Prijedor and Bosanski Novi." I subsequently learned that this story was widely believed in the region.

This revisionism was not surprising; it absolved Dudakovic and his associates of responsibility for the failure to take Prijedor. I suspect the truth is that after the disaster at the Una River the Croatians did not want to fight for a town they would have had to turn over to the Muslims—and the Bosnians could not capture it unaided.

Other parts of the cease-fire agreement were slowly falling into place. The power lines into the capital were steadily being restored as the Serbs and the Croats showed U.N. engineers the location of the mines. However, despite Russian promises, Gazprom continued to delay the reopening of the gas lines into Sarajevo. Finally, after several days of drama, Pickering obtained a serious offer from the Russians: they would agree to await later payment of the unpaid bills, and open the valves, provided the Bosnians agreed not to hold them responsible for any explosions or other damage caused when the gas went back on. When Sarajevo agreed, the gas began to flow (without any serious explosions). On October 11, in a dramatic moment, the lights began to flicker on all over the city, and the first tentative bursts of gas started through the pipes in Sarajevo. A few hours later, wild shooting broke out all over Sarajevo—not fighting, but celebrations. The cease-fire had officially started, although fighting continued for a few more days in the west.

Before leaving for Paris and Moscow, I spent the weekend on Long Island. The President wanted a final discussion, which could not be scheduled until I was already on my way in a car. This led to a surreal scene on the Long Island Expressway. Asked to call the White House on Friday afternoon, October 13, I found myself at the appointed hour trapped in heavy traffic with my family on the Long Island Expressway. The White House switchboard told me not to use a cellular phone for a conversation with the President. I called back from a service-station pay phone, and was connected immediately to Christopher, Lake, and Berger. With the deafening sound of truck traffic in the background, we chatted as we waited for the President to join the call. Two men in a pickup truck drove over, and after a short wait made it clear that in their view my time at the pay phone was up. Their cigarette packs were lodged inside the sleeves of their T-shirts, James Dean–style, and they looked increasingly annoyed. I imagined the headlines in the tabloids if I told them the truth: "Man Attacked in LIE Phone Booth; Claimed He Was Talking to Prez."

Finally, as we waited impatiently, the President came on the line, asking me where I was. "You won't believe it, Mr. President," I said, in a low voice. "Is this the envoy to *The Washington Post*?" he asked with amusement, referring to a favorable editorial a week earlier. "How do you get such an article?" he continued. "I can't get them to say anything nice about me." I replied that the editorial had not been all *that* laudatory, and that it came after "eighteen straight hits on me." "Don't complain," the President laughed. "You won't get many of those.

"Can we get a united Sarajevo?" he asked. "Could we protect it?" "The Serbs want a Berlin with guns," I said. "The two sides have incompatible positions on four or five key issues. Everyone knows that only a peace settlement will bring U.S. involvement. They can't have one without the other."

Areas of Control After Cease-fire, October 12, 1995

SLOV.

HUNGARY

SERBIA

•Zagreb

•Karlovac

CROATIA

EASTERN SLAVONIA

Bosanski Novi
•Prijedor
•Omarska
Bihac•
Sanski Most
Bosanski
Petrovac

Bosanski Samac

Brcko

•Banja
Luka

•Doboj

Mali
Zvornik

Udbina•

Tuzla•

LIVNO VALLEY

•Jajce

BOSNIA-HERZEGOVINA

Srebrenica

Knin•

Kiseljak
•Sarajevo•
Mt. Igman ▲

Zepa•
•Pale
Rogatica

•Gorazde

Split•

•Foca

Mostar•

MONTE-
NEGRO

Dubrovnik•

•Podgorica

0   20 miles
0   20 kilometers

Bosnian Serb–
controlled area

Croat-Muslim Federation–
controlled area

"That's good," the President said. "It's the only dog we've got. Let's use it."

The President was particularly concerned about Yeltsin's support for the peace effort, and spoke with passion about the need to involve Russia in the peacekeeping force.

"We want the Russians in," I said. "But they cannot have their own sector. It would look like a Russian zone of occupation after World War II. Secondly, they cannot have any say in NATO decisions to use force, which they are seeking through some kind of council."

"We should try to involve Russia," the President replied. "It's important. And good luck on your trip."

Moscow. After a short stop in Paris to see Chirac, we landed in Moscow. The Russians were pleased at their first opportunity to act as host for the Contact Group. But the meetings, held at the Foreign Ministry, were confused and shapeless; the Russians, not used to running international meetings, had no set agenda. Foreign Minister Andrei Kozyrev, an affable and decent man, but under pressure from the nationalists in Russia, chaired the opening session.

The French representative, Jacques Blot, announced that it had been "unanimously decided" that Carl Bildt would be the senior civilian representative in Bosnia. Since we had already agreed that the civilian chief would be a European, I agreed to this suggestion despite the odd manner in which it had been sprung on us. To do otherwise would have opened a wide breach within the Contact Group. Besides, we could work with Bildt, whom we had strongly supported in early 1995 as E.U. negotiator.

Kozyrev suggested that the three Balkan Presidents visit Moscow prior to Dayton. His main purpose was to enhance the prestige of the Yeltsin government on the eve of the election for the Russian parliament, or Duma. The Russians promised that if we agreed to this meeting, they would restrict it to a "photo op" with Yeltsin.

I had doubts about this proposal. It risked derailing or delaying the negotiating process, notwithstanding the Russian pledge to stay away from substance. Scheduling would be difficult. It seemed unlikely that the meeting would have much impact on Duma elections. However, I knew Strobe would favor such a trip, and given our recent conversation I assumed President Clinton would also support it—so I told the Russians that Strobe would address it when he arrived in Moscow the next day.

That afternoon I went to the airport to meet him and his team, which included Slocombe and James Collins, the head of State's office for relations with the former Soviet republics.* We headed straight to the Russian Defense Ministry, where we met with a group of grim and skeptical-looking Russian

---

* Collins succeeded Pickering as Ambassador to Russia in 1997.

generals. They listened coldly to Strobe and Walt but seemed more receptive when American military officers spoke, especially Wes Clark; with his crisp military bearing and handsome uniform, he seemed to communicate to the Russians soldier-to-soldier, in a manner that we civilians could not match. When our team left for Belgrade the next day, Strobe asked us to leave Wes behind to participate in their discussions.

In order to join the Bosnia force, the Russians said, they needed joint authority over all decisions. Briefing the NATO Council in Brussels on October 18, Strobe predicted that Yeltsin would "reserve for himself the final say on what has been an extremely contentious issue." This meant the decision would not be made until the Clinton-Yeltsin summit, scheduled for Hyde Park, New York, on October 23.

Congress—and the Twelve–Month Limit. On October 17, Christopher, Perry, and Shalikashvili ran into difficulty during an unusual joint appearance before the Senate Armed Services Committee. Democrats joined Republicans in warning that the Administration had not yet made a convincing argument for deploying American troops in Bosnia.

Like most Americans, affected by endless images on television of U.N. forces killed and wounded in appalling conditions in Bosnia, Congress assumed that American troops would also suffer casualties. This expectation shaped the debate over the next few weeks. Had the public understood that Americans would be sent to Bosnia only in a radically different environment from the one they had seen on television, one that sharply reduced the risk of casualties, there would have been more support for the effort. It was virtually impossible to make the case in the absence of a peace agreement, but Congress demanded that the debate begin *before* the negotiations at Dayton.

Trying to bolster support, Perry told the Armed Services Committee that the NATO force in Bosnia would be "the biggest and the toughest and the meanest dog in town," adding that if it were attacked, "it would bring a large hammer down on them immediately." Still, the Senators were skeptical. "We haven't made the case yet," Christopher said, "but there's a case to be made and we'll make it."

Two issues dominated the hearing. First, would the Administration submit any decision to deploy troops to Bosnia to a formal vote of the Congress and would it respect the outcome of that vote? Senator Robert Byrd of West Virginia spoke for most of his colleagues in a letter to President Clinton that called for "the Congressional majority [to] share full responsibility, from the outset, for any decision to accept the costs and risks of this proposed operation." Other Senators, including John Glenn, Dan Coats, Kay Bailey Hutchison, and William S. Cohen all pursued this same line.

Christopher and Perry had prepared carefully for this. Though they said they would "welcome an authorization from the Congress," they refused to answer repeated questions as to whether or not they would recommend that the President seek such authority and be bound by a vote.

The second issue was fundamental: how long would American and NATO troops be deployed in Bosnia? Although the NATO plan had not yet been formally approved by the President, Perry and Shalikashvili told the Senators NATO would "complete its mission in twelve months and [then] withdraw."

The plausibility of this statement, even when slightly softened by the President a few days later, was widely questioned at the time—and would cause serious difficulty for the Administration later. It resulted from the deeply held conviction of the Pentagon and the NSC that the American people would not support involvement in Bosnia without an "exit strategy." There was merit to this theory, as all students of Vietnam and Somalia knew. Nevertheless, announcing *before the peace talks began* that we would withdraw in twelve months, no matter what happened on the ground, was not an "exit strategy," but an exit deadline—something quite different.

The negotiating team knew that one year was not sufficient to succeed, no matter what happened in Dayton. But we were traveling between Moscow and Belgrade on the day this issue was decided, and after stating once in an earlier discussion that an arbitrary deadline—especially one so unrealistic—was a terrible idea, we were not consulted again. When we heard the news, we feared it would weaken our negotiating hand as well as threaten successful implementation. But the decision had been made, and we had no choice but to defend it.

A Final Systems Check in the Balkans. As Washington announced its decision on the troop commitment, we began our "final systems check," visiting all three Balkan capitals. As a display of Contact Group unity, I asked Bildt and Ivanov to travel with us. It was the only joint trip of the three Dayton cochairmen, and gave us a chance to develop closer working relationships.

It had been almost two weeks since we had seen Milosevic. He began the October 17 meeting with a strong effort to get the sanctions lifted or suspended prior to Dayton. We rejected his request. John Shattuck had called from the Bosnian town of Zenica that same day to report that several thousand Muslim refugees had been driven toward central Bosnia by paramilitary Serb units, perhaps led by Arkan. At the same time, we had received intelligence reports of continued Yugoslav resupply to the Bosnian Serb Army, despite many assurances from Milosevic to the contrary.

Milosevic waved off Shattuck's information. Was the Serbian President lying about what was going on, or was he so isolated that he did not know what his own forces were doing? We did not know, but since he consistently claimed to be uninformed about what was happening in the Banja Luka area, I asked the CIA to prepare a "sanitized" (or unclassified) document that laid out evidence of the ties between Arkan and the Yugoslav Army. We planned to give the document to Milosevic on a second trip to Belgrade on October 19, after Bildt and Ivanov had left. Although the document did not link Arkan directly to the recent events, it was powerful and incriminating.

When I raised the subject again at lunch on October 19, Milosevic tried to brush it off. "No, no, no," he said. "Your information is wrong." At this point, by prearrangement, Pardew pushed our document in front of Milosevic. "Our evidence is all in there, Mr. President," I said.

Milosevic looked away. He would not touch the paper lying directly in front of him. I urged him to read it, but he went on eating. Hill observed later that Milosevic acted as if by touching the document he would be physically connected to the charges it contained. When the meal ended, a Serb official came up to Pardew and said that he had left *his* paper on the table. "No, I didn't forget it," Jim said. "It belongs to President Milosevic."

Hyde Park. On October 23, a gorgeous fall day, a frail Boris Yeltsin met President Clinton at Franklin Roosevelt's home at Hyde Park high above the Hudson. Jim Collins had suggested the beautiful setting in the hope that its reminders of FDR's great wartime alliance with the Soviet Union would encourage a new security relationship, beginning in Bosnia. In a speech to the United Nations General Assembly the previous day, Yeltsin had delivered a blistering attack against NATO expansion and indicated that Russia would not participate in any force under NATO command in Bosnia.

The President's goal was to get Yeltsin to agree to participate in a Bosnia peacekeeping force even if the Russians continued to object to NATO enlargement, on the theory that what we did together in the Balkans would become a partial antidote to Russia's neuralgia about NATO and would, in Talbott's words, "lubricate the NATO-Russia track." Talbott and Perry had spent a great deal of time discussing this nuanced approach to Bosnia and NATO during their frequent trips to Geneva to see Grachev; now, with Dayton only days away, it was up to the President to pull at least the first track—Bosnia—across the finish line while holding firm on NATO.

The President succeeded brilliantly. After hours of intense and often highly personal discussion, the two men agreed that two battalions of Russian troops, totaling about two thousand soldiers, would participate in the force in Bosnia. President Clinton defended the integrity of the Bosnia command structure—a sacred "red line" for NATO, which would rather have a command without the Russians than the kind of messy structure, with separate chains of command, that the Russians sought. The two Presidents did not attempt to settle this complicated problem, instead handing it back to Perry and Grachev, who were scheduled to meet at the end of the week in Fort Leavenworth, Kansas. But they did agree on the size and functions of the Russian contingent, and the meeting set a positive tone for Perry's closing efforts with Grachev.

One other issue concerning Bosnia came up at Hyde Park: Yeltsin's desire for a pre-Dayton summit in Moscow of the three Balkan Presidents. All three Balkan Presidents had told us they would rather not go to Moscow. From their point of view, it would be exhausting, unproductive, and politically undesirable. But Yeltsin was adamant: he did not care that none of the presidents wanted to make the trip to Moscow. Knowing that President Clinton would meet with Izetbegovic and Tudjman the next day in New York, Yeltsin asked him to use "all his influence" to make the meeting happen. Reluctantly, President Clinton agreed.

Izetbegovic and Tudjman at the Waldorf. The day after Hyde Park, October 24, President Clinton met Izetbegovic and Tudjman together at the Waldorf-Astoria Hotel in New York. Seeking to put the Dayton talks in a larger framework, the President began on a high note. "We have seen things in the last few years that we never expected to see," he said. "Israel and the PLO sitting down after thirty years of fighting; the IRA laying down their arms. But what the world wants most is the end of the war in Bosnia." The President praised the Muslim-Croat Federation as essential. "Without the Federation," he said, "I am not sure that the NATO bombing or Dick Holbrooke's diplomacy would have worked."

Seated on both sides of President Clinton, the two Presidents barely acknowledged his point. Rather, Izetbegovic immediately complained about the Croatians. "All parties here support the Federation in words," he said, "but the process of implementation has not taken place as it should." He then listed areas in which the Croatians had failed to live up to their commitments. Tudjman ignored Izetbegovic, and made another strong pitch that eastern Slavonia had to be part of any deal at Dayton. The President agreed. Then the two men took a few more shots at each other, and the meeting ended. Its main value was that it had given the President and his senior advisors a rare firsthand sense of how much these two men disliked each other, and how difficult Dayton would be.

With the formal meeting over, President Clinton asked me and Sandy Vershbow to join him and the two Presidents in a corner. "I want to ask you to do something for the peace process that I know will be hard on both of you," he said to Izetbegovic and Tudjman. "I want to ask you both to go to Moscow before Dayton. It would be better to get the Moscow visit over with before the

Duma elections, and that means before Dayton." The main purpose of the meeting, President Clinton concluded, would be to allow Yeltsin "to send a signal to the Serbs, and to allow the Russian people to see that he is part of the process." Despite their previous misgivings, Izetbegovic and Tudjman agreed immediately. To ease the physical strain on Izetbegovic, President Clinton offered an American plane for the trip; Tudjman had his own plane.

The pre-Dayton Moscow summit, which would delay the start of Dayton by one day, was announced by the Russians and confirmed by the White House on October 25. Two days later, on October 27, Perry and Grachev agreed to put two thousand Russian troops directly under General Joulwan.

This arrangement told a great deal about the complicated mind-set of the Russians in the fourth year of the post-Soviet era. The great World War II alliance of Americans and Russians still echoed in the minds of the Russian military. Having regarded themselves as our only "fellow superpower" for fifty years, they seemed to be ready to accept the U.S. military as a worthy superior or commander in Bosnia. The negotiations over Russia's role in Bosnia thus helped us understand how to approach the next big strategic goal of America's post–Cold War European policy—enlarging NATO.

This was a historic achievement. From the patient negotiating style of Perry and Talbott, strongly supported by General Joulwan, had come an unprecedented command arrangement: for the first time since World War II, U.S. and Russian troops would operate in a unified command. Even Strobe was surprised at the speed with which everything fell into place on the eve of Dayton. "The Russians were unbelievably sanguine about being under American command in Bosnia," he observed later—"but NATO was still a four-letter word in Moscow."

But the same day brought stunning news that temporarily overshadowed the agreement between Perry and Grachev. For the second time in three months, Yeltsin entered the hospital with severe heart disease. Ambassador Pickering predicted that the country was entering a period of crisis and uncertainty. There was, however, a small plus from this frightening development: the pre-Dayton Moscow summit was canceled. As Chris Hill said, "If Yeltsin *had* to get sick, at least he picked a good time from our standpoint." Still, we all knew that a great deal depended on his speedy recovery.

CHAPTER 15

Decisions with Consequences

(October 25–31)

> . . . our theories, like the weather,
> Veer round completely every day,
> And all that we can always say
> Is: true democracy begins
> With free confessions of our sins.
>
> —W. H. AUDEN, *New Year Letter*

> Now the man who has risen to the top [of the military] finds himself with new concerns, political and diplomatic. He is not simply directing the Army or Navy or Air Force. He is consulting with his colleagues and advising his civilian superiors. . . . He is advising them on matters having to do with the goals and ends of peace and war. For this he has certainly not been trained.
>
> —BERNARD BRODIE, *War and Politics*

AS DAYTON APPROACHED, THE PRESSURE INCREASED. It was the most brutal bureaucratic effort I had ever been involved in. Some bureaucratic bruises were made in the process that did not heal quickly. But in retrospect, the amazing thing was not how tough it was to get ready for Dayton, but how hard everyone worked to make it happen. The State Department was swarming with activity. Conference rooms had been turned into messy drafting rooms, where people drawn from various parts of the government were working together, minus most of the normal bureaucratic wrangling. There seemed to be a certain air of destiny, as if everyone working on the preparations for Dayton felt they might be part of a decisive moment in American foreign policy.

The Role of IFOR. However, the Administration remained divided over the most important question it faced: if we got an agreement in Dayton, what would the NATO-led Implementation Force, IFOR, do? Of course, if Dayton failed to produce a peace agreement, such deliberations would be inconsequential. Assuming success in Dayton, however, they would define the most important action in the history of NATO—its first deployment outside its own area, its first joint operation with non-NATO troops, and its first post–Cold War challenge.

There was no disagreement over the first two tasks of IFOR personnel: first, to use whatever force or other means was necessary to protect themselves; and, second, to separate the warring parties and enforce the cease-fire.

But aside from separating the forces and protecting themselves, what else should the peacekeepers do? The disagreement on this critical issue between the "maximalists," like myself, and the "minimalists," mainly at the Pentagon, was profound. With Dayton days away, and our NATO allies sending military representatives to Washington to work out a common position, two high-level White House meetings were scheduled for October 25 and 27 to resolve these questions.

The military did not like civilian interference "inside" their own affairs. They preferred to be given a limited and clearly defined mission from their civilian colleagues and then decide on their own how to carry it out. In recent years, the military had adopted a politically potent term for assignments they felt were too broad: "mission creep." This was a powerful pejorative, conjuring up images of quagmires. But it was never clearly defined, only invoked, and always in a negative sense, used only to kill someone else's proposal.

The debate over mission creep raised an extremely important issue: the role of the American military in the post–Cold War world. The Pentagon did not want to fragment its forces in the pursuit of secondary objectives, especially in the twilight zone between war and peace. Given budgetary constraints, the Chiefs did not think they could pursue these objectives and fulfill their primary missions as well.

America's modern fighting force, primarily the creation and pride of the Reagan era, had handled challenges in Iraq, Panama, Grenada, and elsewhere with courage, skill, and low casualties. But two less pleasant memories still hung like dark clouds over the Pentagon. Phrases like "slippery slope" and "mission creep" were code for specific events that had traumatized the military and the nation: Mogadishu, which hung over our deliberations like a dark cloud; and Vietnam, which lay further back, in the inner recesses of our minds.

Vietnam had affected almost every American who had lived through the 1960s and early 1970s, including myself. But the "lessons of Vietnam" divided people almost as much as the war itself had. The leaders of the military establishment in the 1990s, all of whom had been company or field-grade officers in Vietnam, had derived a lesson substantially different from that of opponents of the war, including Bill Clinton. Colin Powell spoke eloquently for the military in his memoir. "Many of my generation," he wrote, "the career captains, majors, and lieutenant colonels seasoned in that war, vowed that when our turn came to call the shots, we would not quietly acquiesce in half-hearted warfare for half-baked reasons that the American people could not understand or support."[1]

The power of that distant yet living memory was visible on the right shoulder of General John Shalikashvili. As Chairman of the Joint Chiefs of Staff, he was entitled to wear the patch of any military unit on his uniform. He chose the insignia of MACV—the long-decommissioned Military Assistance Command Vietnam. When I first commented on the powerful emotions the once-ubiquitous MACV shield evoked in me, Shalikashvili said he was "surprised a civilian recognized" the symbol. "I spent three years in Vietnam," I explained, "part of it living in a MACV compound in the Mekong Delta." He wore the patch, he said, as a silent tribute to the Americans who served and died in that faraway war.

Despite some major successes, at least three times in the twenty years since Vietnam the military had stumbled. In April 1980, the attempt to rescue the American hostages in Tehran had failed in the Iranian desert, leaving eight Americans dead and contributing heavily to Carter's defeat by Reagan. In Lebanon three years later, 241 marines had been killed when their barracks was bombed, Reagan's worst moment as President. Then, on October 3, 1993, came a new disaster, which rocked the Clinton Administration and traumatized the military. Eighteen Americans, serving as part of the U.N. force in Somalia, were killed in the streets of Mogadishu while trying to capture a Somalian clan leader, Mohammed Farah Aideed. The scars from that disaster would deeply affect our Bosnia policy. Combined with Vietnam, they had left what might be called a "Vietmalia syndrome" in Washington.

To be sure, there were fundamental differences between Bosnia and "Vietmalia." Our goals and stakes were different. The Bosnian Serbs were neither the disciplined, ruthless revolutionaries of North Vietnam nor the drunken ragtag "technicals" who raced around Mogadishu shooting people. But discussion of such distinctions was not welcome: most officials felt they already knew the meaning of Somalia and Vietnam without giving them more than cursory analysis.

In their hearts, American military leaders would have preferred not to send American forces to Bosnia. They feared that the mission would be "fuzzy" and imprecise, like Somalia. Tony Lake, who shared their concerns, argued against a "nation-building" role for the military, and worried aloud about the "slippery slope" in Bosnia. Of course, if they were ordered to go, they would do so quickly and successfully. But the leadership of the military would resist "tasking" for anything beyond self-protection and the implementation of the military provisions of any peace agreement. The JCS and NATO believed that these two tasks would probably absorb all their resources.

American Casualties. Basing their predictions on another misreading of the Bosnian Serbs, as had been the case throughout the war, the military viewed the Serbs as a potent military force that would threaten IFOR as it had the U.N. Our negotiating team, including its two generals, Clark and Kerrick, believed these fears were greatly exaggerated. The Bosnian Serbs were a spent force, and we were confident that Milosevic would no longer come to their aid militarily. We believed that if sent to Bosnia, the U.S. military and NATO would be able to control the situation on the ground with little difficulty or challenge from the Serbs. We would not deploy American or other NATO troops absent ironclad guarantees from all three parties concerning their safety, access, and authority.

I reflected my belief that American and NATO casualties would be low—far lower, in fact, than any official predictions—in meetings and in several interviews just before Dayton. On Friday, October 27, I told Rowland Evans and Christiane Amanpour of CNN that

> While we have to anticipate that it's not a risk-free situation, we're not going to send people into combat. This is not Somalia, and it's not Vietnam. . . . We're not anticipating the kind of casualties and body bags that your question presupposes. *There is no peace without American involvement, but to repeat, there's no American involvement without peace.*
>
> EVANS: Well, I hate to belabor the issue, but this is what Americans are asking themselves. [General] Michael Rose, who ran the U.N. operation for at least a year—and you may disagree with him, but he certainly knows the situation on the ground—estimates that the casualties from this operation that you're planning will exceed the casualties from the Gulf War, which were three hundred and ninety dead. Is he crazy?
>
> HOLBROOKE: He's not crazy. He's wrong. His predecessor in Bosnia, General Morillon, said, "Hit them the first time they challenge you and they won't respond again."*

The Great Debate. Our team argued that after IFOR carried out its primary missions in Bosnia it should undertake additional tasks in support of peace—

* At the end of the program, Evans accurately summarized my views:
Ambassador Holbrooke was very hardheaded on casualties, Christiane. To me at least, he indicated that, if they get what they want from the three parties, there may not be many casualties. He wouldn't say there wouldn't be any, but, Christiane, he really emphasized an aspect of this that may be getting overlooked a little bit here, that the casualties and the body bags, despite Sir Michael Rose's prediction, may not be as bad as everybody here is afraid they will be.

including keeping roads open, assisting in the election process, and arresting war criminals. Without the backing of IFOR, the civilian parts of an agreement—the test of true peace—could not be carried out. And if the civilian provisions of a peace agreement were not carried out, then withdrawal of NATO forces would be more difficult.

In my view, this could create a self-defeating cycle: the narrower the military mission, the longer they would have to stay. But the military saw things quite differently: anticipating a huge security problem that would tie down their forces, they believed that any additional responsibilities would require additional forces, well beyond the sixty thousand troops in the plan.

The disagreement with the military was not personal. My respect for the senior military officers with whom we worked was enormous, especially General Shalikashvili, a friend whose support of the negotiating team had been exemplary. His unusual background added to his charm. He was born in Warsaw of Georgian parents three years before Hitler invaded Poland. English was his fourth language. Once, when several Americans were describing their first memories of Berlin, Shalikashvili quieted the others by recalling his first visit there—in 1943! He and his family came to the United States in 1954 when he was sixteen years old, and he learned English from American movies (especially, according to legend, John Wayne's). His military career had begun in the enlisted ranks, not at West Point.* Low-key but forceful, he was less imposing than Powell, and far less of a public figure. But, like Powell, he conveyed confidence and trust. With a quick smile and a disarming manner— "Call me Shali," he would say to anyone stumbling over his five-syllable surname—he was open and friendly, and universally liked by his civilian colleagues. He never tried to strong-arm or overwhelm civilians in a discussion, but simply stated his position and held his ground as long as possible. That we had good personal relations was important, since we had to work together closely, whatever happened.

With only a year to go until the presidential election, public opinion was heavily opposed to deployments—at that time some 70 percent of the American public did not want troops in Bosnia under any circumstances. The White House was understandably averse to a direct confrontation with the military. If the military openly opposed the deployment, our political difficulties would be vastly increased. We had to have their backing to get congressional and public support for the mission, which meant that they had the upper hand in the debate over what their mission would be.

* It was unusual for the nation's top military officer not to have gone to one of the service academies, but it was also true of two of Shalikashvili's three immediate predecessors, General Powell, an ROTC student at City College of New York, and General John Vessey, who won a battlefield commission on the Anzio beach during World War II.

So the lines were drawn, although not precisely, between two points of view concerning the mission of the peacekeepers: on one side, a narrow approach, backed by the JCS and NATO; on the other side, a broader, more ambitious maximalist approach in which IFOR would support the civilian aspects of a peace agreement if and when it had completed its primary missions.

Less than a week before Dayton, the battle lines were clear. Even after Sandy Berger's Deputies' Committee had resolved many secondary issues, there were still eleven major disagreements between State and the JCS. Some of them were fundamental, as identified in a study by Sandy Vershbow:

1. The JCS wanted to locate IFOR headquarters in Zagreb or Naples, rather than Sarajevo. Quarters suitable for a four-star admiral did not exist in Sarajevo, they said, and they worried about the security of their headquarters. We argued that if the senior American were not in Sarajevo the entire operation would be fatally weakened.

2. They wanted to deploy IFOR only in the Federation, and not in Republika Srpska. State argued that this would turn the Inter-Entity Boundary Line between the two parts of Bosnia into the equivalent of the DMZ in Korea—and effectively partition the country.

3. The Pentagon did not want to place IFOR troops on Bosnia's international borders, despite a strong request from Izetbegovic. We argued that troops had to be placed on the international border to support our position that Bosnia was a single country.

4. The JCS opposed "requiring" that the parties withdraw all heavy weapons from a "heavy weapons exclusion zone." Instead, it proposed that the peace agreement simply "encourage" the parties to withdraw their heavy weapons "on a voluntary basis." We found this position incomprehensible from the military's own point of view. The word "voluntary" did not exist in the Balkan lexicon, and leaving heavy weapons near the IFOR troops would only increase their vulnerability.

5. The Pentagon opposed the cantonment of weapons—that is, the stockpiling in isolated areas open to NATO inspection—by the two sides on the grounds that it was unenforceable. We argued that cantonments would protect IFOR and reduce the chances of incidents.

6. They opposed giving IFOR the authority to investigate "past incidents of attacks, atrocities or human rights violations." We said this was essential.

7. The Pentagon resisted any obligation to respond to "over the horizon" reports of attacks on international civilian personnel or gross

violations of human rights, on the grounds that this would "lead to mission creep and increase force requirements." In plain English, this meant that the Pentagon did not want to go to the aid of international civilian aid workers if a problem arose outside their immediate line of sight. We argued that it was inconceivable that the military could stand by if civilians, some of whom might be Americans, were endangered.

8. The military wanted little or no role in any aspect of civilian implementation, including elections and securing freedom of movement; we argued that its visible presence would be essential for the first series of elections after the war.

9. The Pentagon not only rejected any police functions for themselves, but also opposed giving the International Police Task Force (IPTF) a strong mandate and authority to arrest people. This, they said, would constitute the most dangerous form of "mission creep." If the IPTF got into trouble, the military argued, this could "lead to the assumption by IFOR of police functions throughout the country." I argued that this would weaken the chain of enforcement. Either the military should have arrest authority or else the IPTF should be given such powers.

10. The Pentagon wanted to exclude eastern Slavonia from the IFOR area of responsibility on the grounds that it would require more troops and raise more problems with Congress. We argued that eastern Slavonia, small, adjacent to Bosnia, and directly on the route that U.S. troops would travel to resupply their forces in Bosnia, was an integral part of the region, and would be easy to place under IFOR.

11. Finally, the Pentagon opposed any mandate or obligation to arrest indicted war criminals. Needless to say, I disagreed.

Over the last few days before Dayton we contested every one of these issues, winning some, losing many others. The implementation of Dayton, as it turned out, was determined in these meetings, with decidedly mixed results.

I appealed privately to Perry and Shalikashvili for a more robust IFOR mission. After personal review, Perry and Shalikashvili reversed two of the Pentagon's positions. The first was the location of IFOR headquarters; they realized that it had to be in Sarajevo rather than in Zagreb—a bizarre suggestion that had come up through the chain of command.

They also agreed that IFOR had to deploy some forces in the Serb portion of Bosnia; otherwise we would divide the country instead of unifying it. Perry also agreed to deploy IFOR forces on the international borders, although the number was smaller than we wanted or Izetbegovic had requested.

The first of the two White House meetings on the State-Pentagon disagreement took place on October 25. The JCS agreed to a *required* twenty-kilometer heavy-weapons-free zone adjusted to fit the demarcation of territory, and a four-kilometer zone of separation free of all weapons. This was a significant step forward from the original JCS-NATO plan. (I argued unsuccessfully for a ten-kilometer weapons-free zone.)

Two days later, with the European military representatives already arriving in Washington, we returned to the Situation Room to resolve the rest of our differences. Despite its significance, the debate on October 27 was never personal or tense. In our private meetings, Shalikashvili had promised to look for ways to reduce the gap between State and the JCS. Nonetheless, there were still serious disagreements.

"The issues before us are the ones that will determine the success or failure of the mission," I said. "Elections and the right of refugees to return may not be in IFOR's mandate, but they may be the key. We are deciding here whether or not we will end up with partition or a single country. If we succeed at Dayton, we will then face very tough real-life cases, such as people who want to return to their homes, say Muslims who once lived in Banja Luka—"

Shalikashvili broke in. "That's not IFOR's mission. We can't get every bus through. We should not sign a document we can't implement. I hope police will do their utmost to provide security for returning refugees. If there is an incident and the police are overwhelmed, then the IFOR commander has the authority to assist. But there could be days when he can't do this because his resources are stretched too thin."

Finally, Shalikashvili offered a compromise. "Supposing we accept the 'authority' to do additional tasks," he said, "but not the 'obligation.' " There was some confusion until Shali explained the distinction, which had a clear meaning to the military: if IFOR completed its required missions, it would have the *authority, but not the obligation,* to undertake the additional tasks. "For example, we do not wish to be obligated to arrest war criminals," he explained, "but we will accept the authority to arrest them if we get the chance." This was a big step forward from the military's opening position, which had opposed any widening of IFOR's role. But the meaning of this finely crafted compromise would not be determined until the commanders on the ground decided how to use their "authority."

This compromise was swiftly accepted by Christopher, Perry, and Lake. I did not object. It gave us a unified American position, which was essential for the weekend meetings with our European allies and the NATO Council, and in Dayton.

But had I known then how reluctant IFOR would be to use its "authority," I would have fought harder for a stronger mission statement, although I would probably have lost. But, like all the civilians in the meetings, I believed that IFOR would do more than it did, especially in the critical first year.

The "Silver Bullet." I still did not feel that IFOR's mandate was sufficient. Clark agreed, and he and his staff added a "silver bullet" clause to the military annex. Although phrased in bureaucratese, it gave the IFOR commanders freedom to use force whenever they felt it was necessary, without recourse to civilian authorities. In its final form, it read:

> The Parties understand and agree that the IFOR Commander shall have the authority, without interference or permission of any Party, to do all the Commander judges necessary and proper. . . . The violating Party shall be subject to military action by the IFOR, including the use of necessary force to ensure compliance with the Annex.

On the day between the two White House meetings, October 26, Christopher took the Dayton team and a number of senior officials, including Madeleine Albright, to a government training center in the Virginia hills near Warrenton for a strategy session. By now our team had expanded substantially. Warrenton was a dress rehearsal for Dayton, and we walked through every detail of the talks, presenting to Christopher and his team a ninety-two-page draft peace agreement and volumes of backup material. We agreed on a basic concept: Christopher would open the talks, then return to Washington, where he would remain available for visits whenever his presence might make a difference. After five hours of discussion, Christopher pronounced himself "satisfied and impressed" and we drove back to Washington.

The Consultations Intensify. The Europeans waited impatiently. The civilian implementation structure would be headed by Carl Bildt, and the military force would be at least two-thirds European—yet we had spent almost no time talking to the Europeans while our internal debate proceeded. When the consultations with the Europeans finally began, time was short, and the agenda massive. A visitor to the sixth floor of the State Department that weekend would have seen an unusual sight—dozens of people from at least seven countries wandering up and down a long corridor arguing in small groups over hundreds of pages of draft agreements and backup papers. Kornblum and I moved from room to room, encouraging and guiding the process.

I wish that cynics about government service had observed these meetings. It was one of those lovely Washington fall weekends that make the capital seem invigorating, but inside, oblivious to the weather, dozens of bureaucrats and military officers from many countries sweated through intense, seemingly endless meetings. By late Sunday afternoon, they had resolved many issues, especially those involving the deployment and role of IFOR. But we could not finish work on several key matters, including the authority of the senior civilian in Bosnia, and the role of the International Police Task Force. We agreed to complete our discussions in Dayton.

As the meetings continued, Owen, O'Brien, Menzies, and Jack Zetkulic of the Balkan desk flew to New York with me to talk to the Bosnians. Despite our pleas, they had done nothing to prepare for Dayton. Six weeks earlier, on September 18, I had raised my concern over this issue with Muhamed Sacirbey over a late-night conversation at the Inter-Continental Hotel in Zagreb. "Mo, I'm concerned that your government isn't ready for a peace conference," I had said. "Every time we try to discuss the key issues, you guys disagree with each other. You can't go into a big conference like that."

"We need help," he had replied. One of Sacirbey's charming qualities was his ability to admit, when he was alone, the mess in his government. "You're the Foreign Minister," I had said. "You are going to have to keep your team focused." I remembered his reply: "I know, I know. But it won't be easy." A few days later, Owen gave Sacirbey a list of fifteen international legal experts, but the Bosnians ignored the list and the idea until the last moment. On the eve of the talks, the Bosnians still had serious internal divisions within their government, few clear positions, and no qualified international legal experts, except one overworked and underconsulted international lawyer, Paul Williams.

The meeting in New York was intended to help the Bosnians prepare for Dayton. "Think strategically about what you want to achieve in Dayton," I said. Sacirbey, however, told us his government would not negotiate with the Serbs until we had forced the Croats into a new and better Federation agreement. This threatened our original scenario for Dayton, but Sacirbey had a point.

Negotiating requires flexibility on tactics but a constant vision of the ultimate goal. Sacirbey's demand would slow Dayton down and could even sink the conference, but there was no alternative. Putting the Federation first would give the Sarajevo delegation a chance to settle down, while pressuring us to produce a better Federation agreement.

On Monday, October 30, I flew to Dayton for my first look at Wright-Patterson Air Force Base. Dozens of workmen swarmed over the site in preparation. The Air Force, working closely with Pat Kennedy and Rosemarie Pauli, had repainted and rebuilt parts of the five facing visiting officers' quarters so that the three Balkan delegations, the United States, and the Europeans each had its own building. The Air Force had knocked walls out and created "presidential suites" for some of the participants. They turned over to us the

Hope Conference Center, a two-hundred-room hotel (which we filled completely with administrative and security personnel) with conference rooms. The Air Force had built a high barbed-wire fence around the entire area and had secured the entrances with heavy concrete barricades, which were heavily guarded by military police and security personnel.

With large areas for private walks, many private rooms, and even tennis courts, the final result was close to our dreams for Site X. The Air Force had even built, in the words of Tom Shoup, the deputy director of the 88th Civil Engineer Group that readied the site, a "very lovely meandering walkway, complete with lighting, so that delegates could walk this peaceful path from their quarters to the meeting rooms."* When Donilon saw the facilities, he was impressed. "This is as close as it gets to a perfect setup," he said. "Now all we have to do is get a deal."

Our tour was made more poignant by the vice commander of the Air Force Materiel Command who showed us around. He was Lieutenant General Lawrence P. Farrell, Jr., Joe Kruzel's brother-in-law, whom I had last seen more than two months earlier when he spoke over Joe's grave at Arlington. He was businesslike throughout, but at the end of my visit he told me that he and his family had a special reason to pray for success at Dayton.

That same evening, October 30, the House of Representatives delivered a serious public blow to the Administration, voting three to one for a nonbinding resolution that the Administration not deploy troops to Bosnia without prior congressional approval. Gingrich called the vote "a referendum on this Administration's incapability of convincing anyone to trust them."

Mike McCurry answered immediately. "The President will live up to his responsibilities as Commander in Chief and be true to his oath of office," he said. "If he needs to act to protect America's interests in the world, he will act." While Leon Panetta predicted ultimate congressional support for a deployment, telling *The Washington Post* that "the American people are not going to walk away from a peace settlement," Senator Patrick Leahy of Vermont, one of our supporters, warned that "the President would lose" if it came to a vote right away. The President told the press that the resolution would have no effect on the talks, but there was no denying that if we succeeded in Dayton, the vote's damage would have to be undone.

The Last Briefing. Our last meeting before Dayton was on October 31, with President Clinton and Vice President Gore in the Cabinet Room. Trying to

---

* Two years after the conference, the walkway was formally dedicated and named the Wright-Patterson Peace Walk.

start on a light note, I denied rumors that we had picked Dayton because it was Strobe Talbott's birthplace. Thin laughter. I gave the President a T-shirt from Wright-Patterson showing a dove superimposed over the map of Ohio, and he predicted it would become a collector's item. I noted that Ohio's population included people from every ethnic community of central Europe and the Balkans. "There are more Serbs and Hungarians in Cleveland than any other American city," I said. "The area is filled with Croats, Albanians, Hungarians, Slovaks, and other groups who understand the tragedy of their original home-lands. We hope the fact that they confine their rivalries to the football fields will send a signal to the participants."

This interested and pleased the President. He knew the area well, and spoke with feeling about the way people from different backgrounds lived in harmony in Ohio.

Regarding the talks themselves, I said we were on our own thirty-yard line. "That's not bad, considering we started on our own goal line," I said. "Dayton's a gamble, but the shuttle phase has run its course. Even if we fail, our nation can be proud that we made an all-out effort for peace. But there are practical limits to how long we can keep people cooped up at Wright-Patterson. We'll hit a wall by day ten or fifteen."

The President said that he hoped Dayton would be successful, but if it was he would face the most difficult decision any President has to make: sending thousands of young Americans into a dangerous, possibly lethal situation. "Given Somalia, we must have a clearly defined goal so that there's no mission creep," he said.

"I have especially strong feelings about Sarajevo," he went on. "It would be a mistake to divide the city. We don't want another Berlin. If you can't unify it, internationalize it." Turning to me, he said we should not be "constrained by artificial deadlines."

I said that there was one critical issue I had to raise, even though it was difficult. "If we are going to create a real peace rather than an uneasy cease-fire," I said, "Karadzic and Mladic will have to be captured. This is not simply a question of justice but also of peace. If they are not captured, no peace agreement we create in Dayton can ultimately succeed." There was silence at the Cabinet table.

"We can only go to the Hill with a full agreement," I went on. In the continuing silence, it seemed like a good time to raise some other important issues, even though they would not be resolved that day. "I know that this still concerns the military, but we cannot give up Gorazde and create sixty-five thousand more refugees. Also, there is real tension over what we are doing on the Zones of Separation. If we patrol only on the internal demarcation line, we will be partitioning the country. We must prevent Bosnia from becoming a Cyprus or a Korea.

"Finally, there is a political dilemma. The Hill sees us as replacing the U.N. in the middle of the war, although of course this is not the case. We need to explain better that we won't send troops without an agreement, and we won't participate in an operation like the U.N."

We broke up with many expressions of support. The President led us into the Roosevelt Room, where he told the press, "This is the best chance for peace we've had since the war began. It may be the last chance we have for a very long time." Then he and Vice President Gore posed for pictures with the negotiating team, wished us success, and left.

Our preparations were complete. We drove directly to Andrews and boarded an Air Force plane for Wright-Patterson Air Force Base in Dayton, Ohio.

BOOK THREE

DAYTON

(November 1–21, 1995)

Now sits expectation in the air.
—SHAKESPEARE, *Henry V*

CHAPTER 16

Going in Circles

(November 1–9)

The most gifted man can observe, still more can record, only the series *of his own impressions; his observations, therefore, . . . must be* successive, *while the things done were often* simultaneous. *. . . Actual events are nowise so simply related to each other as parent and offspring are; every single event is the offspring not of one, but of all other events, prior or contemporaneous, and will in its turn combine with all others to give birth to new; it is an ever-living, ever-working Chaos of Being, wherein shape after shape bodies itself forth from innumerable elements. And this Chaos . . . is what the historian will depict, and scientifically gauge, we may say, by threading it with single lines of a few [inches] in length!*

—THOMAS CARLYLE

DAYTON. THE WORD CONJURES UP INTENSE memories: the peace agreement that lasted thirty-seven minutes; our main gathering place, Packy's All-Sports Bar; midnight shrimp and steak dinners with Milosevic; the barren parking lot that separated the buildings where we lived; our cramped quarters, the lack of privacy; the effort of our European colleagues to adjust to diplomacy far removed, geographically and stylistically, from what they were used to; tennis matches with a surprisingly agile Tudjman; the emotional visit of the families of our lost colleagues; "napkin diplomacy" in the Officers' Club; dinner with Izetbegovic and Milosevic under the wing of a B-2 bomber; long walks with Silajdzic in the bitter cold; Krajisnik slamming his fist against a map of Sarajevo; Milosevic singing "Tenderly" with the pianist at the Officers' Club; the family of an imprisoned American journalist pleading his case; Izetbegovic refusing to touch his food during a meal with Milosevic; the stunning breakthrough on Sarajevo; the unforgettable final hours and our ultimatum; Silajdzic bursting into my room, shouting "You've ruined everything!"; Kati finding Milosevic waiting in a snowy parking lot outside my room; Tudjman emotionally telling Warren Christopher to "get peace now"; and Washington—waiting and worrying . . .

We thought we were ready. But nothing had prepared us for the pressure we encountered within the compound at Wright-Patterson. We estimated the conference would last fifteen to seventeen days; surely it would be impossible to keep three Presidents and hundreds of other people cooped up much longer. But twenty-one days later, on the last morning inside the high wire fence, we were facing defeat, with only twenty minutes left before we closed down the negotiations.

"Dayton." Since November 21, 1995, "Dayton" has entered the language as shorthand for a certain type of diplomacy—the Big Bang approach to negotiations: lock everyone up until they reach agreement. A "Dayton" has been seriously suggested for Northern Ireland, Cyprus, Kashmir, the Mideast, and other festering problems.

Those considering other Daytons should proceed with caution. It is a high-wire act without a safety net. Much work must precede the plunge into such an all-or-nothing environment. The site must be just right. The goals must be clearly defined. A single host nation must be in firm control, but it is high risk for the host, whose prestige is on the line. The consequences of failure are great. But when the conditions are right, a Dayton can produce dramatic results.

The translators' booths in the two large conference rooms came to symbolize for me the stupidity of the war. Our system had six language channels on the headsets. The first three were for English, French, and Russian.* Channel 4 was for translation into Bosnian, 5 into Croatian, and 6 into Serbian. This puzzled outsiders, since the same language, with minor differences, was spoken throughout the region. The answer came when one looked at the translation booths a few feet from our table. Each participant from the Balkans could choose his or her channel of preference—but one interpreter translated for channels 4, 5, and 6. When I noted this absurdity to Sacirbey, he said that "Serbo-Croatian" no longer existed—or, perhaps, had never existed. Nationalistic leaders were aggressively developing distinctive vocabularies for each ethnic group. Language, which had once helped unify Yugoslavia, was now another vehicle through which people were being driven apart.

Our goals were ambitious: first, to turn the sixty-day cease-fire into a permanent peace and, second, to gain agreement for a multiethnic state. Many ob-

---

* The Germans did not need, or ask for, a German translator. The French insisted on a French one, even though they all spoke excellent English.

servers believed these were impossible goals. Whatever we did, critics said, Bosnia would eventually divide into three parts, after which the Croat and Serb portions of Bosnia would join their neighboring "motherlands." We could not ignore the possibility that this might eventually happen. But not at Dayton— and not under American leadership. We would not legitimize Serb aggression or encourage Croat annexation. Furthermore, such an outcome might unleash a new round of ethnic and border conflicts in Central and Eastern Europe.

To reach our goal required agreements on many issues: eastern Slavonia, the Federation, a constitutional framework, elections, a three-person presidency, a national assembly, freedom of movement and the right of refugees to return to their homes, compliance with the International War Crimes Tribunal, and an international police force. Finally, we would face our most contentious task: determining the internal boundaries of Bosnia, those between the Serb portion of Bosnia and the Croat-Muslim Federation.

Our governing principle for this daunting agenda was simple: what we didn't get at Dayton we would never get later, so we would try to put everything on paper rather than settling for the sort of short and vague (and ultimately ignored) agreements that had been the products of all previous peace efforts. Better a high benchmark than a weak compromise. Despite the difficulties that implementation was to encounter, this approach proved to be correct. Any lesser goal at Dayton would have resulted in larger problems later. While some people criticized us for trying to do too much at Dayton, my main regret is that we did not attempt more.

The Compound. The size and diversity of Wright-Patterson impressed the participants. We wanted them to see this physical symbol of American power. But the small inner compound where we lived and negotiated was a different story. We placed the American, Bosnian, Croat, and combined Serbian– Bosnian Serb delegations in the four nondescript visiting officers' quarters that faced each other around a drab rectangular parking lot. The Europeans occupied a fifth building off the quad, but only thirty feet away. To emphasize Europe's co-chairmanship of the conference, we gave Carl Bildt a VIP suite directly above mine in the American building. The Bosnians were to our left, the Croatians to the right, and the Serbians and the Bosnian Serbs directly opposite us. The ground-floor windows of my rooms looked straight into those of Milosevic across the parking lot, about sixty yards away, thus allowing us to see if he was in his suite. The buildings were adequate, but hardly elegant. Our rooms were small, sound carried through the thin walls, and the corridor was only about six feet wide. During a preview tour of the facilities for journalists before the talks began, someone compared them to college dormitories. Sacirbey thought they looked like a Motel 6.

These were true "proximity" talks; we could walk from President to President in about a minute. On some days we would visit each President in his quarters a half-dozen times. Our days (and nights) became a blur of unscheduled meetings.

Dayton. There was also a real Dayton out there, a charming small Ohio city, famous as the birthplace of the Wright Brothers. Its citizens energized us from the outset. Unlike the population of, say, New York, Geneva, or Washington, which would scarcely notice another conference, Daytonians were proud to be part of history. Large signs at the commercial airport hailed Dayton as the "temporary center of international peace." The local newspapers and television stations covered the story from every angle, drawing the people deeper into the proceedings. When we ventured into a restaurant or a shopping center downtown, people crowded around, saying that they were praying for us. Warren Christopher was given at least one standing ovation in a restaurant. Families on the air base placed "candles of peace" in their front windows, and people gathered in peace vigils outside the base. One day they formed a "peace chain," although it was not large enough to surround the sprawling eight-thousand-acre base.

Ohio's famous ethnic diversity was also on display. We did everything possible to emphasize the fact that in the American heartland people from every part of southeastern Europe lived together in peace, their competition restricted to softball games, church rivalries, and the occasional barroom fight. Once, as Milosevic and I were taking a walk, about one hundred local Albanian Americans came to the outer fence of Wright-Patterson with megaphones to plead the case for Kosovo. I suggested we walk over to chat with them, but he refused, saying testily that they were obviously being paid by a foreign power.

Our team arrived in Dayton on October 31, in time to greet the Balkan delegations. The wind whipped across the airstrip at Wright-Patterson and there was a cold, light drizzle—weather we would soon become used to. Shortly after 6:00 P.M., Milosevic arrived, proclaiming his confidence that a peace agreement would emerge from Dayton. Then, on an American military plane, came Izetbegovic, withdrawn and apprehensive, who spoke briefly, calling for "peace with justice." Finally Tudjman landed, proud and haughty. Although obviously pleased at the honor guard, he made no statement. From the outset, he wanted to show he had finally become more important than his longtime rivals, and that he was in Dayton only to regain eastern Slavonia. We agreed that he would stay for two days, go back to Zagreb for the opening of the new parliament, and then return.

I accompanied each President to his quarters, then returned to the airstrip to wait for the next arrival. Tudjman and Izetbegovic went directly to bed, but

Milosevic, ever the night owl, was restless as usual, and asked to tour the grounds. I took him, naturally, to Packy's All-Sports Bar.

Packy's was Wright-Patterson's answer to the United Nations Delegates Lounge, and a lot more fun. Pictures of Bob Hope—for whom the Hope Conference Center was named—entertaining American troops in four wars covered the walls. Four giant television screens, tuned to CNN and various all-sports channels, dominated the main room. Each table had its own small speaker, which could tune to any of the four channels, so the room usually resounded with overlapping broadcast sounds. On nights when the Chicago Bulls played, the Croats gathered to cheer their hero, Toni Kukoc; the Serbs waited to cheer Vlade Divac, then with the Los Angeles Lakers.

When Milosevic and I arrived on that first evening, Haris Silajdzic was sitting with Chris Hill. I went over to their table, but Milosevic pointedly held back, shaking Silajdzic's hand brusquely and then turning away to chat with people at other tables. Watching Milosevic turn on the charm, Warren Christopher observed that had fate dealt him a different birthplace and education, he would have been a successful politician in a democratic system.

The waitress serving Milosevic was a pleasant woman who had no idea that she was serving one of the most reviled people in the world. "What's your name?" he asked her. "Where are you from?" Charmed by the attention, she told us she was Vicky. In Milosevic's excellent but accented English, she became "Waitress Wicky." Whenever he came to Packy's, he would ask her to serve him. A local legend was born, and a year later, during the first-anniversary celebrations at Wright-Patterson, I was served by Waitress Wicky herself, now a proud part of the Dayton story.

Milosevic was seething about the press, especially a profile of him by Roger Cohen in *The New York Times* that morning. "It is unbelievable," the Serb leader said, "that such shit can be printed." He singled out the references to his parents—his father, "an Orthodox priest who had committed suicide when his son was 4," and his mother, "a schoolteacher who committed suicide several years later."

"Why do they print such stupid things," he asked, neither confirming or denying their accuracy. "How can you permit it?" Milosevic complained that some of the information in Cohen's article came from within our delegation. This was true, although unintentional, and I made no effort to deny it.

DAY ONE: WEDNESDAY, NOVEMBER 1

"The eyes of the world are on Dayton, Ohio," Warren Christopher said on his arrival at 9:00 A.M. As we drove to the "quad," I warned Christopher that all three sides had hardened their positions in anticipation of the opening bell. This was to be expected at the beginning of such an event. More discouraging was the disarray within the Bosnian delegation and the dissension between the Croatians and the Bosnians over the Federation.

Christopher and I met with each President privately, reviewing once more the ground rules that we had presented to the parties almost a month earlier. The most important rule, of course, was that no one should talk to the press. Carl Bildt had agreed to our proposal that State Department Spokesman Nick Burns would be the only authorized spokesman on Dayton, and he would brief the world from Washington. We did not even have a press briefing officer in Dayton.

Each President made his priority clear in these initial meetings. For Tudj-man, of course, it was eastern Slavonia; he did not even mention Bosnia. We told him eastern Slavonia could be settled only within the framework of a larger agreement. For Milosevic, it was sanctions. Christopher offered a slight change in the American position: we would agree to suspension of the sanc-tions upon *initialing* an agreement, instead of waiting for its formal *signing*. This was significant because we anticipated that about a month would elapse between initialing in Dayton and signing at a formal ceremony. This small change in our position would give Milosevic more incentive to reach agree-ment in Dayton, and simultaneously relieve some of the strain within the Con-tact Group over the sanctions issue.

Izetbegovic and Silajdzic told Christopher again that we had to renegotiate the Federation agreement before the start of serious territorial discussions with the Serbs. We had already agreed to this, even though it would delay us. The Federation was indeed weak, and no peace with the Serbs would work un-less Croat-Muslim tensions, especially in Mostar, were contained. I asked the number-two man in the German delegation, Michael Steiner—the most knowledgeable and tenacious of all the Europeans working on Bosnia—to lead the Federation negotiations, assisted by Dan Serwer, our Federation ad-visor.

With our calls completed, Christopher and I walked the hundred yards to the Hope Center for lunch with the Contact Group. Handling them at Dayton would be a problem. They could, of course, meet whenever they wished with the Balkan leaders. But the real negotiations, with the exception of Steiner's Federation efforts, would be conducted by the United States. "Some of you," Christopher said at lunch in an effort to prepare them for some frustration, "may not be happy with every aspect of the negotiations, but we are all pursu-ing the same result together. Let us not lose sight of that."

Finally it was time to begin. The opening event was planned for maximum symbolic value: a public face-to-face meeting among the three Presidents, the first in more than two years, and the first ever under American auspices. In the

December 31, 1992. With Lionel Rosenblatt, president of Refugees International, in Kiseljak on the road to Sarajevo, just before entering Serb-controlled territory. In the background, a U.N. soldier heads for his compound.

September 1994. In Mostar, standing on the makeshift bridge that replaces the ancient one that was the city's symbol, with General Charles Boyd, Deputy Commander-in-Chief U.S. Forces Europe, during a trip just prior to becoming Assistant Secretary of State.

August 21, 1995. Andrews Air Force Base: Kati, the author, and Strobe Talbott. WASHINGTON *TIMES* PHOTO.

August 21, 1995. A decisive moment: President Clinton pulls the government and the negotiating team back together in a dramatic meeting in a small room behind the chapel at Fort Myer immediately after the memorial service. *Clockwise from the President:* Tony Lake, General Wes Clark, Leon Fuerth (standing), Leon Panetta (partially hidden behind Clark), Warren Christopher, Chris Hill (standing), General Don Kerrick (standing), CIA Director John Deutch, the author, William Perry, Jim Pardew (standing), Madeleine Albright, General John Shalikashvili. Just out of camera range to the left were Sandy Berger and Strobe Talbott. WHITE HOUSE PHOTO.

August 28, 1995. With Bosnian Foreign Minister Muhamed Sacirbey in front of the Crillon Hotel in Paris hours after the marketplace bombing in Sarajevo. We are awaiting word as to whether or not there will be NATO bombing. In the background, Ambassador Pamela Harriman and, far right, Robert Owen. AP/WIDE WORLD PHOTO.

The team on the plane. *Left to right:* General Kerrick, General Clark, Jim Pardew, Chris Hill. STATE DEPARTMENT PHOTO.

October 5, 1995. Outside the Bosnian Presidency in Sarajevo. Carl Bildt (behind author); General Clark and Jim Pardew (right background) conferring with Bosnian officials. REUTERS/DANILO KRSTANOVIC/ARCHIVE PHOTOS.

October 16, 1995. A typical scene during the shuttle, taken leaving the Quai d'Orsay after a meeting with French Foreign Minister de Charette. *Left to right:* Chris Hill, Lt. Col. Dan Gerstein (recovered from his injuries on Mt. Igman), the author, General Clark (on the phone), General Kerrick, Jim Pardew. AP/WIDE WORLD PHOTO.

November 28, 1995. Discussion of U.S. force levels in Bosnia in the Oval Office. Chart shows a possible drawdown schedule for IFOR based on a twelve-month withdrawal plan. WHITE HOUSE PHOTO.

February 20, 1996. Reporting to the Principals Committee in the White House Situation Room, one day after the Rome compliance summit and one day before I left the government. *Left to right, at the table:* the author, Deputy Director of Central Intelligence Admiral Dennis Blair, General Shalikashvili, Secretary of Defense Perry, Vice President Gore, President Clinton. *Left to right, behind the table:* General Clark, Undersecretary of Defense Walt Slocombe, White House deputy press spokesman David Johnson (standing). *Back to the camera:* OMB Director Alice Rivlin. WHITE HOUSE PHOTO.

April 4, 1997. Two guys on crutches, taken during a White House ceremony. (Paul Nitze is in center background.) WHITE HOUSE PHOTO.

August 7, 1997. A meeting of the joint presidency in Sarajevo during a return trip as special envoy. *Left to right:* the author; Robert Gelbard, the implementation "czar" for the United States; and the three "co-Presidents": Izetbegovic, Zubak, and Krajisnik. This photograph was taken at the start of a ten-hour negotiating session that ended at 4:00 A.M. AP/WIDE WORLD PHOTO.

A Dayton Portfolio

October 31, 1995: The core team arrives at Wright-Patterson Air Force Base. *Left to right:* Hill, Kerrick, Clark, Owen (partially hidden), the author, and Pardew. At Pardew's left is Lt. Gen. Lawrence P. Farrell, Jr., base commander and Joe Kruzel's brother-in-law. STATE DEPARTMENT PHOTO/S. SGT. BRIAN W. SCHLUMBOHM.

November 4: Before a private dinner, Milosevic and the author argue over the release of *Christian Science Monitor* journalist David Rohde, who is being held in a Bosnian Serb jail. STATE DEPART-MENT PHOTO/S. SGT. BRIAN W. SCHLUMBOHM.

November 8: Milosevic and Izetbegovic lead a group from the barracks to the Hope Center to begin discussions of the map. The remarkable rapport the two men show—Milosevic laughing, apparently at a comment of Izetbegovic—will disappear within hours, and they will almost never meet face-to-face again. The author is far back, talking to Silajdzic. STATE DEPARTMENT PHOTO/ARIC R. SCHWAN.

Warren Christopher meets with the Contact Group in Carl Bildt's suite. *Left to right:* Christopher, Jacques Blot, Wolfgang Ischinger, Igor Ivanov, Pauline Neville-Jones, Bildt. STATE DEPARTMENT PHOTO/ARIC R. SCHWAN.

An American staff meeting over sandwiches and soft drinks at the Hope Center. *Left to right:* the author, Hill, Kerrick, Ambassador John Menzies, Rudy Perina, David Lipton (U.S. Treasury), Nick Burns, policy planning chief Jim Steinberg, Christopher, Chief of Staff Tom Donilon, Assistant Secretary of State John Shattuck. Also present were Robert Owen, John Kornblum, and Wes Clark. STATE DEPARTMENT PHOTO/S. SGT. BRIAN W. SCHLUMBOHM.

November 12: The core team meets in the author's suite as the map discussions begin. *Clockwise from lower left:* Pardew, Perina, Kerrick (leaning forward), Clark, Rosemarie Pauli, Owen, Hill, the author, Menzies. The issue is the width of the corridor linking Bihac and Sarajevo. STATE DEPART-MENT PHOTO/ARIC R. SCHWAN.

November 14: On a typically windy Dayton day, Christopher and the author, carrying a map, walk from the Bosnia delegation building to see Milosevic. STATE DEPARTMENT PHOTO/ARIC R. SCHWAN.

November 17, 1:00 A.M.: Drawing the map. As Milosevic stares at the high-tech computer screen, the search for a secure path to Gorazde continues. *Left to right:* Kerrick (back to camera), Menzies, Clark, Perina, the author. DEPARTMENT OF DEFENSE.

November 20, 2:00 A.M.: Milosevic and Silajdzic, negotiating in an American conference room, close in on an agreement that would last thirty-seven minutes. *Left to right:* Silajdzic, Milosevic, Clark, Christopher, the author. In the left background, Bosnia's main map expert watches to make sure that Silajdzic does not give anything away. STATE DEPARTMENT PHOTO/ARIC R. SCHWAN.

November 20, 4:05 A.M.: The negotiators toast the Milosevic-Silajdzic agreement, sipping wine from Christopher's personal supply. (Christopher is at author's right, just out of the photograph.) The author watches without drinking, concerned that the "agreement" is somehow flawed. *Left to right:* the author, Clark, Hill, Silajdzic, Milosevic. STATE DEPARTMENT PHOTO/ARIC R. SCHWAN.

November 20, 4:15 A.M.: Ten minutes later, the negotiators relax during the lull before the storm. Silajdzic is asking Izetbegovic's interpreter to wake up the Bosnian President so he can review the agreement. Moments later, Izetbegovic and Croatian Foreign Minister Granic arrive, and the agreement blows up. *Left to right:* Christopher, the author, Clark, Hill, Silajdzic, and Milosevic. STATE DEPARTMENT PHOTO/ARIC R. SCHWAN.

November 20, midafternoon: Reconvening in the author's suite after the disaster of the previous night, Izetbegovic and Milosevic go at it again. Milosevic is pushing hard for an agreement, but as the photo shows, Izetbegovic has withdrawn. STATE DEPARTMENT PHOTO/ARIC R. SCHWAN.

November 21, 11:45 A.M.: Donilon, the author, and Christopher watch President Clinton announce the agreement from the Rose Garden as Christopher works on his own remarks for the afternoon ceremony. STATE DEPARTMENT PHOTO/ARIC R. SCHWAN.

November 21, 1:00 P.M.: The three Presidents meet in Christopher's suite at the Hope Center prior to the initialing ceremony. STATE DEPARTMENT PHOTO/ARIC R. SCHWAN.

November 21: Bildt tries to encourage Izetbegovic before the initialing ceremony. STATE DEPARTMENT PHOTO/S. SGT. BRIAN W. SCHLUMBOHM.

November 21, 3:15 P.M.: The initialing ceremony begins. *Left to right:* Germany's Wolfgang Ischinger (partially hidden), Britain's Pauline Neville-Jones, Milosevic, Izetbegovic (showing his ambivalence), Tudjman, Christopher, Bildt. STATE DEPARTMENT PHOTO/S. SGT. BRIAN W. SCHLUMBOHM.

November 21: After the ceremony, talking to Silajdzic. In the right background, Christopher's executive assistant, Robert Bradkte. STATE DEPARTMENT PHOTO/S. SGT. BRIAN W. SCHLUMBOHM.

B-29 Superfortress Room (each room at the Hope Convention Center carried the name of a military plane)* hundreds of journalists waited behind ropes.

Every detail had been choreographed carefully by Donilon, Burns, and myself. Christopher and I entered first. Tudjman, Izetbegovic, and Milosevic came next, escorted by Galbraith, Menzies, and Perina to their seats at a small round table—a duplicate of the one we had used in Geneva and New York. Then came the most hotly debated and closely watched moment of the day—the handshake among the three men. Christopher and some of his staff feared that they might refuse, embarrassing us in full view of the world's press. I felt a handshake was essential as a symbolic act before we disappeared from public view. After some discussion, we decided to stage a handshake, but when the critical instant arrived, there was, in the words of *The New York Times,* an "awkward" pause. After a moment Christopher rose and asked the three Presidents to shake hands. The photographs—almost the last that would come out of Dayton for three weeks—sent the right signal around the world: the three Presidents were finally in one room and talking, however hesitantly, to one another.

"We are here to give Bosnia and Herzegovina a chance to be a country at peace, not a killing field," Christopher said. He laid out four conditions for a settlement: Bosnia had to remain a state with "a single international personality"; a settlement must take into account "the special history and significance" of Sarajevo; human rights must be respected and those responsible for atrocities be brought to account; and, finally, eastern Slavonia must be resolved. When Christopher had finished his remarks, we adjourned immediately, without letting the warring Presidents make public statements. Nick Burns took a heavy assault from several reporters who understandably wanted more than a short and well-staged public event. But that would have started us off on a contentious note, and we had enough problems already.

Tudjman and Eastern Slavonia. Christopher originally planned to return to Washington soon after the ceremony, but in the first example of a pattern that would emerge at Dayton, we changed the schedule at the last moment so that he could attend a hastily arranged meeting between Milosevic and Tudjman on eastern Slavonia. We met in a small VIP cottage about a mile from the Hope Center. The two Presidents sat opposite each other, while Christopher and I sat side by side on a couch between them; Hill and Galbraith also participated. Their greeting was far warmer than their performance for the press; Milosevic jovially hailed Tudjman as "Franjo." Tudjman called Milosevic "Slobo."

---

* Carl Bildt suggested that we redesignate the rooms with more peaceful names for the duration of the conference, a proposal that was impractical.

Ambassador Galbraith started by saying that he believed the solution to eastern Slavonia, on which he had worked tirelessly, lay in the resolution of several relatively small matters. Tudjman replied testily that these so-called technical problems begged the fundamental question, on which he demanded an answer from Milosevic: would the Serbs accept the full reintegration of eastern Slavonia into Croatia? Milosevic replied that the technical issues were really about another core question: would the Serbs have rights as a minority in eastern Slavonia? Milosevic seemed oblivious to the irony that he was arguing a human-rights case on behalf of Serbs from a region that his army had reduced to rubble. Still, he had a point. The Serbs who had lived in eastern Slavonia and the Krajina for generations should have had the same rights as other dispossessed people in the region.

The conversation began with consecutive translation, but as it heated up, we invited the two men to proceed in their native language (or languages), while we tried to follow with the assistance of an interpreter and Chris Hill. Once they were liberated from the civilizing restrictions of English, the decorum of the meeting rapidly deteriorated. "Franjo!" "Slobo!" They shouted with increasing intensity, half in Serb, half in English. Finally I interrupted. "Let's do something about eastern Slavonia right away," I said. "Mr. Holbrooke, you are too unrealistic," Milosevic replied. "This issue must be settled in the field. I cannot control those people in eastern Slavonia."

Nonetheless, Milosevic agreed to "use his influence," which he continued to claim was nonexistent, with the eastern Slavonian Serbs. Given this small opening, I suggested that Galbraith and the U.N. negotiator, Thorvald Stoltenberg, return with Tudjman to Croatia the next day, in order to seek an agreement among the local leaders. I thought of the stoic Stoltenberg, who was at that moment on a plane en route to Dayton; he would have time only to grab fresh clothes and take a short nap before returning to Croatia.

Although there had been no change in the positions of the two parties, Milosevic had made two important implicit concessions. For the first time, he had agreed that eastern Slavonia would be discussed at Dayton. And he had previously claimed he had no influence over the Serbs of Slavonia; now he seemed ready to "recommend" a solution to the local Serbs.

Tudjman had gained a point. Events had given him a central role in the peace process. Some critics charged that we had made a deliberate decision to overlook Croatia's often brutal policies toward Muslims and Serbs in exchange for Zagreb's support of a peace agreement in Bosnia. The truth, however, was different: we did not empower Tudjman, the situation did. Tudjman could prevent a settlement in Bosnia until he got control of eastern Slavonia, the last piece of Serb-controlled land in Croatia. Given his previous behavior, his threats to go to war again soon after Dayton if he did not get the region back peacefully had to be taken seriously. Tudjman's ability both to prevent a Bosnia agreement and to threaten another war was his primary leverage over Milosevic. His influence over Izetbegovic came from his ability to break up the Croat-Muslim Federation, whose continued survival was essential for Dayton to work. For years Tudjman had been regarded with contempt by Milosevic and hatred by Izetbegovic; now he had the upper hand over his two rivals, and he knew exactly how to exploit it for his own goals.

Warren Christopher. Christopher was appalled by the behavior he had just witnessed. But it was useful that it had happened in his presence; he could warn Washington, as he said, that "it is going to be tough the whole way." Otherwise, he was pleased with the day—more so than I was. It had gone smoothly, and the press coverage appeared to be excellent. Christopher said he would return whenever it was useful, but would leave the timing to the team at Dayton. As we drove to the airstrip, I asked if he was comfortable with the chaotic nature of the process—so alien to his methodical style. "I'm not always sure what you are doing, or why," he replied, "but you always seem to have a reason, and it seems to work, so I'm quite content to go along with your instincts."

I thanked him for his confidence. As he left for Washington, I reflected on the long road we had traveled together. I had known Warren Christopher since 1977, when Cy Vance had made him Deputy Secretary of State and me Assistant Secretary for East Asian and Pacific Affairs. My relationship with him in the Carter Administration had been close, and it became even closer in December 1978, when he undertook a difficult and dangerous mission to Taiwan immediately after President Carter had announced the full normalization of relations with the People's Republic of China. When a screaming crowd of thousands of angry Taiwanese surrounded and attacked his car as he tried to leave the airport, he handled himself with courage and calm.

In the 1980s, Christopher and I kept in regular contact. He invited me to address his partners at O'Melveny & Myers in Los Angeles. We dined together in Los Angeles and New York, and worked on several business deals together. Despite our close association over eighteen years, we were obviously different in style, age, and background. Where Chris was cautious and methodical, I tended to be intuitive and impatient. While he looked at issues as a sort of lawyer-judge, adjudicating the differences between the two sides, I was more likely to focus on the historical causes of the problem and its internal dynamic. He came to Washington from California, a Norwegian American raised in North Dakota; I was a New Yorker with a mixed Central European Jewish background and had lived overseas for many years, on three continents. Almost twenty years separated us in age.

I never felt we were competitors. But starting in 1992, some mutual friends, perhaps trying to stir things up, began saying that Chris viewed me with concern. When Christopher was appointed head of the transition task force for the President-elect, the press printed rumors of friction and rivalry between us. When I raised these stories with him, he dismissed them. Whatever the truth about the past, it was extremely unusual for a Secretary of State to give a subordinate the kind of support and backing Christopher had given us during the shuttle. Now, with identical interests, fate had made us an inseparable team.

That evening, after Christopher left, we handed each Balkan delegation the draft annexes on the constitution, elections, and IFOR. Amazed at the detail and length of the documents, the three Presidents began to realize that when we said we wanted a comprehensive agreement, we meant it.

DAY TWO: THURSDAY, NOVEMBER 2

Trying to create a little order out of chaos, we divided our efforts into six areas:

- First, Michael Steiner, assisted by his diligent German colleague Christian Clages and two Americans, Dan Serwer and Chris Hill, would negotiate a new and tougher Federation agreement between the Croats and the Muslims;

- Second, Bildt, Owen, and I would negotiate constitutional and electoral issues with Milosevic and the Bosnians;

- Third, Clark and Pardew would begin discussions on the military annex with the parties, which I would join later;

- Fourth, we would conduct a two-track negotiation on eastern Slavonia, led by Hill and me in Dayton and Galbraith and Stoltenberg in the region;

- Fifth, we would try to complete unfinished business internal to the Contact Group, with Robert Gallucci taking the lead on two issues that we had not resolved on that last pre-Dayton weekend, the role of the international police task force and the mandate of the senior civilian implementation official, who would be Carl Bildt;

- Finally, we would continue to defer most discussion on the territorial issues ("the map") until we had made progress on other matters.

What Is the Federation? The distinction between the two levels of government—the central government and the entities—was still confusing, even to many people at Dayton. This was understandable: the designations had changed several times during the war, and were poorly defined. The Republic of Bosnia and Herzegovina had been at war since the moment it declared independence in 1992. Its predominantly Muslim government, headed by Izetbegovic, contained some Croats and Serbs, but it had control only over the Muslim part of Sarajevo and the area around Tuzla. Other Muslim areas, such as Bihac and Goradze, were, for all practical purposes, autonomous. The Croat part of Bosnia was run separately out of Mostar by a group of Bosnian Croats whom we considered crooks; they were the people who had waged the terrible war-within-a-war that had torn Mostar and several other mixed Croat-Muslim towns apart in 1993–94. To stop this war and create a common front against the Serbs, the United States, under the leadership of Charles Redman, had created the Federation in early 1994. But after creating the Federation on paper, the United States had not followed up, leaving responsibility in the hand of the European Union. Until the fall of 1994, when we appointed Dan Serwer, no American official was even assigned to work on the Federation.

All this had now changed. Out of makeshift wartime structures, we now sought to create two functioning levels of government: a central government, with its capital in Sarajevo; and two regional entities, one a functioning Croat-Muslim Federation, the other the existing Bosnian Serb entity, but minus any claims to sovereignty. Steiner's plan was for the Federation to turn responsibility for certain functions, such as foreign affairs and finance, over to the new central government, which would include Muslims, Serbs, and Croats. In turn, local matters such as police, education, and internal security would be assigned to each of the entities—the Federation and the Republika Srpska.

For the first week, I turned the problem of the Federation over to Steiner. He and Hill would struggle with Tudjman, Izetbegovic, and Kresimir Zubak, the President of the Federation, while I worked on other issues.

DAY THREE: FRIDAY, NOVEMBER 3

The Contact Group was already restive. We had agreed to meet each morning at 9:00 A.M. The first two meetings were a mess, and we wasted almost two hours on trivial matters. This was not why we had come to Dayton. The Europeans had a great deal to contribute, and would be essential for success. But they seemed addicted to interminable meetings focused mainly on procedure, while the three Balkan Presidents waited a few hundred feet away.

We could not afford to waste so much time, yet we had to keep the Europeans involved. After three days, we dissolved the large daily Contact Group meeting and replaced it with a smaller meeting restricted to the six senior representatives at Dayton: Carl Bildt, Pauline Neville-Jones, Wolfgang Ischinger, Jacques Blot, Igor Ivanov, and myself. For symbolic reasons, I suggested we meet in Bildt's room.

"What Is Europe's Phone Number?" This arrangement reflected a deeper difficulty within the European Union: who spoke for Europe?

This problem had been famously described by Henry Kissinger when someone in the State Department had said that they had better consult Europe on some issue. "And what," Kissinger had rumbled to his staff, "is Europe's phone number?" Now, two decades later, and despite the E.U.'s frequent lip service to a common defense and foreign policy, Kissinger's question was still relevant.

At Dayton, it was a problem from the outset. Although Carl Bildt was one of the three co-chairmen, Pauline Neville-Jones and Jacques Blot told us privately that Bildt could not speak for their governments on certain issues. This made a mockery of both the theory and the practice of having a E.U. representative as co-chairman, and raised other questions. Whom did Bildt speak for? And when? What, in fact, was his authority? Did he represent only the E.U. countries that were *not* there? Where did the Germans, who had not made a similar statement, stand?

No clear answers were forthcoming from Neville-Jones or Blot. In fact, they seemed annoyed when we raised the problem, saying, "We'll sort it out as we go along." It was a sad admission, on the one hand, that the E.U. did not exist as a single negotiating entity. On the other hand, it was not surprising that nations which still aspired to greatness and global influence wanted to retain an independent voice on foreign policy. What troubled us most was the hypocrisy of the European Union in giving a distinguished former Prime Minister such a grandiose title, then undermining and hamstringing him from the outset, and later blaming us for friction in the negotiations. Reflecting on this situation a year later, Carl Bildt observed philosophically, "Europe lacks the capacity to act because of too many competing interests, while the U.S.—when it sorts out its own mess in Washington—has the capacity to act. The Europeans are good at coordinating with each other, while the U.S. is not, but our internal coordination takes up all our time, and you are more decisive when you get your act together."

David Rohde. In the midst of our negotiations, a new problem arose. An intrepid young *Christian Science Monitor* journalist, David Rohde, had rented a car in Vienna and, without telling anyone, set out for Srebrenica, hoping to write a follow-up account of its fall, a story that he had been one of the first to cover. On October 29, showing more courage than wisdom, he began digging in the red dirt of the mud dam near Zvornik, the presumed site of a mass grave. Not surprisingly, he was picked up by Bosnian Serb police. As Dayton opened, he was missing somewhere in Republika Srpska.

Rohde's absence complicated our work considerably. Although he was a private citizen and had knowingly taken great risks—traveling without papers or permission, apparently without the full knowledge of his own editors—we could not ignore the situation. I told Milosevic that while we would continue to discuss the issues, no agreement would be possible at Dayton unless Rohde was found unharmed.

Milosevic was astonished. "You would do all this for a journalist?" he said incredulously. "Yes," I replied. "We would have no choice." It was the beginning of a dramatic subplot at Dayton.

The Bosnian Serbs. The joint Yugoslav–Bosnian Serb delegation at Dayton included Momcilo Krajisnik and Nikola Koljevic, and one of General Mladic's top deputies, General Zdravko Tolimir. Milosevic relegated them to the second floor of the two-story Serb quarters, and treated them with open contempt. This was in sharp contrast to his treatment of Momir Bulatovic, the genial, low-key president of Montenegro, whom he often brought to meetings to demonstrate that the Federal Republic of Yugoslavia consisted of more than just Serbia.

On November 2 and 3, Jim Pardew met with Krajisnik and his colleagues to test their attitudes. The meetings were unproductive but revealing. Krajisnik, an unreconstructed opponent of a single state, proposed that Sarajevo be divided, and that the airport be moved so that the land it occupied could be converted into a new Serb downtown area. After five hours, Jim told them their positions were completely unrealistic, and left.

From then on, the Bosnian Serbs were essentially isolated at Dayton. Dark and brooding, they hovered on the edge of the conference, eating alone at Packy's, avoiding contact with the other national delegations, and trying to communicate with Carl Bildt and Wes Clark, who they thought would be more accessible. Within a few days, Krajisnik began sending us angry letters demanding to know what was going on. I showed them to Milosevic, observing how odd it was for us to receive missives from members of his delegation asking *us* what was going on. Milosevic took each letter, crumpled it up without reading it, and threw it ostentatiously into his wastebasket. "Pay no attention to those guys," he said. "I'll make sure they accept the final agreement."

The Museum Dinner. We constantly looked for ways to break down the barriers of hatred and distrust. The most ambitious effort took place on the evening of the third day: a large dinner for all the delegations at the Wright-Patterson Air Force Museum.

We picked the site with great care. The Wright-Patterson Air Force Base included the greatest military air museum in the world, with a collection that covered the entire history of aircraft, from before the Wright brothers to the cruise missile. Hangar after hangar held priceless airplanes, beautifully displayed. For an hour before dinner, the delegations walked through the exhibition with museum guides. Izetbegovic showed little interest, but the others were fascinated by this brief diversion. With controlled emotion, Wolfgang Ischinger pulled me aside in front of a Messerschmitt. "This was the plane my father flew during the war," he said quietly. "I have never seen it before." Ischinger was a true son of modern Germany—sensitive, urbane, and determined to see his country play a positive role in the world.

Jacques Blot, however, was nowhere to be seen. When Rosemarie called to find him, she discovered that he was boycotting the dinner because the security guards at the gates of Wright-Patterson had stopped his car, forced him to walk around the inspection post, and then searched him using dogs trained to smell explosives.

We put an end to this excessive zeal the next day by ensuring that all senior personnel would be treated with respect and allowed to pass unimpeded through the gates. But it was too late to soothe Jacques Blot's wounded pride. I called him to apologize and promised it would never happen again, but, enraged, he said my apology was insufficient. The insult was not simply to him, but "to all of France." He would not leave the compound for our dinner—but he would make a formal protest to Washington and consider returning to Paris. "I will not," he said, "be sniffed." He pronounced it "sneefed."

Apologizing again, I asked Jacques to come to the dinner. Again he refused. When I offered to send my vehicle, he reluctantly agreed, and arrived at the dinner in a foul mood. When Igor Ivanov heard the story, he laughed, "Blot should not complain until he has been searched at the Kremlin. They used to do it to us every day." But Blot remained angry, and, irritated by other real or imagined insults in the following days, he was dyspeptic throughout the rest of the conference.

We arrived in the last hangar—the largest one in the museum—to find a great array of modern warplanes and missiles. The tables were laid out beneath the wing of an enormous B-2 suspended from the ceiling. Along the wall, in a fortuitous coincidence, was an exhibit that intrigued Milosevic—a Tomahawk cruise missile. Hill and Kerrick took him and some of the Bosnian Serbs over to the missile that had so impressed the Serbs in western Bosnia. It was only about twenty feet long. "So much damage from such a little thing," Milosevic said, almost wistfully, looking up at it.

Kati had come to Dayton for the weekend, along with several other wives. We seated her between Milosevic and Izetbegovic. Bildt and I took our places on the other sides of the two Presidents, and Croatian Foreign Minister Mate Granic, representing Tudjman, joined us, along with the still-seething Jacques Blot and Haris Silajdzic.

As entertainment, Wright-Patterson had provided the local Air Force band, which played World War II songs in the style of Glenn Miller. Three black women sergeants performed as the Andrews Sisters, and as they sang "Boogie Woogie Bugle Boy" Milosevic sang along, while Izetbegovic sat sullenly. The scene was surreal: the warplanes and cruise missiles, Glenn Miller and the all-black Andrews Sisters act, my wife seated between Izetbegovic and Milosevic.

This bizarre feeling increased when we tried to engage Izetbegovic and Milosevic in a single conversation. To break the ice, Kati told Milosevic that in 1980 she had covered Tito's funeral in Belgrade for ABC. When she was growing up in Hungary during the Cold War, she went on, Yugoslavia had represented the best face of multiethnic socialism. "We always admired Yugoslavia so much," she said. "What happened to you?" Milosevic shrugged, as if he had been no more than a passive victim of events.

Kati asked Izetbegovic how he and Milosevic had first met. The two men had been avoiding direct conversation, but this question triggered an exchange. "Alija, I remember calling on you," Milosevic said, "in your office in Sarajevo. You were seated on a green sofa—Muslim green." Izetbegovic nodded, and said that he remembered the meeting well. "You were very brave, Alija," Milosevic said, trying to charm the man he had been trying to destroy. Izetbegovic tried to avoid all eye contact with Milosevic, but the Serbian President was undaunted.

"How did the war start?" Kati asked. "Did you know that your initial disagreements would lead to this terrible conflict?"

"I did not think the fighting would be so serious," said Izetbegovic. Milosevic nodded in agreement, and added, "I never thought it would go on so long."

It was a striking conversation. They both professed surprise at the dimensions of what they had unleashed. Yet neither man had made a serious effort to stop the war until forced to do so by the United States.

DAY FOUR: SATURDAY, NOVEMBER 4

Several participants wanted to unwind on the first Saturday. Sacirbey took Izetbegovic to Louisville for a football game between the University of Louisville and his alma mater, Tulane. I asked Sacirbey several times not to do this, concerned that a football game was not in keeping with the seriousness of the peace conference. In addition, I worried about the added strain on the frail Izetbegovic of a three-hour car ride and the bitter cold and rain of an outdoor stadium. But Sacirbey insisted. With his usual dour expression, Izetbegovic merely shrugged when I suggested it was a bad idea. When he returned, I asked him who had won. "I don't know," he said. "I think it was the people in the red clothes." (In fact, Louisville—the people in red—had clobbered Tulane.)

David Rohde. With Izetbegovic and Tudjman away, the pace slowed down that afternoon. We organized soccer, football, and bowling for the delegations, hoping this would diminish their hostility. But for me the afternoon focused on David Rohde. We received word that he was definitely alive, and being held in the northwest Bosnian Serb town of Bijeljina on charges of illegally entering Bosnian Serb territory and falsifying his ID papers. The Bosnian Serbs had threatened to indict him for espionage. At some personal danger, Walter Andrusyzyn, an officer from the Embassy in Sarajevo, had driven one hundred miles through a brutal snowstorm and forced his way into the Bijeljina jail to see Rohde. It was the first trip by any Embassy officer deep into the Serb portion of Bosnia since the war began. When he saw Andrusyzyn, Rohde became quite emotional. He was in reasonable physical shape but was worried that he would be convicted of espionage.

Violating our rule on no contacts with journalists, I took a call from Ted Koppel, who told me Rohde had worked for him and urged me to make his case a high priority. Then Menzies and I met with ten members of Rohde's family and two of his editors from *The Christian Science Monitor,* who had come to Dayton en masse to plead his case. Menzies had already spent a great deal of time with them, as had Nikola Koljevic, who saw this as an opportunity to ingratiate himself with the Americans. When we arrived at the meeting, the little Shakespearean was in full rhetorical plumage, talking, as he had in Geneva, about his profound love of America and his hopes for peace. Rohde's family did not realize that Koljevic, widely regarded as a drunk and a Milosevic stooge, had no influence over the men holding their relative.

Asking Koljevic to leave, we had an emotional meeting with Rohde's family, whom I liked at once. Mostly from Maine, they had gathered in Dayton at their own expense to impress upon everyone that David was not alone. I told them that we were, in effect, ready to hold up the negotiations on David's behalf—that we would not announce any final agreements while their son was incarcerated.

Rohde's family and his editors, including Clayton Jones, the foreign editor of the *Monitor,* were unsure whether to believe us. Jones wanted us to negotiate with Koljevic over the terms of David's release. This was not a good idea; it would have made Rohde a pawn in the larger negotiations and prolonged his captivity. The best chance for an early release was simply to hold to the line that there would be no Dayton agreements while David was being held. We would not bargain for David's release, we would demand it. I said I was certain he would be freed if we stayed firm. Two of his relatives assailed us for not doing enough, but others in the room seemed more sympathetic. We parted on a hopeful note.

That evening, while Izetbegovic was on his way back from Louisville, we dined at the Officers' Club as the guests of Chris Spiro, an American who was part of Milosevic's delegation. Spiro, chairman of the New Hampshire Democratic Party and an early supporter of Jimmy Carter in 1976, had been an intermediary between Carter and the Serbs, and had become Milosevic's closest American advisor. (He had also run unsuccessfully for Governor of New Hampshire against John Sununu.) I was uneasy about an American in the Yugoslav delegation, but there was nothing illegal about it, and Spiro—a colorful Greek-American who liked to tell us that we "didn't know shit about the Balkans"—did no apparent harm.

Before we sat down to a splendid dinner of lobsters that Spiro had flown in from Maine, Kati cornered Milosevic. Speaking in her capacity as the chair of a humanitarian organization, the Committee to Protect Journalists, she said that if Milosevic did not free Rohde he would face overwhelming pressure from the world's press. Milosevic claimed he did not know where Rohde was, or anything about the case. By prearrangement, I joined the conversation and told Milosevic again that we would not make a final agreement until Rohde was freed. When Milosevic knew the game was up on an issue, he often grumbled and murmured, as if to himself. Now he did just that. "I guess I'll have to see what I can do," he said. I stressed the need for speed; after his visit to the prison, Andrusyzyn had reported that Rohde was "pretty strung out," and urged us to get him released as quickly as possible.

The day ended with tragic news: the assassination of Yitzhak Rabin, Prime Minister of Israel, at the hands of a fanatic Israeli in Tel Aviv. He had been murdered because he had been willing to consider a compromise for peace. The reaction of the Balkan Presidents was cold-blooded and self-centered; this showed, each said separately, what personal risks *they* were taking for peace. None expressed sorrow for Rabin or the Israeli people or concern for the peace process. The only Bosnian who seemed stricken was the Ambassador to the United States, Sven Alkalaj, who was from an ancient and distinguished Sephardic Jewish family from Sarajevo. Izetbegovic let him leave immediately for Israel to represent Bosnia at the funeral. The contrast between Rabin and the Balkan leaders could not have been more evident than it was in the following days, as we watched the funeral on television and simultaneously struggled to find a way forward in the Balkans.

DAY FIVE: SUNDAY, NOVEMBER 5

We were determined not to let Sunday become a day of rest. It was time to intensify the effort. To test this proposition, we asked Izetbegovic to meet alone with Milosevic. With a notable lack of enthusiasm, he agreed. From the reports we received from both sides after the meeting, it was clear Milosevic had made an effort to persuade Izetbegovic that they had mutual interests and could make a deal, perhaps at the expense of the Bosnian Serbs. The meeting was inconclusive, but Izetbegovic later told Chris Hill that he felt that Milosevic was "sincere" in wanting to make peace at Dayton—a small but significant step forward in Izetbegovic's thinking.

That same day, we turned to the issue of Sarajevo—the Jerusalem of Bosnia, the divided city where the war had started. The Bosnian Muslims had never wavered in their quest for a unified capital city under their control. Although President Clinton had publicly supported this goal, it seemed unlikely we could achieve it at Dayton. As an alternative, we devised something we called the "District of Columbia" or "federal" model, in which Sarajevo would be part of neither the Federation nor Republika Srpska. Instead, it would become an independent enclave governed by representatives of all three ethnic groups. The post of chief mayor of the "Federal District of Sarajevo" would rotate among the three ethnic groups.

Silajdzic and Sacirbey were intrigued by this idea, although it provoked some jokes about who would be the Marion Barry of Bosnia. While they still hoped for a unified Sarajevo, they said they could live with the federal model if the Muslims had a majority in all joint commissions. I asked Owen and his associates to draft a detailed proposal for Sarajevo as an autonomous city.

At the same time, we pursued the unresolved issue, left over from New York, on the powers of the presidency and the parliament. Izetbegovic still wanted broad powers for a directly elected presidency and national parliament, while Milosevic continued to favor a narrower mandate without direct elections. But Milosevic left us with the impression that this was a secondary issue to him, and he would bargain it away later.

DAY SIX: MONDAY, NOVEMBER 6

"We've already been here six days. You may be enjoying Dayton, but we Americans want to go home. We can't stay here beyond November fifteenth." It was the first morning of a new week, and I was alone with Milosevic in his suite.

We had made no significant progress on the key issues. In a sense, our efforts to break the personal ice had been too successful. People were too comfortable at places like Packy's All-Sports Bar. Milosevic had a reserved table at the Officers' Club and knew many of the waiters by name, one of whom he jokingly invited to work for him in Belgrade.

Milosevic complained about the confusion on eastern Slavonia, and said that he thought the Galbraith-Stoltenberg talks were not going well. With this, he in effect invited us to negotiate eastern Slavonia in Dayton. We seized the opening. With Chris Hill taking the lead, we wrote a draft agreement based on

Galbraith's original text, reworded and simplified. The Croatians wanted the agreement to make every detail concerning the return of the region explicit—flags, postage stamps, and so on. Milosevic, on the other hand, was trying to soften the fact that he was ready to give up the region. Among other things, he hoped to reduce the risk that Serbia would be flooded with a hundred thousand Serb refugees. Hill had an idea designed to bridge the gap: to place the eastern Slavonia negotiation within the larger context of Croatian-Yugoslav relations. He proposed that the eastern Slavonia agreement be negotiated side by side with a larger agreement on mutual recognition and respect for the international borders that the Serbs had challenged with the original 1991 invasion. Both Foreign Ministers in Dayton—Milutinovic of Yugoslavia and Granic of Croatia—agreed to this approach.

As for Sarajevo, the Bosnians showed increasing interest in the "D.C. model" during long morning meetings. Owen, Pardew, and Miriam Sapiro had reduced the idea to a simple ten-point plan. It contained all the main components of a workable solution: a City Council, a rotating mayor, a unified police force, and local control of educational, cultural, and religious activities—and the demilitarization of the entire city.

I asked Milosevic to join Hill, Owen, and me at the Officers' Club for lunch. We expected the "D.C. model" to appeal to Milosevic, but he resisted it strongly. A joint city, Milosevic said, would involve a degree of cooperation that the parties had not shown. "These people," he said, "would kill each other over who would run the day-care centers." The only way he would consider it was if there was absolute political equality between the ethnic groups in Sarajevo. Milosevic's position was tantamount to killing the idea, since it would neutralize the huge population advantage of the Muslims. Tired of the charade, I grabbed Owen's draft from Milosevic's hands and tore it up. "If you don't like this proposal," I said, dropping the torn paper in the ashtray, "this is what we'll do with it. But that's the end of it. We'll go back to our original position—an undivided Sarajevo under the Bosnians." Owen, who had worked all night on the proposal, looked crestfallen and stared in disbelief at the torn pages of his masterpiece. Milosevic laughed at the theater and said he would reconsider the entire problem.

A Visit by Strobe—and Sanctions. As we had proposed in October, we wanted regular visits from senior Washington officials. Our first visitors were Strobe Talbott and his wife, Brooke Shearer, accompanied by Jan Lodal, the Principal Deputy Undersecretary of Defense. We gave a dinner for the three delegations at Dayton's Racquet Club, the first time we had taken the participants off the base as a group. Through the panoramic windows Strobe proudly showed us landmarks of his birthplace. He brought a fine, conciliatory tone to

Dayton, and added to this graceful stories about Belgrade, where he and Brooke had spent two years while he was with *Time* magazine and she was writing for *The Christian Science Monitor* and *The Sunday Times* of London. At the head table, the mood was spirited and relaxed. The two Presidents, still enjoying the absence of Tudjman, told each other jokes—jokes from Izetbegovic!—and tested Brooke's language abilities. The mood, almost giddy at times, even produced a rare moment of consensus.

The issue that created the good feeling, ironically, was sanctions—but this time with a twist. In the harsh Balkan winter, Belgrade was facing an energy crisis. Milosevic requested permission to import oil to his capital immediately. The humanitarian agencies supported part of Milosevic's request—twenty-three thousand tons of heavy heating oil into Belgrade. In addition, Milosevic asked for help on natural gas, and permission from the U.N. sanctions committee to export a limited amount of grain to pay for the fuel. According to the agreement that accompanied the cease-fire in October, when the gas went on in Sarajevo it was also supposed to have gone on in Belgrade. However, the Russians had not allowed the gas to reach Belgrade, claiming that the United States had blocked them in the U.N. sanctions committee.

These requests kicked off another round of intense discussions between Dayton and Washington. Leon Fuerth, still the main engine in Washington on sanctions, believed that Milosevic's requests far exceeded Belgrade's needs. He estimated that Milosevic's "grain-for-fuel" proposal would give him a profit of between $20 million and $80 million. Still, Fuerth concluded that the problem was real. After a protracted discussion, we reached a common position: we should not let people freeze in Belgrade—but at the same time we should not let the Serbs turn a humanitarian gesture into a profit-making arrangement.

Izetbegovic and Silajdzic told Strobe that the October 5 cease-fire agreement had been intended to permit "unrestricted natural gas flow" to both Bosnia and Serbia. "Millions of people are freezing in both countries," Silajdzic said emotionally, "and with the fighting over, this should be stopped." Milosevic was clearly relieved. It may have been sunny in Dayton that day, he said, but it was already below zero in Belgrade.

It was the first time Izetbegovic and Milosevic had found common ground on any issue. Little surprise then, that we ended dinner hopeful that Dayton's spirit was permeating the drab rooms at Wright-Patterson. Strobe and Brooke left for Washington impressed.

We could not realize it then, but the dinner Strobe and Brooke co-hosted was Dayton's high-water mark in terms of good feelings. Never again would there be such a friendly atmosphere among the warring leaders, and never again would Dayton feel as promising.

DAY SEVEN: TUESDAY, NOVEMBER 7

"All going well," Don Kerrick reported that morning to Washington. "Just unclear where all is going. No evidence anyone—parties or Euros—want to close deal. [Holbrooke] intends to rachet up pressure today."

At our 8:00 A.M. staff meeting, we agreed that while the spirit of the previous evening was encouraging, the parties still seemed to be enjoying themselves too much. We still hoped to end the conference at the end of the following week, but we had no idea how to get there.

The Weak Police. Even some of the annexes remained a problem with the Europeans. The most important was Annex 11, regarding the international police, and Bob Gallucci commuted from Washington to negotiate a deal. NATO continued to refuse to accept any responsibility for arresting people. We could not leave this responsibility solely to the local police, who represented, in all three communities, the worst and most extreme elements. In my view, therefore, it was essential to have a strong international police task force with the authority to arrest people who violated the agreements. The three Balkan Presidents were not opposed to this: since they distrusted one another, they would have accepted an external force that would impose compliance with the agreement.

Regrettably, the problem with the police annex came from within our own ranks, from both NATO and the Europeans. Pauline Neville-Jones, supported by her E.U. colleagues, took the strongest position, saying that British tradition and the legacy of Northern Ireland precluded her government from allowing police officers to make arrests on foreign soil. The connection between Ireland and Bosnia was not clear to us. Supporting the position the JCS had taken in the White House meetings in late October, NATO also opposed giving the international police enforcement power, on the grounds that if they got into trouble the military would have to come to their aid.

Distressed over the deadlock on the police annex, I called Tom Donilon and told him that to get the annex right, we would have to "foot more of the bill." Such a commitment, I said, would allow us to insist on a robust police. A day later, Tom called back with bad news. He had discussed the issue with the White House, he said, and, in light of the crisis over the entire federal budget—the Gingrich assault had reached its height and a shutdown of most of the government was imminent—they felt we could put up no more than $50 million. This meant we could not write the rules. Gallucci had to yield, agreeing to an International Police Task Force (IPTF) consisting of advisers and "monitors"—a favorite Euro-word that could mean almost anything. In addition, the IPTF was put under the United Nations, a change from our previous decision not to let the U.N. play any role in implementation. In the final draft of Annex 11, the IPTF was given responsibility for an "assistance program" *restricted* to:

(a) monitoring, observing, and inspecting law enforcement activities and facilities; (b) advising law enforcement personnel and forces; (c) training law enforcement personnel.

Article V of the same annex further limited the IPTF's effectiveness by imposing on it a convoluted appeal system that did not involve IFOR:

[In the event of a] failure [by the Parties] to cooperate with the IPTF, the IPTF Commissioner may request that the High Representative take appropriate steps, including calling such failures to the attention of the Parties, convening the Joint Civilian Commission, and consulting with the United Nations, relevant states, and international organizations on further responses.

I worried about the police annex from the beginning. Even without Washington's support, I should have fought harder against it, and rejected the compromise with the Europeans. As Clark, who openly disagreed with his own military colleagues on this point, observed, "We are leaving a huge gap in the Bosnia food chain." Events were to prove him right.

That afternoon, Clark, Kerrick, Pardew, and I drove across the base to the national intelligence headquarters of the U.S. Air Force to participate, by closed-circuit television, in a two-hour White House meeting. Milosevic was fuming over the continued delays in getting heating oil and gas into Serbia; he thought the dinner with Strobe Talbott had resolved the problem, and he did not understand why we were still blocking fuel for the freezing people of Belgrade. Izetbegovic and Silajdzic had raised the issue again, in effect on Belgrade's behalf, and urged us to withdraw our "hold" in the U.N. Sanctions Committee on heating fuel for Serbia. Kerrick told the White House the situation was "explosive."

As we watched from Dayton the discussion seemed distant and strange. Twenty of the top people in the U.S. government were debating the amount of heating oil and natural gas Belgrade needed during the winter. None of them knew enough to form an opinion, let alone a policy, yet the argument in the Situation Room became intense. Tony Lake, trying futilely to control the meeting, actually banged his head on the oak table in frustration. To break the impasse, Fuerth finally recommended that we offer Serbia significantly less oil and gas than Milosevic had asked for, and, desperate to move on to some other issue, everyone agreed. But after the meeting Lake put another personal hold on the decision so that he could consider its ramifications again.

The Prince of Darkness. After a week of confusion, the Bosnians finally took a close look at Annex 1-A, the military annex that would govern the role of IFOR. They did not like what they saw. From their point of view, the annex seemed to imply that IFOR would enforce partition rather than create a single state.

The Bosnians had a point. As Don Kerrick put it in a terse message late that night, "[They] will not accept [Annex 1-A] without change. Surprise is length of time it took Bosnians to recognize [the problem]."

To deal with Annex 1-A the Bosnians turned for advice to an unusual source—former Assistant Secretary of Defense Richard Perle, the Prince of Darkness, as he had been called by critics and friends alike during the Reagan Administration. When Washington heard that Perle was advising the Bosnians, reactions ranged from controlled concern (Strobe Talbott) to outright horror (Tony Lake and many of Perle's former associates at the Pentagon).

Richard Perle, originally a conservative Democrat, first came to prominence in the 1970s while a foreign policy advisor to Senator Henry "Scoop" Jackson, the conservative Democrat from Washington State. Joining the government as Assistant Secretary of Defense in the 1980s under Caspar Weinberger, Perle became the leader of the arms-control hard-liners within the Administration.

When the Bosnians approached Perle for advice, he called to ask if I had any objection if he came to Dayton. It was an odd situation, rich in irony: Perle had been a vociferous and influential critic of the Clinton Administration's policies in Bosnia, which he regarded as weak. Only a month earlier he had told a House committee that the American mission in Bosnia was "hopelessly ill-defined." He been a supporter of proposals to give the Bosnians enough military equipment and training so they could defend themselves—an idea to which both the Pentagon and the Europeans strongly objected. His rise to public attention had been greatly aided by Strobe Talbott, whose 1984 book, *Deadly Gambits,* celebrated Perle as one of the leading figures in the shaping of Reagan's arms-control policy. Our relationship—we had known each other for twenty years—had been strained because we were usually on different sides of the political and ideological fence. Yet, to the surprise of most of my colleagues and the press, I urged Perle to come to Dayton immediately. "Richard, the Bosnians need you desperately," I said. "They do not know how to read or interpret a military document, and they are completely disorganized." Perle took the first available plane to Dayton and, with the help of Douglas Feith, a lawyer who had worked for him in the Pentagon, started analyzing the military annex, whose bureaucratic language the Bosnians had been unable to decode. Within a few minutes of his arrival in Dayton, he closeted himself with the Bosnians, showing them the real, often hidden meaning of the jargon in Annex 1-A.

Well after midnight, Pardew, Clark, Kerrick, and I sat down with Richard Perle in the bleak surroundings of the small conference room next door to my suite. Stale pizza and empty Diet Coke cans littered the room after a day of continuous meetings by others. After listening impatiently to our comments, Perle said he would encourage the Bosnians to put the maximum possible pressure on us to make the role of IFOR stronger. In its current form, Perle said, he considered Annex 1-A a "pathetic evasion of responsibility by the Pentagon." He had already begun to identify scores of changes that would strengthen the role of IFOR; I agreed with most of them, but it was not clear how many could be sold to a Washington and NATO bureaucracy that had already gone through a difficult negotiating process and that deeply distrusted Perle. The White House feared he might denounce the Pentagon publicly, which gave him a certain leverage, as long as he did not push it too far. My goal was to use Perle's presence to improve the military annex while keeping him from criticizing the Administration publicly—another subplot of the increasingly complex proceedings at Dayton.

Late that evening, Milosevic asked me to come to his room. When I arrived, he said, "This time you must join me in a drink—because your American journalist, Mr. Rohde, will be released in the morning and sent across the border. This was very difficult."

DAY EIGHT: WEDNESDAY, NOVEMBER 8

We awoke to learn that David Rohde was safe in Belgrade. His relatives, many of whom had stayed in Dayton, were euphoric, and asked to convey their appreciation to Milosevic. Christopher also sent his thanks to Milosevic. It was interesting to watch Milosevic turn the Rohde affair into a public plus for himself by presenting himself as the problem solver, the indispensable peacemaker.

President Clinton, Christopher, and I all spoke to Rohde by phone. He said he hoped he had not "screwed up" the negotiations. A few months later, he sent me a gracious handwritten letter of appreciation from Tuzla which concluded,

> I apologize if my detention complicated your efforts in Dayton. The last thing I wanted was to be an obstacle to peace. You made me a priority when you didn't have to, and I thank you. I saw two survivors here recently. One told me I was a hero. The other told me I was a fool. I think the latter got it right. My family and I cannot thank you enough. I am a very, very lucky person.*

* Rohde won a Pulitzer Prize in 1996 for his articles on Srebrenica, and later joined the staff of *The New York Times*. His book *Endgame* describes the fall of Srebrenica in impressive detail.

The Map—at Last. "Intensive U.S.-led face-to-face negotiations begin in earnest Wednesday," General Kerrick reported to Washington. With progress on the Federation, with political and constitutional discussions moving forward, and with Rohde released, we thought it was time to plunge into the most difficult issue: territory. We called a large meeting of all three sides in the B-29 Room and assembled large maps for discussion.

The meeting was a disaster. Putting the principal actors together in front of maps brought out the worst in all of them. Milosevic participated only after predicting that it would be either a waste of time or a mess. He sat relatively silent most of the time, enjoying the spectacle, which he knew would strengthen his hand. After a six-hour meeting, we had accomplished nothing, and perhaps even set ourselves back. As Kerrick described the ordeal:

> In scene reminiscent of *The Godfather,* two families (don Slobo and outcast Serbs; don Izzy and Federation) held truly remarkable six-hour map marathon. Despite hours of heated, yet civil exchanges, absolutely nothing was agreed. Astonishingly, at one moment parties would be glaring across table, screaming, while minutes later they could be seen smiling and joking together over refreshments. Bosnians presented country-wide 60% map proposal—rejected by Serbs. Serbs will present map Thursday. Saga continues.

Instead of offering an "American map," we invited each side to make an opening proposal. This approach only widened the differences between the sides. The Federation team was composed of Muslims, Croats, and Serbs, who argued continually with one another. As he had many times before—but never directly to the Bosnian Serb delegation—Izetbegovic demanded a unified Sarajevo. This led to one of the most remarkable scenes of the entire Dayton negotiations: the explosive response of the senior Bosnian Serb at Dayton, Speaker of the Bosnian Serb Assembly Momcilo Krajisnik.

As everyone who met him noted, Krajisnik had only one long and extraordinarily bushy eyebrow, which spanned his forehead, creating what looked like a permanent dark cloud over his deep-set eyes. Although Krajisnik had not been indicted by the War Crimes Tribunal—and could therefore participate in Dayton—it was hard to distinguish his views from those of his close friend Radovan Karadzic. Milosevic had often said that Krajisnik was "more difficult" than Karadzic, but we had little basis on which to make an independent judgment. Krajisnik had participated in our epic twelve-hour meeting outside Belgrade on September 13–14, but had said little.

He and Izetbegovic knew each other well, from lengthy meetings in the Bosnian Assembly before the war. Krajisnik owned a five-hectare farm on the edge of Sarajevo, in an area that would probably revert to the Muslims in any settlement, and we often made bitter jokes that the war was really over "Krajisnik's five hectares."

Enraged at the idea of a united Sarajevo, Krajisnik rose from the table, and strode to the huge map of Sarajevo on the easel in front of us. "I've lived here all my life," he shouted, hitting the map with his fist, "and I will never give it up. This land is ours. We cannot lose it." We thought he had hit the map at the point where his own farm was, although we were not sure.

It was evident we could not make progress in such a forum, and we never again assembled so many people in a single meeting. And from that point on, Krajisnik and his Bosnian Serb colleagues were truly nonpersons at Dayton.

Milosevic enjoyed reminding us that he had predicted the failure of the map session. "I told you not to bring those idiots from Pale to any meeting," he said. He had frequently told us that the Bosnian Serbs were a breed apart from the more "civilized" Serbs of the big cities in Serbia itself. "They have more in common with the Bosnian Muslims than with us," he often said.

Meanwhile, Steiner reported gains in his efforts to build a new Federation structure that could run the Croat-Muslim half of Bosnia. His agreement defined which powers would be assigned to the central government and which to the two entities, the Federation and Republika Srpska. It split customs revenues between the Federation and the Serbs, and created a new structure for Mostar, which we hoped would eventually become the capital of the Federation in order to make the distinction between the central government in Sarajevo and the Federation government. To this end, we invited to Dayton the two mayors of Mostar—one Croat, one Muslim—and the courageous European Union chief representative in Mostar, Hans Koschnik, who had survived several attempts on his life. Tudjman would return to Dayton the next day, and his approval of these arrangements was essential. Then, we hoped, Christopher would return to Dayton one day later to announce the Federation agreement.

David Lipton and the Central Bank. One of our main goals at Dayton was to create the framework for a single currency and a central bank. When the Europeans first heard that we wanted to create a single currency, most thought we were wholly unrealistic. In the fall of 1995, the Croat portions of the Federation used Croatian currency, the Serb parts used their own currency or Yugoslav dinars, and the Bosnians also had their own money. Everywhere the German mark was the real benchmark currency. But a single country needed a single currency and a central bank—otherwise it would be a fraud from the outset.

No one on our core team—in fact, no one in the State Department—knew enough to negotiate these goals. We turned to David Lipton, then a Deputy Assistant Secretary of the Treasury. Lipton was one of the most talented young government officials I had ever met. A former Harvard faculty member, he was an expert in the brave new field of converting communist economies to free-market economies. In one of the most satisfying moments of my government career, I had taken him and Dan Fried of the NSC staff to Budapest in the spring of 1995 to present Hungary with a strong, single American voice to urge them to carry out a controversial new austerity plan. Senior Hungarian officials told us later that our meetings had been critical in Prime Minister Gyula Horn's decision to back the unpopular program, which was ultimately successful. Remembering how persuasive Lipton's presentations during that trip had been, I asked Secretary of the Treasury Robert Rubin and his deputy, Larry Summers, if Lipton could come to Dayton, and they agreed. In the final two weeks of Dayton, he would visit us four times, and spend a total of ten days with us.

Lipton flew directly to Dayton from Mexico City, where he had been working on the problems of another shaky currency far more important to the American economy, the Mexican peso. It was the day before his birthday, but he said he would delay his celebration in order to help us. "It will be good to deal with a currency that does not end in a vowel," he joked. As soon as he landed, we went to dinner with Milosevic.

Milosevic, who prided himself on his experience as a banker, enjoyed the discussion with Lipton but said that he did not see how there could be a single central bank. There would be a constant struggle over the ethnicity of its head, and over who got loans. We suggested that the head of the bank be from a Western European country, probably France. Lipton also proposed that the central bank not make loans directly, but restrict its activities to buying and selling foreign currencies. This arrangement, which Lipton called a "currency board," would prevent the Federation from taking loans and imposing the inflation on the Bosnian Serbs. Milosevic, who was familiar with the concept of a currency board from the dying days of Yugoslavia, was delighted with Lipton's proposal. Slapping me on the back, he said, "I like this guy. You diplomats talk bullshit, but this guy talks sense. He is a real banker. I can talk to him." Nonetheless Milosevic expressed doubt that the Bosnians would agree. (He was wrong; Lipton persuaded them over the next few days.)*

Lipton remained in Dayton for another day. He met with Tudjman and Silajdzic, whose understanding of economic issues was better than that of any other Bosnian. Silajdzic was obsessed with the question of his country's debt to the international financial institutions. Although it amounted to only $400 million, he feared that after Dayton the financial institutions would, in effect, foreclose on Sarajevo and bring it to its knees economically. Lipton said this

---

* Lipton's subsequent rise through Treasury was rapid and well deserved: after two quick promotions, he became the Undersecretary for International Affairs. He continued to play an important role in Bosnia, where his proposals, originally regarded as completely unrealistic, gradually were implemented.

would never happen. If there was a viable peace at Dayton and the central banking institutions put into place, he said, then Bosnia would have no trouble recycling the old debt into new lending facilities.

Lipton returned to Dayton after his birthday. He became an important part of the core team. In the close quarters of Wright-Patterson, we included him in small meetings that normally did not involve Treasury officials, and the payoff was enormous.

Nothing was more important to peace in the former Yugoslavia than rebuilding economic ties that transcended ethnic divisions. Shortly before Dayton, the World Bank had drawn up a $5 billion economic reconstruction plan designed to bring the per capita income in the country up to two thirds of its prewar levels by the year 2000. It had, of course, suspended negotiations on the program pending the outcome of the Dayton talks. Lipton and I both called James Wolfensohn, the President of the World Bank, who promised to support our efforts; his representative, Christine Wallich, was already inside the compound at Dayton.

Meanwhile, Perle spent the day with the Bosnians producing a long list of requested changes in the military annex. It ultimately ran to over one hundred suggestions, ranging from tiny word corrections to major changes. In several places Perle simply caught errors in the draft that the rest of us had missed. Elsewhere he and the Bosnians, now following his advice closely, sought significant revisions in the mission of IFOR. Ironically, Perle's proposed changes moved the military annex back toward State's original goals.

Most senior officials in Washington were still unhappy that Perle was in Dayton. Donilon warned me that the Washington consensus was to tell the Bosnians they had to accept Annex 1-A as originally written, and reject all of their proposed changes. "Tell Perle to shove his goddamn changes up his ass," one angry Pentagon official said when I warned him what to expect. "Let's see what they propose," I replied. "We can't reject them all, and some of them make sense."

Perle would depart after three days in Dayton, on November 11, leaving behind the official Bosnian response to the military annex. Although he kept in touch with us by phone, he did not return. When he finished the work on November 11, Clark, Kerrick, Pardew, and I began a careful review of each suggestion, trying to decide how to deal with both the substance and the politics of his proposals.

In Brussels that day, Defense Secretary Bill Perry and Russian Defense Minister Pavel Grachev watched as General Joulwan and General Shevstov signed an agreement that would place Russian troops under the commanding general in the American Sector of Bosnia. As previously agreed, Joulwan signed the agreement with the Russians wearing his hat as the commanding general of U.S. forces in Europe, and not as NATO Supreme Commander. It was, Perry said, "a truly historic moment." This agreement not only made possible the Russian role in Bosnia but also went a long way to ameliorating Russian antagonism toward NATO enlargement.

Every meeting with Milosevic that day turned into an argument about sanctions. "Talbott promised action on the heating oil and gas for Belgrade," he said angrily. "Why hasn't it happened yet?" On this issue, everyone at Dayton was in accord, and Kerrick spent much of the day on the phone with Washington trying to get it done. Finally, late that evening, Lake agreed that the United States would accept the flow of a limited amount of natural gas and heating oil to Belgrade for home use.

Late that night, President Tudjman returned to Dayton. We hoped that his reappearance would lead to breakthroughs on the two matters whose immediate resolution was essential—the Federation and eastern Slavonia. Driving from the airstrip to Tudjman's quarters, I told him that when Warren Christopher returned to Dayton in two days, we had to present him with completed agreements on both issues.

DAY NINE: THURSDAY, NOVEMBER 9

It was one of those days when, despite intense activity on all fronts, nothing significant happened. We used Christopher's impending trip as pressure for concessions from all parties, but with little success. Over lunch at the Officers' Club, Milosevic accepted the new American position on heating fuel with undisguised annoyance, pointing out that it fell short of what even the Bosnian Muslims had supported. On the "D.C. model" for Sarajevo, he remained elusive, neither accepting nor rejecting it. He still sought political equality among the ethnic groups in Sarajevo, a proposal we rejected because it would disadvantage the Muslims, who would be vulnerable to a Serb-Croat coalition or Serb obstructionism. "We will not even submit this to Izetbegovic," I told Milosevic. "It would raise questions about your sincerity." So the question of Sarajevo remained at ground zero.

During the lunch, Milosevic sought to appeal to Kerrick as a professional soldier. With Rabin's funeral fresh in everyone's mind, Milosevic switched from his normal role as the boss of the Serbs to that of a man taking risks for peace. "General Kerrick," he said, "you are a military man, and while America's prestige is on the line, my head and life are at stake, literally." The exchange was fascinating, but it was more theater than substance. Although they often disagreed vehemently, Milosevic controlled the political situation in Belgrade and dominated the Pale Serbs.

Overnight, the Croatians increased the pressure by moving their military forces closer to eastern Slavonia. Tudjman hinted again that he might prefer to conquer the region outright in a military action—as he had in the other three parts of the Krajina earlier in the year—rather than make a deal with Milosevic. On the other hand, because eastern Slavonia was on the Serbian border, Tudjman could not be as confident of the outcome. Tudjman requested that some American troops and an American commanding general be part of a "transition force" that would enforce its peaceful turnover.

Putting a few American troops there as part of an international force under IFOR made sense; it would ensure the successful implementation of whatever was agreed to. And it would be easy: the route from the NATO staging area in Hungary to the bases planned for the American troops in central Bosnia actually ran through eastern Slavonia.

The Pentagon, however, had a different view. Supported by the NSC, they argued that adding a Croatian mandate to the one in Bosnia would create an insurmountable problem with Congress. The White House quickly decided not to send any American troops to eastern Slavonia, a decision I regretted; the additional forces could have been limited to only a few hundred, as in Macedonia, but they would have ensured success in a dangerous sliver of the region.

The Tennis Match. Late that afternoon, Tudjman invited Chris Hill and me to play doubles at the indoor courts at Wright-Patterson. Tudjman, in remarkable condition for a man of seventy-three, took no chances; his official delegation included an outstanding tennis player, a gynecologist from Zagreb. On the first point of the match, with the gynecologist serving, Hill fired a hard volley past Tudjman at net. I walked over to Chris, "Go easy on Tudjman; we need eastern Slavonia," I whispered. Hill, a fine player, nodded. I served again. On my second serve Tudjman rifled a passing shot down the line past Chris. I walked over to him. "The hell with eastern Slavonia," I said, "our national honor is at stake. Let's beat these guys." We lost anyway, 6–2, 6–1, 6–4.

After tennis, we went to the Officers' Club with Tudjman for a dinner with leading Croatian Americans from all over the country. On the margins of this event, which had been planned to show us that the Croatians had significant domestic American support,* we continued to discuss eastern Slavonia. In

---

* There were about 540,000 Croatian Americans, according to the 1990 U.S. Census, with nearly half of them in the Midwest and concentrations in southern California and New York.

many ways the negotiations on eastern Slavonia reminded me of those two months earlier between Athens and Skopje; most of the details were settled, but the political will to solve the problem was still lacking, and a big final push would be essential. The main sticking point seemed to be the length of time a U.N. "transitional administration" would remain in place in eastern Slavonia. Tudjman still insisted on one year, while Milosevic was equally set on three. The obvious answer—a compromise of two years—had been rejected with equal vigor by both men.

Chris Hill stayed up until after 3:00 A.M., working with Foreign Minister Milutinovic. Using the Galbraith-U.N. paper as a starting point, he made progress, although, as usual, Milutinovic said they had to "consult" the local authorities. Meanwhile, Galbraith and Stoltenberg were pressing forward with their negotiations in the region.

We remained deeply concerned with human rights and war criminals; Dayton had to be about more than a political settlement. To this end, I asked Milosevic to extend his earlier support of Shattuck's trips into Srpska. A few days later, this request produced a strange sight: Milosevic's special military security forces escorting Shattuck into Banja Luka, which no American official had visited in several years, as he sought access to mass grave sites of massacres allegedly committed by Serbs. The trip was also designed to answer the charge that we were not sharing enough information with the International War Crimes Tribunal.

We had achieved very little in the first nine days at Dayton. Late that night I expressed my frustration to Kati, telling her I thought our chances of getting an agreement were poor. "There is simply too much work and too little time left," I said. "Milosevic is playing statesman without giving up anything important." My greatest concern that night, however, was with the Bosnians. Their internal splits, which were becoming increasingly acrimonious, were paralyzing us. "They are refusing to give us serious responses on most major issues," I said. "The Croat, Muslim, and even Serb members of the Bosnian delegation are all screaming at one another. Without clear positions from them, it will be impossible to end this negotiation."

CHAPTER 17

"Peace in a Week"

(November 10–17, 1995)

[British Prime Minister] Lloyd George is trying his hand at reaching a settlement with the Italians on the Adriatic Treaty. . . . They all sit round the map. The appearance of a pie about to be distributed is thus enhanced. Lloyd George shows them what he suggests. They ask for Scala Nova as well. "Oh, no!" says Ll. G., "you can't have that—it's full of Greeks!" . . . "Oh, no," I whisper to him, "there are not many Greeks there." "But yes," he answers, "don't you see it's coloured green?" I then realise that he mistakes my map for an ethnological map, and thinks the green means Greeks instead of valleys, and the brown means Turks instead of mountains. Lloyd George takes this correction with great good humor. He is as quick as a kingfisher.

—HAROLD NICOLSON, *Peacemaking 1919*

DAY TEN: FRIDAY, NOVEMBER 10

CHRISTOPHER AND HIS TEAM RETURNED TO Wright-Patterson at 9:30 A.M. on November 10, planning to announce the new Federation agreement that morning. But shortly before he landed, the Bosnian Croats told us they would not sign Steiner's agreement as scheduled because it did not give them enough power. "Blood pressure up"—Kerrick's laconic phrase—was an accurate description of our reaction. Once again, our game plan was scrapped, as we scrambled to prevent an embarrassing setback.

Christopher and I went immediately to see Tudjman, and asked him to get the Croats under control. Without apologizing for the delay, Tudjman said his problem was not with the Federation agreement itself, but with Izetbegovic's refusal to reserve one of the top three posts in the *central* government—president, prime minister, or foreign minister—for a Croat. Tudjman could be brutal at times, but he had a valid point.

We told Tudjman that we would insist that one of the three top posts in the central government be assigned to a Croat if he would support Steiner's Federation agreement. Tudjman assented, and the ceremony was rescheduled for the afternoon. Walking across the parking lot immediately to see the Bosnians, we urged them to accept a Croat as Prime Minister or Foreign Minister of the central government in order to save the Federation agreement. This was the essence of statesmanship, I said, a reasonable concession for a major gain. But this one would add to the tension within the Bosnian camp, already seething with intrigue, since either Prime Minister Silajdzic or Foreign Minister Sacirbey would have to step aside in favor of a Croat. Sacirbey was clearly upset. If anyone had to leave, he knew it would be him, and not Haris, who had a political base in Bosnia.

Less than an hour before the public signing of the agreement, Federation President Kresimir Zubak sent me a letter stating that he would neither attend the ceremony nor sign the agreement. Hill and I immediately went to see Tudjman, who read the letter and laughed. "If Zubak doesn't sign it," he said, "we'll get someone else to."

"That's not good enough," I replied. "Zubak must be part of the event, or else he should be replaced as Federation President. He cannot have it both ways, and we cannot allow him to wreck Dayton." We sent Hill and Menzies to see Zubak. A Croat distrusted by many of the Muslims, he worried that the new agreement would weaken him. We had not paid enough attention to the dapper and normally polite Zubak, partly because he did not speak English well, partly because he was overshadowed by extroverted people like Sacirbey and Silajdzic. He had become difficult, withdrawn, and sullen. Hill and Menzies said that if Christopher and I sat down for a few minutes with Zubak, the problem would be solved. And indeed it was. Flattered by the personal attention of the Secretary of State, who met with him for fifteen minutes, Zubak said he would attend the signing.

Still, the ceremony unveiling the new Federation agreement, while important to the future of Bosnia, was a sour affair. We met again in the B-29 Room, with the press allowed back into the base for the first time since the opening ceremonies. Izetbegovic and Tudjman barely acknowledged each other. (Since the agreement did not involve the Serbs, Milosevic, who mocked the whole process, was not present.) In his prepared remarks, Christopher gave the sort of upbeat speech that the event required. "Today's agreement will bring the Federation to life," he said. "It will create common political and economic institutions that will unite the two communities." He went on:

> The agreement finally gives the Federation the authority to govern effectively. The central government of Bosnia and Herzegovina will keep the powers it needs to preserve the country's sovereignty, including foreign affairs, trade, and

monetary policy. It will transfer most of its other responsibilities, including police, courts, tax collection, health, and education to the Federation. . . . The
agreement provides for the sharing of revenues and a joint customs administration. Internal customs checkpoints, which had marred the Federation before, will
be removed. Finally, the parties have agreed to the reunification of the city of
Mostar under a single administration.

Of course, this impressive agreement was on paper only. After watching the
terrible body language between the two delegations, I was as worried about
the viability of the Federation as about the negotiations with the Serbs. Events
would bear this concern out. Two years after Dayton, much of what had been
announced that day was still not implemented, and Mostar was only beginning
to settle down.

A Semibreakthrough on Eastern Slavonia. Milosevic and Tudjman
were still divided over the time for a transitional period prior to the reversion
of eastern Slavonia to Croatia—a seemingly small issue, but one on which
both men were dug in. After three meetings with each President, neither had
moved an inch. We returned to our quarters to examine our choices. Christopher had to leave in two hours, and while we wanted his day to end with a
breakthrough, none was in sight. "Chris, what about a two-phase approach—
with certain specified events happening in each phase?" I said, adding, half-
teasing, "You're a great lawyer, can't you think of something creative?"

Standing up, Christopher started writing rapidly on a legal-sized yellow
pad. One rarely saw this side of Warren Christopher anymore, yet it was him
at his most typical and best—the skilled lawyer drafting an agreement. "The
transition period shall last twelve months," he read, "and, on the determination
of the Transitional Administration, may be extended for a second period not to
exceed the duration of the first."

It was simple. Christopher's wording used only Tudjman's number—
twelve months—but in fact allowed up to two years, which Milosevic probably could accept, for eastern Slavonia's transition back to Croatian rule.
Tudjman and Milosevic could each present the agreement differently at home,
and the length of the transition would be determined a year hence.

We almost ran to Milosevic's room to present Christopher's idea. Without
hesitation, Milosevic said he would accept the proposal if Tudjman did. "Mr.
President, let's close this now," I responded. "Let's go to Tudjman's room together and work this out before the Secretary has to leave for Washington."

"No," said Milosevic. "Let me see Tudjman alone. I'll come back to you
with a solution." He was suddenly cocky, convinced he could deliver a deal,
and get credit for it.

We returned to my room, where we waited anxiously with our colleagues. Through Milosevic's windows across the parking lot, we could see the two Presidents walking back and forth, gesturing and apparently yelling at each other. An hour passed. Finally, someone glanced out the window and said, in an almost awed voice, "Look at that!"

It was, indeed, an amazing sight. Milosevic and Tudjman were walking side by side, almost shoulder to shoulder, across the parking lot toward our building. The rest of our team quickly slipped out the door, while Christopher, Hill, and I awaited our guests. After a moment the two Presidents entered and sat down facing us on a small sofa. Seated so close that their knees were touching, the two men seemed like schoolboys proudly reporting to the teacher that they had finished their homework. "We have solved the problem, Mr. Secretary," Milosevic said. "We can agree to your formulation. However, we need a few days to work this out so that it looks like the issue was determined by the local leaders in eastern Slavonia." Tudjman nodded, but said nothing.

This did not seem specific enough; experience had shown that if there was an escape hatch, someone would use it. "Excuse me," I interrupted, "but the Secretary of State will return here Monday on his way to Japan. When he gets back, eastern Slavonia must be completed so that we can move on to our main work."

Looking straight at Christopher, Milosevic said, "The two of us pledge that it will be finished, completely finished, in seventy-two hours." Again, Tudjman nodded in agreement. As soon as the meeting ended, he sent one of his closest aides, Hvroje Sarinic, back to Croatia to make sure everything went according to plan.

With the negotiations moving to a new level of intensity, I could no longer reserve an hour or more each morning for the daily Contact Group meeting. The less time I spent with the Europeans the more upset they became, but the more time I spent with them the less we accomplished. But we could not ignore the Europeans, so I asked John Kornblum, who had arrived with Christopher, to remain in Dayton. Although this left the European Bureau almost leaderless in Washington, it freed up a great deal of time for me to work directly with the Presidents, while John handled the Contact Group and other duties. We kept Carl Bildt closely informed of our activities, and left it to him to inform the other Europeans. We knew this would leave bruised feelings among a few Europeans, but there was little we could do about it.

The lesson from Christopher's trip was clear: he should visit Dayton only when a problem was nearly solved, so that he could push it across the finish line. Summarizing the mood in Dayton that day, General Kerrick discerned a cyclical pattern in our moods that he jokingly speculated was "directly linked to tidal Potomac." "Every twelve hours [we are] sure we will fail," he wrote, "only to find real chances for success at next high tide."

When I called Kati late that night, I said that the next week would probably be decisive—but could go either way. "If these guys want peace, they can get it in a week," I said. "If they do not, we could be here for a year. We do not want to return to the shuttle, and I don't want to spend the rest of my life in Dayton."

DAY ELEVEN: SATURDAY, NOVEMBER 11

The weather was miserable. A sleeting rain came down intermittently during the day, and the wind made it feel colder. The short walk from our quarters to Packy's left us shivering and wet.

In the late morning, Tudjman placed a wreath at the Wright-Patterson memorial to the American war dead. Alone of the leaders present, he had remembered that November 11 was an American national holiday—Veterans Day, or Armistice Day to an older generation, which, like Tudjman, would forever know the eleventh day of the eleventh month as the day World War I came to an end. General Clark and I drove with him to the memorial, which was next to a replica of a briefing hut used by pilots during World War II. As we sat on wooden benches in front of an easel showing targets for a 1945 bombing run over Germany, Tudjman made an impassioned speech stressing his own role as a member of the anti-Nazi resistance in World War II. This was part of Tudjman's effort to emphasize that he had been an opponent of fascism, so as to counter widespread international criticism of him for rehabilitating the pro-Nazi Ustasha regime of 1941–45—an action he presented as nationalist but others saw as racist and anti-Semitic. His own television crews filmed the entire scene for home consumption, as the rain pounded on the roof of the small shrine.

Tudjman was feeling good—as Galbraith might have said, he was on "one of his highs." He sat in his room savoring his impending triumph on eastern Slavonia, which would complete his liberation of the territories lost during the 1991 war with Serbia. But reports from Galbraith were confusing; the local authorities in eastern Slavonia had apparently not received the order from Milosevic to sign the agreement, and Peter, shuttling between Zagreb and eastern Slavonia in bad weather, feared that the agreement being discussed in Dayton was not going to be accepted by the local authorities. When Hill and I complained strongly to Milosevic, he laughed at our concern. The deal, he said flatly, was done. Galbraith confirmed this by phone later that day.

For Milosevic, the key to the agreement was that it would be signed far from Dayton by a local Serb leader. While Milosevic wanted credit in Dayton for the breakthrough, he did not want his fingerprints visible in the region. For Tudjman, the results were spectacular: he would get eastern Slavonia back without a war. For the United States, it meant that we had successfully brought a part of Croatia back to its rightful owner without another war, one that had seemed inevitable only weeks earlier. In so doing, we had also settled an issue that was an absolute prerequisite to the broader peace.

The main beneficiaries of the agreement would be the Croatians and a significant number of ethnic Hungarians who had lived in the area before 1991 and would now be able to return to their homes. But the agreement would not have been possible unless the Croatians had also guaranteed the rights of the Serbs in the area, who feared, with reason, that they would be driven out once Zagreb took over. Given the brutal manner in which the Croatians had treated the Serbs in the other areas they had "liberated," this was not an unreasonable concern. The problem was still alive in May 1997, when, during a trip to the region, the new Secretary of State, Madeleine Albright, publicly criticized the Tudjman government for violating the rights of the Serbs of eastern Slavonia and other parts of Croatia.

The November 11 eastern Slavonia agreement gave Dayton instant credibility after eleven days of stalemate. We hoped it would stimulate a productive map discussion. But when the maps came out, we hit the wall again, just as we had during the six-hour map session three days earlier. There was no momentum—no carryover from eastern Slavonia, no value from the progress we had made on political issues.

Milosevic began what Kerrick called "the day of the maps" by presenting us with one that was ludicrous. When I showed Milosevic's map to Izetbegovic, he reacted badly, adding to the tension inside the Bosnian delegation, which seemed to be getting worse. Silajdzic sat in his own room, six feet across the hall, watching us come and go with maps, but he did not join us, so after the meeting with Izetbegovic I went to see him.

"What's going on here?" I asked. "Why aren't you in these meetings? We've started the map discussions and you are not even in the room."

Silajdzic was visibly depressed. His mood seemed to combine despair and barely suppressed fury. "You see what I'm up against! I don't know what's going on in there! You see what a terrible mess they are making of this?"

"You have to get back into this thing, Haris," I said. "Your country needs you, and so do we. In forty-eight hours Secretary Christopher returns here. If there is no progress, I am going to recommend to him that we close this down—"

"Suspend it or end it?" Haris asked, calming down a bit. It was the same question that our team had been debating.

"I think suspend. Maybe resume the shuttle. I'm not sure."

"That's wrong," Haris said emphatically. "Threaten to end the conference once and for all. That will get his attention."

Silajdzic's point made sense. I went directly to Milosevic's room and told him that unless he took the territorial issues seriously, we would consider closing down the conference.

"It's the fault of the Muslims," Milosevic replied. "They are pigheaded and stupid. They—"

"That's not the issue. We need to make progress, or else shut down. The time has come for private, face-to-face talks between you and the Bosnians. I suggest you start with Silajdzic. He's in his room. Will you see him right now?"

I went back to the Bosnians, dropping in on Izetbegovic to get his approval for the meeting. Izetbegovic, seeing the advantage to himself if Silajdzic took the lead—and therefore the risks—on the territorial issues, readily agreed.

As Silajdzic and I walked through the rain and sleet to the Serbian building, with the precious maps covered in plastic, I put my arm on his shoulder and said, "Haris, this may be the most important meeting of your life, and if it works, there will be more like it." He nodded silently. "I'm going to leave the two of you alone," I said as we reached the door of the building. "Just one thing, Haris. Please do not lose your temper. Hang in there. If it is anything like some of our sessions with Milosevic, the meeting may begin to get interesting just when you think it is over."

I went out for a rare treat—a relaxed dinner in town with some colleagues. When we returned late at night, we heard that the two men had spent over two hours alone together. It was too late to learn more until morning, but that, at least, seemed encouraging.

DAY TWELVE: SUNDAY, NOVEMBER 12

The day began with long-awaited news from Croatia: the fourteen-point agreement on eastern Slavonia had finally been signed. There was elation over the agreement in Washington, Zagreb, and Western Europe, and resignation among the Serbs. "I think we have experienced the start of the end of the war in the ex-Yugoslavia," said the tireless Thorvald Stoltenberg, who witnessed the agreement on behalf of the United Nations in the region. President Clinton called it "a major step toward peace."

A Visit from the Families. This particular Sunday would always remain special in our memory because of the visit to Wright-Patterson by the widows and children of Bob Frasure, Joe Kruzel, and Nelson Drew.

Not everyone approved of the visit. Several of my colleagues feared it would divert us from our primary mission or unduly distress the families. The first point seemed wrong; we could handle the extra burden. As for the second, I insisted that we let them decide. All three wives said they wanted to visit, with their children. They wanted to understand better what their husbands had lived and died for, and they wanted to meet the three Presidents. In order to ensure that the trip in no way exploited the tragedy, we told almost no one about it, and the press never reported it. This was a private event.

Jan Lodal, the Principal Deputy Undersecretary of Defense, who had done so much to support our team, brought them to Dayton on a military plane. General Farrell and I met the plane, which landed in a gusty crosswind and freezing temperatures. We took the families—Katharina Frasure, Gail Kruzel, Sandy Drew, and six children, two from each family—directly to the B-29 Room and showed them how the conference was set up. The children reacted in various ways. Some were excited about the visit, but others hung back, still depressed, unable to connect this sterile conference room with the loss of their fathers. After everyone had settled down, I said, "We would not be here today if it were not for Bob, Joe, and Nelson. They are with us here in Dayton at all times." In the midst of our tense confrontations with the parties, it was a suddenly emotional moment, and I had difficulty finishing my remarks.

Rosemarie arranged for each family to have a separate private meeting with each President. At the end of the afternoon, we gave a reception that included all three Presidents. I repeated my earlier remarks, and we ended by asking for a moment of silence. Then the families were gone.

"Shouts, anger highlight map talks," Kerrick told Lake. That was, in fact, an understatement. Even while the three families held emotional meetings with the three Presidents, we were enduring an endless series of setbacks with the same men.

Silajdzic began the day in an upbeat mood. He thought his session with Milosevic the night before had produced real movement. But Milosevic produced another ridiculous map that put five important cities in central and western Bosnia under Serb control. Milosevic also made a strange suggestion—that we present *his* map as an American proposal.

After lunch with the families, we showed Silajdzic Milosevic's map. I first warned him that he was not going to like what he was about to see, but my admonition had little effect. When Silajdzic saw the map he became furious. Waving his arms violently, his eyes darting around the room as if looking for escape, he paced up and back in an extremely agitated manner. He finally calmed down, but his reaction disturbed me. He should not have been so shaken; this was all part of the theater Milosevic was putting on. Was this the "cabin fever" Jimmy Carter and Hal Saunders had warned us about?

We now realized that each map drawn by the parties would be worse than its predecessor. We would have to present our own map—the long-awaited "American map"—the next day. If we did not, we would never move forward.

The "Perle Markup." Although it was now well past midnight, the long day was far from over. I returned to the American building to find almost everyone still awake and working feverishly to prepare for Tuesday, when Christopher would return. While Clark and Pardew prepared our first "made in the USA" map, Chris Hill worked on the final details of the eastern Slavonia agreement. Owen and his team of lawyers continued to draft election laws, constitutional amendments, and various versions of the "D.C. model" for Sarajevo. Meanwhile, Kornblum and I went through the Bosnian response to Annex 1-A, which, for shorthand purposes, we called the "Perle markup."

While many of Perle's suggestions were unacceptable or irrelevant, there was no question that their general thrust was to strengthen the role of IFOR—something we also wanted. In the end, we boiled Perle's 150 suggestions down to about 50 clusters. We recommended acceptance of 35 of these and rejection of only 15. Some of the changes were significant, but to get them through Washington, we needed to downplay that fact. I called both Sandy and Strobe to stress the importance of approving as many of the changes as possible. Sandy Berger scheduled a Deputies' Committee meeting for the next day to give us a final American position.

At the same time, we sent back to Washington the only document the Russians ever produced at Dayton: their review of the military annex. While the Perle markup sought to strengthen IFOR, the Russian draft emasculated it, gave the U.N. a larger role, curtailed the authority of the IFOR commander, and limited the use of force to self-defense only. Since the Russians had chosen to serve under the American commander but not be part of IFOR, it was relatively easy to ignore their suggestions. We handed the problem over to Strobe and Walt Slocombe, and asked them to handle the discussions with the Russians directly.

DAY THIRTEEN: MONDAY, NOVEMBER 13

We pumped ourselves up by telling one another that this would be the decisive week. We noted that we had now equaled Camp David's thirteen days.

It was not a good day. Izetbegovic and Tudjman both withdrew to their rooms, and refused to see each other or Milosevic. Izetbegovic also had ceased talking to Silajdzic. Thus we were back to true "proximity" talks, and every member of our team was in motion, working on annexes, arguing map details, negotiating the Perle markup with the Deputies' Committee in Washington.

. . .

Clark and Pardew represented the delegation in the teleconference with Sandy Berger and his Deputies' Committee on the military annex. Sandy steered them through the document, and the deputies accepted almost all of the thirty-five proposals we had supported. One suggestion they rejected, unfortunately, was to delete the reference to a one-year limit for IFOR. I thought such a self-imposed limit did not belong in the Dayton documents. But the White House and the Pentagon, which had overruled us before on this point, did so again, fearing that its omission would trigger a congressional backlash. The one-year time limit remained in the draft agreement.

The deputies also rejected another major Perle proposal: to create a "mechanism" to investigate suspected war criminals, "in particular all current or former soldiers . . . [and] oversee [their] discharge from such forces." I thought that, while sloppily drafted, this was a creative idea that deserved to be refined and incorporated into the final Dayton agreement. Washington did not agree; it viewed it as a step toward mission creep. In retrospect, it is still odd, and sad, that the Pentagon and NATO so vigorously rejected such proposals, which would have given IFOR greater authority in Bosnia—and greatly aided the implementation of the agreements.

Berger pushed most of the rest of the changes through the Deputies' Committee without much problem. We could now put this important part of the Dayton agreements, which would give the NATO-led forces their authority and the ability to defend themselves, into final form. There was no question about it: the military annex had been improved by Richard Perle's involvement. So valuable was his contribution that I called him a few days later to suggest that he come back to assist the Bosnians on other issues, but his schedule did not permit it.

Engaging the Bosnians. Of the many difficulties we faced that day, the one that disturbed us most was, as I wrote Christopher late that evening, the "immense difficulty of engaging the Bosnian government in a serious negotiation." Desperate to find the key to the increasingly fractious Sarajevo delegation, I took Silajdzic on a long walk at noon. Although it was still cold, the sun was finally out, and as we walked across the quiet streets of the military base, I tried to reach out to this intelligent, remote, often tortured man by appealing to his sense of history. This approach went nowhere; Haris was furious with the Serbs and Croats and gloomy about his own situation within the Bosnian delegation.

Changing my tone, I warned him that Christopher would consider closing down the talks if we could not make progress. We had said this before, but I added that "if the breakdown were attributable to Sarajevo, there would be serious consequences" to their government, including the possible suspension of our plan to equip and train the Federation forces.

This infuriated Haris. "You must never, ever threaten us in such a manner," he said, as we walked past the orderly houses of majors and colonels, trailed by security personnel. "We will never yield to blackmail." There was an almost uncontrolled fury in his voice. "We're not threatening you, Haris," I said, "only trying to convey to you the situation as we see it. We cannot stay in Dayton forever, and we are getting nowhere on the map." I felt sorry for Haris: he was alternately a belligerent defender of his nation and a beleaguered victim of a conspiracy within his own delegation led by Sacirbey.

The Key Map Issues—Defined at Last. We began to move rapidly back and forth across the quad, with Clark carrying the precious maps himself. Each President took hard positions on the key issues, although Milosevic conceded a few areas that were already in Federation hands, such as the Livno Valley linking Sarajevo and Bihac. By the end of the day we had our first clear picture of the most important territorial issues:

1. *Sarajevo.* The "D.C. model" was still on the table; the issue was still unresolved.

2. *Brcko and the Posavina Corridor.* In the original 1994 Contact Group plan, Brcko, the disputed city on the Croatian border on the Sava River, had been "solved" by a complicated proposal that returned the city to the Muslims and narrowed the Serb-controlled Posavina Corridor—the all-important link between Serbia proper and the Serb portion of western Bosnia—to a *thirty-meter* underpass below a railroad bridge. This idea had been "accepted" by Milosevic, who knew it would never be implemented. But that same agreement obsessed Izetbegovic, who insisted it be honored. Milosevic, on the other hand, demanded its widening.

3. *Gorazde.* We had to create a defensible land connection between this last Muslim enclave in eastern Bosnia and Sarajevo.

4. *The Posavina "Pocket."* Not to be confused with the neighboring Posavina Corridor, the Posavina was a fertile area just south of the Croatian border, comprising about 3 percent of the entire landmass of Bosnia. Early in the war, the Serbs had seized it and driven over 135,000 Croats from their land. Importantly, Posavina was near the home of Federation president Zubak.

5. *Srebrenica and Zepa.* Izetbegovic wanted it clearly understood that these two towns in eastern Bosnia, the ultimate symbols of ethnic cleansing, were still on his list of objectives at Dayton. He knew that he would not get them back, but since they were assigned to the Fed-

eration in the 1994 Contact Group map, he did not want to give up his claim to them without something in return.

6. *Bosanski Novi.* This was the town, on the international border with Croatia, where the Serbs had stopped the Croatian Army in mid-September. It was another important railroad junction, as well as a vital link on the river route for goods going down the Sava River to the Adriatic.

There were many other disputed areas, but these seemed to be the most important. Of the six, the most critical were certain to be Gorazde, Sarajevo, and Brcko. And tough as the first two were, we suspected that Brcko would be the most difficult of all.

"Closure or Closedown." Through the day and well into the night the map team and the political-constitutional teams negotiated on parallel tracks with the three presidents and their entourages. Near midnight Silajdzic and I took a second, shorter walk. Haris was in a much better mood than I was. "Today has been the best day so far," he said, to my surprise. "Peace is within sight." He was excited that we were finally engaged on the last and most critical set of issues; I was depressed because of the difficulties that we still encountered at every turn, especially within his delegation.

When we had finished our walk, I sent Warren Christopher a fairly downbeat "scene setter" in preparation for his visit the next day. It was the first time we confronted Washington with our view that if we did not succeed, we wanted to close down rather than suspend. "We have to recast your trip," I wrote:

> Initially conceived of as a possible closer trip, it now becomes a last warning to get serious stopover on your way to Japan, with the clear message that when you return we must have either closure or closedown. . . .
>
> On Day 14, we are about where should have been on Day 8 or 9. Much has been accomplished here . . . but the issues that remain include most of the core issues except elections, where we have made remarkable progress. Most disturbingly, we have had a series of emotional map discussions in which the Bosnians constantly changed their minds. While the Bosnians are the sort of friends that try one's patience, Milosevic has often lied outright about factual data or changed his position after we thought we had locked something in. As for Tudjman, he is fast becoming the King of Dayton. . . .
>
> You can jump-start this conference by a combination of pressure, rhetoric, and direct involvement on some issues where you can break a logjam. . . . All the parties want peace, but they still don't know how to get it. They look forward to your helping them stop killing each other—and so do we.

DAY FOURTEEN: NOVEMBER 14

The struggle in Washington over the federal budget was casting dark shadows over Dayton, hard to define but increasingly noticeable. With the day-to-day operations of the federal government shut down except for "essential operations," the fact that an agreement in Dayton would result in the commitment of twenty thousand American troops to Bosnia at a cost estimated at $2 billion for the first year created conflicting emotions in the White House. On one hand, everyone understood the consequences of failure at Dayton. On the other, the domestic advisors to the President were deeply worried that the Congress and the American people would be doubly resistant to a Bosnia troop commitment in the face of such budgetary problems.

The domestic crisis took its toll in other foreign-policy areas as well. At the last moment, President Clinton decided it would not be appropriate to attend the Osaka summit of Asian-Pacific leaders when many government services were shut down, and sent Vice President Gore and Secretary Christopher to represent the United States. Christopher planned to spend the day with us, then fly to Osaka for the meeting of the leaders of the Asian-Pacific region, drop out of the rest of the Asian trip, and return to Dayton.

He began the day, as usual, with a detailed briefing at the Hope Center, where a suite of rooms was always reserved for him. From then until midnight, he and I crisscrossed the quad, arguing, pleading, threatening, and cajoling the three Presidents. In every meeting, we stressed the new theme outlined in the previous night's memo to Christopher, although he held back from stating that a shutdown of Dayton would be permanent; he wanted to keep open the possibility of a return to the shuttle or a resumption of the talks to Europe. I felt, however, that after Dayton another American shuttle effort would not be effective. Some people in Washington thought moving the talks to Europe would shift the burden of failure from the American hosts to the Europeans, but the core team had gradually concluded that it was all or nothing at Dayton.

Christopher hoped that his visit to Dayton might result in a breakthrough on Sarajevo. But there was no such luck. Milosevic toyed throughout the day with the "D.C. model," trying out on us various unacceptable versions of it. At the end of the day, we had gone nowhere on Sarajevo.

The most difficult meetings were with Izetbegovic. In the last of our three meetings that day, we tried to talk in personal terms to the Bosnian leader. We reminded him of all the benefits peace would bring, and listed the substantial achievements the process had already brought Bosnia: a cessation of hostilities, the lifting of the siege of Sarajevo, the partial opening of roads, the damage NATO bombing had done to the Bosnian Serbs, the $5 billion World Bank package that awaited the country after a peace agreement, the equip-and-train program for the Bosnian Army. Christopher concluded with a drama unusual for him. "President Clinton has put an enormous amount on the line to save Bosnia," he said. "But he will no longer assist your government if you turn out to be the obstacle to an agreement in Dayton." Izetbegovic said nothing in response, and outwardly seemed unmoved by Christopher's statement.

Christopher left for Asia late that night, frustrated that he had spent a day at Dayton and accomplished nothing. To the President, Christopher gave a mixed report. "Dayton," he said, "offered tantalizing hints that a peace agreement might indeed be possible. It is possible, in the good moments, to see the final shape of the map. . . . But it is a very fragile system." He expressed the hope that, in his absence, the negotiators would be able to "fill in the success" of his visit under what he called "Holbrooke's aggressive tutelage." While the "optimistic scenario may well not happen," he added, the "prospect [is] good enough to justify missing the State Visit to Japan." Christopher still resisted the idea of a choice solely between closure and closedown, and told the President that if we had not finished the agreement by early the following week, "it will probably be necessary to suspend the negotiations on the best possible basis."

DAY FIFTEEN: WEDNESDAY, NOVEMBER 15

There was no movement on the core territorial problems, but the negotiators made progress on other issues, including elections. One election issue, however, remained unsolved: how and where refugees should vote. Should they be allowed to vote in their countries of sanctuary, or should they be required to return home? And what was home, for example, to a Bosnian Muslim who had been driven from his house in Banja Luka and now lived in Frankfurt with little prospect of returning? Did he vote in Banja Luka, or for candidates in some Federation area in which he had never lived? On such complicated, but real-life, questions the success of Dayton would depend. During the United Nations–sponsored negotiations on Cambodia in 1992, the problem of refugee voting had been the last issue resolved; we expected a similar last-minute drama on this question in Dayton.

The Germans felt especially strongly about this. With over three hundred thousand Bosnian refugees in their country, Germany wanted to reduce the burden that the refugees had put on its social services and budget. Other countries had similar problems, although not as severe. Bonn had given Wolfgang Ischinger one firm instruction: any agreement must encourage the refugees to return home. Ischinger proposed that the refugees be allowed to vote only if they stated at the time of the voting their intention to return to Bosnia. We incorporated this proposal into the draft agreements, although it was clearly not sufficient for Germany.

Late in the afternoon, Tudjman left for Zagreb to preside over the opening of the new Croatian Parliament. He promised to return in a few days. In our last meeting before his departure, he again asked that an American general officer be put in charge of the United Nations Transitional Authority in eastern Slavonia—a request I promised to support strongly.

We reached agreement that day on another important issue: the relationship between the IFOR commander and the High Representative—although it was not, to my mind, a good agreement. From his headquarters in Belgium, General Joulwan had called Clark and me repeatedly since the beginning of the negotiations to warn that he "would never accept" any arrangement, no matter how weak, that institutionalized a relationship between the IFOR commander and Bildt, who was slated to be the first High Representative. Because, as the Supreme Allied Commander Europe, General Joulwan was not part of the American military chain of command, he had the authority to reject "guidance" from Washington on any issue involving his own command arrangements. His veto of any formal ties between the two senior people in Bosnia was to leave an unfortunate legacy, as Pauline Neville-Jones wrote later:

> Either the High Representative should have been given more authority, or civilian implementation should have been made considerably less ambitious. . . . Much acrimony had surrounded the role played by the senior UN official in theatre, who had come in some quarters to signify civilian interference in the military chain of command. This situation led US negotiators in Dayton to resist including in the implementation structures any sort of body which would provide a forum for the civilian administrator and military commander to discuss and find solutions to problems and issues which spanned their separate responsibilities. . . . Preventing interference should not be confused with promoting cooperation.[1]

Buildup and Build–down. On this, the fifteenth day of negotiations, there was a White House principals' meeting to settle the last outstanding internal issues. Clark, Kornblum, and Gallucci attended by secure video. A decision was also reached on the most controversial and criticized aspect of our policy: whether we should train and arm the Federation, or try to reduce the overall level of armaments in Bosnia.

This was one of our greatest dilemmas. In an ideal world, the several armies of Bosnia-Herzegovina should have been sharply reduced in size and merged into a single force controlled by the central government. However, NATO refused to accept implementation of such a policy as part of its mission. This eliminated any hope, as Pauline Neville-Jones wrote later, "of getting the parties to agree at Dayton to share military power."[2] Sadly, we would have to allow each entity within a single country to maintain its own military force—a fundamental flaw in our postwar structure, but nonetheless inevitable, given the self-imposed constraints on what the outside powers were willing to do.

Thus the most controversial of all programs for Bosnia—to arm and train the Bosnian Muslims—resurfaced. The version under discussion was a postwar variant of the original proposal to arm the Muslims, which had been championed by a powerful group of Senators led by Republican Majority Leader Bob Dole and two senior Democrats, Joe Lieberman of Connecticut and Joe Biden of Delaware. Some bitter Washington debates had been fought over their proposal, which the Administration had opposed on the grounds that it would have violated the United Nations arms embargo.* Facing a defeat in Congress on this issue, President Clinton had pledged that in the event of a peace agreement, the United States would lead an effort to equip and train the Federation in order to "level the playing field" so that it could defend itself. The military hated this idea, which they believed would increase the chances of another war and undermine their desire to be "evenhanded" in enforcing a peace agreement. They also feared that if the United States took part in "Equip and Train," as the program was renamed, its peacekeepers would become targets for Serb reprisals. Our European allies took an even stronger position against Equip and Train.

Despite the commitment of the President, the Pentagon continued in every internal policy debate to oppose military assistance to the Federation. Led by Shalikashvili and Slocombe, they gained agreement during the November 15 White House meeting for a series of measures that did not kill the program but limited American visibility and involvement in it. Specifically, the principals agreed that there would be no active American involvement by American military personnel in Equip and Train, and that the weapons should come from other nations.

To bridge the gap with the Pentagon we added another annex, one that would reduce the level of armaments on all sides—a sort of modified arms-control policy for Bosnia that we called "build-down." Like Equip and Train, build-down was in part a result of congressional pressure. It originated in discussions in late 1994 between Perry and Senators Sam Nunn, Democrat of Georgia, and Dick Lugar, Republican of Indiana, two influential moderates who had supported the Administration's effort to defeat Dole and Lieberman. (It was an interesting feature of Bosnia policy that the congressional debate did not follow party lines.) Whether one supported Equip and Train or not, build-down was an inherently good idea, an indirect step toward disarming the

---

*As recounted earlier, I had advocated a variant of this idea in 1992–93.

swollen armies of Bosnia—provided it did not become a vehicle for weakening the Muslims.

In the end, after much debate in the principals' meeting on November 15, the Administration reached a compromise that confused people at first, but made sense: it decided to support *both* buildup and build-down—that is, an Equip and Train program, accompanied by an arms-control annex. These two programs would be carried out at roughly the same time, according to carefully calibrated schedules and ratios.

We thus added a new annex to the draft agreements for Dayton—Annex 1-B, "The Agreement of Regional Stabilization," commonly referred to as the "arms-control," or "build-down," annex. This annex required the parties to reduce their armaments to ratios that had been carefully calibrated by the Pentagon. Under this concept, a 5:2:2 ratio would be established among Yugoslavia, Croatia, and Bosnia, respectively. The Bosnian allotment would be further divided between the Federation and Republika Srpska, with the Federation getting twice as many armaments as the Bosnian Serbs. These ratios were designed to protect the Federation from ever again being overwhelmed by Serb military power. Unfortunately, the Pentagon once again refused to include an enforcement provision in Annex 1-B. Thus some of the most difficult of all goals—general arms reduction, "restrictions on military deployments and exercises," and the "immediate establishment of military liaison missions"—were left to the goodwill of parties who had no goodwill.

There was one provision I insisted on, over the initial objections of the Pentagon: the "withdrawal of Forces and heavy weapons to cantonment/barracks areas." The Pentagon had objected to every attempt to include cantonment in Annex 1-A, which would have made it an IFOR obligation, but they reluctantly agreed to include it in Annex 1-B, which meant that while it would be a goal it would not be an IFOR task. Months later, when IFOR was on the ground, its commanders finally saw the value of the cantonment provision, and informed the Bosnian Serbs that they would insist on it as part of their core mission. Once IFOR took this line, the Bosnian Serbs began to respond, and, although compliance was never perfect, the cantonment provision proved to be extremely useful.

To many people, these two programs—one to *build up* the strength of the Federation, the other to *build down* the overall military forces in the country—seemed contradictory. But it was the best course available to us. Under Annex 1-B, there was room to build up the Federation forces and stay within the 5:2:2 ratio. But if the Serbs did not respect the annex on build-down, the Equip and Train program was already in place to strengthen the Federation. And when it came time, in early 1996, to set up the Equip and Train program, Christopher and I chose the best possible person to head it—one of its authors, Jim Pardew.

Dinner with Haris. We were still worried about Haris Silajdzic. Menzies, who knew him well, described him as a "caged panther." Frozen out of important discussions by Izetbegovic or Sacirbey, the Bosnian Prime Minister became depressed and increasingly fatalistic. Still looking for ways to reach out to him, I invited him to dinner, and Kati returned to Dayton specifically for the event, since on her first visit Haris had talked to her several times about his dreams for his country and himself.

To emphasize the special nature of the occasion, we took him to L'Auberge, an excellent French restaurant in Dayton. As we ordered caviar and a fine meal, I tried to talk about something other than the details of the negotiation. What were his hopes—personal and political? What did he want for his country? Could he re-engage himself in the talks? Could he negotiate directly with Milosevic?

Relaxing after days of isolation within his own delegation, Silajdzic talked movingly about his family in Istanbul, his young son, and his early days as a student in Sarajevo. But when we said that the future of Bosnia depended on rebuilding multiethnic co-existence, he retreated into an unreachable pessimism. I cited Nelson Mandela as a true leader, a man who could forgive his jailers and embrace power sharing with the very people against whom he had struggled for thirty years. The connection did not seem relevant to Haris. "You don't understand," he said bleakly. "You don't understand what we have been through."

"Perhaps we *don't* understand what you have been through," I replied, "but it was your request that we create a single country, and we are well on the way to accomplishing this. You were one of its chief proponents. Why are we trying to do this if you don't think it can work? Unless you and Izetbegovic reach out to your adversaries, both Serb and Croat, you will isolate yourselves and fail."

Haris did not dispute that he and Izetbegovic had both asked us to negotiate a single country. Instead, he returned to the horrors of 1992. "What you want would have been easier in 1992 or even 1993," he said, "but now it may be too late. Where was the world then? Where was the United States?"

More deaths would not honor the dead—only create more dead, I said passionately. We wanted the war criminals brought to justice, and would not compromise on this issue, but if the Muslims wanted a central government for Bosnia—again, I stressed, *their* own choice—they had to find a way to work with some of the Croats and Serbs, hard though that would be.

These were bleak thoughts, in sharp contrast to the surroundings. Haris was somewhere else, far away. But he had calmed down, and our arguments turned out to have a positive effect on him. Moreover, the evening helped make him feel that he still had an important role to play.

DAY SIXTEEN: THURSDAY, NOVEMBER 16

How much longer could we continue without significant progress on the key territorial issues? The question hung over us during a particularly gloomy 8:00 A.M. staff meeting. Having worked on Silajdzic the previous evening, I decided the next target should be Milosevic, and shortly after 10:00 A.M. Chris Hill and I invited him to take a walk.

It was a clear, dry day—and extremely cold. Dressed in bulky ski jackets and overcoats, we paced the perimeter of the base, trailed discreetly by security guards, for almost two hours. Chris and I put it to Milosevic bluntly: Secretary Christopher was returning to Dayton the next day, and we had no progress to report. Rather than ask for specific concessions, we called for a major gesture of "goodwill" from Milosevic to show he was serious about an agreement. I offered Milosevic two models for Dayton. In one, he could "play Sadat," and show the Bosnians he was ready to make major concessions to get peace. In the other, we could shut down without an agreement, in which case the sanctions on his country would remain in place and the war might resume. Milosevic, in a thoughtful mood, said he would consider "what kind of gesture" he could make.

By a long and roundabout route we arrived at the Wright-Patterson Officers' Club around noon and went to the table that was always reserved for Milosevic. I called Rosemarie, who had taken Silajdzic on a similar walk. She decided to bring him to the club for lunch. Arriving fifteen minutes later, she led Silajdzic and John Menzies to a table at the opposite end of the large central dining room, as far from Milosevic as possible.

Thus the stage was set for an unusual diplomatic effort that was later termed the "napkin shuttle." Leaving Milosevic, I walked across the long dining room to greet Silajdzic. "Are you ready to negotiate right now?" I asked him. "Milosevic is willing to talk about Gorazde." Haris was interested, but when I invited him to join our table, he refused.

I returned to Milosevic, who was eating his steak with Chris Hill. "Silajdzic is ready to discuss Gorazde," I reported. Taking out a napkin, Milosevic started drawing a rough map of the area between Sarajevo and the beleaguered enclave. "We can offer safe conduct along these two roads," he said, indicating the two existing routes between the cities, both now under Serb control. Hill and I objected, saying that the Bosnians would not feel that "safe conduct" would be very safe in light of the last four years. "They will need a genuine, defensible corridor," I said. "Okay, then I will give them a kilometer on each side of the road," Milosevic replied.

Carrying Milosevic's napkin sketch across the room, I sat down with Silajdzic, who, after a moment's thought, replied with a countersketch showing a much wider corridor and substantially more land for the Muslims. As the other diners looked on in astonishment, I walked rapidly across the room carrying the two precious napkin sketches, and sat down again with Milosevic.

This scene was repeated half a dozen times over the next hour. Neither man would move to the other's table, but they eyed each other carefully across the room. Bit by bit, Milosevic yielded land and territory, until the gap between the two men was fairly narrow. Haris went to a phone and called Izetbegovic, who told him to keep negotiating. Finally, I said to Silajdzic, "Don't you realize that you are gaining something important here? You have to sit down with him. If you come over to Milosevic's table now you might get what you need." Reluctantly, Haris followed me to Milosevic's table. The two men greeted each other in characteristic fashion—Milosevic clapping Silajdzic on the back with false camaraderie, Silajdzic unwilling to look Milosevic in the eye.

The other diners gradually left, and by three in the afternoon we were alone in the large room, Milosevic, Silajdzic, Hill, and myself. Rosemarie and Menzies, having delivered their man, had silently slipped away. The two men argued, in English and in their common tongue, over every detail of the area between Sarajevo and Gorazde. The road, the hydroelectric plants, the destroyed mosques, the small village along the road where General Mladic came from—all were discussed with passion and anger.

They did not resolve their differences, and the meeting ended without agreement. *But for the first time the two sides had actually negotiated on a territorial issue.* Our long talks with each man had had an effect; there was a noticeable change in tone. For the first time, Milosevic accepted the need to create a secure land corridor to Gorazde. Once we had crossed this mini-Rubicon—"actually, the Drina," Hill joked—we were, in essence, arguing over the location and width of the corridor. These were negotiable. Although we did not resolve the Gorazde issue in the "napkin shuttle," the meeting marked the first time anyone on either side had shown a readiness to look for territorial compromises.

During the day, Federation President Zubak again threatened to resign. This time his anger was aimed at Tudjman and his fellow Croats, who, he felt, were selling out the Posavina, his home area. He did not feel he could go home again if the territorial agreements at Dayton did not include a Serb "giveback" of some of this land. He felt that the land negotiations were, so far, effectively conceding the Posavina to the Serbs. If this happened, he said, he would have to resign and leave Dayton immediately.

My first instinct was to let him depart. Zubak had been nothing but trouble at Dayton. Susak had always told us to ignore him. But Izetbegovic and Sacirbey both said we should help retain Zubak. After several emotional meetings and a pledge from both Tudjman and Izetbegovic not to ignore the Posavina, Zubak again backed off, and agreed to stay.

It was time for our next high-level visitor from Washington, Tony Lake. Accompanied by Sandy Vershbow, he arrived in the midafternoon at the base. After a briefing at the Hope Center, Tony and I called on the two Presidents. Tony had decided not to try to negotiate during his short visit, but rather to send a strong message, in President Clinton's name, to reinforce our effort.

The meeting with Izetbegovic was fairly routine, but the Lake-Milosevic meeting set off some sparks. Milosevic began with a typical ploy. "I hear you're the most anti-Serb official in Washington," he said. Tony was pleased by what he considered an implicit compliment. At my request, Tony stayed for an early dinner at the Officers' Club so that we could discuss sanctions. Milosevic came right at Tony, making an all-out effort to change American policy, but Tony held his ground, telling Milosevic that while initialing at Dayton would result in suspension, lift could come only with full implementation. This set off a heated debate over what constituted implementation. But Milosevic knew that in real terms suspension of the sanctions would give him what he needed most, immediate relief for his people.

After two brief calls, one on Izetbegovic and the other on Silajdzic, Tony left for Washington. His trip had conveyed the urgency we attached to the negotiations. I summarized his core message late that evening in a memorandum to Warren Christopher: "Tony said there was no second chance for the U.S.; that this was our last, best shot and that Congress was going south on us; that if they didn't reach agreement when you get here we will turn them over to Carl, Pauline, Jacques, and Wolfgang, and our role will greatly diminish."

It had also given Tony and Sandy Vershbow a sense of Dayton. At one point, as we walked alone through the parking lot, Tony leaned toward me and said, "This is the craziest zoo I've ever seen." This was, in fact, exactly what we hoped our colleagues in Washington would remember; it helped if they understood the special weirdness of Dayton.

After Tony left, Hill and I went to see Izetbegovic, hoping he would be encouraged by the progress Silajdzic had made on Gorazde. Instead, I encountered more tension and disarray within the Bosnian camp. The immediate cause was an article by Roger Cohen in that day's *New York Times* in which unnamed "western diplomats" said that Silajdzic, whom Cohen described as "a brilliant, whimsical man with a Hamlet-like tendency to speak in riddles," had emerged as "the key figure—or 'swing vote' in the Bosnian delegation." Seated next to Izetbegovic, Sacirbey began reading excerpts from Cohen's article in a voice dripping with anger and sarcasm. After he finished, Sacirbey paused. "There is only one 'swing vote' in this delegation," he almost shouted, "and that is Mr. President, sitting right here." Throughout this charade Izetbegovic sat motionless, with a slight smile playing across his face. What had happened seemed all too clear: Izetbegovic had been unnerved by Tony Lake's private call on Silajdzic and the direct Milosevic-Silajdzic talks. Encouraged by Sacirbey, he had slapped Haris down—hard.

The Clark Corridor. During the meal with Tony Lake, I had suggested to Milosevic that we resume the negotiation over Gorazde after dinner. After his humiliation, Silajdzic could not continue the negotiation, so we invited Milosevic to our building. We hoped to find a route between Sarajevo and Gorazde that would satisfy the Bosnians. To do this, we decided to introduce Milosevic to PowerScene.

General Clark had brought to Dayton a special unit of the Defense Mapping Agency, personally headed by Major General Philip Nuber. Among other tasks, the map experts were supposed to compute the exact percentage of land that each map proposal gave the sides. They brought with them a highly classified $400,000 imaging system, called PowerScene, first used during Desert Storm. The entire country of Bosnia had been filmed and stored in this extraordinary "virtual reality" machine, visible in three dimensions, accurate down to two yards. Simply by manipulating an ordinary joystick, the viewer could "fly" fast or slow, look straight down, straight ahead, or sideways at any angle. PowerScene was impressive. To foreigners especially, it was a vivid reminder of America's technological prowess.

The Mapping Agency installed its large computers in a room directly across from my bedroom, with a huge sign warning all unauthorized personnel to stay out. Only a handful of people had access to the American building to begin with, so this sign—the only one of its sort inside the compound—naturally attracted endless visitors, who found "flying" the roads and mountains of Bosnia even more enjoyable than Packy's All-Sports Bar. As visitors dropped in, noise from this accidental video arcade often went on late into the night. But the video game would play an important role in the resolution of the Gorazde problem.

Clark and his colleagues had prepared well for the meeting. Flying the land between Sarajevo and Gorazde endlessly on PowerScene, they had found a route that could link the two cities. It was a small dirt track located halfway between the two roads, both now controlled by the Serbs, that had once connected the two cities.

Milosevic arrived alone at the room containing the PowerScene computers around 11:00 P.M. He was fascinated by the technology and spent some time playing with the joystick, "visiting" portions of Bosnia. Then we began an in-

Key Territorial Issues at Dayton

SLOV.

HUNGARY

SERBIA

Sava R.

CROATIA

Drava R.

EASTERN SLAVONIA

Danube R.

• Karlovac

Sava R.

Posavina Pocket

Posavina Corridor

Bosanski Novi •

• Prijedor

Bosanski Samac •

Sava R.

Sanski Most •

• Banja Luka

Doboj •

Orasje • Brcko •

• Kljuc

Mrkonjic Grad •

• Jajce

BOSNIA-HERZEGOVINA

Srebrenica •

LIVNO VALLEY

"The Egg"

Sarajevo •

• Pale

Zepa •

Rogatica •

Mt. Igman

Gorazde •

• Split

Mostar •

"The Clark Corridor"

Drina R.

Drina R.

MONTE-NEGRO

0   20 miles

0   20 kilometers

----- Dayton Agreement inter-entity boundary line, November 21, 1995

Bosnian Serb–controlled area, November 1, 1995

Croat-Muslim Federation–controlled area, November 1, 1995

tense examination of the dirt track that Clark thought we might upgrade. Milosevic began by offering a three-kilometer corridor through the mountainous terrain. This was far too narrow, we told him, and demonstrated the point by showing him, on PowerScene, that the ridgelines had a clear line of sight on the road and his proposed corridor was therefore too narrow to defend.

For almost two hours we examined the maps and "traveled" across the hills and valleys of the Gorazde area, courtesy of PowerScene. The session was made far livelier, even raucous, by the substantial amount of scotch consumed by some of the participants. This later led people to say that Milosevic had made some key concessions under the influence. But, as usual, I saw no evidence that the alcohol affected him. Milosevic knew what he was doing, and he remembered every detail of the discussion the next morning.

Using maps and an old-fashioned technology—crayons—Clark sketched a corridor that cut a wider swath through the hills east of Sarajevo. As he drew the connector, it was no longer simply a narrow, indefensible road. Instead, its width now averaged 8.3 kilometers, and stretched from ridgelines to hilltops so as to minimize the areas in which the road was vulnerable to direct fire from the high ground. After hours of argument, Milosevic offered us a substantially revised, widened version of this route between Gorazde and Sarajevo. It was after 2:00 A.M. We shook hands, and Milosevic drained his glass again, saying, "We have found our road."

We called it the "Clark Corridor," or, sometimes, the "Scotch Road." In his report the next day, General Kerrick said he was "still recovering from scotch exchange with Milosevic [which I drank] for my country—and I don't even drink scotch."

When the lengthy session on the Clark Corridor finally ended, I sent a long message, entitled "Closure or Closedown: The Situation as of 2:00 A.M.," to Warren Christopher, who was about to leave Osaka for the long return flight to Dayton:

> The Bosnians still wish us to believe that they are getting a lousy deal. Yet they know it is not only a good deal but the best they will ever get. Logically, therefore, they should accept. But the dynamics of their delegation make this a very close call. Izetbegovic spent nine years of his life in jail, and is not a governmental leader so much as a movement leader. He has little understanding of, or interest in, economic development or modernization—the things that peace can bring. He has suffered greatly for his ideals. To him, Bosnia is more an abstraction, not several million people who overwhelmingly want peace. Haris, on the other hand, is more modern and focused heavily on economic reconstruction, something Izetbegovic never mentions. . . .
> Milosevic seems to be enjoying himself at Dayton Place, although he likes to intimidate people. Standing up to him when he attacks is the key; he respects

people who act as tough as him. He is always testing us. In order to move him, we must lay down very firm markers and not move them unless we know exactly what we are getting in return. I'll see you at the airport. Have a good trip back.

DAY SEVENTEEN: FRIDAY, NOVEMBER 17

When the Bosnians saw the Gorazde map early the next morning, they were impressed, but did not accept it. This did not worry us: it was standard Balkan negotiating procedure not to accept anything that came from the other side without trying to change it. (This tendency was so pronounced it had become a joke: the best way to confuse someone in the Balkans, we often said, was to accept his initial proposal without change, at which point he would change his own position.) The Bosnians wanted two things: more land south of Gorazde, and firm assurances from the United States that the dirt track would be upgraded into a paved, all-weather road. After discussions with Joulwan and the Army Corps of Engineers, Clark informed us that IFOR engineers would upgrade the road during the summer months and added a key sentence to the military annex: "a two-lane all-weather road will be constructed in the Gorazde Corridor." This satisfied the Bosnians. But they still wanted more territory around Gorazde, especially some land on the south bank of the Drina River, the river that carried so much historical and emotional importance to all former Yugoslavs.*

We planned a day of high-level visitors who would increase the pressure on the reluctant parties. Perry and Slocombe were due at 10:00 A.M., General Joulwan would arrive from Europe at noon, and Christopher would return in the late afternoon. These visits were carefully sequenced: Perry and Joulwan would symbolize American military power and determination, and set the stage for the final push when Christopher returned.

The meetings left a powerful impression on the delegations. Izetbegovic, who knew from Sacirbey and Perle that the Pentagon was opposed to the Equip and Train program, asked for Perry's personal commitment to it. After an edgy exchange, Perry gave Izetbegovic what he wanted, using words that would be cited often by the Bosnians later: "If we get a peace agreement, I will make the Equip and Train program happen." This was no more than a repetition of commitments made by Christopher, Lake, and myself, but it was important that Izetbegovic hear it directly from the Secretary of Defense.

Joulwan joined the meetings two hours later, bringing with him Major General William Nash, the blunt, cigar-smoking First Armored Division comman-

---

* The Yugoslav writer Ivo Andric won the Nobel Prize in Literature in 1961 for his epic novel *The Bridge over the River Drina.*

der, who was scheduled to lead most of the American troops in Bosnia. It was symbolism at its best. With their straightforward warnings and uniforms bristling with medals, the generals made a powerful impression. It was Joulwan's inspired idea to bring Nash, whose no-nonsense style impressed the Balkan leaders; this was, after all, the man who would actually command the American troops on the ground in Bosnia.

With the exception of Perry, the visitors did not get into the details of the negotiations. But they sent a potent message: the physical presence of Joulwan and Nash in Dayton gave NATO a tangible reality in the eyes of the parties, and set the right tone for the final phase of the negotiations, which we planned around Christopher's return. Thirty minutes after they left, at 4:30 in the afternoon, the Secretary of State's big plane touched down from Osaka.

CHAPTER 18

Showdown

(November 18–21, 1995)

Human error is a permanent and not a periodic factor in history, and future negotiators will be exposed, however noble their intentions, to futilities of intention and omission as grave as any which characterised the Council of Five. They were convinced that they would never commit the blunders and iniquities of the Congress of Vienna. Future generations will be equally convinced that they will be immune from the defects which assailed the negotiators of Paris. Yet they in their turn will be exposed to similar microbes of infection, to the eternal inadequacy of human intelligence.

—HAROLD NICOLSON, *Peacemaking 1919*

DAY EIGHTEEN: SATURDAY, NOVEMBER 18

Deadlines. Negotiations have a certain pathology, a kind of life cycle almost like living organisms. At a certain point—which one might not recognize until later—the focus and momentum needed to get an agreement could disappear. *Something* could happen to break our single-minded commitment. Either endless squabbles over small details would replace the larger search for peace, or the Europeans would leave, publicly signaling an impending failure. We worried that if we were still at Wright-Patterson over the Thanksgiving holiday, only a few days away, it would create the impression that we had stayed too long and accomplished too little.

That morning I wrote a short note to myself:

There is a sense here that peace is probably inevitable because of the dangers if we fail. That may be true, as far as it goes. But the critical question—will the Bosnians grasp an imperfect peace or let the war resume—remains unresolved. Their delegation is divided and confused. Silajdzic told me that he had not talked to Izetbegovic in over twenty-four hours. They have let other opportunities for peace slip away before. It could happen again.

Kerrick was even bleaker in his daily report:

Endgame personal dynamics taking downward spiral. Milosevic and Pale Serbs never seen together—rarely speak. Izetbegovic, Mo, Haris continue to amaze us all with their desire to torpedo one another—and possibly even peace.

Christopher did not want to leave Dayton again without a deal. Tired from his quick round-trip to Asia, he had met briefly with Izetbegovic and Milosevic on arrival Friday night, and then went to sleep. The rest of us went to the Officers' Club for another lobster dinner with Chris Spiro and Milosevic. Milosevic seated Tom Donilon next to him to discuss American politics. Tom said that if Dayton failed, the congressional backlash would leave Serbia even more isolated, and the embargo would never be lifted. Donilon's straight-talking style appealed to Milosevic, and he engaged Tom in a sophisticated discussion of American politics, even offering his thoughts on how to handle the budget confrontation with Gingrich.

We thought Saturday would be "the big day, a hell of a day." We told the parties that we wanted to finish the negotiations by midnight Saturday, spend Sunday morning cleaning up final details, and make the announcement later that day. This was obviously unrealistic, but it gave us a twenty-four-hour cushion for our real deadline, which was completion of the negotiations Sunday night and an announcement on Monday.

In the morning staff meeting, we reviewed the status of the negotiations with Christopher. Most of the General Framework Agreement—the umbrella document—had been accepted by the parties, except for the issue of mutual recognition among the three states. Of the eleven draft annexes, agreement was in hand or within sight on nine: the military annexes (Annexes 1-A and 1-B), the constitution—with the exception of the central bank, which was still in dispute (Annex 4); arbitration (5); human rights (6); refugees/displaced persons (7); national monuments (8); public services (9); civilian implementation (10); and the International Police Task Force (11). This was more than we had originally thought possible. But the two toughest problems were still unresolved—the map (Annex 2) and elections (Annex 3):

- *The map*. Of the big issues, only Gorazde seemed close to resolution. Sarajevo, Brcko, the Posavina Corridor, and the Posavina pocket were unresolved. Contrary to our initial hopes, there had been no trade-offs between Dayton's political provisions and the map. We would have to negotiate the remaining map issues literally kilometer by kilometer.

- *Elections*. The problem of refugee voting still stymied us. Milosevic held to his view that voters must register in person in Bosnia. The Bosnians wanted to allow absentee registration and let people vote where they had lived in 1991, the year of the last prewar census of Yugoslavia. In practice, this would mean that Muslims from, say, Banja Luka who were now refugees in Germany would be allowed to vote in the Banja Luka district for a Serb presidential candidate, opening the possibility that Muslims could become a swing bloc in an election between Serb candidates. To the Serbs, of course, this was unacceptable.

Elections and the OSCE. Just before Christopher arrived, we settled a serious disagreement over how to conduct elections. Everyone agreed that an international body should oversee the elections, but there had been an early disagreement over which organization should have the job, and a more serious problem over what the international community's role should be. Organizationally, the choice came down to the U.N. or the Organization of Security and Cooperation in Europe (OSCE). At the urging of John Kornblum, who had served as Ambassador to the organization, the United States opted for the OSCE, which had been created to monitor the 1975 Helsinki Accords.

Known until 1994 as the Conference on Security and Cooperation in Europe (CSCE), the fifty-two-nation OSCE was the only regional "security" organization that included both the NATO nations and all the countries of the former Soviet bloc.* During the Cold War, it had been little more than an occasional forum for meetings, but it was part of our vision for European security to transform the OSCE into a significant component of what President Clinton called "an undivided Europe."

The European members of the Contact Group readily agreed to assign the OSCE responsibility for the elections. But they simultaneously proposed to limit its role simply to *monitoring* the elections. This view ran directly counter to that of President Clinton, who told me, just before Dayton, that "a credible election would be the most important single event" of the first year after Dayton. This would be possible only if the international community ran it; "monitoring," a vague and elusive concept, would result in a stalemate, and either no elections or disputed elections. While an international organization was no guarantee of a "free and fair" election, the larger its role, the better. With the President's words as our marching orders, we insisted that the OSCE *run* the elections. Otherwise, they would either never take place, or be worthless. Finally, after days of argument, we gained agreement at Dayton that the OSCE would "*supervise,* in a manner to be determined by the OSCE, . . . the preparation and *conduct* of elections [emphasis added]."

Although this was still not perfect, I felt this language was strong enough so that the OSCE could interpret it any way it wanted to. Thus the selection of an

---

* Even neutral countries like Switzerland and Malta, and tiny states like Andorra and Liechtenstein, were members. The chairmanship rotated annually, and in 1996 fell to the Swiss, who did an excellent job.

aggressive head for the OSCE mission in Bosnia would become important later.*

That morning, we learned that Muhamed Sacirbey had held a rather casual press conference the night before at the Holiday Inn outside the air base to announce his resignation as Foreign Minister, thus complying with the terms of the November 10 Federation agreement. He would be replaced by an ethnic Croat—Jadranko Prlic—as part of the agreement. This was a necessary step, but it had no effect on the proceedings at Dayton, or on Sacirbey's role.

Sarajevo Breakthrough. Milosevic continued to play with variations of the District of Columbia model, making a series of proposals that would have given the Serbs a voice equal to that of the Muslims in the city. Finally, early Saturday afternoon, I asked Milosevic to take a short walk around the inner compound. I complained bitterly that his behavior was going to cause a breakdown of the talks, and concentrated on Sarajevo. "Some issues can be set aside or fudged," I said, "but Sarajevo must be settled in Dayton." "Okay," he said with a laugh, "I won't eat today until we solve Sarajevo."

A short while later, while I was chatting with Hill and Clark, the door to my suite opened without warning, and Milosevic walked in. "I was in your neighborhood and did not want to pass your door without knocking," he said, smiling broadly. Clearly, he had something important to tell us.

"Okay, okay," he said as he sat down. "The hell with your D.C. model; it's too complicated, it won't work. I'll solve Sarajevo. But you must not discuss my proposal with anyone in the Serb delegation yet. I must work the 'technology' later, after everything else is settled.

"I tell you," he continued, "Izetbegovic has earned Sarajevo by not abandoning it. He's one tough guy. It's his."

These words were probably the most astonishing and unexpected of the conference. As he talked, Milosevic traced on a map with a pen the part of Sarajevo he was ready to give to the Muslims. Immediately Chris Hill objected: it was a huge concession, but it was not all of the city. Milosevic had retained for the Serbs Grbavica, a key area across the river from the center of town. Although a dramatic step forward, Milosevic's proposal did not quite unify Sarajevo.

When Hill pointed this out, Milosevic exploded. "I'm *giving* you Sarajevo," he almost shouted at Chris, "and you talk such bullshit!" We told Milosevic that while his proposal was "a big step in the right direction," it was likely Izetbegovic would reject it.

Hill and I went immediately to see the Bosnian President. Izetbegovic did not acknowledge the importance of the offer, but focused solely on its defects.

---

* This led to an argument with the French a month later. See chapter 19.

"Sarajevo without Grbavica cannot exist," he said with passion. The area that Milosevic wanted to retain for the Serbs jutted directly into the center of the city and was known to Western journalists as "Sniper Alley." Still, we all recognized that the negotiations over Sarajevo had entered a new phase.

Taking a detailed street map of Sarajevo, Hill, Clark, and I went back to Milosevic's suite. We began examining every road and every terrain feature. Milosevic seemed flexible; Hill predicted after the meeting that if we stuck to our position we would get all of Sarajevo the next day. Feeling suddenly encouraged, we adjourned with our hopes soaring.

Joined by Christopher, we reassembled in my suite to assess what had happened. We had not expected this. We agreed to support Izetbegovic's claim to Grbavica and the hills above the city. Then we sat around debating the possible reasons for Milosevic's astonishing decision.

"Why did Milosevic do this?" I asked. "And can he actually make it happen? Has he decided to abandon the Bosnian Serbs? Can he really force the Bosnian Serbs to give up their parts of the city?"

Reunifying Sarajevo Under Dayton

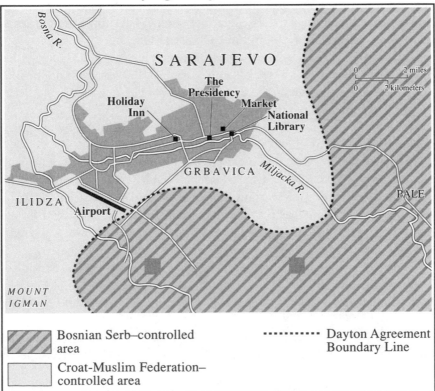

We never fully understood why Milosevic decided to give Sarajevo to the Muslims. But in retrospect, the best explanation may be that he was fed up with the Bosnian Serbs and had decided to weaken their Pale base by giving away the Serb-controlled parts of Sarajevo. By giving the Federation all of Bosnia's capital, perhaps Milosevic wanted to weaken Karadzic and strengthen the Serbs in other parts of Bosnia, especially Banja Luka.

This explanation was consistent with one of Milosevic's main themes at Dayton: that the Bosnian Serb leadership had become an impediment, even though he had earlier made common cause with them. Milosevic had often talked of strengthening the "intellectuals" and businessmen of Banja Luka in order to weaken Pale; now he seemed to be putting this theory into action.

To further weaken Pale, I proposed that the Dayton agreement include a provision moving the Bosnian Serb capital to Banja Luka. Milosevic seemed interested in this proposal, but, to my surprise, Izetbegovic demurred. Even though he hated the leadership in Pale, he seemed to think he could work with them, especially his old associate from the Bosnian Assembly, Momcilo Krajisnik. Izetbegovic also saw value in keeping the capitals of the two entities close to each other so that Sarajevo remained the only important political center in Bosnia. He may also have feared that if the Bosnian Serb capital moved to Banja Luka, which is closer to Zagreb than Sarajevo, it would accelerate the permanent division of the country and strengthen Tudjman.

Whatever Izetbegovic's reasons for not wanting to close Pale, it was a mistake. The mountain town was solely a wartime capital, established by an indicted war criminal and his henchmen. It was the living symbol—and headquarters—of his organization. We should have pushed Izetbegovic harder to agree to establish the Serb capital at Banja Luka. It would have made a big difference in the effort to implement the Dayton agreements.

DAY NINETEEN: SUNDAY, NOVEMBER 19

This would be our longest day. Twenty-two hours after it had begun, we would still be at it—without success.

A Bluff Fools No One. Christopher and I agreed to make an all-out effort to complete the talks Sunday. In an attempt to convince the parties we were serious about this deadline, I asked every member of the American delegation to pack his or her bags and place them in the parking lot where the other delegations could see them. After the bags lay outside for several hours, I asked the Air Force to put them on a truck and take them to the airstrip. Rosemarie began to try to collect the payment of bills from the parties—an effort in which she was entirely unsuccessful.

Of all the gambits we tried at Dayton, this proved to be the most pathetic. Everyone saw through our bluff; nobody else made the slightest effort to prepare for departure. Early in the evening, we gave up and brought the bags back to our rooms.

To bring the conference to an end, in fact, would require much more than a theatrical ruse. We needed to tie up the loose ends on a dozen secondary issues, resolve the question of refugee voting, and settle Sarajevo. But each time Christopher met with Izetbegovic, the Bosnian President pointedly brought up Brcko, referring to the unrealistic 1994 Contact Group map with its railroad bridge and tiny underpass.

The Chart Fiasco. How could we convince Izetbegovic that he was now at the decisive moment? Knowing he was under conflicting pressures from his own delegation, we looked for ways to convince him to take the leap for peace. Through Neville-Jones and Blot, we asked Prime Minister Major and President Chirac to call Izetbegovic. Both men did so immediately, telling the Bosnian President that "if this moment is lost, the opportunity might not easily come again." Izetbegovic conceded to Major that they had made progress, but added that he needed more land to make up for the lost towns of Srebrenica and Zepa. In Ankara, Ambassador Grossman also arranged a call between Izetbegovic and Turkish president Suleyman Demirel, the foreign leader whom Izetbegovic probably respected most.

We asked Menzies to compile a list of everything the Bosnians had already achieved in the negotiations—and would lose if the talks did not succeed. Working with the graphics division of Wright-Patterson, Menzies produced two large posters, listing the "gains of Dayton." On Saturday afternoon—at the same time we were arguing over the Serb portions of Sarajevo—Christopher, Menzies, and I took these to Izetbegovic's suite. In large block letters, they listed everything that had been achieved in the negotiations. Reviewing the charts before we showed them to the Bosnians, Christopher laughed and said, "Well, *I'm* impressed, even if Izetbegovic is not," and added that he did not see how anyone could "responsibly walk away from these gains and allow his country to go back to war."

The posters contained one particularly sensitive item. Measuring the territorial concessions that Milosevic had already made, the Defense Mapping Agency team had determined that 55 percent of Bosnia was now conceded to the Federation. This was a negotiated increase of about 5 percent during the first eighteen days at Dayton over the battlefield situation—and left us with something halfway between an opportunity and a dilemma. The opportunity was obvious: a chance to gain more territory for the Federation. But so was the dilemma: under the 1994 Contact Group plan, all five Contact Group Foreign Ministers and the leaders of all three countries had formally agreed to a 51–49 split of Bosnian territory between the Federation and the Bosnian Serbs.

Were we still bound by 51–49? Given that the Serbs had conquered so much territory through infamous methods, it would have been just for the Federation to control more than 51 percent of the land. Unexpectedly, we had gained 55 percent for Sarajevo. We decided to see if we could retain this higher percentage, since it would significantly strengthen the chance to create a viable country. But we knew that if Milosevic objected we would have little choice but to fall back to the 51–49 formula, given the prior commitments of the United States and the four other nations of the Contact Group. Tony Lake had reaffirmed this as a core American position during his August trip to the European capitals before the start of our shuttle, and it had been included in the September 9 Geneva agreement.

Menzies had placed the dramatic percentage figures in a prominent position on the first poster. We hoped the Bosnians would recognize what a significant achievement it was, and move rapidly to lock it in by finishing the rest of the negotiations. With Sarajevo close to solution, we felt this was possible within hours if we worked fast. But while the Bosnians were fascinated with our charts, they continued to argue over minor issues. Their delay, and what happened next, doomed any chance we might have had to get more than 51 percent for the Federation.

When the meeting was finished, Izetbegovic and Silajdzic asked to keep the charts. Menzies placed them beside the couch, partially concealed. A short time later, Milosevic unexpectedly called on Izetbegovic—in itself an unusual event—to discuss Sarajevo and the need to finish the conference quickly. As the two men talked, Milosevic noticed the top of one of our charts peeking out from behind the couch. On it was written, in bold capital letters: "FEDERATION TERRITORY INCREASED FROM 50% TO 55% DURING DAYTON TALKS."

For the first time, Milosevic realized how far his territorial concessions had gone. Ending the meeting quickly, he walked directly to my room, and entered without warning. I was sitting with Warren Christopher and several of our team. When Milosevic entered, everyone left except Christopher.

"You tricked me," he said angrily. "You didn't tell me that the percentage was no longer 51–49. I asked you but you didn't reply. I saw your charts. How can I trust you?"

At first we could not understand what had happened. Had the Bosnians boasted to Milosevic about the percentage in order to goad him? We had no idea. The truth—that the Bosnians had left the charts partially in view when Milosevic visited them—did not occur to us, and we did not know if it was a deliberate provocation or simply a stupid oversight. (Later, Silajdzic told me that it was just bad luck that Milosevic showed up without warning and saw the charts.)*

"I can do many things," Milosevic said, "but I cannot give you more than fifty-one percent. This is my bottom line with Republika Srpska. We agreed to this before Dayton."

We pointed out that Milosevic had already accepted territorial changes that exceeded 51 percent. "I didn't know what the percentage was," he replied, "and I can't force Pale to accept a deal for less than forty-nine percent. Please believe me. This is the end of the matter."

Christopher and I glanced at each other. The Secretary of State could not renege on a public commitment if any of the parties insisted on sticking to it. Other parts of the original Contact Group map had been changed "by mutual consent," as called for in the plan, but 51–49 had taken on an almost theological force.

Milosevic had a suggestion as to how to return to 51–49—and it was unacceptable. He asked for a widening of the Posavina Corridor from three miles to ten miles. This was, of course, the same corridor that Izetbegovic continually insisted be reduced to a thirty-meter-wide underpass beneath the railroad bridge to the adjoining city of Brcko. The existing corridor, connecting the Serbs of western Bosnia with Serbia itself, hung like a noose around the Serb neck.

Having repeatedly told Izetbegovic that we could not reduce the width of the corridor, we now rejected Milosevic's demand to widen it. But the issue of the Posavina Corridor and Brcko were still not settled, and would, as we had expected, prove to be the toughest of all issues at Dayton.

The day continued with endless meetings over maps. Clark and the military map experts looked for ways to change the percentage from 55–45 to 51–49 without asking the Federation to give up any "important" land. Since a significant portion of the terrain in Bosnia consisted of sparsely inhabited mountain areas ("worthless land," in Silajdzic's dismissive phrase), there was room for some compromise, but not much. Using their computers, the mapping team could measure the land to one one-hundredth of 1 percent (.01 percent!), an absurdly false precision; the thickness of the map lines themselves amounted to at least 1 percent of the land. But, with both sides now obsessed with this issue, the precise percentage of land each controlled was central.

---

* In *The Death of Yugoslavia*, Brian Lapping and Laura Silber's superb six-part documentary for the BBC, Silajdzic recounts this incident in detail. He describes it as an accident, and laughs as he recalls how upset both Milosevic and the Americans were. To those involved in it at the time, however, it was no laughing matter.

The most disturbing aspect of this obsession with 51–49 was that it revealed how little each side trusted the political aspects of the Dayton agreements to which they had both agreed. As Izetbegovic once said, a "mountain of corpses" between the two sides prevented trust. The argument over the land was, in effect, a continuation of the war in Dayton, while the political discussions were a tentative effort to build a political framework for a joint future. We were all too aware of the internal contradiction, but there was nothing that could be done about it.

Milosevic and Silajdzic. The long day dragged on. Milosevic, still fuming over our "clever trick" with the percentages, refused to make any further concessions on Sarajevo or settle the final details on Gorazde. After several hours, he gradually regained his composure, and the talks inched forward again. But Milosevic still held out on the land south of the Drina near Gorazde, on the hills to the southwest of Sarajevo, and, most important, on the Grbavica portion of Sarajevo. Shortly before 8:00 P.M., while Milosevic argued with Hill and me, we looked out the window and noticed Silajdzic walking toward Packy's. The two sides had not met face-to-face since Milosevic had walked out of Izetbegovic's suite after seeing the offending poster hours earlier. Running into the parking lot, I grabbed Haris. "You might get what you want on Sarajevo if you meet Milosevic right now," I said, and pulled him into my rooms. Asking the two men to negotiate face-to-face, I left them alone with Chris Hill, our "language officer."

For hours the three men argued, while Christopher, Donilon, Jim Steinberg, and I waited in another room down the hall. Periodically Hill would appear to give us a progress report or get new maps. A careful man not given to overoptimism about the Balkans, which he knew so well, Hill was now relatively upbeat. As we ate sandwiches in Christopher's room, we thought the end might be in sight. Donilon and Burns began discussing with Washington how to arrange the initialing ceremony.

At 10:00 P.M., Tudjman returned from Zagreb to join the final push. Christopher and I met him at the airport and told him that he had to exert direct pressure on both Izetbegovic and Milosevic. He said he would do whatever he could the next morning, but preferred to stay away from the Milosevic-Silajdzic marathon, already in its third hour.

Under Hill's insistent pressure, Milosevic finally gave more ground near Gorazde. At one point, Silajdzic asked for Ustkolina, a small town near Gorazde, primarily because it held the oldest mosque built in Bosnia. Milosevic laughed sardonically. "Oh, Haris," he said, "don't you know that those idiots"—he meant the Bosnian Serbs—"blew it up?"

"But the location is sacred," Silajdzic replied.

"Haris," Milosevic said, "now you sound like Karadzic." But he yielded, and Ustkolina was Muslim again.

Shortly thereafter, Milosevic agreed to give the Federation a symbolically important strip of land on the southern bank of the Drina. Four days after the napkin diplomacy at the Officers' Club shuttle, Gorazde was settled. We had come a long way from the original U.S. position in July that Gorazde was indefensible and might have to be sacrificed in a negotiation. Gorazde was saved.

The three men shifted back to Sarajevo, drawing lines on the map. Milosevic's lines did not include Grbavica. Silajdzic said that without it, there was no deal; it was an integral part of the capital. Hill drew a line that included Grbavica and said, "This is *our* line, the American line." Suddenly, Milosevic did not object.

Silajdzic demanded land that overlooked the city so that it could never again be used for artillery and mortar attacks on Sarajevo. Part of it contained a Serb cemetery. "Now you want our dead too!" Milosevic exclaimed. But again he relented. Almost without realizing it, the two men had won an undivided Sarajevo.

But, Milosevic said, all his other agreements were contingent on returning to 51–49. Pulling Silajdzic out of his session with Milosevic, Christopher and I told him that we could not hold to the percentages of the posters any longer. This did not surprise Silajdzic, who had always maintained that the quality of the land was more important than its quantity. He agreed to negotiate land readjustments that would get the map back to 51–49.

Shortly after midnight, the three men broke off their talks. Silajdzic, feeling extremely good, went back to his building to consult Izetbegovic and his own map expert.

In the American building, members of our team crowded in the hallway and the small conference room. Stale air and the smell of pizza filled the corridor. In the workrooms, Tom Malinowski, one of Warren Christopher's best speechwriters, worked on two public statements—one for success, the other for failure. I looked at the failure statement, which tried to put a positive face on events, and tossed it into the air. I wrote a new draft that presented failure, if it came, honestly, bluntly, and unapologetically. "To put it simply," the draft ended,

we gave it our best shot. By their failure to agree, the parties have made it very clear that further U.S. efforts to negotiate a settlement would be fruitless. Accordingly, today marks the end of this initiative. . . . The special role we have played in recent months is over. The leaders here today must live with the consequences of their failure.

"The Thirty-seven-Minute Peace." The evening was far from over. Milosevic did not leave our building, but instead moved from my suite to the conference room, where he waited, with Christopher, Hill, Clark, and myself, for Silajdzic to return. Shortly after 2:00 A.M., Silajdzic returned with his map expert. Huge maps had been set up by Clark.

For two more hours Milosevic and Silajdzic argued, yelled, and drew wide, sweeping lines on the maps. Translation was almost unnecessary—the body language, the hand gestures, the emotions told the story. Silajdzic—on the attack, demanding one concession after another from Milosevic, a railroad station here, a hilltop there—was picking up more territory. At one point the Bosnian map expert pointed out that the water reservoir at Faletici northeast of Sarajevo had been left outside the line of Federation control. When Silajdzic raised this, Milosevic said, "I am not a louse," and yielded immediately. It was clear: Milosevic wanted an agreement then and there. But he insisted, at all times, to 51–49.

This was not easy, given the concessions Milosevic had already made. More than minor "shaving" of lesser Federation-controlled areas would be necessary. Well after 3:30 A.M., Silajdzic hit upon a solution that retained for the Federation all the key gains of Dayton but returned to the sacred percentage. He outlined a large egg-shaped area on the map south of Highway 5 in western Bosnia, and offered the land to Republika Srpska. This was a mountainous, lightly populated Serb region south of the town of Kljuc that had been taken during the recent Croat offensive—precisely what Silajdzic had meant when he talked of "worthless land." Because of its shape, Hill dubbed it "the egg," while Milosevic, thinking it resembled Spain, called it "the Iberian peninsula." Both men agreed to calibrate its exact size so as to reach 51–49 for the whole country.

Suddenly Milosevic stuck out his hand. Slightly surprised, Silajdzic took it. Except for some details, the deal was done. It was 4:00 A.M. For a moment, we sat silent, too stunned to react. They talked with sudden ease, and, for the first time, joked. Silajdzic seemed euphoric at his negotiating triumph, Milosevic relieved that it was over. Christopher went outside and asked Bob Bradtke, his faithful executive assistant, to fetch a bottle of his favorite California Chardonnay from the supply with which he always traveled. Out of plastic cups, we drank to peace. (Silajdzic, a practicing Muslim, drank a Coke.) An Air Force photographer came in to record the triumphant scene.

After a drink or two Silajdzic went off to get Izetbegovic, who appeared wearing an overcoat over pajamas and looking sleepy and annoyed. He refused a drink, even a soft drink, while he stared at the map without comment.

As we drank, I had been studying the map, puzzled. Something was wrong, but at first, I was too tired to see what was it was. Then it struck me: all of

Silajdzic's "givebacks" were from Croat-controlled territory—and no Croatians were present. I whispered to Hill to get Tudjman.

Ten minutes later, Hill appeared with Mate Granic. Although it was now after 4:00 A.M., the Croatian Foreign Minister was dressed impeccably and looked as if he had just stepped out of his office on a relaxed day. Sitting down, he politely shared a drink with us and listened to the explanation of the deal. Then, quite calmly, Granic asked to see the map, which was leaning against the wall. As he studied it, an extraordinary transformation came over him. When I thought about it later, it reminded me of the way Zero Mostel had turned himself into a rhinoceros in Ionesco's play. Turning red and barely able to speak at first, Granic slammed his fist into the map. "Impossible! Impossible!" he finally said, walking rapidly around the small room. "Impossible. Zero point zero zero chance that my President will accept this!" He stormed out, almost tripping over Jim O'Brien, who was sitting on the floor in the corridor drinking a beer and chatting with Jim Steinberg.

Within minutes, Granic returned with Defense Minister Susak, who took one look at the map and turned on Silajdzic. "You have given away the territory we conquered with Croatian blood!" he yelled, in English, at Silajdzic, who sat motionless at the table. Milosevic said nothing. Izetbegovic was leaning forward now, listening carefully. This, his body language seemed to say, was getting interesting.

There was still a chance to salvage the evening's gains. If the problem was simply that Haris had given away too much Croat land, perhaps we could redistribute the "givebacks" more equitably between the Croats and the Muslims. I suggested that we try to do just this, "shaving a bit here and bit there."

Izetbegovic still had not said a word. I turned to him, fearing his response, "What do you think, Mr. President? Can we finish the negotiation right now?"

His answer sealed the long day. "I cannot accept this agreement," he said in a low voice, in English.

"What did you say?" Christopher asked, in astonishment.

More loudly: "I cannot accept this agreement."

We sat absolutely silent for a moment. Suddenly Silajdzic took the papers in front of him, slammed them down on the table with great force, and shouted, "I can't take this anymore." Then he stormed out into the cold Dayton night, leaving the rest of us behind.

"Let's deal with this in the morning," I said, and Izetbegovic, suddenly quite animated, walked out, followed by Granic and Susak. We were left alone with Milosevic, who had said nothing during the entire scene.

The "peace" had lasted thirty-seven minutes. We sat with Milosevic for another half hour, utterly spent. The twenty-two-hour day had ended in disaster. Nothing since the Mount Igman tragedy had hit us as hard. Finally, shortly after 5:00 A.M., we parted to get short naps before resuming. We were too exhausted to imagine a way out.

DAY TWENTY: MONDAY, NOVEMBER 20

We rose again after one hour of sleep. (Christopher told me later that he had not slept at all.) The conference was now stalled within sight of its goal, and after the drama of the previous night, emotions were raw in all three delegations. Christopher, Donilon, Steinberg, and I met early in the morning, and agreed that it was time to bring in the heaviest weapon we had: President Clinton.

Intervention (but not a visit) by the President had always been part of our operating assumptions for Dayton, but the questions were when and how. It was important not to weaken the President. The presidential coin is precious, and should not be devalued. The rest of us could rise or fall, succeed or fail, be replaced or repudiated if necessary. But the President represents the nation. There is no higher authority, and his failure or error can hurt the national interest. Thus any involvement of the nation's chief executive is something that White House staffers debate strenuously.

We called Tony Lake, and asked him to arrange two calls—one to Tudjman, the other to Izetbegovic. (No call to Milosevic was needed or desirable.) We recommended a simple presidential message: You are very close to success, and I am asking you, in the name of peace, to work out your differences.

Lake said he wanted to delay any presidential calls until the afternoon, while we made another try to reach agreement. More important, Lake opposed any call to Izetbegovic, on the grounds that the President should not appear to be pressuring the Muslims. Christopher and I felt differently. Both calls, we said, were essential.

Lake was adamant. He would oppose a call to Izetbegovic, he said, even though Christopher and I said that without it the risks of failure increased substantially. When we argued that the call could be couched in a manner that would not be construed as pressure, he still objected.

The core team at Dayton was not happy. Kerrick, using his direct channels to the NSC, tried again, but with no success. Then he wrote the first draft of the "talking points" that the President would use with Tudjman. I suggested that Christopher call the President directly to get him involved immediately and more deeply. But the Secretary was reluctant to get in an argument with Tony over whether the President should call Izetbegovic.

We called on Tudjman, who told us that his ministers had acted with his full support in killing the Milosevic-Silajdzic agreement the previous evening.

"We cannot be the only ones who give up land," Tudjman said. "The Muslims must give up something too."

We saw Bildt at 9:15 A.M. and asked him to meet separately with each of the three Presidents, starting with Tudjman. After calling Spanish Foreign Minister Javier Solana in Brussels, Carl went to each delegation with a simple, but important, message: "Don't hold out for a better deal in Europe. Make it here."

Tudjman walked across the parking lot to see Izetbegovic to see if together they could force Milosevic to accept less than 49 percent of the land. They concluded, as we had, that it would be impossible.

At 11:00 A.M., Bildt came to my room to ask how we were doing. "We are deeply concerned," I said, "that even if Milosevic makes more concessions, the Bosnians will simply raise the ante."

"Do you think Izetbegovic even wants a deal?" Carl asked. It was a question that Warren Christopher had also been asking. "I'm never quite sure," I replied. "Sometimes he seems to want revenge more than peace—but he can't have both." Chris Hill, normally highly supportive of the Bosnians, exploded in momentary anger and frustration. "These people are impossible to help," he said. It was a telling statement from a man who had devoted years of his life to the search for ways to help create a Bosnian state.

It was a beautiful sunny day, clear and crisp, not too cold. People walked around outside to relieve the tension. A sort of "parking-lot diplomacy" took place as people ran into each other and discussed the situation. At one point Bildt ran into Milosevic in the barren asphalt between our buildings, and found him "desperate." "Give me anything," he said, "rocks, swamps, hills—anything, as long as it gets us to 49–51."

At about three in the afternoon, President Clinton made the call to Tudjman. "I am impressed with how much has been achieved in the overall agreement, and with the benefits that will come to all the parties," he said. "A very difficult trade-off will have to be made to resolve the map. I'm calling to ask you to give back a small percentage of nontraditional Croatian territory in western Bosnia in order to bring the map back in line with the basic 51–49 territorial concept of the Contact Group plan."

Tudjman's reply baffled the President and his advisors in Washington, listening in and taking notes. "We have already made such a proposal," Tudjman said, adding that we were only two or three hours from a final agreement. This brought the short conversation to an end.

As soon as Sandy Vershbow, who had listened to the conversation, briefed us on it, Christopher and I went to see Tudjman. Contrary to what he had told the President, Tudjman had made no proposal prior to the call—but he knew that he would have to do so now. "In response to President Clinton's request," he said, "I will instruct my negotiators to give up seventy-five percent of the land needed to reach 49–51." This was good news. But then came two important conditions: "The Muslims must give some of their land up—and I must get back at least part of the Posavina pocket."

President Clinton's call had given us a new lease on life. We returned to Izetbegovic's suite immediately, hopeful that reason would prevail once again. We told him and Silajdzic that, with the President's personal intervention, we had gained agreement from Tudjman that he would "contribute" 75 percent of the land required to reach 51–49. The remainder—just 1 percent of the land—would have to come from them. This would not be difficult to accomplish, we said, especially since the Bosnians would not have to give back any land they currently controlled, only land that they had been given in the last few days by Milosevic—"theoretical land," as we called it.

To our consternation, Izetbegovic refused to budge. While Silajdzic sat silent, Sacirbey argued that the Croat position was still unfair. And, to Christopher's amazement, Izetbegovic began talking again about Brcko, Srebrenica, and Zepa. We returned to my rooms, where Christopher expressed himself in unusually vivid terms on the performance we had just witnessed.

Our next call was on Milosevic. We told him that we could achieve 51–49—but only if he gave back part of the Posavina pocket. Although this request momentarily stunned Milosevic, he understood its importance to Tudjman. Working with detailed maps, Milosevic, Hill, and I started a protracted subnegotiation that went on intermittently for the next six hours. Milosevic finally agreed to return to the Federation a sliver of the Posavina pocket that contained the town of Orasje, which had been the scene of ethnic cleansing of Croats early in the war, and the town of Samac, which lay on the Sava River. A deadlock developed over the exact boundary of Samac. Thinking of Harold Nicolson's negotiators at Versailles, who drew lines on maps with almost no understanding of what they were doing,* I drew a line on the map that ran down the middle of the Sava River, directly on the international border, and then curved around the town's boundaries.

Tudjman accepted this last-minute return of Bosnian Croat land with pleasure. In addition to eastern Slavonia, Tudjman could now show the Croatian people that he had regained some Croat land in Bosnia. And since it was near the home area of Federation President Zubak, it had special value.

By 9:00 P.M., Tudjman had given us enough land in return so that the map stood at 52–48. A shift of only 1 percent, and the deal was done. Yet the

---

* See opening quotation, chapter 17.

Bosnians still refused to share this tiny amount of land. We met in Christopher's room to discuss the situation—Christopher, Donilon, Steinberg, Kornblum, Hill, Burns, and myself. We were depressed and tired. "The land the Bosnians have to give up is only theoretical," I said again. "We are not asking them to give up one inch of land they actually control."

"It's truly unbelievable," Christopher said. "The Bosnian position is irrational. A great agreement is within their grasp, and they don't seem able to accept it."

"What more can we do?" Christopher continued, almost rhetorically. "We have gotten them everything they asked for."

"Chris," I said, "this game has gone on long enough. We must give everyone a drop-dead time limit." I then recommended that we tell Izetbegovic that he had one hour to decide, after which we would close down the conference. "And I really mean close Dayton down," I added. "This should not be a bluff."

It was a huge decision, foreshadowed days earlier in my "Closure or Closedown" memorandum. A heated debate broke out in the room between those who wanted to keep trying and those who thought that our best chance for success was to force everyone to confront failure. The argument went on for close to an hour. Would we resume the shuttle if we closed Dayton down? Would we let the conference continue in Europe under Bildt's chairmanship? It was a gamble. Some people shifted sides, but Kornblum and I held firm for absolute closedown, without resuming the shuttle. Finally, after protracted debate, Christopher agreed that we had to give the Bosnians an ultimatum. We suggested a flat midnight time limit.

"I'd better get the President on board," Christopher said. Over a secure phone line, Christopher told the President what we proposed to do, listened for a moment, and said, "Thank you for your confidence, Mr. President." Then, turning to us, he said, "The President is comfortable with this approach. He will give us complete support."

Kornblum alerted the Bosnians that we wanted to see them immediately, and told Bildt that we were going to deliver an ultimatum. At 10:30 in the evening, Christopher and I walked slowly to the Bosnian President's suite.

Izetbegovic, Silajdzic, and Sacirbey sat in the room waiting for us. Christopher and I took up our usual places next to each other on the couch, and Christopher began.

"Mr. President, we have come a long way in Dayton, and we are very close to a successful conclusion. If you will reduce by one percent the amount of land you claim, we can make a final deal. You do not have to give up any land that you currently control. It's a very good deal, Mr. President. We have obtained almost everything you asked for."

Izetbegovic was visibly uncomfortable. He began to review his grievances—a familiar litany. We tried to reason with him, but he became increasingly obdurate. He mentioned the city of Brcko several times. He felt that he had become the object of all the pressure at Dayton, and he hated pressure. He was tired and beleaguered, and his delegation was about to explode. His eyes narrowing almost to the vanishing point, he looked away from us and mumbled something to his colleagues.

Christopher's famous politeness and patience finally ran out, and he delivered the ultimatum in a tone that conveyed genuine anger. "Mr. President, I am truly disappointed," he said, "at the fuzzy, unrealistic, and sloppy manner in which you and your delegation have approached this negotiation. You can have a successful outcome or not, as you wish. But we must have your answer in one hour. If you say no, we will announce in the morning that the Dayton peace talks have been closed down." We rose to leave, and I added, "Not suspended—closed down. In one hour."

Exhausted, Christopher went directly back to the Hope Center to sleep—his first in three days. I promised we would call as soon as we heard from the Bosnians. Less than a minute after Christopher had left, the door to my room burst open and Haris Silajdzic entered, in a towering rage. "You and Christopher have ruined everything!" he screamed. "How could you let this happen? Don't you know that we can never give in to an American ultimatum—never!"

"You are the ones who have ruined it," I said. "You have at least ninety-five percent of what you wanted, and now you are about to piss it all away, because you can't get your own act together." Silajdzic continued to argue, and I asked him to leave. "Use the next hour to get your President to accept this offer and the war will be over. You will not regret it."

At precisely 11:30 P.M., John Kornblum went to the Bosnians' building to receive their reply. Sacirbey stopped Kornblum in the hall. The Bosnians, he announced, would agree to shave the necessary 1 percent of the land in order to get to 51–49, but they wanted something in return—Brcko.

"You have added a new condition," John said. "You know that we cannot agree." John gave Sacirbey the draft failure statement, and told him it would be issued at 10:00 A.M. the next day.

I called Christopher with the news. "It's over—but maybe it's not over," I told him. "Perhaps confronting the abyss will clear some heads overnight. Please get some sleep, because we are going to have a tough day tomorrow."

Hill delivered the failure statement to Tudjman, who was playing cards with his aides. As befitted a man who already had most of what he wanted, Tudjman laughed, and asked Hill if the United States was really ready to blame the Bosnians publicly for failure. He urged us not to quit.

I sent Kerrick and Hill to deliver the failure statement to Milosevic. Clark, Pardew, Kornblum, and Perina joined the meeting as it went on. Before they left, I told them to make clear that we really were going to close down in the morning—unless Milosevic could save the negotiation. I deliberately stayed away in order to avoid another negotiating session.

It had been, without question, the most depressing day of my professional life. It was hard to believe that the Bosnians would let the agreement slip away over so little, but they seemed ready to do so. I fell asleep quickly, without awaiting the news of the meeting still going on with Milosevic.

Kornblum described the meeting to me later: Milosevic began in a jovial mood, and offered everyone scotch. But when he realized that we would really close the conference the next morning, he reacted strongly. "You can't do that," he said, his voice showing the strain. He became emotional. "We've got this agreement almost done, you can't let this happen. You're the United States. You can't let the Bosnians push you around this way. Just tell them what to do." When the Americans replied that the United States had done a great deal already, but we could not dictate the terms of peace to any party, Milosevic pleaded: "Try some more, don't give up."

Distraught, Milosevic said he would see "Franjo" right away, and propose that the two men sign the Dayton agreements with or without Izetbegovic. Milosevic sent faithful Goran to set up a meeting, but the Croatian President was asleep. Milosevic said he would see Tudjman in the morning. At about 2:00 A.M., the Americans departed, leaving behind a deeply concerned, perhaps even confused Milosevic, who could not believe that we would not be able to force the Bosnians to sign. "Mr. President," Kornblum said as he left, "it's up to you. We've done everything we can."

At 6:30 A.M., the phone rang in our room. It was David Martin, the CBS Pentagon correspondent. It was the first time a journalist had managed to get past the Air Force switchboard since the talks began. "I'm going on the air in a few minutes," Martin said, "and I need you to confirm something. Sacirbey has been at the Holiday Inn all night long, telling everyone that you gave them an ultimatum, they refused, and you are calling off the talks."

Suddenly I was wide awake. "David," I said, "I don't know what Sacirbey said to you, but you can say that we are at a moment of absolute crisis."

"Thanks, that's all I need." A few minutes later, I watched Martin say on television that we had reached "a moment of absolute crisis." It was, indeed. As I showered and dressed, I mentally composed a personal statement to accompany the formal announcement that Dayton was closing down. I would thank everyone for their support, and state that I was withdrawing from the effort, since it was clear that I could accomplish nothing further.

The television was now filled with reports similar to David Martin's. Donilon and Kerrick had briefed the White House, and even as we held our final staff meeting in Dayton the President gathered with his senior advisors. One of the people in the Oval Office that morning—a domestic advisor—later described the scene to me:

> We all woke that morning to hear television reports from Dayton that you had failed. When we gathered in the Oval Office to discuss the situation, there were mixed emotions. Some people, primarily on the domestic side, were relieved, because they knew that if you got an agreement the President would have to make the single most difficult decision of his presidency—to send troops to Bosnia— and then defend it during the 1996 elections. Our polls showed the public overwhelmingly opposed to sending American troops to Bosnia. Yet everyone knew what an enormous amount of prestige we had invested in the effort. The President did not express his own views, but followed the discussion carefully.
>
> I would summarize the general attitude as follows: if Dayton failed, there would be a combination of relief and disappointment. If you succeeded, there would be a combination of pride and apprehension.

Through Tom Donilon, we were aware of Washington's ambivalence about our efforts. Lake had also told us the previous day that "not everyone in Washington wants you to succeed." This neither surprised nor alarmed me; every Administration contains different points of view. The responsibility for failure or success rested with us, and this was no time to worry about Washington's ambivalence.

As I dressed for the 8:00 A.M. staff meeting there was an insistent knock on the door, and Chris Hill came in. "Something's up," he said, excitedly. "Milosevic has just gone to see Tudjman. I think Slobo is going to suggest that the two of them sign the agreement even if Izetbegovic does not."

This did not constitute a breakthrough, but at least they were still talking. After the terrible feeling of failure and exhaustion, I was suddenly, perhaps irrationally, optimistic. As Christopher arrived from the Hope Center for the staff meeting, I pulled him aside and whispered, "We're going to get an agreement!" He looked at me as if I had lost my mind.

The staff meeting was a gloomy affair. Twenty tired people crowded into every corner of the small, messy room. With no more business to conduct, I said this was our last staff meeting, our "shutdown meeting," and started a final statement of appreciation. "The Secretary and I would like to thank everyone for their magnificent efforts. We gave it everything we had, and, no matter what happens today, we should not feel that we have failed, but—"

Suddenly Kati burst into the room. "Milosevic is standing out in the snow in the parking lot waiting to talk to you," she said. For the first time I noticed that it was snowing. She ran back out and pulled him into my room, where Christopher and I met him. He looked as if he had not slept all night.

"Something has to be done to prevent failure," he said wearily. "I suggest that Tudjman and I sign the agreement, and we leave it open for Izetbegovic to sign later."

"That's quite impossible," Christopher said firmly. "We cannot have an agreement that is not signed by everyone. It is not a viable contract."

"Okay, okay," Milosevic said. "Then I will walk the final mile for peace. I will agree to arbitration for Brcko one year from now, and you can make the decision yourself, Mr. Christopher."

Christopher said that he could not personally be the arbitrator. I said we would choose Roberts Owen for the task if we completed the rest of the agreement. I said we had to see Tudjman and Izetbegovic immediately to see if we had an agreement. We ended the brief meeting, and raced to Tudjman's suite.

Tudjman listened intently as I outlined Milosevic's offer. When I finished, he slammed his hands on his knees twice, and, leaning as close to Christopher's face as he could get, said, in English, "Get peace. Get peace now! Make Izetbegovic agree. You must do it now!" Shaking with emotion, he got up, almost pushing us out of his room.

Christopher and I walked back to my suite. I locked the doors so that we could be alone. As we talked, other staff members stood outside, banging on the door, but we ignored them. It was essential to have a single focus for the next meeting, and not a cacophony of voices. This was not a time to consult anyone.

"Chris," I said, "the next meeting may be the most important of your entire tenure as Secretary. We can get this agreement—or we can lose it. Forget Washington. It's entirely in our hands. We must go into the meeting with an absolute determination to succeed."

Christopher listened silently, then nodded. Without stopping to talk to anyone else, we walked directly to Izetbegovic's rooms, where the three Bosnians waited for us. We outlined the offer from Milosevic. Silence. I repeated it, slowly and carefully. There were seven hundred journalists waiting outside the base, I said. They had been told by Sacirbey that the talks were over, and, in fact, we would make such an announcement at 10:00 A.M. unless the offer to put Brcko under arbitration was accepted. Time had run out, and we needed an answer immediately.

There was a long, agonizing pause. We watched Izetbegovic carefully. No one spoke. Finally, speaking slowly, Izetbegovic said, "It is not a just peace." He paused for what seemed like a minute, but was probably only three seconds. "But my people need peace."

Remembering how often things had unraveled with the Bosnians in the past, I did not want to discuss anything else. Leaning over to Christopher, I whispered, "Let's get out of here fast," and rose. Christopher shook Izetbegovic's hand and turned rapidly away. As we reached the door, I said to Sacirbey, "Why don't you come with us and work out with General Clark the final details of 51–49 right now." He said he would be over in a minute, and we left.

Christopher and I called President Clinton from my room, as our team crowded around, excited and relieved. The President offered to fly to Dayton for the announcement. "Mr. President," I said, "you don't want to be anywhere near these people today. They are wild, and they don't deserve a presidential visit." Instead, we suggested that the President make the initial announcement as quickly as possible from the White House, and we rescheduled the ceremony for 3:00 P.M. We also suggested that Secretary Perry and General Shalikashvili fly out to symbolize the Pentagon's support of the agreement.

When he heard that Izetbegovic had accepted his offer, Milosevic came to our rooms. He was in a highly emotional state. As he entered the room, he hugged Don Kerrick, and we saw tears in his eyes. He shook everyone's hand.

There was plenty of unfinished business in Dayton. Focused on the problems that still remained, we could not relax or celebrate yet. A re-energized negotiating team went into action across many fronts at once. Clark and Sacirbey began the tricky process of shaving the map by 1 percent. Kornblum, Owen, and Miriam Sapiro convened the three Foreign Ministers to work out several details of the political annexes. The refugee voting issue was settled by a compromise that permitted people to vote in the area where they had lived in 1991, as the Bosnians wanted, but allowed them to apply to an electoral commission for the right to vote elsewhere, as the Serbs wanted. Two years later this provision would be important, enabling Muslims to elect eighteen members of the eighty-four seat Republika Srpska Assembly.

President Clinton made the announcement from the Rose Garden at 11:40 that morning. "After nearly four years, two hundred and fifty thousand people killed, two million refugees, and atrocities that have appalled people all over the world, the people of Bosnia finally have a chance to turn from the horror of war to the promise of peace," he said. He called on the American people—

and especially Congress—to support the agreement with American troops. "Now that a detailed settlement has been reached, NATO will rapidly complete its planning for IFOR. American leadership, together with our allies, is needed to make this peace real and enduring. Our values, our interests, and our leadership all over the world are at stake."

We briefed the Contact Group, and then brought the three Presidents to Christopher's suite at the Hope Center for lunch and discussion of the remaining details. In order to strengthen our case with Congress, I drafted a letter to President Clinton, which I insisted that all three Presidents sign, in which each man personally guaranteed the safety of the NATO/IFOR troops.

By prearrangement, President Clinton called Christopher's suite during the lunch. The three men huddled around the speakerphone, leaning closer and closer to one another as they strained to listen to President Clinton as he congratulated them. Christopher and I glanced at each other, half amused, half astonished at the sight of Izetbegovic, Tudjman, and Milosevic with their heads almost touching.

Meanwhile, Hill and Kerrick had made an alarming discovery. In conversation with Foreign Minister Milutinovic, they learned that no Bosnian Serb would initial the agreement. In fact, Milutinovic told them, the Bosnian Serb delegation had seen the map for the first time just before lunch. "They went completely crazy," Milutinovic said with a laugh. Milosevic had decided that Milutinovic would initial for the Republika Srpska.

This was unacceptable. What good would the agreement be if the Bosnian Serbs refused to initial? And why would the signature of the Foreign Minister of the Federal Republic of Yugoslavia be valid for Pale? I asked Hill and Kerrick to find Milosevic and tell him that we would delay the initialing ceremony until he got the Bosnian Serb signatures.

Milosevic professed amazement at our attitude. "Why are you making such a big thing of such bullshit?" he asked. "I'll get the Republika Srpska signatures as soon as I return."

"Why can't Krajisnik initial now?" they demanded. Milosevic laughed. "Because he is in a coma after seeing the map."

After further discussion, we decided to accept Milosevic's initials—though not those of his Foreign Minister—in place of Republika Srpska, but on one condition: that Milosevic sign a separate letter, addressed to Christopher, promising that he would deliver the Pale signatures within ten days. He mocked this letter as completely unnecessary. "I guarantee you that I will have the signatures within twenty-four hours of my return to Belgrade," he said. (And he was right; the Bosnian Serbs, including Karadzic, signed the agreement the day after Milosevic returned to Belgrade.)

· · ·

The ceremony that we had not even dared dream about—"a day that many believed would never come," as Warren Christopher put it—began at 3:00 P.M. in the same room at the Hope Center where it had all begun twenty-one days earlier. Facing the press and our colleagues, I could see in the front row Katharina Frasure, Gail Kruzel, and Sandy Drew—proud, silent witnesses to the price we had paid for the agreement. Around them were the members of the Contact Group, our negotiating team, and General Shalikashvili and Deputy Secretary of Defense John White, filling in for Perry.

Christopher began the ceremonies by outlining the positive features of the agreement, but cautioned that the road to full implementation would not be easy. Carl Bildt followed with a short and generous statement of praise for the Americans, with special thanks to the staff of Packy's All-Sports Bar. Knowing that he would now be the senior civilian responsible for implementation, Bildt talked of the "massive effort by the international community" that would be required.

As the third co-chairman of the conference, Igor Ivanov had not played a major role, but he spoke next. To our surprise, he announced that his government would "reserve its position in regard to the military and arms-control annexes." It was a minor hiccup on a day of great achievement, and was soon ironed out. More importantly, President Yeltsin had spoken to the Russian people about his country's support for the basic agreement at Dayton immediately after President Clinton's first announcement, and pledged his country's participation in the effort.

Milosevic was next, his first public words since arriving. He spoke optimistically about the future, calling November 21, 1995, the day that "will enter history as the date of the end of the war." All sides, Milosevic said, had made "painful concessions," but now "the war in Bosnia should be left to the past."

Washington was most concerned about what Izetbegovic would say. Jim Steinberg worried that Izetbegovic would repeat publicly his private comment that the agreement was an "unjust peace," and asked Menzies to try to talk the Bosnians into a positive statement. But Izetbegovic's real audience was in Bosnia, and he was not ready to give unequivocal praise to an agreement that troubled him and that he was not sure the Serbs would respect. After calling this "a historic day for Bosnia and for the rest of the world because the war, we hope, will be replaced by peace," Izetbegovic began the delicate process of gaining support for the agreement at home:

> And to my people, I say, this may not be a just peace, but it is more just than a
> continuation of war. In the situation as it is and in the world as it is, a better peace
> could not have been achieved. God is our witness that we have done everything

in our power so that the extent of injustice for our people and our country would be decreased.

In the crush of last-minute problems and details, I had not thought about my own remarks until after the ceremony was already under way. I therefore had to write my statement while half-listening to the previous speakers. My mood was more one of relief than exhilaration, more weariness rather than euphoria. I could not find a way to share in the joy that some of the participants showed, even though I wanted to. After the behavior we had seen from some of the participants at Dayton, I was more worried than ever about implementing the agreement. As several reporters pointed out the next day, my remarks were notable for their cautionary tone, far more so than that of any of the other speakers that day. They began with a tribute to Bob Frasure, Joe Kruzel, and Nelson Drew, and continued:

> The agreements and territorial arrangements initialed here today are a huge step forward, the biggest by far since the war began. But ahead lies an equally daunting task: implementation. On every page of the many complicated documents and annexes initialed here today lie challenges to both sides to set aside their enmities, their differences, which are still raw with open wounds. On paper, we have peace. To make it work is our next and greatest challenge. . . .
>
> It's been a long and winding road for all of us, and it's not over yet—far from it. The immense difficulties and the roller-coaster ride we have lived through in Dayton over the last twenty-one days, and especially in the last few days, only serve to remind us how much work lies ahead. Let us pledge, therefore, that this day in Dayton be long remembered as the day on which Bosnia and its neighbors turned from war to peace.

BOOK FOUR

IMPLEMENTATION

Between the idea
And the reality
Between the motion
And the act
Falls the Shadow.

—T. S. ELIOT

CHAPTER 19

Slow Start

(November 21, 1995–February 21, 1996)

In 1884, at the International Meridian Conference in Washington, D.C., representatives from twenty-six countries voted to make . . . the Greenwich meridian the prime meridian of the world. This decision did not sit well with the French, however, who continued to recognize their own Paris Observatory meridian, a little more than two degrees east of Greenwich, as the starting line for another twenty-seven years, until 1911. Even then, they hesitated to refer directly to Greenwich mean time, preferring the locution "Paris Mean Time, retarded by nine minutes twenty-one seconds."

—DAVA SOBEL, *Longitude: The True Story of a
Lone Genius Who Solved the Greatest Scientific
Problem of His Time*

AN HOUR AFTER THE DAYTON INITIALING CEREMONY, Kati and I flew with General Shalikashvili to New York. Leaving Wright-Patterson Air Force Base was like release from a comfortable prison; we slowly rediscovered the outside world. Still, after twenty-one days of isolation, normal life seemed far away. The extraordinary public reaction to the Dayton agreement was immensely gratifying, but in the rush of tasks that needed to be done, there was no time to savor it.

Meeting with the President. The next day, November 22, we met at the White House in an atmosphere that combined relief, pride, and apprehension. Lake's opening quip reflected the tone: "We're in a heap of trouble now—but it's the right kind of trouble." The President, arriving with Gore a few moments later, thanked everyone, and joked, "I was all set for a disappointment."

Asked to begin, I said that the arrest of Karadzic and Mladic was the most critical issue that was not resolved at Dayton. I repeated my view that if the two men, particularly Karadzic, the founder and leader of a still-unrepentant separatist movement, remained at large, full implementation of the agreement would be impossible. The President concurred, saying, "It is best to remove both men." Without giving a direct instruction, he asked the military to reconsider the issue.

He then shifted to a more immediate issue: gaining public and congressional support for the policy. "I must be brutally honest with the American people," he said. "When I address the people I must be sure our military and intelligence people have signed off. I must be honest about what we are getting into."

Vice President Gore said Dayton was a gamble worth taking. He paused for a moment, and his face took on a sharp focus. "I want to make an important practical point regarding the JCS and the Pentagon," he said, looking directly at the Defense representatives in the room. "I've had lots of conversations with the Congress. They have told me that our military representatives on the Hill usually leave their audience more uncomfortable than when they arrived. I'm not saying they are trying to undercut our policy, but they are losing us votes up there."

After a brief, stunned silence, Deputy Defense Secretary John White took up the challenge: "We need answers that Shali and his colleagues can all feel comfortable with."

The President stepped in to support Gore. "My sense," he said, "is that the diplomatic breakthrough in Dayton has given us a chance to prevail in Congress and in the nation. People see the stakes and the big picture. But we can't get congressional support without Defense and the military fully behind this. We must show Congress the stakes and the consequences. We can't promise them zero casualties, but we have to convey a high level of confidence in our capacity to carry out the mission and to manage the gaps in the agreement. Your people have body language. It's not a question of being dishonest, but we can't close the deal without the Pentagon's support." He looked directly at Shalikashvili. "I know there has been ambivalence among some of your people—not you, Shali, but some of your people—about Bosnia," he said, "but that is all in the past. I want everyone here to get behind the agreement."

The two men rose to leave, and we all rose with them. Their message would have a substantial effect. When the President and Vice President tell their senior aides to get with the program, and when they say it with vigor and even an unmistakable sternness, it does wonders for a divided or reluctant bureaucracy. I wondered if the two men had coordinated their comments; a year later the President told me that they had.

Congress and the Public. While the public applauded our diplomatic efforts, opinion polls put public opposition to the deployment of American forces to Bosnia at around 70 percent. This was understandable. For almost four years, Americans had watched television pictures of United Nations troops being killed and wounded while unable to defend themselves adequately. Most Americans assumed we were sending our own troops into a similar situation, where they would suffer heavy casualties.

Sending American troops to Bosnia would be the single most unpopular action of President Clinton's entire first term. Although the public was proud of the American diplomatic role in ending the war, we had to convince them that the American deployments would be different from those of the U.N., that NATO would shoot first and ask questions later—and that the deployment was in our national interest. *Newsweek* wryly captured the paradoxical situation in its first post-Dayton issue in an article by Evan Thomas and John Barry:

> Hail Pax Americana! Salute the return of the superpower! Or, then again, maybe not. The foreign-policy establishment may cheer, and Balkan brigands may head for the hills, but ordinary Americans are decidedly wary of sacrifices ahead. . . . Most voters regard Bosnia as someone else's civil war. It will be up to President Clinton to convince them otherwise. . . . Baffled by Bosnia or distracted by domestic concerns, most Americans have not begun to realize the reach and depth of the U.S. commitment made last week in Dayton.

Some important members of Congress immediately came to our support: Senators Lieberman, Biden, and Lugar once again were in the forefront. Some qualified their support by tying it to a tight "exit strategy." Since the Administration had written a one-year timetable into the Dayton agreement, we could not object. Many others opposed the policy outright. Such a position was essentially cost-free, since the Congress knew that the President would send troops regardless of what it did (barring an absolute cutoff of funds, which was very unlikely). Thus members of Congress could take a politically popular position without having to worry about its consequences. Speaker Gingrich predicted that the Administration would win "guarded approval, even acquiescence through inaction" and produced an artfully evasive resolution that allowed his colleagues in the House to vote both sides of the issue; they could give, as he put it, "very strong support for the troops [while objecting to] the president's policy."

In this atmosphere Donilon, Burns, and McCurry coordinated an intense public relations campaign. The President invited many members of Congress to the White House for briefings, and sent Christopher, Perry, Shalikashvili, and me to the Hill. In December we organized two large congressional delegations to the Balkans. Almost seventy members, an astonishing 15 percent of the entire House, went on these trips. Without exception, the members who went came back swayed in favor of the policy, although participation did not automatically mean full support. Cynthia McKinney, a first-term Democrat from an overwhelmingly black district in Georgia, who had previously focused on domestic issues and expressed great skepticism about foreign "giveaways," was typical. She told me later, "The trip changed my life. It made me realize that we have to undertake some of the same responsibilities overseas that we need to do at home, and that we must find a way to do both."

Europe: Applause and Shock. Dayton shook the leadership elite of post–Cold War Europe. The Europeans were grateful to the United States for leading the effort that finally ended the war in Bosnia, but some European officials were embarrassed that American involvement had been necessary. Jacques Poos's 1991 assertion that Europe's "hour had dawned" lay in history's dustbin, alongside James Baker's view that we had no dog in that fight.

"One cannot call it an American peace," French Foreign Minister de Charette told the press, "even if President Clinton and the Americans have tried to pull the blanket over to their side. The fact is that the Americans looked at this affair in ex-Yugoslavia from a great distance for nearly four years and basically blocked the progression of things." But de Charette also acknowledged that "Europe as such was not present, and this, it is true, was a failure of the European Union." Prime Minister Alain Juppé, after praising the Dayton agreement, could not resist adding, "Of course, it resembles like a twin the European plan we presented eighteen months ago"—when he was Foreign Minister. Agence France-Presse reported that many European diplomats were "left smarting" at Dayton. In an article clearly inspired by someone at the French Foreign Ministry, *Le Figaro* said that "Richard Holbrooke, the American mediator, did not leave his European colleagues with good memories from the air base at Dayton." They quoted an unnamed French diplomat as saying, "He flatters, he lies, he humiliates: he is a sort of brutal and schizophrenic Mazarin."* President Chirac's national security assistant, Jean-David Levitte, called to apologize for this comment, saying it did not represent the views of his boss. I replied that such minidramas were inevitable given the pressures and frustrations we faced at Dayton and were inconsequential considering that the war was over.

With two weeks remaining before the formal signing of the agreement in Paris, Karadzic raised temperatures again in the region. Although he had signed the agreement under Milosevic's pressure, he announced that Sarajevo would "bleed for decades" unless we changed the Dayton terms. In response, we said that we would not change the agreement. Defending the most prob-

---

* Cardinal Jules Mazarin, a famously cunning and powerful seventeenth-century prelate, succeeded Cardinal Richelieu as chief minister to Louis XIII.

lematic part of American policy, Perry predicted that "one year will be sufficient to break the cycle of violence in Bosnia." Perry broke the year down into two phases, four to six months to enforce a truce and disarmament, and another six months to create a secure environment. As it turned out, he was overly pessimistic on the first task, and overly optimistic on the second.

There was much work left before the signing ceremony. NATO had to send sixty thousand troops to Bosnia—the largest troop movement in Western Europe since World War II—and deploy thousands more off the Adriatic coast and at a forward logistics base in Hungary. On the civilian side, a series of high-level conferences were jammed into the two weeks immediately preceding the Paris ceremony. First came the annual NATO Foreign Ministers meeting in Brussels on December 5 and 6, which focused heavily on Bosnia. One day later, the scene shifted to Budapest for the annual meeting of the Foreign Ministers of the OSCE, who had to set up the machinery to oversee the elections in Bosnia as called for in the Dayton Peace Agreement. On December 8, the British convened a high-level "Implementation Conference" in London to discuss how to handle the nonmilitary parts of Dayton. Warren Christopher and John Kornblum attended the first two conferences, while Strobe Talbott and Bob Gallucci led the American team to London and Budapest. Meanwhile, I reassembled the negotiating team and returned to the Balkans to pin down the final details for the Paris ceremonies.

This blizzard of diffused activity demonstrated the key difference between the negotiations and the phase that was beginning. The previous fourteen weeks had been highly focused. Now a wide-ranging effort, involving thousands of civilian and military personnel from the United States and other countries, was about to begin. Unfortunately, we had created a structure for implementing Dayton in which responsibility and authority would rest with no single individual or institution. Although Bosnia would play host to fewer agencies than it had during the U.N. days, too many still remained in the process, including NATO, the U.N. and the UNHCR, the OSCE, the E.U., the World Bank, the IMF—and an organization with no precedent, the Office of the High Representative, headed by Carl Bildt.

"Foreign Forces and Elements." When our team met Izetbegovic in Sarajevo on December 8, he was animated and jovial. But his mood darkened when we pressed him on the presence of "foreign forces and elements" in the Muslim portion of Bosnia. These were the Iranians and mujahideen who had been helping the Bosnian Muslims for the previous three years. American intelligence had long known of their existence—they were prominently mentioned, in fact, in my January 1993 memorandum to the incoming Administration—but during the war Washington had not made an issue of their presence since they were helping the otherwise isolated Bosnians to survive. The Dayton agreement required their complete withdrawal within thirty days after the arrival of IFOR, scheduled for December 20. I told Izetbegovic we would withhold our support for the Equip and Train program unless the Iranians and the mujahideen left. The press, aware of their presence, was running stories with headlines that particularly alarmed Congress (*The Washington Post,* November 30: "Foreign Muslims Fighting in Bosnia Considered 'Threat' to U.S. Troops"; *The New York Times,* December 10: "What's Iran Doing in Bosnia Anyway?"). With NATO forces about to arrive in Bosnia, we could not tolerate the continued presence of these people in Bosnia, especially since some had ties to groups in the Middle East that had committed terrorist acts against American troops.

Extremely uncomfortable with this subject, Izetbegovic pledged that the foreign elements would leave within the Dayton timetable "if there is peace." This was only the first of many conversations we would have on this troublesome issue.

In Pale, Karadzic was still giving inflammatory interviews, to our intense annoyance. On December 2, I wrote Milosevic an angry letter demanding that he get the Bosnian Serbs under control. After reading the letter, Milosevic told Rudy Perina that he had been meeting with Bosnian Serb leaders all week, pressing them to "support" Dayton. Six days later, when we met with Milosevic, he told us confidently that he was succeeding. But on the future of Karadzic and Mladic, Milosevic remained adamant; he could not, and would not, deliver the two men to an international tribunal.

I was concerned that we would not get off to a fast enough start. "Everything depends on a vigorous implementation by IFOR *from the first day,*" I cabled Christopher at the end of the trip. "A slow start would be a mistake."

One day before the Paris ceremony, under pressure from the White House, Congress voted on the deployments. In the Senate, with crucial support from Senator Dole, the Administration won a surprisingly easy 69-to-30 victory. In the House, Gingrich's odd approach produced a 287-to-141 vote to oppose the Administration's policy while "supporting" the troops. Coupled with defeats in each house for proposals to cut off funds for the mission, it was enough for Mike McCurry to claim victory. "This is probably the strongest statement of support they could possibly make," he said. "Having voted overwhelmingly not to shut off funding is, in a sense, supporting the President's judgment."

Paris. By the time of the vote, the negotiating team was already in Paris. The day before the ceremonies, in the midst of a gigantic strike of transit workers that paralyzed Paris, I met Foreign Minister de Charette alone to discuss the unresolved issue of whether an American or a European would run the OSCE election unit in Bosnia.

The meeting quickly turned into a general discussion of the relationship between our two countries. I observed that no nation had done more in Bosnia than France. President Chirac's personal intervention with President Clinton during his June trip to Washington had been vital in focusing the Administration. Success in the future depended critically on close French-American cooperation, especially since the French military would be responsible for the Sarajevo Sector, as it had been during the war. Finally, I reminded de Charette that we had kept our promise to have the formal signing ceremony in Paris.

We had agreed to let Europeans head every civilian implementation institution in Bosnia, I said. But there was one exception: we would not yield on the OSCE election unit. The reason was simple: the final wording at Dayton— that the OSCE would "oversee and conduct" the elections—was sufficiently ambiguous that we wanted to ensure a maximalist approach. This required someone of our own choosing.

He and President Chirac, de Charette said, were equally adamant that this position go to a Frenchman. These elections would take place in Europe, and they required a European to head the OSCE team. We went back and forth for a while. I ended the discussion by noting that when President Clinton arrived in the morning, he would take the matter up directly with President Chirac— and he would not yield.

On the morning of December 14, President Clinton and his team arrived in Paris for the signing of the peace agreement. He met in the dining room of the Ambassador's residence with the three Balkan Presidents prior to the formal ceremonies at the Élysée Palace. Two weeks earlier he had made a spectacularly successful trip to both Ireland and Northern Ireland; now he made an eloquent comparison between Bosnia and Ireland. After fifteen months of cease-fire in Ireland, he said, "it is unthinkable for the people to go backward. The whole situation has changed. You need to do the same."

After the meeting, we eased the three Presidents into separate parts of the room, and President Clinton moved among them, spending a few minutes with each. The President told Tudjman that we would send Jacques Klein, a career Foreign Service officer who was also a retired Air Force Reserve general, to eastern Slavonia to oversee the transition of the area to Croatia. With Izetbegovic, the President focused on the dangers posed to the NATO troops by the Iranians and the mujahideen. "If any action is taken against our troops," he said, "it could shatter the whole venture and jeopardize our ability to equip and train your forces. I want to do what I promised, but this could undermine my commitment." Izetbegovic told the President that the bulk of such personnel "had already left," a statement we knew not to be true.

Finally came the President's first discussion with Milosevic. The White House had taken care to ensure that there would be no photographs of the encounter. Still, this was a meeting Milosevic had long wanted; it put him on a plane with other world leaders after years of isolation. "I know this agreement would not have been possible without you," President Clinton said, cool and slightly distant. "You made Dayton possible. Now you must help make it work."

Milosevic said that the key to peace lay in strict implementation of the Dayton agreements. Then he requested full normalization of U.S.-Yugoslav (i.e., Serbian) relations. We swiftly ended the discussion.

Ceremony. Minutes later we were at the Élysée Palace, the home of the President of France, for the formal signing ceremony. First, however, President Chirac wanted to see President Clinton alone. As we waited outside their private meeting room, de Charette approached Warren Christopher and me. "Our President has decided to give you Americans the OSCE election position," he said dryly. "We have our doubts it will work. I hope this is satisfactory to you."

We walked to the ballroom of the Élysée Palace, where we were led to assigned seats facing a long table at which sat the three Balkan Presidents. Behind them stood President Chirac, President Clinton, Chancellor Kohl, Prime Minister Major, and Prime Minister Chernomyrdin, filling in for the ailing Boris Yeltsin. One by one the leaders signed, as either principals or witnesses. The Presidents and Prime Ministers spoke, as did Carl Bildt and, oddly, a man whose actions had contributed so little to the ending of the war, Boutros Boutros-Ghali.

In a strange, almost touching footnote to its sense of injured pride, the French Foreign Ministry called the Dayton Peace Agreement the "Treaty of the Élysée," and asked the speakers to omit any references to Dayton in their remarks. In addition, it seated Tony Lake, Sandy Berger, General Clark, and me near the back of the room, behind many officials and guests who had played no role in the negotiations. This was inconsequential (and Levitte apologized for it later), and if several newspapers had not noted it the next day, it would not be worthy of recording. I did not judge these sad actions by one or two *functionnaires* as representative of the country in which I had lived as a teenager, which had influenced me so much, and for which I had such affection. By wielding the ephemeral power of protocol with such a heavy hand, a few Foreign Office bureaucrats only diminished their country's important contributions to achieving peace in Bosnia.

After the ceremony, we all moved on to the Quai d'Orsay, where Chirac hosted a large banquet. At the end of the meal, the French president pulled me aside for a moment. "*Mon cher* Holbrooke," he said, in great good humor, "you have won your point on the elections, but you will see that it is inappropriate for any American, even any European, to conduct these elections in such a place as Bosnia." I said I hoped events would prove him wrong. At that moment, Milosevic came up to us and, picking up on the subject, told Chirac that he would make the elections work.

Once again the scene became somewhat surreal. Smoking a cigar, Milosevic sought out President Clinton, with whom he engaged in small talk. Milosevic clearly relished the moment; as Pardew told Bill Perry later, "the Serbian President was last seen in the magnificent hall of the Quai d'Orsay puffing on a cigar half the size of a fence post while making one last—but futile—effort to charm the U.S. President."

We flew home on Air Force One, exhausted but awed by what we had witnessed. Despite the minor irritations, the event had been successful in giving the Dayton Agreement the aura that came with a formal ceremony, witnessed by five of the world's most powerful leaders. It was entirely appropriate that it was formally signed in Europe, the continent on which the war had been fought.

The President was in a good mood as we flew home. He came back to the second cabin to ask Clark, Kerrick, and me how we thought implementation would proceed. "We will have far fewer casualties than the public and the Congress expect," I said. The President seemed skeptical; after all, he had heard ominous scenarios from the Pentagon. Clark and Kerrick pointed out that official estimates had to be cautious. But none of us could have imagined just how low the casualty rate actually would be—*zero* American forces killed or wounded from hostile action in the first two years after Dayton.

There was a more difficult discussion I had to have with the President, and about an hour out of Paris I sat down alone with him in his office near the front of the plane.

"Mr. President, the time has come for me to make a tough decision," I began, somewhat stiffly. "I want to ask your support and understanding for my request to leave the government early next year." Before leaving Germany, I told him, I had promised Kati—and told Christopher and Talbott—that, since she could not move to Washington because of her children, I would return to New York within a limited period of time. This had already been extended because of the negotiations, but the time had come.

The President was gracious and compassionate. "Family is terribly important," he said, and we talked about the strains that public service puts on families. This was one of the most difficult decisions of my life—a choice between a job to which I was fully dedicated and a personal commitment that was precious to me, and I was touched by the President's support. He asked me to stay on as long as possible to get implementation headed in the right direction, and requested that I remain available for special assignments in the future.

For Deploys. On December 16, General Joulwan issued the order to begin moving NATO and other forces to Bosnia. It was the first such troop-deployment order since NATO had been formed in 1949.* Most of the U.N. troops already in Bosnia repainted their vehicles from white to a more military-looking olive green, traded in light weapons for heavier ones, and were reassigned to IFOR, the Implementation Force.

American journalists flooded Bosnia to cover the arrival of U.S. troops, led by two of the three network anchors, Tom Brokaw and Dan Rather. Modern journalism requires that if such stars go out on a story, the story has to be good—that is, dramatic. But the only story was the bad weather, which delayed the crossing of the Sava River for several days. Unable to show any tension or conflict between the arriving American forces and the local population, television exaggerated the dangers facing the troops, and covered the arrival in a sort of retro-Vietnam style that misled the American public as to the dangers the troops faced.

Attention would shift away from Bosnia fairly soon, when it became apparent that IFOR was having an easy, untroubled entry. Of course, *this* was the real story, and it was important; there was to be no repetition of the U.N.'s dreadful experience.

A Slow Start for the Civilians. The same was not true on the civilian side. At first, Carl Bildt, now the High Representative, had so little money and support that he was forced to operate without an office or telephones, and used his personal cellular telephone as his primary means of communication. After appeals to the European Union, he received enough funding to open his offices in Sarajevo, where he presided like an elegant squatter over a building filled with wrecked rooms, broken toilets, shattered windows, and almost no staff.

This lag in civilian implementation troubled us enormously, although we shared in the blame for it. While the military, sixty thousand strong, met every early deadline, the civilian side, functioning out of Carl Bildt's cellular telephone, met almost none, and fell steadily behind schedule. For this Bildt was personally criticized, but the fault was more in the structures we had imposed on him, particularly the failure to give him sufficient funding or stronger backing from IFOR.

Furthermore, with a weak police advisory effort, Bildt had no enforcement capability for his task. Now the full consequences of the absurd position taken

---

* Forces normally assigned to NATO were reassigned for use in the 1991 war against Iraq, but Desert Storm was not a NATO operation.

by NATO—opposing a police force with enforcement capability while itself refusing the task—began to come home to roost.

To say that I was concerned would be an understatement. Having announced my early departure, I agreed to a one-month delay at the request of Christopher to help address the mounting problems. I realized later that I should have stayed longer, but by then we were locked into a firm departure schedule.

The President Visits Bosnia. The President wanted to visit the troops as soon as possible, and scheduled a trip for mid-January. The trip was unusually difficult, posing, as one White House official said publicly, "more logistical, security, and weather variables" than they had ever encountered before. I had hoped that the President would be able to visit Sarajevo, but the risks were deemed too great by those responsible for presidential security, so it was decided that the only stop in Bosnia would be the American military base at Tuzla.

On Friday afternoon, January 12, we flew to the American air base at Aviano, Italy, landing before dawn. As the President spoke to American soldiers and their families, bad weather reports poured in from the Balkans, delaying our departure. After two hours on the ground in Italy, we piled into a C-17, a modern, high-performance military cargo plane, for the flight to Tuzla. Four parallel rows of plastic seats facing each other down the middle of the plane created an unusually egalitarian arrangement: the President, his top advisors, and a bipartisan congressional delegation sat almost at random next to journalists, camera crews, enlisted men and women, and a cargo of food for the troops.

With the weather playing to stereotype, we circled over the landing strip at Tuzla for almost an hour. Finally we landed at the American staging area in Taszar, Hungary, where six thousand American troops had established a forward logistics base for Bosnia. We had planned a brief stop at Taszar later in the day, but we arrived almost seven hours ahead of schedule. Moving fast, the American military took the President to a large tent, where he spoke to American troops while we waited for the weather in Bosnia to clear. I wandered around the base, marveling at how quickly the U.S. military could re-create a special universe and culture almost overnight in any corner of the world. The ankle-deep mud, the wooden pathways, the signs stressing communications security and safety, the individual unit insignias, the small PX, the troops, slightly uncertain of what they were doing in Hungary but ready to carry out their mission—all reminded me vaguely of a war thirty years earlier on the other side of the world. But there were also noticeable differences from Vietnam: most markedly the presence of so many women in uniform, and the cleaner, tighter look of the troops.

Early in the Administration, the President had had well-publicized difficulties dealing with the military because of questions over why he had not served in Vietnam, but by 1996 these were a fading memory. A generation of soldiers who were born after the war in Vietnam ended looked at Bill Clinton as *their* President. They seemed pleased he had come to see them, and he was at ease as he chatted with them. The military's greeting of the President, it seemed to me, was genuinely enthusiastic, and the troops filled the tented area with a war whoop—it sounded like they were grunting "Hoo-aa!"—that shook the ground.

Eventually Hungarian President Arpad Goncz, Prime Minister Gyula Horn, Foreign Minister Lazlo Kovacs, and Ambassador Donald Blinken arrived in two small planes. In the chaos and the excitement of President Clinton's presence, no one met the Hungarian officials, arriving on their own soil, except me and, by chance, Dan Rather, covering the trip for CBS. We squeezed the Hungarians and Ambassador Blinken into some mud-caked military vehicles and sped off to meet President Clinton, driving past a row of broken-down MiG fighter planes, a relic of the Cold War. The presence of six thousand American troops on Hungarian soil only four years after the end of the Cold War—and forty years after the 1956 Soviet invasion—was in itself a remarkable symbol of the transformation of Europe. The Hungarians had one message for President Clinton: that they were ready for NATO membership and that the staging area at Taszar was part of that goal. "Stay as long as you like," they said. "Turn this into a permanent NATO installation—and let us join the West."

The weather at Tuzla was clearing, but by the time we landed, just before 3:00 P.M., daylight was fast disappearing, and the Secret Service put an absolute time limit on our stay. A trip originally scheduled for eight hours was now down to less than three; the schedule collapsed into a makeshift set of quick meetings. The President, dressed in a brown leather bomber jacket and khakis, addressed the troops, who had waited for over two hours outside. Under slate-gray skies, as Apache attack helicopters flew overhead and Secret Service sharpshooters followed his every move, he called the troops "warriors for peace" who had the support and prayers of the American people, and gave promotions to five enlisted men.

After the speech and a meeting with senior military officers, we had originally scheduled three important meetings: first, with President Izetbegovic and members of his government; then, with representatives of the leading nongovernmental organizations in Bosnia; and finally, with civic and religious leaders of Bosnia. The last meeting, planned at my request, was designed to stimulate the leaders of the Muslim, Orthodox, Catholic, and Jewish communities to work for reconciliation. The religious leaders of the region had done great damage since 1991, stirring up ancient but long-submerged desires for revenge among their followers. This meeting appealed to President Clinton's sense of the importance of religious leaders for good and bad, derived from his own Southern Baptist background. But with the schedule in disarray, we had to reduce the meeting with Izetbegovic to ten minutes, and combine the last two sessions, turning the plan into a shambles. The President entered a small, overheated room crowded with a diverse group: Catholic priests (including Vinko Cardinal Puljic), Orthodox prelates (led by the Metropolitan Nikolaj), Muslim mullahs, the Muslim and Serb mayors of Sarajevo, Jewish community leaders, Americans and Europeans representing a dozen humanitarian organizations, journalists, and security personnel—and three widows who had lost their husbands during the war. As everyone else yelled and pushed, the President calmly walked through the room, greeting almost everyone individually. Then, as he spoke movingly about the need for religious reconciliation, Harold Ickes, the White House Deputy Chief of Staff, pulled me aside and said that the Secret Service insisted that we leave within five minutes. As the astonished and disappointed Bosnians watched, I almost yanked the President out of the room. Our ambitious game plan to use the trip to begin a multiethnic dialogue had gone down the drain with the weather.

As we were leaving, an American colonel handed me a small plastic bag with something inside it. "A Bosnian soldier found this near the wreckage on Mount Igman and turned it in to the American Embassy," he said. "It's Nelson Drew's Air Force Academy class ring. Would you deliver it to Mrs. Drew?" Sandy Drew has carried it with her ever since.

Another Shuttle—and Problems. A week later, on January 18, our team was back in Sarajevo. While most people were saying that implementation had just begun, I was acutely conscious of a different equation: the IFOR year was already one twelfth over, and nothing had been accomplished on the political front.

Still, the trip from the airport into Sarajevo was exhilarating. For the first time we drove through Serb-controlled areas of the city, cutting fifteen minutes off the trip and using roads that had been closed for years. The city was showing more signs of recovery; in a particularly bold move, one merchant had opened a store with a large plate-glass window.

Our meeting with Admiral Leighton Smith, on the other hand, did not go well. He had been in charge of the NATO air strikes in August and September, and this gave him enormous credibility, especially with the Bosnian Serbs. Smith was also the beneficiary of a skillful public relations effort that cast him as the savior of Bosnia. In a long profile, *Newsweek* had called him "a complex warrior and civilizer, a latter-day George C. Marshall." This was quite a journalistic stretch, given the fact that Smith considered the civilian aspects of the task beneath him and not his job—quite the opposite of what General Marshall stood for.

After a distinguished thirty-three-year Navy career, including almost three hundred combat missions in Vietnam, Smith was well qualified for his original posts as commander of NATO's southern forces and Commander in Chief of all U.S. naval forces in Europe. But he was the wrong man for his additional assignment as IFOR commander, which was the result of two bureaucratic compromises, one with the French, the other within the American military. General Joulwan rightly wanted the sixty thousand IFOR soldiers to have as their commanding officer an Army general trained in the use of ground forces. But Paris insisted that if Joulwan named a separate Bosnia commander, it would have to be a Frenchman. This was politically impossible for the United States; thus, the French objections left only one way to preserve an American chain of command—to give the job to Admiral Smith, who joked that he was now known as "General" Smith.*

Smith treated us like VIP tourists visiting Sarajevo for the first time, offering us a canned briefing full of military charts and vague "mission statements." Close to thirty of his multinational staff sat behind us, saying nothing. On the military goals of Dayton, he was fine; his plans for separating the forces along the line we had drawn in Dayton and protecting his forces were first-rate. But he was hostile to any suggestion that IFOR help implement any nonmilitary portion of the agreement. This, he said repeatedly, was not his job.

Based on Shalikashvili's statements at White House meetings, Christopher and I had assumed that the IFOR commander would use his *authority* to do substantially more than he was *obligated* to do. The meeting with Smith shattered that hope. Smith and his British deputy, General Michael Walker, made clear that they intended to take a minimalist approach to all aspects of implementation other than force protection. Smith signaled this in his first extensive public statement to the Bosnian people, during a live call-in program on Pale Television—an odd choice for his first local media appearance. During the program, he answered a question in a manner that dangerously narrowed his own authority. He later told *Newsweek* about it with a curious pride:

> One of the questions I was asked was, "Admiral, is it true that IFOR is going to arrest Serbs in the Serb suburbs of Sarajevo?" I said, "Absolutely not, *I don't have the authority to arrest anybody.*" [Emphasis added.]

This was an inaccurate way to describe IFOR's mandate. It was true IFOR was not supposed to make routine arrests of ordinary citizens. But IFOR had

---

* Joulwan finally got the command structure that he wanted—the right one—in 1997, when a four-star Army general took over the Bosnia command.

the authority to arrest indicted war criminals, and could also detain anyone who posed a threat to its forces. Knowing what the question meant, Smith had sent an unfortunate signal of reassurance to Karadzic—over his own network.

An hour after our meeting with Smith, we met Izetbegovic and asked him to urge the Serbs who still lived in Sarajevo to stay after the city was unified under Muslim control on March 19. Izetbegovic said he would make the statement, but stressed that it could apply only to those Serbs who had lived in Sarajevo before the war, and not those who had seized Muslim apartments after April 1992, often with a sniper or soldier as a live-in member of the family. Within two months, this issue—the unification of Sarajevo—would emerge as the first true post-Dayton crisis, and the international community would fail it.*

I returned to Washington to warn Christopher and his colleagues again that the civilian effort was already dangerously behind schedule. Christopher talked to Lake and Perry. But bureaucratic inertia and the resistance of the military prevented any serious effort to change the behavior of IFOR. Lake was especially wary of pressuring IFOR, arguing in public and private against anything that suggested that the military should engage in "nation building," a phrase that had been transformed since the sixties from a noble goal to a phrase meaning "mission creep."

Ron Brown. On January 31, I made a farewell call on Ron Brown, the Secretary of Commerce, who had given me exceptional support in Germany and Washington. In addition to thanking him, I asked him to undertake an important mission to Bosnia. Brown had been exceptionally effective in strengthening American exports and supporting business, and I thought his imagination and drive could give a huge boost to the economic reconstruction effort, one of the key long-term tests of our policy. Brown enthusiastically said he could lead a high-level trade delegation to Bosnia in March or April. He asked only that I get Warren Christopher to support the trip with the White House, which I assured him I would do.

Our friendship, like many in Washington, was political and professional, not personal, but I truly liked Ron Brown. He was then involved in several well-publicized investigations into his personal financial affairs, but of these I knew nothing. What I saw was a superb Cabinet member who had made a significant contribution to the resurgence of the American economy. Now he had agreed to launch an essential part of our Bosnia policy. I thanked him for his willingness to make the trip, added that perhaps I might travel with him as a private citizen, and said farewell. I would never see him again. Nine weeks

* See chapter 20.

later, on April 3, his plane, which also carried several other friends and associates, including Assistant Secretary of Commerce Charles Meissner, crashed into a mountain trying to land at Dubrovnik, on the Croatian coast, in a driving rainstorm. Thirty-five people died.

Jacques Chirac. On February 1, President Chirac visited Washington. The mood was strikingly different from his first trip in June 1995, when his blunt warnings had contributed to the re-evaluation of American policy. Now the agenda could focus on other issues, especially bringing new nations into NATO, the Administration's next big policy move in Europe.

In a moving and thoughtful gesture, Chirac held a ceremony at Blair House on February 1 to present the widows of Bob Frasure, Joe Kruzel, and Nelson Drew with the French Medal of Honor. What moved us most was the openness of Chirac's emotions. Standing next to Katharina Frasure as he gave her Bob's medal, I could see a large tear running down the cheek of the President of France.

The Last—and Longest—Trip. This was Warren Christopher's first trip to the region, and my last as a government official. At first, unlike for previous trips, there was no specific objective—only to say good-bye and bring Christopher and John Kornblum, who had been selected as my successor, up to speed. But by the time it ended, seventeen days later, it had become my longest trip, and it ended with a hastily planned Balkan summit in Rome.

We left Andrews Air Force Base on the Secretary's big jet on the morning of February 2, and met with Tudjman late that night in Zagreb. The next morning, after a briefing by Admiral Smith in Tuzla, we flew to Sarajevo. Christopher and his staff were fascinated to see the city they had read about for three years but never visited. Though rebuilding was under way and most of the barricades and wrecked vehicles had been removed, the sight of so much damage stunned them. To his pleasure, Christopher was greeted with cheers and applause when he ventured on a short walk. The next day, after lunch with Milosevic, Christopher headed toward the Mideast, and I took a commercial flight to Switzerland to attend the annual World Economic Forum meeting in Davos. After this, I hoped to launch our diplomatic initiative on Cyprus, accompanied by our Presidential Special Envoy for Cyprus, Richard Beattie, who would carry on the negotiation.*

The Davos conference was a strange affair. Several thousand people, most of them wealthy businessmen, milled around in groups, attending meetings, setting up meetings, skiing, or socializing. The press was everywhere. So were

---

* Beattie, a senior partner at a New York law firm, was appointed under government regulations that allow private citizens to serve on a part-time basis. In June 1997, he became a senior advisor to Secretary Albright for the reorganization of the State Department, and I became the envoy for Cyprus.

Russians and other leaders from the former Soviet Union, who set up shop in one of the many hotels and filled the lobby with the stench of cigarettes and spilled alcohol. The State Department set up a series of high-level meetings for me with leaders from Europe and Asia.

When I returned to my room there was an urgent message from Tom Donilon, who was in Syria with Christopher. "The Secretary has become increasingly concerned about Bosnia since his trip," Tom began. "He would like to take advantage of your last few days in government to ask you to return to the region, assemble the three Presidents, and hold a short follow-up summit, perhaps in Rome. He will join you."

"While Europe Slept . . ." There was one other event of note at Davos. During a meeting I thought was off the record—but nothing is off the record at Davos—I was asked why it took the Americans to solve "another European problem"—a reference to a recent American diplomatic effort that had averted a small war between Greece and Turkey over Imia/Kardak, a tiny islet off the Turkish coast inhabited only by sheep. My answer was honest but undiplomatic. "While President Clinton and our team were on the phone with Athens and Ankara, the Europeans were literally sleeping through the night," I said. "You have to wonder why Europe does not seem capable of taking decisive action in its own theater."

These remarks were picked up by *The Washington Post's* chief European correspondent, William Drozdiak, who used them as a metaphor for the confusion and drift that seemed to have settled over the European Union since the end of the Cold War. Although several European commentators had written similar assessments of Europe's political paralysis, Drozdiak's article kicked up an unexpected furor and provoked a surprising number of articles in the European press. Several European officials complained to Tarnoff, Talbott, and Kornblum. It was clear the mini-uproar was really about Dayton, not Imia. The commentary fell into two categories: first, those who said my remarks were right but rude; and second, those who said that they were right and needed to be said. No one took issue with the basic thesis. As Philip Gordon of the International Institute for Strategic Studies wrote in the *International Herald Tribune* on February 17, the comments "hurt so much because Europeans know that such comments are right."

I never expected these remarks would be so widely discussed and remembered. Two years later, people were still asking me about the "While Europe slept thesis."* Of course, my goal had been not to insult the Europeans, but to

---

* British Foreign Secretary Malcolm Rifkind gently objected to the phrase for a personal reason: he told the press later that he had stayed up until 4:00 A.M. working on the same problem. Introducing him at a speech in New York a year later, I offered a customized amendment to the quote: "While Europe, with the exception of Malcolm Rifkind, slept . . ."

encourage them to deal with the unresolved problems of their own history and the convoluted E.U. system. "My comments were not a criticism of any individual nation or any individual," I told Agence France-Presse, "but of an institutional structure which makes it hard for Europe to use its full moral, political, and diplomatic authority in a coherent and consistent way. Every European in Western Europe knows this. It is no secret."

Drama in Sarajevo. We chose Rome for the first post-Dayton summit as a way of emphasizing the importance of Italy. Christopher proceeded with his Middle East diplomacy, and I visited Poland and Hungary before returning to Sarajevo on the morning of February 11 to set up the Rome meeting.

We arrived just in time to be confronted by an unexpected problem: the local police had arrested two senior Bosnian Serb officers, General Djordje Djukic and Colonel Aleksa Krsmanovic, as they entered Sarajevo in a civilian car. The Bosnians claimed the two men were war criminals.

Since the two men had been apprehended in a manner that violated the free-movement provisions of Dayton, we would normally have insisted that the Muslims release them immediately. But Justice Goldstone complicated matters considerably; from the International War Crimes Tribunal in The Hague, he issued a warrant for the two men—even though they had not been indicted. When Shattuck called Goldstone to find out what was going on, he told us he wanted the two men for questioning and possible indictment.

Milosevic, on the other hand, demanded their immediate release. The Bosnian Serbs said they would not cooperate any further with IFOR until they were freed. The Muslims, meanwhile, threatened to try them in a Bosnian court.

In this tense atmosphere, Clark and I met with Admiral Smith on the afternoon of February 11, and asked if he could get the two men out of Sarajevo swiftly and safely. Smith said he could not guarantee that it would be low-risk, but he would develop a plan right away. For once there was no question about IFOR's authority; Smith saw the danger if they remained in the Sarajevo jail.

Our team flew to Belgrade, where Milosevic again demanded the immediate release of the two men, saying that they were simple soldiers. The general, he added, was dying of cancer and needed medication urgently. We told Milosevic that the two men could not be released. As for the health of General Djukic, we would ensure that if he was as sick as Milosevic said, he would get the proper medication. (It turned out that he did indeed have cancer.)

We returned to Sarajevo early the next morning, February 12, tense with concern. Unexpectedly, our visit had turned into a decision-making trip on a risky operation. At 2:00 P.M., I called Goldstone again. He said he had sent the formal request to IFOR two hours earlier for their removal to his jurisdiction. Smith was back in Naples, but he had authorized General Walker to carry out the operation. Walker described the plan: with the prior knowledge of the Bosnian prison authorities, a small group of specially selected French soldiers would move into the jail at night, grab the two prisoners, and move them quickly to American helicopters for transport to The Hague. The greatest danger, in Walker's view, was that the Serbs would get wind of the operation and try to block it on the roads or shoot the helicopter down, but he felt the risks were acceptable provided they moved fast.

We left Sarajevo just before the operation was to begin. Most of the negotiating team went to Zagreb, while I went to Bucharest for a long-planned visit. The operation went smoothly, but an alert television crew filmed the dramatic nighttime transfer at the prison. The two men were safely delivered to The Hague, where they were held for months by Goldstone before the charges against Colonel Krsmanovic were dropped and General Djukic, now close to death from cancer, was released.

Christopher and I were greatly disturbed by this incident. The seizure of the two men, neither of whom was ever indicted, had disrupted the implementation process and set a bad precedent for the future. We determined to try to prevent any repetition of such an incident before it became a pattern.

Anglo–American Ties. The next three days were a continuous whirl—Zagreb again, then Frankfurt, London, and Paris—before the main event in Rome. My farewell calls with Foreign Secretary Rifkind and Defense Minister Michael Portillo were personally warm, but Ambassador Crowe and I had the sense of meeting government officials who, more than a year before the next election, felt they were already lame ducks.* We had worked together under the most difficult circumstances. When I returned to Washington in September 1994, the strains in the Anglo-American alliance had been at a level that was nearly intolerable, and rebuilding the relationship, which I still believed was "special"—a once-standard phrase that had been banned by the Major government—had been a high priority. At a small farewell dinner at Ambassador Crowe's residence, both Foreign Secretary Rifkind and his predecessor, Douglas Hurd, offered their appreciation for the closing of the gap during the last seventeen months. I repeated my mantra: that when the two nations stood side by side, they could change history, but when they split on an important issue the consequences were invariably disastrous.

Rome. After more farewell calls in Paris, we flew to Rome on February 16 for the first meeting of the three Balkan Presidents since the signing ceremony

---

* Although neither man could have imagined that he would lose his own House of Commons seat in the landslide victory of Tony Blair and the Labor Party in May 1997.

in December. Admiral Smith, who came to Rome for a few hours, took a dramatic step on the eve of the conference to show that he intended to enforce the military provisions of Dayton. Sending a commando team deep into a mountain area of the Federation on February 17, IFOR raided a "terrorist training camp" and captured eleven "freedom fighters" whom they identified as Iranians, as well as sixty heavy weapons, booby-trapped plastic toys, and a model of an American military headquarters building. Stunned, Izetbegovic claimed that he was unaware of the presence of this group until the raid. Joulwan and I told him that it was immaterial whether or not he knew; the presence of such people on Bosnian soil violated Dayton and constituted a threat to the IFOR troops.

With this dramatic event as background, the first Compliance Summit began on the afternoon of Saturday, February 17, with a welcoming speech by Foreign Minister Susanna Agnelli. Christopher and General Joulwan, as well as our team and the Contact Group, sat around a large conference table for the opening session; then we broke down into smaller groups, placing each delegation in separate rooms. For the next two days the corridors of the normally sedate Italian Foreign Ministry reverberated with the arguments of the Balkans—a veritable mini-Dayton. Specific agreements were reached that were designed to get the implementation process back on track: an agreement on what Christopher called the "rules of the road" so that we would never again have to struggle with the consequences of a surprise arrest; a compromise on Mostar that pulled that city, the most explosive in Bosnia, back from the brink of renewed fighting between the Croats and the Muslims; an understanding on improving the performance of the International Police Task Force; and an agreement to hold similar summits regularly.

We returned to Washington on February 19. Two days later, after some more farewell calls and a generous ceremony on the eighth floor of the State Department for the entire negotiating team attended by Secretaries Christopher and Perry, I resigned as Assistant Secretary of State, and immediately signed papers as an unpaid advisor to the Secretary of State. This meant little, except that I would retain my security clearances and be available on short notice to the Administration. That evening, February 21, I left Washington for a new life in New York.

CHAPTER 20

Disasters and Progress

(February 1996–April 1998)

> This even-handed justice
> Commends the ingredients of our poison'd chalice
> To our own lips.
>
> — SHAKESPEARE, *Macbeth*

ON PAPER, DAYTON WAS A GOOD AGREEMENT; it ended the war and established a single, multiethnic country. But countless peace agreements have survived only in history books as case studies in failed expectations. The results of the international effort to implement Dayton would determine its true place in history. And the start was rocky.

The First Setback. The unification of Sarajevo under Federation control ninety days after the establishment of IFOR was the first major political deadline of the Dayton agreement, and in many ways the most important. Before Dayton, no outside observer had thought it could happen, and many still doubted that it would. It was, without question, the first key civilian test of Dayton.

Sarajevo was unified precisely on schedule. On March 18, 1996, a group of ragged Bosnian Serb policemen, their voices barely audible over a scratchy recording of the anthem of precommunist Yugoslavia, lowered their flag from the police station in Grbavica and left for Pale. "We saved this area militarily," said Milenko Karisik, a Bosnian Serb Deputy Interior Minister, "but we lost it at Dayton." The next day, the Bosnian Serbs handed over to the Federation the Serb-controlled portions of Sarajevo. There was no fighting, no attempt to prevent the event.

But at the moment that was one of Dayton's greatest achievements, the Bosnian Serbs exploited the passivity of IFOR and the weakness of the enforcing powers to salvage something for their separatist cause. In the two weeks before Sarajevo's unification, Pale ordered all Serbs in Sarajevo to burn down their own apartments and leave the city. They even broadcast detailed instructions on how to set the fires. (Pile all the furniture in the middle of the room, douse it with kerosene, turn the gas on, and throw a match into the room as you leave.) Young arsonists, mostly thugs from Pale, roamed the streets warning Sarajevo Serbs that if they did not destroy their homes and leave, they would be punished severely, perhaps even killed.

For those Bosnian Serbs who had moved into Sarajevo from the countryside during the war, destroying apartments they would have to leave anyway was easy. But tens of thousands of Sarajevo Serb families had lived in peace for generations in the once-cosmopolitan city. Most were ready to stay had they not been forced to leave. Kris Janowski, the spokesman for the United Nations High Commissioner for Refugees, estimated that before the exodus there were seventy thousand Serbs in Sarajevo, of whom at least thirty thousand wanted to stay. After the intimidation tactics of Pale, fewer than ten thousand remained, many of whom would leave soon thereafter. In the week before March 19, a steady stream of Serbs clogged the roads out of Sarajevo, most carrying furniture, plumbing fixtures, and even doors. Behind them rose the smoking remains of Grbavica and Ilidza. "We must not allow a single Serb to remain in the territories which fall under Muslim-Croat control," said Gojko Klickovic, head of the Bosnian Serb Resettlement Office (and later Prime Minister of Republika Srpska).

Journalists reported nearly incomprehensible scenes: a Serb woman beaten and raped by a young Serb thug before he set fire to her apartment; an elderly Serb couple who survived the entire war in Sarajevo appealing futilely to Italian troops as a Serb thug blew up their apartment. Robert Gelbard, Assistant Secretary of State for International Narcotics and Law Enforcement, was visiting Sarajevo at the time at my suggestion; he watched in disgust as IFOR and the International Police Task Force refused to apprehend the marauding arsonists and IFOR kept its own fire-fighting equipment inside the IFOR compound. Desperate, the Muslims sent their antiquated fire-fighting equipment into the Serb portion of the city, where they were attacked by rock-throwing Serb arsonists. But their requests for IFOR protection were refused. Gelbard watched buildings burn as IFOR troops stood by less than 150 meters away, and observed British General Michael Walker, IFOR's second-ranking officer, coolly reject the pleas of the Deputy High Representative, Michael Steiner, for IFOR intervention. "I was ashamed to be associated with it," Gelbard told me later, "to be unable to get IFOR to do anything." A year later, appointed by President Clinton and Secretary Albright to coordinate the faltering implementation effort, Gelbard would make a difference.

This tragedy could have been easily prevented if IFOR had taken action. But although unchallenged and feared, NATO/IFOR did almost nothing. An IFOR spokesman said that while the burnings were "unfortunate," the Serbs "have the right to burn their own houses." IFOR, said another spokesman, "is not a police force and will not undertake police duties." Shocked by IFOR's sudden passivity, U.N. officials, in an ironic role reversal, now criticized NATO for *its* inactivity. "If [NATO] had been tougher, things would be different," said Kris Janowski. "We're seeing a multiethnic Bosnia being flushed down the toilet."

It was my first month as a private citizen; I realized too late that I had left too early. Watching with growing anxiety from New York, I called Washington frequently, pleading for action, pointing out that Dayton's "silver bullet" clause gave IFOR full authority in such a situation. But Admiral Smith refused to act, repeating his mantra that IFOR was not a police force, that putting out the fires or arresting the arsonists would be mission creep. That IFOR's passivity was endangering fundamental policy goals of the United States and NATO seemed unimportant to him.

Warren Christopher and Bill Perry finally stepped in and insisted that NATO take action. Reluctantly, Smith and Walker ordered their troops to detain a few of the young arsonists and turn them over to the local authorities, while IFOR put out some of the fires. It was too little, too late. "If anyone thinks this is a success," said U.N. spokesman Janowski, "that would be rather silly. There has been millions of dollars' worth of property damaged in looting and fires, and an exodus when we were supposed to see people returning to their homes."

This was the worst moment of the first two years after Dayton. Not only was it a disaster on its own terms, but it ended the sense of hope and momentum that had begun in late November. Pale used the very exodus it had created as an excuse to prevent Muslims from returning to their homes in the Serb portion of Bosnia. Muslims and Croats read the events as evidence that multiethnic cooperation would not be encouraged by NATO. The message seemed clear: leaders and thugs who preached ethnic division would not be punished or constrained.

Stung by international criticism, the military struck back, publicly blaming the international civilian agencies, particularly Carl Bildt, for the "slippage" in implementing Dayton. But assigning blame was pointless. The events of mid-March provided an object lesson in the tenacity and ruthlessness of the Serbs—and the confusion of the implementing organizations in Bosnia. They also illustrated one of Washington's most important but least understood maxims: *good policy badly executed becomes bad policy.*

The Toughest Issue. Until the March disaster, all three ethnic groups in Bosnia, awed by the sight of sixty thousand heavily armed IFOR soldiers, were prepared to do almost anything that IFOR asked. The Bosnian Serbs, in particular, had been so badly battered, both militarily and politically, that they would have offered little resistance had IFOR enforced tough guidelines. Even Milosevic had encouraged IFOR at first to take a firm line, although he would soon cease to do so. Rallying from the despair they had felt since November, the Bosnian Serbs began to resist on almost every nonmilitary issue, while remaining careful to avoid provoking IFOR. It was almost as if they had an implicit understanding with the IFOR command: we will not attack your forces if you leave us alone to pursue an ethnically divided country.

Of all the things necessary to achieve our goals in Bosnia, the most important was still the arrest of Radovan Karadzic. But Karadzic surfaced after a few months of near seclusion and began issuing orders and giving interviews, signaling his followers that they could still safely pursue their separatist goals. With his military forces neutralized, Karadzic used the "special police," a vestige of the communist police state, to threaten any Bosnian Serb who showed support for Dayton. Even though these units were also covered in the Dayton agreement, IFOR pointedly ignored these "police" as they crossed the Serb portion of Bosnia intimidating anyone who cooperated with Muslims or spoke favorably of Dayton. Karadzic's first major target was the first politician to support Dayton publicly, the mayor of Banja Luka, Predrag Radic, whom he prevented from attending the meeting with President Clinton at Tuzla in January.

While the arrest of Karadzic would not have solved all the problems the international community faced in Bosnia, his removal from Bosnia was a necessary, although not sufficient, condition for success. As we had told the President and his senior advisors before Dayton, Karadzic at large was certain to mean Dayton deferred or defeated. Nothing had changed six months later, except that Karadzic was rebuilding his position. While the human-rights community and some members of the State Department, especially John Shattuck and Madeleine Albright, called for action, the military warned of casualties and Serb retaliation if an operation to arrest him took place. They said they would carry it out only if ordered to do so directly by the President; thus if anything went wrong the blame would fall on the civilians who had insisted on the operation, especially on the President himself. This was a heavy burden to lay on any president, particularly during an election year, and it was hardly surprising that no action was taken to mount, or even plan, an operation against Karadzic in 1996 or 1997.

Paradoxically, the same officials who opposed capturing Karadzic supported a tight deadline for American troop withdrawal. The two goals were obviously incompatible; if you wanted to reduce troop levels, capturing Karadzic was essential. Yet still NATO refused to consider arresting Karadzic, arguing that it was too risky and not an IFOR mission.

. . .

I raised the issue with Admiral Smith on my "farewell" trip to Sarajevo on February 11, during the same meeting in which we discussed the detention of the two Bosnian Serb officers by the Muslims. The previous day, *The Washington Post* had published John Pomfret's dramatic description of Karadzic driving unchallenged through four NATO checkpoints—two of them manned by Americans—on a trip from Pale to Banja Luka. When I showed Admiral Smith the article, he tossed it contemptuously to an aide while offering a few pithy comments about interfering, know-nothing journalists. He did not deny the story, however. He remained adamant: his forces would not go after indicted war criminals.

A Letter to the President. When I left the government, President Clinton had invited me to send him my views from time to time. By early June of 1996, I felt that the situation had reached a point where such a message was justified. I sent copies to Christopher, Lake, and Talbott.

Dear Mr. President:

We are at a decisive moment in the Bosnia peace process. I would like, therefore, to take up your request to send you my views:

The success of IFOR so far is now threatened by Karadzic's success in defying the political portions of Dayton. If he continues to thwart the Dayton powers, the peace process will fail.

This would result, at a minimum, in Bosnia's partition, with the real possibility of further division into three parts within a few years—all of which we have said we oppose. While our national interests are not directly affected by whether Bosnia is one country or two or even three, the outcome in Bosnia will profoundly affect our overall role in the emerging *post*–post–Cold War world. . . .

Of the many organizations in the former Yugoslavia in the last five years, only NATO—that is, the United States—has been respected. What NATO/IFOR demands, happens.

But the reluctance of NATO to go beyond a relatively narrow interpretation of its mission has left a gaping hole in the Bosnia food chain. Recognizing this, the Bosnian Serbs have increasingly defied the Dayton powers. In response, the Bosnian Muslims have moved further from a multiethnic state, as Izetbegovic starts building an undemocratic and fundamentally (although not fundamentalist) Muslim state in his half of the country. . . .

The implications of Karadzic's defiance go far beyond Bosnia itself. If he succeeds, basic issues of American leadership that seemed settled in the public's eye after Dayton will re-emerge. Having reasserted American leadership in Europe, it would be a tragedy if we let it slip away again. . . .

It may seem odd that so much can hang on such a matter as the fate of two odious war criminals. But history is replete with examples of small issues leading to the unraveling of larger ones. The question of Radovan Karadzic is such an issue. . . . Our goal should be Karadzic's removal not only from his presidential post, but from power. . . .

There are other things that should have been done earlier—but which, if done now, will still make a difference. Several examples:

—Every day Karadzic uses television and the controlled media to prevent local reconciliation efforts. IFOR has the ability and authority to cut these lines, but has refused to do so. These communication lines should be cut— now. This would be a devastating blow to Karadzic, and popular in the United States. . . .

—Sanctions reimposition. We wrote into Dayton the ability to reimpose sanctions if necessary. This is our strongest remaining leverage. . . . I would suggest Milosevic be given a clear message. . . .

Return to Bosnia. Calls to capture Karadzic and Mladic were mounting. They came from newspapers around the world, and from Carl Bildt and Senator Dole; from Mort Abramowitz, the respected president of the Carnegie Endowment for International Peace; and from the American philanthropist and financier George Soros—who, astonishingly, had spent more of his own money on aid projects in Bosnia than had the United States government.

On the evening of Friday, July 12, the Administration, facing growing international criticism, asked if I would return to the region immediately on a special mission. With the understanding and support of my new colleagues at Crédit Suisse First Boston, I left three days later, after a day in Washington.

The Administration's goal was to remove Karadzic from power or significantly weaken him through diplomatic pressure, thus defusing the pressure for a military operation. As I had written a few weeks earlier to the President, our most potent nonmilitary weapon was the reimposition of economic sanctions against Serbia and the Bosnian Serbs—a right we had carefully retained for ourselves in the Dayton agreement, but only until ten days after the national elections scheduled for September 14.

When I saw Christopher, Talbott, Tarnoff, and Berger separately on Monday, July 15, it was clear that Washington was uneasy about using sanctions. With only hours left before departure for Bosnia, I argued that the threat of sanctions was important if our team was to have a chance of success. When several officials expressed concern that reimposition would upset the Europeans, I reminded them that we would lose the power to reimpose sanctions in only seventy days. "Use it before we lose it," was my slogan for the day.

The key meeting took place with Sandy Berger in the late afternoon. Lake was away; we met in his empty office. He said no consensus could be forged in time for our trip. After close to an hour of intense discussion, Sandy said, "Look, you and I have been friends for twenty years. Don't ask for something we can't give you. Just go out there and do what you can. We know you will make it sound better than it is." He laughed, and clapped me on the shoulder. "That's why we asked you back," he said. On the way to the airport I called Strobe to describe the meeting. He confirmed my impression. "Just use that old creative ambiguity," he said.

"We are here," I told the press when we landed at the Sarajevo airport on Tuesday, July 16, "because we are not satisfied with the degree of compliance we are seeing, particularly on the part of the Bosnian Serbs." Our first meeting was with Robert Frowick, the urbane American diplomat whom we had chosen to head up the OSCE mission in Bosnia and run the elections. He was at a crossroads. So far he had allowed Karadzic's party, the SDS, to take a major role in the election preparations, but he was increasingly troubled by their behavior, which included stuffing the registration rolls and intimidating potential voters. Frowick had the authority to declare any party or individual ineligible. The deadline for a final decision was almost upon him—within three days he had to decide whether or not to allow Karadzic's party to participate in the elections, scheduled for September 14.

Disenfranchising the SDS was tempting but risky. It might provoke a boycott of the elections, but it would remove from the electoral process the party that was, more than any other force in Bosnia, trying to prevent Dayton from succeeding. But before we came to any conclusions, it was essential to find out what Izetbegovic wanted to do; his views would be critical.

Izetbegovic, whom I had not seen in five months, seemed a changed man, cracking small jokes and smiling. He thanked me profusely for what I "had done for Bosnia," and noted that we had kept our promises to his government. When we were alone I outlined the core issue. "Mr. President," I said, "we can disqualify the SDS from the election process if we wish, by declaring that the entire party is in violation of the Dayton agreement. On the other hand, if Milosevic helps us remove Karadzic from power, we can allow the SDS to participate in the elections. What we do next with the SDS is essentially in our hands, and we need to know your views."

This was a huge decision for Izetbegovic, and he said he would have an answer for us when we returned from Belgrade and Zagreb in somewhat more than twenty-four hours.

The next day, July 17, our team met with Milosevic over a long lunch in Belgrade. We were blunt: if we were unable to get a satisfactory agreement, we would "recommend" that sanctions be reimposed and that Frowick disqualify the SDS from the elections. Incredulous, Milosevic was asked to see me alone. Members of our team, including Goldberg and Owen, could hear his voice through the doors between the two rooms, as he angrily charged that we were wrecking the Dayton agreement. I replied that it was Karadzic who was trying to destroy Dayton. Our goal was to get him "out of power and out of country." After a prolonged argument, we agreed to meet again the next day.

We returned to Sarajevo on the morning of July 18. It was another of those meetings whose consequences would be felt for a long time.

"The SDS is the Nazi Party of our country," Izetbegovic began. "But if we throw them out of the elections, they could organize a boycott, like they did the last time. If you can get Karadzic out of power, I think it is much better to let them run. I can work with Krajisnik. I know how to deal with him."

Izetbegovic could work with Krajisnik? The comment was surprising. The speaker of the Pale assembly, the man who at Dayton had slammed his fist into the map of Sarajevo, widely known as "Mr. No," was as much of a rejectionist as Karadzic. But Izetbegovic was worried about the effect of an SDS boycott. While the decision remained ours, Izetbegovic's desire not to throw the SDS out of the elections, his fear that they could wreck the elections, was a powerful message that the international community could not ignore.

Milosevic moved our July 18 meeting to a new venue, a government villa in the residential section of Belgrade. At 4:00 P.M., seated in the garden of the villa, we began a ten-hour negotiating session that mirrored some of the early shuttle drama and produced an agreement that defused the crisis—but at a price.

Milosevic came to the point quickly. "Krajisnik and Buha are upstairs," he said, pointing to windows on the second-floor of the villa. "They are ready to negotiate right now over the future of Karadzic." This tactic, so stunning eleven months earlier when Milosevic had produced Karadzic and Mladic, was no longer shocking. Asking to meet first without the two Bosnian Serbs, we presented Milosevic with a tough document, announcing the resignation of Karadzic from the presidencies of both Republika Srpska and the SDS, effective the next day. Our draft also announced that Karadzic would leave Bosnia and comply with the International War Crimes Tribunal.

Milosevic objected strongly to almost every detail of our draft. Finally, we agreed to bring the two Bosnian Serbs into the discussion. They were in a sullen mood. Krajisnik made not the slightest attempt to be civil; Buha simply sat in silence. But as Krajisnik realized that the removal of his friend and mentor Karadzic would directly benefit him, he became increasingly interested in our proposals. Still, Krajisnik was immovable on the possibility that Karadzic leave Bosnia. "Maybe later, but never tonight, with the world watching," Krajisnik said emotionally as Buha, thin-faced and gaunt, glared at us. "And there is nothing we can do to force him."

"Why don't you send him to stay with his mother and his smuggler brother in his native village in Montenegro?" I asked, half-seriously, half-facetiously. Krajisnik seemed stunned at this reference to the private activities of Karadzic's brother; we believed that Krajisnik was part of the same smuggling operations. I thought of an earlier conversation with a senior Serb official who had told us that Karadzic and Krajisnik had become friends when they were both jailed, one for passing bad checks, the other for stealing cement from public projects. We did not know if this story was true, but, as Phil Goldberg said, "it felt right."

Shortly after ten in the evening, after a great deal of argument, the Bosnian Serbs signed an agreement that removed Radovan Karadzic "immediately and permanently [from] all public and private activities," including his two official positions—President of Republika Srpska and president of the SDS. Mrs. Biljana Plavsic, one of the Vice Presidents of the Bosnian Serbs, would be named President the next day, and Buha would become the acting head of the SDS. Stressing the importance of the pledge that Karadzic also cease "public activities," I cited a number of examples, especially his appearances on television and the use of posters bearing his likeness, that would constitute violations. Although clearly unhappy, Krajisnik and Buha agreed; Karadzic would not appear on television, and his image would not be displayed.

We were still lacking the most important signature, that of Karadzic himself. Milosevic proposed that we obtain it by fax. I rejected this; we did not want Karadzic to claim later that his signature was a faxed forgery. So at our insistence, Milosevic sent his intelligence chief, Jovica Stanisic, to Pale by helicopter to obtain Karadzic's signature personally. After dinner—the best he had ever offered us, lamb, yogurt, and spinach—we left to call Washington. I read the draft statement to Tarnoff, who walked it through "the system" with impressive speed, obtaining Washington's support in less than ninety minutes. We returned to Milosevic's villa at about 2:00 A.M. to meet Stanisic, who presented us with the original document, now signed by Karadzic. Stanisic told us Karadzic seemed "resigned to the end of his political career." But he was not ready to leave Pale, Stanisic said. I wondered aloud if Karadzic's political career had *really* reached the end of the road.

Karadzic stepped down from both posts the next day, and faded out of public sight—even television—for the rest of the year. The world's press hailed the agreement and praised our efforts; in the words of the *Financial Times,* it was "another success."

Our team, drained by two almost sleepless nights and the long flight back from Belgrade, the last hour of it bouncing through violent thunderstorms, drove directly to the White House to join a Principals' Committee meeting already in progress, where we were greeted with a standing ovation that left us moved but a bit stunned. Our colleagues were more impressed with the July 18 agreement than we were. We were ambivalent about what we had done. We had achieved *just enough* to allow elections with SDS participation, and *just enough* to relieve the pressure for the rest of the year for a military operation against Karadzic—an operation I still favored. We might be "whistling past the graveyard," as Strobe put it, but it was just what Washington wanted.

I repeated my earlier recommendation that we close down the SDS television network, but this was again rejected on the grounds that it was either too provocative or impossible to carry out.* I also told the Principals' Committee that we had to move immediately against Pale if there were the slightest violation of the July 18 agreement. But by the beginning of 1997, these admonitions and proposals would be forgotten or ignored, and Karadzic, sensing another opportunity, would emerge once more.

The September 14 Elections. Two months later, I was back in Bosnia, this time as the head of the Presidential Observer Mission to the elections. The team, which had been assembled by the White House, consisted of a group of private citizens and several Congressmen, including two powerful Democrats, John Murtha of Pennsylvania and Steny Hoyer of Maryland, and Peter King, a Republican from New York. Thousands of other international supervisors, observers, monitors, and journalists were crawling all over the country.

The elections chose the three-person presidency and the national assembly established by the Dayton agreement. They were relatively trouble-free, and unquestionably constituted progress—Warren Christopher called them a remarkable success. But none of the winners was in favor of a truly multiethnic government. The election strengthened the very separatists who had started the war.

Many observers later cited this as proof that the people of Bosnia wanted to separate along ethnic lines. I did not share this assessment; the elections took place in an atmosphere poisoned by a media controlled by the same people who had started the war. Advocates of reconciliation in all three communities were intimidated by thugs and overwhelmed by media that carried nothing but racist propaganda. The full costs of failing to close down the SDS television stations now came home. And on the Muslim side, all was not well either; in one particularly ominous incident, zealots from Izetbegovic's party beat up Haris Silajdzic, almost killing him, as he spoke in favor of a multiethnic

* Neither argument against action had merit. Fourteen months later, on October 1, 1997, the NATO forces finally closed down the Pale television transmitters, depriving Karadzic and his party of one of their most powerful instruments of power. Although controversial to the last moment, when it took place the action was accomplished without incident or injury—and had the desired effect.

Bosnia during an election rally. On the Serb side, Milosevic ran a handpicked candidate, but the victory that he had long promised never materialized; Krajisnik won the Serb seat in the three-person co-presidency of Bosnia by a vote of 508,026 to 240,000. Biljana Plavsic won the presidency of Republika Srpska with ease. She was, at the time, the most popular Bosnian Serb. Nothing could have prepared us for the open confrontation she would have with her Pale mentors in less than eight months.

Clinton II and the Together Movement. Bosnia faded as an issue in the 1996 presidential campaign. In addition to the relative success of the effort, Senator Dole also deserved credit as well; he ignored every opportunity to exploit the issue because, as he told me later, he did not want to hurt a policy he now "basically agreed with." Dole even said publicly that he would favor extending IFOR beyond its one-year limit, but the Administration failed to seize this generous opening to get out from under the twelve-month deadline, and, with Dole's defeat in November, it was gone.

Even a re-elected president goes through a transition period, although it is almost invisible to the public eye. Outgoing officials tend to lose interest in the details of policy, as they prepare to return to the private sector. The Clinton Administration effected a smooth transition in most areas, especially at State, where the new Secretary, Madeleine Albright, was familiar with most of the major issues from her U.N. tour, and at the NSC, where Sandy Berger simply moved up (without the need for Senate confirmation) to replace Tony Lake.

Still, the new team—much of it far below the Cabinet level—had to await Senate confirmation. Even the smoothest shifts take time, and in the Balkans events did not pause for our transition. A remarkable challenge to Milosevic unfolded in the streets of Belgrade in December, led by three politicians who banded together into a movement they called Zajedno, or the Together Movement. For weeks, hundreds of thousands of Belgrade citizens braved subfreezing weather to call for democracy. But Washington missed a chance to affect events; except for one ineffectual trip to Washington, Zajedno had no contact with senior American government officials, and the Administration sent no senior officials to Belgrade for fear that their visits would be used by Milosevic to show support. For the first time in eighteen months, Milosevic felt no significant American pressure, and turned back toward the extreme nationalists, including Karadzic, for support. His tactical skills saved him again, and within weeks, the Together Movement was together no more, as its leaders split among themselves.

On Sunday, December 8, three days after Madeleine Albright was named Secretary of State, we met at her house in Georgetown. I offered her my full support, and noted that her well-known tough line on Bosnia made her the ideal person to reinvigorate the policy. She said this was her firm intention. Nonetheless, by April there was a general impression that "Clinton II" was downgrading Bosnia. In Europe, the emphasis was almost entirely on a critical summit meeting with Boris Yeltsin, planned for Helsinki, that would determine the fate of the Administration's plan to enlarge NATO. China also took center stage in internal policy discussions. The comparative silence on Bosnia during the early months of 1997 was broken primarily by the incoming Secretary of Defense, Senator William Cohen, who made a series of statements that the United States would end its troop presence in Bosnia in eighteen months—that is, June 1998. "Are they going to go back to slaughtering each other?" Cohen said. "It's up to them."

Sensing that high-level American interest had declined, Karadzic ventured once more into public view, testing how flagrantly he could violate the agreement I had negotiated the previous July without provoking a NATO response. Finding nothing in his way, he even gave on-the-record interviews to European journalists. His re-emergence went unchallenged by the military, and suggested, as many journalists reported, that personnel in IFOR—now renamed SFOR, or Stabilization Force—were simply counting the days until their departure.

Finally, in April, after a highly successful Clinton-Yeltsin summit in Helsinki—in which President Clinton obtained Yeltsin's acceptance of NATO enlargement—the Administration, led by Madeleine Albright and Sandy Berger, began to focus again on Bosnia. As part of this process, Robert Gelbard was appointed to coordinate all U.S. government efforts to implement Dayton. This made sense; Washington needed a tough, full-time "czar" and Gelbard, who had been working on Bosnia sporadically since I had asked him to strengthen the International Police Task Force in December 1995, was an excellent choice. Gelbard's background was unusually varied for a Foreign Service officer; in addition to both economic and political experience, he had extensive firsthand knowledge of law enforcement and counterterrorism.

An Unusual Birthday Party. Washington is well known as a city where social events can have policy consequences. Such was the case with a memorable party given by Liz Stevens on Friday, April 4, in honor of her husband, the gifted filmmaker George Stevens, and Kati, who shared the same birthday. Without telling us or most of the other guests, Liz had invited the Clintons. We arrived early to find Secret Service agents all over the house. A few minutes later, ahead of other guests, the Clintons walked in.

To be precise, Hillary walked; the President limped in on crutches. Only a month earlier he had famously, and seriously, injured himself in a fall outside the home of the golfer Greg Norman. Less famously, I had injured myself at about the same time, tearing ligaments in my ankle. When we met, I was also on crutches, to the President's amusement, and we spent a few minutes comparing our rehabilitation programs. As he left, the President pulled me aside for a moment and said, "Come by tomorrow and we can do some therapy and talk."

The next day, Saturday, April 5, I presented myself at the White House and was ushered upstairs to the family quarters, where the President was already working out on a bicycle machine. Gesturing me into an adjoining room, he asked his therapist, a Navy commander, to look at my injury. We worked out in silence for a while as if it were the most natural thing in the world, and then adjourned to another room to cool down.

Members of his family, including Hillary and her mother, Dorothy Rodham, stopped by to chat. It seemed simultaneously completely ordinary and completely extraordinary, casual conversation with this nice, average American family—except that one of them happened to be the President. As I was beginning to wonder if we would ever discuss Bosnia, he said, "Let's go downstairs." With that we hobbled down to his office in the family quarters.

It is in the nature of the hierarchical relationship of the Executive Branch that such a meeting would have been almost impossible while I was still in the government. There are simply too many layers between an Assistant Secretary and the Chief Executive, and everyone in the chain of command would have insisted on either being there, changing the nature of the meeting, or preventing such a discussion from even occurring.

"What's going on out there?" the President began. Before the meeting, I had decided, with Strobe's enthusiastic urging, to be completely candid if the opportunity arose. I listed the series of reverses and lost opportunities since December: the collapse of the Together Movement; increasingly public activity by Karadzic; brutal behavior by Tudjman toward the remaining Serbs in Croatia; heightened tensions between the Croats and the Muslims within the Federation, especially at Mostar; and American passivity or worse.

"While NATO policy and your achievement with Yeltsin have been historic," I said, "Bosnia has gone nowhere since Dayton. These issues are interrelated. We said that we'll leave Bosnia in June 1998, which is not possible. People out there are not even sure we still support Dayton, or if we still care what happens in Bosnia. And we are losing irretrievable time."

I urged him to give Albright and Gelbard his full backing. Sensing that he was receptive, I spoke even more bluntly than I had planned, urging him to speak out forcefully on the issue. Finally, the President walked me to the elevator, and then, crutches and all, accompanied me all the way to my car, which was waiting at the South Portico of the White House.

The "therapy session," as Strobe called it, was timely. Both Berger and Albright said later that it was important in getting policy focused and revitalized at a critical moment. Meanwhile, Berger's formal policy review proceeded, and Gelbard "went operational."

The Policy Toughens. With the press filled with stories about Albright-Cohen and State-Pentagon conflicts over Bosnia, the President flew to Europe twice: first, to sign the NATO-Russia Founding Act on May 27 in Paris, which formalized Russia's role in the security architecture of post–Cold War Europe; and second, to attend a historic NATO summit on July 9 in Madrid that invited Hungary, Poland, and the Czech Republic to join NATO. It was a remarkable achievement, defying the predictions of many critics who said that NATO enlargement would do irreparable damage to relations between Russia and the United States.

In May, Berger overrode the doubts of some Pentagon officials; his study reaffirmed a solidly pro-Dayton policy. At the suggestion of several Administration officials, I spoke to the President again on Sunday, May 24, three days before his meetings with Yeltsin in Paris, to argue that if we did not revitalize Bosnia policy immediately it might be too late to salvage Dayton.

Meanwhile, the new British Prime Minister, Tony Blair, and his Foreign Secretary, Robin Cook, made clear that they would follow a more aggressive policy, and urged the same from the United States. When the President, during a joint press conference with Blair in the garden at 10 Downing Street on May 29, was asked about reports of a conflict between Albright and Cohen over Bosnia, he sidestepped the controversy but made it clear that he wanted Dayton to succeed.

As the President returned to Washington, Albright and Gelbard went to Sintra, Portugal, for a meeting of the NATO Foreign Ministers. The NATO countries invited the leaders of Bosnia to Sintra, and, after intense meetings, issued a statement that recommitted them to Dayton. From Sintra, Albright made her first trip to the region as Secretary of State, traveling to Zagreb, Banja Luka, Sarajevo, and Belgrade on May 31. Given her high profile—"the most popular political figure in America," in the words of Joe Klein—her trip brought attention back to American policy in Bosnia. We talked several times before and during the trip, and she called one last time around midnight, from Zagreb, the evening before she went to Belgrade for her first meeting with Milosevic. She was the first Secretary of State to visit Belgrade since James Baker's unfortunate trip in June 1991.

Throughout her visit, Albright showed a deft sense of how to communicate with the people of the region. Perhaps this was a function of her background; after all, she had not only been born in Czechoslovakia but spent part of her childhood in Belgrade. This special understanding was most in evidence when she met Biljana Plavsic in Banja Luka. Albright had added the stop almost as an afterthought on the advice of her closest aide, Assistant Secretary for Public Affairs Jamie Rubin, but the brief visit would have important consequences, emboldening President Plavsic to break publicly with her former mentors in Pale.

Ever since Dayton we had anticipated, even hoped for, a split between Pale and Banja Luka. (It will be recalled that at Dayton we had considered designating Banja Luka as the capital of Srpska, but held back because Izetbegovic objected.) Now it arrived in a most unexpected form. Plavsic publicly attacked her closest colleagues where they were most vulnerable: corruption. Presenting herself as a still-patriotic Serb nationalist, she lashed out publicly at Karadzic and Krajisnik, calling them "criminals" who were living well while stealing from their own people. To almost everyone's surprise, she struck a responsive chord among many Serbs in western Bosnia.

The Team Changes. Major personnel changes were under way within the international effort. Carl Bildt stepped down as High Representative to return to political life in Sweden, replaced by Carlos Westendorp of Spain. I urged Albright and Gelbard to send Jacques Klein to Sarajevo as Westendorp's deputy. In his tour overseeing the transition of eastern Slavonia to Croatian control, Klein had shown a flair for the sort of forceful, even melodramatic performance that impressed the people of the region.

Another appointment changed the equation significantly: President Clinton and Secretary Cohen chose as NATO's new Supreme Commander none other than Wes Clark. In naming Clark, they had, in effect, sent Dayton to NATO— an important signal of determination. At the same time a new SFOR commander, General Eric Shinseki, and a new Ambassador, Richard Kauzlarich, took over in Sarajevo.

Bosnia Once More. On July 18, Bob Gelbard, relatively new in his job as the "implementation czar," asked to have breakfast with me in New York. His drive and focus were impressive, but the situation on the ground was still unsatisfactory—to him as well as to me. Near the end of the breakfast, he asked if I would be willing to make another trip to the region as soon as possible. Its purposes would be to talk to an increasingly obstructionist Milosevic, and help revitalize the implementation effort. Agreeing at once, I proposed that we travel together to show a united front and maximize American pressure. I met Gelbard and his team, including Treasury's David Lipton, in Paris on August 6. President Clinton himself had talked publicly in recent weeks about "saving Dayton," a phrase that disturbed some of his senior advisors but that vividly conveyed his own sense of concern. I had told him that we were about one year behind where we should be.

We flew first to Split to join a meeting between Izetbegovic and Tudjman. They met against the backdrop of highly publicized actions by both the Croat and Muslim communities against refugee return; each had recently mobilized mobs to prevent other ethnic groups from returning to their homes. In the Vogosca suburb of Sarajevo, a mob of Muslim women—many Srbrenica widows—had blocked Serbs from returning to their homes. In Jajce, a Croat mob had done the same thing to five hundred Muslims.

When we were ushered into the meeting room, we were confronted with an unexpected sight. Instead of facing each other with the previous air of hostility, the two leaders were seated side by side at the end of the table, their shoulders almost touching. I remembered the meeting in Zagreb on September 19, 1995, when Tudjman had yelled at Izetbegovic in front of forty people. Now, as one of Tudjman's senior aides explained, they wanted to show us—and a large press corps waiting outside—that they could collaborate without American direction. With great pride, Tudjman and Izetbegovic gave us a joint announcement intended to strengthen the Federation. But it was vague and filled with generalities.

Gelbard and I had never worked closely together before, but we operated easily. I began, "We congratulate you on producing a joint statement. However, if you want us to praise it publicly, you must agree to a second statement with specific deadlines. You must condemn the mob actions against refugee return in both Jajce and Vogosca, and pledge that you will not permit it again."

We presented a draft that we had drafted during the flight to Split, and settled down to a five-hour negotiation that ended with an announcement containing ten new commitments and specific deadlines. As always in Bosnia, one could not be sure that these deadlines and goals would be honored. But based on the pattern of the previous eighteen months, we knew that the best way to make progress was to forge public agreement on specific dates and goals, and then hold the parties to them.*

In a private meeting, Tudjman complained bitterly to Gelbard, Galbraith, and me about his treatment by Washington. He had been hospitalized with a bout with cancer since I had last seen him, but it was in remission, and he showed only a few effects of his illness. But he believed that the United States had leaked information about his health after an examination at Walter Reed Army Hospital in Washington. The United States had also hardened its policy in the face of Croatia's continued expulsion of Serb families from land they had lived on for generations, slowing down or withholding aid to Croatia.

---

* To almost everyone's amazement, the refugees who had been forcibly prevented from returning to Jajce in early August returned peacefully a few weeks later, and more followed after that.

We said that he had to give Dayton more than lip service if he wanted Washington to ease up. I said that we were outraged by the Croat mob in Jajce only three days earlier. "By the way," Gelbard added dramatically, "I know for a fact that Dario Kordic [the most prominent indicted Croat war criminal] was personally directing that mob. You must send him to The Hague if you want things to change between us." Tudjman protested that he had no idea where Kordic was or what he was doing. But he did not really expect us to believe this; he was only testing the importance of the issue. We were immovable; Kordic had to be brought to justice.

Eight weeks later, on October 6, 1997, Kordic and nine other indicted Bosnian Croats "voluntarily" surrendered under pressure from Zagreb. It was an important step forward in the quest for war criminals.* Watching Kordic make his farewell statement on television before flying to The Hague, I noticed a small but revealing detail: Kordic's remarks at the Split airport were translated by Tudjman's personal interpreter, a clear signal that Tudjman and Kordic had reached some sort of private understanding regarding the future.

After our day with Tudjman and Izetbegovic, we spent the night at a resort hotel in Trogir, a beautiful walled city near Split. It was a soft August evening, and my thoughts went back to the last night I had spent in Split, almost exactly two years earlier, before setting out for Mount Igman.

Tuzla and the Generals. The next morning, August 7, we flew to Tuzla at dawn for a meeting with the three senior commanders in the American and NATO chain of command: General Shalikashvili, who had changed his schedule to join us for what was also his final visit to the region; General Clark, now the NATO commander; and General Eric Shinseki, the new SFOR commander. For over a year the Bosnian Serbs had been "cheating" on Dayton by putting military police uniforms on regular soldiers and claiming that they were no longer in the Bosnian Serb Army, even though the military annex of the agreement, anticipating such games, had specifically included "military uniformed police" in the definition of armed forces. These paramilitary police were, I said publicly, "racist, fascist, anti–peace agreement, anti-democratic, and a potential threat to the international community." Yet until Clark took command of NATO, SFOR had ignored them. Clark instructed Shinseki to issue a warning, followed by enforcement, that henceforth the military uniformed police would be treated the same way as regular forces.

When the weather cleared, we headed for Sarajevo, after bidding an especially warm farewell to Shalikashvili, whom I would not see again until his emotional retirement ceremony on the parade grounds at Fort Myer at the end of September. I had never known a military officer of whom I was fonder. It

---

* More voluntary surrenders—including a number of Serbs—followed in 1998.

was impossible to dislike him, and I was grateful for the personal support he had given me even when we disagreed.

Reviving Implementation. The good news in Sarajevo was that the joint institutions actually existed; the bad news was that they barely functioned.

The joint presidency, composed of Izetbegovic, Krajisnik, and Zubak, was one of the most important litmus tests of Dayton. I was gratified to see that our decision to limit the presidency to three people—one from each ethnic group—had been correct, but the joint presidency was still a limited operation. It had been in a state of suspension for over a month as a Serb protest against the British operation on July 10 in Prijedor—the most important military action since Dayton—which had resulted in the capture of one indicted war criminal and the death of another. The dead Serb had been one of Karadzic's closest allies, the Prijedor police chief, a notorious killer during the 1992 "death camp" phase of the war, and his death had been a serious blow to the Bosnian Serbs. Only our trip to Sarajevo had forced Krajisnik to attend.

The meeting began in an unlikely manner. Looking directly at me, Krajisnik said that he wanted to make an opening comment. "At Dayton," he said, "I opposed the agreement. I was wrong. I opposed the deployment of IFOR. I was wrong. Dayton is a good thing for Bosnia. I want to make this clear, especially to Ambassador Holbrooke."

This statement was not as promising as it sounded. Krajisnik's "Dayton" was not what we had in mind; his was a way station on the path to partition, ours was an agreement for a single country. He may have signed the agreement, but he still refused to accept its central thesis.

Krajisnik was immovable on every issue. Fed up, we ended the meeting and asked to see him alone. Gelbard and I angrily told him that his behavior was unacceptable, and obviously incompatible with his opening statement of support for Dayton. I said we had not come all this way just to participate in a meaningless meeting. We scheduled a second meeting for that evening at the National Museum in Federation territory. When Krajisnik protested the venue, we told him that if he did not come to the museum we would assume he was withdrawing from the joint presidency. This startled Krajisnik, and he backed down.

Another All-nighter. We resumed at about ten o'clock that evening, August 7, at the National Museum, and turned immediately to three unresolved problems: creating a single telephone system, agreeing on the distribution of ambassadorships among the three ethnic communities, and getting the Standing Committee on Military Matters functioning.

The meetings ended at four in the morning, with agreements on all these issues. The last carried equally great symbolic value, especially when the Muslims agreed that the ambassador in Washington would be a Serb, while they retained the position at the United Nations.

When the final documents were ready for signature, the acting High Representative, Gerd Wagner, brought them in for Krajisnik's signature. Wagner, whom I had known well in Bonn and Washington, was one of Germany's rising diplomatic stars. Krajisnik clearly disliked Wagner, and instead of signing the agreements, he began to pick a fight with the affable German diplomat. Furious at Krajisnik's abuse of Wagner, I leaned forward across the table and said, "I want to tell you something I have never said to anyone else in this long negotiating process: if you do not sign this paper now, as you already promised in front of witnesses, I promise we will never speak to you or deal with you again." I handed Krajisnik a pen, and he signed the agreements. The next morning, Wagner joined Gelbard and me at a press conference at the American Embassy to announce the agreements of the previous evening. It was a real achievement for Wagner, the highest-ranking German diplomat in Bosnia—but it was one of his last. A few weeks later, he and eleven other people, including five Americans, died when a Ukrainian helicopter crashed into the side of a hill. Once again, as at Mount Igman and Dubrovnik, the enforcing nations had paid the ultimate price for their efforts to bring peace to Bosnia. And once again, the dead were civilians, diplomats, policemen, and aid workers—not soldiers.

A few days later, *The New York Times* would criticize me for having "spent the bulk of [my] time haggling over telephone area codes and designs for a currency and the appointment of Bosnian ambassadors [instead] of dealing with the principal threats to a unified Bosnia." But the front-page article missed one of the main points of our trip, and indeed of the entire implementation process: to create a unified Bosnia, these seemingly small issues had to be solved, one by one if necessary—and this could be done only under external pressure. The parties themselves could not voluntarily agree on anything yet. *The Washington Post* got it right, reporting that "Holbrooke's efforts [were] seen as part of the campaign to end a sense of drift that had settled over the Bosnia peacemaking effort." Our trip helped revive the implementation process, and set the stage for further progress. Bob Gelbard would continue to travel to the region regularly, hammering the parties into slow but steady progress.

Banja Luka and Plavsic. Immediately after the press conference announcing the new agreements on August 8, we flew to Banja Luka to see Biljana Plavsic, who was now receiving international attention for her defiance of both the Pale Serbs and Milosevic. A biologist during the Tito era, she had been a Fulbright scholar in New York and spoke serviceable English. She was on her best behavior, trying hard to charm us. The United States, in turn, had put its weight behind her in her struggle against Pale. Nonetheless, we could not ignore her unsavory origins and close ties to Karadzic.

"I want you to know that while I am still a nationalist, I am also a good democrat," she began. This was a shrewd start. "But what I must ask you," I responded, "is whether you are still a separatist."

"No," she answered firmly, "I do not support a separate Serb state, I support Dayton." Later, although we had agreed to keep our conversation private, her staff made this exchange public. It represented a complete change for her since the days when Bosnian Serbs named tanks after her.

She told us she feared for her life at the hands of Pale thugs. She said that her meeting with Madeleine Albright in May had been critical in her decision to stand up to her former mentors. The day after that meeting, she said, she had gone to Pale to meet with Krajisnik, Buha—and Karadzic. "I told them we should comply with Dayton," she said, "and they attacked me, told me I had betrayed the revolution, and threw me out of the party."

When it was time to leave, the most revealing moment of the day occurred. Over one hundred journalists were waiting downstairs. We had assumed she would keep her distance from us in their presence. Instead, she announced that she would sit with us and participate. In addition, she asked David Lipton to explain to the press the price the Bosnian Serbs were paying in lost international aid because of Pale's refusal to participate in the joint institutions.

Mrs. Plavsic had crossed the Rubicon. It would be difficult for her to scramble back. She had chosen to defy Pale, and was clearly, publicly, counting on American support.

Belgrade, August 8. Once again, Milosevic had moved the meeting place, this time to the "White Palace," a magnificent royal dwelling in Belgrade unused for over a decade. The gardens were splendid, the food significantly better, and the walls filled with Old Masters, including a Rembrandt. But these cosmetic changes only emphasized that nothing else had changed. In fact, the sense of isolation felt greater.

Alone in the palace except for his faithful aide Goran Milinovic and one Deputy Minister, Milosevic said that Dayton was succeeding and that we should be satisfied, except for the troubles that Mrs. Plavsic was causing. We disagreed strongly, saying that Karadzic was now openly violating the July 18, 1996, agreement, and that, by backing Pale over Plavsic, Milosevic was undermining stability in Bosnia. The meeting meandered on, and even a private talk in the gardens was unproductive.

During dinner, Milosevic and I spoke alone in the reception room. "Mr. President," I said, "we have been wasting our time tonight. We are willing to return tomorrow if you wish to bring Krajisnik here so that we can try to make some progress." We finished the meal without any progress.

· · ·

Gelbard and I returned to the White Palace the next morning alone, wondering if Krajisnik would appear. He had told us flatly in Sarajevo that he would not come to another meeting in Belgrade. But there he was, sitting quietly in a chair next to Milosevic, his demeanor quite different from what we had seen two days earlier.

We turned first to Radovan Karadzic, still the overriding issue. I showed the two men an interview that Karadzic had given the previous day to a German newspaper. Both Milosevic and Krajisnik professed to be unaware of the interview, but they readily agreed that it constituted a flagrant violation of the July 18 agreement. We warned that such actions would increase the chances of a military action to bring Karadzic to justice.

"If you take such action," Milosevic said emphatically, "it will be a disaster for all of us. Your nation will regret it." Gelbard and I shrugged. "That is your problem," I said. "You cannot threaten our nation. What happens in Bosnia is important to us, but not decisive. For you these events are life and death."

Krajisnik offered a guarantee that Karadzic "would henceforth comply fully with the July 18 agreement." We rejected this as no longer sufficient. "If you wish to affirm that the July 18 agreement is still valid, you may do so, and we will report it publicly," I said. "But we cannot make a second agreement with you. You signed the first one, and it has been violated."

We concluded the meeting by discussing several other issues that concerned us.* Then, after a press conference, we left for the United States. For the first time since Dayton, I felt that the implementation effort was being pursued with sufficient vigor and determination, thanks in large part to Gelbard and Clark. At a meeting in the Cabinet Room on Friday, August 15, I told the President and other senior officials that we were still far behind schedule, but progress was visible in many parts of Bosnia. At the local level, people were trying to live and work together again. But it was necessary to repeat a warning that was now nearly two years old: as long as the leaders who had started the war remained in power in Pale, the country would not be out of danger, and it would be almost impossible to withdraw our troops.

The President Decides. On December 22, 1997, President Clinton made his second trip to Bosnia. He took with him not only his family and members of Congress but, in a brilliant display of bipartisanship, former Senator and Mrs. Dole. Dole had told me in early September that he would support an extension of the American troop presence in Bosnia, information I promptly relayed, with Dole's blessing, to the President, and the two men, once political

---

* The bulk of the meeting concerned matters that are still "operational," and must therefore be omitted from this account.

adversaries, had found common ground over the need to stay the course in Bosnia.

Two days before his trip, President Clinton held a news conference in which he announced that the United States would keep American troops in Bosnia past the original June 1998 deadline. The President accepted full responsibility for agreeing to the two earlier deadlines, and said he would set no further deadlines.

This was a benchmark decision for the United States. The President had finally made it explicit that we would not walk away from Bosnia. Three days later, he took that message directly to the people of the Balkans.

I talked often to the President and his senior advisors in the weeks prior to his announcement and his trip, and I knew how difficult the decision was at the personal level, especially since his political opponents were determined to take advantage of it. But he knew that the original timetable would have done enormous damage to the national interests of the United States and NATO. We spoke again right after the trip, and it was clear that seeing Sarajevo for the first time had had a powerful impact on him and his family. I had the sense that the trip had reaffirmed in his mind the correctness of his strategic decisions, and clarified for him the difficulties that still lay ahead.

1998—and Milorad Dodik. Once it was clear that the United States would not stick to the June 1998 withdrawal deadline, the pace of implementation picked up dramatically. The first few months of 1998 saw more movement than the two years since the unification of Sarajevo. The common currency coupon, offices handling automobile license plates, rail and air traffic, and the telephone system all began to function.

In a gamble that paid off, the United States backed a proposal by Plavsic to hold new elections for the Republika Srpska Assembly. In our August 1997 meeting, Gelbard and I told Milosevic that we would back these elections over his strenuous objections. Faced with our unyielding position, Milosevic changed course and began to deal with Plavsic, whom he had long ridiculed publicly.

The results of the election, held in September 1997 under OSCE supervision, were stunning. Eighteen of the new Bosnian Serb assembly members were Muslims, elected by refugees voting in their home areas under one of the constitutional provisions hammered out at the last moment at Dayton. These Muslim legislators combined with Plavsic's supporters and those controlled by Milosevic to elect as Prime Minister—by one vote—a previously obscure thirty-nine-year-old businessman named Milorad Dodik. For the first time since the war began, the Bosnian Serb government was not controlled by Karadzic's SDS. While the Sarajevo government watched skeptically, Dodik announced that he would honor Dayton and build a multiethnic Bosnia. The United States, in return, began to release aid funds that had previously been denied to the Bosnian Serbs. The long-awaited dismantling of the Bosnian Serb wartime capital at Pale began as the assembly and government offices moved, one by one, to Banja Luka.

Even the most hardened critics of Dayton were impressed. The American effort in Bosnia was paying off. By March the United States was sufficiently pleased with the situation that it began to "reward" Belgrade for supporting Dodik by removing some of the remaining economic restrictions on Yugoslavia.

Kosovo. In March 1998, violent conflict erupted in Kosovo between the Albanian Muslim majority and their Serbian masters. We had always viewed Kosovo as the most explosive tinderbox in the region—the historic home of the Serb people, the site of the greatest battle against the Turks and of Milosevic's famous 1989 speech. An eruption in Kosovo, which the rest of the world acknowledged as a part of Yugoslavia, could trigger a wider war, involving Albania and Macedonia and perhaps even Greece; this concern had been a crucial element in my efforts in 1995 to reduce Greek-Albanian tensions and to broker a settlement between Greece and Macedonia. By ending the war in Bosnia, we had prevented Kosovo and Bosnia from becoming a single theater of war, but the problem of Kosovo remained.

At Dayton, we had repeatedly emphasized to Milosevic the need to restore the rights of Kosovo's Albanian Muslims, which he had revoked when he absorbed the formerly autonomous province into Serbia. Our warnings at the time restrained him. But the long-feared crisis in Kosovo was postponed, not avoided. By 1998, Milosevic had still not restored the Albanian Muslims' rights, as he had promised to do. When groups of Albanians began to mount guerrilla attacks against the Serb occupiers, Milosevic cracked down ruthlessly, leaving hundreds of Muslims dead. Secretary Albright, determined not to repeat the mistakes of 1991–92, moved swiftly to create a united Contact Group front to put pressure on Milosevic, but, in a replay of Bosnia, it was difficult to gain a unified stance sufficient to impress him. The challenge posed by Kosovo showed again that American leadership, even when it irritated our European allies and Russia, remained indispensable to peace in the region.

CHAPTER 21

America, Europe, and Bosnia

Providence has not created mankind entirely independent or entirely free. It is true that around every man a fatal circle is traced
beyond which he cannot pass; but within the wide verge of that circle he is powerful and free; as it is with man, so with communities.
—ALEXIS DE TOCQUEVILLE

FROM THE BEGINNING OF YUGOSLAVIA'S COLLAPSE, Americans divided into
two groups, broadly defined: those who thought we should intervene for either
moral or strategic reasons, and those who feared that if we did, we would become entangled in a Vietnam-like quagmire. As awareness of ethnic cleansing
spread, the proportion of those who wanted the United States to "do something" increased, but they probably never constituted a majority.

Nonetheless, in only eighteen weeks in 1995—when the situation seemed
most hopeless—the United States put its prestige on the line with a series of
high-risk actions: an all-out diplomatic effort in August, heavy NATO bombing in September, a cease-fire in October, Dayton in November, and, in December, the deployment of twenty thousand American troops to Bosnia.
Suddenly, the war was over—and America's role in post–Cold War Europe re-
defined.

Had the United States not intervened, the war would have continued for
years and ended disastrously. The Bosnian Muslims would have been either
destroyed, or reduced to a weak landlocked ministate surrounded by a Greater
Croatia and a Greater Serbia. Fighting would eventually have resumed in eastern Slavonia. Europe would have faced a continued influx of Balkan refugees.
And tens of thousands more would have been killed, maimed, or displaced
from their homes.

But questions remain: Was American involvement in the national interest?
How did it affect America's role in the world? Did Dayton bring peace to
Bosnia, or only the absence of war? What might we have done better, or at
least differently? Can Bosnia survive as a single multiethnic country, as called
for in Dayton, or will it eventually divide into two or three ethnically based
states? These issues, and others, deserve further attention.

American Leadership. By the spring of 1995 it had become commonplace to say that Washington's relations with our European allies were worse than at any time since the 1956 Suez crisis. But this comparison was misleading; because Suez came at the height of the Cold War, the strain then was containable. Bosnia, however, had defined the first phase of the post–Cold War relationship between Europe and the United States, and seriously damaged the Atlantic relationship. In particular, the strains endangered NATO itself just as Washington sought to enlarge it.

The Clinton Administration was severely criticized for reneging on our commitments to European security and for lowering the general priority accorded to foreign affairs—in short, for weak leadership in foreign policy. These charges deeply troubled the Administration's senior foreign-policy officials, especially when, ironically, they often came from those who opposed American involvement in Bosnia. In its own eyes, the Clinton Administration had laid down a strong track record in post–Cold War Europe: it had built a new relationship with Russia and the other former Soviet republics; started to enlarge NATO; tackled the Irish problem; strengthened American ties with the Baltic nations and Central Europe; and gained congressional approval for the NAFTA and GATT trade agreements. Nonetheless, the perception that Washington had turned away from Europe at the end of the Cold War was hard to shake as long as we did nothing about Bosnia.

Dayton changed this almost overnight. Criticism of President Clinton as a weak leader ended abruptly, especially in Europe and among Muslim nations. Washington was now praised for its firm leadership—or even chided by some Europeans for *too much* leadership. But even those who chafed at the reassertion of American power conceded, at least implicitly, its necessity. As I suggested at the time, this was not a serious problem; it was better to be criticized for too much leadership than for too little.

After Dayton, American foreign policy seemed more assertive, more muscular. This may have been as much perception as reality, but the perception mattered. The three main pillars of American foreign policy in Europe—U.S.-Russian relations, NATO enlargement into Central Europe, and Bosnia—had often worked against each other. Now they reinforced each other: NATO sent its forces out of area for the first time in its history, and Russian troops, under an American commander, were deployed alongside them. "Clinton managed to pull off the seemingly impossible," wrote Russia's former Prime Minister, Yegor Gaidar, "to implement NATO enlargement without causing irreparable damage either to democratic elements in Russia's political establishment or to U.S.-Russian relations."[1] De Charette had it right: "America *was* back."

Strategic considerations were vital to our involvement, but the motives that finally pushed the United States into action were also moral and humanitarian.

After Srebrenica and Mount Igman the United States could no longer escape the terrible truth of what was happening in Bosnia. A surge of sentiment arose from ordinary Americans who were outraged at what they saw on television and from senior government officials who could no longer look the other way. Within the Administration, the loss of three friends on Mount Igman carried a special weight; the war had, in effect, come home.

Despite American pride over Dayton, our own record in the former Yugoslavia was flawed. The tortured half-measures of the United Nations and the European Union had been inadequate, to be sure, but they had kept the Bosnian Muslims from complete destruction for several years. And the Europeans continued to pay the bulk of the bills, without getting sufficient credit from the American public or the Congress, which, immediately after Dayton, told the Europeans that they would have to carry the burden for civilian reconstruction. Thus, the richest nation in the world, in the midst of its strongest economic performance in thirty years, offered the former Yugoslavia a relatively insignificant amount of aid. Furthermore, despite valiant efforts by John Kornblum, implementation of the Dayton agreement was initially halfhearted. Only in mid-1997, with the arrival of Bob Gelbard and General Clark, did the implementation effort begin to show the energy required.

A final report card on Dayton is not yet possible. When President Clinton visited Sarajevo in December 1997, he said, as I had, that implementation was running about a year behind schedule. But there had been no fighting for two years; the three communities had begun rebuilding ties at the local level; Sarajevo was reunified and rebuilding; a large number of Bosnian Serb weapons had been destroyed; four airports had opened for civilian traffic; a few refugee "open areas" had been created; the odious Pale television transmitters had been silenced; and Banja Luka had begun to replace Pale. At the same time, Carlos Westendorp, the High Representative, did what should have been done two years earlier: he simply decreed the design for a new common currency. On January 22, 1998, American soldiers made their first arrest of a war-crimes suspect in Bosnia: Goran Jelisic, a Bosnian Serb who liked to refer to himself as "the Serbian Adolf." If such actions continued, the anti-Dayton forces would be progressively weakened, and the chances of creating a peaceful, viable state would dramatically improve.

Still, while the bloodlust of 1991–95 had begun to subside, it was far from gone; all sides carried deep scars and many still sought revenge instead of reconciliation. Most troubling, the same leaders who had started the war were still trying to silence those who called for multiethnic cooperation. The two most dangerous men in the region, Radovan Karadzic and Ratko Mladic, remained at large more than two years after Dayton. With Karadzic's overt in-

volvement, the rearguard forces of Pale still sought to thwart cooperation between the two parts of Bosnia. They had discovered this strategy almost by accident when, "amid large-scale arson and police intimidation while IFOR
troops stood by," they drove most local Serbs out of Sarajevo in March 1996,
in what one experienced observer called "the greatest stain on the peace
process."[2] As Michael Steiner explained at the end of his tour as Deputy High
Representative in late 1997, "The Pale leadership has only one aim, and that
is to separate from Bosnia-Herzegovina. Short of that, they are fighting for as
autonomous a position as possible within the common state."[3] As long as Pale
had residual powers, the threat would be alive.

Flaws. No one knew the weaknesses of Dayton better than those who had
participated in the negotiations. But these were not necessarily the same as
those mentioned by outside critics, many of whom confused the peace agreement with its implementation. When I looked back on the negotiations, I invariably returned to several key moments or issues:

- The most serious flaw in the Dayton Peace Agreement was that it left
  two opposing armies in one country, one for the Serbs and one for the
  Croat-Muslim Federation. We were fully aware of this during the negotiations, but since NATO would not disarm the parties as an obligated task, creating a single army or disarming Bosnia-Herzegovina
  was not possible.

- A second problem was our agreement to allow the Serb portion of
  Bosnia to retain the name "Republika Srpska."* The decision, it will be
  recalled, was forged in the dramatic late-night meeting with Izetbegovic in Ankara on Labor Day, with the Geneva Foreign Ministers
  meeting only three days away and the resumption of the bombing still
  in doubt. "Republic" does not necessarily connote an independent
  country in the Balkans and eastern Europe, but nonetheless, to permit
  Karadzic to keep the name he had invented was more of a concession
  than we then realized.

- The timing of the end of the bombing will always remain disputed. The
  negotiating team would have welcomed its prolongation for at least another week. But when the military told us in the second week of September that they had only about three days of targets left, we had to
  negotiate before the bombing ended on its own. Warren Christopher
  questioned the military's statement privately, but neither he nor the ne-

---

* See Chapter 8.

gotiating team was able to learn the full facts.* Informal discussion between us and General Michael Ryan, who commanded Deliberate Force, would have allowed more informed decisions at a critical moment. But such contact was apparently barred by Admiral Leighton Smith, even through General Clark.[4]

- The creation of a weak International Police Task Force had especially serious consequences. This was the result of several factors, including European objections to a strong international police force, and Washington's refusal, during a huge budget confrontation with the new Republican Congress, to ask for sufficient American funds for the police. We had identified the problem before Dayton but could not overcome our internal difficulties.

- In his memoirs, Carl Bildt wrote that, in regard to the mandate of the High Representative, "the Americans initially stressed purely military aspects and did not want any cohesive civilian or political authority."[5] Bildt's observation is valid, although the position he criticizes was not that of the negotiating team, which argued this point by phone with NATO throughout the first ten days at Dayton. Even the compromise position we reached with General Joulwan was a mistake. Bildt's mandate should have been stronger. On the other hand, when the Bosnian Serbs defied Dayton, the United States urged Bildt to interpret the authority granted him by Dayton more broadly, at which point, ironically, resistance came from the Europeans, who, having correctly criticized us initially for limiting Bildt's mandate, then reined him in.

- Finally, there were the two arbitrary time limits cited earlier: one year for IFOR; eighteen months for SFOR. They left the impression that the Serbs might be able to outwait the enforcing powers, thus encouraging delaying tactics. By laying out self-imposed time limits, the United States only weakened itself. Everyone closely associated with implementation knew this from the outset. As Madeleine Albright said in a speech in January 1998, "The mission should determine the timetable, not the other way around."[6] When the President dropped the time limits in December 1997, he sent the strongest possible signal that the United States would stay the course, with immediate results.

One Country or Two (or Three)? The most serious criticism of the peace agreement came from those who questioned its central premise, that Bosnia should, or could, be reconstructed as a single, multiethnic country. It was fash-

---

* See Chapter 10.

ionable for critics of Dayton to contend that this was not achievable and that the United States should accept, if not encourage, the partition of Bosnia along ethnic lines. While Dayton was a successful cease-fire agreement, this argument went, its political provisions—giving refugees the right of return and affirming a single country and a central government—could never be implemented. Skeptics—including many old Yugoslav hands—had warned us from the outset that it would be impossible for a multiethnic state to survive in Bosnia. But most of those who opposed a multiethnic Bosnia after Dayton had been proven wrong at least twice: first, in 1991, when they believed that Yugoslavia could be held together, then again when, for the most part, they opposed military action or American intervention.

Still, as implementation slipped seriously behind schedule in 1996–97, some criticized Dayton as a partition agreement, while others criticized it precisely because it was not one. The most distinguished and influential American proponent of the latter view was Henry Kissinger, who argued that Bosnia had never existed as an independent nation and that we should not try to create it now.[7] The negotiating team did not share this view. It was not that we underestimated the difficulties of getting the leaders of the three ethnic groups to cooperate; no one knew this better than those of us who had conducted the negotiations! But every other choice was worse. Dividing the country along ethnic lines would create massive new refugee flows. Serbs, Croats, and Muslims who still lived as minorities in many parts of the country would be forced to flee their homes, and fighting would be certain to break out as the scramble for land and houses erupted again. Thus, contrary to the arguments of the partitionists, the chances of fighting would be increased, not decreased, by partition and the relocation that would follow. In addition, there was a moral issue: the United States and its European allies could not be party to creating more refugees and legitimizing the Serb aggression. As *The Economist* wrote two years after Dayton,

> Partition would almost certainly provoke mass migration and further bloodshed. . . . And the fighting might not be confined to Bosnia. The spectacle of a partitioned Bosnia would hearten every separatist in the Balkans. In areas of ethnic instability like Macedonia and Kosovo, who would listen to the West as it urged the merits of sinking differences and living together in harmony? . . . Fans of partition tend to ignore the situation in central Bosnia, where many Croats live in enclaves surrounded by Muslims. Knowing they would be left in a Muslim-dominated state, most of these Croats dread partition.[8]

Of course, as I had written to President Clinton after Dayton, no vital national interest of the United States was directly affected by whether Bosnia was one, two, or three countries. We did not oppose a voluntary change in the international boundaries in Bosnia-Herzegovina or its eventual division into more than one country—if that were the desire of a majority of each of the three ethnic groups at some future date. Other countries had broken up peacefully in recent years, including Czechoslovakia and the Soviet Union. But this could be decided only by *elections free of intimidation,* something that was not possible in the aftermath of the war, while the ultranationalist parties, preaching separatist ethnic hatred, were in control of the media and the police. With a new election scheduled for September 1998, one could hope that new leaders would emerge. In all three ethnic groups, the men who started the war in 1991–92 were still in power as late as spring 1998. They have to disappear to make way for a new generation of leaders willing to reach out to one another, as Prime Minister Dodik of Republika Srpska has begun to do. If more leaders like Dodik appeared, and survived, then the original Dayton design could work. The connective tissue of the central government could function, something that had not yet happened by the spring of 1998. By then, the greatest threat to a single Bosnia came not from the Serbs, but from the Bosnian Croats.

AMERICA, STILL A EUROPEAN POWER

Even with the Cold War over, what happens in Europe still matters to the United States. This is not self-evident to most Americans, who thought the need for direct American involvement in Europe—and for that matter, most of the rest of the world—would end or decline sharply with the fall of communism.

But American involvement in Europe is not limited to crusades against fascism or communism. Deeper, less tangible factors tie the two continents together. Three times earlier in this century, the United States engaged deeply on the European continent: in World War I, in World War II, and in the Cold War. After each of the first two involvements, the United States withdrew, or began to withdraw, from the continent: in 1919–20, when it decided not to join the international institution President Wilson had helped create, and in 1945–47. After World War II, America's leaders recognized that the country's national interests required a continued involvement in Europe, as well as in Asia.* But when their initial policy, based on the effectiveness of the United Nations, failed because it required the positive participation of the Soviet Union, the Truman Administration quickly recognized its initial misjudgment of Moscow

---

* It is noteworthy that, in contrast to Europe, the United States has maintained military forces in East Asia and the Pacific continuously for one hundred years, since 1898, except when the Japanese drove us from the area in 1942–43.

and entered into the century's third American engagement in Europe, one that led to the collapse of the Soviet Union at the end of 1991.

Then, after fifty years of costly involvement in Europe, Americans hoped to focus on domestic priorities and disengage as much as possible from international commitments. Although understandable, this hope was unrealistic. Well before the Bosnia negotiations began, I argued that "an unstable Europe would still threaten essential security interests of the United States."[9] But, with the disappearance of the Soviet Union, most Americans no longer believed this. There was no clear and present threat to the Western democracies, no Hitler or Stalin. Moreover, for the first time since 1917, Russia and its former republics had to be incorporated into Europe's security structure rather than excluded from it. This new European security structure could not be built while part of it, the former Yugoslavia, was in flames. Settling Bosnia was necessary, although not sufficient, for true stability and long-term economic growth in Europe.

The policies of the last half century produced unparalleled peace and prosperity for half a century—but for only half a continent. With the war over in Bosnia, building a new European security architecture that included both the United States and Russia could finally proceed. NATO, long the private preserve of the nations on one side of the Iron Curtain, could gradually open its doors to qualified Central European nations—in a manner that neither threatened Russia nor weakened the alliance. Meanwhile, a new role for Russia, Ukraine, and the other parts of the former Soviet Union was being defined through new agreements like the Founding Act, which created a formal relationship between Russia and NATO yet did not give Russia a veto power over NATO activities. Other existing institutions, like the Organization for Security and Cooperation in Europe (OSCE), were strengthened and expanded.

Leadership Without Unilateralism. The great architect of European unity, Jean Monnet, once observed, "Nothing is possible without men, but nothing is lasting without institutions." It has become commonplace to observe that achieving Monnet's vision is far more difficult in the absence of the unifying effect of a common adversary. But we should not wax nostalgic for the Cold War. It is now institutional and structural problems that inhibit progress on both sides of the Atlantic.

The United States has survived divided government between the Executive Branch and the Congress for much of the last two decades. But a bloated bureaucratic system and a protracted struggle between the two branches have eroded much of Washington's capacity for decisive action in foreign affairs and reduced our presence just as our range of interests has increased. The United States continues to reduce the resources committed to international affairs even as vast parts of the globe—the former Soviet bloc, China—and new issues that once lay outside its area of direct involvement now take on new importance and require American attention. One cannot have a global economic policy without a political and strategic vision to accompany it, as the 1997–98 economic crisis in East Asia has shown.

If the search for a process that can produce coherent policies is difficult in Washington, it seems to be virtually impossible in the new Europe. Carl Bildt has made a useful observation: the United States, he points out, has to harmonize "institutional views" while Europe has to coordinate "national views." Bildt, who saw the two systems from a unique vantage point, observed:

> In Washington everything has to be formulated and shaped in a continuous compromise between the State Department, the Defense Department, the Treasury, intelligence agencies, and purely domestic factors. The rivalry between these various interests sometimes runs very deep. A great deal of blood can be spilt in the course of inter-agency debates in Washington. *But when this apparatus finally decides on a policy, the United States then has the resources to implement its policy which is almost completely lacking in Europe* [emphasis added].[10]

A QUESTION OF EVIL

Advocates of realpolitik, like three of its most famous American practitioners, Richard Nixon, Henry Kissinger, and George Kennan, have long argued that American advocacy of human rights conflicted with America's true national security interests, amounted to interference in the internal affairs of other nations, and weakened the nation's strategic and commercial interests. In his most recent book, *Diplomacy,* Kissinger portrayed American foreign policy as a constant struggle between realism, symbolized by Theodore Roosevelt, and idealism, as epitomized by Woodrow Wilson. Kissinger, who strongly favored TR, wrote, "The American experience has encouraged the belief that America, alone among the nations of the world, is impervious and that it can prevail by the example of its virtues and good works. In the post–Cold War world, such an attitude would turn innocence into self-indulgence."[11]

Under Presidents Nixon, Ford, and Bush, such "realist" theories were in the ascendancy. (The Carter Administration and the Reagan Administration, after the forced departure of Secretary of State Al Haig, took much more assertive positions on human rights.) But based on personal experiences in the late 1970s with authoritarian leaders like Ferdinand Marcos of the Philippines and Park Chung Hee of South Korea—both of whose corrupt strongman regimes were peacefully replaced by democracies—I came to the conclusion that the choice between "realists" and "idealists" was a false one: in the long run, our strategic interests and human rights supported and reinforced each other, and could be advanced at the same time. In short, American foreign policy needed to embrace both Theodore Roosevelt and Woodrow Wilson. These thoughts were never far from my mind as we searched for a way to end the war.

Throughout the negotiations, I thought often of the refugees I had visited in 1992: how they knew many of the men who had killed and raped their families; how some of the killers had been their co-workers for twenty years; and how they had hardly been aware of ethnic hatred until 1990. Some people offered what had happened during World War II as proof that ethnic hatred was in the Yugoslav bloodstream. But the bloodbath and fighting of 1941–45 were a product of the larger struggle and genocide Hitler had unleashed. The rest of Europe found a path to peace and reconciliation, but Yugoslavia suffered a bad case of arrested development under communism. Them demagogic and criminal leaders seized power.

The killers were driven by ethnic prejudice rekindled by ultranationalists and demagogues. How could adults do such things to their neighbors and former classmates? After a while, the search for explanations failed. One simply had to recognize that there was true evil in the world.

The full ferocity of that evil so stunned most Europeans and Americans that they could not at first comprehend it. Then, as Carl Jung had warned, they did not know "what to pit against it." There was confusion over whom to blame, and disputes about what was happening; this increased as the war continued, since atrocities were committed by members of all three ethnic groups. But although Croats and Muslims were also guilty of atrocities, the Bosnian Serbs remained the primary perpetrators of the actions that made the phrase "ethnic cleansing" a part of the English language.

It was easy to conclude, as Eagleburger did, that nothing could be done by outsiders. Or that Serbs were inherently evil. Such judgments allowed people to justify their own inaction. But drawing either inference would be to share the fundamental mistake of the people of the Balkans themselves, imputing to an entire ethnic group the attributes of its worst elements. For more than fifty years people had debated the degree to which the entire German people shared culpability for the Holocaust, and now a similar question arose: was the entire Serb "nation" responsible for the actions of its leaders and their murderous followers?

I often received letters, primarily from Serbs or Serbian Americans, charging that my remarks, or those of other American officials, lumped all Serbs together with a few indicted war criminals. This was a fair criticism of comments that could not always be precise. In fact, the majority of Serbs in the former Yugoslavia were ordinary people who did not kill anyone, although, like many "good Germans" during the Third Reich, a large number remained silent or passive in the face of something they admitted later they knew was wrong. But others were courageous opponents of the fires that raged across their land, and some even fought on the Muslim side. One of contemporary Europe's great visionaries, Czech President Vaclav Havel, addressed this issue in an eloquent essay:

> I consider it an offense against the Serbian people and betrayal of the civic notion of society when evil is identified with Serbian nationality. But I find it equally misguided when evil is not defined at all, for fear of hurting Serbian feelings. All peoples have their Karadžićs and Mladićs, either real or potential. If such men—as the result of a mix of historical, social, and cultural circumstances—gain greater influence than they have in other parts of the world, it does not mean that they come from a criminal people. . . . [This] is a conflict of principles, not of nationalities. . . . In other words, let us beware of attempts to lay the blame for evil on whole peoples. That would be tantamount to adopting the ideology of the ethnic fanatics.[12]

WAS BOSNIA UNIQUE?

After Dayton we came full circle, back to an uncertainty about how much to invest in Bosnia. Having put American prestige on the line in 1995 to end the war, the United States and its allies were uncertain in 1996 and early 1997 about how hard to try to make Dayton work. The result was halfhearted implementation that led critics and cynics to call for scaled-back objectives in Bosnia. Failure to squash the separatist Serb movement immediately after Dayton, when it lay in disarray, seemed to some to prove that partition was inevitable. Such preemptive defeatism could have led to the permanent partition of Bosnia, followed by more refugees and more fighting. The best course remained vigorous enforcement of the Dayton agreement. At the end of 1997, President Clinton's decision to remove the time limit for U.S. troops dramatically enhanced the chance of success. In 1998 the main constraint was no longer the separatists of Pale, who were beaten, corrupt, and in disarray. Success was within sight, but it would take hard work and a firm commitment from the leaders of the international community—and time.

The circumstances that led to the collapse of Yugoslavia and the war in Bosnia were so extraordinary that it is difficult to conceive of their recurrence. Yet if history teaches us one thing, it is that history is unpredictable. There will be other Bosnias in our lives, different in every detail but similar in one overriding manner: they will originate in distant and ill-understood places, explode with little warning, and present the rest of the world with difficult choices—choices between risky involvement and potentially costly neglect. But if during the Cold War Washington sometimes seemed too ready to intervene, today America and its allies often seem too willing to ignore problems outside their heartland.

There will be other Bosnias in our lives—areas where early outside involvement can be decisive, and American leadership will be required. The world's richest nation, one that presumes to great moral authority, cannot simply make worthy appeals to conscience and call on others to carry the burden. The world will look to Washington for more than rhetoric the next time we face a challenge to peace.

Afterword and
Acknowledgments

But often, in the world's most crowded streets,
But often, in the din of strife,
There rises an unspeakable desire
After the knowledge of our buried life;
A thirst to spend our fire and restless force
In tracking out our true, original course;
A longing to inquire
Into the mystery of this heart which beats
So wild, so deep in us—to know
Whence our lives come and where they go.

—MATTHEW ARNOLD, *The Buried Life*

IN APRIL 1968, AVERELL HARRIMAN AND CYRUS VANCE asked me to join the negotiating team they were assembling for the first direct talks with the North Vietnamese. I arrived in Paris a few days later, a twenty-six-year-old Foreign Service officer caught up in the excitement of the world's most closely watched negotiation. In Paris I read with fascination *Peacemaking 1919,* Harold Nicolson's diary of his experiences on the British negotiating team at Versailles. But, lacking his discipline, I left Paris in the summer of 1969 without having kept any personal record of my experience.

Still, the memories remained—of Averell Harriman, at the age of seventy-seven, tirelessly trying to convince President Johnson to stop the bombing of North Vietnam; Cyrus Vance sleeping on the floor of his office to ease the pain of a slipped disc; secret talks in Paris suburbs with the North Vietnamese; private emissaries from Vice President Hubert Humphrey asking if he should break with LBJ over Vietnam and resign; and visits from a Harvard professor (and Administration advisor) named Henry Kissinger. During the dramatic final week of the campaign President Johnson halted the bombing of the north, and Richard Nixon won a paper-thin victory over Humphrey amidst a welter of accusations over Vietnam. An opportunity to end the war—and not just the bombing—suddenly slipped away, and the conflict continued for another four years. Contrary to most accounts of this seminal period in American history, it was neither foreordained nor inevitable that the war should continue, with another twenty-five thousand Americans and countless Vietnamese dead. A negotiated end to the war in 1968 was possible; the distance to peace was far smaller than most historians realize.

When, twenty-seven years later, President Clinton and Secretary of State Christopher asked me to take over the Bosnia negotiations, my friend and teacher Fritz Stern urged me to keep a detailed personal record. History was becoming harder to preserve and reconstruct, he pointed out; internal memoranda, telegrams, and other traditional forms of communication had been replaced by secure telephone calls and private faxes that were lost to history.

Of course, he was right. But the pace and intensity of the negotiations left me and most of my colleagues with neither the time nor the energy to keep a detailed record, not even at Dayton. My own cables to Washington were extremely rare, and although my Pentagon colleagues did send regular messages to their superiors, these were incomplete, often intentionally so. The best I could do was to dictate a few thoughts occasionally, and preserve a handful of random notes.

But I remembered the failure to record the 1968 story when its memories were still fresh. Encouraged by my friend and agent, Mort Janklow, and guided by the superb editorial team at Random House—Jason Epstein and Joy de Menil, and, until their departures, Harry Evans and Peter Osnos—I set out to tell the story of these negotiations before the details had receded in my mind.

For a better understanding of events, especially those that did not involve our negotiating team, I consulted as many former colleagues (and journalists) as possible. Some simply responded to a specific question; others spent hours going through their records or journals to help reconstruct events. Many participants offered specific suggestions for revision or rewording, almost all of which I accepted. Others—including some not involved directly in the negotiations—took time to read all or part of the manuscript, and made important suggestions.

Valuable work of historical preservation was done in 1996–97 at the direction of Warren Christopher and Tom Donilon. Recognizing that the publication of State Department documents in the annual Foreign Relations of the United States (FRUS) series was no longer adequate alone, they established an experimental unit within the State Department's Historical Division, to produce a history based both on written records and on supplemental oral histories. They chose Bosnia as the first subject for this experiment, and asked Derek Chollet, a young Columbia University historian, to write the study.

When declassified, it will provide an invaluable resource for other historians. I am especially grateful to Derek for his subsequent assistance to me as a researcher, general advisor, and friend throughout the latter part of this project.

I am indebted to many others who offered information, editorial suggestions, or general assistance, including: Morton Abramowitz, Sheppie Abramowitz, Marshall Adair, Madeleine Albright, Walter Andrusyzyn, Kofi Annan, Don Bandler, Marsha Barnes, Reginald Bartholomew, Richard Beattie, Sandy Berger, Carl Bildt, Joachim Bitterlich, Alan Blinken, Donald Blinken, General Charles Boyd, Robert Bradtke, John Burns, Nick Burns, General George Casey, Warren Christopher, General Wesley Clark, Hillary Rodham Clinton, President Clinton, James Collins, Admiral William Crowe, Tom Donilon, Sandy Drew, Linda Bird Francke, Katharina Frasure, Bennett Freeman, Dan Fried, Leon Fuerth, Peter Galbraith, Ejup Ganic, Judy Gelb, Leslie H. Gelb, Philip Goldberg, Vice President Gore, Marc Grossman, Sir David Hannay, the late Pamela Harriman, Chris Hill, Chris Hoh, Robert Hunter, Douglas Hurd, Maxine Isaacs, Wolfgang Ischinger, Cati James, James A. Johnson, Vernon Jordan, General George Joulwan, Lena Kaplan, Sir John Kerr, Major General Donald Kerrick, Joe Klein, John Kornblum, Gail Kruzel, Tony Lake, David Lipton, Jan Lodal, Colonel Robert Lowe, Endre Marton, Ilona Marton, Mike McCurry, John Menzies, Judy Miller, Tom Miller, Tom Niles, Victoria Nuland, James O'Brien, Roberts Owen, James Pardew, Rosemarie Pauli, Rudy Perina, William Perry, David Phillips, Tom Pickering, Sir Robin Renwick, Jamie Rubin, Miriam Sapiro, Aric Schwan, Tom Schick, Arthur M. Schlesinger, Jr., Robert Schrum, General John Shalikashvili, John Shattuck, Brooke Shearer, Doug Shoen, Tom Siebert, Haris Silajdzic, Walter Slocombe, George Soros, James Steinberg, George Stephanopoulos, Fritz Stern, Elizabeth Stevens, George Stevens, Loucas Tsilas, Cyrus Vance, Jon Vanden Heuvel, Sandy Vershbow, Elie Wiesel, Frank Wisner, and Warren Zimmermann.

Jim O'Brien at the State Department and Don Kerrick at the NSC were especially helpful in obtaining the necessary clearances for the publication of this book, and also gave valuable advice along the way.

Among those who offered advice and assistance, I must single out one person: Strobe Talbott, who despite his backbreaking schedule as Deputy Secretary of State gave generously of his time to offer detailed criticism and corrections. I deeply grateful both to him and to his wife, Brooke Shearer, for their support and friendship.

I must also express special thanks to my colleagues at Crédit Suisse First Boston—Rainer Gut, Jack Hennessy, Lucas Muhlmann, Allen Wheat, and Chuck Ward—for their understanding and support. Without their forbearance, especially when this project ran longer than anticipated, it could never have been completed. As always, I owe Beverly Snyder special thanks for carrying out so many administrative and secretarial tasks, big and small but always "urgent," with such skill and charm.

It is commonplace to end acknowledgments with a few words about one's family. In this case it is hard to find the proper words to describe what I owe to my wife, Kati, who lived every twist and turn of this story, often participating directly. Perhaps because she was born in nearby Hungary, she had an almost intuitive understanding of the people of the region. She also played an important role in Bosnia on her own, as chair of the Committee to Protect Journalists, promoting press freedom during several trips to the region. Some of her contributions are mentioned in the text, but not the most important—the intangible ones of love and support.

My two sons, who endured the Carter years as children, are now grown and successful in their own careers. They are a constant source of pride and joy, and their support for my efforts was enormously important. Anthony appeared in this story unexpectedly at a critical moment right after the fall of Srebrenica, and performed with the skill and courage that makes a father proud. His older brother, David, gave me love and encouragement when it was most needed. Kati's two wonderful children, Elizabeth and Christopher, also got into the spirit of the project, even helping with some of the final editing.

I am grateful to everyone for their help. Still, I expect that many readers, especially those who lived through parts of this story, will come forward with suggestions or corrections. I look forward to incorporating them in any future edition of this work.

Cast of Characters

Yasushi Akashi	Senior U.N. Envoy to the Former Yugoslavia (1993–95)
Madeleine Albright	U.S. Ambassador to the U.N. (1993–97); Secretary of State (1997–)
Kofi Annan	U.N. Undersecretary-General for Peacekeeping (1993–97); Secretary-General (1997–)
Arkan (Zeljko Raznatovic)	Leader of paramilitary Serbs
James Baker	U.S. Secretary of State (1989–92)
Samuel (Sandy) Berger	U.S. Deputy National Security Adviser (1993–96); National Security Advisor (1996–)
Carl Bildt	European Union Peace Envoy, High Representative in Bosnia (1995–97)
Jacques Blot	French Representative to the Contact Group (1995–)
Boutros Boutros-Ghali	U.N. Secretary-General (1990–97)
Aleksi Buha	Bosnian Serb "Minister of Foreign Affairs"
Momir Bulatovic	President of Montenegro, Federal Republic of Yugoslavia (1992–97)
Nicholas Burns	Spokesman, U.S. State Department (1994–97)
Jimmy Carter	President of the United States (1977–81)
Hervé de Charette	Foreign Minister of France (1995–97)
Jacques Chirac	President of France (1995–)
Warren Christopher	U.S. Secretary of State (1993–97)

Wesley Clark	Lieutenant General, U.S. Army; Director for Strategic Plans and Policy, JCS (1993–96); Supreme Commander, NATO (1997–)
William Jefferson Clinton	President of the United States (1993–)
William Crowe	U.S. Ambassador to Great Britain (1994–97)
John Deutch	Director, Central Intelligence Agency (1995–97)
Milorad Dodik	Prime Minister, Republika Srpska (1998–)
Tom Donilon	U.S. Assistant Secretary of State for Public Affairs and Chief of Staff to the Secretary of State (1993–96)
S. Nelson Drew	Lieutenant Colonel, U.S. Air Force; Senior Staff member, National Security Council (1995)
Lawrence Eagleburger	Deputy Secretary of State; later Secretary of State (1989–93)
Robert C. Frasure	U.S. Deputy Assistant Secretary of State for European and Canadian Affairs (1994–95)
Leon Fuerth	National Security Adviser to Vice President Gore (1993–)
Peter Galbraith	U.S. Ambassador to Croatia (1993–97)
Ejup Ganic	Vice President, Bosnia-Herzegovina (1992–97); President, Federation (1998–)
Robert Gelbard	U.S. Special Representative for the Implementation of the Dayton Accords (1997–)
Kiro Gligorov	President of former Yugoslav Republic of Macedonia (1991–)
Albert Gore	Vice President of the United States (1993–)
Pavel Grachev	Russian Defense Minister (1992–97)
Mate Granic	Foreign Minister of Croatia (1993–)
Pamela Harriman	U.S. Ambassador to France (1993–97)
Chris Hill	Director, Office of South-Central European Affairs, U.S. Department of State (1994–96)
Robert Hunter	U.S. Ambassador to NATO (1993–97)
Wolfgang Ischinger	Political Director, German Foreign Ministry; Representative to the Contact Group (1994–)
Igor Ivanov	Russian Deputy Foreign Minister; Representative to the Contact Group (1995–)

Alija Izetbegovic	President of Bosnia-Herzegovina (1992–　)
Bernard Janvier	Lieutenant General of France, Commander of all U.N. forces in the former Yugoslavia (1995–96)
George Joulwan	General, U.S. Army; Supreme Commander of Allied Forces Europe (NATO) (1993–97)
Radovan Karadzic	President of Bosnian Serb Republic (1992–96)
Donald Kerrick	Brigadier (later Major) General, U.S. Army; Senior staff member, NSC; later, Deputy to the National Security Advisor (1995–96; 1997–　)
Nikola Koljevic	"Vice President" of Bosnian Serb Republic (1992–96)
John Kornblum	U.S. Deputy Assistant Secretary of State for European and Canadian Affairs; later Assistant Secretary of State (1994–97)
Andrei Kozyrev	Foreign Minister of Russia (1992–96)
Momcilo Krajisnik	Speaker of Bosnian Serb Assembly; later Co-president of Bosnia (1996–　)
Joseph Kruzel	U.S. Deputy Assistant Secretary of Defense for International Security Affairs (1993–95)
Anthony Lake	U.S. National Security Advisor (1993–96)
Jean-David Levitte	Foreign policy advisor to President Chirac of France (1995–　)
David Lipton	U.S. Deputy Assistant Secretary of Treasury for International Affairs (1993–96); Undersecretary of Treasury (1997–　)
Jan Lodal	Principal Deputy Undersecretary of Defense for Policy (1993–　)
John Major	Prime Minister of Great Britain (1990–97)
Mike McCurry	White House Spokesman (1994–　)
John Menzies	U.S. Ambassador to Bosnia-Herzegovina (1995–97)
Slobodan Milosevic	President of the Republic of Serbia (1989–97); President of the Federal Republic of Yugoslavia (1997–　)
Milan Milutinovic	Minister of Foreign Affairs, Federal Republic of Yugoslavia (1995–97); President of Serbia (1997–　)
Ratko Mladic	General, Commander of Bosnian Serb Army (1992–96)

Pauline Neville-Jones	Contact Group Representative from the United Kingdom (1993–96)
Roberts Owen	Legal advisor on shuttle team
William Owens	Admiral, U.S. Navy; Vice Chairman of the JCS (1994–96)
Leon Panetta	White House Chief of Staff (1994–97)
Andreas Papandreou	Prime Minister of Greece (1981–89, 1993–96)
James Pardew	Director, Balkan Task Force, Department of Defense (1995–97)
Rosemarie Pauli	Department of State; Executive Assistant to the author (1993–96)
Rudy Perina	U.S. Chargé d'Affaires, Belgrade (1993–96)
William Perry	U.S. Secretary of Defense (1993–97)
Thomas Pickering	Undersecretary of State for Political Affairs (1997–)
Biljana Plavsic	"Vice President" of Bosnian Serb Republic; Co-president of Republika Srpska (1996–)
Malcolm Rifkind	British Defense Secretary, later Foreign Secretary (1992–97)
Muhamed Sacirbey	Foreign Minister of Bosnia-Herzegovina, Ambassador to the U.N. (1992–97)
John Shalikashvili	General, U.S. Army; Chairman of the Joint Chiefs of Staff (1993–97)
John Shattuck	Assistant Secretary of State for Humanitarian Affairs (1993–)
Haris Silajdzic	Prime Minister of Bosnia-Herzegovina (1992–)
Walter Slocombe	U.S. Undersecretary of Defense for Policy (1993–)
Leighton Smith	Admiral, U.S. Navy; Commander of NATO forces, Southern Europe; Commander, IFOR (1995–96)
Rupert Smith	Lieutenant General, British Army; Commander of U.N. forces in Bosnia-Herzegovina (1994–96)
James Steinberg	Director of the Policy Planning Staff, U.S. Department of State (1994–96); Deputy National Security Advisor (1997–)
Michael Steiner	Deputy German Representative to the Contact Group; Deputy High Representative (1996–97)

Thorvald Stoltenberg U.N. Representative to the International Conference on the Former Yugoslavia (1993–95)

Gojko Susak Defense Minister of Croatia (1992–   )

Strobe Talbott U.S. Deputy Secretary of State (1994–   )

Peter Tarnoff U.S. Undersecretary of State for Political Affairs (1993–97)

Franjo Tudjman President of Croatia (1991–   )

Alexander (Sandy) Vershbow Senior Director for Europe, U.S. National Security Council (1994–97); U.S. Ambassador to NATO (1998–   )

John White Deputy Secretary of Defense (1996–97)

Boris Yeltsin President of Russia (1991–   )

Warren Zimmermann American Ambassador to Yugoslavia (1989–92)

Kresimir Zubak President of the Muslim-Croat Federation in Bosnia; later Co-president of Bosnia-Herzegovina (1996–   )

Notes

Chapter 1: The Most Dangerous Road in Europe

1. Warren Zimmermann, *Origins of a Catastrophe: Yugoslavia and Its Destroyers* (New York: Times Books, 1996), p. 22.

Chapter 2: "The Greatest Collective Failure . . ."

1. "America, a European Power," *Foreign Affairs,* March–April 1995, p. 40.
2. Warren Zimmermann, *Origins of a Catastrophe: Yugoslavia and Its Destroyers* (New York: Times Books, 1996), pp. 151–53.
3. Noel Malcolm, *Bosnia: A Short History* (New York: New York University Press, 1994), p. 252.
4. Zimmermann, p. 174.
5. David C. Gompert, "The United States and Yugoslavia's Wars," in *The World and Yugoslavia's Wars,* Richard H. Ullman, ed. (New York: Council on Foreign Relations, 1996), pp. 122, 134. Gompert's essay is courageous in its candor.
6. James A. Baker III, with Thomas M. DeFrank, *The Politics of Diplomacy* (New York: G. P. Putnam's Sons, 1995), p. 483.
7. Zimmermann, p. 216.
8. Laura Silber and Allan Little, *Yugoslavia: Death of a Nation* (London: Penguin Books/BBC Books, 1996), p. 201.
9. Baker, p. 637.
10. Gompert, pp. 127–28.
11. Silber and Little, p. 166.
12. Ibid., pp. 171–72.
13. Baker, p. 637.
14. Zimmermann, p. 177.
15. Silber and Little, pp. 211–12.

Chapter 3: A Personal Prelude

1. Henry A. Kissinger, *Diplomacy* (New York: Simon & Schuster, 1994), p. 225.

Chapter 6: Pale's Challenge

1. *The Wall Street Journal,* September 20, 1993.
2. Robert Scheer, "Clinton's Globetrotter," *Los Angeles Times Magazine,* February 21, 1995.

Chapter 7: Bombing and Breakthrough

1. Bernard-Henri Lévy, *Le Lys et la Cendre: Journal d'un Écrivain au Temps de la Guerre de Bosnie* (Paris: Grasset, 1996), pp. 464–70. Translated for the author by Kathe Rothe.

Chapter 10: The Siege of Sarajevo Ends

1. Mira Markovic, *Night and Day: A Diary* (Belgrade, 1995), pp. 17–18.
2. Warren Zimmermann, *Origins of a Catastrophe: Yugoslavia and Its Destroyers* (New York: Times Books, 1996), p. 175.

Chapter 13: Cease-fire

1. Laura Silber and Allan Little, *Yugoslavia: The Death of a Nation* (London: Penguin Books/BBC Books, 1996), p. 224.

Chapter 15: Decisions with Consequences

1. Colin Powell, with Joseph E. Persico, *My American Journey* (New York: Random House, 1994), p. 149.

Chapter 17: "Peace in a Week"

1. Pauline Neville-Jones, "Dayton, IFOR, and Alliance Relations in Bosnia," *Survival,* Winter 1996–97, pp. 50–51.
2. Ibid., p. 51.

Chapter 21: America, Europe, and Bosnia

1. *Foreign Policy,* Winter 1997–98, p. 66.
2. Christopher Bennett, "No Flying Colors for Dayton—Yet," *Transitions,* December 1997, p. 37.
3. *Transitions,* August 1997, "Don't Fool Around with Principles."
4. This issue is addressed in a valuable study by the United States Air Force, *DELIBERATE FORCE: A Case Study in Effective Air Campaigning,* a study directed by Colonel Robert C. Owen. In the unclassified conclusion, Colonel Owen writes:
   Contacts between military leaders and some key diplomats did not seem to have kept up with the pace of events just before and after DELIBERATE FORCE. . . . Ambassador Holbrooke and General Ryan made plans and took actions in ignorance of one another's positions in key areas. [Published in *Airpower Journal,* Fall 1997, pp. 21–22.]

5. Carl Bildt, *Uppdrag Fred* [Assignment Peace] (Stockholm: Norstedts, 1997); translation provided by the author.
6. Speech to the Center for National Policy, January 13, 1998.
7. An extended example of the first view can be found in Radha Kumar's *Divide and Fall? Bosnia in the Annals of Partition.* The author's generic criticism of partition from Korea to Cyprus is insightful, but she misstates the goals of Dayton and confuses the Dayton agreement with the way it has been implemented.
8. *The Economist,* December 6, 1997, p. 16.
9. "America, a European Power," *Foreign Affairs,* March–April 1995, p. 138.
10. Bildt; translation provided by the author.
11. Henry A. Kissinger, *Diplomacy* (New York: Simon & Schuster, 1994), pp. 833–34.
12. Vaclav Havel, *The Art of the Impossible* (New York: Alfred A. Knopf, 1997), pp. 232–34.

Bibliography

Air Force Materiel Command. "Special Collectors' Edition." *Leading Edge,* February 1996. Wright-Patterson Air Force Base, Ohio: Air Force Materiel Command, 1996.

Baedeker's Touring Guide to Yugoslavia. New York: Macmillan Company, 1964.

Baker, James A. III, with Thomas M. DeFrank. *The Politics of Diplomacy.* New York: G. P. Putnam's Sons, 1995.

Bildt, Carl. *Uppdrag Fred* [Assignment Peace]. Stockholm: Norstedts, 1997.

Blanchard, Paul. *Yugoslavia Blue Guide.* New York: W. W. Norton, 1989.

Boutros-Ghali, Boutros. *Egypt's Road to Jerusalem: A Diplomat's Story of the Struggle for Peace in the Middle East.* New York: Random House, 1997.

Boyd, Charles G. "Making Bosnia Work," *Foreign Affairs*, January–February 1998.

Brodie, Bernard. *War and Politics.* New York: Macmilllan Company, 1973.

Cohen, Philip J. *Serbia's Secret War: Propaganda and the Deceit of History.* College Station, Texas: Texas A & M University Press, 1996.

Committee on Armed Services, United States Senate. "Hearings on Bosnia," June 7, 8, 14; September 29; October 17; November 28; December 6, 1995. Washington, D.C.: U.S. Government Printing Office, 1996.

Department of the Army. *German Antiguerrilla Operations in the Balkans (1941–1944).* Washington, D.C.: Department of the Army Pamphlet No. 20-243, August 1954.

Drew, Elizabeth. *On the Edge: The Clinton Presidency.* New York: Simon & Schuster, 1994.

Gjelten, Tom. *Sarajevo Daily: A City and Its Newspaper Under Seige.* New York: HarperCollins, 1995.

Glenny, Misha. *The Fall of Yugoslavia: The Third Balkan War.* 3rd rev. ed. New York: Penguin Books, 1996

Gow, James. *Triumph of the Lack of Will.* New York: Columbia University Press, 1997.

Gutman, Roy. *A Witness to Genocide.* New York: Macmillan Publishing Company, 1993.

Hall, Brian. *The Impossible Country.* New York: Penguin Books, 1994.

———. "Rebecca West's War." *The New Yorker,* April 15, 1996.

Havel, Vaclav. *The Art of the Impossible.* New York: Alfred A. Knopf, 1997.

Honig, Jan Willem, and Norbert Both. *Srebrenica: Record of a War Crime.* New York: Penguin, 1997.

Hutchings, Robert L. *American Diplomacy and the End of the Cold War.* Washington, D.C.: Woodrow Wilson Center Press, 1997.

International Commission on the Balkans. *Unfinished Peace: A Report.* Foreword by Leo Tindemans. Washington, D.C.: Carnegie Endowment for International Peace, 1996.

Kaplan, Robert. *Balkan Ghosts: A Journey Through History.* New York: Vintage Books, 1993.

Kissinger, Henry A. *Diplomacy.* New York: Simon & Schuster, 1994.

———. *White House Years.* Boston: Little, Brown & Co., 1979.

Kumar, Radha. *Divide and Fall? Bosnia in the Annals of Partition.* New York: Verso, 1997.

Kurspahic, Kemal. *As Long As Sarajevo Exists.* Stony Creek, Connecticut: Pamphleteer's Press, 1997.

Lampe, John R. *Yugoslavia as History: Twice There Was a Country.* New York: Cambridge University Press, 1996.

Lengvai, Paul. *Eagles in Cobwebs: Nationalism and Communism in the Balkans.* Garden City, New York: Doubleday & Company, 1969.

Lévy, Bernard-Henri. *Le Lys et la Cendre: Journal d'un Écrivain au Temps de la Guerre de Bosnie.* Paris: Grasset, 1996.

Maass, Peter. *Love Thy Neighbor: A Story of War.* New York: Alfred A. Knopf, 1996.

Malcolm, Noel. *Bosnia: A Short History.* New York: New York University Press, 1994.

Markovic, Mira [Mrs. Slobodan Milosevic]. *Night and Day: A Diary.* English translation by Margot and Bosko Milosavljevic. Belgrade: Privately printed, 1995.

Marton, Kati. *A Death in Jerusalem.* New York: Pantheon, 1994.

———. *Wallenberg: Missing Hero.* New York: Arcade, 1995.

May, Ernest R. *"Lessons" of the Past: The Use and Misuse of History in American Foreign Policy.* New York: Oxford Univeristy Press, 1973.

Murray, Rupert Wolfe. *IFOR on IFOR.* Foreword by Richard Holbrooke. Edinburgh, Scotland: Connect, 1996.

Neustadt, Richard E., and Ernest R. May. *Thinking in Time: The Uses of History for Decision-Makers.* New York: Free Press, 1986.

Neville-Jones, Pauline. "Dayton, IFOR, and Alliance Relations in Bosnia." *Survival* 38:4 (Winter 1996–97), pp. 45–65.

The New Republic, ed. *The Black Book of Bosnia: The Consequences of Appeasement.* Edited by Nader Mousavizadeh. Afterword by Leon Wieseltier. New York: A New Republic Book–Basic Books, 1996.

Nicolson, Harold. *Peacemaking 1919.* New York: Grosset & Dunlap, 1965.

O'Hanlon, Michael. "Turning the Bosnia Ceasefire into Peace." *The Brookings Review,* Winter 1998.

Owen, David. *Balkan Odyssey.* New York: Harcourt Brace & Company, 1996.

Powell, Colin, with Joseph E. Persico. *My American Journey.* New York: Random House, 1994.

Quandt, William B. *Camp David: Peacemaking and Politics.* Washington, D.C.: Brookings Institution, 1986.

Remak, Joachim. *Sarajevo: The Story of a Political Murder.* New York: Criterion Books, 1959.

Renwick, Sir Robin. *Fighting with Allies: America and Britain in Peace and at War.* New York: Times Books, 1996.

Ridley, Jasper. *Tito: A Biography.* London: Constable, 1994.

Rieff, David. *Slaughterhouse: Bosnia and the Failure of the West.* New York: Touchstone, 1996.

Rohde, David. *Endgame: The Betrayal and Fall of Srebrenica, Europe's Worst Massacre Since World War II.* New York: Farrar, Straus and Giroux, 1997.

Rose, Gideon. "The Exit Strategy Delusion," *Foreign Affairs,* January–February 1998.

Rosegrant, Susan. "Getting to Dayton: Negotiating an End to the War in Bosnia." A Case Study from the John F. Kennedy School of Government, Harvard University, 1996.

Silber, Laura, and Allan Little. *Yugoslavia: Death of a Nation.* Rev. ed. London: Penguin Books/BBC Books, 1996.

Sobel, Dava. *Longitude: The True Story of a Lone Genius Who Solved the Greatest Scientific Problem of His Time.* New York: Penguin Books, 1995.

Sudetic, Chuck. *Blood and Vengeance.* New York: W. W. Norton, 1998.

Talbott, Strobe. *Deadly Gambits.* New York: Alfred A. Knopf, 1984.

Tanner, Marcus. *Croatia: A Nation Forged in War.* New Haven: Yale University Press, 1997.

Thompson, Mark. *A Paper House: The Ending of Yugoslavia.* New York: Pantheon Books, 1992.

Ullman, Richard H., ed. *The World and Yugoslavia's Wars.* New York: Council on Foreign Relations, 1996.

United States Air Force. *DELIBERATE FORCE: A Case Study in Effective Air Campaigning.* Edited by Colonel Robert C. Owen. To be published by the Air University Press; excerpts in *Airpower Journal,* Fall 1997, pp. 21–22.

Vance, Cyrus. *Hard Choices.* New York: Simon & Schuster, 1983.

Volkan, Vamik. *Bloodlines: From Ethnic Pride to Ethnic Terrorism*. New York: Farrar, Straus and Giroux, 1997.

Wedgwood, C. V. *History and Hope: Essays on History and the English Civil War*. New York: E. P. Dutton, 1987.

West, Rebecca. *Black Lamb and Grey Falcon*. New York: Penguin Books, 1982.

Westendorp, Carlos. "Speech by the High Representative to the Peace Implementation Council," Bonn, December 9, 1997.

Woodward, Bob. *The Choice*. New York: Simon & Schuster, 1996.

Woodward, Susan L. "Avoiding Another Cyprus or Israel," *The Brookings Review*, Winter 1998.

———. *Balkan Tragedy*. Washington, D.C.: Brookings Institution, 1995.

Zimmermann, Warren. *Origins of a Catastrophe: Yugoslavia and Its Destroyers*. New York: Times Books, 1996.

Index

Page numbers in *italics* refer to maps.

ABOUT THE AUTHOR

RICHARD HOLBROOKE began his diplomatic career in Vietnam in 1962, serving in the Mekong Delta and the American embassy in Saigon. After a tour on President Johnson's White House Staff in 1966–67, he wrote one volume of the Pentagon Papers, served as special assistant to Undersecretaries of State Nicholas Katzenbach and Elliot Richardson, and was a member of the American delegation to the Paris peace talks on Vietnam.

Holbrooke was Peace Corps director in Morocco from 1970 to 1972 and managing editor of *Foreign Policy* from 1972 to 1976. He served as Assistant Secretary of State for East Asian and Pacific Affairs (1977–81) and U.S. Ambassador to Germany (1993–94). He was Assistant Secretary of State for European and Canadian Affairs from 1994 to 1996, when he became the chief architect of the Dayton Peace Accords. He is co-author of Clark Clifford's memoir, *Counsel to the President*, and is currently a vice chairman of Crédit Suisse First Boston, based in New York. He is married to author Kati Marton and has two sons, David and Anthony.

ABOUT THE TYPE

This book was set in Times Roman, designed by Stanley Morrison specifically for *The Times* of London. The typeface was introduced in the newspaper in 1932. Times Roman has had its greatest success in the United States as a book and commercial typeface, rather than one used in newspapers.

SOULS
IN THE
GREAT
MACHINE

SOULS
IN THE
GREAT
MACHINE

SEAN
McMULLEN

TOR®

A TOM DOHERTY ASSOCIATES BOOK

NEW YORK

SOULS IN THE GREAT MACHINE

Copyright © 1999 by Sean McMullen

This book is printed on acid-free paper.

Edited by Jack Dann

A Tor Book
Published by Tom Doherty Associates, Inc.
175 Fifth Avenue
New York, NY 10010

Tor Books on the World Wide Web:
http://www.tor.com

Tor® is a registered trademark of Tom Doherty Associates, Inc.

Designed by Lisa Pifher

Library of Congress Cataloging-in-Publication Data

McMullen, Sean.
    Souls in the great machine / Sean McMullen.—1st ed.
        p.   cm.
    "A Tor book."
    ISBN 0-312-87055-8
    I. Title.
PR9619.3.M3268S6   1999
823—dc21   99-21934
                                                     CIP

First Edition: June 1999
Printed in the United States of America
0 9 8 7 6 5 4 3 2 1

To
Jack Dann,
who has made
so many things
possible in
Australia

ACKNOWLEDGMENTS

Jack Dann
John de la Lande
Peter McNamara
Trish Smyth

PROLOGUE

The girl moved with the calm confidence of a thief who knew that she would not be disturbed. The crew of the three-hundred-foot tower had deserted the beamflash gallery at its summit, and the great eye of their receptor telescope stared blankly at a tower on the eastern horizon. Although mounted to look perpetually east for signals from the Numurkah tower, the communications telescope could be moved through a few degrees for adjustment and servicing. Unclamping the control wheels of the telescope, she spun them, slowly turning the glass to where the moon was rising. A reciprocating clock on the wall tinkled as it reached 9:45. The calendar wheels beside it declared that it was the 26th day of September in the Year of Greatwinter's Waning 1684.

The lunar surface was the familiar jumble of craters and mountains, along with a faint tracery of ancient strip mines. A few deft twists detached the standard eyepiece, but her own array of lenses and caliper screws took longer to install and adjust. The clock rang out the tenth hour past noon. The moon was 5 degrees above the horizon when she finished.

The increased magnification gave a washed-out image that danced in the air currents. Because the moon was a little past full there were shadows near the edge, exactly where she needed them. She adjusted movable crosshairs within her eyepiece, glanced at the clock, then measured the length of a shadow cast by the cut of a strip mine. She gasped, then fought down her excitement.

She repeated the measurement, then made it again with her other eye. The readings were identical. The clock announced 10:15. She scrawled down the figures, selected another shadow, and took more measurements. By 10:30 the elevation was nearly 10 degrees. Time seemed to accelerate as she measured a third strip's shadow—and suddenly one of the wheels raising the telescope reached its maximum elevation and jammed. The vista of lunar strip mines slid out of the field of the eyepiece.

She was aching to look back to her measurements as she lowered the telescope, reinstalled the standard eyepiece, and focused on the beamflash gallery at the summit of the Numurkah tower. Some rough calculations verified what she had already worked out in her head: the first of the three strips that she had measured was significantly deeper than it had been a year ago.

With a final glance around the beamflash gallery, she left for the stairwell and began the long descent. All the way down, her mind was racing with the

implications of a 5 percent deepening in a scratch on the lunar surface. Walking into the deserted streets of the river port, she paused to look up at the moon. It was such a momentous discovery, yet she could tell no one. Her entire life was becoming a catalogue of secrets she could not share.

"Fantastic, even after two thousand years their machines still work," Zarvora Cybeline said aloud; then she turned to the jumble of moonlit buildings that was the Echuca Unitech's library. "Time to build my own machine."

CHAMPIONS

Fergen had not noticed a suspicious pattern in the pieces on the board by the seventh move. Champions was his best game and he had even its most exotic strategies and scenarios memorized. The Highliber advanced a pawn to threaten his archer. The move was pure impudence, a lame ploy to tempt him to waste the archer's shot. He moved the archer to one side, so that his knight's flank was covered.

The Highliber sat back and tapped at the silent keys of an old harpsichord that had been cut in half and bolted to the wall of her office. Fergen rubbed plaster dust from his fingers. All the pieces were covered in dust, as were the board, the furniture, and the floor. The place was a shambles. Wires hung from holes in the ceiling, partly completed systems of rods, pulleys, levers, pawls, gears, and shafts were visible through gaps in the paneling, and other brass and steel mechanisms protruded from holes in the floor. Occasionally a mechanism would move.

Fergen gave the game his full attention, but Highliber Zarvora tapped idly at the harpsichord keys and seldom glanced at the board. A rack of several dozen marked gearwheels rearranged their alignment with a soft rattle. The mechanisms were part of a signal system, the Highliber had explained. Libris, the mayoral library, had grown so big that it was no longer possible to administer it using clerks and messengers alone.

The Highliber leaned over and picked up a knight. With its base she tipped over one of her own pawns, then another. Fergen had never realized that she had such small, pale hands. Her knight toppled yet another of her pawns, then turned as it finally claimed an enemy piece. Such a tall, commanding woman, yet such small hands, thought Fergen, mesmerized. The knight knocked another of its own pawns aside; then his king fell.

For some moments he stared at the carnage on the board, the shock of his defeat taking time to register. Anger, astonishment, suspicion, incomprehension, and fear tore at him in turn. At last he looked up at the Highliber.

"I must apologize for the surroundings again," she said in the remote yet casual manner that she used even with the Mayor. "Did the mayhem in here disturb your concentration?"

"Not at all," replied Fergen, rubbing his eye. Behind it the early symptoms of a migraine headache were building. "I could play in a cowshed and still beat anyone in the known world in less than fifty moves. Do you know when I was last beaten at champions?"

The question had been rhetorical, but the Highliber knew the answer.

"1671 GW."

She tapped again at the silent keyboard. The little gears marked with white dots clicked and rattled in their polished wooden frame.

"And now it's 1696," he said ruefully. "I've played you before, but you never, never made moves like these."

"I have been practicing," she volunteered.

"You take a long time between moves, but oh, what moves. I have learned more from this game than my previous hundred. You could take my title from me, Highliber Zarvora, I know mastery when I see it."

The Highliber continued to tap the silent keys and glance at the row of gears. The same slim, confident fingers that had harvested his king so easily now flickered over the softly clacking keys in patterns that were meaningless to Fergen.

"I am already the Highliber, the Mayor's Librarian," she said without turning to him. "My library is Libris, the biggest in the world and the hub of a network of libraries stretching over many mayorates. My staff is more than half that of the mayoral palace. Why should your position interest me?"

"But, but a Master of the Mayor ranks above a mere librarian," spluttered Fergen.

"Only in heraldic convention, Fras Gamesmaster. I enjoy a game of champions, but my library means more to me. I shall tell nobody about your defeat."

Fergen's face was burning hot. She could take his position, but she did not want it! Was an insult intended? Were there grounds for a duel? The Highliber was known to be a deadly shot with a flintlock, and had killed several of her own staff in duels over her modernizations in the huge library.

"Would you like another game?" asked the Highliber, facing him but still striking at the keys.

"My head . . . feels like it's been used as an anvil, Frelle Highliber."

"Well then return later," she said, typing her own symbols for / CHAMPIONS: ELAPSED TIME? / then pressing a lever with her foot. Fergen heard the hum of tensed wires, and the clatter of levers and gears from within the wall.

"I could teach you nothing," he said in despair.

"You are the finest opponent that I have," replied the Highliber. "I think it—"

She stopped in midsentence, staring at the row of gears.

"You will excuse me, please, there is something I must attend to," she said, her voice suddenly tense.

"The gears and their dots have a message?"

"Yes, yes, a simple code," she said, standing quickly and taking him by the arm. "Afternoon's compliments, Fras Gamesmaster, may your headache pass quickly."

Fergen rubbed his arm as the Highliber's lackey showed him out. The woman had all but lifted him from the ground! Amazing strength, but to Fergen no more amazing than her victory at the champions board.

Zarvora slammed a small wooden panel in the wall aside and pulled at one of the wires dangling from the roof. After a moment a metallic twittering and clatter arose from the brass plate set in the recess.

"System Control here, Highliber," declared a faint, hollow voice.

"What is the Calculor's status?" she snapped.

"Status HALTMODE," replied the distant speaker.

"What is in the request register at present?"

"MODE:CHAMPIONS;COMMAND:ELAPSED TIME?"

"And the response register?"

"46:30.4, Highliber."

"Forty-six *hours* for a twenty-minute game of champions, Fras Controller?" shouted Zarvora, her self-control slipping for a rare moment. "Explain."

There was a pause, punctuated by the rattle of gears. Zarvora drummed her fingers against the wall and stared at a slate where she had written 46:30.4.

"System Controller, Highliber. Both Dexter and Sinister Registers confirm the figure."

"How could both processors come up with the same ludicrous time?"

"Why . . . yes, it is odd, but it's the sort of error that even skilled clerks make sometimes."

"The Calculor is not a skilled clerk, Fras Lewrick. It is a hundred times more powerful at arithmetic, and with its built-in verifications it should be *absolutely* free of errors. I want it frozen exactly as it was during that last calculation."

"That's not possible, Highliber. Many of the components from the correlator were exhausted by the end of the game. They were relieved by components from the spares pool."

Too late, thought Zarvora. "We shall run a set of diagnostic calculations for the next hour," she said. "Do not change any tired components. If some fall over at their desks, mark them before they are replaced."

"Highliber, the Calculor is tired. It's not wise."

"The Calculor is made of people, Fras Lewrick. People get tired, but the Calculor merely slows down."

"I'm down inside it all the time. It has moods, it feels—"

"I *designed* the Calculor, Lewrick! I know its workings better than anyone."

"As you will, Highliber."

Zarvora rubbed at her temples. She too had a headache now, but thanks to the long vibrating wire beneath the brass plate her discomfort remained unseen.

"You are trying to tell me something, Fras Lewrick. What is it—and please be honest."

"The Calculor is like a river galley or an army, Frelle Highliber. There is a certain . . . spirit or soul about it. I mean, ah, that just as a river galley is more than a pile of planks, oars, and sailors, so too is the Calculor more than just a mighty engine for arithmetic. When it is tired, perhaps it sometimes lets a bad calculation through rather than bothering to repeat it."

"It is *not* alive," she replied emphatically. "It is just a simple, powerful machine. The problem is human in origin."

"Very good, Highliber," Lewrick said stiffly. "Shall I have the correlator components flogged?"

"No! Do nothing out of the ordinary. Just check each of the function registers on both sides of the machine as you run the diagnostic calculations. We must make it repeat its error, then isolate the section at fault. Oh, and send a jar of tourney beer to each cell when the components are dismissed. The Calculor played well before that error."

"That would encourage the culprit, Highliber."

"Perhaps, but it is also important to reward hard work. The problem is a hole in my design, Fras Lewrick, not the component who causes problems through it. We could take all the components out into the courtyard and shoot them, but the hole would remain for some newly trained component to crawl through."

Libris was Rochester's mayoral library. Its stone beamflash communications tower was over 600 feet high and dominated the skyline of the city. Unofficially, the Highliber of Libris was second only to the Mayor in power, and she controlled a network of libraries and librarians scattered over dozens of mayorates and thousands of miles. In many ways the Highliber was even more powerful than the Mayor. There was no dominant religion across the mayorates of the Southeast, so the library system performed many functions of a powerful clergy. The education, communication, and transport of every mayorate in the Southeast Alliance was under the discreet but firm coordination of the Highliber of Rochester.

Rochester itself was not a powerful state; in fact, the other mayorates of the Southeast Alliance deliberately kept it as no more than a rallying point, a political convenience. Neighboring mayorates such as Tandara, Deniliquin, and Wangaratta held the real power, and wielded it shamelessly in the Councilium Chambers at Rochester. Mayor Jefton of Rochester was the constitutional Overmayor of the Councilium, but in practice he was of little more consequence to his peers than the servants who scrubbed the floor, dusted the tapestries, and polished the broad red rivergum table at which the meetings were held.

Libris was the very reason that Rochester was kept weak. A powerful mayorate controlling the vast and influential library network would quickly become strong enough to rule the entire Alliance. The Councilium was wary of that. Zarvora had been appointed recently, replacing a man eighty years her senior. She had become a Dragon Silver at twenty-four, and after two years had jumped

the Dragon Gold level to be appointed Dragon Black—the Highliber's rank. There had been some luck involved: Mayor Jefton also happened to be young and ambitious, and was weary of elderly men and women telling him what he could or could not do. Zarvora offered him the chance to make Rochester powerful, and outlined some radical but plausible ways of doing it. He proposed her name to the Councilium, giving her the chance to address the Mayors in person. She promised to make both Libris and the beamflash network pay for themselves within three years or resign. The Mayors were impressed and appointed her.

Zarvora became Highliber in 1696 GW and massive changes followed. The Tiger Dragons, Libris' internal guard, were tripled and a branch of them was turned into the Black Runners, a secret constabulary. Parts of Libris were rebuilt and extended, and staff and books were moved into other areas. In the workshops of the expanded library artisans toiled through twelve-hour shifts, day after day, month after month, making strange machinery and furniture. Carpenters, black-smiths, and clockmakers were recruited from far afield, and the edutors at the University were contracted to solve odd problems in symbolic logic. Large areas of Libris were sealed from outside scrutiny.

Zarvora explained that Libris had become too big to govern manually, and that a vast signaling and coordinating division of clerks, lackeys, and librarians had been set up to manage its books and coordinate its activities. Indeed the efficiency of Libris' activities improved dramatically in only a few months, and by the end of 1696 GW the Mayor could see real savings set against the Highliber's expenses.

There were also drastic changes in the staffing of Libris. Examinations for Dragon Red and Green were changed to favor candidates with mathematical and mechanical backgrounds, rather than just knowledge of library theory and the classics. No recruit was older than thirty-five, and several accepted options to study further at Rochester's University. The changes did not go uncriticized, but the Highliber was dedicated and ruthless. She lobbied, fought duels, had officials assassinated . . . and even had the more numerate of her opponents abducted for a new and novel form of forced labor. When those obstructing her had been outside Libris, it had been necessary to arrange other means to push them aside. In the case of Fertokli Fergen, Master of Mayoral Boardgames, she had used humiliation.

The Call moved across the land at a walking pace, visible only by the creatures that were swept along by its allure. It moved southeast, and within its six-mile depth were dogs, sheep, an occasional horse, and even a scattering of humans. Although it had begun far away in the Willandra Drylands, none of the animals it had first gathered were still walking within its influence, or even alive. Few creatures drawn away by the Call ever reached its source.

Ettenbar was a Southmoor shepherd, living a precarious existence near the

border river between his Emir's lands and the Rutherglen Mayorate. His sheep grazed placidly in a ragged circle, all tied to the central stake that he had knocked in that morning, while his emus walked free among the sheep with great mincing steps, all neck, legs, and shaggy feathers. Striped chicks ran about at their feet.

A movement in the distance caught Ettenbar's attention: a stray ram wandering without a tether. Untethered sheep carried rewards, and unbranded strays were the property of those who caught them. Releasing himself from the tetherstake, he began stalking the spiral-horned merino.

It was wary. It trotted away to a comfortable distance as Ettenbar approached. He circled off to one side, untying his bolas and shaking them loose. The stray still kept its distance. Ettenbar crept closer, driving it to where there were clumps of bushes to cover his approach. The ploy worked. Within fifty yards he began whirling the bolas, he cast—and tangled the stray by the hind legs. As he strode forward to collect his struggling, bleating prize, the Call rolled over him.

For the most fleeting of moments Ettenbar had a choice, yet it was a choice with only one possible outcome. He betrayed himself, he accepted his weakness and wallowed in it, all within a single thought. His discipline and control collapsed, his steps slowed, and he turned to walk southeast. The stray ram also struggled to follow the beckoning, but could not move as fast as the Call with its hind legs entangled in the bolas. Ettenbar's sheep were also drawn by the Call, but got only as far as the length of their tethers. His emus studied them quizzically, cocking their heads with avian curiosity. In spite of being so much larger than a sheep, they were birds and so were immune to the Call. All mammals larger than a big cat were drawn away, but never birds or reptiles.

Only dimly perceiving obstacles, Ettenbar walked on. He waded streams, tumbled down steep hillsides, climbed walls, and stumbled through ploughed fields. He passed a farmer who was straining to walk southeast with the Call. The man was held by a body anchor that had been released by a rawhide timer ten minutes after the Call had caught him. The farmer would live, but Ettenbar was already lost to the world, dead because he was walking freely. Ahead was the broad, brown river that marked the border. Ettenbar waded in and began to swim. Not one-quarter of the creatures drawn along by the Call survived the crossing, but Ettenbar reached the south bank and staggered on.

Three miles into the Christian mayorate of Rutherglen he crashed blindly into a dense thicket of blackberries. The heavy shepherd's leathers and boots that had nearly caused him to drown in the river now protected him from the worst that the thorns could do, but he could not maintain even the slow walking pace of the Call. It continued to beckon to him and he struggled to follow it as thorns tore at his face and hands. Finally his legs became so entangled in thorny branches that he could not move. After three hours the Call finally passed, releasing him.

Ettenbar awoke. He was cold, wet, bleeding, and exhausted. The sun was

low, almost smothered behind gathering clouds. One moment he had been striding to collect the ram that he had snared, and now . . . The Call had spared him! With bleeding fingers he drew his knife and cut his legs free from the thorny branches. He stumbled back out of the grove of grasping thorns, prostrated himself, and gave thanks to Allah for the return of his life.

From the setting sun he took a bearing for northeast and began the journey home. He felt ashamed for being caught without his tether, but otherwise walked along proudly. The Call had released him, he was blessed in the eyes of Allah. It was only when he reached the river that he realized where he was.

"Hei, Callshewt!" shouted someone behind him. He hesitated, then bolted for the riverbank. A gunshot barked out and soil sprayed up in front of him. Ettenbar stopped and turned, his hands high.

Three bearded, gore-encrusted spectres approached. They were not border guards but river gleaners—scavengers looking for livestock drowned in the river while trying to follow the Call. Ettenbar saw that only one of them had a gun, and realized too late that he could have run on before the musket was reloaded. They wore stained oilcloths and swenskin breeches, and stank of mutton fat and blood. Three pairs of scabby, dirty knees showed through ragged holes. They had been dragging freshly drowned sheep from the water and butchering them for the Rutherglen markets when Ettenbar had appeared.

Prakdor reloaded his gun while Mikmis and Allendean examined their prize. Although their leader, Prakdor, let Mikmis do most of the talking. He had been in his mayor's army once, and knew the fate of the loud and vocal.

"Southmoor sheepshagger," Mikmis observed as they bound Ettenbar's wrists and hobbled his ankles.

"Hold 'im? Ransom?" Allendean asked.

"Ransom? A sheepshagger? We'd not get the price of the rope. Better march him to Wahgunyah and sell him to a bargemaster as a rower."

"Wahgunyah. Long trek," Allendean grumbled.

"He's strong. He'll fetch twenty-five silver nobles if he gets one."

While they argued Ettenbar looked across the river to the fields that were home. Until this day he had never traveled more than twenty miles from where he had been born, but now he was unlikely to ever see those fields again.

"Jorah," he murmured.

"What say?" snapped Allendean.

"Jorah, it's Southmoor for the Call," said Prakdor. "It means Changer of Lives."

"Shewt, he got that right," chorkled Mikmis. "Kiss your sheep goodbye, sheepshagger." The three river gleaners burst into hoarse, raucous laughter.

"I—hey, can he count?" Mikmis suddenly exclaimed.

"Southmoor sheepshagger? Give break!"

"Can you count? Er . . . Prakdor, do you know how they say—"

"Vu numerak, isk vu mathemator?" Prakdor asked in the dialect of the neighboring Southmoors.

Ettenbar nodded proudly. The local mosque had a fine school.

"So, he can count! I've heard the Warren pays one gold royal for Southmoors who can count—two if they speak Austaric."

"Sheepshagger nayn't," Allendean grumbled.

"Shewt pighead, it's still four times what he'd fetch as a rower."

They turned to Prakdor who considered, then nodded. "We'll take him to the camp and clean him up. Mikmis, go to Wahgunyah, see the Warrenmaster."

Nothing symbolized the power and authority of Libris better than the tall beam-flash towers that stood in every town. In Rutherglen the tower was within the grounds of the Unitech, but some distance from its library. Lemorel had been walking purposefully down the cobbled streets of the Unitech, yet something made her pause to gaze at the tower.

It was wooden and whitewashed, gleaming starkly against the clouds of the late-winter afternoon. White fumes poured from the outlets at the summit as magnesium flares powered the beamflash equipment in the absence of direct sunlight. A signal was going west, to Numurkah, from where it would be relayed southwest to Rochester. The distance that a message could travel in moments might take Lemorel months, or even years. . . . but no matter. Today she would take another step on her journey to the capital.

She was saved from abduction by being a librarian. Five men in shabby oilcloths loitered near the gates of the Unitech, staring at a sheet of poorpaper that might have been a map. They seemed to be itinerant farmworkers trying to find their way around an unfamiliar town.

"Lemorel Milderellen, Dragon Yellow Librarian," one of them muttered as Lemorel walked through the gates.

Another shook his head. "Let her go."

"She won the Unitech prize for mathematics," insisted the first.

"Abducting even a Dragon White Librarian is a good way to get us shot. Who is this next one?"

"Joakim Skinner. Assistant edutor in Accounting."

"That's more like it. Mark him down."

"Five. He makes five."

"Five is enough. Two gold royals for each of us."

"That Constable's Runner is staring at us again," their tall, gaunt lookout reported.

"Then let's find a coffeehouse and bide."

They had not noticed the color of the armband that the librarian had been

wearing. Lemorel had been promoted to Dragon Orange rank only that afternoon. The rise in rank could not have come at a better time, as there was a Regional Inspector visiting the town. Libris recruited librarians from outside Rochester at the level of Dragon Red and above. She had a minimum of two years more before she became eligible for the exams, yet there were now ways of hastening promotions with Highliber Zarvora in charge.

Rutherglen had been the vineyard heartland since the earliest records began, and the rhythm of life was closely tied to the grape harvest and its cycles. This was late winter, a time for repairs and barrel building, for hunting wild emus in the open woodlands to the south, and for long philosophical discussions in the evenings over old vintages beside fires. Bright flags, ribbons, and bunches of evergreens hung from the lintels of most houses and shops in celebration of the Drinkfest. Out of sight on some roof a band was practicing. Lemorel noted that the cornetton was slightly out of tune and the two snailhorn players were probably drunk. Smoke from cooking fires hung over the streets, mingling with genuine fog and hinting at stews and baking. Overloaded lever-pedal tricycles on unsprung wooden wheels creaked and rumbled along the Callside of the road.

There had not been a Call for over three weeks, Lemorel reminded herself as her clockwork Call timer clattered its warning of a minute's grace. She reached down to her waist, twisted the reset dial to a half hour, and wound the mainspring. A Call was due soon, and she hoped that it would not interrupt her interview. The houses on the north side of the street were all blank walls of abandonstone, tarbrick, and red shingle: no street had two sides. If a Call came, those inside houses would walk to the blank wall at the back and wander there mindlessly, but in safety. No windows or doors ever faced in the direction of the Call. Just like the people themselves, open and welcoming on one side but blank and unassailable on the other, Lemorel mused. Those who recognized her quickly looked away and found something to be busy with. She fantasized about being the source of the Call itself, a godling that people protected themselves against with their blank sides. Even though it was an old and tired fancy, it was her only armor against the townsfolk who shunned her.

In the distance she could see the Wayfarer's Rest, a hostelry for the better class of traveler. The Regional Inspector was waiting there. Her appointment was for 4 P.M. The single arm of the clock on the Mayor's palace was touching the numeral but the chimes had not yet begun. She slowed her pace. Whether it was passing exams, arriving for appointments, or shooting in duels, timing was all important.

For Lemorel this was a chance to escape with dignity. Being a librarian with a reputation for shooting straight meant that she might bypass the lengthy rounds of protocol maze-running to get into Libris. The new Highliber was as refreshingly young as her predecessor had been stultifyingly old. Traditions that dated

back centuries were being uprooted and opportunities were being made for the young and competent.

Lemorel was with the Rutherglen Unitech library, and like all libraries in the Southeast Alliance it was affiliated to Libris. When Lemorel had been appointed as a Dragon White, the lowest librarian ranking, the Highliber of Libris had been in office forty-one years and was 106 years old. He had died within a year and was followed by Zarvora Cybeline.

Zarvora was dynamic and dedicated, had an edutorate in applied algebra from Rochester University . . . and was twenty-six. She had killed the Deputy Highliber's champion in a duel a day after gaining office and within a month had sent three-quarters of the executive staff into exile. All at once Lemorel's temporary job within a hidebound profession became a marvelous opportunity to get ahead.

Lemorel glanced at the clocktower and shivered in the still, cold air. The arm was right over the numeral four. The trip rod on the hour gearwheel would be pressing against the release lever of the horlogue barrel by now. Weights on a pulley would soon rotate the barrel, and studs on its surface would move another set of levers that would trip spring-loaded hammers to strike a tune on brass bells. Lemorel's father had maintained the mechanism for years, and some of her earliest memories were of the inside of the mayoral clock. Now there was a proscription on him working there and the mechanism was slowly going out of adjustment. There was a distant, muffled clack, and the chimes of the horlogue began. Heart racing, Lemorel entered the hostelry taproom and caught sight of a portly man in casual maroon robes wearing the silver badge of the Inspectorate Service. He was twirling the waxed beardspike on his chin and frowning. The last chime sounded as she crossed the room.

Vellum Drusas had a round of vineyard towns that he went to some trouble to visit in the winter. It was a good season, as people had time to spare and were glad of company from outside the mayorate. There was, of course, the matter of the business that justified his travel in the first place, but while Drusas might have been indolent, he was not stupid enough to abuse his travel allowance. If he worked minimally to justify trips to his favorite vineyards, at least he worked.

The taproom was full of growers and artisans from outlying areas, gathered together for the Winter Drinkfest. This was also the reason that Drusas was in town. Smoke from the sunflower-oil lamps and numerous pipes hung on the warm air, and the talk was loud and strident. The speakers were not so much drunk as used to bellowing to each other across open fields. The farmers squirmed and scratched, unaccustomed to the feel of starched tunics and brushed cotton stovetrews. Some suspiciously eyed the reciprocating clock that had replaced the sun, moon, and stars to mark the passage of time. Drusas watched the clock too, shaking his head. If the librarian arrived late he would have no time to mix with the grapegrowers and wheedle an invitation to the wine-tasting competition that

night. "To 1681!" someone shouted, and most goblets were raised. That had been a fine year; in fact, Drusas had nine bottles of the famous Barioch '81 Shiraleng in his cellar—the tenth had been uncorked the day that he became a Deputy Overliber. Their value had increased fifteen times since he bought them.

Outside, the horlogue began striking, and on the fourth stroke of the hour a girl seemed to materialize before Drusas. He saw large, dark, intense eyes in a pleasantly round face framed by severely pinned and braided black hair. Her tunic was the rather pale shade of violet prescribed by the Regional Overliber and her oilcloth raincape had seen a lot of use. She bowed with a brisk, birdlike movement and presented her papers. Drusas accepted them, noting that she wore no jewelry aside from her hairclasps, and that her gunbelt was severely functional. Typical new-blade career librarian, he decided.

"Frelle Milderellen?" he asked.

"Yes, Fras Inspector."

"You know me by sight?"

"You conferred my Dragon Yellow rank last year in a ceremony at Wangaratta."

"Ah yes, but there were many presentations and only one presenter. Or perhaps I was especially memorable, eh?" He gave a wink and a coy leer. Lemorel did not react, not even to blush. Drusas hastily looked down at her papers. A diploma from the local Unitech, a weapons license . . .

"Dragon Orange," he said, eagerly picking on an obvious mistake to show that he was alert. "Your petition of this morning stated that you were Dragon Yellow."

"I was regraded today, Fras Inspector."

"With no ceremony?"

"No, Fras Inspector. I petitioned for the grading tests against my Overliber's wishes. Because I passed I was entitled to regrading, but—"

"But because you were regraded by petition you automatically renounced the increase in salary and the right to have a conferral ceremony. Ah, congratulations anyway." He settled back and took a sip of frostwine from a blue crystal thimblet. He read further, and felt his stomach sink as he reached the magistrate's report. She was noted to have survived trial by combat. They had warned him that there was a strange one in Rutherglen, and this had to be her. Lemorel noticed the color drain from his face. She took a deep breath and clasped her shaking hands behind her back.

"Frelle Milderellen, you have an exceptional record," he said slowly. "Top marks in your year at the Unitech, small-arms champion at the regional fair— twice—and Dragon Orange at nineteen. Your petition is to transfer to Libris at your present rank, but to remain on the staff of the Unitech. That is not possible."

Even the raucous banter of the other drinkers could not fill the chilled silence of the moments that followed.

"The Unitech Overliber assured me that it can be done."

"Oh it can be done, but only if he permanently transfers your position as Dragon Orange to Libris as well as your person. Libris has been swallowing a lot of librarians from the regions lately. Your Overliber might be willing to let you, Lemorel Milderellen, go, but I doubt that he would give up the right to replace you."

"Does that mean that my petition is rejected?"

She was polite and deferential, but something about her rattled the rotund and comfortable Drusas. It was not so much the threat that she might shoot him from some dark alleyway so much as her remembering him in two decades when she was a Dragon Gold in Libris.

"Rejected? No, heavens no," he laughed. "We just need to discuss your case in more detail. There are many paths to follow, and you must take the right one. If you don't, I will be to blame as your adviser. Here, sit down. Frostwine? Honeycakes?" Lemorel sat down beside him, as wary and sinuous as a cat with a stranger who smelled of dog. She selected a honeycake. "Now, what we need to do is to get down to basics, Frelle. Just why do you want to go to Libris? To follow a lover, to escape nagging parents, or perhaps even to genuinely further your career?"

"Does it really matter, Fras Inspector?"

"Yes indeed. Going all the way to Libris is a drastic step. What exactly are your circumstances?"

Lemorel took a moment to gather her words together, words that could not be softened unless she lied. She had already decided not to lie.

"I've shot nine men and one woman during the course of two duels and one vendetta. I was also mentioned in my lover's suicide note. I'm under the protection of the magistrate, but my family has been proscribed in five mayorates by the families of the dead. My father's business is suffering, Fras Inspector, but if I go into exile and go sufficiently far, the proscription will be lifted."

Drusas shivered, then gulped down the remains of his frostwine. It suddenly seemed no stronger than sweetened water, so he called for a shot of black barrel brandy.

"These, ah, shootings . . . I presume that they were all done within the rules of the Disputes and Reconciliations Act of 1462 GW?"

"Yes, Fras Inspector."

The Disputes and Reconciliations Act was a legacy of the old Riverina Empire, and had been meant to reduce the incidence of violence by channeling it and swathing it in rituals and regulations. The carrying of guns was not so much confined to the educated, administrative classes, it was required of them. Guns were the symbols of judgment and power, so that those who were expected to exercise power and judgment had to wear them and be proficient in their use. The ultimate appeal against a judgment was trial by combat, where either the

disputants or their nominated champions would engage in a legal duel. The death penalty was automatic for anyone going outside the system of mediated duels, and there was a ruinous system of follow-up fines for their families. It was not often that disputes got to the dueling stage, but it was known to happen.

"Ah, well now, why Libris?" Drusas ventured. "Why not some library in a closer mayorate, one that does not proscribe your family?"

"I'm well known in the nearby mayorates. Libris is big enough and sufficiently distant for me to lose myself."

That made a lot of sense to Drusas. "Dragon Orange," he said, then paused and stared intently at his brandy. "That makes a difference."

Lemorel leaned forward, eager, ravenous. She would be like this if she were dueling with me, thought Drusas, flinching back. In a way that was precisely what she *was* doing.

"I can't change the rules, but I can recommend candidates for the grading exams at Libris. You are a Dragon Orange, so you are in theory eligible to sit for Dragon Red at any time. Your Overliber would probably not approve, but if you get into Libris that hardly matters, does it?"

"The minimum wait is two years, according to the regulations."

"No, the *recommended* minimum is two years. There was a case in, ah, 1623 where a candidate had been unfairly kept as Dragon Yellow for forty-seven years. When the case was finally brought to the attention of the Regional Inspector, he was promoted to Dragon Red after only a few minutes as Dragon Orange. Your case is different, of course, but it would be possible for you to depart for a Dragon Red test at Libris as soon as you could pack your bags. Pass that test, and you would be promoted. Your former Overliber would still have your Dragon Yellow position to fill again, so everyone would be happy."

He sat back and smiled magnanimously. Lemorel took an instant to comprehend that he was going to help her.

"Fras Inspector, thank you—"

"No thanks yet, please. I have to be convinced that you have at least a ghost of a chance of passing the tests. Now, how is your weaponcraft—ah no, that could hardly be in question. Your subjects at the Unitech include mathematics, good, the Highliber likes that. Just a credit in Library History, and only a pass in Heraldry . . . but that may not matter. Lackey!"

A gangling youth in his mid-twenties with thick, wire-frame spectacles clinging to his nose hurried up from behind Lemorel carrying a writing kit. He snapped the legs down, uncorked the ink jar, and presented Drusas with a selection of newly trimmed goose quills. The inspector chose one with a great deal of show and flourish, then began writing.

"Do you have valid border papers?" he asked.

"Yes, Fras Inspector, I can leave tonight."

"Tonight? Well, so be it." He scribbled out notes as his lackey lit a taper

in the fire and melted some wax for his seal. "Lackey, take this to the beamflash tower at the Unitech and have it transmitted tonight. Lemorel, this is for you."

Only nine minutes after leaving the hostelry tavern Lemorel was packing in an upstairs room of Milderellen Fine Lenses and Clockwork. Petari Milderellen hovered anxiously at the door.

"But the train leaves at five, Lem. You'll never have time to buy a ticket."

"I met Jemli on the way home and sent her to the railside to pay for a cell."

"All this haste, you're sure to have forgotten something."

"The next train leaves in a week, Dada, and I can't wait."

She buckled the pack's straps and hefted it. Suddenly Petari caught her excitement.

"Well hurry then, run for the railside. I'll come after you in a minute."

Lemorel clattered down the stairs with her heavy pack, barked her fingers on the doorframe, then jogged awkwardly down the street while struggling to get her arms through the pack straps. Petari rummaged in his shop, then bolted the door and ran after his daughter.

"Lem, this is for you," he called as he caught up with her.

It was a Morelac twin long-barrel 34 bore. Lemorel stopped, eyes wide with surprise.

"Keep going, move," he panted, unconsciously holding the gun in front of her like a carrot before a donkey. "From the style of the filigree on the grip I'd say it dated from the late fifteen hundreds. It's a gift . . . gunsmith owed me a favor . . . made that tournament scope for the Mayor of Tocumwal. The barrels . . . finely wrought. He's replaced the original ramlock strikers with modern flintlocks."

The gun was old yet stylish, and had a good name with librarians and administrators. It was much heavier than the 25-bore pistol that she had shot her way to infamy with, and while not as expensive as the guns of the elite, it would suggest that she had gone to some trouble to find and refurbish a rare pistol with a name for accuracy.

"Thank you for everything, Dada," Lemorel gasped. "You've really been good to me. I brought you just . . . trouble and pain. Will you please—"

"Flowers for the graves of your mother and Jimkree . . . I'll do it," he wheezed, his breath beginning to fail. "If the Highliber . . . has any contract work in lenses and clockwork . . . mention my name. Oi, they're starting to pedal. Hurry now, goodbye Lem."

The galley train was about the height of an average man and built of waxcloth over a wooden frame. It was shaped like a streamlined, articulated worm on wheels, and had a walkway with a light railing along the roof. Being human-powered, it accelerated slowly. Lemorel scrambled over the stone wall of the

platform with Petari pushing at both her and the pack. She turned to give him a brief spasm of a hug, then turned and ran beside the accelerating train to where Jemli was waiting. Jemli gave her the boarding ticket and a small cloth pouch, and the sisters said goodbye as Lemorel stepped onto the train's roof. Jemli ran along beside the train, wishing her good luck until the platform came to an end. Lemorel dropped to one knee, gasping for breath and waving back. As the train rolled out among the houses of Rutherglen, the conductor showed her to a cell and she entered through the hatch in the roof. She settled into the seat and he zeroed the counter beside her pedals with a key.

"Know the rules?" he asked through the hatch.

"Two hours pushing and an hour to rest, for as long as the train is moving."

"And any extra will be credited. Likewise you will be debited if you decide not to pedal. First stop in five hours."

The train rumbled on through the town and Lemorel looked through her cell's shutter for her father's shop and the buildings of the Unitech. Easily visible was the lifeline of her hopes and ambitions, the beamflash tower.

"Failed again," muttered Lemorel as she sat perspiring. "Didn't say goodbye to Dada, didn't kiss Jemli."

They passed through the outer wall and into the countryside, rolling through vineyards and fields of tethered sheep and free-range emus. She knew the country well, but not from the angle of the paraline track. For some moments she stared at a large whitewashed barn with a bark and shingle roof. Such a large building, surely all the buildings in Rochester would be at least as big, she thought, even while a faint alarm began to clang at the back of her mind.

Why was the barn familiar? Off to one side was a much smaller shed, where a farmer was pitchforking hay into a loft from his cart. It was close enough so Lemorel could see that his horse was tethered to a fence while the farmer had his own timer and anchor. That was foolish. If a Call came he would step straight off the cart, risking damage to his timer. If that happened, only a broken leg would save him. The shed was familiar too—she had seen it before, at night, by distant torchlight!

With a sudden shudder of revulsion Lemorel slammed the shutter closed and gritted her teeth as she fought back a wave of nausea. She doubled over. Horror seemed to crawl over her with myriad spiders' feet as the galley train swayed and clacked along the paraline. Click, click, click, click, the counter unit between her legs reminded her that she was not pedaling. How long had she been like that, she wondered amid the flood of unwanted images. The more she pedaled, the faster the train moved, she told herself as she lay back in her seat and pushed hard against the pedals. Gears whined somewhere beneath her.

"It must be Libris. It must be Libris. It must be Libris," she chanted softly to the clacking of wheels on rails.

It was dark inside her cabin with the shutters closed, as dark as it had been that night in—"No! Think of something else, anything!" She felt for the little cloth pouch that Jemli had given her. Inside was a silver star with eight points on a fine, clamp-link chain, the sort of slightly tasteless jewelry that an unsophisticated teenage sister might be expected to give. Lemorel fingered the little star with a rush of nostalgia and regret. She was indeed trying to escape from two very bad years and regain lost innocence. She leaned forward for a moment and clipped the chain around her neck. As she settled back to pedal, the star sat cool and fresh against her skin.

The Call that had torn Ettenbar, the Southmoor shepherd, out of his life and flung him into a new destiny bore down on Rutherglen about ten minutes after the pedal train had left.

Vellum Drusas had been staring after Lemorel in the hostelry taproom when the Archbishop of Numurkah joined him.

"Combining pleasure with business, Vellum?" said the Archbishop stridently as he laid a hand on his shoulder.

Drusas gave a start, but did not spill his drink.

"Ah James, the day's fortune to you," he said, half rising and kissing the ring on his finger. "It's been . . . two years!"

"Eighteen months. The harvest blessing at Shepparton."

"How could I forget? Redsker decked his barn with gum mistletoe and dressed his field hands as vine sprites."

The Archbishop took the seat beside him after dusting it with the tassels of his sashtrail. If dressed identically they might have been mistaken for twins.

"So who was the Dragon girl?"

"Oh just Lemorel, the local problem child. I've certified her for Dragon Red exams at Libris."

"Lemorel? Lemorel Milderellen?"

Drusas nodded.

"My dear Vellum, she was the one who sent most of the Voyander household to meet the good Lord well before their allotted span ended."

"It was a legal vendetta."

"Oh but still, such an old and noble family and they made such wonderful honeywine—was it wise to send her to Libris?"

"It might be the wisest course of all, dear Archbishop. She will soon get shot by someone's champion. Strange girl, very like the Highliber herself. Perhaps she might shoot the Highliber. I live in hope."

"Come now, Vellum, that's hardly the Christian attitude," laughed the Archbishop, wagging his finger.

"Good Fras, you have no idea what that woman has done to the library service. Libris itself is being torn apart. The most worthy and noble senior Colors have been shot, exiled, or demoted."

"Has anybody noticed their passing?"

"James! How could you? The foundation stones of your cathedral do no more than sit quietly in their places, yet where would the rest of the building be without them?"

"Oh I agree, but there's more to a building than foundations. Good Fras, *you* are still in your old position, so virtue must still have rewards." He sprawled back along the bench and regarded Drusas through bushy eyebrows. "What are your plans for tonight? Not business, I hope?"

"Well, there is the wine-tasting competition. Were you invited?"

"Oh yes, a matter of course . . . but I'm working. Such a cruel life, dear Vellum. I have to ride out to the Broadbank estate to do some private buying for the Episcopal Consensus."

Drusas' eyes widened and his heart pounded with anticipation. "Your dedication leaves me breathless," he said guardedly, aware that he was playing a large fish with a thin line.

"I had hoped to enlist you as a taster, Fras Vellum, but seeing that you have a trophy to win—"

"Fras James, what is a trophy beside friendship? I should be delighted to assist."

"We leave within the hour."

"Splendid. Do you fancy a frostwine to keep the palate charged?"

"Such temptation, you might be the Call itself. Get behind me, Horned One!"

"Since when has the Call been from the Fiend?"

The Archbishop frowned. "Fraenko's heresy has surfaced again. There's to be a Council of Overbishops to pronounce upon it. Of course I am merely an archbishop, but I can tell you that nothing will change."

"So the Call is still meant to come from God?"

"Yes and no. 'Thou shalt not take pleasure from the allure of the Call' and 'Thou shalt not despair at succumbing to the Call' will remain in the catechism. The Call is seen to be like the allure of a bottle of excellent wine: your own bad intentions maketh the sin, yet the bottle and the wine are blameless."

"And what measure of sin is it?"

"From me, oh, five silver nobles in the almsbox and reciting the Miserablia twice a day for a week. Confess to one of the New Fraenkites and you might have to donate two gold royals to their campaign funds and spend a month in a hair shirt."

"That's about the difference between masturbation and adultery."

''So, you've had occasion to atone for both? Shame on you, and congratulations—''

The Call rolled over the taproom. The Archbishop surrendered in a private, well practiced blaze of forbidden pleasure. Drusas was able to assure himself that he could do nothing about what he was feeling before plunging into the same reverie. They slowly stood and mindlessly walked southeast across the taproom. Farmer, Archbishop, librarian, serving wench, cook, and vintner: all crowded against the wall, unable to think to cross the room to the door in the northwest wall, so blind and unreasoning was their desire to walk southeast.

Two blocks away the five strangers who had earlier considered Lemorel as potential quarry were safe in a coffeehouse. Being still during business hours, most people were indoors or safely tethered. A lamplighter was caught in the open, and he mindlessly turned southeast, walking through the streets and lanes, then out through the city gate. Moments after he passed, a Call timer tripped a release and the gate rumbled shut by itself. He walked across open fields, beside a dog that had trotted beside a certain Southmoor shepherd only hours earlier. Blood from the blackberry thorns was congealed in its fur.

Even though he had joined the procession of death, the lamplighter was safe. At his waist a clockwork timer ticked steadily, already forty minutes into its one-hour cycle. He was walking through a vineyard when the time expired and the timer released a grapple on a strap. It snared a training post and he stopped, straining against his tether to walk southeast. The Call lasted three hours. It was after sunset when it finally passed, and the lamplighter shook his head, cursed, then reset his timer and began the trek back to town. In a way he had been lucky. The Call always stopped for part of the night, still holding its victims. He might well have remained in the cold, open fields until it moved on in the morning if it had not passed him by then.

Thickening cloud blotted out the stars, adding to the gloom of evening, and there were no lamps lit to cast even a feeble glow at the street corners. A chill, misty drizzle discouraged people from venturing out of doors, and many retired to bed early. The strangers left the coffeehouse, winding their timers as they went.

''Perfect timing for a Call,'' chuckled one as he untied their hired pony dray.

''Aye, and such a surprising number of people will have been careless with their tethers,'' said the tall man.

Jaas was a stores clerk from the railside warehouse. He was unmarried, middle-aged, and lived alone, and had just reached home when the Call had rolled over him. He awoke in his house, cold, hungry, and in darkness. He spent ten minutes finding the tinderbox he had dropped three hours earlier, then lit a pottery thumblamp. By the smoky olive-oil flame he took a mutton and port sausage from the pantry, dragged his favorite chair to the table, and sat with his feet up. The

shadows of his feet made the caricature of a head on the wall as he carved off a slice of sausage. The shadow head had been his silent and faithful companion for years.

"Why be a free man if ye can't dine casual?" he asked the shadow, and it nodded gravely as he rocked his feet. There was a knock at the door.

"Call census!"

"I'm here," he called.

"Call census!" insisted the voice.

"Fagh dummart," Jaas muttered, lowering his feet from the table and walking to the door. "Here I be, th'art satisfied—"

As he flung the door open and stood outlined by his own lamp a fist slammed into his plexus, dropping him quietly and neatly. Within a minute he was gagged, bound, and tied in sack. Mabak left a broken tether strap clipped to an outside rail beside the firewood pile as the others loaded Jaas onto their dray. When the real census clerk came past he would conclude that Jaas was the victim of a faulty tether.

Jemli's edutor was working late in his office to make up time lost to the Call. Expecting only his students, he called "Enter" at the knock on his door, and did not even turn to face his visitors. A tax collector's clerk on the abductors' list went the same way. For the last two there was no stealth. The dray was tied up outside the Constable's Watchhouse and three of the abductors entered. Their papers had the seal of Libris, a book closed over a dagger. The Constable himself was on duty, and his hands shook as he broke the seal and read the order. Two writhing bodies were carried out in sacks as the Constable wrote out "Escaped just prior to a Call without wearing tethers" against both of their names in the Watchhouse register.

As the lamplighter began his rounds the pony dray had already left on the five-mile trek down the flat, fog-shrouded road to the river wharves at Wahgun-yah. The real census clerks were busy on their rounds too, checking for missing citizens. They reported a terrible tragedy, five souls lost to the Call, and the Mayor of Rutherglen issued a proclamation about the proper use and maintenance of Call tethers and body anchors. This was shouted about for a half hour by the criers in the foggy streets. Christian, Islamic, and Genthic services were held in memory of the five, and prayers were said that they might be forced out of the Call by some fence, thicket, or mercy wall.

An oarbarge was being held ready at the Wahgunyah wharves, and a bribe had insured that no questions were being asked. When the pony dray arrived, five sacks were unloaded and stored under cover. The abductors pushed the barge away from the wharf and began rowing into the gloom. The tall man wiped condensation from the bowlamp's concave, then turned up the wick. A dim but focused beam swept the river ahead for shoal buoys and snags. Once the barge

was out of sight of the wharves, the sacks were opened and the prisoners were made to help with the oars.

"I'm not built for a life of rowing," said Jaas sullenly. "There's not a bargemaster on the river as would pay good silver for me."

"Rowin's not the value on you," said the tall man.

"What then?"

"You all can count. The Warren pays gold royals for those as can count."

"The Warren!" exclaimed the tax clerk. "Since when has the Warren been across more than stolen drygoods?"

"The price is two gold royals for souls as can count and speak Austaric. We've done well baggin' Southmoor teachers from mosques near the border. Got seventeen over the past five months, an' nine of them spoke Austaric. That's twenty-four gold royals—"

"Mabak!" barked the leader. "Hold your talk or wear a gag."

The tall man snorted and spat into the river, but obeyed.

One hundred miles to the west, in Rochester, the machine that would soon swallow them was being shut down for the night. Having given the Highliber her victory at champions it was dissolving into its exhausted components.

As the door of the cell thudded shut behind them the four men collapsed, two onto the lower bunks and two onto the straw that covered the flagstones.

"Told you this would be a bad day," said ADDER 17. "Whenever the whole nine dozen of us are assembled in the late afternoon, you can be sure that the correlator components will be worked like a harlot's doorknocker."

MULTIPLIER 8 lay on the floor with his eyes closed and his fingers twitching. "We need more multipliers," he said. "When the load is on it all comes to us for verification and we can't keep that sort of pace up for long."

They lay there in silence for some minutes, then ADDER 17 sat up on the edge of his bunk. He reeled slightly from the movement, then shook his head and stood up.

"Anyone interested in a meal?" he asked, but received only groans and mutters by way of reply. He shuffled through the straw and pulled the slatted pantry door open.

"A pot of hot stew!" he said in surprise. "With fresh bread and a jar of beer."

"Mayoral Standard?" asked PORT 3A.

"No, just tourney beer."

"It's always tourney beer. Why can't we have something strong?"

"For the same reason that kavelars in a tournament have to drink it," said FUNCTION 9. "We need to be refreshed, not drunk. Could you pass me a bowl of stew, ADD?"

As the lowest-ranking component in the cell, ADDER 17 was servant and housekeeper to the rest. He began to ladle out the meal.

"Clean straw, clean blankets, and sulphur's been burned to kill the vermin," he remarked. "They're rewarding us."

"I expected a beating," said MULTIPLIER 8, rubbing his hands together to steady them. "The way they questioned us in the training hall after leaving the Calculor had me thinking the machine had failed."

"Nay, I remember an orderly HALTMODE coming up on my frame," said PORT 3A. "They use FREEZE if something's wrong."

They ate in silence for a while, and a Dragon Red Librarian looked in briefly for the evening inspection. She told them that some repositioning was to be done in the Calculor room before the next working session, and that there would be a training run to accustom them to the new arrangement.

ADDER 17 mopped out his bowl with a crust, then poured a measure of beer into it. The others were still eating, as their hands were too swollen and painful to handle spoons easily.

"I keep wondering what it's all for," he said after his first sip.

MULTIPLIER 8 gave a groan of derision and held out his hand for the jar of beer. "To torture us, what else? A new punishment for felons," he said as he mixed beer with his stew.

"I disagree," said FUNCTION 9. "I was an edutor in Oldenberg University, and I'd never stolen so much as a copper—or made a political statement. There I was, walking in the cloisters after dinner when clout! When the blindfold came off I was here."

"Some rival may have wanted your job."

"There was not that sort of rivalry for the chair of Arithmetic Fundamentals. No, I think I was kidnapped especially to work here. Seven of the ten FUNC-TIONS were kidnapped from provincial colleges, and all prisoners who work here used arithmetic in their work. Then again, most of the people here are those with backgrounds that . . . well, nobody would miss them greatly. Felons, the lonely, the friendless, those whose loved ones are too poor to have proper inquiries made, and those wastrels whose loved ones are rich enough to bribe officials *not* to have proper inquiries made. Anyone who can be easily trained to work the beads, frames, and levers of the Calculor has a welcome. For many it's the best home they ever had."

"Surely someone with your background would be missed," said MULTI-PLIER 8.

"Not so. My wife had a lover, a romantic dandy with no money. With me gone they got the house, my library, and an estate worth thirty-five gold royals—as well as each other. No, I would not have been missed. Someone did their homework well on me."

PORT 3A was asleep, his beer untouched, as ADDER 17 began to collect the bowls. He lifted the exhausted man's legs onto the bunk, covered him with a blanket, then drained his beer. The gong rang for a half hour to lights out.

"Anyone have time for a game of champions?" ADDER 17 asked as he stacked the bowls in the pantry.

"Got plenty," said MULTIPLIER 8. "The magistrate gave me nine years."

"And for manipulating shipping registers, as I recall," added FUNCTION 9. "It was a very clever scheme, as you explained it. The rectifier who caught you out must have been a skilled mathematician."

"Never met the bastard," he said as ADDER 17 set up the board and pieces. "Right out of the blue the Constable's Runners turned up with a couple of dozen sheets of poorpaper showing how I'd managed to pocket one gold royal for every thousand I handled. The churls I worked with stole from the shipments too, but none of them are here. It's damn unfair!"

"They were of no interest to the Calculor's master. You stole using arithmetic, they just pilfered from the cargoes. You are here because you showed skill with numbers in your crime."

MULTIPLIER 8 turned to the board and drew a straw from a pair in ADDER 17's fist. It was the longer, and he sighed with satisfaction as he shifted a pawn for his opening move.

"At last something went right for me today," he said.

FUNCTION 9 climbed up to his bunk and began leafing through a slim training book.

"Did it ever cross your mind, MULT, that the rectifier who caught you out was actually the Calculor?" he asked casually.

It had not. MULTIPLIER 8 gave such a start that he upset the champions board.

"I—yes, yes, that makes sense," he said in wonder at FUNCTION 9's powers of deduction. "It would not take long for the Calculor to unravel it. But why pick on me?"

"It probably examined the figures from every shipping register from every river port for a couple of months, looking for anomalies. Your scheme was invisible to human checking, because nobody would have the time to look at the registers in such detail. The Calculor, however, has greater patience and power than the mortals who comprise it—us."

"The devil you say!"

"There's more likely to be one very clever edutor or noble behind the Calculor than the devil. Just think of it. If the Mayor can plug the many thousands of holes through which his taxes and shipping levees are diminished, why he could double his income."

"So *that's* what the Calculor's for," MULTIPLIER 8 said in awe, turning

back to help ADDER 17 set up the board again. "You know, it makes me feel proud in a way. It's like serving the Mayor as a soldier."

"Except that you gets shot at in the army," said ADDER 17, extending his forearm to display a well-healed but ugly scar.

"Hah, try to escape and see who gets shot at. You start this time, ADD. It was I who tipped the board."

In seven moves MULTIPLIER 8 moved a knight to crush two pawns and tilt his opponent's bishop. This exposed his own bishop to an opposition archer, who had a "ready" weighting. ADDER 17 rotated the archer through half a circle, then removed the bishop.

"Damnhell, but I always forget what archers can do," MULTIPLIER 8 grumbled. "What I need is the Calculor to work out the choices for me."

"But then it wouldn't be you playing," said ADDER 17.

"Nonetheless, the idea is sound," said FUNCTION 9, looking up from his book. "In playing champions you are always dealing with patterns and values. Anything that can be reduced to numbers can be handled by the Calculor."

MULTIPLIER 8 checked the status of his own archers but found that none of them had a worthy target. In peevish frustration he reversed one and shot down a pawn.

"I bet the Calculor could give the Mayor's Gamesmaster a run for his money," he muttered.

"It will probably never happen," said FUNCTION 9. "If it can snare felons it can be used to do far more important things than playing champions."

"Such as?"

"I'm trying to work that out at this very moment. Just what can one use a huge capacity for arithmetic to do? One of the few surviving fragments from before Greatwinter mentions that calculating machines were used for everything from guiding ships to toasting bread. Most edutors would tell you that the writer was constructing some sort of allegory, but after spending a year in here I'm not so sure anymore."

FUNCTION 9 lapsed into thought. MULTIPLIER 8's knights took an enemy keep, but he forgot about an archer that ADDER 17 had used two moves to give a three-quarter wind—so that it could shoot diagonally. It shot his king across six spaces. MULTIPLIER 8 damned all archers, and the duty Dragon Red arrived to quench the lamp that illuminated their cell through a heavy glass block.

"I have a prediction," said FUNCTION 9, and a questioning grunt floated up from the darkness below. "Before long the Calculor will be made at least three times bigger. What is more, it will run for twenty-four hours every day, in shifts."

"What use is that?" muttered MULTIPLIER 8 sleepily.

"What use is a Mayor who never sleeps?"

2 CAPITAL

Lemorel caught sight of the Libris beamflash tower an hour before she could see the walls of Rochester. She was gazing at the forest through the slot beside her headrest as the galley train rounded a long curve, and suddenly there it was, like a mighty pointed spearhead above the trees. After savoring the sight of the white tower for a moment she pushed harder against the pedal bars, adding slightly more impetus to that of the other passengers on the train. Its speed was not great. This train's passengers had a higher than usual proportion of the old, unfit, or indolent, and those who were either willing or able to pedal were being worked particularly hard.

Some minutes later they reached the border of the Mayorate of Rochester. The city of Rochester itself might have been the capital of the Southeast Alliance, but the mayorate was a tiny scrap of territory. The forward and rear gunners screwed down the brakes and the train shuddered to a halt as the clamps pressed against the wheels. Lemorel slumped in her seat, her tunic cold with perspiration. She was unsteady on her feet when she finally stood and stretched. The railside accountant came striding out of his office, a thin, angular man who reminded Lemorel of the wading birds that lived by the irrigation canals of Rutherglen. He took the logbook from the rear gunner and looked over the figures, then inspected the stroke counters of the leading passengers. He came to Lemorel last. As he stooped to read her stroke counter his head lunged forward while his shoulders remained still, as if he were pecking the figures off.

"Excellent, excellent, excellent," he said as he straightened. "Strong, strong girl, eh?"

Lemorel nodded in reply.

"The train's log says . . . says you should finish the trip with a credit—a credit, at least five silver nobles. Now, now, you rank third on the train, but first among the female passengers. So you may go first. Go first! Go, go."

She shambled off to the railside privy. Hard work was rewarded with more than just journey credit. Priority use of facilities at each railside was a further incentive to pedal harder to drive the train. She unclipped her hair before the mirror beneath the skylight. This would be the last chance to touch up her appearance before she reached the terminus at Rochester. She peered at herself carefully. No lines on her face as yet . . . but a gray hair. And another! She plucked another five before rebinding and fastening her hair. She reeked of per-

spiration and her clothes were damp, but at least she would not look disheveled. By the time she had brought water and pineseed cakes at the kiosk the Inspector of Customs was checking her rollpack. If the railside accountant was a stork, this man was a ferret: small, agile, and sharp-eyed.

"You can afford a Morelac twin-barrel, yet you travel in the galley train?" he said, turning the worn but polished weapon over with nimble, dancing fingers.

"A gift from my family, Fras Inspector," she replied, carefully casting her eyes down to the platform rather than locking stares with him.

"Hah! Rich family, then, but that's none of my business." The inspector opened her border pass. "Dragon Orange, and you're only nineteen. Impressive." The clockwork timer of Lemorel's body anchor clattered a warning, and she reached down to reset and rewind it. The inspector laughed. "No need for that now, Dragon Orange Milderellen, you're in the Rochester Null Zone. The Call never comes to *this* little mayorate."

"No Call, Fras Inspector?" she asked, for no better reason than to practice small talk with a stranger.

"No Call, Frelle, but plenty of danger. The scum of the southeast gather in Rochester. Those who come here because they are too lax to wind a Call timer are too lax to mind their morals either. Rochester suits them. I spend time in neighboring mayorates every year, so that the Call can put strength back into my heart. Everyone should do it, especially a young innocent like you. Are you to work in Libris?"

"Yes," she whispered, almost beside herself with pride at being called innocent.

"Then take my advice and live in the Libris hostelry. Stay out of the city. Perdition, so much perdition in Rochester." He handed back the flintlock. "If some town rake accosts you in an alleyway and makes lewd suggestions, just shoot him with your fine gun. Don't even bother to talk. You're a Dragon Librarian, the magistrates always believe the word of a Dragon Librarian. Can you shoot?"

"Why of course, I—I passed the test for Dragon Orange."

"Ah yes, but always keep practicing. Never be afraid to shoot in your own defense, especially in Rochester."

"It's a comfort to know that not all Rochestrians are bad, Fras Inspector," she replied.

He blushed. His lackey wrote out a customs ticket at his portable desk and the inspector peered over his shoulder as he worked, calling out items and values from memory.

"I marked down the value of your Morelac," he said as he handed the ticket to her. "The modern flintlock mechanism obviously reduces its value as an antique." He winked at her. "You are only a poor country girl whose family probably saved a long time for that gun."

"Thank you, Fras Inspector, thank you so much. I shall be very careful in Rochester."

As she strapped herself back into her seat Lemorel tried to come to terms with what had just happened. Someone had read her name without asking if she was *the* Lemorel Milderellen. Could she shoot, he had asked. Wonderful! Perhaps she really had come far enough to escape her past. She fingered the little eight-point star at her throat. The inspector had probably been a Gentheist. They believed that the Call was sent by their gods to strengthen the character of the human race.

"At the ready!" the rear gunner cried, and Lemorel strained against the pedals. The front and rear gunners unscrewed the brakes and the five-carriage train began to ease forward. "Under way!" cried the rear gunner as the brake pads came clear of the wheels. The train began to gather speed.

So they were in the Null Zone. To Lemorel, life without the Call was unimaginable. How could she live with the idea of never having to be vigilant against wandering off into oblivion? Could she afford to lose her survival habits while staying in Rochester? How long would she stay? Did she really need to leave Rochester every so often?

Rochester stood on an immense plain of low eucalypt forest, but the area close to the city was cleared for farming. The paraline abruptly emerged from the forest into ploughed fields and vineyards, with a scattering of fortified manors. So, they must have freebooter raids even here, Lemorel thought to herself as she surveyed the walls and gunslits. A small beamflash tower stood in the grounds of each manor.

The walls of the city were streaky gray abandonstone capped with slitted battlements. The city proper was on an island at the center of a shallow lake, with a wooden roadbridge and two paralines on trestles crossing it. Lemorel looked to her travel book as she pushed at the pedals and the train rumbled smoothly through the fields. The walled inner city was roughly elliptical, and five miles by eight. Surplus population had spilled into a band of suburbs halfway around the shores of the lake.

At the outer wall a switcher joined the train, and guided it through a maze of points and signals in the shunting yards. Great wind-train engines towered over them, with spiral painted rotor towers spinning lazily in the slight breeze. The burly crews of navvy engines looked across contemptuously from their stocky, powerful shunters. Suddenly the jangling confusion gave way to the trestle bridge across the lake, and the ride was smooth again. The city entrance was an archway in the wall, and the train was at dead slow as it passed through. The Rochester terminus was a long roofed railside sheltering the platforms and a maze of gates, fences, and small offices.

Lemorel unbuckled herself from the seat and stiffly paced beside the train

while she waited for her meter to be read by a railside accountant. After the gate tax and weapons levee she had made three silver nobles on the trip. Walking slowly, her legs like lead weights, she made her way past inspectors at the platform gate, customs gate, tax gate, City Constable's gate, and finally the railside gate. Amid the gaggle of signs with names that people in the crowd were holding up was one that read MILDERELLEN—DRAGON ORANGE. Lemorel walked across to the woman holding it. She was five or six years older than Lemorel, with braided brown hair. Her gray librarian's uniform had a Dragon Blue band on the right arm.

"Evening's fortune to you, I'm Lemorel Milderellen," she said, summoning the enthusiasm to smile and putting her roll down.

The other smiled back but did not reply. Instead she held out a card. MAY THE PROMISE AND FORTUNE OF THE MORNING/AFTERNOON/EVENING BE WITH YOU. I AM DARIEN VIS BABESSA, DRAGON BLUE. I HAVE NO VOICE, FRELLE, PLEASE BEAR WITH ME. I AM TO TAKE YOU TO LIBRIS. IT IS TWO MILES AWAY.

"Two miles," echoed Lemorel, who was having trouble even standing up.

What would a genuine country girl do? Break down and cry or suffer in silence? She decided to suffer. With a deep breath she shouldered her roll. Darien gestured to the road and began walking. Once they were clear of the terminus she showed Lemorel another card.

TAKE THE NEXT TURN ON THE LEFT. ENTER A COFFEEHOUSE NAMED THE RAILSIDE WELCOME.

"I'm right to keep walking," Lemorel replied, but the words were forced.

I MUST BRIEF YOU ABOUT LIBRIS BEFORE YOU ARRIVE was on the back of the same card.

Lemorel needed no more persuasion. The shop was of scrubbed redbrick with abandonstone slabs on the floor, and Northmoor tapestries glittering with gold thread on the walls. Incense, coffee, and half a dozen varieties of smoke-weed smothered her senses as she entered. Her eyes were streaming as a waiter in a jezalakan saw them to a table by the window. It was not until she had half finished her mug of Rockhampton Ebony that she remembered her mute escort.

Darien was sitting patiently, fingering a fan of cards and watching the traffic passing outside the window.

"Do you know the Portington sign language?" Lemorel asked.

Darien's head snapped around, her formerly placid eyes bulging with surprise. "Yes, yes," she gestured back at once. "How do you know it? It is taught only to the mute and deaf."

"The parents of a friend of mine were both deaf-mutes. I picked up enough to hold a conversation."

Darien sat rocking back and forth in her seat, her hands moving in little

circles as she searched for words. "I have been in Libris for nine years," she signed, too overcome to think of anything else.

"I've been a librarian for two years," Lemorel replied.

"In all of Libris there is none fluent in sign language but you and me." There was something approaching hunger in Darien's face. "I hope we can be friends, Frelle Lemorel. I would love to put these damn cards away sometimes."

A friend. The prospect appealed to Lemorel more than she dared admit.

"I'm not on the Libris staff yet, Frelle. I came here to take the Dragon Red test. Where can I find a hostelry?"

"There is a spare pallet in my rooms in the Libris hostelry," Darien signed so quickly that Lemorel barely caught the meaning.

"I couldn't impose—"

"No, no, I insist. Please, agree to stay."

"Well . . . it would be a relief not to worry about finding lodgings before the examination. When will it be, do you know?"

"Tomorrow afternoon."

Lemorel gripped the edge of the table as she felt herself sway backward. "As soon as that?"

"There are problems with the internal workings of Libris, Frelle Lemorel. We need new staff urgently. The Highliber has a . . . a secret machine that most people know about but which none but the most trusted have seen. This machine is said to handle beamflash signaling with unheard-of efficiency, but it has been making errors recently."

"If they gave me a few days to rest and study I might have a better chance of passing the examination and joining the staff to help with the machine."

"Maybe so, Frelle, but the examiner is available only tomorrow. He has to work on the machine as well. Come now, I shall take you to my rooms, then show you the bathing chambers and the refectory. When you are washed, fed, and rested you may feel happier about the examination."

"No bath can replace study," said Lemorel as she stood up. Darien signed a paper bearing the Libris crest that the waiter brought, and then she picked up Lemorel's packroll. She staggered a little under the unexpected weight as she swung it across her back; then they set off down the cobbled streets to Libris.

Outside the coffeehouse the shadows were lengthening as evening approached. Nobody wore Call anchors, Lemorel noted, but then if a Call swept over the city the walls would prevent people from going very far. Still, it was like being the single clothed person amid a gathering of nudists—and even in the notorious nudist estate at Hansonville the patrons were reputed to still wear their body anchors. Here there were no body anchors, no tether rails, no mercy walls, nothing! The very thought was somehow wanton. Perhaps that was why people's morals seemed looser in Rochester.

An ebony Kooree carrying a nine-foot spear and wearing no more than a loincloth walked past talking animatedly with two merchants and a man wearing the uniform of a paraline guard. Robed, veiled Southmoor women strolled in groups; packrunners trotted past with impossibly balanced loads on their heads. Pushtricycles towed buggies laden with the gentry of the city, while armed escort runners warily surveyed the crowds for ambush. Lemorel noticed that she was not being jostled. She had expected to have to fight her way through the evening rush, yet the two librarians were given a clear path wherever they walked.

A Gentheist preacher wearing a ragged jezalakan shouted in a hoarse yet strident voice to a small crowd of idlers.

". . . and woe unto ye who would shun the touch of the Call and let thy souls grow so soft that . . ."

His voice was quickly lost in the background din of the cries of the vendors of fine cotton, fine silk, fine wool carpets, fine tomatoes, fine blood-beans, fine sandals, and fine gunpowder. Ahead through the crowd was another preacher, a backwoods Christian Foundationist by the look of his black gamberloid and buckleshield hat.

"God in his wisdom allows this place of perdition to exist so that honest folk might see what life can be like without the Call to guide them along His path. Now ye have seen, friends, so I say unto ye, leave this place of Satan's comfort, turn thy backs on . . ."

"Fine pastries, macaroons, pineseed cakes, roast macadamia nuts."

"Strikers, new flint strikers."

Darien nudged Lemorel for attention, then gestured. "It is a wild part of the city, but it is the shortest way."

Gangs of navvies from the rail yards roamed in groups. Their legs were distorted with muscle from pedaling the shunting engines, and bulged against the trews of their blue uniforms. Harlots lounged at the upper windows, each flagged with a guildsign while pimps carrying the corresponding guildsign flags ran among the passing crowds. Hellfire preachers shouted doom and brimstone at the women, who responded with flashes of breast or backside. Someone tugged at Lemorel's arm.

"Southmoor girl, handsome Fras, the escaped concubine of a Wimmeran and skilled in—" The pimp stopped with something between a gasp and a cough as Lemorel turned and he realized his mistake. He bowed, ducked, and backed away babbling, "Pardon Frelle. Mercy Frelle. Evening's Fortune unto you Frelle."

Darien was laughing soundlessly.

"I can't look as bad as that," said Lemorel. Darien shook her head.

"It is the Rutherglen uniform. In the half-light it resembles that of a shunting-engine navvy."

In the center of the road five navvies cheered some unseen companion in an upper-floor bedroom. Booming laughter and outraged squeals about dirty hands echoed down. From a neighboring window a buxom girl bared a pair of jiggling breasts painted like bull's-eyes at the navvies, then at Lemorel.

"Must buy a new uniform," muttered Lemorel, but Darien had sharp hearing and she caught the words.

"I'll lend you one of mine," Darien's fingers replied.

The offer of something as intensely personal as a uniform sent a curious, thrilling sensation shivering through Lemorel's exhausted body. A group of enormous Central Confederation navvies approached them in a line, then suddenly split to let them pass, bowing exaggeratedly and calling, "Breil, breil Frelle hufchen," to Lemorel.

"They're calling you a pretty girl," signed Darien, trying to be helpful, but Lemorel knew enough of their language to realize that they had taken her for a female shunter.

Above the rooftops the huge beamflash tower of Libris beckoned, and before long they reached the wall of the library complex. Darien signed them both in and they went straight to her rooms. While Lemorel bathed, her new friend took measurements from her uniform. By the time the refectory bell rang Darien had tack-sewn a Libris uniform of her own to Lemorel's size. Feeling nervous and vulnerable in a borrowed bathrobe Lemorel took the gray clothing and dressed behind a paper frame screen painted with stylized Warialda flowers. Darien clapped as she emerged.

"I'm not on the staff yet," she said doubtfully. "Tomorrow some examiner will be trying hard to make me change back into my old uniform."

Darien held her fingers up to the lamp and began gesturing. "I know your examiner, Lem. Do not be afraid of him. He is a bit abrupt but very fair. Just remember, it is in our best interests to recruit you."

"I may not be good enough. I'm weak on heraldry."

"So hire a herald. I have three working for me. Heraldry can be waived if you are outstanding at mathematics."

"Really? It can?"

"It can. The Highliber is desperate for Dragon Librarians with skill at mathematics."

"But that will surely cause imbalances in the running of Libris."

"It already has, Frelle Lemorel. Shall we go to the refectory instead of cooking here?"

"Just one more question. You said that you have three heralds working for you?"

"Yes."

"How many more staff do you supervise?"

"Twenty-five."

"Yet you came to meet me, a base recruit at the paraline terminus? A senior Dragon Color like you?"

"A newcomer's first impressions are the impressions that last most strongly. The Highliber's faction could not afford to let some inexperienced junior babble nonsense to you, any more than we could allow a minion from the Libris restorationists to pour lies into your ears. We value you, we want you to know that."

Highliber Zarvora had taken charge of Libris two years after the death of Mayor Jefton's father. She had gone to great trouble to gain the boy's attention and trust, amazing him by predicting lunar eclipses and delighting him by breaking the secret codes of the nobility. When she began to promise great wealth and real power, he was ready to listen. The Highliber was officially one of the monarch's private edutors, so nobody wondered at the long tutorial sessions in her office.

"We need a glorious war to restore the throne's dignity," he declared as Zarvora tried to explain a new scheme to snare tax evaders. "I grant you that it is comforting to see the treasury filling for a change, but that inspires no respect. Look at this decoded dispatch: they call me Mayor Miser the Mouse!"

"That was from Tandara's mayor. Very rude of him."

"I want to be treated with respect."

"He is a dangerous man. Better to have him treat you with contempt and ignore you, than treat you with respect and send assassins."

Jefton caught his breath. Zarvora continued to tap at her keyboard. Her attitude was beginning to annoy Jefton.

"I am considering a campaign against the Southmoors," he announced in a loud but forced voice.

"You have insufficient troops and kavelars," Zarvora patiently explained without showing any trace of surprise. "The Rochestrian nobles and kavelars would come to your aid if the Southmoors seemed likely to win, but if you had caused the fighting in the first place you would find yourself kneeling before a headsman's block while your own nobles and the Southmoor envoys watched to make sure the job was done properly."

Jefton flicked the wing of a mechanical owl in frustration. The row of dotted gearwheels rattled into a new pattern in response.

"Please do not fool about with the Calculor, Mayor, it is easily disturbed. One day it will provide you with an army that nobody can stop."

He petulantly flicked the wing again, but Zarvora had already typed a HALT-MODE command into the keyboard, so nothing happened. It was symbolic of his reign: whatever he did would be countered.

"I apologize, Highliber," he said, walking to the window and staring out

over the slate roofs to hide his shame. "I dream out loud when I talk of war. Dreams are the only place where I can break loose from my peers. Even if I had the money for a bigger army I could not raise one, for they would rip up the decree ordering its recruitment before the ink was dry."

"You may not need a bigger army," said Zarvora as she tapped out a new set of instructions. She let the words hang. After a moment Jefton turned.

"Is this an idle promise?" he demanded.

"Have I ever made an idle promise?" she asked, still typing. "I could give you a demonstration, if you care to sit down before the champions board. The Calculor is a skilled player, and I shall demonstrate—"

Suddenly she stiffened, staring at the rack of marked gears.

"Champions?" exclaimed Jefton with amazement. "It can predict eclipses, catch felons, break secret codes, and now you have taught it to play champions too? It's like having a tame god at my command."

"There seems to be a problem," muttered Zarvora, scowling at the rack of gears. "The god may be tame, but it is not entirely well just now."

Jefton thought for a moment. "You mean it's made an error? Perhaps it was distracted by all the book-organizing work that it does for Libris."

"The Calculor has no background tasks just now, Mayor. It is dedicated to the tasks that I have invoked from this office."

Zarvora continued to type test calculations. From the way that her eyes widened and her fists clenched it was obvious that the Calculor made several more errors.

"Its reliability seems to be in question," ventured Jefton. "If it cannot perform simple calculations how can I trust it with questions of the defense of the realm?"

"It has already brought you more extra income by snaring dishonest clerks than a one-third tax increase would have," Zarvora explained with strained patience. "What is more, it has brought popularity too. Your people have not been out of pocket, yet they have seen the unjust punished. It also lets you spy on your nobles by the very secret codes that they use to conceal matters from you."

"Perhaps the Calculor gets careless when it is tired. Rest it more often. That could solve the problem. My advisers often fall asleep when meetings drag on."

"You do not understand, Mayor. The Calculor does not get tired like we do, and cannot make a mistake. If the felons who perform the operations inside it grow tired it will work slower, but its accuracy should not change."

"Should not?"

"Will not, once I find the problem. When it is fully functional it will be made up of three teams of components who will be swapped every eight hours. The Calculor will then be an adviser to you which will never sleep or die. Even better, it will have no personal opinions or interests to color its advice."

Although young, and born to his position, Jefton was as astute as many far more experienced rulers. He always thought through the consequences of advice offered to him with great care, but acted decisively once he was convinced. The advantages of the expanded Calculor had not taken long to win his confidence.

"I must have the services of the Calculor available by the end of the month," he announced after a few moments of thought.

"But Mayor, the source of the errors—"

"The errors do not concern me. If they tend to appear when the components are tired, the problem will disappear when the components are rotated before they actually become tired."

"But the weakness will still be in the system."

"I know you, Highliber Zarvora. You are a perfectionist, and such people do more than is needed to accomplish a task. So the Calculor can play champions, eh? I have noticed that Fergen has been in a very bad mood lately, and my lackeys tell me that he has been visiting this office. I suspect that champions has been played in secret, and that the Calculor has thrashed him soundly."

"I had meant to tell you once the error had been—"

"Excellent, excellent! If it can play champions so well than it can unravel political intrigues too. Remember, the end of the month, Highliber. If you cannot get it working I shall send in a committee of edutors from the University."

Zarvora was lost for words. A committee of edutors! The idea of anyone discovering what the Calculor could really do made her shiver.

"I must return to the palace now, Highliber. What should I do about that insulting dispatch?"

"Take heart from it, Mayor. It means that they acknowledge that you can manage your treasury and will not be running to them for loans. As long as you seem harmless and thrifty you will be left free to govern Rochester as you will."

Zarvora signaled for the Calculor hall to be cleared as soon as Jefton left; then she hurried down the seven flights of stairs from her office to inspect the place in person. System Controller Lewrick was waiting when she arrived.

"Everything must be checked," she announced. "Every gear, wire cable, register, transmission line, and decoding chart. Every bead on every abacus and every cog in every translator."

"Another error, Frelle Highliber?"

"Five errors, and while I was demonstrating it to the Mayor."

"Ah, I see. Is he losing faith in our machine?"

"On the contrary. He was so impressed that he wants it fully operational by the end of the month. In his opinion, the errors will cease if the shifts are changed before the components tire."

"A good idea, the Mayor is a bright lad."

Furious, Zarvora seized the little man by the tunic and lifted him until their faces were level.

"I have been keeping very accurate records of the failures, Fras Lewrick, figures timed by the reciprocating clock in my office. The errors are turning up progressively *earlier* in the shifts. Do I make myself clear?"

He smiled nervously and nodded. She put him down.

"Well, well, the little monster seems to be growing lazy," he said as he straightened his clothing.

"It is *not* alive! There is a defect, and it is getting worse. If the Calculor becomes operational before we find it, Jefton will get some very stupid advice—which he will follow blindly because he trusts the Calculor too well."

"Serves him right for meddling with our work," said Lewrick with a shrug. "After the first big mistake he will leave us alone."

"After the first big mistake he'll send in a committee of edutors from the University," said Zarvora, smiling grimly in anticipation.

"Edutors? In here?" cried Lewrick in disbelief that became horror as he realized what the full consequences would be.

"Edutors, in here, Fras Lewrick."

"Godslove, no! They wouldn't understand. They would try to prove that it couldn't work. The secret would be out, damn nobles and relatives would try to liberate some of our best components."

"It will only happen if the errors are not stopped. Come, we shall begin by checking the abacus frames on each desk."

They started at the back row of desks on the right-hand processor of the Calculor and gradually moved forward. After an hour they had found no more than a hidden bag of walnuts and some obscene graffiti.

"The mechanisms are in excellent condition, Fras Lewrick," said Zarvora as they reached the partition that separated the FUNCTION section from the common components. "You are to be congratulated for maintaining the machine so well."

"I love the Calculor, good Frelle," he confessed as he checked the gears in a translator. "When I think of some rabble of edutors violating this hall, babbling their ignorant opinions, poking their grubby fingers into her gearwheels . . . it makes me shake with rage. I think I'll clean my gun and spend some time in the gymnasium tonight."

"Admirable loyalty, Fras Lewrick, but your time would be better spent finding the defect. We know that the same incorrect answers come from both Dexter and Sinister processors, yet these are separated by two cloth partitions ten feet high—and the corridor between is patrolled by Dragon Colors. Still, components on the two sides *must* be communicating with each other."

"Would you fight a duel rather than let the Calculor be violated, Frelle Highliber?"

"I already have. Now, if two components had a tiny mirror each they could flash coded signals on the ceiling of the hall. Have the components stripped naked and given new uniforms as they enter. Nothing reflective must be smuggled in."

"Yes, Highliber."

"Coughs, or the humming of tunes, could be code as well. Have all components gagged for the next shift. I would like to put the two processors into separate halls, but that would take months of rebuilding, and would slow the processing time. Have the components well rested, Fras Lewrick. There will be a ten-hour series of tests tomorrow."

The Assessor of Examinations was barely ten years older than Lemorel, and did not conform to her image of Dragon Silver Librarians. He was graying, haggard, and unshaven. His robes were disheveled, and looked as if he had been sleeping in them. There were ink and coffee stains on his sleeves.

"Dragon Orange Milderellen?" he asked, glancing up from a nest of forms and other paperwork as she entered.

"Yes, Fras Assessor."

"Please sit down," he said, opening her file. "Good marks in mathematics, in fact honors. You topped your year three times, I see." Suddenly he frowned. "Won the regional shooting championship twice and shot the magistrate's champion in a duel: that's a worry."

Lemorel felt a surge of horror, and suddenly wondered if she would be given a test at all. Without another word he closed the file and fished out two lists of questions from the mess on his desk.

"Please complete these tests when I tell you to start," he said as he handed them to Lemorel with a slate for rough work. "Married?"

"No, Fras—"

"Just as well. I was married, but my wife left me. Thought I had another woman in Libris, because of the long hours I work. Hah! I should be so lucky. Lackey!"

A short girl with large eyes and long black hair came mincing in from another office. She smiled at Lemorel. Her tunic bore the twin bars of the library-assistant grades.

"Rosa, this candidate is to be examined before two witnesses for a Dragon Red upgrade. Bring your work in here and give the Frelle anything that she needs—coffee, headache powders, all that."

Rosa took Lemorel over to a desk where an hourglass with a calibration seal stood at one corner.

"Pay him no mind," she whispered. "He works too hard and doesn't get enough sleep. Now, you have exactly one hour to finish, from when I turn the hourglass. Ready?" Lemorel nodded. "Start . . . now!"

There were ten questions of moderate difficulty on the first sheet, and five really hard questions on the second. Fighting down waves of panic, Lemorel scanned for the easiest questions, marked them in order of difficulty, then started.

The first four she did mentally, juggling figures and scrawling down answers without bothering to verify anything. The sand drifted down into a pile that grew ominously. Group theory, integral calculus, and division of matrices: some of the methods she could only guess at, others she had studied. She rounded off results for convenience, wrote in numbers remembered from tables and made approximations from roughly chalked graphs. In the background the Dragon Silver muttered to Rosa.

"Working us like slaves, how can she expect me to fill these quotas? Does she think Dragon Greens grow on trees? For every ten components we need one Dragon Green equivalent in the support staff, yet she wants the machine up to a thousand components in ten months."

Lemorel was desperate by now, and as the sands ran out the final question was still unanswered. The Dragon Silver continued to mutter about workloads and not having time to spend his apparently generous salary.

"Time's up!" Rosa announced, reaching across to take the papers and slate back from Lemorel. She handed them to the Assessor. He sat up, stretched, and began to mark the answers.

She would be sent back to Rutherglen now, to Lemorel there was nothing more certain. She forced herself into a cold, calm state to keep the tears back.

"Now . . . first paper, ninety-six percent, that's good. Second, fifty-two percent. A bare pass but good enough," he concluded with a flourish of his pen, then looked up with a smile. "Congratulations, that was short notice, but informality is in vogue here."

"Have I passed, Fras Assessor?"

"Of course, welcome to Libris."

"But that was only mathematics."

"Frelle, we have to work under pressure to keep the Highliber's needs satisfied. Look at my desk: a staff of nine used to do all this, but now there's just me and a couple of assistants."

He scribbled on a form, then signed it and handed it to Lemorel.

"Fras Dragon Silver—"

"Dargetty, Tarrin Dargetty."

"Fras Tarrin, this means so much to me, I just have to tell you. Working in Libris has been my dream for years."

"I'm glad to hear that, Frelle Lemorel, because you won't do anything else but work in Libris—except for sleeping and eating, if you're lucky. Now, lovely to meet you, but you'll have to hurry if you are to catch the Registrar's lackey before he closes up for the afternoon."

"Fras Examiner Dargetty, don't you even know Libris office hours?" Rosa cut in. "It's not even four as yet, she has over an hour."

Tarrin sat perfectly still for a moment, then slowly looked up at the reciprocating clock. He turned to Rosa.

"Did you just make Frelle Milderellen do two exams in one hour?" he asked slowly.

Lemorel blinked, too numb to comprehend. Rosa gasped.

"Oh—shewt! Er, well—well you didn't tell me!"

"You're paid to think as well as follow orders," said Tarrin, putting his head in his hands. "A red header on one paper, a green header on the other."

"I don't follow," said Lemorel anxiously. "Am I a Dragon Red?"

"Only for as long as it took me to mark the second paper. You're Dragon Green now. Ah shewt, where are the regulations? 'When a candidate faints, suffers a heart attack, gives birth or is otherwise unable to complete a paper for any justifiable reason the mark may—at the discretion of the examining officer—be increased by a percentage of the mark obtained equal to the percentage of the time remaining.' That's one hundred four percent in your case . . . no, that will never do. Anyway I'm not sure if that clause covers shoddy supervision."

"Giving birth seems unlikely."

"Not at all, the stress of the exams seems to trigger it. Apparently happens every couple of decades—on average."

"Why not add the two marks together and take an average?" Rosa suggested. "That way she gets two credits instead of a distinction and a pass."

Tarrin looked up and clasped his hands together. "I know, she could do another paper for Dragon Green. Frelle Milderellen, what do you think of—Rosa, catch her!"

They helped Lemorel back onto her seat. Rosa sat with her while Tarrin went outside to find a lackey to bring coffee. In a few minutes she was feeling better.

"Met the Registrar in the corridor and told him what happened," Tarrin announced as he placed a steaming mug of black coffee in front of the new Dragon Green. "He said he'd sanction a distinction for Dragon Red and a credit for Dragon Green, with an option of sitting the exam again if you wish."

"A credit's quite enough, Fras Tarrin. Are you sure there are no other tests?"

He rubbed his face with one hand and sat on the edge of the desk.

"You just passed the test for Dragon Green, Frelle, and there's an end of it."

"But what about heraldry and advanced cataloguing?"

"Mathematics has become everything in Libris, at least for the work that you will be doing. You've passed mathematics at Dragon Green, so you are a Dragon Green Librarian. I know there are rituals and ceremonies that ought to go with this honor, but there's no time for all that. Ah yes, I'm sorry. I remember my own Dragon Green ceremony, with a thousand Dragon Librarians, edutors, and library assistants presided over by the previous Highliber in the old Investiture Hall, but now the Hall has been given over to—well, you will see soon enough. Now Rosa, try to make up for what you did to Frelle Milderellen by taking her papers over to the Registrar's lackey."

"What *I* did to her? *You* were the one who—"

"Just take the papers over and come back with her green armband. Please?"

"Just one question," Lemorel asked when Rosa had gone. "When you read about my dueling record you seemed to have doubts about me. Will, ah, my past count against me here?"

"No, quite the opposite. If you had come in as a Dragon Red with that sort of shooting record Vardel Griss would have claimed you for her Tiger Dragons just as fast as she could petition the Registrar. She's under pressure to meet recruitment quotas too. Now, however, you're too senior to be a Tiger Dragon recruit so I can send you to Systems Design."

Lemorel was too drained to reply, and just stared at the cooling mug of coffee. Tarrin flinched nervously several times, then gritted his teeth, stood up, and came around the desk. He put a hand on her shoulder. His touch was light and trembling, and he smelled of stale clothing and coffee. Here's someone with even worse graces than me, Lemorel told herself. He coughed and cleared his throat.

"Frelle Lemorel, trust me, this is a better path for you. Five years in Systems Design and you'll be a Dragon Silver, I guarantee it. By the way, I want you to enroll at the University for some postgraduate work."

"I—ah, yes. How long is the course?"

"Three years, normally, but I'll arrange for the exams to be earlier. I need eleven new Dragon Blues to act as senior regulators in the, ah, Highliber's special calculation section, and you need to have at least partly completed a degree to be made a Dragon Blue."

Rosa returned and announced that Lemorel could not be awarded her green armband by proxy. Utterly exhausted, she shambled to the Registrar's office, where a Dragon Blue tried to comply with a fragment of the old ceremony by reading some lines of the formal presentation and giving her the green armband on a faded red cushion that had been on his chair a moment earlier. Tarrin, Rosa, and the librarians waiting in the queue for their pay envelopes clapped.

"Where are you staying?" Tarrin asked as they walked out into the bluestone corridor.

"In the hostelry," replied Lemorel, her words slurring. "Darien vis Babessa . . . letting me stay with her."

"The Dragon Blue, linguistics expert. Ah yes. No real talent with figures. Rosa, escort Frelle Milderellen to her rooms, she looks terrible. Sleep late tomorrow, Frelle, don't turn up for work until seven A.M. I'll introduce you to your superiors and have you sign the Capital Secrets Act."

"As in Rochester the capital?"

"The word 'capital' refers to capital punishment, Frelle."

Closter and Lermai pushed their overloaded book trolley down the long passageway that led from the backlog store to the Cataloguing Chambers. Normally they would have made one such trip every two months, but for several weeks past the rate had climbed to nine trips per day. The two elderly attendants were grimy with dust and sweat.

"Soon there'll be no backlog at all," said Lermai as Closter complained about their workload. "Then things will ease."

"No backlog? No backlog?" retorted Closter. "What's a Cataloguing Department without a backlog? The new Highliber has no respect for tradition. She's just too . . . new."

"Not so new, Closter. She's been here three years."

"Three years? Hah! Her predecessor was here ninety-five years. He came here as a mere boy and worked his way up. Forty-one years as Highliber! Tradition meant something under him."

They trudged on in silence for some yards; then Lermai sneezed into his sleeve. A cloud of dust billowed out, causing Closter to sneeze in turn.

"It's all because of that signaling machine," grumbled Closter as he waved at the dust. "All books have to be in the main catalogue because the machine can only find books that are catalogued. Men and women slavin' for a machine! Hah! The whole of Libris is turning into a machine. And what are we?"

"Library Attendants, Class Orange, Subdivision Five—"

"No, no, dummart, we're machines, I'm meaning. Even though we're breathing, talking, sneezing people, the Highliber's turning us into machines."

As they opened the door to the Cataloguing Chambers they instantly knew that something was wrong. Along the rows of overcrowded desks not a single cataloguer was moving. A heated argument could be heard in the Chief Cataloguer's office.

"The Highliber's here," whispered a Dragon Yellow, holding a finger up to her lips.

"I do not request, I order!" shouted Zarvora from behind the office door.

"My department! I'll not run it to please your daf-shewt machine," the Chief Cataloguer shouted back in a high, reedy voice.

"My library! You will do what my system demands."

"I challenge your system, I challenge you!" shrieked the Chief Cataloguer. At the word "challenge" the cataloguers cringed, and Closter and Lermai took refuge behind the trolley. The door to the office was flung open.

"Meet me in the dueling cloisters at dawn or report for exile to the paraline chain gangs," called Zarvora as she strode out.

She passed Closter and Lermai without a glance and slammed the door behind her. The Chief Cataloguer emerged from his office holding some torn, grimy pages. His face was red with fury and his gray hair disheveled.

"Tore up my copy of the cataloguing rules!" he shouted at a burly young Dragon Blue. "Horak, you must stand in the dueling chambers as my champion."

"Against Highliber Zarvora?" replied Horak without standing up. "Sorry, good Fras. I'll duel for you, but suicide is another matter entirely."

The Chief Cataloguer's blue eyes bulged so alarmingly that Horak recoiled. "Traitorous wretch! I appointed you to your Color, and I can break you down to Dragon White."

Horak marshaled a grim smile. "Better a live Dragon White than a dead Dragon Blue."

The Chief Cataloguer flung the tattered pages in his face. "Get out! Now!" he cried, pointing at the door. Horak left his desk and walked across to the main door.

"Enjoy your new appointment to the paraline gangs," he called as he pulled the door closed behind him. The Chief Cataloguer snatched up a thesaurus and flung it after him. It fell short, striking a pile of books on the trolley and spilling them across the floor.

"The Highliber's angry about something," whispered Closter as they picked up the books, "and it's not the cataloguing backlog either. They say something's wrong with her signaling machine. They say a bad spirit has possessed it."

Lermai opened his mouth wide in astonishment. The Great Machine was only a signaling system as far as the librarians and attendants knew, but it was so complex and large that they had begun treating it as a living—and senior—member of the staff.

"Why not call in a priest to perform an exorcism?" asked Lermai.

"Why? Why? Because there's not been a machine like it since before Greatwinter," replied Closter, feigning exasperation. "The art of exorcising machines has been lost for so long that we have not a single book of prayers and ceremonies concerning it."

Observing the drama from a corner of the cataloguing room were Tarrin and Lemorel, trapped during the new Dragon Green's tour of the Libris departments. As Closter and Lermai picked up the fallen books Tarrin took his recruit by the arm and hastened her through a side door and down a service corridor.

"We see a lot of that," Tarrin said with a shrug once they were out of earshot. "The Highliber is introducing reforms that certain factions in Libris dislike. People have to work to schedules and deadlines now, people who have never worked to a schedule or met a deadline in their lives. As you have just seen, our complaint system is a little dangerous. A complaint against the Highliber must be addressed to the Highliber herself before it can be addressed to the Mayor. The Highliber can choose to challenge—and that means a duel. Now, you could name a champion, but if the Highliber kills your champion, then she has the right to demand a retraction. If you refuse, you have to fight her in person."

"That's the same as everywhere in the Southeast Alliance."

"Yes indeed, but in Libris there's been a lot more of it lately. The Highliber's killed nineteen champions and two Dragon Golds who chose to duel in person. She's a deadly shot and has a bad temper. On the other hand, us younger Dragon Colors love her. She makes everything move, she gets things done."

They came to a newly renovated area with whitewashed walls and skylights. Tarrin had to sign them in with the guards at three separate doors, and they finally entered an office with the title System Controller stenciled roughly on the door. Tarrin introduced Lewrick, who smiled and kissed Lemorel's hand, then called for his lackey to bring coffee. He had a faint smell of bath salts, and impressed Lemorel as the sort of person that one could not help but like.

"Milderellen, yes, that paper on the directional distribution of the Call," Lewrick said as he carried a cane chair over for her. "Excellent work. Did you work out the mathematics yourself?"

"Yes, Fras Lewrick. It took five months."

"Months? It would have taken me decades—by myself, that is. Of course I could do the work in days using the Highliber's, yes, ah, what you are about to see." He rummaged about among the papers on his desk, then brought over a form on a clipboard. It was headed Capital Secrets Act.

"You are about to learn of a secret machine, and the secret is a close one," Tarrin explained. "Please read this form and sign where indicated."

Lemorel read. It was an act endorsed by the Mayor, but was internal to Libris. Something known as the Calculor was mentioned in nearly every clause, and most of the penalties for breaches of the rules were death. Those that were not involved a life sentence in the very same Calculor, but the text gave no clue to the Calculor's nature. Taking the goose quill that Lewrick held out, Lemorel dipped it in a porcelain ink jar held in a silver dragon's jaws. A drop spattered the poorpaper form.

"Don't worry, Frelle, you can be shot whether you sign the form or not," said Tarrin, reaching for a jar of powder.

Lemorel signed.

"Welcome to our family," declared Lewrick as Tarrin dusted powder on the wet ink. "Firstly you must meet the most important member of all—"

"Who eats Dragon Colors faster than I can recruit them," interjected Tarrin. "I've seen it all before, I'll stay here." He sat behind Lewrick's desk and tugged at a cord hanging from the ceiling, then picked up a reel of perforated paper tape and began to read the code directly from the patterns of holes.

Lewrick unlocked a thick ironwood door and took Lemorel down an unlit corridor lined with limestone slabs. It opened into another chamber. Two Tiger Dragons saluted as they emerged, alert and hard-muscled youths who were armed with two double-barreled flintlocks each. Lemorel could see that they were not for show.

"The Highliber's machine is called the Calculor, and is a calculation engine of really prodigious power and versatility," Lewrick explained as he gestured to a small door hung with thick felt curtains. "It can process tasks in days that any lone clerk might labor over for years."

He held the curtain aside and Lemorel walked out onto an observation gallery. It was set high in one wall of the Calculor hall, right above the double partitions that separated Dexter and Sinister processors. Wildly differing impressions swept over Lemorel. A hall full of students doing exams, the weaving championships at the regional fair, a vineyard crowded with pickers at harvest time . . . but there could be no real comparison with anything else. The Calculor was an echo of something all but incomprehensible from the distant past. It was an engine like a river galley or galley train, yet so much more. This was not just a device to move cargo, it multiplied the *skills* of whoever used it.

"So, Frelle Lemorel, what do you think of our Great Machine?" Lewrick asked eagerly, like a proud parent presenting a gifted child.

"It—a device to enhance the mind, just as a telescope enhances the eye," she said slowly, mesmerized by what she saw.

"Very good, a good analogy!" Lewrick exclaimed. "I'll note that one. Come now, let's return to the office."

He began explaining some elements of the design as they walked, but they were back with Tarrin before he had even covered the logistics of shiftwork for the Calculor's components.

"As a Dragon Green you will be working in Systems Design—ah, that is when you are at work. When you are not at work you will be studying at the University, I hope?"

"She has been enrolled already," Tarrin assured him.

"Splendid, our expansion activities require more Dragon Blue librarians in a year than Libris used to promote in a century."

"Which brings me to my interesting news," said Tarrin.

"Could I sit at my own desk as you tell me?" asked Lewrick hopefully, rubbing his hands together and bowing a little.

"Oh, my apologies," replied Tarrin, mopping up a coffee ring with his sleeve as he stood up. "You are about to get the services of the Chief Cataloguer."

Lewrick frowned suspiciously. "As a Dragon or a component?"

"A component."

"Splendid, splendid!" exclaimed Lewrick, slapping his hands on the leather facing of his desk. "Whatever his faults he does have a head for figures. He can be a trainee function in Sinister—"

He was interrupted by a sharp knock on the door, and before Lewrick could speak the door was flung open. Highliber Zarvora strode in.

"Fras Tarrin, the guards said that you were here—who is this?"

"Dragon Green Lemorel Milderellen," Tarrin said as Lemorel stood up and bowed smartly.

"Milderellen . . . *Demographic Analysis of the Call Vectors in the Southeast*, yes a good paper." She turned to Tarrin. "But I remember seeing her name on the Dragon Orange promotions listing only last month."

"I tested her the day she arrived and double-promoted her," Tarrin explained. "Gave you quite a shock, didn't I, Frelle? Quite an ordeal, she fainted in my office."

"Put this on and try not to faint," said Zarvora, throwing a band of gold cloth to Tarrin. "The Chief Cataloguer challenged, but was unable to name a champion. You are now Chief Cataloguer."

Tarrin opened his mouth and his jaw worked, but no words formed. Zarvora turned to Lemorel.

"It is a shock when you get an unexpected promotion, yes?"

"Yes, Frelle Highliber."

"But my work as Examiner, there's nobody qualified to take over," Tarrin protested.

"Then you will have to carry both positions. Make your clerk a Dragon White. She knows your basic office procedures. Send her to the local Unitech to study administration, raise her salary, anything, just keep both offices working."

"Couldn't I make her Chief Cataloguer?"

"No."

Lewrick laughed. "Chief Cataloguer, may I be the first to congratulate you?"

"Highliber this is impossible—"

"Fras Tarrin, it is very easy. Just get the cataloguers working. Break up the entrenched groups and send any troublemakers to the Calculor."

"Oh yes," said Lewrick, "they'd be most welcome."

"It's not as easy as that, Frelle Highliber!"

"Fras Tarrin, listen. Cataloguing *must* be made an extension of the data-storage register of the Calculor by the end of the year. My lackey has some papers for you to sign and a charter for your office wall."

"There will be challenges."

"So? Do what I do: shoot them."

"I'm a terrible shot."

"Engage a champion."

The Highliber left. Nobody spoke for a full minute.

"A wonderful lady, the Highliber," said Lewrick. "Were I thirty years younger I might propose a liaison."

"You're either mad or senile, or both," said Tarrin, rubbing his temples. "Frelle Lemorel, I'm afraid that I cannot complete your tour of Libris, but I did manage to get you as far as your Department Head, Dragon Gold Lewrick MacKention."

"See you on the Executive Committee," Lewrick called as Tarrin left. The newly appointed Chief Cataloguer slammed the door behind him.

"This is all a strain, my dear Frelle," Lewrick said kindly as he sat back at his desk. "The Highliber needs calculating power for both the Mayor's projects and her own researches. Expanding the Calculor is proving disruptive enough, yet there is something worse. The Calculor has become unreliable and we don't know why. Frelle Zarvora's temper is strung tight enough to play a tune upon and we, her staff, are being run ragged."

I've met the Highliber herself, thought Lemorel, barely following his words. And the Highliber had actually seen—and remembered—her paper on Call vectors.

"How long has the Calculor been operational?" she asked, abruptly pulling herself out of the reverie.

"It isn't. We have been running tests for many months and have even done some important projects for the Mayor, but it's not operational. There were plans for a commissioning ceremony, but they have been held over. It has begun to make strange errors—but more of that later. Come now, let us find a desk for you. People need their own desk, just as they need their own bed. Desks are intensely personal things, don't you think so?"

The sun had been down two hours when Lemorel finally returned to Darien's rooms, flopped onto the spare bunk, and blanked out. After another hour Darien entered, looked at the limp figure sprawled on the bunk, and shook her head. Lemorel did not wake as her boots were pulled off and a blanket was draped over her.

3 COURTSHIP

FUNCTION 9 recognized the sequence of numbers as they appeared on the wheels of his reception register. The Calculor had been through the same sequence a dozen times already, but now there was a slight rounding error. A lot of testing was being conducted, the Calculor's masters were very agitated about something, and other components had been flogged for both oversights and initiatives. FUNCTION 9 was too skilled for oversights, and he preferred his initiatives to be invisible.

He performed his operations on the numbers, then sent the results to the Dragon Green who was in charge of the correlator components by setting a register of levers to represent his answer and pressing the transmission pedal below the desk. The Calculor was designed so that the independent Dexter and Sinister sides checked each other's work. Their correlation subsections passed results to the Central Verification Unit, and if the results differed that particular calculation would be repeated. FUNCTION 9 had a good memory and he knew that some of the tests being performed on the machine were invalid because of rounding errors and such, yet they did not come back for reprocessing. He knew it was odd, but he did nothing about the errors. He did not want a flogging.

The correlator sat behind a screen several feet away from FUNCTION 9's desk, and the component could hear the clacking as he fed the data into his register for transmission to the Verification Unit—then there was a faint thump and hum of tensed wires. A moment later he heard a thump from the correlator on the other side, but the accompanying chord was not quite the same. Another thump, and this time the chord matched that of his own side. FUNCTION 9 smiled as much as his gag would allow.

From the Verification Unit the results went to the System Control Room, where Lewrick and a team of Dragon Greens and Blues analyzed them. The librarians in the Calculor were carefully isolated from those who were checking the output, and of course none of them knew why the tests were being performed.

Lemorel's initial work in Libris was part of this massive check of the system. Tables of figures were fed in and processed, with both Dexter and Sinister processors alternately disabled. The results came out roughly as expected: the two processors made randomly different mistakes. Teams of Dragon Librarians were used as components, and they could find no way to break the system after getting an insider's view. The Calculor was returned to normal operation, but after a

week the errors began to reappear. The backlog of important work continued to pile up.

Even in the atmosphere of impossible workloads, frayed tempers, and impenetrable secrecy, Lemorel was happy. She was new to the place and relatively junior, so she was assigned nothing more than analysis of the Calculor's output. While others exchanged insults and argued about the demarcation of duties, Lemorel did her calculations quickly, accurately, and anonymously. At last her past had lost her; she could merge with the Highliber's machine.

She decided to accept Darien's offer to permanently share the twin-room apartlet in the Libris hostelry. It was a long climb to the top floor, but they had a good view of the mayoral gardens, the lake, and the farms and forests beyond. Lemorel and Darien got along very well, in part because they had the bond of sign language, but also because both knew what it was like to be an outcast.

The Rochester market lay between the paraline terminus and the University, and helped to divide the city between the affluent classes of the eastern side and everyone else. Through the market one could travel the known world, and even go a little farther. Southmoor carpets woven from dyed wool and emu down hung from terraced frames to form a gaudy little city of façades. Finely tailored clothing from Griffith insured a permanent crowd at the Central Confederation's stalls, while the clockwork and gunsmiths' stalls of the Wangaratta, Shepparton, and Rutherglen mayorates attracted more foreigners than locals. There were fresh vegetables from local farms a mile or two distant, beside Northmoor coffee from the northernmost regions of the known world.

Darien and Lemorel visited the market on their scheduled free days. After buying food they went to the vagary stalls at the University end. Darien always came away with books in obscure languages or classics in older variants of Anglaic, while Lemorel searched for books on mathematics and natural philosophy. The dealers put some of the more interesting volumes aside for them.

Lemorel now wore her hair down, retiring behind the dark, wavy cascades that nobody in Rutherglen had ever seen unbound. A change in image could not go without a change in appearance, after all. Darien persuaded her to buy a brightly patterned Cargelligo scarf, and to have the Libris uniform run up in Cowra silks by a master tailor who was the endorsed tailor to members of the Libris Executive. As the weeks passed the newest Dragon Green began to think about new weapons.

''A pair of duelers' throwing knives, or a long-bore matchlock that has seen better days,'' Lemorel said as she stood before Tantyrak, former Powdermonger to the Emir of Cowra. ''I can throw a knife, and they seem elegant.''

Darien held up her hands. ''Would you ever enter a duel with a knife?''

''Oh no!''

"Then don't buy them."

"Then it must be the musket."

"What good is a musket to a librarian?"

"It has Inglewood filigree work along the barrel, and greenstone inlay on the stock. It might get me into ceremonial guard squads."

"More likely you will be put into firing squads for important felons."

Lemorel lifted the musket down from the rack. Tantyrak smiled, bowed, and rubbed his hands together.

"It once had a ramlock mechanism, you can see by the holes here and here. The mechanism was removed and replaced by a matchlock fuse for use by a musketeer from Deniliquin. See the pokerwork Deniliquin crest on the stock that someone has tried to file away?"

"It was probably looted from a body on some battlefield. Why would he have the ramlock removed?"

"Reliability and ease of reloading. A smoldering fuse means a shot every time. A weak shower of sparks from a ramlock or flintlock means click when your life depends on boom. On the other hand, a well-maintained ramlock under a rain sleeve can allow you to shoot even when all other guns are washed out. Fras Tantyrak, how much?"

"Ah, very fine gun, Frelle, special rebuilding of mechanism as matchlock. Forty-nine silver nobles."

"Terrible gun, I hate matchlocks. Smelly fuse smoke, always going out. Do you have the original ramlock?"

"Alas Frelle, the faithless pestilent who owned it previously had no regard for the elegant and virtuous principle of ramlock sparking."

"Fifteen nobles."

"Fifteen nobles? Frelle, the greenstone in the stock is worth more than fifteen nobles."

Ten minutes of haggling secured the musket for thirty-seven silver nobles, and Lemorel insisted that she had been robbed even when out of earshot of the merchant.

"It should take me three months to rebuild the ramlock."

"You?"

"Why not? I have a toolkit of files, demi-saws and such. I'm a clockmaker's daughter, after all."

"Why not have the Libris workshops do it for you?"

"Darien, I use my head all day. I need to do something with my hands to relax."

They stopped at a metal foundry, and Lemorel ordered blank plates and springs to be made for her ramlock. As the metalsmith took measurements and made drawings Darien looked around the shop. There was a tiny forge fired by

anthracite, as prescribed by law and holy scripture. Chain links for pedal tricycles hung on pegs, and the shelves were piled with gears, sprockets, cams, and axles. Several larger, heavier chains hung waiting for repairs, chains that could only be from galley trains. So, there was more work than the paraline workshops on the northern edge of the lake could handle. That usually meant fighting somewhere, or fighting soon to be. Wind trains ran for practically nothing, but they were slow and depended on the weather. Galley trains were expensive but fast, and speed often won wars.

A troop of armed runners marched past outside, escorting the Market Rectifier and his accountant. Tall orange plumes marked them above the undulating sea of heads, and their butt-leather armor creaked as they marched, brass-tipped swagger sticks rapping the cobbles in unison at every second step. The Rectifier carried his standard of office, while the accountant walked behind him with the leather and giltwork Register of Merchants beneath his arm. Several lackeys followed carrying record boxes, and behind them were more runners and a sullen prisoner. Darien did not recognize him, but noted that he was wearing a bargecap of the river-merchant service. An agent of the Warren, quite probably. Catcalls and hisses sniped at him from the onlookers.

The Rectifier had been unraveling fraudulent dealings at an astonishing rate in recent months, so much so that two underground cartels had been forced to disband and even the mighty Warren was reduced to no more than a few legal fronts. The crushing of organized crime in the Rochester market had lowered both prices and overheads, so that honest traders were better off.

''Could you take this back to Libris, Dar?'' Darien turned from the door and Lemorel thrust her musket and a wicker bag into her arms. ''I have to go on to the University now.''

With her hands full Darien could not reply.

The University was a mile or so from the walls of Libris, and was nearly as old as the library itself. Its beautiful gardens were famous, and both mayors and highlibers had been educated there for over a thousand years. Lemorel was comforted by its size. Nobody knew her there, and she could just sit quietly and listen to the edutors expound theorems and proofs as if she were the respectable young daughter of rich parents from the southeast quadrant of the city. She was indeed being given a second chance at life.

In Libris she was set dozens of incomprehensible tasks in symbolic logic and set theory each day, and was even trained as a component in the Calculor. Tarrin looked increasingly haggard, and Lewrick snapped at anyone who spoke the word ''edutor'' in his presence. Once Lemorel had even seen the Mayor himself coming out of the Highliber's rooms. Months passed, but whatever the problem was, it moved no closer to resolution. Her ramlock mechanism slowly took shape over dozens of nights by the fireside, and by December she was testing the fully restored musket in the practice range of the Libris dueling chambers.

· · ·

"The Calculor really is alive," insisted Lewrick as Zarvora paced the floor in front of him.

"I designed it, right down to the last bead on the lowest component's abacus," she replied listlessly. "It cannot be alive."

One hundred and thirty yards away a marksman squinted down the tunnel sight of a flintlock musket as he crouched beside a gargoyle on the Libris roof. His target was pacing constantly, so he could not aim well enough to be sure of a kill.

"Highliber, you used fragments of the old science, and we know that before Greatwinter some machines really were alive. Perhaps the *patterns* of the machines were alive, rather than the beads and wires. By using the old patterns you may have accidentally re-created some sort of life. Perhaps the data that you play into the Calculor's keyboard is educating it. Some of it is astrological, remember."

"No, no, no!" insisted Zarvora, sitting down before the champions table and pounding the edge. "Only *astronomical* data has been fed into the Calculor: positions of the planets relative to each other, motions of the moon, motions of lesser bodies. The equations to describe their movements are modern Southmooric, and are based on all orbits being elliptical. It is exact, measurable science."

"Astrological influences may—"

"No! This is astronomy, not witchcraft."

The marksman aimed slightly above the seated Zarvora's head and waited for a slight puff of wind to disperse. Counting slowly, he squeezed the trigger. There was a sharp click as the flint hit the fizzen, but the flashpan cover did not lift and the gun did not discharge. Zarvora stood up and began pacing again. With a soft but eloquent curse the marksman took a small screwdriver from a ring on his belt and loosened the bolt in the pancover's bearing.

"I have a theory about Greatwinter, that its return can be predicted from planetary motions," Zarvora explained as she resumed her pacing. "Using the Calculor I worked out when a second Greatwinter will come."

Lewrick stared at her, aghast. "But it can't!" he exclaimed. "It was caused by ancient weapons, bombs that caused 'nuclear' winters around their victims. The bombs were used too often, so that the whole world froze for decades."

"Wrong, Fras Lewrick. It can and will happen again, and soon. We are very lucky."

"Lucky! How can annihilation be lucky?"

"Being forewarned about a great disaster is worth more than wagonloads of gold, and brings more power than the mightiest army. I need a more exact date for Greatwinter's return, but even the Calculor will take years to provide it. For such long and complex calculations, even one error per month is intolerable. The

Calculor's administrative work slows my research even further, but it pays for its own running.''

''Perhaps if you talk to the Calculor, Highliber, request that it be more careful.''

''If I thought that it was alive I would threaten it, not plead. Still, it is just a glorified abacus.''

''Highliber, how can I convince you? You sit up here and play in your instructions, yet down in the Calculor hall one can see rhythms in the patterns of beads on the large abacus frames above the rows of desks. The whispering of the moving beads often seems to form real words, yet I cannot quite catch their meaning. There are harmonious chords in the wires when the two processors of the Calculor are in agreement, yet discords when they arrive at different answers and have to repeat everything. One can hear life pulsing all around the hall.''

''Chords, Fras Lewrick?'' cried Zarvora, whirling to face him so abruptly that he sat back with a start. The distant marksman took aim at Zarvora's chest, because a crossbeam obscured her head. ''Come down now, and show me where I might hear—''

The bullet smashed through a pane of leadlight glass and struck the back of Lewrick's skull just as he stood up. A moment later the assassin saw the window explode outward through the cloud of smoke from his shot. He gasped with surprise, unable to guess what had happened. Instead of scurrying down his escape rope he stood up beside the gargoyle for a better view. What he saw was the Highliber kneeling on the roof amid shattered glass and lead strip, and the flash from the muzzle of her flintlock.

Six hours later Zarvora was still shaking as she stood between the two processors in the Calculor hall. Lewrick's killer had not been a member of the Libris staff, and nobody could identify the corpse. There was, however, not the slightest doubt that the System Controller had stopped a bullet meant for her. The forces of tradition in Libris were going beyond petitions, resolutions, and even duels to halt her modernizations.

Behind the screens on either side of her the components of the two processors worked hard at a diagnostic problem. As Lewrick had said, the Calculor made a whirring, bustling mixture of sounds when working at full capacity, and there was nothing else in the world that was even remotely like it. The hiss and click of tens of thousands of abacus beads underlaid the soft rattle and clatter of gears and register levers, while the many banks of transfer wires hummed in weird chords that were sometimes strung into unsettling melodies.

Zarvora stood absolutely still, breathing shallowly. A deep chord sounded close by as the output wires from Dexter processor strained against the gate of the Verification Unit. A gear whirred for a moment; then a rack of levers was released for the wires to pull them into ''yes'' or ''no'' positions. While the levers were clacking into place, an identical chord sounded from the output wires

of Sinister. Both processors had arrived at the same answer to some part of the diagnostic calculation.

Those in charge of the output registers were Dragon Green Librarians, not prisoners. Zarvora had earlier decided that this work was too important to entrust to components, but perhaps she had been mistaken. Dragon Colors were free to conspire in secret—over dinner, in taverns, in bed. Dragon Colors did not live in the same fear of punishment as the components. They could get lazy.

Again the chord sounded from Dexter processor's bank of output wires, but this time there was a slight mismatch in the sound from Sinister! Zarvora's lips parted slightly in anticipation. Before the gear on Sinister had released its bank of levers the left's wires slackened again, and from behind the left screen there was the clicking of a register being reset. Again the wires from Sinister were tensed, but this time the chord from it matched that from Dexter. The Dragon Green on Sinister was matching his output to that from Dexter by tuning the sound of the transfer wires while they were under tension.

Lemorel noticed unusual activity on the Libris upper floors and roofs as she was escorted from the Library complex by a grim-faced pair of Tiger Dragons. Nothing unusual had happened within the Calculor, in fact it was still in operation as far as she knew. The Highliber had walked past her desk moments before the Tiger Dragons had arrived, but there was nothing unusual about that. Just beyond the main doors was a group of thirty or so librarians milling about uncertainly, and she recognized Hirolec Var from Systems Design. When the Tiger Dragons released her the others crowded around.

"Hirolec, what's happened?" she asked.

"We thought *you* might know," he said, clearly disappointed.

"Overliber Jandrel's lackey said she heard two shots and the sound of breaking glass," said one of the Dragon Reds from Reference.

"Some say the Highliber's been killed," said Hirolec.

"But I saw her not five minutes ago, she walked past my desk," Lemorel countered.

There was a collective exclamation, many different words superimposed. Lemorel did have news after all: the Highliber was alive. They waited in the plaza before the main doors. Another twenty Dragon Greens and Blues were ejected, singly and in groups. From these they learned that the Highliber had survived an assassination attempt. Gargoyles leered down at them in the late-afternoon light and Tiger Dragons patrolling the roof cast them an occasional glance. Extra guards were brought in from the mayoral palace, and they marched across the mosaic starburst of the plaza with their ceremonial halberds, wearing yellow slashwork uniforms that flashed strips of red as they swung their arms.

Lemorel left after an hour. She was clearly not wanted on duty until further

notice and the sun was low in the sky, so she returned to the hostelry. Darien was already there, but knew nothing more about the afternoon's events.

"Two shots, and some broken glass near the rooftop offices," Lemorel said as she chopped a parsnip for the soup. "The Highliber's still alive, in fact all the senior Dragons from that level have been seen alive since the shots were fired."

"Perhaps the Tiger Dragons shot an intruder," Darien signed with flour-caked fingers.

"Possibly. The Highliber would be badly rattled if any intruder managed to get as close to her chambers as that. She likes total control."

"Any progress on the Calculor's fault?"

"Not as yet. It's very discouraging but we can't give up."

Lemorel poured part of a jar of Rutherglen Broadbank '91 into the soup and Darien put her honeycakes into the ovenbox to bake. Other librarians knocked on the door from time to time, asking for news or sharing rumors.

After dinner Lemorel stripped down her ramlock mechanism to file the lever slot wider. Darien tried to read, but could not concentrate. Instead she unpacked her body-anchor belt and Call timer, and dismantled it for a service. The mechanism was in good condition, so the work did not take long.

Lemorel reassembled the ramlock, and when she drew back the ramstud and pulled the trigger the ram snapped forward to spray a shower of sparks into the flashpan. The musket that she had bought months ago was now unrecognizable. Its barrel had been polished until it gleamed like a weapon of the palace guard, and she had carved a new stock, one tailored to fit her arms and shoulder.

"I often wonder about the Call," Darien signed with languid, oil-stained fingers. "I just feel a quick plunging away, then I wake up. It seems unrelated to anything else in my experience, yet there's still a thrilling feel to it."

Being relaxed and feeling pleased with her work on the ramlock, Lemorel replied without thinking.

"There's something in my past akin to the Call. Whenever it sweeps over me, I'm taken back to that very moment. I . . ." She suddenly caught herself. "I wish that I could scour the feeling away with sandsoap."

Darien sat up. "Tell me, Lem. Was it a lover?"

"Not just one lover, I—Do we really have to talk about it?" She cocked the ramlock again and fired a shower of sparks at the stars beyond the open window. "I wish that I could point a gun at my memories and blast them away."

Darien crossed the room and put a hand against Lemorel's cheek, gently turning her head away from the window.

"There was a bully boy who lived in my street when I was young," she signed, her fingers very close to Lemorel's face. "He would chase me and do cruel things because he knew I could not cry out. Fear of him gave me nightmares, and I became frightened to go outside. I spent more and more time indoors,

reading. I became so good at schoolwork that I won scholarships. Five years ago I saw him again, on a visit to my family. He was a brushwood carter, fond of the drink and with a long history of time in the stocks. I was a Dragon Blue.''

''What are you trying to tell me?''

''You need to look back at old problems every so often, even if it hurts. They always diminish with time.''

''My own past is worse than a nightmare, Dar. There's a blood-spattered demon—''

''He cannot have hurt you too badly, you have no scars.''

''The demon is me.''

Darien stepped back, wringing her hands together. Cradling the musket as if it were her only friend in the world, Lemorel closed her eyes and leaned against the wickerwork back of the chair.

''I'd rather not add you to the people who fear me,'' she said, even as a hand began to stroke her hair. The touch was curiously soft, the soothing caress of a nurse rather than the tingling play of a lover. With her eyes closed, Lemorel felt herself speaking into nothingness. ''I'll tell you what reminds me of the Call,'' she finally decided.

''During my last year of median school I had a boyfriend named Semidor. He was . . . a bit precious: a poet, an artist. If you could imagine someone who was not a great scholar, but loved the idea of being a scholar, then you would have him. At that time I was a studious girl with a gift for mathematics and tightly bound hair. My mother had died when I was eight, and my father raised me and my sister like apprentices. I became quite a good shot from testing gun mechanisms, I knew about clockwork and the mathematics of lenses, and I suppose I neglected my appearance a little.

''So, I was an ideal match for an eccentric scholar like Semidon, and we held hands and kept company with each other for about two years. To me it was just a comfortable friendship, but to him it was quite a lot more. I was, unfortunately, too young to understand that. Gradually I outgrew him. While he dreamed of being some sort of mendicant songwriter and bard, I dreamed of entering the service of the Dragon Librarians. For a country girl with a brain it's either the convent or the library, nothing else. Still, we stayed together, perhaps by habit. We passed our median-school exams and I was recruited to the Rutherglen Unitech library as a Dragon White. I studied for my first letters in my spare time. Semidor's parents paid for him to study there too, perhaps to distract him from becoming a wandering songwriter.

''After a time I began to make friends among the Dragon Librarians. They encouraged me to be a little more sociable, and even to go to the regional fairs and dances. Semidor refused to go. According to him, serious scholars did not do that sort of thing. On the final day of the harvest festival there was a small-

arms shooting match, and I won. At the revel that night I became a little drunk, and a youth named Brunthorp began paying me court.

"He knew his business, as I realized later. He gave me all of his attention, flattered me in seemingly unconscious ways, and listened to everything that I said and built upon it. After being an audience of one to Semidor's scholarly discourses and poetry for years, I found this a pleasant change. Soon we had our arms around each other, we kissed, and he steered me outside the barn and into a nearby field. There was a hayloft in a small shed, and he made a show of being surprised at finding it. We lay down and began to fondle each other very ardently. I thought of Semidor. I wanted to be loyal to him, but in a strange moment of surrender I made myself angry with him, convinced myself that he deserved me to be unfaithful. That's what reminds me of the Call, that little moment of surrender, that decision to do something reproachful. The Call is *knowing* that I shall always surrender, and I hate it." Lemorel opened her eyes and looked up at Darien. "So now you know."

"You hate the Call but still you study it?" she signed.

"I study it to break its grip."

"Was it so very bad in the hayloft?"

Lemorel looked out through the window to the night sky again.

"I said 'Yes.' He ran his hand up my leg and rolled on top of me. I was very tense and tight, in fact it was quite painful. He asked if it was my first time. I admitted that it was and said that I hadn't thought it would hurt so much. He said that I felt wonderful to him, but his words did not really cheer me at all. That was it, I suppose. Pain, mess, and a lot of guilt over betraying Semidor as soon as it was over.

"In the days that followed I was torn apart with fear and remorse, and I decided that if I had become pregnant, it should seem to be by Semidor. That was not as easy as it might sound. He had some odd notions about the purity of romantic love. It took several nights of awkward urging but I finally seduced him. Through sheer luck I did not become pregnant to either my seducer or my seducee. Semidor soon decided that passion had a place in pure romantic love after all—but not babies. We began to use sheepgut armor for all our dalliances. Everything seemed to settle down."

Lemorel opened her eyes and turned to Darien. Her fingers whirled briefly. "Semidor must have found out."

"Semidor certainly did, and things went badly wrong. I threw myself into my Unitech studies and my Dragon Yellow regrading. Luck was with me. I had a natural talent for mathematics, and just then Highliber Zarvora was scouring the known world for librarian-mathematicians."

Away in the distance they could hear boots on a stairway, marching in step.

"Enough of my past," Lemorel concluded. "How were you first seduced?"

Darien blinked in shock and hid her hands behind her back. The boots were louder now, in their wing of the hostelry.

"Let me guess, was it one of the Libris Dragons?" Lemorel speculated with a knowing leer.

Darien's hands reappeared. "I was quite in control for the whole time. I rendered him staggering drunk first, and to this day he does not know what he did."

"Ah Darien, what a wise little girl you were."

"Little girl? It was last January!"

Lemorel burst out laughing and Darien clapped her hands. The marching boots were at the landing of their floor now, and the two women suddenly sat up in alarm as the marchers tramped down the corridor and stopped at their door. The knock was an insistent pounding, the blow of a fist rather than a polite rapping of knuckles. Lemorel handed the unloaded musket to Darien and walked to the door. Three Tiger Dragons were outside, all male, all armed. They were clearly tense, but not about being at that particular door.

"Lemorel Milderellen?" asked the squad leader.

"Yes, that's me."

"You're registered as a reserve magistrate's champion in the Mayorate of Rutherglen as a result of ordeal by dueling."

"Correct."

"Change into full Dragon Color uniform, Frelle Milderellen."

"I—can you tell me why?"

"Highliber's orders. By law, civil firing squads must be captained by a magistrate's champion."

They escorted Lemorel to Libris. In one of the small assembly rooms close to the Calculor hall she was put in charge of a squad of twenty-three Dragon Blue Librarians. The Libris Marshal entered, unlocked a gunrack, and handed a Tolleni matchlock to each of them. After they had checked and loaded their guns the Marshal took them back, added a musket that he had been holding, and removed another. The lackey distributed the guns again.

"One may not be loaded," the Marshal explained as a Dragon Red walked along lighting the matchfuses with a taper. It was not necessary to elaborate further. Lemorel eyed her gun suspiciously.

Tarrin entered, carrying a blue armband. He walked across to Lemorel and asked her to hold out her arm.

"This is an acting promotion," he declared as he pinned the cloth over her green armband. "According to our records you're a registered magistrate's champion and executioner. According to Libris internal regulations, only a Dragon Blue can act as captain. The Highliber wants a firing squad in a hurry and nobody else with the right qualifications can be found at such short notice." He raised

his voice. "Before these witnesses I hereby elevate you, Lemorel Milderellen, to the temporary rank of Dragon Blue, until such time as the Highliber of Libris shall review your standing."

The Marshal, the fuse lighter, and the rest of the firing squad gave three cheers amid swirls of fuse smoke. With each promotion the ceremony becomes less formal and more bizarre, Lemorel decided.

The components were assembled into cell groups at the back of the Calculor hall. The area occupied by the desks of the Calculor was no more than the first quarter of the other end. They were in two separate groups, to the left and right of the center. The Highliber paced impatiently between the two rows.

"Bet it's a talk on some damn new configuration," muttered MULTIPLIER 8, and PORT 3A nodded wearily.

Suddenly a side door opened, and two dozen Dragon Blues filed in carrying matchlock muskets. The fuses in the strikers were already alight and smoking. Even as the components were exchanging puzzled glances the four Dragon Green Librarians who took turns to operate the output registers were marched in. Their hands were bound and they were gagged. They showed signs of recent torture.

"They be Dragon Colors," hissed ADDER 17.

"They're senior Dragon Colors," observed MULTIPLIER 8.

"They're tying them to the retaining rail," gasped PORT 3A.

"They're going to shoot them," whispered FUNCTION 9.

The Highliber gave another order, and the musketeer Dragon Colors formed into two rows of twelve, the front row kneeling.

"Attend the Highliber!" shouted the System Herald.

"System Officers, Dragon Colors, processing components, all souls who comprise the Calculor," Zarvora began, her words echoing from the stone walls. "You have been gathered to witness punishment on four Dragon Colors. These librarians, all trained and skilled, did conspire to degrade the performance of the Calculor. Their motives were based in neither greed, nor treason, but in pure sloth. When errors appeared at the end of long processing sessions, they contrived to falsely verify mismatched results, so that calculations would not have to be repeated.

"You!" she barked, pointing straight at MULTIPLIER 8. "If you were a soldier and were found asleep on sentry duty what would the sentence be?"

MULTIPLIER 8 glanced hopefully around, but there was nobody behind him. "I, ah, very severe," he spluttered.

"Service in the Mayor's Calculor is no different from service in the Mayor's Army," continued Zarvora. "The sentence for dereliction of duty is the same, too." She turned to the musketeers. "Form to! Present arms!"

The two lines of musketeers held their weapons out for the Highliber to

inspect. ''Release guards!'' The terrified prisoners struggled against their bonds as two dozen trigger bars clicked free.

''Take aim!'' shouted Zarvora, and the matchlocks came up in a silent swirl of blue fuse smoke.

Although two of the matchlocks misfired in the volley that followed, four bodies hung from the retaining rail by their bindings as the smoke cleared. A Dragon Blue cut the ropes that held them; then two elderly, terrified attendants loaded them onto a book trolley and trundled them out through the side door. Zarvora addressed the gathering again.

''I can tolerate a great deal from both Dragon Colors and components— amorous dalliances, the black market in luxuries, all that is officially forbidden in prisons but tacitly allowed. You are worked hard here, and I am not above rewarding good work. What I shall *never* tolerate, however, is meddling with the Calculor.''

She paced between the two groups with her hands clasped beneath her cloak. But for a slight swishing of cloth, there was silence.

''Those Dragon Colors tampered with the system to make their work, and yours, easier,'' she said, pointing to the pockmarked wall and smears of blood. ''For some months they made my own life a lot harder, however, and they have paid for it. Do not follow their example. You are dismissed, return to your cells.''

The components streamed out of the hall while Zarvora conferred with Lewrick's successor. FUNCTION 9 felt a nudge in his back.

''Yes, MULT, what is it?''

''The name's Dolorian,'' murmured a pretty Dragon Yellow. ''Would you care for some voluntary duties with me, Fras FUNCTION? The Highliber tolerates it, you know.''

There was a separate assembly of Dragon Greens and Blues once the components had been herded out of the Calculor hall. Lemorel stayed with the Dragon Blues as they waited for the Highliber in the anteroom. Many were clearly distressed, as it was the first time that they had fired a shot in anger—or killed. When Zarvora returned she was much calmer.

''As you may have gathered, we have just made an important breakthrough with the Calculor's reliability,'' Zarvora explained. ''The Calculor is the most secure secret in all of the mayorate. Even courtiers who could tell you how many times the Mayor mounted his mistress last night could not give you more than a vague account of the nature and purpose of the Calculor. The Calculor is a strategic engine of immense power, it can multiply the wealth and power of Rochester a hundredfold and for that reason it must be kept the closest of secrets.

''My machine is destined to become indispensable to the prosperity and security of Rochester. In a few days, after more testing, it will be declared opera-

tional and will be run continuously with three shifts of eight hours each. This will require both components and Dragon Colors to supervise them. All of you will be expected to work in shifts, but duty on the unpopular shifts will be rotated.

"All of you are vital to the reliable working of the Calculor. That is why you have jumped decades of seniority in a few years. You have mathematical ability, and the Calculor will boost that ability in the same way that a bombard can allow one artillery crew to smash down a castle wall. You will have more to do with running the mayorate than the Mayor himself, but breathe so much as an afterthought about it to any but your colleagues here and you will find yourself looking down twenty-four barrels instead of squinting down the sights."

"Five days without a single error," said Zarvora as she presented Mayor Jefton with a large silver key on a cushion. "We can trust the Calculor now, and put our faith in its results."

The modifications to her office were complete, with all the mechanisms and controls installed and polished, and the dust cleaned up. The window had been repaired, and there was a strong smell of oil and wood polish on the air. Jefton picked up the heavy key and looked at it doubtfully. Shelves of little silver animal caricatures stood ready to signal their messages, and colored velvet pulley cords hung down from the ceiling.

"It goes into the slot here, Mayor," Zarvora explained, "then you give it a half turn clockwise."

"I feel that I should give a speech," said Jefton. "This thing is so important and ingenious. Its commissioning should be before the whole court, not with you as the only witness. Still, secrecy is our only shield at present. For the greater glory of Rochester, I accept the service of this machine."

Jefton turned the key. A rack of gears moved, then moved again.

"That's all there is to it?" asked Jefton, who had been expecting a more diverting display. "Can't you make it move those mechanical animals, or ring the little bells?"

"It's already busy with important work," explained Zarvora, holding out a tray with his goblet of wine. "I configured it to begin designing your new army as soon as you turned the key."

They raised their goblets of wine and water, toasting the Calculor.

"There will be no more errors, I trust?" said Jefton.

"Felt dampers have been put on the transmission wires, and four FUNCTION components have replaced the dead Dragon Green operators. Willful souls make up the Calculor, but it has no will of its own."

"A tame god, and ours to command!" exclaimed Jefton. "What is the name for those who rule the gods, Highliber?"

"I cannot say, Mayor," replied Zarvora, staring at the coded patterns that

the gearwheels displayed every few seconds—that only she could read. Jefton stared too, but his eyes were glazing.

"Are you sure it can do all you promised?" he asked, nervous at his own incomprehension.

"Very easily," she replied with a reassuring smile. Jefton continued to gaze blankly at the rack of gears, not yet aware that Rochester had a new ruler, and that he was now just another soul for the Great Machine to command.

"I have the business of my mayorate to attend now," Jefton declared, closing his eyes and shaking his head. "You will of course represent me at Lewrick's funeral and present the Shield of Honor."

"It will be my pleasure," Zarvora replied, picking up a silver medallion rimmed with star points from the side of the keyboard.

As Jefton was turning the key Lewrick's body lay at the back of the Calculor hall, guarded by six Tiger Dragons. The green and gold wattle pennon of Rochester and the black and white striped pennon of Libris lay across his coffin, which was at the end of the curtained corridor that ran down the center of the Calculor hall, visible only to the guards in the corridor and the controllers in the two observation galleries. Although he had not lived to see the Calculor become operational, he had been there on the day.

When a person engaged in the most secret of projects is killed in the line of duty it is not easy to provide a funeral with full state honors. The Calculor's work continued as always, but a regular and distinct rhythm began to build up between Dexter and Sinister processors: Zarvora had programmed the machine to play a halt-step drumroll. Zarvora, Tarrin, and Griss stood in the rear gallery as a procession of Dragon Silver Librarians emerged from the far door, halt-stepping along the corridor between the curtains, unseen by the components in either of the processors. These were followed by the ranks of Blue, then Green, then Red, all marching in single file past the coffin, with those who were particular friends of the dead System Controller placing a red flower on the lid as they passed, but without breaking step.

Tarrin could see tears gleaming on many faces, and he dared not turn to look at Zarvora as she broke ranks with the other mourners and laid a sash with the Shield of Honor pinned to it along the length of the coffin. He looked down at the medal, which was like a small star on the lid. Lewrick was the first Dragon Gold to be given Rochester's highest civilian award for the whole of the century. Poor Lewrick, he'd never have guessed it, Tarrin thought. Not even the Highliber had the Shield of Honor. In Dexter and Sinister processors the first of the Dragon Blue marchers were replacing the Dragon Red regulators who were on duty among the components, and these now marched down the corridor. Finally, with a Tiger Dragon escorting each of them, came five components who had been

particularly close to Lewrick. All five were wearing blindfolds. When the last of the marchers had passed, the six Tiger Dragons returned their long-barrel Morelacs to their holsters and lifted the coffin, then marched out to the half-step rhythm of the Calculor. Tarrin heard the door below him thud shut, and the half-step rhythm vanished from the background sounds of the Calculor moments later.

The Libris chapel was not large, and Lewrick's brief service was restricted to his immediate friends and relatives. After a short Christian service those who had not signed the Capital Secrets Act were escorted out. Five blindfolded components were escorted in as Zarvora walked to the lectern.

"System Controller Lewrick died in the service of the Mayor, Libris, and the Calculor," she began in a steady voice that emphasized her odd, precise accent. "He died in the Calculor's defense, and as he died he gave me the clue that I needed to correct the last of the flaws in the machine's design. Lewrick was a good friend and colleague, and the first System Controller of the first Calculor. Not one aspect of its design or operation does not have his mark upon it. Goodbye, my friend. Sleep well."

As a blindfolded Southmoor was escorted to the lectern a single thought was being shared by nearly everyone in the chapel. It was the first time that any of them had heard Zarvora refer to anyone as a friend.

Ettenbar, a Southmoor component from Dexter processor, was able to speak passable Austaric by now, but for the service he had rehearsed some grammatically perfect lines.

"I speak for the components of the great machine that is known as the Calculor. Although we are prisoners, the Calculor has enriched our lives. Not long ago I was a shepherd tending sheep and emus. Now I have risen to be a trainee FUNCTION. I have rank, authority, and important work. I live in comfort, I have many friends, and my Islamic faith is tolerated. Lewrick gave us our comforts. Lewrick wrote the prayer times of Islam into the Calculor's schedules. Lewrick made life for a component in the Calculor tolerable. If the guards were ever removed, many of us would not flee. Thank you, master, and goodbye."

When I die what will they say of me, wondered Tarrin as he and Vardel Griss walked to the coffin and placed two yellow roses amid the red flowers that covered the lid. Zarvora was last, with a black rose whose genes carried alterations dating back to the early twenty-first century.

The service was the end of the funeral. The six Tiger Dragons carried the coffin down several floors and into the maze of passages under the mayoral gardens that were the burial chambers for senior Dragon Librarians killed in the service of Libris. Tarrin and Griss still escorted the coffin, with Zarvora following. Behind her were a dozen more guards. The stone-lined corridors seemed to go on forever; the gilt lettering of hundreds of plaques gleamed in the lamplight as

they passed. At last a lamp came into view ahead of them, glinting highlights off the silver buckets and trowels of the burial masons.

The niche for Lewrick's coffin had already been cut into the rock. He was pushed in feetfirst, and then the stone plaque was mortared into place by the masons. Tarrin seemed to come awake, suddenly realizing that his colleague was already behind the stone. He read the gold lettering, noting that Lewrick had been only forty-nine years old. He had seemed older. Now he was gone. Tarrin could not remember consciously touching the coffin. He lit a wax taper from a lamp's flame, inverted it, and let wax run down the plaque and pool at the projecting ledge. Zarvora raised her ring seal and pressed it into the soft wax. "Rest now, Fras Lewrick," said the Dragon Black softly; then she turned and strode back down the corridor.

Those who made up the Calculor soon rediscovered a fact that had been well known nearly two thousand years earlier: while a computer center with a malfunctioning machine is the very embodiment of bedlam, a well-behaved computer is utterly boring. Figures and records arrived in oilcloth bundles sealed with impressed wax, and results were neatly written onto reedpulp cards by the output lackeys. Nobody understood the figures.

News of neither the assassination attempt on Zarvora nor the execution of the Dragon Greens had been made known generally, and the rumors that did circulate were gilded by the factions to their own advantage. Conditions improved for the Cataloguing Department. Tarrin paid little attention to his duties in Cataloguing because the Calculor was now reliable enough to expand. The aim was two registers with a thousand components each, and a separate, experimental machine was to be set up to test new designs.

Work commenced on improved coding tables for the parts of the beamflash network under Rochester's control. Those tables soon enabled the transmission rates to be tripled while lowering the error rates. The value of the tables quickly became apparent to other alliances, such as the Central Confederation and the Woomera Confederation. There were tests, then negotiations between the beamflash administrators of Griffith, Woomera, and Rochester. The tables exchanged hands for a sum reported to be over a hundred thousand gold royals, yet the administrators went home happy. The tables would quickly pay for themselves.

In Cataloguing, it was as if Libris had returned to the rule of the previous Highliber. The backlog began to build up again, arguments about fine points of classification, categorization, and book numbering dominated staff meetings, and the practice of reading entire books to gain a good feel for the contents crept back.

Bernard Wissant had become Deputy Overliber to Tarrin when he had been appointed, but Peribridge, the previous Deputy, held the real power. They soon

realized that Tarrin intended to rule them on the basis of their own reports, so those reports were falsified. Books incorrectly catalogued and returned for more work were counted twice or more, parts of multiple volumes were counted as separate titles, and the Backlog shelves were renamed 'Updating.'

"She's frightened," Peribridge declared to Wissant as they drew up the monthly report for June. "These figures are a full restoration of our rights and autonomy."

"Do you really think the Highliber has backed down?" Wissant asked, his voice quavering in spite of the smile on his face.

Peribridge lay back in the enfolding leather armchair and drew her Toufel flintlock. It had a reliable mechanism, but was badly balanced. This did not matter to those who did little shooting. No more than a reliable discharge was needed for ceremonial volleys.

"This had never been used in a duel, Fras Bernard, and I have no champion, yet I always get my way. The Highliber can do what she likes in the dueling chambers, but there are other places to die. Lewrick died on the floor of her inner sanctum."

"And now the roof swarms with Tiger Dragons."

"So? There are yet other ways. Libris runs by tradition, and that tradition cannot be swept away with a decree or two. It was established during Greatwinter itself, Bernard. It is older than our dating system."

Certainly the office reflected that. The abandonstone floor was so worn that embedded steel bars showed through in places, yet frail, vulnerable books of the same age lined the shelves intact. The names of more than two hundred Chief Cataloguers were carved into slabs of blackstone on the south wall, each picked out in gilt. At the year 1192 GW there was an elaborate flourish. This was when Cataloguing had become a separate department.

The Deputy read at random, noting that the names of the Overlibers reflected the way the language had changed. Wilson dij Soulfarer had been what was then called Sayer of Types from 97 GW to 105 GW. The year of his death was that of the Genthic Crusade. Rochester had fallen to the Gentheists, but had the Sayer of Types died in the fighting or been executed? Perhaps he had died in bed. Wissant doubted it.

"We must always defend our department," he said with a rush of pride, "even though the methods of fighting change."

Peribridge slid her flintlock back into its holster. "Highlibers come and go, but Libris will always be here. Highlibers are meant to make Libris more secure, not change it beyond recognition. The Highliber is damaging Libris, she's failing in her duty. Libris should cut her off like a diseased toe, and *we* are Libris!"

•   •   •

Several times a year Zarvora reviewed the strategic implications of what she was doing. By the winter solstice holiday in June the Calculor was settling down after its fifth major expansion, so it was time to refine other facets of Libris. A large, green register with CATALOGUING stamped in gold lettering on the spine lay beside her keyboard as she typed in data. A warning flag dropped beside her paper tape punch and she reached over to wind the spring with a polished brass lever. The mechanical hens began to peck furiously. After examining the pattern of holes in the output tape she crossed the room to where a row of colored silk ropes hung from the ceiling. She tugged at the second from the left.

Tarrin was at the door several minutes later.

"Now, about your cataloguers," Zarvora began, handing the tape to him. "Here I have a sample of forty-five books catalogued recently. Six are on the shelves. The rest have been withdrawn for 'special updating.'"

"Updating is for books catalogued under archaic cataloguing rules," Tarrin said suspiciously.

"I know. Such books have usually been in Libris for over two hundred years. That either means you have introduced major changes to the cataloguing rules since last April or cataloguing output is about a seventh of what it seems."

"So, they're back to their old ways," he sighed. "Well Highliber, if you have one Dragon Gold carrying two positions this sort of thing is bound to happen. There are others who could run Cataloguing."

"There is nobody else that I trust but you."

"Well, you'll have to learn to, Frelle Highliber. After all, did you trust *me* before Lewrick was killed?"

"I miss him, Fras Tarrin," Zarvora said wistfully as she stared at the harpsichord keys. "In all the world nobody understood my design so well. Funny little man, he actually loved the Calculor like a doting father. To me it is just an engine."

Tarrin did not know what to say. "I'm dedicated to the work," he said uncertainly. "Is that good enough?"

"Good enough? Fras Tarrin, that is actually better. Lewrick was emotional, but you are more like me. Yes, I know that many of Lewrick's solutions were truly inspired, but you actually think more as I do. That is an advantage of a different kind."

"Does that mean that I'll not be taken off the Calculor?"

Zarvora looked up and nodded. "You will be relieved of your duties as Chief Cataloguer, if that is what you mean. You are to be the new, permanent System Controller."

"Thank you, Frelle Highliber," he said brightly, not making any attempt to hide his relief.

"You seem to be standing straighter already."

"The weight is gone from my shoulders, or some of it at least. Who will take charge of Cataloguing?"

"Oh I could not possibly decide that," she said impishly. "I am far too paranoid, you said so yourself. You decide. You have a month from today."

Tarrin thought for a moment.

"A difficult choice, Fras System Controller?" Zarvora asked.

"I'm trying to think of someone I dislike sufficiently, Frelle Highliber."

Music echoed in from the distant city streets, where the solstice celebrations were reaching a climax. Zarvora glanced at her clock, then went over to the Southmoor leadlight door, unlocked it, and stepped out onto the roof. She beckoned for Tarrin to come with her. They followed a narrow walkway past two guards and emerged onto a flat area of sandstone beside the Libris observatory. The tip of the shadow from a wedge of rock was approaching the solstice point of an inlaid brass analemma at their feet. Not far away a noon sundial's shadow on the observatory wall was near the low summer mark. Zarvora stood with her hands on her hips.

"There we are, summer begins," she said. As if on her cue, bells, cheers, and gunshots sounded in the distance. "I have work to do on the Calculor, Fras, and you need not return to my office. Use the lightwell stairs. Is there anything else that I should know about?"

"Highliber, I could serve you better if I knew what the Calculor is meant to do—besides the schemes to uncover felons, decode secret messages, and administer Libris and the beamflash traffic."

"It keeps track of the Cataloguing statistics."

"Highliber!"

"Well then, to predict the return of Greatwinter and unravel the secret of the Call for the amusement of the Mayor and the greater glory of Rochester."

Tarrin scratched so violently at his tousled hair that several strands came away in his fingers. He brushed his hands together and shrugged with resignation.

"If you wish to keep your secrets, Highliber, that's your business. All that I ask is that you treat me exactly as you would Lewrick. I need to be well informed to do my work properly."

Zarvora looked out over the city.

"It is no joke, Tarrin," she said quietly. Tarrin turned to face her. "I have done studies in some of the oldest of our archives, and I discovered clues of grand projects before Greatwinter. I cannot say more than that for now."

Tarrin was silent for a moment. "Who else knows?"

"Only you."

"Not even the Mayor?"

"No. He thinks that I designed the Calculor to control the beamflash network, but that I discovered some interesting extra uses that profit him as well. The truth

is that the Calculor was built to forecast Greatwinter's return, or at least to forecast it to a thousand times the accuracy that I could manage myself. As I once explained to Lewrick, knowing the date of Greatwinter's return can bring great advantage.''

To Tarrin it sounded like the ravings of a street-corner prophet, and he could hardly believe that it was the brilliant, rational Highliber speaking. He preserved an expression of polite attention and said nothing.

''Greatwinter was the end of the world for billions of people and its return could be the end of our world too,'' she continued, regarding him with the intense gaze of a bird of prey tutoring a chick. ''Just think of it: if there is great cold then crops will fail and stock animals will die. Imagine crystals of frost as high as your knees that last all day to grow higher by the next morning. Animals could not graze, and the ground would be too hard to plough. What would happen if rain only fell as hail? Fruit would be pulverized on the trees before it could ripen, crops would be flattened instead of being watered. Wind patterns will be different, too: will the winds be too violent for the wind trains to run without being totally rebuilt? So many questions, and only one Calculor to assist me.''

''Highliber, we might all die,'' replied Tarrin, now genuinely uneasy.

She stepped across the shadow cast by the stone sundial, as if taking charge of cosmic motions and matters.

''I have begun to take measures. Stores are being put aside: Rochester is stockpiling grain, dried fruit, nuts, oils, and seeds for all manner of plants. Cloth and pelts, too.''

''So . . . you think Greatwinter is as close as that? Will it be next year? Will it start with ice falling from the sky?''

''Actually I am being dishonest with you, Fras Tarrin. My figures indicate around five years, but the cooling will be over another five again. The stores are to help hold the nation together in the times of anarchy when the sign of the second Greatwinter appears in the sky, to help us through the transition as we learn farming methods for colder weather. Deputy Overliber Kenlee and two assistants have been sent to study farming in the Talangatta Mayorate in the border highlands. The weather is colder there, yet they still grow crops and raise animals.''

Tarrin again ran his fingers through his untidy hair. He looked at Zarvora in silence as he tried to tried to assemble his feelings into words of at least token diplomacy. He was not able to do it.

''Highliber, what you're doing is monstrous!'' he forced himself to say in a voice that came out loud and flat.

''People have been calling me a monster ever since I can remember.''

''But, but Highliber—''

''There you have it Fras Tarrin: Highliber. I am Highliber. Go out into the

streets and you will find a dozen hairy, hysterical nobodies foretelling Greatwinter's return before you have even reached Buttermilk Terrace. What is the difference between me and them?''

"I . . . well, your great power—and scholarship.''

"No, Fras, just power. Some of the prophets of doom are also very well read and educated. When I realized that Greatwinter was returning I was fourteen. I joined the Libris Dragon Colors because apart from convents and advantageous marriages, it is the only place where women can advance themselves in our society. I worked my way up to where I am today and all the while I gave people great profit in return for letting me do things my way. Look at me now. I have Rochester and several other mayorates partway prepared for Greatwinter without them knowing it. If I were to declare my true motives I would be branded a loonbrain by every one of my rivals and enemies, and within weeks I would be just another powerless street-corner prophet. People in power cheerfully prey on visionaries to gain more power, Fras Tarrin. I do not intend to be preyed upon.''

Tarrin could not deny any of what she had said. He had spent too much time in the offices and corridors of power himself.

"So the deaths of millions are inevitable?'' he said as he began to pace, clenching and unclenching his hands behind his back.

"Perhaps I have been unfair to you, Fras. You are an administrator, not a mere ruler. You really care about the systems that you serve. Look at it this way. If Greatwinter returns and civilization collapses, millions will die. Should some mayorates manage to maintain their farms, paralines, abandonmines, artisan guilds, and armies, millions fewer will die. One small life raft can hold two dozen above the surface of a river if they just hold on to the edge. I care about civilization too, Fras, but in a broader way than you.''

Tarrin ceased his pacing and leaned against a sandstone wall. His legs wobbled like the mechanism of a reciprocation governor, yet he remained standing. Zarvora stood with her arms folded, as if she were a sergeant assessing the spirit of a musketeer recruit after a forced march.

"Propped up by Libris, like everything else,'' he said, fingering the ears of a weatherworn gargoyle cut into the stone. "So what can I do to help? Conquer the Southmoors at the head of an Alliance army? Girdle the continent with beamflash towers? Devise a way to defy the Call itself?''

"Any or all of those things would help, Tarrin, but in all the world nothing is so important as keeping the Calculor in operation and expanding it with all possible speed. Nothing! Not the Mayor, not the Overbishop, not Rochester, not Libris, and especially not the cataloguers. Fras System Controller, with the aid of the Calculor I intend to fling thunderbolts into the sky and smash the ancient Greatwinter engine!''

Even as she spoke Zarvora realized that she had said too much. Without

another word she returned to her study. Tarrin stood dazed by her astounding outburst of sheer hubris. Brilliant she might be, but sound of mind she was not.

Inevitably, Tarrin's choice of an outsider to succeed him as Chief Cataloguer was not popular with the senior Cataloguing staff. Taking his lead from the Highliber, he decreed that dissension would be ignored, then set about preparing to hand over his office. A petition was circulated and an indignation meeting was called, to be attended by everyone in Cataloguing. Tarrin decided to attend as well. It would be a good place to bid the department farewell.

John Glasken was not alarmed to hear a surprised shout and cry of pain somewhere in the darkness ahead of him. Just drunks fighting, he thought, but he still shifted his grip on his swagger stick as he walked confidently down the alleyway. A gunshot shattered his complacency, and even as he stood frozen in midstride he was confronted by the outline of a jumpslash. The alley was narrow and Glasken saw the glint of a knife held for stabbing. His reflexes took over. He parried the blade up, using his swagger stick like a quarterstaff, then drove the stick's butt hard into the man's forehead. Even before the Southmoor had hit the cobblestones another figure dashed into the alley.

"Hold!" There was a flintlock backing up the command. Glasken let his swagger stick fall and raised his hands. Even in the darkened alley the cut of the figure's clothing showed her to be a Dragon Librarian.

"He attacked me, Frelle, I acted in defense."

She glanced at the figure on the ground, then back at Glasken. "Your pardon, Fras," she said, then lowered her gun. "Will you be good enough to drag him out into the street?"

Around the corner another Southmoor lay dead in the slops gutter that ran down the center of the street. Over near a pile of empty barrels were two more Dragon Librarians. One lay unconscious on the cobblestones, the gold band on his torn sleeve distinct in the lamplight. Amid the background reek of wine slops, piss, and pony dung was the scent of blood.

"My name is Lemorel Mil—ah, I'm a Dragon Green, from Libris," the girl said as she examined the jumpslash.

"Glasken, Johnny Glasken, final-year student of chemistric at the University of Rochester, at your service."

She seemed to ignore him as she examined his victim. "Another Southmoor, they're both Southmoors." Lemorel turned to her colleague. "How is Tarrin, Dar?"

Darien gestured in the dim streetlight with bloodstained fingers, then tore a strip of cloth from her cape to bandage Tarrin's arm.

"Can I have that jar of wine at your belt, Fras Glasken?"

Glasken gave her the jar and she sprinkled a little on the Dragon Gold's face.

"Can you hear me, Fras Tarrin? You're safe, it's Lemorel and Darien." Tarrin groaned, but remained insensible. "He may have hit his head as he fell, I saw the live one trip him."

"Your shot will bring the Runners," warned Glasken, who was anxious to leave.

Lemorel looked across to the bodies of the Southmoors and stood up with his jar of wine.

"Then let's learn what we can before the due processes of the law get in the way," she said as she emptied the wine over the surviving Southmoor's face. He groaned, and as he opened his eyes she pressed the twin barrels of her Morelac hard against his nostrils. "Who paid you?" she demanded.

"Poor man, poor man," he babbled. "Have to steal, feed family. Three wives, nine little ones—"

Lemorel pulled one trigger. There was a click and a shower of sparks but no blast. The Southmoor screamed.

"Mercy! Pretty Frelle, merciful Frelle."

"The other barrel is loaded," she warned.

"The Warren, Frelle. They beat me, threaten my family. Evil men, evil women. Told me kill Dragon Gold."

"Who spoke to you?"

"Woman in purdah, evil woman. No see face, no see face."

A Constable's Runner arrived, attracted by the gunshot. He blew his whistle and another four soon appeared. The surviving Southmoor was taken off to the Watchhouse and his comrade was loaded onto the coroner's cart. Glasken carried the wounded Dragon Gold to the nearby University Infirmary, where the gashes on his arm were cleaned and stitched. The medician told them that he should rest there until morning.

Lemorel was still keyed up and alert as she stood on the Infirmary steps with Darien and Glasken. She regarded the student obliquely while searching for words. Most shadowboys and bullies who carried swagger sticks stood with them across their shoulders and their arms draped over the ends. Glasken stood with the stick held out to one side and the tip resting on his boot. It was the stance of a gentleman, a student from a good family. Lemorel wanted words, but none came. Glasken twisted his foot on its heel, as if about to go.

"This is Frelle Darien, she has no voice," Lemorel almost shouted as she grasped at the omitted introduction. Glasken smiled and bowed to the Dragon Blue.

"I am honored, Frelle, and charmed besides. I should invite you to my room at Villiers College for coffee, but it is not in a state for such senior Dragon Librarians to see."

"Oh no, Fras Glasken, it is we who are in your debt. Where is there a coffee-

house near here, Dar?'' Darien gestured with her fingers and Lemorel beamed with pleasure. ''The Golden Casket, just the place.''

Glasken blinked in surprise, for the Golden Casket was beyond the means of the general run of students. Words came more easily to Lemorel as they began to walk.

''That was fine stickwork against the Southmoor, Fras Glasken. Have you done town-fencing at an academy?''

''Johnny to my friends, Frelle Lemorel, and no.''

''Ah, but you know . . . ah, good stickwork.''

''Thank you.''

Again the words petered out. They walked a few steps in silence before Glasken came to her rescue again.

''And are you a graduate, Frelle Lemorel?''

''Only of Rutherglen Unitech, Fras, ah, Johnny. But I'm studying for an edutorate in Rochester. Mathematics, vector modeling.''

''Vector modeling? Ah, a lot of wearisome calculations, you must be a very patient person.''

''Oh I have, ah, a lot of help, Fras Johnny.''

Darien tugged at Lemorel's sleeve, then flashed a series of gestures at her in the dim light. ''He knows what a vector model is. Impressive.''

''So you understand sign language too?'' asked Glasken.

''Ah, yes. Darien asked if you are, er, studying full time.''

''Alas, no, I study as I can, Frelle. I'm paying my own way, you see. I work in the taverns of the city, earning silver nobles by keeping order.''

''Hence your skill with a swagger stick,'' Lemorel added, as if satisfying herself about something.

In the Golden Casket they bought Glasken a dinner of roast emu cuts in orange sauce, and potatoes stuffed with cream cheese and crushed nuts on a bed of savory brown rice. Lemorel replaced his jar of wine with another worth somewhat more than the original. After that they sat drinking coffee and eating candied locusts and honeynut pastries until the University clocktower chimed 9 P.M. By now a winter rainstorm had set in and was lashing the deserted street outside.

''Frelle Darien cut up her cape for a bandage,'' Glasken said as he reached up to pin his cloak into place. ''Please, take mine, good Frelles.''

''But Fras Glasken, what about you?'' replied Lemorel.

''Libris is nearly two miles away, and my college is only a few hundred yards.''

''No, wait, we'll go with you, then return under your cloak to Libris.''

''Dragon Librarians visiting the room of a common student? There would be talk about town, and we must protect your reputations from that.'' He dashed out into the rain and took several loping strides into the storm before turning back

for a moment. "Return the cloak to Villiers College when you will, Frelle Lemorel," he called, then he was gone.

Darien laughed soundlessly.

"What's so funny?"

"You like him, but deny it," her fingers fluttered.

"Like him? Absurd. Why he's . . ."

She could not think of any reasons. Darien's fingers moved again.

"He's big, handsome, well educated, and gentlemanly. If he is poor, then so what?"

Lemorel touched a carefully mended saber cut in Glasken's cloak. "This has seen action," she said.

Darien held her fingers high, where Lemorel could not miss what they were saying.

"He combines the best of Semidon and Brunthorp, does he not? Big and handsome, yet a scholar. He seems a true gentleman as well, braving discomfort for our welfare."

Lemorel looked into the lamplit rain, but sighed through clenched teeth. "He was brave enough to confront an armed Southmoor and skilled enough to drop him. That's all." She turned back to Darien.

"The nightmares are a long way behind you, Lem. There will be reasons to see him again. Return his cloak yourself."

"Why do you have such an interest?" asked Lemorel impatiently as she held up the cloak and spread it to cover Darien and herself.

"I can see the way you reacted to him. I am only telling you what you will not admit to yourself."

By the morning of the indignation meeting Tarrin was well enough to attend, but his arm was still in a sling and his head was bandaged. He walked with a limp from twisting his ankle when he fell, and his Dragon Gold armband was still smeared with dirt from the cobblestones.

The cataloguers gathered in the Millennium Auditorium, which had been used for Dragon Color presentations and other Libris ceremonies since the Calculor had been installed in the only larger hall. The clock behind the lectern clacked as the arms of its reciprocator swung back and forth. 9 A.M. came and went, yet numbers were slow to build. By 9:30 Peribridge checked the rows of faces and frowned. The senior cataloguers were still not there, and many of the others who had pledged their support were absent. The clock clacked with relentless regularity. Finally at 9:40 Tarrin entered, with Lemorel behind him wearing his champion's colors. He stood at the door without calling for attention, but by now the cataloguers were so uneasy that the buzzing conversation quickly died away. He shambled to the lectern, his hair tousled and dark circles under his eyes.

"Now, who is in charge of this meeting?" he asked in a soft, hoarse voice, seeming a little puzzled.

Peribridge stood up as if jerked by invisible puppeteer strings. "Deputy Overliber Wissant, Senior Classifications Cataloguer Cobbaray, and Senior Liaison Cataloguer Nugen-Katr were to be the meeting coordinators, Fras Overliber."

"*Fras* Wissant, *Frelle* Cobbaray, and *Fras* Nugen-Katr will not be available to address any more meetings henceforth."

Tarrin seemed almost apologetic with the news. Peribridge sat down. Tarrin cleared his throat before continuing.

"I'm pleased that you are all together here, as I have an announcement from the Highliber. Due to pressures on the staff of Libris caused by her special project, certain cataloguing staff have been, well, redirected to other work." He allowed a lengthy pause before adding "Any questions?"

Feet shuffled. A Dragon Yellow raised her hand.

"Please, Fras Controller, but how many cataloguers have been redirected?"

"One hundred and twenty-six."

There was complete, breathless silence. Tarrin waited. By now even the least perceptive in his audience had realized that his façade of weariness and defeat concealed a very dangerous loss of patience. At last someone at the far corner of the auditorium stood up.

"Ah yes, you have a question?" Tarrin asked gently, as one might encourage a nervous candidate in an exam.

"Please, Fras Controller, but I was just leaving to attend some urgent work," the Dragon Orange replied. At this another dozen stood up, and more joined them as they made for the doors. The doors were locked.

Tarrin held his hand up for silence.

"Regrettably I must concede that Frelle Costerliber, Deputy Overliber of Accessions, has been declared not acceptable in a petition signed by two hundred and ninety-seven of the Cataloguing Department. That's very impressive: everyone from Fras Wissant the Deputy Chief, to Fras O'Donlan the assistant cleaner. In view of such opposition, and seeing there is nobody else suitable to run Cataloguing, I have secured the Highliber's approval to abolish Cataloguing as a department. Cataloguing is to be made a section of Acquisitions—as of this morning."

There was a collective gasp of shock. "But Cataloguing's been a separate unit since 1192," someone called.

"Five hundred and five years without a reorganization is far too long. Are there any more questions? No questions?" There was silence. "Very good, very good. Now, Frelle Vardel Griss, Chief of the Tiger Dragons, wants to have a few words with you as well."

Lemorel tapped the door in a prearranged code. There was a loud clack from

outside as a bolt was drawn back, then Griss swaggered in a few paces and faced the audience with her hands clasped behind her back. She had the alert yet relaxed stance of an experienced dueler, and just the faintest hint of a frown on her face.

A squad of twelve Tiger Dragons filed in and lined up behind her, muskets shouldered and matchlock fuses smoking. Lemorel drew her Morelac and stood beside Tarrin.

"Stand to Alert!" snapped Griss, and the Tiger Dragons brought their weapons to point just a little above the heads of the cataloguers.

"I shall be quite clear about it," said Griss in a tone as hard as gunbarrel steel. "Cataloguing as a department has ceased to exist. What is more, *you have no rights!* None! Understand? Work well and you will not be harmed. Try to resign, run away, or shoot at the senior staff and you will be redirected instantly. I am not above punishing ten innocent cataloguers to catch one who is guilty. If you hear anyone plotting, remember that your own freedom is at stake if you remain silent. Report every suspicious word to my Tiger Dragons at once."

She went across to where Tarrin was leaning against the lectern. "Any more names for me?" she asked quietly, but not inaudibly.

Tarrin unbuckled the lid of a hide pouch at his belt and took out a list. "Twenty-five more for indolence," he said as he handed the folded square of poorpaper to Griss. "Oh, and add Peribridge as a special. She was showing a suspicious degree of leadership earlier."

Peribridge was well skilled at listening in to conversations at a distance. She sat calm and serene as Griss ordered the cataloguers to file out one by one past her guards at the door. Lemorel stood with Tarrin beside the lectern.

"This will mean open warfare," she whispered amid the echoing clatter of feet on the ashgum floorboards.

"So? I stopped the first blow," he said, rubbing his bandaged arm with his free hand. "In time the worst of those remaining can be weeded out."

Peribridge comprehended what was happening all too well. Even the façade of the rules had been abolished. The battle had been fought before she realized it had begun, and now prisoners were being taken. She was among those marked down to vanish into the out-of-bounds area of Libris, the black pit from which nobody returned. She let her hand rest against the butt of her Toufel flintlock. Tarrin was five rows of seats plus fifteen paces away. Too far. It had been three years since she had been to the target gallery, and that had done no more than prove that her stubby Toufel was badly aligned and woefully inaccurate over more than a few yards. Lemorel was beside Tarrin, her gun in her hand, as wary and deadly as a bush cat. Peribridge knew that she would have to shoot at the scrawny Dragon Gold without even taking a bead on him. That was hopeless. Lemorel would kill her and get the credit, and Tarrin would live. Do nothing and the Highliber has me as slave labor, Peribridge grimly reasoned. Nobody will profit by my fall.

She reached down and scratched her leg. As she brought her hand up again she cocked the striker of her Toufel.

"You shouldn't be too strict," said Lemorel, scanning the auditorium but expecting no trouble. "Who will do the cataloguing?"

"A mere fifth of those left could catalogue all the books that come into Libris, provided they work diligently."

"So the rest go to the Calculor?"

"If any are truly untrainable they can be sent to lay paraline rails on the new Loxton bypass."

"They say war is—"

Peribridge stood up to leave, drawing her gun in the same movement. Lemorel raised her Morelac and shouldered Tarrin off-balance with the sinuous grace of a Genthic temple dancer just as Peribridge raised her Toufel flintlock and pressed it against the side of her own head. The cataloguer's gun blew the top of her head off just as Lemorel's shot hit her squarely in the throat. Peribridge crashed to the floor amid overturned chairs and fellow cataloguers diving for cover. Slowly the smoke cleared to reveal Lemorel, Griss, and the Tiger Dragons at the door with their guns aimed into the auditorium.

"The rest of you raise your hands and continue to file out," Griss ordered. "Walk slowly, no sudden movements."

Tarrin got to his feet, clutching his bandage. Blood was seeping through his fingers. "Anyone else attempting suicide will also be shot," he muttered to himself.

The stiches in Tarrin's gash had been torn open by his fall, but he stood beside the others with blood dripping from his arm while the last of the cataloguers left the auditorium. Many were splattered with brains and blood, and all were wide-eyed and ashen-faced. Tarrin collapsed into a chair as the last of them left. Griss left to find a medician as Lemorel used her gunbarrel and Tarrin's sling as a tourniquet for his arm.

"What were you saying about war?" Tarrin asked, glancing across at the remains of Peribridge.

Lemorel had to stop and think for a moment. "Lameroo and Billiatt are threatening war over the Loxton paraline bypass."

"War at Loxton, ah yes. For a moment I thought you meant here."

CAPTIVE

Being a linguist, Darien found her career in Libris continually nudged toward the Inspectorate. With war threatening in the westernmost mayorate of the Alliance, she finally accepted a commission as a trainee Inspector. Her first assignment was to the assist with the opening ceremony of the bypass paraline between the towns of Morkalla and Maggea. The laying of this new track meant that the paraline west was now on the territory of the Southeast Alliance until it reached the Woomera border. The independent castellanies to the south were thus faced with a big loss of customs revenue, so there was large military buildup where the new paraline skirted the border.

Darien's only warning that fighting had begun was a heavy lurch as the wind train that she was traveling in toppled from its tracks. The lightly built engine and carriages crashed down and split open beside the paraline. Darien sat up on what had been the wall of her carriage, dazed and in pain. Her first thought was to crawl out of the wreckage, but Morkundar, one of her small escort squad of Tiger Dragons, barred her way. Bright red blood was oozing from above his hairline and trickling down the black skin of his face.

"Stay down, Frelle Darien, this is no accident," he said urgently as he wiped blood from his eyes. "The train's been attacked."

He led her to where the other Tiger Dragons were assembling and as they arrived a patter of shots began. Survivors who were already outside screamed as they were hit, and bullets tore through the flimsy woodwork of the wrecked coach. The Tiger Dragons lay low and checked their guns.

"They'll charge at any moment," Morkundar's voice warned from somewhere beyond a pile of seats and luggage. "There's no cover east of the paraline, so they must be all on the western side. All of you, line up along the breach in the roof."

Even as he was speaking nine dozen regulars from the Billiatt Castellany charged from their cover waving sabers and cheering. Morkundar watched through a split board.

"Steady, steady . . . Up, aim, fire! Second barrel . . . fire!"

Like Darien, every one of the Tiger Dragons had a double-barrel flintlock, so forty shots tore into the Billiattians as they reached the wreckage. Darien fired blindly the first time, but aimed for one of the officers with her second shot. He

reeled, the saber fell from his hand, and he collapsed. She dropped the gun and drew her dagger, then stood petrified. Someone dragged her down under cover and she came to her senses with the envoy from the Brookfield Castellany to Renmark slapping her face and shouting at her to reload.

The shock of sudden disciplined fire at the Billiattians was made worse by the loss of their five most senior officers among the seventeen killed. "A trick, an ambush, fall back!" someone shouted, and they broke ranks and fled for cover.

One minute had passed since the derailment.

"Synchronize Call anchors," Morkundar shouted as they began to reload. "A quarter hour drop, and reset on my command or timeout. Counting, three, two, one, reset!"

It took some time for Billiatt's troops to regroup and organize return fire. The three trained snipers in the Tiger Dragons had meantime unpacked their long-barreled muskets and were picking off any Billiattians who tried to get a closer look. Darien reloaded her flintlock and lay ready for the next order. Two more surviving passengers now joined them, but they were both wounded.

Darien touched the envoy's arm. As he turned to her she shrugged and bowed.

"That's all right," he said. "First time under fire?" She nodded. He was a thickset, balding man of about fifty, a little like one of her uncles. "I'm afraid too," he said, turning back to peer through a hole in the smashed paneling of the carriage. His tone became mixed with anger. "They must have invaded across Brookfield territory, they couldn't have got here so fast otherwise—uh, here they come again."

The sharpshooters dropped two officers just as the charge began. Darien stood and fired, once, felt the tug of a ball passing through the shoulder pad of her tunic, then fired again and dropped back under cover. She had no idea what she had shot at or whether she had hit anyone. Her right breast felt clammy. Blood from a gash in her shoulder was soaking her uniform.

The volley from the train broke the wavering line before they had advanced more than a few yards, even though their own marksmen were laying down covering fire ahead of them. The enemy musketeers began to shoot blindly into the wreckage from cover. A Tiger Dragon was hit as he sat reloading his gun.

Morkundar gave Darien a cloth soaked in eucalyptus oil and told her to stuff it under her tunic and against the wound. She winced with the sting of it.

"The pain helps close your blood vessels and slows the bleeding," he said. "Stay low now, the train's too flimsy to give us cover."

"Seats," said the envoy. "Use luggage and seats as a barricade."

Fire from the Billiatt muskets continued to rake their overturned carriage.

"Ready with anchors, three, two, one, reset!" Morkundar called.

"I don't understand it," said the envoy. "Why attack this train, why violate

Brookfield territory? Billiatt and Brookfield were at peace. My Castellan will be
screaming for reparations when he hears of this.''

"The beamflash link," Morkundar replied. "My guess is that the Castellan
of Billiatt has laid siege to the Maggea railside, also with troops sent across the
Brookfield borders. This force here has been sent north to cut the beamflash link.
They may have bombards to smash a tower, or they may just light grassfires to
cloud the beam. By breaking both the beamflash and paraline the Castellan will
show that he has a stranglehold on whatever the Alliance wants to do. The more
timid mayors will want to pay him his customs money again.''

"But there's barely a hundred musketeers out there.''

"The main force will be up ahead, and probably visible from the paraline.
We were bombed to stop us overtaking them and raising an alarm.''

Morkundar spilled a little gunpowder on a scrap of poorpaper and drew back
the striker of an unloaded barrel. The shower of sparks ignited the powder and
set the poorpaper alight. Darien looked on in alarm, silently shaking her head at
him.

"Careful, this carriage will burn like kindling," warned the envoy.

"That's why I'm setting it alight.''

"What? But it's our only shelter.''

"The wind engine is lying close by, and is built more solidly. We must run
for that and take shelter beneath it. The smoke from this carriage will alert lookouts in the beamflash towers. Patrols will be sent to investigate and they will
discover the main force of Billiatt raiders.''

"That main force could turn back to help that lot over there put out the fire.''

"So we must attack instead of just surviving.''

Darien wept with frustration. Her cards were gone and none of them knew
sign language. There were probably flares somewhere in the wind engine, but—
but Morkundar was a good leader and she had no voice.

"If we just stay here those musketeers will leave to join the main force,"
the envoy pleaded. "We can't attack. There's five of them for every one of us.''

"Then we'll die defending a burning carriage.''

Die. Darien felt herself convulse at the thought. The envoy turned to her.
"Frelle, you're the most senior Dragon Librarian here, and the Fras Tiger Dragon
must have your approval. What is your word?''

Her word? Darien put a hand over her eyes and laughed her silent laugh,
close to hysteria, nearly in tears. The envoy's balding head suddenly went crimson
and he tried to splutter an apology. Morkundar's face remained grim.

"Well, Frelle Darien?" he asked.

She pointed to Morkundar and nodded.

Lemorel had hired a good lawyer when she heard that Glasken was in trouble. It
paid off. There had been a drunken brawl in the street outside a tavern, and when

the Constable's Runners had arrived Glasken was one of those lying unconscious on the cobblestones. The city prosecutor cited Glasken's poor record, but the defense cited Glasken's role in saving Tarrin's life as proof of his good character. After his release Glasken returned to his college at the University with Lemorel beside him. His head was bandaged, and there was a red stain where the blood had seeped through.

"I used to think that justice in my own yoick-town mayorate was backward, but not anymore," fumed Lemorel. "That magistrate went out of his way to weight the evidence against you."

"Justice is like having big muscles," Glasken said without rancor. "Some people just have more than others and it can't be helped. I work as a swaggerman, so I get into a lot of fights. Because I get into a lot of fights, I see a lot of the magistrate."

"But soon you will have a degree, Johnny, and will be working in safer places," Lemorel said hopefully.

"I majored in explosives, Lem. Does that sound safer than rioting drunkards?"

"Well, whatever you do, I'll do what I can to make your life easier."

By now they had reached Villiers College in the University grounds. It was an old, solid, and comforting building of ochrewash abandonstone. The main doorway was shrouded with vines, and their footsteps echoed on the boards of the hallway as those of students had for centuries.

Glasken had a room upstairs. Lemorel glanced around approvingly as she entered. The place was orderly and well swept, with the books in a straight row on the shelf and the bunk made neatly.

"Not very inviting, I'm afraid," he apologized.

"It's wonderful," she responded. "I expected you to have the squalid habits of most young men living away from home."

"So, you have had occasion to see their bedrooms?" he asked at once, although playfully.

"Only late at night."

"Oh so, pray continue."

"And only after the Tiger Dragons had broken down their doors and taken them away for questioning."

Glasken gave a slight choking sound before realizing that it was probably a joke.

"There are better ways to get questions answered," he suggested, sitting on the edge of his bunk.

"Those being?"

"Tap lightly on the door, then enter the room with the top button or two of your tunic undone. You should also be sure to have a jar of plumb brandy with you."

"Why plum brandy?"

"Because it is upon you before you know it," he said, raising his hands like claws. "It slips the knots on lacings just as surely as it loosens tongues."

Lemorel turned away, a little unnerved at the wordplay. She examined the books on his shelf, then noticed a small lemonwood box with a deacon's pledge stamp bearing the date 14th April 1696. She lifted it with two fingers. There was a tracery of hearts and arrows all around it in pokerwork.

"And what is in here that has been sealed away for a year and a half?" she asked, frowning slightly. "Love letters, perhaps?"

Inwardly she prayed that it was not so.

"The armor of lovers," Glasken replied.

Lemorel dropped the box with a gasp. The seal broke as it hit the floorboards.

"Fras Glasken, I didn't think you—that is, I thought you too much of a gentleman . . ."

"And so I am, lovely Frelle. Take note of the date."

"But—"

"Lemorel, sweet Frelle, just think of what would happen should I find myself with some lovely young girl and both of our passions running amok. The deed would soon be done, yet what is in that box could make the difference between a harmless frolic and a pregnancy that would be anything but harmless."

He reached down and picked up the box.

"Hmm, the seal pledged before the deacon is broken," he observed.

Lemorel considered this, then flicked the top button of her tunic. It popped undone.

"How many buttons did you mention earlier, Fras Glasken?" she asked.

He stretched out on the bunk, like a big, languid cat. "To win my heart, Frelle, none at all. To win my body . . . as many as feels comfortable."

Glasken lived up to his promise as a lover, in spite of the narrowness of the bunk and the fact that he had been clouted over the head the night before. This is the way that virginity really should be lost, Lemorel thought as a clocktower nearby clanged the hour past noon. Down below on the lawns she could hear students chattering as they went from their lectures and tutorials to the college refectories. Lemorel had missed a lecture on applied calculus to be where she was, but was feeling smugly superior about it.

Her new lover was lying with his head on her shoulder and a leg sprawled across her thighs. She caressed the hair above his bandage, suddenly troubled by something about him. He was good-looking, considerate, intelligent, strong, and sensible . . . but slightly dull. It seemed a terrible thing to admit, yet the man did everything right: nothing was colored by foolishness or mistakes. How tolerant would he be? Lemorel shivered to think of dead lovers, cold in their graves. How would John Glasken react to her past, were it ever revealed to him? She could

be open to blackmail unless their liaison remained a secret. Now she realized why such a prize as he was unpartnered: when you are too good to be true, very few others can come up to your standards.

She gently shook him awake.

"Johnny, I must go now,"

"Umm? So soon?"

"I have work to do in Libris. There's always too much work in Libris."

He admired her from the bed as she pulled on her trousers then sat lacing her boots on his guest chair.

"Fras Johnny, it's not that I don't feel proud of you . . ." she began, but the rest of her words did not line up properly in her mind. She looked down at the floor, pressing her lips together.

"A Dragon Green Librarian should not be seen to be liaising with a student," Glasken said in a kind, level voice.

"No, it's not like that—"

"Ah, but it is, Frelle. Think of your reputation, it's quite reasonable."

"You don't mind?"

"If Libris knew, Libris would send people to spy upon every move that *I* make. Those in the taverns where I keep order would soon think that the spies were really working *with* me. I would not live long."

Lemorel was still sensitive on the subject of dead lovers. Still naked from the waist up, she flung herself over him, imploring Glasken to give up his work in the taverns, even offering to pay his expenses herself.

"Generous Frelle, I cannot accept money for nothing," he said as he held her against him, "but I am quite safe if our love remains a secret. It's in both our interests to be discreet."

"So you understand that I'm not ashamed of you?"

"Of course. Now off with you, to Libris and the service of the Mayor."

Lemorel got up and buckled on her gunbelt and dagger. Glasken clapped in appreciation as she struck poses with her breasts thrust out; then he got out of bed and shouldered his swagger stick like a musket.

"Were you to dress like that for duels, men would challenge you just for a dying glance at such breasts," he said as he dropped his swagger stick and fell to his knees, clutching his heart.

"Come on now, Johnny, back into bed—no, stop that."

But Glasken did not stop, and Lemorel did not emerge from his bed again until five in the evening. This time she put the tunic on before buckling on her gunbelt.

"What will you tell them at Libris?" asked Glasken as he stifled a yawn.

"That I fell asleep while studying at the University."

"That will be enough?"

"I have a good record, they owe me a few lapses."

"And ex-lovers in high places?"

Lemorel shook her head. "I've had only one affair since joining Libris, and it was nothing special. I prefer affection, so I stay out of the political dalliances on offer there. And what of your ex-lovers? Don't try to tell me that this afternoon was your first time."

Glasken lay back in the bunk and clasped his hands over his chest. "Lovers, yes I've had several. Silly, frilly wenches who saw only a body of passable allure. Lust without affection is like taste without food: you feel good while gradually starving. One of them hurt me deliberately, just before an important exam. That's when I saw the deacon and sealed that box."

"Lucky me," said Lemorel as she kissed him goodbye.

Rochester was suddenly wonderful as Lemorel returned to Libris through lamplit streets crowded with evening traffic. Perhaps Glasken was still a little more staid than she would have liked, but she would quickly bring him out of himself. The criers were going about, some with their tools and wares, others with dashpapers.

"Auction of fine horses. Auction of fine horses."

"Flour, fine ground flour by the bag."

"Clayware, buy a fine mug or lamp."

She stopped and glanced at the stall. The symbolism of her buying a lamp to light up Glasken's hard life appealed to her.

"War with Billiatt. Fighting on Loxton paraline."

Lemorel crashed down out of her reverie and ran over to the young crier girl. The dashpaper that she bought told of actions that had taken place that afternoon and been reported by beamflash. It was a series of headline phrases, no more. "Beamflash link saved from attack due to bravery of Dragon Green Justin Morkundar." He had been the Tiger Dragon in charge of Darien's escort, one of several koorees working for Libris. So what of her friend? While she had been in Glasken's arms Darien might have been dying on a battlefield. "Whatever I do, there's always guilt to dog me," she muttered as she scanned the rest of the dashpaper. "Brookfield enters war on Alliance side. Brookfield envoy saved during wind train ambush by Dragon Blue Darien vis Babessa."

Lemorel gave a cry of delight, then seized the girl selling the dashpapers and whirled her around, sending papers fluttering in all directions. She gave the startled girl three silver nobles and kissed her, then ran all the way back to Libris.

After some days of savage fighting, the war over the bypass developed into a standoff that dragged over weeks. As was usual in wars, the Call wreaked a heavy toll on the confusion of the battlefield, claiming more victims than disease or fighting. Billiatt was too small to fight an extended war and because its first attack

failed, the Alliance mayors had time to decide on a united response and fall in behind Renmark and Rochester. The paraline west was reopened within a fortnight, and after his army suffered five thousand casualties in two battles attempting to sever it again, the Castellan of Billiatt sued for peace. The terms of the peace treaty were humiliating, but he signed nevertheless. Were his army to be further weakened, his own throne would not be long in falling. Buffer strips of territory were ceded to Renmark and Brookfield to insure the safety of the paraline bypass.

For Rochester it was a narrow but important victory. The initial attack had been beaten back more by luck and bravery than sheer strength, so the other Alliance mayors still did not see Mayor Jefton as a serious new rival. Rochester was the keeper of Alliance accounts and that was that.

Throughout the Southeast Alliance general prosperity followed the war. The citizens of Rochester were too busy making money to notice the minor changes to the mayorate's central library, and even within Libris itself a stability of sorts developed as the Calculor established itself as a strange but useful member of the staff. Only an elite few realized that its influence extended far beyond Rochester and over much of the known world.

The Calculor's impact on the Central Confederation was subtle but profound. Gradually it worked its way into the running of the paraline network, coordinating rail traffic and optimizing carrying capacity with new timetables that were almost miraculous in efficiency. It also made itself indispensable to the beamflash network, generating codes and translation tables faster and more reliably than the Griffith Beamflash Academy had ever managed, and optimizing beamflash traffic in parts of the network under Rochester's direct control.

By the time the political implications of Rochester controlling such vital resources became clear to the other mayors it was economically impossible to return to the old ways. Everyone was making more money than before and the services were far more reliable. If it came to the worst and Mayor Jefton tried to hold the paraline and beamflash services to ransom, his mayorate could easily be crushed by a combined army of the other mayorates.

All librarians working on the Calculor were subject to random surveillance by the Black Runners, and once it became operational they were required to sleep in the Libris hostelry and nowhere else. This suited Lemorel very well. Libris protected her from outside inquiry, and her only contact with her past was the letters she exchanged with her father. His news was all good: business was booming and Jemli had married and left home. Lemorel spent long hours in the Calculor rooms, studied diligently at the University, and kept Glasken a secret.

They saw each other so infrequently that the Black Runners had no mention of Glasken on Lemorel's personal file. Both worked for a living, Lemorel with the Calculor during the day and Glasken in the taverns at night. When they

did meet it was between lectures. At the end of 1697 Glasken failed a subject and was faced with another year of study. Lemorel was relieved. The arrangement of their liaison suited her well. Having Darien away suited her too. She knew that it would be difficult to be quite such a close friend to her as before now that John Glasken had entered her life.

As Libris took over more and more of the paraline scheduling, the Dragon Librarians became deeply involved with far-flung lines and nations. Although she had no voice, Darien was an accomplished linguist and as long as there was someone who could read her cards she could communicate in many languages.

Two months after the defeat of Billiatt, Darien was brought back to Rochester and made a Deputy Overliber, and she and Morkundar were decorated by Mayor Jefton for bravery in his service. Being both a war hero and a Kooree, Morkundar was made Rochester's ambassador to the Woomera mayorates where there happened to be a Kooree overmayor in office. Darien had dragged the Brookfield envoy to safety when he had been shot in the dash to the cover of the wind engine, and the Highliber was anxious to give the heroes on her staff as much public exposure as possible. Darien spent only weeks in Rochester before being sent west again as a fully commissioned Inspector. This time it was to work on an even bigger project to link the beamflash terminus at Peterborough to Woomera's beamflash network. Three immense stone-and-timber repeater towers were to be built, and her task was to reconcile the transmission protocols and linguistic differences between the beamflash networks of the two systems. At the opening of the link on the summer solstice of 1699, Darien stood beside the Highliber in the beamflash gallery of the Rochester tower while Mayor Jefton exchanged pleasantries with the Mayor of Woomera. The link between them was eleven repeater towers and 660 miles in length. Rochester was becoming the center of the world in a very real sense.

Darien was only given a month to write her report on the project before she was assigned to something even more remote and ambitious: the linking of the railside towers on the immense Nullarbor paraline to forge a beamflash link to the mayorates of the distant west. Long sections of the line were already linked, but the number of towers had to be reduced to make high-speed traffic economically viable. A prime site for a massively upgraded tower was the Maralinga Railside, over 300 miles west of Woomera.

The Call was intense at Maralinga Railside, and came as often as once in five days. Maralinga was the biggest, most remote and most beautiful of the outposts on the Nullarbor paraline. It was a magnificent sight from the approaching wind trains, standing tall and bright, like a gleaming cluster of pinkish salt crystals on the flat, scrubby Nullarbor Plain. It was built from sawn limestone blocks, with one tower twice as high as the others to monitor the approach of distant wind trains.

When Darien arrived it was by wind train. A legacy of Greatwinter was that the wind was almost continuous on the Nullarbor Plain, and the rotor engines hardly ever had to be augmented by expensive navvy power. The slatted rotors would turn no matter what direction the wind came from, and although the trains were sometimes slow, they were never becalmed. Balance booms extended to either side, and eight staggered rotors spun in the steady southwest wind.

The driver's cabin was set back from the buffers, and he glanced over the readings on his dials as the approach stones passed on his right. He called readings to the engineer, who in turn shouted orders to the gearjacks at each of the rotors. The train lurched and shuddered as gears bathed in sunflower oil clanked into lower ratios and the speed diminished. A pinpoint of light flickered at the summit of the highest tower, and on top of the cabin the train's watchman began a heliostat exchange.

/ POINTS SWITCHED FOR DOCKING OF WESTWARD HI09 / the tower announced.

/ ACKNOWLEDGED—SWITCHING TO LOWER RATIOS FOR AP-PROACH / the watchman replied.

/ ARRIVAL OF DEPUTY OVERLIBER DARIEN VIS BABESSA EX-PECTED / the tower inquired.

/ CONFIRMED / the watchman assured the Maralinga signalers.

Deputy Overliber Darien was the lowest-ranking, most recently appointed Overliber in the known world, yet a woman of quite some importance nonetheless.

None of the railsides on the Nullarbor paraline were heavily fortified, despite evidence of a distant but warlike civilization beyond the northern desert. The Call reached as far as that, yet the desert robbed it of most of its victims and hardly a week passed without the watchman in the Maralinga tower sighting new corpses. There were dead camels with harnesses of woven green silk and gold thread, bearing dead riders buckled into saddles encrusted with lustrous black opal plates. Some dead warriors clutched saberines made of steel that even the advanced technology of Rochester's artisans could not duplicate, and their camels' sand anchors contained very fine clockwork. In the saddlebags were brass telescopes, silk veils woven with the images of fortified towns cut into cliffs of red rock, and books. A powerful, alien civilization, but too remote to be a threat, or to trade with.

The train rattled over the points as it turned off into the Maralinga siding; then the gearjacks spun their crank handles to screw down the brake blocks against the wheels. The train came to a screeching but smooth stop with the buffers of the wind engine within inches of the emergency retainer. The rotors continued to free-spin in the steady wind, waiting for the gears to be engaged again. The guard blew his whistle, signaling that the doors could be opened in safety.

Darien stepped onto the platform first, sweating in her Inspector's uniform

of black tunic and britches. The silver armband of her Dragon Silver rank gleamed in the sun, and she carried her Overliber's commission to present to the Stationmaster. She was greeted by six controllers, half of the Maralinga staff. They were honored to have such an important guest; in fact they were honored to have a guest at all. Because she had no voice they chattered nervously.

"Here comes the shunting engine," the Railside Master said, and he pointed to a short red wind engine with two white rotor towers that was approaching from the staging yard. "It will take your personal coach from the back of the train and pull it to a siding."

The shunting engine clanged into the coach's couplings, and the crew unhitched it from the train. With a crash the gearings beneath both wind rotors were switched to reverse and her coach was drawn off. She was committed to stay now, and her welcome was the heat, the flies, the fine gritty dust on the relentless wind, the stench of rancid lubricating oil, and the chatter of six nervous strangers. Other passengers began to disembark for a brief walk on solid ground before the train pulled out again. The porter opened the shutters of a little kiosk filled with souvenirs, candied fruit, and jars of cistern water. A crowd quickly collected.

"You can take off your body anchor, Frelle Overliber," the Watermonger said as they began to walk from the platform to the buildings of the railside. "There's a mercy wall to the south, and a Call is unlikely for several days."

She turned. A great circular wall encircled the railside, with interlocked wings to allow wind trains to pass through. At the southernmost point was a tiled shelter. The Call always came from the south here. If it had come at that very moment, they would have all blindly walked south until reaching the mercy wall and been directed to the shelter. She unbuckled her body anchor and the Watermonger proudly carried the ticking mechanism for her.

The railside was amazingly cool within. Gleaming limestone walls reflected the worst of the sun's heat away, and convective ventilation ducts were built into every building. They climbed two floors to the observation terrace, where the Provindor had laid out the coffee setting at a table overlooking the shunting yard. As the Railmaster went through the formalities of the coffee ceremony Darien watched the wind train preparing to depart. The shunting engine was returning and a few passengers were being herded back aboard. The little engine crashed into the rear carriage's couplings with an echoing boom, the guard blew his whistle, and the rapidly spinning rotors on the express engine suddenly slowed as the gears were engaged. Slowly the line of green-and-yellow-striped carriages began to back out of the buffers, and the train rumbled back onto the main line, rattling over the points and stopping with a shudder of brakes. The shunting engine was uncoupled, the yard inspector blew his whistle twice, and the train moved off, resuming its journey west. The shunting engine pushed for a few yards, then dropped behind to return to the staging yard.

"... Which brings us to your business, Frelle Overliber. What can we do to assist with your visit?"

Darien had a folder full of cards already prepared. She selected the appropriate card and handed it to him.

I APOLOGIZE FOR HAVING NO VOICE. THANK YOU FOR YOUR TROUBLE. I SHALL NEED ONLY SOME SPACE IN YOUR LIBRARY AND ACCESS TO THE ENTIRE RAILSIDE. I HAVE A SURVEY TO DO. THE MAYORS OF ROCHESTER AND WOOMERA REQUIRE THIS RAILSIDE TO BE EXTENDED.

He handed the card onto the Watermonger, and it was passed among the others as he continued the conversation.

"Frelle Deputy Overliber, I am gratified that my requests for extensions to the yards, cisterns, and warehouses have been recognized by His Highness the Mayor and your own monarch. I shall prepare a memo of thanks at once for you to take back to court."

Darien had not been briefed about his request, so now she had to correct a misunderstanding. She began writing on a blank card with a charblack stylus. The monitors waited eagerly, yet she would not let herself be forced into undignified scribble. At last she handed the note across.

THE EXTENSIONS ARE NOTHING TO DO WITH YOUR REQUEST, ALTHOUGH WHAT YOU PROPOSE IS ENCOMPASSED BY THEM.

While he puzzled over the words she selected another card.

THE MAIN SIGNAL TOWER IS TO BE TRIPLED IN HEIGHT. THE STAFF WILL BE INCREASED TOO. OTHER FACILITIES WILL BE EXPANDED ACCORDINGLY.

"But that's wonderful!" exclaimed the Railmaster. Before he could say anything more she handed him yet another prepared card.

MARALINGA RAILSIDE WILL BE RECLASSIFIED AS A FIRST-CLASS OUTPOST. IF ANY CURRENT MEMBERS OF THE STAFF WISH TO RETAIN THEIR RELATIVE RANK THEY WILL HAVE TO SIT FOR EXAMINATIONS.

The mood changed abruptly as the card made its rounds, almost as if the controllers had allowed themselves to be struck dumb in honor of their mute, distinguished guest.

Darien based herself in the library for the next four days, as she made a detailed inspection of the main tower against the original plans. Her findings confirmed what the planning consentium in Libris already suspected. The foundations were inadequate to support a new structure, and much of the existing stonework was built to interlock on the existing height-to-weight ratio. It would be quicker and easier to dig new foundations and build a new stone tower. On the other hand a timber extension could be added without straining the foundations. It could also be completed in a tenth of the time that a new stone tower would take.

The bearers of bad news are never popular with those who suffer the con-

sequences. Apart from meals and formal coffee Darien was shunned by the sulking controllers, and she spent the evenings going through the library's collection of books found with the bodies in the desert. The enigmatic books were in what she knew as a dialect of the Northmoors, Ghan nomadic. They painted an exotic but severe picture of the distant society. Honor, service, loyalty, and ruthless discipline among warriors held the various nations together in a harsh and arid land. Women and children were cloistered and protected past the point of imprisonment. Much of the romantic poetry was about yearning and longing, of love unfulfilled, of secret notes smuggled past watchful elders. Women could only travel by cart or sedan chair if they ventured beyond the compound of a building. It was fascinating yet repelling for Darien. She was, after all, a powerful woman, holding the careers of a dozen men in her hands as she wrote out her recommendations and reports.

On the morning of the fourth day she had just dressed and was preparing for the day's work when the Call swept over the railside. There was a sweet and familiar feeling of falling away into surrender, followed by waking to bruises and torn fingernails. It had caught her in a corridor, but she had been attached to a shackle rail by her waist tether. Buildings were dangerous. Without a tether one might walk to the southernmost window and fall several floors during a Call. Darien awoke on the thick carpet of the library, bound hand and foot!

It was impossible. Nobody could have walked about freely while the Call swept over the railside. The others were awake and calling out now. The Railmaster, the Watermonger, the mechanics, all were shouting that they had been bound during the Call. Then she heard slow, shambling footsteps in the cloisters outside. A thing out of a nightmare stopped at the doorway and peered in at her through mirrors set a handspan apart on its face, its eyes gleaming in the depths of the reflections.

"So, one woman among twelve men," it said in a deep, muffled voice. It was a language borrowing heavily from the North Mulgarian tongue in accent, but was pure Ghan nomadic in structure.

"Your people's language makes no sense to me," the thing went on, yet she could have done nothing but stare in reply, even if she had had a voice. A man completely enmeshed in living vines, vines that were trained, grown and woven to cover him like a suit, a man wearing a jacket of olive-green leaves and thick, cumbersome knee-boots which smelled of wet soil and mulch. His arms tapered into mittens of finely woven tendrils.

The Call beckoned to all living things larger than a cat, so that a man walking about freely during a Call was no less amazing to Darien than levitation. The black Kooree nomads of the northern deserts were known to go into a trance when the Call seized them, collapsing to the ground for two hours. Thus they escaped the Call, but they did not resist it. Darien stared in amazement. The man

wore a living robe: did that make him immune to the Call's allure? She had been bound during the Call, what else could explain it? The consequences screamed within her mind: his suit was a weapon that nothing could stand against.

Very soon other Ghans swarmed into the railside. They were dressed in robes like those of the bodies in the desert, and they reeked of perspiration and camel. Darien was carried into the cloisters with the railside's staff. None of the Ghans could speak their tongue, and none of the staff could understand the Ghans. This was established after an hour of beatings, kicks, and shouting. They also realized that Darien was mute, but not that she understood everything they said.

"So this is the source of the Call," declared Kharec, their captain. "It comes from the strips of iron in the desert."

"Not so, Captain," said the man clothed in vines. There was a sudden hiss of many breaths sharply drawn, and Kharec turned on him.

"You question my word, vineman?" he snapped.

"I would never question your *informed* word, Captain. It is just that I know what you do not. I saw a feral goat in the grip of the Call cross those metal rails and continue south. You could not have seen that, being in the Call's grip yourself."

Kharec turned away from the man of vines and mirrored eyes, and the tension dissipated. He had saved face and was satisfied. Kharec was powerful and dangerous, yet the other had the confidence of one who knows that he is indispensable.

"Frelle Overliber, can you understand them?" whispered the Railmaster, who was lying beside Darien. She shook her head as Kharec strode up and kicked him in the face.

"So you can't speak the Alspring tongue!" he shouted at them. "Well that's sign language for *no whispering*."

Darien was taken away to the Railmaster's quarters, where she was chained to the eyebolt beside the bed. Kharec strode about the room, puzzling over the equipment, books, and maps; then he stood staring at her.

"A woman with no voice, a woman who cannot answer back. Such a luxury." He said this to another who never left his side, a small, relaxed, but observant man who seemed more of a spy than a bodyguard. Darien had expected to be ravished then and there, but they left without another word.

The Ghans hastily fortified the railside, posting lookouts and barricading outer windows and doors. There were forty of them, including the vineman. Darien was forced to cook and wait upon them, and thus she heard most of their discussions. They argued about the nature of the paralines, about the source of the dried meat and fruit in the stores, even about the limestone blocks that the railside was built from. The vineman stayed outside in the sun while the others gorged themselves on the stores and water. They had taken three months to reach

the railside, and had come due south across an immense expanse of sand, stunted scrub, and saltpans. There had been very little water along the way, and almost no game. Some of the Kooree nomad tribes had attacked the Ghans and had killed at least a dozen.

After the evening meal on the first day Kharec held a council with his officers. Darien served water from the deepest, coldest cistern . . . and coffee. They knew coffee, but it appeared to have the value of gold in their society. She learned that Kharec was looking for new lands to conquer. The Ghan kingdoms had been at peace for eighteen years, and their rulers wished to retain that peace. Thus ambitious nobles could not better themselves by conquest, and because Kharec was the youngest son of a noble family he could expect little from inheritance either. If he could find unaligned cities to attack, however, he could have conquests without violating any truce. Oddly enough, the Ghans were officially on a scientific expedition, and were funded by a woman whom they called the Abbess. Both the man who shadowed Kharec and the vineman were her personal agents, but Kharec was the commander.

They could make little sense of the railside or paraline. The wind engines, wagons, and carriages were made to roll along the rails, but there were no camels to pull them!

''The place is built as solidly as a fort, yet the gates and doors are wide and undefended,'' Kharec declared, scowling. ''If their towns are as badly guarded, we could make quick strikes and carry off enough gold to raise a force of five hundred lancers. Then we could return and conquer these mice and make a new kingdom. It seems too easy. Why haven't others done it already?''

''But where are the cities?'' asked Calderen, the oldest officer. ''There are no roads, only that pair of iron bars laid from horizon to horizon.''

''I have found maps. There are marks and lines that cannot be anything else but cities and roads.''

''But we cannot read them, and none of these people here speak Alspring. We don't even know which dot on a map is *this* place.''

''There is a way. Yuragii has made a discovery.''

Kharec let the words hang. The officers looked from one to the other, then back to Kharec. Before the short, thin officer could explain, Kharec clapped twice for Darien's attention, then pointed to a tray of food and gestured to the observation terrace where the vineman sat basking in the horizontal rays of the sunset.

She walked out of the hall, changed her tether to the outside shackle rail, then climbed the stone stairs to the terrace.

''Ah, someone remembered me,'' the vineman said as she stood before him with the tray. He did something with the vines and tendrils over his mouth, then lifted a flap to reveal his lips.

''A good and simple system,'' he said, taking a goblet of water from the

tray. "If a Call comes while I hold the flap open, I will drop it even as I respond to the Call, and so will be protected by this suit again. Hmm, such a serious little face. You do not understand a word that I say, do you?"

Something in his manner was reassuring, and Darien smiled at him.

"A smile for me. How pleasant. Not many people smile at me when I wear my vines. The last to smile for me was a lady in Glenellen, a very important lady. She is the abbess of a great convent, one of our centers of learning. Ah yes, she smiled at me, but then she is very strange herself. She eats grilled mice on toast and washes her hair in oils of nightshade. Such hair, it hangs in black curls and reaches past her waist."

A woman who could rise to such a position of power in his society would be truly remarkable, Darien thought. He began to eat, taking dates and roasted nuts from the tray and crunching them beneath his mask of woven vines. The sun struck crimson highlights from the mirrors and tubes that led down to his eyes, then winked beneath the horizon. In the gathering shadows his human outline was even less distinct, and he became an animate plant preying on the dates and nuts with deliberate, rustling movements.

"Has Kharec raped you? I should think not, Makkigi watches him like a hawk. Our patroness is the Abbess of Scalattera Convent in Glenellen, and she paid for this expedition. She said that an expedition with a woman as its patron must not result in any other woman being raped. Makkigi was sent along to make sure that Kharec complies. I am watching him too."

Darien lit an olive-oil thumblamp with her striker and held it up for him to eat by. He leaned closer, and his mirrors peered at her face. For an instant she saw two eyes, gleaming at the bottom of the dark tubes by the smoky flame; then he straightened again. There was cursing and rowdy singing echoing down the corridors.

"Isn't that a funny story? A pity that you cannot understand me, it would reassure you a little. Ah, you are perhaps thirty-three, I can see that: your face is beautiful with experience, rather than innocence. Do you hate me? Yes, you must, but I am not like the rest. I am a scholar, would you have thought it? My teacher is the great Abbess Theresla of Glenellen herself."

The one-sided conversation continued until he handed the tray back to her and gave a rustling bow. Then, as she picked up her thumblamp he took her by the wrist and raised her little lamp to one of his mirrors. All at once light glowed from beneath the woven vines that covered his face, reflected by the mirrors just below his eyes. His eyes and the upper part of his face were visible, as if through a veil lit from behind. His grip was gentle; he wanted to reassure her that a human lived beneath the woven vines.

"I am blinded by the flame," he said as he lowered the lamp and released her. "How ironic. I must be dazzled so that you may see my face."

. . .

The vineman turned out to be right about Kharec. For all of the time that the Ghan lancers were at Maralinga Railside he did no more than slap Darien about and force her to do menial tasks. A Deputy Overliber under the protection of an abbess hundreds of miles away: the irony was not lost on her. Only the night before the Call had come she had shuddered at the strictures on women in the distant Ghan society as she read their books.

The screaming started on the morning after the railside had been invaded. It was the Provindor's voice at first, then it was joined by that of the Railmaster, and soon all the staff were screaming in agony. As the hours passed the voices grew less and less recognizable. The cries were pleading yet hopeless, the cries of those tortured pointlessly. Darien did not realize that they were being tortured to reveal just who had been translating passages of Ghan books in the library.

At the end of the second day Kharec called a meeting of the Ghan officers to discuss what they had learned—which was nothing. Two of the Railside staff were already dead and three more would not last another day, yet still nobody would answer them in their own language. Darien served, cowered, and was ignored. The days passed, and although her reward for feigning slow wits and incomprehension was kicks and slaps, she alone was not tortured. When not cooking or serving she was kept in a hostelry room overlooking the observation terrace where the vineman sat sunning himself.

At mealtimes she always took food to the vineman as he sat in the sun, reading books from his saddlebags and writing notes on reed-pith paper with a charblack stylus. He always had a few words for her. On the evening of the third day his patience with Kharec ran out.

"It is as well that you understand none of this," he said as Darien gave him his tray of dried fruits and water. His voice was so low that it was almost inaudible beneath his mask of woven vines. "Kharec is torturing your people because he knows someone here can speak our language. A copy of one of our holy books was found in the library with a partial translation into your language beside it. Your people are brave, none will admit to it."

Horror crawled over her with tiny, icy feet. So *she* had been the cause of all that the controllers were going through. She could stop it at once by merely writing a note and showing it to Kharec, yet she knew what he wanted, too. He wanted maps translated and interpreted so that he could find settlements to attack. Let the torture continue or betray her own people: she struggled between the ghastly alternatives for a moment before the vineman came to her rescue.

"I killed them, just now," he went on, looking south. "I gave each of them water laced with enough banegold crystals dissolved in it to kill a camel. Your people were staked out in the sun with their fingernails and toenails torn out, and ants feeding on the wounds. I ended their agony."

Now he turned to Darien and saw the tears on her cheeks.

"You are crying," he said gently. "Do you think I'm a monster? But you cannot know what I am saying, so . . . why? Are you afraid of this man of rustling vines and leaves? A monster!" She sat very still. "Monster. Do you know monsters?"

He gestured to himself, then to her head, then reared over her with his arms up. HIM—I THINK—MONSTER, Darien guessed, then managed a smile and shook her head.

"You don't think I'm a monster?" he exclaimed.

She pointed to where his mouth was, then to her ears, then stroked one of her hands with the other.

"Ah, you think I've got a kind voice. Well, thank you." He bowed with a great rustling of leaves and tendrils. "How deceptive voices can be. I confess to murder, yet I do it in a kind voice and a strange language, so you think me not a monster. If you knew that I'd poisoned your people you would feel differently. They did nothing but scream and plead in your language no matter what the torturer did to them . . . so I killed them through kindness. How I wish that the truth went no further than that, but there were greater issues guiding my fingers to the poison jar.

"Had your unknown linguist broken, it would have endangered the expedition. Kharec would have learned where your towns are and would have turned aside to plunder them. I could not allow that, so I had to kill. The Abbess Theresla wants us to find out where the Call comes from, so we must continue south. I am the right hand of the Abbess, I can reach across the harshest deserts and over the edge of hell for her. To be the instrument of her will, ah, it makes me become alive. When she looks out over the edge of the world into the very lips of the Call, it will be through *my* eyes. How lucky for me that she was born female, and that I must see, hear, fight, thirst, starve, and kill for her."

He shook a mass of verdure that might have been a fist, and his mirrors turned to the south as if he were defying the source of the Call. Darien could see the strength and pride within him, but she could also see a woman of immense power and charisma behind him. He turned back to her.

"Do you want to know how I killed them? Ah, I was very clever. I told Kharec that your people would not live long enough to have their wills broken, what with the way they were being treated. I offered them water from my own waterskin, but Kharec had me seized, unlaced the vines masking my lips, and forced me to drink half of my own water. All morning he had me watched, yet I did not drink any phial of antidote, and I did not die. At noon he called me the turd of a diseased camel and left to bathe in the cool waters of one of your cisterns. The guards let your people drink from my waterskin, then gave it back to me. Here it is, here."

He raised the nearly empty waterskin and drank what was left.

"Only a few drops, yet enough to kill you two or three times over, my pretty flatterer. Hah, but I have been adding a little banegold to my water for years, so to me it has become just an exotic flavor. How long have we been here now? Three days? Soon Kharec will lose patience and decide to move on. You will be slain before we leave, he has already ordered that. Now there is irony for you: under the charter of the Abbess you can be killed, but not raped."

Darien's heart seemed to plunge through the flagstones as he spoke. She was going to be killed, yet his voice was level and calm. Decades of life, study, struggle, love, and achievement were going to become nothing with the slash of a blade, yet he did not care! He stood up and loomed over her. Seeing fear in her face, he chose to interpret her terror as fear of him.

"You fear me, pretty, nameless scullion," he said gently, then backed off a pace. "Very silly of you. Not only will I not hurt you, but I shall make sure that nobody else does. I am not a man, you see, I am the hands of the great Abbess and she would always protect you."

He was being casual about her death because he was going to save her! The swirling vortex of emotions within her suddenly broke Darien's self-control. Tears left shining tracks down her cheeks in the light of her little lamp. She hung her head and began to sob. The vineman stepped forward again and the leaves rustled loudly as he patted her shoulder. She looked up.

"You must help yourself, though. I shall make sure that Kharec is the first out of this strange fortress. When you get free you must run and hide. Understand?"

He made a cutting motion over her tether, then did a lumbering run on the spot. She nodded that she understood.

"It is good to be within stone walls again," he said, looking out over the desert. "At Glenellen we have a fine city, all cut out of red stone. Deep red sandstone walls, as red as the blood from an enemy's artery and reflected in the cobalt waters of the gorge. You could not imagine how pretty it is. The black Kooree nomads call it Jupla, they say that it is where the first humans emerged from the earth. The road to the governor's palace is lined with macrozamia cycads to signify long life to our rulers, and the courtyards and terraces of the convent are shaded by livistona palms and drooping ironwood trees. Covered stone irrigation canals water orchards of date palms, while grapevines grow in terraced gardens right up the side of the gorge. The suit that I wear is descended from a grapevine. It was fashioned by the Abbess Theresla.

"I am her hands, her legs, her ears and eyes. By our sacred laws she can go nowhere and I can go everywhere. I am devout, my pretty one, I read our sacred scriptures every day and I follow them to the very word. Yet . . . I also like being a protector, I do not do it just to obey the holy word. You are helpless, so I shall keep you safe. I am the right hand of the Abbess, reaching out to protect you."

The deaths of the controllers bought Darien extra time. Kharec had the two lancers who had been guarding them seized and tortured. They quickly confessed to the killings, yet could not say where they obtained the banegold poison. Their torture continued through the night and into the next day.

The vineman was also under suspicion, yet his value was too great for him to be harmed. Kharec ranted and fumed and threatened, and finally had him confined. A Call tether was threaded among the large stem vines at his back, and padlocked to an eyebolt in the courtyard where he passed the hours sunning himself. Darien watched them arguing from the window of her hostelry room, listening carefully to the distant voices.

"I don't like you being free during Calls," Kharec said as he impotently paced the gleaming white flagstones.

"But during a Call only I can move freely. Who will now creep into enemy fortresses and lay them open for you? Who will rescue your men if their camels' sand anchors fail during a Call?"

"You place too much faith in your value, vineman. These people are as timid as rabbits, and easily conquered. As for rescues during Calls, I think the men have come to depend too heavily on you. Having you confined will give them reason to maintain their sand anchors and timers better." His voice was raised: his words were meant as much for the unseen ears of his lancers as for the vineman.

The vineman could now only move beyond the courtyard by tearing the vines of his suit, or by unlacing the front and getting out of it. If he did either during a Call he would be as vulnerable as any other mortal. Darien left the window and lay on her bed, but the voices still reached her clearly above the light bluster of the desert wind.

"If I have no more value, why bother to keep me?" the muffled voice of the vineman asked calmly.

"Kill you when you may be innocent? I am deeply hurt, vineman. You may be under suspicion, but no more than that. I am a fair and just leader."

"Besides, using me you can open up any fortress without losing a single man, or risking your own—"

"Don't press my patience, vineman. You will not be tortured, but your baggage will be searched. If banegold poison is found among your bundles of books, instruments, and fertilizer then—"

A Call swept over Maralinga Railside. Darien tumbled away from the horrors of her captivity into oblivion, then awoke with her waist chaffed from struggling against her locked tether. Outside the lancers stirred and cursed. This Call had been the first since the Ghan raid on the railside.

"Captain Kharec!" someone suddenly cried. There were other cries of "Gone!" and "His tether must have snapped."

The vineman's muffled voice shouted for their attention.

"Listen to me, listen well! The Captain's tether was carelessly fastened. I saw it come apart, I saw him go south with the Call."

"But you should have stopped him!" someone bellowed.

"He had me fastened here by the very vines that make me immune to the Call. What could I do?"

Now Calderen cried out. "Go down to the mercy wall at the south, he will have been stopped under the shelter at the junction." Three lancers hurried off to fetch Kharec. They returned in great distress.

"One of the camels broke free from the stable and was guided into the apex shelter by the mercy wall," one of them wailed. "Captain Kharec must have climbed onto its back, then reached the roof of the shelter. The tiles were broken where he got through and over the wall."

Calderan took command, yet the vineman was the real leader. He ordered his tether cut, then had the two tortured guards released. Calderan was a loyal and dedicated officer, and was adamant on one matter: Kharec had to be rescued. Oddly enough, the vineman seemed eager to help.

"The sweep of the Call is six miles deep, and once you enter it you will be trapped in the Call yourself. I am the only one who can save him."

"You must leave now, take a squad of ten and ride hard—"

"No! This is totally unknown country, so we must remain at full strength when we leave. Tonight the Call will stop, and become a malaise zone. We will keep moving in the darkness, until we reach the edge of the malaise, then I will go on alone."

"But you might not find him in the dark, over all that area."

"Precisely, that is why we must leave together. The search may take many days and nights, and could be dangerous. We may not even be able to return this way."

"What about that mute woman?"

"What about her?"

"She could write an account of what happened here for her own people. Send someone to kill her."

His words stabbed through Darien like a knife through her breast, as sharp as the blade that would follow in a few minutes. She sat up, thinking only of staying alive. Soon someone would come and she had to escape, hide, or fight. She could jam the bed against the door, gain a few moments. She would die fighting! She turned to the bed—and there was a key and a double-barreled flint-lock lying beside it!

Even as Darien snatched up the gun the outer latch rattled and the officer Yuragii entered. He was leering, already gathering up the front of his robes. She held the gun behind her, fumbling to draw the strikers back to be fully cocked.

"Now don't be afraid, you don't know how lucky you are," he crooned in a genuinely pleasant voice.

I'm only afraid of the recoil, she replied to herself. The gun had half-inch-bore barrels, far larger than any she had been trained to use during her Overliber accreditation. Suddenly his gaze turned to the bed, where the key to her tether still lay. At that moment she brought the gun around, gripped it in both hands, and fired.

Only one barrel went off, but Yuragii slowly doubled over amid clouds of gunsmoke. The others were slow in coming, thinking that the shot had been his. As Yuragii hit the floor Darien snatched up the key and was soon safely hidden in the maze that was the railside.

She watched the Ghan lancers leave from a hidden vantage. Calderen was in the lead, terrified of actually being in charge after a lifetime of orders from others. Makkigi seemed lost, now that he did not have Kharec to spy upon. She counted the riders: thirty-seven, with three camels being led. A telescope revealed that two lancers rode unsteadily, obviously the guards who had been tortured . . . and sure enough, one lancer was a straw mockup wearing robes. Somewhere in the railside there was a lancer, hidden and aware that she was dangerous. He would be an experienced, ruthless warrior, and he would shoot to kill if he caught sight of her.

Darien began to write on a sheet of parchment, choosing her words carefully. The first lines were for whoever found the note:

"On the authority of Deputy Overliber Darien vis Barbessa of Libris in Rochester, this note is to be sent by beamflash to Rochester with the highest priority."

Some coded blocks of routing information followed, along with a valid beamflash authority number. After that was a thousand words of neatly written code which would be intelligible to anyone using the Calculor.

That night Darien crept out to the wind-engine shed. The shunting engine's brakes were screwed down tight and its rotors collapsed down into the primary drums and locked against the wind that blew through the double-ended shed. Working in total darkness she slowly cranked the tubular rotors up to their full height and unlocked them. The wind spun them up to a good operating speed. She tied a thin cord to a buffer to hold the engine steady on the rails and rigged the timer from her body anchor to the gearlever of one of the rotors. She set it for just after dawn, then unscrewed the brakes. Before she stepped off the engine Darien tied her parchment note to the master gearlever with bright red ribbon. The next person to enter the cabin could not miss it.

She settled down to wait in the kiosk on the railside's platform. Somewhere in the railside a lancer was hiding, waiting for her to emerge. All the food had been cleared away, probably to the kitchens. She would have to eat eventually, and he would be hiding somewhere with a good view, waiting. The sky brightened. She had the platform bell and two long sniper muskets on the floor beside her. Sunlight streamed over the horizon. It would shine in the eyes of anyone running after the shunting engine.

There was a dull clang as the timer released the gear lever, which engaged the forward rotor. The wind engine snapped its cord as the tubular rotor powered the wheels and it moved forward with a deep rumble. Darien began to ring the railside bell, but stopped as the shunter rattled over the points and east along the main line. In the distance she saw the Ghan lancer scramble out of the railside entrance and run across the staging yard, robes flapping and musket held high as he stumbled over the rails.

It was all so simple for the Ghan. The engine was moving, so she was obviously escaping on it. Luckily it was slow enough for a running man to catch. Women were such easy opponents, he panted to himself with satisfaction; they knew nothing of tactics or feints. He was thirty feet away when Darien squeezed the trigger. The wind scoured the smoke away to reveal his body sprawled in the pinkish sand. She aimed the second musket and took a bead on his head, shivering with revulsion at the idea of shooting a dead man, yet . . . click-boom!

Darien emerged from the kiosk holding the vineman's double-barrel red flint-lock and approached the body. The right side of his head was a bloody mess; he was definitely dead. She turned the body over. There was no other wound, the first shot had missed! Great, gasping sobs burst through Darien's self-control, and she collapsed to her hands and knees. Her tears left dark craters in a drift of powdery, pink limestone sand.

The wind engine rumbled off into the distance and Darien made no attempt to stop it. With a particularly good wind and no coaches at all it rapidly gathered speed and rolled past Irmana within three hours. The duty switchman only realized that there was nobody on the engine when it was too late, and nothing could be done to stop it. The switchman at Jumel was caught by surprise as well, but this time there was a beamflash link to the next railside. At Warrion they were ready when the runaway arrived.

The switchman set an iron lever in a slot beside the track and nearly half a mile farther on a driver was waiting. The engine hurtled out of the west, and the trackblock brake's release arm clanged into the iron lever beside the track. Hard-wood blocks swung down to jam under the rear wheels, yet the engine was traveling so fast that the blocks belched smoke and burst into flame with the friction. In half a mile the engine had slowed to a walking pace, its rotors straining to drive it forward while smoke streamed from its wheels. A driver ran beside the track and easily swung himself aboard. When he disengaged the gears to the wind rotors he noticed the note tied with red ribbon, and as he took the engine into the railside's siding he read Darien's instructions.

Because Warrion was within the newly expanded beamflash network it took only a few minutes for the first phrases of Darien's message to be routed to the clearing center at Woomera. Soon it was passing through the galleries of the towers that Darien had helped to establish; then its header crossed the border of the Southeast Alliance at Renmark and flashed east across the grasslands and

eucalypt forests to the tower at Rochester. Here one of Darien's codes routed the message straight down to the Calculor's receptor. It was decoded, and soon an astonished operator sent an alarm to the Highliber's study.

As Zarvora was reading the first decoded words, the eastbound express train was approaching Maralinga and Darien was waiting to flag it down. There were ten reserve musketeers among the passengers, and they stayed to guard the railside with her while the express continued east for help.

Three days later help arrived in the form of a wind train from Woomera carrying twelve dozen more musketeers and twenty lancers. More important, there were also six demi-terriers that were too small to be affected by the Call. The dogs were trained to attack anything not mindlessly straining to wander along with a Call, such as rats that had learned when humans were helpless. The vineman would no longer have the world to himself during Calls, and if only one of the small dogs was able to tear a hole in his suit that would be the end. The demi-terriers were taken to sniff at the place where the vineman had sat sunning himself, and they learned his scent quickly.

 **CODING**

As Darien's message was traveling east, another message began its beamflash journey southwest at the market town of Canowindra in the Central Confederation. Initially it was just a table of figures, a record of network traffic at the Canowindra terminal tower. A clerk used a code book to encrypt the figures, then handed the slate to the transmission supervisor, who took it to the beamflash gallery at the tower's summit. Here he checked the encryption, broke it into ten packets of data, calculated a checksum for each packet, then gave the slate to the relay.

The relay looked through a large telescope pointing east to the Wirrinya repeater tower, sixty miles away. He pressed a key, two long flashes, two short. A concave mirror on the roof focused sunlight through a series of lenses to the shutters attached to the key. The flashing beam of light traveled over the town's markets, the fortified walls, a scatter of vegetable gardens, then rolling hills covered in dusky, olive-green eucalypt forests to the 540-foot Wirrinya tower.

Wirrinya's receptor noted the POLL signal from Canowindra and told the eastward relay to flash the READY code. Canowindra's relay noted the faint, sharp flashing in the blue haze on the horizon, and only now began to key the encrypted table of figures into flashes of light.

•   •   •

Hundreds of miles to the south Lemorel Milderellen sat in the cloisters of Rochester University with John Glasken. Her face was pale, and she was anxiously holding his strong, broad hands.

If Lemorel had lived two thousand years earlier she would have been a doctoral student in computer science, but in the year of Greatwinter's Waning 1699 her thesis was in observational philosophy. Its subject was the shape and movement of the bands of alluring nothingness known as Sweeps of the Call. The movements were those timed and reported by the network of beamflash towers.

"The beamflash traffic table is due to be sent about now," she said in a soft, apologetic voice. "If the figures deviate from the mean, then I must see the Dragon Lady herself."

"So why are you afraid?" Glasken said without concern. "The Highliber's lackey and her cleaner see her every day."

"But not for the reasons that may bring *me* to petition her. I'm just a scholar doing research, yet my research is taking me into international politics. I hate it! I wish that I had your drive and confidence, Johnny. It's you who should be seeing her."

"Lem, you need to go through trials like I have or you'll never develop confidence. Come, let me start you on your way."

It seemed to Lemorel that he always said the wise and right thing, and she felt stronger just being with him. They stood up, and he began to walk her through the cloisters. Glasken cut an impressive figure, tall, strong, and dressed in the height of fashion with blue tunic, possum-fur codpiece, and black academic cloak. He was a desirable accessory for any girl, and she could hardly believe her luck to have him.

"I'll miss your graduation revel," she said sadly. "I'm sorry. I must begin waiting at ten o'clock, and Highliber Zarvora may keep me waiting until evening. Where will you go?"

"Alas, Lem, my friends are taking me to some secret place. I can say nothing for I know nothing."

"I'm glad to have at least attended your graduation ceremony. So you have been John Glasken, Bachelor of Chemistric, for an hour. How does it feel?"

"Not nearly as good as it does to be with you."

They kissed long and gently; then she strode off through the University gardens, past lattices entangled with flowering honeysuckle and jasmine, a small figure in the new black uniform of Libris. A blue band on her upper sleeve showed her acting promotion confirmed.

From the Wirrinya repeater the message was sent fifty-two miles southeast to the Tallimba repeater. Below the signal's path the rolling hills flattened into plains, and the trees of the eucalypt forests became more sparse as the country turned

into dry, scrubby grassland. Another fifty-three-mile stretch took the twinkling flashes across increasingly settled and irrigated land to the great beamflash center at Griffith.

The network of communication towers was vital to the prosperity of the Central Confederation. Its thirty-five nations were scattered over an immense, parched area of the continent, so that anything which reduced the need to travel was a blessing. Why move cattle, gold, dried fruit, or rice between distant centers when debit and credit could be juggled on beams of light? Further, driving herds of cattle was made very difficult by the Call. Its enigmatic beckoning swept across the land at semiregular intervals, luring both herded and herders away. Better to move goods and livestock only when it was unavoidable.

The beamflash towers also helped predict the Call. When a relay stopped sending a regular polling flash, the neighboring tower's receptor knew that a Call was approaching. A bell was tolled, and all within earshot would fasten their Call shackles.

Eight major beamflash lines converged at the gallery of the Griffith tower. There was a duty supervisor for each line, and the Canowindra line's supervisor studied the encrypted message on the receptor's slate as he copied it down.

"The checksums match the message packets for a change," he remarked with mock surprise.

"Be fair, they get most of 'em right," the receptor replied.

"The error rate on the Canowindra line is still four times the average for Confederation towers. There should be an investigation. Backsides should be kicked."

"So? Will it happen?"

"Wait for my annual report. There'll be a big shakeout."

He noted the message in his logbook, then passed the slate to the Rochester line's relay. From Griffith the signal went almost due south, over the yellow tiled roofs of the prosperous city, over flat pasture and tethered flocks tended by tethered shepherds to the river that marked the border with a Southmoor emirate. It crossed grassy plains dotted with the tents, sheep, donkeys, and camels of Southmoor nomads until reaching a tiny, isolated Rochestrian enclave.

The Darlington repeater was fifty-one miles from Griffith, on a plot of land about a mile square. The Southmoors were an Islamic sect that proscribed— among other things—the use of beamflash equipment. A beamflash signal could cross the Sweep of a Call without being affected, and because the Call was suspected to come from God, that was possibly blasphemy. The Emir of Cowra nonetheless leased a little plot of his territory to Rochester for a beamflash repeater tower at Darlington, preferring the Mayor's gold to a clear conscience.

At Darlington the receptor wrote down the message on his slate—but decoded it in his head as he worked. Smiling, he noted the correct checksums, then

unrolled a table of his own and checked the figures. He shook his head. Definitely not for the eyes of Rochester, he decided. His modifications did not take long, and soon the altered message was being flashed over another fifty-six miles of dry, flat Southmoor grasslands to the border tower at Deniliquin.

In the time that it took for the signal to be flashed from Wirrinya to Deniliquin, Lemorel walked the uneven cobblestone streets of Rochester from the University to Libris. Deniliquin was on the border of the Mayorate of Rochester, and a last hop of fifty-eight miles took the signal over a great plain of eucalyptus forest to Rochester City's beamflash tower.

In the Rochester tower's gallery a transceiver keyed pulses of reflected sunlight down a system of mirrors in the core of the tower itself and into the beamflash clearing room. Here a clerk copied the encrypted message onto slates, noted the routing instructions, and passed the slates to a Dragon Red Librarian. This Dragon Red typed the message with a soft pattering of coachwood keys on felt buffers, and beyond the keyboard, the Calculor decoded and stored the table of figures that had begun its journey of nearly 330 miles less than an hour before.

A few minutes more passed; then an array of mechanical hens began pecking holes in several feet of paper tape being drawn beneath their beaks. Lemorel stood beside them, reading the figures in the rows of patterned holes. As she suspected, the data was impossible. She would have to confront the Highliber.

"The beamflash traffic data has been tampered with," Lemorel insisted, timid but brave, saying to herself that this is what John Glasken would have done. She offered a sheaf of papers to Highliber Zarvora. "I need to travel to Griffith to check their beamflash traffic registers. I could also check the Darlington tower on the same trip."

"I'll not sanction a trip to Darlington," the Highliber replied. "Our position there is precarious already. As for Griffith, what you propose is almost as bad. We have spent years convincing their Guild of Relays that the Rochester network can be run by Dragon Librarians alone. If you go across there now and imply that they do not know how to run a beamflash network, they are likely to respond by closing the Griffith-Rochester link."

It had been a long shot. The Highliber would not risk religious riots or diplomatic incidents by allowing a student researcher to blunder about in sensitive areas.

The interview was being held in the study where Zarvora had her personal terminal to the Calculor. Dozens of little metal faces seemed to smirk at Lemorel from the shelves as she sat pleading her case.

"Highliber, someone out there is modifying beamflash-traffic data, data that I need for my thesis on the Call. How can I convince you?"

"You do *not* need to convince me, Frelle Lemorel, I agree," she said, smiling for the first time that Lemorel had ever seen. "When your written petition reached me I did some research of my own using the Calculor. I found anomalies too."

"With the Calculor?"

"Yes. I confirmed in a morning what took you months to—just a moment."

A rabbit had raised a red flag while the fox beside it struck a bell. The Highliber began to tap at her keyboard. Lemorel had never been given unlimited access to the mighty calculating machine itself. So much power! Lemorel thought hungrily. If she had the Highliber's access she could solve her network data mysteries without leaving Rochester.

Abruptly the Calculor dumped several lines of decoded message onto the binary wheels mounted above the keyboard. Lemorel missed part of the message, but not the important part:

/ MARALINGA RAILSIDE SEIZED DURING—REPEAT DURING—CALL. RAILSIDE RETAKEN. REQUEST INSTRUCTIONS. /

The Highliber gasped, then hit the RESET lever for the display wheels. "I have a journey to make, I must leave now," she said as she tapped the TERMINATE switch and turned to Lemorel. "Write out the rest of your submission on the beamflash problem, then let yourself out. I shall tell the guards to give you as long as you want."

Then she was gone in a swirl of black cloth, slamming the door behind her and shouting down the corridor for her lackey. Lemorel could not get the short message on the display wheels out of her mind. A railside outpost seized during a Call, impossible . . . yet if not impossible, fantastic. People who were able to move about freely during a Call could conquer the world. No wonder the Highliber had rushed off to investigate for herself.

Lemorel stood up and took a step toward the desk before stopping in midstride. The mechanical bear above the TERMINATE switch was still holding his flag up: the Highliber had not pressed the switch hard enough and her connection to the Calculor was still active.

Lemorel felt her mouth salivating. Here was a pot of cold ale being held before a thirsty drunkard, here was a thief confronted with an unattended pile of gold royals. By using the Calculor the Highliber had duplicated Lemorel's months of work in hours. It was not fair. She walked slowly across to the keyboard and ran her fingers along the inlaid and inscribed keys.

Tampering with the Calculor carried the death penalty, nobody knew that better that Lemorel. A spasm of fear and elation wriggled through her body as she stood staring at the little mechanical bear holding a flag marked ACTIVE aloft. The Highliber would not be back for days, at least.

It was like the time she had been seduced by Brunthorp: an overwhelming temptation with dire consequences if anyone else found out, yet one little step

led to another until the deed was done. The Highliber's connection was still active and the Highliber's priority on the Calculor was absolute. Lemorel sat down on the console chair, shivering with the thrill of twisting the dragon's tail. It was her duty to deactivate the Highliber's connection, but . . .

She typed—with one finger at first.

/ COMPOSITION REGISTER /

The console display wheels rattled into a request for a destination.

/ DENILIQUIN/ TEXT/ REQUEST CHECKSUM ERROR LOG FOR PAST WEEK /

Her finger hovered over the COMMAND key; then she depressed it with a soft clack. The Calculor began assembling her command into encrypted code, then routed it up to the beamflash tower. Moments later the receptor at the Deniliquin tower was reaching for his code book.

This is already enough to get me shot, Lemorel thought grimly, yet what more could they do than shoot her? She studied a map of the beamflash network until the reply from Deniliquin arrived with a rattle of wheels on the binary register. She checked the figures against her notes. Identical.

By now her nerve was beginning to fray. She was risking her life to conduct tests that she could do more slowly through official channels. What was the point? If my Johnny was to risk his life, he would do it for a sensible reason, she told herself. She fought down a rush of panic as she typed in a plain text request to the node at Griffith. Again she was presented with statistics that she already had. One more test and she would give up. She repeated her previous request to Griffith, but this time used an obscure code and requested that the reply be similarly encoded. The Calculor decoded the reply, but this time the figures pecked out on paper tape were different.

Lemorel stared at the checksum error rates, then checked them against her projections. They matched: the anomaly had vanished. She looked back at the map. Only the Darlington repeater stood between Griffith and the secure parts of the network. Somebody there was altering the statistics. What else was he altering? He. They were all male at the Darlington tower: the Southmoor treaty saw to that. Even as she scratched her head the tape machine rattled into life again. It was an amendment to what she had just received, informing her that there had been an error in transmission, and offering the old, anomalous figures by way of correction.

''Nice try,'' she whispered between clenched teeth, then gasped. They had no code book at Darlington, it was only a repeater! The encoded message had to have been broken then recoded in four or five minutes. No human could have done that, only the Calculor . . . no, only *a* calculor could do that. Another calculor, and in a place where inspections could be done only twice a year!

She had been working for barely an hour, yet what a discovery. One hundred

fourteen miles to the north there was another calculor, and it was being used to filter messages being passed to Rochester. Why? She looked over the figures for the seven lines going into Griffith and saw the anomaly at once. There was a massive checksum error rate on the eastern line.

The operator at Darlington was aware of her now, and she would not get another message past him. Not in the same way, at least. Lemorel composed a request with every third letter missing, had the Calculor encrypt it into decoy text, then sent an amendment after it with a higher priority. The request was for a dumpout of the message log at the Canowindra terminus. She also requested that it be headed as dried fish subsidies.

This time the wait was much longer. She could not disconnect because she did not know the Highliber's password. Half an hour became an hour. Lemorel read through the Highliber's manuals on operating the Calculor. At ninety minutes she helped herself to shortbread and cold coffee from the study's little pantry, then put the Calculor through some exercises in data encryption. By two hours Lemorel was becoming restive, and she checked the log of the afternoon's traffic. Everything looked normal.

The operator of the Darlington calculor would be using it to break the code of Lemorel's amendment message without realizing that it was just a useless bundle of corrections. The public clock built into the beamflash tower clanged four-thirty. The evening beamflash traffic would be reaching a peak as users tried to beat the sunset. She composed another split message, this time to Griffith, and launched it into the afternoon datastream. The message would be matched with its amendment at Griffith—and be revealed as an amendment to send to Canowindra. With the deluge of traffic, her opponent at Darlington might not bother to check everything in great detail.

The reply appeared after forty minutes. The figures meant nothing in their raw form, but a few keystrokes had the Calculor comparing them with its own records. It made interesting reading: every message that had been concerned with troop movements and the transport of strategic supplies for the past five weeks had been returned to Canowindra for verification. Not only that, but there had been instructions that all amendments should be sent in decoy code. Naturally enough, the resends had not been reported to Rochester.

Lemorel scanned her notes as she munched a piece of shortbread. All reports of military movements had been amended. She examined the Highliber's list of Calculor commands, then worked her way through the options marked MILITARY. Several programs estimated troop movements by correlating other factors, such as stores requisitions, travel restrictions, and missing market figures from specific places. She ran three such programs, but no warnings or alerts were flagged.

The conclusion was clear. Southmoor troop movements were being disguised

by someone at Darlington. Why? Perhaps the Emir of Cowra was moving an army south for a surprise attack on Alliance border forts. Perhaps Southmoor armies were already massed along the border, poised to overwhelm the Alliance forces while the Highliber was away. Had the Highliber been tricked into leaving?

Lemorel could only warn of impending war by revealing how she had learned of the threat—and that would get her shot. Still, the issues seemed more serious than a single life's value, she thought as she drank cold coffee straight from the Highliber's demijar. War. Her lover would be taken away to fight. What would Johnny do if he was in my position? she wondered. She recalled his advice to her: never let a problem beat you, even if you have to work at it all night. Well, what was good enough for him was good enough for her.

Records were being changed at Darlington. Darlington was also requesting double-encoded repeats of records from Canowindra. This did not follow. Why request correct information if you were changing it? Lemorel studied the map again. The eastern line was short and simple: the node at Griffith went through the Tallimba and Wirrinya repeater towers to the terminus tower at Canowindra. Canowindra's tower was known to contain a monitoring corps in the pay of the Mayor, a corps that returned data on Southmoor military movements. The operator of the Darlington calculor was taking care to get correct data past those two repeaters. Why?

The leadlight windows glowed red with sunset. That meant the end of heliostat transmissions through the beamflash units. Expensive flares would be needed from now on, and flare requisitions would show up on network accounts. There could be no more work, yet she was so close. If the moon was near full, though, the beamflash could still be used without being powered by flares, although at a slower data rate. She checked the almanac. The moon was a day off full! Lemorel retired to the Highliber's private toilet, taking the almanac with her. The moon would be sufficiently high for transmissions in another half hour.

The room was dark enough for her to need lamplight as she returned to the console. Today had been John Glasken's graduation. His friends were taking him on a secret revel to celebrate. Lemorel felt a pang of loneliness, she wanted to be with him so very much. This was the very day that she should have been with him! She stared at the white and black keys . . . keys of power! Keys to order the Libris Black Runners to find a student named John Glasken. With a shivery thrill of excitement she invoked the RUNNERS function.

/ LOCATION:JOHN GLASKEN/ STUDENT OF CHEMISTRIC/ UNIVERSITY OF ROCHESTER/ REPORT STATUS ONLY /

They would probably find him within the hour; then she would have them deliver a sealed envelope with a little note of greetings. She wriggled with delight to imagine his surprise.

She continued to examine the Highliber's private library by lamplight while

she waited. There were records of everything that happened on both the Alliance and Confederation networks, right down to details of rosters for each tower. The rosters for the eastern-line towers, the Griffith and the Darlington towers showed nothing out of the ordinary over the past month. She went back two months and suddenly the Wirrinya tower stood out. Eight of the eighteen communicators there had arrived over a two-week period. The roster also showed that six of the new arrivals monopolized the day shift, while both the dusk and dark shift always had one of the new communicators on duty!

Infiltration! Nobody had ever dreamed that a tower might be systematically infiltrated by qualified relays and receptors. A tower could never secretly fall to direct attack; there was a set of alarm codes that every relay had memorized, and these took only seconds to transmit. Within a day a relief squad of cavalry would be on its way from the nearest fortified town.

The Guild of Relays was huge. Each of the dozens of major towers and hundreds of minor ones had an average of ten relays, and for every active relay there was another involved in teaching, research, or administration. Relays did more than transmit messages at the tops of towers; they were also librarians, teachers, medicians, and merchants, they were pillars of local communities and the point of contact with the outside world. In other societies their role might have been filled by priests.

All shifts at Wirrinya were covered by the new communicators, and they had total control of day shift. Day shift carried most traffic, and relays liked to avoid it if possible. It was ideal for a group that wanted to take over and exclude all others. There were also observers on the other two shifts, just in case something important came through—but how could they read the codes? Repeater towers did not have code books. A calculor could break codes. Did Wirrinya have a calculor too?

Someone at the Darlington tower was carefully checking all data that was being sent from Canowindra, and was smuggling encoded corrections back past Wirrinya, then on to Rochester. Was he an ally? If so, why did he not denounce Wirrinya outright instead of just correcting their data? Wirrinya was in the Forbes prefectory, an independent, unaligned state. Any alert to arrest the conspirators in the tower would have to come over the beamflash line, and at least one of them was always on duty. They would have time to escape . . . but surely exposing the plot was more important than catching the plotters.

The reciprocating clock's weighted beams rotated back and forth with a clack-click, clack-click. In fifteen minutes transmission by lunar light would be possible. Lemorel opened the Highliber's drinks cabinet and poured out a shot of apple brandy. Zarvora never drank alcohol; the jars were only for her guests.

What was there to do? Telling the Highliber anything that she had learned would also involve telling her how she had learned it. That alone would have

Lemorel chained to a wall and staring down the barrels of two dozen muskets in less time than it took a beamflash message to reach Canowindra. The proper channels would take months . . . but she could also do nothing. Perhaps that was best. She was only a small cog in a vast machine, and a cog in the wrong place, too. She sipped at the sharp, sweet brandy and pondered the moonlight on the roofs of Libris. Finally she made up her mind to wait for the message from the Black Runners about the location of her beloved Johnny, then run to his side and forget the mess.

Almost on cue, a mechanical bellbird raised a wing and whistled, then the battery of silver hens began pecking at the paper tape. It was a plain text message from the Libris Black Runners. Lemorel jumped from her chair, her heart pounding with joy:

/ SUBJECT: JOHN GLASKEN, UNIVERSITY STUDENT
LOCATION: A BACK ROOM IN THE *TOAD AND TANKARD*, ALEHOUSE.
COMPANION(S): SERVING WENCH NAMED JOAN JIGLESSAR, ALSO KNOWN
    AS JIGGLE.
ACTIVITY: FORNICATION—SPECIFICALLY, HE HAD HER BENT OVER A TA-
    BLE AND HAD MOUNTED HER IN A POSITION REFERRED TO IN THE
    EROTICAREN COMPENDIUM AS THE BULL AND COW.
UNUSUAL OR SUSPICIOUS ACTIONS: WHILE FORNICATING, GLASKEN WAS
    SEEN TO DRINK FROM A JAR OF BLACK ALE, AND HEARD TO BELLOW
    LIKE A BULL.

By now Lemorel's hands were shaking so much that she could not hold the tape steady. She rushed to the window and stared out at the lights of Rochester, eyes blazing with rage and mortification. So *that* was what he was doing for his innocent revel—it probably explained a lot of his late-night study too! She would have the Black Runners kill him that very night—but no, that would undoubtedly lead back to her.

She closed her eyes and leaned against the window frame, burning with shame. While she had been longing to just hold his hand, that toad had been grasping handfuls of breast and buttock. A minute passed, and Lemorel grew curiously numb. It was as if everything soft had been burned away inside her. She returned to the tape machine, picked up the tape and read on.

ACTIVITIES SUBSEQUENT TO BEING LOCATED: AFTER COMPLETING THE
    ACT OF FORNICATION BUT WITHOUT RE-BUCKLING HIS CODPIECE HE
    RETURNED TO THE TAPROOM AND PISSED INTO THE FIRE. THIS
    CAUSED COMPLAINTS FROM OTHER PATRONS. WHEN INSTRUCTED TO
    "PISS OFF" BY THE VINTNER, GLASKEN AND TWO FRIENDS SET UPON

HIM WITH THEIR SWAGGER STICKS. THE CONSTABLE'S RUNNERS
WERE CALLED, AND GLASKEN AND HIS FRIENDS TRIED TO LEAVE
THROUGH THE BACK DOOR. THIS DOOR WAS FOUND TO BE BOLTED—
BY JOAN JIGLESSAR, WHO WAS STILL GETTING DRESSED. ALL THREE
STUDENTS WERE ARRESTED.

CURRENT LOCATION: GLASKEN IS ASLEEP IN CELL 15, CONSTABLE'S
WATCHHOUSE, CHARGED WITH RIOTOUS BEHAVIOR, ASSAULT, THEFT
OF A JAR OF BRANDY, INDECENT EXPOSURE, AND URINATING IN A
PLACE LICENSED FOR THE SALE AND CONSUMPTION OF FOOD AND
DRINK./

/CONTINUE SURVEILLANCE? /

Lemorel pondered for a moment, then typed DISCONTINUE. Someone must
have enjoyed compiling *that* report, she thought. She pondered Glasken's earlier
court appearances. Doubtless the other times that he had asked her for bail and
character references had not been due to mistaken identity while he rescued innocent citizens from shadowboys. Blind rage welled up within Lemorel again.

"Filthy, fornicating, drunken sot," she muttered to the shelves of mechanical
animals as her carefully cultivated façade of gentle and well-spoken sweetness
crumbled. "Lies! I'll give him lies!"

A stooge. She was the perfect character witness to get him out of the sort of
trouble that he was in now. She stamped about the study, seething with impotent
rage. She could repay Glasken by leaving him to the mercy of the magistrate this
time, but that was not good enough. She wanted to hit someone now! Her eyes
fixed on the pages of tables for the Wirrinya repeater.

"A tower full of Glaskens," she said slowly. "I'll get them! I'll make them
squeal like pigs."

Eight relays conspiring together, living a lie for five weeks and trusting their
lives to each other: violate that trust, or even call it into question, and one might
touch off a heated argument at the very least. Relay towers were not especially
private places, and a fight would quickly be noticed by the tower marshal.

Lemorel jabbed at the Calculor's keyboard, doing a search of bank tally
registers held in Rochester. None of the Wirrinya relays held one. She shrugged,
composed a fictitious tally number, credited seven hundred gold royals against it,
then sent it to the output buffer with the name of the Wirrinya day-shift supervisor
appended. After checking the Highliber's record of the Wirrinya roster again,
Lemorel encoded the names of the dusk- and dark-shift relay conspirators and
appended TERMINATE. The word TERMINATE had no function attached to it
in the Highliber's manual of commands, but it carried alarming implications.

What else would foster fear, suspicion, and doubt at Wirrinya? The truth was
probably no more their ally than it was Glasken's, so she would give them a dose

of it. She accessed a random sample of Southmoor military-movement records from the Canowindra terminus, records that had been corrected then smuggled past Wirrinya by whoever was running the Darlington calculor. She instructed the Calculor to encode them in a standard encryption, then transmit them to Canowindra. That was enough for the eyes at Wirrinya—but there was still the matter of getting it all past Darlington.

Thirty minutes passed, thirty minutes of fuming about a drunken chemistric graduate in the Constable's Watchhouse. In the morning he would send her a message that he had been unjustly arrested by the Constable's Runners while defending a little old lady against a pack of shadowboys, but Lemorel would ignore him. The magistrate would throw the book at him after all his earlier escapes from justice, and he would spend at least a week sampling rotten fruit, eggs, and fish in the public stocks.

Then it would be her turn. What to do with him, to him, about him? How to make him pay? She would be waiting when he was released from the public stocks, she would give him such a beating that he would never again dare to make a Dragon Librarian his stooge.

Lemorel forced her thoughts away from Glasken. Eyes at the Darlington tower would be reading her message by now. Was it causing a fuss, she wondered? Appended to some dummy data had been a note for the calculor operator there:

/ TO THE GENIUS IN DARLINGTON REPEATER, GREETINGS. NO THANKS TO YOU I NOW KNOW ABOUT THE SECURITY VIOLATION AT WIRRINYA. YOU WILL ALSO KNOW THAT THEIR MASTERS MUST BE GETTING THEIR ORDERS TO THEM VIA SOME SECURE CODE. WHAT IS THAT CODE? GELDIVA. /

Over one hundred miles down the beamflash line, Nikalan Vittasner smiled and shook his head.

"Geldiva, Goddess of the Brewarrina Pantheists," he said to himself. "Geldiva, Weaver of Illusions. Clever girl."

Quickly but carefully he composed a reply.

/ WHY SHOULD I TELL YOU? SIVA, DESTROYER OF ILLUSIONS AND GOD OF THE ANCIENT HINDUS./

Within half an hour he had his answer.

/ SIVA, I DEDUCE THAT YOU DO NOT HAVE A MASTER CODE BOOK IN YOUR RELAY TOWER. IF YOU HAD THAT CODE BOOK THEN YOU WOULD KNOW WHICH CODE THEY ARE USING TO COMMUNICATE WITH THEIR MASTER. IF YOU HAD THAT CODE THEN YOU WOULD HAVE SENT THE FOLLOWING MESSAGE TO WIRRINYA BY NOW. GELDIVA /

Nikalan nearly burst out laughing at the message, a combination of unaltered military data that should have been altered, with a tally for a fortune in gold royals against the name of the infiltrator who was day-shift supervisor. The tally was for a Rochester bank.

He composed another reply.

/ MESSAGE UNDERSTOOD AND ACCEPTED, GELDIVA. I DO NOT HAVE THE CODE, BUT I HAVE A SAMPLE MESSAGE THAT HAS BEEN ENCRYPTED IN IT. THE SAMPLE FOLLOWS, ALONG WITH MY AT-TEMPTS SO FAR AT BREAKING THE ENCRYPTION. GOOD LUCK. IF YOU CAN BREAK IT, THEN WHEN YOU SEND THE MESSAGE TO THE TERMINUS, FLAG IT GELDIVA, AND I SHALL PASS IT ON WITHOUT DELAY. IN THANKS, SIVA. /

Rochester had a register of all master codes, but this code was not among them. It would take months for an individual to break, not the Calculor. Lemorel consulted the manual and found a command named CODEBREAKER. She typed in the sample, along with the work that Siva's calculor had done. His had perhaps a tenth of the power of the Highliber's machine, that was obvious. The task would take only a few hours, as Siva had given her a head start.

What to do about Glasken, she wondered as she sent the message off to be decoded. Beating was a crude, common vengeance, in fact it would be a public humiliation for her as well. She had been his dupe, and she did not want the world to know it. As she looked down at the keyboard she thought of the Libris Black Runners. Fear? Lemorel had the power of the Highliber now. Apart from having to spend the night in the watchhouse Glasken had not a care in the world, the world was his for the taking . . . but that could be changed.

Another message, this time to have a search made of Glasken's room at the residential college. They would probably find little more than filthy sketches and stolen brandy jars, yet he would see that a search had been made. There was one sign of Libris that everyone in Rochester knew, the red stamp of a book closed over a long dagger. That stamp meant that you had offended, and that you had been given an unspecified number of days to make amends. Lemorel looked through the manual and found the command to use the stamp. It could be used as a genuine option to warn of impending assassination, or merely to frighten. She typed, then sent off the command. The Calculor was slow to respond, due to the load of the decoding task.

While the Black Runners were ransacking Glasken's room and putting the red stamp of fear on his pillow, Lemorel was reclining in the Highliber's reading chair and drinking apple brandy. Her thoughts returned to the Wirrinya problem, and of her own precarious position. Records would have been kept of her work on the Calculor, and there was no other master user other than the Highliber— but there was! The one who called himself Siva at the Darlington tower. Some of Lemorel's own early work had proved that the Libris Calculor could be op-

erated over the beamflash network, and the Highliber had since used that very facility when touring the provinces. It might be possible to make it look as if Siva had somehow taken control of the Libris machine.

It was four in the morning before the Calculor had the code broken, and Lemorel was jolted awake by a mechanical owl striking a bell. Using the Wirrinya conspirators' code she assembled a message that read like a mistake by their own masters, words meant for their leader's eyes only but sent when a minion was on duty. Finally she typed the encrypted message into the output buffer, with 'GEL-DIVA: PLEASE REMOVE THIS' appended in plain text. She struck the SEND key firmly.

Lemorel stretched and looked up. Stars were visible through the windows. This was the message that would shatter the conspiracy at the Wirrinya relay tower, but she was not the Highliber. As much as the Highliber might approve of Lemorel averting a costly war, her gratitude would probably not extend to forgiving a blatantly illegal use of her Calculor. Even if she escaped the firing squad, she would have her career in Libris brought to an untimely end.

For the next hour Lemorel worked her way through the internal records of the Calculor, changing housekeeping entries so that tasks originating in the Highliber's study seemed to match messages sent from Darlington. Finally she cleaned up the crumbs and washed the glass she had used, covering her tracks so well that the Highliber's lackey would not suspect a thing. As she finished, the mechanical hens began to peck out a brief message from the Black Runners:

/ TASK: SEARCH OF COLLEGE ROOM OF JOHN GLASKEN, WITH STAMP OF
    FEAR TO BE LEFT ON HIS PILLOW AS A WARNING
CONTENTS OF NOTE: *ONE FLINTLOCK PISTOL, REPORTED IN THE CONSTA-
    BLE'S REGISTER OF FIREARMS AS HAVING BEEN STOLEN FROM THE
    MASTER OF THE ROARING BOAR (ALEHOUSE) DURING EQUINOX FES-
    TIVAL * 2 GOLD ROYALS* 19 SILVER ROYALS* ONE DEACON'S PLEDGE
    STAMP SET AT 14 APRIL 1696 GW* ONE BAR OF SEALING WAX* 11
    PROPHYLACTIC DEVICES, NEWLY WASHED, OILED AND LAID OUT TO
    DRY* A SKETCH OF LIBRARIAN CLASS DRAGON BLUE LEMOREL MIL-
    DERELLEN (NUDE) SIGNED WITH HIS NAME* FIVE MARKED CARD
    DECKS* ONE PAIR OF LOADED DICE* 87 SHEETS OF DOGGEREL VERSE
    LOVE POEMS DEDICATED TO 37 DIFFERENT GIRLS* 327 LOVE LETTERS
    FROM 52 GIRLS /

Lemorel fought down a wave of nausea, then ripped the tape off the mechanism. Her whole wonderful romance had been a shabby trick. He had a stamp to reseal that accurse box of condoms every time that he wanted to impress a prospective conquest with his virtue and common sense. How many had pre-

ceded—and followed—her along that path to his bed? She returned to the key-board and composed a message.

/ INSTRUCTIONS RELATING TO JOHN GLASKEN, STUDENT
*CONFISCATE HIS PISTOL, MONEY, CLOTHING, DEGREE, THE DEACON'S
    STAMP AND EVERYTHING ELSE NOT OF IMMEDIATE USE TO HIM AS
    A STUDENT
*BURN ALL SKETCHES, POETRY, AND LETTERS, AND BURN THE LIST OF
    WHAT WAS FOUND IN HIS ROOM
*CUT THE TIP OFF EACH OF PROPHLACTIC DEVICES /

Lemorel disengaged the Highliber's keyboard as the sky brightened outside, then left the study and sat on a bench in the corridor outside. She tried to doze, but thoughts of Glasken intruded. Was Joan Jiglessar a new sweetheart or some casual dalliance? What did she have that Lemorel did not? There might have almost have been two Glaskens: one wise, sensible, and honest, the other with a taste for drink, brawling, and the most gross and tasteless amorous frolics imaginable. Presently the sheer exhaustion of the night claimed her. She fell asleep sitting upright, her head slumped to one side and her hands folded in her lap.

"Superlative actor," she muttered in her sleep, "and all love is acting."

When the Highliber's lackey arrived for the day's work he found Lemorel waiting patiently outside his door. He assumed that some mixup by the guards had allowed her through, and quickly explained that the Highliber was away.

In Wirrinya the conspirators began knifing each other just after the 7 A.M. change-over to day shift. As Lemorel sat gathering her thoughts in the honeysuckle-and-jasmine-scented gardens of the University, a vertical shootout developed between the conspirators and the Wirrinya tower marshal and his guards—who had come to investigate the commotion. Two conspirators survived, and after moderate torture confessed to being in the pay of members of a Southmoor religious faction that objected to the Darlington beamflash link traveling over Southmoor territory.

The modified data had been meant to make Deniliquin's mayor think that the Emir of Cowra was massing troops for a secret attack. Had it not been for the efforts of Siva at Darlington, the Mayor would have reacted with a preemptive strike, provoking a war that would have seen the Darlington tower razed as one of the first actions. Diplomatic messages flew thickly, and the Emir's executioner spent several busy days at the public block. Meantime, far away to the south, John Glasken was sentenced to a fortnight's humiliation in the public stocks.

Highliber Zarvora had to interrupt her journey west and return to Rochester. Lemorel was called in by the Highliber to determine if the Calculor could be

operated over the beamflash network by someone using the master password, and she assured the Dragon Black that it was indeed possible. Zarvora muttered something obscene about ducks in ancient Anglaic. A day later Lemorel was promoted to Dragon Silver and put in charge of a project to tighten Calculor security. She was the youngest librarian to hold the rank of Dragon Silver for the entire century.

Newly released from the stocks, Glasken was subdued as he returned to his college. Even though he had washed his face and hair in a public fountain, he still reeked so badly that people raised handkerchiefs to their noses as he passed them in the street. Upon reaching Villiers College he went straight to the laundaric annex.

"Linen to wash, Fras Glasken?" inquired the ancient clerk at the desk.

"A bath, if you please," he replied quietly.

"But ye've had one this month."

"So, I'm having another!" Glasken snapped.

The clerk suddenly wrinkled his nose and peered over his spectacles at the abrasions on Glasken's neck. He smiled toothlessly.

"Ah, there's nothing so bad as a spell in the stocks, eh Fras? Locked into the wooden frame and a target for rotten fruit and slops by day, then chained up and not able to scrape off the muck by night. Did a spell in 'em meself back in '47 for, ah . . ."

"Is there hot water?"

"Aye, ye can have five buckets of hot and nine of cold . . . That's it! I'd dressed up in the Rectifier's clothing, such as he'd left at my laundaric."

"I have no coin to hand, charge it to my college expenses."

"Treated meself to ale and cakes at nine taverns before the real Rectifier chanced upon me."

"Bath salts and a towel, if you please."

"Why'd they lock yer own neck in the stocks, young Fras?"

Glasken straightened and thrust his chest out. "I confessed to a crime to save a lady's honor," he replied wistfully.

The clerk scratched his head. "Ach, doesn't sound like your sort of lady, Fras Glasken."

Forty minutes of soaking and scrubbing cheered Glasken considerably, and he resolved to bathe at least once a fortnight henceforth. Wrapping himself in a threadbare college towel he left his clothing with the clerk for washing and padded upstairs to his room, carrying his boots. The key was oddly stiff in the lock, and as soon as he pushed the door open he sensed that something was wrong. Things had been rearranged in subtle ways. However dissolute Glasken might have been, he was neat and orderly in his domestic routines.

Dropping his boots he pulled a drawer open. His money, border pass, loaded

dice, and marked cards were gone! He jerked the cupboard door wide: no riding gear, swagger stick, flintlock, saber and clothes, nothing. The pictures were missing from the mantelpiece, even his newly awarded degree had been taken. As he looked around in dismay, he was uneasy as well as angry. Ordinary thieves would have left the place in a shambles, and would have taken only what could have been sold in the night market. This was methodical, malicious, even vindictive. His sheepgut condoms were still neatly laid out along the windowsill, but their tips had been cut off. That gave him a fearful pang.

He sat on the edge of the bed and resolved to lie down and think through what had happened. If he reported this to the magistrate, the thief might be caught. How then would Glasken explain marked cards, loaded dice, and a pistol that he was not licensed to own and that had been stolen in the first place? What to do? It required calm thought. He pulled back the covers and was about to let his head fall to the pillow for a much-needed rest when he caught sight of something like a smear of fresh blood.

At the center of his pillow was the Mark of Libris! Glasken's world stopped, his entire consciousness focused on the red stamp of a book closed over a dagger. The Mark was well known but rarely used, it was the stuff of cheap adventure novels . . . yet there it was, the legendary warning of impending doom. They were going to kill him unless he heeded the warning and made amends for—what? He had stolen wine, brawled, and fornicated, but neither he nor his crimes were important enough to deserve the Mark. A mistake, perhaps, surely that was it. He had been mistaken for someone else. What he needed was a senior Dragon Librarian to speak on his behalf.

Suddenly a chasm opened up inside him. He felt light and hollow, as if a breeze could blow him away. Lemorel! She had dealings with the Highliber. He tried to think back to their last words with each other. She had been about to tell the Highliber about some problem with the beamflash towers. What had the Highliber told her in turn?

That had to be it. Lemorel had normally testified in his favor whenever he had been hauled before the magistrate, but she had ignored his notes this time. Glasken shuddered. That was the trouble with having a powerful mistress. Her patronage had been wonderful, yet her revenge was this thunderbolt.

"Who did she hear about?" he asked the row of decapitated condoms on the windowsill. "Was it Joan Jiglessar, Carole Mhoreg, that wench from the refectory, or perhaps even some girl from last week?"

Glasken reached under his bed, fumbled for a moment, and drew out a short length of stiff wire. "Hah, they missed my greatest treasure of all," he chuckled, kissing the wire with a flourish.

Still wearing only the towel, he methodically checked his room for anything else of value. Everything that might help him to travel was gone; someone clearly

meant him to stay in Rochester. They would expect him to be in a helpless panic—or perhaps a towering rage. He stamped out of his room and returned to the laundaric.

"I say there, Palfors, my room's been burgled," he declared loudly as he entered.

"The devil ye say!" exclaimed the clerk. "Lose much?"

"Clothes, money, and papers. Some petty vandalism, red ink splattered over my bed, that sort of thing."

"Sounds more like students than shadowboys from outside. Ye'd best see the Rector."

"Not in a towel I can't. How long before you can have my clothes clean and dry?"

"They're soakin' just now, Fras, but I could put 'em through the pedal agitator then dry 'em in front of the furnace. Two hours, at most."

"Two hours, then. I'll wait in my room. Did you happen to see anyone unusual lurking about the college over the past fortnight, Fras Palfors?"

"Ah . . . only some Dragon Red Librarians."

"Late at night?"

"Aye."

"Well, we all know what may be done with stolen laundry, don't we then?"

The man nodded, eyes suddenly wide and mouth open; then he shuffled away to work on Glasken's clothing. Glasken leaned over the counter and read the tags on several bundles.

"Matheran, Chan-ye, MacLal, Orondego, Lorgi—ah yes, Fras Lorgi, a man of just my excellent stature."

Glasken walked from the laundaric in Lorgi's clothing, his face muffled against the unseasonally cold October evening by a knitted scarf. He had decided on instant flight, a dash into oblivion so fast that even Libris with all its resources could not begin to trace him until he was long gone. He felt a lot more confident now that he was clothed again, but money was the key to everything else—and money was there for the bold to take. Snapwire in hand, he made his way down to the College Purser's office. The dinner bell was ringing as he knocked smartly to make sure that nobody was within. It took Glasken only moments to get past the simple two-tumbler lock. Leaving the door slightly ajar behind him, he crept across the darkened room to the strongbox.

Its lock was more difficult, but presently the tumblers yielded and he lifted a bag from the box and hefted it. About fifty coins, more than enough to get him . . . where? With this sort of money he could hire an unwitting decoy to journey south while he took a wind train west into lands beyond the reach of Libris. Suddenly the door was pushed open and light flooded into the room.

"I say, Stoneford, are you there? Hey, who—?"

Glasken clubbed him over the head with the bag of coins. Pulling the door

behind him he dashed out into the corridor and crashed blindly into the evening procession of cloaked edutors bound for the refectory high table. The bag slipped from his hand, sending gold and silver coins spilling before him in a jingling cascade.

By the tenth hour Glasken was sitting in a cell in the Constable's Watchhouse. The edutors of Villiers College had turned him over to the University Warden, accusing him of breaking into the Purser's office, stealing fifty-one silver nobles and six gold royals, and striking the Rector unconscious. He was then handed over to the Constable's Runners, who took him before a magistrate and had him charged formally. Due to his obvious skill with locks he was shackled to a ball and chain by a heavy rivet after being stripped naked and clothed in striped trews and a blanket.

Some days later he awoke to the door being unlocked, and he looked up to see Lemorel being shown in. He stood up at once and began to put out his arms to her. She was not smiling. That was bad sign. He turned the offer of an embrace into an imploring gesture.

"Ah, Lem, dearest, I have been unjustly—"

"They say that virtue is its own reward," she interjected. "I see that the rewards of vice are more appropriate." Contempt dripped from her words like poisoned honey.

"What do you mean?" Glasken asked nervously.

"I have been promoted to Dragon Silver Librarian, Glasken, and I don't want rumors of our liaison hanging over my career. I am not without influence and there is much that I can do to make your life unpleasant. I can even arrange that the last four seconds of it are spent falling down the center of a beamflash tower. The idea of having been your dupe revolts me, the thought that a sketch of my nude body was pinned above your bed while you were in it with Joan Jiglessar makes me want to retch."

Glasken contemplated this. He had bedded Joan in many places, and many other girls in his college bed, but never *that* particular girl in *that* bed. Whatever Lemorel's source of information, it was fallible, he concluded with some relief.

"Lem, please, I need your good testimony just once more. I'm charged with violence to a gentleman. Do you know what the magistrate will say to that? Death, either by hanging or musket fire, according to his mood. If it's been a bad week for assaults, I might also get a spell of public torture first."

This time Glasken was quite sincere. He could practically feel the straps on his wrists and hear the ratchets clicking. Lemorel's eyes narrowed and she smiled.

"Tell anyone that we were ever more than vague acquaintances and I'll kill you myself. Keep silent, and I'll see that you're not killed or tortured—for these offenses, at least."

"That's all?"

"That's all."

Glasken gave an indiscreetly loud sigh of relief and agreed.

The following morning Glasken was tried, found guilty, and sentenced to death. The magistrate let the words hang, and Glasken stood trembling in the dock, sweat trickling from his armpits and running down his ribs. The magistrate cleared his throat and adjusted his wig.

"John Glasken, when I sentenced you to the stocks not three weeks ago I felt I was the happiest man in all of Rochester," he said as he looked out over the courtroom. "It was small satisfaction after the way you soiled the honor of my granddaughter—"

"That's not true, Your Honor," interjected Glasken. "She was nineteen years old, and I'd met her in the Toad and Tankard—"

"Order!" Glasken was silent at once. "So, as I was saying, imagine my delight at being able to prescribe death for yet another of your crimes so very soon. Unfortunately, however, you will not get a chance to sow dead man's seed below the gallows. Clemency has been granted to you by reason of the Mayor's birthday."

Glasken drew breath for a mighty cheer, then thought the better of it. The Constable and his two attendant runners grinned, but then they were not facing the magistrate. The clerk of the court stopped with his goose quill poised to scribble out the new sentence.

"Fras John Glasken, by the power invested in me by the Mayor of Rochester I hereby commute your sentence of death to one year in the blazing deserts of the west . . ." Glasken was incredulous, he barely stopped himself cheering. ". . . for every coin in the bag with which you struck the Rector." Glasken reeled, and would have collapsed had he not seized the railing of the dock. The magistrate grinned openly as he continued. "It should come to fifty-seven years. Am I correct?"

"Yes, Your Honor," the clerk of the court replied.

"Have you anything to say, Fras Glasken?"

"I'd like to wish Mayor Jefton a happy birthday and thank him for his present," Glasken said in a tone colored more with sarcasm than defiance. The magistrate's face went dark red with fury, but Glasken was quite familiar with courtroom procedures. Sentence had been passed, and now could not be varied. Congratulating the Mayor on his birthday was not contempt of court, even if it had been done specifically to antagonize the magistrate.

"May you live another fifty-seven years, Glasken," the magistrate said as he handed his silver mace to the Constable to dismiss the court.

Glasken was marched from the courthouse by two runners and chained inside an armored wagon. The trip to the paraline terminus took nearly an hour, and there the prisoner was taken, still carrying his chain and ball, to the office of the

Inspector of Customs. The official signed for him, and Glasken was held under guard until he was to be handed over to the train's warden.

He sat in silence, limp and apprehensive. Although he had narrowly avoided death, life was about to become decidedly unpleasant. A man that he took to be from the train entered, a scroll in his hand. He sent the guards out of the office, and two armed, uniformed men replaced them.

"Prisoner Glasken, I have a few details to check," he said genially. "You have a degree, I see here."

"I'll be the best-educated prisoner on the chain gang," Glasken sighed.

"Perhaps not. You have a technical degree, including articles in arithmetic with a good pass."

"Yes, but chemistric is—"

"Splendid," he said, smiling more broadly and rolling the scroll up. He turned to the guards. "Gag and bind him, then back the wagon up to the door."

Even as she was gloating over the freshly signed order to induct Glasken as a component in the Calculor, a summons arrived for Lemorel to sit on a special panel of experts. The matter was so urgent that two armed Dragon Reds had been sent to fetch her. A youth of about Lemorel's age was sitting in shackles in one of the seminar rooms, and the subject of the inquiry was so sensitive that no guards were present. His gaze was intense and penetrating, yet it was more an expression of ravening curiosity than aggression. Zarvora paced restlessly as she addressed her four advisers and the prisoner.

"A few days ago this relay, Nikalan Vittasner, slipped away from the Darlington relay tower in disguise and rode to the border at Deniliquin. Using false papers he crossed the border and took a pedal train south to Rochester. This morning he demanded an audience with me."

With her face blank, Lemorel frantically grappled with her surprise and terror.

"He claims to have helped expose the Wirrinya conspirators, and has provided me with documents to show what he did. He also claims to have had help from someone in Libris named Geldiva, who processed a difficult encryption for him."

The Highliber paused. She wanted an opinion.

"Recent investigations show that he could have used the Libris Calculor," Lemorel ventured in a flat voice. "Evidence exists that there is a separate, smaller calculor in Darlington, so he would have had the experience to learn your Calculor's command structure."

Zarvora nodded. "The evidence supported that idea until a few hours ago, but not now. My tests show that Nikalan here has the most extraordinary powers of mental calculation that I have ever encountered. They are a significant fraction of the Libris Calculor itself. He denies all knowledge of *any* Calculor."

"If you please!" Nikalan interrupted.

He stood up. He was as tall as Glasken, yet very lean and fit, with no comfortable bulges from ale and indolence . . . and very, very bright. He's like Glasken with all the warts removed, Lemorel decided approvingly in spite of herself.

"You seem confused about me, Highliber. With your permission, could we talk openly?"

Zarvora nodded. Lemorel shivered.

"Two years ago a tower outpost called Ballerie Vale was attacked and burned by Northmoor freebooters. It was less than a node but more than a relay, just important enough to have a master code book. The relays and tower staff were slaughtered."

"I read the report," said Zarvora. "The relays got off a number of messages about being under attack before smokebolts were fired into the tower gallery from crossbows. The response was quick, and the Marshal of Walgett arrived with two hundred lancers while the fires were still burning but the freebooters were gone. It was a cruel, pointless raid."

Nikalan shuddered, then pressed his lips together and frowned. When he regained control his tone was softer, more neutral.

"Not so. I searched and searched for one particular body, a body with an inscribed copper bangle on the left wrist. The bodies of those killed in the open were dead only a few hours, Highliber, but the charred bodies inside the burnt-out buildings had been dead at least a week. I sewed Mikki's remains into the shroud myself. Her flesh was full of charred maggots, she had been dead many days. Two dozen more were just like her."

He paused to let the implications register. The tower had been in operation for about a week under the control of the raiders. People with relay experience had captured a tower, stolen the master code book, and practiced on the beamflash line for a week. Then they had left, killing those who had not died in the initial attack and burning the evidence.

"The Marshal chose to ignore the maggots. Perhaps he had been bribed." Suddenly his composure shattered. "My beautiful Mikki was killed by them!" he shouted.

There was stunned silence. The last person to shout at the Highliber had been the Chief of Cataloguing, and he was now a multiplier.

"Please go on," said Highliber Zarvora quietly.

"My brilliant Mikki," moaned Nikalan without apologizing. "If you think that I'm a skilled calculator, O Highliber, my abilities are nothing beside hers. I knew that they would strike again, and that this time they would try to keep control of a tower for months, or even years. To do that they would probably pose as genuine relay recruits and infiltrate the staff at some isolated repeater.

"With the stolen code book they could wield the power of Mayors by tampering with supposedly secure messages. They could make fortunes for people, ruin careers, start wars . . . but they did not know I was stalking them. I had been

working in Walgett tower during the week that Ballerie Vale was in their hands, and I remembered some of the odd quirks in the data traffic from when those murderers had been in control. I arranged a transfer to Darlington, a relay tower with a lot of traffic.''

"Why not the great node at Griffith?'' asked Lemorel.

"No, Darlington was an unpopular and isolated tower where I could quickly become a supervisor. I needed to be a supervisor so that I could falsify entries in the data-traffic logs. Since then I have watched and waited.''

Lemorel was staggered by his bravery and dedication. Nikalan's quest to avenge his sweetheart had led to him gaining as much power to manipulate the network as the Wirrinya conspirators, yet he had remained true to his purpose: avenging the death of his lover. He could have made himself a Castellan and amassed a fortune, yet he was faithful to his dead Mikki. Why couldn't any of her own lovers be so faithful, Lemorel wondered with a pang that almost made her convulse.

"Opinions?'' asked the Highliber. Lemorel took two deep breaths to steady her voice.

"It's possible,'' she agreed. "Tracts copied from a master code book were found at Wirrinya. I suggest that Griffith be advised. The master code book of the Central Confederation must be replaced.''

"That will be done,'' said Zarvora, "but there is something important that puzzles me, Nikalan. Why did you merely clean up the Wirrinya messages? Why did you not alert the Marshal at Griffith and have a squad of cavalry sent to capture them?''

"*Me* trust a *Marshal*, Highliber? Spies would have alerted the conspirators before the Marshal's squad had left the city gates. The bastards would have been into the Weddin Mountains and across the Southmoor border in no time. I wanted revenge, and I was only a week from breaking their masters' code when someone here beat me to it and set them killing each other.''

"Beat you to it?'' said Lemorel. "But you were the one who ordered her—I mean it—to break the code.''

"No, no . . . she *helped* me to . . . avenge Mikki.''

He sat down and rubbed his face in his hands. After years of stalking the conspirators the daemon that had driven him was finally gone, leaving him exhausted and directionless. All that he could think of now was the fantastic possibility that there was another like Mikki. Only Lemorel knew that his ally was a chimaera of herself and a fantastic machine.

"If you are telling the truth . . .'' Zarvora began, then she paused. "I don't know what to think.''

"Highliber, please let me meet her. I never dreamed that there could be another like Mikki, yet there she was at the other end of the beamflash line.''

"But *you* issued the commands—''

"No! She came to my aid. Highliber, I could have fled to the Confederation. Instead I've given up everything to meet this lady. Please, let me meet Geldiva, the Weaver of Illusions."

"Meet her? Impossible!"

"You owe it to me!"

It was clear that he was close to a nervous breakdown, and that threats would have no effect on him. Lemorel withdrew her hands into her sleeves so that nobody could see that they were shaking. Tarrin cleared his throat.

"I suggest that we, ah, introduce them, Highliber. That should bring him to his senses."

"Yes, yes, take me to her now!"

"Meet the Calculor?" exclaimed Zarvora, shaking her head in exasperation. "You are sounding like Lewrick."

"No, no, let's just take him to the duty controller's gallery and let him see for himself."

Zarvora looked to her other advisers, but only Lemorel shook her head. "Highliber, one look at the Calculor, and—well, its obvious what will happen in his present condition. Let him rest for a few days."

"No! Don't listen, Highliber. Let me meet her now."

Zarvora thought for a moment, then shrugged and beckoned for them to follow her. They walked the short distance slowly, to the rhythmic jingle of Nikalan's shackles. Two armed guards unlocked and unbolted an ironbound redgum door, and as it opened the distant cacophony of whirrs, clicks, and humming wires that was the Calculor's heartbeat spilled out. Almost frantic with apprehension and guilt, Lemorel seized Nikalan's arm as the others entered.

"I tried to warn you," she whispered, but he scowled and pulled away.

They entered the gallery and looked down over the railing.

"There is Geldiva," said Zarvora. "A thousand people chained to desks and split into two cross-verifying arithmetic processors. Eight hundred abacus units, two hundred higher functions, and several thousand yards of communication wires on pulleys to carry the data—are you all right?"

Nikalan was slowly sinking to the floor of the gallery. His mouth was open, his eyes were bulging, and tears were on his cheeks. Zarvora knelt beside him.

"This is what you call Geldiva. One machine made of a thousand souls. Many of them are convicted felons. Could this be the wonderful lady who helped you?"

"No," Nikalan said very softly.

"Now, how did you learn the command structure of my machine? Was it by monitoring my remote sessions during my visit to Griffith last year?"

"No, no, no! Mikki—Geldiva! Where are you? Geldiva!"

The sanity was already gone from Nikalan's voice as his mind leaped into

its own abyss to escape from this second terrible loss. His screams turned every head in the hall. For a moment the entire Calculor interrupted its work to stare up at the gallery. The guards dragged him away, but he would not stop screaming. Lemorel took a deep breath.

"Highliber—"

"Yes, you were right, that was horrible—but precisely *what* has been going on? Walk with me."

Nikalan's screams stayed within Lemorel's head as they slowly walked the corridors. Zarvora was disturbed and baffled.

"Mathematics, love, and revenge," she muttered with her head bent forward. "What an incredible romance."

Lemorel had walked the precipice and survived—but at Nikalan's expense. She had won prizes in mathematics and optics, yet her calculating skills were not in the same class as those of Nikalan or Mikki. She had gained his love while directing the greatest calculating machine in the world, but without it she could not be Geldiva. Glasken had betrayed her, and now she had betrayed Nikalan. She was down in the same pigsty as Glasken, and there was only one way to climb out: she had to become Geldiva.

"His devotion touched and disturbed me," Zarvora was saying.

"And me, Highliber."

"I did not think men like that existed. Why cannot *I* meet them?"

"You just did, Highliber."

"Have you ever had such a romance?"

"My liaisons have all been failures, Highliber."

"There must be others. Must one post a notice at the University? MAN WANTED: MUST BE YOUNG, HANDSOME, BRAVE, HIGHLY ROMAN-TIC, GOOD IN BED, AND A BRILLIANT MATHEMATICIAN SPECIAL-IZING IN APPLIED NUMERICAL VECTORS AND LOGIC."

"You could look in the Calculor, Highliber."

"Very funny. You may return to your work. Try to write something coherent about the past hour and have it on my desk by this afternoon."

Alone in her study, Zarvora activated her Calculor console, rubbed her fingertips together, stared out the window, deactivated her console, then paced in circles around her mechanical orrery. Abruptly she flung off her cloak and tunic and stared at herself in a mirror, bare to the waist and with her hands on her hips. Her body tapered to a very narrow waist from moderately sized but well-formed breasts. She leafed through an art book and held up several sketches of nude women for comparison, giving each a rating out of ten. She stared at herself again.

"Realistically speaking . . . eight!" she concluded with relief.

After getting dressed she rang for her lackey.

"I want the personnel files of all FUNCTION components in the Calculor: all shifts plus the spares pool," she ordered.

"That's six hundred and twenty files," he gasped.

"Correct. I want them in my office in a quarter hour, then I want complete privacy for the rest of the day."

6 CALL

Maralinga had been transformed from a railside to a garrison within a week of the Ghan raid. There were never fewer than four wind trains parked on the sidings at any time, magnificent with their high white rotor towers painted in red and gold spirals, and they had brought musketeers, engineers, new railside staff, and the Assistant Commissioner of the Paraline Authority himself.

Maralinga was part of the Woomera Confederation. Although Woomera controlled more land than the Southeast Alliance, it had only a twentieth of its neighbor's population. Much of its defense strategy was based on isolation. It had used the desert as a shield for its northern boundaries, but suddenly the shield had crumbled. If nations beyond the red desert were developing the ability to strike over immense distances, then Woomera would need allies.

Rochester was a convenient, if distant, ally. The Highliber sent a galley train with troops and beamflash staff to rig up an emergency link between the Tarcoola and Maralinga railsides. Military observers in the other mayorates of the Alliance were alarmed by the operation. How had Mayor Jefton managed to secretly develop the prefabricated wooden beamflash towers, and the new segmented, self-propelled military galley trains that could carry materials and troops a thousand miles within days? Three weeks after the raid was reported, Maralinga was commissioned as a permanent part of the beamflash network.

The strategic implications of the feat caused sleepless nights for many mayors and their advisers. Zarvora had been reluctant to deploy the towers because the operation would display little Rochester's astonishing new strengths. The trains and towers had been kept ready as disassembled piles of stores and inventoried as parts of unrelated civilian equipment. The Calculor coordinated the assembly and packing of the trains at speeds beyond the comprehension of shipping clerks. Because the towers were made of interlocking parts that required no specialist artisans to assemble them, the work was done by military engineers using manuals that they had studied on the trip west.

Each of the galley trains was pulled by three galley engines, and each of

these was propelled by a hundred navvys. The machines had been derived from the smaller civilian trains and shunting galleys. They were independent of the wind, carried their own rail-repair equipment, and could move a small army to the most remote railhead in days. No sooner had these swift military machines rumbled across their territory than many mayors hastily passed laws limiting the movement of such trains in the future. At the same time they began programs to develop and construct their own galley engines.

The Marshal of Maralinga was from the Woomera Paraline Guard, but took his orders from Rochester. Eager to learn anything about the way that the Call had been defied by the raiders, Zarvora also rushed a team of edutors to Maralinga. Darien was put in charge of the investigation. The raid was an open secret among the mayorates, but the fact that it had taken place during a Call was known to only Zarvora and a few of her advisers.

The investigations at the railside were thorough. Scraps of vine, dead leaves, and hairs were collected and sent to the Highliber under guard. Rubbish and broken equipment left by the raiders was examined and sketched, and the weapons and timer from the lancer that Darien had shot were sent to the Overmarshal of Woomera for evaluation. Trackers traced the trail of the Ghans back north until they reached where they had emerged from the sand dunes, confirming that they had been traveling directly south when they had seen the railside. The trackers were sent along the paraline for two hundred miles to either side of Maralinga to confirm that the remaining lancers had not crossed it again on the way north. Observers in the portable beamflash tower monitored the southern part of the plain for the returning Ghan lancers, but saw nothing.

Sentry posts were established a mile out of Maralinga at each point of the compass. They were no more than wooden barricades under an awning, each manned by five Woomeran musketeers and a Rochestrian sergeant. Two terriers were assigned to each post, and the northern post doubled as a Call-warning station.

The western post was beside the paraline, and the sentries were not surprised when a hermit came tramping along beside the rails from the west. There were several dozen hermits scattered along the length of the paraline, all earning their supplies by doing occasional maintenance on the rails. This one set the demi-terriers barking. It was the morning of the 15th of October 1699 GW, a month after the Ghan raid.

"Something about his scent," said the Rochestrian sergeant. "Dirbok, keep the dogs on a head-hand switch. Jaysec, train your musket between his eyes."

"But Fras, he wears no vines," said Jaysec.

"He has a body anchor and robes like those from the lancer that the Deputy Overliber shot," said the sergeant.

The hermit stopped, nervously smiling and bowing.

"Fras, hermits scavenge from the bodies in the desert," said Jaysec. "There are some flea-ridden scavengers dressed as richly as mayors along this part of the paraline."

The sergeant stroked his beard. He walked forward, leaving a clear line of fire for Jaysec's gun.

"A paraline hermit should know our languages. You! Speak Austaric?"

The hermit smiled and bowed again but said nothing. The dogs continued to bark.

"The dogs think he's the vineman, Fras," Jaysec decided, coming over to the sergeant's opinion.

"Perhaps the dogs bark at what smells like a Ghan lancer," said Dirbok.

The sergeant held up a length of rope and put his wrists together. The hermit hesitated, then comprehended the gesture and held his hands out to be bound.

"Fagh! Smells of camel," said the sergeant. "But he's scabby like a hermit."

Jaysec escorted the hermit back to Maralinga. The Marshal was informed, and after inspecting the enigmatic newcomer he decided to present him to the Deputy Overliber. The hermit was stripped naked and issued with trews and a tunic, then shackled to a bench in the library while Darien was sent for.

"His face and hands are burned and peeled, as if he's unused to the sun," the Marshal told Darien as they walked along the pink limestone cloisters to the library. "There was something odd about his behavior, too. He gaped and gawked in wonder at the wind trains when he was brought inside the walls. Paraline hermits know wind trains as well as their own fleas. Some are even members of the Peterborough Train Spotters Brotherhood."

Darien nodded, then bowed her thanks at the library door. As the Marshal unlocked the door she scribbled out a question with a charblack stylus.

HAS HE BEEN GIVEN FOOD AND DRINK?

"Frelle, he's only a hermit. He smells like a camel's fart."

IN ROCHESTRIAN SOCIETY POLITE HOSTS, NO MATTER WHAT THEIR RANK, ALWAYS GREET TRAVELERS WITH FOOD AND DRINK.

"As you will, Frelle."

The Marshal tramped off, muttering to himself. He returned with a pitcher of water and lime juice in a demijar, and a plate of seedcakes and dates on a tray.

Darien took the tray and the Marshal's keys after gesturing to him not to follow her.

"Frelle Deputy Overliber, he might be dangerous,"

Darien shrugged and faced the door. The Marshal opened it, glared at the shackled hermit as Darien entered, then pulled it closed.

In Ghan nations, only servants served the food. Being a Ghan, the hermit took Darien for a servant at once, in fact a servant that he already knew. His

peeling, gaunt but handsome face was not familiar to her and his voice was no longer muffled, yet she recognized him and smiled. His eyes were bright with apprehension until she put a finger to her lips, smiled again, and shook her head. She unlocked his shackles, and noted the way that the muscles of his jaw untensed and his shoulders sagged with relief.

"So, you are not going to denounce me," he said, taking the drink that she offered him. "Thank you. I'm glad you survived. Did you know that Kharec's officers actually argued over who had the right to kill you? You have no voice, and nobody would return to see your body. Ah yes, rape was promised to he who killed you, yet death was the real reward that lay in wait. How I smiled, beneath my mask of leaves. Now I am the prisoner of your people, and nobody can understand what I say. What will happen to me? How can I plead for mercy when I have no words, my pretty? You of all people should know . . . yet you cannot understand my language."

He munched a seedcake and stared through a window at the wind trains in the sidings. One was being readied to return to Woomera, and the engine was slowly shunting carriages, driven by the gleaming rotor towers, which spun in the ceaseless wind. The crewmen were dwarfed by the great vehicle, and the carriages clanged together like distant bombards firing. On a siding beside it was a dark, sleek galley train. Light bombards protruded from low turrets on its roof. The vineman shook his head.

"All those huge machines that roll along the iron bars, and carry hundreds of warriors without camels. Kharec could never have known your people's real strength."

She stood behind him, watching him watch. He turned with a neat, sinuous motion and stared at her, then pointed to himself and shrugged his shoulders. She nodded and stepped forward.

"I look different without my vines, don't I?" he said, and Darien stroked his cheek with her fingertips. "Ah, so you think I have a kind face, too. Such a pity that you cannot understand my words. Kharec and his raiders are all dead, I wish that I could make you understand that. The hand of the Abbess Theresla struck them down."

She took the pitcher and poured him chilled water and lime juice. He raised his eyebrows at the taste.

"Ah, you know that limes can ward off the scurvy that comes from long journeys and poor food. How very civilized. And you give it to me, but hid it from Kharec. How very flattering. Where is your civilization, I wonder? At the end of those iron bars that cross the desert?" He sipped again from the stoneware cup. "Ah, but I wish that I had some of my banegold poison to go with this. I miss its flavor."

A flea drinking his blood would probably die, Darien thought. Every move

that he made seemed to bring a smile to his face. That was understandable, for he was free of the vines at last.

"Do you wonder how I killed Kharec and the others? Hah, you don't even know that they are dead. Look here." He held up all ten fingers, four times over, then made motions as if he were riding a camel. Finally he drew a finger across his throat. Darien was careful to stare at him, wide-eyed with shock. "All dead."

She pointed at him, then stroked the back of her hand. "So you still think that I am kind, even without an explanation. Well then, I'll tell you everything. I need to tell someone, and the only other person in the world that I could trust is far away, in a Glenellen convent. You would not like her. She eats sparrows roasted on skewers, and sends letters to me by carrier bat. For all that she is a great scholar. Because of it, perhaps. It helps to repel suitors, for her hand in bethrothal would be a great prize. I have killed five of her suitors myself. I am her right hand."

He had just walked out of an unspeakable ordeal, the skin of his face and hands was blistered and scabby with exposure, yet he sparkled with vitality. If he was the right hand of the Abbess of Glenellen, what would the rest of her be like? Darien wondered.

"But you want to know how I killed Kharec and his elite warriors—or you would if you could understand me. The Sweep of the Call is as wide as a two-hour march, and it stops each night for its victims to eat and rest. They remain in a trance, while plant eaters eat plants and meat eaters starve. I led the lancers to the boundary of the Call, then left them there while I walked on into its realm. There I found Kharec. He was chewing on the leaves of a bush, just like a camel. I bound his hands and led him back out of the Call, to where his men were waiting.

"He regained his senses at once, but instead of being grateful the wretch had me seized. He accused me of duplicity and mutiny, without a shred of evidence. Still, he was right. He had his men extract me from my suit of vines, and he had his own worthless body strapped and bound into it instead. It was his intention to come back here and wait for the camel train that supplies you. Camel trains, hah! One glance at your mighty travel-machines and he would have fled all the way back to Glenellen.

"Kharec forced me to walk as punishment, yet that slowed them as they rode north again. If you could understand my words, pretty one, you would know that as we started back for here, four days had passed and a Call was due. I was counting on that to save me.

"Events moved a little faster, however. Early in the next afternoon Kharec's men noticed that the suit of vines was dying. The leaves were wilting, the tendrils hung limp. His lieutenant, Calderan, mentioned it to him. I was dragged before Kharec's camel and commanded to speak—with a blade pressing against my throat.

"I explained that the suit could only be worn and kept alive by me. I have been taking a little of my banegold for years, and can resist a goodly dose of it by now. My vines had been growing dependent on it by absorbing it from the sweat on my skin—not from the water at their roots. If Kharec drank enough poison to keep the vines alive, he would die. If he did not, the suit would die.

"At this stage I raised the stakes a little. I told them to check the timers on their body anchors and the camels' sand anchors: I had done more than release Kharec and leave you a key and pistol when the last Call had passed over this outpost. I had also taken the finely machined gold release pins from every sand anchor in the entire squad and hidden them. So, their sand anchors could no longer save them from the Call, and only I could wear the suit of vines and keep it alive.

"I had Kharec by the balls, my pretty. A repulsive thought, is it not? He could do no more than give me back the suit of vines because only I could save them from the next Call.

"Do you think his pride would allow that? Oh no. He tried to cut me down, but his men defended me for fear of losing the one person who could preserve their own lives from the Call. He killed five, because they could not slash at him for fear of damaging the vines that he wore. When he finally made a break and rode north, all the others streamed after him. Once they were out of sight I caught a camel that belonged to one of the dead lancers and rode south.

"Yes indeed, I rode south. No sand-anchor timer, no suit of vines, yet I rode south. I am the eyes of the Abbess Theresla, after all, and she wished to learn the source of the Call. It was after another day that I noticed the horizon begin to change. It became a jagged edge below a flat boundary between earth and sky. There was a trace of salty mist on the air, and a deep rumbling somewhere in the distance. I was about a hundred paces from the edge of the cliff when I realized what it was and tripped the manual release of my camel's sand anchor. In this place there was a weak Call that seemed never to stop, yet it was only a few hundred paces wide. I dismounted and crept forward on all fours."

Darien poured him another drink, struggling to maintain a bland but puzzled expression on her face. He had seen the source of the Call! It was miraculous, fantastic. It was known that if one followed the Call for a sufficient distance one came to a region where the allure never ceased, the Calldeath lands. Observers had been sent up on tethered hot-air balloons at the edges of these regions, and reported only forests, mountains, and ruins as far as their telescopes could reach. The paraline skirted one of the Calldeath lands at Peterborough and a balloon flight there only the previous year had shown that there was a vast lake in the distance.

There were references to immense bodies of waters called oceans in the earliest surviving books, but these oceans had been out of sight for so long that they were now no more than subjects for scholarly debate. The most popular

theory was that because they lay in the direction of the Call, they must be associated with it. Many religions located hell in those legendary oceans, but now this man had walked into the very nightmare itself and calmly gazed upon . . . what? Darien was about to become the second person in all the world to know the Call's true source. She felt her legs trembling and knew that her excitement must be blazing out like a beacon. The vineman was sure to notice soon—but he turned to stare out through the window at another wind train noisily shunting as he continued with his tale.

"The flat plain fell away in a sheer drop to an enormous lake that stretched all the way to the horizon. Great waves broke against the base of the cliffs in showers of spray and seething foam. Can you imagine it? The waves on the waters of the Alspring gorges are never more than a handspan in height, yet these were huge beyond telling. The water was blue-green, and among the waves I could see streamlined bodies gliding and dorsal fins slicing the surface. Larger, darker things were herding them, keeping them in orderly rows that patrolled the edge of the cliff. Try to imagine a fish from a river or lake that has grown to the size of your travel-machines. Further out were more of the bigger creatures, splashing and spraying water high into the air. Is this the edge of the world, I whispered to myself, and is this the face of the Deity? In some places there were rocks at the base of the cliffs, and these were piled high with whitened bones.

"I took a little telescope from my robe and studied the sleek shapes in the water. Shepherds and sheep, no doubt of it. Were they also angels and souls? If hell was fire, was paradise water? I watched for a long time, and as I did, a full-strength Call came, swamping the little guard Call that suffused the air around me. There was a sudden surge of tingling, yearning ache, a summons to be seduced, yet I could resist it."

He turned back from the window now, his eyes closed and his smile beatific. The jaws of death had closed upon him, but he had nimbly stepped between the teeth. He was justly proud of what he had done—yet he had been wearing no vines! He immediately answered Darien's unspoken question so precisely that she almost gasped.

"Ah yes, I had no need for the suit of vines at all, it was nothing more than a ruse to disguise my real secret. Remember when I had been fastened by my vines at the outpost? When the Call came I slipped from the suit in moments and went about my work naked. Oh yes, I stood before you naked as I put the key and gun on your bed. Would you have liked my body?"

He was looking straight at Darien as he spoke, and she blushed as crimson as the sunrise. His smile broadened, yet it was a teasing smile, not at all evil.

"You blush. You know that I am saying something naughty but you do not know what it is. Do not worry, nameless lady. I am the hands of the Abbess Theresla, and she would never molest you. Ah but here I am talking about my

nakedness when I could be talking about what lies beyond the edge of the world. Which would you find more interesting? I wonder.

"After I had been watching for some time I heard the sound of camels behind me, and I turned to see four riderless beasts trotting straight for the edge of the cliff, a little to my right. As I watched they suddenly broke into a gallop, and all four of them hurtled over the edge, their legs still working in midair. They hit the water well beyond the rocks at the base of the cliff amid cascades of spray which turned to bloody foam as the huge fish tore them to pieces. Now a kanger came bounding to the edge, one that had grown just big enough to be snared by the Call. It too splashed to its doom, and was consumed within moments. The thirty surviving lancers soon appeared, and plunged into the jaws of the living mincers. Then came a pair of goats, a dingo, another kanger, and even an emaciated donkey. One last lancer approached the cliff, a rider clad in ragged greenery.

"Beast, warrior, elder, all are meat for those great sheep in the deep, green water. Kharec's camel broke out of its trot and into a full gallop. And of course it had to be a charge over the last few paces: the bodies must fly clear of the edge and hit the water, not fall to the rocks at the base of the cliffs where they would be out of reach. Harvest home, chaff for the sheep—or perhaps fishmeal for the pigs. As the fishing nets drift through the waters of the gorges in the red Alspring mountains, so too does the Call drift over the land.

"As the moving Call passed I watched as the torrent of flesh poured over the cliff and the shepherds moving their charges past in an orderly feeding pattern. When it ceased I noted that the group of larger shapes further out from shore disbanded first, then the ranks of feeders moved away. More sickening than the sight of the carnage was the thought of the waste: for every beast that reached the cliff at least a thousand must have perished in the desert.

"I crawled back to my camel, and once I had rested I made notes and sketches. Kharec had helped me. The fish that had bitten him in half was four times the length of his body, so that I had an idea of its size. I led my camel out of the guard Call and tethered it to graze. Just outside the guard Call I found a cave, a deep hole in the plain. Here I lived for two weeks, and I observed several more Calls reach the edge of the cliffs. Between Calls I climbed down the cliffs on a rope and took samples of the water. It is salt, at an undrinkable concentration. On the rocks at the base, among the bones of those animals that had not reached the water, I found tattered cloth and jewelry, and piles of human bones in shells of red rust that had once been armor. All along the cliffs it was the same.

"Slowly my cave became a treasure trove, and then I found the greatest prize of all. One skull wore a gold headband with eight claws holding a magnificent green emerald. The skull was so, so small, and even though it was nothing but

whitened bone I saw the beauty that had once clothed it. I knew it to be the body of the sad, legendary Ervelle, who had been banished into the Call many years ago for . . . the saddest of crimes. The lovely girl would have died of thirst and rigor only a day or two into the Call, but her camel had followed it all the way across the red deserts to the cliffs and plunged over the edge. I gathered her bones, rings, and jewelry and buried them in my cave, beneath all the other jewelry that I had collected. At the mouth of the cave I carved ERVELLE deep into the limestone. Just think, my pretty, I rescued Ervelle herself from the Call, I showered her with riches, I built her a palace and I slept beside her. I actually became part of her sad legend.'' Tears glistened in the vineman's eyes, and he dabbed at them with a napkin. "It is as well she will not find out,'' he added with a rueful grin.

"There were other wonders at the base of those cliffs, but why bore you with words that you cannot understand? After fifteen days I packed my gear, rolled my notes and sealed them in waxcloth, then mounted my camel and rode north. It's tethered a long way from here: I could hardly play the mendicant hermit and own a camel, could I? And why have I returned?

"Yes, you would guess it if you could understand me. I returned to take you with me to Glenellen, to lock you away and protect you forever. Nameless one, I am devoted to the service of the Abbess, yet she is not one who could be petted and adored. You are so very vulnerable, and I yearn to give you my vows of protection so very much. Alas, I am not a warrior, and even if I returned during a Call that pack of little dogs with poisoned metal fangs strapped to their jaws would defeat me.''

He was proposing marriage, or at least its equivalent in his society. For him the idea of protection bordered on an erotic fantasy, and Darien was not only female, she was also mute. He seemed genuinely distraught at being thwarted. After a few moments of wringing his hands he changed the subject.

"How did I resist the Call? That is very hard to explain. You have to *be* a certain way or else . . . you cannot. I learned my techniques from the Abbess Theresla, who in turn built on the techniques of the Kooree nomads. They have a different sense of time to us, they can dream different types of time at will. That is part of the secret. And how did she move among them when she is not permitted to leave the Glenellen Convent? Ah-hah, I am her keen ears and sharp eyes. I lived with the Kooree nomads, learned their wisdom. It requires immense concentration and self-discipline, and years of training. The likes of Kharec would not accept that, they would torture me for the secret, yet the secret cannot be put into words. The Call is not material, you see, it seduces the mind.

"I am so proud of being the senses of the Abbess Theresla: if you work for the gods, you live like a god—or so the Diarec heathens say. So, having learned to resist the Call, she then wanted to know what caused it. I am her hands, ears,

and eyes, so I would have to go south, through the hot, red deserts. I needed a strong escort. The Kooree there would kill a lone rider exploring their lands, but a squad of lancers would keep me safe. That is why Kharec was hired, and why the deception of the suit of vines was invented. The suit was too clumsy and undignified for a warrior to bother with except in the most extreme circumstances. My lady is clever, isn't that so? Will I ever see her again? Now I shall have to cross Kooree lands alone, and without the cover of the Call as I travel north. It has never been done, but then I have already done much for the first time, so who knows?''

Now that he had finished his story the vineman lay back on the couch, the first furniture that his back had touched in months. Darien fed him dates and seedcakes with saltbush tiens. A cool breeze played through the window, and sand paintings misted themselves into fluid landscapes as their frames tumbled on brass bearings in the breeze. Away in the distance they could hear a dull, continuous rumble as the wind train finally pulled out to return to Woomera. Through the window Darien could see the rotating towers painted with spirals that rippled forever upward as they spun to drive the gears that turned the wheels. The vineman sat up and watched the train depart.

''Now I understand,'' he whispered. ''Those travel-machines move along the road of steel bars without the need of control. If a Call sweeps over the machine, it travels along as before, while the people that it carries are safely tethered inside. You must have cities at either end of the iron bars. Big, wonderful cities.''

She turned. He put his hands on her shoulders and slid them together to caress her face.

''You . . . are lovely. I wish to lock you away and protect you from the horrors of this world,'' he said gently. ''Yet that cannot be. It is too dangerous to abduct you, and the journey back over the red desert past hostile Kooree nomads will be more dangerous still. You will never meet the abbess who eats grilled mice with banegold chutney and washes her hair in oils of nightshade. She has killed many suitors by dipping her hair in their drinks.

''My name is Ilyire, beautiful lady. It means grape grower, man of the vine. My noble father once seduced the daughter of a poor farmer. Ah, and the settlement turned him into a rich farmer. Could you guess it, but I am the half-brother of the Abbess Theresla? That is well known, and it is why I may come and go at the convent with impunity.

''Now, take this to remember me by. This is the gold pin from the sand anchor of Kharec's camel. If I am released by your people I shall return to my camel and vanish forever from your life. In my pack is a sealed roll of notes and sketches that I must present to the Abbess Theresla.''

Darien held the pin to the light, as if she did not understand what it was, then with a sudden inspiration pushed it into the braids of her hair. Ilyire laughed

and clapped. After a few minutes more of gestures and smiles there was a sharp, urgent rapping on the door.

"Frelle Deputy Overliber, are you all right?" called the Marshal. "If you're not out within another fifty heartbeats, I'm coming in."

She gestured to the shackles, and Ilyire let himself be restrained again. Before picking up the tray she dipped the edge of her scarf in the water, wiped the center of Ilyire's forehead, and kissed him. Ilyire cried out in astonishment.

"My lady, no!" he shouted. "To mock the strength of men is sinful, the scriptures teach—Haargh!"

The Marshal burst the door open with his shoulder in time to see Darien empty the pitcher over the prisoner's head, laughing soundlessly all the while.

"Frelle, Frelle, what did he say, what—"

She held a finger to her lips and gestured that Ilyire was to be washed and fed. The Marshal smiled maliciously and saluted smartly.

"I'll get the five strongest engine-scrubbers in the railside to fill a tub with chilled water," he said to the uncomprehending Ilyire before marching out.

The Ghan stared at Darien. "You seem to be more than a servingmaid," he whispered, his voice so soft that Darien scarcely caught the words. With a final kiss to his forehead she left him to his fate.

Ilyire's clothing and packroll were held for examination in one of the hostelry rooms while he howled and cursed in his bath on the terrace. There was nothing out of the ordinary within the packroll, except for the roll of reedpaper pages wrapped in protective waxcloth. It was an account of what he had discovered at the source of the Call, written with a charblack stylus. The text paralleled what he had told her in the library, with certain notable omissions. Darien left instructions that the hermit was to be locked in a cell until the morning, then released with all his possessions and as much food and water as he wanted.

The climb to the gallery of the beamflash tower was all by ladders. The tower's prefabricated extension had no luxuries such as pulley lifts, and the sensitivity of Darien's message was such that she had to key it herself. The sky was cloudless, and it was almost noon. The beamflash heliostat would throw a strong signal east on its first leap toward Rochester.

What had crossed half a continent as twinkling pinpoints of light was pecked into a strip of paper tape by the Highliber's battery of silver hens. As the message reeled out into view, Zarvora had her back to the mechanism and was speaking to Vellum Drusas.

"The libraries of the Southeast have been squeezed dry, Highliber," Drusas said as he spread his open, empty hands.

"There are more Dragon Librarians in the mayorates of the Alliance than there are in Libris," she replied unsympathetically. "I am talking about another hundred Blues and Greens out of more than a thousand."

"But Highliber, they have duties that *must* be performed. Beamflash towers to run, classes to teach, books to distribute and collect, even ceremonies to perform. The mayors are already complaining about you taking their best people. I have formal complaints from the mayors of Hopetoun, Warracknabeal, Litchfield, and Tandara. Libris is becoming unpopular."

Zarvora reached behind her and tore off the paper tape, but did not look at it.

"The Warren has contacts in the Central Confederation," she said as if she considered it a reasonable option. Drusas was aghast.

"You would have them abduct *Dragon Librarians*, Frelle Highliber?"

"Could it be done?"

Drusas took out a handkerchief and mopped at his face. She had listened patiently to his opinion on the recruitment problems, and the abduction alternative was clearly meant as a reasonable suggestion.

"Yes, perhaps, in a limited way . . . yes," he replied reluctantly, aware that it would be dangerous to give her too many negatives. "It would have to seem like random kidnappings, and be over a vast area, otherwise we would be detected."

"How many would that gain us?"

"I could promise thirty or so of mixed ranks. No more."

"That is barely a third of what I require."

"Please Highliber! The Central Confederation is our ally and trading partner, and all prisoners would have to be brought across Southmoor territory. If the Emir found out that Confederation citizens were being abducted by us he would fall over himself to shout it to the whole Southeast. He has had to make many concessions over that business of the rogue beamflash tower, but this would help him save face."

Zarvora had begun to read the message as he was talking.

/ MARALINGA <> DARIEN VIS BABESSA <> CODE CY900 <> VINEMAN SURVIVED THE JOURNEY AND SAW THE SOURCE OF THE CALL. ALL OTHER GHAN LANCERS ARE DEAD. THERE IS A CHANCE TO RECRUIT THE ABBESS HERSELF. MAY I PROMISE HER A DRAGON RANK IN LIBRIS? /

She looked up. Drusas was opening a folder of letters bearing a bishop's crest.

"Highliber, abductions from the Central Confederation are so risky as to not be worth the trouble. Once again, I implore you to consider the monasteries. Monks are diligent, well educated, and disciplined, and the Archbishop is willing to offer us very generous terms."

"What about the ban on them living in Rochester?" she said dreamily, reading the holes in the paper tape over and over.

"For a reasonable fee per recruit, perhaps he could justify it to the College of Peers."

"Arrange a meeting with him."

"He cannot come to Rochester."

"I shall go to him."

Drusas sat back, puzzled. He had never seen her so agreeable.

"Is there good news on your paper ribbon, Highliber?"

"Yes, Fras Inspector. I took a great gamble and won."

While Drusas saw the Highliber's lackey about arranging a visit to the Bishop, Zarvora keyed a message for the beamflash address of Maralinga and coded it CY900. It read /ACT AS I WOULD / and was directed to Darien vis Babessa.

Darien returned to the beamflash gallery in the late afternoon, when the Highliber's reply was due. As she expected, Zarvora had lost no time in replying. It was a short message, only four words, yet it gave her a free hand. Back in her room she began to write out her own account of the raid on Maralinga Railside. It was midnight before she was finished. As she wrapped the pages at the core of Ilyire's own roll of notes she paused to reread the final page, laughing silently at the words.

John Glasken had also been recruited into the Highliber's service, but under very different circumstances. Blindfolded, bound, and gagged he was bundled into a wagon and driven away from the paraline terminus and through the streets of Rochester. From the street cries, sounds of working artisans, and challenges from guards he could tell that he was being taken to the area of the palace and Libris, then inside. The air around him became cold as the doors rumbled shut behind the wagon, and he was lifted from the tray by someone of great strength and held upright. His shackle was struck off with a chisel; then he was carried for some distance, through doors and past the challenges of several guards. They ascended two flights of stairs before he was put down on a hard bench.

His hands and feet were untied, and his gag and blindfold came off last of all. Before him was a burly Dragon Red Librarian, armed only with a heavy truncheon. He was obviously what Glasken was meant to see first, an incentive to behave. The room was small, with a barred skylight in the ceiling. On one wall was a blackboard and box of chalk. A door on his right opened and a thin, middle-aged Dragon Red came in, a striped uniform over his arm.

"I am your instructor," he said, throwing the uniform on the bench, then standing back with his arms folded. "Put those on."

Glasken had only the watchhouse britches to remove. The new uniform was clean and comfortable.

"Prisoner John Glasken, you have been redirected from six decades on a chain gang because of your training in arithmetic," the librarian told him as he took a piece of chalk from the box. "You will be well fed and clothed, and there will be no heavy work. You will work hard, however. The Mayor needs calculation and arithmetic, and you will provide it."

He turned to the board and drew five small circles in a row, then another just above them.

"This top circle is myself," he said, pointing with the chalk. "These down here are people like you. Now, I have been given a long calculation, one that would take me ten days of tedious arithmetic. Instead I take half a day breaking the task into five parts then share them among my five assistants. They work for two days. I spend a half day putting the results together, and I have the task done more than three times faster. Do you follow?"

"Ah, yes, Fras Dragon Red."

"Good. Now, I can work no more than twelve hours a day, and neither can you. If I have ten people available, I could have another shift working while you sleep, and the solution would take only two days. What would you do to get the solution even faster?"

"Get twenty people?"

"Fool!" he spat, flinging his chalk in Glasken's face. "It still takes me time to split the task up. What I must do is have the task split up by another team of calculators, and then I can get better speed. If I get two people to split up the task into twenty parts, *then* I can increase the speed. What good would it be if I had the task calculated in a few minutes if it takes me a day to prepare it?"

Something more agreeable than six decades in the desert was obviously on offer, and Glasken was anxious to please. "What sort of problems are calculated?" he asked, hoping to sound intelligent.

"Does a rower ask where a battle galley on the river is being steered? Would the knowledge help him row better? What we have here is indeed very like a river or a paraline galley, Fras Glasken. It is a machine of a thousand people, with three shifts to spread the work. This machine has hundreds of times more calculating power than an individual. It never sleeps, gets sick, or dies."

"But what if someone makes a mistake in the middle of one of the big team calculations? How would you know the answer is wrong?"

"The machine is divided into two identical halves, and these run in parallel. If the answers are different then they repeat the calculation until both halves agree. I am now going to train you to be the most basic component of all, an ADDER. You will also cease to be John Glasken. You are ADDER 3084-T."

And so it went, seemingly for hours. Glasken was told the punishments for mistakes and misbehavior, taught the daily routines, taught the ranks of guards and Dragon Librarians, and had the tasks of his fellow prisoners outlined to him.

He was given trials at a desk with a large frame abacus and three rows of

levers, and taught to recognize a number from a row of metal flags in various combinations of up and down. He had to take the numbers specified by the top row and put them onto the abacus. He would then press a pedal and another number would appear on the row, and he would add this to the first on the abacus. When the list was complete all the levers on the flag row clicked to the top position, and he keyed his answer into the bottom row of levers and pressed a pedal. When the next list was due all the levers on the top row fell to the bottom position, and when he pressed the pedal, the first number appeared. He learned about the other levers later.

Although the skylights showed day and night, he began to lose track of time. He was told that the guards who patrolled the aisles were called regulators. They punished, kept order, and sorted out problems with equipment and components. During his training Glasken saw nobody except his instructor and some silent prisoners who brought meals. The meals were constipating and the drinks infrequent, except after training sessions had just finished. Privy breaks were not encouraged during the sessions, each of which were four hours long. At the end of each day he was locked in a small room with four bedcells, and he would collapse into one of the low cells as exhausted as if he had been breaking stone.

One day, without warning, he was sent down a new corridor and into a vast, brightly lit hall. It was the Calculor itself, not a training rig. Glasken was awe-struck. There were dozens of rows of desks and wires crisscrossed above them. Some wires carried little message cylinders from point to point, others hummed under tension. What really made him uneasy was that there was no conversation, in spite of there being so many people. The only sounds were a continuous swishing of beads on wires and a clacking of levers like a field of muted crickets in the evening. After puzzling over the partition curtain that ran down the center of the hall Glasken suddenly realized that he was seeing only one of the huge machine's processors.

He was shown to a seat at the rear of the Calculor, and was shackled to a bench by irons padded with leather. The chains were light and bound with felt to muffle the clinking. Every care had been taken to keep the components comfortable and free from distraction. Glasken's instructor stood behind him and pulled a lever from NEUTRAL to STAND READY.

"You will have light work for the first two hours, while you adjust to the routine," he said quietly, his voice barely more than a whisper. "If you perform up to your training standard, you will be put on the full rate until the half-shift break. While you have your coffee we will assess your work, and after that you may be classed as an installed component."

"What happens if I don't perform well enough?" Glasken asked, ever anxious about the consequences of failure.

"You will be given another week of training. If that does not do any good, you will be discarded."

"Does that mean I go to the deserts to lay paraline tracks?"

"I'm afraid not," he said gravely, shaking his head. Glasken shivered visibly. The instructor moved the lever to ACTIVE.

The sweat soaked Glasken's tunic as he began to work, but after a while he realized that the work was easier than what he had been doing at the training desk. When the rate went up he was able to cope with no trouble at all. At the half-session break three Dragon Reds came over, smiling and nodding, and unpinned the 'T' on his badge. By the end of eight hours Glasken was weary, hungry, and desperate for a trip to the privy, but sure that he would not be discarded. His instructor congratulated him, then led him off to a different cell. He was to share this one with three other men, all from his shift.

Two of them were in their mid-thirties, and the other old enough to be quite grey. Meals were handed to them in tin bowls.

"So you're new, then?" asked MULTIPLIER 901.

"My first shift today," Glasken said between mouthfuls of stew.

"Congratulations," said the old man, CONVERTER 15. "Some new components don't get through the tests the first time. A few never get through, apparently."

"Does being discarded mean what I think it does?" Glasken asked. CONVERTER nodded.

"Have you ever heard of the Calculor outside, ADD?" asked PORT 72. "Thought not. None of the newcomers ever have. That means that none leave here alive, or there would at least be rumors."

Glasken paused between mouthfuls and belched contentedly. "I suppose that means we're in here for life."

"Nay, in here until you cannot perform at least as a basic component," said CONVERTER. "But don't worry, lad. They give you reasonable repair time when you get sick, and there's a pool of spare components to relieve us on fortnightly rest days or when we're sick. Watch your health and you could live to a ripe old age and die in bed before your quota of repair days is used up."

Glasken was unsure whether or not to feel relieved. CONVERTER went to a corner and began to use the piss-jar.

"Has anyone tried to escape?" the Calculor's newest component asked MULTIPLIER.

"Aye. Every so often someone thumps a guard and runs down the corridor, but they get caught and clubbed down. Get past the clubs and there are guns. Ever hear of anyone getting to the guns, CON?"

"Last one was in '97, not long after the Calculor was set up," he said over

his shoulder. "Before my time, mind. I'd say, oh, twenty or more have been discarded for becoming doubles, though."

"Doubles?"

"Trying to escape twice, ADD. Any component doing that gets discarded automatically."

That was a pity, thought Glasken. One could not build up escape skills by trial and error.

"Just one more question," Glasken said as he scraped up the last of his stew. "Who are you all—you for example, PORT?"

"I used to be a money changer," said PORT. "Then I got caught for shortchanging. Been here four years. We're all petty felons, ADD, just like you. Nobody misses us."

Glasken pondered that for a long time. It hurt, but he had to admit that it was true.

Ilyire's journey north was far more arduous than when he had been going south with the squad of lancers. Being immune to the Call offered little protection when one was moving against the Call's direction. He detoured a long way east, to avoid the Kooree tribes that Kharec had fought with. The journey lasted a year, as his camel died in the parched wilderness and he was forced to walk. He hunted, hid, and fought when cornered. At last he reached Fostoria, which he had once considered to be on the edge of nothingness. Slowly he recovered, and while he looked for work as a driver on a caravan returning to Glenellen he noticed that there were at least two men in the oasis who spoke a language very like that of the people beyond the southern deserts. Ilyire speculated that perhaps there might be safer routes south than the one he had taken.

It was another two months before he stood before his half-sister and presented the sealed scroll that described the source of the Call. She had not changed at all, but Ilyire was scarred and tanned by the long and harrowing expedition. They embraced briefly and formally, as was prescribed in the scriptures, yet Ilyire trembled with his eagerness to tell of how he had carried out her orders so very well.

"I am pleased to see you alive, Ilyire," said Theresla, mocking the formal, prudish restraint of Alspring manners.

"I have survived to stand before you again, half-sister," he replied with a sinuous flourish of his hand, joining in the game.

"Had you died I would have lost my right arm."

"Your right arm is as strong as ever," he said proudly, sweeping back his sleeve and flexing his hard, stringy muscles.

Theresla sliced the waxcloth open and unrolled the pages. The distant chanting of her nuns was punctuated by birdsong as Ilyire sat back to bathe in her

praise. She read quickly, but it was a long account. Water tinkled in a small fountain somewhere out of sight, and a sun engine blew a gentle breeze through the garden of vines, cycads, and sandstone pillars. Ilyire knew the desert well and could survive there as well as anyone, yet he did not love it. The cool shade and greenery in the convent was far more to his taste. Spray from a nearby fountain drifted across his face and he closed his eyes. It was now Theresla who was out in the blazing deserts that he had endured for sixteen months, but she was safe from the heat and danger, and would return in the time that it took to read his words. Suddenly she began to read aloud.

" 'Abbess Theresla, where are you reading this? It must be in the shady red sandstone cloisters at Glenellen.' "

"I didn't write that!" Ilyire exclaimed, sitting bolt upright with a convulsion of alarm.

Theresla held a finger to her lips. She was reading from extra pages at the core of his roll.

" 'Ilyire must have just returned, the sole survivor of the squad led by Kharec. He has presented a roll of papers sealed in waxcloth to you, but there are twelve extra pages enclosed, close written, with this at the start. Yes, I gave written orders for Ilyire to be held for the night while I wrote all this out. Abbess Theresla, greetings from Deputy Overliber Darien.' "

By now Ilyire was sitting on the edge of the wicker bench, wringing his hands and writhing in mortification. Even though he had dreamed of nothing else but returning to the terraced gardens of Glenellen for over a year, he now wished that he could be anywhere else in the world. Theresla looked up from the page again. Her large, violet eyes held his gaze for a moment, just long enough to assert her authority.

It was a very, very complete account of all that Darien had seen of the lancers and the vineman, from the raid on the railside to Ilyire's enforced bath on the railside terrace. Theresla read aloud, slowly and clearly, so that Ilyire would not miss a single word. She was standing beside a red sandstone table whose inlaid black opal grotesquery seemed to mock him. On the table lay a long, thin knife with a bloodwood handle, holding down the waxcloth wrapper that it had sliced open half an hour earlier. He toyed with the idea of lunging for the knife and cutting his throat to end the humiliation.

The voluminous black robes that Theresla's hair cascaded over were meant to enhance her helplessness as a woman, yet she wore them as if they were shackles that barely restrained her. There were stories about her, stories that she prowled the roofs and parapets of the convent at night, naked, but smeared with lampblack and mutton fat. She was Ilyire's mad god, and it was exhilarating to serve her. She was also his bottle imp, but the cork that confined her was crumbling.

"This makes amazing reading," Theresla said as she finished the main part of the text. The smile on her intense, bone-white face did nothing to calm Ilyire, whose suntanned face was also more pale.

"She understood everything I said," he whispered, utterly desolate, his hands pressing against his cheeks. "A linguist without a voice!"

"I am proud of you, Ilyire. Your hands did as mine would have—more or less."

"I swear that I behaved with honor!"

"And I believe you. I have Darien's word on it, after all. Now shush, there is a little more to read."

"I must end with a warning, and my warning is the reason that I have written this long story. The Mayor's hold on his western states is weak, and the dispatches that I have seen suggest that he may resort to something terrible, now that Kharec's raid has shown the west to be vulnerable. He has a weapon, a terrible and ultimate weapon. The Mayor could have five hundred camels brought to Maralinga Railside and loaded with poisoned meat. When these camels follow the Call and feed those huge fish many of them will die, and their retribution will be swift and terrible. The Call will reach out to your inland kingdoms, and it will last for weeks, not hours. Your people will strive to answer it until they starve in their Call shelters or at the ends of their tethers. Do not credit us with too much power, however. We know only a little of the Call's origin from our histories, just enough to manipulate it.

"I am committing treason by writing this to you, for I am giving warning to an enemy of the Mayor. Gather your loved ones together, train as many as you can to resist the Call. Organize those people to care for those in the grip of the Call but who are as yet untrained. With luck you may save perhaps a few dozen lives. I wish to help you out of gratitude, yet can do no more than give this warning for I am only a Deputy Overliber. One offset by a dozen.

"Yours in hope and shame, Deputy Overliber Darien vis Babessa."

They sat in silence for long minutes. Leaves and cycad fronds stirred slightly in the breeze from the sun engine. Theresla absently plaited strands of her deadly black hair as she puzzled over writing on the back of the page.

"That is all," she declared at last. "There is some writing in their language on the back of the last page, but I cannot read it. What do you think, Ilyire? Could those people beyond the red deserts destroy us by using the Call?"

"Yes, they could do it," replied Ilyire in a choked whisper. "They will strike before we have enough warriors who are trained to resist the Call. Imagine how they see us now: they think we are training an army that can fight through a Call. Such an army would be almost invincible. They will hit us with the Call itself,

and we'll be wiped out. They had a year to prepare while I was returning." He stood up and paced the red flagstones restlessly. "But why do it this way? She could have shown me these pages back at the Maralinga Railside."

"You told her many intimate things, Ilyire, thinking that she did not understand. She may have feared your anger."

"Feared my anger? I was the soul of kindness with her, I lavished such affection on her that—ah . . ."

Theresla raised her eyebrows and smiled. "Perhaps my hands have been up to more than either you or Darien have confessed."

"No! I swear—"

"I'm sure you do, but let us return to her warning. Something will have to be done."

Ilyire walked to the edge of the terrace and looked out over dark blue waters of the gorge, past the red sandstone cliffs and buildings, and to the south. Theresla came up beside him with a soft rustling of cloth and put an arm around him.

"What is your plan, half-brother?"

"I could go south again. I could lie in wait at the cliffs and cut the poisoned loads from the camels. Five hundred camels . . . yes, perhaps I could manage."

"And if they booby-trapped some of the loads with gunpowder? No, my dear brother, there is only one way to save the beautiful people and cities of Alspring. This Mayor must learn my secret of resisting the Call. Then he would not fear us enough to exterminate us."

"But you are the only teacher, Theresla."

"Very true, and once I leave this convent I shall be condemned as a renegade and a wanton by the Council of Elders. I shall go south and you will be my guide."

"Leave? You?" exclaimed Ilyire, horrified. "No! Absolutely not! You're an abbess, you're a noble's daughter—you're a woman!"

Theresla leaned on the stone railing and looked out across the blue waters of the gorge.

"Remember the last time that you said those three words to me, Ilyire?" she asked.

Ilyire shuddered. "You pushed me over the railing and held me by my robes for at least ten minutes."

"It was a few seconds."

"It seemed like ten minutes. All those neophytes on the terrace below looking up at my, ah—"

"Do not avoid the issue, half-brother. I held you with one hand, and pulled you back with one hand. I am very strong."

"After all those years of climbing about in the roofs, hunting sparrows, I'm not surprised."

"I am strong and resourceful, and I shall go south," she stated. "You will be my guide."

"No! Scripture is quite specific. 'Protect thy women from the beast in the soul of man. Cloister thy women and children from unjust harm. Adore thy women as the vessels of destiny. Protect—"

"—thy women from their own follies.' Yes, Ilyire, I know the scripture as well as you, if not better. The third dictate is the reason that I must go. This is a matter of destiny. Either I go with you to Maralinga or there will be total destruction."

"It would be a violation of scripture."

"The destruction of the Alspring people would be the greatest possible violation of scripture. *You* would be killing thousands of women and children, Ilyire. Could you stand before the Deity and explain why you allowed that to happen?"

He squeezed his eyes shut and shuddered.

"You taught me, I can teach others," he said in desperation.

Theresla smiled, then lashed at him teasingly with her black tresses. "Excellent. I shall call a neophyte, and if you can teach her how to resist the Call within a week, I shall let you go alone."

Ilyire stood with his head bowed while Theresla waited for an answer. At last he shook his head. She patted him on the back.

"Besides, I taught you nothing."

"What?"

"Never mind. Hurry, we shall need two riding camels, four pack camels, and enough stores to last us three months . . . ah yes, and robes to disguise me as a mercenary lancer. We shall leave tonight."

"It would be better to go during a Call."

"But Calls are cast as far inland as this only two or three times in a year, and we cannot afford to wait. If the Deity is pleased with what we intend to do, he may send a Call."

Ilyire went to buy camels and stores, while Theresla returned to her cell to pack. There *would* be a Call to cover their flight, there was no doubt of that. She had refined her knowledge of the Call in Ilyire's absence, and could now detect the approach of one within twelve hours. Soon she would tell him that, and more. Soon, but not yet.

By the light of a smoky olive-oil lamp Theresla unfolded the last page of Darien's letter. It was a coded message, which she had hastily unraveled in her head while in the garden. Now she wrote it out carefully, to be quite sure.

"One offset by twelve, Frelle Theresla, such a simple code, yet I doubt that Ilyire will break it. In the pages you have read you have seen that women of talent can

reach positions of great power in our nation, yet enjoy much freedom as well. That is half of my reason for telling this story. The other half is to frighten Ilyire into helping you come to us if you wish. Are you happy with such a cloistered and restricted life, even as an abbess? Do you wish to continue to live and explore through Ilyire? If not, I can offer you escape, Frelle Theresla.

"There is *no* ultimate weapon, I made up that scheme of poisoned meat and the Call. Before Ilyire gazed over that cliff we had no idea what lay behind the Call either. If you are happy with your lot as abbess, then decode this for Ilyire, laugh at my guiles, and go on with your lives. If you wish to exchange your rank of Abbess for that of Overliber Dragon Silver, then Highliber Cybeline herself has authorized me to bid you welcome. How do I know this so soon, when Libris is many days away, even by wind train? Come to us and find out. Combine our command of physical machineries with your mastery of the mind, Theresla, and we may even break the curse of the Call itself. Think about it, then come to Maralinga Railside and ask for your friend and servant,

"Frelle Deputy Overliber Darien vis Babessa."

Theresla smiled at the words.

"In all the world there are now two women and one man who know the source of the Call," she told the reedpaper page, then touched its edge to the flame of the olive-oil lamp. The material burned slowly, reluctantly, as if it disapproved of her decision.

7 COUP

To the older staff of Libris it seemed that the end of the century was bringing with it the end of their world as well. Under Highliber Zarvora books were no longer revered as the symbol of civilization's former greatness and ikons of unattainable power: they had become mere tools for answering questions. There were no long, leisurely committee meetings about the finer points of cataloguing, no ceremonies in the cloisters to celebrate important lost books being recovered, and no excursions of senior staff to examine Rutherglen's libraries during the annual Drinkfest. Life in the new Libris was full of production schedules, timetables, relocations, and messages on paper tape punched full of holes. The number of staff had doubled in just three years, yet everyone was doing more work. The fastest-working cataloguer had processed two hundred *times* the weekly average of five years earlier, yet even his record would probably last a mere month.

The matter of just what the extra staff were doing remained unclear. The library network now effectively ran both the beamflash and paraline networks, and provided a host of other services to the Mayor's administration. During a brief but savage border war with the Southmoors at Talangatta it was again clear that Libris played an important role in Rutherglen's small but well-equipped army. Astute observers realized that the little mayorate's real military potential might be hidden from sight. Again its military galley trains and portable beamflash towers had materialized out of uninteresting piles of spare parts in less than a day when the Southmoors had mounted what they thought was a surprise attack. What else lay waiting to be assembled in Rochester?

Spies from other mayorates noted that far more food went into the Libris signaling annex than the staff listed as working there could eat, and rumors of a vast team of calculating lackeys had even spread as far as the common folk of the city. That team was known to be hungry for new recruits. Men and women in all walks of life professed ignorance of mathematics for fear of being recruited by a blow on the head during some moonless night. Enrollments for mathematical subjects in schools and universities across the Southeast Alliance fell to a tenth of what they had been a year before, and students had to be granted the status of Dragon White Librarian before they would set foot in a mathematics class or lecture. Many mathematics edutors fled to the Central Confederation and even the Southmoors. They could not be persuaded to return until Mayor Jefton proclaimed them all to have the rank of Dragon Red and to be under mayoral protection.

The Calculor demanded ever more components, however. The Highliber's military galley trains had poured reinforcements into the battle zone at an unheard-of rate to crush the Southmoors at Talangatta, generating a lot of goodwill toward Libris. Zarvora's inspectors had been allowed to comb the Islamic prisoners for those who were numerate. Seven hundred recruits were culled from five thousand prisoners, along with ninety bilingual translators. To accommodate the extra components almost a fifth of the books in Libris were moved into the mayoral palace for storage, together with a complement of Dragon Librarians and lackeys.

Lemorel learned from Tarrin that the Southmoor prisoners had been assembled into a little dual processor unit housed where the Classics and Epics bookstacks had been. There were 150 components per processor running in two shifts, but the Highliber was negotiating for yet more numerate Southmoors from the sporadic fighting on the Deniliquin border. This Calculor, the Islamic Machine as the librarians called it, was particularly fast with control and decoding calculations, and freed up time on the main Calculor for the Highliber's work.

The nature of that work remained a mystery. Some of it involved the calculation of all lunar and solar eclipses for centuries past, and other processing work had Dragon Whites and lackeys searching card drawers and books for references to astronomical events. Then there was the work on orbital mechanics.

Calculations on the production of tiny orbiting blocks, and calculations on ge-ometries of particles with strange vectors acting on them. Neither components nor librarians understood what was behind their calculations.

Lemorel's work on Call vectors, historical drifts, and changes in Call paths continued to have a low priority, although she had improved rights of access on the Islamic Calculor. She was a Dragon Silver, and her research work produced verifiable data. That carried weight. As Tarrin was always saying, the Highliber did not have much in the way of idle conversation, but she took note of results.

A very strange decree was delivered by the System Herald one day when Glasken was about to finish a shift. Henceforth all regulators, managers, and guards were to wear masks over their eyes while working with the Calculor's components, and were to be known by codes and numbers. Lemorel was MAN-AGER 37, he noted as a list was read out for the first and only time.

Vellum Drusas was careful to keep in contact with everyone that he had ever helped, yet he also subscribed to the old saying that fish and visitors grew stale after three days. A large number of librarians throughout the Alliance saw him only occasionally and briefly, yet held him in high regard. Lemorel was a prime example of Drusas' friends; indeed, he considered his decision to send her to Libris to be one of the wisest moves of his career.

"Lemorel Milderellen, author of nine papers on the Call, and soon to be Lemorel Milderellen, EdR in Observational Philosophy," Drusas said as they sat together on the balcony of the Dragon Silver refectory. "Just three years ago who would have known it?"

She folded her arms and sat back, still a little nervous at his overfamiliar mannerisms.

"I had thought you suspected some talent in me when we met in Rutherglen, Fras Vellum. Why else would you have recommended me for the Dragon Red tests?"

"Genius is a fine balance, Frelle. It is easily upset, yet if given a chance it can soar above the clouds. That's what I love about my work as Inspector. I may be on the heavy side and as slow as a river barge, yet I can give others a chance to fly. When do you present your thesis?"

"June 1700 GW. My father will be traveling from Rutherglen for my grad-uation."

Drusas laughed affably and snapped his fingers for another drink.

"I'm glad of, it does my heart good. With the exception of Dragon Yellow all your librarianship ranks have been presented in a rather makeshift fashion. That's bad for tradition. Libris has changed so much and so quickly. Why, every one of my own regradings was carried out with full ceremony: processions, oaths, dinners, robes, everything."

"Tradition must give way to need sometimes."

"Perhaps, perhaps," he conceded, arching his eyebrows and stroking the multiple folds beneath his chin. "But surely when need is great and the work is so hard, one should work hardest at preserving a little tradition and ceremony. Think back on the three most precious moments of your life, Frelle—now, right away!"

He gave her a moment to think, looking away at the petals cascading from an ornamental apple tree in the light breeze.

"Now, at least one of those moments was your Dragon Yellow ceremony, am I not right?"

"Yes Fras, but—"

"Yet you have received more promotions than that. You remember Dragon Yellow because of the ceremony."

"Where is this leading, Fras Vellum?"

"Nowhere in particular. I just want you to remember that Highliber Zarvora will not be here in a century, but Libris will certainly endure. Spare a little time for tradition, pay a little heed for the old ways. I have worked in Libris during the full glory of the old traditions and it was indeed glorious."

REGULATOR 45 nudged REGULATOR 317 as five Black Runners sauntered along the aisles of Dexter processor on a security inspection.

"I know THETA and EPSILON, but who are the others?" she whispered.

"PI and OMEGA are visitor tags," he whispered back.

"And BLACK ALPHA?"

"The word on her is *don't even ask*. Very, very senior."

With her inspection over Zarvora dismissed the four Black Runners and made for the components' cells. Behind her mask, makeup, indigo lipstick, and with her hair tightly braided and beaded she hoped that she looked anonymous, but she felt as if she were stark naked. Opening a folder, she read the personnel evaluations one more time.

FUNCTION 5: too old; FUNCTION 26: seldom washes; FUNCTIONS 214, 646, 614, 620: notorious bores; FUNCTION 587: has pimples; FUNCTIONS 79, 450, 333, 390, 471, 569, 598, 606: have the pox; FUNCTION 247: works well when cornered like a rat in a trap; FUNCTION 9: dangerous security risk; FUNCTION 490: should not be allowed to breed; FUNCTION 34: lock up your silver; FUNCTION 92: apart from arithmetic, out of his depth in a puddle of spilt beer.

Zarvora had been hoping for better from the twenty best male FUNCTIONS in the Calculor. All struck her as unpleasant or unsuitable, not the sorts of men that she would willingly share a romantic coffee with while they discussed numerical methodology and optimization theory. FUNCTION 9 was actually dangerous! Why had he not been shot? she wondered. She selected his brief. His latest exploit had been to reconfigure the register wires to play "Happy Birthday" ten days earlier. Why was October 17th so familiar . . . ?

"My birthday!" Zarvora gasped.

So, FUNCTION 9 was dangerously clever, but perhaps not dangerous as such. She decided to assess him first. She adjusted her robes, checked what could be seen of her face in a small mirror, swallowed, squeezed her eyes shut, and took a deep breath.

"I command eleven thousand staff and provide services to fourteen million souls," she whispered. "Why is *this* such a problem?"

FUNCTION 9 and his cellmates looked up as a guard unlocked their door; then BLACK ALPHA appeared. She silently pointed to FUNCTION 9 and beckoned. He followed her to the isolation cells. REGULATORS often took components there for discreet dalliance, but ALPHA was carrying a personnel file, not a jar of wine and chocolates.

"Your pranks have been brought to my attention," ALPHA began in an unusually high voice. "They caused disruption."

"I apologize," ventured FUNCTION 9, bracing himself for the worst.

"The Highliber was furious—" Zarvora caught herself. "But was flattered at the birthday greeting."

FUNCTION 9 sighed with relief.

"How did you do it?"

"Too easily."

Zarvora swallowed and fought for patience.

"Why did you do something so, so blatantly . . . blatant?"

"To get the Highliber's attention. To show her holes in her security procedures big enough to drive a wind train through."

By now Zarvora had almost forgotten why she was there.

"But—but you are a prisoner!"

"That's no reason not to protect the Calculor. It's a wonderful machine."

Suddenly it dawned on Zarvora like the light of a magnesium flare: this man was at least as exceptional as Nikalan, but in a very different way. Definitely a good prospect—but now what?

"Your loyalty and diligence are impressive, FUNCTION 9. I—we want you to be working with us more directly."

"Uh, thank you."

"I have been studying your file. You are one of REGULATOR 42's five lovers."

"What—*five*?" he exclaimed, then sat back frowning and shaking his head.

His reaction gratified Zarvora. She had at least known something that he had not.

"On my word your security rating could be regraded to that of a MANAGER and you could be given a pool password. You could be punished, but I, ah, take a personal interest in you and, ah, should you be—that is—attracted to me—that

is, my proposal I could, ah, give you those powers and more. That is, of what you want.''

FUNCTION 9 could neither follow the thread of her argument, nor deduce her real intentions. He thought he was being interrogated about breaking passwords.

''The pool password is 999POOL, the System Controller's is XX99XX, but the Highliber's is proving harder. Do you want to know how I found out?''

Something inside Zarvora shattered. He knew the passwords. He knew the Calculor better than she did. I have nothing to offer him, she thought. How mortifying.

''Uh, yes. Please prepare a report, mark it for BLACK ALPHA.'' She stood up, her movements jerky and uncoordinated. ''I should go. Thank you. You saved me from public humiliation. I am grateful. More than grateful, you must understand . . . or perhaps not.''

Only now did FUNCTION 9 realize what was being played out between them. She was a master of security, but he had made her look like a rank amateur. Now she was being gracious enough to acknowledge it rather than having him shot and trying to cover up the evidence. She was also, possibly, trying to seduce him out of gratitude. Well, I've had a short but interesting life, he thought as he stood up and reached out to take BLACK ALPHA's hand.

''BLACK ALPHA, thank you for shielding me from the Highliber,'' he declared, looking into the eyes behind the mask. ''Your tolerance is almost as attractive as your figure.''

He had intended to kiss her hand and hope for the best, but she surged forward and wrapped her arms around him before he could move, clinging to him more out of relief than lust.

''You are a dear, dear man,'' she said after a long time. ''I have been watching you. You are infuriating but . . . cute.''

Four hours later Zarvora was in her office, lying on the couch with her hair brushed out and a wet cloth over her eyes. Her lackey knocked.

''It's Vorion, Highliber.''

''Enter.''

''Highliber, are you not well?'' he asked as he caught sight of her.

''I have just had the most harrowing afternoon since my interview with the mayors for the Highliber appointment,'' she mumbled.

''Surely not the cataloguers again?'' replied the lackey.

''No. There is a man I hold in high esteem. I thought he might despise me, but he treated me with great kindness.''

''May the Deity bless him, Highliber.''

''So I seduced him.''

''You what?'' exclaimed Vorion, who had never thought of her as anything other than as neuter and dangerous as a lightning bolt.

"I seduced him, Fras Vorion. What do you say to that?"

"Congratulations?"

"Fetch me a blanket, then wake me in fourteen hours. Why did you knock, anyway?"

"It's October twenty-seventh. Mayor Jefton is here about the Tandara situation's briefing."

"Tell the Mayor to roll his briefing up very tightly and—"

"Highliber!"

"Then tell him to prepare for war. Now go away and stop bothering me."

The Mayoral Advisers Council was led by Gamesmaster Fergen. In this role he was ever watchful of the Mayor's moods, and in this meeting the Mayor's mood worried him. For most of his short reign Mayor Jefton had been talking vaguely about wars to establish credibility of one sort or another for the Mayorate of Rochester, so it was no surprise to find that topic on the agenda again. Rather than being jaded and in need of excitement, however, the young Mayor was now nervous, hesitant, even frightened.

"What are our chances in a war with Tandara?" Jefton asked.

A lackey standing beside a large wall tapestry map of the southeast pointed to the powerful Tandaran capital with a white cue.

"Tandara borders on Rochester," Fergen replied. "Whatever you do is of interest to its mayor. If you were to, say, side with Deniliquin against the Emir of Cowra in the Finley border dispute, then Tandara's Mayor Calgain might allow you to rail certain wargoods through his territory in return for an impost against Cowran sanctions on the Balranald paraline."

The lackey dutifully indicated each of the principalities, cities, and paralines in turn. Mayor Jefton did not answer immediately, and his hands twitched as he sat gazing up at the map.

"I meant Rochester *against* Tandara," he finally admitted.

Fergen spluttered, loudly and involuntarily. The other advisers sat up as if they were puppets jerked on strings.

"Suicide—with respect, Mayor. Tandara has twenty times our land area and thirty times our population."

Jefton continued to gaze at the map. "Tandara controls all our major trade, paraline, and beamflash routes. Rochester is charged for the privilege of running the Alliance for the benefit of Tandara and the other thirty mayorates of the southeast. That is hardly fair or just."

Archbishop James interjected for the first time. "Christian mayorate fighting Christian mayorate is repugnant to the eyes of God without there being good reason," he warned.

"Tandara has the biggest army," said Overhand Guire, yet his tone was not entirely dismissive. "Mayor Calgain is very unpopular. There are factions within

the Tandaran council that are sympathetic to us. If his army were to be defeated, well, he would be in serious trouble. His army is his power base.''

The Gamesmaster quickly stood up, snatching the cue from the lackey.

''Mayor, look there at the map. Deniliquin and Wangaratta are very powerful, but have a long border in common with the Southmoors. It is in continuous dispute, and takes up most of their regular forces. Offer them help and they will greet you with open arms. Ask for help and you'd get silence. Nathalia and Kyabram are very small and run by cowards. Propose an alliance and they'd denounce you to Tandara just as soon as it takes a lackey to run to the local beamflash tower. Shepparton has no kind feelings for Tandara and they want the annexed Kyneton province back, but the mayor there is no fool: he wants to side with a clear winner. If it comes to that, Deniliquin would like to see Tandara put in its place before Mayor Calgain raises paraline customs duties again and seizes more border castellanies. The only problem is that they'd rather not help with the fighting.''

''Then the Overhand's analysis is sound? Tandara does have weaknesses?''

''No, no, Mayor you're missing the point. Look, in a general sense, yes, the Overhand is right. If the Emir of Cowra allied himself with Mayor Gregory of Deniliquin and crushed Tandara there would be few capitals that did not have dancing in the streets. With respect, however, you are neither the Emir nor Mayor Gregory.''

''Indirectly, I control about the same area as the Emir.''

''Granted, but at least some of his states are united behind him, Mayor. Rochester is no more than an administrative convenience. It's a neutral area where the business of the Southeast Alliance can be run from without disruption from the Call. We have the biggest library system in the world, and our librarians provide a lot of useful services, but that's all. The mayorates of the southeast pay Rochester to provide services. Try to go beyond that and they would replace you as easily as sneezing.''

''Our librarians provided those galley trains to rush troops to the Talangatta fighting,'' said Overhand Guire.

Fergen put the cue down and folded his arms, openly sneering at the Overhand. ''How many mayors would put troops on those galley trains for a war against Tandara?''

Mayor Jefton flung down the transcript of his Advisers Council meeting in front of Zarvora and stood back with his hands on his hips. She in turn gazed at him steadily until he looked away, turning his attention to the window. It did not take her long to scan the transcript.

''There is nothing new in here,'' she observed. ''We have already discussed all this.''

"The facts are the same, but the opinion is different. A war would destroy Rochester."

"A defeat would destroy Rochester, Mayor. A war—"

"A war with Tandara and a defeat are one and the same."

"Tandara gives us an opportunity to assert our strength. We cannot bother with a lot of petty squabbles between little states. Defeat Tandara in the name of prosperity and stability, and the whole of the Alliance would rally behind you."

"No! Highliber, you have served the mayorate well, but this is too much. Rochester would be crushed. Mayor Calgain would make this land a Tandaran province and rule the Alliance."

"I could defeat Calgain with my Tiger Dragons alone."

"No! Not another word. Say anything more and I shall consider it a challenge."

Zarvora straightened in her seat, then slowly put both hands on the desk. The reciprocating clock behind her clacked seven times. Jefton stood trembling, his eyes staring wildly at the rows of mechanical animals that spoke for the Calculor. He was clearly terrified, yet he held firm. Zarvora nodded slowly to herself, surprised at his bravery.

"Mayor Jefton, you have no choice."

Jefton turned to face her, then held his gaze against hers. To him it had become a choice between fighting the Highliber and losing his mayorate.

"I accept your challenge," he said, his words forced, almost a wheeze.

"Will you be representing yourself or naming a champion?" Zarvora asked in a neutral tone.

Humiliation stung Jefton like the slash of a whip.

"The mayoral champion will do what he is paid to do," he said, feeling as if disembodied hands were squeezing his throat.

Like Libris, the mayoral palace had its own dueling chambers. Bluestone paving extended a hundred yards to either side of a thin white inlay of marble. To either side of the central line was an armored gallery equipped with plate-glass mirrors for the judges. Lackeys polished the mirrors while the judges positioned themselves and checked the field of view.

Stevel Coz limbered up beside the gunrack as the moderator looked on. As the Mayor's champion, and the challenged party, he had the right of choice of weapons and he intended to weight that choice to the fullest advantage. The rows of dueling pistols gleamed in the light filtering between the grooved marble arches that framed the strip of level bluestone. Across the chambers, beside the other judges' gallery, Zarvora and Vardel Griss stood waiting.

Zarvora had chosen the head of the Tiger dragons to be her second as much for her loyalty as her rank. Griss was not an exceptionally tall woman, but was

lean, severe, and sharply groomed. Her hair had been bowl-cut that morning, she was wearing her nine medals, and she smelled faintly of scrubbing soap. Years ago a musket ball had passed between her lips, smashed two teeth, and passed out through her right cheek. Zarvora noted that she had buffed up the ragged scar to make it stand out all the more. Without speaking, she spoke for the Highliber: This is my second, so be all the more fearful.

Somewhere out of sight a razzlehorn fanfare blared, and heavy doors boomed open.

"His Eminent Supremacy, the Mayor!" called a herald, and the mayoral party entered to the strains of a band playing the Rochestrian anthem.

"Technical breach of protocol, it should be his personal anthem," whispered Griss. "You're challenging the Mayor, not the state. I'll note it down."

The judges assembled at the center line with the moderator. Archbishop James and Overhand Guire stood on one side, Gamesmaster Fergen and the City Marshal on the other. The moderator was the Chief Magistrate himself.

Zarvora and Coz stayed on their respective sides of the chamber as their seconds walked forward to the Chief Magistrate.

"I am obliged to beseech you in the name of God, the people of Rochester, and my own office of Chief Magistrate to consider further arbitration. I place my services at your disposal, here and now."

Jefton, standing beside his champion's second, barked "Never!" then coughed immediately. Griss replied, "Thank you, but no."

"As the challenged party's champion, Stevel Coz may choose the weapons," the moderator ritually informed Coz's second. A pair of matchlocks was selected from the gunrack and presented to the moderator on a tray. "Choose one pistol for the challenger," Griss was instructed. She inspected both weapons and chose one. "Return to your stations."

"Dussendal short-barrel matchlock," Griss whispered urgently as she reached Zarvora. "Heavy, big grip, rifled bore but no sights. You aim it by the weight and feel of the weapon."

If you were experienced with it, Griss neglected to say. Zarvora had small hands, and was known to favour medium-weight guns. Griss loaded the gun and lit the fuse, then handed it to Zarvora. The moderator called them to the center line as two handlers wheeled in a target pinned to a haybale frame.

"Stevel Coz, fire at the target and may mercy guide your hand."

Coz raised the Dussendal above his shoulder, then swept it down and fired in a single movement. Booming echoes reverberated as the smoke cleared to reveal a dark hole precisely midway at the top of the outer ring. "Bad form," whispered Griss to herself. Coz was making a show of giving the Highliber every possible chance to fight.

"Zarvora Cybeline, unless you can better that shot you must forfeit the duel and consider yourself the loser. Proceed."

Zarvora knelt, steadied the gun with both hands, closed each eye in turn, and squeezed the trigger. Her shot showed dark on the middle circle. The moderator conferred with the judges for a moment.

"I declare this duel legal by the laws of this mayorate and the powers invested in me," he announced. "Judges, proceed to your posts. Chamber marshals, clear the dueling range. Seconds, load the weapons again and stand clear."

Griss handed the reloaded gun to Zarvora, whispering, "Call short, turn fast, but shoot with both hands on the gun."

Zarvora hefted the Dussendal clumsily and the Coz had to pause in his breathing exercises to suppress a smile. She did not like the weight, and there was no sight. Unless she chose to save face by calling a distance beyond the range of the matchlocks she would be killed. A call of ninety paces would save face. Twenty paces meant she wanted a fight, but would be at a disadvantage because of his experience. Below twenty would be dangerous to them both, with the speed of the turn deciding the duel. Zarvora was fast, but the gun was heavy and would overswing in inexperienced hands.

Zarvora stood back to back with the Mayor's champion, the thin line of marble between their heels. The moderator wound his metronome.

"Attend me. At each strike of the metronome you will take one pace. The number of paces is to be decided by the challenging party, Highliber Cybeline, and at her word the count will begin. You will call a number at my words 'Call the distance.' Is that clear to both parties?"

"Yes," they replied in turn, their voices sounding a cadence that echoed like the "amen" of a hymn in the chambers.

"Ready. . . . Highliber Cybeline, *call the distance!*"

"One!" snapped Zarvora.

Coz hesitated with surprise as the moderator's metronome clacked out for the first time. Zarvora stepped a fraction earlier than Coz but precisely on the count. As her foot touched the ground she swiveled her body and slapped the barrel of the Dussendal into her free hand to steady it, firing as Coz was completing his famous sweep-turn. Zarvora's shot caught him high in the rib cage as he pulled the trigger. The ball from his gun tore a short furrow through her collar, but he was already dead as he hit the ground at her feet.

The moderator strode forward, calling for a medician and the seconds. Griss brushed at Zarvora's collar, where smoldering wadding from Coz's shot had lodged. The Mayor's champion was pronounced dead. The moderator collected the guns, gathered the judges together, and led them to his chambers beyond the white arches.

"Wonderful, masterful, that was superb," Griss babbled, shaking with relief as if she had been in the duel. "I know I advised you to call short, but only a single pace!"

Zarvora closed her eyes as Coz's body was lifted onto a stretcher.

"Such a waste, Frelle Vardel. Still, I am alive."

"And the winner, Frelle. You beat the Mayor's champion, you rule Rochester now."

"Rule Rochester? No, there will be more fighting before that. Fortunately I have a champion who owes me several duels."

"A champion, Frelle Highliber? *You* need a champion?"

"A champion, Frelle Tiger Dragon, a deadly champion."

The razzlehorn announced the return of the moderator and judges. They walked with visible tension, strain showing in their faces. Jefton appeared between two arches, face white, and flanked by five of his personal bodyguard.

"As moderator in the duel between Mayor Jefton III of Rochester and Highliber Zarvora Cybeline, I hereby declare the judges tied on a foul. Two of the judges maintained that because the moderator had instructed the Highliber to call the number of *paces*, she was obliged to call more than a single pace."

A foul declared by a majority of judges would have had Zarvora executed for murder that very afternoon. Instead the vote was evenly split, and would have to be referred to the next meeting of the mayors of the Southeast Alliance in— eleven months. They would decide if any of the judges had been unfit to preside at the duel. If all were declared fit and proper judges, then the mayors would declare a winner on the basis of further deliberations.

"Highliber Cybeline, you are to surrender yourself into the custody of the Marshal of Rochester. Have you anything to say?"

"I hereby petition for an immediate meeting of the mayors of the Southeast Alliance," she said briskly.

"Only the Mayor can answer such a petition," replied the moderator, turning to Jefton.

"Denied," Jefton called confidently. "An extraordinary meeting of the mayors can only be called in times of great danger to the mayorate. This is no such time."

"Who shall act as Highliber?" Griss whispered urgently.

"Who indeed?" answered Zarvora. "But tell Fras Tarrin TURING-17-ADA. He will understand."

Zarvora was led away by the Constable's Runners and Griss hurried to Libris with the news. A meeting of the Dragon Gold Librarians was called for that evening to decide who should act as Dragon Black while Zarvora was in custody. Sternley, the Head of Reference, was chosen for his seniority, according to tradition. Tarrin was left in charge of the Calculor.

With Zarvora gone the pace suddenly changed dramatically for those working in and with the Calculor. There were no new schedule tables for the week to come, so work was suspended until the appropriate Dragon Librarians drew them up.

When they were assigned, a sizable number of staff found themselves with nothing to do. Some did nothing. Lemorel asked Tarrin for control of the Islamic Calculor and set it to work on her thesis. Months of her planned work suddenly evaporated, but the edutors at the University were not to know. Another request to Tarrin for runners and lackeys to do reference work was welcomed with open arms—literally. The support staff at Libris had been suddenly starved of work with the Calculor taking so long to set up. A request for scribes to write up the results as they were processed also met with instant approval. Lemorel began to think in terms of submitting her thesis by the middle of January and writing "EdR" after her name by March.

The unaccustomed surfeit of leisure time confused the other middle-rank librarians. Some were reduced to working two hours or less per day, and spent their time reading books, chatting in taverns, or even programming the Calculor to play other games besides champions. The Black Runners recorded an extraordinary increase in amorous affairs among librarians, especially at levels Red, Green, and Blue, yet the acting Dragon Black was too busy to read their reports.

Lemorel experimented with the Islamic Calculor, pioneering methods to allow a single processor to check its own results by introducing calibrated process checks tied to checksum verifications. The Highliber would have been interested, but the Highliber was allowed no visits from the Dragon Librarians of Libris. Growing bolder, the bored Dragon Silver experimentally seized control of the beamflash node at Griffith one afternoon and changed some minor routing tables. Nobody noticed. She spent whole nights playing champions against the main Calculor itself when assigned to oversee the night shift. Somewhere within it was Nikalan, she knew that from the rosters, and the same rosters revealed that Glasken was currently asleep. She took great satisfaction from the knowledge that he slept alone.

Outside Libris the effects of the Calculor's subtle failures were dramatic and alarming. First the beamflash decoding became scrambled. Felons were set free at random by mayoral order and wind trains were scheduled at one-minute intervals: investigations revealed that sections of beamflash traffic were being decoded into random characters. Hand-coding and decoding would take an order of magnitude longer, and the traffic volume had grown enormously owing to the capacity of the Calculor for encoding and decoding.

Within twenty-four hours Rochester was all but cut off from the rest of the southeast. Much of the life of the city was also guided by the wires and beads of the Calculor. The Constable could no longer check records of the felons in his custody and the jails soon filled with prisoners that the Calculor then set free at random. Tax records were found to be missing. The Calculor knew where they were, but to allow a human down that trail would take weeks of decoding and audits. Diplomatic messages were no longer being decoded, so that Jefton no

longer knew what was being said in his own court. Freebooters from the Heath-
cote Abandon raided a customs post, and there were other troop movements on
his borders that he did not understand.

Thirty drayloads of sheep manure were delivered to the palace kitchen, while
a herd of pigs was turned loose to ravage the palace gardens. The palace provisions for a week were delivered to the city stables, and Jefton had to send lackeys
to a nearby tavern to buy his dinner. Jefton signed an appointment for the new
Minister of Finance only to be told a day later that Atholart, his appointment,
was a prizewinning stud goat. The news that the appointment had been officially
commended by the Council of Envoys did little to comfort Jefton. He decided to
visit Zarvora in her cell.

"Rochester is plunging into chaos," ranted Jefton, infuriated. "How are you
doing it?"

"Rochester can no longer function without the Calculor, Mayor, and the
Calculor requires maintenance. I designed it so that only I can perform that maintenance."

"But Rochester will be ruined."

"Mayor, I have been walking a long and difficult tightrope for some time. I
am weary of idiots like you jiggling the ends for their amusement."

"Idiots! Did you say—"

"Idiots, yes."

"I could—"

"Do what you like, but you will do it without the Calculor."

Jefton ordered the Libris staff to restore the Calculor to full functionality. It took
six hours for the Dragon Gold Consentium to explain to him why this was impossible without the Highliber's cooperation, and even then he was not sure that
he understood. A group of edutors from the University was called in to inspect
the Calculor, but after getting over the shock of the machine itself they declared
that it could not possibly work. This enraged the desperate young mayor even
more. When Tarrin declared that the edutors could not be allowed to go free now
that they had seen the Calculor, Jefton was not inclined to dispute his decision.
The edutors were added to the Calculor's trainee intake.

Jefton was finally forced into action when Mayor Calgain of Tandara annexed
the Hunter Triangle. This was a tiny slab of land at the south of Rochester, and
Calgain declared that freebooters were using it as a base to raid his territory. It
contained a registered customs post for a Tandaran paraline, however, so this
would no longer bring in revenue for Rochester. The breakdown of the service
functions of the Calculor had by now caused sufficient chaos to justify calling an
extraordinary meeting of the Alliance's mayors. Even the mayors themselves

wanted the services restored, but like all such high-level meetings it took time to convene.

A month after the Highliber's arrest Lemorel decided that Libris was sure to collapse back to half its current staff, and that those who had been promoted on the basis of mathematical skills alone might soon be looking for other work. Getting work as a magistrate's champion seemed a good option, and she decided to polish up her targetry skills in the Libris dueling chambers. The gun-lackeys were well trained and brisk, loading and cleaning the guns with efficiency, resetting the targets quickly, and carefully recording the scores. In spite of the echoing blasts and reek of sulphur, the atmosphere was one of calm concentration.

One morning Lemorel arrived early and was surprised to find the Dragon Red Dolorian standing with a 20-bore matchlock. She glanced uneasily at Lemorel, who nodded affably and settled down to watch. When it was quite clear that she was not only to have an audience but one that outranked her, Dolorian turned to the target bale, standing square-on and squinting down the sights of her pistol with one eye. She pulled the trigger, then teetered back a few steps on her tower heels as the gun went off. The shot did not even strike the haybale behind the target. A lackey emerged from his shelter, shaking his head and pointing to a fresh hole in the paneling behind the bale. The Dragon Red's eyes flickered to Lemorel again as she called for another gun. Brave enough to risk humiliation, concluded Lemorel approvingly.

Dolorian was a career librarian of the old school, and was still a Dragon Red in spite of being over thirty. Her mathematics was weak, but she had a chance to achieve Dragon Green rank if she showed up well over the full range of subjects. Targetry was one of them. Her figure was sinuous yet very well curved, and she dressed to show it to full effect. While she wears weapons as jewelry she will remain a Dragon Red, Lemorel decided as she watched. Again Dolorian aimed, fired, and staggered back. Lemorel dived for the floor with her hands over her head as the ricochet whined above her. The gun-lackey emerged from his shelter and pointed to a groove in a marble archway some yards from the target.

"Frelle Dolorian, that was atrocious," said Lemorel as she stood up and dusted her uniform. Dolorian gave her a cornered, desperate stare, then looked down at the flagstones. "Please take your boots off," Lemorel ordered.

One did not disobey a Dragon Silver. Dolorian started for a moment; then, with a self-conscious grin, she sat down on a bench. Her boots reached all the way up to her tunic, and her tunic of the day was very short. With seeming concentration she began to unlace the boots. Her legs were gleaming white and bare beneath them. Lemorel looked down at her feet, then kicked off her own shoes.

"Our feet are about the same size, Frelle Dolorian. Put these on. Lackey! Reload the Frelle's gun—no, bring her a twenty-five-bore, with flintlock action."

The lackey jumped as if he had been whipped.

"Frelle Milderellen, my wrists are too thin for the recoil from such a big bore."

Lemorel held out her own wrist. There was very little difference.

"Six weeks of pushups and floor-bars and you won't know yourself, Frelle. Firstly, stand side-on, feet apart by a shoulder's width and a half. Bend the back knee for balance against the recoil. Your grip should be with two hands, while you get confidence. Squeeze the trigger: jerking it is the commonest mistake in beginners."

The lackey brought a loaded pistol. Lemorel held Dolorian's hands and guided them down to a firing position. Her hands were warm and soft, while her breasts were as firm as rammed-cotton cushions. It was little wonder that she had an entourage of admirers.

"Now, do it by yourself, and shoot this time."

"But what about aiming?"

"The Dragon Green test is dueler's freeform, not target shooting. You must hit through reflex, not squinting down the sights. There's no time for that sort of thing in a real duel. And keep your eyes open. You always close them when you shoot."

Dolorian swept the gun down and fired. Through either genuine skill or chance the shot knicked the boundary between the inner circle and the bull. Her big green eyes bulged unblinking as she stared at the neat hole in the target through the dispersing powder smoke. It was her first shot to hit the target that morning. The lackey called "Bravo!" and clapped.

"That suggests that my advice has some value," said Lemorel, turning back to her pupil.

Standing with her legs bare and wearing flat, scuffed dueling slippers, Dolorian still seemed to have grown visibly in stature as she called for another gun. This time she hit the median circle.

"I expected you to at least hit the target bale, but this is even more promising," said Lemorel as the smoke cleared. "You have to practice a lot more. Fifty shots per day at least."

"But my hearing—"

"Wear wax plugs, as I do." The flagstones were cold beneath her feet, and she stepped back onto a mat. "Lackey, another gun."

Dolorian never bettered her first shot that morning, but she at least hit the bale or target paper every time. After seventy shots Lemorel called an end to the lesson.

"But Frelle, did *you* not come here to practice?"

"Ah yes," said Lemorel, drawing her twin-barrel and firing one side. The shot hit the bull slightly high. "Yes, I need a little practice, but not today. Could I have my shoes back?"

They went out into the city together, to the markets at North Junction. Lemorel supervised while Dolorian bought two pairs of low-heeled goat-leather ankle boots and a pair of cloth dueling slippers. The selection of a proper pistol took somewhat longer. Dolorian traded her 18-bore ornamental matchlock for a 32-bore target flintlock. Lemorel insisted that 34-bore was the ideal caliber for her and that she would regret the choice as her wrists became stronger.

"A heavier gun means more weight to take the recoil," she explained as they went through a gate to the green between the wall of inner Rochester and the lake. An open-air tavern was serving boating parties from the lake, and the day was bright, cool, and windless. They sat at a table, watching the light pedal trains rattle across the trestles and into the inner city. Dolorian took the new gun out of her woven shoulder bag and turned it over doubtfully.

"This looks . . . bulky and gross, if you'll pardon my saying so. To me it says 'This person cares only about function and nothing about style.' "

"On the contrary, Frelle Dolorian, to me it says that the wearer knows guns, and is someone to reckon with. Polish the metalwork. Oil the wood, rub in scent if you like, and have hot poker tracery burned into it. That will all personalize the gun, but the style is already there."

Dolorian considered this, then decided that her new instructor was right. While she strapped the holster on and adjusted the straps Lemorel leafed through a book that had spilled from Dolorian's bag, *The Highliber's Courtesan*. She read the last few pages.

As history it was mostly fabrication. Highliber Charltos had been 106 years old and suffering from dotard's sickness when he died in his sleep. The book had him being stabbed by a beautiful Dragon White wielding a poisoned hairpin in mid coitus. The only points in common with the truth were his name and title, and the fact that he died in bed.

"It's a tasty little story," said Dolorian, by way of explanation rather than apology.

"I'm told that Charltos was a mousy classics scholar whose idea of a wild time was a midnight sherry party with the Dragon Golds. Do you read many of these, ah, romances?"

"Oh yes. There's nothing better than a mug of Northmoor coffee, an easy book, and a bed piled deep with cushions after a bad day in Libris—except for a man of talent in the bed, of course."

"You should have any number of offers, what with working in the Calculor as a regulator."

"That I do, but I pick and choose very carefully, Frelle. Once every so often

I treat myself to a demijar of frostwine, and I treat myself to men in much the same way. The act of love should not be a chore, and I go to some pains to make it special each time.''

''You have no one lover?''

''I swore not to have one special lover until I reached Dragon Green in rank. With my looks and figure, Frelle, it's hard to get men to take me seriously. Were I a Dragon Green, men would be forced to admit that there was more to me than bottom, breasts, long hair, and a pretty face.''

Lemorel pondered this while Dolorian strode about awkwardly in the low-heeled boots and struck poses to show off her new flintlock. A shunting engine rumbled across the trestles and the navvys whistled to a boatload of girls. A servingman brought two mugs of coffee.

''Have you come across the component John Glasken?'' Lemorel asked.

''I only know them by their numbers, Frelle.''

''3084, and he's currently MULTIPLIER.''

''The one who has an embargo on him against dalliance?''

''That's him. What do you think?''

''He presents well, and plays the lutina passably. He's due for an upgrade to FUNCTION in two months. His body is impressive, but I've found that impressive bodies are too often guided by unimpressive brains.''

''He has a degree in chemistric.''

''Has he? Well, if the embargo comes off I shall keep him in mind.''

Lemorel considered her words.

''One night long ago, Frelle Dolorian, I found myself in mortal danger. While I was fighting for my life I learned that my supposedly faithful lover had a tavern wench bent over a table with her skirts around her ears.''

''MULTIPLIER 3084?''

Lemorel nodded.

''Tasteless . . . but rampantly lustful,'' said Dolorian, pouting. ''As long as you know what to expect—''

''Ah, but I did not expect it. Glasken had played the virtuous and faithful romantic to me. I had him sent to the Calculor, and now I make suré that he draws his weapon for nothing more than passing water. Three months. It's probably the longest he's been without access to the nest of paradise since he learned the facts of life.''

''But Frelle, all manner of men would do the same. I've been betrayed too, but with more discretion.''

''Glasken knows no guilt, that's his difference. I want him punished, but before she was imprisoned the Highliber was considering a limited release for him. He knows chemistric, and she needs graduates of that science to help develop a new type of beamflash flare. All the magnesium in the known world comes

from a single pre-Greatwinter warehouse in a Central Confederation abandon. The price is going up as stocks run low, yet beamflash traffic at night is increasing. I don't want Glasken free.''

Dolorian squeezed her hand.

"How old are you, Frelle Lemorel?''

"Nearly twenty-two.''

"Nine years my junior. Let the years pass and you will learn not to bite so hard.''

"My friends call me Lem. I do have friends, believe it or not.''

"Mine call me Lori, and I have fewer *good* friends than you'd think. Was 3084 your only betrayal?''

"In a manner of speaking. In my very distant past . . . I had a lover and it was I who did the betraying. Perhaps Glasken was the payback that fate owed to me. On the other hand, perhaps I was the payback that fate owed *him* in turn. He sampled women like warm, succulent pies: now he gets bread and water.''

"So you too have been a betrayer, Lem. I can't imagine you doing anything beyond the rules.''

"I've learned my lesson. A roll in the hay with the village stud is not a good reason to betray yourself or anyone else. For me it was calamitous.''

"One infidelity? A few tears and sharp words are nothing.''

"I've never talked about this . . . but it hardly seems to matter these days, so why not? I had a lover in Rutherglen. Nothing was consummated, then one night I let myself be seduced by somebody else. It was all so stupid.''

"If nobody was hurt then why worry?''

"Somebody *was* hurt, Lori, believe me. Brunthorp, my seducer, had another girl, yet he could not abide the fact that a weedy little sod like my lover Semidor began bedding the girl that he had deflowered. He courted me again, urging me to leave Semidor. I refused. He told Semidor about what I had done with him. That very evening Semidor killed himself.

"It was an evil, hideous night. Before he learned that Semidor was dead Brunthorp came over and told me that he'd told my poet-lover who had taken my virginity—and under what circumstances. I ran to Semidor's parents' house at once, but found him dead. There was an inquiry, but Brunthorp was exonerated. That was not good enough for me. What would you have done, Frelle Lori?''

Dolorian was sitting and listening very quietly, knees together and hands clasped, hunched over a little as if pressed down by the weight of the story.

"Nobody has ever killed themselves over me. Once I discovered that a lover was playing me doubles and I poured rancid fish oil along the length of his bed on the evening that he had hoped to share it with another. That was when I was younger and less resigned to the ways of the heart. What was your revenge?''

"I killed a great number of people.''

"Lemorel!"

"It shocks you?"

"It does indeed. Why bother? Was justice achieved? Was the world a better place for it?"

"Three questions . . . to which I say I don't know, yes, and no. Will you hear the full story?"

"If you wish to tell it. This is like some lurid novel come to life."

"After Brunthorp was exonerated I registered a challenge with the magistrate. Brunthorp and I were called to the dueling chambers for a formal hearing. His father was a friend of the Mayor, and the decision went against me. I challenged the decision. The magistrate's champion entered, and I was shown the weapons of settlement. Still I did not withdraw. The champion selected a gun and aimed at a target. He hit it two points below the eye at forty paces. I took a gun and aimed—there would be no case if I could not better him—but I hit the bull squarely.

"Both the champion and Brunthorp were badly shaken. During my childhood my father let me test the guns whose mechanisms he had repaired as contract work for gunsmiths. I became a very good shot, I probably have a natural talent. I stood back to back with the champion, he called, oh, thirty paces. We walked, turned, and fired. I hit him squarely in the center of the chest. His ball raked my side and broke a rib. With blood trickling down my side and half crazed with pain, I challenged Brunthorp.

"It was like the night that he took my virginity. Pain, guilt, and blood on my skin. Perhaps the memory of it made me spurn the formal apology that Brunthorp delivered on his knees. I wanted to kill him, and I'd earned the right to a judgment duel. He was white with fear. In spite of his hale and manly image and the pistol that he wore in public, he was not a good shot. He called fifty paces, perhaps hoping that we would both miss. I did not miss. I hit him just above the right eye, and his head burst like the melons that I had been practicing with. I dropped to my knees and threw up. When I stood again I was dizzy from loss of blood.

"When we emerged from the dueling chambers the magistrate was bound to silence by law, but not me. I let people know why I had challenged, and how Brunthorp had pleaded for his life. By law I was the victor in a trial by combat, yet I was marked from then on. I was dangerous, I was a killer. The horrible thing is that I had not loved Semidor so very much. Oh, he was a sweet little sod, but he was also rigid, opinionated, and a terrible poet. If he'd showed any sort of initiative over the previous year he could have had what Brunthorp had appropriated. Instead, I dragged him closer to me, so close that he would be terribly hurt when Brunthorp exposed our sordid little romp. Perhaps Semidor would not have fallen so hopelessly in love with me had I not introduced him to the pleasure and closeness of sex, but who is to know?"

Dolorian shivered. The air was cold, and sitting very still while Lemorel talked was chilling her as surely as the tale itself. Lemorel took a sip of coffee and scratched at a heart carved in the tabletop.

"I wonder why I'm telling you this, Frelle Dolorian. I came to Libris to escape from that past, to make myself over. Now I'm telling a stranger who might gossip it all over Libris."

"You need an artisan of the heart. As you know guns, I know passions."

"So what is your advice?"

"First, could you tell me what happened after the duel?"

"More deaths. Brunthorp's family were newly rich merchant nothings and were relieved that I didn't pursue them for damages. Not so his girl. She was an estatant's daughter, and she sent her brothers out on an illegal vendetta. My brother died by a bullet meant for me. I was granted a legal vendetta from the magistrate, and I went to the estate and killed four guards, the three brothers, and the girl herself. Her parents petitioned the magistrate for peace and gave half of their estate to the mayorate in fines.

"Once more I had won, but at a terrible price. People shunned me henceforth. While other girls had their sweethearts, the boys—justifiably, I suppose—feared me. I had to leave Rutherglen, and the library system was my path. Now here I am, in Libris. The present magistrate's champion in Rutherglen is technically my deputy and I still have an executioner's practice, would you believe that?"

Dolorian sat shivering and rubbing her arms.

"What do you think of me now, Frelle Dolorian?"

"Lem, what can I say? You're hopeless. Listening to you is like watching me trying to shoot. People . . . people in my life have never taken dalliances as seriously as that. I'm truly sorry for you."

Lemorel smiled ruefully, then gave a soft, breathy laugh, the laugh of an exhausted soul.

"Glasken is getting off lightly compared to other men in my past."

"We need to find you a wonderful lover."

"Oh but I have met someone wonderful."

"Oh-ho, now the full truth comes out. Who is he, what does he do?"

"He's a guest of the Mayor of Rochester, and he's doing life."

"Oh Lem! You can't go on like this."

"Then what should I do?"

"Keep company with me, learn to take men and the games that we play with them less seriously. Agreed?"

"Done—but look at the sun. It's time I was back in Libris. Now, what do we owe—no, put away your purse, rank pays today."

After Dolorian had left, Lemorel sat thinking for a while. Her friendships with women were so civilized, while her dealings with men turned into such disasters. Down near the shore of the lake a troupe of itinerant players was re-

hearsing a street burlesque. Acting! That was it. With men she tended to play a role, with women she was Lemorel. Was acting to blame? Was she at fault for trying to be what she was not?

She took a breath, tried to whisper her thoughts but found she could not. She resolved not to breathe out until she had spoken.

''I'm proud of what I am.''

The admission did not sound as foolish as she had feared, and came as a great relief. Many people liked her for what she was, and if others did not, it was their loss. The servingmen had begun packing the tables and benches onto a cart as she paid for the coffee.

The walk back to Libris took Lemorel through a city very different from the one it was before the Highliber's arrest. The riot shutters were up on most buildings, and the street stalls that were still open were guarded by varying numbers of armed men. The Constable's Runners were in disarray, and were more interested in protecting their own homes from the increasing chaos than obeying the orders of a mayor who was clearly demented. They were good times for the preachers of doomsday, however, and religious orators of every kind were attracting anxious crowds and fueling their worst fears. Lemorel noted that the message of every orator she passed was the same: Rochester was a null zone, it was never swept by the Call. It was an evil place where the hand of heaven never culled the guilty.

Religious opinions differed about Rochester. The smaller fundamentalist groups wanted the entire area abandoned, but established faiths all had churches, temples, and shrines in the null zone. The inhabitants of the mayorate needed ministering to, after all, and senior church officials vied with each other for the right to suffer the torment of Rochester's pleasures. The library system had no need for such justifications. Having no Calls to interrupt work meant that the part of the beamflash network controlled by Libris handled more traffic and coding than even Griffith. Rochester did Call tracking and forecasting for the whole of the beamflash network now, even for areas where predicting the Call was seen as thwarting the will of God.

The guards saluted as Lemorel entered Libris, but behind the façade of security and order the situation was, in a subtle way, worse than outside. The systems that Zarvora had designed were falling apart. Tarrin was working frantically to keep the Calculor services going, but he was at best only a diligent administrator and was not equal to the task. Walking out onto the observation gallery Lemorel gazed down at Nikalan as he sat at his FUNCTION desk. She still felt guilty about him. He had been such an admirable person before his breakdown. Still, she was done with acting so there was no point pretending to be someone else to make up for what she had done to him. Lemorel thought of exercises that she had run against the Calculor using her own brain and nothing

more. She was good, but she could never compare to Nikalan—or Mikki. How could she win his admiration, and perhaps his love, as she was? By being clever in her own way, perhaps? By making the Calculor far more than the Highliber intended it to be? It was an interesting thought.

She sought Tarrin and told him that she had some ideas about restoring the Calculor to a more reliable state. He gave her the master password with something akin to relief. Now she sat in the Highliber's study without fear of arrest, playing at the keys of the silent harpsichord and reading the messages of the gearwheels and mechanical animals. Zarvora's lackey hovered about constantly. He had meals brought to Lemorel, had a bunk moved into the study, and cleaned the place only when she took her daily break to meet Dolorian in the shooting gallery. It was yet another revelation for Lemorel: elite people had elite servants.

Getting the Calculor functioning for specific tasks was not as hard as she had feared, and after a few days she had it restored for reasonably efficient stand-alone operation. Its relationship with the external world was the real problem. Lemorel decided to begin by going over the records of her illicit session on the Calculor. The bank-tally reference archives were held in Libris. They contained encoding checks, simple checksum digits which were meant to guard against errors, rather than tampering. Lemorel accessed the account that she had created in September with seven hundred gold royals. The seven hundred gold royals were still there.

Those seven hundred royals did not exist, of course. She had not altered the grand tally register to increase it by seven hundred, but that would never be checked unless someone tried to draw on the account. The owner of the account was dead, however, but it could not be reclaimed into the Mayor's Consolidated Revenue for another seven years, because he had been a foreigner. Some accountant would then throw up his hands in horror, but the trail would be cold. To guard against even that danger she would have had to alter the grand tally itself, and that was not an option. It was held in too many reports and documents, and too many accountants had the monthly grand tallies for the past ten years committed to memory. Lemorel had certainly remembered *that* tally for *that* month with no trouble. She tried to access the tally to check her memory, but accidentally set the Calculor adding the individual account registers to arrive at the figure. When it arrived it was seven hundred royals *short*!

She sat up straight in surprise, popping the joints in her spine. The message on the wheels of the output register was clear, but not possible. She remembered particularly that the last three digits should have been 777, the incorrect figure. Now they were 077, matching the real tally. Seven hundred gold royals sponged from somewhere. The actual amount was too much of a coincidence for it to be theft by some Dragon Librarian.

The grand tally did not have a checksum digit because it was known to the

public and verifiable. All the individual tallies did. A few strokes on the keys set
the Calculor verifying checksums against tally amounts. The task estimate came
in at three hours, not because of the processing involved, but due to the bottleneck
of lackeys having to copy figures from tally cards.

Now she turned to the thornier problem of restoring the Calculor's contact
with the outside world. The mail register was full of communications data and
coded requests that Tarrin could not translate into instructions for the Calculor.
Lemorel read through the index, hoping to pick out patterns that might group the
requests into like types. The patterns were certainly there, although unraveling
them would be no easy task. She stopped abruptly at the name of Deputy Overliber Darien vis Barbessa. Her message was a dozen pages long, and had come
over the beamflash with a high-security code. Darien's letters to Lemorel had
been bland and friendly, and emphasized that she was working very hard in a
particularly boring railside. Twelve pages of expensive beamflash time seemed
unlikely if the far west was really as quiet as Darien made out. Lemorel typed
/ACCESS/ and waited for the file runner to arrive.

The file arrived in a sealed red folder, and Lemorel signed for it. Tarrin had
given her a free hand, so why not? Maralinga Railside was a familiar name, but
the account quickly expanded to Alspring, Glenellen, the Ghans, and the alarmingly strange Abbess Theresla. There was a man who could defy the Call by
wearing a suit of living vines—a suit which he turned out not to need at all. Then
came the description of the source of the Call. Had Darien lost her mind?

"This is too fanciful for words," Lemorel told a mechanical owl.

The last page revealed that a copy had been sent to Abbess Theresla. It was
as much a report to the Abbess as to the Highliber. If true, it was beyond the
wildest imaginings of the greatest philosophers in history.

There were other notes in the file. Zarvora had been doing research using
the vast resources of Libris. There was the transcript of a sixth-century chroni-
cler's account of a crude experiment with the Kooree nomads. A warrior philosopher from the cave stronghold at Naracoorte had led several dozen lancers to
raid a Kooree tribe, and after a sharp, intense battle five of the nomads were taken
prisoner. They were held in the Gambier Abandon, where tests with tripwires and
tethers were done during seven Calls. There was no question of it, the Kooree
were able to make themselves collapse as the Call passed over them.

Attempts were made to learn the Koorees' secret, and these attempts escalated
into torture. The warrior philosopher sent a detailed letter back to his mayor,
reporting that although some of the Kooree were trying to cooperate, their explanations involved concepts that were too alien to grasp. Nothing more was heard
from him. When a squad of lancers arrived at the abandon later they found evidence of an attack by a larger group of Koorees, but no graves or bodies. There
were, however, the smashed remains of sixty-two anchor timers.

A brutal and ruthless way to confirm a legend, thought Lemorel as the output bell rang, and the hens pecked data into their paper tape. She tore off the tape and held it to the lemon glow of the oil lamp. Seven hundred gold royals had been debited from the bank tally of Archbishop James of Numurkah, but the checksum digit did not match. That was the only anomaly in the whole scan, but the recalculated grand tally was still seven hundred royals short of the original total. The credit on Lemorel's bogus account and the debit from the archbishop's account should have canceled to give the correct total. Someone had tried to implicate the archbishop in the Wirrinya-tower incident, and they had assumed that the seven hundred royals had already been included in the grand tally.

The monthly aldirectum revealed that Archbishop James of Numurkah had been appointed as adviser to the Council of Mayors at Rochester in 1698 GW. He lived in the grandmanse at the east end of the mayoral palace . . . and had the status of duel judge to the Magistrate of Rochester. He was one of those who had presided over the Highliber's challenge against the Mayor. There was, of course, no record of how he had voted.

An incompetent robbery by means of the Calculor, or an attempt to frame the Archbishop? The data was encoded, so that the human lackeys did not understand the figures that they read and wrote on the orders of the Calculor. Thus the changes could have only been made *through* the Calculor—but who would do such a thing?

Zarvora? Tarrin? Aside from them, there was only Lemorel herself. Tarrin was floundering badly in his attempts to program the Calculor properly, and Zarvora would not have neglected to change the checksum digit for the bank tally. A full inquiry by the Council of Mayors would result in the bank records being decoded and released to a team of clerks, and these would relate the bogus account to the Archbishop's. They would also discover the bungled changes and conclude fraud by persons unknown. Archbishop James would be declared an unfit judge, and the Highliber's case would be thrown open again.

Lemorel looked from the keyboard to the rows of mechanical animals, then at the silver hens poised to peck at the paper tape. She unlocked the door, nodded to the guards, and made her way to the observation gallery above the Calculor. The machine was oblivious to the problems it was causing across the mayorates of the Alliance and beyond. If it was given rubbish to process, it returned results that were rubbish. She walked to the data-exchange chambers, where lackeys and runners retrieved and copied data from miles of handwritten cards for the Calculor, then on to the Reference exchange, where runners were sent to the bookstacks of Libris itself to answer the Calculor's questions. Such a grand concept, such a mighty tool.

The main Reference Center in Libris was an immense domed cylinder, with

the walls lined with bookstacks that extended back beyond view. It was night, so there were no external readers working there, just runners on the Calculor's business. She stopped and gazed around, aware that she was standing within the memory of a vast brain. It was hers to command; should the Highliber lose her case, Tarrin would gladly give it to her . . . yet only Zarvora could develop it and make it grow. Lemorel understood its usage, but not its design. She watched the runners going about their business all the way from the ground to the ninth floor. Some of their work was on her own thesis, yet if the Highliber was released she would quickly learn what had happened from the shadow logbooks that were updated at noon each day.

The walk back to the Highliber's office seemed far longer than her tour of the entire Calculor.

The Archbishop was discovered to have an association with the Wirrinya conspiracy in the investigations leading up to the extraordinary meeting of the Council of Alliance Mayors. True, the evidence was slim, not enough to have him tried for treason, but still enough to discredit his credentials to serve in Rochester. All decisions that he had made on matters of law subsequent to the Wirrinya conspiracy were invalidated, and this included his judgment in the duel between the Highliber and the Mayor's champion. It was disclosed that he had voted against the Highliber, but with his vote removed the verdict favored her two votes to one. Zarvora was freed immediately, and the Council of Alliance Mayors met a week later to declare Jefton a constitutional monarch. Zarvora Cybeline was to run the mayorate as Prime Councillor—for life.

Lemorel received a summons to the Highliber's study in Libris not long after she had been freed.

"I have been examining logs of certain recent work on the Calculor," Zarvora began ominously. "Tarrin's knowledge of checksums is limited, yet a certain transaction that he made, ah, outside the usual procedures, turns out to have had the checksum corrected."

"Fras Tarrin is lucky to have loyal and competent staff, Frelle Highliber," Lemorel replied.

"So am I. You cleaned up after Tarrin while acting as System Administrator."

Lemorel swallowed. "Yes."

"Why?"

Lemorel swallowed again. "To strengthen your case with the Council."

"Why?"

"Curiosity, Highliber."

"Explain."

"The Calculor can do extraordinary things, yet I know nothing of its real

purpose. If the tool is so very wonderful, the reason that you built it must be quite fantastic. I defended you to discover that reason. It is not to schedule trains and decode messages.''

Zarvora considered this while looking through Lemorel's personal file. ''Your reason is hardly flattering and is not based on loyalty . . . but I am grateful. How can I reward you? Promotion? Power? Wealth?''

The Highliber was pleased. Lemorel felt as if she were melting with relief.

''I would like to help you more directly, Highliber. In your absence I redesigned parts of the Calculor to reduce the need for checking and speed up processing. Tell me more of your projects and I can design better ways to run them on the Calculor.''

Zarvora peered into a glass case where a brass orrery was standing. She moved a lever at the front of the case and it whirred and clicked into motion. ''This is the year 3931 Anno Domini, that is, in the old Anglaic calendar,'' Zarvora said slowly as she watched the planetary motions being modeled by the clockwork. ''Greatwinter's Waning 1699 is 3931 AD, and the original Year of Greatwinter's Waning was 2232 AD.''

Lemorel thought carefully.

''If you please, Highliber, but scholars have been arguing over those dates for centuries. How can you be so certain?''

''It's nearly dark enough to use the observatory. Come with me.''

She slid the lever back and the orrery stopped. Her lackey Vorion hurried up to lock the study as they left.

''Just before I was imprisoned the Calculor completed a massive project of sorting and correlating all the Greatwinter data known from all sources and texts. It gave me three possible dates, and using those dates and a number of pre-Greatwinter references to solar eclipses I did a series of double checks. One date verified to within minutes, and I was able to fill in the missing years. This is the year 3931 Anno Domini, there is no doubt about it.''

The observatory was an onion-shaped dome, whose sides hinged down like petals as the telescope rotated within to follow the movement of the sky. The eleven-inch refractor was driven by pulleys powered by weights deep below in Libris. A mechanical regulator within the observatory clicked out to the gears that drove the telescope. Zarvora spun a brass wheel and the instrument dipped until it pointed to a part of the sky opposite the vanished sun. While Zarvora adjusted the focus and checked the calibration of the alignment dials, Lemorel looked out over the city, bathed in the day's afterglow. The Wanderer star Cobleni was moving rapidly among the fixed stars. It reached the Earth's shadow and winked out.

''The objective glass in this telescope was made in 1880 AD, yet here it is, still faithfully serving astronomy,'' Zarvora said as she selected an eyepiece.

"Strange how a piece of glass could outlive so much, yet still be as good as it was the day it was made. It will probably outlive us as well."

Lemorel continued to look out over the city. Midsummer was past, but the days were still long and hot. Water boys went about in the mayoral gardens, keeping exotic plants alive. Pleasure craft moved languidly on the waters of the lake, and music floated over from some distant beer party beyond the walls of Libris. An horlogue in the observatory beat out the eighth hour since noon. Zarvora clipped an eyepiece into position and stared through it.

"Please observe," she said finally, standing beside the screen and folding her arms.

Lemorel peered into the eyepiece, in which a faint, coppery star glowed steadily. It seemed dispersed, almost oval.

"It's Mars, badly focused—but no, Mars is away over there. It's another planet, or perhaps a comet. Yes, a comet. That would account for the odd shape and fuzzy outline."

Zarvora shook her head. "It is a reflection from the inside of a vast band encircling the Earth. The bright spot is from the sun's rays being focused by some sort of texturing on the inner curvature. Sometimes it appears as a starlike point, sometimes it is a thin bar of light."

A shiver passed through Lemorel, although the night air was warm.

"What is it? Something to do with the Call?"

"Three weeks ago it was not visible, but now it has begun unfurling. Do you recall the output from that particularly long Calculor run just before I was arrested? It was a date, December the twenty-seventh, 3931 AD, which is 1699 GW. It is the date of Greatwinter returning, the date of the band becoming active."

Lemorel stared into the eyepiece again. The faint, fuzzy oval was unchanged.

"Which theory of Greatwinter do you believe in?" asked Zarvora.

"There are many theories. I favor a physical explanation rather than divine punishment. A failed experiment in the engineering of weather, perhaps."

"An open mind, good. I shall tell you what I have pieced together. The entire world was heating up in the twenty-first Anno Domini century. Then the Call came. In the panic and anarchy that it caused, the stronger of the Anglaic nations fired things called nuclear winter bombs blindly, thereby generating dust that veiled the Earth and made summers like the coldest of winters."

"So the Call caused Greatwinter—indirectly?"

"Yes, but in that century the world was actually being threatened by a Great-summer, could you believe it? One mayorate, Japan was its name, proposed to erect a huge, thin band between Earth and the moon, a shield to weaken the sunlight a little. Its plan was to send tiny machines to the moon where they would replicate themselves out of moondust. Hundreds of rockets were to seed the moon, but only one prototype had been launched by the time the Call arrived and shat-

tered civilization. Ever since then the tiny machines from that single rocket have been building copies of themselves as well as the modular parts for that sunshield, sending them out into orbit where they have been circling as a diffuse cloud. Now they are interlocking and unfurling into a vast band.''

"But the Earth is no longer warming up," said Lemorel.

"Quite correct, Frelle, but the machines on the moon do not know that. We now have that band whether we want it or not.''

"So the Earth will cool.''

"Yes, Frelle Lemorel. In four hours' time we shall have a new year, 1700 GW and 3932 AD. The fuzzy star that you can just see will become plainly visible in a few weeks, and its nature will be deduced. 1699 is the last year of Greatwinter's Waning, 1700 is the first year of a new Greatwinter.''

Zarvora made a few observations, measurements, and drawings, then returned the telescope to the rest position. Lemorel helped her to close the dome.

"It is the eve of the new year and century," said Zarvora as they stepped out onto the roof. "Do you plan to join in the celebrations tonight?''

"I surely will, Highliber. It may well be the last such new-year revel. Tell me, though, what are all your studies of that band in the sky leading to?''

"Just before Lewrick was shot I told him part of the answer: to be warned of a disaster is to gain great power.''

"And the other part?''

"I am not totally without altruism, Frelle Lemorel. Greatwinter threatens civilization, and civilization is very much to my taste. I have been researching ways to prevent the worst effects of this second Greatwinter happening, and possibly to even stop it.''

"Does that involve the Call, and a strange abbess from beyond the deserts who eats grilled mice?''

"So you have been reading my beamflash mail. The penalty for that is death.''

Zarvora did not sound as if she meant it.

"I had official use of the master password, Highliber.''

"Not guilty, then, and case dismissed. As to the Call and the Abbess of Glenellen, yes, I have hopes of making use of them.''

The world had changed completely since Lemorel had walked into the observatory. She descended the external stone steps past the guards as Venus dipped below the horizon and a clocktower somewhere sounded half past the ninth hour. By the tenth hour she was walking the streets of Rochester. The holiday was in full cry, with dancers, drinkers, and rowdies seeming to have replaced the rest of the population. Dolorian was away in Inglewood and Lemorel did not want to be alone as the new century began. She bought a mask from a stall and removed her armband of rank.

By midnight she was at the University, where revelers were throwing each other into an ornamental pool. As the clocktower struck out the hour there was a countdown, then a cheer as the new century began. Lemorel kissed several dozen revelers, and lingered with one young man who seemed unattached. They wandered back to his undergraduate lodgings, where they removed all but their masks and made love on his hard bunk. Not an act this time, she thought as they lay there. This is really me.

With her lover for the night asleep, still masked, she slipped from the bed, dressed, and vanished from his life forever. Outside, the dawn was twenty minutes or so away, and she strode hurriedly through the streets and back to Libris. As she reached the roof she saw that the Highliber had returned there, too.

"Come," Zarvora said, and they went to the base of the beamflash tower.

The lift took them to the apex in a few minutes, and Zarvora led her up to the beamflash gallery's roof.

"We shall see the new century first from here, Frelle Lemorel. See the glow on the horizon? It will be there. How was the city last night?"

Lemorel hesitated, wondering if the Black Runners had been watching her. She decided that it could not possibly matter.

"I went to the University and seduced a stranger. I . . . need to be taken at face value sometimes."

"Are you still pining for your dead lover?" Zarvora's face was blank as she looked out to the brightening northeast.

"I'm pining for a lost lover, Highliber."

"John Glasken?"

Outrage and revulsion surged through her. "Highliber!" she exclaimed angrily.

"Do not worry, I know of your liaison, but the official records have had the references sponged clean. I could not have one of my senior librarians having someone like *him* in her past, could I?"

"Thank you Highliber, but . . ."

"But?"

"You offered me a reward yesterday. Now I claim it: Please don't release Glasken for your project to replace magnesium beamflash flares."

"Granted," declared Zarvora once she had stopped laughing.

"Thank you," said Lemorel, feeling very relieved. "How did you spend the evenight, Highliber?"

"I need to be alone a great deal, there is so much to think through," Zarvora replied—although I had company last night, she added in her mind.

A brilliant bead gleamed on the horizon.

"There, we are first. Look at the way the light moves down the beamflash tower, and at the land lighting up."

They watched the dawn of the first morning of 1700 GW spread down to the rooftops and walls of the city below. Distant cheers of a few hardy revelers on rooftops floated up to them.

"Because you did not stay for breakfast with your young man—yes, I know that it was a young man—perhaps you will eat with me," Zarvora offered as they descended the stairs to the gallery. "I have some matters to discuss about the Calculor."

"Greatwinter calculations?"

"Military calculations. There is to be a war."

The word had a shocking urgency.

"With the Southmoors?"

"Tandara. I have been planning it for some time, and it underlay my dispute with Mayor Jefton. As you know, following my arrest Tarrin falsely implicated Archbishop James in that Wirrinya conspiracy, guessing that he had voted against me. After the Archbishop was disgraced and I was freed, Inspector Vellum Drusas came to see me on a very urgent matter."

Lemorel blinked at the name. "I know him, he's a friend. A librarian of the old school."

"The old and conservative school. The Archbishop offered to make him Highliber."

Drusas as Highliber. Lemorel gasped audibly.

"When Drusas asked Archbishop James on whose authority he would do so, he cited the Mayor of Tandara. When James fell Drusas was anxious not to fall too, so he told me everything. Thus by tampering with the Archbishop's bank tally Tarrin accidentally uncovered a dangerous spy. The Mayor of Tandara knows of my intention to attack his mayorate, and he is both on his guard and making his own preparations. My preparations involve the Calculor and yourself, Frelle Lemorel Milderellen. The two of you are to build me a weapon that has not been seen on a battlefield for nearly two thousand years."

8 COMBAT

Being in charge might confer authority, but it did not create resources. Even with a dozen edutors from the university in the FUNCTION pool and quite a few of Jefton's personal staff and guards added as menial components, Zarvora still did not have the processing power that she needed. Her biggest problem was that of recruiting Dragon Color staff. Dragon White, Yellow, Orange, and Red could

be scoured from other mayorates or from the University, but above that one needed either talent or years of experience. She and Lemorel had to work three weeks of eighteen hour days, but it was not until mid-January that the Calculor had finished designing the new calculor.

"The tests took until the beginning of March," Lemorel told the meeting of Dragon Golds. "Now the battle calculor will be trained and put through its paces. It should take eight weeks."

"We have four weeks," Zarvora interjected. "In four weeks the rail extension from Barhan to Cohuna will be complete. Add the Hunter Triangle paraline and Tandara has a huge loop of rail to supply any war that its mayor chooses to start. I've been in contact with the Mayor of Deniliquin. He thinks that there will be a showdown with the Southmoors over Finley very soon. Tandara will attack just then and seize the whole northwest. We must strike before that."

Lemorel looked back at her figures and nodded reluctantly. "It could be done, Highliber, provided we had no serious problems at all."

"There is the small matter of treaties," Griss pointed out. "We can supply weapons to our ally Inglewood, but no troops."

"No troops, and only one weapon," said Zarvora. "One single, devastating weapon."

Lemorel sat back, weary but triumphant. She could not match Nikalan or Mikki, but she had become a mother to a child that was their peer. She had built a new calculor and Nikalan was to serve in it. He could not fail to be impressed, she was absolutely sure of it.

Glasken quickly became a model component and was promoted to MULTIPLIER after only a few months. He was made to study to become a FUNCTION, a component with a number of special mathematical skills that could not be easily shared through a team. Components had two hours of free time daily after the extra work of cleaning the cells and passages, cooking, repairing damaged calculor equipment, and exercise. He used some of that time to study equations in probability and the theory of charts. FUNCTION components had a status only just below that of a Dragon Librarian, but were still prisoners. Finally he was made a trainee FUNCTION, which meant that he was apprenticed to a senior FUNCTION.

His first impression of his master was of a vague, dreamy youth of about his own age. Nikalan was now FUNCTION 3073 and Glasken shared a cell with him. His new master was agreeable but bland company, someone who did not understand the most basic of jokes, yet was brilliant at mathematics. Other components told Glasken that FUNCTION 3073 was nursing a great hurt: his sweetheart had been murdered.

•   •   •

" '84, there's something strange happening," Nikalan mentioned one evening.

"Strange? It's bloody horrible," Glasken sighed as he lay on his bunk. "Five system generations in a week, then all those simulations for the subcalculor group. You'd think they had better use for a marvel like this."

"They're experimenting with a smaller machine. Each system generation was for a different size, and it was followed by tests to determine performance peaks. I noticed that the equipment was confined to small desks. Runners took the results from calpoint to calnode."

"I know, '73, I know. All the components in the last generation were FUNC-TIONS, so we had to do our own menial addition and multiplication. No justice, I say. We slave away to become FUNCTIONS but when we're promoted they remove our lackeys."

"You're missing the point," Nikalan said patiently.

"Well, what's your idea?"

"They are designing a mobile calculor."

Glasken sat up, his mind racing already. A mobile calculor might be taken outside Libris.

"They're using me a lot in the tests, that must mean I'm being considered for it," he said hopefully. "That's good. There are aspects of Libris I really hate."

The aspect that Glasken hated most was that of sex—or the fact that others had access to it while he did not. With several thousand people of mixed sexes in the Calculor it was no surprise that opportunities often arose, yet they never arose for him. There was always a guard about to spoil things when fortune beckoned. There were women who looked willing, yet assignations always went wrong. Getting a female component pregnant was a serious offense, and he knew one component who had been dealt with in a chillingly severe way for doing just that. Still, there were means available to prevent such accidents. Why me, why me alone, Glasken wondered, sometimes hundreds of times a day.

The regulators in the Calculor were men, but there were a few women sprinkled among them. One in particular caught Glasken's eye, a woman with a particularly fine figure who often wore thigh-length boots. He decided that she had style, unlike the shy, uncertain girls of the University or the loud, ribald wenches from the taverns and bawdy houses. Glasken almost drooled whenever she strutted past wearing tunics and blouses tailored to show her figure to best effect. He especially liked her in boots with tower heels, and tight black fencing britches. He had never known anyone like her, and was desperate to broaden his experience.

He did pushups and situps by the hundred to shape up, sewed his uniform tight in strategic places to bulge impressively, sang his heart out whenever he could borrow a communal lutina, and sketched the beautiful Dragon Red many times from a distance. He did this for a good many other women among the

components and regulators as well, but REGULATOR 42 remained his fondest hope for amorous conquest.

The day after he was upgraded to FUNCTION status he was sitting in his cell alone when he heard a tap at the bars.

"Shift check," said a husky voice.

"Check," Glasken replied before looking up to see REGULATOR 42. She had never been on cell duty before, and he hastily added "Frelle 42, are you permanent on this shift now?"

"No, just relieving," she said, folding her arms under her breasts, and not without some difficulty.

Glasken made a show of sighing. "Such a pity, 42. The sight of you is all that makes this drab place bearable."

His look of pathos had been practiced for long hours in front of a mirror. She smiled, a soft, open smile. The rate of his pulse shot up. Her tunic was of crushed red velvet, showing a great area of cleavage and fastened by one clasp above a row of buttons. He moved his hand, and the shadows of his fingers fondled her white skin.

"You're a handsome, clever beast, 3084," she observed, looking down at the shadows. "And my name is also Dolorian."

Instead of swirling the honey-brown cloak to cover herself, she merely put a hand up to the clasp. He brought the shadow of his hand down to cover hers. As he moved the shadows, her fingers followed. On impulse, he moved them back to the clasp, then motioned them to tug. The clasp popped open. Each of the buttons below seemed in turn to depend on the clasp. Two quite large breasts with small, pink nipples surged out with such force that Glasken stepped back from the bars in surprise.

"Now you will have to put them back," she purred.

"My—my shadow hands are so clumsy, Frelle Dolorian. Perhaps . . . if you stepped closer?"

She did. The pleasure of touching her flesh made his pulse race so hard that he could feel real pain in his temples.

"For all your cleverness you cannot work simple buttons, 3084," she said, folding her arms behind her back.

"It's the bars, lovely Frelle. Come inside and I shall show such skill with your clothing as you have never seen."

"But you may take my keys and escape."

"I'd never escape from wherever you are."

There was a slight jingle behind her back, and Glasken realized that she was going to come in. There was at least a full half hour before the morning shift began. Sheer anticipation made him giddy. After all those months of deprivation he was about to plunder the greatest prize of all. The assembly bell began to ring.

In a silent, dancing swirl she drew back out of his reach, swept the cloak around to cover herself, whispered "Later," then melted into the shadows. When another REGULATOR came by some moments later Glasken was still frozen in midgrasp.

"Reaching for something, FUNCTION?" he asked, stopping to stare with his hands on his hips. Only then did Glasken let his arms flop. "Come on, get your act squared. The Highliber's to make an announcement."

All off-duty FUNCTIONS and the elite of the lower components were herded into the back of the Calculor hall. Glasken stood with his hands slightly out from his body, savoring the lingering feeling of Dolorian's breasts on his fingertips. The System Herald rang twice on the bell and cried "System hold!" At once the whispering of men, women, and beads on wires tapered away in an orderly shutdown and the partition curtains swished back. The Highliber entered and climbed the stairs to the System Controller's rostrum. Several Dragon Reds, Blues, and Silvers were lined up on either side of her. Lemorel was there, and over near the edge was the rebuttoned Dolorian. A double squad of Tiger Dragons flanked the components, the fuses in their matchlocks smoldering.

The System Herald banged three times on the floor with his staff of office and called, "Attend to the Highliber, Zarvora Cybeline."

"Components of the Libris Calculor," Zarvora began in a sharp, clear voice, "I am the Highliber. I designed and built the Calculor."

She paused to let them assimilate the words. She had not addressed the Calculor's components since the four Dragon Greens had been shot for degrading its performance, and many components had never seen her.

"Some of you are to be given a change of scenery. We are building a new, mobile calculor to assist the Mayor's army in battle. It will consist of only a hundred components. Those selected for the battle calculor will step aside as their names are called out and be mustered for immediate departure."

The System Herald began to read out a list. Nikalan was first. Lemorel winced as if slapped. There were no women selected, or any components with less than two years' experience as a FUNCTION. The list came to an end without Glasken's name being called. He was not disappointed. After the morning shift REGULATOR 42 would return to his cell, and the thought of what would follow made him pant so hard that the components on either side of him turned to see what was the matter. The Highliber was speaking again.

"The Inspector of Examiners also has a list of less experienced FUNCTIONS who are nonetheless strong, fit, and suited to life on the battlefield." Lemorel walked across and gave the herald a list.

"FUNCTION 3084" was the first name that was read out.

Glasken gasped so hard that he began coughing. Lemorel smiled demurely and Dolorian looked down with a grin. "Conspiracy!" hissed Glasken as he

pushed the component next to him out of the way and stamped off to join the other components of the battle calculor. He tried to stare Dolorian down, but she was not looking his way. He found that his eyes kept dropping to the gates of paradise that had been slammed shut in his face. The additional names on Lemorel's list brought the total number of components selected to 110. That was fewer spares than Zarvora had wanted, but the Libris Calculor could not spare more FUNCTIONS. A squad of Tiger Dragons marched the components of the battle calculor out into a courtyard, where they were gagged and chained inside covered wagons.

Basic military training took only a fortnight, as the components were only being taught to keep up with the musketeers and to defend themselves as a last resort. They ran many miles in helmets and light ringmail, each with foraging pack, weapons, and calculor desk strapped onto his back. Glasken excelled in saber and musket and was fairly adept in the use of most other weapons, but Nikalan had trouble with everything. They were no longer known as component numbers, but by their real names: on a battlefield it would be much easier to shout a name than a number.

Glasken was grimly pleased that all the others were now subject to the same celibacy as had been forced upon him in Libris. The camp was on a cleared field about twelve miles from the walls of Rochester, and was used by the mayoral army as a shooting range and skirmish ground. The perimeter was well guarded, but Glasken felt there was little point in trying to escape. He was safe, well fed and clothed, and in a part of the army that would be as far from the front line as any slacker could wish.

The battle calculor was quite different from the thousand-component Libris machine. Each component had fairly complex functions to perform, and there were runners to go between them as they worked with problems and data passed about on slates. The battle calculor would be of most use when applied to a set-piece battle where enemy forces could be easily assessed. Clerks would draw a quick map on tentcloth and set it on the ground. Colored blocks represented groups and types of fighters, and were moved according to orders from the battle calculor, or reports from scouts.

The machine's advantage was that it treated fighting as a game, like champions or chess, and was quick, accurate, and flexible. Unlike human commanders, it had no emotions or expectations as it ordered when to move, where to stand firm, and what to shoot at. Signals were sent by coded trumpet calls, whistles, heliostats, and signal flags. There were observers on mobile observation poles to provide a good overview of the real scene, but these were a favored target with enemy marksmen, and had to wear full plate armor.

At last they were put into the field with two groups of a hundred soldiers

and officers of roughly equal skill. At first the practice team led by officers alone outflanked the battle calculor's team every time, and the troops jeered the components. Soon the calculor's officers began to get a feeling for the machine's power to make quick and accurate decisions, in spite of the unfamiliar form that the instructions took. The battle calculor's team was winning one mock engagement for every one that the others did by the end of the second day, and during the third it won them all. The odds were doubled, then tripled, and in a week the battle calculor's team could beat odds of five to one in set-piece engagements.

There were other tests, such as when a party of "enemy" soldiers was allowed to break into the battle calculor. The components repelled them with the aid of the Calculor guard, compensated for "dead" components, and resumed operations. Once the components were even required to solve problems while drunk, and again when they were hungover. The results led to a total prohibition on alcohol. There were still more tests on how fast they could pack the calculor desks onto their backs, move a few hundred yards, then unpack and become operational again.

For all the training in tactical methodology that Glasken had been given in the Libris Calculor, he was quite unaware of the strategic value of the battle calculor. He paid little attention to the number of musketeers from Inglewood training illicitly with the Rochestrian troops, and it was fortunate for the Mayor and Highliber that none of the neighboring monarchs were any more observant than Glasken. Inglewood was, like Rochester, a small sliver of territory dominated by the Tandara Mayorate, which separated the two states and maintained a strict embargo on the transfer of troops between them. Rochester and Inglewood had once been part of a much larger and very powerful mayorate, one with proud military traditions. Those traditions were, in miniature, still very much alive.

With no warning the components were marched out of the camp one afternoon, stripped naked, and dressed in striped prison tunics. Next they were taken to a railside and put aboard a wind train with a consignment of felons being sent to work on the Morkalla paraline extension. At the Elmore railside the Tandaran customs guards came aboard. The train was searched for undeclared weapons, and the Rochestrian guards were changed for leased Tandaran regulars.

The train skirted the ghostly Bendigo Abandon, then went west across the Inglewood border, where the guards were changed again. All at once the components were given fresh uniforms and calculor desks, and set free from their shackles. By now most of them understood the Highliber's plan. Inglewood was limited by treaty to a tiny army of a thousand musketeers, fifteen mobile bombards, and sixty lancers. Nine mounted kavelars led them. The battle calculor could boost the power of that small force many times over.

Glasken and Nikalan were summoned to the tent of Field Overhand Gratian

of the Inglewood forces, an angular, reserved man with a hatchet face and a penetrating stare. He was also a first cousin of Vardel Griss.

"Vittasner, Glasken, we are about to put the battle calculor to its first real test. Inglewood has declared war on Tandara."

Glasken felt his bowels go to ice. That was about as mismatched as putting him against the Libris Calculor in a mathematics contest.

"Vittasner, you are to be the chief of components during the fighting. All will obey your orders with regard to the working of the battle calculor. Your title will be Chief. Not an imposing title, but we're making this up as we go."

"Yes Fras," he mumbled.

"Glasken, you are to head the Components' Militia, and will have the title of Captain. You will be subject to the Chief's orders until such time as the battle calculor comes under direct attack, in which case everyone will obey you. Is that clear?"

"Fras! Yes Fras!" Glasken barked, having absorbed something of military discipline already.

"Both of you have already been trialed in these duties, and found to be best out of the components. Return to your men and prepare them. Dismissed."

"Fras!" they chorused.

Badges of rank were pinned to their arms, a black CC on a silver background for Nikalan and the same with a CM for Glasken. That was the equivalent of Dragon Silver rank, and Glasken wished that Lemorel could have been there to see him with a rank equal to hers. On the other hand, he knew that she would eventually find out. He gloated over fantasies of the scene as he walked.

They called the components together and Nikalan gave a talk about an actual battle being no different from the training runs that they had been doing. Then it was Glasken's turn.

"Okay folks, who can tell me what happens to a component who loses sleep or gets drunk and can't perform up to benchmark?"

"Firing squad!" came the ragged chorus.

"That's it. Anyone planning to drink a hidden jar of wine better remember that. All those out there in the firing line tomorrow will be depending on us. Also, if our side gets minced, the enemy isn't going to believe that we aren't regular musketeers. We have the most to lose if the attack fouls up. Everyone will want a piece out of us."

It was the first speech of his command! A rambling, disjointed little farrago, it was true, but it made the important points in words that all could understand. The components had to be frightened into being absolutely trustworthy. Unlike the Libris Calculor, this one had only one processor, so there was no parallel processor to verify each calculation. The work had to be fast and accurate on one pass.

They began marching well before dawn the next morning, and came within sight of the castle that was their objective in the first hour of light. The weather was dry and sunny as they passed the boundary stone for the Tandara Mayorate. Castle Woodvale stood among low, rolling hills and sparse woodland. A light wind was blowing from the north.

The fifteen bombards were of recent design, with brass-alloy barrels. They had a good range and fired cast-iron balls with lead cores instead of stone. Thus they could do great damage from just outside the range of the cheaper bombards that were standard in Tandara's castles. They had cost twenty times as much to build as a normal bombard, and had come close to breaking the military budget of Inglewood.

At the border eight hundred Inglewood musketeers and bombardiers joined their group, and after another hour they were set up on a low hill as the troops split up to block the paraline on either side of the castle. Glasken could already see a message pulsing from its beamflash tower, and the Tandaran capital was only four hours' march away—less by wind train or horse, and less still by galley train.

Scenario slates were given to the components. These had been worked out remotely at the Libris Calculor and transmitted in code by beamflash. They included the wind strength and estimated train speeds. Extra squads of irregulars were marching with the Inglewood musketeers carrying spades, axes, and bundles of pikes.

The attack began while they were setting up the battle calculor and observation masts on a scrubby hill some distance from the castle. The Inglewood bombards were brought to bear on the castle's walls and beamflash tower, and an early hit smashed the gallery of the beamflash tower. News of the attack had been flashed north to the capital before the first shot had been fired, however, and relief forces were already in the mustering grounds. Galley trains were being shunted into place to transport them. Zarvora had, of course, cut off all the Calculor's paraline coordination for Tandaran trains. Glasken looked up in alarm at hearing a massive explosion some miles to the north, then another to the south. Seconds later a scenario slate informed him that the paralines had been blown up with wagons of gunpowder.

The castle's bombards were quickly silenced; then troops withdrew, leaving only a token squad to cover the gate. The battle calculor calculated the movement times for the troops on both sides. It was already an hour and a half from the first alert, and the cavalry from the capital were visible to the lookout on the field mast. Galley trains with foot soldiers were following.

Lookouts and scouts soon reported that eighteen hundred heavy lancers were riding hard down the highway from the north. They dispersed into two broad blocks to pincer the northern line. Scout lancers with hand heliostats warned the

battle calculor's lookouts that two thousand musketeers were marching up the road from galley trains halted by the shattered rails to the south. The Tandarans had timed them to arrive with the lancers but now they would be rather late.

Glasken scanned the colored blocks being moved about on the cloth map and wondered if any of the enemy blocks would ever materialize into real soldiers. Inglewood's musketeers were outnumbered five to one. The components calculated odds, times, numbers, and possible tactics based on which commanders' pennons had been reported by the scouts. The battle calculor ordered six hundred musketeers into the southern trenches, while only bombard crews, lancers, and peasants armed with pikes faced the horde to the north.

Glasken contemplated life as a Tandaran prisoner of war as the blocks representing the groups of lancers formed up. There were weak points in the stake wall, even he could see that. The lancers charged in a line, ignoring the obvious traps at the weak points. The moment that they charged, the battle calculor ordered firepots to be cast into the grass before the southern trenches, then sent its musketeers running north. The bombards poured grapeshot north at the lancers, cutting down those who broke through the defenses and ignoring those floundering against the more heavily fortified stretches.

Soon the main body of lancers broke through, but instead of ordering the bombardiers to stand and fight the battle calculor ordered them into full retreat. They ran before the lancers, met with the musketeers from the south, then turned to present a triple line of eight hundred muskets to the lancers. Orderly volleys slashed through the lancers as they reached the bombards and tried to move them—but they were chained to rocks, and the battle calculor had ordered the excess powder drenched so that they could not be spiked. The lancers faltered, unable to do anything with the bombards that they had just taken. Musket fire still tore through their ranks.

On the groundsheet map Glasken could see the Tandaran musketeers charging through the fires at the now empty southern trenches, but the lancers could see nothing but smoke. With perhaps five hundred dead or disabled littering the field, they broke and retreated. Now the musketeers broke through the flames and dropped into the shallow Inglewood trenches, but discovered that they were dug sheer on one side and sloping on the other. The triple line of Inglewood musketeers turned, and had a clear line of fire at an enemy backed against the trench walls and outlined by flames. Not a single Inglewood death was yet registered on the scoreslate.

For twenty minutes the withering volleys went on, with one Inglewood musketeer dropping for every ten of the Tandarans. The bombard crews had been ordered back, carrying dry powder, and as the lancers tried to rally they were fired on again. The battle calculor ordered the irregulars out to strip weapons from the dead as the Tandaran musketeers retreated over the smoking grass stubble.

At last someone on the castle's walls thought of coordinating their two groups using handheld heliostats, and at this the battle calculor ordered the remaining musketeers into a triangle, with one side formed by the line of bombards. It need not have bothered: the signals were ignored by the confused Tandaran commanders on the battlefield.

The most desperate part of the battle came when those left in the castle charged out, adding another five hundred to the odds against Inglewood. The battle calculor ordered its own guard of two hundred men into the fighting. Suddenly there were a hundred components guarded by only ten regulators, yet they did not rebel. They were in charge and they were proud of it. The Inglewood troops out on the battlefield were *their* men fighting impossible odds.

The calculor guard caught the garrison troops between the gate and one side of the triangle. Fired on from both sides and unable to retreat they broke and ran south, only to be fired upon by their own people. The battle calculor made its assessment from the reports of the lookouts and heliostat signals from the field, then calculated from the disposition of troops that the enemy would not be able to rally within at least an hour. Secure with these parameters, it ordered its bombards unchained and brought to bear on the castle. A dozen shots had the main gate reduced to splinters and the few Tandarans left inside surrendered. Until now Glasken had seen no action directly, apart from the shot that disabled the beamflash tower. It was a strange, detached way to fight a war.

Messages poured in about casualties, approaching Tandaran reinforcements, and exhaustion quotients for both sides. The battle calculor ordered itself moved into the castle along with all the Inglewood bombards and musketeers; then the gate was blocked solid with stone rubble. Ten of its most expendable FUNCTIONS, including Glasken, were ordered into the decapitated beamflash tower to rig up a communications link with Inglewood—and hence to the Libris Calculor. More trains began arriving from Tandara at the paraline breach, and this time the enemy really meant business. Lookouts estimated eleven thousand enemy troops outside by late evening.

During all this Glasken labored among the flies, dust, and occasional musket balls to nail a wooden beamflash gallery together at the top of the tower while three Dragon Red Librarians set up a mobile beamflash machine and telescope. With a link established to the Derby tower, and hence the rest of the beamflash network, tactical data poured in. Rochestrian troops had attacked over the border and taken Elmore, then gone on special galley trains to secure the main line all the way to the Bendigo Abandon and the junction railside at Eaglehawk. They might have been stopped by Tandaran reinforcements from the north, except that these were not able to pass the broken track and hostile bombards at Castle Woodvale. All the while, there was no Call. Lemorel's work on Call vectors and times had been used to schedule the battle for a window of days when there was unlikely to be a Call.

· · ·

By the next day the fighting had died down, so much so that the battle calculor was running at half strength as a local decoder. The spare FUNCTIONS were resting and taking turns working in the beamflash tower. The heavy strategic processing was being done on the Libris Calculor now, and orders were beam-flashed to individual overhands. Nikalan and Glasken were assigned to the early-afternoon shift. Glasken stared through the telescope at the distant tower, copying out the messages in the distant flashes of light.

"They'll never let us go now," Glasken complained as he mechanically scribbled on a slate. "The Highliber's machine worked, she's tripled her territory, and she will probably demand client status from Tandara's mayor. Tandara's allies will be too frightened of the battle calculor to squawk."

"An elegant contest," Nikalan replied as he worked the beamflash key to send a separate message outward. "Did you know the battle calculor was used to only sixty-five percent of its capacity yesterday? We could have won against even greater odds."

Glasken shuddered. "So, what will the Highliber have us doing next, I wonder? Fighting the Southmoors? I hate being a component, I hate being a part of a machine's brain, and I hate not even knowing what's in these coded messages that we're handling."

"Oh, but I know all the codes," said Nikalan vaguely. "These are but simple messages. This one I'm sending mentions that no battle calculor components died."

"Change it," Glasken said listlessly. "Tell 'em I'm dead."

"But I would be disciplined—"

"So tell 'em you're dead too. Ah, the Derby relay is closing down for lunch. Wake me when they start again."

Glasken dozed. He dreamed of the heady pressure of Dolorian's big, firm breasts pressing against his bare chest instead of being at arm's length. Nikalan shook him awake just as Dolorian had opened the cell door.

"Wake up, Johnny, you're dead."

"Piss off."

"No, it's true and so am I. Libris has replied to our message. NEW COM-PONENTS BEING SENT TO REPLACE GLASKEN AND VITTASNER. THE BODIES TO BE RELEASED FOR BURIAL."

Glasken sat up, horrified. "What?" he cried, seizing Nikalan by the tunic. "You really *did* change the message?"

"Yes."

"And Libris accepted it?"

"Well, yes. The code was simple, and I only had to adjust the wording so that the checksums matched."

Glasken released him and leaned back. "Don't you know a joke when you hear one? We really are dead now. The Highliber will spit hellfire when she finds out and . . . did you say released for burial?"

"Yes."

Mountain ranges of breasts trembled within Glasken's grasp, forests of thighs bid him come exploring.

"Could you change that to just 'RELEASE THEM'?"

"Well . . . no. The reply code is different, based on a checksum total requiring the same number of letters."

Glasken thought frantically for a moment.

"How about GLASKEN AND VITTASNER TO BE RELEASED?"

"But I don't want to be released. I like working in calculors."

"But I need your name to make up the wordage!"

"I'd really rather stay."

The urge to fling him over the edge of the tower was almost beyond Glasken's control. In hindsight Glasken realized that Nikalan could probably have had them both released from the Libris Calculor months ago.

"Well, nice thought while it lasted, good Fras," he said as he stretched then adjusted a screw on the telescope. "One favor, though: could you show me what the message might have looked like in code?"

Glasken struck him over the head the moment he had finished, then cried out that Nikalan had fainted and called for a relief team. Before Nikalan had revived the Overhand's lackey came to see them with releases so fresh that the ink was not dry. Glasken poured a phial of salts of nightwing down Nikalan's throat to keep him quiet.

War is a great time for opportunists, and in spite of the watchful eyes of the calculor regulators, Glasken managed to loot two gold royals, sixteen silver nobles, and two border passes in the confusion. He paid five silver nobles for a captured Tandaran horse and they set off for Eaglehawk.

The Eaglehawk railside was only five miles south, and aided by the chaos caused by the war, Glasken's stolen papers, ten silver nobles for two fares, and one gold royal for a bribe, the escapees managed to board a freight wind train by nightfall.

Glasken had planned to ride the Nullarbor paraline to the Western Castellanies, but his train turned due north to Robinvale while he slept. The ensuing months were not kind to the escapees, but they survived.

Glasken sprawled in the desert sand, very drunk and nearly asleep. The campfire had burned down to glowing coals, yet the captain of the Alspring camel train called encouragement, urging Glasken to finish his tale of beamflash towers, wind trains, and calculors.

"Good sir, pray finish your wonderful story. I'll not sleep at all if I do not hear the outcome."

Glasken looked up at the sky, where the stars were shining brightly, then lifted a jar of date-mash brandy to his lips to inoculate himself against the cold of the desert night.

"Ah, not much to tell after . . . wind train . . . got diverted to Robinvale. Things got really bad. I shot the Robinvale Inspector of Customs when he refused a bribe, then fled with Nikalan into the Southmoor Emirate. He had some idea of traveling to the Central Confederation, but alas, the fool got us auctioned in the slave market at Balranald while trying to buy a camel. Our owner was a caravan master going north. Oh how we suffered . . . attacked by freebooters . . . stole camels, fled into the desert. Nearly died . . . wandered into this oasis . . ."

Glasken drifted off to sleep. The Captain gestured to his scribe.

"Did you get the whole of his story?"

"Yes Captain."

"Then append this before it."

He cleared his throat and thought for a moment.

"To His Serene and Merciful Eminence, Ziran Hoantar:

"Whenever I lead a camel train to the edges of the known world, master, I take particular care to work closely with my drivers and strappers. Knowing their moods, fears, and needs can be the difference between harmony and mutiny. We were encamped at the Fostoria Oasis after crossing the great desert of pebbles when I came upon a strange character called John Glasken. This man was nineteen metric tall, with a thick black beard and uncommon broad shoulders. He spoke the Macadalian tongue clumsily, and hung about the campsite selling proscribed spirits and herbs.

"On the second night of our stay Glasken became most disgustingly drunk with some of my infidel drivers. As I sat at their campfire carousings to insure that none of the talk became mutinous, Glasken began to relate such a strange tale that I soon sent for a clerk to copy it down in dashscript. The tale ended when Glasken fell asleep and began to snore swinishly, but the essence is there. You must agree that his story is far too consistent and detailed for such a wastrel to have dreamed up, so that there must indeed be barbarian nations with very advanced sciences beyond the red deserts. If so, dare we ignore their works?

"I had the drunken infidel bound and taken to my tent, then sent armed strappers to fetch Nikalan from his tent near the counting house in the marketplace. I am now pleased to report that we are returning to Glenellen. This scroll will precede us with a courier squad.

"Read Glasken's tale now, master, read to understand why I am returning to Glenellen with all possible haste. Master, were you to gather a hundred souls of moderate ability with the abacus in some place that cannot be spied upon, we

could use these two components to build our own battle calculor, for the greater glory and prosperity of your royal house. Might I suggest the fortress at Mount Zeil as an admirable site?

"I am your humble and devoted servant, Khal Azik Vildah."

The Call was no respecter of life. Cluttered below cliffs throughout the land were the whitened bones of humans and animals that had followed its allure blindly. For those few who could resist the Call, however, it offered great advantages. To travel within its sweep was to be invisible, and to be immune to human attack.

Theresla and Ilyire left the convent as soon as a Call swept over Glenellen, but they guided their camels along established roads rather than just allowing them to go south. They fled along the steep, narrow roads of the MacDonald Mountains, through palm-filled valleys and regular grids of date-palm plantations, then out into the flat, scrubby drylands beyond. At the Henbury Gatefort they turned onto the ancient trail south after taking generous stocks of water and stores, and even fresh camels while guards and merchants strained mindlessly at their tethers to follow the Call.

It was a day's journey farther south, near the Erldunda market town, that they encountered a large camel train. It was stopped on the road, anchors manually released by each rider. Theresla and Ilyire reined in their own Call-allured camels.

"The caravan has stopped in a very orderly manner," Theresla observed.

"They probably used a Call scout," Ilyire explained. "When a caravan travels north or south on straight stretches, a lone rider with a pilot flag is stationed ahead or behind to ride in view of a sentry. If a Call seizes the scout he lets the pilot flag fall. The caravan master immediately orders all sand anchors to be released and the caravan stops dead. When the Call has passed, the caravan continues on with minimal disruption. Only the scout and his camel wander south until the clockwork timer in the saddle releases the sand anchor. The greatest danger to the scout is from attacks by freebooter bands or Kooree nomads while riding to rejoin the caravan."

The caravan was silent, except for the tinkle of the harness bells and the creaking of leather straps as the camels struggled against their Call anchors. The riders were buckled into their saddles, unable to think to release themselves.

"They have prisoners," observed Theresla. "Those two there have their hands tied, and their camels are tethered to pack animals." She peered at the two men. "They're tall, as you describe the men of Maralinga to be."

"Indeed they are," agreed Ilyire, struggling to keep his camel under control. "In fact I know them from Fostoria! The scrawny one worked in the market, calculating quantities and exchange rates for the merchants and caravan masters. His name is Ni-kalan. A little crazed in the head, but he taught me some basics of the Austaric speech while I regained my strength."

"Could they be explorers from the southern Austaric nations? Might they have sent expeditions looking for us as a result of Kharec's raid?"

"No. More likely they're outlaws or fugitives who wandered into the desert and were lucky enough to reach Fostoria."

"Why are they prisoners, I wonder?"

"Perhaps they attacked the caravan."

"Two against sixty?"

"They may be survivors from a bigger force of freebooters that was wiped out. The skinny one, Ni-kalan, looks unwell. He may have been wounded."

"But the big, brutish one is very healthy."

Theresla had unwittingly touched a nerve.

"Him? Filthy, drunken, lecherous swine. He's tupped every whore in Fostoria, and any number of cloister-wives and their daughters besides. He's a ravening beast that devours women instead of protecting them. He has no morals, no honor, no discipline, and no shame! Jorn Gla-escen, yes, that was his name."

She stared at the vacant face of the broad-shouldered prisoner for some moments while their camels strained and danced against their reins to follow the Call. He had a heavy black beard and was wearing soiled, greasy robes in the style of the Outland camel drivers. With a swift, supple movement Theresla drew her saberine and slashed his camel free of its tether. Ilyire laughed his approval.

"That's right, dear and just sister, feed him to the Call. A fair trial for his crimes is too good for him."

"Hurry now, we must stay with him," Theresla called as she gave her camel its head to go south again.

"I—what! What do you mean?" spluttered Ilyire, hauling his camel's head about so hard that it nearly stumbled.

"I have a use for him."

"Him? Gal-escen? Are you mad?"

"Yes."

"But he's big, bigger than even me! Once out of the Call we could have a fight on our hands."

"But we shall not be leaving the Call for a long time, Ilyire. We are travelling within it for protection from freebooters, the Koorees, and our own people. In just the same way it will protect us from him. Gla-escen will be as docile as a lamb."

"Until we leave the Call. Then what?"

"Then, dear half-brother, he will depend upon us to survive."

"But why bring him at all? He's good for nothing but tupping. Even the camels wouldn't be safe!"

"He will teach us to speak the Southerners' Austaric language fluently."

She had been urging her camel faster than its Call pace all through the argument, and now she seized the trailing tether from Glasken's camel.

"Don't reach for that arrow, Ilyire," she shouted without turning around as she tied the tether to her saddle frame.

"What? And waste a charge of black powder on him?"

"Kill him and I kill you, brother or not. Swear that you will not kill him."

"But—"

"Swear to it!"

There was a lengthy silence. Theresla continued to observe Ilyire in a tiny mirror on her camel's harness, but he did not reach for his weapons again. She began to count the rhythmic sways of her camel, and had reached eighty-three before Ilyire replied.

"All right, then I swear—but only if you untether his camel from yours."

"Why is that? His camel must be kept with ours."

"The tether between your camels is—too much for me. It's a symbolic union of filth and purity, the sight makes me gag."

Theresla laughed. "You would have him tethered to your camel?"

"It's punishment for my sins," Ilyire muttered before lapsing into silence for the rest of the day.

They journeyed on with the Call, down through the Cavanagh Outpost, past the turnoff to Fostoria, and on into the unexplored drylands that Ilyire had traversed with Kharec's lancers nearly a year and a half earlier. Traces of an ancient bitumen road remained, threading through clumps of ruins thousands of years old. There were no inhabited towns here, so there was no more water and food for the taking. They began to snare and butcher animals caught in the Call to supplement their supplies, and their waterbags grew less taut.

The road veered due east, but they continued south into the desert, following the Call and covering their tracks to elude any pursuers following in the Call's wake. Theresla's compass showed that the Call was taking a slight westward bias, but Ilyire said that such variations were not unknown so far south. By his calculations they would join the route of Kharec's expedition just north of Maralinga Railside, but there was a long way to go as yet.

Now that they were off the road the camels began to show signs of strain as they struggled across the mulga- and mallee-bush-covered dunes of red sand. The fixed pace of the Call was too much for them, but Ilyire postponed dropping the sand anchors until the last possible moment. It was clear that nobody could be following them, and that the country was too parched to support more than a small scattering of Kooree nomads, yet it was only when their supplies of water had dropped to dangerously low levels that Ilyire reluctantly made the decision to drop the sand anchors and let the protective Call zone go on ahead of them.

Ilyire drew a flintwheel long-barrel from his saddle frame and jumped to the stony ground. He unbuckled Glasken, then stood clear and smiled as he clambered from the saddle, fell, and began to shamble south.

"Catch him, tie him to a bush," ordered Theresla, still in her saddle.

With the sensation of a clammy fog dispersed by a warm breeze, the trailing edge of the Call passed over them. Glasken shook his head and tried to stretch. His hands were still tied in front of him . . . he was standing on hot, red sand and rock, tethered to a mallee bush! Where was the caravan? The land was still dry, red and parched, but was a different kind of desert from where the caravan had been.

There were camels tethered nearby, yet only two Alspring camel drivers were with them. No, not drivers, more like the camel lancers of the Fostorian town guard. Their clean, well-cut robes and gearsacks, their very self-confidence warned him that they might even be some type of elite warrior. They were clearly to be assessed with great care before . . . suddenly it dawned on him! They had freed him from the caravan, so they *had* to be friendly! The bonds on his wrists were an understandable precaution.

"Ambicori, gratico. Johnny Glasken ibi," he said in the language that he had been learning in Fostoria. He forced a broad smile and bowed deeply.

"Macadalian dialect, I recognize it but barely speak it," said Ilyire at once. "No good to us, Frelle sister. Free him and let's be gone."

"Not so fast, Ilyire, I understand enough Macadalian to know that he speaks it awkwardly. His native tongue might be Austaric." She held a hand up in a slow, friendly gesture. "Gal-escen. Can speaking Austaric?"

"I—yes!" Glasken stammered in Austaric. "Quite well, my native tongue in fact, and I have letters from the University of Rochester, I am well educated—"

Ilyire spat a curse and Glasken was silent at once. "That's Austaric, Frelle, you were right," he sighed, "I recognize it, even if I don't know the words." He barked at Glasken in Macadalian to hold out his hands. The saberine hissed out in a flat arc, slicing the knot from the prisoner's wrists. Glasken gasped in fright, then began to rub his wrists very slowly, careful not to make a sudden move.

"We speaking little Macadalian. Ilyire, calling me. This Abbess Theresla. Sister mine. Touching her you, remove balls. Understanding?"

Glasken smiled and bowed, still rubbing his wrists and trying to stare at Theresla without seeming to stare.

"Gla-escen, ah, knowing Maralinga fort?" she asked.

Her voice was a low but powerful contralto, and full of authority.

Glasken did not know Maralinga, but he thought quickly. They were in the desert, and if Maralinga was not too far away it was probably a fortified railside guarding cisterns and stores. Only the Nullarbor paraline was serviced by fortified outposts as distant from civilization as this, and the Alliance did jointly control a few of the railsides there with Woomera.

"Maralinga, I know it well. A fortress with deep cisterns, a fine place on the

paraline that carries the wind trains west to the great underground cities at Kalgoorlie.''

His words were a jumble of Macadalian grammar and Austaric nouns and verbs, but again Ilyire had to grudgingly nod to Theresla.

''Soldier? You?''

''Soldier, yes, I'm a soldier. I was stationed at, er, Maralinga, but I got lost in the desert while on patrol—with my companion Nikalan, that is.''

''Good,'' she said, turning back to Glasken. ''Reaching Maralinga five weeks. Maybe. You teaching Austaric us?''

''Teach you to speak Austaric?'' he exclaimed, relieved to learn the nature of his value to them. ''Yes, yes, my pleasure. I'll teach you to speak as well as the Highliber herself.''

''Highliber! Knowing Highliber?'' demanded Theresla eagerly.

''Frelle, I worked for the Highliber of Libris for seven months,'' Glasken replied. Mind you I'm not saying what the Highliber *did* to me for those seven months, he thought.

''Go Maralinga,'' said Ilyire. ''Desert, salt lakes, Kooree warriors, snakes, scorpions, us to kill. You fighting? Knowing weapons?''

''Can I fight? Fras, Frelle, I've been in the army of Overhand Gratian of Inglewood.''

Ilyire tossed him a sheathed saberine, a quiver of arrows, and a recurved bow.

''Reaching Maralinga, you free. Helping go Maralinga.''

''Yes, yes, Maralinga. My people are there. I'll introduce you.''

Glasken bowed as he buckled on the saberine; then he slung the quiver over his back. He bent back the bow between his legs and strung it, then pulled the string. ''Seventy pounds, very good,'' he said as he unstrung it again. Ilyire frowned, disappointed that he knew what he was doing with the weapon. At last my luck has changed, Glasken thought. He would be dropped on the Nullarbor paraline, free to go on to the Western Castellanies, the very place that had been his destination when he had escaped the battle calculor. He suddenly remembered Nikalan.

''Where is Nikalan?'' he said to Theresla. ''The other prisoner.''

''Thin man, sick?''

''Ni-kalan, we leave,'' Ilyire cut in. ''Executing?''

''Ah, maybe.''

''Friend? Yours?'' asked Theresla.

''Yes, a friend. We've been through a lot together.''

''Leaving Ni-kalan, very sorry,'' said Theresla, who was growing impatient with her lack of Austaric vocabulary.

Must not seem annoyed, Glasken thought to himself. ''You must have done

what you have thought was right,'' he finally said with a broad smile. He glanced at the sun, then turned to what he thought was north and waved. ''Farewell, and good fortune, Nikalan,'' he called.

Ilyire untethered Glasken's camel from his with obvious relief.

''Riding, now!'' he snapped.

Glasken took the reins. ''Kush! Kush!'' he said confidently, and the camel knelt at once. He stepped into the saddle, buckled in, and checked the sand anchor and timer. ''Shill, shill,'' he said, and the camel stood. Ilyire spat into the sand, then mounted his own camel. He was sullen as they rode along behind Glasken, and he muttered to Theresla constantly.

''He is lying to us. Probably a deserter from some army.''

''Well then, he should be a good fighter,'' she replied with a smile. ''He seems well educated and articulate.''

''Perhaps Ni-kalan was a senior officer. They could have deserted together, taken refuge in the Fostoria oasis, then been captured by the caravan's lancers. They were to be questioned about the military arts of the Austaric cities and empires—Yes! Surely that was it.''

''Gla-ssken. A strong name.''

''Perhaps he will be shot for desertion when we reach Maralinga,'' Ilyire said hopefully.

''Come now Ilyire, we must speak with him constantly and learn his language.''

''I saw him glancing at you, ogling the curves beneath your robes. If he so much as gestures to you I'll cut his hands off.''

The journey was all heat, boredom, and red dust, punctuated by a few spasms of alarm when the Kooree nomads confronted them. Ilyire had by now refined a tactic of looking to be retreating while tacking along in their original direction. Thus the encounters seldom involved more than an exchange of shouts and brandishing of weapons. To the Koorees, the invaders were seen to be driven off, honor was satisfied, and nobody was hurt. It was so different from the bloody battles by which Kharec and his larger force had hacked their way south.

Ilyire knew how to survive in the desert now that they were not hastening along with the Call. He could read the subtle signs that showed where to dig soakholes for water, and he used a sheet of translucent membrane over a pit of leaves to collect very pure water when it was safe to stop for any length of time. Glasken was acutely aware that he was being watched for any signs of lechery toward the Abbess. Theresla was quite obviously the leader, but without Ilyire they would have been hard put to survive. Theresla was rather hard to work out: fit, supple, and potentially more of an asset in any fighting than Ilyire, yet sometimes Glasken noticed her staring at him out of the corner of an eye. She definitely gave him little smiles, but they were always fleeting.

The country varied little from day to day, so that even the crossing of a dry riverbed became a big event. The small, tenacious bushes and trees gradually thinned, but never completely gave way to the red sand and broken rock. Harsh country meant fewer Koorees, as Ilyire explained every time Glasken asked if he was sure he knew where he was going.

As the days became weeks Glasken worked at the Austaric lessons as if his life depended upon them. In a sense it did. They could get along without him, and Ilyire clearly would have preferred it that way. Glasken's dilemma was one of staying friends with the Abbess without seeming to be familiar and so arousing Ilyire's anger. The Glenellen fugitives quickly learned the words for flies, sand, heat, danger, and the most minute aspects of camel saddlery. Conversations involving mathematics, literature, and the technology of the Southeast Alliance inevitably swerved to fat lizards, dangerous snakes, and the estimated distance to Maralinga. At night Ilyire always took the watch, and during the day he spent a lot of his time in the saddle dozing while Glasken taught Theresla Austaric ballads—and sometimes love poetry—and explained the basic tenets of physistry and chemistric as taught in the University of Rochester.

"Many ladies must have, ah, cried for your leaving," Theresla said one morning as they plodded across a dry lakebed encrusted with salt. It was the first time that the subject of dalliance at a personal level had been raised. Glasken had been patiently awaiting such an inquiry for weeks.

"I had many admirers, Frelle Abbess, I cannot deny that. As to my departure, it was probably a puzzle to them. One particular girl, a mean and poisonous wench, became obsessed with me and sought to make me all hers. She was from a very rich and powerful family, and it would have profited me greatly to marry her. Nevertheless, I refused to trade my freedom for anything other than true love. She flew into a rage and paid a shadowboy gang to abduct me. I laid out five of them with my swagger stick, but they finally beat me to the ground and bound me tightly. I was taken far away and sold as a slave, but eventually I escaped into the desert with my friend and fellow slave Nikalan. We suffered terribly before we stumbled into the oasis at Fostoria."

"So. You are not soldier?" Theresla asked, playfully rather than as an accusation.

Cursing himself for the slip, Glasken wove his words quickly to cover up the rent in his story.

"Frelle . . . how could I have explained such subtle affairs of the heart before, when we had practically no words in common?"

This seemed to satisfy Theresla, and she rode on in silence for a time. After checking that Ilyire was a safe distance behind and still asleep she guided her camel beside Glasken's again.

"Why did caravan master . . . taking you prisoner?"

''*Take* me prisoner. We were merely strange fugitives from unknown lands. We were to be questioned by your elders in one of the Alspring cities. Perhaps they want to find new lands to trade with or invade.''

By the time they emerged from the dunes onto a vast, treeless plain of bushes and tufty grass on pinkish limestone, Ilyire and Theresla were reasonably fluent in simple conversational Austaric. Ilyire smiled for the first time that Glasken had seen as he unrolled a map and indicated their location. Maralinga was close. They decided to make camp early, and the sun was still well above the horizon as they ate.

Theresla volunteered for the watch, and Ilyire reluctantly agreed. He seemed unusually tired to Glasken and was soon deep in sleep and snoring. Theresla stretched out on her sandmat, with her head resting on a pack. The hem of her robe had ridden up a little, and both of her calves were exposed. Glasken glanced at her legs, then hurriedly stared hard at Ilyire.

''Crystal of oblivion, ah, put in drink,'' Theresla explained, gesturing to Ilyire.

Glasken's head snapped around. ''He cannot wake?'' he asked, his loins stirring even as his mind scrambled to interpret her words.

''Not for . . . ah, many minutes.''

For once a seduction was moving too fast for Glasken. He looked into her smiling face, then back down to her legs. She stretched again, and slid forward. Her robe rode up above her knees.

The urge to reach down and fling her robe right back was so strong that Glasken could barely fight it back. He moved slowly forward and knelt beside her. She put a hand out and stroked his beard.

''I thought she was afeard,

Till she stroked my beard,

And we were both wondrous merry.' ''

''What is that?'' she asked. ''Austaric poem?''

''A few words of a student song. An old, naughty student song.''

''Our students . . . all from religious orders. They sing chants, only. Sometimes, ah, moral epics.''

Slowly, cautiously, Glasken reached out and stroked her hair, then ran his fingers along her chin. She trailed her fingers down his chest, through the black hair there and along his ribs. His hand dropped cautiously to her side. Theresla smiled. His fingertips caressed the lower curve of her breast . . . and her smile remained. The gates of paradise are wide open, his mind shouted.

''How long will he be—''

''As long as need.''

''You're sure?''

"No needing hurry."

The magnitude of the prize and the fear of who she was blunted Glasken's haste enough to prevent him bundling her out of her robes with no more ceremony whatever. He was still half-fearful as he fumbled with the knotted belt at her waist, but then she did likewise with his own knot. At the feel of a smooth leg against his own he suddenly threw caution to the desert winds and rolled on top of Theresla, but with a sinuous movement she was suddenly on top of him. Her breasts hung enticingly, slowly descended, then the nipples caressed his chest.

"Not so much fast, Fras Glasken. Just little more longer."

"In Greatwinter's name, Frelle Abbess! Why hover above the altar of ecstasy when you could just—"

A Call swept over them, blotting out Glasken's consciousness, yet . . . he did not move. Theresla hovered above him on her hands and knees, exploring subtle feelings, tensions and energies.

"You are part of a great experiment, Fras Glasken, you should feel honored," she said softly in Alspring.

Slowly she raised herself, so that her breasts barely touched Glasken's skin— and then rose clear. With no contact at all between them Glasken still did not wander away with the Call.

"Your lust defies the very Call itself," she said in genuine wonder. "In all the world, not another lust to match yours, I would wager . . . but this is enough for now. I have much to think about."

Theresla suddenly rolled clear, and Glasken heaved himself up to walk south at once. She lashed out a foot and tripped him, then tied a tether to his waist. As she dressed Glasken struggled at the end of the tether, his face blank, his interest in her gone. It took her some time to get him dressed again, as he had no interest in anything except wandering south. Finally she parted Ilyire's lips and tipped a drop of liquid from a small phial between them. She counted fifty heartbeats with his pulse, then shook him roughly.

"Ilyire, wake up! A Call."

Ilyire's muscles rippled but he opened his eyes without jumping up or saying a word. Seeing only Theresla he rose slowly from his sandmat and looked to the sun.

"Nearly sunset, that's good. The Call will stop soon and become a null zone right over us. We'll be protected for the night. Maralinga Railside is not far now. We can throw this turd on their dung heap and be about your business with their mayor."

Theresla lay stretched out on her sandmat in much the same position that she had been in when Glasken had tried to bestride her, gazing at the ruddy furnace of the setting sun amid the flaming ribbons of cloud. The air was already noticeably cooler.

"We're so close to the Edge of the World, it seems a pity not to go on," she said as Ilyire began to repack the dried meat. "The wind trains will take us far away, to see the Mayor and Highliber."

"But I have seen the Edge for you," quavered Ilyire, like an artisan whose craftsmanship had been questioned.

"I must go there myself. I have tests to perform."

"I did every test that you ordered."

"But I developed new tests and techniques to probe the Call while you were away. I can sense a Call coming, did you realize that?"

Ilyire stared at her with suspicion. He had not realized it, and with a sudden twinge of horror he twisted around to look at Glasken—who was still struggling mindlessly at the end of his tether. No, not possible, he concluded, and turned back to Theresla.

"All right then, we go to the Edge. We can leave this maggot of a camel's turd tethered within sight of Maralinga."

"He will come with us to the Edge."

"With—never! Give me one good reason."

"There is a thin black band across the sun."

Ilyire turned and stared at the sun, which was just touching the horizon. Across its disk was a thin, black line which had been swamped by the glare while it was higher in the sky.

"What is it?" he asked, wide-eyed and incredulous.

"The end of the world, and the reason why Glasken must come to the Edge with us."

"It's just a cloud."

"Have you ever seen such a cloud?"

Wringing his hands, Ilyire looked from the sunset to Glasken. "Theresla, dearest sister . . . I've seen him glancing at you, running his eyes under your robes. Every time he licks his lips I just know that he dreams of running his tongue over your nipples, his filthy mind is filled with thoughts of defiling—"

"So what would you have him do, Ilyire? Ogle *you* instead?"

"What? I'd shoot him for a sodomite!"

"So you'd kill him whatever the case. Why not kill him now, while he's helpless?"

"Ladyship, sister, honor forbids that. He just needs to learn his place—"

"And he *does* know his place! Why else would he be furtive about glancing at me? Be sensible, half-brother. The man is a rascal, but we have learned much from him. Besides, I need him for some experiments at the Edge."

Ilyire jumped to his feet. "What? You? Him? Experiments? What sort of experiments?"

"Experiments that require someone not trained to resist the Call."

"Use a camel! Anything would be better than Glasken."

Theresla thought for a moment, looking across to the rapidly vanishing sun. Ilyire followed her gaze.

"There is a risk, of course. A risk that my experiments will fail, and that Glasken will be drawn over the Edge by the Call."

Ilyire was torn between hope and disbelief. "In what manner?" he asked, twisting strands of his beard until the roots hurt.

"I mean to hold him against the Call without a tether."

The disk of the sun winked out below the horizon, taking the black stripe with it. Ilyire's shoulders sagged with relief with it out of sight. He turned back to his sister, but she was solemnly shaking a finger at him.

"It is still there, my brother, an arch of black nothingness where the stars are obscured."

Ilyire shut his eyes tightly. "All right, all right. I understand nothing, but Glasken can come with us."

9 CATASTROPHE

Early the next morning they broke camp as the Call began to move, and before the sun was high they were within sight of the pale, gleaming walls of Maralinga Railside. As they reached the rails of the paraline Ilyire pointed to a dark shape in the distance, and they could hear a rumble above the wind. They crossed the paraline and let the camels go a hundred paces farther south before reining in and looking back.

"See, that long, low thing with the striped cylinders pointing to the sky?" Ilyire said as he pointed to the machine approaching from the west. "That is a travel machine."

Theresla stared as it drew near, amazed as its sheer size grew increasingly apparent. The rumble in the air seemed to beat against her, and she could hardly believe that there were no horses or camels pulling it. It passed them, an immense complexity of tubular rotors, balance booms, wheels, and masts, and behind it were coaches as featureless as the engine was complex. " 'Great Western Paraline Authority,' " Theresla read from the Austaric lettering beneath the windows. They watched it dwindle away toward Maralinga Railside.

"How does the machine's driver resist the Call?" Theresla asked.

"He doesn't. It runs by itself until it's required to stop. Watch, listen."

As it reached the railside's outer mercy wall, there was a clang as a brakepost

beside the rails tripped a lever protruding from the engine. It began to slow at once as the dropchocks gripped the wheels, screeching and belching smoke, but soon all except the spinning rotor towers and masts were obscured behind the wall. There was an echoing boom from the impact of the train against the buffers that had brought it to rest.

"All automata, no humans needed," explained Ilyire, attempting to seem casual about the wonder of it all.

"The sheer scale of their machines is a wonder," said Theresla with undisguised awe.

They stopped again just before noon, and while Ilyire tethered Glasken and the camels, Theresla found a boulder that was passably level and set up a brass crosspiece on screwdown feet and adjusted it with a spirit level. As solar noon passed she noted the length of the edgepole's shadow and direction on a pair of marked scales.

"I have an absolute north from the noonshadow, Ilyire. Come and adjust your compass."

He was pouring a little of his drinking water on his hands, a ritual that he performed each time he was forced to touch Glasken.

"What is our parallel of latitude?" he asked as he loosened a clamp and nudged the reference arm on his compass.

"Thirty-one degrees, six minutes."

He paused to estimate figures and distances. "Our southwest bearing is five-two, and we are following the Call's new bearing precisely, so . . . the Edge is thirty-five miles away."

As she began to dismantle her sighting platform she held up a brass plate with a tiny hole at the center and projected an image of the sun onto the rock face. Compared to the previous sunset and the morning's sunrise, the band across the sun had moved a little higher, and was thicker.

"Hold this for me, and hold it still," she said to Ilyire.

He muttered something about blasphemy but did as she said. Theresla took out a pair of dividers and measured the band's thickness and its position on the solar face.

"The Call that we travel in will stop for the night perhaps six miles from the Edge, am I right?" Theresla asked.

"That is probable."

Theresla gave him her most unsettling smile. "Good, good, that suits me very well. You say that the Call sweeps across this treeless plain quite often?"

"Yes, every three or four days. It's odd, because there are very few animals here. Perhaps the great fish who project it are somehow aware of the Austaric speakers in their wind trains."

•   •   •

Theresla set a timer to wake them two hours before dawn the next day, and they dragged their camels along before the Call began to move. The waning moon rose with Venus to light their way through the stunted bushes and broken rock. Glasken gave a yawn truncated by a gasp as they passed through the stationary leading edge of the Call.

"A Call!" he shouted in alarm, and Ilyire laughed.

"A Call, Fras Glasken. Too right, you are."

"It's *You are right*," Glasken angrily corrected him as he glanced about. "But I was lying—ah, in a camp, and it was daylight. Now it's night and—look at the moon! I must have been mindless for days. What has . . . I mean, I don't understand."

"You are slow, even with all studying," laughed Theresla. "Phase of moon show one passing day only."

"And you anchored us out of the Call so we are going . . . north? No, the Call doesn't move at night. Besides, look at the stars: we're going south!"

"Very good," mocked Ilyire.

"But how can anyone escape a stationary Call? It's not possible, unless an anchor holds you until the Call moves on."

"Have you not, ah, realized, Fras Glasken?" said Theresla. "Asking how did rescue you from camel train during Call? Call does not touching me and Ilyire."

Her revelation silenced Glasken as he recalled breasts of the most exquisite shape and symmetry hanging above him, breasts which then descended to press lightly against his pectorals. Then the Call had blotted it all out. What had he done as the Call had struck? Obviously Ilyire had stayed asleep: his head was still attached, he thought as he rubbed his neck.

It was dawn when they stopped. Theresla took sightings from the rising sun and measured what seemed to Glasken to be an oddly regular band of cloud across its face. There was a strange, rhythmic rumble in the distance and tang of salt on the air.

"The Edge is very close," Ilyire whispered to Theresla in Alspring, and pointed out an odd parallel below the horizon.

"Time to unpack and secure the camels," Theresla decided.

"Hey, lazy turd of camel have anus disease, you carry rocks, make Call shieldwall," Ilyire shouted to Glasken, who sullenly obeyed.

Theresla unpacked a length of rope and some instruments; then she and Ilyire walked toward the Edge.

"A band of perpetual Call extends a few hundred paces back from the Edge," Ilyire explained. "That cairn marks it, I built it last year."

"Yes, I sense it," Theresla agreed. "If the moving Call is like a net, this one is like a fence. Whatever is beyond the Edge does not want to be seen."

Glasken watched them walk some way toward the odd, double horizon, then vanish. Clearly there was a cave in the plain that they had entered to explore, but that was none of his business. He dropped the last of the rocks to complete the V-shaped deflection wall and piled their gear behind it. When the Call came past later that morning they would not be trampled by passing animals . . . except that Theresla and Ilyire were immune to the Call. That perplexed him, yet he was curiously heartened as well.

He reached down to lift one of Ilyire's saddlepacks—and was alarmed to feel air rushing past his hands. As he stood frozen the air rushed back the other way. A giant down there, breathing, he thought for a moment. A flat, pink rock beneath the saddlepacks appeared to be covering the mouth of a small cave. Ilyire's gear was right over it . . . very significant. Glasken grinned and looked to the horizon. No sign of them. He moved the saddlepacks and seized the edge of the rock. It was heavy, but he was strong and raised it without much trouble. There was Alspring writing cut into the lip of the little cave, and he recognized Ilyire's script.

Glasken found the entrance a tight fit, and his eyes took some time to accustom themselves to the gloom. He went in a short way and stopped. The place was suffused with the soft gleaming of gold and swirling cloudscapes of blue opal, shot with sparkles of gemstones. For a time his mind seemed to blank out; it was almost as if he was in a Call. The trance passed and his thoughts raced. Two pack camels could carry the lot, he could flee north and flag down a Great Western wind train on the paraline . . . but Ilyire was fast and deadly, and more to the point he was immune to the Call. He stared at the piles of wealth again, this time assessing and estimating. The air in the cave continued to move, as if he were in the mouth of a breathing dragon. It continually underlined the danger he was in.

His saddlepack was not full, and he could stuff the remaining space with enough gold coins and small jewelry so that the loss from the hoard and the change in his baggage would not be noticed. Even that would be the worth of the crown jewels in some small mayorates. He could go to the Emir of Cowra as a refugee Islamic prince from the far west, buy an estate with farmlands, buy five wives, buy enough wine to—but wine would be a problem with the Southmoors. Better to flee west as a refugee prince from the east. He made a hasty but careful selection of items and emerged from the breathing cave. The others were still out of sight.

After replacing the flat rock and Ilyire's gear he carefully hid the wealth of the Call victims in his saddlepack. As he pulled the final strap tight he noticed that Theresla had emerged again, and was hurriedly pulling up a rope from somewhere.

She walked back with brisk strides, casting a long shadow in the morning sun. The rope was coiled about her shoulder.

"Where were you, Frelle Abbess?" Glasken asked.

"Climbing over Edge . . . the world, of."

"Climbing over *the* edge *of* the world—you were *what*?"

"I were—was—making experiments. Watching marvels are, not for your eyes. My Austaric is bettering?"

"Is *better*, yes, but, but—"

"Ilyire is, ah, left down, under ledge, near water. Ilyire is ordered to experimenting for me." She slipped the rope from her shoulder and held it up. "Ilyire is not happy."

Glasken returned her little grin with a knowing leer, yet his mind was racing all the while. With Ilyire out of the way he could bind Theresla, then empty the treasure cave and take the lot north on the pack camels. The Abbess would fetch a good price in the slave markets of the Southmoors, and he could buy a small mayorate for what was in the cave. But first . . .

"Fras Glasken, we have business for finishing," she prompted, as if reading his last thought.

"Please, Frelle Abbess, no lengthy preamble this time," he said, tugging at the knot of his belt.

She spread a sandmat on the pink dust and broken stones, then began to undo her robes. Glasken stood naked facing into the morning sun as she stood with her back to it, holding her robes open.

"Come to me Fras Johnny Glasken. Come do what you will—"

The front of the Call rolled over them. Passion, pheromones, animal and mental cues mingled and balanced. Glasken's muscles crawled and twitched . . . but Theresla held him against the Call across a narrow gap of air, using no physical tether. In a different age, in a different science, it would have been called a tuned circuit.

What was set up between Glasken and Theresla was more than just an invisible tether; it interacted with the Call itself and tuned signals out of the world's two-thousand-year-old affliction. The Call was from the voices of the Callers, and as Theresla had hoped, they used the voices to communicate. It had always been known that the Call did not affect birds or reptiles, or mammals under a certain size, but nobody had ever traced its allure to sexuality. Most people surrendered to the Call as if being seduced, and Theresla had developed a theory that some rare individuals might surrender to sex so completely that in some circumstances even the Call could not quite draw them away. Glasken was the living verification of her theory, and she knew that she could use him to modulate and amplify the voices behind the Call into speech.

Theresla listened, her eyes unfocused. There were feelings and concepts rather than words at first, but she knew that they came from the shapes in the water beyond the cliffs. Or some of them, at any rate. Ilyire had been right. Sheep and shepherds. Shepherds calling food for their sheep with fantastic horns that

were heard without ears. Meat for fishes. Animals being dragged along by the Call were bounding past now, but the deflection wall kept Theresla and Glasken undisturbed. She noted distant bodies tumbling over the cliff. Small, sharp sensations of satisfaction came to her, and the taste of blood in the water. These would be those sleek and fantastic sheep bleating with pleasure.

The sensations of the shepherds were softer, but more complex. At first she just noted the patterns and feelings without understanding them, but as speech it was simple, she came to realize. These were not elite scholars, they were as simple as human shepherds, she told herself. The patterns were odd, but would not be hard to project. There was a temptation to shout to them, but she hesitated. A sage or yogi seeing a huge fish emerge from a river and speaking a jumble of human words might well recognize a fellow intelligence and try to converse. A simple shepherd would probably reach for his foxgun. Theresla listened, watched through other eyes, felt herself float and swim. Words began to match with understandings and perceptions. The shepherds were conversing idly while projecting the Call. They were ideal for Theresla's purpose.

Sooner than she wished, the Call ran its course. She felt the trailing edge approaching, reluctantly broke her self-induced trance, and waited. Her back had been to the sun as she held her robes open, so she had been well protected. Glasken had stood facing her, totally naked, for hours. He was sunburned deep pink.

As his mind returned he cried out in pain and surprise, then collapsed as Theresla swept her robes back across her nakedness. He had sunburn all down the front of his body, although slightly more on the right than the left because of the angle of the sun. She splashed some water from a skin over his head.

"Get dressed, Glasken. Ilyire to be getting rope back."

"Galloping Callbait, I'm roasted," he groaned. "What, how?"

"Dressing. Quickly!"

"My cod! It burns like a dose of pox."

She threw his tunic to him and he put an arm into one sleeve.

"Argh, no. The cloth's agony to my skin."

"Suit yourself," she said simply, picking up a tether. "Now be still, this be for your good health." Glasken howled as the strap rubbed against his skin.

By the time Ilyire crawled back over the Edge Glasken was still lying naked on his back.

"What in the name of—he's naked!" Ilyire thundered as they approached.

"A painful experiment, you should be pleased," Theresla explained.

Glasken continued to groan. Suddenly Ilyire gasped, then smiled beatifically as he realized that Glasken was burned only on the front of his body.

"Darling, wise, just, beautiful sister, you staked him naked in the sun for the whole of the Call! How could I ever have doubted you? Please, will you ever forgive your silly brother?"

Theresla forced back a smile. "You can start by rubbing ointment on his skin and bandaging him so that he can stand to be clothed again."

"Touch that maggot of a camel turd? Ah, a cruel punishment, sister dearest, but I bow to your wisdom—no, no, don't tell me: You want him saved so that you can do this again."

"Why Ilyire, you read my mind."

"Dearest, wonderful sister!" Ilyire composed a few words in Austaric and knelt beside Glasken. "Camel turd, I bring ointment and rub on with cloth. You lie still or I rub on with saltbush branch. Yes?"

It was another two days before Glasken was fit to travel. Ilyire found another cave in the limestone plain and Glasken sheltered from the sun inside it. Theresla spent the time making observations and drawings at the Edge. She explained that the supposed breathing of the cave was probably caused by waves at the base of the cliffs washing in and out of some vast labyrinth beneath their feet.

The journey back to Maralinga was slow because the blistered Glasken needed to rest quite frequently. He had lost all interest in sex and at first was barely able to keep croaking out his lessons in Austaric, but was much improved when they reached the paraline. When they caught sight of Maralinga's beamflash tower the sun had just set. They could see a light twinkling at its summit, which was trailing flaresmoke into the wind.

"Another two hours, sister," Ilyire reckoned.

"Say all in Austaric," she ordered.

"Traveling two hours. Camp here. Go on tomorrow. In dark get shot, perhaps."

"Am wishing arrive tonight," she replied.

"I agree," said Glasken.

"Camel turds have no—"

"Quiet!" snapped Theresla, gesturing to the sky in the gathering gloom. "Look up."

There was a thin band, a slash of starless blackness which bisected the firmament. In the west a copper-colored, fuzzy light was rising. Like a comet without a tail, it was at the very center of the band.

"So?" grunted Ilyire.

"Important I go Maralinga now. No time losing."

"*To lose*," added Glasken, anxious to be free of both of them. "I'll ride on ahead and risk getting shot."

"First good suggestion you make—" began Ilyire.

"We go together," Theresla decided.

The Highliber realized that the chance of Ilyire and Teresla ever returning to Maralinga was probably remote, yet she had ordered the railside to be fitted out to prepare for them. They were challenged at the southern sentry post two hours

before midnight, and once the sergeant of the watch realized who they were he lit a green flare to alert the railside. The Marshal had assembled the staff and troops of the entire railside for a lavish welcome ceremony that he had been planning ever since he had been appointed. Only the beamflash crew was absent, and they were already transmitting messages to the Highliber.

By the time Theresla, Ilyire, and Glasken were being escorted through the railside cloisters to a hastily prepared open air banquet, the Highliber's reply was being decoded in the beamflash gallery. A lackey brought it down in a pulley cage and ran to the courtyard where the Marshal was raising the first toast to the travelers. He broke the seal with a flourish and held the poorpaper up to a lantern.

"A message from the Highliber," he began grandly. "She sends her greetings to the Abbess Theresla and the intrepid warrior Ilyire, and bids the good Abbess go to the tower gallery at once to speak with her over the beamflash."

"A message?" exclaimed Theresla. "I am told . . . Highliber is living, ah, very distant."

"It's the signaling towers that I tried to explain about," said Glasken. "They relay messages to anywhere within minutes."

"Fras Glasken is nearly right, but we are so remote here that a securely coded exchange with Rochester takes almost an hour," added the Marshal. "Unfortunately Overliber Darien vis Babessa had been recalled to Rochester—"

Ilyire gave a loud sigh of relief and Theresla giggled. The Marshal paused with his mouth open, then went on.

"Luckily a beamflash inspector from Rochester is visiting the railside to explain some new codes and procedures. She will code and decode for you."

Theresla squirmed, then shivered. She was not used to being with so many men, and the relative familiarity of even the most respectful of them was unsettling.

"Where to speak with Highliber?" she asked.

"You could give a message to me, Frelle Abbess, and I would have it taken to the beamflash gallery at the top of the tower for transmission," said the Marshal hopefully.

"An hour exchanging, more minutes for up and down tower," Theresla said aloud as she looked across to the immense stone and wood structure. "I am wishing to say, ah, very secret things. Highliber says go to gallery, so do I. Is Inspector of gallery trustable?"

"She has a higher security clearance than me," the Marshal assured her.

"Then I go. Up tower. Please to have me taken."

Leaving Glasken and Ilyire to eat, drink, and listen to the speeches and music, the Marshal escorted Theresla to the tower's lift cage and worked the drive clamps. He was in full parade uniform while his distinguished guest was still in reeking, travel-stained lancers' robes. The contrast made his skin crawl.

"You have men pulling . . . cage up?" Theresla asked as the lift ascended the center of the tower.

"The cage is lifted by counterweights, Frelle, as in a reciprocating clock."

"Re-cipro-cating. Don't know word. Counter-weight machines, yes, we have them. What resets counterweights?"

"A rotor tower driven by the wind provides enough rewind for twelve ascents and descents per day. We seldom need even half of that."

The beamflash gallery was mostly enclosed, so that the operators' eyes would remain sensitive as they looked through the telescopes and read the signals from the distant towers in daylight. One telescope pointed east and another west. The beamflash network had been extended west by another three towers since Ilyire had last been there, and Kalgoorlie would be linked to Rochester within another year.

The beamflash crew sat ready at their equipment and the Inspector met them at the cage landing. She was a cheerful but brisk woman, dressed in a black uniform and wearing a Dragon Silver armband that gleamed in the soft light from the lanterns. As the first high official from Libris that Theresla had encountered, she made a good impression.

"Marshal, another request," said Theresla as they stood before the lift's door. "Man with me is great value. You protect with all cost. Yes?"

"Which man, Frelle Abbess?"

"Big, strong man, Fras John Glasken."

"At your word, Frelle Abbess. Shall I hold him in chains?"

"No, no. Just keep safe. No sexing with women, too. Yes?"

"He will be treated like a mayor but watched discreetly. Now, may I introduce you to Beamflash Inspector Lemorel Milderellen, Dragon Silver, EdR. Frelle Milderellen, this is the Abbess Theresla of Glenellen."

The librarian bowed stiffly in the gloom of the beamflash gallery, her eyes bulging wide and gleaming in the lamplight. There was no longer a smile on her face.

"The day's fortune to you, Frelle Abbess," she said in a cold, controlled voice.

The Marshal stepped back into the lift cage and descended. Theresla was used to people being nervous in her presence, but Lemorel's abrupt change in manner surprised her particularly. After reflecting for a moment she decided that the librarian's sudden coldness was probably something to do with Libris discipline. Lemorel began to show her around the gallery and explain the equipment. Theresla frowned at some of the words.

"Frelle Abbess, I have become reasonably fluent in your language with the help of Overliber Darien. Should we speak in Alspring?"

"No. Austaric speaking please."

Lemorel shrugged and guided her to the beamflash transmission desk. "Now, do you have a message ready for Highliber Zarvora?" she asked.

Theresla had rehearsed any number of greetings for the Highliber, but in spite of Glasken's account of beamflash technology she had not been prepared for this. Lemorel made some adjustments to an encryption machine, then linked its output lever to the beamflash key. Theresla spoke some thoughts and formalities in her limited Austaric and Lemorel wrote them into a consistent message.

"How does this sound, Frelle Abbess? 'I am honored to greet you, Frelle Highliber. Your machines and science are astounding. I know the basics of your language. I met a man who once worked for you, John Glasken. He was a prisoner of my people, but I freed him. He taught me some Austaric while we traveled south.' "

"Seeming right," Theresla decided. "Send."

"Is that all, Frelle Abbess?"

"Ah . . . yes."

"With respect, Frelle, there is nothing of substance in your message for the Highliber. Do you have anything important to tell her? Remember that her reply will not reach here for at least fifty minutes."

Something important! Theresla frowned for a moment, but could think of nothing else besides the Call. She began to explain what she had seen and done. Finally Lemorel read the text back.

" 'I have been to the Edge of our world. I have looked upon the source of the Call. It is made by huge fish. I have listened to their speech with a special machine of my own making. Is this of interest to you? I know nothing of your sciences and philosophical researches. You must ask many questions. What do you know of the band across the sky?' "

"Is good, you send," Theresla decided.

Theresla watched Lemorel typing, mesmerized by her fingers flickering over the keys of the encription device. The message clicked into pulses of light focused from a flare above the gallery. There were twenty-one beamflash towers between Maralinga and Rochester, and the message would accumulate as much as a minute's delay in each of them. In the clear night air of the Nullarbor there were few transmission errors, and the turnaround times were more like fifteen seconds. By the last word of her message the first pulse of light was only four towers from Renmark, at the western edge of the Southeast Alliance. Dispersing fog and the smoke from a grassfire at Robinvale would introduce errors after this, and there would have to be retransmission.

The Marshal sent a change of clothing up for Theresla. She washed and changed in the beamflash operators' tiny washroom while her message was making its journey. She emerged wearing a black tunic and trousers, with a Dragon Silver armband. Lemorel watched her pace about hesitantly, stiffly, with her arms folded across her breasts.

"Is something the matter, Frelle?" asked Lemorel.

"Feeling bare. Like breasts exposed, legs naked."

"In our society this is modest dress. You could wear a cloak, but it would look odd in this hot climate."

"No, no cloak. Better feeling naked than looking odd." She ran her fingers along the well-tailored fabric. "Very lucky. My size and form, ah, matching uniform here."

"The Highliber sent a hundred uniforms across. The fittings ranged from small and thin to tall and fat. The Marshal's hospitality lackey is trained to estimate fittings by sight alone, then choose the correct uniform. We have gone to great trouble to make you feel welcome."

Theresla searched Lemorel's cold, composed face, increasingly nervous at her manner. "I disappoint you? Yes? No?"

"It's not my business to make judgments, Frelle."

"You seem, ah, distant."

"Do I, Frelle? I'm sorry. I work so much as the extension of a machine that perhaps I have come to resemble one."

Lemorel turned a smile on instantly. Theresla laughed with relief just as a bell clanged. A receptor began to work the keys of his paper tape punch. Although ten feet across the room, Lemorel closed her eyes and typed into the decoder.

"You not read paper tape, Frelle?" asked Theresla.

"I recognize his keystroke patterns," said Lemorel tersely, her eyes still shut.

A second strip of paper tape reeled out of the decryption box, and this contained the decoded message. Lemorel ran it past a frosted glass screen lit by a lamp.

"From Highliber Dragon Black Zarvora Cybeline, EdR, the day's fortune to you, Frelle Abbess. I have read an account of Ilyire's journey to the Edge of the land written by Darien vis Babessa. I wish to hear your account from your own lips, so we must meet at once. Instruct the Marshal to get a galley train ready. What is the nature of the machine by which you can hear the Call beings? The idea of communicating with them is of great interest to me. Our world is in danger from a machine left over from the old civilization, but while the Call scours our lands and cities we cannot easily stop it. Glasken was declared missing and presumed dead more than half a year ago. As to the band in the sky, I can only tell you to your face.' "

Theresla pouted and cleared her throat. "I speak, you type. My Austaric only improve with using."

"As you will," said Lemorel, her fingers poised above the keys of the encryption machine.

"Frelle Highliber, you right. We need speaking together. My machine is, ah, human energies. Explaining later. John Glasken, vital part. His, ah, lustings so much, I never see similar. Must protecting Glasken. Costs no matter. I find, I free

him from Alspring traders. I not free companion, ah, Ni-kalan, also of—Frelle Lemorel, you are unwell?''

Lemorel had almost doubled over, clenching her fists, her face contorted. Almost as rapidly she straightened and took a deep breath, but within her head she had plunged over an Edge and down into insanity. For months she had tortured herself for putting Nikalan into the battle calculor and sending him to his death. She had even transferred to the Inspectorate to try to rebuild her shattered life. Now the truth had ridden out of the desert, and it had Glasken's leering face!

''A slight cramp, nothing serious,'' muttered Lemorel. She began to type again, speaking Theresla's words aloud. '' 'I encountered, but did not free, Glasken's companion Nikalan.' Please continue, Frelle Abbess.''

''No more, thank you. Please to call Marshal on, ah, voicewire box?''

Lemorel listened carefully as they spoke.

''Preparing . . . travel machine for Rochester,'' Theresla began.

''A galley train,'' twittered the distant Marshal's voice.

''Whatever. Leaving tonight. Teacher of Austaric come also.''

''Consider it done, Frelle Abbess. Is there anything else?''

''Yes. Murder wish Ilyire has for Glasken. Ilyire hating. Ilyire has strong morals, Glasken has no morals. Glasken on galley train to come. Is vital.''

''That may not be wise. Glasken is badly burned and has sun-exposure sickness. Further travel so soon may harm his health.''

''Ilyire might soon kill Glasken.''

''Take Ilyire with you.''

''Ilyire has work. Here. For me.''

''Once Glasken can travel again I'll be his personal escort. As for Ilyire, I swear I shall keep Glasken and him well apart.''

''Ah, is good.''

Theresla broke the connection, leaned back in the chair and stretched. By now it was past midnight. She removed the pins from her hair and it burst free in a black cascade. Lemorel sat with her hands clasped in her lap as Theresla began to comb out the tangles.

''Frelle Lemorel, my words to Highliber seeming strange, yes?''

''The Highliber's work is never dull, Frelle Abbess.''

''More exciting than secret of Call?''

''I cannot comment. It's the discipline of the service.''

''Discipline? Very good. Discipline not so much in Alspring cities. No discipline . . . no . . . towers, trains, speech machines.''

Lemorel nodded agreeably, then called for a lackey.

''Take the Abbess to the Marshal,'' she told the youth, then stood and bowed to Theresla. ''I bid you the fortune of tomorrow, Frelle Abbess.''

Theresla imitated her bow. Lemorel watched the roof of the life cage de-

scending for a moment, then returned to where Theresla had been sitting. With the aid of a lantern she picked four long, black hairs from the floor. She sat at the encoder and typed.

/ HAIR SAMPLES SECURED FROM ABBESS. BARBER HAS HAIR SAMPLES FROM VINEMAN AND GLASKEN. SAMPLES WILL BE SENT IN SEALED BAG WITH TRAIN'S CAPTAIN. /

She tore off the tape and walked across to the beamflash crew.

"Send this to the Highliber," she ordered.

"Can it wait until dawn, Frelle, or should I light another magnesium flare? We have orders to conserve them."

"Light a flare, Fras Captain. The Highliber will want to know this."

It took what remained of the night to insure that the almost becalmed westward express was shunted clear of the main line and into the siding at Tarcoola. Theresla did not sleep until she was aboard the galley train with her saddlepack of notes and instruments. As she began the journey east, Zarvora requisitioned a galley engine with the Mayor's personal carriage and set off west, taking Darien with her as linguist and translator. After two days the trains converged on the junction town of Peterborough. Constant, intensive tutoring had improved Theresla's command of Austaric somewhat.

Theresla's train arrived first. Ever curious about the strange and exotic Austaric civilization, she left her carriage to climb to the gallery of the control tower of the Peterborough shunting yards with her translator. The Overswitch had been told only that an important guest of the Highliber had arrived. He went through his usual tour description as they walked around the circular stone gallery.

"Peterborough's always been the junction of three major paralines, but now, with the recent linkup of the Rochester mayorates through the new Loxton tracks, aye, traffic is double or more."

Theresla looked down at her own train. The galley engine was on a turntable, being turned for the trip back to Rochester. The exhausted navvy pedalers crew had already been relieved.

"So much steel," Theresla said in wonder as she looked out over the rails. "Hard to believe . . . so much steel."

"Oh yes, these are big yards, Frelle. The rails here have been salvaged from abandons hundreds of miles away."

She looked at a large compass rose set amid the tiles of the floor. The Austaric word for Call was right on the west point, and the names of the three main lines were also on the rim.

"Rochester is south now, yes?" she asked, disoriented.

"No, Rochester is southeast. The paraline runs due south for a way, then veers east at Edunda. Ah, see that galley train on the southern paraline? Very

high priority on that one. It carries the Highliber. I've got nine wind trains ready to leave, yet they've been held for two days while you and the Highliber were converging. Seven of them are from the Central Confederation. Ah, but there'll be sharp words between mayors over that. You must be very important, Frelle.''

"I am," said Theresla, watching the red and green engine with its gold coach pulling into the shunting yards.

There was a distant screeching of brakeblocks being screwed down, and the train began slowing near Theresla's coach.

"Dummart, she's stopped on a proceed," shouted a signalman from across the gallery. "Right across trailing points, too."

"Switch out the paralines, then halt all traffic on accident alert," the Over-switch called. "Aye, and send a runner to the captain of the Highliber's train to ask what her pleasure is. As Highliber asks, Highliber gets."

Theresla's keen eyes picked out the captain of her own train walking across to the newly arrived galley engine. He was carrying a black dispatch bag.

"We should go down to the Highliber, Frelle," Theresla's interpreter suggested, but she shook her head. Too many people were jumping at the Highliber's word, barely pausing to ask how high. She would make her wait.

Far below, Zarvora broke the seal on the dispatch bag from Maralinga and took out Lemorel's papers. Most of it was reports that expanded on what had already been said by beamflash, but there were also three slim packages that also bore Lemorel's seal: they were marked THERESLA, ILYIRE, and GLASKEN.

She broke the seals and unpacked a brass microscope from her instrument case. Under the objective, lying together on the slide, the Ghans' samples looked like long, fine feathers. Zarvora sat back and folded her arms, nodding to herself. She took a little scalpel from the instrument case and cut the end of one of her own hairs. Laid between those of Theresla and Ilyire, it became another long, fine feather in the eyepiece. Glasken's hair was a plain rod, like that of any human.

There was no fanfare or ceremony for the meeting of Zarvora and Theresla. The Overswitch assumed that Theresla was a senior Dragon Librarian reporting to the Highliber on some matter of the highest importance, but he was puzzled by his visitor's odd ignorance of geography. The Highliber's galley engine was being reversed on the turntable. It would not be long before the shunting yards were back to normal, he thought with relief.

Zarvora was standing with Darien beside her as Theresla and her interpreter entered the coach. Theresla folded her arms, then swept them open and to her sides, palms outward. Zarvora bowed from the waist.

"Is men's greeting in Alspring," Theresla said as she walked forward. "Forbidden to women."

"I shall not report you," Zarvora replied. "How confident are you with our language?"

"Having words for to order bat for breakfast, or lackey beheaded."

"That seems sufficient. Frelle Darien, would you take the Abbess' interpreter to the next compartment and take her report—but be ready to return should we need you."

Darien nodded and turned for the door, but Theresla seized her arm.

"You are Darien, with no voice. My brother, ah, besotted with you."

Darien blushed, then held up a card with THANK YOU written on it.

"We speaking later, yes?" said Theresla as she released her.

Alone with Theresla, the Highliber sat at her desk beside the window while her guest lay on a leather couch on the other side of the coach.

"Moving palace," Theresla observed, looking over the opulent fittings.

"It belonged to our Mayor, but is now surplus to his needs."

There was a heavy rumble as the galley engine rolled backward off the turntable, building up to a heavy lurch as its couplings crashed into those of the coach and engaged them. Moments later the coach was moving forward, rattling over a set of points. Theresla watched the vista of trackwork and parked trains passing the window and seemed disinclined to speak.

"You have never been able to teach anyone but Ilyire to defy the Call," Zarvora stated flatly, not trying to disguise her impatience.

Theresla looked around slowly. "You cannot know, Frelle Highliber."

"I did not go to so much trouble to make you welcome just to endure a display of pouting and posing, Abbess. Either we act as equals or I shall have you returned to Maralinga and turned loose to do as you will."

Theresla looked out of the window again, in time to see the train pass through the gates in the town wall. Beyond was scrubby grassland grazed by tethered sheep.

"But we are not equals, Frelle Highliber," she said without turning back. "I can defy the Call, like this Call . . ." She raised a hand. "Now."

She dropped her hand. Almost at once a deadhand alarm clanged somewhere at the front of the train as the Call swept over them.

"Ah, you can anticipate the Call," said Zarvora. "A good trick, Frelle Abbess, you must teach it to me some time."

Theresla cried out in surprise and whirled around so fast that she lost her balance and tumbled from the couch, thudding to the floor. Zarvora was sitting at her microscope, calmly peering through the eyepiece.

"Why are you sitting on the floor with your mouth open, Frelle Abbess?" she asked, glancing up. "It does not become you."

"But how? I, I—you . . ."

"I was born with latent resistance to the Call, as were you and Ilyire. You

have much to offer, but not a method to resist it. If we are to work together, we need some mutual respect. Agreed?"

Theresla remained sitting on the floor, speechless. Her wildest fantasies of this meeting had not included anything like this.

"You have rankings above me . . ." she began; then her pride smothered the rest of the admission.

"In your patriarchal society you dealt with those with power over you by keeping them guessing, playing the part of a deranged genius. You see, I am not so very insensitive, am I? Frelle Theresla, you do not need to do that anymore. Dragon Silver confers status, freedom, and power. What more do you want?"

By now Theresla was back on the couch, but she sat hunched forward, staring at Zarvora intently. Zarvora noticed a glistening at the edge of her eyelid.

"Frelle Zarvora, very hard, this, for me. I never trust. Not even Ilyire. Having no equals."

"Neither have I, Frelle. Now then, do you understand microscopes?"

The train had finally rolled to a halt, its crew and navvy pedalers all in the grip of the Call. Theresla walked over to Zarvora's desk.

"Wish Ilyire been sister," she said, putting an arm around Zarvora's shoulders.

Zarvora reached up and gave her hand a short, convulsive squeeze. "At least you had a brother to love, Frelle. I had nobody." She gestured to the microscope. "Please, look through the eyepiece."

Theresla squinted down the tube. "Looking as would . . . three emu feathers, ah, with string across them."

"The feather on the right is a length of your hair, collected by the beamflash inspector at Maralinga. That on the right is from Ilyire, the strand in the middle is one of my mine, and the plain one lying across them is from a human."

Theresla straightened, then walked to a window and looked out at the tethered sheep, all straining to walk east. Emus were walking among them, quite unaffected.

"Birds feel no Call. You, I feel no Call, have feather-hair too. We bird-human, are, yes?"

"Yes. When did you learn that you could resist it?"

"Turning twelve. Am older than Ilyire. I tried teaching him. No good. Suddenly, he learn. Was fourteen. I tried teaching my nuns. No good."

"Just as I thought, the skill is linked to puberty. I was eleven years old when a Call swept over me and did no more than give me a sort of shivery tingle. Over the years I have examined the hair of hundreds of people, but not one strand was as mine is. Not that of my parents, nobody."

Theresla sat on the edge of the desk, then suddenly lay out flat across Zarvora's papers and closed her eyes.

"Is ancient word for blasphemy against Diety's will. Gen-kehic, tamper in godworks."

"It is in my books as genetics, a medical skill. Today medicians could, say, cut off your ears, but before Greatwinter the medicians could change you inside so that your children would be born without ears too. Perhaps when the Call first began some medicians put some of feature of birds into a few humans so that they could resist the Call. Every so often an echo of that work arises, and beings like us are born."

"But why ancients, ah, not change all people to be as birds?"

"There was a war that caused Greatwinter. Many arts and sciences were lost. I have rediscovered the art of building calculation engines, calculors, but only by using thousands of slaves. The ancients had calculors called computers that worked by, ah, the essence of lightning, as from clouds in a storm."

"Elt'ronik. Essence of devil. Deity sent angel. Angel scouring elt'ronik from Earth. Scouring still, or so scriptures tell."

"Libris has books talking about an 'EMP' cannon, which destroys electroforce machines. I do not know what the letters stand for, but the same book mentions that they were installed on 'orbiters.' 'Orbiter' is an ambiguous word, but it can mean artificial moon."

"The dawn and dusk travelers that wander among the fixed stars?"

"The Wanderers. Some of them appear to be ancient weapons, designed to detect and destroy electroforce devices. They are why our attempts to build simple electroforce machines always end with the wires glowing red and melting soon after they are activated."

Glasken had eluded his guards by climbing out of a window, and disguising himself by shaving off his beard. He had an assignation. She was a Dragon Orange, a plump, jolly girl with a very pretty face. She alone had been willing to defy the prohibition on dalliance with him that Theresla had ordered. It had not been easy. Winks, simpering looks, and finally notes had been exchanged. Glasken crawled along the stone guttering, then dropped to a courtyard and made his way to the stables.

As Weldie had promised, the stablehands were gone, even though it was only late afternoon. A soft voice called from the hayloft, and Glasken scrabbled up the ladder. Weldie was there, out of her accursed Libris uniform, and wearing a cotton blouse and a lyre-print skirt.

"You escaped, Fras Glasken, I knew you could do it."

"Darling Weldie, call me Johnny."

"Hoo! Johnny, so very ardent!" she exclaimed as he ran his hands up her legs.

"Please Frelle, please none of this foreplay business, just this once. I have been tortured for months by foreplay without afterplay."

"Johnny, Johnny, of course. I love to be desired by a man who can't wait to have me."

"Then I'm your man. Oh, you're soft, you're paradise."

"Fras Johnny, my hero warrior."

In spite of the heaving and thrashing in the hayloft, nobody came to investigate.

Across the continent, to the east, it was already sunset. Zavora had ordered the train stopped so that she and Theresla could make accurate measurements of the band across the setting sun. The Tiger Dragons paced uneasily, their weapons at the ready. They were on a stretch of track that was not visible to lookouts on the beamflash towers.

"Its thickness seems stable now," Zarvora concluded.

"Is wobbling in orbit," said Theresla. "Soon to leave face of sun, then return. You predicted band, Frelle?"

"Yes, but from sparse clues. I found a reference to a thing called a 'nano-composite constructor,' an electroforce machine that does certain work but also makes copies of itself. One was sent to the moon just before Greatwinter."

Zarvora explained the rest as they packed up the telescope.

"What is plan, you have?" Theresla asked as they walked back to the train in the sunset's glow.

"The band in the sky is an intelligent machine. It was built to serve us, so perhaps it can be persuaded to disassemble itself if we can contact it. Otherwise, I shall attack."

"You?"

"Me."

"Attack that?" Theresla exclaimed, pointing to the setting sun's bisected disk.

"Yes."

"You being demented as me, but more. We to be getting along, ah, fantastically."

They climbed back into the mayoral coach, and the captain ordered the brake-blocks unscrewed. The train began accelerating slowly and smoothly.

"I want to contact more people like us," said Zarvora. "I have begun with a survey of all the, ah, slaves in my Calculor. My study is piled deep with hair samples, just now. They will take days to check."

"Fetch other . . . microscope, is name? I help."

"Well, thank you. I need help to explore cites in the Calldeath lands for the ancient weapons and machines. Radios, Fa'eighteens, rockets, plasma cannons."

"Working, would they? Two thousand years is old."

"Something called shrink-wrap prevents aging, or so I have read."

"Speaking to Call creatures, maybe I can. Stop Call over Calldeath abandons. Glasken is key. Call using lust as hook. Glasken having lust with no relenting. Have developed technique with lusting tension."

"Glasken. The name is vaguely familiar. I shall check with my Calculor and find his history."

"With only Glasken, it works. Tried others. Guarding carefully, Glasken."

"Inspector Milderellen will do that, have no fear."

Glasken and Weldie had been in the hayloft for an hour when the butt of a twin-barrel Morelac obliterated his reverie. Weldie had been kneeling in the hay while Glasken introduced her to the bull-and-cow position. She heard a heavy thump and Glasken had slid off her.

"Sorry I could not get here earlier," said Lemorel as she turned Glasken's body over.

"That's all right, Frelle Inspector. Shames me to say that I quite enjoyed him."

"There's no accounting for taste. Help me get him back into his trousers."

"I made sure that he kept most of his other clothes on."

"Up, lift, push him down the chute—there. Now go! There's ten gold royals waiting beneath your pillow. Forget this ever happened."

"Good fortune, Frelle Inspector. You'll not kill him, will you? I mean, he was, well—"

"I need him alive more than you could believe. Now go!"

For all her skill with a flintlock, Lemorel was not exceptionally strong. Glasken, clubbed and bound, still weighed over 220 pounds. The camels padded about restlessly as she dragged him across the stables.

"Down! Down, damn you!" she hissed at the Alspring camels—that did not understand commands in Austaric and remained standing.

"Permitting me help, Frelle," said a voice from the darkness.

Lemorel dropped at once and rolled behind Glasken's body, the Morelac in her hand.

"Shooting not, Frelle. Sound bring soldiers."

The voice was soft, conspiratorial.

"Come out where I can see you" was all that Lemorel would concede.

Lemorel watched as Ilyire emerged from a corner and into the light diffusing in from the lamps outside. He tugged at a camel's reins and softly barked "Kush! Kush!" It knelt at once. He took Glasken under the arms and heaved him into the saddle, then strapped him securely to the frame.

"Shill! Shill!" he hissed, and the camel stood up. "Kush, down. Shill, up. Remembering, please to. How to saddle and load others, you did?"

"I had a stablehand to do it hours ago. There's nothing suspicious about strapping saddlepacks onto camels."

"Ah, but camel turd Glasken suspicious, yes? Why you wanting him?"

"To guide me to a man named Nikalan."

"Sickly one, Ni-kalan? Glenellen, is taken there. All I know. Making Glasken maggot rescue Ni-kalan?"

"Glasken's the guide, I'll do the rescuing."

Ilyire's composure slipped, and he seemed really aghast.

"You? Woman rescuing? Pervert acting, no, no, scriptures tell *protect women.*"

The light was bad, and he barely noticed Lemorel's hand flicker. A palm-sized metal star thudded into a post beside his head. He gasped and jerked aside, leaving several hairs stuck to the post.

"Fras Ilyire, in Austaric society you must choose the people that you insult with exquisite care. Insults lead to duels, and duels are to the death."

"Frelle, I . . . warn, only. Scriptures say protecting of women." He took a breath and swallowed. "You dress as man, act as man, yes? If not, bad morals. Priests lock you in convent, nuns reading scriptures to you, many years."

Lemorel nodded, and began to relax. "So your people have some sort of protection rule, like the purdah of the Southmoor women. I see your point. I must dress like a man to move freely in the Alspring cities. Meantime, you should take care who you insult. Understand? Insults kill."

"Gratitude for lesson. Make Glasken turd teach Alspring. Has few words useful."

"But I speak Alspring," Lemorel said, suddenly realizing that her grasp of it was better than Ilyire's Austaric. They changed languages at once.

"Where did you learn Alspring?"

"A linguist friend of mine gave me lessons."

"A linguist without a voice?"

"Yes, as it happens. Darien."

"I must meet her again, I love her."

"I think she has a lover in Rochester, but—"

"I kill him!"

Glasken groaned and tried to move against the saddle straps. Lemorel reached up with a pitchfork handle and beat him over the head. He slumped in the saddle again. Ilyire's teeth gleamed in a smile.

"Good Frelle, listen carefully. Go north to the sand hills then northwest, for five days. Then north, for a long time, months. The land is harsh, so there are not many Kooree tribes to avoid. Avoid them, try never to fight, that is their protocol. It took me a year last time and I had many battles, but the badwill from Kharec's crossing was fresh then. Fifty days, it may take you fifty days. Dress

as a man, ask the way to Glenellen when you meet anyone. Tell them that Glasken is your eunuch. Better still, make it true.''

"Why haven't you killed him if you hate him so much?'' Lemorel asked as she climbed the railings and stepped into her own saddle.

"I gave an oath to my sister not to harm the camel turd.'' He gave a low, oddly deep laugh. "I have kept my oath to the very letter.''

"That you have, Fras. Now open the gates, if you please.''

"Frelle Inspector, you will make the camel turd suffer, please? Fortune be yours.''

At Lemorel's suggestion the Marshal and other senior officers of Maralinga had gathered in the beamflash gallery for a small but exclusive celebration. A lackey brought around a tray with a jar of wine and polished silver goblets as they waited for her to arrive.

"The Inspector is pleased,'' the Marshal declared to the beamflash captain. "The Abbess is safely with the Highliber and the upgrade of the beamflash procedures is complete.''

"But where is the Inspector?'' asked Captain Burla.

The Marshall glanced around the crowded gallery. "Delayed with work I presume.''

"Perhaps a little toast before she arrives?''

"Why not, she is surely sour company,'' he whispered, nudging the Captain in the ribs before raising his voice. "Your attention, good folk,'' he said as he raised his goblet in a toast. "Listen carefully while I—''

A flash of light from down in the shunting yards was followed by a heavy detonation. Flaming debris arced through the air above the shunting yards as shots popped like fireworks in the darkness.

"An attack!'' barked the Marshal. "Quickly, light a flare and alert the Irmana tower,'' he called to the beamflash captain as he hurried to the lift-head. The pulley ropes were gone, and the voicewire had been cut.

"Marshal, the flares are gone from the locker!'' someone cried a moment before another explosion blew away part of the emergency stairway in the center of the tower.

Lemorel had not realized that there were tripwires with bells some distance to either side of the northern sentry post. Someone with a megaphone tried to hail her, but she ignored him and rode on. Shapes began moving, dimly outlined by the starlight and the distant fires at the railside.

She led the guards another mile north before anchoring Glasken's camel and attacking. In the gloom they did not realize that she was coming back, dodging from bush to bush. Her first shot barked out, hitting a guard hit just below the

collarbone. In a panic the other two fired at where the flash had come from, but she had dropped her musket and rolled aside, drawing her twin-barrel. The flashes from their own muskets betrayed their positions as her two shots echoed theirs.

Ten miles farther north she drew alongside Glasken's camel and removed his gag.

"Damn you Lemorel, they'll have us back by morning," he spluttered as he shook his head free of the cloth. "They've got trackers who can work by moonlight."

"But there's no moonlight, it's the time of the new moon. The railside staff think that they're under attack, but once they realize that the shots were only fireworks they'll have to catch the camels I released and scattered."

The whites of her eyes gleamed with mania. Glasken shivered.

"They'll have to wait until dawn, then they must find our trail. Should they manage to do that, they can take you back over my dead body, and that should be difficult."

"I'll testify to the magistrate, I'll have you facing a squad of musketeers—"

"From now on, Fras Glasken, whatever you say must be in Alspring. Understood?"

"Alspring? I barely know a word of it."

"Then search your memory *very* hard."

"Alspring's months away, through a bloody desert!"

"You learned survival skills from Ilyire. You'll teach them to me."

"And what will you use for Alspring money?"

"The coins and jewels I found in your saddlepack when I searched your room."

"You stole my treasure?" screamed Glasken so loudly that tiny animals scurried away in the darkness.

"Yield to fate, Glasken. You falsified beamflash transmissions and made me think that Nikalan and you were dead. You ripped him out of my life, now I want him back! You *will* help."

"You! Nikalan?" Glasken exclaimed, incredulous.

Mirrorsun was high in the sky, but its weak, coppery light gave them no more than a bearing as they rode north. They reached the dunes well before morning, and the wind obliterated their tracks in the shifting sands as they turned northwest. As the banded sun rose over the desert, the man who was the key to the very Call itself vanished without a trace.

A month later, to the very day, Theresla and Zarvora boarded the mayoral coach at Rochester's paraline terminus. The coach behind it carried several guards and nineteen men and women who were nervous, wide-eyed and apprehensive. The train moved off, and had absolute priority on the paraline south.

"Twenty Call folk among the Calculor's components!" Zarvora declared in triumph to Theresla. "Twelve from a group that lives within the Calldeath lands. They call themselves aviads."

"But why they were living among humans?" asked Theresla, who had not helped to question them.

"Aviads are prey to the Call until puberty. The children cannot live as vegetables in the Calldeath lands, so they are raised among humans. The twelve in the Calculor were teachers. There are thousands of them there! We no longer need Glasken."

"I am not needed, perhaps, either," said Theresla, drawing the conclusion out further.

"Nonsense. You have an outlook very different to mine, Theresla, you see what is not obvious to me. The teacher aviads are taking us to their town, Macedon. It is south of the Bendigo Abandon. The other seven want to join them."

"Is nineteen. Found twenty."

"Ah yes, FUNCTION 9. I need him—that is, his talents, in the Calculor."

"Is long journey? Coronation next week."

"Being crowned Overmayor of the entire south is less important than winning the trust of the Macedon aviads. The coronation can wait."

Hastian followed the arm of his watchman, who was pointing to a pair of camels approaching from due south. His Neverlander warriors wound their Call timers and checked their guns as they stood up. One of the riders was strapped into his saddle, the other was oddly dressed and carried guns of an unfamiliar design.

"The greetings of the day," came an oddly shrill voice. "We seek Glenellen."

The voice. Breasts. And she was wantonly wearing trousers.

"Ai-ya, seize the witch!" called Hastian, scandalized.

Two of his Neverlanders started forward, but the witch's gun miraculously fired two shots. Both men dropped. The others fired, her camel reared and collapsed, but she emerged from behind its body with more of the infernal, multishot guns. Five men fell to six shots, and another two to her saber. A pointed metal star thudded into Hastian's knee, and the pain was such a shocking thunderflash that he fell convulsing to the red sand. Time seemed to stop.

A knee came down on Hastian's chest and a twin gunbarrel was rammed into his screaming mouth. The face looking down at him was female, but something in her eyes was more unsettling than the gaze of a tiger snake.

"My guide rode off," she snarled. "You guide me now."

Hastian gurgled. She withdrew the gun and stood.

"Who?" gasped Hastian, without moving, tasting blood.

"I am dark side of Ervelle's soul, returned from Call for vengeance."

He looked around. Nine of his invincible Neverlander warriors were lying dead. The two other bloodied survivors were prostrating themselves in the dark red sand. To Hastian there was no doubt of it. This thing was what she claimed to be. He was blessed. One of the gods was calling him to service.

 ## CHRYSALIS

In the four years following Zarvora's coronation as Overmayor the south of the continent united in the most powerful union since the fall of the Anglaic civilization. Her rule was intelligent, tight but fair, and economies boomed. Armed conflict practically ceased, and thanks to the expansion of beamflash and paraline networks no bad harvest was ever followed by famine. There were rumors that the surplus wealth of this golden age of prosperity was being fed into some mighty project to revive yet another marvel from the Anglaic civilization and prevent another Greatwinter, but only Zarvora knew the entire truth. That truth was not her only secret, but it was easier to conceal than a more immediate problem.

"You, Highliber, are pregnant."

The Libris medician had come to know Zarvora quite well over the years because of her headaches, but he was nervous about how she would react to this particular diagnosis.

"I have been a little nauseous and put on weight," said Zarvora impatiently. "That means nothing."

"And missed four periods."

"That too."

"My advice is—"

"This is highly inconvenient. Leave!"

When he was gone Zarvora sat staring at the Calculor console. In all the world there was nobody she could confide in. She stared at a silver owl with ENCRYPTION ENABLE engraved on the plate beneath it.

"I rule half the continent, yet I am pregnant by a man who does not know it, and does not exist, in a machine that does not exist, but which I nevertheless designed. Constructive suggestions are welcome."

The owl remained silent.

"I have never felt so very alone. Everyone will gloat and laugh, they all want to see me pulled down. Did you hear the one about the component who got

his beamflash tower stuck in the Highliber's input buffer? No, because everyone who tells the joke gets shot!''

She flicked the lever that enabled the voicewire box to her lackey. As the felt damper lifted free and she opened her mouth to speak the voice of the medician echoed out.

''I am not making insinuations, Fras Vorion. The fact remains that she is pregnant and unmarried. A woman of her power and in her position—''

''You're saying Frelle Cybeline is not married?'' retorted Vorion.

''Yes! It's a fact! Public knowledge! The Overbishop is Christian, rain falls from the sky, and the Highliber is unmarried. Now my advice—''

''Frelle Cybeline's husband is a senior engineer working on a secret machine far away—in Kalgoorlie. Gah, now I've already told you too much! Get out before I call a guard. Go. Go go go go!''

Zarvora disabled the voicewire, thought for a moment, smiled, then tugged at one of several dozen tassels hanging from the ceiling. Moments later Vorion was at her door. His face was flushed from his exchange with the medician.

''Fras Vorion, how did you know my secret consort is an engineer stationed in Kalgoorlie?'' she asked.

Vorion was thunderstruck. The man that he had conjured out of the air not thirty seconds earlier had suddenly come to life.

''Highliber, I, I, I must have heard you say something.''

''Well next time ask my permission before saying it to someone else. Sumeror is a good medician but an even better gossip.''

Vorion's legs wobbled as the color left his face. He fell to his knees.

''Highliber, I can only tender my regrets and my resignation.''

''How long have you served me?''

''Nine years.''

''And you are still only a certified lackey.''

''Yes. That is—yes.''

''Arrange a train for me to Kalgoorlie. I want to be with my consort for the birth.''

''Yes, of course.''

''Then report for retraining. In seven months I want to be at the ceremony when you are presented with Dragon Red. Any subjects that trouble you can be waived.''

It took several shots of expensive brandy before Vorion could string a coherent sentence together again. He poured out his story of being a classics graduate whose career in Libris had been stillborn because of Zarvora's new promotion criteria. He was currently the happiest man in Libris, and possibly the continent.

''I ruined your prospects, yet you serve me so well?'' she said, not comprehending.

"Highliber, you don't understand. I am nothing, but you share greatness with me. I adore you, I would die for you. I lied about your unscheduled absences when I thought you were having an affair."

Zarvora swallowed. "Fascinating. Have another drink."

"I even forged documents to protect you. I found out about Archbishop James—oh I have friends who know people who get told, well, intimate things. Bitchy bag of lard, but I cut the balls from *his* little scheme when I put those seven hundred gold royals against his name—"

"What? I thought it was Tarrin."

"Tarrin? That walking soup stain with delusions of adequacy? He carries on like a eunuch, but I've heard that . . ."

Vorion had heard a great deal, and Zarvora listened for a long time. When she finally spoke she had very little to say.

"Vorion, I—I do not deserve your service, but fortune must favor me. Now, book my train, then take the afternoon off and read the Dragon Red syllabus."

Alone again, Zarvora pondered the servant who had saved not only her pride and reputation, but her life as well. Tears rolled down her cheeks, yet her world had suddenly brightened. She was certainly in strange company, but she was not alone or without allies.

Several years in the mayorates of the south had not changed Ilyire. As he paced the floor of a tavern in Kalgoorlie he seemed merely an intense, distraught man in an emu-leather bush jacket and hobnail boots, but within his soul, he was still a Ghan warrior. Seated at a nearby table was Darien, the bands of her Dragon Silver rank displayed on a clasp that fastened her ochre traveling cloak. Although they were arguing, the other afternoon patrons heard nothing. Darien and Ilyire were fluttering their hands through the words of Portington sign language.

"I am going back to Libris with the Overmayor because you have not changed in half a decade," Darien signed with slow, emphatic symbols, then thumped the table for emphasis.

"Me? No change?" he signed in reply. "I learn your history, language, this sign language, everything for you. I learn your cultures and religions."

"But you do not even *like* to speak Austaric, Ilyire. *Your* grammar is all over the place, yet your sister can now speak Austaric as well as the Overmayor."

"I fix."

"It's not just grammar," she signed with impatient flourishes. "It's jealousy and Alspring protectiveness. All that I did was go out for a drink with the Merredin envoy and there you were, smashing up the tavern and beating him senseless."

"You not tell me about official business. Seem like funny business."

"You should have trusted me."

"I not trust *him*!"

The gesture for "him" was a violent, slicing stroke, and had a saber been in Ilyire's hand, the movement would have been no different.

"Ilyire, I am leaving. The Overmayor's wind train departs tonight and my berth is reserved. You are violently overprotective. I cannot stand it."

"Wrong. Am restrained."

"No. You will not accept me for what I am: a fully grown woman. Men have slept with me, have made love with me—"

"You tell who, I kill them!" Ilyire bellowed at the top of his voice, abandoning sign language.

Several other patrons spilled their drinks in alarm. Ilyire held onto a stay-beam beneath a shelf while he fought his temper back under control. Darien drummed her fingers on the table until Ilyire sheepishly made a gesture of apology.

"So that is an example of your new restraint," she signed. "I have accepted the position as Overmayor's aide, Ilyire. I go where she goes, or where she sends me. Just now she is going east, so goodbye."

The other patrons had their hands on their swagger sticks as Darien stood up and dropped a copper beside her pewter goblet, but Ilyire did not attempt to stop her as she walked out. The vintner sighed with relief as Ilyire left a minute later.

"The Constable's Runners can have 'im if he's wont to raise hell in the streets," he said to a serving boy.

"Skinny sort of shadowlad, but strong as ye'd never think, Fras," the boy replied. "That stay-beam's splintered where he gripped it."

The vintner whistled as he scratched at the slivers of wood. "Ee, that be kauri, too. Still, a bullet would stop 'im, and if he carries on like that again it's a runner's bullet he'll be getting."

Ilyire did manage to control his behavior, however. He went to the stables around the corner and got his horse, then set off to the west for the Calldeath lands. He rode slowly, knowing what awaited him there.

The landscape below the red upland cliffs was laid out like a scatter of colorful cloth scraps on a Northmoor carpet of pink-and-olive designs. From their vantage on the clifftop three riders observed the aftermath of a battle and made their own judgments about what had happened between the armies of two Alspring cities. They were dressed as Neverlander nomads, swathed against the pervasive red dust in robes, veils, and head shrouds of ochre, light orange, sienna brown, and dappled olive.

"Glenellen is again victorious," said Overhand Genkeric as he lowered his

brass-inlay telescope. "That infernal calculating machine fights their battles for them now. It has made them invincible."

The man on his right continued to scan the scatterings of color on the land-scape below, using one of the new twinoculars that split the light from one lens into two eyepieces.

"Glenellen's battle calculor, I see it!" he suddenly exclaimed. "It's off to the left, just near those observation masts. Just a group of scribes at desks! Who would ever guess what they are, or what they can do?"

"An invincible machine, Captain Lau-Tibad. Whatever the odds the dam-nable thing multiplies its men's effectiveness to match. What hope do our Nev-erland tribes have against it?"

"I see them folding their desks away. The desks are white, no—about a third of them are red."

"Gah, shut up will you! You're not with the bird-watching convial now. This is war."

"My apologies, Overhand Genkeric," he said as he lowered the twinocular and let it dangle from the strap around his neck.

"We are nothing, that's what has protected us so far. As nomads we Nev-erlanders are just a minor bother to Glenellen's expansion, but the raids of our brother tribes must become a serious problem eventually."

"To Glenellen? They're the bite of a flea. There's plenty of room for all on the desert, and what do we Neverlanders have but our tents and camels?"

"The day will come when Glenellen scratches its fleas. We must stop biting, and persuade the others to do the same . . ."

His voice faded as he realized that the third rider had looked away for a moment from the patchwork of despair and triumph below the cliffs, and was regarding them with eyes that were at the same time quizzical and impatient.

"If only you could hear yourselves," she said.

The voice from behind the heavy red cotton veil was measured, sarcastic. While the two officers sat proudly erect in their saddle frames, the Commander turned away from them again, and hunched over, intent upon the scene below.

"But, Commander, our numbers are small and we are untutored in such advanced arts of war," replied Genkeric. "That machine multiplies their numbers twentyfold, and their numbers already exceed ours."

The Commander laughed, and it was a long, mirthless, unsettling laugh with a light but hollow pitch. "That machine is nothing more than a highly developed book of tactics. I helped to build the first one. I should know."

"Commander, I know how a crossbow works, but that will not stop an enemy shooting me with one."

"Oh so? Well, I too know how a crossbow works, and that tells me where to stand to be out of range, and how much time I have to charge at a bowman

who is reloading. I say that any skilled officer could have done what that battle calculor just accomplished.''

''Profound apologies, Commander,'' said Captain Lau-Tibad, ''but if that is the case, why did Glenellen's forces triumph so convincingly just now?''

''Because there are few good officers among those dandified, overdressed lapdogs that pass for the military command of the Alspring cities.''

''The Gossluff army was three times bigger—''

''The battle calculor is a strategic weapon. It has some tactical uses, but they're limited. It's vulnerable, so very vulnerable that it could shatter its own army as easily as granting it victory.''

The Overhand raised his telescope and began examining the battlefield again, as if looking for something he had missed earlier. Captain Lau-Tibad did likewise with his twinocular.

''Do you have the squadrons of lancers, archers, and musketeers I need?'' the Commander asked without turning.

''They await you within a day's ride, Commander,'' the Overhand replied, hastily lowering his telescope.

''Good, then we leave. I must begin training your lancers before someone realizes that the battle calculor is a fickle ally.''

''But, Commander, what advantage will that be to us Neverlanders? We want food, caravan routes, and land.''

''And we *shall* get land, my puzzled Overhand. All the land from here to Rochester, and beyond.''

The gusty wind of a late-summer thunderstorm spun the tubular rotors of the wind engine Victoria as it rumbled into the paraline terminus at Peterborough. The sun was down and the lamps of the terminus were glowing brightly. Waiting on the platform was a squad of Woomeran musketeers and all the senior paraline officers of Peterborough. Zarvora Cybeline, Overmayor of the Southern Alliance and Highliber of Libris, was on this train. The gauge of the paraline track changed from seven foot to four eight and one-half inches at Peterborough, so she had to change trains. There was actually a chance she would spend a few moments with them on the platform.

The Overseer of Yards, the Terminus Master, the Presiding Engineer, and the Logistics Supervisor stood around the door of the Great Western Paraline Authority coach as Zarvora stepped out. She hurried under the platform awning to where there was a salute followed by an inspection of the musketeers. The hood of her raincape was thrown back to reveal her black hair, braided and pinned by silver orbile combs. Her face was pale and gaunt, and she seemed weary.

''We had arranged for a band, Frelle Overmayor Cybeline,'' explained the Terminus Master, ''but then this unseasonal storm began.''

"No matter, Fras," replied Zarvora. "This is no state occasion."

"Did you have a good journey across the drylands and Nullarbor Plain from Kalgoorlie, Frelle Overmayor?" asked the Logistics Supervisor.

"Yes. The broad-gauge coaches of the Great Western trains are like palaces."

The Presiding Engineer gave a slight bow. "Frelle Overmayor, you will be pleased to learn that the extension of the broad-gauge rails is now within five miles of Morgan. Next week the broad-gauge wind trains will be able to run as far as the Morgan yards and railside. The Great Western Paraline Authority will be operational from Southeast Alliance territory, you will not have to change trains here in Peterborough."

"Good progress," she said, favoring him with a smile, "but rest assured, gentlemen, that I shall always stop at Peterborough for a few words with you. The paralines stitch my overmayorate together as surely as the beamflash towers that transport its messages. Peterborough is a linchpin of both networks."

They reacted with discreet smiles and sideways glances, and the Presiding Engineer drew breath for his carefully rehearsed reply. He was interrupted by shouted curses and the sounds of a scuffle. The Overseer of Yards snapped his fingers and pointed, and a lackey in parade uniform immediately dashed off along the rain-lashed platform toward a crowd of gearjacks and riggers.

"The usual problems with broad-gauge and narrow-gauge gearjacks fighting over which system is better," he said with a shrug and a graceful flourish. "The trains' captains have orders to keep them in good discipline, but this still happens."

"I cannot understand this," said Zarvora. "I have witnessed half a dozen such fights on my many journeys between the Alliance and Kalgoorlie. Why are crews so emotional about the width of a paraline track? The Great Western trains give a fine ride, that is why I authorized the broad-gauge extended to Rochester, but . . ."

She was interrupted by the young lackey returning, his uniform of green felt and gilt braid now soaked.

"Where are the captains, why hasn't that fight been stopped?" demanded the Overseer.

"It's the captains as is fightin'," replied the lackey.

The squad of musketeers was dispatched into the rain, and presently they returned with the two disheveled, soaking-wet captains. Both were still cursing each other and struggling against their captors as they approached Zarvora and the group of officials.

"It's frogs and fishplates, and thus it's been for two thousand years!" shouted the captain of the Alliance and Midlands Paraline's galley engine.

His opponent bawled back defiantly. "Fishplates! Fishplates! Fish don't use plates! As for frogs, if I comes upon frogs on my track I squashes 'em."

"Just as your overgrown brute of a windfarm damages all trackwork as it passes over."

"Broad-gauge trackwork is all balks, transoms, and screwpins, it can't be damaged."

"It doesn't have fishplates."

"Replace your sleepers with balks and you don't *need* fishplates."

"Replace our sleepers with balks and it'd be easier for *your* poxy Authority to convert us all to broad-gauge rubbish."

"And what's wrong with that? Mr. Brunel invented balk-and-transom track-work twenty-one hundred years ago and—"

"Pox take Brunel!"

A scream of blind rage burst from the captain of the Great Western wind train, his standard reaction to any insult whatever to the memory of Isambard Kingdom Brunel. He did not so much break free of his musketeer captors as drag them with him until he was close enough to deliver a solid left hook to his rival's eye. The musketeers took some moments to restore order, and had to form a line between the officers, gearjacks, riggers, and pedal navvies of the two trains. Zarvora and the paraline officials remained beneath the shelter of the platform's slate-shingle awning as the musketeers did their thankless work.

When the captains began yet another exchange of insults, Zarvora interjected.

"Are you two quite finished?" she demanded.

The noise of the struggle faded into the hissing of the rain and the rumbling of the free-spinning rotors of the wind train.

"He said my wind engines were fit only to grind corn."

"He called my navvies mice in a treadmill."

"Rats in a treadmill!"

"There! There! You heard him!"

"He started it."

"Both of you, stop it!" Zarvora shouted.

Suddenly realizing that the most powerful ruler in the known world was angry enough to shout at them, the two captains came to their senses.

"I have a wagonload of work waiting in Rochester, I have not seen my husband for six months, the Council of Mayors of the Southeast is waiting for me to preside over their annual meeting, and what do you two do? You, top-link captains of two of the most advanced and powerful machines in the world? You roll about in the rain trading punches and insults, and arguing about—what were they arguing about, Fras Overseer?"

"Frogs and fishplates, Frelle Overmayor."

"Galley Engine Captain Songan, Wind Engine Captain Parsontiac, call your crews to attention."

"In the rain, Frelle Highliber?" asked the Overseer.

"In the rain, Fras Overseer."

Zarvora entered the railside's operations room, where a fire burned in the grate and refreshments were laid out on one of the tables. She shrugged off her raincape and accepted a towel from the Terminus Master.

"What else can I get you?" he asked.

"Good weather, sane engine captains, and my husband's company."

"I didn't know that you were married, Frelle Overmayor," he remarked as she dried her tightly pinned and braided hair.

"Sometimes I almost forget it myself, Fras Terminus Master."

He smiled sympathetically. "I understand, Frelle Overmayor. Since the Unification there has been work beyond imagining for everyone."

Tarrin Dargetty was escorting an important visitor through the complex of halls, corridors, bookbays, workshops, dormitories, and cell blocks that was the interior of Libris. Jefton was now merely the Mayor-Pretender, the deposed monarch of Rochester, but he still had status.

"The place has changed since I was last here," observed Jefton, ducking under a pulley rack that was humming and swishing with taut wire cables.

"Those original systems of 1700 seem so old as to be unusable compared to what we have now," reflected Tarrin. "The Highliber can run the Alliance quite smoothly from fifteen hundred miles to the west in Kalgoorlie."

"And she runs it better than I could," Jefton said with a hint of annoyance. "Why should I even bother to sire an heir?"

"There is more to running a mayorate than collecting taxes, controlling the army, maintaining the roads and paralines, and having the turds carted off to the farms. The people need a face for ceremonial occasions, a royal love life to gossip about, and a figurehead to complain to."

Jefton shrugged his podgy shoulders, sending tremors across the rest of his generously fleshed body. "They can throw rotten fruit at felons in the stocks if they have anger to vent. What has this to do with me?"

Tarrin did not answer, for they had reached a guarded door. The Mayor-Pretender had to be signed into a register. Beyond that door, and the door behind it, was a balcony overlooking the Calculor hall. Jefton crossed to the edge of the balcony and looked down over the stone railing, overawed.

"It has grown to fill the entire hall," he observed after a time.

"Yes, and there is some dispute among the Libris planners on whether a floor should be added ten yards up for future expansions, or whether more calculors should be built elsewhere for specialized tasks."

"This is impressive, but why did you bring me here?"

Tarrin made a spiraling gesture to the Calculor, then gave a parody of the mayoral bow. "Would you be willing to sit on the throne of Rochester if the Highliber ruled you as Overmayor?"

In spite of his expanding waistline and general look of dissipation, Jefton had retained the sharpness of his mind. "She wants me as a figurehead? I'm to be restored as Mayor?"

"As Mayor-Seneschal, actually. She has the same arrangement in Tandara, Yarawonga, some western castellanies, and the former Southmoor province of Finley."

"I'm not sure I like the title of Mayor-Seneschal."

"So you prefer Mayor-Pretender?"

Jefton did not answer that, but glared away into the bustling complexity of the Calculor. Tarrin scratched at soup stains on the sleeves of his robes.

"The title is generally abbreviated to 'Mayor,' " Tarrin explained casually, not wanting to give Jefton the impression that anyone was desperate to have him back. "When the Overmayor is present you would be announced as Mayor-Seneschal. The title would be on all official documents and letterheads, but you could move back from your villa at Oldenberg and live in the mayoral palace. New rooms have been built for the Overmayor in Libris, you see."

Jefton folded his arms on the rail and looked up at the skylights of frosted glass. "How often is the Overmayor actually in Rochester?"

"No more than one week in nine. Most of her time is spent traveling the other mayorates, and across in the far west at Kalgoorlie. She works a great deal with its mayor."

Jefton's decision was visible before he spoke it. He suddenly stood up straight and threw his shoulders back in a pose of mayoral dignity that he had not allowed himself for many years. Tarrin heard joints popping.

"I accept!" declared Jefton brightly.

Tarrin was not surprised by the sudden change in mood

"Well then, very good . . . *Mayor* Jefton," he replied, this time with a deep, formal bow.

"Not yet, Fras Dragon Gold Librarian. There are papers to be signed, I know the procedures."

"Now that you have agreed, the articles will be scribed up for a ceremony this evening. The Overmayor is currently visiting Rochester, so your status as Mayor-Seneschal will be law by the time you climb into bed tonight."

Down below in the Calculor itself the shift change began, with fresh components diffusing in to relieve those who had just completed eight hours of work. Tarrin glanced down at the battered old clockwork on his belt, and checked the changeover against it.

"Now you must excuse me, Fras Mayor, I have another pleasant duty to perform."

"Nothing could be so pleasant as the scribing of my articles of office."

"Oh, I'll order the work commenced as I am escorting you out."

"Then please, get me out of here."

Lackeys with clipboards and slates bustled along with Tarrin and Jefton as they returned to the main reception lobby of Libris. Tarrin gave Jefton into the care of a herald to arrange further details such as robes and forms of address.

"Just what is that other pleasant duty you have scheduled?" asked Jefton as they stood on the vast point-flower mosaic in the lobby.

"Something very auspicious. The first public release of a nonfelonious component from the Libris Calculor."

FUNCTION 9 had just returned to his private cell and was sitting alone when Tarrin arrived. At thirty-five, FUNCTION 9 was not the oldest component in the Calculor, yet he was one of the longest-serving. As a FUNCTION he had advanced as far as he could. None of the younger recruits had overtaken his early records in mental arithmetic, and he had even invented methods of improving the workings of the very Calculor in which he was imprisoned.

The clanging of a swagger stick drawn across the bars brought his head up from a book of pre-Greatwinter mathematics. He recognized Tarrin, the System Controller.

"You work diligently in your free time," observed Tarrin.

"Free time is only for the free, Fras Controller," he replied with bored forbearance. "I have to survive within this rat race of a Calculor, and you keep introducing younger and faster rats."

Tarrin clasped his hands behind his back and studied the component. FUNCTION 9 was well groomed, and dressed in clothing that paralleled the fashions in the city. He had sewn the robes himself, or so the regulators reported. Highly intelligent, and definitely not broken in spirit, Tarrin mused to himself. Defiant and proud, but not a rebel.

"May I come in?" Tarrin asked as FUNCTION 9 turned back to his book.

"That depends whether you have the key," he said without looking up.

FUNCTION 9's head jerked up as he heard the creak of tumblers. Tarrin stepped into the cell, leaving the door open. His cloak was drawn aside to display a flintlock in his belt. He sat down on the bunk and drew the pistol. Reversing it, he placed it on FUNCTION 9's writing desk.

"Very nice, Fras Librarian, but please take it away. We components are executed if guns are found in our possession. You should know, they're your rules."

"But you are not a component, Fras Denkar Newfeld," said Tarrin as he drew a scroll from his sleeve.

Taking the pillow from the cell's bunk, he placed the scroll on it. He stood up, bowed, and presented it to the still-seated component. FUNCTION 9 regarded him steadily, then slowly reached out and picked up the scroll between his thumb and forefinger.

"The Highliber's seal," he observed as he broke the wax. "Hmm. Be it known to all the usual time-serving lackeys and their constable lapdogs that the guest of the Mayor of Rochester, designated as FUNCTION 9, is a free man, and is henceforth to be known as Fras Denkar Newfeld."

"Not quite Overmayor Cybeline's words."

"Except for the substance. So, is this a joke, then?"

Tarrin produced another scroll, which was unsealed. "I have here your Articles of Release from the Calculor. You are the first to have the opportunity to sign them. In fact I only had them drawn up this morning."

FUNCTION 9 unrolled the second scroll and read the Articles carefully. Tarrin ran his swagger stick along the bars again, then tried to balance it on the tip of his finger.

"Insufferable legal babble," Tarrin said as he noted that FUNCTION 9 was reading the text for the third time. "In short it says that you must agree never to speak of the internal workings of the Calculor to anyone outside Libris under pain of death—without permission from the Overmayor. You must accept that you were mistakenly imprisoned here, and will consider the matter closed for a sum of three hundred gold royals. In her roles as both Overmayor and Highliber, Frelle Zarvora Cybeline expresses her regrets."

"Regrets! She keeps me here nine years, the best nine years of my life, then gives me a bag of gold and throws me out on my ear with only regrets?"

"What more do you want?"

"Nine years of seniority at Oldenberg University. I'd be lucky to get work as an accounts clerk after moldering in here for nearly a decade."

"So you don't accept your Articles of Release?"

The scroll trembled slightly in FUNCTION 9's hands, and he felt the beginnings of tears welling in his eyes. Fight it down, don't show weakness in front of this ratty little librarian, he thought as he smothered gratitude with anger.

"Of course I do!" he exclaimed, snatching a quill from a clay grotesque on his writing desk. He checked the cut then scratched out his signature in neat, even loops at the bottom of the Articles.

"One final scroll, now that you are Fras Denkar Newfeld again," said Tarrin. "This is an offer of employment that goes some way to restoring your lost seniority."

Denkar read, then slowly looked up. His color and composure were both gone. "Now this really is some twisted little joke," he said in a clipped whisper. "You want to employ me as a Dragon Green Librarian in the embassy at Kalgoorlie? That's on the other side of the known world!"

"It's a good salary, and they speak the same language."

"I like it here. What about work in Libris?"

"Ah now, in Libris we have no vacancies pending."

Denkar replaced the quill. ''No, thank you. Freedom by itself will do nicely.'' He picked up his pillow, placed the scroll upon it, and handed it back to Tarrin. Denkar had already picked the badges of Calculor rank and numbers from his uniform as they left the cell, leaving only patterns of thread. Several Dragon Red guards challenged Denkar, then saluted in amazement as Tarrin held up the scrolls. Denkar paused by the regulators' canteen.

''May I?'' he asked, gesturing to Tarrin's flintlock.

Tarrin stared back at him for some moments, then reluctantly drew the pistol from his belt and handed it to him butt first. Denkar cocked the striker, then entered the canteen. Several regulators of Red, Green, and Blue rank were sitting around a table playing cards and drinking beer. Denkar gripped the gun with both hands and fired at a ceramic jug of black beer on the table. It shattered amid gouts of foam, and the librarians burst back from the table. A moment later nine guns were trained on Denkar's head.

''Fras Tarrin, did he take you hostage?'' gasped a Dragon Blue as she wiped the foam from her face with her free hand.

''Lower your guns,'' replied Tarrin. ''Do it! Fras Denkar Newfeld has been released by decree of the Overmayor.''

There was devastated, incredulous silence. Denkar savored the moment.

''Remember, I'll not be the last component to be released,'' he warned before turning his back on them and walking out.

''Why?'' asked Tarrin as he hurried after him.

''To improve their behavior toward the other components,'' replied Denkar without breaking stride. ''A parting gift to my former comrades in slavery.''

''You escaped death by no more than good luck!'' barked Tarrin. ''Why did you really do it?''

Denkar stopped and whirled around so suddenly that Tarrin nearly collided with him. The former FUNCTION's expression was one of unsettling perception.

''There's more going on than just my release from the Calculor, or you would be marching me straight back to my cell after my canteen trick. What is really going on?''

Tarrin stared at the floor. ''The Overmayor only tells me—''

''Very little at best, and nothing if she can help it. All right then, what is *your* theory?''

''Many important components in the early Calculor were, like you, ah . . .''

''Kidnapped.''

Tarrin stepped around him and continued down the corridor with his hands clasped behind his back. Denkar stared after him for a moment, his hands still on his hips, then he shrugged and strode after him.

''We prefer the term conscripted,'' said Tarrin. ''Yes, I admit that several dozen components were inducted without being felons. We needed their skills,

both to run the Calculor and to train the felons. The battle calculor has been known to the outside world for years and the Libris Calculor has become an open secret. There is no point in keeping you here either to protect a secret, or for skills that are no longer unique.''

"So even the mighty Highliber-Overmayor can no longer keep innocent components imprisoned—as opposed to criminal components?''

"That's the gist of it.''

"Well, Fras Tarrin, I don't believe you, but that's hardly relevant to anything, is it? Meantime, let's get me paid off and outside the walls before the urge to shoot at a Dragon Librarian seizes me.''

"Again.''

Thousands of miles to the west another captive was about to find freedom, although it would be by escape rather than release. A procession of burlap-clad figures trudged in single file across the desert landscape of frost-shattered pebbles and red sand. Leading them was the abbot of Baelsha Monastery, and their objective was a cairn of rocks containing a shallow cave. The abbot walked around the cairn once after they arrived, then entered the cramped alcove within it. Presently he had satisfied himself that all was in order. The monks went to work as he stood back.

The place was swept clean, and the heavy cistern bolted to the wall of the shelter was checked. Two of the monks unpacked flatbread and dates wrapped in greasepaper and stored the food on a rock ledge that served as a pantry. Finally they unlaced the necks of four goatskins of water and emptied them into the cistern.

Venturing back outside, the abbot gestured to three other monks who had been waiting in the intense sunlight. The tallest of them began to strip off his clothing of burlap and cotton, and finally surrendered his flat wicker hat. A gesture from the abbot sent the other monks running to make a row behind their now naked companion. They stood to attention with their feet together.

"Re!'' barked the abbot, and all bowed from the waist.

The abbot took a small book from the slingbag across his back and beckoned the naked monk to step forward. He handed the book to him, then stepped back. They bowed to each other again.

"Brother Glasken, you are embarking upon the most important ten days of your life,'' the abbot said sternly as Glasken stood before him, clutching the book. "This is the culmination of five years of celibacy, abstinence, prayer, fasting, freedom from the vices of the world, and training in the ways of our pure but demanding martial arts. There were many times, Brother Glasken, that I thought you would fall from our regime but you proved me wrong. Here now is your final and greatest test.

"In five days or so, the Call will come. When the seductive touch of the Call reaches into your soul, you must resist it with no more than your mind and willpower, as we have taught you. With no tether, sand anchor, trained Call terriers, or Call walls, you will resist its allure. You have nothing to wear, and only straw to sleep beneath in the cold of the desert night. The cave faces south, and nothing hereabouts can be used to tether yourself. Brother Glasken, do you wish to take this final test?"

"I do, Your Reverence."

"Brother Glasken, you can return with us to Baelsha Monastery. The hamstring tendon in your right leg will be severed, but nothing more will befall you and you can live out your life as a gardener with us. It would be an honored existence of prayer and meditation. Do you wish to step back from this final test?"

"I do not, Your Reverence."

"Brother Glasken, should you resist the Call you will become a monk of Baelsha, bound by your vows of poverty, chastity, and obedience, bound to my authority, and bound by death should you ever try to leave. Should it be God's will that the Call prove too strong for you, you will follow it into the desert and die. Do you wish to step back from this final test?"

"I do not, Your Reverence."

"Then by your own free will you challenge the Call. Re!"

They all bowed from the waist again. The abbot stepped forward with a broad smile and shook Glasken's hand.

"Please, get out of the sun and into the shelter, Brother Glasken," he said genially. "Pray and prepare yourself, but have no fear. Should you fail, you will be in paradise within a few days."

"But if I should resist the Call, Your Reverence, it would put the rest of my lifetime between me and paradise. You make failure sound attractive."

The abbot put a fatherly arm across the naked monk's shoulder and gestured to the shelter. "I know what you mean, Brother Glasken, but hold the set of your mind very carefully. Should you have a desire to surrender to the Call, why that would be suicide. That would be jumping into hell!"

"Your Reverence, I understand. Even after all these five years at Baelsha sometimes a little joke slips past my guard."

"Ah, Brother Glasken, guard against laughter. Remember, all laughter is at the expense of someone, and in this case it is yourself. Should the devil make you chuckle just as the Call arrives, you may have his company for all of eternity."

"Your warning is the staff with which I shall beat him, Your Reverence."

"God's will be done. Work hard and pass the test, Brother Glasken. You have been my greatest challenge."

Five figures left the cairn, this time in a less formal step. The abbot's head was low as he walked.

"Five years ago he crawled out of the desert, starving and crazed with thirst," the abbot said to the others. "Could he really have come all the way from the Alspring cities, as he claimed? And if so, what drove him to face the immensity of the desert?"

"A fugitive from justice, Your Reverence?" said the monk carrying Glasken's clothing and hat.

"Perhaps. Or perhaps he really is what he says he is: a lost philosopher and explorer, who had been charting the extent of the land. A strange and . . . a *driven* man is Brother Glasken."

Glasken watched the monks fading into the heat shimmers at the horizon. He was gibbering softly to himself.

"Alone at last, alone for *ten days*. Soon there will be others I can talk to—aside from myself. Myself! The only civilized company at Baelsha, that's what you are, Johnny Glasken. Ah . . . I've kept myself sane by talking to you for five years, but soon Glasken will talk to Glasken no more."

Once he judged that the monks really were gone he darted into the shelter. Reaching into the cistern, he stretched down until his head was almost submerged. There they were! Dozens of pebbles wrapped in squares of cloth, and ten tightly tied leather bundles. Glasken fished them out by the handful, giggling.

"Ten little waterskins of rat, cat, and bird, thirty squares of cloth, and the thread and thonging that bound them while they traveled within the waterskins. Now, little prayer book, answer my prayers." He eased back the cover boards of the prayer book and peered between the spine and the binding. "A scrap of razor and a needle—everything's here, everything!"

He began to sew the squares together, his fingers flashing along to leave well-practiced stitches. He muttered dementedly as he worked.

"My magic carpet to carry me to the western mayorates: to women, wine, revels, seduction, women, money, gambling, women, more women . . ."

Once his kilt and a suncape were complete, Glasken used the razor to dress some of the straw, which he quickly wove into a wide conical hat. His water pouches seemed depressingly small as he filled them, but he also gorged himself on water, dates, and flatbread. Every so often he checked outside, making sure that the abbot had not decided to return.

Using some of the thonging, Glasken strapped several pieces of flatbread and some dates between the hat and his shaven head. He carefully left the book in a corner, open in midprayer; then he rumpled the straw as if he had been sleeping in it. Stepping outside, Glasken estimated that the sun had less than an hour to set. He looked to the west, where the abbot and other monks had gone. He laughed loudly and spoke to the horizon.

"Careful you were to inspect me, Abbot Haleforth, but you never thought that I'd break into *your* rooms and inspect *your* pack, aye, *and* put a needle and razor into that little book you've been torturing me with for five years. I know you packed a telescope, you scabby old fox, I know you're sitting out there squinting back at me. Well roast in the sun while I recline and feast in the cool of my stone verandah. Roast, for when you set forth for your monastery at sunset, I'll set forth too, but I'll be going south. Roast, all you lazy lackey monks who wondered which kind and charitable soul had already filled those goatskins with water when you came into the kitchen at dawn—aye, and laced up the necks good and tight!"

As the last glow of the sun faded from the sky Glasken drank from the cistern until he was almost sick, then set off for the south. He moved at a slow, shambling pace to leave tracks as if he were in the grip of the Call. As he walked he glanced to the west, where Baelsha lay.

"Goodbye, Baelsha," said Glasken with a wave to the faintly glowing horizon. "Give me long enough and I'll bed a wench and drink a pint for each and every one of you, aye, even though you number twice twelve dozen."

Using the stars and Mirrorsun as clock and compass, Glasken continued south. When the waning moon rose to augment Mirrosun's orange light he broke into a steady jog-trot across the rocky sand. Often he stumbled, sometimes he fell, but he pressed on in high spirits.

Denkar stepped hesitantly through the gates of the Libris forecourt and into the streets of Rochester. The sky was luridly bright after ten years inside the huge library and he shaded his eyes as he walked. There would be eyes watching, he was sure of that. He bought a honey pastry with a gold royal and told the astonished vendor to keep the change. At the paraline terminus he booked a passage to Oldenberg, but the pedal train was not due to leave for hours. Tarrin had given him a voucher for the Café Marellia, an expensive eatery just across Paraline Square.

I'm meant to go here, Denkar decided. As he reached the door he beckoned to a man standing in the street.

"Did you mean me, Fras?"

"Yes, come in, call all your friends who are watching me from greater distances."

"I don't understand, Fras."

"Of course you do. I want my shadows to have a coffee with me. I'll pay, of course."

The man turned and walked away briskly. Denkar entered the café, and a waiter hurried across to him, wax gleaming on his hair and long mustache like dark, textured wood that had just been varnished.

"Lady in reserve bower, Fras," he murmured, his eyebrows arching. "Liking your company, she is."

Denkar was well beyond surprise by now. "Indeed. But I may not be liking *her* company, Fras waiter." He winked and pressed a silver noble into his hand. "Tell me, is she pretty?"

The waiter smiled knowingly. "Thank you, generous Fras. Beautiful lady, Fras, beautiful lady. Fine, delicate face, with bushy black hair untied—and such eyes! Expensive silver orbile combs in hair, hah, from rich husband too busy making money, yes?" He nudged Denkar's arm. "Big eyes like velvet—"

"Stop! Enough. Either she tipped you more than I did, or she really is all these things. Tell me, though, is she a Dragon Librarian?"

"No uniform, Fras."

"Indeed. In a way I'm disappointed, but I'm relieved as well. Lead the way, Fras waiter."

They walked among chunky but polished redwood tables and benches, at which a cross-section of the bland, bored upper class of Rochester was seated before their eggshell coffee cups and dainty squares of bread with emu liver paté. Denkar noted that body-hugging shirts with loose sleeves were the current fashion.

The reserve bowers were a row of rooms running down the center of the café, with doors on either side. The waiter gestured to a lattice door, then left. Denkar rapped at the door, and a resonant, honeyed contralto voice responded, "Enter." He pressed the latch down and opened the door to the candlelit bower. Her face was partly shadowed, but there was absolutely no doubt of her identity.

"Highliber!"

"Close the door behind you, Fras Denkar."

Denkar sat down warily on the leather of the bench seat, the horsehair padding scrunching in the silence like the crackle of kindling in a fire. Zarvora's hair was unbound and bushy, embroidered with a few gray strands and pinned to frame her face. Her face was relaxed and remarkably winsome in the privacy of the bower. He had only ever seen her being rigidly formal at official announcements, or with her features contorted by rage when she had visited the Calculor in a vile temper because of some malfunction. Here she was now, the very wellspring of his enslavement. He noted with odd detachment that no hate was blazing up within him. She was like Tarrin, or the door of his cell: just a thing that had once confined him. Unlike Tarrin, however, she was very attractive.

"Do you wish me to apologize for your decade of slavery, Fras Denkar?" she asked after an awkward silence.

Death hovered just behind Denkar, awaiting the one word of defiance. He swallowed, steadied his breath, then replied.

"Yes."

Death's scythe began to swing.

"Then for you alone, I apologize."

The scythe was checked. Denkar felt giddy. In spite of his quite justifiable bitterness he somehow wanted to be pleasant to her. She had apologized. Now what?

"I wish to become the Dragon Gold in charge of the Calculor."

"The post is not vacant."

"You are Highliber—and Overmayor."

Zarvora considered for a moment, then stood up.

"So I am," she said as she left the bower. Moments later she reappeared and sat down again.

"How do you find freedom?" she asked awkwardly.

"Pleasant beyond telling, but . . ."

"But?"

"The years in the Calculor were fascinating. I learned such skills at mathematics as I could never have done at Oldenberg, and I made discoveries in calculating theory, too. I have friends in there, I may even meet them again, yourself willing."

She nodded, her eyes never leaving him. Denkar held her gaze for a moment, then looked down, unsettled.

"Interesting," she said. "Now what are you going to do? Return home, drink in the taverns, chase wenches?"

"Home, well . . . they may even remember me there. I'd certainly like a pint of black beer. You forbid that to your components."

"Black beer? That must be an old regulation from earlier, more desperate times. It will be repealed by tomorrow."

Denkar inclined his head. "You're generous. As for wenches, I do have a . . . ah, request to make in that regard."

Zarvora said nothing, but continued to watch him. It seemed to Denkar that she was preparing to pounce and snatch something away. He took a deep breath, then another. Finally he leaned toward her, defiantly looking into her dark, intense eyes. "I have—there was a Black Runner who would visit me in the darkness of the confinement cells."

"Ah yes, the solitary confinement cells. Do you know that they have never once been used to punish anyone by solitary confinement for the whole existence of the Calculor? They are rather heavily booked for private assignations between librarians and components, however."

"Highliber, I never saw her face but she was lovely beyond telling. I intend to stay in Rochester to try to meet her as one free citizen to another."

"Stay in Rochester! So, Tarrin was right. Denkar, I left some very important business in Libris to meet with you like this. I really want you in Kalgoorlie."

"I want to stay."

"I am used to getting my way! Kalgoorlie—"

"Highliber, I'm serious. If not in Libris, I could work as an edutor at Rochester University. You see, I do love Black Alpha. I think that she loves me, and she knows what I look like. If I stay in Rochester she will see me one day. She will come to me, I know it."

"She has work elsewhere."

"So you do know her!" he exclaimed, his arms laid along the table, his hands open and pleading. "Please, what is her name?"

She shook her head.

"You—you free me, then you bind my life as tightly as if I were still a prisoner." He rose to his feet, the menu he had been fiddling with crushed in his hand. "Well, you can have me dragged back to the Calculor for all I—"

"Denkar! Please lower your voice and sit down—and notice that I said please. Thank you. Now hold out your hand—please."

Denkar felt a slight crawling of revulsion as she reached out her small, bone-white hands. She took the crushed menu and placed it with her own. He had expected her skin to be moist and as cold as porcelain, yet it was very warm and dry, somehow familiar. She leaned forward until her face was very close.

"I love you too, Fras Denkar, and I am touched by your devotion to me."

There were no words that could have possibly had a place in the moments that followed. For a time he sat staring into her huge, green eyes; then he reached out to touch her hair. It was oddly bushy, very much like his own. He closed his eyes as his fingers caressed her face. His fingertips told him that there was no doubt at all.

"It *is* you," he whispered. "But your voice, it was much lighter."

"You mean like this?" she chirped.

In spite of the intensity of the moment, he found himself giggling. "Oh, Highliber."

"Frelle Zarvora, although you can continue to call me Black Alpha. I prefer Zar."

"But—Frelle, ah, Zar—Highliber, why me?"

"Why you, Denkar? Come around to my bench and sit beside me, there is much to tell." Denkar hesitated only for a moment, then shuffled awkwardly around in the cramped space. Zarvora took his hand again. "Firstly, why you? That is not easy."

Zarvora put her hand to his cheek, then ran her fingers through his hair. Although she was trying to explain some important matters, the heady sensuality of her presence made it hard for Denkar to concentrate. The huge green eyes, the warm, dry tingling touch of her fingers, the musky, feathery scent of her hair . . . With an effort he brought himself back to what she was saying. She explained

about aviads and the Call, and about his own hair. Finally she explained about their romance.

"You were such a challenge, you could make me laugh. I liked to be with you so much." She began to fiddle with a strand of her own hair, twirling it around her index finger.

"So, you released the other aviads in 1700 but kept me as a pet."

"That was stupid of me. I—I was worried. I walk a tightrope, I need certainty. With you in the Calculor I could at least be certain of something in my life. I can make it up for you."

"You spied on me and Dolorian. You sent her away."

"I promoted her into the beamflash network. A real tyrant would have had her shot."

Denkar closed his eyes and ran his fingers through Zarvora's bushy hair, trying to recapture what she had once been to him.

"Everything around me has been controlled. I . . . don't know what to say."

"Denkar, darling, for years what I did was actually controlled by *you*, if that makes you feel better. Once I kept the Alliance mayors waiting four hours because you wanted me to stay longer. When I had to start spending so much time away in Kalgoorlie I was torn between being separated from you and telling you everything and risking . . . risking a bad reaction."

"The mighty Highliber and Overmayor, frightened of her slave?"

"Frightened of losing what we had." She pressed her lips together, then looked down at the crumpled menu. She began trying to smooth it out, as if it was an allegory of Denkar's life. "Concerning your time in the Calculor, all that I can do is apologize. I needed raw calculating power very quickly back in 1696, and you were one of the thousands that I enslaved to get it. Several dozen of the best early FUNCTIONS were as blameless as yourself, I admit it."

He pondered for a time while Zarvora stroked his hand.

"It was courageous of you, telling me this," he concluded. "You could have lied."

"Den, I want you of your own free will. A galley train is waiting for us at the Rochester terminus." She slid her arms around his neck and placed her forehead against his. "For some time now I have been telling people that I have a consort. Many are anxious to meet my mysterious husband who is too busy to bask in the glories of court life."

"Me?"

"Yes."

"You, you want me to transform from an unknown slave into the consort of the most powerful ruler in the known world—in twenty minutes?"

Zarvora had not thought of it quite that way. "Ah, well . . . yes," she ventured. "Will you come with me?"

"Life is hell for the nobility," sighed Denkar, smiling grimly. He turned away to clasp his hands together on the table and shake his head slowly. "Frelle Overmayor . . . no. I cannot forgive you. I am very angry, I want someone beaten for my nine years in the Calculor, and—"

Zarvora stood up and snapped her fingers. The door of the café was slammed open and there were shouts and shrieks as a squad of guards tramped in. The door to the bower was not so much opened as torn from its hinges and flung aside. Tarrin stood before them, held firmly by two guards and gagged. As Denkar watched he was stripped of his robes and insignias of office, which were placed on the table.

"Four blows," said Zarvora, folding her arms.

As Denkar sat wide-eyed with astonishment Tarrin was turned side-on to face a burly guard whose helmet's rim shadowed his eyes. A right cross smashed into Tarrin's jaw, followed by a left to his eye. He was now standing only because he was being held. A blow to the stomach doubled him over. He was released, and fell. The guard kicked him in the ribs as he lay on the floor. The guard turned back to Zarvora.

"Five blows," she ordered as she came around the table.

Denkar braced himself for the beating, but nobody seized him. The guard nervously rubbed his fist and shifted his weight from foot to foot.

"Five blows!" Zarvora demanded.

The left cross to her jaw sent her reeling back to sprawl over one of the open area tables and its terrified patrons. The waiter and owner were scrabbling to hide behind each other as she picked herself up and returned to the guard.

"The jaw again," she ordered, and his right cross knocked her into a shelf of crockery that clattered down and smashed around her. Slowly she got up, blood trickling from a split lip.

"Highliber!" shouted Denkar. "Stop it! What is this?"

Zarvora's jaw gave a loud click as she opened her mouth. "Your order, System Controller Denkar. A beating for those who enslaved you. One blow for every year. Four for Tarrin, five for me."

"I never meant this!"

"For me there is black and white, Fras System Controller," she replied coldly. "Nothing else. I asked what would make up your lost years and you told me. I believe we are up to 1702, Fras Executioner."

"Stop!" shouted Denkar. "You. Take your boot off that man's neck and give him back his robes—and office. Then get out—Zarvora, not you!"

They faced each other in absolute silence as twenty-five pairs of terrified eyes looked on. Zarvora's jaw clicked again.

"I am serious about needing your forgiveness—" she began.

"I forgive you! I forgive you, sincerely, I really do." He dropped a few gold

royals on the table then held out his arm. Zarvora placed her hand upon it. "So where is our damn galley train, then?"

Crockery fragments crunched beneath their feet as they made their way to the door, and Denkar realized that Zarvora was unsteady on her feet and leaning heavily on him.

"Thank you, c-call again," stammered the waiter.

Denkar saw that BY APPOINTMENT TO OVERMAYOR CYBELINE had already been chalked on the door.

The Calldeath lands were marked by a drystone wall snaking across the hills. The boundary's location sometimes moved a few miles, however, so no wall could be really effective. When Ilyire's horse suddenly became less responsive and settled into a steady walking pace, he knew that he had crossed the boundary. At sunset Ilyire was seven miles into the Calldeath lands and within sight of a wooden stockade. Its angles and colors were starkly geometrical and vivid against the overgrown leafy jumble of the Calldeath countryside, and it drew his eyes as he approached. He did not pay sufficient attention to an overhang of branches dripping with vines.

The dirkfang cat that waited in the vine-shrouded cover weighed nearly thirty pounds and had fangs over an inch long. Seven hundred generations ago its ancestors had sat purring upon human laps and eaten canned pilchards in aspic from saucers on newspapers. The evolutionary predilection for cats to grow heavy and develop huge fangs had been boosted more than anyone could have guessed by the procession of large, entranced animals passing through the Calldeath lands on the way to the sea. Weight was required to pull them down, and large fangs to flay them open to die of blood loss. The balance was delicate. Those dirkfangs that grew too heavy were themselves drawn off by the Call. Lately something had altered in the equation, however: some of the humans could fight back.

The cat sprang with precision rather than surprise in mind, expecting to subdue its prey with a few slashes and bites. Ilyire brought up his well-padded arms as it sprang, then twisted from the saddle as it made contact. The dirkfang was thrown clear in a flurry of dust and scrabbling paws and it regained its feet to be confronted by a human on his knees and very much aware of what was happening. Ilyire slowly drew a flintlock from his belt and cocked the striker. The big cat mewled and began to inch forward on its belly. Ilyire smiled, then uncocked the striker and returned the gun to his belt.

The cat sprang, but Ilyire executed a turn-dodge, snatching at one outstretched paw, whipping the cat off-balance and slamming it to the ground. Claws slashed through leather, cloth, and skin as Ilyire used his superior weight to pin down the animal. He slammed the heel of his hand into the dirkfang's throat. Standing back, he watched the cat writhing and gasping its life away.

Now his own lacerations began to assert themselves with sharp pain. The Call anchor on his horse had dropped when his weight had left the saddle switch, and the grapples were snagged on a vine-smothered bush. He bent over the dirk-fang, seized its head, and twisted. The sun was down by now, and the glow of Mirrorsun was rising above the trees in the east. Tonight it was a glowing red oval in the middle of the band. There was also a faint orange corona. By the ruddy light, Ilyire saw a single aviad emerge from the stockade as he led his Call-enraptured horse toward the gate.

"Cutting it fine tonight, Fras Ilyire," said the man, who was in his early fifties. "The cats here still don't know to avoid us."

"Unlucky," said Ilyire, heaving the body of the dirkfang off his saddle. "Cat not kill me."

Ilyire dragged his horse into the stables and the older aviad whistled as he examined the dead cat.

"How did you kill it? There's no cuts."

"Bare hands. Very macho. Yes?"

"Yes, yes indeed, Fras Ilyire. You'll be wanting the pelt and fangs, so—"

"So nothing. Needed good fight. You keep body."

Ilyire entered the stockade's little hall. He removed his torn leathers and unrolled a medician's kit. The air grew sweet with the scent of eucalyptus oil as he cleaned his scratches. The other aviad brought a kettle of hot water over from the grate and poured it into a bowl beside him.

"So, you are depressed again, Fras."

"Hurt from claws dulls hurt in heart."

"More fighting with your sister, Theresla?"

"Always fighting with sister. This . . . something else."

"Another woman, a romantic interest?"

"Honor holds me silent."

"Now then, I—ah, I hear the others. They have the counter-Call wagon quite close now. In a day, perhaps two, we can leave the Highliber's precious rockets for the Callbait humans beyond the boundary wall."

Ilyire was glad of the change of subject.

"We had rockets in Alspring. War rockets. Two yards, brass. What special about ancient rockets?"

"They're bigger, Fras. They be built in three pieces that boost each other higher, and the biggest piece is thirty feet long."

"Thirty feet! Big indeed. Do they fly when so old?"

"Oh they're just strong tubes that you fill with fuel. Simple, fantastic things, they are. The metal seems as strong as ever after two thousand years in that museum. Making the fuel will be difficult."

"Black gunpowder plentiful."

"Ah no, the explosive must be much more powerful."

"More powerful than black gunpowder! Hah! Wonder indeed."

The other aviads were inside the stockade by now, dragging and prodding their Call-bemused horses into the stables and exclaiming at the body of the dirkfang. Soon three men and two women entered the hall. Ilyire recognized Sondian, a councillor from the Macedon settlement in the Southeast Alliance.

"Ilyire, you're back in the west again," Sondian said as he caught sight of the Alspring Ghan by the fire. "Did you kill that dirkfang out there?"

"Was me. Where my sister?"

"Not with us. She's much farther in, at the Perth Abandon. How did you kill—"

"Who is with her?"

"Nobody."

"Then how you know where she be?"

Sondian's welcome rapidly chilled. "She stayed here. She told us of her plans. Then she traveled on alone."

"Where did she sleep? Who slept with her?"

Sondian slowly drew a well-worn flintlock and pulled back the striker until there was a soft click. He cradled the gun in both hands as he stood leaning against a kauri pillar.

"Listen and listen carefully, Ilyire of Glenellen. You may be twice as strong as a comparable man, faster of reflex, and immune to the Call, but remember that we're all aviads here. Everything that makes you special is just ordinary. If you want to live among us, then observe our manners and courtesies."

"Will not have my sister defiled!" Ilyire shouted, flinging down his mug and standing.

Sondian looked at him for a moment, then gently released the striker and tossed his gun to one of the women. At this signal the three other aviad men began to close in on Ilyire.

"Best not to reach for your gun, Fras," said the woman holding Sondian's flintlock.

Ilyire lunged, throwing a punch at Sondian, but the Ghan's reflexes were attuned to dealing with humans and Sondian easily dodged him. Seizing Ilyire's arm he threw him over his shoulder and onto a chair, which smashed. Ilyire was pinned down and disarmed at once.

"Throw him out," said Sondian.

"The stables?" asked one of the aviad men.

"Right outside. He should be safe enough if he can kill dirkfangs with his bare hands."

Ilyire was stood up and marched to the gate with his arms pinned. Sondian strode up behind him, and without warning delivered a bone-jarring kick to his backside with his hobnailed boot. Ilyire cried out and collapsed.

"Get out, crawl," snarled Sondian. "There are too few aviads and too many humans for us to fight among ourselves. I'll beamflash the guards at the counter-Call wagon to shoot to kill if you come too close."

Ilyire turned his head. "You defiled my sister—"

Sondian bent down and backhanded Ilyire across the face, striking him so hard that the Ghan lost his senses for a moment. When he revived Sondian was gripping him by the hair.

"Listen well, you pathetic little worm. Not only did I not touch your strange and demented sister, but I am greatly insulted by the insinuation that I might have. Now take your filthy, twisted, diseased, perverted little mind and go!"

Ilyire spent the night beside the stockade, huddled by a fire of offcuts left by the carpenters and wainwrights. He kept watch as shapes warily prowled in the distance and spent his time making a crutch and fire-hardened T-spear. In the morning he turned his back on the rising sun and limped off into the west.

Sondian watched from the gallery of the beamflash scaffold.

"If we're lucky the dirkfang cats may eat him."

"From what I've seen of his sister, *she* may eat him," said the watchman.

"Compared to him she's civilized. At least she tries to mask her weirdness."

"Sometimes. What of his horse?"

"Release it with the anchor pinned, the Call will lure it west along the road. He may catch it."

"Generous of you, Fras."

"Well, his sister may be hungry."

Ilyire limped along slowly, now careful to watch for lurking cats and other predators. Presently he encountered the transport wagons. Musket barrels followed him as he approached, and until he was out of sight. The wagon containing the rockets was the biggest that he had ever seen, but the ancient devices themselves were swathed in tarpaulins. The counter-Call wagon that pulled it was far more striking. It was long enough to accommodate twelve horses, in pairs on the tray. They were being strapped into their frames as Ilyire went past and he noticed that they faced backward to the west, where the Call was luring them. Their hoofs drove two articulated treadmills, which in turn drove the wheels through a gearbox. The horses mindlessly strained to walk west, but the engine-wagon traveled east, pulling the wagon loaded with rockets behind it. Some time later Ilyire's own horse caught up with him. He was mightily glad to ride again, even though it hurt to sit in the saddle.

It was another day before Ilyire reached the Perth Abandon. He surveyed the overgrown buildings and towers, looking for evidence of habitation. There it was, fluttering in the wind from the sea. A flag, the one object that could not have lasted two millennia and could only have been put there by an aviad. It was on the new littoral that had extended into the streets of the Perth Abandon. Ilyire

blew his whistle to announce himself, then dismounted. His horse strained to continue west, and into the water.

"Can't drag you all the way back," he said as if in apology, then pulled his saddlepack off and released the reins.

The horse immediately set off for the water, splashed in and began to swim. He watched until its head was lost amid the greenish-gray waves of the bay.

"A cruel experiment," observed a voice behind him, and Ilyire jerked around to discover Theresla watching him.

"Sister!" he exclaimed.

She was staring at him from barely three yards away, a girl-woman with her hair pulled into a bushy ponytail. She was dressed in the tie-cotton green and red tunic and trews of the other aviads, Ilyire noted with instant disapproval. Her expression was odd: intense, calculating, almost hungry, and somehow devoid of the mischief and mockery that she always reserved for him.

"What of my books?" she asked.

Ilyire took a package from his saddlepack and tossed it to her.

"You don't want them," he said sullenly. "You wanted me away, only."

"Think what you will," she said, turning and gesturing for him to follow.

Theresla began to walk and Ilyire fell in beside her. The trees were loud with the buzzing and clicking of insects in the heat of the day. Miraculously, some of the ancient towers had retained their shape over two millennia and looked like oblong, sharp-edged hills under their mantles of green vines.

Theresla explained that a dirkfang had been stalking Ilyire as he watched his horse swimming away. She had sent it off, but Ilyire was not grateful.

"Why you live here? Dangerous place."

"I am alone, Ilyire. Surely that should please you."

"You should be safe. Safe from dangers. Safe from desires."

"What do you suggest?"

"Return to Kalgoorlie. Set up convent. Spread our great Alspring Orthodox Gentheist faith."

Theresla stopped and gestured to the vine-smothered mounds.

"In the eastern Calldeath lands the Anglaic buildings have been looted by aviads over the centuries, but aviads are never born among the peoples of the western mayorates and castellanies. Thus in these Calldeath regions the buildings have been undisturbed for nineteen centuries. We can learn a lot."

"Pah. Anglaics walk on moon, now trees grow in their roads. So what? Nothing by sinful mortals be built is lasting."

"That is not the point. Now that Zarvora has secretly brought aviad settlers across from the southeast, there will be plundering and disturbance, even with the best of intentions."

Ilyire snorted impatiently, then stopped to look out over the bay.

"Those things like blocks in water, over west," he said, pointing. "Ancient beamflash towers. Nothing new."

"They are too close together."

"Used water for defense against freebooters?" he ventured.

"According to old maps, those towers were once on dry land. The water is higher now."

"So what?" grunted Ilyire.

She raised her eyes to the sky. "So I am wasting my breath," concluded Theresla. "That building there is a museum, and it has survived the years well. Come."

They entered warily, looking for predators. The museum was a series of high-ceilinged, spacious hallways, but they were now dark caverns due to vines and mosses smothering the windows. Most exhibits were either crumpled piles of corrosion or encrusted with mold and bat droppings. Those that survived were incomprehensible to Ilyire. There was a musty, feline scent, and the flapping of bat wings high above them. Theresla unclipped a tinder-lock from her belt, lit the fuse to a paper-wrapped charge, then tossed it ahead of her. The blast was a sharp, echoing whiplash, and two tabby shapes frantically scrambled from their lairs and streaked out of the building.

"The dirkfangs can be befriended, but it takes time," she explained. "Those rockets on the counter-Call transporter came from here. Something of their workings was described on that slab of very hard polished rock over to the left."

There were a dozen rockets left in the display, with their nose cones partly cut away to display the complexity within. Ilyire surveyed them with no comprehension.

"Two thousand years old," said Theresla. "Most materials of the old civilization are brittle and useless after so long, but not the metal of those rockets."

"So, men came here with reverse-wagon?"

"To remove four of the rockets, yes. Zarvora was here a week earlier. She studied the rockets and their plaques for an entire day before deciding upon which to take. She intends to make them work again."

"Where the men sleep?"

Theresla stared at him, hands on hips. "You amaze me. People come here to revive the glories of the old civilization and all that you can think of is who slept with your sister."

"There! You said it!" Ilyire cried. "You slept with one. Sondian, I know it."

"Sondian, a fine man and a good leader, an example for other aviads to—"

"He defiled you, then he beat me. Know his kind. Domination pervert. Power and sex same for him. I hunt him down, I kill him."

"Ilyire, I did not unload my virginity on him or anyone else. Leave Sondian

alone. He's the leader of the colony here, and they need his wisdom and leadership.''

"I bring his head in bag, I show you. Rent he put in your honor be fix. Where guns? You give me one you carry.''

Theresla drew the flintlock from her belt. Ilyire started forward eagerly, then froze as she cocked the striker and pointed it at his chest. It had a short barrel, but a bore of at least 45 points.

"You have turned yourself into a thing, half-brother. Things are easy to kill.''

She fired, looking straight into his eyes. Ilyire saw a flash before Theresla vanished behind the cloud of smoke that belched out between them.

Ilyire awoke in the late afternoon, lying where he had fallen. Needles seemed to stab at his chest each time he breathed, and the pain increased when he sat up. His hidden metal breastplate had absorbed the impact of the shot, but not before buckling inward and breaking two ribs. There was an impressive hole in his tunic.

Using his knife he cut the straps of the breastplate away, and the pain lessened. He looked at Theresla's footprints in the dust and felt an unfamiliar numbness. There had been death in her eyes; then she had shot him. She had not laid his body out in the way prescribed in the scriptures. She had meant to shoot him all along. His world was suddenly empty, his passions quenched.

"I . . . am dead,'' he said experimentally, and his voice echoed through the ancient gallery.

Brother John Glasken, late of the Baelsha Monastery, had traveled an incredible sixty miles at the end of his first two nights and one searingly hot day as a free man. Five years of monastic training and discipline had given him quite extraordinary powers of endurance. His routine in the days that followed was to sleep during the hottest part of the day, with his makeshift cloak rigged as a sunshade. Glasken was experienced in desert survival after his three ordeals a half-decade earlier, but although raw lizards and snakes supplemented his flatbread and dates, his water diminished faster than he had planned. His rate of progress dropped to thirty miles per day.

On the eighth day a pile of whitened bones appeared ahead. Glasken limped toward them, then squatted to examine the skeleton. It had been partly scattered by scavengers, but lying beside the pelvis was a dagger with the Baelsha cross engraved on the blade. A little purse nearby had rotted to reveal six coins from the Kalgoorlie Mayorate. Glasken scooped up the dagger and coins, then noticed something long and straight lying half-buried in the sand: a staff!

"Alas, Brother, I mourn for you,'' he said as he knelt in the sand, his hand on the skull, "and may your soul rest in peace. How did you ever get all these things past that old devil and his watch-monks? Perhaps you brought these at the expense of food and water-skins. Very foolish, but I appreciate your sacrifice.''

Glasken stood, leaning gratefully on the staff. "I'll buy a candle for you in that underground Christian cathedral at Kalgoorlie, then I'll drink to your memory with a pretty wench in some tavern. Meantime, I'd best be limping on. The Great Western Paraline is still sixty miles away, and my water just ran out."

The wind train was nothing more than a speck amid the shimmers on the horizon as it came into sight from the platform at the Naretha railside. A small group of people stood watching as it approached, its array of tall, tubular rotors and their framework of masts and rigging distinct above the flat, sleek body. The Railside Master looked at the register in his hand, then at the schedule plate. Away on the wind train, at the forward masthead, a twinkling of light began, and almost at once a bell clanged for attention at the base of the station's beamflash relay tower. The Railside Master strode over, trying to seem neither casual nor anxious. The register board bore the code of Overmayor Zarvora.

"That's it, the Overmayor's train."

The railside's militia scrambled to take up guard positions, leaving a single traveler waiting on the platform and a crowd of gangers watching from the stone fence. The rotors of the train had been disengaged and were spinning freely as it approached. Its brakes squealed and shuddered, and as it came to a stop the gearjacks jumped down and ran with cans of sunflower oil to the oil traps at the axle heads of the coaches while others crawled beneath the wind engine to attend to the bearing wells. They felt them for overheating first, then topped up the lubricating oil. Fires in badly maintained traps were not so much possible as likely. Each of the huge steel-rimmed, wood-laminate mansel wheels was inspected for warping and slippage, while high above them the riggers adjusted and tuned the ropes, masts, and spars that held the spinning rotor tubes vertical.

Two passengers stepped out onto the platform, glad of a chance to be on solid ground for a few minutes. The Railside Master stood nervously with his clipboard, noting that one of the passengers was a tall woman dressed in an Inspector's uniform of the Libris Beamflash Network, and with her black, bushy hair clipped back from her face with silver orbile combs. She nodded to him, just a single, curt nod that all was in order and satisfactory as far as she was concerned. The Railside Master threw a quick salute back, then busied himself with his board, writing, "Inspected by Overmayor Cybeline. Found to be satisfactory."

As the crew began to load water and supplies aboard, the traveler who had been waiting patiently walked up to the overgear.

"Greetings of the afternoon, honorable Fras Overgear," the tall, tanned man said in a strange amalgam of Southeast and Kalgoorlie accents. "I wish to work a passage west, I wish to serve aboard your glorious broad-gauge Great Western Paraline wind train."

The overgear looked him up and down. He was big and strong, with muscles in good proportion. His patched olive trews, tunic, and cap were the type that the paraline gangers wore, but his sandals looked several sizes too small. When he removed his cap for his bow's flourish there was about a fortnight's stubble visible on his scalp.

"Were you thrown off another train's crew?" the overgear asked.

"I've not worked on a wind train for years. I was once a cabin boy and runner, then an apprentice gearjack."

"You're hardly a cabin boy now. We need extra hands for rotor windlass and gearjack work, but have no time to spare for training. What can you offer us?"

"Strength to wind the rotors up and down, and to screw down the brake-blocks. I can tell when an oil trap is running hot on the axle head, and when a rim or flange has slipped its seating on the mansel." Mind you, thought Glasken, I only learned all those words by listening to gearjacks and riggers singing tuning shanties in the Rail's End tavern years ago. "I've also worked in beamflash towers, so I know the unsecured codes."

The overgear was more impressed that he showed. Too much enthusiasm and the stranger might expect to be paid.

"Aye . . . well that's a start. We're short of a relief beamflash monitor . . . and you're strong besides. You'd have to work the gears and handles on order, then take over at the beamflash seat as needed."

"Aye, I'd do that."

"How did you get out here?"

"I've been in the desert to the north, meditating. Now I want to return to Kalgoorlie."

"So, a hermit. And what is your name?"

"Jack."

"Just Jack?"

"Jack Orion."

The overgear considered. He was experienced at picking fugitives and troublemakers, but this one had no obvious hallmarks of either.

"Well then, Fras Jack Orion, you're on approval. Start by loading those boxes beside the warehouse into the supply wagon."

The overgear went over to the Railside Master as Glasken got to work.

"What do you know of him?" he asked.

The Railside Master scratched the back of his neck, then looked across to where Glasken was working. "He arrived about a week ago, wearing rags and crawling along the paraline from the west. He was raving with thirst. Once he had regained his senses he said he was a student of Cordabeldian theology. He got so engrossed in his meditations at some sacred ruin that he ran out of supplies. He had money, though."

The overgear rubbed his chin as he looked across at Glasken, who was obviously working hard to impress him.

"So you had no trouble with him?"

"Oh no, he's worked well. He can do the work of ten men—in fact when I did my noon inspection yesterday there were ten men sitting idle and only Orion working, yet still the rails, balks, and transoms were stacked in good order by the evening."

"I'll watch him, but he could be a rare good recruit. We had to crew this train in such a hurry that full shifts could not be covered." He bent closer and winked. "Like to know where this broadline engine was engaged?"

"Why, Peterborough—oh no! You don't mean to say that the broad-gauge track has reached Morgan."

"No less, but it's not official. I'd best be aboard. Long life and broad gauge, good Fras."

"Long life and broad gauge."

Glasken joined the gearjacks as they unscrewed the brakeblocks and released the wheels. The overgear waited for the captain to ring through for primary torque; then the brass arrow of the dial slipped forward a notch. At the overgear's signal each gearjack pushed back the clutch lever-rack and engaged the gearboxes to the bank of rotors that spun in the wind. The rotor engines strained forward against the couplings, and then the train began to roll. There was a ragged cheer from some waving gangers who had come to see Glasken off, all of them looking the worse for the night before.

From inside the luxurious mayoral coach Denkar noted the sendoff. "Someone popular seems to have joined us," he remarked to Zarvora.

"The overgear recruited an extra gearjack," she replied, without looking up from an ancient text.

"He's being farewelled by a lot of badly hungover men."

"If he is a rake and drunkard named Glasken, a reward of a thousand gold royals has been on his head for five years."

Denkar turned from the window. "Who is Glasken?"

"FUNCTION 3084."

"Ah yes, one of the only two components ever to escape from the calculors. Well, from what I remember of him, if he were still alive he would surely have been arrested by someone for something by now. Were that the case, you would soon know."

"True, too true. Fras Glasken could not have been kept out of trouble for five years without being gelded or dead."

She put down her book and patted the seat beside her. Denkar walked across the gently rocking floor and sat down with an arm around her shoulders.

"Now, to continue your briefing on Kalgoorlie sciences," she said. "We in the Alliance are ahead of them in calculor technology, optics, code theory, and a few other related areas. They have nothing like Libris, either. It is a treasure house of ancient texts."

Denkar bent and peered into a microscope that was bolted to a bracket in Zarvora's desk. Beneath the objective, a human hair lay beside one of his own and one of Zarvora's. The latter two certainly had a fluffy, feathery appearance.

"When can I meet more aviads?" he asked.

Zarvora thought for a moment. "There are not many where we are going. For some reason aviads do not arise among the peoples of the west, but I have arranged for some aviads from the secret Macedon community in the east to come over and do some work. In return, they have a whole, new, unoccupied Calldeath area to explore and settle."

"What work is that?"

"There are things in the half-drowned abandon of Perth that I need to transport to the paraline terminus at Northam. Big, heavy, ancient rockets, mainly."

"Rockets?"

"I shall explain later. It is a vast and complex undertaking."

After the vast expanse of the Nullarbor Plain, Denkar welcomed the occasional scatter of trees that soon thickened into an open eucalypt forest as the train slowly rumbled west, a light breeze spinning its rotors. An Inspector of Customs came aboard at Coonana, but he did no more than exchange pleasantries with the Overmayor. John Glasken watched with puzzled relief from his hiding place behind the rear-starboard gearbox in the primary rotor engine as the Inspector strode past down the access corridor without the slightest attempt to search for aliens who lacked border papers.

"Someone important aboard," he muttered, unable to break the habit of talking to himself that had kept him sane for five years.

They rolled into Kalgoorlie two days later, after being delayed by particularly light winds. The sun was down, the railside was lit up with lanterns of all colors, and a brass band played the Overmayor's personal anthem. On the platform the waiting crowd cheered as the sunflower-oil running lights of the huge wind train came into sight, the vertical blades of its mighty rotors flashing and gleaming.

Inside the rotor engine the Purser realized that the pennants for both Highliber and Overmayor of the Southeast Alliance were still furled, just as the cheers of the welcoming crowd and the blaring of the band became audible above the rumbling of the wheels and rotors.

"You, take these!" he cried as the bare-chested and sweating Glasken finished winding down a rotor drum. "Climb the front of the rotor engine and stand by the port railing. Hold these pennants up as we pull into the railside."

"But, Fras Purser, my tunic—"

"*Do as I say!* Be dignified, and whatever you do don't drop the pennants!"

Glasken had not seen himself in a mirror for over five years, and had no idea of how the ordeal in Baelsha had changed his physique—which had previously been impressive, if slightly chubby. Gasps mingled with the cheers of the crowd as the magnificent, bare-chested pennant bearer at the front of the rotor engine was illuminated by the lanterns and torches of the railside. Sweat glistened on his skin, and the dancing flames highlighted the outlines of his muscles with dark shadows. Glasken began to catch comments as he rolled past the crowd on the platform.

"Look at that figurehead."

"Fanciful carving."

"Nay, he's real, he smiled at me."

"Does gearjack work do *that* for you?"

"I'm joining Great Western."

Girls in white togettras showered the puzzled Glasken with rose petals and mint leaves meant for Zarvora and Denkar. The train came to a smooth stop with the engine facing into the darkness of the marshaling yards beyond the railside. Glasken crawled back through the access hatch with the pennants. The Purser was elsewhere, but his dustcape and slingpack were still there, abandoned beside the flare locker.

"I know I agreed to work my passage, but I'm worth a bonus," he muttered as he rummaged for the feel of a purse in the slingpack. The purse was large, and contained mixed gold and silver. He reached in for a generous handful, then returned it to the slingpack.

Moments later he was on the platform with his packroll under his arm and his tunic over his shoulder. Several girls in the crowd recognized him as the pennant bearer from the front of the train.

"Fras, Fras, are you a Tiger Dragon?" one of them called breathlessly.

"Sweet Frelle, I am also not at liberty to tell you," he replied in a deep, educated tone that marked him as something more than a gearjack.

"Fras, are you off duty now?" her companion asked. "The Mayor's guards are here to protect Frelle Overmayor Cybeline and her consort."

Cybeline? *Highliber*—now *Overmayor*? Glasken got such a fright that his knees nearly buckled, and he did actually drop his rollpack.

"Fras Tiger Dragon, are you all right?" squeaked the first girl.

Glasken was careful to steady himself on her arm as he scooped up his rollpack. The other put her hands against his chest, her eyes wide with concern. The feel of smooth, soft female skin against his after so long nearly made him pass out again.

"Just . . . weary. A good meal will set me right."

"Fras, have you eaten, will you drink?" called a portly man wearing a vintner's striped sash. "My tavern is but close by. Come, bring your Frelle lady friends, honor my humble establishment."

Not a hundred paces away Zarvora and Denkar stepped from the train as a fourteen-bombard salute began to boom out and fireworks streaked into the sky. Denkar noticed an olive-skinned man of short but powerful build in bead-point and ray robes. He was approaching at the head of a large retinue that seemed to have at least one member of every race that Denkar knew of, then more besides. A racial mixing bowl of peoples, Kalgoorlie was well known for that. One of the courtiers was leading a tiny pony that was being ridden by twin boys of toddler age. They were dressed in the Rochester pennant colors.

Zarvora squeezed his arm and her indrawn breath hissed between her clenched teeth.

"Denkar, I had meant to tell you before. I am sorry."

"What? I can't hear with the noise."

"Shh. Mayor Bouros, my dear friend!" she called.

"Overmayor Zarvora, my fulsome pleasure to greet you again," Bouros declared loudly as he stretched his arms out to embrace Zarvora.

"Mayor Bouros, I have missed your hospitality. This is—"

"Fras Denkar, your consort. Fras! A pleasure."

Denkar, crushed in the Mayor of Kalgoorlie's embrace, wheezed, "Delighted." Bouros stood back to regard him.

"Ah yes, reserved, and keen eyes, intelligent eyes. Don't tell me, Frelle, but he is an engineer. No, the mighty Frelle Zarvora Cybeline, Highliber of Libris, Mayor of Rochester and Overmayor of the Southern Alliance, could take none other but an engineer for a consort. Tell me, Fras, what is your field?" he said, putting an arm around Denkar's shoulders.

"I—ah, applied mathematical systems."

"Mathematics and engineering! The Empress of Sciences and—" Bouros suddenly raised a hand, then put a finger to his lips. "Ah, Frelle Zarvora, how could I be so indiscreet? An engineer of systems that . . . cannot be spoken of Fras Denkar, I too am an engineer, but merely of structures, and of fluid dynamics. I am a graduate of the University of Oldenberg."

"I taught there for five years," Denkar exclaimed.

"You taught at my old university?" Bouros said, his voice booming out again. "Frelle Zarvora, your good taste never ceases to amaze me. Ah, but what manner of barbarian am I? You must be desperate to greet your magnificent twin sons yet I stand blocking the path. Dahz!"

"What's this? Are you a widow?" Denkar hissed to Zarvora behind his hand.

Zarvora whispered urgently back in Denkar's ear. "Please, just play along.

Say that you like the names. Bouros helped choose them, and he is a fanatical admirer of Brunel.''

''Brunel?'' whispered Denkar. ''Was he your husband?''

Her elbow dug into his ribs. ''No, you are my only husband. These are *our* sons.''

''Frelle Zarvora, Fras Denkar, here are your boys, safe and hale,'' Bouros announced proudly.

Zarvora lifted the toddlers from the pony and the bewildered Denkar was glad that he had to kneel to embrace them. ''Charles, Isambard, this is your father,'' Zarvora said gently while Mayor Bouros led the cheering. The twins were still at an age when they greeted all strangers without reserve, and they hugged and kissed Denkar at once.

''This Daddy?'' Isambard asked Zarvora, who nodded.

''Isambard was my humble suggestion, after Brunel,'' explained Bouros. ''Zarvora named Charles after the legendary Babbage. But come now, I have had a welcome prepared for you both for a day past, but the winds saw fit to thwart me.''

Bouros led them to a cable terminus where his private tramcar was waiting. The tramcars worked whether the Call was sweeping over the city or not, and were powered by a wind pulley farm backed up by a water-dropwheel station. The capital was situated over a complex of old mineshafts, and much of it had been built down rather than up. The most prominent exception was the mayoral palace and its soaring beamflash tower.

''Oh, my head,'' Glasken groaned, wincing at the pain of his hangover.

He could not bear to speak again. Where am I? he wondered. Big arches, incense, drapes and pictures on the walls, colored glass in the windows . . . looks like a church. Maybe I'm dead. Wonder who the mourners will be . . . but this is a bed. Haven't slept in a proper bed since . . . 1701?

''Fras Tiger Dragon, are you awake?'' whispered a light female voice from somewhere under the covers beside him.

''Ah—aye.''

An arm and a leg snaked over him, and black hair washed across his face. Almost at once the opiates of arousal began to blunt the ferocity of Glasken's headache. He noticed a gold wirework coronet still tangled in her curly hair.

''I have never, never met a man like you,'' said the woman, who looked to be in her late twenties. While not actually fat, she had certainly had access to fine food and drink for most of her life. Glasken found the effect quite pleasing after the privations of Baelsha. Her skin was light brown, its natural color rather than from tanning. ''Do you still like me, Jack, now that it is morning?'' she crooned.

"I always choose with good taste, Frelle."

"But, dear Fras Jack, would you have chosen me from all those others were I not the sister of the Mayor?"

Glasken's hangover vanished, sucked down into an enormous chasm that had opened up at the bottom of his stomach. He was thankful that he was already lying down, and that she was whispering into his ear and not watching his face go pale. The sister of the Mayor! He did not even know her name. He did not even know the Mayor's name if it came to that.

 **CANTRIP**

As the Glenellen lancers formed up against the Neverland freebooter cavalry, the city's battle calculor made an outline assessment of both the terrain and the enemy. Scribes pushed colored blocks about on the scenario groundsheet, and runners hurried about with weighting cards that identified the speed, weapons, and experience of the various blocks of fighters. Senior components studied tactical cards detailing freebooter behavior in past battles. Glenellen's battle calculor was no longer a novelty in the Alspring cities; in fact, this was its fourth use in anger. Its record was thus far flawless.

Overhand Baragania frowned and tugged hard at his beard as he surveyed the scenario groundsheet.

"The Neverland freebooters are a weak but difficult enemy," he said to his deputy, Mundaer. "Their ranks are open and they are lightly armed and armored, yet they are fast." He shrugged and spread his fingers. "They can do us little damage, but we cannot catch them."

"Except in a trap," said Mundaer smugly, straightening his ochre robes.

The Boardmaster was hovering beside them with his cue ready. "Would they but come here, to this plain south of the hills, we could let them exhaust their attack parameters on our heavy brigades," he said eagerly. "All the while we would be encircling them with mounted archers disguised as lancers."

"Except that they are not obliging us," replied Baragania simply.

"But it's their move!" exclaimed the Boardmaster, as if it were a game of chess.

"But they do *not* move. We are stuck here, with the heat, flies, and red dust."

The Boardmaster cursed sharply, then flung a block in the Neverlander colors to the ground and stamped on it.

"Sympathetic magic, Boardmaster?" asked Mundaer mirthlessly.

Mundaer walked around the scenario groundsheet several times while the Overhand and Boardmaster stood watching. Scribes respectfully moved back and forth out of the way as he paced, and he occasionally bent to tap terrain pins and nudge blocks with his riding whip. Moving and reconfiguring the groundsheet was not easy, and the scribes and Boardmaster were as anxious as the Overhand and his deputy to confront the Neverlanders with a decisive battle.

"With respect, Commander, but why not move our trap?" Mundaer said with a flourish of his whip.

"We need to fight on a plain, otherwise we can't maintain our communications, as the battle calculor requires. The ground is hilly where the Neverlanders are sheltering."

"But we can *make* a plain! If we send in a dozen small units of heavies with heliostats to take the hilltops and dig trenchforts, they will have a view of the whole area. The Neverlanders may attack one individual hilltop with overwhelming numbers, but meantime we can use the cover of the hills to guide in our mounted archers unseen—the battle calculor can give us the optimal path."

"Hills that are really a plain, invisible archers . . . this is all very appealing, but it relies totally on the heliostat signals."

"How can they fail, Commander? The sky is cloudless, the air is still, and there is little grass for the freebooters to set afire."

Baragania glanced from the map to the hills, then back to the map. Five weeks of desert skirmishes and discomfort had worn down the resolve of his troops and lancers, but for the Neverland freebooters the parched, dusty landscape was home. There was a subtle danger, of course. The freebooters could swamp one of the hilltop positions and annihilate the troops there in a fast and furious strike, then retreat and claim a victory. A Glenellen position wiped out by freebooters: the emotional impact on the Glenellen Makulad was likely to be far worse than the military significance. Overhand Baragania fingered his neck nervously at the prospect of explaining something like that to his master.

"Major-Director Mundaer, have the battle calculor work out times for every possible route the mounted archers would need to reach each hill. Tell me the longest."

"Already done, Commander. Nineteen minutes is the longest."

"As long as that? Too long—but wait. If the mounted archers could be split into two groups and deployed at either end of the hills, then that time would be halved and they could arrive in time to blunt any attack. Meantime, the rest would arrive as a second wave. Yes, I like that. Tell the calculor translators what we want, then begin the deployment of our men in the hills."

The deployment took five hours, which was roughly what the battle calculor had predicted. Both the Glenellen officers and their men were eager for a fight, so eager that they were willing to look for one.

"There now, a heliostat signal," said Baragania. "Mundaer, what is it?"

"Neverlander movement, Commander. Grid 44 by 79 with a vector of A9 at 40 degrees."

"That threatens our battle calculor!" exclaimed the Boardmaster as he moved his blocks and scanned the overview of the battlefield. "They're coming here, through those smooth, shallow gullies." He jabbed at charblack shading on the groundsheet.

"We're dug down behind lancers and archers," said Baragania. "We stay."

The Neverlanders did not attack the battle calculor. Instead they rode for the line of sight between Baragania's command group and the hills. They appeared to be leading packhorses, and as the Glenellen officers watched, the freebooters cut the packs free and abandoned them. Smoke began to belch from the fallen packs: thick, acrid, black smoke.

"Smokepots?" wondered Mundaer, scratching his neck at the base of his helmet. "But they can scarcely hide behind—"

"Regroup, here!" shouted Baragania. "Transmit the message now!"

"Commander?"

"Do as I say!"

Mundaer barked an order to the heliostat operator and Baragania listened to the click of the mechanism while watching the nearest hilltop through his telescope. Tendrils of smoke began to drift across the field of view.

"What are they waiting for?" he shouted, then he saw a faint twinkle through the smoke. "What was their message?"

"REQUEST CONFIRMATION," replied the observer at the large telescope beside the heliostat mirror.

"Send confirmation!" called Baragania frantically, but heavier billows of smoke were already across the field of view.

"The battle calculor has worked out six possible scenarios," began Mundaer, unsure of what was unfolding.

"Damnation to that, we've lost already!" said the Overhand quietly, shaking his head. "Our signals are cut and our men are trained to fight only under instruction. Their first blow was a gash above our eyes to blind us with our own blood."

"There!" cried Mundaer, pointing at a dust cloud. "Something in those gullies, look at all that dust! Freebooter cavalry, about six thousand, at least half of their force. They're going to hit the calculor."

"Break post, go, move! Get the battle calculor moving. Make for the smokepots first. We'll use their own smoke as cover, and then dash for the nearest hilltop."

The battle calculor and its escort were already moving when scouts reported that the dust was being raised by a few dozen freebooters trailing ropes and

sacking behind their horses and camels. Baragania decided that the nearest hilltop, the one designated by the scribes as Hill Alpha, was still the safest position. In the distance they could hear trumpets and whistles, and the sounds of a conflict. The smokepots were flaming out as they passed them, and the air was clear to the hill.

Abruptly arrows began to pour down from Hill Alpha. The freebooters had captured it behind the screen of smoke. Overhand Baragania led them to a rocky outcrop that was within sight of the hills but still held by his own men.

"They can't have taken more than one hill," insisted Mundaer, who was struggling to understand what was happening. "The battle calculor proved there was no time."

"Masterful," said the Boardmaster. "They took the very hill that would cause us the greatest delay setting up the battle calculor again. What say the heliostats?"

"We're just getting their attention," replied Mundaer. "Green flare, fire when ready."

The arc of green smoke drew heliostat reports from two hilltops, and the twinkling signals began to tell their story. Hill Alpha had been attacked almost as soon as the pall of smoke had gone up, smothered in a suicidal charge by Neverlanders who had paid with casualties of at least ten to one to buy their victory. The smokepots and riders trailing dust-raisers had added to the confusion, but the other eleven hills were secure, as were the two groups of mounted archers.

Mundaer began to regain confidence when he realized that very little real damage had been done to the Glenellen forces, aside from the loss of the men on Hill Alpha. The Overhand Baragania was less optimistic.

"Signal the archers to converge to this outcrop," ordered Baragania. "Then we'll go from hill to hill, collecting our garrisons in greater strength."

For a moment the Overhand's composure cracked. He seized the Major-Director by his pennant scarf and shook him roughly. "Of all the stupid . . ." Then, just as quickly, his control returned. "Where are the Neverlanders?"

"On Hill Alpha," replied the confused and uncomprehending officer, "and riding about with dust-raisers and smoke bombs."

"I say that only ten percent of Neverlander men are accounted for there."

"There's more than that. The battle calculor estimates that eleven point two percent of their known forces are all that are required for—"

"Damn you, Major-Director! Can't you see? All those dozens of men with their cumbersome folding desks, cards, and abacus frames can better my experience by only one point in a hundred! Gah, the battle calculor can screw itself, I'm done with it. Now get the archers back here before something else goes wrong for us."

The mounted archers of his first group rode to skirt a ridge adjoining Hill Alpha. The ridge had not been adequately scouted for the Glenellen archers, yet they chose to skirt it as the shortest route available to regroup. As they were riding through the neighboring gorge a cloudburst of arrows descended upon them from the main force of Neverlander freebooters, who had been concealed there. Within minutes there was blind panic among the Glenellen archers. Many fled up the slopes of Hill Alpha, forgetting that it was in freebooter hands. These were slaughtered. Others reached the summits of Hills Beta, Gamma, and Delta. The second group of archers made it safely to the outcrop of rock where the Overhand was sheltering.

By late in the afternoon the Neverlanders had brought in more smokepots, and were again disrupting the signals between the hilltop positions and the Glenellen Commander. Scouts and messengers were ridden down and slaughtered by what appeared to be elite freebooter squads assigned specifically to that purpose, yet some Glenellen messengers managed to reach their assigned hills with their messages. By morning, Hills Kappa, Mu, Theta, and Lambda had been evacuated and the garrisons consolidated with the main group. It was a feat of desperation that seemed to surprise even the Neverlanders.

"They're treating this like the Surgeon's Gambit in the champions board game," Baragania told a meeting of his officers and nobles. "Who can tell me what that is?"

A captain from Hill Lambda shook a tasseled lance with his unit's colors. "Esteemed Overhand, the enemy's forces are mostly left on the board until the king is ready to fall."

"Right, and that king is ours! We need to get our remaining hilltop garrisons back together, but I estimate six thousand of the enemy are in the hills in a rapid-strike force. We have been evacuating hills singly, and I think that they will rush to the next garrison that shows signs of movement. Instead, we shall move all seven remaining garrisons at once. One or two could be trapped and wiped out, but that's better than losing them all one by one."

The Neverland freebooters had another surprise. They were known not to have bombards, only siege rockets that were lighter and could be transported in racks by camels. These had not been modeled on the scenario board, as they were notoriously inaccurate. At extreme range they could barely hit a 100-yard-diameter circle . . . yet the main Glenellen encampment was significantly bigger than this. The first of the rockets plunged down and exploded among the Glenellen men a quarter hour after the tactical meeting. The warhead flung deadly metal shards into humans, horses, and camels.

By the time the consolidation order went out from the Overhand's heliostat there was rebellion in some of the garrisons. They did not want to add their own bodies to a shooting gallery for the Neverlander rocket artillery. At last three

garrisons were convinced to rejoin the main force, but two were mauled by the freebooters. Rockets continued to plunge into the main Glenellen encampment at the rate of one every five minutes.

Overhand Baragania finally decided to cut his losses and return to Glenellen. He had over half of his original force, which was still double the Neverlander numbers, and his men were adequately provisioned for the three-week journey back. Their morale improved at once, for they would now be out of reach of the siege rockets.

"This is a miracle," declared Baragania as he rode. "This morning I expected to be lying dead in the sand by noon, yet here I am at the head of an orderly retreat of over half my men."

Mundaer was looking back toward the hills. "There! Another puff of smoke. They're using the siege rockets on our four rebel garrisons."

"Good, it will keep the Neverlanders occupied while we run and it saves us the trouble of executing our own traitors. Boardmaster, what estimate would you give for reaching Glenellen?" he called.

The Boardmaster rode his camel over. "No less than two weeks, no more than three, Overhand."

"We shall, of course, be executed for our trouble. The invincible battle calculor has been humbled. There's been four men out of every ten dead, and a great boost to the confidence of the Neverlanders."

"Why then are we returning?" asked Mundaer morosely.

"Why? To deliver ten thousand troops to the city for its defense and for the protection of our families from ruin and slavery."

"I can't understand what went wrong with the battle calculor!" exclaimed the Boardmaster.

"Ah, but nothing went wrong. From what I can tell, however, the Neverland freebooters were commanded by someone who knew exactly what a battle calculor can do, and what it cannot. *That* was what defeated us."

The gardens of the mayoral palace of Kalgoorlie had been designed by the grandfather of the current Mayor, and specifically with dalliance in mind. There was a true maze of hedges, bushes, and hidden alcoves, surrounded by a cloister square fifty yards on a side. Couples not only had privacy, but they could hear others approaching by the crunch of pebbles underfoot. To Glasken, the gardens were also a discreet and direct route from the main gate to Varsellia's rooms, and he had become quite familiar with them since arriving in Kalgoorlie. To Ilyire, the gardens were a place where he could be alone without leaving the city, and he needed to be alone increasingly often.

One clear, bright autumn day Ilyire did not move quite fast enough. Glasken had been slipping away from the palace in the late afternoon, all spruced up for

a night of reveling in the market quarter of the city. He almost walked straight into Ilyire in the deserted garden maze, appearing like a phantom amid the tall topiaried hedges. Ilyire had been dozing on a small rectangle of lawn, but he jackknifed to his feet at once.

"Glasken!" he exclaimed, incredulous.

Glasken began to ease back, holding his swagger stick before him in both hands. Ilyire had a swagger stick too.

"So, first time I glad to see you," Ilyire added, stepping slowly but confidently toward the bigger man.

Glasken eased back another step, glancing around.

"Can't say I share the feeling," he replied in an oddly casual tone.

Ilyire advanced on Glasken with confident contempt, yet he was unsure of what he actually intended to do. Theresla wanted Glasken recaptured, but Ilyire was no longer in her service. Zarvora had a big reward posted for Glasken, yet Ilyire held money in contempt. Ilyire basically resented the fact that Glasken existed at all and wanted to do no more than humiliate him. Glasken did not share his indecision.

Ilyire reached out with a feint, at which Glasken twisted and took the first step of a headlong flight—except that his back leg swung up and around in an arc as his arms counterrotated. His foot caught Ilyire squarely in the face, sending him sprawling, stunned, and with a cheekbone cracked. The Ghan hit the path in a shower of polished quartz stones. Glasken swung a blow at his knuckles to make him drop the swagger stick, but missed as he slid in the pebbles himself. Seizing the advantage, Ilyire rolled a blow at Glasken's face, but his old enemy rotated, easily deflecting the blow upward with his forearm. Ilyire spun with his own momentum. Glasken's knee slammed into his ribs, but Ilyire snatched at Glasken's arm. Glasken let himself be caught, then twisted. Ilyire's arm was wrenched around, levering him into another fall. The impact winded him and his arm was twisted behind his back as scarlet waves of pain washed past his eyes. Presently Glasken released his very precise grip on a nerve in Ilyire's neck, yet he kept him pinned to the path.

"You dirty, *filthy* wretch," Glasken said smoothly.

Ilyire tried to struggle, glaring at Glasken out of the corner of one eye.

"You wanting to ravish my sister!" Ilyire panted. "I kill you."

Again Glasken jabbed at the nerve, and again Ilyire was racked by such pain that he could barely draw breath.

"I've visited your treasure cave at the edge of the world," said Glasken as he released the nerve again. "The one with ERVELLE carved at the rim."

"Swine—" Ilyire began, then caught himself. Horror chilled him. He stared at the terra cotta gutter beside the path, suddenly desperate to turn into water and flow away to hide.

"Swine? Me?" Glasken was saying. "I discovered a fair princess in your foul clutches. You slept with her bones."

"Liar, I kill you," whined Ilyire, trying to fan anger through the cold shroud of shame.

"I sleep with the Mayor's sister, and that gives me access to all sorts of interesting documents. I read Overliber Darien's transcription of your boasts. On your first journey to the Edge you discovered the bones of a girl named EVA NELL. I suppose that the Frelle Overliber could be forgiven for a few mistakes in recalling such a long and rambling tale, but *I* saw the original cave."

"I kill you, I kill you," squealed Ilyire, despair in his voice.

"But Ilyire, surely it's obvious that I'm a vastly better fighter than you now. I could kill *you*, just by pressing your neck, here, for a minute. Nobody would ever suspect me."

Ilyire's breath came now in short, wheezing gasps. "As I live, I live to kill you."

"But only to keep the world from finding out about Ervelle. That's not the vendetta of honor, that's the sting of a guilty conscience."

"Not true!"

"You slept with the bones of Ervelle herself, the most revered legend of the Alspring cities. Poor girl. You despise me for the rogering of such maids as would have me, yet you did *that* to a helpless shade who could not even scream for help?"

"No!"

"No woman has ever screamed for help while in my arms, Fras Ilyire. They've screamed for a few other reasons, though. *I* am a good lover. *You* are a pervert."

"No, no."

"You're desperate to kill me," Glasken said as he slowly released Ilyire and stood clear, "but have you heard of lawyers?"

Ilyire looked up at Glasken, his expression a study in hopelessness.

"So, you have. I've had to engage a few in my time, so I know what they can do. They can hold sealed letters in trust, to be sent to such people as the town crier, your sister, or the Alspring trade envoy at Maralinga in the event of my death. Kill me, Fras Ilyire, and your private perversions will become *exceedingly* public. Remember what you used to call me? Camel turd, penis pustule? Imagine what *you* will be called: bone buggerer—and with the very bones of Ervelle herself."

"No! No, never, I lay close to her bones to guard her, I only wanted to give her the protection that she never had in life. Please, please, believe me, Fras Glasken, Fras John Glasken. I couldn't live if, if . . ."

Ilyire was on his knees with his hands clasped in supplication, tears streaming down his face. Suddenly he bent down and began to strike his forehead against

the pebbles. Glasken unfolded his arms, surprised at the abrupt completeness of Ilyire's collapse. It was not often that he found himself in a morally superior position, and he could not carry it off very well. He reached down and seized the devastated man by the arm.

"Stop that, your forehead's bleeding," he said as he hauled Ilyire up. "Get up and piss off."

"Deserve to die. Here, take knife. Kill me."

"Put it away and—"

Ilyire twisted out of his grip. "Then I kill myself!"

The toe of Glasken's boot flickered out delicately to send the knife spinning high into the air, across the garden and out of sight. It stuck in the buttocks of a wooden cherub in the cloisters' gargoyleresque, where it remained undiscovered for several months. Glasken stood with his hands on his hips looking down at Ilyire, who was curled up on the path with his hands over his head, weeping hysterically.

"Come along, I can't leave you like this."

After some persuasion Ilyire stood up and wiped at his eyes with his sleeve. "What—where we going?"

"Off to a medician's shop."

Ilyire threw up his hands, tearing at his hair. "No philtre, no medician could help."

"This shop is where souls are healed, Fras Ilyire. It's called the Green Dragon's Tankard."

The retreating Glenellen army was within a day of the city and riding as fast as their horses and camels could manage when the Neverlanders made their challenge. The ground was largely open, but bounded by wide gullies.

"This terrain is optimal for a battle calculor," suggested the Boardmaster as Overhand Baragania stood in the stirrups of his camel's saddle frame, studying the Neverland freebooter movements ahead of them.

"There will be no use of the battle calculor," replied the Overhand firmly. "Now then, over there: the heavy brigades will chase the Neverlanders along those gullies and tear their rear guard to shreds, while our mounted archers come across to outflank them."

"The men are not trained for such fighting, Commander," pleaded the Boardmaster. "They would be out of sight, having to make decisions themselves without the benefit of the battle calculor."

"Precisely. The enemy is not expecting it."

They watched the heavy brigades stream into the wave gullies in a wide, leisurely pincer movement. Presently the distant thunder of hooves gave way to battle cries, whistles and the clash of weapons, interspersed with occasional gun-

shots. The Overhand sent out scouts with heliostats, only to have them run down by small, fast squads of freebooter lancers.

"Again, they hack at our communications," said the Overhand. "They try to keep us blind and deaf."

"Commander, the advantage is still ours, we outnumber them and we're on open ground," Major-Director Mundaer insisted.

"I hope you are right. See there, our archers riding across on their correct vector. Come now, let us move toward the wave gullies ourselves. Keep my pennon high. The helioscouts need a focus for their signals."

As they began to move at a leisurely canter a lancer suddenly appeared over the edge of the wave gullies and rode furiously for the center of the plain.

"One of the heavies, a deserter, by Dalahrus!" the Boardmaster exclaimed.

"Neverlander squads are after him," said Baragania.

"He's trying to use a hand heliostat," Mundaer observed through his telescope. "It's impossible on a galloping horse."

As they watched, the lancer glanced again at his pursuers, then reined his horse in. As they closed the gap he began to signal in the direction of the Overhand's pennon. Moments later he was obliterated in a swirl of dust and flashing weapons.

"Brave man, he gave his life for that message," said Mundaer. He hawked and spat into the red sand. "Well, did you get any of it?"

"It was the codes for 'archers' and 'trap,' " said the Boardmaster.

"Ah, he was calling for our archers to be sent in to trap them quickly," said Mundaer, turning to the Overhand.

"Not 'archers-trap,' " said the Boardmaster. "That's a separate code, it cannot be confused with the others."

"A man with death at his back has a right to confusion."

The Alspring archers had reached the wave gully now, and were vanishing over the edge.

"Three Neverlander squads, behind us!" cried the captain of the Overhand's escort. "See there! Cutting us off from the square."

"Make for where the heavies are!" ordered Baragania.

"We outnumber them, Commander, we could turn back and charge," suggested Mundaer.

"That may be what they want, they could be trying to distract us. Forward, ignore them unless they attack."

They changed to horses in anticipation of the fighting ahead. As they rode, the squads of freebooter lancers gradually closed in. When the Overhand finally realized that he had to fight and closed with the nearest and weakest group, a reserve squad of lancers came out of the wave gully. The final conflict was drawn out and savage, and lasted for more than twenty minutes. The Overhand and

Boardmaster were taken prisoner, but Major-Director Mundaer died in the fighting. Most of the battle calculor components had been sent on ahead, however, and reached Glenellen safely.

The Neverland freebooters dressed very much alike, but as soon as their leader spoke Baragania knew it had to be the she-demon herself, the one known as Lemorel. She treated him with courtesy.

"I know about your battle calculor," she said as they rode toward the nearest wave gully. Baragania looked over the edge, and was speechless with shock.

The gully was a scene of carnage. The heavy brigade had been set upon by Neverlander archers disguised as lancers: exactly the tactic Baragania had used to try to ensnare the Neverlanders in the previous battle. The archers had shot down the horses of the Glenellen vanguard, plugging the gully so that those behind floundered under a rain of arrows. By the time the Alspring archers arrived, the Neverlanders were ready for them.

"Never let your enemy choose the battlefield," said Lemorel to Baragania from the shadows beneath her heavy veil and hood.

"I tried not to," replied Baragania with undisguised exasperation. "That was why I retreated from those hills in the north."

"A good move, a brilliant move. I thought I had you, but you slipped away in good order. Was that your battle calculor's advice?"

"Calculor? Pah!" He spat, with a dismissive cut of his hand. "My horse could have advised me better." He patted the horse's neck, then spread his hands and shrugged hopelessly. "No, that was experience guiding me. The battle calculor brought us disaster."

"Calculors can do that when used incorrectly, Overhand. You must not stop thinking when you use them, or you will surely be lost. Behold," she said with a gesture to the gully. "All lost."

Baragania was silent at the sight of the gully filled with dead and dying. After a moment he hung his head and closed his eyes.

"And yet the machine worked before," he said slowly, unsure of what fundamental point he was missing.

"Ah yes, but through luck and good leadership as much as the battle calculor itself. The Highliber of Libris designed the original machine as a strategic weapon, not a tactical aid. It brought the entire resources of the mayorate behind the action over scenarios spanning hundreds of miles. Oh it can be used tactically too, if the enemy has never fought one before. When set against a force commanded by someone who knows its limitations, well, nobody knows the consequences better than you."

"You annihilated us," he breathed.

"Not intentionally. My Neverlanders fight only as much as they have to. Life in the desert is short enough without throwing warriors away in futile combat. I

stopped the fighting as soon as your force was broken, and not a minute later. Had your Major-Director not been hell-bent on fighting to the death, you would not have lost a single one of your personal staff. I am recruiting, Overhand Baragania. Consider it.''

"You want me to join you?'' asked Baragania, looking up at once.

A subtle twist in the skin about her eyes betrayed a smile beneath the veil.

"An uncommon offer from a truly exceptional enemy,'' he concluded.

"You have a choice. Become a prisoner, and perhaps your family will ransom you. You can also become one of my probationary overhands, but if you do that there is no going back. One desertion, one betrayal, and the consequences will be unimaginable. I need clever people like you. I shall have captured all the Alspring cities very soon. After that, there is a world beyond to take. My spy-merchants are out and at work there already. You could grow with me, Overhand Baragania, think upon it.''

"I shall treat your offer very seriously, My Lady Commander,'' he said in a level voice.

She put her whip gently but firmly across his chest. "Just Commander, when speaking to me.''

As the Glenellen overhand was being led away to join the other captives, one of Lemorel's own Neverlander overhands moved in closer at her gesture.

"Glenellen lies before you,'' he said with flamboyant enthusiasm. "Take it and there will be rich pickings.''

Her riding whip thudded against his chest. It was not a heavy blow, just a caution.

"We are not petty thieves, Genkeric. If you want to scavenge, I can arrange for you to tend a rag and bone cart.''

"Commander, I meant only for the men.''

"No! You're still thinking like a raggy nomad, a petty thief. Glenellen is a symbol of strength. I want it to be mine and I *don't* want its power weakened by looting and pillage. With Glenellen fallen, Ringwood will join with me against Alspring itself. I'll no longer be just another freebooter warlord. Go after that Glenellen overhand there, give him a tour of our forces. Be polite, be friendly: he may be fighting beside us in the next battle.''

Some days later Overhand Genkeric died in a confused, minor skirmish not far from Glenellen's walls. He was quickly replaced by a senior officer from the ranks of the Glenellen prisoners: Baragania.

Dawn was in the sky but the lamps at the street corners were still alight as Glasken and Ilyire returned to the mayoral palace. Mirrorsun was just above the western horizon, spilling its light in between the spires and towers bordering the square, and the nightly shape-changing glow was that of a six-rayed star. Glasken pushed

the brake chocks on the stolen costermonger's cart down onto the wheels as they emerged into the square before the palace gates. Ilyire was lying on the tray, singing incoherently with his legs hanging over the frontboard. Glasken had some quiet words to the three girls who had been helping with the cart, and they departed into the predawn shadows, each leaving a kiss on his cheek. Two of them also kissed Ilyire.

"Frash Glashken, you good man," Ilyire bawled emotionally as Glasken helped him out of the cart and onto the cobblestones. "Help man into gutter, who is."

"That's *out* of the gutter, Fras Drinking Apprentice."

"Everyone dis-pishes, er . . . Ilyire."

"Shame on them."

"Sister shot me."

"Lucky she missed."

"She didn't."

"Lucky you're tough. Look, we're home."

Ilyire began to sing in ancient Anglaic: "I belong te Glascow, Dear old Glascow town."

"Shush! The guards'll think we're drunk."

"Where's Glascow?"

"Long way away. I think it's a Northmoor city."

Ilyire lurched free of Glasken's supporting arm and stood with his hands on his new friend's shoulders.

"Did you robert my sister?"

"Roger your sister."

"So you did! Filthy swine," Ilyire paused to emit something between a belch and a sob.

"I never did it," said Glasken, fanning the air between them.

"You didn't? Why not?"

"She wouldn't let me."

"You lucky, she's weird. Eats mice, poisons suitors, shot me."

"Ilyire, it's nearly dawn, we're at the palace, and you're going to bed. I'm going to clean myself up and visit the lovely Varsellia."

"Fine, fine girl. What's she like?"

"Stop that!"

"Like ride on haycart with broken axle, yes?"

They meandered toward the main gates and the six increasingly uneasy guards. Ilyire suddenly lurched to a stop.

"Frash, friend," he said, confronting Glasken again. "You I give treasure cave. Jus' one promise."

"What sort of promise? If it involves your sister—"

"No! Never. Poor, shamed myself, never return there. Friend, take all trea-

sure, but gather bones of Ervelle. Bury at Maralinga. Graveyard there for Ghans. Ghans who die in desert, following Call. Do it, Frash. Please.''

"A noble gesture," said Glasken, taking off his cap to Ilyire with a wobbly flourish.

"Not gesture! Her soul you put to rest. Hero needed for that. You hero. Me? Just worm."

"I . . . dunno, worms have all the fun," said Glasken, elbowing him in the ribs.

Ilyire collapsed with a cry of pain. Glasken helped him up.

"Sorry Ilyire, what did I hit? Lovebite?"

"Fras Glasken, Johnny . . . big jokings."

"Do you have a map of how to reach the cave?"

"No."

"Can you draw one?"

"No. Navigated by, ah . . . innuendo? Intercourse? Intuition! Yes, yes. Only Theresla made maps."

"Well, can you take me there?"

"No, Fras. Shame, the shame."

"Gah, dummart! How do you expect me to help?" Glasken waved to the guards. "Will ye help him inside?" he called.

"We know you both, Fras Orion," replied the duty officer. "You take him in. We can't leave our posts."

"Thank God," murmured the gate sergeant.

They watched them totter past, and presently heard the rattle of a pulley lift's mechanism. The six guards relaxed visibly.

"They're the floor domo's problem now," the officer said with relief as he noted their entrance in the gate register.

"Thought the Ghan didn't drink," said the sergeant, who was staring at the abandoned cart across the square.

"After three weeks of watching Fras Orion arrive back here at strange hours in stranger company, I've ceased to be surprised by anything," the duty officer replied.

Zarvora was awakened by the sound of distant shouting and smashing crockery. She shook Denkar awake. "Listen!" she hissed.

"Some cook throwing a tantrum," he muttered sleepily, pulling the covers over his head.

"It does not sound like that."

"Zar, I've been up until four A.M. converting your trajectory equations into binary on punch tape. Unless the palace is on fire, I'm asleep."

Zarvora strained to hear words in the distant argument.

"Filthy wretch, get out!" shrieked a female voice.

"I'm going, don't shout," pleaded a man.

"I'll shout what I want! You're not a Tiger Dragon, you're a damn gearjack. You lied to me!"

There was a series of percussive smashes and inarticulate cries of rage, then running feet.

"Drunk! Drunk every night!" Something like a very large vase smashed. Fragments skidded and tinkled.

"And when you've not been mounting a tavern bench you've been mounting my serving maids!"

A door slammed, sending booming echoes through the corridors and cloisters. For some moments there was silence, but this was broken by another smash and a cry of surprise.

"And take your filthy rye whisky with you! Nobody dupes the Mayor's sister!"

Zarvora raised an eyebrow. "But somebody appears to have, nonetheless," she concluded.

She settled down again, but could not get back to sleep. Such outbursts were rare in the palace, and one of the parties involved had been Varsellia. The other . . . a Tiger Dragon? A gearjack? Zarvora pushed back the covers and stood up, stretching for a lingering moment before stepping into the drench bath. Wrapping herself in a towel, she went into the next room to check her sleeping sons. She drew the curtains against the sunlight, so that they would not wake early and disturb Denkar.

Although she had arisen to investigate the disturbance, Zarvora was in no hurry. It was indeed prudent to let Varsellia calm down a little before calling by to speak with her. She dressed in her working clothes of gray cotton trews and tunic, then went down to the palace kitchens for breakfast.

"Frelle Varsellia seemed a little excitable this morning," she mentioned to the servingmaid who brought the tray of coffee and freshly baked raisin bread.

"The good lady discovered that her lover was not all that he claimed to be," the maid replied.

"Apparently he claimed to be a Tiger Dragon."

"Most of the palace heard that, Frelle." The maid looked to the floor and blushed a little. "I can tell you, though, that Frelle Varsellia has discarded a rare accomplished lover."

"Does experience speak?" asked Zarvora, daintily cutting up a slice of warm bread.

"Fras Jack was generous with his affection, Frelle."

"Jack, an ancient name," said Zarvora, before taking a sip of coffee.

"Aye, Frelle, but nothing else was ancient about Jack Orion."

On her way to Varsellia's rooms Zarvora noticed heavy snoring from the room occupied by Ilyire. The door was ajar, which was unusual for the paranoid Ghan. She pushed it open to find him on his back and snoring, sprawled across his bed and still fully dressed. His trousers and codpiece were on backward, however, and a fashionable shade of women's ruddy cheek-ochre was smeared over his face and collar. What appeared to be claret stained the ruffles down the front of his orange tunic.

"Ilyire."

There was no reaction whatever. She shook his leg, which should have made him leap to his feet with a knife in his hand. He did not stir. Finally she took a ray-stipple pitcher of water from the sideboard and poured it over his head. Ilyire spluttered, and his eyes opened.

"Ah, sister . . ."

"I am the Overmayor."

"Wasser difference? Both shout at me. Both strange as . . . devil's codpiece."

"Have you been drinking?"

Ilyire raised his head slightly, then cried out in pain and flopped back onto the pillow. Zarvora pulled open the towel drawer in the sideboard beside the bed, only to discover that he had vomited into it. She left, returning some minutes later with another pitcher of water, a towel, and a glass tumbler containing some white powder.

"Get up, drink this," she said, splashing more water over him.

"Lemmedie."

"Head up. Drink this."

"No! No, that's wha' Fras Glasken sayn' all night. Drink this, drink that."

Glasken. Zarvora froze. Jack Orion, lecher. John Glasken, lecher. She suspected that they had everything in common.

"Drink! This is salts of willow for your headache and soda for your stomach."

Ilyire drank, but threw up almost at once. Zarvora skipped back from the foul torrent, then forced him to drink pure water until he had ceased to vomit. After that she gave him more of the mixture, and eventually he lay back, panting with exhaustion but reasonably lucid.

"Who were you with last night?"

"Can't remember . . . much. Woman! Soft as silk."

"You?"

"Embarrassed. Knew no positions. Belgine, good teacher. Know some now."

Zarvora lifted two generous lengths of sheepgut sheath from his half-open pouch with the tip of her dagger.

"Poor sheep. Died fr'a good cause. Women's thighs . . . heavenly. You know that, Highliber?"

Zarvora blinked. "I shall take your word for it. So, you spent a night drinking and wenching with John Glasken?"

"Fine fella, misjudged him . . ." mumbled Ilyire, pulling a sheet over his face.

Zarvora pulled it away again. "How long has he been Varsellia's bobble-boy?"

"Dunno. Arrived . . . your wind train."

"*My* wind train?"

Zarvora could get no more sense from him. An inquiry to the palace guard revealed that Ilyire had arrived at the gate on a costermonger's cart. A check with the Constable's Runners turned up a report of three women and a tall, strong-looking man pushing someone singing in a foreign language on a stolen cart. A check of the Felonies Register at the Constable's Watchhouse led her to the fruit and vegetable markets south of the paraline railside. She began asking after a girl named Belgine at the nearby taverns, and at the Green Dragon's Tankard she finally met with success. Glasken—as Orion—was staying at the tavern, but was in no condition to see anyone. Apparently he had company.

"Has he committed a felony?" asked the tavern master, rubbing his hands anxiously as he stared at the official braiding on Zarvora's tunic.

"No, but I want him watched," said Zarvora as she opened her hand to display three gold royals on her palm. She tipped them onto the counter. "Report his movements to the Constable's Watchhouse. Tell them WATCHBOOK SE379G with each report."

He swept the coins from the beer-seasoned counter and wrote down the reference. "By my life, Frelle, I'll guard him as a son."

Returning to the palace, Zarvora sat down to write a coded message to Theresla.

Riots were unusual in Kalgoorlie, as were civil disturbances of any kind. Thus the chanting mob drew a crowd of spectators bigger than itself, and so gained the strength to intimidate further by that very increase in numbers. The number of people was no more than a thousand, yet that was enough to intimidate the nearby merchants, vendors, and artisans. The leaders carried banners bearing the Gentheist symbol of a wreath of green leaves surrounding a blue disk and they were chanting a mixture of prayers and slogans. Zarvora could not see the mob outside the palace walls, but she could distinguish the dominant chant of "No steam!" among all the others as she swung herself up into the saddle of her horse.

"It shames me that you must travel on horseback when a cable tram is available," said Mayor Bouros to Denkar, who was having difficulty with his mount after ten years out of the saddle.

"A group of riders gives them nothing to focus on," Zarvora explained. "They think to attack the escorted, not the escorters."

"Why not send out lancers to clear the way?" Denkar asked.

"They have women and children mixed in among them," Bouros replied.

"An old trick of the Gentheists in the Southeast," said Zarvora. "Human shields. Hurt them and you are called a butcher."

"Oh so! That's where a lot of these Gentheists are from, even though they wear the robes of my Kalgoorlie subjects."

"If they attack us, what then?"

"I'm prepared. If there's fighting, stay with the rest of us and no heroics if you please."

Zarvora slashed the air with her swagger stick, then rested it over her shoulder while Denkar experimentally rode his horse around the courtyard. The gates were pushed open and the forty riders moved out toward the crowd of protesters. The Gentheist leaders held back at first, looking for a carriage or cable tram behind the horses, but when the gates closed behind the last of the riders they led a surge toward the horses.

With the exception of Denkar and Zarvora, all of the riders were cavalry guardsmen, and when fringes of the crowd began to close in front of them chanting "No steam! No steam!" they brought their swagger sticks to the ready and rode straight for them at a trot. Those in front tried to push back, but those safely behind them continued to advance. The leading riders reared their horses, which had been trained to lash out with their hooves.

This was the cue for fighting to break out, for the Gentheist leaders had deliberately set up the confrontation with violence as an end. Screams and blood were added to the jostling swirl of bodies. The riders were all dressed in cavalry leather and ringwork, except for the Mayor, who also wore his heavy gold chain of office over his armor. Swagger sticks and sabers clashed, but the riders had the advantage in terms of arms, armor, and horses. The column made steady progress through the crowd.

The gunshot itself was barely audible, but a rider beside Mayor Bouros flopped forward and began to slide from his saddle. Denkar reached over to hold him up as something whizzed past his head, followed by the bark of a second shot.

"That's two!" shouted the Mayor, lifting a whistle to his lips.

At his signal the riders drew flintlocks and began firing birdshot at those rioters who were half a dozen back from the horses. The rout began almost immediately, while scattered gunshots continued from farther back in the crowd. The distant gates of the palace compound suddenly opened again, and a far larger squad of cavalry poured out, cantering straight into the rioters and laying about them with sabers. Barely six minutes from when the first blow had landed, the riot was over. One of the Mayor's officers and nineteen rioters were dead. Two of the dead were women, and another three were children.

·   ·   ·

The wind train journey did not get off to a good start for Glasken. Eastward K207 had been listed to leave on time until he had booked himself aboard. Immediately the schedule was put back an hour. Glasken cursed, spat on the platform, and made for a nearby tavern. As he sat sipping his ale beneath a vine-smothered pergola he noted that several of the loafers near the station were strutting slowly, rather than just casually wandering about.

"Black Runners," he said to the serving girl who was removing his empty tankard.

"Indeed, Fras?" she said with polite skepticism.

"Hah, you doubt me," he said, putting an arm around her waist and raising his free hand. "Oi, Black Runners! Ye stand out like tits on a bull!"

Of the dozen people who turned at his shout, two moved with a distinctly martial reflex.

"Surely they're not all Black Runners, Fras?"

"World's full of 'em," replied Glasken. "Well, time for a stroll down Tumble Street," he said as he stood up.

The girl squeaked with indignation, then ran off. Glasken shouldered his rollpack, twirled his swagger stick, and sauntered off toward a tangle of shabby buildings and alleyways. A half hour later he reappeared, a slash across his rollpack and his swagger stick splintered. As he arrived at the platform he stopped to remove a tuft of hair from the toe of his boot. Darien was on the platform, dressed in a neutral ochre kaftan that blended in with the Kalgoorlie crowd.

"Frelle Darien, so you're the Dragon dignitary they held the train for," Glasken bawled as he strode through the gate. "I suppose you're on hush-hush work, so I won't bother asking."

Glasken's appalling pun had been accidental, but was not lost on Darien. She swung a slap at him, but again Baelsha's training came to his rescue. A quarter-step twist-dodge allowed Darien's hand to sweep harmlessly past his face, and she spun and stumbled with her own momentum. Without looking back at him she picked herself up and ran from the platform. One of the men who had tried to ambush Glasken in Tumble Street came stumbling through the gate holding a bloodied kerchief to his head.

"Oi, she forgot her journey cases," Glasken called to him, tapping the brass-bound wooden luggage with his swagger stick. The man glared at Glasken, then pocketed his kerchief and snatched up the journey cases. "I've owed that to you bastards since 1699," Glasken added.

The man stalked off, with blood starting to trickle down his face again. Glasken felt a touch at his arm.

"Varsellia!" he exclaimed.

She held a finger to her lips, then drew Glasken back away from the crowd. The Mayor's sister was dressed as a common goodwife. Ochre sun powder had been heavily applied to her face, giving her the guise of a much older woman.

"Surely you are not leaving forever?" she said anxiously. "I do apologize for throwing you out—though I still think the blame was not all mine."

"Pah, worse has been done to me."

"You were naughty for drinking every night in the taverns."

"And you're guilty of parading me as your pet man."

They stood contemplating their respective sins and staring down at the red flagstones of the platform.

"So we are both sorry, Fras Reprobate," Varsellia conceded, and Glasken nodded.

"Did Ilyire pass on my message?"

"Yes he did, but why are you here, Frelle?"

"To see you off with a sweet memory of Kalgoorlie, lonely boy."

"Pah, I'll not be gone long."

Her face brightened into a wide smile. "So you're not leaving forever?"

"Weeks, at most. Lately I have been feeling an odd urge to be . . . more settled."

"You?"

"Me. I spent five years in a very isolated, ah, outpost doing . . . contract work. All that time I dreamed of girls, wine, and jovial times, but now that I have all that I find myself wondering if there is not more to life. I hope to raise some, well, venture capital for mercantile dealings during my trip."

"Hmm. A more settled Jack Orion could be even more attractive to me. Mercantile dealings, you say? As the Mayor's sister I can give you some important introductions. Am I forgiven?"

"As long as I am."

When the wind train finally pulled out, it was with a galley shunter pushing it until it was clear of the city and able to take better advantage of the light and uncertain breeze. Near the outskirts of Kalgoorlie the houses were smaller and lower, neat little jumbles of red-on-white blocks. Finally they passed through the paraline gate in the immense curve of the city's outer defensive wall, but there were still whole suburbs of nomad tents and shanty dwellings before the train reached the irrigated patchwork of farmland.

"Thae sae Mirrorsun's weakening ther winds," said the Merredinian cook as Glasken bought several jars of ale.

"As long as I'm not pushing pedals in a galley engine, Fras, I don't care," Glasken replied as he flipped a copper from his change to the man.

"Think thee that Mirrorsun be Deity's disapproving of wind trains, Fras?"

"I think Mirrorsun's the Deity's way of lighting drunks home on moonless nights."

Strangely enough, however, Glasken's daydreams were of being a rich merchant and building a splendid villa, rather than of drinking ale, fighting in taverns, and seducing serving girls with the aid of handfuls of gold. His brief taste of

court life and his five years at Baelsha had changed him more than he wanted to admit.

Zarvora and Denkar's trip to the University was postponed until the Mayor called a Noontime Magistrade in the square before the palace. Two Gentheist priests and five others had been caught and identified as being leaders of the rioters. All but one were foreign nationals, four from the Southeast Alliance and two from Woomera.

A massive scaffold wagon was wheeled out from the stables, and the gibbets folded out and locked into place. As a crowd of Kalgoorlie citizens gathered, the bodies of the dead were laid out on stretchers before the gallows. A small group of Gentheists began a chant, but they were immediately surrounded and their leader escorted away to stand with the others on trial. The Mayor ascended the steps of the scaffold wagon and began to read from a scroll.

"My loyal subjects, justice rests with the Mayor through the text of the Mayoral Charter. Though I delegate my authority in justice to the magistrates of this city and mayorate, I retain authority to pass sentence when I have personally witnessed an act of felony. In this case, I saw a crowd led by these men attack cavalry escorting myself, appearing as Mayor and wearing my chain of office. This is treason. During the fighting shots were fired that killed one of my loyal officers. This is murder. When more riders came to rescue us, these members of the crowd laid out here were trampled to death. As you can see, several are women and children, and these were made part of the crowd by the cowardly Gentheist leaders who used them as shields to fight behind. This is also murder."

The square was in silence. A clock in a tower began to ring out the count for noon. A herald with an agenda board climbed the steps and stood beside the Mayor.

"On the charge of treason I find these men guilty, but commute the usual sentence on my discretion. On the charge of murdering my officer, I declare the charge to need further investigation and pass it to the City Constable. On the charge of inciting a riot that led to the deaths of these people before you, I find these men guilty. I have been in contact with their mayors via beamflash and have obtained orders of extradiem proxian. I sentence them to death. Carry out my order, Constable."

The swift retribution caught both the Kalgoorlie citizens and the Gentheist extremists by surprise. Seven men were wrestled to the gibbets and into their nooses. One by one the platforms beneath their feet fell away, leaving them spinning and dangling. The single latecomer stood wide-eyed and horrified as the Mayor turned to him.

"For incitement to riot within a public gathering I find you guilty, and sen-

tence you to three hundred strokes of the sunrise and fifteen years in the Bonelake Penal Garrison. Carry out the first part of the sentence at once.''

The Gentheist died after two hundred strokes, and was left bound to the triangle set up beside the scaffold wagon and its grisly display. The City Constable's report showed that two-thirds of the rioters had been from outside the mayorate, and deportation proceedings for the remaining Gentheist militants were begun.

It was not until late afternoon that Mayor Bouros and his two guests finally reached the University and entered the walled research park.

Wind rotors and windmills spun in the dry, warm breeze, and there was the steady rush of water being pumped into reserve tanks to provide back-up power. The smell of burning alcohol and vegetable oil was on the air, mixed with more exotic chemical scents.

"This is our power field," said the Mayor as they walked between the pumps and rotors. "It drives the cable trams in the city, the water pumps and lifts in the underground shafts, and the bellows in some of the smelters."

"It smells like a brewery," said Denkar.

"Close. It's a distillery. We make alcohol here for fuel export. The Gentheists maintain that we also have steam engines hidden down in the shafts and burning alcohol, but that's all nonsense, isn't it?" The Mayor arched an eyebrow and— unnervingly—smiled on only one side of his face. "Alcohol burners are maintained at the bottom of the shafts, and they circulate air from the surface by convection. Some of the rising hot air also turns turbines that power small generators in Faraday cages half a mile down."

"Convection engines, Denkar," Zarvora said. "They are weak, but have been accepted by all the major religions as not coming under the steam and explosive gas proscribium."

"Not quite, Frelle," said Bouros. "The Gentheists are still arguing among themselves about convection engines."

"They seemed united when they attacked us," Denkar pointed out.

"Ah no, Fras, that was nothing to do with convection engines. Their spies have gleaned word of two beautiful triple-expansion, high-pressure steam engines that also burn alcohol and vegetable oil and reside at the bottom of my deepest shafts. After all, I have to have a reliable source of power, don't I?"

The Edutor-General of Physistry met them as they stepped out of a lift that dropped so far that Denkar's ears popped constantly with the pressure difference during the descent. Vegetable-oil lamps gave the shafts the scent of an enormous kitchen, and Denkar was reminded of Libris. They toured several workshops first. These were filled with artisans at benches and desks, which were piled with wire, glassware, and vats of beeswax.

Warm, rushing air was everywhere, laden with the scent of alcohol and sun-

flower oil. Faraday cages were built into several tunnels, so that no electromagnetic signals leaked out to attract the attention of the orbiting Wanderers—and conversely, so that any electromagnetic thunderbolt from the ancient military satellites would be absorbed.

"Mayor Bouros has been experimenting with ancient electroforce devices of the old civilization," Zarvora explained. "When I came over two years ago on a . . . diplomatic visit I discovered that he was very advanced in his work. Much of what I thought I would have to pioneer myself in electroforce studies was already done. He has a spark-gap or sparkflash transceiver that can send an invisible signal across empty space."

"I have a two-hundred-yard length of tunnel fully shielded for my electroforce experiments," Bouros said proudly. "There's nothing else like it in the known world."

"Well in Oldenburg we had the Loyal Company of Electroforce Studies," began Denkar.

"Pah! Faraday cages the size of broom closets and pedal-powered generators no bigger than a tinderbox. This is *real* electroforce, just like the ancients had it."

His steam engines were nothing like the soot-belching, wheeled juggernauts of admonitory religious texts. They chuffed and hissed busily and steadily, and their brasswork was polished so that it gleamed with dozens of highlights in the glow of the lamps. There was a dull roar from the burner in the alcohol and oil mix boiler, and an insectlike whirr from the generators spinning beside both engines. Denkar noted two cables in varnished wooden trays, both insulated with poorpaper soaked in beeswax and bound down by woven mesh.

"Come this way," said the Mayor, putting a thick arm about Denkar's shoulders and gesturing along the mesh-shielded tunnel. "Along here we have the greatest triumphs of my sixteen-year rule and patronage of this laboratory. I have prepared demonstrations of an arc lamp and a type of beamflash signaler called a clickwire that uses shielded copper wire and electromagnets that produce clicks. It can replace beamflash mechanisms, it is not affected by fog or smoke, and wires can travel over the horizon and beyond the line of sight."

"The Loyal Company tried that back in 1681," said Denkar. "Shielded wires were slung between two houses containing Faraday cages, but a currawong landed on one of the wires and disturbed the foil and pitch shielding with its claws. A Wanderer passed overhead as they were testing it, and flash! It became all smoke, flames, melted wire, and beeswax."

"Hah! Foil and pitch shielding indeed. We use woven mesh over poorpaper and beeswax. Still, that was a noble effort, and one day we may make such things operational. It's only a matter of engineering of course."

"Of course."

"Now then, I also have a sparkflash radio to demonstrate, an electroforce engine that drives a water pump, and best of all, a model electroforce tramway. First, however, I have been working with your good wife on a tiny but clever device that she calls a dual-state, electromagnetic relay. It can store the status of something like an abacus bead—"

"Why yes! An electroforce abacus frame, and you could have dozens of relays for each component to use," Denkar exclaimed, suddenly catching on. "Each frame could be connected to the central correlators by a bundle of wires. Why, with a few hundred component people you could outperform the entire Libris Calculor."

"Well . . . that is possible, but it was not our approach," said Bouros. "Behold this device here."

To Denkar it looked like nothing at all. Layers of polished wooden racks and metal struts were draped with wires and springs, and made a sound like the Calculor of Libris in miniature.

"This is a calculor," said Zarvora. "Although less versatile than my first Libris Calculor, it is faster and more accurate in tasks of pure calculation."

"It's the Highliber's design," the Edutor-General added. "She calls it an Induction-Switch Relay Calculor. It's powered by electroforce from one of the generators you saw earlier. This one has the equivalent of two hundred fifty-six component-steps per timed cycle. Originally there were four cycles per second, but that has been speeded up somewhat."

"In terms of raw calculating power it is roughly the same as the Islamic Calculor in Libris," said Zarvora.

"The calculating power of over two hundred and fifty-six people in a machine the size of a haywagon?"

"Ah, but this is a tiny device, Fras Denkar," said Bouros grandly. "Frelle Zarvora has designed a machine of over four thousand ninety-six component-steps in capacity. That's more than the great Calculor of Libris itself can boast. All that slows us down is the lack of sufficient artisans to build switches as fast as we can install them, but we are recruiting clockmakers from wherever we can."

"Unbelievable," Denkar said in awe, running his hand along the frame of the electroforce calculor. "When does work start on the big machine?"

"We still have two thousand relay units to make," began Zarvora, but Bouros waved her silent with a flourish that ended with a finger on his lips.

Taking Denkar by the arm, he led him to tall double doors in the rock wall, which the Edutor-General hurried ahead to open. Beyond it they passed along a short archway cut in the rock, then into a hall-sized cavern as alive with clattering and clicking as the insistent pounding of hail on a metal roof. The thing itself was a metal lattice of scaffolding draped with wires and cables, and the warm air

reeked of beeswax and ozone. The roof gleamed with metal mesh, and a half-dozen people were tending a complex bank of instruments on a raised platform surrounded by a railing.

"Here now is my little wedding present for you two dearest of my dear friends," said Bouros, coming up behind them and putting his arms around their shoulders. "It's a little late—when did you say you were married, Zarvora?"

"I . . . two years—no! Three years ago."

"We forgot to date—that is, we keep forgetting *the* date," added Denkar.

"Lucky man," said Bouros, grinning broadly and wagging a finger, "having a wife who doesn't bother about silly things like wedding anniversaries. We decided that this calculor can be made partly operational with a mere two thousand forty-eight units, so here it is, all ready at half-power."

"My need for calculating power has exceeded even what the Libris machine can offer," said Zarvora. "Unfortunately it has also exceeded my ability to do the development and research to improve it all by myself. I have decided to begin to bring the cream of the FUNCTIONS of the Libris Calculor across to help with the work, starting with you. Would you like to take charge of this machine's development while I continue with other researches?"

Denkar had been following the signs and wires festooned from the steel racks, trying to make some sense of the architecture.

"Where are the correlator registers?" he asked.

"Why it's that board stretching along the wall there. A dozen regulators plug and unplug the wires according to instructions that arrive from above via that paper tape punch."

"I designed a harpsichord keyboard in a Faraday cage that sends impulses down a half mile of shielded wire," added Zarvora.

"Why not replace all those plugs on the board with a bank of relay connections?" asked Denkar.

"Why, because . . ." The Mayor scratched his head, then turned to Zarvora. She shrugged. "Look, there is a coffee room with a chalkboard just past that rack to the right. Would you like to repeat what you just said while I scribe up a diagram?"

As they were leaving Zarvora whispered in Denkar's ear. "We had better think up a plausible date in 1703 for our marriage. I can beamflash a message to my lackey in secured code and he can enter some forged records in the Libris data store."

"Don't bother him," Denkar whispered back. "All I have to do is prepare a numeric string to go down the beamflash and straight into the Libris Calculor."

"You do not understand, Den. We need someone with a password to—"

"No, no, I broke your Calculor's transmission conduit codes back in 1697. I've been able to do whatever I wanted to in your data store for eight years."

Zarvora stopped dead in her tracks. "You what?" she shrieked.

Bouros and the Edutor-General stopped and turned. Zarvora waved them on.

"I can write a numeric string to go down the beamflash network and take over the transmission conduits so that the data following is automatically acted upon by the Calculor."

Horror stabbed through Zarvora, horror that was real, physical pain. "You— you were able to control the Libris Calculor for *eight years*?"

"I confined myself to a few experiments. I was afraid to tell, ah, Black Alpha."

"You could have started wars, ruined the economy, destroyed my power and credibility completely, yet, yet . . . you did nothing?"

"You almost sound disappointed, Zar."

"But . . ."

"I'm not a vandal."

Zarvora's shock sublimed into warmth and adoration, and she suddenly realized that she could unreservedly trust someone for the first time in her life. So this is what it is like to be rescued from a dragon by a handsome kavelar, she thought as she flung her arms around Denkar's neck.

Bouros and the Edutor-General again looked back to where Zarvora and Denkar were standing in the golden lamplight of the tunnel.

"Just look at them, kissing and embracing," said Bouros.

"It must be a very exciting day for them," agreed the Edutor-General. "Why, getting such a magnificent wedding present as this must melt away the years and make it seem as if they have only just been married."

"Aye, true. Now what could I fashion for my own wife so that our romance would blaze up as fiercely as with those two?"

Glasken bought another rollpack and swagger stick at the railside market at Coonana, along with a cap that sported a wicker frame eyeshade and goose feather painted with one of Mirrorsun's many shapes. He also bought a reel of white ribbon and a handful of lead shot. The wind had begun to pick up by then, and the train made 120 miles per day thereafter. Just beyond Naretha Railside he dropped a padded bottle of ale through his window into the darkness. It was unlikely that any other refugee from Baelsha would find it before some paraline ganger came by, but Glasken was happier for the gesture.

As the train rolled through Cook Railside on the fourth day, Glasken was reclining in drink-shrouded contentment, sipping delicately at macadamia-mash brandy and watching the treeless expanse of the Nullarbor Plain passing the window. Sensibly, he was chained to the shackle rail on the wall. He had by now checked the passenger register for unattached women, and there was one, in a private compartment at the back of the train. He thought through various pretexts to meet with her, then decided that lethargy was his wisest option.

Glasken was roused as someone walking past stumbled at the open door to

his tiny compartment. He caught a flash of green and red needlework woven with gold thread into black fabric very like fine cheesecloth. A woman's robes! She wore a veil of blue gauze that hung from just below her eyes but only reached down to her chin.

"Ta'aal baek, Frelle," he said politely, assuming that she was Islamic, and that a husband, father, or other guardian would be close to hand.

"But surely you are not a Southmoor," the woman replied. Glasken sat up at once.

"No, I'm of the Southeast Alliance, Rochester actually, Jack Orion's the name, do come in—should you feel my hospitality is honorable."

She stood regarding him for a moment, and he noted what beautiful eyes she had. With the expertise of a practiced lecher he also noted that the nipples of her breasts were beginning to stand up under the cloth. As if to confirm his observation she sinuously slid down into the seat across from him.

"I am Wilpenellia Tienes, from the Carpentarian Mayorate of Buchanan."

"I don't know it," he replied easily. "Is it west of Kalgoorlie?"

"No, it's directly north."

"Alspring?" exclaimed Glasken with surprise.

"No, not those barbaric nomads!" she replied, throwing her hands up in mock horror. "Carpentaria's mayorates are to the north of even Alspring. Have you not heard of the Northwest Paraline Authority, and the link through the Great Sandy Desert?"

Glasken had not, but the idea seemed plausible.

"So, what faith do you follow?" he asked.

"Reformed Gentheist, not the Orthodox Gentheist of those Alspring Ghans. I am a scholar, on my way to work on some rare texts at the great library of Rochester, Libris. You look to be a man of learning, have you studied in Libris?"

"Libris, I know and love it well. Why, when I worked there I simply couldn't get out of the place. Lately I've been settling family matters to the west: an unfortunate death of a distant relative that involved a great deal of wealth."

With these words Glasken stretched out along his seat like a large and languid cat.

"Ah, a man of means," she said.

"And do you like train travel?"

"I hate it. I have a tent that my servants set up every two days or so. There I stay in comfort until the next wind train arrives."

"An eminently civilized strategy, Frelle. And when is your next stop?"

"Oh, I thought to disembark tonight, possibly at Maralinga Railside. Have you been there?"

"Years ago. A boring place, you might say."

"Boring? Ah, but, Fras Orion, what glorious peace there is in the desert. Not

a sound but the wind, none of the bustle of towns and cities, nor the rumble and rattle of the trains. Have you ever slept in the desert, Fras?''

She drew breath rapidly, so that her veil outlined the pouting lips beneath. Glasken found the effect unsettlingly erotic.

''I . . . have been known to. Would you drink to such a thing?'' he asked boldly.

She batted her eyelashes at him for a moment, let him dangle, then caught him.

''Only from a glass tumbler, Fras. We must be civilized, whatever the beauty and tranquillity of the wilderness.''

Glasken jerked the service cord for a new jar of brandy and an extra tumbler. Once the conductor had gone they drank to the Nullarbor Plain and the tranquillity of the desert. Glasken was already ahead by an entire jar, but felt obliged to match her drink for drink. He did not notice her squeeze something into her mouth while feigning to politely stifle a belch.

Wilpenellia slid over to his bench with a flowing rustle of cloth, and Glasken's arm snaked under hers to seize and fondle her left breast. She immediately lifted her veil a little and planted her lips against his, sliding her tongue into his mouth in a lingering, passionate kiss. The nightwing solution in her mouth—that she was immune to—worked surprisingly quickly on even such a large and powerfully built man as Glasken.

In an unexpected bonus for the aviad woman, a Call rolled over the train while it was still a mile from the Maralinga Railside. As the train thumped into the safety buffers she already had Glasken on a lead. She dragged him to the stables and appropriated two camels, which she loaded with packs from the train. Glasken was too large and heavy for her to strap into a saddle, so she let him walk south beside the camels on the end of a rope. When the Call stopped for the night she fed him, and the food was mixed with salts of nightwing. It took an hour to maneuver him into the saddle frame of a kneeling camel; then she led their camels out of the stationary Call zone and south, toward the Edge.

Glasken awoke with dawn seeping through the fabric of an ochre-colored tent. His head was muddled with something that was neither sleep not drink. There was a sweet, pleasant scent on the air, and the ground was strewn with blankets and air cushions.

''Where's the train?'' he said to nobody in particular, but was not surprised to be answered.

''Long gone,'' a woman's voice purred from the other side of the tent. ''Was I right? Was my tent indeed more comfortable than the train?''

Glasken raised his head, to see the veiled face of a kneeling, naked woman across the other side of the tent.

"Wilpenellia?"

"Oh, Fras, but you hold the spirits rare well. What a rare and wonderful time we had."

Glasken considered. His head was muddled rather than splitting with a hangover, but his lusts seemed as rampant as if he had been abstaining for days. She slowly raised herself to her knees, confirming that she was naked except for the veil. Her skin was faintly honey-brown. Glasken got to his knees as well, noting that he too was naked.

"Frelle, you'd best remind me," he said, affecting a suave leer.

Some people never forget a face, a voice, or a pair of eyes, but for Glasken it was breasts that always burned themselves indelibly into his memory. Before him was a smallish yet perfectly formed pair of breasts in the Davantine classic shape. Theresla. He had suspected as much from the first.

"Wait!" she said, holding up a hand. "Wait, please, Fras . . ."

He sat back, selected a grape from a bowl, and ate it.

"It's only a cramp, it will soon pass," she added, surprised by his sudden indifference.

Glasken had no doubt that a Call was close. Theresla would wait until it was nearly upon them and say, "Come to me, Jack Orion. Come do what you will."

"Ah, the pain has passed. Come now, Jack Orion, do what you will."

"Actually I'd rather prepare for the Call, Frelle Abbess," he said as he sat back in a lotus position.

Glasken slammed down mental shutters developed and nurtured in him by the abbot of Baelsha over many, many celibate years. He squeezed desire from himself like water wrung from a sponge as the Call's front rolled over the tent. Glasken was torn by allurement that he did not think possible clawing at everything that made up his being, yet he remained hunched over with his fists clenched, shivering and gasping for breath. It's getting easier, he noted. Theresla stared down at him in amazement.

"You resist it," she whispered. "A *human* resisting the Call."

Glasken did not reply. There were hours to go.

"You now resist the Call by yourself, my allure has nothing to do with it," Theresla continued. "How can you do it?"

"Sheer spite," whispered Glasken.

Slowly she tilted his head up. His eyes were open. He was aware of her nipples a tongue's length from his face, yet she no longer allured him.

"Spoiled," she said glumly as she sat back.

The trailing edge of the Call passed the tent, and Glasken slumped to the blanket, limp and exhausted.

"That was amazing, Fras Glasken," breathed Theresla.

"Getting easier," he panted.

"Please, have a drink."

"More sleeping potions?"

"I'll partake first."

"You probably drink a little every day to become immune."

"Oh take it, damn you!" shouted Theresla, flinging the waterskin across to him. "You have nothing I want anymore. How? You must be the only human in the world who can remain aware and awake during a Call."

"I've had lessons."

"From who?"

"Truly horrible people. Eventually I surpassed them. Where are we?"

"Not far from the Edge itself, the very spot where I did my experiments with you over five years ago. We can return to Maralinga whenever you like."

"I like now," said Glasken.

He caught sight of his clothing in a corner and crawled across to retrieve it. Theresla frowned with the strain of some decision, then tossed her veil aside and stretched out among the cushions.

"We are far from anywhere and alone," she said simperingly. "I have in-experience on offer—"

"You'd better let another relieve you of that inexperience, Frelle," he said as he checked that his purse and pockets had not been looted. "No slight on your wonderful body of course, but I cannot trust *anything* you say. Not after what you did with me five years ago, and just tried to do again."

"Nobody has *ever* denied me!" snapped Theresla, abruptly sitting up.

Glasken shrugged, pointedly holding his bundle of clothing across his loins. "Still, it's happened," He reached for his flintlock pistol, then presented it to her butt first. "Here, kill me. Prevent the world from learning that a man has rejected your advances."

Theresla pouted and echoed, "Still, it's happened." She slumped back on her haunches, her head turned to one side. "Get dressed, I'll leave you alone."

Glasken unlaced the tent flap and stepped outside, looking around as he began to dress. It was the flat, treeless semi-desert of the Nullarbor Plain, and off to one side were the Edge cliffs. The dark blue of the ocean horizon lay beyond. Nearby was the crude Call wall that he had built back in 1700 . . . and close by was the flat stone covering the hole in the ground that was the entrance to Ilyire's treasure cave.

An incredible stroke of luck, he thought. Theresla had brought him to the very place that he had been seeking, the place to which Ilyire could not return. Theresla emerged from the tent fully dressed.

"Apparently Ilyire has a treasure cave somewhere nearby," she said as she joined him. "Darien mentioned it in a letter."

"I'll wager it's well hidden," replied Glasken casually.

"We could search for it."

"Plunder my friend's treasure? Not I."

"Your friend? Ah yes, *you* got him rolling drunk then had him laid a-bed with a couple of hopsicles at the Green Dragon's Tankard."

"*You* shot him."

"The man was a toad. Now he has changed, too."

Glasken walked over to the camels and checked the gear and harnesses. "Bloody camels," he muttered. "Even when they're standing up you feel like you're falling."

Theresla was packing the tent away as he returned, but he stopped dead as she pointed his own flintlock pistol at him. He raised his hands.

"More nuttery in the name of scholarship?" he asked wearily.

"Fras Glasken, I've tried to give you my body, I've tried to give you wealth, but now you are going to get my third gift whether you want it or not. Walk toward the Edge. When you enter the narrow Calldeath region, do whatever you do to resist it."

Theresla put the gun down as Glasken entered and began to fight the weaker, permanent Call. Theresla walked beside him, ready to trip him if he suddenly lost control. They reached the edge of the cliff. It dropped sheer to rocks pounded by the ocean waves.

"Stop here, Fras Glasken, and look out across the water. Those dark shapes out there, note them well. They are the source of the Call. See there, one breaks the surface and blows water into the air. No human has ever seen such a sight as this, and not many aviads have either. Look near the rocks, see that great dark thing? It is one of the Call creatures' livestock, a fanged fish as long as a wind-train carriage. The Call creatures are even bigger. Come back now, and I shall take you back to Maralinga. There will be no more tricks."

On the streets of Glenellen there was apprehension as the first day of the month of Gimleyat began. As the eastern horizon brightened the vendors in the market were already doing a heavy trade in foodstuffs, particularly food that could be stored. Nuts, dates, sultanas, dried mutton, candied apricots and figs, salted white-fish, rice and seedflour commanded outrageous prices from customers who were nonetheless relieved to buy anything at all. The vendors of cloths, perfumes, utensils, and Call-anchor belts sat idle at their respective stalls, watching the nearby bedlam over their red cotton veils as the sunlight spilled over the horizon, painting the towers and cliffs fluorescent red.

"So, the great day is here," said Emzilae, the nomad cloth merchant. "The mighty Commander Lemorel rides into the city at the second hour past dawn."

Heczet, the vendor of Call-anchor belts, reached over and set a clockwork

release to one hour. "One hour, then I pack my stall and hide. There will be looting."

"Looting? How so?" asked Emzilae, brushing at a moth with his emu-feather whisk.

"The Commander's Neverlanders," drawled Zeter from his perfume stand. "They're barbarians, they've never been in a city. They don't understand money, they take whatever they want."

"One hour," declared Heczet again. "Then I pack my stall and hide it. When I watch the parade enter the city gates I'll be wearing rags and have a pox badge."

"Ah, but the city will be full of beggars when the Commander enters," said Emzilae. "I saw it happen at Gossluff, Tempe, and Ayer. The same thing, every time."

Emzilae stood up, stretched, then clapped his hands. A youth with a wispy, pubescent beard scuttled around from the back of the stall. He was unveiled, the sign of an apprentice who has as yet no means or skill to guard a sanctum of his own.

"Master?"

"It's time, Da. I want twelve dozen camels, twenty handlers with their own weapons, and six strong eunuchs to pack and carry. All to be here in two hours."

"Aye, Master."

When the boy had disappeared into the bustle of the market Zeter sauntered across to Emzilae's stall and fingered a bolt of deep blue cloth.

"A-he, fine Northmoor cotton," said Emzilae. "A fine, fine bargain at—"

"You have only enough to pack two camels."

"Alas, such cloth is rare, my friend."

"So, a pack beast for Da and another camel for you, others for the handlers and eunuchs: that leaves a hundred and fourteen excess camels."

"A-he, they are needed to carry dried fish, candied fruits, roasted almonds, spiced walnuts, and the like."

Zeter jerked a thumb at the melee across at the food stalls, then gestured to the blue cloth between them. "You would be lucky to trade a whole bolt of this cloth for a single dried fish."

"A-he, but within two hours I will buy that same fish for a copper. Nomads know the cities better than you think, my worthy perfumier." He gestured to his chest, his fingers spread. "This nomad has seen the Commander enter half a dozen cities. Her warriors are highly disciplined, and to show that nobody should dare attack her she never has more than a hundred of her personal guard escorting her."

Now Heczet walked over to the stall. "But only yesterday you were standing on a fish barrel, shouting to all who would listen about scenes of bloody horror in Gossluff. Youths cut down in the street for sport, girls stripped and raped in

their very sanctum rooms, looting and burning, followed by starvation for those who survived. What of that?

"People listened. Just look at the boom in foodstuffs across the way."

Zeter suddenly straightened, his hands on his hips. "Oh so, then what is to come may not be so bad?"

"A-he, such suspicion."

"What really happened in Gossluff?" asked Zeter.

Emzilae's face split in a wide, knowing grin. "Why, the Commander entered with a few dozen lancers and rode through the boulevard to the Palace of the Makulad. She was met there by the Makulad and his College of Elders, who surrendered the city. Without dismounting she shot the Makulad through the heart, then killed his son. The rest of his family and some of the Elders were led off into slavery, but that was the worst of it: two killings. No looting, no rape, no murder."

"By the noontime heat!" exclaimed Zeter. "So who rules Gossluff now?"

"An exiled pretender, whose family lost power in that city centuries ago. The Commander said she was reinstalling him as the rightful Makulad. Later this morning the fugitive Prince Alextoyne will ride through the gates at the right hand of the Commander, and when she has shot your Makulad he will ascend to the throne. There will be new taxes to fund her wars—"

"Prince Alextoyne?" exclaimed Heczet. "The descendant of Makulad Moyzenko, who lost the throne for love of the beautiful Ervelle?"

"None other."

"An inspired choice. This is a legend coming alive, the Golden Age of three hundred years ago being restored."

Emzilae smiled enigmatically, looking across to the crowds fighting over the dwindling stocks of food.

"You have no broad vision, friends. In two hours those fools will realize that the Commander will do no more than tax them. Those who have spent their savings on food will want money for the tax, especially since those with no money must provide mounts, weapons, or sons for the Commander's army." Emzilae patted the coin bags of his float. "When they come streaming back with their bags of dates, rice, and dried meat, I shall be here to buy, and what I buy I shall take to Alspring to sell at twenty times its value when the Commander lays siege to the city."

Heczet and Zeter stood back, stunned.

"But such a rich caravan, you will have. Surely freebooters would fall upon you without a ruinously large escort."

"My friend, no freebooter would dare touch me. I am under the protection of the Commander."

"She uses you?"

"But of course. I spread fear, then she enters and shows mercy. The mood of the people becomes one of great relief. The Commander gets another undamaged city to support her wars. A pillaged city is of no value to a conquerer."

"So the great Lemorel is not such a demon after all," said Heczet, stroking his beard.

Emzilae frowned. "Demon she can be, rest assured. There is a nameless town, a place of five thousand souls not far from Olgadowns. It was proud and fortified, and they resisted her for five weeks. I passed through the place two months after the fall, and it was a horror such as I could never describe. Not a man, woman, child, or beast was spared, and the surviving officers were tortured to death before the rulers of Ayer, Olgadowns, and Tempe as a warning. Every pot was smashed, everything that would burn was torched, then the town was left just like that, as an example. Bones lie in the streets still, and the houses are all burned-out shells. Commander Lemorel has an evil temper when resisted."

Zeter was wringing his hands nervously, glancing to the crowd then back to his own stall. "I, ah, should make a presentation to the Commander, a blend of my rarest fragrances in a phial of Carpentarian porcelain. I will say that it is to refresh her after the heat and dust of her ride."

"A-he, she will like that," said Emzilae with a shallow nod. He inclined his head toward Heczet. "I also happen to know that she is a great judge of fine lenses and clockwork."

"Truly?" exclaimed Heczet. "Then I shall buy a fine chronograph and sextant set. Morgyo has one to sell at a very low price, what with the silly panic about buying food."

Later that morning Lemorel Milderellen rode into the city on a war camel at the head of ninety lancers. As Emzilae had predicted, she shot the Makulad dead, dispersed the women of his family into various convents, and had the men and boys gelded before being taken to the slave markets. Prince Alextoyne was made the new Makulad of Glenellen, and for his gift of perfume Zeter was made Royal Hospitalier in the palace. Heczet's gift had him appointed official agent of Glenellen to supply Lemorel's army, a position which brought him wealth, property, a royal title, and—eventually—the attention of loyalist assassins.

Emzilae did indeed spend the afternoon buying food stores at the market at a fiftieth of what had been charged in the morning, being ever careful to undercut the local vendors who were charging even more ruinous rates. The city was almost back to normal by then, except that Neverlander guards were in charge of the palace and their wardens were stationed at every watchhouse.

Servants thronged about Emzilae's stall, laden with sacks of food to be sold for coins to pay the war tax, while camels carried sacks away to the pens just outside the gates of the city. Emzilae supervised, sometimes bargaining, sometimes carrying sacks, and even driving camels through the crowds. The citizens

wore an odd mixture of beggars' rags, disguises, and fine robes, and most were in a festive mood. The mud hovels, redstone houses, and even towers were decked out with Neverlander pennons and colors, while veiled women waved coyly to passing nomads from balconies, some throwing flowers.

The journey back to the paraline took Theresla and Glasken several days. They exchanged stories of the preceding five years, ranging from her explorations in the Calldeath lands to Ilyire's first night on the town. Glasken was reluctant to talk about his time in Baelsha, but under persistent questioning he eventually outlined some of his training, trials, and torments.

"I begin to understand," Theresla said as their camels swayed along together. "The monks taught you to meditate on an object like a mandala, something that symbolized the Call's greatest hold upon you. That symbol, that mandala-object, was almost certainly me."

"Perceptive," agreed Glasken.

"You, Fras, are highly, even grotesquely oversexed. I once used your drives to attune myself to voices within the Call. Now you have been trained to use my image as a channel to divert the allure of the Call past you. You know within the deepest recesses of your mind that you will never let yourself have a consummation with me. That is your strength."

Glasken nodded agreement and sat up a little more erect in the saddle. He knew that he was exceptional in his resistance to the Call, but to be considered unique was something more like an honor.

"The Baelsha monks and the Kooree nomads merely drop down unconscious at the touch of the Call, but I can remain awake. Why is that?"

Theresla thought about this for many minutes, staring straight ahead. Glasken surreptitiously dropped yet another length of white ribbon weighted at one end with lead shot.

"Because *you* are extraordinary. Live long, Fras Glasken," she concluded. "Do not get yourself killed for a very long time."

"Well, the same to you too, Frelle."

"And don't trust me. Never trust me."

They both began to laugh.

"I went to a lot of trouble over you, Glasken."

"All the girls say that."

"It took the word of Mayor Bouros himself to convince the Great Western Paraline Authority to depart from their precious schedule for even one hour."

A white smudge was by now visible on the straight-edge horizon, and Glasken realized that they were approaching Maralinga. He hurriedly checked a little compass concealed in his hand while pretending to cough.

"Tell me now, if you were a woman, and were you interested in . . . initiation, what would you do?" Theresla asked.

"Find a man."

"By my age, the alluring men are all taken. Those that are left have been left for a variety of very good reasons."

Glasken thought for a moment. "Theresla, if you're really determined to bed someone for its own sake, then just select a nice Fras who is already taken. Get him to a hostelry one afternoon with a couple of jars of the great leveler."

"Fras Glasken! That's . . . that's worth further thought. How were you deflowered, if I may ask?"

Glasken nearly dropped his compass in surprise. He glanced across furtively to Theresla, but she had turned away, giggling.

"When I was fourteen I was quite a good hand with the lutina," he said, firmly refusing to smile. "The local hicks would hire me to serenade their Frelles for them. One night the girl at the upstairs window invited *me* in. When I went inside I found she had more in mind than a couple more songs and a honeycake."

"That's lovely," Theresla laughed as Glasken dropped another white ribbon. "Couples get together in such silly and unsuitable ways, yet those unions can lead to mighty alliances of mayorates, advances in scholarship, anything and everything. Just one awkward, vulnerable moment, one desperate gesture when pride, dignity, and self-respect are offered to another in one's trembling hand."

"One gently pinched bottom that does not result in a slap?"

Theresla pouted at him, her eyes narrowing. "You have a way of going straight for the crude fundamentals."

"I am a rake. I deal in crude fundamentals."

"It is said that rakes love sex and conquest, but not women. You, Glasken, are not a rake. Your heart is in the right place, even if the rest of you is . . . wherever it is."

Maralinga had grown into a fortified garrison post and beamflash relay, with a nomad market and even a hostelry. With Theresla safely on a wind train that was vanishing west into the heat shimmers, Glasken strode over to the stables to equip himself for a second—and this time lone—expedition. As he fumbled for coins to pay for stores and camels he felt a square of poorpaper at the bottom of his purse. He unfolded it, then read it again.

"Fras Glasken: Theresla is return palace. Highliber tell her of you. You go paraline Great Western. Theresla know. I fix. Your drinker friend, Ilyire."

"Lucky she didn't find that," said Glasken as he dropped the paper into the coals of the stables' forge, where it ignited with a soft pop. It had been a desperate gamble, but it had paid off. Theresla had taken him where Ilyire could not bring himself to return. This time Glasken had been careful to drop markers as they returned to Maralinga.

12 CLOCKSMITH

Glasken spent several weeks on the Nullarbor, stripping Ilyire's treasure cave clean. He re-secreted three-quarters of the contents in other caves, then removed Ervelle's bones and wrapped them in a saddle blanket. Finally, he stood in the cemetery at Maralinga Railside early one morning, seeing to it that Ervelle's remains were buried properly and played the old Alspring tune "Ervelle's Farewell" on a borrowed lutina. A Reformed Gentheist lay minister from the beam-flash crew—the closest equivalent of the Alspring Orthodox Gentheist religion that Glasken knew of—read a service.

"Ilyire begs forgiveness," Glasken said in Alspring as he sprinkled a handful of pinkish limestone dust into the open grave.

The headstone bore Ervelle's name in both Alspring script and Austaric Roman, as well as the dates of her birth and death. It had been sent out on a wind train by Ilyire. Glasken stood watching the hired paraline navvies shoveling limestone rock and sand into the grave, and a plume of dust streamed away from the hole on the hot, blustery wind like a tenuous white soul that was free at last. He raised his cap a fraction.

"Glad to be of service to such a legend, Frelle," he whispered. "Perhaps one day I'll meet some girl as wonderful as you were said to be. Preferably today."

He sighed. All of his seductions had been conquests, yet he had never been any girl's hero. Legends were full of virtuous heroes, evil villains, and vulnerable heroines, but there were never any harmless rakes who were merely fun to be with. Could he only ever enter a legend as Ervelle's undertaker? Could he be loved for being himself and not some insipid alter ego? Now he had the riches to do whatever he wanted, but he had no idea what he wanted to do.

A wind train was due in the afternoon, and Glasken wandered about the railside looking at the changes that had taken place in the years since Lemorel had abducted him. What surprised him most was the scatter of Alspring Ghans who were living in a small encampment to the east of the railside. There were fifteen or twenty of them, and about sixty camels munching on fodder in wooden troughs. Two Kooree men were lounging in the shade of the warehouse, speaking to one of the uniformed railside staff. Glasken could draw his own conclusions easily enough: the Ghans had negotiated caravan rights across Kooree land, and were now trading with merchants on the wind trains. Coffee

would be of great interest to the merchants from the inland, but he doubted that any political contacts had as yet been established. He did not spare a thought for Lemorel.

Wandering past the railside's cemetery Glasken noticed that three Ghan merchants were prostrating themselves before Ervelle's grave and wailing softly in unison. He recognized some words of a a prayer of reconciliation. The ticketmaster came up to him as he stood watching.

"It took them only minutes to discover that grave this morning, Fras. They've been wailing there in rotation ever since. Just whose bones did you bury?"

"Ervelle was an exceedingly beautiful young Alspring woman who was mistakenly sentenced to death and turned loose into a Call, strapped to a camel. I chanced upon the bones, and was familiar with the legend. She is revered by the Alspring Ghans, as you can see."

"I certainly do. Fras, you may have made Maralinga some sort of holy place. Your name should be on the headstone too."

"Oh no, no, good Fras, I have no place in legends."

"As you will. Now, this afternoon's wind train west has no vacant A-class compartments left, according to the beamflash."

"Damn and hellfire! I couldn't sit up in a B-class seat all the way to Kalgoorlie, not after five weeks on a camel."

"Fras, Fras, let me finish. I expect that several will be vacated when the train arrives. There are always a few coffee merchants on each train, they come to trade with the Ghans."

The wind train was later than expected, so Glasken indulged in a bath and shave, luxuriating in cool water from the cisterns for a half hour. The glow of the sunset faded in the west as Mirrorsun rose in the east. Its form this night was a dull bar of reddish light across the band in the sky, and the band was actually visible right across the sky owing to Earthlight. He was staring up at the sky when he realized that he could hear the rumble of the wind train.

Glasken stood back as the front rotor engine rolled past, its brakeblocks squealing and its rotors disengaged and spinning free. In the lamplight it looked like some enormous, unwieldy insect. The Alspring Ghans rushed about, shouting their wares to the merchants emerging from the coaches, and the quiet railside rapidly became a bustling night market. Merchants' lackeys unloaded bags of coffee beans and a variety of spices. Glasken was about to push his way through the crowd to one of the carriages when he noticed Darien stepping down from a carriage.

He eased back into the shadows beside the kiosk and watched while a robed Alspring Ghan went up to her and addressed her after an elaborate flourish. The mute Darien selected a card from a small satchel on her belt and handed it to him. He read, bowed, then gestured toward the camp. Glasken was puzzled, but

relieved that she was going away. The railside's ticketmaster met him at the door of the A-class carriage.

"Fras Orion, you're in luck. The Purser's board shows that several A-class compartments are now free. I assigned A-one to you, I'll just mark your ticket."

Glasken was pleased. He wanted privacy whenever he opened his rollpack, quite apart from his own privy and the luxury of having a folding bunk to stretch out along. The whistle blew for departure. Glasken boarded and held up his ticket to an approaching conductor, but the rotund and splendidly dressed man brushed past him without a word. He was dabbing essence of hedgerose on his face from a small bottle, and his freshly waxed mustache might have been carved out of blackwood and oil-polished. Glasken wondered why the man was wearing a parade uniform in the middle of the Nullarbor Plain.

The train began to roll slowly along the rails with a smooth and gently rocking motion. Glasken checked his ticket: compartment A1. He noted that compartments A5 up to A2 were vacant, with their doors open, but A1 was shut as he reached it. He assumed that it was something to do with it being reserved for him, and he slid the door aside and stepped in without breaking stride.

A woman in her mid-twenties was reclining on the bench seat. She was very tall, but with a well-curved and attractive figure beneath her plain dretan of sienna cotton. Her face was a pleasant oval, framed by honey-brown hair that was unbound and cascading down to the seat and as far as the floor. She had scuffed clogs on her feet. At the sight of Glasken she shrank back in alarm.

"Oh—I'm in here!" she squeaked in surprise, then snapped in a much deeper voice: "Now you get out!"

Glasken was quite weary, and in no mood to be pushed around. He sat down heavily beside her, footsore from pacing the platform and depressed from the funeral.

"Indeed you are in here, Frelle, but A-one has been assigned to me." He held up the ticket, which had been marked to A1.

"A-one was not booked," she insisted.

"I just boarded."

He noticed a large, battered artisan's toolbag and overnighter in the corner. Her accent was Eastern Highlands but stronger than Lemorel's.

"The conductor gave me to A-one," she insisted. "You get out or he'll throw you off."

Glasken began to rub the muscles along the back of his neck. "It's my bet that you're about to see more of him than I ever wish to. Artisans like you can't afford A-class tickets. *You* get out. I'm going to report the two of you to the Purser."

A subtle sag of her shoulders showed that his retort had hit home. With her lips pressed together she stood up and hoisted her bag's strap to her shoulder.

"Good Fras, I—I, please, I apologize, I'll go." Her tone was now subdued. "My miserly clockmaker husband gave me only enough for B-class fare, but conductor said he'd let me ride in a vacant A-class tonight. Please, good Fras, don't report me. I'm not up to a fine, and they'll impound the tools of my trade, I'd have to sell my hair."

Suddenly Glasken imagined himself in her position, staring down with her hurt, frightened, brown eyes. The woman was tall, so she would have had trouble sleeping in the B-class seats. Just because you're big, everyone assumes it doesn't matter if you're hurt, he thought. She began to sidle out, giving a deferential little bow at each step. He thrust his foot out to block the doorway.

"Frelle, you stay here, I'll move to A-two. If anyone else gives you trouble, just call me and I'll punch some manners into him."

Glasken stood up, unfolding and straightening to his full six feet five inches. He blinked with surprise to find that even when standing he still had to look up slightly to meet her eyes.

"You—you're leaving?" she asked.

"A-two to A-five are still vacant."

"You'll not report me?"

"No harm done, pretty Frelle. Nothing a mere smack on the bottom wouldn't set right."

He grinned wearily at her. She grinned back, yet something subtle had changed in her expression. Her face hardly seemed to belong to the same woman as she regarded him coyly over her shoulder.

"So, you'd be liking to smack bottoms, Fras?"

"Only if I be allowed to rub them better again, Frelle," he quipped, finding the words out of his mouth before he was aware of speaking them.

She put her free hand on her hip, then presented the curve of her left buttock to him with a slow, rolling motion.

"Well Fras, I'm waiting," she said, batting her unusually long eyelashes at him.

Glasken did a double take: he had not even been trying to seduce the woman, and she was also still free to share a vacant compartment with the conductor. He reached for her hand, then brushed it with a kiss. She dropped her bag and slid her arms about him.

"Fras, you've just been more gentleman to me than any man. Ever. Please don't go, or I really will be hurt."

Glasken put his arms about her and squeezed gently. Her lips hovered close to his, and after another moment they drew each other into a long, soft kiss. Her skin was slightly moist, and he could feel her heart pattering wildly. Their eyes were almost level as they stood with their foreheads pressed together.

Nearly an hour later Glasken rang for service. The conductor made a note in

his pocketbook and walked briskly away down the narrow corridor to the galley as if he was anxious to have some unpleasant duty out of the way.

"A jar of Sundew leg-opener for the pair in A-one," he snapped to the cook. "Not that they need it."

"So, Fras, your arrangements for the night have gone awry?"

"Gah, and I overheard the most *ridiculous* proposition in the history of the Great Western Paraline Authority. Well I suppose I can do nought but pray for strong winds."

Daily life in Glenellen was little different under Lemorel's rule from that of the former Makulad, except that the punishments for rebellion were devastating. The whole family of any offender was punished, giving households the incentive to become unofficial extensions of the Neverlander wardenry and keep rebellious members in check. With Glenellen fallen, only the great city of Alspring remained against her. Unknown to everyone, however, Glenellen itself had been her real objective. The greatest moment of her life was close.

With the proclamations done, Lemorel secured the palace and had the seneschal summoned. He was a tall and dignified man, wearing a heavy red veil below his eyes as a mark of his duty to protect the palace. Lemorel paced before him, her riding whip held behind her back. It seemed to him that she was steeling herself to do something that was bound to be distressing, yet he could not imagine what it could be.

"There is a device in this palace," she said at last, continuing to pace with restless, driven strides. "It is a device made up of some two hundred people with abacus frames and known as a calculor. Where is it?"

"In the great median tower, on the tenth level, Your—ah, Majesty."

"My title is Frelle Commander."

"Frelle Commander."

"Now take me to the calculor."

The calculor hall was on two separate floors in the tower, and the components worked in very cramped conditions. Nikalan was one of ten FUNCTIONS at the front of the hall, and the machine was whirring and clacking through a calibration task as Lemorel entered. She recognized him at once, but her face was veiled.

"System halt!" shouted the Chief Regulator, and the tasks being performed tapered away into silence as an orderly shutdown was performed.

"A fascinating design," said Lemorel as she picked her way through the maze of wires and struts. "Components sitting at desk-frames stacked atop each other five high. That means much faster transmission speeds, and faster calculation times for the same number of components."

"My own innovation, Frelle Commander," said an Elder who had been standing beside the Chief Regulator. "There were areas of the original design that were too concerned with neat layout. They neglected efficiency."

Lemorel regarded him coldly, yet her veil hid her expression. "The man who designed this for you. Bring him to me."

"That man is myself, Frelle Commander," replied the Elder.

"I shall not ask again. A prisoner was brought here from the Fostoria Oasis five or more years ago. His name was either FUNCTION 3073 or Nikalan Vittasner. Bring him to me!"

Interpreting Lemorel's tone as anger with Nikalan, the Chief Regulator decided to gain favor by presenting the component to Lemorel in person. He took the keys from the System Warden and strode over to a complex of desks where he unlocked a shackle on a thin, white leg in the second row up. He reached into the desk, dragged Nikalan down by one arm, then marched him to where Lemorel was standing. He forced Nikalan to his knees, then pushed him in the back with his foot, to prostrate the component before Lemorel. Looking up for the Commander's approval, he saw a twin flash as her double-barreled flintlock discharged. For the first time in her life she had lost control so badly that she had fired both barrels together.

"Nikalan, my poor, shattered Nikalan," she crooned as she knelt and held him in her arms. "This is Lemorel. Lemorel here with you again."

"Lemorel? Will you take me back to Libris and the Calculor?"

Lemorel looked into the vacant eyes, her control again slipping away like a greased rope in her grasp. He knew her, but she was not enough. Only as part of a bigger machine could she ever be what he could love. With a great effort she caught herself.

She had conquered over a million people for this moment, yet her long-sought holy grail was no more than a handful of shattered pieces. As she knelt with him she suddenly saw her new self for the first time. She was larger than life now, she was vast and powerful. Nikalan was no more than the scrap of smoking fuse cord that had unleashed the power of a mighty bombard. By the time she stood up again, Nikalan had become nothing to her.

"The Libris Calculor is very far away, Fras Nikalan, but give me time," she said in a bland tone. "I shall take you back to it, I promise."

She helped him to his feet and gestured to the Seneschal, who trotted over quickly.

"Have Fras Nikalan Vittasner bathed by the concubines and eunuchs of the former Makulad. By the time he is clean and dry I want the palace tailors to have a suit of the Makulad's robes altered to his fit, then see that he dines better than *any* other in the palace. He is to be veiled as protected by my sanctum. Nikalan is to be put in the Makulad's bed tonight."

"But, Frelle Commander, what about Prince Alextoyne?"

"Have him serve at Fras Nikalan's meals. He can sleep in the guest rooms."

"Yes, Frelle Commander."

"Seneschal, allow Nikalan to be harmed, and I will do something so point-

lessly hideous that you will die as much from disbelief as pain. I am insane, Fras Seneschal. Never forget that! Nikalan, go with this man.''

''But my shift is not over.''

''You have been promoted to System Controller, and you must rest before beginning your new duties.''

When they had gone Lemorel gave the body of the Chief Regulator a vicious kick, then seized the Elder who had built the calculor. She held him by the hair and made him stare at the corpse, which had been decapitated above the eyes.

''Clean that up before the components get upset,'' she snarled.

''At once, Frelle Commander, at once.''

''And another thing. If I *ever* hear *anyone* refer to you as more than a lackey who helped Nikalan to build this calculor, I shall have you diced into pigmeat, starting at your toes.''

With a kick to his buttocks she sent him sprawling, then walked from the calculor hall without another word.

The following morning Glasken and his companion lay together on the narrow bunk in compartment A1, she watching the brightening sky and almost featureless panorama of the Nullarbor Plain through the window of the compartment, and he regarding the shape of her breasts pressing against his chest.

''Can you be breathing under my weight, Fras Jack?'' she asked yet again.

''Stay there, pretty Frelle, please. I can feel you all the better from below,'' he said as he caressed her long and sinuous back.

''I'm two hundred pounds.''

''So? I'm two hundred and thirty.'' He peered at a passing milestone and frowned to see the train making good time. ''So, is your clockmaker husband in Kalgoorlie?''

''No, he's in Rochester doing contract work for big library.'' She stretched out with her hands against the bulkhead. ''He heard of need for clockwork in Kalgoorlie but was worried about leaving secure employ. I said I'd go see what was what. I've skill in clockwork, as Dada was a clockmaker.''

''Oh, so will you be needing someone to tend the springs of your clockwork?''

''Yesss. Be your key free for winding, Jacky?''

Glasken rolled on top of her. ''Aye. You'd best send your husband bad reports of Kalgoorlie while you are there.''

''Pah, I'm never going back to Southeast. Damn strutting Dragon Librarians and Constable's Runners.''

''Surely you've not been a felon, Frelle?'' asked Glasken, at once nervous about his bag full of gold on the floor.

She put a hand theatrically to her forehead, then flung both arms in the air before squeezing Glasken again. "No, but my sister's as you'd never believe. Brains of Family, that's as Dada called her. Went about with damn stupid depressed poets. I hate poets. You're no poet, are you, Jacky?"

"Not damn likely."

"Dada made me his apprentice and saved money for schooling her to median level. 'What of me then?' I asked. 'Oh no,' says teachers to Dada. 'She's too dim, look at her.' What the fykart did they expect? I was six feet tall when I was eleven! I looked eighteen and stupid, while being eleven and bright."

"Dummart bastards," Glasken sighed.

"Unfair, Fras, unfair. It really—There's a thought. Where's privy in A-class?"

Glasken rolled to one side and pointed to what she had taken for a wardrobe. "All self-contained luxury in here, Frelle Jemli."

She rummaged for something in her bag, then sidled through the narrow door of the privy. Within her now open bag Glasken could see three books. Suddenly he sat up on the bunk with a start. It was not so much the title, *Encyclopedia of Mechanical Physistry*, that had alarmed him, as the embossed red letters declaring LIBRIS READING ROOM REFERENCE: DO NOT REMOVE. Jemli emerged and washed her hands in the demi-drench with a little bar of scented soap.

"Are you a Dragon Librarian traveling incognito?" demanded Glasken.

"Absolutely not, Fras."

"But there's books from the Libris Reading Room in your bag."

"Oh those?" she said dismissively. "I stole them."

"But, but, but—you can get shot for picking your nose while reading in there, and *you* stole *books*?"

"Aye."

"Gak—" Glasken was speechless for a moment. "But why? You can't sell them."

"I needed them for studies! I'd no money for transcript sheets and no time for scribing what I needed for studies."

"Studies? For your guild?"

"My guild? Pox take guild, though no guildsmen could raise it long enough to catch pox. It's Rochester University I was in, studying by night and tending clockwork by day. Eight years, eight subjects."

"Extraordinary."

"I'm transferring to Kalgoorlie University, I'll graduate in four years. Then it's divorce and into the beamflash service for me. Tower captain, I'll be one day, you mark it. I love the towers, they're like us, Jacky: damn-hell tall and proud of it!"

"Uh, divorce?"

"Aye, Dada matched me to one of his smelly old guild friends. He died, and his money went to my sister. Ach, what a waste, Jacky."

She put out a hand and stroked his head gently. Glasken immediately snaked his arms around her and held her tightly, his chin resting over her shoulder.

"You're just beautiful, beautiful all the way through, the most beautiful woman I've ever met," he said with tears in his eyes.

He pulled back a little and rested his forehead against hers, gazing into her chocolate-brown eyes. Jemli rubbed his temples, feeling both confused and nervous. Glasken was no less confused. What am I doing? he wondered. I have the Mayor of Kalgoorlie's sister waiting for me when I return, yet my heart is slipping away to a clockmaker's wife with hardly a copper to spare. Damn you, Theresla, you cursed me to fall in love.

"I'm sorry if I shot off my mouth a bit there, Jacky, but I've had nobody to tell all that to for eight years. Once it started, out it came."

Jemli wiped his eyes with her brown hair, then draped it over his shoulders.

"I've always wanted to do that with someone, but nobody's been special enough until now," she said, stroking his head.

"Your hair is exquisite."

"It's nice enough, but it's also three months of University fees if the trade in Kalgoorlie is not up to promise. Long hair is a blessing, it's like a purse that nobody would think to steal."

"Never!" exclaimed Glasken angrily. "Don't say it, don't even think it!" He put his hands over his ears.

Jemli shrank away, alarmed. Glasken swung his legs off the bunk, undid the laces of his rollpack, and rummaged within it for a moment. To Jemli's astonishment he pulled out a gold coin and dropped it into her open bag.

"Here's gold, say when more's needed," he said in a parody of her Eastern Highlands accent.

"Fras! That *is* gold. It could keep me in food, fees, and rent for a month."

He cupped her jaw in his hands and looked into her eyes. "Jemli, you're wonderful. Wanton but canny, brave but sensible."

"Fras Jack, that's all the things I see in *you*."

"Ah well, we must be suited to each other. Will you stay?"

"Stay? Jacky, even without such fittings as you it's heaven in here. Are you sure? I'm not used to getting things free."

"I meant with me, after we arrive at Kalgoorlie."

"Oh, Fras, do you really mean that? If you do, my heart is as big as the rest of me."

Glasken swallowed and walked two fingers along the edge of the bunk, then took a deep breath.

"I . . . may have a few nights occupied . . . sometimes. Business contacts of a female kind. In the mayoral palace. Would you be jealous?"

"After what we've been up to, and me a married woman? Business contacts are to be cultivated."

"Done!" exclaimed Glasken. "I rather fancy myself owning a tavern, actually. Let's look over the prospects when we arrive in Kalgoorlie."

"Done! Then we can have a really big revel for free. Ah Jacky, you're my hero and you're such fun to be with."

A hero and fun to be with! So it really was possible, he thought hopefully. Perhaps all the real people in legends had been expunged by dour, boring scholars.

Lemorel was forced to undergo purification and penance for shooting a man in the head, an act proscribed under the Orthodox Gentheist religion of the Alspring cities and Neverlander nomads. The head was seen as the link between the Deity and the human soul, and as such was held sacred. Enemies could be poisoned, shot through the heart, even decapitated, but the head itself could not be harmed. Lemorel's sacrilege was tempered, however, by the romance of the circumstances in the eyes of her followers. She had found her long-lost beloved, but he was dead—and she had shot his murderer. A great commander was expected to be passionate, so the incident had actually worked in her favor.

Within a week she was again with her army, leading them east to Alspring's checkerboard walls of red and white stone blocks. As this was the last of the great cities of the inland region, her Council of Overhands was anxious to know what would happen after it had fallen. Lemorel had also made her Council of Overhands members of her personal sanctum. She gathered them in her circular tent of red ochre and yellow stippling, and as the tent flap was drawn she slipped the ties of her veil, then let her outer robes fall to the ground. The effect was startling for the Ghan men, both Neverlanders and those of the Alspring cities. Straight hair cut sharply at shoulder level, painted red lips, and eyes traced out in ebony liner. Her skin was powdered a slight shade pink, rather than the tusk-white of Ghan erotica, and she wore black riding trousers and a black shirt unbuttoned to display her cleavage as did no other Ghan woman. Two double-barreled Morelacs and two daggers were at her belt. Seductress and daughter, child and warrior, nun and fiend, protector and protected: to them Lemorel was all these in one. Although she was entrancing, they could not see her as one of their own women or comprehend her by any familiar values.

"A drive south, to conquer the fat, soft lands of Woomera and the Southeast Alliance," she told the gathering as they sat cross-legged before her.

There was no muttering, but an uneasy shifting and rustling of the men in their varied but colorful styles of robes, head windings, and veils.

"But Commander, where will the time be to enjoy what we have con-

quered?'' asked Baragania. ''Even the Neverlanders among us are hungry to enjoy the newly won lands and riches.''

''Then you can enjoy them under infidel rule,'' she said in a carefully understated voice.

All of them knew her ways of speech by now. When a thing was so because it was beyond her control, she always said it softly. When Baragania did not reply, she took a small white cylinder from her sleeve. She slipped the string from its rim, and it unwound a long streamer of paper tape, all punched with little holes.

''This is a machine message taken by my spies in the Woomera Confederation. The former Abbess of the Scalattera Convent in Glenellen has just married the consort of the Overmayor of the Southeast Alliance, to become their invel-spouse. The wedding was in Kalgoorlie.''

Again she was silent, and she paced before them while they muttered among themselves and speculated about the consequences of such a union.

''Do you know what that means?'' she suddenly shouted, flinging the streamer of tape at the cross-legged half-circle of men. ''It means that Overmayor Zarvora can claim associative rule in Glenellen. Since the Abbess' father died she is the heir to his seat as an Elder, and the Overmayor can claim the right to restore her as a member of the College of Elders.'' Lemorel paused again to let her words be discussed and assimilated. ''I shall not restore any part of the previous Makulad's dynasty or College of Elders, so the Overmayor has the excuse she needs to attack.''

''Commander, the rights of the Abbess Theresla are forfeit because she deserted the protection of her sanctum keeper, the Marshal of the Convent,'' began Baragania.

''Wrong!'' shouted Lemorel. ''Under the convention of the Forgiveness of Ervelle, one of your most respected laws, any woman who deserts her sanctum keeper under the protection of a male member of her family, and in order to marry for love into a union above her station is—come on, someone tell me now, who can tell me?''

''Is blameless under the eyes of the Deity and the rule of law,'' came the quavering voice of an aged overhand from Ayer.

Lemorel stood with her hands on her hips, triumph in every angle of her posture. ''Theresla has opened the way for the southern Liberal Gentheist infidels to stream north. Her invel-sister the Overmayor has already gathered Kalgoorlie into her mighty web of alliances. She wants wants nothing less than rule of the entire continent.''

Now the muttering and hand-waving of the overhands was bright with marvel at Lemorel's breadth of vision and foresight.

''I have no particular liking for a bloody conquest of the South. It was my

home, my dear parents and brother are buried there. My surviving sister dwells in contentment there with her devoted husband, and doubtless there are many children clinging to her robes and looking to her for protection. *I* do not want to attack my home, but I have no choice. The safety of my new home and you, my people, comes first. The Deity cries out for it. The Deity is even slowing the winds that drive their wind trains as a sign of disapproval. What other sign do you want? Mirrorsun torn asunder?''

By Coonana the Nullarbor Plain had given way to open eucalypt forest that was interspersed with patches of grassland and dotted with water holes. Nomads were visible from the wind train, some with camel caravans, others in painted wagons drawn by mules. The town itself was a major interchange for the wind trains, one of the places where east- and westbound trains were able to pass on the paraline. The paraline railsides such as Maralinga and Naretha were exotic and isolated, but Coonana was the cultural beachhead of the Western Mayorates. Jemli marveled at the colorful pageant beyond the wind train as it slowly rumbled into the railside. The eastbound train was in a bypass, waiting for a clear line.

"Kalgoorlie is much warmer, drier, and windier than Rochester," Glasken explained. "Coonana is a foretaste."

"What are all those colorfully dressed people?"

"The locals and nomads have a market whenever trains arrive. They stay for only a few hours, but a lot of money changes hands. It is said that the latest fashions always arise among the stalls of Coonana before they are seen on the streets of Kalgoorlie."

Jemli stared longingly through the window as Glasken stood behind her, thoughtfully running a finger along the drab brown cloth on her back.

"We should dress you in Kalgoorlie style."

"Oh, Jacky, how could I pay?"

"By letting *me* pay."

They visited the sugar-fruit stalls, then bought small bags of nuts and pastries for the remaining journey. Jemli discovered the metalwork stalls next, some of whose products had traveled as far as the Libris Calculor, to be incorporated in the mechanisms in Zarvora's study.

"Fras Glasken—er, Orion—fancy meeting you here!"

Glasken closed his eyes before he even began turning. He knew Theresla's voice all too well.

"The day's fortune to you, Frelle. Travelling east, I hope?"

"Oh yes. My train is on the bypass beside yours."

He opened his eyes to see her dressed in the current style of mirror-inlaid cheesecloth dyed dark blue, with a lyrebird picked out in highlight beads. The

cut of the cleavage did not suit her, for her breasts were not especially big.

"Kalgoorlie was wonderful in the autumn festival," she said with her hands on her hips. "*I* seduced a man!"

"Poor devil," replied Glasken, folding his arms and arching his eyebrows.

"I think he enjoyed it. I did."

"Is he still alive?"

She gave him a little push, and giggled.

Glasken suddenly remembered Jemli, and quickly glanced around. She was watching from beside a metalwork stall with large, unblinking, and worried eyes, her hands clasped together. He hurried back to her, reluctantly beckoning Theresla to follow.

"Frelle Theresla, this is my . . ." He took a deep breath and gathered Jemli close against him. "My mistress, Jemli."

Theresla noted the plain brown dretan and blackwood clogs, then looked up at Jemli's very nervous face. Theresla was not a short woman, but her forehead barely came up to Jemli's chin.

"Frelle Theresla is an editor, a woman of science, and, ah, quite a lot more besides," Glasken babbled desperately.

"So this is why you went back to the Alliance, Fras Orion. What a lovely, lovely figure you have, Frelle."

"Why, why thank you, Frelle Theresla," stammered Jemli, still nervous and overawed.

"Frelle Jemli has a husband—"

"And you stole her away? Were I a man I'd steal her too. Well, come on Jemli," she said, linking arms with her. "We'll soon have you out of those Rochester drabs and into Kalgoorlie fashions."

Glasken stood staring after them, then suddenly realized that he was gnawing the butt of his swagger stick. An hour later Theresla returned to join him beneath the awning of the vintner's tent. Jemli was still at the clothing run, as most of her purchases had to be altered or custom-sewn. He snapped his fingers for the serving maid and called, "Chilled half-jars, Mergeline white!" They poured the little jars into each other's goblets and toasted Theresla's future. Glasken allowed himself a smile.

"Your dalliance in Kalgoorlie . . . did it weaken your psychic ears?"

Theresla looked up from swirling her goblet. "Thanks indeed for your concern, Glasken. It changed me, it attuned me differently. We always need to change when we think we are perfect. You taught me that."

She flipped a copper coin into the air. It landed with a splash in Glasken's wine.

"Nice shot," he said without moving.

"Pure chance," she replied. "Look after Jemli, you never will get another chance like that."

"I can afford to." Glasken reached slowly for her hand and squeezed it. "Thank you for leading me to Ilyire's treasure cave."

Theresla snatched her hand back. Her face turned red, then white, then red again. "Consider your face slapped," she muttered.

"The hardest part was trusting you with my life, Frelle Abbess."

"Remind me to be less trustworthy in future, Fras Glasken."

The Rochester Overmagistrate banged his staff for order and laid it in the rack across his desk. He took his seat; then the Constable of the Court took the staff and banged it once more for the court to be seated. The Overmagistrate picked up his highlight scroll and adjusted his spectacles. Tarrin sat glumly on the back bench as the representative for the accused.

"Case of the morning: the Family of FUNCTION 22 against the Mayorate of Rochester, in the matter of false imprisonment for nine years in a device known as the Libris Calculor."

"Are the assailed's representatives present?" called the Constable after banging the staff on the floor twice. A man and two women stood up.

"Fal Levey, attorney for the assailant, present."

"Pakul ak-Temros, Rochester Association for Human Rights, present."

"Gemile Levey, wife of the imprisoned, Endarian Levey."

"Objection, Fras Overlord," exclaimed the man beside Tarrin. "The legal name for this man is FUNCTION 22, and this is a court of law."

"Endarian is my husband and not a number, you librarian bastard!" screamed Gemile Levey. "He was christened Endarian James Levey, and if you think—"

"Order! Order!" bellowed the Constable, pounding the floor with the Overmagistrate's staff until there was silence.

"Frelle Levey, another ourburst like that and I shall have you expelled from the court until such time as you are called as a witness," admonished the Overmagistrate. "As to the objection, overruled! This court is sitting to determine the legality of ah, the assailed's incarceration, and the name FUNCTION 22 is a product of that incarceration. Henceforth the prisoner will be referred to as Fras Endarian James Levey, which may be abbreviated to Fras Levey. Constable, proceed."

"Are the defendants present?" called the Constable.

Tarrin and his attorney stood.

"Tarrin Dargetty, Dragon Gold Librarian, the mayoral library of Libris in the Mayorate of Rochester. I am representing the mayorate on behalf of the Mayor and office of Highliber."

"Holward Derris, attorney for the defendant, being the Mayorate of Rochester."

"The court will be seated," the Constable concluded.

"He's not sympathetic," whispered Holward as Tarrin sat preparing himself for the ordeal ahead. "My objection should never have been overruled, the law is the word of the Mayor in decree until challenged and—"

"Order!" warned the Constable.

"Fras Overlord, I wish to call my first witness," said the attorney for the assailed. "Fras Tarrin Dargetty."

Tarrin and his attorney ordered emu steak and kidney pies for lunch as they sat in the taproom of the Drunken Wizard. Both were nursing a fist-shot of macadamia whisky.

"He should be free by now," grumbled Holward.

"Didn't even want to be free," muttered Tarrin. "Told me as much. He has an . . . understanding with MULTIPLIER 417—lovely woman."

"His wife's been sleeping with her attorney. The Scribe of the Court told me."

"Then why free FUNCTION 22, ah, what's his name again?"

"Fras Levey." Holward stared into his fist-shot whisky. "The attorney has now created a precedent by freeing a component who does not want to be freed. That means he can mount a class action to free all components who are not held in the Calculor against a specific felony or who have served out their original sentences. That will be a major professional victory, as well as giving him a big share of the damages that the Overmagistrate awards. Drink up, here come our pies."

Two large pies were placed before them, but Tarrin seemed not to notice.

Holward smiled up at the serving wench. "Thanks, Frelle, oh, and two dog-heads of ale at your convenience."

"We're doomed," said Tarrin morosely.

"Oh no, not at all. A class action will take time to assemble, and will apply only to Alliance citizens who were not felons. That means all Southmoors are excluded until the Emir signs an extradition treaty, and that's not happened in two centuries. The felons still serving their original sentences are also excluded."

"But the felons who have served out their original terms are not excluded, and if they go, then the heart of the Calculor will be cut out. Our most experienced components are those most likely to be released."

"Ah, but how many of those are of military service age? Even though it's peacetime you can still have a goodly number for five years of military service—fighting for the Mayor and mayorate by working in the Calculor. Now, should the Overmayor start a Class-A war, we would have the right to demand five years of military service from everyone, felon or nay."

"A Class-A war is an invasion," said Tarrin, shaking his head. "There are no states left that would contemplate that. The Southern Alliance has become too powerful."

"Well, whatever, but as you can see, there's no cause to give up hope. The Calculor may grow a little lean, but it's by no means broken."

"Overmayor Zarvora will be furious nevertheless."

Holward began to cut into his pie. "Fras Tarrin, the problem is that the Overmayor's power is being eroded by her own innovations. For example, the Mayors are learning to move troops by galley train and use the beamflash towers to their advantage. They have their own calculor teams, as they call them." He washed down his pie with a mouthful of newly arrived ale.

"I know what you mean, and it's another reason to drag us through the courts," said Tarrin as he at last took a bite from his pie. "The Libris Calculor is the greatest source of trained components in all of the known world. I have heard rumors that the Human Rights people are being funded by a secret group of mayors, all of whom are anxious to build up their own calculors with experienced people."

"But surely the Overmayor will not put up with that? What are her plans to fight the releases?"

"She says that she needs the Calculor and has instructed me to fight the releases all the way. Pah, she spends most of her time in Kalgoorlie and sends her data over the beamflash network. I feel used and abandoned, Fras. The Calculor is in decline and nobody seems to care but me."

The Bullfrog's Rest was in the railside quarter of Kalgoorlie. Denkar wandered about the tavern's rooftop beer garden as he awaited the landlord's arrival, sweltering in the white mask of an auditor. The shady rooftop garden was cultivated from both local and rare, imported plants, all strange and subtle. Goldentongue shrubs attracted swarms of bees, which provided a soothing yet busy background as mixed and complex as that of the city streets below. The landlord kept hives, and the big tavern was famous for its mead. Ferns grew in stone tubs amid the bushes in whitish limestone soil, and their fronds were soft and lurid green in the shade of the garden's follystones. Beneath these were subtle, spidery plants with flowers about the size of a small pea, but with no leaves. Bending close, Denkar noted that each of the flowers was fringed with a frill of red tendrils that ended in a sticky drop of fluid. One of the flowers had a tiny insect struggling in its grip.

"A sundew," announced a voice behind him.

"Yes, yes, a carnivorous plant," said Denkar, neither turning nor getting up. "I've seen them in illustrations."

"Where I was born they grow wild. Welcome to the Bullfrog's Rest, Fras

Auditor, home of the finest mead and chardontal white in Kalgoorlie.'' He gave
a formal bow. ''I'm Jack Orion.''

Denkar bowed, they shook hands, exchanged script cards, and rattled through
the Business Morality Oath together. Lackeys came running with wickerwork
chairs and deep cellar mead. Denkar sat back with a clipboard against his knee
and began to scribble with a charblack stylus.

''Now, how have I sinned?'' asked Glasken.

''There's nothing to fear, Fras Orion. So, you bought this tavern six weeks
ago?''

''That I did,'' replied Glasken, gazing at the bees at work in the golden
tongues. ''A fine investment—nay, more than an investment, a real home.''

''You seem rich, for someone so young.''

''I come from a good family.''

''You paid for this estate with gold bars. I see that you also have a fine
collection of Alspring gold coin, as well as personal and harness jewelry.''

''Ah, so you have heard of it too. It's been the pride of my family for
generations. Would you like to see some pieces?''

''Certainly, but later. Some weeks ago a diligent clerk in the Rochester treasury noticed an increase in unregistered gold bars in the intermayorate repository.
Fearing that they were adulterated, he had them examined. It was quite a desirable
sort of adulteration, as it happened. The gold in those bars turned out to be of an
even finer grade than either Alliance Standard or Kalgoorlie Benchmark.''

''Is this not a cause to celebrate?''

''Indeed, but on inspection of the standards and sample tables by the Calculor, the gold turned out to be identical to that of the gold coins originating in
the Alspring Cities.''

''Ah-ha, I know what you are going to say, but rest assured that I have not
been robbed, Fras Auditor. Not one gold coin, not a single ring of my collection
is missing.''

Denkar leaned back, holding his clipboard out at arm's length. He looked up
at his host's face again and nodded to himself. Glasken gently brushed away a
bee that had alighted on the rim of his polished silver goblet; then he took a sip
of mead. Denkar finally held up a sketch.

''Oh, very good!'' exclaimed Glasken. ''Such an excellent likeness of me—
although is my expression really so somber today?''

''Take it, it's yours.''

Denkar leaned forward and handed the sketch to him. After a moment Glasken's eyes bulged as if he were being strangled.

''By your expression, Fras, I gather that you have seen the caption at the
base.''

Glasken began to read again, but aloud this time. The words were slow and

deliberate: "COPY OF CALCULOR COMPONENT FILE SKETCH / COM-PONENT NUMBER 3084, FUNCTION. FEBRUARY 1700 GW. DRAWN BY THE HAND OF WILBUR TENTERFORTH, PERSONNEL LACKEY, GRADE 2."

"I have a very poor way with art, Fras Glasken. I merely added your month's growth of beard. Do not panic, all that I want is the answers to a few questions. I am Denkar Newfeld."

Glasken slowly lowered the sketch to his lap.

"If it's about the gold—" Glasken began, but Denkar shook his head and reached for his goblet of mead. He took a mouthful before replying.

"It seems that we have something in common, Fras Glasken," he said, rummaging in his sleeves. He held up a strip of punched tape. "You and your friend Nikalan were the first components to escape from the Calculor, while I am the first component ever to be legally discharged from its service."

"You do seem familiar," said Glasken, peering at him more closely now. "A senior FUNCTION, were you not?"

"I was FUNCTION 9 for nine years, two months, three weeks, six days, fourteen hours, and twelve minutes."

"And they let you go?"

"They did."

Glasken frowned doubtfully. "In my limited experience in the Calculor's ranks, Fras, the better that you performed, the more they wanted to keep you."

"In mine, too, but here I sit."

Glasken clasped his hands together and stared intently at Denkar. "What was demanded from you in return?"

"I was offered other work, which I accepted."

"To me it sounds more like you rogered some highly placed Dragon Librarian and pleased her mightily."

Denkar gazed at him steadily, his eyes unblinking.

"Fras Glasken, you have a grubby mind, but then the world is a rather grubby place. Now to business: services are required of you."

"Really? What manner of services?"

"The enhancement of explosives and some calculor work—as a regulator, not a component. Additionally, you are an escaped felon with a half-century of sentence outstanding."

"That's no worry, Kalgoorlie has no extradition agreement with the Southeast Alliance," said Glasken smugly.

"As of last night, wrong."

Glasken's smugness evaporated. "That's a worry."

"However, Overmayor Zarvora signed a provisional pardon for you last night."

"A pardon? The devil she did!" exclaimed Glasken, then his eyes narrowed. "Where's my copy?"

"Uh-uh, it will be given to you and registered with the Constables' Presidium once you sign her contract. The Overmayor needs experts in the chemistric of explosives, especially those who also understand the programming of calculors. At the contract's end you will be granted a full pardon."

"Can I have that in the contract?" asked Glasken eagerly.

"I . . . don't see why not."

When the constable of the watch arrived at the chapel of the Liberal Reformed Gentheists the priest was waiting by the door. He beckoned to the constable, then led him to the alleyway beside the chapel, where a large handcart was blocking the narrow gap entirely. There was a tarpaulin over the load, and the ties were sealed with red wax and an unfamiliar guild imprint.

"I found it after this morning's Call," said the priest. "The glazier was to repair a leadlight window beyond, and he couldn't get past with his ladder and kit."

"Aye, and the wheels be strapped as well," observed the constable, bending over with his hands on his knees.

"The alley is maintained by the parish," explained the priest. "Nobody but me can approve standing rights for carts, and I didn't approve this one."

The constable looked at the wax seals, lifted his hat, and scratched his head. "Don't know the guildhouse as uses these."

"They can be looked up in the register later. I just want it moved."

"Suppose I can impound it, but I'll have to go find hauliers."

"Pah, don't trouble yourself, I have two volunteers from our Youth League ready to move the thing. All we need is authority to move it."

"Aye, I'd say there's a case for moving."

The priest left, and presently two young men arrived. They unstrapped the wheels as the constable watched, making sure that they did not tamper with the load. Lifting the pushbeams, they strained to set the cart in motion.

A thin cord attached to a spoke tightened, pulling against a catch which in turn released a spring-loaded lever. The lever slipped free, ramming a flint against a striker and sending a shower of sparks into a pan of gunpowder beside a barrel. The ensuing blast was heard across the entire city.

The priest and glazier had been just around the corner of the alleyway and although thrown many yards they were not badly hurt. The wall of the chapel was blown in, bringing most of the roof down with it. The stables on the other side were totally demolished. Dust and fragments were still raining down as the priest got to his feet, his ears ringing. All around him were groaning, screaming shoppers, tradesmen, and merchants who had been hit by flying debris.

For the size of the blast it was amazing that only five had been killed. The constable, the two boys from the Youth League, a worshiper in the chapel, and a stablehand in the other building died, but more than sixty others were injured. Before the hour was out the synod of the Liberal Reformed Gentheists was blaming the blast on Mayor Bouros, while the local bishop held a service in the ruins and railed against machines and mechanisms of all kinds. Watching from a distance were two merchants from the mayorates to the west.

"A passionate speech, Fras Sondian," commented the taller of them, "but the blame is misplaced."

"That does not matter. The priest and glazier survived, and they know the cart was not there before this morning's Call. When the priest is fit to preach again you can be sure it will be against Call demons or whatever they call us here."

"They have no name for aviads in the western mayorates, Fras Sondian."

"Ah, but they will soon, and it will be an unpleasant name, too. Aviads are at a threshold, Raleion. We are more organized than ever before, but we need unity too. War with the humans will provide it."

Denkar and Glasken interrupted lunch upon hearing the blast. They watched the cloud of smoke and dust dispersing from the rooftop garden of the tavern. Glasken speculated that some militia's powder store had blown up. Jemli sent a servant after them with their goblets and another jar, then returned to the management of the tavern.

"Impressive Frelle you have there, Fras Glasken," Denkar remarked as they were descending to the master parlor. "By her accent, I'd say she is from the Eastern Highlands."

"That she is, we met on the train. She's quite presentable and charming until someone says 'librarian' or 'poet' in front of her—and she's a wonder with accounts."

"She hates librarians?"

"Aye, so don't let on that you are one. She has a tongue like hellfire. When I bought this place I flicked through the accounting papers and settled down to a drink with the vendor. Before I'd finished my pint—and I'm not a slow drinker—she's gone through all the columns in her head and uncovered six hundred Kalgoorlie royals worth of outstanding debts and more botched entries than a whorehouse gets on old folks' day. Well, you never heard anything like what followed! I got the place for twenty-nine hundred, and now I give her five percent clear for managing the books and minding the staff. So, what have you been about since you were FUNCTION 9?"

"Performing certain tasks on a new type of calculor."

Glasken shuddered, picked up the jar again, and discovered that it was

empty. He rang for another two jars. "I hope you're easy on the components."

"They don't complain. More recently I have been confronted with a certain Frelle Theresla: Dragon Gold, Edutor of the Chair of Call Theory at the University of Rochester, Personal Adviser to the Highliber Zarvora—and weirdo."

Glasken seemed to shrink a little into his chair. "Does she still eat grilled mice on toast?"

"When there is toast available. I was approached by her one morning at the Kalgoorlie mayoral palace. We had coffee in her rooms, during which she made her intentions toward me very plain. She is quite attractive and fascinating of course."

"Of course." Glasken allowed himself a smile.

"I pointed out that my wife, Overmayor Zarvora, was very dear to me, and that it would hardly be fair to cheat upon her."

"Very generous of—Hell and Greatwinter! You're the *Overmayor's* consort?" exclaimed Glasken, jolting bolt upright and spilling his newly arrived drink.

"Correct. I left for the University where I am developing . . . various things. Fourteen hours later I rolled home reeking of sweat and burned beeswax insulation, covered in grease and soot, and near-blinded by a migraine, only to be met by Zarvora and Theresla. Theresla had asked Zarvora for permission to become my invel-spouse. Zarvora had agreed to give up her right to invel-husbands if I would wed Theresla."

Glasken thought for a moment. Liberal Gentheism allowed multiple spouses, but only to one partner or the other. Zarvora would have given up her right to other husbands so that Theresla could marry into their partnership.

"Should I ask?" Glasken said with a shrug.

"Oh I agreed. I was almost surprised that they bothered to consult me. Two weeks later we had a full mayoral wedding: Theresla in white, Zarvora and I in gold."

"New-star-in-the-morning-sky symbolism. Very traditional."

Glasken closed his eyes and exhaled. A clock began to ring out the hour with cool, pure chimes.

"So, ah—look, did you actually roger her? That is, in the classic sense?"

"Well yes, as a matter of fact. There was one odd thing about it, though."

"Only one?"

"One in particular. Although she was consummate at little social niceties and the general banter that precedes the act of seduction, she was . . ."

"Was something of a virgin?"

Denkar smiled broadly. "I've never encountered any degree of virginity other than a hundred percent or nil, Fras John, but yes. Her behavior was strange in some ways, but perfectly civilized in others. Now Zarvora wants

me to go east and seek her out over some business that I cannot discuss with you.''

Denkar drained his goblet and placed it upside down on the tabletop in the Kalgoorlie gesture for farewell.

''I am sincerely delighted by this meeting,'' Glasken said as they stood up together.

''You have changed since you were 3084,'' Denkar said as he shook Glasken's hand. ''Thank you for your hospitality. May your tavern thrive.''

''May your components be ever sober, Fras.''

''And speaking of components, Fras Glasken, call in at the palace and ask for the Highliber tomorrow morning at the tenth hour, or you may find your name changed back to FUNCTION 3084.''

They shook hands, bowed, and made their way out into the street. Denkar mounted his horse and gestured to his escort to set off.

''Fortune be with you, Fras Glasken.''

''Fortune be with you too, Fras Denkar.''

To say that Glasken was apprehensive as a palace lackey showed him into Zarvora's meeting parlor would be like saying paraline rails are parallel.

''Fras Glasken, the very man I wanted to see,'' she said genially, ''but I am sure all the girls say that to you.''

A joke! Coming from Zarvora it seemed almost a contradiction in terms. Glasken tried to force a grin, but the contortion looked more like he was trying to swallow a hot pepper.

''A graduate in chemistric, with experience in the Libris Calculor. Fras Glasken, you are a rare combination and I need that exact combination just now. How would you like some months of contract work translating experiments with explosives into calculor input? I might offer, say, twenty gold royals per month.''

''Twenty-five,'' croaked Glasken in a desultory attempt to seem awkward.

''Done! Oh, and here's a pardon for hitting the Rector of your old university college with that bag of coins. There are still fifty-six years of your sentence outstanding on that conviction. So, you own a tavern and have an importing business. You can change it to Glasken Enterprises now.''

''I want to settle down and become established, Frelle. There's been too much running in my life. I need to feel wanted.''

''Wanted. Well as of now you are no longer wanted in every Constable's Watchhouse in the Southern Alliance, but doubtless you can live with that. I was impressed with that trick you used to escape my battle calculor. Persuading the Libris calculor to release you by tampering with the transmission codes was very clever. You will not try to feed any more creative data strings to the new calculor at the University, will you?''

"I am your loyal, obedient, and dedicated employee," declared Glasken with a bow.

"What of Lemorel?"

"I escaped her during a Neverlander attack. She probably died."

"Pity. She was brilliant, if twisted. And then?"

"I lived with the Kooree nomads for some months, then left them when I saw Baelsha. Big mistake."

"Where did you get the Alspring gold?"

"A chance find in the desert. I used it to buy my tavern."

"I'm surprised. I would have expected you to have spent it all on the greatest revel of the century."

"I *was* tempted, Overmayor, but revels have gotten me into any amount of trouble in the past. Besides, I fell in love—sort of—by accident."

"Fras Glasken, I know the feeling."

Denkar did not journey all the way from Kalgoorlie to Rochester, but left his galley train at the Bendigo Abandon. Disguising himself as a Gentheist pilgrim, he began a journey south, on foot. The Calldeath lands south of Rochester had been colonized by refugee aviads for a century, although less formal groups had lived there for much longer. Macedon was a town of about two thousand aviads, and had been built behind abandonstone walls on the slope of a lopsided mountain. It was surrounded by farmlands, and its principal buildings were the university and technologium, although the artisan quarter was growing rapidly.

Denkar noted everything with voracious fascination as the Deputy Mayor, Guidolov, took him on a tour.

"Our numbers are small here, Fras Denkar, so we use machines wherever we can. In this building here, for example, we have a steam engine fired by alcohol and crop tailings to mill grain for bread."

Denkar looked the building over, approving the clean, compact efficiency of the mill compared to the inefficiency of humans.

"Have you any problems with the religious aversion to steam power?"

"Fras, every aviad here would be killed by the humans for merely being immune to the Call, so we have no respect for their laws. We are a pious and religious community, however, and we follow the Gentheist principle that we should use no more than we can grow and that all should be in balance. Within that context, steam machines are allowed."

"What else is run by steam?"

"Water is pumped for irrigation, wood is cut in the sawmill, and there are two small mobile engines driven by steam traction that pull carts along the roads of the farm grid."

"Amazing. And you say there are other towns like this?"

The Deputy Mayor beamed with pride. "There are five more over a thousand, and another twenty settlements bigger than a hundred. We estimate twelve thousand aviads live in the Calldeath lands fringing the Southeast Alliance, and we have explorers extending our influence to the settlements in the north. You know about the exploration and colonies in the far west, I presume."

"Yes. The Overmayor transported two hundred of your people to the west in return for two steam engines and the labor to get her rockets out of that museum in the Perth Abandon."

"The Overmayor has been of great use to us. We modified our town charter to base the Council on a library structure, and are planning a beamflash network. Our weakness is that aviad children are affected by the Call from about two until they reach puberty. That means we can either keep them here as vegetables for their first twelve years, or we have to live in human lands in secret to bring up our children."

Later that day they took a ride on a steam tractor to the edge of an abandon that was being mined for building materials. There was a crew of ten using a steam crane and a steam crusher, and their output was that of a crew of hundreds of humans. They are building a whole new world, reflected Denkar proudly, and I am one of them.

"And farther down that path?" he asked, pointing south along a partly restored road.

"It leads to the salt water, the ocean, the sea, whatever name you like to use. That particular road leads to Phillip Bay, and beyond that is the limitless ocean."

The idea of virtually unlimited water both perplexed and allured Denkar. "Have you ever seen the Call creatures?" he asked.

The Deputy Mayor shook his head casually, and did not seem interested. "There is no clear and close vantage to watch from. We have seen animals and humans walk into the water and vanish. Sometimes their bodies are washed back ashore, dead. Occasionally we have seen dark fins and a splash."

"Do you ever follow them out with boats?"

"Not anymore. It was tried at the Gambier Abandon in 1617, and the two boats used just disappeared in a swirl of spray. Smashed planks bearing the marks of huge teeth were later washed ashore. Fifteen of our best edutors and warriors died that day, and we have always been too few in number to waste lives like that. One aviad is living on the shores of the Phillip Bay at present, though."

"Would she be a rather strange woman named Theresla? My invel-spouse?"

"Yes, and she had your genototem release signed by Pandoral the Gentheist Bishop, and the Highliber herself, of course."

"Genototem release? What—oh never mind. When can I be taken to her?"

"Your pardon, Fras, but I have nobody to spare at present. You must wait a week."

"A week! I'll find my own way."

"That is not possible, Fras. There are too few of us aviads. We cannot allow a single life to be risked in traveling the Calldeath lands alone."

"But Theresla—"

"Theresla is different. You are a gifted mathematician, you must be protected."

They returned to the town, where the sentries were told that Denkar was not permitted beyond the walls. Other than that, he was free. He explored the town. The architecture was not on a grand scale, except for one auditorium in the university that could accommodate a thousand people. The houses were a mixture of terraces with woodlace trim, decorator-artline bungalows, and functionalist revival cottages. At the center of the town, beside the university, was a little square shaded by gum trees. There was a scatter of cafés under canvas awnings in the dappled light. The incongruity of a cobbled square with outdoor cafés serving coffee and seedcakes in the middle of the Calldeath lands was not lost on Denkar. Student couples strolled hand in hand in the weak winter sunshine, or sat at tables gazing into each others' eyes, their cups and plates forgotten. Three youths sat at another table, gesturing first at the faint band of Mirrorsun in the blue sky, and then at a diagram that one of them had chalked on the wooden tabletop. It could easily have been Rochester or Oldenberg.

Denkar ordered a jar of beer beneath the awning of a small tavern, noting that the currency was Rochestrian royals, nobles, and coppers. Very soon he was surrounded by curious edutors and students. He had worked in the Calculor of Libris, after all. They were operating a primitive calculor in the university, but it had only sixty components and only ran twice a week in five-hour sessions. He did not have the heart to tell them about the new machine in Kalgoorlie. The senior edutor of Physistry took him to the university and showed him a Faraday cage whose floor was ten yards square, and which housed an electroforce laboratory. Denkar quickly recognized the equipment for a sparkflash transceiver, a simplified version of the Kalgoorlie design.

After an afternoon of being quizzed and questioned on calculor theory and architecture, Denkar made his way to the modest abandonstone cloister-plan house where Guidolov, his wife, Nayene, and their family lived. For all his frustration at being held there, Denkar certainly felt better for a meal—of roast emu steaks in orange sauce on a bed of rice and nuts, with a large bowl of Rochester salad in the center of the table. Their two teenage daughters were well-educated and friendly, having been brought up at a villa near Oldenberg. Their other three daughters were still at the same villa. The two teenagers had some odd conspiracy of nudges, giggles, and snickers that their parents either frowned at or tried to ignore. Nayene had the figure of comfortably approaching middle age, and was wearing a low-cut Northmoor print in a style that was currently all the rage in Kalgoorlie.

"A Kalgoorlie import, Frelle?" asked Denkar.

"Why thank you, Fras, but no, the pattern was sent along the beamflash in a numerical string. All that I did was select the cloth to suit it, and adjust some seams to my own figure."

"Tailored to perfection, Frelle," replied the weary Denkar, his manner friendly and gracious, but automatic.

"Now then, Fras, you have no silly qualms about genototem hospitality?" asked Guidolov genially. The two girls giggled.

"Fras Deputy Mayor, your hospitality is my rule."

"Splendid! Come now, young Frelles, off to your rooms and into your coding exercises—now! You will excuse us?"

Nayene took Denkar by the arm and led him from the table to his own room. It was a generously large room, tastefully furnished with a double bed at the center. He turned to see that Nayene had dropped her robes to stand before him wearing only kid-leather lounge boots. Denkar nearly choked on his own gasp of shock, took a step back, and fell over onto the bed. Nayene followed eagerly, and climbed onto him at once, pinning him to the softness of the bedcover.

"See there, your genototem release has been pinned above the bed and inspected by Bishop Pandoral herself," she said brightly. "We allow no lewdness in such intimate and sensitive matters, Fras Denkar, we are a very pious community."

Suddenly the precise meaning of genototem hospitality dawned upon Denkar. He spread his arms in disbelief as he lay there. Nayene took it as a gesture of welcome. She slid her arms beneath him and squeezed, then began to unfasten the ties of his robes, trews, and codpiece.

She sighed, her head against his chest. "Five daughters, Fras Denkar, but not a single son. I have great hopes for you, though. Your genototem trace is very promising."

It was all very logical, he realized as they climbed between the cool and scented sheets of the wide bed. A small population trying hard to expand, yet constantly in danger of inbreeding. Hence this scheme of systematic mixing of bloodlines, "genototem hospitality." If only Glasken had been an aviad, he thought.

Lemorel's strategy with the city of Alspring was tailored to suit the siege conditions that were being played out there. The city had sealed itself tightly, with stores laid in and well-trained warriors on guard, all armed with the finest weapons available. In one sense Lemorel was sweeping all before her, but in another she was very vulnerable. Time was not on her side, and she had little but conquest to offer her followers. If the conquests stopped, disillusion might set in.

True to her style, she had thought strategically. A year earlier she had ar-

ranged the purchase of five bombards from Inglewood, a mayorate so remote to her followers that none even knew that it existed. The barrels were shipped in cases marked as coffee to the paraline railside of Maralinga, then trekked by eight-camel sling across the deserts to a stronghold where they were mounted on gun carriages. Using contract artisans in several cities, including Alspring itself, she had secured a large supply of precisely wrought bombard balls, but until now the bombards themselves had only been used in test firings. The other cities had sent their armies out to meet her, as her forces always seemed weaker than was the case. Thus the finely made bombards were of no special advantage. Until now.

It was not enough to lay siege to Alspring, she had to break the defenses quickly. The walls were far thicker and better defended than those of any other Ghan city. They were encrusted with bombards, and these could belch copious grapeshot to shred all opposing infantry or cavalry. Against Alspring many other aspiring conquerors had been tested and found wanting. Lemorel had to defeat Alspring, or her aura with the Neverland nomads would begin to fade.

The first volley of shots caught the Alspring defenders totally by surprise. They were fired from twice the range of the bombards on the walls, and they smashed among the red and gold domes and spires of the palace. After that a pattern set in, with a shot every two minutes that was sure to land with mathematical precision. Only the palace and one section of wall were being targeted, and the bombardment continued through the night. Presently the palace became a shambles, while the famous checkerboard-pattern city walls were ragged and crumbling along the southwest face.

As it became harder for the defenders to mount their own bombards on the southwest wall, the Neverlanders moved in conventional bombards and began pounding the wall at close range. Casualties were heavy among the bombard crews on both sides, but the wall slowly crumbled and fell under the sustained battering. Within the city the word was spreading: Commander Lemorel was only interested in their Grand Makulad, she always spared the common people when she conquered a city. This was the opposite of the message that her spies and agents had spread in Glenellen, but then this was a full siege. The evidence was the smashed towers and domes of the palace, and the untouched temples, houses, and shops of everyone else. Siege engines began to appear in the distance, but the ground before the walls was trenched, mined, and littered with obstacles. All defending forces were concentrated near the disintegrating part of the wall in preparation for the attack to come.

"We shall lure them into our city like a mouse into the jaws of a cat!" the infuriated Grand Makulad of Alspring ranted to his Elders, senior officers, and other advisers. "She shattered my palace, she smashed my treasures. I want her in the stocks, stripped naked with a waterfall of pig dung and offal pouring over

her. We shall fight street by street, sponging up their lives in the ruins until her army is bled dry, then my elite Palace Lancers will ride out and crush those cowards that dared not venture inside.''

It was a fine, fighting speech, but the audience went its way in small groups, all animated with anxious discussion. Commander Lemorel showed mercy when a city surrendered in the face of overwhelming odds. Commander Lemorel was unspeakably cruel in the face of pointless resistance.

A gunshot echoed through the rubble-strewn corridors and halls of the palace. Someone shrieked inarticulately; then another shot barked out.

''Muskets!'' exclaimed the Overhand of Artillery. He and his adjunct rushed back into the Grand Makulad's throne room to find the monarch shot dead before his throne. Nearby was the Overhand of the Palace Lancers, lying dead with two flintlocks beside him. A scroll was tucked into the sash around his waist. The Overhand of Artillery read the words aloud:

''Commander Lemorel wants no life but that of the Grand Makulad. In the Name of the Deity I offer it to her, with mine, for the protection of the women and children of Alspring.''

By now other overhands, Elders, and advisers had rushed in, along with the throne-room guards.

''Where the hell were you and your men?'' the Overhand of Artillery demanded of the guards' captain.

''We were ordered from the room,'' he replied in a strong monotone.

''Ordered? By whom?''

''The Overhand of Lancers.''

''But you answer only to the Grand Makulad.''

''He gave his consent to it, sir.''

''His consent. I see. And you left the Grand Makulad with a man armed with two loaded pistols?''

''The pistols are the symbols of his protection for the Grand Makulad, sir.''

''Once again, I see. As the senior overhand I am the Grand Interim for now. Sub-Overhand Dalin, you can command the Palace Lancers. Stay with me. The rest of you, out!''

When they were gone the Overhand indicated the barrel of one of the flintlocks on the floor with the toe of his boot.

''What is that sticking to the barrel?'' he asked.

''A white down-feather, sir.''

''Yes. Do you think that he discharged that gun into the backside of a chicken and then forgot to clean it, or might someone else have fired it into a feather pillow to muffle the blast?''

''Sir?''

''Look there, a jagged, messy hole in his forehead and the back of his head

blown out, yet there are no powder burns around his face. Could he have shot himself from a mere handspan away?''

A Neverlander artillery shot whistled down in the distance, to land with a muffled boom followed by a clatter of heavy masonry.

''A conspiracy, sir?''

''Very probably. My guess is that somewhere nearby a cushion is being burned, and that two guards are frantically reloading their muskets. There were four shots, Dalin, but these two flintlocks were fired into a cushion after the Overhand and Grand Makulad were already dead. I thought at the time that I'd heard muskets, not pistols.''

The Overhand went to the fretwork shutters and pushed one open. Beyond the palace the city remained undamaged. Suddenly a bombard shot whistled in and they both recoiled and threw themselves to the lavish carpet as it impacted close by.

They picked themselves up and dusted plaster off their robes.

''The conspirators were right, Dalin,'' said the Overhand, ''whatever the morality of what they did. Run up the orange and white pennants for a truce and assemble a delegation to meet with Commander Lemorel. You will lead it, and you will surrender the city on my behalf.''

''Me, sir? A mere sub-overhand? Surely Commander Lemorel would be insulted if any less in stature than yourself were to go?''

''I want to remain here and insure that some hothead does not seize command and resume the siege. If Commander Lemorel is insulted, I offer my life in atonement. Unlike a few of the hypocrites in this place, I really am willing to offer my life to protect the innocent of this city. See to it.''

''Yes, sir, Overhand and Grand Interim.''

The Overhand turned away to gaze through the window over the city as Dalin began to walk away.

''And Dalin!''

''Sir?''

''Discreetly arrange a tragic accident for the throne-room captain and those six guards if you manage to survive the next couple of hours.''

''Sir. As good as done.''

Denkar's escape from Macedon went horribly wrong about fifteen miles from the walls. He had thought the huge lizard to be a log until it charged out at him from a collapsed and overgrown ruin in the abandon. Partly by reflex, mostly by panic, he fired both barrels of his Morelac 50-point into its mouth, and one of the lead balls tore through the great reptile's brain. He sought open ground, and kept his improvised lance across his knees as he sat reloading the pistol.

He was about to leave when Theresla seemed to materialize from the bushes at the edge of the clearing. She was panting heavily as she gazed intently at him.

In spite of her emu-leather bush jacket and lace-up boots, she still looked svelte and shapely.

"Denkar, you're here alone," she said in a disapproving tone. "Why did the Mayor of Macedon let you come here without an escort?"

"How about something like 'Welcome, Fras Invel-Spouse'?" he replied.

She halted a few paces away and regarded him with hands on hips. "Take it as said," she said impatiently. "Why did they allow you come here alone?"

Denkar remained seated. He was somewhat annoyed at his blunt reception. "They didn't. I was to wait with them for a week while some men could be freed from digging an irrigation canal, and soon that week stretched beyond a fortnight. In the meantime their edutors were anxious to get me involved in the development of their calculor, and as for my sleeping arrangements!"

"Ah yes, very . . . hospitable. Zarvora and I decided that you would have enough on your mind without . . . anticipating your reception at Macedon."

"Very considerate of you."

Someone in the early twenty-first century had built a very solid dwelling, even to the point of using steel beams and interlocking terra cotta tiles for the roof. It still provided shelter with a view after two thousand years, and Theresla had cleaned out the accumulated creepers and nests. Denkar was surprised at how neat and orderly the place was, given her behavior in human society.

"Vermin accumulate after a time," she explained. "Every month I seal the doors and windows and light a fire on the ground floor, using the branches of certain trees and bushes. I also move my bed around. I am nomadic within my own house."

He glanced about approvingly. The lines, space, and lighting were well evident, even after two millennia.

"A pleasant house, too."

"A house built of greed, Fras Invel-Spouse. Only four people lived here, yet it can hold thirty."

"Thirty! But four would be needed merely to maintain it."

"No, they had machines to do that. There are piles of overgrown rust and oxides that were once their vehicles, there is a tiled cistern that they appeared to use for swimming, and there may even be a flying machine behind the house. The building that sheltered it has collapsed and been overgrown by blackberry tangles." She went to the wide window and stood proudly framing herself against the scenery. "There are thousands of similar dwellings nearby, and more under the water."

They had a meal of nuts, raisins, and wild oranges on a balcony overlooking the bay. Theresla explained about her explorations and researches. Her estimate was that the Melbourne abandon had once housed three million people.

"That seems fanciful," he said, rubbing at his temples. "No city could sup-

port so many people in such a small area. The place should be covered in the remains of paralines and beamflash towers.''

A dirkfang cat jumped into his lap and began to purr. Theresla lay down on the rugs and cushions beside him and held up a complex lump of corrosion about the size of her hand.

''Remember that they could use electroforce devices like this might have been, and that they had personal carriages driven by steam and turbine cycle engines.''

''Three million people with their own steam tractors!'' he scoffed.

''Yes, and this city was no exception. It is hardly a surprise that so many of the surviving books speak of the air being rank with fumes. There is hardly any evidence of books, however. No bookcases in the houses, no neighborhood libraries, only one huge library in the central city area. I've checked it, but those books that survived the mold, insects, rats, and mice for two millennia have been taken by other aviads. It seems to have been more of a museum for books than a working library as we know them. I don't know what to make of this city, Denkar: such a huge, advanced yet illiterate society.''

''Not so illiterate as you may think.''

''How so?'' she asked, lying up against him with an arm draped over his chest.

He ran his fingers idly through her hair, straining to assemble complex thoughts into common language. ''I've done some experiments on that electroforce calculor that Zarvora and Bouros built at Kalgoorlie. I took a thousand words from a romantic novel and keyed them into what I have called the volatile memory, to be stored as positions of switches held either open or closed by electromagnetic relays. I could read the entire text back on the display.''

''As on paper tape with punched holes?''

''No, I designed a row of one hundred thin wheels on a common axle, each with the letters of the alphabet, numerals, and common punctuation painted on the rims. They are spun by gears connected to the calculor to present a line of text at a frame window, just like a line of text in a book or scroll. I read my thousand words of text back with no errors at all. Next I tried moving some words from one place to another, like letters in a printing press. That worked equally well.''

''An expensive way to store a page of words.''

''Indeed, but with a hundred years of development one may reduce such devices to the size of a small room and store thousands of whole books within them. When I switched off the electroforce current to the calculor, the switches were all reset to a zero representation and my page was lost. Think upon that.''

Denkar gingerly lifted the dirkfang cat and sat up to pour out some more of the soupy yet flavorsome tea that Theresla had brewed out of local herbs. The ceramic pot was a priceless Anglaic artifact that she had found somewhere, as

were the matching cups. His head was still pounding from being denied coffee for more than a day, and he attempted to use a Southmoor breathing technique that Ettenbar, the new System Controller of the main Kalgoorlie calculor, had taught him. The afternoon was becoming overcast, and a light wind had made the water of the bay choppy.

Theresla sipped quietly at her tea, her mind turning over possibilities. "You are saying that the Anglaic publishers put all their books into electroforce calculors," she said at last. "When the supply of electroforce stopped, the books were all lost."

"There is more to it than that, but—"

"A stupid idea, even *their* engineers must have been humble enough to accept that even the best machines have failures. Still . . . I have met a lot of stupid engineers since I came south from the Alspring cities—present company excepted. It would explain why books were already rare even before Greatwinter. Zarvora has told me of a legend that people actually mined a huge library in the Canberra Abandon for books to burn."

Denkar put his finger to her lips. "As I was trying to say, I think there was more to it than that. In another experiment I channeled my thousand words of magnetically held text onto a reel of paper tape."

"Pointless. You can read the symbols represented by the punched holes without a calculor."

"Yes, but the calculor can read it too, and present it back in a much more readable form than punched-hole code. Just imagine a vast library of paper tape reels connected to as many as a hundred calculors. If these calculors were connected by wires to a device in a house like this, then those living here could read whatever they wanted in that library without ever having to open a book or even walk out of the door."

Theresla was impressed by the idea. "Cumbersome . . . but it makes sense."

"It did until the anarchic wars of Greatwinter. Some mayorates must have built the Wanderers in order to cripple the electroforce libraries of their rivals."

"So their governments were based on libraries too, just as ours are now?"

"Undoubtedly. With the calculors gone, the books and documents were just too hard to read directly from paper tape. Chaos and anarchy followed. Without books their ideas and sciences quickly became distorted and went into decline. There must have been other factors as well, but that would account for the lack of books."

"But what of the religious proscription upon heat engines?"

"Just think: the furnaces of three million steam cars in a city such as this would produce a lot of heat. Perhaps the combined steam cars of the whole world were heating and poisoning the air. I hope it is not true, for I have a weakness for engines."

Some time later the sun set amid a scatter of clouds with a slash of Mirrorsun

band across its disk. Theresla and Denkar were in each other's arms beneath a blanket, already settled down for the night.

The following morning Theresla took her visitor down to the new foreshore, where a chill steady wind was driving heavy waves onto a jumble of sand, rubble, and ruined buildings. They had taken a small telescope with them.

"Be careful of any concealment like those walls over to the left," she advised him. "Large, amphibious carnivores that the ancients called sealions keep up a sort of patrol here. They are clumsy but powerful, and the cetezoid Call creatures use them as we use guard dogs."

Denkar was peering out to sea through the telescope. "I see a dark, sleek body from time to time, and sometimes a jet of water."

"They are the dolphins that have this bay as their territory. They generate what is known as the Rochester south Callsweep. They have some sympathy for us land animals, and dislike the sealions."

"They lure thousands to their death, yet they have sympathy for us?"

"Be grateful, Fras Denkar. They deliberately start their Callsweep at Elmore instead of farther north. That is why Rochester and Oldenberg never feel the Call."

He looked around at her, astonished. "By heaven—the great mystery of two thousand years, yet you toss it to me as casually as a bone to a dog?"

"Your explanation of why books were in decline before Greatwinter was no less wondrous to me, my clever and resourceful lover."

"So you can communicate with these, ah, dolphins?"

"I have learned to, yes. One needs a very nonhuman attitude, but it can be done by someone like . . . me." She snapped her teeth at him, but he did not even flinch. "I have studied the dolphins near the Perth Abandon as well, and the situation with them is the same. They are forced to cast the Call by other, larger creatures. Those are called cetezoids, and they appeared in the oceans about the time of Greatwinter. The dolphins are treated like tenant shepherds or peasants, and my Bay Dolphins resent it. At the edge of the Nullarbor Plain the cetezoids themselves make the Call. It is a special place where they give birth."

"What do the Bay Dolphins think of us aviads?"

"They are fascinated, they want to know more. I am actually negotiating the casting of a null zone over Macedon, so that aviad children can be brought up free from the dangers of contact with humans. See that large lump in the seaweed across there? Watch."

Theresla made a series of hissing, sibilant sounds and Denkar thought that he heard something pattering through the bushes. Presently a small, tabby form emerged from nearby cover, crawling with its belly against the ground, stalking toward the dark shape in the seaweed. The cat sprang and sank its long fangs

into the blubber of the sealion's back. There was a roar that sounded more like outrage than pain, and the cat bounded away as the sealion reared up. With a surly glance at the two aviads it turned to shuffle away toward the water.

"It was stalking us," Theresla explained.

"And the cats obey you?"

"Well . . . I'm their leader, one might say."

They walked down to the water's edge. Denkar splashed his hand in it and tasted salt. He shivered in the stiff wind.

"Are we going to meet your Bay Dolphins?"

"Not today. They are easily confused and worried by new sounds, scents, and tastes. Their speech is all clicks, whistles, touches, and postures. The cetezoids use other means to communicate. I have devised other means to study the Call and overhear their thoughts. They speak with thought exchange, and that is why we use the older dolphin language here: we cannot be overheard. The cetezoids do not approve of fraternization."

"Cetezoids. Where does the word come from?"

"It was a thought-form that I learned in my first attempt to eavesdrop at the Nullarbor cliffs. It is their name for themselves, but it also seems to be an old human word."

13 CHAOS

Glasken entered the control room of the Kalgoorlie calculor and received two surprises. Firstly, it was no more than a medium-sized room cluttered with the familiar half-harpsichord input keyboards, some very functional paper tape engines for output, and a wall full of gearwheel registers. Only a half dozen operators were on duty, chatting and drinking the bitter local coffee sweetened with banksia honey. The second surprise was the System Controller.

"Fras—ah, Fras . . . FUNCTION 795?" stammered Glasken from the doorway. "No, 797, that was it."

The System Controller left his work desk and came across to greet him. "Ah, Fras FUNCTION 3084, it is indeed a pleasure to meet with you again, and praise be to Allah that your life was spared over these years past. But your name: you are Fras John Balmak Glasken now, the great Frelle Overmayor sent me a personal communication that you would be arriving."

"Yes, but FUNCTION—no, please, what is your real name?"

"Ettenbar Alroymeril, good Fras. Ettenbar to my friends. Ha-ha, Fras Glas-

ken, I have not yet given up my hope of converting you to the path of Islam, or have you already forgotten?''

Glasken thought of his years in Baelsha and shuddered at the prospect of yet another future without alcohol.

''Well, that could be harder now. I have spent five years as a novice in a strict Christian monastery.''

''Fras Glasken! You?''

''Brother Glasken, actually, but Fras is good enough between friends.''

''But you were born a Gentheist.''

''Correct, but I was raised as a Christian, and that was sufficient for Baelsha.''

''Well then, Fras, what are you doing here?''

''My last and most difficult test, Fras Ettenbar. I must spend a year abroad in the world, alone while I fight the temptations of the devil. Greed, the drink, and the lovely form of the female body combined with the enchanting female face anticipating the feel of female skin against my own while—''

''No, no, Fras Glasken, please do not torture yourself to demonstrate your great faith.''

Glasken dropped his pack to the floor, then stretched the stiffness out of his shoulders as he looked around.

''So where's this calculor, then? In the basement?''

''Not so, Fras, it lies a full half mile below us in ancient tunnels.''

''In tunnels! Poor devils, I say. I may be free, but I'll always feel sympathy for the components.''

''Ah, but these are happy components,'' said Ettenbar slyly. ''Their work is faster than that of the Libris machine, even though they do not have the same FUNCTION versatility as in Libris.''

Glasken stared at him intently. ''Is this a test of intelligence, and am I failing?''

''No, Fras, but there are certain matters about its architecture that I may not divulge to you.'' Ettenbar took him by the arm and whispered conspiratorially in his ear. ''It only has one processor, but makes no errors at all.''

''The devil you say! Only one processor! Hi then, are there any pretty components or regulators?''

''For shame, Fras, and from you who aspire to the clergy!''

Glasken quickly settled into his duties of converting chemical test data into optimization-curve programs for use in the underground calculor. He, like everyone else on the project, assumed that Zarvora was designing new weaponry for the Mayor of Kalgoorlie. He was surprised at the power of the explosives, as well as their instability. After nearly blowing his foot off with a single drop of liquid

he decided to leave the mixing of glycerine and concentrated acids to whoever else was foolish enough to volunteer.

The rocketry tests were done on the dry bed of Lake Cowan, generally with rockets no more than a yard in length. There were several impressive explosions, and several more rocket flights where the little missiles flew right out of sight and could not be found again. All the while Glasken carefully invested in the property market of Kalgoorlie, maintained his liaison with Jemli, and paid an occasional visit to the Mayor's sister. Life was becoming comfortable and prosperous, yet there were some habits that never left him.

He trained at the martial-arts exercises he had learnt at Baelsha for two hours every day without fail, and the sight of a monk of any denomination or creed would make him duck for cover. Whenever Calls swept over Kalgoorlie he practiced balancing the allure against his self-discipline. In all of the world Glasken was the only human who could maintain even limited movement and control when the Call swept over him, and the talent was growing all the time.

Living up to her reputation, Lemorel taxed Alspring heavily in terms of wealth, weapons, livestock, and recruits, but there were no atrocities that could not be attributed to criminals taking advantage of the disruption. She was now the undisputed ruler of the entire center of the vast continent.

As an exercise in logistics, she soon launched what she termed a thunderbolt strike to the north, at the Carpentarian cities. Rather than following tradition, with all supplies carried on the attack camels, the lancers were backed up by armed supply caravans that stood well back from the fighting. Several Carpentarian patrols were wiped out or captured; then a regional city was captured within four days. The shock caused the other cities to seal themselves into siege law, leaving the countryside, roads, farms, and canals in the hands of Lemorel's invaders. Each city was isolated, then led to believe that all the others had fallen. Mere brigades of lancers gathered groups of tens of thousands of Carpentarian peasants near the besieged cities, giving the impression of enormous armies. Surrenders were generally swift, and within three months every city was under Lemorel's administration. A population of 900,000, which was not even registered on the Libris Calculor's data cards, had been subdued at the cost of 860 lives.

To the south of Alspring was a gap in a rocky ridge known as Call Funnel, where a mercy wall had been built to save people in the grip of the Call from wandering south into the desert. At the center of the curved wall was a stone speakers' platform which was used for religious orations, reedpipe concerts, military reviews, and public executions. It was known as the Red Stage, both for the executions held there and for the blood-red stone from which it had been cut.

Lemorel strode the Red Stage alone, wearing robes of red ochre that were

tied and bound to make her look as small and sharp as possible. She had selected her attire to seem both small and in need of protection, yet hard, sharp, and unkillable, like a saber ant. The veil below her eyes was of such a thin gauze that her face was quite distinct to those standing close by, but it allowed her voice to carry farther than the more mundane type. The nine thousand in her audience were the elite lancers and officers of her army.

She started by congratulating them on conquering all of the Alspring cities in the six years since she had led her first band of Neverlander freebooters into the battle, then went on to rant against the Overmayor in the distant south. They were cheering spontaneously by the time she told them that they were all united as Alspring Ghans now, led by the Neverlanders. She reminded them that talk of other groupings was treason. To become an officer was to become a Neverlander, and to become a Neverlander was the highest honor of all.

"I once told you that the Center would tremble at your name, and now it is true. I once told you that you would rule the cities that treated you with contempt, and now it is true. I once told you that nations would surrender at the mere dust of your approach, and now it is true."

It was several minutes before the cheering, shouting, and discharging of muskets had subsided. Lemorel was patient; she was happy to see them exuberant. They had just won an exhausting race, but they were about to be told that they had to run several times farther.

"Now you are mighty. Now you are rich. Now each of you has many invel-wives to protect and you are all blessed in the sight of the Deity."

She paused for emphasis. Her entire appeal to them had been based on headlong and unstoppable expansion, and not one expected that they would be told to go home and tend their newfound prosperity in peace.

"Now I tell you that every overhand will soon be a prince. Every officer will be an overhand. Every lancer will be rich enough to live in a mansion and own a hundred camels. This very day I had word from my envoys that many cities and mayorates to the southeast are begging to be our clients so that together we may subdue the sprawling lands beyond the red and rocky deserts, lands where the water never dries up and the grass is green all the year. Neverlanders, nomad lancers that are my mighty and invincible right hand, this day I shall begin to muster an army of a quarter of a million to sweep south—"

The sheer scope of the adventure raised such euphoria that the rest of her oration was lost in deafening cheers and commotion.

That afternoon Lemorel met with Overhand-in-Chief Baragania and the four logistics overhands who managed the care, feeding, supply and transport of her troops. Scribes had already produced renderings of the routes south from the caravan maps, and details of states beyond the deserts had been culled from maps smuggled north in bags of coffee.

"This is all soft, undefended land," she explained in a hoarse voice as her fingers brushed across the names of states that few of them had known existed until recently. "They rely on the desert to keep them safe, yet the desert can be as fickle and unfaithful as a Rochestrian suitor. This land can be crossed by an army of lancers, men able to live in the saddle, carrying all that they need to survive on a minimal number of spare camels. Our spearhead will be camel lancers, but horses will soon be provided by the Southmoors. Large herds are being moved to the northwest of the of the Balranald Emirate, by secret agreement. We shall get them here, north of the Barrier Grasslands."

"And cities, great lady? Soft, rich cities like the great explorer Kharek promised to us?" asked a logistics overhand.

"Rich, lazy cities, with no skill in our type of war."

"But they have powerful machines and deadly weapons, Commander Lemorel," Baragania warned.

"Their machines are easily bypassed, or even turned to our use. We shall use their wind trains and beamflash towers, just as we have built a superior calculor. As for their weapons, ours are better. We have camels that carry lancers, water, and supplies faster than an army can march, and our long and secret preparations will be a knife in their back."

With a nod of heads the logistics overhands indicated that they were satisfied by her explanation. The discussion moved on to specific invasion scenarios, as modeled by the Glenellen Calculor. The figures were encouraging, and the group became eager. When they had finally gone, Lemorel sat alone with Baragania, who was one of the very few that she treated as anything like a peer.

"How is Nikalan?" he asked as Lemorel rolled up her maps.

"Improving, but still little more than a shell," she said after a moment, as if she had been struggling to recall a distant memory. "The finest physicians in Alspring agree that he has been allowed to do nothing but work on Glenellen's calculors for far too long. When Nikalan was wandering free with—" She exhaled, then inhaled again. "—with Glasken through the deserts to the Fostoria Oasis, he was forced to live a varied existence and his mind was slowly healing. He had lost a great love, and the trauma had unhinged his mind. When made to do nothing else but calculor work, his mind retreated again into a smooth, pure shell and he slipped further away from our world."

Baragania watched her closely, noting that she now spoke more openly about Nikalan. Perhaps her own heart is healing itself? he wondered.

"And how are you, Commander?" he asked. "You came to our lands to rescue him, you conquered us during that rescue, then you found that he lives as if dead. This is the day of your greatest triumph, but are you happy?"

"I am happy," she said after a pause to think the question through. "Could you imagine it, but one physician attending him employed a harlot who is especially good with very aged clients," she said, then giggled. "The woman ac-

tually coaxed a response from him. No less than three times, I have been assured. She calls him a sweet little boy, even though he is about thirty-five. He can again cut his own bread and pour juice for himself . . . yes, the repairs to his mind are proceeding apace.''

"That is hardly a life.''

She dropped her gaze, then looked up at him again. There was still a measure of pain in her eyes.

''I know, but can you suggest anything better? Baragania, he was the goal that set me on the road, but now that I have him I find that the road is more important. Nikalan was like a finely bred racing camel: superbly suited to a very specific course, but hopeless for use elsewhere. I bumped him once, and he fell to the ground and shattered. Had it not been me, it would have been someone else.''

''But what drives you now, Commander? Why, in the moment of your greatest triumph, are you not at the celebration?''

''Why, you ask? Because there is work to do, preparing the strike south. The Overmayor is a fool. She built her entire power base on calculors and some long, frail networks of paralines and beamflash towers. If I cut her precious infrastructures at strategic points, I can seize two-thirds of the continent in less than a year. It is like when I spied upon you and your Glenellen Calculor, many battles ago. You were so very vulnerable, I simply could not wait to engage you, lest someone else realize how very easily you could be defeated.

''My agents have organized joint operations with the Southmoors and have infiltrated the beamflash and paraline networks. I have even been chipping away at the mightly Libris Calculor itself by financing civil actions to free its components. In fundamentalist Gentheist circles my people have been dropping hints about steam power being used in Kalgoorlie. Baragania, what does all this suggest to you?''

Months of campaigning with Lemorel had taught him to think as she did when the occasion required it. ''The war with the Southeast and Woomera has already begun, but in a subtle way,'' he speculated.

''Precisely, superbly observed and reasoned, my friend. The war has begun. I have insured that every single merchant who travels to Maralinga is a trusted agent. Those same agents have been negotiating right-of-way across Kooree lands for my armies as well. Add all of that activity together, and it becomes a highly noticeable operation. All that it will take to alert the Overmayor is a blunder or two, an accident, or even a traitor's word. We must move now. If we do not take our enemies by surprise, they will be far too strong for us.''

The first of Zarvora's ancient rockets left Kalgoorlie amid a noisy festival in honor of the glory of technology. The first stage was firmly bolted to a flatbed

truck and painted a bright green with red bands. Two galley engines pulled the flatbed and its attendant cars, while another five carried relief crews and the support equipment. It had been arranged that Denkar would stay in Kalgoorlie and provide calculor backup over the beamflash line as Zarvora required it. On the paraline platform Glasken was saying goodbye to Jemli, who was by now his business partner.

"When the Golden Jar comes up, begin the bidding at a thousand royals."

"A thousand! That's too much."

"But don't go over fourteen hundred without asking me."

"But you will be in Woomera, Glassy."

"Use the beamflash."

"The beamflash? It's a royal per thousand words!"

"A royal, be buggered. Hey there, sonny, catch."

"Glassy! That was a gold royal."

"You don't make royals by skimping on coppers, you're too much of an accountant, Jemmy. Besides, I know about a few embarrassing matters that I can threaten to reveal if I have to. Beamflash me, all right?"

Zarvora had been standing nearby with the galley engine's captain, checking the freight lists and timetables. Presently she walked along to the door of her personal carriage, where Denkar stood gazing at Glasken farewelling Jemli.

"Don't they look the sweetest pair of lovers you ever saw?" he remarked.

"Apparently she has a tongue like a machine-crossbow," replied Zarvora doubtfully.

"Apparently she never flays Glasken with it."

"I overheard him trying to persuade her to have an affair with Ilyire while he is away."

"What?"

"It makes sense. Ilyire is one of Glasken's . . . vassals, if I can use the term so loosely. Glasken probably feels he has control over whatever she gets up to while he is away. She is ambitious, Den. Although she professes hatred for librarians, she has been simpering about with the minor nobility at court and going out of her way to show off the results of her elocution lessons. Soon she will have a degree as well. Will she still want Glasken once she no longer needs him?"

"Glasken is Glasken, he will never be short of women," replied Denkar, but now he was frowning.

"Really? All his life he has left a trail of Frelles with the breath knocked out of them and their skirts about their ears, yet look at him now."

"Without Glasken you'd have died in that explosion at the test range, like those five engineers. It left his left ear and back quite a mess."

"I know. He saved my life so now I worry about him."

Mayor Bouros' personal band began to play as the trains were made ready to go. Denkar and Zarvora touched foreheads in farewell.

"Why Woomera?" Denkar asked yet again, shouting above the cheering and music.

"I am unsure myself," Zarvora replied. "The ancients also used the Woomera site to launch rockets into space, so they may have known something about the location that we cannot even guess at."

The train moved out of the railside slowly and smoothly amid showers of petals and streamers, but the tumult died away rapidly once they were into the suburbs of the great inland city. Ettenbar was with Zarvora in the mayoral coach, finalizing arrangements for returning data to the electroforce calculor via beam-flash.

"These galley engines are an expensive way to move freight, Frelle Over-mayor," he said as he watched the houses give way to fields and grazing cattle on group tethers.

"The rocket has to be launched from a precise place at a precise time, little worrier. Expense is no object."

"I could help better if I understood, exalted Frelle. If I understood, I would give my life to insure that your results were satisfactory."

"And that is one of the reasons why I am telling you nothing. If you do not know what results I hope to get, you cannot bend the actual results to please me."

Ettenbar laughed and waggled his finger. "Very cunning, exalted Frelle, but shame upon your suspicious nature."

She pulled at a green tassel that hung from the ceiling, then spread diagrams of a launching gantry on the folding table. Moments later there was a scream and a slap just outside the door; then Glasken entered rubbing his cheek.

"I swear, the train lurched just as I walked past her—"

"Come in, Glasken, and sit down," said Zarvora. "In a week we shall be in Woomera, and from there the rocket stages and support equipment will be taken by mule cart to where the launching gantry has been assembled. During the unloading and mule cart ride the rockets will be your responsibility. Guard them as you would guard your life, guard them as you would guard your testicles—"

"—for the latter will surely be forfeit if there is any sort of accident," said Glasken in quite a good parody of her tone and accent.

Zarvora looked up and stared at him for a moment, neither smiling nor frowning. "Fras Glasken, I think that we are beyond threats of that sort by now. I would have said please if you had let me finish."

"Your pardon, Frelle Overmayor. Where will you be?"

"I shall ride ahead and insure that the gantry and other equipment is prepared

for the rocket's arrival. I shall be in charge of its assembly, arming, and launching. This is the most difficult and ambitious endeavor since the fall of the Anglaic civilization, Fras Glasken, and it is a thousand times more important than the Calculor of Libris.''

It was long after sunset, and the plains to the northwest of Woomera were illuminated by the glow of that part of the Mirrorsun band opposite the sun. This time the Mirrorsun glow was from sixteen bright points arranged in a square of twelve enclosing a square of four. It was a most intriguing spectacle, yet this night's display, like all the others, had no explanation. Many edutors had written erudite papers on the changing Mirrorsun configurations, but all remained pure speculation.

Lamps outlined a structure that rose from the dimly illuminated plain like a huge weapon, and yet for all its size it seemed insignificant against the vastness of Mirrorsun in the sky above. Lanterns glowed and moved amid shadowed woodwork structures, indicating dozens of people hard at work. A green flare arched up into the sky and began to fall.

The ancient rocket ignited with a howling roar, and it shot up through the framework of the launching gantry like a thunderbolt out of a giant crossbow. It flew free from the apex rails and the glow of the brilliant gleam of its exhaust jet quickly dwindled as it ascended, leaving dark, dispersing exhausts to occlude the stars. Zarvora and her engineers and technicians watched together, raising their telescopes as the glow faded. When the rocket was barely a speck in the sky, the first stage burned out and separated and the second stage ignited. Presently the rocket was nothing more than a point of glow. There was a slight break as the second stage burned out and the third ignited.

"It looks good, but it is out of our hands," said Zarvora to the sky.

She turned to the horizon but did not use her telescope. The Rangemaster continued to watch its progress through his own device, calling the reports out as he was given them.

"Fourth-stage ignition reported from the downrange telescopes. The rocket is reported as little more than a moving star. It's too high to track reliably."

Zarvora released her breath explosively. "Give the order 'Transmit,' to the four beamflash towers," she ordered, and added more softly: "Let us draw attention to ourselves."

The Rangemaster gestured to the nearby beamflash crew, who ignited a flare in the transmission rig and began to send out the enigmatic order.

"With respect, Overmayor, but whose attention do we wish to draw?"

"I do not know, Fras Rangemaster, but should my electroforce beacon devices in those beamflash towers begin to smoke and melt, we shall have been successful."

"And the rocket, Overmayor?"

"A complex and desperate gamble, Fras Rangemaster."

"And if it fails?"

"We shall return here in a month or so and try again." She lifted her telescope to her eye again, and focused toward the southern horizon. "Ah there, a signal from beamflash tower South," she said as she gazed through the eyepiece. " 'TRANSMITTER COILS BURNED THROUGH HOUSING AND MELTED.' "

"Overmayor, beamflash West—"

"Is reporting the same thing?"

"Yes."

"Then a Wanderer is interested in what we are doing. Let us hope that it is also . . . enthusiastic. Too enthusiastic."

High above the atmosphere the fifth stage of the rocket flew smoothly along its trajectory. When its fuel had been exhausted a fuse had burned through a tether and released a timer that ticked out the seconds. Hundreds of miles away in space, an ancient orbital fortress detected radio emissions on the ground and shot EMP bursts down until all four sources had been silenced. There had been more than one source, there might be more remaining, its AI command module decided. It remained on alert.

The timer in the rocket's payload engaged the first setting, and a circuit closed. DIT DIT—DIT DIT. The circuit opened again. The transmission had taken less than two seconds. The orbital fortress had not fired, but it tracked the fifth stage as it moved along its ballistic curve. It had transmitted for a moment, and the fortress' control logic had tagged it as suspicious. DIT DIT—DIT DIT— DIT DIT, the signal commenced again, and the fortress spat a pulse adequate to silence it. A fuse burst, the timer ticked on, then the little radio transmitter began again with a new, heavier fuse.

The fortress spat another EMP, but the coils of the transmitter in the rocket were built to withstand a moderate pulse and the DIT DIT continued. Again the fortress fired at the tiny fifth stage, this time a sustained pulse. The circuit finally melted under the load and was silent, yet the fortress continued to follow it with its beam of electromagnetic energy. Zarvora's rocket drew the beam across the limitless backdrop of space . . . until it slashed across the band of the nanotech shield that orbited thousands of miles farther out. Circuits melted and died in their trillions, and the ribbon was cut right through. Each tiny slab of Mirrorsun's fabric was a separate, versatile machine, with a small amount of onboard intelligence and powered by solar radiation. The sum of all the parts was sentient.

The AI command of the fortress traced through paths of logic not run for millennia, then reached a conclusion. A radio source traveling above the atmo-

sphere had resisted EMP attack for an unusual period. It might still be live. A railgun swung around and received its programming, then spat a cloud of alloy spheres on an intercepting trajectory with the fifth stage. Seconds ticked into minutes. The last stage of Zarvora's rocket was pulverized under a hail of metal that then plunged into the upper atmosphere and streaked into trails of glowing ions.

The orbital fortress moved on and vanished over the horizon as the fragments of the rocket fell into the atmosphere and burned. The fortress noted the disruption in the Mirrorsun band, but continued to ignore the glow from its electroforce activity, as it always had. Nothing like it was in the ancient mission parameters, and it had not shown any sign of hostility. Each of the old weapons platforms classified Mirrorsun as an unidentifiable but harmless natural phenomenon.

On the ground there were cheers in the Woomera observatory as the monitors observed the first signs of the rent in the band. The Rangemaster congratulated Zarvora on ending Greatwinter's second coming.

"You reached out and slew the gods themselves," he declared grandly, for he had been in the student theater ensemble at Woomera University.

Zarvora was pensive as she looked through the eyepiece of her telescope. "Slew it, Fras Rangemaster? I wonder. But perchance I merely annoyed it a great deal."

The Rangemaster put his hands on his hips. "Overmayor, you cut the band."

"It may recover. The question is one of whether it takes centuries, decades, or merely years."

"So you will launch the second rocket?"

"I shall keep it ready."

Zarvora inspected the initial measurements of the flight, then handed them to Darien to take back to the beamflash tower in Woomera to transmit west to Kalgoorlie. The hardcopy accounts would follow on the paraline, but they were only for verification, and the archives.

High above the Earth, the band's collective consciousness enhanced itself into a neural network to deal with the rent in its body. Over the days that followed, meteor damage lines formed out of chains of nanocells, then whiplashed across the gap to join the two ends and draw them back together. By that time the gap was thousands of miles across, but six weeks after the breach the band was whole again. The network now turned its attention to the cause of the trauma that had cost it so dearly in energy and resources. Slowly, ominously, the band began to restructure itself.

Zarvora observed the activity with initial dismay, then she noted that the band was putting itself through strange and unprecedented configurations. It was

seeming to experiment with localized concaves in its greater curve, and the localized concaves were focused on the Wanderers. Zarvora knew that she had failed in her attempt to cripple Mirrorsun for at least a few decades, but she dared to hope that something even better might come from her ambitious and desperate project. She decided that it might be worth attempting to antagonize Mirrorsun just a little more.

Glasken had learned to travel light during his many journeys. Thus when called upon to travel with the Highliber's train, he packed a change of clothing, his undercottons, a swagger stick and cheap Gilmey 40-bore, his seal, and some money. He reasoned from past experience that if he was to be robbed, swindled, or otherwise set upon there was little point in taking anything of value.

"I find that possessions travel better than I do," he explained to Ettenbar as he poured wax into the seal countersinks of a wooden crate and pressed his seal ring down hard. Within were calibrated circuits that had been damaged by the electromagnetic pulses from space.

"Perhaps bags and trunks do not have enraged husbands, fathers, and Constable's Runners in pursuit of them," Ettenbar suggested.

"Very funny. Throw me that strap. There, all sealed for the customs bald heads at Coonana to see."

"What is your design's meaning, worthy Fras?" asked Ettenbar as he helped. "The barrel and sickle framed by leaves?"

"The Kalgoorlie Guild of Master Vintners."

"I did not know that you are a master vintner."

"I'm not. That cost me five hundred gold royals. Look upon it as patronage. I may not be a master of the guild, but I *employ* two masters to tend my investments."

"Fras, your logic is convoluted indeed."

For Glasken it had been a quiet trip—it was free of people trying to abduct, murder, torture, enslave, or imprison him. Much to his surprise the Highliber had granted him the temporary rank of a Dragon Blue Librarian. He did not mention it in his beamflash mail and letters to Jemli.

"Another rocket due in a week," he said to Ettenbar as he snapped his fingers for a waiter in the refectory. "Two weeks more and the third rocket arrives, and then I'm free to drink, sing, and get my face slapped by nonlibrarians. Ah, waiter! Um, plistebi grep enfola, bieratel, salavou kremti, eti—Gah, how does one say 'Islamic menu' in Woomeran?"

"Viadatem Islam, good Fras," responded the waiter.

"Why the hell didn't you say you spoke Austaric? Lucky for you my Frelle isn't here. Now, a pie, beer, and salad for me, and your Islamic menu for my friend here."

The waiter scribbled the order on his slate and hurried away.

"Well, Fras, I suspect that my own days tending the calculors of the Highliber are over as well," Ettenbar confided as they sat waiting. "Now that this glorious project with the rockets is close to completion, my intent is to return to the Southmoor province of my birth and design a calculor for the university."

"So what about women?"

"Ah-ha-ha, Fras, you think that I am all working and no passions, but you are wrong. I have been in discreet contact with my family and . . . there is talk of an arrangement with a girl who would be a highly suitable match."

"An arranged marriage?"

"A suitable marriage."

"You're mad."

"Fras, Fras, you are on a different path, but that does not make you any the worse."

"Look here, my pie and your menu. Where's my beer? Gah, different waiter! Speak Austaric? Thought not. Bieratelissi?"

"Numeren vor eti dwel, da ke," said Ettenbar to the waiter.

"Bloody hell, Ettenbar, why didn't you say you spoke Woomeran?" exclaimed Glasken.

"I thought you wished to make good the chance to practice, Fras."

"Dummart. One day I'll be *your* overseer, then we'll see some smart work."

"Ah, whatever else you are, Fras Glasken, you are never boring as company. When the third rocket has gone its way and we have gone ours, I shall miss you."

"Just as well. Most folk seem to hit me without any trouble."

"Ah-ha-ha, you have the jokings again."

A week later the second rocket had arrived from the paraline terminus, and was mounted on the railings of the launching frame. This was to be a daytime launch, for reasons determined by Zarvora's calculations of the Wanderers' orbits. The time for the passing of the orbital fortress approached, and the Rangemaster monitored a little windmill attached to a friction axle.

"The wind seldom drops below ten miles per hour, Frelle Highliber," he reported.

"The ramp should be safe at that speed."

"But it's gusty wind, 'untidy' wind, as the paraline engine drivers would say."

"So what is your opinion?"

"If a gust was to catch the rocket while it was just emerging from the tower and still moving slowly it could alter its course very slightly."

Zarvora weighed up several factors, political as well as technical.

"Prepare for a launch in four minutes, by my authority," she finally ordered.

A technician set the timer at the base of the rocket, then ran for his bunker a hundred yards away. The mechanism clicked, the wind gusted . . . the wind gusted just as the igniter flared, distorting the launch tower very slightly. The second rocket rammed itself into the slightly distorted rails, and the watchers saw the top of the ramp shatter in a plume of rocket exhaust and smashed wood. The force snapped the rocket between the first and second stages, and the burning first stage slammed at full thrust into the desert with a boom that shook the observers in their bunker. The upper stages did not fire, but crashed to the ground in a lesser cloud of dust.

Zarvora climbed into the remains of the ramp as soon as it was declared safe. It quickly became clear how lucky they had been. The supporting structure was nearly intact, with only the upper framework and guide rails wrecked. The technicians and engineers estimated a fortnight was needed to make repairs.

"The upper stages of the rocket are badly dented and twisted," the Rangemaster reported as Zarvora descended to the ground. "They'll have to be taken apart, defueled, and beaten back into shape. The armorers and mechanics think four months is needed."

"But meantime there is a third rocket on the way from Kalgoorlie. Damn and damn hell, this was my fault. I should have had tests done for wind distortion. We only have four rockets, we cannot afford to waste any."

A far-off movement caught Zarvora's attention, and she glanced around to where a boundary rider had appeared, driving his horse as hard as he could over the limestone sand and broken stone. Nobody rides like that without news of disaster, she said to herself.

The rider called to the guards as he reached the shelter tower, and they pointed to the launching gantry. As he rode up to her, Zarvora could see that one of his arms hung limp, and was soaked in blood.

"Hostile lancers and musketeers on camels and horses, Frelle Overmayor," he cried, sitting upright only with difficulty.

"Warriors? Out here?"

"Aye, and making right for the towers and ramp. They must have noticed the explosion. I was shot as I rode from them."

"A patrol from Woomera," ventured the Rangemaster. "A mistake."

"There were hundreds."

"And to the northeast?" responded Zarvora. "Unlikely—wait! How were they dressed?"

"They were swathed in robes of red, vermilion, and orange, Frelle Overmayor."

"Alspring Ghans, come all the way across the desert."

"They tried to ride us into a pincer-trap, but their camels were too slow for our horses. Even so, they shoot well, and only I have survived out of five. We may have accounted for three of them," he added with pride.

"And they broke off the pursuit?"

"Aye, when we were in sight of the towers. They might have thought that this is a fort. They were bringing up horse cavalry."

Zarvora ascended a few steps and peered to the northeast. There were camel lancers in scattered groups, and a central knot of perhaps fifty. Behind them was a vast dust pall from a far larger force.

"The Ghans are said to strike hard and rapidly," she said, shading her eyes against the glare as she leaned away from the timber rails. "I can see them scouting this place. . . . Yes, they will attack before the main force arrives. They have surprised us, and they will want to take advantage of that. Ilyire told me that their commanders value surprise highly."

"We have sixty lancers and nine Tiger Dragons," said the Woomeran marshal. "We should be able to stop a mere eight or nine dozen Ghans, no matter how fierce they may be as warriors."

"There's as many as ten thousand Ghans behind 'em," the rider insisted.

"Pah!"

"Ten thousand, Fras. Probably more."

"Pure fancy," said the marshal dismissively. "What do you think, Frelle Overmayor?"

"How far away is the main column?" she asked the rider.

"Seven miles, no more."

"Assume the worst." She stepped down from her vantage point, and there was a look of grim determination on her face. "Glaetin, take two lancers and escort this man to Woomera, take him to the Overhand."

"Frelle Highliber, he bleeds freely—"

"Well, patch him as you ride, but move! A lot more will bleed otherwise. Marrocal, douse the gantry with spirits, then set fire to it. I shall set fire to the papers, drawings, and tables in the bunker. Rangemaster, set the timers on the upper stages of the rocket. Make sure that they ignite and wreck themselves. Understand?"

"Aye, Highliber."

"After that, ride for Woomera as hard as you can. Captain Alkem, take the sixty lancers and the Tiger Dragons and set up a rear guard when I ride to the south quadrant tower. Make it seem as if you are defending this burning gantry."

"But, Highliber, we could outpace them if we all left for Woomera right away."

"Fool! Obey orders! I need ten minutes in the beamflash tower to alert the network and clear all wind trains from the paraline. If they capture a wind train they will move like a bushfire, they will shatter our undefended outposts, be in Kalgoorlie within a week, and Peterborough even sooner. Ten minutes, by your anchor timer. After that, ride for Woomera."

Three minutes later Zarvora was pounding up the steps of the wooden beam-

flash tower, glancing north to where the lancers were riding to intercept an enemy marked only by a cloud of dust. She burst into the beamflash gallery and pushed the transmitter from his seat.

/ POLL: PRIORITY DRAGON BLACK/she keyed. Seconds passed, then the reply came.

/ ACKNOWLEDGED: BEGIN TRANSMISSION /

/ SATURATION TRANSMISSION: ALL BEAMFLASH LINES: IN-VASION FROM ALSPRING NATIONS FROM NORTH OF WOOMERA. ESTIMATE AT LEAST TEN THOUSAND LANCERS, UNKNOWN AUXIL-IARIES, SEVEN MILES NORTH OF OUTPOST HARTLAK. CLEAR ALL WIND AND GALLEY TRAINS FROM THE PARALINE FROM NARETHA TO WOOMERA, PETERBOROUGH AND BROCKNIL: ALL RAILSIDES MOVE TO FULL WAR ALERT: BURN ALL BUILDINGS AND EQUIPMENT THAT CANNOT BE MOVED BEHIND THE FORTIFIED WALLS: FIRE ON ANY WIND TRAIN THAT DOES NOT ANSWER CODE IN REFERENCE 2T-3GK: BE ALERT FOR OTHER INVASION COLUMNS COMING FROM THE NORTH ANYWHERE FROM NARETHA TO BROCKNIL: ACKNOWL-EDGE THAT TRANSMISSION HAS BEEN PASSED ON. /

There was an unnerving delay of nearly a minute, followed by a twinkling of light in the tower to the south. /ACKNOWLEDGED: AWAITING FURTHER ORDERS /

Zarvora turned to the beamflash tower's captain and pointed to the north.

"What has been going on over there? Did our lancers hold the invaders back?"

"They're still fighting, Frelle, but they seem to be in trouble."

"In trouble!" exclaimed Zarvora, astounded. "But they're our finest lancers, part of my personal guard."

"It's what I see, Frelle Highliber."

Zarvora thought for a moment, then clicked / BURN YOUR TOWER AND EVACUATE TO WOOMERA. She did not wait for an acknowledgment, but seized a lamp and smashed it down on the floor beside the bench.

"Evacuate to Woomera, now!" she barked, then ignited a flare with its fire-strip and flung it into the spilled oil as the crew began to clatter down the steps. For a moment she hesitated, glancing north to where the savage battle between the two groups of elite lancers was raging. Her anchor timer read eight minutes: two minutes more would ensure her safety, yet . . .

"Cowardice is punishable by death," she reminded herself, then she took a gabriel rocket from the flare box.

The flames were blazing up around her as she swiveled the launching tube around to point north. She thrust the wick into the flames, then dropped the smoking rocket into the tube and ran for the stairs. As she reached the ground

the rocket shrieked away, howling its message to retreat over the red sand and frost-shattered rock. The tower captain was holding her horse ready. As she mounted she pointed south.

"Every man for himself, Captain, and every woman too," she cried as she dug her heels into the horse's flanks.

His reply was lost in the detonation of the flarebox high above. The tower's gallery disintegrated, flinging smoking debris around them. They traveled at a gallop at first, then Zarvora eased back to a canter and glanced back to the north.

"Why are they not retreating, I see only a half dozen—"

She caught herself, horrified by the truth: her elite lancers had been all but wiped out by the time her rocket had shouted its orders. Other riders were streaming across the plain, Ghan lancers on horses from other squads. The tower captain drew a flintlock.

"No!" shouted Zarvora. "Give me your loaded guns."

He drew alongside and handed them over to her, then drew his saber and rode alongside her. The horses were beginning to tire, and a squad of a dozen Ghans was slowly closing with them. Zarvora turned in the saddle and fired with a smooth sweep of her arm. A Ghan lancer threw up his arms and fell from his mount. She flung the gun away and drew another from her belt. This time she hit a horse and it sprawled amid the sharp stones, flinging its rider down. The next shot missed. Zarvora dropped the third gun and drew her fourth. Turn, sweep, fire—the head of the leading lancer exploded as the heavy lead ball found its mark. The remaining nine suddenly lost their resolution and slackened pace.

In the distance to the south Zarvora noticed that the beamflash relay tower was on fire, trailing a plume of dark smoke into the light wind. Their pursuers began to fire their muskets, and a shot tugged at Zarvora's robes as she reached for her last gun, a stubby Westock half-inch. More riders were closing from behind to join the Ghans—then the pursuers broke into a confused, wheeling, shouting gaggle as the newcomers hacked into them with their sabers.

"The last of our own lancers," shouted the tower captain.

"Then turn, here's enough of fleeing."

The wild scramble that followed lasted no more than a minute, but six Ghans and the beamflash captain lay dead before Zarvora and the three surviving lancers from her personal guard set off for the south again.

"Wild, savage warriors," shouted the man beside her. "We were evenly matched, but we barely held our own. A second squad hit us just as your rocket came over."

They rallied with more surviving lancers at the burning relay tower, then set off for Woomera again. They reached the fortified capital in the late afternoon. The towers of the city rose against the blue sky with the darker blue of the Mirrorsun band arching across like a mighty sash. The band had drifted into an

eccentric orbit as it strove to repair the damage from the Wanderer's beam, so the glow was easily visible late every afternoon.

"I changed the very heavens, yet look at me now," Zarvora muttered under her breath as she rode for the west gate of the city.

Zarvora's lackey was shouting messages from the beamflash network to her even as she dismounted from her exhausted, trembling horse.

"Force of two thousand on the Great Western Paraline at Warrion, laying siege. Another force reported at Hawker, but no numbers as yet. Yuntall Railside under siege by a force of over five thousand—"

"Yuntall! But that's on the Barrier Paraline to Brocknil."

"It's confirmed, Overmayor. Wirramina reports three thousand Ghan lancers crossing the Great Western Paraline and moving south, but not attacking."

"A pincer movement. They will meet at the south of Lake Tyers, cutting Woomera off from the Southeast Alliance. They move fast, and to our most vulnerable points. How do they do it? Did that escapee Vittasner build them another battle calculor? Take me to the paraline depot, now."

The City Overhand of Woomera caught up with Zarvora at the depot, just as she was trying to find a galley engine and crew.

"The Ghans are burning the scrub between our beamflash towers to blind us," he said as he followed her about. "Soon all links with east and west will be gone."

"The beamflash network has done its job already," Zarvora assured him. "Your fortified towns have been warned and secured. Most could withstand a limited siege from a few thousand attackers."

"But Hawker is under attack by ten thousand, perhaps twelve."

Zarvora stared at him in astonishment. "As many as that?"

"And they have bombards. I've requisitioned a galley train to relieve them. Four hundred troops and a dozen bombards of our own."

"That does not seem enough, but how can we know? I must be on that train."

"If you wish, Frelle Overmayor, but to be anywhere outside a fortified town or city is dangerous."

That night, as the galley train reached the southern tip of Lake Tyers, Zarvora ordered it stopped. She had a horse unloaded in the darkness, then ordered the captain to proceed without her. As the train moved out over the trestle bridge she sat alone on her horse, watching the wagons dwindle into the distance by the light of Mirrorsun. The Calldeath lands were quite deep here, and were only a quarter-hour ride from this part of the paraline. She set off slowly across the bed of the dry lake.

Suddenly there was a faint flash of light to her left, followed by the sound of a distant blast. The bridge had been mined. I would have done that, Zarvora thought as she rode on. After another twenty minutes a faint tingling feeling warned her that she was entering the Calldeath region. Her horse grew eager to go south, and for a time she let it have its head. Now she was safe from human attack, and she could follow the Calldeath strip all the way to Peterborough.

As she rode, a name kept echoing through her mind. Lemorel, Lemorel, Lemorel. Several coded dispatches had referred to Commander Lemorel, the leader of the Alspring Ghan invaders. Lemorel was most certainly not a Ghan name. Lemorel Milderellen had abducted John Glasken and gone in search of the Alspring cities a half-decade earlier. Lemorel had also been one of her most trusted and promising young Dragon Librarians. No wonder the Ghans knew exactly where to strike in order to do the most damage.

The whirring and swishing sound of the Libris Calculor room began to take on a regular rhythm as the diagnostic program ran its course. There were no anomalies, the Libris Calculor was in perfect order. MULTIPLIER 8 and PORT 3A cleared their frames, and MULTIPLIER 17 sat back from his frame as he tapped the floor pedal with his foot and sent his last calculation away to the local node. The sound of the huge machine began to fade, as if they were leaving a shift and walking away down a corridor.

" 'Tis running down, PORT," said MULTIPLIER 17, but the components nearby only turned to glare at him. A regulator walked up, rested her cane on his shoulder, and held a finger to her lips.

The noise faded further, until there was nothing but the swish of polling signals being sent at five-second intervals. Input had ceased, there was no more work being entered. The System Herald stood up and banged the floor with his blackwood rod.

"System Hold!" he called clearly and firmly. The polling signals stopped, and there was silence. Four thousand pairs of eyes were upon him. "Components attend! Shift terminated. Announcement to follow."

Buzzing coversation welled up throughout the Calculor. The regulator beside MULTIPLIER 17 sat down and began sobbing softly. He put an arm over her shoulders, and she put her head on his chest and began to soak his tunic with tears. He scarcely felt any happier himself.

"Some damn major reconfiguration, I'll bet," said MULTIPLIER 8 to PORT 3A.

"Don't be a dummart," he replied. "They're going to shut down the Calculor."

They sat in silence for a moment. "They can't do that," said MULTIPLIER 8. "What about our work? Who's to do it?"

"Contract labor? Perchance the mayorate itself is no more, perchance the Southmoors have crushed the mayoral armies and are advancing on the capital."

"None of that's in the beamflash traffic. Things is quiet, and prosperous—except that inflation on the royal is up to three point two percent."

"Then this is it, then . . . the end of the machine."

"No, it's a new configuration."

As he spoke there was a deep clack at the back of the Calculor hall. The heavy curtains that divided the hall began to be drawn back along the wires. As they bunched up at the wall, the double doors between them opened. A lackey entered carrying a scroll bound with a black ribbon and sealed with black wax. It was a decree from Tarrin, and the System Controller appeared following behind him. He was going to read it in person.

When Tarrin reached the rostrum the System Herald banged his rod for attention in spite of the near-complete silence. "Attend the System Controller!"

"My fellow souls in this great machine, the Calculor of Libris," he began, breaking the seal on the scroll. "I have here a decree from Mayor-Seneschal Jefton, in his capacity as the ruler of Rochester. It reads thus: 'Be it known to all magistrates, servants and officers of the Mayor, and citizens of the dominions of Rochester, the machine known as the Calculor of Libris is hereby declared to be decommissioned. All components who were formerly felons are hereby granted a mayoral pardon. All components who might have been pressed into the Calculor's service although not felons will be granted their freedom, fifty gold royals, and full restoration of their property. Your service in the Calculor of Libris has changed the very world itself. Accept my thanks.' "

He lowered the scroll and surveyed the Calculor Hall. There was no movement amid the ranks of faces focused on him. He raised his voice again.

"There will, of course, be administrative assistance for those components who have difficulty in readjusting to life outside Libris. All Dragon Librarians who are acting as regulators will be redeployed to other duties with no loss of rank. Please go to your cells and pack your possessions. The doors will no longer be locked. Components of the Libris Calculor, on behalf of the entire Libris staff, goodbye and good luck."

He stepped down from the podium and began to walk back along the corridor through the center of the Calculor. A component stood up as he passed.

"Fras Controller, what will replace us?" the component pleaded, his hands open and extended.

"This is our home," called PORT 3A from nearby. "This is our mayorate, our world. You can't take it away from us."

There was a rumble of assent that rippled out across the Calculor. Tarrin shrugged hopelessly as he looked from component to component.

"There are smaller calculors, and even mechanical devices. These have taken over much of the work of beamflash decoding and records control."

"We won't go!" shouted the component in front of him, and his shout was echoed by both the walls and scores of other components.

"There's stores down in the vaults to last months," cried the regulator who had been sitting beside MULTIPLIER 17. "We can stay here."

"This is none of my doing. I fought hard and long for the Calculor. The Mayor will have us removed if we don't go."

"We can arm the components!" cried a regulator. "Twelve thousand components is a fearsome army!"

"Aye, and most of us has been felons," bellowed a gruff voice. "We can shoot, hit, an' stab wi' the best of 'em."

Tarrin looked about him, bemused. "But most of you must want to go!"

"Those who want to go are welcome to go," PORT 3A shouted out across the ranks of the components. "We choose to stay!"

The cheering that erupted was deafening, and components and regulators closest to the doors ran off to tell the off-duty components what was happening. Tarrin was surrounded by angry, shouting components, and was unable to move.

Beyond the gates of Libris, the delegates and supporters of the Rochester and Southeast Alliance Human Rights Association waited in vain to welcome the newly liberated components of the Libris Calculor. When an hour passed with no result they demanded to send in a delegation, refusing to believe that the components had barricaded themselves inside, and that the regulators and guards had joined them. The delegation was beaten up and ejected. The candles in their party globes began to burn out; then it began to rain. The letters in the banners that they carried began to run, and were soon illegible.

The siege of Libris lasted only a few hours, during which the Libris Calculor was again made operational. A message arrived under the Overmayor's personal code, and it declared the entire Southeast Alliance to be in a state of general mobilization. Civil rights were now subject to the provisions of martial law, and the Calculor was most definitely not to be disbanded. Tarrin was carried shoulder high from the Calculor Hall by the components, all grateful for his long series of court battles to keep them where they were.

John Glasken emerged from the beamflash public office after three hours, too exhausted from arguing with the clerks and lackeys to feel rage. Ettenbar joined him and they strode off down the road.

"Morgan! They shipped that bloody third rocket to Morgan and the only reason that it didn't get as far as the marshaling yards in Rochester is that the gauge of the rails changes from broad to narrow at Morgan and they didn't have a suitable flatbed available with narrow bogies! Misrouted beamflash message, that's what the Controller of the Morgan Paraline Shunting Yards said. The beamflash system really is letting standards slip."

"The Overmayor will not be pleased!"

"The Overmayor will blame *me*! Fools and incompetents, they're all around me—present company excepted. I'm going to get that rocket back to Woomera on time if I have to strap a saddle to it and ride it there."

"A trifle extreme, Fras 3084?" Ettenbar ventured.

"STOP CALLING ME THAT!" Glasken shouted, his voice hoarse.

"Ah, yes, and I am sorry, Fras Johnny. Under stress I tend to revert to the serenity and discipline of the Libris Calculor. Still, you prevailed."

"That I did, and now I'm going to have a drink, then catch the next wind train to Morgan Railside."

The tavern was packed with patrons, and after another long and infuriating wait Glasken emerged with their pies and his tankard. They sat on a pile of roofing shingles and began to eat.

"Lot of worried folk in there," said Glasken between mouthfuls. "Something about an IW10 code. Everyone was saying it was an IW10 code. Come to think of it, there was mention of it in the beamflash office as well."

Ettenbar turned to him at once, eyes wide. "That is Invasion War alert at level ten."

Glasken frowned, put down his pie and took up the tankard of black ale. "War, eh? There's always a war somewhere, I bet it's the Southmoors at Finley. It's as inevitable as the Call. Or maybe some castellan's sent his gamekeepers to shoot at his neighbors again—hope it's not one of my old man's neighbors. The last thing I want on my doorstep is refugee parents." He took a thoughtful swallow of ale.

"Fras Johnny, level ten is a very large war, with an invasion force of above fifty thousand."

"Fifty thousand!" Froth sprayed over the edge of Glasken's tankard. "There's never even *been* an army that big. I—Etten, what's wrong? The Call got to you?"

Glasken followed his gaze. Ettenbar was looking down the street, to where a lone rider was slowly approaching on a lame horse. It was a tall woman, with her hair roughly bound back, and wearing a ragged wayfarer's cloak. Soiled bandages covered her left arm, and dark splotches of blood showed through. As she drew near they could see that she had bound a saber into her injured hand, and there were fang marks in her boots and the flanks of her horse.

"Overmayor!" shouted Ettenbar, dropping his rice pie and running out into the street. Glasken followed, tankard in hand.

Zarvora reined in her horse and looked down at them, but her eyes seemed unable to focus. "Beamflash tower," she managed in a slurred whisper.

Having stopped, the horse was unable to walk any further. Glasken called for a stabler as he helped Zarvora from the saddle. She could hardly stand, but after a sip of his ale she regained her senses.

"Beamflash, take me there."

"Frelle Overmayor, you need the attention of a medician first," began Ettenbar.

"Take me to the nearest tower at once," she replied emphatically, a contralto
tone returning to her voice.

That was enough for Glasken. "Aye Frelle," he said as he lifted her in his
arms and began to walk toward the beamflash tower. He was surprised at how
light she seemed, just as Ilyire had been when he had lifted the drunken Alspring
Ghan into a stolen cart. Ettenbar followed, and behind him was a small crowd
who were muttering about it being the Overmayor.

"Overmayor, do not be afraid," said Ettenbar reassuringly. "We are your
loyal servants, two FUNCTIONS of the Dexter Register."

"Calculor FUNCTIONS? I can hardly believe it," she mumbled.

"He's raving, Overmayor, it's Glasken and Ettenbar," added Glasken.

At the beamflash office Glasken suddenly found himself given far more deference than had been forthcoming for the previous three hours. The deputy captain
of the tower ushered them straight into the counterweight lift and they were raised
to the beamflash gallery itself. Glasken was still holding Zarvora in his arms. The
tower captain met them as they stepped out into the gallery.

"What news is there?" Zarvora asked. "I have been traveling two days."

"Hawker has just fallen," said the captain, assuming that Glasken and Ettenbar had a high security clearance. "Before the signal was lost there was word
that Wirrinya was under attack and unlikely to last another day. There was a
fierce attack on the walls of Woomera itself, but grapeshot from the bombards
drove the Ghans back. The Great Western Paraline's railsides received a destruct
order from Kalgoorlie last night, so the rails have been blown up and the rolling
stock burned as far west as Naretha."

"Good, the desert will do Kalgoorlie's fighting for now. What else?"

"The Barrier Paraline has been taken from Nackara to Cockburn, and the
Ghans have captured at least two galley trains and several wind engines. The
citadel at Brocknil had held, but the city proper and the railside have fallen. Also,
the Southmoors seem to have an alliance with the Alspring Ghans. The Darlington
beamflash tower was destroyed by Southmoor bombards yesterday. Contact with
the Central Confederation has been lost."

In the background Glasken and Ettenbar listened to the litany of disaster with
near incredulity.

"The Ghans attempted to cut off Peterborough, but for once their lines were
overextended. The Peterborough Mayoral Musketeers Cavalry stopped them in a
battle ten miles to the east."

Zarvora shambled over to a map on the wall where she ran her finger over
the names of several towns.

"So, someone is a match for them," she said with her finger poised over Peterborough.

"There is one more piece of good news, Highliber. A suicide squad of about fifty Ghans got all the way to Morgan. They blew up a section of paraline track and detonated another charge against the wall of the beamflash tower before the militia killed them. Luckily they had used too little powder, so the tower is still standing and in operation. Also the paraline track that they blasted turned out to be a shunting line, so traffic is still getting through."

Just then a medician emerged from the lift to tend her, and as her hand was being unwrapped she accepted a honeycake from one of the beamflash crew.

"Without help they could not have moved so fast and far in three days," she said to the tower captain. "There must have been advance parties sent out, all coordinated to act at the same time. There *must* also have been help from within our own system. How many galley engines are there here at Peterborough?"

"Two, Frelle Highliber. Three others were ordered north on the second day of the fighting, and were destroyed on the line near Hawker."

She removed two of the four pistols from her belt and handed them to Ettenbar. He immediately began cleaning and reloading them.

"Tell the Mayor to seal the town, begin rationing, and prepare for a long siege. Assemble all sheep and horses that cannot be fed out of stores and send them overland to Morgan. They must not fall into the hands of the Alspring Ghans. Set the gangers destroying track to the north and east of the town. Put as much rolling stock behind the two galley engines as they can pull at low speed, and load the train with all the noncombatants that it will carry: women, children, and wounded. I shall take it south to Burrat."

The tower captain nodded at each of Zarvora's instructions, but his manner had no sense of urgency. "Overmayor, that would be unwise. The townsfolk look to you for leadership. Your place is here, defending your dominions against the invaders."

Zarvora waved his objections aside with her newly bandaged hand. "That would see me isolated, Fras Captain, for this town is surely to be besieged by the invaders."

"So you will leave us, Frelle Highliber?"

"Yes. Now obey my orders."

In spite of his misgivings, Glasken decided that being close to the Overmayor represented his best chance of survival. He and Ettenbar were sent to make sure that all was in order with the galley engines and to pass on Zarvora's instructions. By the time they reached the streets the town had erupted into bedlam, with the truth about the invasion finally common knowledge. Prices had increased tenfold

within minutes, women and children were being hurried along toward the hastily assembled train by grim-faced men, and agitators were shouting to the crowds that Rochester and the Overmayor had abandoned them. The train was standing ready, with the galley engines Firefly and Iron Duke coupled to pull it. The crowd around it was unruly, a mixture of weeping women, hysterical children, and uncertain men being harangued by yet more agitators.

"Good old Glasken, you've picked another winner," Glasken said aloud as they left the cabin of the lead galley engine after delivering Zarvora's messages.

"Friend Johnny, this is no time to think upon horse racing," admonished Ettenbar.

"Ettenbar—look here, have you ever been in a war?"

"Why, no."

"I have, but it wasn't like this. A few hours ago people were worried about whatever was happening with this rumored war, but they were still loyal. I should know, I stood farting and complaining with them in the queue at the beamflash office. Suddenly there's all these men shouting the same message against the Overmayor. This isn't a spontaneous rabble, this is organized."

They arrived back at the beamflash tower as the sun was setting and the clerk in the office rang a message for Zarvora to come down. She emerged from the pulley lift limping but looking better than when they had left. They walked along the streets to the jeers of those who recognized her.

"Run from the Ghans, ya coward!" bawled someone in a hoarse voice, and something flew through the lamplit gloom and splattered on her ragged cloak.

"Stay an' fight, ya bitch!" This time the voice was female, and from a balcony. "Us women belong here, with our men."

"We'd rather welcome the Ghans than fight 'em. Death to the Overmayor!"

Glasken and Ettenbar flanked her as they made their way through the thickening crowd.

"Pay no attention, Frelle Exalted Overmayor," said Ettenbar, marching proudly erect with a scattershot gun at his shoulder.

"Aye, Frelle Overmayor," agreed Glasken. "Folk have been calling me a coward all my life, but—Stand back, ye buggers!"

"They call abuse well in Austaric, although this is a Woomeran town," remarked Zarvora. "I know mobs, and this one is better organized than the Great Western Paraline Authority's schedules."

Zarvora went straight to the lead coach after pushing through the angry, restless crowd at the railside. People began banging on the outside of the coach, while within were shrieking children and their wailing mothers.

"Go to the Firefly and tell the captain to wait," she said to Glasken and Ettenbar. They immediately made their way forward.

Captain Wilsart of the Firefly, the lead galley engine, helped them through the forward access hatch.

"If this train starts to move there'll be a riot," Glasken warned. "The Overmayor says wait. Who's behind this trouble?"

"Whoever 'tis, the Overmayor can count on the Great Western Paraline Authority," replied Captain Wilsart calmly.

Glasken looked out of the driver's window slit, and noted that the track ahead of the train was relatively free of people. A small knot of men with muskets stood on the balks and transoms, and one of them had a sledge hammer and bolt-wrench over his shoulder. Glasken turned at a commotion behind them. Zarvora was climbing up into the driver's cabin, filthy with grease and dirt, and panting heavily.

"Highliber! Did the crowd beat you?" gasped Ettenbar.

She shook her head. "No, I crawled from the lead carriage under the Iron Duke, then entered by the floor access hatch. At my word, prepare to leave. Put your crew and navvies on alert, Captain."

"But what of the Iron Duke?" asked the captain of the Firefly.

"I uncoupled it as I crawled here. I also unpinned the safety catches on its brakes and jammed them."

"Very good, Highliber," he said as he unclamped the brake lever and engaged the Ready signal.

"Who are those men on the tracks up ahead?" exclaimed Zarvora. "One of them is removing rail bolts!"

Captain Wilsart seized Glasken's shoulders. "Glasken, go down to the forward gunner, tell him to fire the grapeshot barrel at anyone who fires on us when we begin moving. Quickly!" He turned to the driver. "At my word . . . Forward!"

The Firefly moved smoothly away, with little more noise than the rumble of its wheels on the rails as a warning to those ahead on the track. Some members of the crowd cheered, thinking that the galley engine was abandoning the carriage with the Overmayor still in it. One of the gangers looked up to see the galley engine approaching and shouted a warning to his companions. He raised his musket and fired at the driver's window slit. The bullet glanced off the heavy armored glass; then the forward gunner replied with grapeshot. The blast annihilated the group of men, and a moment later the Firefly jolted over shattered flesh and weapons. The loosened rail held as the galley engine passed.

It was not until the exchange of shots that those in the crowd realized that anything was wrong. A peppering of fire lashed out at the departing Firefly as people fled or flung themselves behind cover. The leading agitators stormed aboard the Iron Duke, but the crew were all loyal Great Western Paraline employees and they feigned confusion. By the time the forward bombard had been unclamped and run out, the Firefly had disappeared around a bend.

"The town has been filled with hired churls and churlenes from the independent castellanies, probably in the pay of the Alspring Ghans," Zarvora said grimly to Captain Wilsart. "The beamflash tower crew was with them, too. I could tell by the pattern of clicks from their instruments that they were sending out orders contrary to what I was saying."

"But what will—"

Across the darkened rooftops the gallery at the top of the beamflash tower exploded in a ball of lurid flame. Glasken gasped in horror, but the gunner beside him did not even turn to look. Zarvora climbed down from the access walkway to join them.

"The town walls are ahead there, gunner," she said as the Firefly rattled over a set of points. "If the gates are shut you will get but one shot at them, and that must hit the transverse beam or we are all dead."

"Not te worry, Frelle Highliber," he replied. "Just tell me what speed we do."

"Twenty-five of your speed units."

"They be miles per hour, Highliber. Good enough for Brunel, good enough for us. Now then, closed the gates be, and twenty-five, ye say. Thet's a three-nick elevation, and a true of four point five."

On the town wall, two of the militia watched the galley engine approaching with more than purely military interest. In spite of the darkness the two members of the Peterborough Train Spotters Brotherhood were sufficiently expert to be able to identify it from little more than the sound that it made on the paraline's rails and the outline of its shape from its running lights.

"There be a GWG-class galley engine of five-segment configuration," said musketeer first class Mansorial.

"Firefly, that be the Firefly, GWG-409/5," replied his companion, Prengian.

"No sighting on a number, we can't claim a confirmed sighting without seeing the number."

"No carriages or wagons, now that's worth a note."

"Leave the gates closed, we can hold up a lantern to the number as they wait. Have you got the sightings book?"

A rocket flew straight and true from the Firefly's forward tube, striking the gates a little below the transverse bar and exploding. Instead of breaking, the bar was blown clear of its clamps, and it came down just as the Firefly was butting through the splintered gates.

"Firefly shot out the gate!" cried Mansorial in disbelief.

"I'm a-notin' it in the book," Prengian called back excitedly.

The great wooden beam crushed the rear roof of the galley engine's last two segments as it butted through the heavy swinging gates and the Firefly slowed as

it dragged the bar clear of the gates. Amid the cries of injured navvies Glasken worked alongside Ettenbar, Captain Wilsart, and Zarvora to cut through the tangle of bar, fabric, and ashwood frame with hatchets. They were puzzled that the militia on the wall had not opened fire.

"Do we call this sighting an accident or an incident?" asked Prengian.

"Accidents is unintentional, incidents is intended in part," was the reply.

"Looks to be elements of both here. An incident what results in an accident."

"We should put it to the next monthly meeting of the Peterborough Train Spotters Brotherhood," said Mansorial excitedly. "Good Lord, now look at that! They're convertin' it, they're detachin' the last segment right there on the track."

"You're right!" exclaimed Prengian, "GWG-409/5 has become GWG-409/4. Does this merit a new entry in the book, or is it part of the incident report?"

At last the navvies were able to push the bar and wreckage onto the paraline. The rear of the engine was so severely mangled that its wheels were jammed, but galley engines were built from articulated modules. At Captain Wilsart's word the rear third of the Firefly was evacuated and unclamped, and the galley engine rumbled forward as if it had been freed from a leash.

"Ah, Prengian," said Mansorial tentatively, as if remembering something important.

"Aye?"

"GWG-409/4, Firefly, has just shot out the gate we're a-guardin'."

"Aye, but as GWG-409/5."

"Shouldn't we have fired on it?"

There was a short, awkward silence.

"Ach, that would never do. It's a Great Western Paraline Authority engine, GWG-class! The Peterborough Train Spotters Brotherhood would have us expelled before a single day was past for a-doin' that."

"But the Gate Captain will have us shot for not doin' so when he gets across here."

"Aye, you're right. Let's put a shot or two from the bombardiette into the wreckage that's left."

The little bombard had a flintlock striker instead of a fuse. Mansorial withdrew the safety pin, aligned the sights with the dark mass on the paraline, and squeezed the trigger. A one-pounder ball was spat from the barrel. It struck the canvas and ashwood wall and smashed into the rocket locker for the rear tube. The damaged segment was blasted apart as the warheads exploded, mangling the mixed-gauge rails and in the process rendering the paraline impassable for at least an hour. By this time the Firefly was lost in the darkness of the overcast night.

"Five crew dead and fifteen injured," Ettenbar reported to Captain Wilsart as they passed the tiny railside of Gumbowie. "Twenty-seven pedal mechanisms are

smashed or lost, and a quarter of the roof destroyed. The rear grapeshot bombard and rocket launcher are gone too, with the rear of the engine.''

''What about rockets?' asked Zarvora.

''The main store was at the rear.''

''Damn. How many rockets are left at the front?''

''Three, Frelle Highliber.''

The Firefly rolled swiftly along through the night. Zarvora had the relief crewmen relocate the bow rocket launcher and bombard on the roof, so that they could be fired in all directions. At last there was no more to do. Zarvora, Glasken, Ettenbar, and Captain Wilsart retired to the driver's cabin, where they sat cleaning and loading their muskets and pistols in the lamplight.

''Soon we shall fire a rocket into the tracks behind us,'' said Zarvora. ''We must cut the track where we can.''

''Good work, Frelle Highliber,'' replied Captain Wilsart easily, ''but there be better ways.''

''Better ways? And you are not upset at the damage?''

''As Overmayor you authorized extension of the broad-gauge all the way to Rochester, Frelle, and you named your son after Brunel. You can do no wrong.''

The answer was not what Zarvora had expected.

''What is it about you Great Western Paraline people?'' she said, sitting back with her arms dangling beside her. ''Why this fanatical loyalty to some pre-Greatwinter engineer who we know practically nothing about—and his seven-foot paraline gauge?''

''Because it's the best, Frelle. We always ask what Brunel would have done. Oh and by the by, it's seven foot and one-quarter inch.''

Zarvora smiled at the correction. ''Was Brunel a general too? If he left any writings on battle tactics I ought to look at them.''

''He were a man of peace and building, Frelle. Our motto at Great Western Paraline is: Look To Functional Requirements. Just now your functional requirement is to tear up as much track as can. One rocket would take out a mere rail or two, and take a ten-minute to fix. I'll show you a scheme to do better.''

Zarvora sat thinking and resting for some minutes, while the Firefly's captain began to sketch a mechanism at the back of the galley engine's logbook. He handed it to her and she held it up to a pinlamp.

''Have you ever thought of becoming a Dragon Librarian, Fras Captain?'' she asked as she realized what he was proposing.

''Nay, Highliber. Train work is the only real work. No offense, mind. Libraries have their place and someone has to mind books and such like, but I count myself lucky that it's not me.''

Zarvora had killed everyone in the Peterborough beamflash tower before she had even lit the fuse to the charge that blew its gallery apart. Thus the final set of

messages sent out across the beamflash network was as she intended them to be, and in particular there had been no false orders sent south to Burra and Eudunda. Burra was actually a fortress of the old Spalding Castellany, and was well equipped for any siege. It had not been targeted by the infiltrators, and the local governor was loyal to the Southeast Alliance.

The Firefly rolled into Burra without further incident. The governor and a small group of dignitaries were at the railside to greet Zarvora and receive their orders.

"Send an unmanned wind engine north," Zarvora instructed the Burra governor. "Attach a balkdrop truck and put mines with timers on the sliprails. Set them to drop right on the paraline every seven miles, and set each timer to explode after one minute. Have one large mine to explode in the engine after the last drop is made."

The injured from the Firefly were taken into the fort, and mechanics swarmed through the damaged section repairing and replacing mangled pedals and rigging up canvas streamlining. Before the work was complete, a crewless wind engine began its journey north, pulling its truck laden with mines. Zarvora was in the beamflash gallery of the Eudunda-facing tower when there was a flash of light to the north, followed by a distant boom.

"That's the first mine dropped," said a beamflash receiver, peering through the telescope facing north. "I can still see the rear running light of the wind engine. You know, Overmayor, the flash of the Peterborough gallery blowing up gave me quite a start. Had spots before my eyes for a good quarter hour."

"If they want war by infrastructure, I shall give it to them," Zarvora said grimly.

The receiver continued to stare through his telescope's eyepiece. "I can see the glow of Peterborough clearly, and streaks like signal rockets above it. All sorts of colors. A big party to welcome the invaders, it looks to be. Now that wind engine—Argh!"

The flash of light had even caught Zarvora's unaided eyes. She pushed the dazzled receiver to one side of the telescope as the boom reached the tower gallery.

"Fires, burning trees. Damn timer for the main charge must have gone off early—but wait! Burning carriages, all smashed and tangled, at least a dozen of them. They must have sent a galley train in pursuit of us from Peterborough. Your uncrewed wind engine slammed straight into it."

The receiver massaged his eyes. "A good job, too," he said, "and by a Great Western machine."

Twenty minutes later they were traveling south again, with the Firefly repaired and a full, fresh crew at the pedals. Glasken was unimpressed by the cold wind in the cabin from the open side windows.

"Can't you have this thing glassed in like the South and Eastern Standard's wind engines?" he asked as he sat shivering beside Captain Wilsart.

"Oh no, Fras. The feel of the wind gives you the mind of the land and weather. I mean, those SES ruffins would take a wind's strength from the gauge on the roof."

"Seems reasonable to me."

"But Fras, it's quality of wind that ye want. Is it steady wind, or is it blustery? What of direction? Is the direction changing from minute to minute? How cold is it?"

"Well tonight it's damnable cold! I thought your galley engine is independent of winds."

"Why yes, Fras, but the Firefly presents a profile to a headwind, and even a more of a profile to a vectored wind. The gears that you select and the pace of the crew depends on the wind—taken with the gradient of the track and the loading of the train as well. In a galley engine we must be optimal in our selection of the gearing between the pedals and the drive wheels to balance speed and torque while at the same time not wearying the navvies who push the pedals. As captain, one must become part of the train, Fras, you must feel the wind as the train does. Now Mr. Brunel—"

Zarvora interrupted. "This Brunel engineer, he is pre-Greatwinter, yet you know a great deal about him."

"Aye, Frelle, he died two thousand eighty year ago next September, and those damnable traitors in the Britanical government destroyed the last of the broad gauge track in 1892 of the old calendar."

"Britanica, I have read about that in one of your paraline verse epics." Her eyes narrowed for a moment. "Now, how long ago would that have been?"

"Two thousand forty-seven years, Frelle Highliber."

Zarvora sat upright. "But that is exactly right. Do you know the date that the Call began?"

"2021 of the old calendar, Frelle. One thousand nine hundred eighteen years ago."

"Correct, all correct. Did you get it from my published papers in the 1702 Astronomical Transactions?"

"Nay, just from good bookkeeping and logs, Overmayor. Mr. Brunel specified that good records must be kept. Some of our paraline epics and sagas help too, for when disorderly mayors made wars and burned our archives over the centuries, our epics were used to keep the records alive and preserved. Drop into our Kalgoorlie offices sometimes and you can check any entries and dates in our archives. We also have there the original pre-Greatwinter model diorama of Pangbourne Station in 1885. It's thirty-six feet long, and in four millimeter to the foot. Nearly all our knowledge of the original Great Western trackwork comes from that model."

Zarvora closed her eyes and lay back. Glasken mixed some of his Naracoorte brandy with some water and held it to her lips. She sipped, coughed, then sipped again. Captain Wilsart went aft to check on the navvies, and Ettenbar had by now fallen asleep.

"Glasken, John Glasken," Zarvora murmured.

"Aye Overmayor?"

She regarded him quizzically in the dim light from the navigation board pinlamps. A long thin scratch across his forehead was beaded with drops of dried blood.

"You stayed with me when you could have turned me over to the mob. As for the explosives wagon disaster last August, well I would be dead without your heroics. What drives you, Fras?"

The question caught Glasken off-guard. He sat hunched over, wringing his hands with the cold in the weak light.

"I'd not stopped to think, Frelle Overmayor. I suppose I've been in the stocks for more felonies than I can think of, but . . . well, I may be a bastard, but I'm not a traitor. I mean, you're the Highliber and Overmayor, and the Southern Alliance is my home."

Zarvora lay back against the ashwood and canvas wall of the galley engine to think. She stayed that way for several minutes while the train rolled along the tracks to the rhythmic clatter of wheels on rails and the shanty-cycle chant of the navvies who provided its power.

"The Ghans seem to know where to hit us to do most damage," she said at last. "Our strength is in infrastructure and they hit us there. Why is that, Glasken?"

"They've studied us, I suppose."

"No, I think not. They are being led by Lemorel Milderellen."

Glasken sat up at once with a loud gasp. "Frelle Overmayor! She—I mean I—surely you don't think that *I'm* working with her?"

"Not anymore. An evil, difficult war has broken out, Glasken. I did not foresee it, but I managed to escape to rally my armies. The trouble is that there will be no quick and convincing victories through my innovations and ingenious engines, just a lot of desperate men shooting muskets at each other in fields. Still, what is the alternative?"

Glasken began to reply, then seemed to think better of it. He hunched over again, almost collapsing in the gloom. Zarvora watched him carefully.

"What were you going to say, Fras Glasken?"

He raised his head and looked directly at her. "I lived among the Alspring Ghans, at one of their desert outposts. They're not monsters. Should it matter if they conquer and rule us?"

Glasken expected an outburst, but she was pensive at his proposal.

"I have friends who are Southmoors, Glasken, and I suppose I could live

under Southmoor rule, yet still I have fought many wars against the Southmoor cities and states. As for the war with Tandara, why they were neighbors.''

''Agreed, Frelle.''

''There is more to this than just a stupid struggle for power, Glasken. I sometimes feel as if I am trapped in a pit and trying to build a ladder to escape, yet my fellow prisoners keep trying to snatch the wood away to stoke their fires. It annoys me intensely.''

Zarvora said no more, but slowly pulled herself up by the cabin Call railing and stood beside Captain Wilsart, who had returned from his inspection. They stood talking, looking out into the darkness ahead of the galley engine. Glasken rewound his Call anchor's timer, then joined them.

''The Firefly is traveling at its top endurance cruise speed,'' the captain commented, a strangely dispassionate inflection in his voice.

''Are you worried about the Ghans or their agents tearing up the tracks or laying mines,'' said Zarvora.

''Were I a Ghan, that I'd be doing.''

''But it's not a Ghan leading the Ghans, Fras. Their leader knows the value of trackwork and captured rolling stock for the transport of her own troops. I'll wager that they cut only the track near Burra or Eudunda, or even mount an attack on the bridge across the river at Morgan. They need transport between towns more than we do, so out here we should be safe.''

Glasken moved across to the open side window and stood in silence, reassured yet shivering with more than the chill of the night air. He had told Zarvora only part of the truth. He had really gone to her aid because she was female. Theresla was right. He liked women in general, not just sex. If it had been, say, Mayor Jefton, he might have been able to rationalize an excuse to run. He looked across at Zarvora, standing beside Captain Wilsart in the gloom. Zarvora: inhumanly strong, unnaturally light, but still a woman. Now she was being civil to him, she actually seemed to respect him. Glasken had to admit feeling pride and loyalty.

''Pride and loyalty can get you killed,'' he murmured to himself, but the words were insufficient to stoke his fears.

''One last matter, Fras Glasken,'' said Zarvora as she returned. She led him down to the now unmanned gunner's chamber. ''There are spies within my great system of paralines and beamflash towers, yet I have my own agents too. Using them, and carrier pigeons, I can get messages through to Kalgoorlie. At Morgan I shall be sending a message back with a lot of coded instructions. You are on intimate terms with an artisan from the Southeast named Jemli Cogsworth.''

''Ah yes, a fine—''

''—tall figure of a woman who is probably quite entertaining in bed. I can find no records of Jemli using beamflash transmission, except on your business.''

''That's right, she thinks the charge per word is too high.''

"All of her communications with her husband in Rochester are by letter, and those letters have all been checked. They carry false reports about the working conditions and cost of living in Kalgoorlie. Meantime she runs your mercantile interests rather well and she has made friends with your other lover Varsellia. She is living in the mayoral palace itself just now."

"They probably talk about me all the time."

"You flatter yourself. Has she ever asked you about calculor programming, or my rocket-fuel development, or the electroforce experiments in the old mineshafts of Kalgoorlie?"

"Only in terms of how long I would be away, whether I was in bed with other women, and if I was would it change things between us. Oh, and those metal and coil switches. She once asked if the market for them was liable to trail off in the near future."

"Did she? Was that all? Did she ask you for figures? What did you tell her?"

"I had just asked her to be assistant manager of the newly renamed Glasken Enterprises and Imports. I was offering her ten gold royals a month to forget clockmaking and work for me full time. I was more than fair, and I also offered her—"

"—a twenty-percent partnership and seneschal status if your growth index exceeded fifteen percent in the first year. Anything else? Dealings with my staff, edutors, or other associates?"

"She once said that she fancied Ilyire."

"Ahhh, yes."

"What? What do you know?"

"Everything."

Glasken's blush went unseen in the gloom.

"Well as I once said to her, better him than some riffraff churl with the pox. I trust Jemli as I trust no other woman, Frelle Overmayor, in the counting room as well as in bed. She has a strategic outlook and an excellent head for figures."

"She ought to. Her maiden name is Milderellen and her sister is Lemorel."

Zarvora shot out a hand and caught Glasken as he reeled and fell from his seat. Some minutes and quite a lot of brandy later he was recovering. Zarvora held his face into the windstream from the side window. As they sat back she held up a folded square of poorpaper.

"After I intercepted this I decided that the worst of my suspicions were correct, and that Jemli was a spy for Lemorel, that she was trying to wheedle her way into places where she could do damage at the highest of levels. I drew up and signed the order for her death, Fras Glasken, but your words saved her life. Just as well, I did not want to kill a woman who is five months pregnant."

She took the death notice from her jacket and dipped it down the funnel of

a pinlamp. It burned quickly, flaring up bright in the dark of the cabin. Glasken sat watching, barely comprehending.

"Highliber, your wisdom and mercy—Pregnant? Jemli?" Glasken held up his fingers and began to count. "January, December, November, October, September—oi, then I'm the father!"

Glasken suddenly realized that he was embracing Zarvora. He hastily released her and backed off a step; then she handed the square of poorpaper to him.

"It is a beamflash message. It has been chasing you around the beamflash network for some days. I just happened to notice it in the routing buffer while I was in the Peterborough beamflash gallery. Varsellia's pregnant too. It should have a bad effect on Ilyire's sex life."

Glasken unfolded the poorpaper, fumbling with both haste and confusion, then he dropped his hands and stared at Zarvora. His face was a study in baffled amazement, and he shook his head as if struggling out of a dream.

"I don't understand you, Frelle. You joke about a woman whose death order was in your pocket until just moments ago."

She smiled and touched his arm. "Fras Glasken, I had to turn Jemli into a thing before I could have her killed. Now I need to turn her back into a person. Turning people into things is dangerous, Fras. I thought of the Calculor components as things for many years, then discovered that I loved one of them. That shook my nerve, and I can no longer kill and imprison so easily."

"Lemorel will scream hellfire when she finds out about me and Jemli."

"If she ever conquers Kalgoorlie . . . ."

Glasken raised his hands. "That's enough, I'll fight in your army."

Morgan was on full war alert when they arrived there at 3 A.M. Several suspected Ghan agents and agitators had been lynched from the paraline signal towers, and the bodies swung in the Firefly's slipstream as it rolled into the railside. Zarvora went to the beamflash tower and established a link to Tarrin at Rochester. Her hope had been to bring the Libris Calculor straight into the war, but the process was slower than she had planned. The Calculor itself had been saved by the siege of its own components, but civil lawsuits had released many components and forced the introduction of several inefficient work practices. On Zarvora's instruction, Tarrin began to restore the vast machine to what it had once been, but that process was disruptive in itself.

Without the Libris Calculor it was difficult to route military trains through the system optimally and new, secure beamflash codes could not be generated fast enough. Resource and stores inventory cards and punched tapes were beyond access, except through the Libris Calculor, yet Tarrin had taken some initiatives of value. The strategic resources and garrisons communications throughout the Southeast Alliance were temporarily transmitted in unsecured beamflash codes to

the War Assembly of Mayors. His reasoning was that it was better to risk disclosure to the enemy than not to use the resources at all. Zarvora agreed, having no choice.

Beamflash reports confirmed what she already suspected. The invaders were isolating the cities and towns while dominating the countryside. Zarvora acted at once to neutralize the Ghan strategy, ordering the destruction of all bridges and paraline links in isolated stretches of track. Beamflash towers were to be defended most strongly of all. Supplies that could not be carried into towns were to be destroyed, and cattle in farms threatened by the Ghans were to be shot or turned loose to be taken by the next Call.

The third experimental rocket was located in the marshaling yards, and Zarvora immediately ordered that a narrow-gauge coach be demolished down to the base frame to take the rocket on to Rochester. Glasken and Ettenbar joined in the work, along with Captain Wilsart of the Firefly.

"Nothing I like better than smashing up narrer-gauge rolling stock," Captain Wilsart laughed as he swung his axe in the lamplight.

"Well mind the base, we want that left usable," called Glasken. He was already supervising a team of carpenters who were rigging a cradle for the cumbersome first stage.

"What's this rocket for anyway?" Captain Wilsart asked.

"If I knew I'd be shot for telling you. Ettenbar, have the men clear that wood from the line. Captain, have the Firefly haul the rocket out of the marshaling yards and bring it alongside this wagon."

Another half hour passed, and the eastern sky began to brighten. Glasken saw the Firefly moving through the yards across sets of points and heard the muffled shanty of the navvies as they pushed the pedals. Captain Wilsart was down on the tracks, throwing the switches in person, while he communicated with his driver via signals from his shutter lantern.

The Firefly was turned on the turntable, and finally began to rumble toward them. Glasken saw Captain Wilsart suddenly work the lantern frantically, then drop it and dash along the tracks in the path of the train. As he knelt between the tracks and began striking at something a shot rang out from a nearby carriage, then another. The captain slumped as Glasken aimed for the window where the gunflashes had been and fired at the varnished canvas just below the window shutter. He was rewarded with a thin scream, then he ran for where Captain Wilsart was crawling from the tracks. The Firefly approached, its brakes beginning to squeal and its gears grinding as the driver tried to engage reverse gearing.

Glasken was too late. The Firefly's forewheel passed over Captain Wilsart, nearly cutting him in two before the huge machine shuddered to a stop.

Glasken came running up with two of the carpenters as the crew of the galley engine jumped to the ground. The captain was still pinned beneath a wheel.

"Easy with him," said Glasken as they tried to make the man more comfortable. Captain Wilsart was breathing, but there was nothing that anyone could do for him.

"Mine, between tracks," he whispered. "Jammed dagger . . . into release . . ."

Glasken looked between the tracks and noted the dark lump just behind the forewheels. In the distance the last of the Ghan raiding party was being hunted down by a squad of Zarvora's Tiger Dragons. Glasken swore softly to himself; then, as sunlight began to spill into the marshaling yards, he crawled beneath the engine and examined the mine. Gingerly he peeled the covering cloth back from the spring-loaded trigger transfixed by Captain Wilsart's dagger. The design was Rochestrian. He reached in and unscrewed the detonator, then returned to the bloodied figure of Captain Wilsart. As Zarvora arrived he held up the detonator.

"How is he?" asked Zarvora, although Captain Wilsart's fate was beyond question. Glasken drew a finger across his throat and shrugged.

"Captain, I shall never forget what you did for the Alliance and for me," Zarvora whispered to him.

Captain Wilsart coughed blood, which dribbled down his chin and onto his collar. "Died . . . for *her* honor," he said, reaching up and patting the traction wheel that was pinning him to the rail. "Glad it wasn't one o' those damned narrer-gauge engines as done it," he declared with his last breath.

Zarvora sat back, Captain Wilsart's blood on her hands, and soaking the knees of her trousers. "Brunel? Broad-gauge paralines? Now he dies for his engine's honor."

"But you fought for your Calculor's honor," observed Glasken.

"I fought for control of my Calculor, not its honor. This is . . . incomprehensible! I am surrounded by lunatics, madmen, and fanatical engineers."

"True, Frelle Overmayor, but at least we're loyal to you."

Lemorel had known from the start that the invasion of the Southern Alliance would be an order of magnitude more difficult than all of her previous campaigns, yet her army was larger than ever before and she was striking across desert, across the very country that her enemies had relied upon for a shield. Her spies and agents had also prepared her targets well.

The Woomera Confederation was in her hands within nine days. The city of Woomera itself was besieged, along with a few fortified beamflash towers, but nearly every big town had fallen in the surprise of the first onslaught. Some beamflash towers along the paraline had fallen to her men and bombards, but the price had been high. The towers were equipped with even newer Inglewood bombards than Lemorel's, and they had a greater range. Maralinga was the westernmost point of her conquests, yet it had fallen to guile instead of assault. A hundred

Ghans posing as coffee merchants had infiltrated the place and had seized it at the command of a coded message on the beamflash network itself.

The broad-gauge paraline was almost undamaged from the Lake Tyers bridge to Maralinga, and Lemorel used it to fortify Maralinga against invasion from Kalgoorlie. The deserts and the Nullarbor Plain combined to channel everything that passed between east and west along the paraline. Kalgoorlie was powerless to ship troops or send messages farther east than Fisher.

It did not go all Lemorel's way, however. Even faced with torture and death the staff of Great Western Paraline Authority were nothing less than obstructive. The Ghans were finally reduced to pulling trucks of supplies along the paraline to Maralinga using camels and horses. A scant twenty miles farther west the wind and galley trains were running along newly repaired track, supplying a military barricade that would require the full weight of the Ghan army to breach, and providing materials to repair beamflash towers that had been incapacitated out of precaution. Out in the deserts, the western Kooree tribes were unhappy about the Ghan raiding parties dashing across their land, and were quick to fight back. There could be no Ghan invasion of the western mayorates for a long time.

Zarvora had expected that the invaders would attack Morgan and Renmark, but Lemorel had another surprise for her. Over the following fortnight she moved directly east across the Barrier Grasslands, sending squads of lancers ahead to spread havoc. She met with Southmoor envoys and the Central Confederation agreed to remain neutral while the Southmoors and Alspring Ghans fought the Southern Alliance. In return for the dry and sprawling Balranald Emirate, the Southmoors would be given all the Alliance Mayorates as far west as Rochester, and Ghan troops and lancers would advance no further than the Murrumbidgee River. The Southmoors would strike at the eastern border while the Ghans hit Mildura, Wentworth, Robinvale, and all the western paraline and beamflash links.

Unfortunately for Lemorel, Zarvora was not above preemptive strikes either. In March, and against the advice of her War Assembly of Mayors, she launched a massive assault across the eastern border, striking deep into Southmoor artisan centers, smashing bridges and physically removing paraline rails on such a scale that Southmoor transport was reduced to a tenth of normal capacity. She had timed the strike with beamflash network reports of unseasonally heavy rains arriving from the west. The Southmoor prohibition on beamflash communication worked against them, and they were unable to coordinate their defenses with the Ghans. Meantime the Ghan offensive in the west had been brought to a miserable, shivering halt, as they were unused to fighting in cold, continuous, torrential rain in lushly vegetated country.

By April, Zarvora had earned some respite and was fighting back in ways that the Ghans found bewildering. When the Ghans struck deep into enemy territory to frighten the cities into siege mode, the Alliance lancers would strike at

their supply depots and harass them until they were forced to withdraw. Ghan victories became hard-won, bloody, and transitory, rather than glorious, quick, and decisive. Try as she might, Lemorel could cut neither the beamflash nor paraline links any farther east than Morgan.

For all her successes, Zarvora remained objective. Her ever-rebellious western castellanies had gone over to Lemorel without a fight, and the Southmoors were slowly beating her troops back out of their lands in the east. In mid-April the city of Woomera fell, and Lemorel shocked even her own overhands by burning the stubbornly defiant capital of the Woomera Confederation to a warren of smoking shells without allowing any inhabitants to escape. The end of the siege freed seventy thousand Ghan troops and siege engineers. She decided to bring them to bear against Robinvale, a key beamflash link whose capture would isolate a third of Zarvora's territory.

Meanwhile there were numerous inconclusive strikes and probes for weaknesses. At Dareton a hastily trained line of musketeers faced and broke a charge by five brigades of Ghan lancers. A pin bearing crossed muskets was pressed into Zarvora's wall map to denote the battle, while a scribe added crossed sabers to a map in Lemorel's distant command tent. Within the Libris Calculor, a large vector was added at Dareton for the 105th Calculor Musketeer and it was assigned several parameters of movement.

The sun was setting on the Dareton battlefield, and the sky above was clear with the promise of a chilly night. Beside a burned-out farmhouse in the red mud of Dareton the exhausted captain of the 105th Overmayor's Heavy Infantry leaned against a fence post and drained a mouthful of sour wine from a jug, then dropped it into the ashes. Two plucked chickens dangled from his forage belt, and he was wearing the grubby jacket of a Great Western Paraline conductor and boots looted from a dead Ghan lancer. His corporal-adjunct sat on a nearby wool bale, patiently reloading their muskets.

"Captain Glasken, I still say that it is immoral to loot—"

"For the last time, you rambling Southmoor ricebrain, there's a difference between foraging and looting. This is for the good of the Alliance war effort."

"You stole that conductor's jacket at Morgan. That did not assist the war effort."

"That's different, I don't like conductors and anyway, it's my size. What a nightmare, did you ever see so many lancers trying to kill you?"

"Until Peterborough, Fras Captain, nobody has ever tried to kill me."

"Can't even remember what I said."

"You said 'Wait for my whistle ye—,' then you called their parentage into question."

"Why not? Mine certainly is."

"Six hundred and twenty dead or gravely wounded, Fras, and us with barely a scratch. We are certainly favored in the eyes of Allah."

"Speak for yourself, look at my neck—and the piece out of my helmet. Cost me sixty-five silver nobles at Loxton. Hullo, there's the trumpet. One long, two short, long, two short. That's . . . regroup and report to the railside."

Glasken took his musket back and shouldered it as they tramped back across the broken ground to the rally pennant. In the western sky the Mirrorsun band had partly eclipsed the new moon. It was much thinner than before, except for three dishlike thickenings spaced about 40 degrees apart across the sky.

 14　CASUALTY

Theresla was marched through the gates of Macedon in chains, with two dozen aviad musketeers escorting her. Her bearing was confident, however, and she was even smiling enigmatically. The Mayor met her in the town square, where most of the citizens had already been gathered. There was no doubt that this was to be a public humiliation.

"Always such a pleasure to meet with you, Mayor," Theresla declared as she walked up to him. "I came as fast as my chains would allow."

"The Overmayor has closed the school estates where our children are being raised," he declared loudly, as much for the benefit of the crowd as Theresla. "As her invel-sister you are to be held until our children are free."

"The message that reached me was that the children can return whenever they wish. Only their teachers are being held."

"You know what I mean! Our children cannot return here until they reach puberty, else they would live as vegetables under a perpetual Call."

None of Theresla's captors were particularly anxious to touch her, so she was free to climb onto a low wall where all could see and hear her easily.

"The sea creatures have a complex society," she began. "It is more advanced than ours in many ways, yet it is still driven by politics and factions. There are groupings of like-minded thinkers, power struggles, factions, and even duels. At least I think that they are duels. Most of their concepts are beyond both Austaric speech and my vocabulary. To them, we are all creatures of the land, creatures with puny mental powers but mighty tools. They have legends of when humans hunted them and nearly drove them to extinction."

"But *we* are not human," said the Mayor, climbing onto the wall beside her.

"To look, who would know? The Overmayor is fighting a war against very

stupid but annoyingly strong forces. The sea creatures do not want to intervene in a war between factions of their old enemies. They wish both sides a quick trip to 'the Chasm'—of hell, I suppose. The aviads of Macedon could fight for her, however, sabotaging Ghan positions when the Call sweeps over the battlefields.''

"There would be deaths," cried the Mayor, raising his arms. "I am opposed to anything that endangers the lineage and the genototem strength that we have cultivated so carefully."

"So you prefer to play spouse-swapping in safety while your allies and benefactors are blown to pieces? You might find that the Ghans are less liberal about the movement of citizens than Overmayor Cybeline. When you find access denied to the school estates you will really squeal."

"We have lived for two thousand years in hiding," retorted the Mayor. "We can do without the school estates, there are other ways."

"But not as good as a null zone over Macedon."

This was the stuff of aviad dreams and fairy tales: a null zone within the Calldeath lands, where children could be raised but that humans could not reach. The Mayor stared at her, his mouth hanging open.

"What sort of desperate lie is this?" he sneered.

"*I* am not desperate, but *you* are. As I said, the sea creatures are not a unified force, and the Phillip Bay dolphins are more sympathetic to us than the others. I have been negotiating a null zone over Macedon, and they are agreeable to it. There is a price, however, and that is aviad blood. Are you willing to fight for your children?" she demanded of the crowd.

Within an hour Theresla walked free through the gates of Macedon. Behind her the Mayor had already set up a recruiting office in his chambers.

Zarvora pondered the maps and charts that hung on the walls and littered the floors of a Libris hall that had been converted into her command headquarters. Vardel Griss, who was now her Overhand-in-Chief, was pointing to maps of the Great Western Paraline link to Kalgoorlie while Tarrin monitored a punched tape mechanism.

"Our spies tell us that several miles of track have been torn up just west of Maralinga, but nowhere else," said Griss as she gestured with her swagger stick. "If we could coordinate an attack from the west, it would force the Ghans to put some of their strength into a second front, giving us a chance to regroup and advance."

"Not a hope," said Zarvora.

"But Overmayor—"

"Tarrin, explain the problem."

"It's one of strategy," Tarrin began. "The western mayorates would depend on the paraline to move their troops across the Nullarbor. The Ghans are more

mobile on their camels and horses, and the paraline is impossible to defend along its entire length. A few hundred Ghans could tie down ten thousand Kalgoorlians by a series of quick strikes on the paraline. The desert would make slow traveling for an army using the road, and that army would be fighting heat, distance, and supply lines under constant attack by raiders appearing out of the desert.''

"Our spies also tell us that the Ghans are overextended in the west and fighting the Koorees as well,'' said Griss.

"It could be a ruse, a feint. The Ghans pretend to be weak, we advance, then we get shredded. We're holding them in the west. We must be satisfied with that.''

Griss glared at him, but was unable to fault his reasoning. Feints were indeed a Ghan tactic. She turned back to the map.

"You talk like we have already been defeated, Fras.''

"Strategically, we have,'' replied Tarrin in a flat detached voice. "Lemorel knows our strengths too well, and has hit us precisely where it hurts most. The time is right for a negotiated truce.''

"Pah! Tactically we have many advantages,'' said Griss defiantly.

"Name one.''

"The Southmoors will not sanction beamflash communications, so Lemorel's commands move slower than ours. With transport, our paraline grid and galley trains are running far more efficiently than those in enemy hands.''

"But their cavalry is far more mobile and versatile.''

"But not invincible,'' insisted Griss. "They sent five brigades against us at Dareton, but our musketeers broke their charge with discipline and steady shooting.''

"And they've learned from that! A Ghan overhand was shot by Lemorel herself for what happened at Dareton. Now the Ghans use mobile brigades whose officers choose their own ground for each battle while the Southmoors fight from well-defended trenches.''

"We can move resources faster.''

"But our resources are limited.''

With the exchange played out, they turned to Zarvora, who was standing before a map of the southeast.

"Griss is right, up to a point,'' she said slowly. "We can move faster, so we can choose the battlefields. From the paraline at Robinvale we shall strike near Balranald, the weakest Emirate among the Southmoors.''

"Weak? What about the hundred and fifty thousand Ghan cavalry that are hitting us along the entire length of our border with Balranald?'' asked Griss.

"Ah no, Balranald's political ties with the other Southmoors have always been weak,'' Zarvora pointed out offhandedly.

"If I were the Emir of Cowra, faced with an unreliable client in the northwest and a strong invader and ally in the same area, I would probably hand over

everything north of the line between Balranald and the Central Confederation's border. We know that the Emir of Balranald has declared the city closed, which is unusual considering that we are nowhere near the place. He fears his Ghan allies.''

"Seize the land between the Confederation and Balranald, and the Ghans would be cut off from the Southmoors.''

"The Ghans would just invade the Central Confederation,'' warned Tarrin. "A truce—''

"But the Confederation has a strong beamflash grid, as well as cavalry that's used to plains-country fighting,'' interjected Griss. "The Ghans do not want multiple fronts.''

"Yes, and a lot of Balranald territory is still controlled by its Emir,'' said Zarvora, tapping at that part of the map with her swagger stick. "If he and his subjects closed ranks against the Ghans, we could hold that strip indefinitely.''

"But if we lose that strip, a wedge will be driven right through our heartlands,'' said Tarrin. "The Ghans will be setting up their bombards on the shores of the Rochester lake moat itself within a week.''

Sondian was waiting under guard in the anteroom when Zarvora returned to her study. He stood and came forward as she reached her study door, and after turning the key in the lock she turned her back to the door and faced him.

"The greetings of the day, Fras Sondian. What can I do for you?''

"Why nothing, I know you are hard pressed. I came to offer help.''

"When I want a church, hospital, or market bombed during a Call you will be the first I contact,'' replied Zarvora in a light, cold voice. "Now go.''

"Some of my Aviad Radicals and their people have suffered terribly under the humans. They seek retribution, but I restrain them as best I can. How can we help in the war?''

"Help? Your Radicals would commit a few atrocities of doubtful military value, then claim half my territory as a reward after the war. My answer was, is, and will always be no. Guards, see him to the gate.''

The Mirrorsun band around the Earth had been transformed into a thin cable anchoring three immense concave dishes—pale red disks that shone with dull and metallic light as they traversed the night sky and faded into the blue of day. Zarvora watched the band changing on each night that was clear. She was sure that her first and only successful rocket had been responsible, and she had a good idea of what was soon to happen. Mirrorsun was going to hit back at the Wanderer battle satellites, something that might allow an entirely new technology onto the battlefields of the southeast. Even before the invasion she had freighted electroforce devices from Kalgoorlie to Rochester.

With no warning at all, the elements of the Mirrorsun dishes rotated in unison and at precisely programmed angles, each of trillions of facets showing a reflective facet to the sun. One of the orbital fortresses had caused damage to its fabric months earlier, and thus they were all classified as requiring elimination. An area a quarter of the moon's face punched the sun's radiation back in a beam that focused on an orbital fortress that had just cleared a landmass and was over the Pacific Ocean. The fortresses had not been attacked in millennia and their self-repairing and maintaining extensions had evolved vulnerabilities. Cooling vanes melted, pipes ruptured, internal circuits fried, and then the fortress detonated in a flash that lit up the Earth beneath it. The heavy shell continued to orbit amid the dispersing cloud of debris. An ancient comsat in geosynchronous orbit was next. A flickering change in direction of trillions of facets sent three searing cones of heat converging. The comsat became ash and vapor.

So far no alarm had gone out. High above the north pole another orbital fortress blazed brightly like a tiny, intense sun in Mirrorsun's beams, then exploded into an expanding sphere of debris and ionized gas surrounding the tough, dead shell. The Mirrorsun facets switched to above the south pole, where another fortress was passing the axis of rotation of the Earth. Its solar collectors melted and disintegrated first; then coolant burst through heat-weakened walls, internal systems failed, and the internal structure of the fortress blew into space as thousands of shining fragments.

By now the two other comsats on the far side of the earth were trying to poll the third. A malfunction was the first conclusion, but when they tried to poll a dead fortresses their alarms shrieked through space. The AIs of the surviving fortress satellites conferred briefly before the immense mirrors of Mirrorsun focused on the two comsats in turn. Their initial conclusion was an attack from an immense laser projector on the Earth's surface.

The fourth fortress was scanning the Earth when it became a bead of brilliance drawn across the night sky, and its AI fought to turn its weapons on bearings that were already melting. As it died the fifth fortress' AI was analyzing the configuration of the Mirrorsun band and it reached the correct conclusion. An EMP pulse slashed across one Mirrorsun dish, but although it left a thin black line in its wake, it did not sever the fabric. The default setting of the nanotech units was now LOCK. The mirror focused more slowly, but the beams played full on the fifth fortress. Its solar panels degraded and failed and the AI switched to battery backup. More pulses tore across the three dishes, leaving a tracery of black scars. Huge areas of the mirror dishes went dead and their combined beam weakened.

The sixth orbiter now joined the fight. Not being under attack, it played the full fury of its EMP cannons on the mirrors, analyzing the command structure in Mirrorsun's fabric by the pattern of failures on its surface. The fifth fortress broke

off the attack, realizing that it was being aided. It began to rotate itself with an internal gyroscope, trying to spread the heat dispersal over more of its surface.

Further out in space the cable that had seemed only an anchor for the three dishes had been far from passive. Like an immense particle accelerator it pumped a cluster of nanotech units up to 400 miles per second and spat them out into space. The sixth fortress was warned by its Doppler radar of the approach of the particles and it spun a cannister to pump a shield of particles to protect its flank. The nanotech units burst and sparkled in the cloud, yet they kept coming in an endless stream. Particle reserves fell to 50 percent, 40 percent, 30 percent. The AI realized that the stream was not self-directing, and it concluded that it could protect itself very simply. A moment later its ion rockets nudged it sideways in its orbit. Mirrorsun deployed a beam of focused sunlight that was a quarter of its former intensity. The fortress furled the arrays and began to rotate. Its AI noted that heat dispersal was tolerable, and that 90 percent of the solar cells had survived.

Far across the face of the Earth the AI of the fifth fortress began to cycle through damage-assessment routines. Its solar arrays were gone, its external sensors fused and blinded; the EMP weapons were jammed and their batteries almost drained. It still had control of its engines, however, and it could use its reserves of fuel to reach the orbit of the band and self-destruct. Its AI was still comparing optimal trajectories when a cloud of nanotech particles slammed into its outer armor, vaporizing themselves as they flayed it open to the backup cloud only milliseconds behind.

The sixth fortress nudged itself back into its original orbit as another cloud of particles hurtled toward it. They continued along their now harmless trajectory—then exploded! Debris intersected its orbit, raking the skin of the last fortress, tearing away armoring and solar arrays, and damaging one ion engine. Another cloud approached, and the orbital fortress pumped more shield particles out as it changed orbits again. The nanotech units exploded, absorbed by the cloud. The AI ran through an analysis: the resources of the Mirrorsun band were nearly infinite, while its own fuel and defenses would not last beyond the hour. It detached its armed engine module and fired it just before another wave of nanotech units pounded into the armored shell, destroying the AI.

Mirrorsun noted the engine module moving to a higher orbit and it directed a new stream of nanotech units to intercept the new trajectory. The module slipped behind the Earth, then climbed to meet the band, slowly and under constant attack. Hours later it passed through the band, flaying it with EMP bursts and particle clouds, tearing at its fabric until it was reduced to orbiting nanotech rags. As the module began the fall from apogee its command chip noted that it would now pass through the top layers of the atmosphere on the descent to perigee. The hail of nanotech units continued, exhausting its protective particle clouds and smash-

ing its remaining engines. Hours later the toughened cylinder plunged through the atmosphere, skipped back into space briefly, then dropped to earth, pulverizing itself in the Andes.

Slowly Mirrorsun began to reassemble itself. A third of its fabric was dead, but reserves were already being pumped up from the moon's surface.

"Strange lights in the sky," Glasken observed as he lay on his drop cloth. "Something's changed with Mirrorsun, too. It looks tarnished and ragged."

"The Wanderers have halos, Fras Captain, that is another point," said Ettenbar from where he too lay looking upward. "There! Look at Theten."

Glasken snorted. "Well, so what? In a few hours we'll be dead, as likely as not. What word of the Southmoors?"

"The Call of this morning scattered them worse than us. Perhaps their timers were set to a longer interval, so we were less affected."

"We'd not have been affected at all without this prohibition on beamflash Call warnings."

"Ah but that is vital to allow the people of Balranald to ally themselves with ourselves, who use beamflash communication."

"I've never worked out why Islam prohibits Call warnings."

"No, no, Islam prohibits nothing specifically to do with the Call. We merely recognize that the Call is an unknown to be treated with respect until such time as it is understood, that is where the prohibition on artificial Call warnings originates. Were the Call discovered to be from a mundane source, why we Southmoors would construct the finest beamflash grid in the world because our mathematics and lensware is the finest—"

"But that's unlikely to be before dawn tomorrow?"

"Regrettably."

Early the next morning they marched to a point where the highway neared a wide river. Rochester's small, shallow-draft battle galleys had penetrated all the way to the customs chain at Haytown, and the only bridge between Balranald and the Confederation had been demolished. Ghans lancers had appeared on the northern banks and fired at the galleys, but the boats were armored against small-arms fire and their grapeshot bombards scattered the lancers. Soon the access to the border was secure, but heliostat messages told them that an attack was coming at Ravensworth Junction. Southmoor mounted musketeers had ridden forty miles through the night, along the back roads from Wanganella. They were now beginning to dig in.

Overhand Gratian of the Alliance forces called a hurried conference of his captains. The officers were grimy and haggard, but still well disciplined as they gathered around him in the drizzle that had ended a brief period of sunlight.

"The only viable bridge between Balranald and Haytown is here at Ravensworth," the Overhand began, "and if the enemy can rebuild it the Ghans will

pour across to join the Southmoors. They have two dozen medium bombards on the banks and those could sink our battle galleys. We have to take the bridgehead and defend it. Captains Fitzen, Alluwanna, Kearley, Glasken, Ling-zo, and Richards will lead their companies in the attack on specific points in Ravensworth, then strike north to the bridge. Intelligence reports that their trenches are about five hundred yards from the river, so that's to our advantage. If we dig in there we can use bombards against their bridge repair crews.''

"A question, sir.''

"Glasken?''

"Won't we be in range of *their* bombards?''

"As a matter of fact, yes, and our battle calculor at Balranald estimates that *no* aid will be available to us. Everything the Alliance has in this sector will be thrown into an offensive north from Deniliquin against the Southmoor reinforcements. We here are facing very bad times.''

"But if the floodwaters subside the Ghans can rig up a pontoon bridge out of range of our bombards and there's a hundred and fifty thousand of them.''

"Correct, Captain Glasken, but nothing's certain in war.''

The Alliance attack began about an hour past noon, with bombards pounding the higher buildings of the town to deny the Southmoors an overview. The infantry advanced in open order across scrubby pasture and at Glasken's whistle Jay Company started forward with Dunoonan holding the regimental colors and Ettenbar playing the regimental march on his zurna. Heavy, sustained fire burst from the distant buildings of the town and men began to cry out and drop before they had gone a dozen paces. To the right a line of two dozen knelt, aimed, and fired a ragged volley at the houses before rejoining the march. Another line knelt, fired, and stood, but the respite was transitory. Dunoonan staggered for a moment with the standard, then limped on, and the butt of Glasken's musket shattered along one edge as a ball caught it. Something tugged at Glasken's sleeve and stung his arm. Even as he was wincing, the back of Sergeant Condolonas' head burst with a sharp wet thud from a ball that had entered by his left eye. Glasken was splattered with warm, wet flesh, and his mesmerized determination to continue the lumbering charge was suddenly broken.

"South-Twenty, all to cover, charge!'' he shouted, then broke into a run. Moments later they were pinned down behind an earth wall by sporadic but accurate fire from the outlying houses of the town. Glasken lay panting on his back with his eyes tightly shut, aware that blood was trickling down his sleeve, and that it was probably his. He opened his eyes to see Ettenbar beside him, trying to tighten the reed of his battle zurna.

"Damn hell, Ettenbar, couldn't you play something they liked?'' panted Glasken, at last looking down at his own blood-soaked sleeve.

" 'Campbell's Farewell to the Red Rock' is the esteemed—''

"That's 'Campbell's Retreat from the Red Castle'! What the hell do you mean playing a retreat during a charge?"

"With all deference to your rank, Fras Captain, it is 'Campbell's Farewell'—"

"It's 'Campbell's Retreat,' you stupid little Southmoor bastard! It's an old Scottish tune. I was born in Sundew, I grew up in Sundew, and my people moved there from wherever Scotland was two thousand years ago. I spent the first eighteen years of my life wearing kilts, eating porridge, playing the bagpipes, and learning bloody Highland dancing even though there weren't any highlands within two hundred miles of the place. I say it's 'Campbell's Retreat'!"

"Is regiment's tune," insisted Ettenbar sullenly.

Glasken noticed that sixteen dozen pairs of eyes and ears were following the argument with interest. He stared back, his mind full of jagged, jangling confusion. I know what they're thinking, he told himself. Every one of them is thinking, "If these two loons keep arguing about musicology I might live an extra few minutes."

"Well?" he asked them.

" 'Campbell's Farewell to the Red Castle,' " chorused the men. Glasken flopped on his back again, unable to face them. They had all just faced death and many more would be dead within seconds of his next order.

"Is not retreat!" muttered Ettenbar, still fiddling with the reed.

"Gah, shaddup! Poll the men."

Of the 250 men who had started across the field, 195 had reached the shelter of the earth wall.

"And nine men can go no further due to injured legs, Captain," Ettenbar reported.

Glasken thought for a moment, then unfolded his tower scope and peered at the houses. "Maybe two hundred Southmoors," he muttered.

"But Fras, the rate of fire was far above that."

"They probably have three guns each, and doubtless they're elite musketeers. There's a whole swag of tricks like that for overextended forces: have spare guns to hand, shoot straight, load fast, but . . . yes, but I know tricks too. Get those nine wounded together, over there, to the left. Give them a dozen spare pistols each from the others. The rest are to drop their muskets and forage packs and carry only sabers. They're to scrape the mud from their boots, too."

"But, Captain, this is unheard of. The men need their packs."

"There's fifty behind us who still have their packs but don't need 'em. Do it."

Glasken gave his officers and sergeants a short and unconventional briefing.

". . . and when the command to *really* charge comes, it will be this white kerchief pulled from my jacket, waved twice and flung down. Everyone's to watch

for that, then it's straight over the top without a yell. Run like the whirley-clappers for the Southmoor cover. Total silence, understand? The bastards won't expect that, they'll think their eyes are playing them false because their ears hear nothing. We'll be over that ground before they get more than two volleys into us, then it's sabers as has the advantage. Lieutenant Jendrik, if I'm dropped, they're yours.''

The group started to break up, and Glasken pretended not to notice for a moment.

''Oi, I've not finished,'' he called so that all of the musketeers could hear. ''Any of you caught fighting over prisoners or loot and it's fifty lashes each. Mark your gear so you can find it without arguing when you come back. There'll be too much to do what with digging in.''

Bloody pathetic bravado, Glasken thought to himself. Anyone who's not stupid will see right through it. On the other hand, we must all be pretty damn stupid to be out here in the mud getting shot to pieces, so who knows?

Some minutes later the Southmoors heard Glasken's whistle, and a scatter of shots flashed atop the earth wall to their left. The heads appeared all along the wall and the Southmoors opened fire at once. The heads withdrew, then there was more whistling and cursing. The battle zurna brayed ''Campbell's Farewell to the Red Castle'' again, but the tune was cut short. ''Rebellion,'' several Southmoors muttered. Again a few Alliance musketeer heads appeared. Another volley, the heads fell back—then more figures silently swarmed over the bank and came running across the field unnaturally fast.

Glasken had guessed well. There were three muskets to each Southmoor. One more hasty volley tore into the Alliance men; then the Southmoor fire became irregular as some tried to reload and others drew their flintlock pistols and delivered a less coordinated volley. There had been no time to dig stake trenches, and Glasken's unencumbered company flashed through the vegetable gardens with unexpected speed and agility, ducking, dodging, and scattering the cowering poultry.

Glasken's reflexes took over as he burst in among the Southmoors with his saber and demiblade whirling, slicing and punch-chopping with a half-decade of Baelsha training behind every movement. Now that the fighting was hand-to-hand, the versatile and battle-hardened men of the 105th had a distinct advantage, even though two dozen more had been sliced from their ranks by Southmoor fire. Jay Company of the 105th took their sector of the town after forty minutes more of bloody, desperate fighting, then went to the assistance of the others. Overhand Gratian was impressed. He assigned hundreds more men to Glasken, then left him to dig in and make sure that the bridge stayed down. Balranald was in need of as many musketeers and officers as Gratian could take there.

Glasken's mind had begun to move in slightly more strategic channels during

the course of the war, and he treated his Southmoor prisoners accordingly. While his officers called for all prisoners to be shot, Glasken ordered them stripped to their trews, then had their right hands struck one hard blow each with an axe handle before turning them loose to return to the Southmoor lines.

"A merciful gift, that of life," said Ettenbar.

"Nothing of the kind. They're weaponless and with broken fingers to boot. They'll tax their own army's support but help them not at all. A pity if any were lutanists or pipers, though."

He noticed that Ettenbar had removed the reed from his battle zurna, and was corking it into a bamboo tube. Glasken broke a twig from the peach tree above him.

"Oi there, Corporal Ettenbar, hold out your hand."

"Yes, Fras Cap—Ach!" he cried as the blow landed and he snatched his hand back.

Zarvora had begun to operate her transmitter even before the fifth and sixth orbital fortresses had been destroyed. She had watched the rapid changes and damage in the Mirrorsun band, then noted that one of the Wanderer satellites was surrounded by a dispersing cloud of sparkles. She incorrectly concluded that all the Wanderers had been destroyed, but this was soon to be the case. The fortresses were by then too preoccupied with Mirrorsun to bother with her puny signals.

She sat at a bench in a darkened room with an array of batteries powering the coils of her tuned circuit while she tapped at a modified beamflash key. Tarrin stared at a tiny air gap through a lens, frowning in the darkness.

"I don't recognize the pattern that you are sending," he said as the hour chimed out from a distant clocktower. "What is this thing meant to do?"

"Flash to you."

Tarrin sighed and squinted at the gap. "I see sparks now." His eyes widened. "UNDERSTOOD AND ACKNOWLEDGED is the message, in standard calibration code."

"Undamaged," sighed Zarvora with relief, standing up and wringing her hands together so hard that her knuckles crackled. "Requisition a galley engine. I must go to Oldenberg with all this machinery."

"But it would fill two trucks or more, Frelle Overmayor."

"I know, it filled three when I had it shipped from Kalgoorlie, before the invasion. Now move!"

When he had gone Zarvora began to work the key again. As soon as she had noticed the rapid, ominously purposeful changes in the Mirrorsun band, she had sent a message to Denkar through her agents and carrier birds. He was to watch the skies, and if the Wanderers suddenly changed or vanished he was to connect a sparkflash transceiver to an unprotected external antenna and await her signal.

INSTANTANEOUS COMMUNICATION WITHOUT BEAMFLASH, she

typed. REPLY. SPEAK TO ME. I LOVE YOU. TELL ME ABOUT KAL-
GOORLIE.

After only seconds the sparks began to crackle faintly beneath the eyepiece
of the receiver.

I LOVE YOU TOO. THE SUN IS SETTING AND THE SKY IS CLEAR.

"It works!" shouted Zarvora, leaping to her feet and waving her fists above
her head. "It works, it works, the war is won, the universe is changed." She
caught herself, then glanced around, thankful that she had not had an audience,
then sat down and tapped a reply.

THE SUN IS HOURS DOWN IN ROCHESTER. SUMMON MAYOR
BOUROS. WE MUST DISCUSS THE WAR. I WANT CONTACT NAMES
FOR THE LOYAL COMPANY OF ELECTROFORCE STUDIES OF OLD-
ENBERG.

It was midnight before Zarvora was interrupted by Tarrin, who had organized
a galley engine and three trucks for her. Reluctantly she powered down the spark-
gap transceiver and supervised its packing. Down in the system console room of
the Libris Calculor she found that Dolorian was visiting to discuss a problem
with beamflash protocols.

"Frelle Dolorian, just the Frelle I need. Rouse a lackey to find the six others
on this list. In two hours you are all to be packed and ready to leave at the
paraline terminus on the military platform."

"I—*Military*, Frelle Overmayor?"

"You have just joined my army, Lieutenant Dolorian. You rank ninth in
Libris Gallery Lists, so you must know one end of a gun from the other."

"Yes, but, but—"

"You have the key beamflash codes and Calculor protocols memorized. Because of your former association with Lemorel Milderellen you have also been
so thoroughly scrutinized by the Black Runners that your security rating is within
a point or two of *mine*. I shall explain the rest on the train."

Parsimar Wolen was dragged from his bed by the Oldenberg Constable's Runners,
who had broken down the door. With his wife screaming that he was seventy-
three, innocent, and suffering from arthritis he was bundled into a pony gig wearing only his nightshirt. At the assembly hall of Oldenberg University, Parsimar
saw that the other eight members of the Oldenberg Loyal Company of Electroforce Studies were also there, huddling together in their nightshirts.

"Jarel, what's happened?" he asked as they stood shivering together.

"Don't rightly know, Fras Parsimar. Boteken thinks that electroforce studies
has been declared a heresy, an' that we're to be burned at the stake."

"Heresy's only punishable by exile, and besides, burnin' at the stake was
struck off the books in 1640."

"We'll all be shot, then. I told you we should have stayed a secret society."

It was very cold in the hall, and Parsimar was shivering.

"Ah, Sergeant?" he quavered.

"Yes, Fras?"

"Might—might I have a blanket, please?"

"Certainly, Fras, and slippers too?"

"What? Ah, yes, thank you."

"The coffee and bread rolls will not be long. Seems we caught the University refectory by surprise."

The runner marched off smartly, leaving the two elderly guildsmen staring after him.

"He were civil to us," said Jarel incredulously.

"Doesn't sound like we're felons," Parsimar concluded. "Looky there! It's the Overmayor herself."

Zarvora had the hall cleared of the runners. Soon only the nine guildsmen remained, and she gathered them around her.

"These are the plans for a sparkflash radio transceiver, and out in the marshaling yards three paraline wagons are standing by with a disassembled working model. I want you to build seven more transceivers, each small enough to fit into four horse-drawn military wagons. I want them working, and their operators trained, within a fortnight."

The guildsmen gave a collective gasp.

"But, Frelle Overmayor, the blight of the Wanderers—" began Parsimar.

"I have destroyed the Wanderers."

For a moment they were speechless.

"Three cheers for the Overmayor," shouted Parsimar in a thin, reedy voice.

When the last of the wheezing cheers had died away, Jarel raised his hand. "The cost will be great, Frelle Overmayor. No less than five hundred gold royals."

"You can have *five hundred thousand* gold royals, you have *unlimited* resources, Fras, understand? *Unlimited.* The Rochester Home Guard has sealed the city, the artisans of the paraline workshops, the Guild of Watchmakers and Call Timers, and the University workshops and laboratories are being roused at this very minute. Two hundred artisans, mechanics, engineers, and lackeys are on their way from Libris in Rochester to assist you. Who is Fras Parsimar Wolen, your Guildmaster?"

"I, I—"

"Delighted to meet you," she said, shaking his hand. "You are Overseer, reporting directly to me. If anyone deliberately obstructs you, have them shot. Anyone! The City Constable, the City Librarian, the City Undermayor, *anyone.*"

Parsimar was dizzy with what was flooding past him. Listening to the Overmayor was like trying to drink from a waterfall.

"But, Frelle Overmayor, I'm seventy-three—"

"Happy birthday. These drawings are an overview of the sparkflash, and I want to spend the morning reassembling the unit from Libris here, in this hall, to familiarize you with the design."

"I need my pills and tonics," Boteken interjected.

"The University's Faculty of Medicians will suspend all teaching and re-search work to tend your health. *Nothing* is as important as having those seven transceivers completed in two weeks. Ah, here is Lieutenant Dolorian. She is in charge of training."

Dolorian was carrying a sheaf of files under each arm. She was wearing a borrowed jacket, which she had unsuccessfully tried to button over her breasts. The effect was quite arresting. Parsimar goggled, then hastily tilted the lenses of his bifocals.

Zarvora left to finish the mobilization of Oldenberg behind the project. Do-lorian continued the briefing from notes that Zarvora had dictated on the train.

"The six Wanderers were ancient military machines," Dolorian began, her hips swaying slightly as if to the beat of an inaudible tune. It had begun as a nervous mannerism when she had delivered her first public speech, but she soon realized that it was guaranteed to secure the undivided attention of every man in the audience. "Their purpose was to detect and destroy electroforce devices of the enemy."

"So the Wanderers were weapons that operated for two thousand years, Frelle?"

"Amazingly, yes. Just before the Ghan invasion, the Overmayor brought the Wanderers into conflict with whatever controls the Mirrorsun band. Less than a day ago there was a second battle in the sky and Mirrorsun was the victor. We can now use electroforce machines in war, and the present war is going badly for us. Sparkflash radio wagons will give us instant communications, and they can move with our armies."

On the other side of the world, Brother Alex of the Monastery of the Holy Wisdom near Denver was listening to the thunderstorms in the mountains to the west. More precisely, he was listening to radio emissions from lightning far be-yond the horizon. Using a rectifier made from a crystal of galena he had built an unpowered tuned circuit a decade earlier and was developing a system to predict storms' movement without the need for sailwing patrols by wardens.

Today the storms were very distant, he could hear only the faintest of light-ning bursts. Faint but regular. Very regular. His hands rose to press the coilmuffs hard against his ears. This was no thunderstorm, he realized.

"Electroforce signaling," he whispered. "Dear God in Heaven, an electro-force machine!"

In all of Mounthaven's wardenates there was not another working on tuned circuits, while those in the Callhavens to the south could not even build aircraft. That meant somewhere farther away. Perhaps from the legendary continents of Asiaire or Australica. But surely the moving Sentinel stars would burn any electroforce device. . . .

Brother Alex suddenly recalled the strange events in the sky of some days past when Mirrorsun assumed strange, portentous shapes and the Sentinels moved through the skies surrounded by the most exquisite haloed clouds of sparkle. Everyone had assumed it to be some message of great astrological import, but now Brother Alex had his doubts. Suppose it had not been a glorious cosmic fiesta. Suppose it had been a war. Suppose the Sentinels had been vanquished.

For the next two hours the monk copied down the faint, coded transmissions from beyond the oceans, then reluctantly decided that he needed to spend time with the ancient textbooks in the library. As he walked through the cloisters clutching his sheaf of papers, a flock of gunwings from the nearby wingfield droned through the clear spring sky in formation, their compression engines straining as they gained height.

"The universe has changed on this day in May, Anno Domini 3939," Brother Alex said to the wardens high above in their tiny fighting machines.

The seven transceivers took nearly a month to be made operational, but Zarvora knew that she had to accept the delay. The stalemate in the east was starting to work against her now, as the Southmoors had adapted better to trench warfare. Winter mist interfered with beamflash links, while the thick cloud often hindered the use of heliostats on the battlefield. Finally the Black Runners brought an unconfirmed report that the Ghans and Southmoors were to merge several divisions for a thrust from Deniliquin down to the Calldeath lands. Rochester was to be split in two.

Five of the seven sparkflash tranceivers were deployed in the west, northwest and northeast. One was even smuggled across Southmoor Territory into the Central Confederation. Troops freed from defending the beamflash towers were moved by paraline to Robinvale, where they were assembled into a new army. Dolorian was assigned to this force, with the seventh sparkflash squad. The objective was to fortify a strip of land that Alliance forces had captured, a strip that reached all the way to the Central Confederation's border.

It never happened, for a horde of Ghan lancers and mounted musketeers appeared, seemingly from nowhere. Zarvora later estimated that some of the Ghan units had been brought from seven hundred miles away in no more than a week. The exhausted but well coordinated Ghans prevailed over the unprepared Alliance musketeers in a battle halfway between Robinvale and Balranald, yet Overhand Gratian somehow gathered the remains of his divisions into

an orderly retreat. At Balranald they crossed the flooded river and destroyed the bridges.

"The Ghans were warned," Zarvora announced at the new Sparkflash Command Center in Oldenberg. "Someone who knew about the paraline movements deduced that troops were to be concentrated at Robinvale."

"That spy could be one of thousands," Vardel Griss replied. "The paraline system is vast."

"In three months it will be more secure. We shall have a sparkflash unit on every galley train and in every fort, but until then we have to use the beamflash system, and that system is not secure. The codes were good, yet they were broken and used against us."

"Another calculor, Frelle?"

"Even the Kalgoorlie machine would take two years to break our new codes. No, we were betrayed, as were the fifteen thousand dead musketeers at the Battle of Robinvale. Damn. Still no report of Dolorian and Sparkflash Seven."

Griss looked at the wall map, and its seven green pins. The pin marked with a 7 was just north of Balranald. Zarvora returned to where the sparkflash operator sat.

"She may not be captured, and if she is moving she cannot transmit. The sparkflash gear takes five hours to set up and tune."

"Let us hope so—uh! That's odd."

Zarvora began to copy out characters from a sparkflash signal. Griss looked over her shoulder, shaking her head.

"Very, very faint," said Griss. "I've never seen anything like it."

"It's familiar, I saw something similar in the fragments of texts in Kalgoorlie. It could be an ancient system of letters and numerals known as Morse Code, which depicts them in two types of strokes, short and long."

Zarvora reached for a book of tables. "It spells DENVER YANG-KI over and over."

"That's not any place I know. It—it could be from beyond the Calldeath lands."

"So it would seem, Frelle Griss. Ours may not be the only civilization."

"Yang-Ki. It sounds like a name from old China. Will you reply?"

"What can I say? Thanks awfully for calling, but we are very busy so please go away."

"Something simpler, Frelle Overliber. It never hurts to be friendly. Give them a pre-Greatwinter place name, something big. What is the name of that huge abandon to the south of here?"

"Melbourne. Well, why not?"

Zarvora tapped: OVERMAYOR ZARVORA. MELBOURNE. HEARING DENVER YANG-KI.

The ensuing exchange was less than productive, for American and Australian English had drifted apart during two thousand years of isolation. Zarvora keyed END OF TRANSMISSION several times, and presently the transmitter on the other side of the world signed off too.

"WE something FOR PEACE was their last message," said Zarvora.

"They won't find it here, there's a war going on," said Griss.

Away to the north Dolorian and Major Hartian, who was commanding the Spark-flash 7 unit, were hauling rafts carrying the sparkflash wagons across the Murrumbidgee River in the driving rain while Alliance bombards on the south bank raked the attacking Ghans with grapeshot. The river was in flood and still rising and muddy water swirled about the wheels of the last of the wagons as it was hauled up the bank to safety.

"Are you all right, Lieutenant?" the driver of the transceiver wagon called down to the mud-encrusted figure who was pushing against the transverse beam.

"Only just," panted Dolorian, who was soaked, her long hair partly free of its bindings and plastered to her face by muddy water. "Hairpins at the bottom of the river. Nearly went with them. We're safe now, though."

"Not so, Frelle Lieutenant," called a runner who was waiting. "New Southmoor advance, word just came by dispatch rider. It's going to be all running battles. The Major wants to know your needs. He's at the pennant pole."

"Six silver hairpins and a Cargelligo orbile comb, dry clothes, hot chocolate, and a month's leave—oh, and a rich and handsome suitor who can play the lutina."

"Can't help, Frelle," panted the runner, who looked to be all of a weedy and pockmarked eighteen. "He wants to know what you need to get Sparkflash Seven working."

"Five hours in secure territory."

"There's a fortified trench square guarding what's left of the bridge pillars at Ravensworth."

"Ravensworth? That's liable to be the place of the next major attack as the Southmoors and Ghans try to link up. Better to destroy the wagons here, before they're captured. Riding hard we could reach to Central Confederation in a day, at most."

"At Ravensworth they're dug in securely and they have bombards, Frelle Lieutenant. Their captain fought at Dareton when they broke that cavalry charge. Glasken, that's his name. John Glasken. They say he's a good 'un to be under. Brave, a great leader, and seen action."

Dolorian sagged against the muddied wheel of the wagon. Unconsciously she flicked open the top button of her wet, filthy jacket, then walked two fingers slowly along a spoke as the rain pelted down on her. Bugles sounded assembly in the distance.

"More action than you'd ever suspect, Fras Corporal," she said huskily, then pushed away from the wheel and tramped through the red mud toward the pennant pole.

Captain John Glasken of the 105th Overmayor's Heavy Infantry was in his command tent when the wagons of Sparkflash 7 and their escort arrived at Ravensworth. Major Hartian supervised the selection of a site for the wagons, then set off for the command tent. He noted that there was no guard, then entered. There was a piercing scream and he backed out again.

About a minute later Glasken emerged, buttoning his shirt and carrying his saber and scabbard under his arm. As he approached, a woman darted from the tent behind him with a coat over her head and vanished behind a pile of logs in the direction of the orderlies' area.

"I was, ah, taken with a fever," Glasken explained. "A nurse was tending me."

"A nurse wi' paraline conductor's coat over her head?" asked Major Hartian.

Glasken watched the unpacking of the radio wagons with perplexity as the Major briefed him on the requirements of Sparkflash 7.

"There are two mast wagons, a power wagon, and the transceiver wagon," he explained as Glasken struggled to understand what the thing was. "The mast wagons must be fifty yards apart, and they extends collapsible masts to a height of fifteen yards. Between them is strung a double wire called an antenna, after the ancient Anglaic word 'antenna.' "

"But they're the same word," said Glasken.

"Fras Captain, manual says antenna is named after 'antenna,' so antenna is what I says. I 'ad two days of training from Overmayor herself—"

"Agreed, agreed. What's it to do?"

"It replaces beamflash towers, that's what. You can call all the way to Rochester direct for orders."

"But the towers are far too short to be useful. A man on top of one of them might as well be up a tree."

"They're not workin' on light flashes, Fras Captain. They pick waves out of the air itself by that wire."

"Waves? Like on a river or lake?"

"Aye, that's right. Now—"

"But where's the water?"

"See here, are you ignorant or somethin'? Once the waves are picked up the operator sees the message at the spark gap. The little flashes of light are like beamflash transmissions—"

"But you just said it's waves and wires, and now it's back to light flashes and beamflash codes."

"Fras Captain, this is a major scientific advance."

"Well I have a scientific degree!"

After a further ten minutes of argument and exposition the two officers parted on less than amicable terms. For the next hour Glasken stripped and cleaned his rifle and pistols while he watched the masts being erected and braced with guy ropes. The double wire between the mast-top insulators was almost too fine to see. The cover of the power wagon was removed to reveal ten sets of pedals from a galley train mechanism, with the gearing connected to a barrel-shaped thing with wires trailing off to the transceiver wagon.

More hours passed, and the rain began again. After a tour of inspection Glasken returned to watch Sparkflash 7 working. There was an odd buzzing sound and the same smell of ozone that followed thunderstorms. Presently his curiosity got the better of him. He made his way over to the transceiver wagon, which was dark inside and filled with a buzzing, crackling sound. A Dragon Librarian sat in one corner; Glasken could see the blue armband of rank above her military stripes. Her head was obscured by a baffle but her breasts were not. They were alluringly large. He cleared his throat.

"Captain John Glasken of the 105th reporting," he declared. The woman beckoned him in without looking away from the spark gap.

"You are just in time, Captain," she said in a husky voice. "I am in contact with the transmitter at Oldenberg, with the Overmayor herself."

Glasken slid onto the bench beside her and peered past her head into the spark-gap box, where a violet light was flickering on and off. The space was confined and he draped his arm over the operator's shoulder to see past her head. The sparks had a familiar pattern about them.

"I say, that's beamflash protocol, with standard code," he exclaimed with surprise. "CALIBRATION TEST 5 COMPLETING."

"Good work, Captain, I see you are an experienced operator," his companion purred approvingly.

Glasken realized that although his hand was resting on her left breast, his face had not been slapped. He gave an affectionate, experimental squeeze.

"Just as I can tell distant operators by their keystrokes, I can recognize you by your touch, Johnny Glasken."

"Frelle, I have never worked your switches before, enchanting thought though it be."

"Ah but you have, Fras Johnny," she said as she turned away from the spark gap.

"Dolorian!" cried Glasken, and he turned to stumble and crash his way out of the wagon at once. "Guards! Guards! Guards! An Alspring spy. Guards! Damn you, here! Quickly."

The Major arrived to find Dolorian standing beside the wagon with her hands in the air and ringed by a dozen of Glasken's infantry. Glasken watched from

a distance, calling for them to be careful and to shoot to kill if she moved.

"What in hell goes on?" demanded Major Hartian.

"Alspring spy," said Glasken, waving in Dolorian's direction with his saber. "A personal friend of Lemorel, their maniac leader."

"She's also the most experienced sparkflash operator besides Overmayor herself," the Major shouted back.

"All the worse! A spy at the heart of our command."

"I have the Overmayor's security clearance," began Dolorian.

"That she does, Fras Captain."

"But she knows Lemorel. Lemorel taught her to shoot, they went shopping together, they were friends, and well, who knows what else?"

Dolorian raised her eyes to the sky for a moment. By now there was an audience of several dozen muddy musketeers gathered around them. "Well *I* never slept with her, Captain Glasken, which is more than you can say!" she said in a soft, clear voice.

"*You* slept with the Alspring Horde's *supreme commander*?" asked the incredulous Major.

"Ah, well, just a student dalliance," stammered Glasken. "And only once."

"From July 1697 to September 1699," Dolorian corrected him, "when she discovered that you had been cheating."

"You *cheated* on the enemy's supreme commander?" exclaimed the Major, scarcely believing what he had just heard.

"Three cheers fer Captain Glasken!" called an onlooker, and the musketeers cheered loudly.

Since taking Ravensworth, Glasken's force had demolished the bridge across the river right down to the stone foundations, then dug in at the edge of their own bombards' range. The bombards were finely made, the latest Inglewood type that shot calibrated lead balls with great accuracy, and thus outreached the enemy bombards across the river. The Alspring engineers tried to float their own bombards across on rafts, but the turbulent floodwaters and Alliance bombardment frustrated them. They gave up after the fifth bombard was lost.

All the while the Southmoors had been pouring cavalry along the roads from Wanganella, and in spite of sabotage and cavalry raids across the border it was only a matter of time before the gun carriages arrived. With Balranald in Alliance control and Haytown supposedly neutral, the importance of the Ravensworth bridge grew by the hour. One hundred thousand Alspring lancers and their support forces were building up on the north side of the bridge. Major Hartian ordered the eight female nurses of the 105th to be escorted north, to the neutral Confederation's border and internment for the rest of the war. The medician remained.

Dolorian worked the sparkflash radio constantly, sending estimates of en-

emy strength to Oldenberg and getting new intelligence through from the transmitters at Balranald and Robinvale, as well as the secret transmitter that had been smuggled into the Alliance embassy at Griffith. Using the Confederation's beamflash system, spies at Haytown alerted the embassy when a senior delegation of Alspring leaders arrived from the west. In particular, it was noted that the pennants of the Ghans' supreme commander were flying over the governor's mansion.

"Lemorel's there to demand access to the Haytown bridges," Glasken concluded when a runner brought him the message.

Hartian was doubtful. "Why should she bother talking? She has a division besieging Balranald, and Haytown is not nearly as well fortified. Two days at a forced march and she could have Haytown in her purse."

"Good tactics, bad strategy," replied Glasken. "To crush Haytown would get her the Central Confederation as an enemy. The Confederation has a lot more strength in its lancer divisions than the Alliance, and they're a match for the Ghans in dryland fighting. It also has a long border near the Alspring supply lines. No, she'll bluster and threaten, then offer them some compromise they couldn't refuse."

Major Hartian looked at the map on the folding table between them, then read through the radio transmissions again.

"Over the river there are a hundred thousand Alspring Ghans, who are particularly anxious to rebuild that bridge. On this side there are eleven thousand Southmoors on the roads from the south, and already there's a buildup of five thousand surrounding us. We have nine hundred men and three pathetic bombards."

"Those brass-alloy bombards are the finest that my taxes can buy," said Glasken indignantly.

"But there's still only three of them—what's that?"

A rattle of small arms fire broke the peace.

"An attack!" said Glasken, seizing his musket and lancepoint helmet.

The Southmoors had been expected to attack from the Ravensworth side of the Alliance trenches, and to pound the place with artillery first. Instead they had sent nearly the whole force of dismounted cavalry crawling through the open fields to the west and east until they were in a position to attack the Alliance bombard emplacements from two sides. The thin wedge of trenches held at first, then began to take breaches under the weight of suicidal attacks. In a half hour of fighting the bombards were cut off, and the Alliance troops retreated to a second line of trenches while their trapped comrades fought on in isolation.

Dolorian had been following the developments from the shelter of the power wagon when a runner found her. He indicated a ragged rally pennant.

"That's the forward command post," he panted. "You are to report there."

Dolorian crawled miserably through the cold, red mud, trying to stay as low as possible and for once in her life wishing that her breasts were a little smaller. Ettenbar called to her from a foxhole, and she made her way across to him while shots flew waspishly overhead. He had been promoted to sergeant by now.

"All gone, Frelle Lieutenant," he cried. "Captain and Major, trapped with the bombards."

"Out there? They're cut off?"

"Lieutenant, you are the communications officer, the senior officer left here." He gave her as crisp a salute as he could manage. "Pleased to give orders, Frelle Lieutenant?"

"Me? But my commission is administrative."

"Orders, Frelle? Please? We are desperate. We want a leader with orders."

Dolorian raised her head to survey the field of struggling men, gun flashes, drifting smoke and mud-encrusted corpses.

"And I want a pile of cushions, my high-heeled boots, filtered coffee, and caramel cream chocolates."

"Regrettably, Frelle, those things are not in supply here."

"I want to die in bed, and of old age, preferably with company—"

A shot kicked up the mud between them, and they crouched down again.

"Ah, death, Frelle. Now I *can* accept that in your place. You give the order, I lead the attack."

Dolorian could feel tears welling from her eyes and mixing with the mud on her cheeks. There was a heavy blast in the distance as a spiked bombard exploded.

"Fras Major and Captain are destroying the bombards, Lieutenant."

"Sergeant Ettenbar, if the Southmoors break through, the incendiary bombs in the sparkflash wagons must be ignited. Meantime, I want an attack to relieve the bombard crews."

Ettenbar smiled as he drew a double-barreled flintlock.

"Your orders, my duty, Lieutenant. Might I suggest that a nurse's jacket and headband are in the captain's tent. Southmoors are chivalrous, a nurse would be treated with honor—"

Dolorian reached out and snatched the gun from him.

"You'd look silly as a nurse, Sergeant."

"No, no, Frelle, I mean—"

"*I* lead the charge, *you* stand by to burn the sparkflash wagons."

The third bombard had just been spiked when another onslaught of Southmoors fell on the doomed position, but the Alliance men were well armed and the Southmoors could not coordinate their superior numbers. They were lancers, trained to fight from horses. Major Hartian lit the fuse to the bombard's touchhole, then made a flying leap for the corner beside Glasken. The barrel jammed with

wadding exploded. The shattering blast left their ears ringing, and the Southmoor attack faltered. The line of white cavalry uniforms smeared with red mud and began to fall back.

"That's all bombards, we have nothing they want," shouted Hartian above the ringing in Glasken's ears.

"They'll have the bridge up in ten hours, now that we can't blast it any more," Glasken replied.

"Let 'em. We'll not last an hour, but main square could hold out for a couple more days. The Ghans don't know about sparkflash wagons. I'm guessing they'll pass us by, leaving a small force of bombards to pound us. Lieutenant Dolorian can call their numbers out to Overmayor for all time that's left."

"Listen!" barked Glasken. "A Southmoor battle zurna."

"Just tryin' to rally their men."

"No!" exclaimed Glasken. "It's 'Campbell's Farewell to the Red Castle,' the 105th's march. That's Ettenbar!"

"They're attacking to relieve us! Fools! The Southmoors will hit their wedge from both sides."

"Major, we should break out and meet them. Major?"

Glasken glanced around, but saw only bodies encrusted with red mud. One of them was probably the Major. A stray shot no doubt, he thought. Back in command of the encampment he blew his whistle in the code of the day: RALLY—CHARGE—AT MY SIGNAL. The men gathered as the rescue force began to march over from the distant trenches.

"We're to link up with 'em, then retreat to the main square. Ready . . ."

Glasken blew his whistle and they began to scramble out of their trenches and stumble south over the broken ground and corpses. The Major was not dead, however; he was away piling barrels together in the powder well, a smoking matchlock fuse between his teeth. At Glasken's final whistle he smashed the top of a barrel in with the butt of a musket, took the fuse from his teeth, and plunged his dagger into a calico bag of granulated gunpowder.

"Good man, Johnny, now here's a sendoff to hasten ye," he said as he held the fuse above the black granules.

To Glasken the blast was the earth lifting beneath his feet and a brief sensation of flying. It was a strangely serene feeling.

Dolorian was picking herself out of the mud in Ettenbar's foxhole when the explosion of the powder dump enveloped her like a thunderclap. Blood was streaming from a cut above her hairline where Ettenbar had clouted her with his heavy brass powder horn, and it was running into her eyes and mouth. She wiped her face, then pulled on her lancepoint helmet. Ettenbar had taken her saber, so she drew the Blantov 32 flintlock from her belt, slipped and stumbled over the muddy lip of the foxhole, and ran crouching into the battlefield.

Smoke and sulphur fumes were billowing out from the explosion and dirt was still raining down from the sky. Groups of men were struggling and hacking at each other all around her, and there were no organized volleys of fire. Off to her left she could see a Southmoor pennant at which an officer was rallying his men, waving his saber and blowing a tambal. A hundred yards, she estimated. Still feeling dizzy, she dropped to her knees, cocked the striker of the Blantov, then flopped forward into red mud that was cold, and acrid with human blood. Raising herself on her elbows she took aim, gripping the gun with both hands.

"Must not aim high, must try to hit something," she whispered to herself. As Lemorel had taught her seven years earlier in Libris, she squeezed the trigger gently.

The Southmoor officer toppled, shot through the neck. His men hesitated, then broke and scattered. Dolorian forced herself to stand, her head pounding, then stumbled dizzily through the mud and bodies to where her victim had fallen. She was alone. What to do, what—her whistle! It also marked her as an officer. She blew the three quick blasts for RALLY, and almost at once shapes began gathering around her in the dispersing smoke: bleeding, limping, battered musketeer infantry with broken saber blades and muskets with splintered butts.

"Lieutenant Dolorian!" exclaimed a short bearded man.

"Status, what status?" she cried, not knowing what to do next.

The men shambled in closer, their weapons hanging limp, their eyes huge and round through masks of red mud. She noticed two bands on the sleeve of the bearded man. They were not listening to her or responding, she thought in despair.

"Corporal, what status?" she shouted, almost sobbing.

He pointed between her feet and she looked down to see that she was standing astride the body of the Southmoor officer that she had killed.

"Frelle Lieutenant, that Southmoor—"

"Well so bloody what?" she cried in exasperation. "I shot him. He's the enemy, isn't he?"

"Frelle Lieutenant, he's an Overhand. You just broke their attack."

The Southmoors were in too much disarray to mount another attack that day, so the Alliance troops had the battlefield to themselves. The medician found Glasken in a row of Alliance wounded behind their trenches. He was semiconscious and crying for black ale with no head and a proper chill. He revived when medicinal rye whisky was poured between his lips, and although he had no deep wounds, he had bad lacerations all down his left side.

"Ettenbar, where is he?" Glasken spluttered. "Damn-fool ordering that attack. I'll have his balls for—"

"Best hurry then, Fras Captain," said the medician. "Sergeant Ettenbar is dying."

Glasken was helped to somewhere midfield, where Ettenbar had fallen. His battle zurna was beside him in the mud. The medician said that he had been shot high in the chest, and that his lungs were filling with blood.

"You bloody dummart!" sobbed Glasken, beating the mud beside Ettenbar with his fists. "I told you not to attack, I told you to defend the sparkflash wagons."

"The Frelle Lieutenant . . ."

"Dolorian? Dolorian ordered the attack?"

"Her order . . . she tried to lead, but . . . I hit her. I led."

"You what?" cried Glasken. He carefully raised Ettenbar's head to help clear the blood.

"Can't . . . have lady endangered, Fras . . . bad form. Besides . . . she couldn't—"

Ettenbar began coughing, and blood streamed from his mouth and nostrils. Just like the captain of the Great Western galley engine, Glasken realized. The words of the sergeant who had put him through basic training eight years earlier returned to him: once they bleed from the mouth, don't bother.

"She . . . couldn't play the zurna."

Glasken covered his face with his free hand. "In the Deity's name, Ettenbar!" was all that he could think to say.

Ettenbar coughed again, but more weakly. Glasken looked down to see that he was smiling, and his face was no longer contorted with pain.

"Fras Johnny, may Allah . . ." Ettenbar began, but he could not manage another breath. Glasken lowered his friend's head to the mud, then sat back on his haunches.

"I know, I know, old friend. Put in a good word for me in the afterlife, whether it is Allah, God, the Deity or whoever. I'll need it when I get there, and that's liable to be soon."

With the Alliance bombards destroyed, the Alspring engineers resumed work on rebuilding the bridge. By evening they had the understructure and beams in place on the stone foundations. Dolorian reported to Oldenberg that the enemy was working through the night, laying planks by lantern light.

There was talk of a ghost, a shadowy Southmoor who carried wounded off the battlefield. Glasken gave the story no credit.

"Think what you will, Fras Captain," said Sergeant Gyrom, "but you were one of those he rescued."

Glasken's eyes widened. "All this death about us, I'm surprised there's not more ghosts. Ach, now Lieutenant Dolorian's coming over. Why do I keep bumping into her?"

"Wish she'd bump into me," he said, nudging Glasken's arm. "Should I leave?"

"Yes. No! Yes . . . I suppose. Check if the medician wants for anything, then catch sleep."

Dolorian and Glasken paced slowly around the sparkflash wagon. Mirrorsun was glowing luridly bright through the dispersing clouds. Its configuration was like three large, bright eyes.

"Fras Captain, I only want to apologize," she insisted.

"Apology accepted, now leave me alone."

"I don't have to grovel, Fras Captain."

"Well don't."

"I could have my pick of any man in your 105th!" she snapped, stamping her foot in the mud.

"Sergeant Gyrom!" shouted Glasken. The sergeant hurried out of the medicians' tent and made his way to them through the Mirrorsun-tinted gloom.

"Fras Captain?" he said as he stopped and saluted.

"Sergeant, arrange for the Lieutenant to have her pick of any man in the 105th."

Dolorian's temper flared, and she delivered such a slap to Glasken's face that she broke a fingernail and left a short, deep gash in his left cheek.

"Sergeant, leave us!" shouted Dolorian as Glasken reached into his pocket and pulled out some circles of wadding paper to hold against the cut.

"Fras Captain?" asked Gyrom.

"Dismissed," grunted Glasken.

Gyrom saluted smartly, turned on his heel, and left, decidedly glad to be away from them.

"Both of us should feel ashamed," said Dolorian quietly when the sergeant had gone.

Glasken grunted, but did not disagree.

"Fras, why are you so cold to me?" she suddenly burst out.

"You showed that you are cruel enough to dangle me on a string, then to let the string go."

"So? You made passionate vows to any number of women, all the while courting others."

"So they did not know about each other. That was all done in affection."

"That was all lies, too. Over the past six years I've met fourteen girls who were at University with you. Your line was that you had been celibate for two years past before meeting each of them. Were you really at Rochester University for twenty-eight years? You would have had to have entered the university at four years old."

"Very funny."

"Perhaps . . . we could take up where we left off?" she ventured.

"Oh ho, and to raise me to the level of MULTIPLIER 37, FUNCTION 12,

FUNCTION 780, ADDER 1048, FUNCTION 9, PORT 97, MULTIPLIER 2114—and who was that short one with the bald head who liked to use pine-scented bath salts? MULTIPLIER—no, FUNCTION 1680, he served in the original battle calculor with me so he must have been a FUNCTION. Then there was that Confederation ADDER, what was his number now? 3016 or 1630?''

Dolorian stamped her foot with anger, but she had been standing in a puddle, and splashed them both. It reminded Glasken of Jemli as she farewelled him on Kalgoorlie's paraline terminus.

"You know their numbers better than I do," Dolorian said sharply.

"I had to watch as you sauntered past with them to the solitary-confinement cells. I had to listen while many of them boasted about it later. I had to shrug and shake my head when they asked what I thought of you. I had to look away to my book of conversion protocol codes when they winked and made droopy signs with their fingers."

"Fras, I'm—"

"Let me finish!" exclaimed Glasken, throwing his hands into the air. "I know that you were doing it to rub humiliation in my face, and for no better reason than to please Lemorel. For all of my dalliances, Frelle Lieutenant, I never once ever deliberately humiliated or hurt any Frelle that I bedded. You ought to know that, you quizzed a few about me. Your face actually frightens me, the form of your breasts makes me feel ill. In my long years of celibacy in a night-mare monastery I had to do no more than whisper your name to send my lusts yelping away in terror."

Dolorian was unused to having to do the courting, and even less familiar with apology: being caught out was entirely beyond her experience. She hung her head, and the tear that ran down her nose and dripped from its tip was for genuine sorrow.

"Your point is made, Fras Captain. I have always loved life, but now I feel I want to die. Good night."

When she did not turn away, Glasken did so instead. Glasken's arms hung loose and limp, blood ran from the cut below his eye like a stream of dark tears.

Glasken visited the medician to have two stitches put in his cheek, then returned to the command tent. Sergeant Gyrom entered sometime later, carrying a sheaf of poorpaper. Glasken looked up from the papers on his pinlamp-lit table.

"I told you to catch sleep."

"NC briefs from Rochester, Fras Captain."

"Leave 'em with me."

"If ye don't mind me sayin', Fras Captain—"

"I probably will."

"A ravagin' beauty is that Frelle Dolorian."

"The word is 'ravishing,' Sergeant."

"I think she likes you, Captain. Tomorrow may be the end o' ye, and—"

"That's true of every battle, Sergeant. The death rate is highest for captains."

"What I mean is that the Frelle Lieutenant . . . well, she's in the sparkflash wagon and is cryin' a lot, and I'm sure it's over your cross words."

Glasken stared up at him for a moment, his chin cupped in his hands, then he reached for his pack and pulled out a jar.

"Share this among the men, and have a swig yourself. It may not make their last night on Earth as delightful as Frelle Dolorian undoubtedly could, but it's the best I can do for a few of you. Now leave me alone."

Around 3 A.M. the Alspring mortar-bombards were in place, and they began to fire ranging shots into the Alliance square. Glasken woke from an exhausted sleep to the sound of the first mortar shell exploding, and he made his way to the power wagon, where a team was standing ready to pedal. Dolorian was already with them, the white bandage around her head seeming to hover in the blackness as it gleamed in Mirrorsun's light.

"The final attack?" she asked.

"No, but if they have the bridge repaired well enough to take the weight of a siege mortar then they must be pouring their lancers across too."

"How long do we have?"

"Oh, they'll keep us awake like this, then bring up the Southmoor heavy infantry. They'll do what the dismounted lancers could not and we'll be a minor entry in the history books by noon."

"Perhaps a Call will come?" Dolorian suggested hopefully.

"The Alspringers use mobile heliostat towers, they'll have warning to anchor down. Use the sparkflash, tell the Overmayor about the bridge being repaired. When the square begins to break tomorrow run to the medician. I left a nurse's coat and headband with him for you."

"Thank you, Fras Captain, but I'm sure the buttons would never fasten across *my* chest. Besides, I'm meant to be a soldier so I should act like one."

Glasken sighed. "The offer's there, Lieutenant. Now go your post."

Dolorian did not turn away, but put a hand out to Glasken's arm. In the light of Mirrorsun, he could see that her face was clean, and that she was wearing her lipstick, ochre face powder, and ebony eye shadow below the bandage on her forehead. Without doubt, it was for him.

"Thank you for caring, Fras Captain," she said gently. Glasken's shoulders slumped.

"Very sentimental of me, Frelle Lieutenant," he said with his eyes downcast. Without another word she slipped a hand behind his head and drew him

closer. Their shadows blended into one for a moment as they embraced and kissed. A chorus of hoots and whistles broke from the watching pedal crew on the power wagon; then they saw Glasken striding toward them as the distinctive form of Dolorian made for the sparkflash wagon. There was a discreet snickering above the distant thump of mortar-bombards being test-fired by the enemy. Glasken put his hands on his hips.

"Now there's only one thing I want to say to ye buggers before you get pedaling and that's—Mortar! Jump for it!"

The explosive shell scored a direct hit on the wagon, flaying the crew with shards of iron and wood splinters. Dolorian picked herself out of the cold mud, her ears ringing. She scanned the roil of smoke, descending fragments, and running men by the light of Mirrorsun, after-images of the flash dancing before her eyes. Voices were calling for the medician.

"Captain Glasken!" she screamed. "Johnny."

There was no reply, not even a groan. She climbed into the sparkflash wagon, and in the darkness pulled a heavy switch across to BATTERY mode. After clenching her hands to steady them and taking several deep breaths, she began to key out her message.

RAVENSWORTH OUTPOST OF 105TH TO ROCHESTER. RAVEN-SWORTH OUTPOST OF 105TH TO ROCHESTER. POWER WAGON DE-STROYED. BATTERY MODE ONLY. NO POWER FOR RECEIVER. MESSAGE TO FOLLOW. ALSPRING ENEMY HAS REPAIRED BRIDGE. SURVIVING ALLIANCE FORCE IN 200 YARD SQUARE AROUND TRANS-MITTER. ESTIMATE 150,000 ENEMY WITHIN 7 MILE RADIUS OF TRANSMITTER. 300 ALLIANCE SURVIVORS. ALSPRING AND SOUTH-MOOR FORCES CLOSING IN.

She checked the battery dial in the dim light of her pinlamp. It was nearly down to the red band. Another mortar shell exploded nearby, shaking the wagon.

BATTERIES FAILING. BOMBARDMENT INTENSIFYING. ESTIMATE ONE MORTAR SHELL IN FOUR IS NEW EXPLOSIVE TYPE. REPORT BY LIEUTENANT DOLORIAN JELVERIA, SPARKFLASH 7, FIRST ALLIANCE SPARKFLASH CORPS.

She hesitated a moment, then took a deep breath and added SENIOR SUR-VIVING OFFICER. END OF TRANSMISSION.

As Dolorian stepped from the wagon she suddenly remembered that there were two fully charged batteries in each of the mast wagons. If what remained of the encampment square held until daylight, she could make another transmission. The Overmayor would at least know what forces were crossing the bridge, and have a last estimate of enemy strength. The batteries had only to be unclamped and carried to the sparkflash wagon. She blew her whistle amid the dim forms of scurrying musketeers.

"I want four strong men here, at the double!" she shouted in a hoarse voice.

"Should we form a queue?" Glasken called from somewhere in the confusion.

Dolorian slid to the mud beside the sparkflash wagon, giggling uncontrollably. Presently Glasken came over and sat beside her.

"I nearly choked. Keep your mouth open in case an explosive one comes down, that's what they told me: saves your eardrums. Well the bugger didn't mention the risk of swallowing a pint of mud and horse turds, did he?"

Glasken had a deep but short shrapnel wound in the lower leg. Medician Torumasen cleaned and sewed the gash, and in spite of Dolorian's protests he managed to walk a few experimental steps with a staff and bar crutch.

"I thought you were dead," she admitted as she supported him. "I—I reported it to Oldenberg. I said I was in command."

"No matter, Frelle. Leave it a few hours and both of those may become true."

She helped him to the command tent and he lay with his head in her lap while she stroked his hair and teased out the gritty knots.

"Now what manner of woman could capture your heart, Fras? I would guess one who is very pretty, but not so much as to catch the eye of too many men, one who is bright enough to appreciate your very real talents but not so bright as to overshadow you. Well off for funding, and . . . you would probably expect a virgin as well."

"As a matter of fact I did lose my heart," replied Glasken dreamily. "She was pretty, intelligent, ambitious, poor, and someone else's wife."

"Fras, my word! I *was* unfair. Who was she?"

"Jemli Cogsworth. Milderellen is her maiden name."

It was some moments before Dolorian recovered her breath and composure.

"Is—"

"Yes."

"Enough! Too much! Far too much!" Dolorian exclaimed with her hands over her ears. "Change the subject, anything."

"Ah . . . I'm told you are a fine shot," ventured Glasken.

"Oh, I practiced my pistol work for years in Libris. It got me through promotions and regradings, and helped keep me out of duels."

"How so?"

"I've had five challenges to legal duels, but each time I hit the target more squarely than my challengers. That denied them the right to the duel."

"How many were over the poaching of other Frelles' men?"

"All," admitted Dolorian. "Lemorel's sister," she marveled with her next breath.

Glasken raised himself on one arm, then pressed his forehead against hers in the universal gesture of relaxed affection.

"I'm proud of you, Frelle Dolorian, and I think you lovely. Hardest of all to say, but I forgive you too. Does that help?"

Dolorian put her arms around him and kissed the remains of his left ear.

"Darling Fras, sweet man," she whispered.

"You no longer wish to die?"

"Not unless it's for you."

An hour passed, during which the bombardment slowed to a shell every ten minutes. Dolorian was dozing when a flickering blue light blazed up outside the tent. It was followed by a deep hum mingled with a vast crackling in the air. She came back to her senses with a start.

"Callshewt! My batteries!" she shouted, seizing Glasken's raincape and darting outside. At the sparkflash wagon, two technicians were standing staring at the horizon. "It's a short-circuit, you're draining the power!" she called. "Cut the cables, use your saber."

"We haven't even got the insulator caps off, Frelle Lieutenant," one of them called back.

"You—" There was a distant rumbling explosion, followed by another, and another. "Then what was that noise . . . and that smell in the air, like thunderstorms?"

"The sky lit up like lightning, Frelle. Aye, it may be a storm, you can hear the thunder." The man did not sound convinced by his own words.

Dolorian looked to the horizon, which was glowing red. "By the Call, are they the Alspring campfires?"

"Can't say as I've noticed, Frelle Lieutenant. Been busy wi' the clamps, as was glued down by some loon back in Oldenberg."

"They's cover fires," speculated a deeper voice behind the wagon. "The blue flash were probably a signal flare, a signal for 'em to all start fires together for smokescreen before dawn. Mark my words, Frelle Lieutenant, they's been told of us as havin' this manner of sparkflash. Those fires are to blind us from reportin' their numbers before they flay us te pie meat come dawn."

Dolorian looked to the horizon again, not fully convinced by the explanation. Beneath Glasken's raincape she was shivering, and her feet were bare in the cold mud. "I'll note it down for when we can transmit again," she decided. "Carry on."

"Ah, Lieutenant?"

"Yes?"

"We . . . we just wanted to say what a great shot that was you did."

"What he means is, Lieutenant, is that we're with you."

"You an' the Captain, too."

When Glasken awoke the sun was just above the horizon, but glowed pale and cold through a pall of smoke. The mortar-bombards had ceased to fire during the

night and there was not even sniper fire. Dolorian briefed him on what had happened while he slept. Glasken sniffed the air.

"Charred meat," he said in a flat voice, as if he was in a dream.

"They must be burning their dead," replied Dolorian.

"No, no . . . Strange, silent stillness. Not normal, not real. Perhaps *we're* dead. Was there an attack? Were we killed?"

His questions surprised Dolorian. She put a hand to her face and said, "Your only death was the little death." She kissed the wound on his cheek that she had made the night before.

"They should have attacked at dawn, when the sun from the eastern horizon was in our eyes. Is the sparkflash wagon working?"

"Several coils and joints melted last night, probably because some terminal was connected awry in the dark. My crew should have it live in a quarter hour."

Glasken stood up with the aid of his crutch and looked out of the tent into the swirling smoke.

"There's nothing alive beyond the trenches," he said. "No noises, no shouts, no jingles of gear and harnesses. How long has it been like this?"

"Hours. Since long before dawn."

"Your command, Lieutenant," he said as he began to limp toward the trenches facing the bridge. "I'll not be long."

"Johnny, get down!" she shouted, running in front of him and trying to push him back.

For all his wounds, Glasken resisted. "There's no alarm, Frelle Lieutenant," he said dreamily. "They're all dead. Your command, mind the square." He limped on.

"All dead?" she said aloud, then beckoned to Sergeant Gyrom. "Go after him, drag him to the ground at the first shot!" she hissed. "We'll stand ready with covering fire."

"Frelle!" said the sergeant with a crisp salute, then he went after Glasken in a crouching run.

They made their way past the dogleg in the trench line, then out into the no-man's land of the previous day's fighting. They reached charred scrubland. Many of the trees were still burning, and the blackened grass was brittle underfoot. Glasken passed several corpses, charred and smelling obscenely succulent. Dark trenches gashed the red earth, and the reek of roasted flesh was even more sweet and pervasive.

"Captain, Fras Captain, come back!" Gyrom whispered, tugging at his arm. "This is an evil, devil place. The Ghans have sent daemons against us."

Glasken shook him off and tried to lift a heavy, charred plank that was lying at his feet. The effort made him reel, and he could feel his stitches tearing.

"Sergeant, help me lay this across the trench," he said softly, as if fearful to break the stillness.

Beyond the trench they walked down the road in utter stillness and silence. Nothing moved, nothing made a sound. Men, animals, insects and birds, all were dead. Smoke drifted and swirled like cream stirred into coffee. They reached the bridge. The railings had been burned away, but the boards had been covered with wet sand and gravel as a precaution against fire bombs. Down on the river a galley wrecked in fighting days earlier was burning where it had been grounded. Bodies floated on the water. Glasken walked out onto the bridge.

"Fras Captain, the bridge isn't safe," called Gyrom.

"Walk in the middle, as I do," replied Glasken, neither stopping nor turning.

"But the Ghans' camp is just beyond the bridge."

"That's where I'm going."

Not far from the bridge was a vast field where the Ghan camp had been made. Glasken looked across the field but did not walk any further.

"Captain, they are all gone."

"Not so, Fras Sergeant, tents burn easily. They are still here."

Gyrom stared more closely at the nearest mound, then took a few steps toward it. He scrambled back. "You're right, Captain Glasken, these are all bodies. Thousands of men, with their horses and camels. Look over there, that great hole: thunderbolts from the sky."

"No, that was an ammunition dump exploding in the heat that did all this. Some ancient weapon, perhaps. A glass that concentrates the sun so as to burn . . .''

"But this happened at night."

"Then I don't know what to say. Whatever has been turned loose here has made no distinction between Ghan and Alliance warriors, except for a circle a couple of hundred yards in radius . . . centered somewhere near our sparkflash wagon." He scratched at his stubbled jaw. "Sparkflash seven was at the very center."

Glasken gestured to Gyrom to return. The sergeant hurried after him and they crossed the bridge again.

"Have the men bring a barrow of gunpowder here," Glasken said as they stepped back onto the south bank. "Tell them to place the barrels low in the supporting framework, make sure that the walkway cannot be as easily rebuilt as last time."

Later that morning the explosion that shattered the bridge echoed out across the blackened land. A cloud of smoke and debris rose into the air, then silence returned.

"Annihilated!" the sergeant was crying over and over again as the cart returned to the circle. "It's the Overmayor. How did she do it?"

The forty riders that made their way through the charred landscape were evenly divided between Ghan, Southmoor, Confederation, and Alliance representatives.

A truce pennant fluttered above them on the lance of one of the Confederation officers. They rode uneasily at a brisk trot, surveying the desolation and fearful that it might come again. It was with considerable relief that they reached the untouched Alliance square at Ravensworth.

In a sense Lemorel had the advantage at Ravensworth, because she still had fifty thousand lancers just outside of Haytown. It would have taken but a word from her for the Alspring forces to break the treaty and pour through Haytown unopposed, crossing the river. In another sense time was running out. The renewed rain and unending mud and cold were draining the morale of her men, and now the circle of char seemed to be a warning that the Alliance was favored by the Deity. The truce delegation was a way to check just what was happening near Ravensworth. If the Alliance forces had some advanced weapon, then it was all over. If the catastrophe was something else, the drive to cut the Alliance in two would go ahead.

"Just as I suspected, no mighty weapon," she said to Overhand Baragania as they approached the Alliance encampment. "This was some natural disaster. Haytown will offer no resistance if my lancers cross their bridges without attacking the town. The Central Confederation will demand reparations, but their Overmayor wants to stay out of the war if possible."

Baragania was wide-eyed and ashen-faced. He rode hunched over, as if he expected to be shot at without warning. "Commander, this horror could well have been an act of wrath by the Deity. How can you be so sure of yourself?"

"It's obvious what has happened. The blocking of our way at the Ravensworth bridge meant that a huge buildup of metal weapons and cooking fires took place in a very small area. Why do you think that steam engines and the like are proscribed by all major religions, and why is industry now spread thin over the countryside? Metal, heat, and smoke. If they become too concentrated in a small area . . . well look around you. When my army was compressed into this tiny area, it became like an industrial town in the ancient civilization. Old Anglaic writings talk of industry causing 'greenhouse warming.' Now we can see what that mysterious term 'greenhouse warming' really means."

Baragania looked about him. Her explanation was plausible, but the sheer magnitude of the forces that had been unleashed was still terrifying.

"Why were the Alliance forces spared?" he asked.

"I say they were not. This was but a pocket of a much larger Alliance unit, the rest of which was destroyed. As for this little area, well, why will nine of a city's spires be struck by lightning in a thunderstorm while a tenth is untouched? Pure chance."

"You will have to convince a lot more followers than me, Commander. The men are cold, homesick, and frightened. The war has gone from a triumphal promenade to a slow, bloody, hard-fought nightmare. Of late there has been talk

of the Deity sending all that rain to blight us as a sign of displeasure. Now . . . this.''

''I explained it to you!'' snapped Lemorel, growing impatient.

''I am an educated man, Commander. I can trace out the mathematics of planetary motion and explain the optics of a telescope. Thus I can accept what you say, but there are no more than a few hundred like me in all of your remaining army.''

''Then the educated elite will have to convince the others.''

''This is just my concern, Commander. The elite, as you call them, have the strongest sense of honor and chivalry. Violate the truce at Haytown or behave dishonorably in any otherwise, and you may find that the nails that hold your army together are pulling loose.''

''I am a ruthless hammer, Overhand.''

''You are a leader, even if your title be Commander. If none follow, you cannot lead.''

''That's enough! You're treading a dangerous border.''

''Commander, if you do not hear this from me, nobody else will tell you. Meantime the fears and mutterings will still be there. I shall say this once more because I really am dedicated to your service: behave with honor and do not lose the respect of your officers. We are on the balance, and the needle is finely poised.''

''If you want to see honor dragged in the mud, just observe the Alliance captain in this encampment ahead. My spies have warned me that it is John Glasken, the very incarnation of dishonor.''

''This officer cannot be the man you have spoken about. By all accounts he's a brave and popular leader whose men would follow him to hell and back.''

Lemorel cut her riding whip across his arms with a sudden swoosh. Baragania flinched at the stinging blow.

''That's enough,'' she said between clenched teeth.

The incident was not lost on John Glasken, who was watching their approach with a heliostat telescope. The veiled one in blue, he thought to himself. Only their Supreme Commander would whip an Overhand: it just has to be Lemorel. If he could insult her sufficiently, she might just take offense and challenge him to a duel. She was said to be fond of personally executing senior officers who failed her and killing those who challenged her in duels.

''Let's hope that I live up to your small-arms training, Abbot Haleforth,'' Glasken whispered as he lowered the telescope.

Dolorian met him back at the command tent. ''I made another transmission to Oldenberg,'' she reported. ''They know about the charring now.''

''Lemorel's with that delegation, and disguised,'' he explained hastily with

a flourish of his telescope. "When I meet them I'll drop a few choice Glasken-isms, try to goad her into challenging me to a duel."

"Duel with Lemorel?" Dolorian cried in alarm. "Even if you were Frelle Zarvora I'd advise you to think again, Johnny. And how can you pace out a duel while walking with a crutch?"

"I can manage—but yes, the crutch would be a good prop to give her false confidence. After she bites at the bait I'll drop the crutch, have my leg bound with splints and walk flatfooted. If I die, you're in charge. Make for the Confederation. They're neutral, and there's said to be no chocolate shortage."

"Good fortune, sweet Fras, and shoot straight."

"Good fortune, sweet Frelle, and do nothing that I would not be proud of."

Glasken chose to meet the truce party beside the sparkflash wagon. The Confederation officer bearing the truce pennant rode up and saluted him. The other thirty-nine representatives gathered in a wide semicircle.

"Are you in charge here?" he asked Glasken in Austaric after noting the standards and pennons flying over the camp.

"Captain John Glasken, I'm the most senior officer left alive," replied Glasken, supporting himself with a staff and bar crutch. "What are you doing here?"

"We heard an explosion two hours ago. We made for the cloud of smoke."

Glasken leaned more heavily on his crutch. "I'll put it another way. What are you Confederation neutrals doing out here with those Ghans and Southmoors, and why won't those Alliance officers speak with me?"

"We are here only to observe."

Glasken bit his tongue, barely intercepting an obscene and sarcastic reply. "Is all that out there enough fact for you?" he snarled.

"We rode through it for seven miles. They're all dead, tens of thousands. How did you do it?"

"Me? With three hundred infantry, a medician, and six signalers?"

"Thousands died last night, Captain, roasted instantly. You must have a weapon."

"Balls. We were preparing to be overwhelmed. I want to speak with the Alliance officers in your party."

"No. That would violate the terms of the truce sealed under that pennant," he said with a gesture upward. "There can be no exchanging of tactical information that could benefit either side."

Glasken made a desultory flourish in the direction of the command tent.

"All right then, so how can I help you? A formal coffee? Dancing girls? A troupe of Alspring eunuchs to draw you a hot bath and lay out a change of undercottons?"

"Fras, I understand what a strain has been upon you—"

"Then get to the point."

The Confederation officer glanced about, puzzled and disappointed that there was no ancient superweapon to be seen in the scruffy but defiant little outpost. He turned his attention back to Glasken.

"Last night the Ghan commanders summoned us to demand the use of the Haytown bridges. We were in their camp when the sky to the south was filled with a blue, flickering glow. A vast humming followed, then fires began below the horizon. It lasted only a few heartbeats. The Ghans sent scouts out, and they said everything was burning within seven miles of the bridge near Ravensworth. It seems now that a small circle at the center of that circle is the site of your camp."

Glasken felt himself go hollow inside, but tried not to show it. "It was not us."

"The Alspring Ghan delegation cites evidence that the Overmayor Zarvora was bringing ancient weapons to life."

"The Overmayor's experiments are pure science." He turned and pointed at the Ghans. "You Ghans, you attacked her testing ground at Woomera and killed her engineers and scholars. Can you swear by the Deity that you found anything there like this vast expanse of charring?"

The Ghans remained silent behind their veils.

"If this is the work of the Deity, however, then *we* were spared while the Ghans and Southmoors were annihilated," Glasken concluded.

An uneasy tone entered the pennant bearer's voice. "Why should the Deity favor you? What special righteousness and virtue does the Alliance have?"

"Look for evil, not righteousness," cried Glasken, turning back to the Confederation's pennant bearer. "Look to the Alspring leader who brought this calamitous war upon us. An Alliance renegade and outlaw, who wins her victories by stealth and betrayal. It is *her* the Deity is displeased with."

"Fine words from the man who ravished our Commander when she was a girl," Baragania interjected, riding forward from his group.

Glasken rounded on him sharply. "I have never ravished anyone. My charm alone has always been sufficient, and my charm seduced Lemorel—But why look to my own sorry encounter with her? In our countless nights together her sister, Jemli Milderellen, told me—"

Lemorel's shot silenced Glasken. An instant later five dozen muskets were trained on the truce delegation, yet several of the Ghans had their own flintlocks trained on Lemorel as well. She extended her arm outward, then dropped her Morelac to the ground, one barrel still unspent. Glasken lay in the mud, shot side-on, high in the chest. The dark splotches of blood across his left bicep and chest mingled with the red mud that already smeared him.

"Medician!" someone called from the Alspring musketeers.

"Don't bother, I never miss," snapped Lemorel, tearing her veil away and sliding from her horse, but her face was pale and fearful. She had killed to cover her own lies, and now she had to conjure a very convincing reason. Dolorian noted her former friend's expression with grim interest, then walked forward to stand protectively astride Glasken's body.

"He abandoned me to the desert," Lemorel shouted in an Alspring dialect to Baragania. "He defiled me, then he defiled my sister!"

"You shot our commanding officer under the cover of a truce!" Dolorian screamed in Austaric.

"Austaric, all speak in Austaric!" demanded the Confederation's pennant bearer.

"As Captain Glasken's second-in-command I demand satisfaction," cried Dolorian. She shrugged off her jacket and stood before them in a blouse stained with river water from several days past. "Name your seconds and have them search me for hidden armor," she said with her hands on her hips and her breasts thrust out.

Lemorel raised her eyebrows, but did not smile. "You should know better than to challenge your teacher. This is a joke."

"Afraid of me?" asked Dolorian.

"Commander accepts!" shouted Baragania.

Lemorel whirled around in fury and glared at him. He stared back steadily.

"Do you need a second, Commander?" he asked calmly.

"What good is a dead man as a second?" she replied. "I'll fight alone."

She tore off her outer robe, then strode across to Dolorian who held her arms out as she approached.

"Impressive breasts, Frelle Dolorian," said Lemorel as she checked for hidden armor. She stood back and held her own arms up for Dolorian.

"Medician, check her for armor," said Dolorian, folding her arms beneath her breasts as well as she could. Lemorel's face contorted at the slight, and something like a muffled squeal escaped her.

Because a Confederation truce had been violated, the pennant bearer was declared overseer by acclaim. He named four observers.

"As the challenged party, choose the weapons," he said to Lemorel.

"Amnessons. Your officers have them as standard issue."

"Nice choice," Dolorian replied, rolling her hips for the benefit of the onlookers. "Long barrel, lightweight, and a friction trap for the recoil."

Lemorel sneered to hear her own lessons of seven years earlier quoted. Two guns were selected and brought over. Lemorel snatched one weapon and slashed the air with it, feeling the weight and balance. "Your target, Frelle Challenged," urged Dolorian.

Gyrom had found a sheet of poorpaper and some colored pins in the com-

mand tent. The Confederation officers watched carefully as he pinned the paper in place, with a wide, black shield pin at the center.

Lemorel hefted the gun again, then walked to the target and paced back. Without warning she whirled and fired, and a hole appeared beside the black pin. She was giving Dolorian the chance to better it if she could.

Dolorian pouted. She went down on one knee, supporting her left elbow with it as her hand steadied the long, functional barrel. Slowly she squeezed the trigger. The blast echoed into the silent, charred landscape. The shot smashed the pin.

"That was stupid of you, Frelle," snapped Lemorel, who had never before been beaten at the target. "You bettered my shot so you have the right to fight me, but do you think that I'll give you a chance to kneel down and aim like that?"

"No, Frelle, but I'll still try."

"You never learn, do you? Never discuss tactics with your enemy."

They stood back to back. Reloaded pistols were returned to them.

"Call your distance, Lieutenant Dolorian," the overseer said clearly.

"One hundred and fifty," said Dolorian, and there was a faint hiss of breath from Lemorel.

It was a very, very long call. The count began, and took quite some time. ". . . one hundred forty-nine, one hundred fifty!"

As Lemorel whirled she judged the distance, noted that Dolorian was beginning to kneel, then fired—just as her opponent suddenly bobbed up straight. Her shot took Dolorian low in the rib cage, a little to the left—but below the heart, where Lemorel had been aiming. The image of Dolorian falling was hazy through the gunsmoke as Lemorel lowered her arm. She shook her head, then turned to the overseer for a verdict . . . just as the clearing smoke revealed Dolorian lying flat, and bracing her elbows in the red mud as she took aim. Her shot hit Lemorel side-on, in the right of her chest. The ball passed through her heart. She toppled to the red mud, her face a death mask of surprise.

The overseer looked to the observers, who inspected the two women. Lemorel was dead. Dolorian was still alive, and thus declared the winner. Medician Torumasen tore the fabric away from an ugly wound below Dolorian's left breast.

"Not good with pain," she whimpered through clenched teeth, tears flowing across her mud-stained cheeks. "But . . . got her!"

"I've checked the Captain," said Torumasen as he pressed cotton wadding soaked in eucalyptus oil against the wound. "He's alive. The shot passed through his arm, smashed the shaft of his crutch and deflected, then broke a rib and tore a furrow through his skin. He's in shock and unconscious, but he'll live. Lie still, your bleeding is very bad."

"Tell him . . . feared reaching forty. Worse ways to go."

"Don't talk. Relax and you will bleed less."

Dolorian looked into his eyes. "Fras Medician, you can . . . rip my blouse . . . anytime."

"Not unless you're alive," he replied, feeling his heart wrench. "Don't drop your pack. There's everything for you to live for."

She pouted at Torumasen, then closed her eyes as he brushed his lips against hers. Moments later she was dead. As Torumasen pumped at her heart and breathed into her lips, the attention returned to the delegation.

"I appear to be in command," Sergeant Gyrom said to Overhand Baragania. "Are you through with spying on our defenses under the cover of truce, or should I line my men up for inspection?"

"We go," Baragania said, folding his arms and looking sadly down at Lemorel's body. "War with honor I understand. Not this. What happened here is . . . evil, obscene thing."

"Follow a devil, and such like will befall you."

"Devil has good disguises."

"You should have looked for the forked tail."

"Is hard to see when her hand be on your shoulder." The Overhand gestured across to Lemorel's body. "You bury our Commander?"

"Why not? I've become good at it, thanks to her."

One of Dolorian's crew transmitted the news back to Oldenberg. Within two days the fighting had stopped everywhere and the opposing armies were pulling back to truce lines. Lemorel was buried on the battlefield, with all the other dead. Dolorian's body vanished.

The Southmoors ceded a buffer province to the Southeast Alliance that reached to the Central Confederation, while the Balranald Emirate declared itself independent of the other Southmoor nations. Other matters were not settled so easily. The Ghans who were holding the Woomera Confederation's cities refused to give them up. After annexing all independent castellanies as far as Peterborough, Zarvora's forces laid siege to the town, then sent three brigades north to Hawker and took that town in a surprise attack.

Tarrin sat in Zarvora's Libris study, listening in amazement while she finally explained the workings of her radio system to him, and how she had used it as a parallel and secure command network in the closing weeks of the war. There was also the matter of what had happened at Ravensworth.

"It was linked to the sparkflash, of that I am sure," she said. "The Mirrorsun band was involved. I think that it was an intense, hollow cone of heat, probably what it used to destroy the Wanderer stars."

"You mean it attacked the sparkflash yet spared the very center, where the wagons were positioned?"

"Believe me, Tarrin, I have given it a great deal of thought. My feeling is

that it could be a matter of aiming. Aim at a target using a drop-compensator sight, and the bead of the sight will cover the target itself.''

''But why cover what you are shooting at?''

''The Wanderers were big, they may have been more than two hundred yards across. A direct hit would be a kill, even if the center was spared.'' She waved her hands in circles, then let them fall. ''That theory will have to do for now.''

Tarrin was less than convinced. ''But the sparkflash transmitters have been used since the Night of Fire.''

''Yes . . .'' Zarvora frowned at her mechanical orrery as she assembled a few of her speculations into the bones of a theory. ''Perhaps there was some code used that made the Mirrorsun identify Sparkflash Seven as one of the Wanderers. That code triggered the response . . . and it could happen again. I have set the Calculor analyzing Dolorian's last transmissions for clues, and when the fighting to free Woomera is done I may conduct experiments in the desert using cleared areas and a single transmitter. Until then, I have had all sparkflash wagons returned to Oldenberg, where they are to be kept under guard.''

''Until the end of the war?''

''That will be soon. My overhand at Peterborough predicts capitulation within three days. I shall go there to preside over the treason trials. Peterborough will be the interim capital of the Woomera Confederation until the city of Woomera is set free.''

''But Lemorel had the Mayor of Woomera killed when the city fell, Frelle Highliber.''

''His heir was studying at Rochester University at the time. Guard my sparkflash wagons well while I am away, Fras Tarrin. If fools or traitors get hold of them it could be truly horrendous.''

Glasken spent three weeks in a hospitalry near the slave markets at Balranald. His left arm was heavily bandaged, but his leg was soon well enough healed to carry his weight. On the day that he was due to be discharged and return to the 105th he was visited by Vellum Drusas of the Libris Inspectorate.

''Fras Glasken, the great hero of Ravensworth,'' boomed the inspector in a mellow and cheery voice. ''Are you recovered enough to be honored?''

Glasken was sitting on the edge of the bed, easing his boot on over the bandages. To anyone who knew him well, he looked rather subdued.

''If truth be known, I'm feeling just a trifle flat,'' he said as he drew the laces tight. ''My closest friends in the brigade were killed, and I've been three weeks in an Islamic hospital where I can't get anything stronger than coffee and the only nurses they let near me are men.'' Glasken fell silent, his fingers idle on the boot laces, then he looked up at Drusas. ''All that sorrow leaves me sickened.''

Drusas put a hand on Glasken's shoulder and adopted the positive tone of a

good counselor. "Well Fras Glasken, I can cure a little of that. I'm here to take you to the paraline terminus and send you to Rochester for a great and fabulous ceremony. It's not only your own medal. The late Frelle Dolorian's parents have asked that you accept her medal and honors on her behalf."

Glasken picked up his packroll. He looked around one last time, as if he was about to leave something of great importance forever; then he limped out of the room with Drusas.

"Doesn't seem fair," he said as he signed for his musket, saber, flintlock, and dagger at the locker desk. "There's many as did braver than me. I just survived."

The hospitalry staff and many of the patients saw him off, hailing him as the liberator of the Emirate of Balranald, the man who held the bridge at Ravensworth against odds of a hundred to one, the man whom Lemorel could not kill, the man who broke the army of the Ghan invaders. Drusas had a gig waiting, and an escort of a dozen lancers.

"Balranald's like home," said Glasken as they drove along the streets. "It's a paraline terminus town like Sundew, a big place with lots of industry and wind trains taking crates and bales away to places with wonderful names." He gazed about at the turbulent bustle of town life, letting his nostalgia for Sundew wash over the memories of war. "Look there, the slave markets where I was sold for three hundred silver rikne—that's nine royals—back in 1700 after I'd escaped the battle calculor with Nikalan."

"Hah, a real bargain," laughed Drusas.

"And there, a rail-capping foundry, just like Sundew's. I was born in a lathe-and-mudbond tenement like that one over there. My father was a paraline ganger."

"Well he obviously found better times," said Drusas, genuinely impressed and trying to show it. "Saving the fees for University is not common among gangers."

Glasken seemed hardly to hear him. "Look, a narrow-gauge paraline truck with Great Western colors and markings. It must be from their mixed-gauge paraline."

"The war scattered rolling stock widely, Fras."

"Aye, like people by the Call. That's how my stepmother died. One day I was in school and the Call rolled over, but we were tethered so it was nothing special. Then some lad burst in and said my mother was taken. I hardly cried, I just felt numb. A few weeks later Dad told me that we'd come into a lot of money. He also told me that I was a bastard—a real one, that is. My real mother was a big, jolly woman who cooked well and went in beer races. He married her once we were out of mourning and bought a share in a vineyard. It was odd, but I always remember how my first mother used to be so proud of me whenever

I got honors at that ratty little alms-school near the railyards. I always thought that those big sad eyes of my first mother only brightened when I studied well. Eventually I won a Mechanics Institute Scholarship to Rochester.''

Drusas was unprepared to hear someone with Glasken's reputation speaking like this—and at such length. His own replies sounded awkward and forced, and he was very surprised to find his usual eloquence failing.

"But why did it take you eight years to get a four-year degree?''

"Not sure. In Rochester I had a lot of time to myself, and that led to thinking that whatever I did, my first mother would not be there when I graduated. Drink, revels, and wenches were there on offer, so that's why I'm what you see today.'' He sat up straight and clapped Drusas on the shoulder. "Here now, the paraline terminus.''

"And here I must leave you, my remarkable scholar and man of action,'' said Drusas with some relief. "In your exalted future, spare a thought for old Fras Drusas.''

"I'll even spare you a drink, Fras.''

With Glasken aboard the train Drusas drove through the city to the new Alliance embassy where he filed a sheaf of forms. He also collected a purse and spent an entertaining night watching the dance festival in the market sector of the city with two shadowhands ever close behind to guard his purse and back. While they were with him he had no fear of darkened lanes and shadowed doorways.

The night was enjoyable, yet there was no wine to be had in the Islamic city. The dancing was a wildly exciting spectacle, however, starring nomad performers from the north, many of them from Christian and Gentheist tribes. For the first time in many months Drusas felt a stirring at his loins as the show whirled to a climax. At his request one of the shadowhands indicated which streets might harbor harlots, and Drusas hurried along between the narrow, darkened buildings, sniffing at traces of perfume and gaping at forms outlined against gauze shutters.

Suddenly something made him stumble and he careered into the gloom of a deep-set doorway. Drusas was appalled to find an arm hooked under his chin and his feet free of the ground. By the Mirrorsun light he could make out a dagger point before his eyes, and there was wet blood gleaming on the blade.

"Glasken where?'' said an accented voice. "Embassy say returned to regiment. Not so. *Don't* struggle. Shadowhands dead.''

"Know—nothing,'' gasped Drusas frantically, his fingers scrabbling at a thin, hard arm.

"Order for Glasken from Overmayor. Go to occupation army at Peterborough.''

"I'm only an Inspector. I just filed forms.''

The blade point dropped, to begin pressing into the skin over his heart.

"Business with Glasken. Where is?''

"I, I can't. . . .''

The dagger point was through Drusas' skin and pressing deeper.

"Try."

"Train. To Rochester."

"With who?"

"Darien. Darien vis Babessa."

15 CONVERSION

Peterborough had been badly mauled in the siege to dislodge the Alspring agents and sympathizers. Not a single building had escaped damage, yet it was still an important town—and thus became Zarvora's new headquarters. In spite of the ruins and devastation beyond the windows of the Mayor's palace, however, it was a handful of beamflash reports from far away that filled Zarvora and Denkar with dismay.

/ SEYMOUR BURNED, EXCEPT FOR TEN YARD CIRCLE AT TOWN CENTER. HUGE CHARRED CIRCLE. EVERYTHING DEAD. MARTIAL LAW DECLARED./

"There are more details, but the pattern fits everything we know about the way Mirrorsun attacks," Zarvora said.

"So it was Tarrin," said Denkar with a scowl as he shook his head slowly. "The Acting Dragon Black of Libris was a spy for Lemorel. No wonder she got our defenses handed to her on a golden platter."

"Not quite. The original plan must have been to capture me, but I reached safety. All he could do was sabotage and spy, but now he has an invincible weapon. He must have smuggled a sparkflash wagon into the town and had it broadcast whatever that trigger code happens to be. He could annihilate any town or city like that."

"Four wagons, Zar, not one."

"Not so, Fras Husband. Research in Oldenberg has continued, although at a less frantic pace than at first. By the end of the year Tarrin will have a transmitter that will fit into a one horse gig and be powered by a single operator with a pedal generator. He could smuggle one into Kalgoorlie, here, anywhere. Look at this report: the central circle is only ten yards across. He must have found a way to fine tune what Mirrorsun can do with its weapon."

"We're not defenseless!" exclaimed Denkar, appalled by her sudden depression. "We can seal every road and paraline from the southern Calldeath lands to, to . . ."

"To where? The Northmoors? The Carpentarians, who are subjects of the

Alspring Ghans anyway? Disassembled transmitters could be carried on camel caravans across the deserts and we would have no way of knowing.''

''But not yet. Tarrin's position is weak.''

''Weak? Most of Woomera's territory is under Ghan rule, the Southmoors could be rallied within days, and the Southern Alliance would plunge into civil war if forced to choose between myself and Tarrin. Look at his demands. Full control of all beamflash towers, all paralines to be restored, his galley trains to be given total freedom of movement with no inspections.''

''No! Galley trains can carry the transmitters even at their present size and weight!'' cried Denkar, appalled at the idea. ''He could kill whole cities with what he already has.''

Zarvora had been fighting too many enemies for too long, and having victory snatched away after such a hard-fought war was nearly more than she could take. Tarrin knew her well, perhaps better than Denkar. He knew what would drive her to the wall.

''You think we should fight for time?'' she asked wearily.

''Yes! Definitely yes!'' Denkar shouted, frantically trying to revive the famed aggression in his wife.

''But Tarrin is just another ruler, little different from me. Why kill thousands, even millions, just so I can be Overmayor?''

''Because you have a vision and Tarrin is a damn lackey! I'd follow you to hell and back, Zar. Glasken fought odds of a hundred to one in your name, Dolorian faced Lemorel across the line of honor for you. They did that because they knew *you* would never break. Lead us, because as sure as the pigeon craps on the statue nobody else can!''

Zarvora seemed not to hear. She sat staring at the messages, unmoving, her eyes unfocused. Denkar paced before her for a time, then went to a chalkboard and began drawing circles and figures. Suddenly Zarvora shook her head.

''The circle of char is seven miles in radius, so its center could be observed in safety from the gallery of a nearby beamflash tower,'' she said.

Denkar drew a tower symbol beside one of his circles. ''Yes, yes, cunning. Tell Tarrin that you will accept his terms if he can put a char circle exactly nine miles south of the Culleraine tower.''

''We could watch in safety.''

''Not just watch. Mayor Bouros has developed a sparkflash that fits into a single wagon. When Tarrin sends a four-wagon sparkflash to Culleraine we can monitor the code and have a dozen wagon-sized units ready to—''

''No!''

''We could be ahead of Tarrin within a single day!''

''No! I'll not destroy my people to rule them.''

''Tarrin is a lackey, he has no guts for a fair fight. Look, you could have a

gig-sized transmitter smuggled into Rochester or Oldenberg within a fortnight, ready for the code and your order.''

"*My* order. Precisely. Glasken has been abducted to Rochester. Could I kill him after he has fought so hard for me?'' She stared at his chalkboard circles. "Tell me this: why Culleraine?''

"We can observe it easily.''

"Then why Seymour?''

"I—I don't know. It's Tarrin's most secure territory, he had to invite us to send observers after Mirrorsun's fire descended.''

"Precisely.''

Glasken's blindfold and gag were removed once he was within the walls of Libris. When he was finally unbound he found himself in the very induction room that he had been taken to in 1699. This time Tarrin was waiting to meet him, flanked by two Southmoor guards.

"Welcome home, FUNCTION 3084,'' said Tarrin as Glasken rubbed his wrists.

"I thought there's a new law against this sort of thing,'' replied Glasken.

"Not for you.''

"What? The Overmayor—''

"Overmayor Zarvora has been assassinated in Peterborough. The Ghans took heart and renewed their invasion, so I was forced to sign a truce. I do not have the late Overmayor's talent to wage war.''

Glasken shook his head. The news was like a slap across the face. Zarvora had seemed unkillable.

"So, why am I here? I'm a good officer, but a pretty average component.''

"For your own safety, Glasken. The Ghans want you dead. Lemorel died in a duel fought over your questionable honor, you held up her advance at Ravensworth when victory was at her fingertips, and you called down the fire that annihilated two-thirds of her army in her very moment of triumph. How did you do it?''

"The guards—''

"Cannot speak Austaric. Tell me how to call the fire, Glasken. I can save the Alliance with that secret.''

Glasken scratched at the newly emerging stubble on his jaw as he thought over Tarrin's words. Victory at her fingertips, her moment of triumph: put together, the words said more than Tarrin had intended.

"You rogered Lemorel.''

Tarrin went sheet-white, then lunged forward and backhanded Glasken across the face. The Southmoor guards moved in to seize Glasken, but he did not attempt to move.

"You filthy defiler," ranted Tarrin. "I should hang you by your testicles and lower you headfirst into a vat of boiling banegold. What was the text of Lieutenant Dolorian's last transmission before Mirrorsun's fire?"

"You mean you don't have it?"

"There was a thunderstorm over Oldenberg on that night. Parts of the message were lost."

Glasken stretched his legs and settled back in his chair, regarding Tarrin thoughtfully. Something about him was as suspicious as another man's trousers on the bedroom floor.

"I don't know what Dolorian transmitted."

"But you tupped the woman, you slept with her!"

"Ah-ha: tupped, slept. Important words. Did *you* discuss beamflash traffic with Lemorel while you were rolling about under her desk—"

Tarrin backhanded Glasken again.

"She didn't put that last message in her transmissions log, probably because you were in such a hurry to bundle her out of her trews. There *must* have been pillow talk."

"I was wounded, I soon fell asleep."

"Lies!"

"Lies? You've never been wounded, you wouldn't understand. Even a flesh wound from a small-bore musket can leave you gibbering for days. I was blown up twice in the one day, I had nine gashes down one side and a piece of metal the size of your thumb pulled out of my leg."

"But you were Dolorian's commanding officer, she *must* have briefed you," insisted Tarrin, pacing in circles with his hands clasped over his head. "Think! The Alliance is hanging by your words."

Glasken scratched his head, then carefully folded his arms.

"Dolorian thought I was dead at the time. She typed that the Ravensworth bridge was repaired, and that the Ghans were pouring across."

"I have the gist of that already. She added estimates of Ghan numbers, said your square was about to fall. What else? Something extra, some odd phrase?"

"As the eunuch said to the abbess, I'd oblige if I could, but I can't."

Tarrin met the fully reinstated Mayor Jefton in Zarvora's old study. Jefton looked about in distaste, for Tarrin had let the room slide into a chaos of files, scrolls, maps, and punched paper tape. Some Calculor display mechanisms and mechanical animals had fallen out of adjustment or were broken. Plates of food scraps and coffee mugs were all over the place, and Jefton shuddered at the mouse droppings and trails of ants. He cleared some files from a chair, dusted it with his fly-whisk, and sat down.

"Glasken was no help with the text of that message, damn him," Tarrin reported.

"Then just transmit combinations of what we do have until Mirrorsun sends the fire again," Jefton suggested. "We only lack a dozen or so letters."

"No. Zarvora has new receivers from Kalgoorlie. If she overhears us bumbling about she'll suspect the truth and be down on us like a trainload of mortar shells."

"Not so. All the combinations will take less than a day to transmit."

"No!"

"I order you to!"

"*Nobody* gives me orders!" shouted Tarrin. "I gave you back Rochester. Don't forget that I am Highliber and Overmayor. You serve *me*, Fras Jefton, don't forget it."

"And do not forget that Zarvora is still alive, whatever you told Glasken!" Jefton retorted sharply, sitting forward and gesturing with his fly-whisk. "You are no more Highliber or Overmayor than I am until you have Mirrorsun at your beck and call." He sat back and smiled accommodatingly. "Why not do as I say?"

Tarrin smashed his fist down on the keyboard. A blow from Zarvora would have splintered the wood, but Tarrin's fist just bounced off. He gave a yelp and sat rubbing the reddened skin, his eyes tightly closed.

"Well, why not?" asked Jefton again.

"Because I may not have all the combinations, and I'm not good enough at codes and mathematics to be sure that what the FUNCTIONS and regulators tell me is true."

Jefton sat back, impressed yet appalled by the admission.

"Well, use the University's edutors."

"Then *everyone* will have the full text. If they master the true code it will only take one rebel with one transmitter, and this city will be ash."

"We could rule in safety from the Libris cellars."

"But what would we rule, Mayor Jefton?"

Across in Peterborough, Denkar reread the full text of Dolorian's last message before the char, then shook his head. He was striding down the platform with Mayor Bouros, who had arrived on the first galley train from Kalgoorlie since the paraline's restoration.

"Tarrin must be better at coding than I thought if he can make sense of this," he admitted. "Are you certain about the words?"

"There was a little interference, but our filters and directional antennas are very fine, Fras Denkar. The duty operator is convinced she got the full text."

"Poor Dolorian," said Denkar, handing the transcript back to Bouros. "There's something so sad, so compelling about her words."

A lackey showed them to where the Firefly was standing, now repaired and rearmed. They inspected a guard of honor, and the galley engine's new captain saluted them as they came aboard.

"The track's repaired, so I can take ye as far as Maldon," the captain explained. "After that there's . . ." He swallowed. "There's narrer-gauge available."

"Thank you, Captain. Have the line cleared, then wait until Overmayor Zarvora arrives. She will travel with us."

"The Overmayor, Fras?"

"The Overmayor, Captain. She insisted that no other engine but the Firefly should carry her."

Practically bursting with pride, the captain left to get clearance for the line ahead while Denkar and Bouros waited in the control cabin. Mayor Bouros clamped his spectacles to his nose and read Dolorian's message again. As he finished he flicked the edge of the page. "I have seen this so many times that I'll soon be able to recite it, my friend."

"Pah, I already can," said Denkar with an elaborate orator's flourish. He proceded to recite the full text.

"Splendid work," said Bouros, applauding.

"Ah, you never met her, Fras Mayor. She was very full of figure and had long, lustrous hair. She had style and a roving eye, yet she was discriminating."

"You had a little dalliance with her perhaps?" inquired Bouros.

"Quite a memorable dalliance. That was before the Overmayor and I met, of course."

"I . . . suspect you were once a component in Libris."

Denkar considered, but felt no alarm. With so many components who had known him being liberated, it would be impossible to maintain the public version of his past for long. He turned away from Bouros to study the levers, dials, and pulley switches that controlled the galley engine, then patted the stopper in the speaking tube to insure that those in the pedal chamber could not eavesdrop.

"I stayed in a prison with an open door for love of my jailer."

"Hah, a strange and wonderful romance."

"Poor Dolorian. Always poor Dolorian. When I first saw the incomplete transcript of her message, why my heart nearly broke. I wanted to rush across with an army to save her."

"Ah, Fras, we all wished we could have gone to her side to fight the Ghans. Even I, who never laid eyes upon her. Name me anyone who would not have—"

Denkar had slammed both hands down on the gear exchange panel, then turned to stare at Bouros with his eyes protruding as if pushed from behind.

"I *cannot*, Fras Mayor, and you are a genius!" he exclaimed, beaming as if he had just discovered one of Glasken's caches of gold.

Bouros looked back doubtfully. "If you have some brilliant insight, my friend, then you are the only genius in here."

Denkar grasped him by the shoulders and shook him as he spoke, his voice blazing with excitement.

"Dolorian reached out and touched my heart, and yours—and *Mirrorsun's*! The greatest of the ancient calculors were said to be sentient, and the Mirrorsun band must be controlled by ancient calculors. It heard her transmission and saved her."

Bouros sat dumbfounded for a moment, then dug a piece of chalk from his robes and began scratching on the cabin's floorboards.

"The area of char is the same as that she defined the enemy to occupy in her message, with a circle at the center where she was said to be! Yes, yes indeed, Fras Denkar. The figures support you."

Just then the captain returned with Zarvora behind him. Denkar waved them away from the figures on the floor.

"Frelle Zar, you must have read my mind," he cried, spreading his arms wide over the figures like a priest performing a religious sacrament.

Zarvora dropped to her knees beside Denkar and hugged him.

"Darling Denkar," she cried. "Next time I ever talk about giving up, kill me!"

"I—ah, so you have good news too?" replied her astonished husband.

"Wonderful news. I decided to check certain matters in depth, so I sent a message through to the aviad town of Macedon. They sent observers to a border peak in the Calldeath lands that has a clear view of Seymour. With a powerful telescope they discovered Seymour to be untouched, although sealed off by units of the Alliance army. They also noticed the burned-out ashes of huge bonfires in practically every paddock."

"A bluff, by Greatwinter!" exclaimed Bouros.

"A bluff indeed, the cunning little rat!" added Denkar. "We were about to tell you the same thing."

They explained their theory of Mirrorsun and Dolorian to Zarvora as the Firefly glided out of the station and rattled over the pointwork in the Peterborough shunting yards.

"I have ordered a blockade of all mayorates under Tarrin's control," continued Zarvora. "He will have trouble holding anything other than Rochester city for more than a day or two. I already have an army moving into place and I shall do what Lemorel did at Alspring: lay siege and bombard only the mayoral palace."

"Libris is close by," said Denkar. "We owe the people of the Calculor too much to risk their lives."

Zarvora shook her head. "Starving Tarrin out could take years, and many others will suffer before he does."

"There may be a better way," suggested Bouros. "Glasken is back in the Libris Calculor as a FUNCTION, according to reports. The aviad friend of his, Ilyire, is familiar with Libris and he knows Glasken by sight. Can you smuggle Ilyire into Libris, Overmayor?"

"Perhaps. Our double agent, Darien, is known to Ilyire. She could deliver the necessary papers and instructions and help him gain access to Libris. She goes by the name Parvarial Konteriaz when working for me, but her own name when about Tarrin's business."

"Is she trustworthy?"

"I think so—but so does Tarrin. She accidentally delivered Glasken into his hands."

Denkar stood up and looked through the forward window slit as they rolled south. His right hand was waving beside his ear, as if trying to coax an idea out of his head.

"Make ready to do all that we have discussed, but first get me to Phillip Bay and Theresla with one of the new sparkflash transmitters on a wagon. Mind, it's vital that I not be delayed for genototem games at Macedon."

Guided by Zarvora's other agents, Darien found Ilyire at a tavern in a hamlet just east of Echuca. Tales of his transformation had been filtering through to her over the months, but at first she suspected that he had merely been spreading rumors to lure her back. Now even Glasken had confirmed that Ilyire had lost his fanatical protectiveness and she was eager to give him another chance.

The Bargeman's Jar was a low, rambling, ancient place that served as the hamlet's hostelry as well. Darien paused cautiously as she caught sight of the sign. She stared into a polished draper's plate to comb her hair and smear a film of scarlet onto her lips. In spite of the winter chill and mist she wore her traveling cape thrown back, and she even undid two buttons of her blouse.

At the taproom she presented a card to the maid, but the girl could not read. She fetched the vintner, who laboriously worked out that Darien could not speak, that she wanted a private room, and that she wanted Ilyire sent there. As she sat waiting, a Call warning bell began to ring in the distance. Ten minutes to a Call. She reached down and wound her timer, then clipped her tether to a rail in the gloomy room. The latch of the door clacked. Ilyire entered.

Darien held up her hands and began to sign a greeting, but Ilyire shot out a hand and twisted her arm up behind her back. She struggled silently, her face contorted with pain. He grasped her other arm and bound her hands behind her, and only then did he walk in front of the Dragon Silver Librarian. Her eyes were wide and white with fear, and she was shaking her head from side. He spoke to her in Alspring Ghan.

"No? You shake your head for no. Only yes and no are left to you, my little assassin, my dangerous vixen. Your voice is crippled, but you are deadly. You betrayed my master, Fras Glasken. Drusas delivered him to you and you gave him over to that filthy worm, Tarrin. Poor Master, betrayed after fighting so valiantly and suffering so much."

Darien shook her head again and struggled against her bonds.

"Darien, Frelle Darien, I am disappointed in you, and in myself. You are a traitor, but I love you still. Still, I must kill you. You once wanted me to break my slavish, perverted adoration for you and I have done just that. Alas, you will die because I have changed into what you wanted me to become."

He examined the papers in her slingbag, and in her pockets. There were sealed orders for Glasken which seemed to be genuinely from Zarvora, but when he broke the seal the contents were in some military code that he could not follow. Other papers and border passes were made out to himself, and there were detailed instructions for breaking into Libris and locating Glasken. Most of the papers referred to Parvarial Konteriaz.

"Who is Frelle Parvarial, and how did you kill her? Poor girl. You had a mind to lure me to Rochester with genuine papers for my master from the Over-mayor, then deliver both papers and myself to Fras Pretender-Liber Tarrin. Well then, the papers will reach my master, but your Tarrin will be disappointed."

He pocketed the papers.

"A Call is close, Frelle Darien. Very soon your mind will be lured away and I shall unbind you and turn you loose to wander south to your death. Perhaps the Deity will spare you as he spares one in a thousand, that is the only chance I can give you. By rights I should plunge a knife into your heart—but I cannot do that."

He closed his eyes and concentrated for a moment.

"Not long now. I—I want to kiss you goodbye, but that would be obscene. Darien, Darien, do you wish for me to be as I was?"

The question was rhetorical, but to his surprise Darien gave a weak smile, stared straight at him, and shook her head. A moment later the Call blotted out the intelligence behind her eyes, and she was mindlessly striving to go south. Ilyire untied the cord that bound her wrists, unclipped the Call tether that held her to the room's railing, and led her outside. He held her facing south down the street, then released her. She walked away at a steady pace, never once looking back.

"Even facing death you loved me just a little," he said to her distant back, then he turned away, his face in his hands.

Glasken looked up from a copy of *Systems Enhancement Abstracts* as the hooded regulator turned a key in the lock of his cell. Without a word he beckoned Glasken to follow, but not any of his cellmates. They went to an empty tutorial room. The regulator latched the door and turned to face Glasken—who exclaimed in disbelief as the hood fell back.

"Ilyire!"

"No less, Fras Master. My humble self."

"Theresla, she sent you."

"My silly sister? Hah!"

"Just wait a minute! What's this Master bit and who really sent you?"

"Overmayor . . . little bit, Fras Master."

"Zarvora was assassinated."

"Not so. Still alive, still unpleasant."

"Tarrin! That lying fykart Tarrin told me she was dead."

"Is more. Men in cassocks and sandals seek you. Come to Kalgoorlie, go everywhere, even palace. Want you."

"Baelsha and its bloody abbot, I should have known. Nobody ever escaped from Baelsha before me. Are they far behind you?"

"Long way, Master. Killed five."

"You managed to kill five monks from *Baelsha*?"

"Not easy. Spending weeks to recover."

"Unbelievable. Can you get me out of Libris?"

"Mmmm . . . can do, but stay first. Overmayor instructions for to follow."

"I was afraid of that. Ah, my friend, it will take a long night of drinking to tell you *my* story."

"Not so, Fras. I with you since Woomera."

"What?"

"I see all. You rescue Highliber at Peterborough, lead charge against Southmoors at Ravensworth, roger Frelle Dolorian. I carry you from battlefield, Master."

"What? But why?"

"You bury bones of Ervelle at Maralinga. Now I repay. I vow any man threaten master, I cut out his heart. Too late I discover Vellum Drusas false."

"What did you do?"

"I cut out his heart."

"Oop—That's it, no more! What do I have to do for the Overmayor?"

Ilyire handed across the coded instructions to Glasken, who read them slowly and carefully.

"A bold and delicate scheme, Fras Ilyire, and quite a role for you as well. Listen carefully."

Glasken sat at the specialized FUNCTION desk in the Calculor, trying not to look suspicious or guilty but feeling as conspicuous as an emu in the stocks. Contrary to the falsely embellished tales of continual grinding work in the great machine, there were extended periods of inactivity for many of the components during a normal shift. An algorithm written in by Zarvora in 1696 rotated the workload across components to keep the loadings even, but it had not been updated in twelve years. Now the Calculor was forty-six times larger. Glasken knew

that he would have five or ten minutes of slack once a particular pattern of work was cleared.

The bypass scheme that Denkar had developed in 1698 had not been updated either, and Glasken wondered whether it would still work. Sighing as if he had been hard done by, he began to set patterns of values in his transmission registers according to the instructions that Ilyire had brought. It took two minutes, according to the reciprocating clock above the observation gallery, and he silently thanked whoever had installed a minute hand since he had last worked there.

With three minutes left the status flag snapped to the ENTER position, giving Glasken such a start that he flinched on his seat and muttered ''Fykart'' under his breath. FUNCTION 12472 looked around. Glasken muttered ''No fykart peace for wicked'' by way of explanation as he flicked the beads back and forth to code a message that existed in his mind alone. FUNCTION 12472 wrote his name in her disruption complaints log and put a cross against it. He dumped the last of the code patterns to the output registers, then added the routing protocols for Rushworth, Seymour, and, and . . .

He could not remember the name of the beamflash tower that sat on private land south of Seymour, on the edge of the Calldeath lands. There were nine such towers, he did remember that. Only one thing to do, he decided as his input register flag snapped up to signal that legitimate work had arrived: he followed SEYMOUR with COMMON.

A request from Zarvora to Theresla via Macedon went out to nine stations. This is it, thought Glasken as he worked the beads for a paraline routing problem between wind and galley trains at the Euroa interchange. There was a half hour to go before the end of the shift; then he had study time and a meal break. It would take only minutes for the message to reach each of the outpost towers, and while the local lackeys were scratching their heads over the odd code one tower in particular would be sending it on to Macedon. By the time he was leaving his shift a decoded transcript would be strapped to the back of an emu running from the township to the Melbourne Abandon, where Theresla lived. How long would that take? Hours? Days? Glasken was uncertain about distances beyond the Calldeath boundary. And if Theresla was not home? Then what?

''Can a bloody bird work a letterbox?'' he asked out aloud, and FUNCTION 12472 frowned and put another cross against his name.

His mind returned to the other eight outpost towers while his fingers and feet did their Calculor work. By now the more conscientious operators would be reaching for their code books. Ten, fifteen minutes remained at most. A few would assume it was a military transmission gone astray and destroy it. Someone would have returned it to the beamflash tower above him by the time he was walking out of the hall. Someone else would put it aside in the Inwards Anomalies basket. After an hour, perhaps two, but no more than four, it would be put to the Calculor

for decoding. In very little time it would show up as uncrackable to the decoding routines. There would be a trace of the message, which would end up back at the output buffers of the Libris Calculor itself. I must be clear of the place by then, he reminded himself.

The System Herald declared the shift ended. Glasken stood up and stretched after locking his registers. He winked at FUNCTION 12472, who colored and made to put yet another mark against his name before she realized that he had not actually caused a disruption that time.

In his cell again, Glasken found that his cellmates were asleep. The door was locked, as Tarrin had brought back the old, penal Calculor conditions. Minutes passed. Ilyire did not come. Glasken waited until the regulators had ceased to walk past before extracting a snapwire from its hiding place and turning to the lock. After several minutes the lock had not yielded and his patience was beginning to fray. He carried on a running dialogue under his breath as he continued to work the lock.

"What sort of fykart administrator wouldn't change the fykart algorithms in twelve years but spends a bleeding fortune of my fykart taxes on new fykart locks to keep dummart components in fykart cells that they're not wanting to leave anyway—"

"I have key, Fras Master," murmured a voice under his bunk.

Glasken leaped aside, bringing his guard up, then collided with the cell wall and fell across his writing desk.

"Ilyire! Damn you! The others will wake."

"They bound and gagged, Master."

"I—Well then, let's hurry. The bloody place will be down about our ears in four hours."

"Did message reach Theresla?"

"Aye, but in a damn sloppy way. It's four hours before the screaming starts, I figure, just after midmorning coffee break. The security regulators had better be wearing their brown trews, that's all I can say."

"I don't understand, Fras."

"Ach, just give me the key. Do you know where we can hide?"

"Yes Master."

When they were securely hidden in a stores loft Glasken began to relax.

"Nothing to do but wait," he said. "One matter, though. Where is the agent that Zarvora sent with you? She had better be safe and secure somewhere, for real chaos starts soon."

"She was traitor. I avenged you, Master. I send her into Call."

"The devil you did!"

"Once—still—love her."

"You love—Darien!" Glasken suddenly went pale in the dim light.

"I—"

"Gah, shaddup. Fargh Alspring fykart dummart. Did you *read* what the Highliber said in my instructions?"

"In code, Master."

"But, but—no, I'm not about to tell you in case you do some fykart dummart thing as is worse."

Glasken sat in silence, thinking and weighing up risks. Ilyire became increasingly restive.

"Ilyire, how many guns have ye?"

"Two twin-barrel Morelacs."

"Aye, the Lemorel special. Give 'em here—and that throwing knife."

"Master, what to do?"

"Get myself killed, dummart, that's what."

"Not without my helping!"

"Thank you for the kind offer, but—Hey, who's that?"

"Where?"

Glasken brought the butt of a Morelac down on Ilyire's head as he turned away. He caught the Ghan as he fell and eased him to the floor.

"Call's touch, but it still feels good to do that after Maralinga in 1701."

Brother Alex stared at his notes and transcriptions, his mind almost numb with horror. The Australicans were fighting a war with over a quarter of a million warriors and tens of thousands had been killed within a few months. In Mounthaven the wars were highly ritualized, being fought between Airlords and flocks of wardens, and to very strict rules. No more than a few dozen rich noblemen would die in any conflict in Mounthaven, but the Australicans were burning whole cities.

As if that was not bad enough, the strange and distant continent's people had a religious revulsion for fuel-burning engines, yet Mounthaven's entire society, economy, and nobility was founded on diesel-powered gunwings and sailwings of the nobility, and the steam trams used by merchants and commoners. Chivalric air combat went back over a thousand years, yet here was a vast and populous continent that regarded them as heretics and devils.

Worst of all had been the contact with a group calling themselves the Radicals. They said they were a persecuted minority, that they wanted Mounthaven technology. Their weapons were flintlock guns, but Brother Alex had unwittingly told them of gunwings armed with reaction guns that could fire 300 shells per minute. They wanted to know more, they wanted details, specifications, and ideas . . . They wanted to kill their enemies by the millions.

Brother Alex disconnected his transceiver from its power pile, methodically dismantled it, and smashed the components. Into the fire in which he burned the boards and coils of his radio he dropped his neatly stacked and sealed notes,

diagrams and tables detailing both how to build the equipment and what it had revealed to him. Behind him young Brother James swept up the stray fragments, slowly shaking his head at both the waste and loss to scholarship. He was pleased with himself for having secretly copied out a few key passages and diagrams.

Work in the Libris Calculor was never so pleasant that components would go out of their way to do two shifts in one day. Thus there was no procedure to catch a component returning for a second, consecutive shift. Glasken hurried down the corridors, then slowed at the sight of the registration desk. There were four Dragon Orange guards there and a Dragon Red seated on the corner of the desk.

"And where might ye be goin'?" he asked as Glasken smiled and made to pass.

"I, ah, had to see the medician. Ah—headache."

The Dragon Red turned to the register. "No names listed as is taking leave of the Calculor hall during this shift."

"I was, that is, I was in so much pain that I was carried out. I couldn't sign."

"Were that the case yer escort would have signed for ye, and there's no signature by anyone. Where's yer escort?"

"He stayed with the medician. He's . . . got a headache too."

"And now ye haven't?"

"Ah, well it's a good medician you've got here, nothing but the best for us components."

The Dragon Red slid from the desk and advanced on Glasken. Garlic was strong on the breath that he exhaled up at the much taller component. Glasken backed away until stopped by the wall. The Dragon Red's eyes were close-set and red-rimmed, and when he held a hand up to wave his finger in Glasken's face, he exposed a dotted line around the wrist with CUT HERE, SOUTHMOOR CALLBAIT tattooed beside it.

"I think ye're just late, FUNCTION 3084, I think that ye're so late that ye'll break the record set in 1699. Get over to that book and sign in under the red line on the Inwards column!"

Glasken signed. The five who were guarding the door were enjoying themselves, and were unlikely to search him.

"Ye'll get a demotion at next Humiliation Day," said the Dragon Red as Glasken straightened. "Now get in there and rattle the beads."

Instead of making for the FUNCTION desks or the relief pool room, Glasken went straight to the privies and entered the door reserved for FUNCTIONS. It was nearly four hours into the shift, and not far from the beginning of the staggered coffee break. He took DISABLED signs from the mop closet and hung them on all privy doors but one. In this one he waited until the sound of approaching footsteps announced the first FUNCTION. There was an exasperated curse from

outside and then his door was pushed open. Glasken's fist slammed into the man's midriff; then he hit a precisely chosen spot on the FUNCTION's jaw with the point of his elbow. Within seconds he had removed the DISABLED signs from the other doors and returned to the cubicle to tie his unconscious victim and appropriate the desk identification badge from his tunic. In a gesture of compassion he unlaced the man's trews and propped him over the dump-hole, then jumped the locked door.

The desk assigned to his victim was in LOCK mode and as Glasken returned it to ACTIVE he glanced to the FUNCTIONS either side of him and tapped his forehead. They nodded back, satisfied that he was from the spares pool and replacing a component with a headache. A scan of the registers showed that heavy diagnostic work was in progress using decoding algorithms. They were already on to him. He suspected that traps had been set for the code pattern that he had used to send the message to Seymour, but he had to use the same pattern, and even the same addressing, if he wanted to contact Macedon. His fingers flew over the beads; then he set the registers, broke into the data-transmission stream, and began to set up his output registers to transmit to the beamflash network. They were sure to stop the message at the gallery above him—then he stopped and thought. Was there a direct link to Euroa? He set up a routing string through Euroa that might have only existed in his conjecture. Reaching under his tunic, he pulled back the strikers on both Morelacs. There was an emphatic click as he dispatched the contents of his output register.

Glasken's legitimate work was piling up by now, and it would not be long before a regulator was sent to check on him. He tried to drag recollections of beamflash procedure manuals out of a memory that had never been particularly willing to accept them. In normal routing practice—no, but this would be war routing, and there would be a contingency check before any transmission. The follow-up would catch his use of the same anomalous code, and they would send a HOLD command directly to Seymour. Unless, of course, something distracted them. He frantically typed the first two lines of a Rochester University drinking song in the code pattern and routed it directly to Seymour and the nine towers beyond. He dispatched it.

Almost at once a bell jangled somewhere high above him in the observation gallery. They had picked up the message. Regulators would be sent to detain him within seconds. What else to do? He drew a Morelac and fired at the gearbox of the main reciprocating clock.

Amid the screams and cries that erupted with the echoes of the shot, something whizzed past Glasken's ear and smashed into his output register. Automatically he turned and fired the second barrel at the observation gallery. A guard tumbled over the stone railing, screaming as he fell, and crashed to the desks below. Senior, unchained components were now dashing about in a panic while lower-level compo-

nents struggled to hide under their desks and benches. Another guard fired, dropping a FUNCTION to Glasken's left. They're shooting at random, he thought as he took out the second Morelac and checked the strikers. His shot hit another guard in the gallery, who collapsed over the stone railing. The others backed off out of sight. Another figure appeared at an access hole cut in the brickwork for extensions that had never been continued because of the Kalgoorlie calculor's success. A Dragon Librarian clothed in black. Tarrin! Glasken took aim and squeezed the trigger. The flint striker shattered, but the gun did not discharge.

"Fargh dummart gunsmiths, pox 'em all!" shouted Glasken as he frantically unclamped the flint from the other striker. By the time he was ready for another shot, Tarrin was nowhere to be seen . . . and a fantastic headdress of gunmetal barrels and wooden stocks ringed Glasken's scalp, all with guards or regulators at the other end. Glasken lowered his Morelac to the floor very, very slowly.

It was late in the afternoon before anyone saw fit to get back to Glasken. Two guards and one FUNCTION were dead. Over a hundred components had been injured, and a lot of damage had been done by trampling feet and components smashing mechanisms under desks as they sought cover. The Libris Calculor had been disabled for the longest time since its commissioning. All of those who would have questioned Glasken were needed for the repairs.

Glasken's first message reached Theresla on the shores of the Phillip Bay. Its simple instruction was BEGIN, because aviad agents were ready in Rochester. She entered the water at once to communicate with the dolphins and relay to them a request for help. The dolphins deliberated, decided, then acted. A Call rolled over Rochester for the first time in recorded history.

The city had not been designed for safety during a Call. There were no mercy walls, Call rails, watchbirds, or trained terriers, and nobody wore anchors and timer belts. Ilyire raced through the corridors of Libris opening doors and unlocking gates amid crowds of mindless, shambling people who could do nothing but walk south. Librarians, technicians, guards, senior staff, and readers wandered into the streets of Rochester and joined the crowds making for the south of the city. A ring road inside the wall led to the south gate and out across a wide stone bridge over the shallow lake and into the suburbs. The main gate was closed, and only a trickle of people were getting through the access door beside it. Ilyire hurried to the gatehouse, where he threw levers and chopped ropes until he could raise the dropgate. Once it was two yards clear of the ground he jammed the windlass using the gate captain's halberd of office. The crowd poured under it and across the bridge.

This Call did not last two or three hours, as it did everywhere else on the continent: it continued for five. Libris emptied, the mayoral palace emptied. The Constable's Watchhouse, the markets, the University, the shops, the houses,

the hostelries, the taverns, the brothels, the blockhouses of the fortifications, every part of the city was purged of its citizens. A few were left, trapped in blind laneways and corners, or locked in watchhouse cells or the stocks. Those locked in the cells of the mayoral palace and Libris were all of unquestioned loyalty to Zarvora and were mainly Dragon Librarians.

Ilyire wheeled a cartload of gunpowder into the middle of the main bridge after four hours had passed; then he released the main dropgate and secured it. The cart blew a span out of the heavy stone bridge. There were other bridges across the lake and dozens of boats, but the south bridge was wide and strong, a perfect route for a massed attack.

Suddenly the aberrant Call ceased. Most of the people of Rochester, Oldenberg, and all of the small towns in the null zone that was the Rochester Mayorate found themselves in open fields, about fifteen miles from home. All at once a rush began in the opposite direction. Tarrin managed to rally several hundred Dragon Librarians and lead them to the forefront of the horde of citizens. Their only weapons were pistols and sabers: those with muskets had dropped them the moment that the Call began.

"Nothing like it's ever happened," panted Tarrin as he jogged along with the others.

"Could the enemy be commanding the Call?" asked a Dragon Gold.

"Impossible," puffed the already winded Tarrin. "We must be first back. At least nobody else was better prepared."

But the loyal Dragon Librarians that Ilyire had just released from the Libris and palace cells were far better prepared. Ilyire had freed and armed them as soon as the Call ceased. The Calculor components had been just as safe, being imprisoned as well, and Ilyire had disarmed and chained up their regulators. The Dragon Librarians loyal to Zarvora were outnumbered, but they had the advantage of being behind high walls and having all the bombards and muskets that they could use. They also had the leadership of a hero of Ravensworth bridge: Captain John Glasken.

Zarvora had also been ready, with small sparkflash transceivers stationed at the four compass points around Rochester. As soon as the extraordinary Call began she was informed, and commenced moving her troops in from loyal centers by galley train. For several days the fighting continued in the outer suburbs of Rochester and around the lake, but once Zarvora's troops had fought past paraline centers under Tarrin's control the end was a foregone conclusion. Tarrin was no warrior and for once the situation needed tactical rather than strategic skills. He was caught, tried, and sentenced in very short order, and was already hanging dead on a scaffold by the time Jefton was found hiding in a farmyard shed near Euroa. The Mayor-Seneschal of Rochester could only be tried and executed by his peers, and it would be many months before the assembled Mayors of the

Southeast Alliance sat in judgment over him, then knelt in their splendid robes and raised their muskets at the command of Overmayor Zarvora Cybeline.

The street-to-street fighting was still raging in Rochester's suburbs when Zarvora entered inner Rochester across one of the footbridges. With her were Denkar, Bouros, and several dozen Tiger Dragons. Glasken was nowhere to be seen, but was said to be directing bombard fire at rebel concentrations in the lakeside suburbs from the inner city walls. Zarvora's group split up after a hasty conferral and Bouros made for the artillery position. The Mayor of Kalgoorlie had never actually set eyes on Glasken, and he also had the mistaken idea that his own fame was so widespread that everyone knew him by sight.

"Where is that Glasken who got my sister with child?" he said to the bombardiers.

Muskets appeared from everywhere, pointing at Bouros.

"You leave Captain alone, an' back away," snarled a strong east Highland accent.

"Yes, mind your place, Kalgoorlie Callbait," added an educated Rochestrian voice.

"Touch our Captain we blow ugly head off," called a Southmoor.

Bouros thought for a moment. Rule one in engineering, he thought to himself: Meet the functional requirements.

"Fras Glasken!" bellowed Bouros at the top of his lungs. "Your lady's in labor. Get to the beamflash tower!"

A tall, powerfully built man gave a start, then bolted in the direction of the tower.

Glasken stumbled out of the lift into the beamflash gallery, panting and flushed.

"Glasken!" shouted Zarvora from the beamflash transmitter mechanism. "Do you take Jemli Milderellen as your lawful primary wife?"

"Who, me? But what of her husband?" Glasken called back.

"The Black Runners located him last week and persuaded him to sign an adultery admission," said Zarvora as she rubbed her temples. "They are divorced."

"Then yes!"

Denkar led him to where Zarvora was tapping out a beamflash transmission.

"And now we wait," she concluded.

"Wait for the beamflash to Kalgoorlie?" cried Glasken. "My child will be born, grown, and halfway through University—and still a bastard—before the reply returns."

"Not so, Fras," Denkar assured him. "A sparkflash unit stands at the base of the Kerang tower and it's linked to another at the Kalgoorlie palace."

Zarvora was trying to massage a migraine from behind her left eye and she seemed to have aged several years in a matter of weeks.

"I am legitimizing your child because I owe you a lot, Glasken," she said hoarsely, "but in the name of the Deity will you settle down and sort out your love life?"

Zarvora gazed patiently through the eyepiece of the beamflash telescope as Denkar rubbed a wet towel across the back of her neck. She read the sparkles of code from the distant tower's heliostat out aloud, not bothering to work the key of the tape punch. Glasken was lying against a nearby pillar.

"Baby girl, Jemli well, weight at birth . . . thirteen pounds! The poor woman. Hmm, wrong blood type for Ilyire, but right for you."

"Can you send a reply?" asked Glasken.

"And an aviad," Zarvora continued, looking worse with each passing minute. "What is her name to be?"

"Call her Lessimar, after my stepmother."

Denkar rattled the door of the medician's closet. When it did not open Glasken drew his Gimley 40-bore and blew the lock off. Zarvora slowly lowered her hands from her ears, drew a key from her jacket, and tossed it to the flagstones beside Glasken. Denkar pulled the shattered lock away and took a jar from the closet. After pouring some whisky into two measure-glasses he tossed the jar to Glasken.

"Lameroo Medicinal Rye?" Glasken commented as he removed the cork. "What's this for? Changing my bandages?"

"To Lessimar Glasken," declared Denkar, holding up his measure-glass. Zarvora delicately dipped a fingertip into her measure-glass and licked it. Glasken swallowed several mouthfuls.

"Jemli and I tested as human," gasped Glasken once he had finished coughing.

"So did my parents," Denkar assured him. "It's rare, but aviads can be born to humans. Genototem scholars can explain it."

"As Overmayor I also have a magistrate's authority. I picked up this blank marriage certificate on the way here, so . . ."

She scratched at the parchment with a goose quill from beside the gallery's attendance roster, then handed it to Glasken. Moments later he was gone, in search of better company for a revel.

"Although pregnant, Jemli has been keeping company with estatiers, Costassian in particular," Zarvora remarked in a flat, cool voice.

"Ilyire is no longer there to occupy her," replied Denkar.

"Wrong. Glasken introduced her to life above her station, he taught her to mix with highborn, rich, vindictive nobodies with no dreams or vision. Now she wants an estate and a rich husband with a title."

"Glasken meets those criteria. One day he will be a mayor, too."

"And will still be Glasken. She will eventually demand refinement, Den, and that will cause grief. Still, for now I rewarded him with what he wanted, even if what he *needed* may not be her."

There were many treaties and arrangements signed over the weeks following Tarrin's defeat. The Southmoors broke into a number of small mayorates and emirates, leaving the Emir of Cowra in charge of his immediate emirate and nothing more. Many of the new and smaller states were well disposed to the Southern Alliance.

The Alspring Ghans began returning to their desert cities, not so much in defeat as with the promise of something better than conquest. Six months of trying to control the staff of the Great Western Paraline Authority had backfired very seriously. Many Ghans had become hopelessly entranced by broad-gauge wind and galley trains, and they were scouring the desert for ancient iron rails and suitable track routes. A seven-foot-gauge paraline was to be built linking Alspring to Woomera, but in the meantime camel trains were opening up a flourishing trade.

The strange annihilation at Ravensworth was the subject of a great number of studies, and early in August an intermayorate conference of edutors at Griffith concluded that it had been caused by an excess of conductive smoke from many cooking fires combined with ionized paths traced by mortar shells and the proximity of a great deal of metal weaponry. It had induced a type of massive and localized lightning, providing proof that the prohibition on steam engines was based in physics and not religious mysticism. Metal, steam, and smoke were pronounced a deadly combination. It was definitely unwise to concentrate heavy industry in any one place or use steam engines to power trains.

Zarvora, Denkar, and Bouros knew differently, but chose to remain silent. They knew that Mirrorsun, the huge band with a potential surface area greater than that of the entire moon, was alive and conscious. With the war over they turned to the problems of communicating with it. It took time, but contact was established and a translation code agreed upon.

The Mirrorsun band had heard their sparkflash radios in an otherwise lonely cosmos. When Dolorian sent out her message from Ravensworth about defeat and death being close, Mirrorsun interpreted the words as allies of the Wanderers attacking one of its fellow intelligences. It focused a massive blast of radiation on the area that Dolorian had radioed as being covered by enemy forces.

Nor was Mirrorsun the only voice on the radio bands. On another continent, Col-Arado had a single transceiver, operating from a Christian monastery. Before suddenly going silent it had told of a great and strange civilization in what had once been the Rocky Mountains of America. The gathering together of the ancient civilization's legacy accelerated beyond Zarvora's wildest dreams.

"Nobody but you should hold the key to Mirrorsun," Denkar told her. "I would have used its power as a weapon, but you would not. That earned you the right to deal with it."

"That may have just been my weakness," she countered.

"Then it's a weakness that we can all learn from. Where do we go from here with Mirrorsun?"

"More study and better communication. I shall use a Bouros calculor for an encryption interface. It can be housed in the old Calculor hall."

"But the hall still contains the Libris Calculor, Zar."

"It is no longer sufficiently fast or accurate, it must be decommissioned. The components can be given a general amnesty and a bag of royals each."

"But Zar, many don't want to go, remember? Tarrin tried to disband them on the eve of the war and they barricaded themselves inside. They saved the Libris Calculor for your use in your war with Lemorel and there are still five thousand components who want to stay. That's a lot of skilled, talented people, Zar."

Zarvora looked at him as if she were seeing him for the first time. It took her some moments to gather together the words of a reply.

"To me it was just a tool . . . yet you are telling me that it is a whole world to those living within it."

"Perhaps not a world, but a home."

"All right, I did not fight the war to throw my troops out of home. Tell me what would please them."

The components of the Calculor were subdued and morose as they obeyed the SYSTEM HALT command and gathered, along with those off-duty, to attend Zarvora's briefing. When it had been the Rochester and Southeast Alliance Human Rights Association attempting to destroy the Calculor they could imagine there was a mistake. With Zarvora, there could be no doubt about it.

"Wish it was some new configuration," said PORT 3A sadly as they sat waiting.

"We could get together outside once in a while," MULTIPLIER 17 suggested. "You know, meet with abacus frames and run the machine."

"Oh yea, it could be in the meeting hall of the Echuca Library. We could invite some Dragon Librarians to walk among us with canes, hitting anyone who makes a mistake and dragging an occasional component off to the broom closet for some solitary confinement."

"A few of us have not thought it such a stupid idea—Ah now, here she comes."

This time there was applause for Zarvora instead of cowering and terrified silence. She mounted the rostrum, then spoke in a more muted voice than they were used to. Many cupped hands to their ears to listen.

"Components of the great machine known as the Calculor, today is a day of destiny for you all. Today you will go free, but being free does not mean that you cannot work in the Libris Calculor."

At this there was a flurry of whispers.

"Some of you may know that a new electroforce calculor has been brought from Kalgoorlie. It is a thousand times smaller than the Libris Calculor, yet a thousand times faster. Now, imagine your Calculor in its current form being expanded a thousand times. The demand for regulators and technicians would be enormous. In a way, the electroforce calculor is no different. I have great need of experienced folk to convert programs written in Calculor Conversation Protocol to the electroforce calculor's language, CIND—Calculor Instruction Numeric Dialect. This will be a massive task, yet there is more again. Mayor Bouros of Kalgoorlie estimates a two-hundredfold increase in calculor speed by this time next year."

There was another wave of incredulous whispers.

"Those of you who stay in Libris will be paid as regulators to tend the new, electroforce calculor. It will be harder work, with no more blind following of instructions. You will have to think. Take my offer seriously, you have five days to decide. Thank you once more for all the work that you have done here as souls in the great machine, the Libris Calculor. You changed the world."

The components had begun talking among themselves already. For the first time in over a decade, Zarvora had found herself ignored.

"So, it be a new configuration after all," said PORT 3A.

"New configuration be buggered, it's a complete rebuild," replied MULTIPLIER 17. "Do they have any manuals or diagrams, I wonder?"

"Look there, by the door. It's FUNCTION 9."

"Hey there, FUNCTION 9!" called MULTIPLIER 17 as they both hurried over to Denkar. "Where have you been for the past eighteen months?"

"3A, 17, the day's fortune to you. Will you stay?"

"Oh aye, they'll need me," said PORT 3A. "It's all very well for a toy-sized model, but not on the scale of the Libris Calculor."

"Not so. We've had prototypes working for months. I've been developing the CIND language myself. It's faster for writing programs because you can write out the whole thing in numerical symbols."

"Numerical?" said MULTIPLIER 17. "When can we see it?"

A crowd was beginning to gather around them by now, both regulators and components. Zarvora called for attention.

"I want volunteers to carry in boxes, pedal on the galley wagons, and to break up desks to make room."

A forest of arms shot up. The Great Calculor of Libris thus came to an unceremonious end, with its components chopping away the desks, wires, frames,

and mechanisms while others carried in boxes of relay units, plugs, and insulated electroforce cables. Assembly began under Denkar's direction, and continued for several days until the first test calculations brought the relays clattering into life.

With the help of the electroforce calculors in both Kalgoorlie and Rochester, Zarvora composed a string of messages in the ancient ASCII code and keyed them through her sparkflash transmitter to the Mirrorsun band. This established protocols to render exchanges impenetrable to eavesdroppers elsewhere. It was unrewarding work at first, with hesitant and confusing transmissions between two intelligences quite alien to each other. The band had to work in Japanese, then English, then extrapolate the English into Austaric. This was why it had taken so long between Dolorian's desperate message to Oldenberg and Mirrorsun's burning the greater part of the Southmoor and Alspring armies. Under Zarvora's tuition the standard of Mirrorsun's Austaric improved, yet the concept of life at ground level was difficult for Mirrorsun to comprehend. In the end it was Zarvora who provided the solution.

Glasken peered through the curtains of his room in the Rochester mayoral palace. Four floors below, in the Courtyard of Triumph, the Overmayor was presenting medals conferred during the war. Ilyire stood behind Glasken, hearing only the cheering and band music.

"Oi, there goes one of their secret agents, wearing a mask," said Glasken. "Can't see the medal from here." He turned back to Ilyire. "Come and see, you don't know what you're missing."

"My place is here, Master."

"Still guarding my back?"

"It has enemies, Master."

"And your back?"

"I guard for guarding you."

Glasken parted the curtains again and looked down to where Sergeant Gyrom was accepting medals from the Overmayor on behalf of himself and Dolorian's family. There was a medal for Gyrom as well.

"What a life. I can't accept a bloody medal in public or go to my family for fear of Baelsha monks a-watch for me. How can I have a public invel-wedding to Varsellia?" He looked back to Ilyire, who was standing relaxed yet alert, his eyes always on the move for threats. "You don't have to be part of this, Ilyire."

"But, Master, I am."

Ilyire looked either hurt or guilty, Glasken was not sure which. He gave Ilyire a reassuring slap on the shoulder, forgetting how little his aviad friend really weighed. Ilyire stumbled, but Glasken caught him by the arm.

"So, you want to live as a fugitive, protecting me because I am the only one

that you wronged who is still alive! You really need Darien to occupy your time, don't you?''

"Master, is done what is done. I killed her, Master. Evil mistake, now only memory to love."

Glasken looked through the curtains again. "Oi, the herald stumbled while backing away from the Overmayor! Bouros caught him. Now he's up again, but his hat's on backwards. Pompous fop." Glasken closed the curtains. "Ilyire, I admit I enjoy having you around to deflect the blades and bullets from my unworthy body, but I'm not selfish. If I bring Darien back from the dead will you promise to leave me alone and guard, say, Frelle Cybeline instead?''

"Master, do not blaspheme."

"Promise?"

"The dead are dead."

"Promise!"

"I promise."

Ilyire closed his eyes, and Glasken knew that he was shutting out the topic. Ilyire opened his eyes again. Darien was standing with her hands pressed against her cheeks and her lips parted in an unfathomable expression. There was a gleaming medal on a green ribbon pinned above her left breast.

"Master, master, you bring her back from dead," Ilyire babbled, but Glasken was gone.

Darien held up a card in Glasken's writing.

LOOK AFTER EACH OTHER. LOVERS ARE EASY TO FIND, BUT LOVE IS RARE.

Glasken had slipped a message into the beamflash network to Macedon, asking the aviads to watch for Darien on the Call tracks. The aviads' way was not to help humans passing through the Calldeath lands, but they owed Zarvora some favors.

The shadowy figures from Baelsha kept watch around Libris for several days after the ceremony. A confirmed sighting of Glasken at Elmore eventually drew them south, but before they could close in on the fugitive a Call swept over the little railside town and lured Glasken away. The monks followed the trailing edge of the Call, keeping the anchorless figure of Glasken in sight, but they broke off the pursuit upon reaching the Calldeath lands. Glasken was as good as dead.

Zarvora watched the sky above Phillip Bay, while Theresla's dirkfang cats prowled about, guarding her. The sky was clear blue, with not a cloud or bird to be seen. She did not know what to expect, but Mirrorsun had agreed to this exact time and place. Thunder rumbled somewhere in the distance. Thunder from a clear sky! That had to mean something. She scanned the sky again with her brass and silver twinoculars.

When she finally caught sight of the object it was already quite low, and perhaps a mile away. A tiny white sphere was descending beneath a red, parasol-

shaped thing, like the seed of some featherdown plant floating on the wind. It approached the horizon, stood out sharply against the waves, then splashed undramatically into the water.

About forty minutes later several dolphins became visible towing what looked like a vast red tent through the waves. Behind it a scorched white sphere bobbed sluggishly on the dark water. Theresla was visible as a dark figure being towed by one of the dolphins. She waded ashore, white skin showing in places through her grease and blacking.

"We must remove the fabric that broke the sphere's fall, it's smooth as glass and my dolphins are disturbed by it. They dragged it here only to get it out of their water."

They hauled the white sphere from the water and carried it to the ruins of a nearby hut. Zarvora tapped an array of numbered studs near where the parachute had been attached and the top of the sphere hinged open. Inside were white, cubelike packages, which she removed and began to put into her rollpack.

"What are these?" asked Theresla.

"Devices to communicate better with Mirrorsun, a type of sparkflash that nobody can spy upon. The cloth that broke its fall can generate electroforce essence if left spread out in sunlight. Even the cords that attach it are electroforce connectors. Mirrorsun and I are about to explore each other's worlds."

Zarvora studied the markings on several of the boxes, then opened one and took out something like a bracelet. It was a plain, coppery color, but slightly flexible to the touch. A number of studs and square panels were inset.

"This is for you," said Zarvora as she read instructions on a sheet of smooth, skinlike material. "Hold out your hand."

Zarvora cleaned the grease and lampblack from Theresla's left wrist with medicinal rye whisky and a cotton cloth. At the touch of a stud the band shrank and bonded with her wrist.

"So this is the same as a sparkflash transceiver the size of a wagon?" asked Theresla, holding her wrist up and regarding the unlikely-looking machine skeptically.

"Oh more, much more. It transceives sounds and pictures, and draws power either from your blood or body heat. You turn it off thus, with this stud."

"So I am linked to you wherever I go, Frelle Invel-Sister?"

"And to Mirrorsun, just as I am to be."

Zarvora attached her own bracelet, and they went through a few trials in local mode. Finally they changed mode to give Mirrorsun its first view of the Earth from a human perspective.

Glasken had surrendered himself to the Call at Elmore, and wandered south in an unresisting, mindless rapture, safe within the Call from the pursuing monks of Baelsha. A prearranged beamflash signal had been sent south, and like Darien he

was rescued by the Macedon aviads and escorted through the Calldeath lands. He came to his senses as if walking through an invisible curtain and found himself at the edge of a small town. It was a cool winter's morning with the sun bright in a cloudless sky. The place was a gaudy splash of terra cotta roofs, orderly and incongruous against the green fields and bushland of the Calldeath. There to meet him was Theresla.

"This is a null zone like Rochester," she explained as they walked the streets, "except that we are within the Calldeath lands."

Glasken noted that Theresla spent a lot of time with her left hand up to her neck or shoulder. There was a strange-looking bangle on her wrist.

"A pleasant town, and some pretty goodwives," he commented, trying to show enthusiasm as they walked.

"Ah-hah, now here is Bishop Pandoral," she said as they met with a tall, lean, but kindly-looking woman. "What a trio we make: Bishop Lessimar Pandoral, Abbess Theresla, and Brother John Glasken."

"My son, I have always followed your progress," said Lessimar, "mostly with pride."

"Uh, thank you . . . but why me?"

"You are my son."

"What?"

"Your father lied to you, Glasken," said Theresla.

"No, I checked the records."

"The records were altered. Lessimar was being beaten by an angry mob—as an aviad—just before a Call. She escaped to Macedon and a new life. Your father had the town records altered to show that you were the child of an adulterous liaison with Jolene."

"The scrawny old goat!"

Lessimar held out her arms, but Glasken's knees buckled. They finally embraced kneeling together in the dusty street.

"Brother Glasken, they say you're as hard to kill as I am," said Lessimar with her arms around his neck. "I have always watched over you."

"Always?" quavered Glasken.

"Always. All those women, all that fighting and drinking—"

"But at least I got my degree!"

Theresla stood by for a time with her arms folded, her left wrist facing outward. Presently she wandered off with the Mayor as the crowd around the reunited mother and son grew bigger.

"An impressive fellow," the Mayor declared. "A pity that he turned out to be human. We could, ah, use him."

"True. His hair tests as human and he is not as strong as most aviad men. Although he has been trained to resist the Call in a limited way, he is as susceptible as any human."

"Well, he should be a great asset to the humans, whenever it's safe for him to return."

"He is Alpha Two Positive Gamma Negative."

"His genototem? Well, that's no surprise. We must monitor his offspring among the humans to see if any turn out to be aviads."

"His first is, Mayor. Gamma Negative, Mayor, remember what that means? With human women there is a significant chance that he can sire aviads, but any couplings he has with aviad women will result in aviad children. Exclusively."

The Mayor's eyes suddenly widened, and his mouth hung open as he stroked his chin. "I . . . shall get the medician to draw up a little list, I think. Thank you, Frelle Theresla. Thank you well indeed."

An hour later Theresla was packed and ready to leave. She called past Lessimar's house, where the preparations for an evening revel to celebrate Glasken's reunion with his real mother were under way.

"You should stay for the evening at least," Glasken insisted as Theresla kissed him on the cheek and tweaked his mustache. "You're the real guest of honor here."

"I am not one for revels, Fras. I am going north, to the Sydney Abandon. The cetezoids think of it as a holy place."

Glasken was surprised. "The Sydney Abandon? We know it to be huge, but nothing connects it to the sea creatures."

"All the more reason for me to go there. Take care, though. In the years ahead I shall be watching you."

"I was afraid you might say that. Still, I'm not going anywhere with Baelsha bogeys after me. That will make it hard to see my family."

· "Do not fret, Glasken. Mayor Bouros will be off to see Baelsha's abbot in a fortnight, and he has some strong bargaining points for lifting the death order on you."

"Aye now, that's fantastic news. Two weeks, you say? Good. I'll be able to leave for Kalgoorlie. I suspect that Varsellia does not want her invel-wedding over either the beamflash or the sparkflash. But what of you? When are you to leave?"

"Fras Glasken, remember how you vanished as soon as Ilyire and Darien turned their backs upon you?"

"Aye."

"Well I shall do the same. Let us say goodbyes now. Quickly, a last Glasken grapple."

"Look to yourself, and don't eat any strange mice," he said as they hugged each other.

"And stay out of trouble, Glasken. It is my turn for stupid heroics now. Ah

look here, the Macedon medician, his lovely wife Vivenia—and their beautiful little daughter who is walking already! Hullo, hullo.''

The child cowered away from Theresla, who only laughed.

''Fras Glasken, you will be staying some weeks in Macedon, I hear,'' began the medician. ''Vivenia and I were wondering—''

''Fras Medician,'' interjected Theresla, ''this man does not yet know the term 'genototem hospitality' or the difficulties you have had to keep inbreeding out of the aviad genototem. I could think of no better edutors than yourself and Vivenia, however. Why don't you all go for a walk in the gardens of the beamflash tower?''

Theresla was gone before Glasken returned. She traveled swiftly north through the Calldeath lands, escorted by creatures that struck fear into the hearts of everyone else. Days later she emerged into the farmlands of humans, and changed into the robes of a Libris Inspector before entering the town of Seymour.

Sondian's inner council was not pleased by Zarvora's near-absolute victory, and saw in it a real danger to their own interests. As they met in a fortified collective in the Calldeath lands near the Gambier Abandon they were grasping for ideas rather than reporting progress.

''The bombings should continue,'' suggested Theta 9. ''They keep hostility between the two species alive.''

''But do not build advantage for us,'' Sondian pointed out.

''Some devices from Mirrorsun do reach us by sympathizers,'' said Beta 2.

''Devices that cannot be disassembled and copied, and devices in very small quantities,'' scoffed Sondian. ''Think! We have to do better than this.''

Delta 7 lifted a little globe of the world from the table and held it up before her. It was grimy and battered with the millennia, but the continents were still clearly visible.

''Cross this gaggle of islands to the north of the continent and there is land for thousands of miles across, ah, China and Siberia,'' she said. ''One more tiny strait and we reach the American continent with its flying machines and reaction guns. Remember what the monk with the sparkflash implied? There are *no* aviads there. A few of us could rule them.''

''Crossing the water is a major obstacle,'' Beta 2 pointed out.

''There are hot-air balloons.''

''They can ascend for barely an hour, and are at the wind's mercy.''

''Macedon's engineers have developed a small, light, high-speed steam engine fired by oil—''

''But it was still too heavy for the biggest balloon possible.''

Sondian raised his hand, one finger pointed upward. The others fell silent.

"Put that engine in a light canoe, however, and it could outpace the fastest fish or cetezoid. A crew of six could carry it when there is land."

"But Fras Sondian, it would take a decade to reach Mounthaven and Denver that way," said Theta 9, tracing the path on the little globe.

"Well then, there is no time to lose," replied Sondian with a nod of approval to Delta 7.

The eleven years that followed the end of the war saw things change beyond recognition yet remain very much the same on the surface.

The aviads isolated themselves in thriving towns and farms in the Calldeath lands, and Mirrorsun supplied a huge solar powered sailplane from its fabricators. Originally designed to cruise high in the atmosphere and generate ozone, the template had been altered to accommodate aviad explorers. Offshore islands were discovered and colonized, providing sanctuaries forever beyond the reach of humans. Zarvora remained the sole contact with Mirrorsun, and controlled the bounty from its fabricators with a very firm hand.

The humans remained oblivious to all these developments, and life in their cities and mayorates went on as before—more or less. Sparkflash technology was withdrawn and replaced with a few dozen small, sealed transceivers from Mirrorsun's fabricators. They were efficient, tight-band devices with a hundred channels each, but they could not be adjusted or duplicated. Zarvora would say only that skilled artisans built them in secret workshops. The wind and galley trains continued to run, markets thrived, combustion engines remained anathema, and the electric calculors slowly increased in speed, efficiency and size.

Sondian's expedition to the North American civilization vanished without a trace. In distant Mounthaven the wardens still put on jewel encrusted flight jackets and ascended in tiny gunwings to patrol their lands and duel with rivals. They were unaware that the Wanderers had been disabled, Mirrorsun was a total mystery to them, and there was not a single aviad on their entire continent. Half a world away, Sondian continued to recruit and train agents by the hundred and drew up new plans to destroy Zarvora's power and enslave the humans of Australia. The weapons and tiny aircraft of Mounthaven still featured heavily in his plans.

One chilly winter's evening in 1719 GW, Zarvora alarmed her Tiger Dragon escort by slipping away from a diplomatic reception and vanishing into the streets of Griffith. Try as they might they could not find the Overmayor, and the woman she was visiting was dead. It had taken Zarvora eleven years to track her down.

"It is true, I am a deserter," explained Torumasen, the former medician of Glasken's 105th. "I also brought Dolorian here, to neutral territory."

He was wearing the medal won over a decade earlier but only presented

minutes ago. They were standing in a small courtyard behind his house, the centerpiece of which was Dolorian's grave. A splendid, life-size, marble nude of the woman reclined on a red granite slab carved in the shape of a large bed, which was sheltered beneath a slate roof.

"Very nice, but not quite what I had in mind for one of the two greatest heroes of the Milderellen Invasion," Zarvora decided.

"It is what she wanted, Frelle Overmayor: to be remembered as beautiful, sensual and in her prime."

"How could you know that?"

"Because she did not die in the battlefield mud. I dragged her back to life, put her on a river galley and brought her here to Griffith. Dolorian lived thirty-one days and was recovering, but . . . alas, Milderellen's bullet had grazed a major artery and it finally burst. She died in a comfortable bed, asleep, and beside me. By then I *had* learned what she liked, Overmayor."

Torumasen raised his goblet of wine, then Zarvora clinked her goblet of spring water against it. In spite of the cold they remained standing beside the exquisite likeness of Dolorian.

"Why did you contact me?" asked Zarvora.

"I have a new love now, and we are soon to be married. I could not in fairness bring my bride home to, well, all this, so I wanted to ask you to move Dolorian's remains and memorial to the Shrine of Heroes at Rochester."

Zarvora gave a rare laugh.

"The Shrine's custodians will scream nine flavors of hellfire . . . but why not? People need to know that soldiers who love life are no less brave than those who love killing. Perhaps, though, there should be a mosaic of Dolorian working the sparkflash in the background. Yes?"

"You have a deal, Overmayor," said Torumasen, taking a sip of his wine. He saw that she was looking up into the sky.

"She charmed even Mirrorsun," Zarvora said wisfully.

"The band in the sky remains very thin," said Torumasen, all the while wondering whether Dolorian might have been responsible for that as well. "Does that mean Greatwinter will not return?"

"Yes."

"Just yes?"

"Greatwinter is a complex term, Fras Medician. The Anglaic civilization had accidentally changed the climate, and when the Call first appeared the seasons were already hotter. Mirrorsun was a vast enterprise to give the world a sunshield, but we have grown used to a hotter climate. In the Sydney Abandon there is a ruin called the Miocene Institute. We have discovered that the ancients were experimenting with the genototems of sea creatures, just as they altered themselves to make us. Apparently they built a race of aquatic creatures with enhanced intelligence, so—"

"To what end?" interjected Torumasen, who became philosophical after three drinks and was now up to his fifth. "Why breed more intelligence into a beast? Better wool or more milk, of course, but intelligence?"

Zarvora sighed and shrugged. "We breed more intelligent emus and terriers so they can be better trained to restrain shepherds gripped by the Call. Perhaps these sea creatures were meant to herd and tend fish in the same way as our drover emus and terriers look after herds and flocks on land. The experiments probably got out of hand, the creatures developed the Call, and here we are."

"But what about the wars between humans?" whispered Torumasen. "The nuclear bombs that caused nuclear winters?"

"I have commissioned detailed maps of our continent. At only two abandons are craters where the ground is turned to glass, as the bombs were reputed to do. Extend that to the rest of the world and you have a terrible war, but not a catastrophe. In the confusion and panic following the first Calls the humans must have blamed each other and sent their flying machines to attack in revenge."

There was a chorus of yelping terriers in the distance.

"Ah, my zealous Tiger Dragons and their tracker terriers are closing in," remarked Zarvora. "I should leave your house and return to them."

"I am truly pleased to meet you, Overmayor Cybeline," said Torumasen as they bowed in the darkness. "I once thought you just another despot. Now I see that you have vision."

"Although I remain a despot," concluded Zarvora.

She drew a strange, soft band from her jacket's pocket.

"Live well and long with your new love, Fras Medician, and take this as my wedding present."

"It's . . . I don't appear to have one," he replied, holding up the flaccid band.

"It is Mirrorsun material. If ever again someone is as precious to you as Dolorian is in the grip of death, put this around their neck. Mind, however, it can only be used once."

Zarvora slowly walked away from the house along the dimly lit street. In the sky Mirrorsun was gleaming steadily, but the first traces of fog were gathering. From a balcony garden a marksman followed her head with the sights of his musket. He was breathing regularly, slowly. He exhaled, paused, and began to squeeze the trigger.

Ilyire's knife plunged into his back and tore through his heart. As Zarvora walked on, oblivious, the Ghan pulled some strands of his victim's hair free and rubbed them between his fingers.

"Aviad dummart," he whispered as he noted the texture, then he dropped to the street and caught up with Zarvora. As he fell in beside her he held up a bloodied hand.

"All your own work?" asked Zarvora.

"Another Aviad Radical," warned Ilyire. "They want to kill you and take

over Mirrorsun's fabricators to fight the humans. One day my eyes will not be sharp enough, Overmayor. Then you will die. You must take more care and help me to protect you.''

''Ah, but you are wrong,'' replied Zarvora, draping an arm over his shoulder and gesturing up to Mirrorsun. ''I am not only safe, I am immortal too.''

''Another of your visions, Overmayor?'' he sighed glumly.

''The creation of my vision, Fras Ilyire. For the second time I have become the first soul in a great machine.''